OF EMPIRES AND DUST

OF EMPIRES AND DUST

BOOK FOUR OF
THE BOUND AND THE BROKEN

RYAN CAHILL

READING ORDER

The reading order for The Bound and The Broken series is a highly contested thing. So, keeping that in mind, I have decided to provide you with two suggested reading orders, Both are named after sword movements within the series.

If you prefer to jump headfirst into a world, letting the action and high stakes consume you, then the svidarya is the path for you. If you are the kind of reader who prefers a slower burn, immersing yourself completely in a world, learning the intricacies and terminology as you go, then fellensír is the correct course.

It is highly recommended that all currently published novellas are read prior to Of Empires and Dust.

SVIDARYA

The Fall

Of Blood and Fire

Of Darkness and Light

The Exile

Of War and Ruin

The Ice

The Blood that Burns the Winter Snow

Of Empires and Dust

FELLENSÍR

Of Blood and Fire

The Fall

Of Darkness and Light

The Exile

Of War and Ruin

The Ice

The Blood that Burns the Winter Snow

Of Empires and Dust

Of Empires and Dust

Book Four of The Bound and The Broken series

First Published in 2025 by Ryan Cahill

Cover Design by: Stuart Bache

Map by: Jack Shepherd

Typesetting by: Kate Cromwell

Illustrations by: Peng Lu

ISBN: 978-1-7396209-7-4

www.ryancahillauthor.com

To Ella, my daughter, whose screams were the soundtrack to this book.

You will always be loved.

To Milky, my friend, your loss will never heal,

but your kindness is immortal.

THE STORY SO FAR

A full glossary, along with a quick, high-level refresher of the events in all previous books is available on www.ryancahillauthor.com

CONTENTS

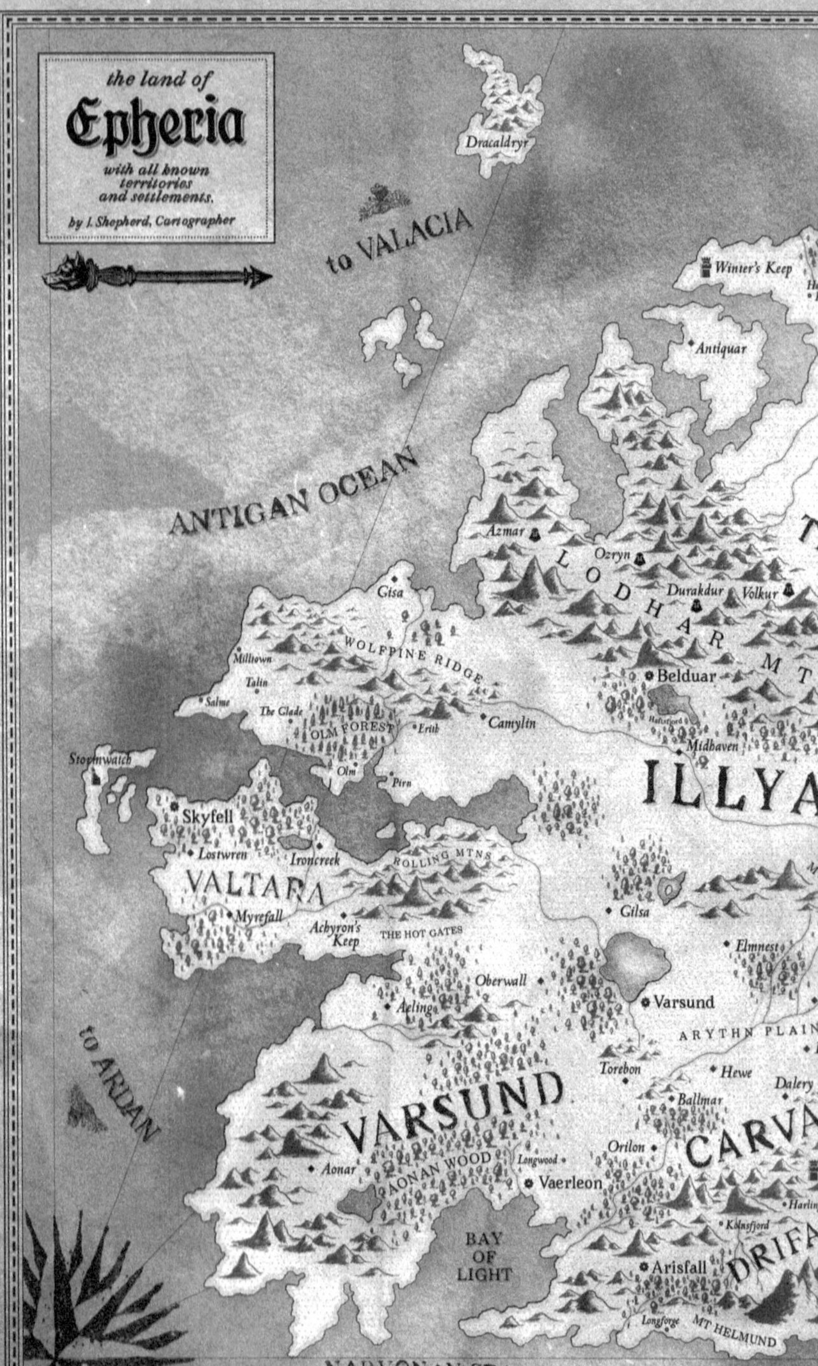

the land of
Epheria
with all known
territories
and settlements.
by I. Shepherd, Cartographer
to VALACIA
Dracaldryr
ANTIGAN OCEAN
Winter's Keep
Harke's
Ride
Antiquar
Azmar
Ozryn
LODHAR MTN
Durakdur
Volkur
Gisa
WOLFPINE RIDGE
Belduar
Milltown
Hafsfjord
Talin
Midhaven
Salme
The Glade
OLM FOREST
Erith
Camylin
ILLYA
Olm
Stormwatch
Pirn
Skyfell
Lostwren
Ironcreek
ROLLING MTNS
VALTARA
Gilsa
Elmnest
Myrefall
Achyron's
Keep
THE HOT GATES
Oberwall
Varsund
Aelinge
ARYTHN PLAIN
to ARDAN
Torebon
Hewe
Dalery
Ballmar
VARSUND
Orilon
CARVA
Aonar
AONAN WOOD
Longwood
Vaerleon
Harling
Kolnsfjord
DRIFA
BAY
OF
LIGHT
Arisfall
Longforge
MT HELMUND
NARVONAN SEA

SEA OF STONE
Catagan
Dead Rock's Hold
Highpass
Merchant's Reach
Khergan
FIRNIN MTNS
Fort Harken
Elkenrim
MTNS
Steeple
Greenhills
Holm
Gildor
Bromis
erona
LORIA
Arginwatch
Ravensgate
LICHENING COAST
Copperstille
MAR DORUL
Easterlock
T LANDS
LYNALION
THE DARKWOOD
Kingspass
A
ARGONAN MARSHES
Falstide
Driftstone
Fearsall
Baylomon
VELORAN OCEAN
Stonehelm
Narrith
Cardend
Lensa
ARKALEN
Hirane
Aerilon
Yarrin
Bayfort
Seaside
THE STORMWOOD
Land's End
to KARVOS

CHAPTER ONE

PICKING UP THE PIECES

5th Day of the Blood Moon

Five miles from Aravell – Winter, Year 3081 After Doom

Calen dropped to his knees, the blood-soaked mud squelching beneath his weight. He rested his helmet beside his gauntlets, tilted his head back, and closed his eyes, the burble of the stream settling in the back of his mind. He drew a long breath, the smell of spilt blood and burning wood filling his nostrils. A sigh of sweet relief escaped his throat as he dipped his hands into the water and splashed his face, pressing his fingers into his skin and dragging them through the sweat and grime that marred his cheeks and forehead.

"We're ready to march." Vaeril's words were softly spoken, almost tender. The elf didn't approach, for which Calen was thankful; he needed a moment. In truth, he needed a lifetime, but he'd settle for a moment.

The first thing Calen saw when he opened his eyes was the Blood Moon's crimson light sparkling in the stream's shifting waters, battling against the purple glow that shone from the runes in his armour. The moon had hung in the dark sky since the night it had bled into the world. The sun rose and set each day, but its light was dim, as though tempered by Efialtír himself, the world painted with an unyielding crimson hue.

The second thing Calen saw was the bloodied water dripping from his face onto his hands, then the bodies. Uraks, elves, Angan, and humans alike floated in the stream, lifeless and broken.

He allowed his gaze to linger on the aftermath of the ambush before pulling his gauntlets from the mud and sliding them into place over his hands, watching as the runes on his armour glistened and the metal melded together. The armour had saved him ten times over already.

Calen grabbed his helmet, then rose.

Vaeril stood a few feet away, his helmet in the crook of his arm, his golden hair reflecting the moon's light and the emblem of the white dragon emblazoned across the breastplate of his armour.

"Casualties?" Calen hated how plainly he asked the question, hated that death had become such a common part of each passing day. It was never a matter of if, but how many. And with the Blood Moon in the sky, the Uraks were stronger than Calen had ever seen them.

"Two hundred and eighty-three."

Calen nodded sombrely. He approached Vaeril and gestured towards the trees and where the rest of the army waited.

Vaeril inclined his head and turned to walk with Calen. "Dann is arranging the recovery of the bodies. They'll be brought back to the city, where they can be mourned with the others at the Eleswea un'il Valana."

The Ceremony of the Lost. Calen had only heard fragments of the ceremony in Therin's teachings, but Vaeril had explained it more thoroughly in the days since the battle. It was only ever performed during times of unspeakable death. A waypoint in history, a marker in time. It was one of few pieces of culture shared by the Jotnar and the elves.

"Good." Calen wanted to say more, wanted to *feel* more, but he was just so tired and numb. Five days had passed since they had routed the Lorian armies attacking the city of Aravell, five days since he and Valerys had burned thousands alive. He'd heard them scream, watched them thrash as the flames consumed their flesh and turned them to blackened husks. He'd lost a piece of himself as he'd watched… and more pieces in the days since.

They'd had no choice—No, that wasn't true. They'd had a choice, and they'd made the only decision worth making. A decision they'd make again to protect the ones they loved. But that didn't mean Calen didn't hate himself for it. It didn't mean he hadn't taken thousands of fathers, mothers, daughters, and sons from their families.

His throat tightened, images of fire and smoke filling his mind. Blood-curdling screams resounded in his head. Shrieks, cries. Men made inhuman sounds when burned alive. Sounds that had etched themselves into Calen and Valerys's shared soul.

Vaeril stopped just as the voices and footfalls of the others drifted through the trees. "May I ask?"

"Vaeril, you don't have to ask permission every time. We're past that."

The elf stared back at Calen, holding his gaze, his expression unchanging.

Calen sighed. "Yes." Exhaustion seeped into his voice. Elven customs were infuriating at times. "Ask."

Vaeril inclined his head. "Are you well?" He shook his head before Calen could answer. "My apologies. I know you are not well. None of us are, but I just—"

"Just tired." Calen rested his hand on Vaeril's pauldron, mustering what must have looked like the most insincere of smiles, all while the screams still rang in his head. "Let's gather the others and get back to Aravell. It's been a long few days, and I'd have a night's rest under my belt before the ceremony."

The truth was, Calen wanted nothing less than to return to Aravell and deal with the unceasing, unrelenting politics and questions that had erupted in the wake of the attack and King Silmiryn's death in the fighting. But there were problems that needed to be solved, and he'd been away from Ella and Valerys for too long. At the thought, the dragon rumbled at the edges of his mind, the pain from his wounds flaring.

A moment passed in which Vaeril stared into Calen's eyes as though waiting for him to say something more, but then the elf nodded, and they started off through the trees.

They emerged into a clearing newly forged out of the dense, all-consuming canopy of the Aravell woodland. Thanks to the Dragonguard, the ground was now laden with char and ash, the earth open to the skies above. Bones protruded from blackened animal carcasses, and the trees and brush lingered as brittle husks. Around the edges, fires still burned, dark smoke pluming into the air as the Blood Moon loomed in the star-dusted sky.

Urak and Lorian bodies lay scattered amidst the ashes, the gemstones set into the Uraks' blackened weapons pulsating with crimson light. The beasts had taken Calen and the others by surprise while they'd been scouring the area for the Lorian remnants, falling upon them in the dark.

Just short of a thousand warriors stood in the clearing. Some were arranged in columns, ready to march, while others moved about, checking the injured and loading bodies onto hastily lashed-together sleds, drawn by the giant, white-furred stags that were the Dvalin Angan. Many of the warriors – those whose armour Valdrin and the smiths had finished – were garbed in silver plate and chainmail, the symbol of the white dragon peering through blood and dirt.

Calen didn't think he would ever look upon that marking and not feel strange. These warriors looked to him; they fought in his name, bearing Valerys's likeness on their breastplates. They had charged at his back on the night the Lorians attacked Aravell, and they had never faltered. In the days since, they had done so again and again as they routed the Lorians from the woodland and the areas around and pushed back the Uraks that ventured into the Aravell from Lodhar.

It was a strange feeling – to owe a debt of loyalty to so many. But they were willing to die for him, and he was willing to do the same in return. If his father had taught him anything, it was to protect your own; and he would. The people of The Glade never stood alone, and nor did they allow others to do so.

As Calen looked out at the clearing, six figures pulled away from the others and approached: Dann, Tarmon, Lyrei, Ingvat, Narthil, and Harken Holdark.

The elf, Narthil, was the first to speak. Calen had not spent much time with him before the attack on the city – Haem had selected the captains – but in the past few days, Narthil had proven himself more than capable, if a little rigid.

"Draleid," he said, bowing slightly towards Calen before inclining his head to Vaeril. "Narvír."

Commander.

"Two hundred and eighty-three casualties. One hundred and seventy-two elves, one hundred and nine humans, two Angan," Narthil said matter-of-factly.

"Just the count, Narthil." Calen's tone was sharp, sharper than he'd intended, but he gave no apologies. He knew the elf meant nothing by it, but after everything that had happened, they could not afford to see the differences between them. They needed to stay united. It was humans who had burned this woodland. Humans who had attacked Aravell. It would be all too easy for those facts to take root in elven minds.

Narthil gave a slight nod before continuing. "Two hundred and eighty-three casualties. By our count, at least six Bloodmarked are dead and over one hundred Uraks along with all Lorian soldiers. Despite the Urak ambush, the pursuit was successful."

"Tell that to our dead." Dann's eyes were fixed on the ground, his arms folded, jaw clenched. "I'm sure they'd disagree."

Calen allowed his gaze to linger on Dann. "Where are Atara and Aelmar?"

"They took fifty soldiers to scout the area for stragglers." Harken stepped forwards. The Rakina towered over the others, his face and hands still smeared in blood, his long hair tied in a braid that fell over his shoulder and down to his hip. The man had thrown himself into the thick of the fighting, and the soldiers had rallied around him. "They will follow us to Aravell. The Uraks grow bolder, Calen. And if the past is any indication of the future, they will continue to do so as the Blood Moon waxes. We should pull our forces back, closer to the city, where the remaining Nithrandír stand guard. We were lucky. Had their numbers been greater, we would not be standing here drawing breath."

Calen nodded. "We'll discuss it with the others. For now, we need to move."

THE THRUM OF THE SPARK in the air reached Calen before the southern gates of Aravell came into view, like lightning crackling over his skin. The Craftsmages had begun the city's repairs a few days prior, though with the chaos that had followed the attack, progress had been slow.

Calen's heart ached as he once again set eyes upon the devastation that had been wrought on the ethereal city. Shattered veins of glowing erinian stone glittered like fragments of broken stars strewn across the crater-filled courtyard that fronted the gates. Uprooted trees as tall as towers lay amidst chunks of wall and cliff that had been broken free by the Lorian mages. At the very least, the bodies had been cleared, the elves prepared for the ceremony, the Lorians fed to the forest.

The repairs to the courtyard may have been neglected in favour of higher priorities within the city, but the enormous white gates that had been blown apart during the attack were now resurrected, and several watchtowers of white stone now stood about the courtyard's perimeter.

As Calen and the others led the column of warriors across the rubble, the Highguard who patrolled the yard in their silver plate all stood to attention. Each bowed their heads, whispering 'Draleid' and tapping the butts off their glaives against the stone as Calen passed.

At any other time, Calen would have expected Dann to make a smart remark about it, but Dann had been different since the attack, quieter, more withdrawn. Alea and Baldon's deaths had hit Dann hard. He had grown close to them both. Calen wished he knew what to say, but it had always been Dann who'd comforted *him*. Rist would have known what to say; Rist always knew what to say. He might have taken a bit longer to say it, more time thinking and weighing each word, but in the end, Calen could scarcely think of a time when Rist hadn't been proven right... eventually.

The simple thought of Rist set a pang of guilt in Calen that manifested as a tangible ache in his chest. With each day that passed, the hope that Rist was alive withered; not that it had been a large hope to begin with. Calen grabbed hold of the guilt, shoved it down into the dark abyss of his mind where he kept all the things that clawed at him, and kept walking.

In truth, he feared the moment he stopped and dwelled on the things he couldn't change would be the moment they swallowed him whole.

Once they passed through the gates, Harken, Narthil, and Ingvat led the warriors to the makeshift barracks that Queen Uthrían had gifted them in the eastern section of the city. Meanwhile, Calen and the others carried on to Alura.

A dark mood hung over the city of Aravell like a dense fog. Thousands had been lost during the attack, ripped apart by the Spark and steel, crushed beneath falling rubble, butchered by the dark spirits of the Aldithmar, burned alive in dragonfire. The loss of life was at a scale Calen still struggled to comprehend. In The Glade a death was a significant event. The mourning of the loss and the celebration of the life could carry on for weeks. The entire village ached. One single death. This was thousands upon thousands.

He and the others walked through the city in silence. Aravell's residents flowed around them carrying lanterns and wreaths in their arms as they prepared for the ceremony the following night. Many of them stopped in their tracks and bowed their heads at Calen's approach. The elves of Aravell had treated Calen with respect from the first moment he'd stepped foot within the walls, but since he and Valerys had fought in the skies over the city, that regard had only grown. They had all lost so much, and yet still they stopped, still they bowed their heads and whispered 'Draleid'.

Calen tried to be grateful, but the truth was he felt only guilt. Simply by his presence he was forcing these elves, bound by their honour, to halt their grieving and acknowledge him. The thought made him sick. All he wanted was to let the shadows swallow him whole. Instead, he stopped and bowed his head in return to each and every soul that passed.

As they moved through the city, Dann, Lyrei, Tarmon, and Vaeril each mirrored Calen, not one grumbling at the slow pace they set.

"You do them a great honour," Vaeril whispered in Calen's ear. "It will not be forgotten."

"I know what it is to lose the ones you love," Calen answered as he inclined his head to an elven woman holding the hand of a small child. "It's they who honour me. I brought the death here. They suffered its wrath… because of me."

Vaeril grabbed hold of Calen's arm, locking their gazes. "This was always coming. The empire was never going to leave us here, and neither were we going to stay put. This is known. It has been accepted for a long time. You were not the cause, but on the night the Dragonguard flew over this city, you rose to meet them."

Calen sighed through his nostrils, giving Vaeril the faintest of nods before pulling his arm free and carrying on. He understood Vaeril's words, but they brought him no comfort.

Eventually, the crowds thinned and Calen and the others made their way through the city and across the bridge that separated Aravell from Alura.

Calen stopped at the archway that led into Alura while the others carried on, not noticing he'd lagged behind.

In his moment of solitude, Calen looked up at the words carved into the rock. He swallowed, his hand resting on the coin pommel of the sword at his hip.

"Draleid n'aldryr, Rakina nai dauva. Ikin vir vänta. Ikin vir alura. Marai viel alanín til ata ilynír abur er kerta." Calen whispered the words, as he had done the first time he'd read them. Now, though, with all he had seen, they held new meaning.

Dragonbound by fire, Broken by death. Here we wait. Here we rest. Until we are called to make whole what is half.

The first time he'd read those words, he'd seen them as a resignation: 'This is where we rest until we can finally die.'

But when Ithrax and the other dragons had sacrificed themselves to save Calen and Valerys, they had shown him how wrong he'd been. It wasn't a resignation. It was a proclamation: 'We will fight until our dying breath. We will not be bowed. We will not yield.'

They were guardians until their last.

A deep sorrow flooded into Calen's mind from Valerys's, so powerful it brought tears to his eyes. There were so few dragons left in the world. And, somehow, finding that Valerys wasn't alone, only to lose so many more, cut far deeper than if they had never known at all.

"Calen?" Dann walked back through the archway, concern in his voice. "What's wrong?"

"Nothing."

Dann followed Calen's gaze to the words etched into the stone, his expression softening. "Therin told me what that means."

Calen pulled his stare from the words and looked at Dann. Tear drops still rolled over his chin as his lips curled into a brittle smile.

"I've got some of those jugs of whatever the elves think passes for mead stashed away in my room," Dann said, the smile on his lips brittle. "How about tonight we sit in the Eyrie with Valerys and get piss drunk? I'll have a bit too much, and you'll have to stop me from wandering off the edge."

"That sounds… perfect." Once again, there Dann was when Calen needed him. Despite his own loss, despite his own grief, Dann was always there. "Dann, I…"

Calen searched for the words, but Dann shook his head.

"No." Dann swallowed hard, his lips contorting, the half-smile fading. The pain in his eyes twisted Calen's heart. "Not now. Later. I'm not drunk enough for the sappy shit."

A STRANGE SENSE OF RELIEF swept over Calen as he stepped from the archway and onto the platform that overlooked Alura, taking in the structures of white stone blending into the rock face that swept outwards in a circle and sloped towards the enormous courtyard at the bottom.

Bodies moved to and fro across the many bridges and along the grass paths that wound their way around the spark-carved basin within which Alura was built. Even from that distance, in the courtyard a hundred or so feet below, Calen recognised Thacia's blood-red hair and bluish skin. The Jotnar sat with her legs crossed by the trees on the central platform, a clutch of others around her, the hulking frame of Asius at her side.

Across the way, eight spark-wrought homes of pure white were set into a massive alcove at the back of the enormous plateau the elven Craftsmages had created when Calen and the others had first reached Aravell. Each home rose several storeys and flowed naturally into the rock face as though part of the mountain itself. In one of those homes, Ella lay still, Faenir watching over her, as he had done since the day she'd collapsed.

The elves of Aravell had bowed to Calen and paid him respect as though he and he alone had saved them from death. But it was Ella who had sacrificed herself to save them. Ella who had paid the price. It was she who deserved their thanks, not him.

Calen had never really given her the credit, but when Haem had not returned from Ölm Forest, his sister had watched over him like a mother hen. She had been the anchor that had stopped him floating adrift, the guiding hand that had kept him on course. She had done so with the combination of mockery and love only a sister could give, but still, she had been there.

As Calen and the others made their way along one of the paths towards the plateau, they passed the Healer, Kiko Sander, leaning against the white wall of one of the homes, her palms pressed against her knees. The mage lifted her gaze, her eyes tired as she smiled at Calen and the others, sweat slicking her needle-straight hair to her head. Before she could say anything, another of the northern rebels, Loura, burst from the doorway in a fluster.

Calen didn't catch any of the words that passed between them, but the smile vanished from Kiko's lips and the pair darted back inside without a word.

"I should go help." Vaeril looked from Calen to the doorway. "We're losing more injured every day. The infirmaries are full. My people's Healers can't keep up. Kiko hasn't slept."

"Go," Calen said, nodding towards the house. "And Vaeril."

The elf raised a curious eyebrow.

"Don't overextend yourself." Calen hesitated. "You can't save everyone."

The words were as much for himself as they were for Vaeril.

Vaeril's mouth stretched into a grim line, but he gave Calen a nod before setting off into the house.

"Aeson and the others are back then," Tarmon said as they reached the plateau. He gestured towards where Surin sat on a low bench before the leftmost home. The Craftsmage had been one of the captains sent with Aeson and Erik to clear the northern wood of Lorian remnants while Calen and the others took forces to clear the south.

As soon as Surin saw Calen and the others, she rose, patting her robes down and collecting herself before approaching and regaling Calen with a full account of what had happened with Aeson and the forces sent to the northern wood. Calen cared little for what came after the words 'no casualties', but he let Surin continue.

"Thank you, Surin. It's good to hear nobody was lost."

Appearing to sense Calen's desire to press onwards, Surin bowed deeply. "On your leave, Warden."

The woman turned, picked up a journal and pen she'd left on the bench, and stepped inside the house.

"The Warden of Varyn," Tarmon said, giving a downturn of his lip. "It's a powerful title."

"Hmm." Calen shook his head. Surin, Ingvat, and the other rebels from Berona had taken to the name over the past months, but in the wake of the battle, it seemed to be spreading.

"Whether you like it or not, let them have it. Legends are powerful. Not just for those who fight at our side, but for those who would stand against us. Fear wins more battles than steel. And fighting against the Warden of Varyn, who rides into battle on dragonback, could strike fear into the hearts of many."

The thought didn't comfort Calen.

"I feel a new poem coming on," Dann said, stroking his chin. "The Warden of Varyn, his name is not Karin. He—Argh!"

A swift slap to the back of his head from Tarmon cut Dann short.

"What was that for?"

Tarmon raised an eyebrow and folded his arms. "Hmm."

"You're just jealous of how quickly I found a word to rhyme with Varyn."

"Marin."

"Well, you've had some time to—"

"Barren, heron, faren, zarin."

"That last one's not even a word."

"It means 'gold' in Ardanian."

"Since when do you speak Ardanian? You can barely speak the Common Tongue."

"I'm going to check on Ella," Calen said, cutting across Dann and Tarmon.

The mood changed at the mention of Ella's name, and the emerging smiles on Dann and Tarmon's faces melted away. Even Lyrei shifted uncomfortably, meeting Calen's gaze for a fleeting moment.

Tarmon gave a sombre nod. "I'll check on Valerys, make sure he's fed and looked after, and get a briefing from Erik. I'll find you in the Eyrie later. I heard Dann say something about mead." He grasped Calen's forearm, staring into his eyes for a long moment. "Suffering alone serves no one. Remember that."

As Tarmon left, Dann leaned in closer. "Do you want me to come?"

Calen shook his head.

"Well, that's awkward because the mead is in my room… which is in that house… because that's where we sleep."

Calen shook his head and pulled Dann into an embrace, their armour clinking as he squeezed him tight. Calen's breath caught in his chest, a sudden wave of sadness washing over him. "I'm not sure what I'd do without you."

"My clothes are in there too. I can't walk around in this armour all day." A smile spread across Dann's face, and he grasped Calen's shoulders. "Go. Lyrei and I will see if we can find us some more mead, keep the supply in my room for a rainy day." He looked down at the white dragon on his breastplate. "I'm pretty sure I'll get a better price with this on anyway."

As Dann made to leave, he turned once more and met Calen's stare. "She'll be all right, Calen. Ella's just like you. All of you Bryers. You're harder to get rid of than weeds."

Calen nodded in return, barely managing to muster a brittle smile as Dann and Lyrei made their way back up towards the archway that led to the main city.

Finally alone, Calen turned towards the tall white building that he supposed was now his 'home', though he didn't think he could ever truly see it that way. His home was The Glade, as it always had been. He felt the touch of Valerys's mind from where the dragon rested in the Eyrie and opened himself to it.

Warmth spread through him, filling his bones and soothing the aches in his muscles. But more significant than anything was the way Valerys's soul filled the gaps in Calen's; it made him whole and complete and left him wondering how he had ever existed before the bond.

I'll come to you as soon as I've checked on Ella.

Calen could feel Valerys shifting in place at the thought of Ella. Concern and worry seeped from the dragon's mind. Valerys's injuries from the battle had left him unable to leave the Eyrie without assistance, and with his size, the Healers could only do so much at once. Even still, Valerys's only thoughts had been of Ella – of his family.

Calen had barely opened the door when the warm aroma of braised lamb flooded his nostrils. Somehow, that familiar scent, that smell of home, pulled the fear and anxiety from his bones and at the same time set a deep sense of loss and longing in his heart. He closed his eyes for just a moment, picking out the rosemary, the thyme, the roasted tomatoes. It was as though, all of a sudden, he was back in The Glade, his mam standing over a cast iron pot, cooking a meal to warm their bellies.

That moment of comfort – of warmth – was followed by tears welling in his eyes.

"My sweet boy."

Calen snapped open his eyes, hearing the sound of his mother's voice. But it wasn't his mam he found himself staring at, it was Elia Havel.

Rist's mam rested her fingers against the side of Calen's cheek and brushed away the budding tears with her thumb as delicately as though he were made of paper. Grey still streaked her hair, exhaustion still carved dark wells under her eyes, and she still looked as though she weighed little more than a child, but the joyful, bright woman that Calen had always known was slowly returning.

"Come," Elia said, pulling her hand away and gesturing for Calen to follow. Unlit candles sat in small alcoves all about the walls, crimson-touched moonlight drifting in through the windows while the fireplace set into the wall on the other side of the room roared. A long wooden table abutted the wall to Calen's right, stretching halfway into the room, sturdy chairs lining its length on both sides. Elia rounded the table and stood by an enormous cast iron cookpot suspended over the fire. She grabbed a thick cloth and lifted the pot's lid, drawing in a long breath through her nose.

"I've tried for years to braise lamb like your mother. Never quite succeeded. I—" Elia's head twitched to the left, and a shiver spread through her shoulders and back; a remnant of her time beneath Berona. Tarmon said he'd seen it in many a warrior, their bodies reliving trauma long past. Some learned to suppress it, others never did. Elia drew a slow breath and shook her head. "I thought it might put a bit of warmth in you."

"It smells just like how she made it." Calen moved beside Elia, letting the scents of the lamb fill his nostrils. "Thank you."

Calen stared down into the massive pot, watching the bubbles form and burst, the oils swirling in the juice. He reached for the ladle and received a firm slap on his wrist.

Elia raised her eyebrows and pursed her lips, daring Calen to try a second time.

Calen laughed, but that laughter faded as he thought of Ella. "How is she?"

Elia sighed and rested her frail fingers on Calen's pauldron. "No change. Tanner is with her now. He's been by her side since you left – him and Yana. Why don't you go up and tell him to have some food and a rest. I'll bring some lamb up when it's done. It's still missing something."

Calen nodded, finding his words caught in his throat. He made for the stairs, but Elia called him once more.

"Oh, and Calen."

Calen raised an eyebrow, turning back.

"Take your armour off and bathe before you go to your sister. You're covered in blood."

CHAPTER TWO

A WORLD BETWEEN

5th Day of the Blood Moon

Aravell – Winter, Year 3081 After Doom

Calen paused at the door to Ella's room, the handle cold against fingers still warm from the bath. He'd only bathed long enough to scrub the blood and dirt from his skin and hair. He could still see dried crimson beneath his nails. No amount of scrubbing would ever truly leave him clean.

The smell of lavender stopped him in his tracks as he entered. That scent always reminded him of home. Sure enough, sprigs of lavender sat in a terracotta vase upon a small table to the left of the door. Calen had no doubt Elia had left it there. Despite everything she'd been through, everything she'd suffered, all she ever seemed to do was care for others. He supposed it was a motherly thing, though he'd known some that hadn't shared the trait.

Tanner Fjorn – who sat in a tall chair by Ella's bed with his legs outstretched and his arms folded – lifted his head.

Calen found it hard to look at the man and not see Rhett's face. They were so similar they could have been father and son instead of uncle and nephew; the same jet-black hair, the same broad shoulders, the same look in their eyes as though they'd known you their whole life.

Aside from Tanner, the enormous mound of fur and muscle that was Faenir lay curled into a ball at the foot of Ella's bed, his snout resting on his paws.

The wolfpine lifted his head, a soft whine sounding in his throat as Calen approached.

"Calen." Tanner straightened himself in the chair, smiling softly and unfolding his arms as he stood and grasped Calen's forearm. His eyes were bloodshot and ringed with purple. "How did it go?"

"We were ambushed." Calen reached out as he spoke, scratching at the side of Faenir's head, the rough hairs of the wolfpine's outer coat bristling against his skin. He forced himself to look down at Ella, taking her hand in his and running his thumb across her knuckles. "Uraks. They must have come down from the Lodhar Mountains."

"Did we lose many?"

"Almost three hundred." He squeezed Ella's hand gently. "With the glamour gone, the Blood Moon in the sky, and so much of the Darkwood burning, they're testing their limits. The Nithrandír should hold them back from the city."

"This is it then," Tanner said, folding his arms.

"This is what?"

"The North is burning. The Darkwood is burning. The southern provinces are in rebellion. The Blood Moon has come again. We now stand in the heart of this Age's great war."

Calen sighed, looking down at Ella. "It's not like the stories."

"Nothing is ever like the stories. If the stories told the truth, people would never pick up swords."

A moment of silence passed between the two men, broken by Calen. "Where is Aneera?"

Tanner nodded over Calen's shoulder to the back of the room behind the door. "She's been like that since the sun rose."

Aneera sat on the ground with her long, fur-covered legs folded beneath her, eyes closed and clawed hands resting on her knees. At first, Calen couldn't understand how he hadn't noticed her there, but the Angan were like shadows when they wanted to be.

The last time Calen had seen Aneera, she had told him she would reach out to others of her kind – and the druids. It had taken Calen more than a second to process that. There were more druids alive. According to the Angan, what happened to Ella was not the first instance of such a thing. And there were those who may be capable of bringing her back to the waking world.

Calen allowed his gaze to linger on Aneera a moment before turning back to Tanner. "Elia says you're to go down for some food and rest. I'll stay."

For a moment, Tanner looked as though he was going to argue, but instead he gave a short nod.

"And Tanner."

"Hmm?"

"Thank you."

"Rhett was my family," Tanner said, resting his hand on Calen's shoulder. "He loved her fiercely, and I can see why. That makes her family too. Your sister has a fire in her, Calen. When she decided to come find you, there was no stopping her." Tanner squeezed Calen's shoulder. "She will find a way back."

Tanner let out a soft sigh, then stepped from the room.

With Tanner gone, Calen dropped himself into the chair beside the bed. The closer he looked at his sister, the more the worry gnawed at him from the inside out. Beneath her shifting lids, he knew her eyes were white from edge to edge.

Before Haem had been forced to return to the knights, he'd told Calen that Aneera had said Ella's mind was fragmented. That it had shattered and split between two worlds: the mortal plane and a place called Níthianelle – the Sea of Spirits. A world between worlds.

Calen had no idea what that meant. All he knew was that he wanted his sister back, he wanted her to be all right. He'd only just gotten her back, and now she was taken from him once more.

He leaned forwards, taking Ella's hand in his. An anger bubbled within – an anger at Haem for leaving him alone again while Ella needed them – but he held it down. Like everything else that seemed to be going on around him, Calen didn't understand Haem's oaths, but he knew the knights had suffered great losses when the Blood Moon had risen. And one thing he did understand was being there for the people who fought at his side. Haem could do more good with them than sitting here by Ella's bedside, twiddling his thumbs. Even still, he prayed to Varyn – or more rightly to Achyron himself – that it would not be long before he set eyes on his brother again.

Letting out an exasperated sigh, Calen lifted Ella's hand and kissed her knuckles. "Please come back to me..."

Darkness.

Everywhere Ella looked, all she saw was unfaltering, unending darkness.

No sounds reached her ears. No scents touched her nose. She was falling. How long had she been falling? For some reason she couldn't remember. She could barely remember anything at all. The passing of time was a blur. An hour might have been a day, might have been a year, might have been little more than a second. She could have been falling for a lifetime or no longer than the blink of an eye.

Her only memory was of panic flooding her, consuming her, yielding to despair in a hazy blur. But now... at that precise moment of awareness, something was different. Something had shifted in the fabric of this place, and she was conscious.

"Please."

The voice echoed endlessly. She couldn't tell if it came from the world around her or from within. All she knew was that she recognised it.

"Come back to me..."

The second time was clearer, the voice stronger, the words resounding.

"Calen?" Ella called out with all the strength in her lungs. It had been her little brother's voice. She was sure of it. "Calen?"

Ella's call echoed as though she stood at the foot of a mountain, a great valley opening before her, but no answer came. And still, she fell.

The darkness was a physical weight on her soul. It pressed down into her, flooded over her, choked her. It threatened to swallow her whole, to devour everything that she was.

Something burned deep inside her, something screaming from her core. No, not screaming. Howling. Clawing. Fighting.

Her jaw twitched, blood burning as the wolf rose within her. A part of her fought it. A part of her called it forth. The wolf was as much a piece of her as the soil was of the earth, and it heard Calen calling just as she did – their family. Their pack. They would not go quietly into the darkness.

Ella closed her eyes, drawing in deep breaths, focusing her mind. As she did, the wolf howled in her blood, growing ever louder, a red mist slipping over her eyes. Her muscles tensed, the cry of the wolf rising to a crescendo until it consumed everything she was. Her skin itched and burned, her blood boiled, her lungs choked.

And then, without warning, the world stopped falling, and Ella found purchase beneath her feet.

Her entire body trembled, chest heaving as she dragged in ragged breaths. Slowing her breathing, she opened her eyes.

Before her, Ella's fingers and hands shimmered with an ethereal white light, wisps of luminescent smoke trailing as she waved her hand back and forth.

"Níthianelle," she whispered. The Sea of Spirits. The world between worlds. She looked down over her body, seeing it glow with the same light, wrought not from flesh, but spirit itself. But why was she there? How was she there?

Ella tried to think back, but everything was a blur. The last thing she remembered was the battle in Aravell. She had shifted with the dragons and flown to help Calen. Memories flitted through her mind: fire, lightning, claws, blood. Everything was jumbled, untethered, unstable. What had happened? Why couldn't she remember? Was Calen all right?

She tried to reach out and feel her body in the waking world, as she had before. But she felt nothing... nothing at all. Panic flared in her heart. Was she dead? Why couldn't she feel her body?

Ella's chest tightened at the thought, her lungs feeling as though her ribs were trying to crush them. Her lungs pulled at the air, but each breath caught in her chest. She had to resist the anxious urge to claw at her skin. She crossed her arms, clasping her shoulders and trying to steady her heartbeat, trying to calm her racing mind.

Ella had only felt like this twice in her life: the day she learned Haem had died, and the day she watched Rhett bleed into the dirt. It was a feeling like no other. Like the world was collapsing and burying her beneath its weight. Like the oceans had risen around her and she kept swallowing water, scrambling to keep her head above the surface.

That was it... She was drowning.

"That's it, Ella," she remembered her mother whispering as they sat on the bed all those years ago when Haem had been taken from them. Ella had lain on her side, curled into a ball, her knees tucked to her chest, her arms wrapped around her legs. She had cried for so long and so hard that her eyes had burned, and her head had pounded with a fury. Even breathing had hurt.

"Listen to my voice. Focus on my words." Freis had moved to lie behind Ella in the bed, gently draping her arm across Ella's shoulder, sheltering her from the world. Ella could still remember the warmth of her mother's breath on the back of her neck, the tenderness of her voice. "You are strong, my girl. We will get through this, together, as we always have."

Even just remembering her mother's voice helped settle Ella's mind, her breaths slowing.

"But he's gone… he's…" Ella's sobbing had smothered her words.

"He is never gone, Ella. Your brother is too stubborn to ever leave us. We might not see him, but he is there, watching over us from Achyron's halls."

Back then, all Ella had seen was her own loss, her own anguish. Her big brother had been ripped from her and she'd never even had the chance to say goodbye. Haem had always protected her and Calen, had always been there whenever they'd needed him. And then, one day, he was gone, and he had left Ella to take his place, to look after Calen. She had been furious, and distraught, and broken, and empty… and just… numb. So many emotions all at once.

It was only now, as she stood in the void of Níthianelle, her memories the only thing keeping her from being swallowed whole, that she realised how strong her mam had been.

Freis had lost a son that day – her eldest son, her firstborn, life created from her own blood. And she had turned her agony inwards so as to protect Ella and Calen from its touch.

"You are not ready… You will not give up."

Those words sent a shiver through Ella. They were not a memory. Her mother had never said that.

Shaking, Ella pulled her hands from her shoulders, watching the white light pulse and wisp as her fingers trembled. "Mam?"

"You will not give up."

The words were spoken in a whisper, and yet they echoed, moving around Ella as though resounding off walls.

Ella's mouth grew dry, her heartbeat slowing to methodical hammering thumps. She spun, seeing only emptiness wherever she turned, a never-ending sea of black. The last time she had entered Níthianelle, she had been able to sense the souls of all the animals around her, been able to feel the essence of the world. Now, she felt and saw nothing.

"Mam?" Ella roared, lungs burning, eyes stinging. "Where are you?"

"No daughter of mine…"

It was her mother's voice, of that Ella had no doubt.

"No daughter of mine lets the world control her." The voice grew clearer, firmer. "You are strong, Ella. Just as you were then, you are now. You are strong."

Ella continued to turn, searching the ocean of black and finding nothing. She let her voice drop to a whimper. "I don't want to be alone…"

"You will never be alone."

"Mam… what am I?"

The wolf howled in Ella's blood as she asked the question, scratching at the back of her mind. She looked down to see claws lengthening from her fingernails, forged from white light.

"What am I?" she whispered again.

"You are a Blooddancer. A guardian of the gods."

Ella's heart stopped, the hairs on her arms and neck pricking. Those words had not echoed, not resounded in her mind like a ghostly whisper. They had been spoken aloud. They had come from behind her.

Ella turned slowly. "Mam?"

Calen jolted awake to the sound of Ella screaming at the top of her lungs.

"Mam!" Ella was writhing in the corner of the bed, her eyes open, white as clouds. Faenir stood over her, hackles raised, snout crinkled in a snarl.

"Ella!" Calen threw himself forwards from the chair, his knees cracking against the floor, the pain dulled by worry. He reached for Ella but yanked back his hands as Faenir snapped at him.

A deep rumble resounded in the wolfpine's throat, golden eyes shimmering as he stared at Calen.

"Faenir…" Calen swallowed hard, reaching out tentatively, his gaze flickering from Faenir to Ella – who now convulsed at the edge of the bed against the wall. "It's me."

Calen stared into Faenir's eyes, the eyes of the creature who had been everpresent in his life over the past five years. But something was different, something had shifted in the wolfpine. The way he stood over Ella, the way he protected her. Faenir would kill anyone or anything who dared to come near Ella.

In the back of Calen's mind, Valerys roared. Pain seared through the dragon as he cracked his wings, trying to lift himself into the air. Calen urged Valerys to stay in the Eyrie, but doing so was like trying to stop a hurricane with his bare hands. He could feel the dragon's talons raking the earth, wounds cracking and bleeding as he attempted to haul himself airborne. Valerys's rage seeped into Calen, but Calen pushed back against it, his stare flickering between Faenir and Ella.

The door swung open behind Calen, bouncing off the wall with a crack. Footsteps charged in, voices shouting and calling.

Yana Veradis – Tanner's partner – was the first to Calen's side, her eyes wide with panic, her arms spread. "Ella!" she roared, looking from Calen to Ella to Faenir. She grabbed Calen's arm. "What happened?"

Lasch and Elia Havel followed after Yana, Tanner just behind them.

"I don't know." Calen stared into Faenir's golden eyes as he spoke. "I fell asleep—"

"You fell asleep?" Yana pulled at Calen, cold fury in her eyes. "How could you fall asleep?"

"Yana." Tanner placed a hand on Yana's shoulder, but she swiped it away and pulled at Calen once more.

"How could you—"

"This isn't about me." Calen cut Yana short, his voice like steel. "Or you."

The woman's mouth hung open, but she didn't speak. Calen turned back to Ella and Faenir. Ella had stopped writhing and now lay still and slumped in the corner, her eyes closed.

Faenir stood tall over her, his head bowed, hackles still raised, teeth still bared.

Beside Calen, Lasch Havel had taken a few steps forward and opened his arms with his palms out. "It's all right, boy. Easy."

Calen moved to stop Lasch from getting any closer, but the man moved past him and stared into Faenir's eyes.

"Easy now. We need to make sure she's all right." Lasch's words held a calm and level tone, as though he were speaking to a child and not a wolfpine that could rip him limb from limb. "All we want is to keep her safe."

Calen inched closer, his pulse pounding. But then, as though the air had suddenly changed, Faenir lifted his head, his eyes softening, his snarl fading. The wolfpine whimpered and leaned forwards, pressing his snout into Calen's open hand.

Calen closed the distance to Faenir in a heartbeat, pulling the wolfpine's head to his chest and scratching at the back of Faenir's skull. He looked past Faenir at Ella.

Yana, Elia, and Tanner rushed past Calen and fussed over Ella, checking her for injuries and pulling her lids back to peer into her milky-white eyes.

With all the care of a mother wolf, Tanner picked Ella up – one arm behind her head, one arm beneath her knees – and placed her back in the centre of the bed, pulling the sheets up to her stomach.

With Faenir still whimpering against his chest, Calen turned his head to look at Aneera.

The Angan sat cross-legged in the same spot, betraying no sign that she had even heard Ella's struggle. Calen prayed to Varyn that she could find a way to bring his sister back.

CHAPTER THREE

STRANGE FRIENDS

5th Day of the Blood Moon

Nithianelle – Winter, Year 3081 After Doom

"Mam." Ella stood in the void of Nithianelle, her voice echoing, her heart fluttering.

The woman that stood before her was not her mam, and what's more, her body wasn't wrought from white light as Ella's was. A luminescent mist drifted from her clothes and skin, pulsing with every movement of her body, but she looked very much flesh and blood.

She was a little shorter than Ella, with a lean frame and dark hair tied into a single thick braid. A heavy leather coat adorned her shoulders, and two axes hung from loops at her belt.

"Who…" Ella subconsciously drifted closer to the woman. Her heart thumped, the panic still clawing at the back of her mind, the darkness closing in around her. "Who are you?"

"My name is Tamzin Aurielle." The woman took a step closer. "I am an Aldruid, a daughter of Kaygan. I've been searching for you."

Ella pulled back reflexively, hackles rising, the wolf bubbling to the surface, her nails hardening to claws. "How did you know to look for me in the first place? How do you even know who I am?" A growl crept into Ella's voice. She trusted nothing in this place. "Answer me."

The corner of Tamzin's mouth twisted upwards, and she raised an open palm. "Calm yourself, Wolfchild. When you fragmented, it sent tremors through this plane, as it always does. I came to you as quickly as I could. Though in truth, I had feared I was too late."

"Fragmented? What does that even mean? How... Why would you come to me? How are you..." Ella gestured at Tamzin, at her clothes, her skin and flesh – her body. Ella had too many questions for her mouth to process. "How are you like that in here? We are in Níthianelle, are we not?"

Tamzin gave a downturn of her lips. "So you do know of this place. Good. That goes some way to explaining how you are still alive." She reached out her hand, that white mist drifting from her fingers. "There is much for you to learn and little time to learn it. We are not safe here. Time itself is your enemy, one amongst many."

In the short time Ella had spent in Níthianelle, she'd never once stopped to consider what dangers the place might hold. Ilyain had spoken to her of the Sea of Spirits, told her what he'd known. But he was not a druid. He only knew what Andras had told him. Ella looked down at Tamzin's hand but didn't take it. She knew nothing of this woman. "Do you know what happened? Why I'm here? Why I can't remember how I got here? Why I can't leave?"

A hint of sadness touched Tamzin's eyes. She shook her head but kept her hand outstretched. "I don't know what you did to fragment yourself, but I do have some theories. I can help you, but you need to come with me."

"Fragment... Why do you keep saying that word?"

Tamzin reached her hand out further, visibly irritated, the muscles in her jaw clenching. "I will explain, but I need you to come with me."

"And if I don't?"

"Then you will die here. Your body will waste away and wither in the mortal plane while your soul drifts endlessly through the sea. You will lose your sentience and become a wraith, wandering without reason or purpose."

The words sent a shiver through Ella, one that swept over her skin. Another thought set in: she couldn't feel Faenir. The wolfpine had become an extension of her, a piece of her heart, and without him she felt strange and alone. She swallowed hard. "How can I trust you?"

"You can't. But you don't have a choice."

Ella stared back at Tamzin. Even though her body was not her own, her mouth still felt dry, her throat tight. She hated the feeling of being helpless. That was how she had felt when Rhett had died, and it was something she never wanted to feel again. "Does the name 'Andras' mean anything to you?"

Tamzin didn't shift her gaze from Ella's, her hand still lingering in the air. She shook her head. "It does not." She took another step closer. "We need to move."

"He was a druid," Ella continued, ignoring Tamzin's words.

"There are others who may well know his name. If we can repair your mind, I will take you to them, but right now we're out of time. I'm not the only one who felt you fragment, not the only thing looking for you."

The wolf rumbled in the back of Ella's mind, a sense of resignation within it. She didn't trust this woman, but she had little choice. She tried to pull herself back to the waking world, just as Ilyain had said Andras had described: by closing her eyes and willing it so. But nothing happened. The only other time she'd left Níthianelle was when she had shifted with the owl… and that hadn't ended particularly well. Besides, she couldn't sense the spirits now like she had then.

Ella moved forwards, drawing a long breath and rolling back her shoulders. "Where will we go? There is nothing…" She looked around. "Anywhere."

"Your eyes are closed, Wolfchild. I can open them."

It seemed impossible to Ella that her lips could be dry considering they were made of light, but that was exactly how they felt. She nodded slowly, uncertain. The wolf within her bowed its head in acquiescence. "Do it."

Tamzin reached out her hands, looking keenly into Ella's eyes. The woman's nails were strange, thick and tapered to a point, curling slightly, thin scars lining the skin at the centre of her fingertips.

"I am a daughter of Kaygan, one of his guardians." Tamzin's eyes flickered from deep brown to sapphire blue, her pupils stretching to slits. Her nails extended out, the scars on her fingertips opening, claws curling. "This continent hunted our kind to near extinction. Used us as weapons, as tools. But here we are, alive and free. You are not alone anymore, Ella. And you never will be again."

Ella felt the wolf within her whimper, a strange sense of belonging radiating from it.

"Do not be afraid," Tamzin said, a sincerity in her voice. Her pupils widened, rounding and growing larger as she looked at Ella. "Too many of our kind have died from being alone and afraid. We were never meant to be that way."

Ella clenched her jaw and pressed her hands into Tamzin's, wrapping her fingers around the woman's wrists.

"Close your eyes." Tamzin moved closer, the blue in her eyes seeming to shift and change like a raging storm.

Ella did as she was told, nodding more to herself than Tamzin.

"When a mind fragments," Tamzin said, "it loses its grounding, loses its bond even to Níthianelle. Focus on your breathing. Feel your chest expand and contract. Feel the air enter your lungs. Listen to the sound it makes."

Once again, Ella did as Tamzin commanded. The swelling of her lungs rushed in her ears, each breath like thunder against the silence around her.

"Now focus on your heartbeat. Not just how it thumps in your chest, but how each beat sends a pulse through your blood, how it feeds life to your body. Feel it, become conscious of how it flows in your veins."

As Ella followed Tamzin's words, a sense of calm came over her. The panic from earlier was gone. Each breath of air, each beat of her heart, settled her mind.

"Feel my hands on your skin. Feel the touch of my claws."

Ella suddenly became aware of a warmth that flowed from Tamzin's grip, of the sharpness of Tamzin's claws pressing against her skin. It wasn't that she hadn't felt it before, but now it seemed clearer, more tangible.

"Níthianelle has many secrets, Ella, many layers, many truths, and many lies. It is a mirror of the mortal plane, a place where souls are tethered. This realm is as real as anything you've ever known. You are here, just as you are there. It will take many moons and many summers for you to understand the depths of what you can do here, but for now I need you to reach out with your mind, to feel the world around you."

Ella wished people would stop saying that: 'reach out with your mind'. It wouldn't irritate her as much if someone actually explained how to do it. Her mind wasn't a limb. She couldn't extend it like she could her arm.

Letting out a sigh of frustration, Ella attempted to do what she was asked, despite still not quite knowing how. She drew a long breath, then tried to imagine the world around her, the real world, the waking world – the mortal plane.

All she could see were images, memories, things she had witnessed in the past. A dirt road. Plumes of grey smoke wafting from chimneys in The Glade. The white walls and red slate rooves of Midhaven. Calen's face. Rhett's eyes. The lines at the corners of her mam's mouth whenever she laughed.

She stopped for a moment, a lump forming in her throat, but then she pushed forwards.

"Tell me what you feel, what you see."

"Nothing." Ella did little to hide the frustration in her voice.

Tamzin gave a short laugh, her hands pressing a little tighter against Ella's. "You're as iron headed as I was. Let go. Let your mind paint a picture of the world around you. Don't force it, just set it free. Bind yourself to this place, find your feet. Your subconscious knows more than you realise."

Ella sucked in her cheeks and nodded. It was easier said than done, but at least Tamzin had given her some actual instructions this time. Once more, Ella focused on her breathing and the beating of her heart, then looked outward and began to paint.

"There's a forest," she said after a moment, a sense of relief as the tall trees and broad leaves took shape in her mind. "And a stream. It's rushing... I can hear it."

With each piece that slotted into place, each leaf and rock and branch that formed in her mind's eye, Ella's excitement grew.

"Good. What else?"

"A mountain. I can see it through the canopy. And..." Ella allowed her voice to trail off as a doe appeared in her mind's eye, lifting its head from the stream, its eyes watching her. The creature was as it would be in the waking world, its fur white and brown, its nose black, ears pricking up. But just like Tamzin, a glowing white mist drifted from its body.

"What is it?" Tamzin asked, urging Ella to continue.

"A doe... drinking from the stream." Even as the words left Ella's lips, she noticed more creatures trickle into life around her: birds darting among the trees, fish glinting in the river, bees swarming around a hive between two rocks. She didn't just see them, she could feel them, their hearts and their souls.

"Open your eyes, Ella."

For some reason, Ella felt something she hadn't expected: fear. What would happen when she opened her eyes? What if nothing had changed and she was once again left floating in the vast emptiness.

Her pulse quickened.

"You're not alone." Tamzin squeezed Ella's hands, repeating herself. "Open your eyes."

Ella let out a long breath, feeling the wolf prowling in the back of her mind, rumbling in her blood. Whatever darkness they faced, they would face it together.

Ella opened her eyes. The darkness was gone, the emptiness eviscerated. Everything she had seen in her mind now stood before her. Both she and Tamzin were in an open forest with towering broad-leafed trees and a stream that rushed past behind them. The doe still stood by the water, its eyes fixed on her, two fawns at its side.

The world was not as it had been in the mortal plane, though. Pearly white mist drifted from every surface, light shifting as the leaves rustled and the water flowed.

"What is this?" Ella looked to Tamzin, finding the druid's pupils now dominated the whites of her eyes. Ella's gaze fell on her own hands, which still gripped firmly onto Tamzin's wrists. The light that had comprised her body was now flesh, the same white mist wafting from her skin. "Even before, it was never like this. How?"

Tamzin's lips curled into a broad smile, revealing two pairs of long fangs among her top and bottom teeth. "Like I said, this place holds more secrets than you could begin to imagine. Your eyes were closed, now they are not. Now, come with me. We must find somewhere safe. Then I will answer your questions."

Ella made to step after Tamzin, then hesitated. "Why?"

"Why what?"

"Why are you helping me?"

"Because I've been you. Now come."

ELLA FOLLOWED TAMZIN THROUGH THE woodland for hours. Every tree, every branch, every blade of grass moved with that same ethereal glow. The ground beneath her feet was as solid as anything, the bark of the trees felt as it should – rough and harsh. Even the wind felt right as it swept Ella's hair back. It was the same as the world she knew, and yet it was not.

Not a moment passed where she wasn't aware she walked through the Sea of Spirits. Every creature radiated their emotions and thoughts.

She could feel the single-minded determination of the spider weaving its web, the hunger of the young fox, the contentment of the kat curled in the high branches of a nearby tree. And at times, she felt darker things… eyes watching her, hungry and wanting. She thought she saw dark shapes floating amidst the trees, shifting and twisting like clouds of black smoke, their faces almost human. But as soon as she saw them, they weere gone.

"This is not the Níthianelle I know," Ella said, feeling the waxy texture of a leaf as she ran her fingers along its surface. "Before, all I could sense were the animals. They were nothing more than lights, spheres of energy. Is any of it real?"

"Oh, it's real," Tamzin said, springing onto the trunk of a fallen tree. She reached back and extended a hand to Ella, heaving her up and onto the trunk before dropping down on the other side. "Your eyes are simply open wider now than they were before. This is a reflection of the mortal plane."

Ella jumped from the trunk, landing with a thud, her feet pressing into the soft earth. "I can sense things I couldn't before… things that send a chill through me. They're—"

"Wraiths," Tamzin said before Ella could finish. "Those who were lost here, their souls doomed to wander endlessly. Some simply drift… others hunger." Tamzin pointed to the base of an enormous tree with gnarled roots that lifted from the ground. "We will rest here. We've moved far enough. Tiredness affects you here just as it does in the mortal plane, though you won't have to worry about food."

The woman turned and leaned against one of the thick roots, folding her arms and fixing her gaze on Ella. She pointed towards a rock nestled near the tree's base. "Sit."

"I'm fine standing."

"Suit yourself." Tamzin bit at her lip with a fang, drawing a long breath through her nose and exhaling slowly. "So, you've entered Níthianelle before?"

Ella nodded. "The first time, I shifted with an owl. Its ribs were crushed and I…"

"You died. That's a rough first time, but you were lucky."

"I didn't feel lucky."

"This isn't a game," Tamzin said, gesturing at the world around her. "If you shift with a creature's soul and that creature dies in the mortal plane, it can harrow you, it can scar you, but it won't kill you. But if your soul dies in here, your physical body will waste and wither like a hollow shell left to rot, your soul cut adrift, unable to sense or feel or touch. Time unending. There is no worse fate. Many of our kind have met their end this way. Without a guide, without someone to teach you, Níthianelle is the most dangerous place in existence."

Tamzin looked towards the sky, then dropped to the ground, folding her legs beneath her in a single smooth motion. She gestured for Ella to sit across from her. This time, Ella obliged.

"What do you know of what you are?"

Ella looked at the dirt, shaking her head absently. "Nothing. Not truly. Until recently, all I'd heard of druids were stories. I still don't know if that's what I am, but—"

"It is." Tamzin leaned across and rested her hand on Ella's knee. "You are what our kind call a Blooddancer. A druid of the warrior blood. In millennia past, we were the guardians of the gods – Fenryr, Kaygan, Dvalin, Bjorna, Vethnir… There were more once upon a time, so many more. And as our gods died, so did we." She squeezed Ella's knee. "You are a druid. Simply proved by the fact that you are here. But even if that were not so, I can feel it in your soul."

She leaned back, once more staring up towards the canopy with a broad smile on her face. "There is so much to teach you. So much about our people, our history, our gods. It's been many years since we've found new blood." She opened her palms. "Where to start?"

"You can start with what happened to me and who else is looking for me."

Tamzin nodded. She pressed her two hands together, leaning forward and resting her chin on her index fingers. After a moment of silence, she lowered her hands. "Your mind was fragmented. Split and shattered. It is something that happens to young Aldruids who run before they can walk or older ones whose arrogance outweighs their ability. You pushed yourself too hard, and now… now the tether between your body in the mortal plane and your soul in Níthianelle has been torn."

That familiar drowning feeling washed over Ella, her lungs struggling to draw breath, her heartbeat faltering. "What does that even mean?"

"What's the last thing you remember before this place."

"The battle…"

"What battle? Where?"

Ella hesitated for a moment. "In the Darkwood. The Lorians were attacking the city." Ella's hands shook, and her voice trembled. "Calen needed me. He was going to die… I had to do something…"

Tamzin leaned forwards once more, clutching Ella's hands between hers and looking into her eyes. "Ella, I need you to breathe slow. Look at me. Look into my eyes." She slowed her voice, emphasising each word. "What did you do?"

"Calen needed me…" Ella repeated, staring into the whirling blue of Tamzin's eyes, black slits staring back. "The dragons… I could feel them. I could feel the hollowness in their hearts. They were missing pieces. They wanted to fight. Every piece of them wanted to, but they couldn't. It was like they were frozen. Afraid, alone, filled with rage…"

"You shifted with a dragon?"

The shock in Tamzin's voice set a panic in Ella. "Five."

"That's not possible…" Tamzin let go of Ella's hands and leaned back, staring at Ella as though she were Efialtír himself. "Even just one would have ripped your mind to pieces."

In that moment, Ella realised how truly foolish she had been. She did not understand anything about Níthianelle, about her abilities, about who she was. She had reached into those dragons' minds without understanding anything.

"Not even in the legends passed down have I heard of an Aldruid shifting with a dragon. There are tales of people who tried and of how the dragon's spirit tore them apart. It's no wonder you were fragmented…" She leaned forwards, eyes wide, curiosity in her voice. "How… how did it feel?"

"Terrifying." Ella thought back to that moment. "They were broken somehow, damaged. They held so much sadness in their hearts it almost broke me too. But when they let me in, when our souls were joined, it was as though together we were almost whole. Not quite, but almost."

"Incredible." Tamzin stared at Ella, shaking her head, her shoulders slumping.

Ella thought back, remembering how it had felt when her mind had connected with those of the dragons. How she had seen through all their eyes at once, how she had felt the power in their muscles, the beating of their wings.

Memories flooded back. Dragons crashing against dragons. She remembered burying her talons into a dragon with shimmering silver scales, smashing its skull into the side of a cliff, ripping it to pieces, the smell of ash and char filling her nostrils, the iron tang of blood on her tongue. Then she remembered dying, again and again and again.

"I felt them die," she whispered, just loud enough for Tamzin to hear. "Each one was like a bone snapping, like a shard of me splintering."

Tamzin nodded slowly. "That's how it happened. When a Blooddancer shifts and experiences too much trauma before they're capable of handling it, their mind fragments and cracks. When that happens, their soul is sheared free from their body, connected by only the loosest of threads. You didn't just run before you could walk, you flew."

"How do I… How do I fix it?"

"Most druids who fragment can never centre themselves. You did. You brought yourself back, stopped your soul from drifting endlessly. That's a start."

"I heard my brother calling to me."

"We can re-tether you," Tamzin said, leaning forwards. "But we must get you back to Níthianelle's counterpoint of where your body rests in the mortal plane. We can move much faster here. The distances are… different. But the Darkwood is still almost a week's march."

"A week? Where are we?"

"When I found you, your soul was drifting. We are about thirty miles east of Elmnest in Varsund – or at least its counterpoint. I will not be able to stay here. Even with Kerith guarding me, I will have to return to eat and drink."

"What about me?"

"If you are still alive, that means there is someone tending to your body, likely a mage sustaining you with the Spark. But eventually your body will give out."

"And what about leaving me alone here? You said there are people looking for me? Things looking for me?"

"So long as we keep moving, you'll be all right. I promise, Ella, I'll get you back."

The next question was one Ella had been waiting to ask. One she had held back until Tamzin had answered the others. "How do you know my name?"

Tamzin's pupils sharpened to thin lines, her body tensing.

That was all Ella needed. She lunged forwards, calling to the wolf in her blood. It answered with a howl as she slammed into Tamzin and pressed the woman down into the dirt, wisps of glowing white mist whooshing into the air. She wrapped a hand around Tamzin's neck, her clawed nails pressing into the soft flesh, luminous white blood trickling. Tamzin just lay there, still as a board, eyes fixed on Ella.

"I never told you my name," Ella growled, her voice low, the wolf snapping in the back of her mind. "Who are you, really? And who is looking for me? Remember, if you die here, your body dies there."

"You truly are of Fenryr's blood," Tamzin said, dragging in a ragged breath through the pressure of Ella's hand. "I did not lie to you. My name is Tamzin Aurielle. I am a Blooddancer of Kaygan. I was born in Carvahon thirty-four summers past, just outside Vaerleon. My druidic blood ignited when I was eleven. When your mind fragmented, it sent a pulse through this place. I was sent to come and find you – to save you if I could. With each passing year, our bloodlines grow thinner. There are so few of us already. If our kind is to survive, we must find each other. We must stand together."

"Who sent you?" Ella leaned in, coming nose to nose with the woman, her top lip pulling up in a reflexive snarl, baring her teeth.

Tamzin stretched her neck out, her pupils shifting from thin to round, but she made no attempt to free herself. "There are some who never lost the old ways, who can trace their lineage for thousands of years, back to Terroncia and when the gods walked freely amongst us. They took me in on my fifteenth summer. They are rebuilding, readying for when the Lorian Empire falls. That is who sent me. I speak no lie. But we are not the only ones. There are others. Zealots of Bjorna still clinging to the old wars, purists who would see the other gods dead – see us dead. Vethnir Hunters and factions who would kill you just because I got to you first. And then there are those who would have us hide who we are until time itself crumbled."

Ella loosened her grip, not much but just enough to allow Tamzin to breathe more comfortably. The fact the woman held no fear in her eyes despite Ella's claws being wrapped around her neck was more than a little unsettling. "How do I trust you? How do I know anything you have said is true?"

"Because." Tamzin's lips curled into a half-smile, exposing her fangs. "Like I said already, you have no choice. Sleep well, Ella Bryer. I will return soon. Sleep in the tree, and if something comes for you, run. The wolf in your blood will keep you safe until I get back."

Ella made to speak but instead fell forwards, her hand pressing into the earth as Tamzin evaporated in a mist of white light.

CHAPTER FOUR

IN GODS WE TRUST

5th Day of the Blood Moon

Temple of Achyron – Winter, Year 3081 After Doom

Brother Ormin screamed as Kallinvar laid him on the long stone table at the northern edge of the Heart Chamber. The stone groaned beneath the weight of Ormin in his Sentinel armour, dust falling from the table's joints.

Watcher Gildrick, along with his shadow of a ward, Tallia, and two healers swarmed around Ormin, attempting in vain to hold him down amidst his thrashing.

"We need the armour off." Gildrick checked Ormin's knee, where the plate of the Sentinel armour had been cracked, blood pumping through the gaps. Several other gashes marked the plate at Ormin's shoulder and his left arm. A Soulblade had been used to carve through the otherworldly metal.

"Brother." Kallinvar laid his hand on Ormin's chest, his gauntlet clinking against the metal. "I need you to recall your armour so Gildrick and the healers can see to the wounds. Pain is the path to strength."

Ormin's only answer was a grunt, followed by the man's Sentinel armour flowing over his skin like molten steel and returning to the Sigil marked into his chest.

Brother Gildrick grimaced at the sight of Ormin's shattered knee while Tallia turned and vomited.

"Achyron tests you, brother," Gildrick said, cupping his hand at the side of Ormin's face, forcing the knight to look into his eyes. "Will you rise to his test?"

Ormin clenched his jaw and gave a sharp nod. "Yes, Watcher," he said with a grunt, speaking through gritted teeth.

Kallinvar rested his gauntleted hand on Ormin's bare leg. Snapped bone pierced the skin in several places, pale as snow, torn flesh dangling. With the power of the Sigil flowing through Ormin, and the restorative gifts of Heraya's Well, he would walk again, but the bones needed to first be set.

The two healers poured Altweid Blood into Brother Ormin's open mouth and got to work. The liquid was to pain what water was to fire.

"How is he?" Brother-Captain Gandrid, the knight who took Illarin's place as Captain of The Seventh after he fell at Ilnaen, appeared by Kallinvar's side, Sentinel armour coating his body from the neck down.

"He'll live," Kallinvar said, resting his hand on Gandrid's pauldron. "Torebon?"

"Safe, for now. Six of Efialtír's Chosen bound into bodies of Bloodspawn and more Bloodmarked than I could count. The mages held them at bay, but the city will fall eventually. The Bloodspawn are simply too many, and the light of Efialtír's moon turns those Bloodmarked into demons. And the Chosen… We've never faced anything like this, Grandmaster."

"And yet here we are." Kallinvar kept his tone level, attempting to radiate the same sense of calm that Verathin had always possessed. "Our duty remains unchanged, does it not, brother?"

"Protect the weak," Gandrid said, nodding to himself. "Forgive me, Grandmaster."

"There is nothing to forgive, brother. This path was never meant to be easy. It will test us, push us beyond our limits, and it may even break us. We were given a second chance so that we may protect this world. If our lives are the cost of victory, then so be it. We have already given them."

Gandrid exhaled sharply, then met Kallinvar's gaze. "What news from the North?"

"The Bloodspawn have poured from the Burnt Lands and Mar Dorul, razing Arginwatch and Copperstille. Kingspass still stands, but only just. Lyrin's eyes and ears in the city tell us it will soon fall. The Lorian Empire are on their heels, but this war is far from over. Ilnaen changed everything." Kallinvar hesitated but pushed onwards. "I will summon the knighthood to the great plateau once the others have returned. There is something that must be discussed."

"At your command, Grandmaster."

"You did well, Gandrid. Illarin would be proud."

The man simply nodded, then turned to his wounded knight. It had been Illarin who had been given the honour of granting Gandrid his Sigil over three hundred and fifty years prior. They had been like blood.

With the Altweid Blood taking effect, Ormin's screams faded as Kallinvar made his way to the war table at the centre of the chamber. Four more knights lay about on cots and tables, wounded and broken, healers and Watchers tending them before they could be moved to Heraya's Well.

This had been the way in the days since the Blood Moon had risen. Sixty-three knights still drew breath, almost thirty fewer than before that night.

This war will take everything from us.

"We will avenge them, my child," Achyron's voice echoed in Kallinvar's mind.

"It was you who led them to their slaughter," Kallinvar answered.

"What was that?" Gildrick appeared at Kallinvar's side, wiping blood from his hands with an old cloth.

"Nothing." Kallinvar shook his head, resting his hands on the edge of the war table. Much to Gildrick and the other Watchers' displeasure, he'd had Sister-Captain Arlena rip the table from the floor of the war room and shift it into the larger Heart Chamber. "What news from Poldor and the Watchers?"

"Your description allowed us to locate several old texts. They talk of the Chosen as Efialtír's champions in the realm of the gods – the Vitharnmír. They are the warriors who held the armies of the other gods at bay so Efialtír could cross to this world and plant his seed in the crust of the earth. They also mention the other name you spoke of – the Urithnilim, the Fades. They are lesser souls, servants of the Traitor, created from his shadow, if you would believe it. But the Vitharnmír are more than that. They are demons carved from Efialtír's flesh, empowered by his soul, given life through his blood. Most of it reads more as mythology than history."

"The two are one and the same more often than not, Gildrick. Have you found anything that would give us an idea of Fane Mortem's plan? Why would he bring the Vitharnmír through the tear in the veil?"

"Efialtír is to cross, my child. He seeks the Heart of Blood. It is hidden, even from me."

Kallinvar closed his eyes and shook his head, releasing a calming breath.

"Are you all right?" Gildrick asked.

Kallinvar pried his lids open, finding Gildrick staring at him with a curious expression. He drew a short breath and let it out in a sigh. "Look for references to a 'Heart of Blood'."

Gildrick raised an eyebrow.

"Just do it, Gildrick. Search through the texts. Have the cooks bring meals on the hour, Tarkin Stem, ale, tea – whatever keeps the Watchers awake. Sleep comes later. We have no time for it now." Kallinvar leaned in close, lowering his voice to avoid Tallia's prying ears. "We need to know how Fane plans to help Efialtír step through the veil between worlds. He will make his move before the Blood Moon has faded. We must stop him."

"It will be done, Grandmaster." Gildrick bowed and made to leave.

"Gildrick."

"Yes?"

"What news of Tarron?"

"Still nothing, old friend. And I do not believe we will find anything in the texts we have. If he still lives, it is not in the mortal plane." Following Kallinvar's lead, Gildrick bent his head so Tallia couldn't hear. "He speaks to you still? Perhaps that is where you may find answers."

Kallinvar nodded. "Barely anything of use. He speaks, but he does not answer questions. It's more like the ramblings of a madman."

"Give it time. Wars are not only fought in this realm, old friend. Achyron fights for us. We must allow faith to be our armour."

"Hmmm." Kallinvar returned to the war table as Gildrick took his leave, Tallia close behind. Faith was all well and good, and Kallinvar had faith, but there was only one reason a god would ask a man for blind faith, and that was control.

He shook his head, attempting to loose the thoughts from his mind. Doubt was the true killer of men, and he had no time for it.

Porters, servants, Watchers, and healers flitted about the room, the din of their footfalls and chatter fading to the back of Kallinvar's mind as he looked over the war table. Over half the knights were on task, holding back the flood of Bloodspawn that poured from their mountain holds across the continent. Regardless of whether the Blood Moon was only the beginning or not, while it dominated the sky, the Bloodspawn flowed across the continent like locusts. Some cities were strong enough to hold back the tide - barely – but others would be swallowed whole if the knights didn't come to their aid. The next few weeks would change the continent forever.

Ruon, Arden, Ildris, and the others fought near the base of the Marin Mountains where the Bloodspawn had overrun the city of Elmnest. Thousands were dead, the city in ruins. But without the knights, those fleeing would be picked off and harvested. More knights were scattered across Epheria, doing all they could to slow the tide.

The only saving grace was that the Lorian Empire had been silent since that night, and so the knights were fighting on one front and not two. But Kallinvar knew that if Fane Mortem was silent, it was because he was scheming. That man never did anything without a purpose.

He couldn't shake Achyron's words from his mind. "The Alignment will happen, my child. It is inevitable. You cannot stop Efialtír's harbinger from widening the tear in the veil. Too much has been set in motion. But you must meet him when he does. You must limit the crossing and close the tear. Then prepare the world for the war to come."

Prepare for the war to come.

For four hundred years, Kallinvar had been readying himself for the Blood Moon, readying himself to face the darkness that had ripped the world apart during The Fall. And now the Blood Moon was here, and all his preparation was for nothing. The knighthood was stretched thin as parchment, their numbers almost cut in half. Efialtír's Chosen had already crossed. Fane Mortem was even stronger than he had been then. For all his efforts, all his sacrifice, all Verathin's sacrifice, the world was a darker place and closer to the precipice of oblivion than it had ever been.

"I've failed…"

"It has not even begun, my child."

"Well, then give me some damn answers!" Kallinvar slammed his fist onto the stone war table, garnering looks from all those about the chamber. A pulse rippled through his Sigil, and he had no time to worry about the looks the porters, servants, and Watchers gave him.

His Sigil burned, his skin turning to ice as he summoned the Rift, the green light of its rim glowing against the cold stone, its centre black as night.

Ruon was the first through, the black liquid of the Rift rippling in her wake. Varlin followed close behind, her Sentinel armour washed in crimson.

The pool of black bulged outwards, and Arden charged through, cradling Sylven in his arms. The woman was unconscious, her arm severed just below the elbow, blood flowing freely.

"Help!" Arden roared, Ildris stepping through the Rift behind him. "Gildrick!"

"Here, Brother Arden." Watcher Poldor sprinted across the room, sweeping stacks of scrolls and old books from atop a table. "Lay her down." He turned to Watcher Timkin. "Brimlock sap, catgut, needles, Altweid Blood, and a stick."

Timkin hesitated, his mouth open.

"Go!"

The young Watcher scuttled away, panic in his eyes.

Kallinvar understood. To the people of Ardholm, the knights were akin to the gods themselves. In the past four centuries, it was the rarest of things for a knight to return to the temple with so much as a scratch upon their skin.

Brother Arden laid Sylven atop the table as though she were made of glass.

"It's going to be all right," Arden whispered, standing over her, one hand at the back of her head. She was completely unconscious.

"It will." Kallinvar rested one hand on Arden's shoulder, placing the other on Sylven's chest. He could feel the pulse of the woman's Sigil like a heartbeat in his mind. Drawing in a deep breath, Kallinvar reached out through his Sigil. Just as he had read in the journals of Grandmaster Telemanus, he focused on Sylven's Sigil and commanded it to recall her Sentinel armour. Within seconds, the armour had begun to recede, exposing the gruesome wound of Sylven's severed arm and allowing Gildrick and the healers to get to work.

Unless necessary, it was not something Kallinvar thought he would do again. It felt like a violation of Sylven's very soul.

"Report," Kallinvar said to Ruon, no longer wanting to look upon Sylven.

"We held the Bloodspawn off long enough for most of the survivors to flee towards Varsund. The city's garrison stood with us and now march with the refugees. The Chosen appeared, and the Bloodspawn consolidated to the city. All the souls left within…"

"You did what you could." Kallinvar clasped his hands at the side of Ruon's head and brought their foreheads together. "That's all Achyron can ever ask of us. The Shadow is rising, and we will be there to meet it."

Ruon drew a deep breath, then pulled away, nodding.

He passed his gaze over Ildris, Arden, and Varlin. He could sense the pain and exhaustion emanating from their Sigils. "Go and rest yourselves in Heraya's Well. Lyrin waits for you there. He returned from Catagan only an hour past. We are to meet on the plateau once the rest of our brothers and sisters are with us."

"Please, Grandmaster. Send me back out." Arden's helmet receded and he looked into Kallinvar's eyes. Sweat streaked Arden's face, and he was breathing heavily, but his eyes were unwavering. He swallowed, then took a breath. "Every minute we spend here, more people die. I can help them. I can save them…" He shook his head. "You didn't see it… You didn't see what those monsters did." He drew a sharp breath and steadied himself. "Please. Send me back. We are not done there."

"If you don't rest, Arden, you, too, will die."

"I already died. I was given this chance so others wouldn't have to die the way I did. The duty of the strong is to protect the weak. I ask you again. Please. Send me back."

"Heal your soul in Heraya's Well." Kallinvar stared into Arden's eyes as he spoke. He understood the young man's frustration. "There is more at play here than you know. The duty of the strong is to protect the weak, Arden. All of them, not just a few. When you have recovered your strength, I will send you and Lyrin to Aravell. We will need their aid, and the Draleid is still important in what is to come."

The hardness in Arden's expression dissipated at the mention of Aravell and of his brother. "Yes, Grandmaster." He bowed his head, his breaths still heavy. "Grandmaster, may I ask, the western villages of Illyanara?"

"Your people are safe." Kallinvar drew a long breath. It was often difficult for knights to dwell on their past lives, but for Arden in particular the past was still blended with the present. Kallinvar did not doubt his commitment, but he was wary of the weight he might place on the young man's shoulders. "From Lyrin's last report, many of the remaining villages and towns were abandoned in favour of Salme. They have gathered in large numbers and have erected fortifications. They are holding back the Bloodspawn."

"Thank you, Grandmaster."

As Arden, Ildris, and Varlin left the chamber, Kallinvar grasped Ruon's arm. "Walk with me?"

Much like in the Heart Chamber, porters, cooks, servants, and priests filled the corridors of the great temple, their footsteps and shouts echoing. Every face spoke of fear and worry.

"I will address the village once I have spoken to the knights."

Ruon gave a downturn of her bottom lip, nodding. "It would go a long way. They are terrified. The crimson twilight of the Blood Moon is all they've seen in days."

"I should have done it sooner," Kallinvar admitted.

Ruon shook her head, then gave a slight bow at the sight of Watcher Hildan. "No," she said, looking back at Kallinvar. "Time is a luxury we've not been able to afford. But the knights could use a rest, even a few hours."

The pair walked in silence through the temple, eventually arriving at the Soul Vault. Candlelight warmed the stone of the one hundred alcoves carved into the far wall. The last time Kallinvar had been in the room, all but three alcoves had been empty. Now thirty-seven Sigils rested in their places, metallic green surfaces glinting in the candlelight.

A priest garbed in white and green robes bowed deeply to Kallinvar and Ruon before lighting two freshly placed candles and slipping from the room.

Kallinvar's steps echoed as he walked through the chamber. He stopped before the wall of alcoves, reaching out a hand to touch a Sigil. "This one belonged to Verathin."

"Kallinvar…" Ruon's words faded as her steps bounced off the stone.

"This was Mirken's," he said, moving to the alcove six spaces over, then to the alcove beside it. "Daynin's… Illarin's."

"Kallinvar, it's not on you. We all chose this."

"I can feel them, Ruon." Kallinvar turned to look into Ruon's eyes. Those eyes had stared back at him for centuries, kept him sane, kept him grounded. Ruon was his keystone, his anchor. With Verathin gone, she was his reference point in the world, the thing around which time flowed. Ildris, Tarron, and Ruon. The three of them were part of Kallinvar's soul, shards of who he was as a man. But Ruon was… different. She knew him like no other.

"We will find Tarron," she said, resting a hand on Kallinvar's arm. "We must trust Gildrick and the Watchers. They will find a way. Have faith in Achyron."

Kallinvar sighed, his fingers lingering on Illarin's Sigil as it rested in its alcove. "I hear him, Ruon."

"Illarin? What do you mean you can hear him?"

"Not Illarin." Kallinvar pulled his hand away from Illarin's Sigil, then took a step closer to Ruon. His mouth suddenly felt dry as sand. "I can hear Achyron's voice in my head. He speaks to me."

Ruon didn't answer. She tilted her head sideways, narrowing her eyes, examining every line on Kallinvar's face. He could feel his heart pounding slowly against his ribs under her gaze.

"I've not lost my mind," Kallinvar said, moving closer. "I should have told you sooner, but I didn't know how. How do you tell someone you can hear a god's voice in your head?"

"What does he say?" Ruon's gaze never left Kallinvar's.

"Many things, but not enough. He told me the Blood Moon was only the beginning, that there was a war to come. He said that… I'm sorry, I know how this sounds. I know it seems like I've lost my mind—"

"Kallinvar." Ruon shook her head, cupping her hands to his cheeks.

"What?"

"I believe you." She pressed her fingers into Kallinvar's neck, her thumbs resting under his cheekbones. "I always have, and I always will. You know that. I trust you."

Kallinvar nodded softly, leaning his cheek into Ruon's left hand. "I don't know what I'd do without you."

"You'd keep fighting." Ruon leaned forwards and pressed her forehead against Kallinvar's. "Just as you did before me, you will do after."

Kallinvar leaned into Ruon, closing his eyes, feeling the warmth of her skin against his. He did not want an 'after'. Without Ruon there was no after. Then, as the weight on his shoulders felt that little bit lighter, he jerked backwards, the Sigil in his chest burning once more, reminding him the world was on fire.

"What is it?" Ruon asked, her touch lingering on his arm.

"Emalia is ready to return. It is time to carve the path forward."

CHAPTER FIVE

PURPOSE

6th Day of the Blood Moon

*Salme, western villages of Illyanara – Winter,
Year 3081 After Doom*

"Hold the breach!" Dahlen roared, rain sheeting down, thunder clapping overhead. He charged towards the shattered section of the palisade wall that ringed Salme. Bodies lay in the mud, men and women who had been thrown from the ramparts as the wall had erupted inwards and the three Bloodmarked had crashed through in a frenzy.

Smoke billowed from the glowing runes carved into the beasts' skin, their obsidian claws tearing through flesh and steel without distinction. His father had told him of the beasts, but before Salme, he'd never witnessed them with his own eyes. Monstrosities forged to kill mortal men, demons born of fire and death.

Dahlen's boots sucked and squelched with each step. The rain had fallen for days without end, turning the ground to slop. Every muscle in his body ached, and every breath he drew stung. The twenty surviving former Kingsguard who had travelled with him from Belduar fell in at his side, their usually pristine plate tarnished with dirt and blood. The Urak attacks had been as unrelenting as the rain, their numbers swelling with each passing night, but this was the first time they had breached the walls.

"Form up! We need to stem the flow!" Dahlen's throat burned as he barked orders, doing all he could to raise his voice above the din of the fighting and the raging storm above. "Neck, heart, head! Killing blows!"

More Uraks flooded through the opening, swarming around the three Bloodmarked and tearing through the warriors who had been first to the breach. Though, the term 'warrior' was a stretch. Many of Salme's defenders were little more than town guards or people who'd fled from the surrounding towns and villages, picking up spears to defend the last bastion of the west. The people of the villages were hardy, but most were nothing more than farmers or fishermen or craftsmen.

Three heartbeats passed, and then Dahlen crashed into the mass of bodies that surrounded the breach, the Kingsguard at his side.

He caught the swing of a blackened sword with his left blade, the vibrations jarring his arm, then drove his right blade up through the Urak's neck. His momentum carrying him forward, Dahlen slammed into the Urak's chest with his left shoulder.

With his blade still lodged in the Urak's neck, Dahlen's boot lost purchase in the mud, and he fell with the beast. The ground rose to meet him with a slap, mud pulling around the Urak's body. Moving swiftly, he hauled himself upright, ripping his blade free in a spray of blood.

"To me!" Dahlen called out to the townsfolk, trying his best to pull them into some semblance of shape. He sidestepped the thrust of an Urak spear, swinging his right blade up the shaft and slicing through fingers. As the creature stumbled forwards, howling, two of the Kingsguard fell upon it.

A bolt of lightning illuminated the carnage, mutilated bodies sprawled in the blood-soaked mud, severed limbs, and snapped bones.

Two more Uraks charged at Dahlen, two more fell. The sword forms took hold, flowing through him like water, his father's teachings burned into his blood. But for every Urak he killed, the beasts took four townsfolk with them. Beneath the light of the Blood Moon, the creatures were more savage than they had ever been.

Dahlen sheathed the sword in his left hand and grabbed the collar of a young woman covered head to toe in blood and dirt. She held a spear in her fist, her fingers white from squeezing, the rain streaking her face and soaking her hair. Her eyes held nothing but terror. He had seen her before the attacks. She worked the fishing boats by the coast. "Run to the western wall. Tell Nimara and the mages they're needed here. Tell the riders to wait for the horn."

The woman nodded frantically, her hands shaking on the spear shaft. Her voice trembled, teeth chattering. "Who... Who is Nimara?"

"The dwarves," Dahlen said, trying to level his voice to calm her. "Get the dwarves and the Lorian mages."

She nodded, eyes wide, hands still shaking.

"Go!"

The woman turned and ran, using the butt of her spear to stop herself from tumbling in the mud.

"To me!" Dahlen roared again, the Kingsguard pulling in around him, others following. He left his second sword sheathed and snatched up a circular wooden shield from the ground, sliding his arm through the strap and gripping the handle. Through the chaos he could see clusters of the town guards in their various colours fighting side by side, while the villagers fought like cornered kats, stabbing wildly with their spears.

"Move together," Dahlen called to the Kingsguard at his side. They pushed forwards through the thick of the fighting, gathering stragglers as they did. They would not be able to hold the breach – the Urak push was too strong – but they could gather as many as they could and fall back, pull the beasts into the open where their flanks were vulnerable.

Ahead, Dahlen watched as an enormous, grey-skinned Urak drove its spear through a young man's belly, twisting the shaft as the man thrashed and screamed. The beast grabbed the back of the man's head and dragged him along the spear shaft, then clamped its jaws around his neck and ripped out his throat in one motion. The gemstone set into the Urak's spear pulsed with a crimson light that glistened in the pools of blood and rain.

The creature spat a chunk of flesh into the mud, ripped the man's body free of its spear, and threw its arms in the air, unleashing a visceral howl that echoed in the night.

Even Dahlen felt the pull of fear in his gut at the sight. These creatures were monsters. They cared for nothing but death. Around him the defenders were close to breaking. He could see it in their sunken eyes, hear it in their wavering shouts. Cries of 'run' broke out, screams following as Uraks tore through flesh and bone.

"No…" Dahlen whispered. If they routed, if they gave these monsters their backs, they were all dead. The Uraks would not show mercy. They would slaughter them to the last. "Hold your ground!"

Those who had gathered with Dahlen stood firm, if only just, but many of the others began to break, slipping on the sodden ground as they tried to escape the melee, trampling each other as they went. But there was no escape. Only the endless waters of the Antigan Ocean lay at their backs. If the Uraks pushed through to the centre of Salme, thousands would die: the children, the elderly, the infirm. There was nowhere to run. But fear had a way of killing rational thought, and so the men and women who had not long before tended fields, held nets from boats, and felled trees ran for their lives.

"Fall back slow and steady," Dahlen instructed the Kingsguard about him. "Give them a wall to rally behind. We need to bait the Uraks further in, but we can't allow them to push through in force."

Grunts were the only responses Dahlen received, but the Kingsguard stayed tight, their shields linking, the mud squelching beneath the weight of their armoured boots. The men and women in burnished steel and purple cloaks were one of the few legends he had seen with his own eyes that had lived up to the stories. They were hard, disciplined, and unyielding. The Kingsguard of Belduar were pulled straight from the stories of old.

At the sight of Dahlen and the Kingsguard holding firm, some of the town guards joined their line, hefting shields and pulling tight.

The Uraks crashed into them, blackened weapons hacking and slicing. Dahlen caught a sword with the top of his wooden shield, turning the blow upwards. As he did, he dropped low and stabbed into the creature's exposed belly. Intestines slopped into the mud as he ripped his blade free. No sooner had the Urak fallen than another took its place.

One of the beasts charged into the man beside Dahlen, its shoulder slamming into his shield. The shield's rim smashed into the Kingsguard's face, shattering his jaw and snapping his teeth. The man collapsed into the mud, his howls muffled and choked. The guards that had rallied behind Dahlen hacked at the Urak, and the Kingsguard closed the line, but the beasts kept charging. The creatures were simply too strong. Again and again they crashed through the line of shields with little thought for self-preservation. With every charge, more men and women fell, but the Uraks didn't stop.

"Where the fuck are Nimara and the mages?" Dahlen's shield rim splintered, an Urak claw tearing through the wood as though it were paper, missing the meat of his arm by a hair's breadth. He staggered back a step, then swung his arm forwards, slamming the remainder of the shield's rim into the creature's jaw, then driving his sword through its open mouth.

"My lord!"

Before Dahlen could retrieve his blade, the Kingsguard to his right – Altmin – leapt across him. Dahlen turned his head just in time to watch an enormous obsidian claw smash into Altmin's face. Smoke plumed from the Bloodmarked's runes as Altmin stumbled and fell into the mud, his jaw ripped away, his face a mangled mess of torn flesh.

Dahlen pulled his sword free, ducking in the same motion to avoid a swipe of the Bloodmarked's claw. He pulled in close to the beast and drove his blade into its chest, the hilt clicking against the monstrosity's stone-like skin.

The creature roared and swiped its clawed hand at Dahlen, who only just raised the remnants of his shield in time to dampen the blow.

Dahlen hit the ground with a wet slap, sliding through the mud until his skull cracked against something hard. Stars flitted across his eyes, his vision blurring. His head throbbed, and the left side of his body felt as though he'd been kicked by a horse, his shield shattered and reduced to nothing.

"To Lord Virandr!" a voice called out.

Dahlen slipped in the mud as he pulled himself to his knees. His head spun, blood trickling into his eyes. Red light spilled through the haze of his vision, the outline of the Bloodmarked charging towards him. The clang of steel and the roars of men and beasts pounded in his ears.

The Bloodmarked clapped its hands together, unleashing a shockwave of fire that tore through the defenders.

Dahlen planted one foot in the mud, sliding his second sword from its sheath. He stumbled backwards, narrowly avoiding a swipe of the Bloodmarked's claw. The creature towered over him, the runes carved into its dense muscle glowing, its eyes blood red.

Once more, the Bloodmarked swung its obsidian claw, and Dahlen brought his blade up to meet it. Steel clattered against claw, the force of the blow knocking the sword free from Dahlen's grasp and sending it splattering to the mud. Dahlen again staggered backwards, just managing to keep his footing.

A roar sounded to his right, and a mountain of a man charged through the fray, swinging a mighty warhammer. The weapon crashed into the back of the Bloodmarked's knee, exploding forwards in a spray of blood and bone.

The runes on the creature's body ignited in a blinding light, black smoke billowing. It fell forwards, its shattered knee collapsing. And as it did, the man swung his hammer back in an arc, smashing the creature's jaw to pieces.

The man followed through with a downward hammer swing, cracking the Bloodmarked's skull against the ground like an egg. The runes burst to life one last time before fading entirely, the creature going still.

Before Dahlen had even a second to think, more shouts and roars erupted to his right and he turned to see a cavalry charge smash into the Urak flank, curved swords carving through grey hide.

As the cavalry carved a path through the Uraks, the reinforcements from the western wall filled the gaps left behind. Dahlen spotted Nimara, Almer, and Yoring charging in the vanguard, the other dwarves at their side.

Dahlen reached down and dragged free the blade that was still lodged in the Bloodmarked's chest, nodding to the man who had saved his life. He rolled back his shoulders and roared. "Forwards!"

The rain had slowed to a trickle when Dahlen walked among the dead. His boots sucked into the blood-soaked mud, his gaze passing over the twisted faces and broken bodies. About him, men and women hauled the corpses into carts, salvaging weapons and armour as they went. He wasn't sure how many they'd lost. A hundred or so, likely more. There wouldn't be time for a count before the next attack. There would just be faces never seen again.

"I believe this is yours." Nimara appeared at Dahlen's side, holding out a mud-covered sword with a triangular pommel.

"Thank you." Dahlen inclined his head as he took the sword and slid it into its sheath across his back. "I wasn't looking forward to having to search for that."

"You need to learn to hold onto it better," Nimara said with a half-smile. Even with her blonde hair streaked with blood and dirt, the gold, silver, and bronze rings tied through her braid gleamed in the crimson moonlight. She held his gaze, a soft smile curling her lips. "You fought well."

"I'd have died well if not for you and the Lorian cavalry." Dahlen glanced over to where the Lorian riders were tending to the horses. They had arrived a week or so before, along with four mages and some two hundred infantry. Their auxiliary force had been caught in an Urak ambush when trying to relieve Camylin, and the survivors had fought their way back to Salme.

Beside him, one of the Belduaran captains, Camwyn, spat into the mud. "We should have left them to the Uraks."

"Aye," another, by the name of Thannon, said. He glared at the Lorian soldiers, his hand resting on the pommel of his sword. "There's still time."

A grumble of agreement spread through the Belduarans – fifteen of whom had survived the battle.

"Without them, this battle would have been lost." Dahlen too had wanted the Lorians turned away and left to the Uraks at first, but the council had granted them access to Salme so long as they defended its people. He didn't trust them as far as he could throw them, but at least they fought well. And if his enemies would die to keep him alive, he would let them.

"Respectfully, my lord—" Camwyn clenched her jaw, twisting her neck to look at the Lorian cavalry "—those pieces of shit burned my home to the ground. They murdered thousands. Men, women, children. They didn't draw lines, they just slaughtered. I watched my brothers and sisters of the Kingsguard give their lives as we fled down the Wind Tunnels. I will neither forgive nor forget."

"I'm not asking you to. All I'm asking is that you let them give their lives instead of yours, that you let them fight and die defending this place rather than bolstering another Lorian army."

"That I can do. But if I get the chance, I'm telling you now, I will burn them all alive, just like their dragons did to us."

Dahlen only grunted at that. What could he say? If it had been his city, his home that had been torched in the Lorian dragonfire, his friends and kin burned alive, he would have felt the same way. Truth was, he already did.

"Captain Nimara." Almer's voice broke the rising tension as he strode through the mud, Yoring and three of the other dwarves at his side.

Nimara inclined her head.

"The Uraks have fallen back, and the perimeter is secure. I've set dwarves on watch while the breach is rebuilt, but there are not enough of us and the human captains seem content arguing amongst themselves – something about a market from last winter."

"I'll speak with them," Dahlen said with a sigh. It had been the same ever since he had arrived at Salme. With so many souls gathering from across the western villages and beyond, the chain of command was nigh on non-existent. The village councils had banded together and elected representatives, but on the field of battle they were scattered. There was no plan, no strategy, no system. Each night they fought with only one thing in mind: survival.

"See that you do." Nimara's green eyes held on Dahlen's, her tone sharp. "We cannot carry on like this. If we're not organised before the next attack, we may as well roll over and die."

"I'll speak with them." Dahlen ran his fingers through his saturated hair, letting out a long puff of air. "Still no word from Kira or Oleg?"

Nimara shook her head. "Not since the news of King Lakar's election in Azmar."

Dahlen nodded slowly, pressing his fingers into his cheeks. It hadn't been long since Oleg's last letter, but he couldn't shake the feeling that something was wrong. It was that same feeling he'd had since before leaving the Freehold. There was more going on there than any of them realised. He was sure of it.

"My queen can handle herself. As can Queen Elenya. They will look after the Belduarans." Nimara brushed her hand against Dahlen's, only for a moment, but long enough to make his heart flutter. "I'm going to walk the wall, make sure there are no gaps in the guard." She stepped closer, holding his gaze, her voice a whisper. "I could use a warm bed tonight."

Dahlen inclined his head, and the dwarf smiled as she pulled away. Before Nimara turned, she nodded towards something over Dahlen's shoulder.

Dahlen turned to see the same mountain of a man that had saved him in the fighting. The man stood a head taller than Dahlen, a chest like two oak barrels, shoulders as wide as a draught horse's. He still held the warhammer in his right hand, the dual-sided head floating just over the mud.

"Thank you."

The man raised a curious eyebrow.

"For saving my life."

He grunted. "You lead well. The Belduarans follow you, as do the others. My life is easier with you alive, and my people are safer."

"My name is Dahlen Virandr." Dahlen reached out his arm, which the enormous man grasped.

"I know who you are, Lord Virandr. There's barely a soul here who doesn't. You arrived with the Belduarans and the dwarves. Had you not, we would all have been dead the night the Blood Moon rose, or even before." The man stared at Dahlen for a moment. "Erdhardt Hammersmith."

"Ahh…" Realisation set in. "Fellhammer. I should have known it was you."

Erdhardt grunted. The man's eyes were sunken and dark, and scars littered the sun-bronzed skin of his neck and forearms. Short, white-grey hair did nothing to alleviate the severe sharpness in his face.

Dahlen had heard tales of Erdhardt Fellhammer since the first time he'd set foot in Salme, though he'd not fought beside him in the attacks. The people spoke of him as though he was tall as a Jotnar, with the strength of five men, and that his presence alone struck fear into Urak hearts. One woman had even claimed he swung his hammer with the power of Achyron himself. Having seen the man fight, Dahlen now saw the tales weren't as exaggerated as he'd thought.

"Erdhardt!" a voice called.

Two men and a young woman approached, each staring about the scattered dead as they did. One of the men had a sword strapped to his hip, but he walked as though he wasn't yet accustomed to its weight. The other had a bow slung across his shoulders and a quiver at his hip. The woman wore leathers but no weapon and kept her fire-red hair tied back with string. Mud caked her shins and knees, and blood smeared her chest, stomach, and hands.

The man with the bow grasped Erdhardt's forearm. "The council have called the night's meeting at the great hall. Ylinda is already there, but she's got the sense this one will be important – seeing as we all came within a rat's tail of losing our heads. She's asked us all to attend. She's asked that you attend. You're no use drowning yourself in your cabin."

"So be it." Erdhardt gestured towards the other man with the sword. "Dahlen Virandr, this is Jorvill Ehrnin, village elder of The Glade."

The Glade. The name floated in Dahlen's mind. He knew the place, but it took him a moment to remember why: Calen.

Erdhardt moved on, inclining his head towards the young woman. "This is Anya Gritten. She has taken on the role of healer for our people. And this," he said, returning to the man with the bow, "is Tharn Pimm."

Pimm. Dahlen narrowed his eyes. "You're not by any chance Dann Pimm's father?"

The atmosphere shifted, even Erdhardt's stony expression cracking. Tharn Pimm went white as a ghost. "You know my boy? Is he... is..."

"He's alive. Last I heard, he was with my father and brother just north of Argona." Dahlen wasn't sure how much he should say of the elves for now. He'd not heard a word from either Aravell or Durakdur since the Blood Moon had risen. "Calen is with them. Calen Bryer."

Anya's jaw dropped open. "Calen?"

"My boy..." Tharn Pimm muttered.

"They're both alive?" Erdhardt turned his body to face Dahlen, the darkness lifting from his eyes. "What of Rist, Rist Havel? He was with the others when they left."

"There's a lot you all don't know. After the council, we'll talk."

THE GREAT HALL STOOD ON a rise that overlooked Salme's port. It was five times as long as it was wide, comprising thick wooden beams and a roof of grey stone slabs. Just inside the enormous double doors, four tables ran parallel to each other along the hall's centre, stretching for what had to have been almost thirty feet, a series of fire pits set between them with lanterns hanging from the rafters above.

A large circular table sat at the end of the hall, eight chairs around its perimeter. All but two of the chairs were filled: Nimara's and the council representative for Salme itself. As an envoy from the Lodhar Freehold, the other members had granted Nimara a seat at the table, but rarely did they seem to care much for her opinion. This was their home, not hers.

"They're scared," Camwyn whispered. Along with Thannon, the woman had taken up position as one of Dahlen's captains on the journey from Durakdur. Both were former Kingsguard and fine warriors. It felt strange to think of them that way: 'former' Kingsguard. But it was the truth. Belduar no longer had a king. The ancient bastion had fallen, the city gone, the crown broken. Belduar was no more.

"They ought to be," Thannon whispered back, scanning the room. "The Uraks are testing us. Whittling us down." He leaned towards Dahlen as they made their way along the table at the hall's left side. "Any word from your father? We could use reinforcements here."

Dahlen shook his head, not moving his gaze from the circular table at the far end of the room, taking note of those who stood about it. "Still silence since the Blood Moon."

Dahlen tried not to think on what that might mean. He had intended on making his way to Aravell almost a month ago, but when he'd seen the state of Salme and the increasing frequency of Urak raids from Wolfpine Ridge, he'd decided to stay longer. This was where he was needed. He could make a difference here.

As he and the others approached the circular table, he spotted Erdhardt, Jorvill, Tharn, and Anya standing behind Ylinda Pimm. Dahlen had seen Ylinda speaking at each of the council meetings, but it was only then he realised that she must also be related to Dann, likely his mother, judging by the years marked into her face. She was a sharp woman with little time for pleasantries, but she rarely spoke anything that wasn't sense.

Erdhardt inclined his head at Dahlen, a gesture Dahlen reciprocated.

"He's almost as big as the Uraks," Camwyn said, inclining her head towards Erdhardt.

"The man's a demon on the battlefield." Thannon folded his arms. "I've heard stories that the beasts killed his wife a few moons ago, and now he only emerges from his home to spill their blood."

"Stories are just that," Dahlen whispered. "Stories."

"One thing I know for sure, he only goes where the fighting is thickest. I saw him on the night the Blood Moon rose. He leapt from the walls, swinging his hammer like a madman. He has a death wish, one the gods won't grant – thankfully for us."

As Thannon spoke, Nimara walked past, Yoring and Almer at her back. Each of the dwarves nodded in greeting as Nimara took her seat. Over a hundred people were crammed around the table by the time the elders of Salme arrived, late, as tended to be their way.

The gathered crowd parted for the three elders: a broad-chested man without a hair on his head; a short, lithe woman with dark hair; and a woman with bronzed skin, a shaved head, muscular arms, and two missing fingers. Each of them had a number of brass rings looped through their nose and ears.

The woman with the two missing fingers pulled back her chair languidly and set herself down, barely raising her eyes to acknowledge the others.

Lanan Halfhand. She was a strange one indeed. On appearances alone Dahlen would have thought her aloof and disinterested, but his experience had been quite the opposite. It was, after all, by her allowance that the refugees from Belduar and the other towns and villages around Ölm Forest had been allowed safe haven in Salme.

After a few moments, Lanan raised her hand in the air, and the chatter stopped. She lifted her gaze and cast it about those gathered.

"Another night passes, and still we draw breath." As though emphasising her point, Lanan pulled a long breath in through her nostrils, held it, then released slowly. "Long have the people of the western villages supported one another. Our children come of age together in The Proving. Our people survive together in the harsh winters. Our history is alive in the stories we share. But now, we welcome more into the fold – the people from Belduar, the dwarves of Lodhar..." She sucked in her cheeks, then clicked her tongue off the roof of her mouth as her stare settled on the Lorian mages and the cavalry commander who stood to the right of the table. "... and the warriors of Loria."

Murmurs spread through the crowd, along with a number of spitting noises. Dahlen didn't envy the woman. In taking in the Lorians, she had undoubtedly made enemies. But that decision had saved every soul within Salme's walls twice over.

"We don't need a history lesson, Lanan," said a man, tall and thin, sitting four seats to Lanan's left. He was the representative of Pirn, if Dahlen remembered correctly, and he seemed to have a problem with just about everything. "We need—"

"Hold your tongue, Benem," snapped Kara Thain, Erith's representative. In the short time Dahlen had known the woman, he'd found nothing but respect for her. Each of the elders participated in Salme's defence, though some less enthusiastically than others. But he'd seen Kara on the walls more than once, fighting from the front. "We don't have time for your groans tonight. Let Lanan speak."

Benem looked as though he was ready to leap from his seat, his cheeks flushing, fingers grasping the edge of the table. But his gaze flashed across the table and he pulled himself back in his chair. Dahlen followed the man's stare to see Erdhardt glaring at Benem, his hand resting on the pommel of his hammer that stood with its head on the ground.

"We have always been close," Lanan continued, her gaze lingering on Benem. "But the times are changing, and we must become more – we must become one. We cannot weather this storm divided."

"What are you saying?" The man who spoke was Yarik Tumber of Ölm.

"She's saying that now that we're at her mercy and living within her walls, with the Uraks breathing down our necks, she wants to seize power." Benem pushed his chair back and stood, leaning forward and resting his palms on the table, his eyes fixed on Lanan. "You think it will be that easy?"

The woman returned Benem's stare, one eyebrow raised, a look on her face as though she were staring at a child who had tested a mother's patience. After an awkward silence, within which the entire hall stared at both Benem and Lanan, the woman bit her lip, then spoke. "I have no desire to seize power. I wish only to unite us so that we may defend this place as one. Salme is your home now, too. I'm sure you've seen it from where you stand in the thick of the fighting, but as it stands, we are a hair's breadth from losing everything."

Slowly and purposefully, Lanan pushed her chair back and rose. She met Benem's gaze, then looked about at all those gathered. She turned to Ylinda and then Erdhardt. "When the people of Talin and The Glade came to our gates, their homes burned, their loved ones in Heraya's embrace, what did we do?"

"Welcomed us with open arms." A half-smile cracked Ylinda's face, and she inclined her head towards Lanan. "You fed us, watered us, and helped us build homes."

"And we're all the stronger for it, are we not?"

"We are."

"Had Erdhardt Fellhammer not stood on our ramparts these past months, Salme would be nothing more than rubble and bones. I have lost count of the men and women whose broken bones have been set and wounds stitched by young Anya Gritten. No healer I've ever seen roams the battlefield while it rages and drags the wounded from the fray. Once more I say, we are stronger together. What of Erith, Kara?"

"Aye. We will forever be grateful for the shelter you gave."

"And in return, what did we ask?"

Kara shrugged, sitting back in her chair. "That we fight for this place as we would Erith. That we bleed for it – and we have."

Lanan nodded her thanks. "And Milltown, Ölm, Pirn?"

"You've made your point," Benem snapped. The man pulled his hands from the table and stepped back, walking around the perimeter towards Lanan. "You've always been good with words, Lanan. You twist them and shape them, but they still mean the same thing." The man pointed his finger at the Salme elder. "You see an opportunity, and you're taking it." He jabbed her in the shoulder with his finger. "I for one won't be letting you spin your webs like the spider you are. Who will lead this new city, this new people? You don't have me fooled…"

Benem trailed off, his finger still prodding into Lanan's shoulder, his stare fixed on Erdhardt, who had left his hammer standing on its head and now walked towards the man. "What? You can't intimidate me, Erdhardt."

"Sit down, and let Lanan speak. Some of us need to rest so we can fight again tomorrow. We can't all stand in the back, using the mud to prop up our spear."

Benem moved towards Erdhardt. "I've known her for over forty years. I don't need to hear what she has to say because venom is best left in the fangs."

"Take a step closer and I'll put you down. I'm in no mood."

Benem rolled his eyes, still moving towards Erdhardt. "We've all lost people, Erdhardt. Your wallowing is not unique. Aela was—"

Erdhardt lashed out with an open hand, striking Benem in the throat. The man staggered backwards, grasping his neck as a number of the representatives jumped to their feet, gasps of shock spreading through those gathered.

"Don't say her name." Erdhardt's voice was cold and level. He was only an inch or so taller than Benem, but his shoulders were twice as broad. "Sit back down, and let the adults speak. If you'd been at the breach tonight, you wouldn't have the energy to talk all this shit."

"You…" Benem coughed and choked, his eyes watering as he held his throat. "Stupid fucking oaf." The man stood tall, rolling his shoulders back and puffing out his chest before launching himself at Erdhardt.

The resulting fight lasted all of three heartbeats.

Benem swung his fist. Erdhardt leaned his neck backwards, avoiding the blow. He grabbed Benem's head and slammed it down against the wooden table with a crack, causing the representatives from Ölm and Talin to jump backwards.

Benem slumped to the ground, mumbling, blood streaming from his nose and forehead.

The entire hall went silent.

"Please, continue." Erdhardt gestured towards Lanan as though nothing had happened.

For a moment, the other elders from Pirn looked as though they were about to cause a riot, but one look at Erdhardt made them think better of it. Instead, they hauled Benem into his chair, checking his wounds and slapping his cheek to keep him awake while he groaned.

Erdhardt looked from Benem to the other elders, shaking his head. "I don't even know how many of us died tonight. We're too tired to count the bodies.

We've lost hundreds in days. The likelihood is each of you in this room has friends you spoke to today but will never speak to again. None of us, not one soul here, has seen darker times than these. And still, this fool wants to squabble and argue over who has 'power'. None of us have power. We are not fighting for control, we are fighting for survival. We are fighting so that our bloodlines are not ended here, so that fear is not the last thing our children know. My boy died of the blood lung when he was no more than five. My wife, the only piece of me that was worth anything, died the night I lost my home. I fight for all of you, in the hope that you never know my pain. If any of you have a problem with that, speak now."

After a tense moment, Lanan straightened. "Let us no longer fight as men and women of Salme, or The Glade, or Talin, or Pirn, but as kin. The western villages have long shared blood and honour and promises. But now, let us share oaths. I do not wish to become your lady or your ruler – that is not our way. I wish to recognise this point as the moment we chose to stand together. I propose we formally recognise the members of this council not as representatives of separate peoples but of one people. That we lead together with a clear purpose – to survive. I know it seems an insignificant thing at a time like this. Pointless, even. But it's not. We must see each face around this table, each face within these walls, as kin, as one of our own. All those in favour?"

Kara Thain was the first to raise her hand. "It is long past time."

The other elders of Erith followed suit, with Ylinda Pimm and Yarik Tumber close behind. Eventually, all those gathered, with the exception of Benem, had done so. After a few moments, and some harsh muttering from the other Pirn elders, Benem raised his hand.

Dahlen, Camwyn, and Thannon remained silent with their hands at their sides, as did the Lorians.

Nimara was the only one still seated at the table. "What of the Belduaran refugees?"

"They have come here seeking a new home, just as the others have." Lanan rested one hand on the table. "They have fought and bled with us. They have earned their place, as have your dwarves. We stand together or we break. If they want their new home, they will have to save it."

Nimara nodded.

Lanan drew a long breath, then looked to the Lorians. She pinched her top lip with her bottom teeth. "And what of you, Exarch Dorman? What of the Lorian soldiers under your command?"

The man glanced to his companions, then around those gathered. "We have sent hawks to the Twenty-Third Army stationed near Argona and north to Antiquar. We will stay until relief arrives."

"With the Uraks holding everywhere between here and Camylin, you don't exactly have a choice, do you?" Thannon leaned forwards, giving the Battlemage a flat stare, the elders turning their heads at his interjection.

Dahlen tensed as the mage's eyes sharpened, and he took a step forward. Dahlen had faced enough mages to know if it was Dorman's will, Thannon's heart would cease beating in a matter of moments.

"Speak plainly, Belduaran." The mage stopped only a foot or so from Erdhardt, unblinking.

"What he meant to say, I'm sure," Lanan interrupted, stepping between the two, "was that we thank the Lorian Empire for its aid, and we will gladly accept your steel for as long as you can spare it."

"Hmm." The mage drew a slow breath through his nose, then inclined his head to Lanan. "To protect is our duty. Thank you for taking us in."

"Now," Lanan said, turning back to the table as the mage took his place by his companions. "If we are to be one people, we must swear it under the eyes of the gods."

"And what would be the name of this new union? If we build a city here, what do we call it?" one of the Erith elders asked.

"A name means little if we're all dead," Erdhardt said with a shrug.

"True words." Lanan gave Erdhardt a smile of agreement. "For now, we will swear to abide by the decisions of this council, to treat each other as kin, and to defend our home as one. A name, we can choose later."

When each of those present had sworn the oaths, Erdhardt raised his hand, letting out a short cough.

"What is it, Erdhardt?"

"There is none more eager to put these talks to rest than I, but there is one last thing that must also be discussed."

"Which is?" Yarik Tumber asked, not bothering to hide the irritation in his voice.

"Just as we must be one as a council and a people, we must also be one in the defence of our new home. Swearing oaths to each other in this hall does nothing for us on the field of battle – as sweet a sentiment as it is."

"Go on." Lanan gestured for Erdhardt to continue.

"As their first act, I would ask the new council to choose a commander for Salme's – or whatever we're calling this place – combined forces. We are too scattered. There are a hundred voices on the battlefield, each yelling a different command, each trying to save a different thing. The men and women of Pirn fight in one place while those of Talin fight in another. The leaders from Salme insist on one plan without thinking of its impact on another. Tonight, we came moments from defeat because we were too slow to react to the breach in the wall. We need a single strategy, a single focus, a single voice."

"And do you have any suggestions for this 'commander'?" The representative from Milltown had barely spoken through the entire meeting, but now he stood with his arms folded, one hand scratching at his thick beard. "Let me guess, Erdhardt, yourself? Fellhammer, the defender of Salme."

A smile spread across Erdhardt's lips as he shook his head. "I can swing a hammer, but I know nothing about true warfare. No, I suggest Dahlen Virandr."

Dahlen straightened, his eyes wide as he realised the entire hall was now staring at him. Nimara turned in her chair, her smile so wide it almost touched her ears.

"Have you lost your mind, Erdhardt?" Yarik Tumber moved his stare from Dahlen to Erdhardt. "You would suggest we trust the defence of our home, of our families, to a foreigner? An outsider? To someone who shares no blood with these lands?"

"I would suggest, Yarik, that we trust the defence of our home to a man who understands battle. Dahlen and those with him from Belduar are warriors. Warfare is a craft they have dedicated their lives to. What are the men and women of Ölm? Farmers, fishers, woodsmen? Putting weapons in our hands does not make us warriors in the same way that putting a chicken on a horse does not make it a rider. Despite not 'sharing blood with these lands', Dahlen Virandr and the Belduarans have fought at our gates every night the Uraks have attacked. They have shown their loyalty, painted it in the blood they have shed."

Yarik stared open-mouthed at Erdhardt. The look on the man's face mirrored how Dahlen felt. This had been the last thing he'd expected.

"Does anyone have an alternative candidate?" Lanan asked, looking about the room.

Dahlen looked to Nimara, but the dwarf shook her head, mouthing the word 'you'.

He turned his attention to Thannon and Camwyn, but they both pulled closed fists to their chests and inclined their heads.

"You pulled us through Durakdur, my lord," Thannon said. "You'll pull us through this."

A few heads turned towards the Lorians, but none dared say anything. To suggest a Lorian soldier take command of Salme's defences would have started another argument, one that Dahlen was certain would have ended in more corpses.

In the end, it was Kara Thain who spoke. "I second Dahlen Virandr. It was he and his warriors who held the breach tonight when others broke. His shouts that rallied us." The woman looked to Dahlen and inclined her head. "I will follow you."

"As will I," came another voice from amidst the crowd.

A few more mumbles of agreement sounded, and Lanan raised her hand.

"Are there any who object?" She looked at Benem, who sat slumped in his chair, hand clasped to the side of his bloodied head. The man simply glowered and gave a grunt of acquiescence.

"Well then, Dahlen Virandr, do you accept the mantle of Salme's protector?"

Dahlen had no idea what to say. He was a warrior, true, but he was not a leader of men. He'd never been a leader of anything in his entire life. All he'd ever done was follow and and carry out his father's commands. The only things he knew about leading he'd learned from Aeson. And the core of it was to not ask anyone to do something you wouldn't do yourself and to never ask anyone to bleed for you if you are not willing to bleed for them.

Camwyn elbowed Dahlen sharply in the back, then whispered, "If you're going to answer them, Lord Virandr, I suggest saying yes, otherwise we'll be fighting under the command of a sheep shearer."

Dahlen drew a long breath, then nodded slowly. "I accept."

"Well then," Erdhardt said, wrapping his fingers around the pommel of his hammer. "Can I go to bed?"

CHAPTER SIX

A RAY OF LIGHT

6ᵗʰ Day of the Blood Moon

*Somewhere in the Dwarven Freehold of Lodhar – Winter,
Year 3081 After Doom*

Kira sat with her back against the wall of the cell, her hand pressed to her ribs, her lungs burning with each breath. She swallowed, tasting the tang of iron on her tongue.

It had only been a matter of days since Hoffnar had revealed himself and butchered Elenya and Lakar. She wasn't sure how many. Hoffnar's guards hadn't allowed her so much as a drop of sleep. As soon as her eyes were shut, the cell door would swing open and pain would follow.

She still couldn't wrap her mind around what had happened. Elenya was dead. There had once been a time when Kira had thought that dwarf unkillable. And yet now the memory of the axe splitting her old friend's face in two haunted her every waking moment. She could still hear the sound of Elenya's teeth snapping, feel the terror twisting in her chest.

Even King Lakar's severed head held residence in her thoughts. She'd not known the dwarf long, but he'd not deserved a death like that.

Kira groaned as she arched her spine, agony igniting along her lower back. She lifted her hand, her breath catching as she touched the short tufts of hair at the side of her head.

They'd sliced her long blonde hair with a knife on the first day, taken away the rings of service she'd spent her entire life earning.

Her pride, her honour, her legacy.

That coward Hoffnar hadn't even had the courage to do it himself. She supposed he'd wanted to disgrace her, to make her a traitor by more than simple words alone. Or perhaps he meant to break her, crush her spirit. If that was his aim, he had clearly never taken the time to truly learn who she was.

She clenched her jaw as she fingered at the remnants of hair that sprouted from her scalp.

Kira let out a short laugh, coughing at the pain. If she ever got out of this place, she would give Hoffnar his own braid and his own ring when she took his head from his shoulders. She would wear his death like a trophy, dye a scarf with his blood, and make a necklace from his bones. She would carve the beard from his face and toss it into the forge fires, watch his rings melt amidst black smoke.

Metal creaked and groaned, Kira's pulse quickening at the sound of the door's bolts opening. She pressed herself harder against the cold stone wall, clenching her jaw.

The door swung. Kira hissed, raising a hand to her face as the greenish blue light of Heraya's Ward sprayed through the passage, blinding in the darkness. Two silhouettes followed, indistinguishable against the light, the sound of armoured boots clinking.

Kira waited for the dwarves to draw close, then hurled herself to her feet, roaring. Pain flared in every muscle, burned in every fibre of her body. She buried it. She would not make this easy for them.

She bunched the fingers of her right hand tight, then struck out at the closest of the two guards. The top of her hand scraped against the bottom of the dwarf's helmet, stripping skin. But she followed through, her knuckles slamming into his throat.

The dwarf staggered backwards before his companion rammed a heavy steel gauntlet into Kira's stomach. She doubled over, the blow dragging the air from her lungs and conjuring blood. A second strike crashed into her cheek, steel crunching against bone.

Kira crashed against the wall at her back, her head spinning, stomach turning. Her head pounded like an anvil. With her vision blurred, she caught a flash of motion and threw herself to the side. A violent *clang* sounded as the dwarf drove his fist into the wall where Kira's head had been.

Before he could recover, Kira launched herself at him, sliding her fingers into the gap between his collar and helmet and wrapping her hands around his throat. She squeezed, throwing her weight forward, and they fell together.

Kira's grip loosened as the dwarf smashed into the ground and she fell on top of him, the vibrations jarring her starving body. She squeezed the dwarf's throat with every ounce of strength she had, losing herself in the effort.

Something stirred deep within her, a primal call, an unyielding urge that lit a fire in her belly. The call of the bersekeer – Hafaesir's rage in her veins. Finding power deep in her bones, she tightened her grip and lifted the dwarf's head from the floor before slamming it down as hard as she could. Again and again, she beat the dwarf's head against the ground until his helmet skittered across the stone.

That same primal call roared in her heart, a fervour consuming her, and she continued to smash the dwarf's skull against the stone. Cracks and snaps sounded in her ears, but she didn't stop. Her hands were covered in blood, shards of bone twisted with brains and gore splattering the stone.

When the dwarf's skull all but crumpled in her hands, Kira fell backwards, her chest heaving. Her heart felt seconds away from breaking through her ribs. She looked about the cell, seeing the other guard still lying on the ground, gasping for air, his hands clasped around his throat.

The flowerlight flooded in through the open doorway, painting the scene in hues of green and blue.

Her eyes landed on the two bearded axes strapped to the hips of the dwarf whose skull was now smeared across the ground. Her body still crying out in agony, she scrambled across the floor and pulled the nearest axe from its loop, then turned and brought the blade down against the chain that connected her to the floor.

Steel clanged against steel, and the axe head skittered. She swung again, arms shaking. The sound of clinking chainmail and hurried footfalls rang through the corridor outside.

She swung again, chipping away at the steel links.

The footfalls were joined by shouts.

"Hafaesir, if you bear any love for me..." Another swing, another clang of steel on steel.

A voice sounded at the door. "What in the..."

Kira didn't turn to look. She swung again, the fury of the bersekeer rising in her, sweeping through her like a flood. The axe connected with the chains and cleaved the steel link in half, the head jarring off the stone beneath.

Kira scrambled to her knees, the shackle still locked around her ankle. But as she tried to pull herself to a standing position, a weight crashed into her and she lost her grip on the axe. Once more she collapsed to the ground, her head smacking against the stone.

She tried to pull herself up, but a boot connected with her stomach, causing her to curl into a ball and gasp for breath. A second boot slammed into her face, her vision blurring, pain splitting her skull.

"Traitor," a voice spat.

Fingers grasped the loose, torn tunic at her neck and hauled her upright, before a punch to her gut sent her back to her knees.

Just as they had before, the kicks came swift and unyielding until she was coughing blood and spewing vomit onto the stone. When the guards were done and the door creaked closed behind them, Kira lay on the floor, battered and bloody.

She curled up on her side, pulling her knees close to her chest, and sobbed. Every piece of her screamed in agony. Her nostrils were so filled with blood she could barely breathe.

After a few minutes, she dragged herself upright in opposition to her body's protests. Even just holding herself in that position threatened to make her pass out. It was then, as her head pounded like virtuk hooves on stone, she saw a thin strip of fabric on the ground.

With a grunt, she dragged herself across the floor, dropping flat on her stomach as she reached the fabric, her arms refusing to keep pulling her weight.

Her breaths grew heavy, her eyelids drooping as consciousness slipped from her grasp. Kira shook her head, letting out a short breath, then lifted the piece of fabric into her hand.

In the dim light that crept in around the doorframe, she could barely make out the fabric's crimson colouring. She knew its touch: the smooth linen of her Queensguards' cloaks.

Kira had personally hand-picked every member of her guard. They had been family to her, and now even they had betrayed her. The thought called that primal fury back to the fore, the pain ebbing at the corners of her mind. But then, as her bloody hands shook, she noticed something: the fabric had not been torn, but neatly cut.

It had not been ripped free in the fighting. It had been cut and placed – with a little haste, by the looks of it, but intentionally.

They wanted me to find it.

Kira allowed herself to drop back onto the stone, her muscles crying out in relief. She drew heavy breaths, every inch of her body throbbing, her head pounding, and her right eye swollen shut.

But as she lay there, her fingers tightening around the strip of red linen, a smile crept onto Kira's face.

They were coming for her.

CHAPTER SEVEN

GUARDIANS

6ᵗʰ Day of the Blood Moon

Aravell – Winter, Year 3081 After Doom

alen stood in the eyrie connected to Alura. In the distance, the Blood Moon's crimson light sprayed over the rocky cliffs, igniting the thin clouds in an incandescent fury.

Before him, Valerys's snow-white scales glistened, tinted with a ruby hue. In the dragon's attempt to fly to Calen, he had reopened several wounds sustained in the battle and now groaned in discomfort as the elven Healers pushed themselves to exhaustion trying to sew the injuries back together with the Spark.

The four elves applied healing salves to the open wounds on Valerys's underbelly, wings, and legs, threads of each elemental strand swirling around them. From what Calen understood, the concoctions helped to take the burden off the Healers, allowing them to work for longer. Even with the salves, lethargy seeped into their movements with each passing moment, the drain sapping at them as they worked.

From what Vaeril had told him, when it came to healing with the Spark, the larger a creature, the more complex their workings, the deeper the wounds, the more energy it required to heal. Dragons, as Vaeril had explained to him, were the most difficult of all, and Valerys was not the only dragon that had sustained deep wounds during the fighting.

Off to Calen's right, on another of the Eyrie's platforms, the two surviving Rakina dragons – Varthear and Sardakes – lay curled together, enormous masses of blue and black scales.

"I told you not to come," Calen whispered as he looked into Valerys's lavender eyes. He cast his gaze over the dragon, feeling Valerys's pain in every breath. Calen hated seeing him like this. "You need to rest."

Valerys lifted his head and shook his neck – much to the dismay of the elven Healers – letting out a warm breath of air that smelled of smouldering coals, a defiant rumble in his chest. He pushed his snout into Calen's chest with enough force that Calen had to brace himself to stop from falling backwards. No words were needed. Calen could feel Valerys's intent: *you should not have put yourself in danger.*

"Faenir wouldn't have harmed me."

The images that flashed in Calen's mind let him know that Valerys disagreed with that assessment. Would Faenir have done him harm? It was near-impossible to imagine, but the wolfpine was different than Calen remembered. Larger, more savage. There had been something in his eyes as he stood over Ella – a ferocity.

Calen let out an exhausted sigh. So much had changed in the last two years. Everything he had known about the world had turned on its head. Why was it so hard for him to believe Faenir was any different? Probably because he had known Faenir since the wolfpine had been nothing but a pup, small enough to hold in the crook of his elbow. Calen remembered the first night that tiny ball of fur sat in his arms by the fire. Faenir had spent the whole night whimpering, so much so that Calen had left his bed and slept on the floor with the pup all night, and every night thereafter for a week.

Allowing the memory to linger, he rested one hand on Valerys's snout, then ran his other along Valerys's scales. Calen's fingertips slipped into the cuts and gouges that marked the dragon's body, tracing over the rough edges. Valerys's scales had once been smooth as polished stone, and he, too, had been as small as Faenir had been. That seemed so long ago now.

He looked down at the discoloured scar on the back of his own hand where the lance of stone had ripped straight through his palm during the battle for the city. The Healers had offered to rid him of the mark – it had been fresh enough to heal fully. He'd been tempted, but ultimately, he'd refused, just as Dann had when the Fade had struck him with lightning in Belduar. Some scars were worth keeping, if only to remind a person of how close they'd come to Heraya's embrace.

Lucky didn't come close to encapsulating what Calen had been the night of the attack. Had Tivar and Avandeer not appeared, he and Valerys would have been ripped to pieces.

If Ella hadn't roused the Rakina dragons. If they hadn't caught Eríthan by surprise. If the Dragonguard hadn't been so sure of their advantage.

If. If. If.

All that had separated Calen and Valerys from death was an ocean of ifs. Sensing Calen's thoughts, Valerys nuzzled his snout harder against Calen's body. The dragon matched Calen's gaze, unblinking. Those enormous lavender eyes shone as they stared at him, images flooding from Valerys to Calen: Dann, Haem, Erik, Tarmon, Vaeril, Ella… so many more.

The images, no, the memories continued to flow like a river through a broken dam.

The white spires of Aravell, the crashing waterfalls, the trees, the elves.

It took a moment, but Calen finally understood what Valerys was trying to tell him: it didn't matter what could have happened or what should have happened. All that mattered is what *did* happen. Their friends, their family, and their new home were safe. Tens of thousands drew breath who otherwise would have burned alive in dragonfire.

Calen leaned forwards and pressed his forehead against the dragon's scales, closing his eyes and allowing Valerys to take his weight. The dragon's warmth seeped into him, easing the pain in his soul. "Du aendret myia viël, Valerys. Myia nithríen. I denír viël ar altinua."

You changed my life, Valerys. My soulkin. In this life and always.

A deep rumble resonated in Valerys's throat, the dragon's scales seeming to grow warmer to Calen's touch. They stayed like that, unmoving for minutes until a gasp broke the silence.

Valerys and Calen broke apart, shifting to see that one of the elven Healers had collapsed on his side, limbs splayed in all directions.

The other Healers knelt beside him, lifting his head and checking his eyes.

"He has nothing left, Draleid," one of the Healers – an elf by the name of Namír – said as Calen approached. The elf bowed at the waist. "I will send for porters to carry him back and for another to take his place."

"No." Calen looked down at the collapsed Healer.

Namír stared back at him in confusion. "But your soulkin, Draleid. He still suffers. He cannot—"

"We all suffer, Namír. There are thousands of injured in the city that need a Healer's hand. You could save hundreds with what you give to Valerys. He will heal. All he needs is rest. Your gift to him is time, your gift to others is life. Valerys will not need any more healing."

"But, Draleid…"

The elf trailed off as Calen shook his head, then gestured towards the collapsed elf. "Go. Ensure that he gets seen to. Valerys is strong enough to make his way to the ceremony."

The elf gave a brisk nod, keeping his eyes fixed on the floor, then turned back towards the others.

"Namír."

The Healer looked to Calen, more than a touch of apprehension in his eyes. "Du haryn myia vrai." Calen inclined his head to the other Healers. "Du aillin ata."

You have my thanks. You all do.

Namír's generally severe expression cracked, a half-smile touching his lips. He clasped his hands and inclined his head. "Du gryr haydria til ourín elwynar."

You bring honour to our hearts.

As the Healers packed their things and set off, Calen dropped to the ground beside Valerys. He leaned against the dragon's scales and took that precious moment of peace where there was nothing else but him and the other half of his soul. That peace was short-lived though as he lifted his gaze to the crimson orb in the sky.

In the days since the battle, he hadn't had much of a chance to truly let that fact settle in, to truly think on what that red moon meant, the gravity of it. Much like everything else that had happened in the past two years, the Blood Moon had been nothing but a legend to Calen, a myth, something conjured by bards to lend weight to a tale. From all the stories, and from what Chora and the others had said, it was the herald of death and devastation, and it would taint the skies for a full month.

Calen pushed his chest forwards, his back cracking, tense muscles stretching. And as he did, a roar tore through the night, echoing off the rock.

Calen sat up straight and Valerys shifted behind him. The dragon lifted his head, a blend of anger and sorrow seeping from his mind and causing Calen to clench his jaw. Across the way, both Sardakes and Varthear had stirred, their gazes fixed on the same thing as Valerys's: a passage in the rock on the western edge of the Eyrie.

A second roar followed the first, resonating in the mountain basin. It reeked of pain and suffering.

Valerys pushed himself upright with his forelimbs, a deep rumble in his chest, his limbs screaming out in complaint.

"After the ceremony," Calen whispered, standing. He rested his hand on the old wound from the Fade's lightning that had marred Valerys's side since Kingspass. "They will not have to wait much longer."

A third roar erupted from the passage.

Valerys turned his head and looked to Calen, only for a moment, anguish and rage in his eyes. The dragon turned back to the passage and unleashed a roar of his own in answer. Calen's entire body shook from the vibrations that travelled from Valerys up through his hand and arm. And with Valerys's roar, two more joined. Sardakes and Varthear now stood tall on the other plateau, their scales sparkling in the crimson light. The entire Eyrie shook, the dragons' roars sounding like a thunderstorm raged in the basin.

The sight of all three dragons roaring set every hair on Calen's body on end and caused his pulse to quicken. He clenched his jaws, curling his fingers into fists as Valerys's fury overwhelmed him.

When the roars died out and the rage ebbed, the sound of crunching dirt reached Calen's ears. He turned to find Aeson, Chora, Atara, and Harken approaching.

Atara and Harken inclined their heads to Calen, pressing closed fists to their chests, while Aeson gave the shortest of nods and Chora ignored him entirely. They hadn't spoken since Calen had discovered both Tivar and Avandeer had survived the battle and Chora had insisted on imprisoning them both until a decision could be made on the path forward. Calen understood the choice on a practical level, but it didn't mean he agreed with it.

Chora's gaze moved to the three dragons as she wheeled towards Calen, a pensive look in her eyes. She stopped near Valerys, seemingly lost in thought as she blew a strand of straw-blonde hair from her face. "Fascinating."

"What?"

"I've not seen either Sardakes or Varthear show this kind of emotion since before they were Broken. I've not seen it from any dragon who has become Rakina. Not even Ithrax."

Calen took a step towards Chora, allowing some of Valerys's anger to burn in him. "You have one of their kin in chains – one of ours."

"A traitor," Chora snapped, her demeanour shifting in an instant. She glared at Calen. "The both of them."

Valerys reared behind Calen, fury burning away the pain of his wounds. The plateau shook as the dragon approached and lowered his head over Calen. Calen glared at Chora, his and Valerys's anger blending.

Both Atara and Harken stared up at Valerys, visibly tensing. Chora, however, returned Calen's stare without flinching, not even glancing at the looming dragon.

Calen spoke with a level tone, but his voice was ice. "If it weren't for those *traitors*, we would all be dead. Every one of us. Every elf, every human, every Angan and Jotnar – every soul in this city. And you wouldn't be here to cast sentence over them. You owe them a debt."

With an eerie sense of calm, Chora placed her hands on the wheels of her chair and pushed forwards until she was a foot from Calen. "Those traitors and others of their kind are the reason we've spent the last four hundred years hiding." Even with Valerys's warm breath blowing her hair, Chora did not waver, her eyes cold and hard. "You think Tivar and Avandeer are any different to Farda, or Ilyain, or Hala, or Eltoar Daethana himself? They have slain both dragons and Draleid. They have laid waste to armies and levelled cities. They are the reason my Daiseer lies cold in the ground. They are the reason the ones I loved no longer draw breath." Chora's voice grew harsh and dark. "They are the reason my world burned. One noble deed does not balance a lifetime of darkness. I owe them *nothing*."

Calen's breath trembled as he stared back at Chora. Since meeting the woman, he'd found her to be stern, at times harsh, but always with glimpses of levity. That was gone now; her eyes held only fury and loss.

"This is not the time nor the place." Aeson stepped between the two of them, tilting his head and raising his hand. He locked his gaze on Calen's for a moment before staring at Chora. "We said we would hold off on the decisions until after King Silmiryn's successor was announced and the mourning ceremony was held. We still have respect for the dead, do we not?"

Chora ground her teeth, fingers pressing against the bone-white plates at the side of her chair's wheels. She looked as though she was about to challenge Aeson but instead she gave him a sharp nod.

Aeson looked to Calen, who mimicked Chora's gesture.

"Good. With the Blood Moon in the sky, the elves of Lynalion burning the North, and the imperial armies marching across the South, decisions must be made swiftly. Fane and the empire will not take this defeat lying down. We must be ready. But before that, we must ensure our house is tidy. After the ceremony, we shall reconvene here along with the others. This is the time we've been waiting for."

"Agreed." Harken folded his arms, dense muscle bulging through his shirt. The man was so large he looked as though he were part Jotnar. He flashed a glance across the Eyrie towards the passage to where Tivar, Avandeer, and the others were being held. He nodded softly, as though accepting something, then sighed. He looked to Calen. "With that, we must make haste. The mourning ceremony will begin shortly, and our lateness would bring great dishonour. Valerys has recovered enough to attend?"

"He has." Calen reached up and brushed his fingers against one of the horns that framed the bottom of Valerys's jaw. "It'll be a few days before he's ready to truly take flight, but he is strong enough for this."

"Let us be gone then," Harken said, turning as he spoke. "King Galdra is not known for his patience."

"Give me just a moment," Calen asked, inclining his head and making his way across the Eyrie to where Sardakes and Varthear occupied a plateau of thick grass.

The two mighty dragons watched Calen approach, a brightness in their eyes that had not been there the first time he'd entered the Eyrie. They shifted as Valerys moved behind Calen. Both dragons were at least twice Valerys's size, but even still he stood tall, a deep growl in his chest.

Sardakes, with his flight taken from him when his soulkin died, hadn't fought in the Battle of Aravell. But he had not moved from Varthear's side from the moment she had returned. His scales were black as polished obsidian, his eyes a vibrant blue.

"Sardakes moves only to eat and drink," Calen remembered Chora saying when Calen had first come to Alura. Those words had proven true over the months that had followed. Along with the others, Sardakes's listless despondency had broken Valerys's heart. The dragon may not have fought in the battle above Aravell, but something had changed in him nonetheless.

Beside the black-scaled dragon, the only survivor of the Rakina dragons who had come to Calen and Valerys's aid, Varthear, was a canvas of scars and fused scales. The Healers had mended the tears in her brilliant vermillion wings, but the deep wounds of body and flesh would take longer to recover.

As Calen drew closer, Sardakes pushed past Varthear and stood over Calen, lips pulling back to reveal rows of spear-like teeth, the sapphire-tinged frills on his back pricking. The dragon's warm breath blew over Calen's face, the familiar smell of ash and char filling the air. With jaws wider than Calen was tall and his dense, scale-covered chest puffed out, Sardakes looked every bit the terrifying creature of legend that Calen had always known dragons to be.

Valerys loomed over Calen, the purple light of his eyes shining against Sardakes's scales. Both dragons leaned their necks forwards, snouts only feet apart, chests rumbling. Sardakes may have dwarfed Valerys, but Valerys cared little; he would protect his soulkin even if Efialtír himself stood over them.

Calen swallowed hard, staring up at the two dragons. Doubt crept into his mind, but he took another step forward, and as he did, Varthear growled and pushed her head into Sardakes's neck, knocking the black dragon off balance.

Sardakes snapped tamely at Varthear, but then backed away, bowing his head.

Calen could hear every beat of his heart thumping against his ribs, every breath his lungs drew.

Varthear craned her neck forwards so her snout hovered just off the ground only a foot from Calen. The dragon could have swallowed him whole with ease. Some of the horns that stretched back from her jaw were longer than Calen's legs.

She stared at him with eyes red as liquid fire, warmth radiating from her scales.

Calen drew a calming breath and extended his right hand. He allowed his fingers to float inches from Varthear's cobalt scales. Exhaling slowly, he rested his hand along a fused scar that stretched upwards from the dragon's lip. A moment of warmth spread through Calen's hand before the familiar ringing sounded in his ears and his vision blurred, fading to black before bursting with white light.

Just as they had when Queen Uthrían had grasped his forearm, memories flooded Calen's mind. Memories that were not his own. Images of a time long past, fleeting and broken.

A light filled his eyes, then faded, feelings of comfort, warmth, and safety overcoming him as he stared up into the eyes of a young elf.

"Draleid n'aldryr, unwë ayar," the elf whispered, cradling him in his arms. "Din navn væra Varthear."

Dragonbound by fire, little one. Your name will be Varthear.

More memories flitted through Calen, emotions crashing into him: anger, joy, fear, hope. His pulse raced, his breath trembled, his heart sank. Of it all, one thing rose above all else: Varthear's love of her soulkin, Ilmirín. The Draleid had been fierce and strong, yet gentle. Wise and learned, but always willing to listen. It was his heart that had taught Varthear how to love, his soul that had shown her what kindness was. She would have given anything and everything to have kept him safe. She would have given her life a hundred times over, endured any pain the world could conjure… but instead, she had been cursed to watch him die.

The world flickered, flashes of fire and lightning igniting the darkness around Calen. He was swerving through thick clouds, a storm raging on all sides. Panic and fear permeated every piece of his shared soul.

A bright flash illuminated the sky before him, and he watched as a dragon covered in brilliant yellow scales ripped another from the sky, blood dancing with the rain.

He swerved to avoid a column of dragonfire, its light burning through the dark. All around him, Draleid and dragons tore each other to pieces. Brothers and sisters, lovers and friends. Everything he had ever known was crumbling before his eyes.

The world blurred and shifted once more, and now he was on his side, solid ground beneath him. A blinding pain burned where talons had carved through his scales. But his pain was nothing, not compared to the terror that wracked his bones.

His soulkin lay bleeding on the rocks not fifty feet from him. Ilmirín had been ripped from Calen's back and thrown through the air. He could hear Ilmirín's heartbeat faltering, feel his consciousness fading.

Calen pushed himself upright with his forelimbs, urging every drop of strength he had into Ilmirín. If he could get his soulkin to a Healer, he could save him. No matter how many traitors filled the sky. He would carry Ilmirín through the void if he had to.

A heartbeat passed, the world flickering once more. An enormous weight crashed into his side, talons slicing through his shoulder, jaws wrapping around his neck.

He knew the dragon who attacked him. Hrothmundar, soulkin to Jormun Stonefist. Large as a mountain, with a heart that smelled of burning blood.

Calen thrashed and roared, swiping at Hrothmundar with his forelimbs, but he was wounded, his strength ebbing. Jaws closed around his throat. And while Hrothmundar held him against the rock, Calen felt Ilmirín die.

The world broke. Calen's heart shattered. His soul sundered. There was not a word spoken in the tongues of living things that came close to the grief, agony, and emptiness that became him. He was hollow, and numb, and nothing.

As Hrothmundar tore into his side, all Calen could do was stare at Ilmirín's lifeless body, blood seeping onto the stone.

A roar thundered overhead, and then Hrothmundar was lifted off Calen and sent crashing into a boulder. Two dragons plummeted from the sky, rivers of dragonfire pouring down over Hrothmundar and Jormun.

Listlessly, Calen pulled himself upright. He was empty, the world around him dull and faded. He hobbled to Ilmirín's body and nudged his soulkin with his snout. Ilmirín simply lay there. His warmth was gone. His smile stolen.

Calen lowered himself, draping his wing over his soulkin's body and resting his head on the ground. There was no joy without Ilmirín, no warmth or purpose.

The world spun around Calen once more, shifting and changing, flashing forwards. Something nudged him but he didn't move. There was no point in moving, no point in breathing.

A pair of ice-blue eyes appeared before him, scales dark as the deep ocean: Lyara. Her heart smelled of lightning and fresh rain, her warmth was that of the morning sun. Lyara whined, pressing her snout into Calen's jaw, begging him to rise, pleading with him.

After a moment, a hand rested on the scales of his cheek. "Din saleere er ourín saleere, Varthear. Din nithír er ourín nithír. Vir væra kanet tiastri du."

Your pain is our pain, Varthear. Your soul is our soul. We will not leave you.

Calen stared into Aeson Virandr's eyes before the world shifted again.

Time passed. Aeson kept Calen safe, brought him to the elves. Years turned to decades, turned to centuries. Every moment of life was devoid of purpose, or joy, or meaning. It was apathy unending.

Until one day something changed. A soul reached out to his. That soul offered purpose. It asked him to be a protector, asked him to save the ones it loved. The soul's words stirred something within him, lit a fire long extinguished. He was still Rakina, still Broken, but now he was more. He was a guardian of one who was loved – all that Ilmirín had ever wanted to be.

Once again, the world faded to black and burst forth in a flash of incandescent light.

He was in the sky, rain pummelling against his scales, death all around him.

Ahead, a smaller dragon with scales of pure white tumbled through the air with a much larger beast – Hrothmundar. A rage unlike anything Calen had felt in centuries ignited within him. As he tore through the sky towards the two dragons, a pillar of fire poured from the white dragon's jaws, consuming Hrothmundar's soulkin. A pang of sympathy flared within him, but he quickly snuffed it out. They deserved to feel the same pain they had caused.

In that moment, Calen watched the smaller dragon clamp their teeth around Hrothmundar's neck and rip out his throat.

One final time, the world shifted, and Calen was standing in the Eyrie, sweat cooling on his skin, lungs heaving, heart pounding. With his hand still resting on Varthear's scales, he stared back at the dragon and dropped to his knees, his breath misting in the air before him.

Above Calen, Valerys leaned forwards, the side of his snout brushing against Varthear's, tender and warm.

There, in Alura's eyrie, the light of the Blood Moon tainting the sky, all three dragons roared so loud as to rival thunder itself.

CHAPTER EIGHT

THE BEGINNING AND THE END

6ᵗʰ Day of the Blood Moon

Temple of Achyron – Winter, Year 3081 After Doom

Kallinvar stood at the edge of the great plateau, his loose shirt flapping in the wind. Dark clouds streaked the sky in lazy brush strokes, mottled with pink and grey. The Blood Moon, full and clear, was a wound in the world, leaking across the night.

He could have summoned the knights to the war room or the Heart Chamber, but this was where he wanted them. He needed them to look upon Efialtír's mark, needed them to *feel* The Shadow, to understand what it was they truly faced.

To Kallinvar's left, Ardholm spread out across the mountainside, set into an enormous horseshoe-shaped inlet. Smoke wafted from the chimneys of the many homes, lanterns illuminating the hundreds of windows carved into the rockface. In the time from when Kallinvar had taken the Sigil until that moment, Ardholm's population had grown tenfold, if not more. He had always known it as a village and still called it as such, but in truth, it was a city. And as the city's numbers rose, they pushed deeper into the mountain, carving new homes, stores, chambers. He would do anything to protect this place, to protect its people, *his* people.

Ruon moved so she stood at his side.

"They will follow you wherever you lead," she said, gesturing over her shoulder at the knights – what was left of them – gathering on the plateau.

Kallinvar nodded, pulling a lungful of air in through his nose.

"I need more…" he whispered. The words weren't for himself or Ruon, but for Achyron, for the god who held them all in the palm of his hands. "I don't know what I'm doing. I need more."

"Come to me, my child."

Just as it had before, the Sigil fused with Kallinvar's chest ignited with a furious energy, sending a ripple through him. A brilliant green light burst across his vision, obscuring the world before him, and everything fell silent.

One heartbeat. Two.

A shriek pierced the silence, followed by a second and a third. A thunderous explosion roared in Kallinvar's ears, screams and shouts, the clang of steel, the raging of fire and the wails of death.

Slowly, the green light faded.

Kallinvar stood on the rise of a hill covered in blades of grass that glistened like emerald shards. Hundreds of warriors surrounded him. Each was garbed in armour of shimmering green steel, the Sigil of Achyron emblazoned across their breastplates. Not one looked to be from a race Kallinvar knew. Their appearance was almost human, but the smallest was over a head taller than he, with skin the colour of terracotta. Its face was sharp and angular, its nose flat, eyes green from edge to edge with pupils that looked like beaded black slits.

A few of the warriors glanced in Kallinvar's direction but gave him no heed. They looked out over the hill's crest, towards a battlefield like none Kallinvar had ever seen.

A crush of bodies swarmed at the base of the hill. No fewer than a hundred thousand. Even from where Kallinvar stood, he could see the pulsing light of thousands of Soulblades in a myriad of hues. Arcs of lightning and plumes of black fire streaked through the mass while monstrous creatures as large as dragons tore through swells of bodies.

With every second Kallinvar stared, he saw something new: gargantuan warriors in red plate swinging axes larger than his body, creatures four times the size of a horse with three horns jutting from their skulls, winged creatures with dark jagged scales and ferocious mandibles crashed down again and again.

As Kallinvar watched in awe, a figure marched up the hill, armour-clad warriors at his flanks.

Kallinvar dropped to a knee, pulling his hand across his chest. After the disaster at Ilnaen, after so many of his brothers and sisters had been taken from the world, souls sheared, an anger had burned within him at the god who spoke in his mind. But still, in Achyron's presence that fury melted away, replaced with shame for ever having doubted his god.

"Rise, my child."

Slowly, Kallinvar lifted his gaze to see Achyron standing before him in the same green plate with pauldrons in the shape of blazing suns. Blood-covered armour. At least, Kallinvar thought it was blood. It wasn't the deep crimson hue with which he was so familiar, but white and blue and glistening gold. Splodges of black marred Achyron's cheek, a viscous luminescent purple dripping from his gauntleted fingertips. The god held a scintillating green Soulblade in his right hand and a shield wrought from the same light in his left.

Kallinvar made to speak. His lips moved, but no sound came. This was the god of legend. The god that had saved him from the brink of death. The god whose halls all souls wished to enter. This was The Warrior.

Achyron looked to the others around him and to those who had been waiting beside Kallinvar, then gestured towards the battlefield. Soulblades burst into life, their light reflecting in the emerald grass.

"Anatarion." Achyron looked to a warrior with onyx black skin, streaks of marbled blue running diagonally across his face. Kallinvar had never seen the like before. White horns protruded from the front of Anatarion's skull, wings of leathery blue at his back. "Take the Rhunîr around the western flank. Crush the Urithnilim from the rear. This battle ends now. Efialtír has pushed too deep into our lands. I will permit it no longer."

"As you command, Blessed One." Anatarion inclined his head, then set off down the western slope of the hill, the others moving at his back.

Achyron stared after them a moment before looking back to Kallinvar. "I told you the Alignment was only the beginning, my child." He gestured towards the battlefield. "Can you see that now? This war does not solely blight the mortal plane. Efialtír has spent millennia waiting for this moment. He seeks to hold us here while his Vitharnmír work to cross him to your realm. And all the while, my kin feign blindness." Achyron drew in a slow breath. "This battle is but one of a thousand raging across our world. He throws everything he has at us. The war in this realm is not one he needs to win. It is simply one he needs to wage. My brothers and sisters will soon see that they can no longer stand back and watch, but by that time, it may be too late. They will not act outside this realm until Efialtír crosses and, in doing so, breaks the last vow. But no matter the oaths, no matter the cost, we cannot allow that to happen."

Kallinvar pulled his closed fist across his chest once more. Every shred of anger and doubt that had touched his mind was now gone, obliterated in Achyron's presence. "Tell me what it is you need from me. It will be done. I am your sword."

"Efialtír seeks to cross into your world, to take a form of flesh and blood. That has been his wish ever since the birth of the first life in the mortal plane. He achieved it once, millennia ago, breaking the sacred oaths we swore. On that day, he sowed his seed into the crust of creation and formed the tether that connects our worlds, the conduit that allows his power to seep through the veil – and to harness the essence of life that flows back. That was the day he earned his name. With his Chosen now in the mortal plane, he is closer than ever to crossing once more."

Achyron folded his arms and looked out over the battle that raged below. "The Urithnilim we have captured alive speak of something called the Heart of Blood. It was difficult to tell through their screams, but from what we know it is a well of life Essence so large that in the hands of Efialtír's Chosen, it contains the power to carry him across the veil. His harbingers do not possess the Heart, for if they did, your world would already be ash and dust. But they search for it ceaselessly. I need you, Kallinvar, and my children to find the Heart and destroy it. And failing that, I need you to keep it from Efialtír's hands while the Alignment continues. This is not the same as his last crossing, my child. The fabric of everything will change if he succeeds."

"We will not fail you." Kallinvar lifted his gaze. He paused a moment. How did one address a god? That was a question he would need to ask Gildrick. For now, he mimicked Anatarion's words. "Blessed One, how am I to find such a thing? A single stone across an entire continent."

"Feel for his corruption, feel for the Taint that tarnishes the world. Follow it, and you will stand between Efialtír and his desires."

Kallinvar nodded slowly. "It will be done, but… my brothers and sisters, our numbers are few, and the Chosen, they are not like us… They are stronger."

The world seemed to shift around Kallinvar, blurring. A green light spread across Achyron's body, and when it faded, the god stood no more than a head over Kallinvar, his eyes misting that same green light. "The Vitharnmír are Efialtír's sworn champions, born of his own flesh and blood. They are amongst the mightiest of his warriors. In their crossing, they shed some of their strength, but godsblood still flows in their veins. They are creatures of this realm."

Achyron reached forward and placed his open palm against Kallinvar's chest.

"I cannot forge you into what they are, nor do I want to. You are Voran Thrace, son of Hallain and Yor Thrace, brother to Lok, Allay, and Sanira. You are the son of a fisherman and a basket weaver. You spent your childhood defending your sick brother and earning every penny you could to help put food in your family's mouths. When your mother died, you swore yourself to the Amendel Royal Guard and sent all your coin to your father. You rose to become the queen's shield, her most trusted warrior. And that is where I found you, the breath aching in your dying lungs, the blood spilling from your veins, the city burning around you, and the queen and her family alive because of your strength. You have spent your life giving everything for others. At every turn, every fork in the road, every branching path, you chose to shoulder the burden so that others would not have to bear its weight. I choose my champions with care, Grandmaster Kallinvar. And I chose you."

Achyron turned back to look at the battle below. "As for your numbers. It is time for you to replenish. War consumes your world. I will allow the dying voices to speak to you. Find those who are worthy and give them the chance to save it. Let them bear the weight of my Sigil."

A blinding purple light burst into life on Kallinvar's left, and a voice boomed. "What is the meaning of this, Achyron?"

Achyron's jaw clenched. He looked to the light, which had forged itself into the shape of an archway, then back to Kallinvar. "This is it, my child. All paths end here. This task was always yours. It was always meant to be you standing at the precipice. Do not doubt." He glanced back towards the archway that had formed from thin air, wisps of purple mist sweeping forwards. "Go now."

Kallinvar's Sigil pulsed and that same sharp noise sounded in the back of his mind. "Please, before you send me back—" Kallinvar clamped his hand to the side of his head, trying to drown out the high-pitched sound. "One of my brothers was pulled into the tear in the veil when it closed."

"Brother Tarron." Achyron inhaled slowly, looking over his shoulder at the dark figure now stepping through the archway. "He is alive. I can feel his soul tethered to mine. But I do not know where. Something masks it. You must go."

Kallinvar wanted to ask for more, but the piercing noise grew louder, an unending shriek, and green light once more filled his vision. In a heartbeat, a cold breeze rolled over his cheeks, air filling his lungs.

He opened his eyes to the Blood Moon etched into the night sky, its light piercing charcoal clouds that blanketed the horizon. Kallinvar pressed his fingers against his shirt, feeling the cold metallic touch of the Sigil in his chest. Something was different. *He* was different. Voices called to his mind, faint, weak, and muffled. Some lasted only seconds, while others clung on, unwilling to be silenced.

"Sigil bearers…" Kallinvar's jaw slackened as he realised the voices were souls of the dying, the last calls of those who still clung to life.

He drew several long breaths, trying to calm the chaos in his mind.

"Kallinvar?" Ruon's voice sounded from over Kallinvar's shoulder.

He allowed his gaze to linger on the Blood Moon for a moment longer before turning to her.

"You walked to the edge," Ruon said, looking past Kallinvar to where he had been standing only moments before. "You looked as though you were in some kind of trance. I called to you, but… you just stared out at the clouds."

Kallinvar clasped his hands on Ruon's shoulders. "I was there, Ruon."

"You were where?" she asked, eyes narrowing.

"In the realm of the gods."

Ruon slowly lifted her gaze, looking into Kallinvar's eyes. Her lips moved, but no sound came.

Kallinvar nodded to the unspoken question. "I was there."

More knights ascended the stairs to the plateau, falling in around Kallinvar. He spotted Ildris, Lyrin, Arden, and the others of The Second amongst them.

Kallinvar looked into Ruon's eyes for a moment, then stepped forwards, casting his gaze over those gathered. He caught Gildrick's stare from among the other Watchers and priests.

As silence settled, shuffling feet coming to a stop, murmurs fading, eyes fixing on Kallinvar, he drew a breath, then spoke. "I have called you all here, under the light of the Blood Moon, to tell you that our time is now. Each and every one of you has suffered loss and hardship. For some, hundreds of summers have passed before your eyes. We have watched our homes burn and fade into the annals, our loved ones die, our bloodlines wither. And we have stood by, keeping our creed. But we were, each of us, chosen. For our strength, our will, our hearts. We carry this burden because we are the only ones who can. We carry it so that others need not know its pain. We are the Knights of Achyron. We stand when others kneel. We fight when others falter. And we charge when others yield. It is our duty to protect those who cannot protect themselves, to defend this world against the coming shadow. I am not Verathin, nor will I ever be. I assure you, if I had the choice, I would take his place in a heartbeat."

The wind whistled and gusted, sweeping dust across the stone plateau. Kallinvar settled himself with a breath, rolling back his shoulders. He had spent hours preparing a speech, thinking on how he would tell the others that he heard Achyron's voice in his mind, how he would convince them that he wasn't within insanity's grasp, that a god had truly spoken to him. But all that melted away as he looked out over the gathered crowd of knights, Watchers, and priests.

"Achyron has spoken to me."

Murmurs spread. Shock clear on many faces, confusion on others. But within seconds, the murmurs had died and Kallinvar saw only expectation. All eyes were on him.

"He spoke to you?" Sister-Captain Emalia of The Tenth stepped forwards. There was no scepticism in her voice. Her gaze was fixed on his.

"He did." Kallinvar nodded. "I can hear his words in my head even now. He took my soul to the Godsrealm, showed me the war that wages there, and gave me our path forward. I know how it sounds… I thought I had lost my mind at first…"

Sister-Captain Olyria dropped to one knee, a closed fist drawn across her chest. She lifted her head so her gaze met Kallinvar's, but not a word left her lips.

Brother-Captain Gandrid knelt beside Olyria, with Armites, Darmerian, and Airdaine following suit. Ruon moved past Kallinvar and joined the others, a soft smile curling her lips.

The last of the captains to step from the gathered crowd was Sister-Captain Arlena of The First. She had fought at Verathin's side for centuries, been his sword and shield – his friend. The sound of her armoured boots clipping against the stone rose above the silence. She walked past the others, stopping before Kallinvar. Arlena stared into Kallinvar's eyes, the green of her irises swirling with specks of brown and gold.

"You are not Verathin."

The words lingered in the air, hanging heavy, but as Kallinvar made to speak, Arlena continued. "But nobody could be. I trust you with my life. Your word is without question, your deeds without equal. It has been my honour to fight at your side and answer your call. And when my soul finally leaves this world, I will walk into Achyron's halls telling The Warrior himself that I died fighting alongside Grandmaster Kallinvar, alongside one of the greatest souls I have ever known."

Arlena knelt, resting her two palms across her bent knee, then lifted her chin to look at Kallinvar.

"We were not given our lives to spend them sitting next to a warm hearth and getting fat on ale and cheese. Tell us where Achyron needs our blades. Even if it is to the void itself, we will follow you."

As Arlena spoke, the rest of the knights across the platform knelt, resting their hands across their knees and looking to Kallinvar. Even the priests and Watchers followed.

A surge of pride swept through Kallinvar, and for a moment, he felt as though Verathin stood beside him, a hand on his shoulder.

I never thought I would do this without you, old friend.

"Achyron asks us to find an object of great power – the Heart of Blood. A vessel that holds the Life Essence of hundreds of thousands. We are to find it and destroy it so that Efialtír can never cross into our world," Kallinvar called. "And if that cannot be done, we are to ensure that the Heart never falls into the hands of The Traitor's followers while the Blood Moon holds sway over this world. We will strike every convergence of the Taint, burn it out root and stem wherever it dares rise. We will scour the lost city of Ilnaen, strike into the heart of Mar Dorul, storm the mountains of Wolfpine Ridge and Kolmir. But we will not do it alone..." As Kallinvar looked out over those gathered, he saw the faces in his mind of those they had lost: Verathin, Daynin, Mirken, Illarin, and so many others. "Achyron has opened my ears, and the voices of the new Sigil Bearers call to me. We cannot bring back those we have lost, but we can ensure their loss was not in vain."

Kallinvar stepped forwards and summoned his Soulblade. As the green light burst from his closed fist, he thrust his hand into the air, allowing the light of Achyron's soul to carve through that of Efialtír's moon. "The Godwar has begun, my brothers and sisters, and each of us has a part to play."

CHAPTER NINE

OLD TRICKS

6ᵗʰ Day of the Blood Moon

*Lost Hills, northwest of the Rolling Mountains – Winter,
Year 3081 After Doom*

Dayne stood at the top of the rise, his hands clasped behind his back as he looked down into the open valley. This was the highest point of the Lost Hills, just before they joined the Rolling Mountains, thousands of feet above the level of the sea. The march was an exhausting one, particularly for an army moving quickly with heavy armour and weapons.

Which was why Dayne had marched his five thousand warriors there two days beforehand. There would still be many aching muscles between them, but they would be far fresher than the host of seven thousand Thebalans hurrying to join the new head of their house, Aldon, at Achyron's Keep.

Aldon's father Miron, whom Dayne had killed in the siege of Myrefall, had commanded a force twice as large. Many had died in the siege, the survivors splitting in the aftermath. Some three thousand had joined Aldon and the rebellion, the rest scattering to the wind. Once word had spread that Aldon had followed his father's wishes and betrayed the rebellion, the other banners had gathered and marched to meet him at Achyron's Keep.

"I still think you should have taken the ten thousand your sister offered." Belina stepped up beside Dayne, sucking in her cheeks as she surveyed the land. The valley cut through the hills and forked, dense woodland bearing down on all sides. Something about having her there made the weight on Dayne's shoulders that little bit lighter.

"Five will do. With the ten thousand sent with Joros to retake Myrefall, Alina needs as many spears as she can muster to hold her position, lest Loren try to overwhelm her." It had been Dayne's plan. With the remnants of House Thebal's forces leaving Myrefall to join Aldon, the city would be vulnerable. A two-pronged attack, with Alina and the bulk of the free Valtaran forces holding position three days' march from Achyron's Keep. They needed to secure their rear before moving forward. But just because it had been his plan didn't mean he liked the idea of being so far from his sister, especially after what had happened the night of the betrayal.

"I like the sound of ten thousand a lot more than I do five. Oh, also, I have to admit, that armour looks good on you. Though I'm not sure how I feel about the skirts and those white crests." She nodded at the bronzed helmet Dayne held in the crook of his arm, the white horsehair crest of the Andurii running from front to back. "They do kind of break the first rule of ambushes."

"The first rule of ambushes?" one of Dayne's captains, Iloen, asked, raising his eyebrow curiously.

"Ignore her." Dayne shook his head.

The smile that spread across Belina's face was one which Dayne had grown far too accustomed to across the years. "Be a bush."

Iloen narrowed his eyes. "What?"

Dayne pressed his face into his palm. There would be no stopping her now.

"Where do you find these people, Dayne?" Belina looked at Iloen as though he were an idiot. "The first rule of ambushes, Ilan—"

"Iloen."

"Yes, Ilopen, like I said. Anyway, the word ambush comes from being able to say 'I am a bush', as in to blend in with your natural surroundings. So the first rule of ambushes is to *be* a bush. What bush wears white and orange skirts with a crest of white horsehair? That sounds a lot more like a flower to me. Damn attention seekers."

Iloen opened his mouth as though he were about to say something but thought better of it and pursed his lips.

"Sometimes it's best just to pretend she isn't there, Iloen."

"That's a lie," Belina whispered in Dayne's ear. "You missed me."

"Like a horse misses a flea."

"You're calling yourself a horse," Belina said with a shrug.

Dayne ran his free hand through his hair and let out a long, exasperated sigh.

"She's not entirely wrong." Dayne hadn't heard Mera approach. Alina had given her the command of twelve Wyndarii to assist in the ambush. She moved to Dayne's right, running her hand along the small of his back, giving him a soft smile. Her blue eyes stared into his for a moment before she looked out at the valley. "Once they enter the valley and we break through the trees, every second will count. The skirts and the helmets should stay behind."

"I told you." Belina shrugged again, holding her open palms out. "I can't help but be right. It's a curse."

Dayne just grunted, biting at the inside of his lip. As much as he appreciated the brief moment of levity around him, he could not share in it. He had no doubts that with the Andurii and the wyverns, his five thousand would carve through the Thebalans' numerical advantage. But still, many would die.

He hunkered down, running his fingers through the dry grass and pressing into the cracked earth beneath. It hadn't rained in weeks. He narrowed his eyes, surveying the valley, all the while rubbing dry dirt between his fingertips. "Mera, your scouts reported that the Thebalan ranks comprised vast numbers of cavalry, yes?"

"They did."

"How many?"

"Three thousand heavy horse with lances and shields, another six hundred light cavalry. Enough to turn the tide of any battle."

Belina crouched beside Dayne, looking at the dirt between his fingers. "What are you thinking?" She lowered her voice. "And why are we crouching?"

Dayne frowned at her. "You remember south of Elkenrim, about six years back?"

The smile on Belina's face vanished, replaced by a grim line. "Where I killed my father."

Dayne drew a slow breath and nodded in return. "The armies that march here wear thick armour and carry heavy ordos and valynas. They've been marching double for days on end and through the Lost Hills for the past two nights. They're completely exhausted. Add three thousand heavy cavalry to that…" Dayne pulled on threads of Earth and Water, feeling the elemental strands pulsate in his mind. He pressed his hand to the earth and pushed the threads into the ground, loosening the clay and pulling the moisture from the depths. Within seconds, the soil was thick and gloopy.

"It will be chaos," Belina said, her lips twisting into a grin. "My favourite."

"What are we doing?" Mera asked, staring down at Dayne and Belina.

"We're going to trap them like rats in a bucket," Dayne said, rising. He turned to Iloen. "Bring me the other captains and my bow. And Iloen?"

"Yes, Andurios?"

Dayne looked to Belina for a moment, still not quite believing what he was about to say. "I need every man and woman to cut off as much foliage as they can and lash it to their ordos."

Belina's face lit up. "*Be* the bush!"

SOME HOURS LATER, DAYNE KNELT about three quarters of the way down the slope towards the flat of the valley, looking out at a column of torches marching in the ever-present twilight of the Blood Moon. His ordo – or more so, his father's ordo – was driven into the earth before him, branches and leaves lashed to its front. Dayne gripped his bow in his left hand, two quivers of arrows waiting where the shield connected with the ground.

Half his forces were spread out along the hill beside him, stretching off for hundreds of feet, masked by the same foliage strapped to their shields. The other half were positioned across the hill on the opposite side of the valley, with Mera's Wyndarii waiting in the rear.

Ileeri and Dinekes knelt to Dayne's right and left, half the Andurii around them. Several valynas were laid out at each warrior's feet. The spears weren't typically used as missiles, but they would punch through plate as though it were dry wood.

Dayne almost leapt out of his skin as Belina whispered in his ear. "Why don't I get a shield?"

The woman had an unrivalled ability to move without making the slightest of sounds.

"Do you want a shield?"

"No, but that's not the point."

"Belina."

"It's just nice to be asked."

Dayne allowed himself a half-smile, staring down at the grass beneath him. He lifted his gaze, meeting Belina's. "Thank you for coming."

Belina's expression hardened, the perpetual note of levity abandoning her voice. "Always." She leaned forwards and grasped Dayne's arm. "I told you I would be here, and I am." Belina shook her head as though trying to stop a tear, then let out a short laugh. "Look at me. I think I've grass in my eye."

Dayne grasped the back of Belina's head and pulled their foreheads tighter together. "By blade and by blood."

"You Valtarans are so dramatic. Has anyone ever told you that?" Belina pulled away, wiping the back of her hand against her eye, then met Dayne's gaze once more. "I'll help you free Valtara, Dayne… or I'll die horribly."

"I'd rather you didn't die at all."

"No promises."

Dayne turned his head at the sound of shuffling feet to find Tarine Valanis dropping to one knee beside him. "Andurios. The Thebalans are entering the valley. Our forces are in position."

Dayne turned to Ileeri and Dinekes, who both gave him short nods.

"By blade and by blood, Andurios. They won't leave this place," the pair chorused.

Reaching for the Spark, Dayne pulled on threads of Air and Spirit, weaving them through his voice and mimicking an owl's hoot. The sound carried through the valley, amplified by the threads. Within seconds, shuffling feet and heavy breaths sounded around him. He wove the thread of Spirit through his eyes, adding Fire and granting himself moonsight. Across the valley, he could see the rest of the forces readying, the foliage strapped to their shields helping them blend seamlessly with the hillside.

He glanced towards the encroaching column of Thebalans at the mouth of the valley, the light of the torches like a river of blurred fire to Dayne's moonsight-enhanced eyes.

Dayne drew his breaths slowly, cold air filling his nostrils, warm air rolling over his lips. His pulse was steady, his heart well used to the anticipation of battle.

As the column marched forwards, Dayne closed his eyes, picturing twisting elemental strands in his mind, their light pulsing. He allowed his chest to swell with air, the slow thump of his heart sounding in his ears. In the darkness of his mind, he plucked heavy threads of Earth and Water. The hairs on his arms pricked at Water's cool touch, the weight of Earth filling him. He pushed the threads outwards, down the hill, and into the valley floor.

He could feel the touch of the dried, cracked clay, the grass brittle and dying. After a few moments, he found what he'd been looking for: a wealth of water gently flowing through the layers of deep rock and dirt hundreds of feet below.

"Wait for it," Belina whispered in his ear. "Waaait."

"Belina."

"Sorry. Old habits."

Dayne blocked Belina out. He needed to focus. Letting out a breath, he wove his threads into the water and drew it upwards, careful to follow the paths of least resistance through the rock. The Spark was a delicate thing. If he drew the water up too quickly or through a channel of dense rock, he would find the energy sapped from his bones in a few beats of his heart.

He drew the water up slowly, allowing it to soak the earth, turning it to mud so dense it would pull at boots and sap the energy from already tired legs. The speed of the Thebalan horses would suffer tenfold.

Below, the Thebalan forces slowed as they trudged through the dense mud, shouts and commands echoing in the natural acoustics of the valley. For a moment, Dayne feared they might turn back in favour of a better route. It's what he would have done. But their march was too urgent, and so they pushed forwards into the valley that would be their tomb, under a crimson-touched sky that was to be the last sky they would witness.

Dayne cast another cursory glance at the opposite slope. Even though he was looking for them, the other half of his forces were all but impossible to see. Masked by the foliage and aided by the night, they truly blended with the hillside.

Dayne hooted twice more, amplifying the sounds with threads of Air and Spirit. Around him, the sounds of shuffling signalled the others reaching for arrows or pulling valyna spears into their grasps.

Dayne slipped an arrow from the closest quiver, his fingers brushing the wild turkey feather fletching, black and grey striped. The wood was cedar, the sweet fresh scent lingering. He'd had the arrows made only a week prior by Tula Vakira's best fletcher. For some reason, knowing the heart of something, the core of what comprised it, gave Dayne a soothing sense of calm. Particularly if it was a weapon with which he was to take a life. And he would take many lives that night.

He nocked the arrow, and Marlin's words echoed in his head. The words the man had spoken the day Dayne had lost everything. No, the day Loren Koraklon and the empire had *taken* everything. Words that reminded him of his purpose.

"War is no different to peace. It is simply more honest. Do not hesitate, do not contemplate mercy. Remember everything I have taught you."

"Valtara will be free," Dayne whispered. "Even if I have to wade through a river of their blood. Valtara *will* be free. May the gods forgive me."

Dayne peered over the rim of his shield, watching as the column of torches continued their march.

Just a few more paces.

They needed to wait until the Thebalans had slogged far enough into the valley they would be entrenched in the mud, unable to flee while Dayne's warriors fell upon them. Dayne had never liked fights like this. A man should know how and why he died; that was a belief Dayne held close. But if doing it this way saved more lives in his charge, then so be it. Besides, the Thebalans had known why they would die the moment they'd betrayed their people. They'd sealed their own fates long ago.

Dayne twisted a little, pressing his boot into the ground to make sure he had solid purchase. He lifted himself more upright, angling his arrow above his shield's rim. Once more drawing in threads of Air and Spirit, Dayne let out a sharp whistle, drew his bowstring, picked his target, and loosed.

The snap of bowstrings sounded all about him, the soft whistle of arrows gliding on the air. Grunts followed as men and women heaved valynas, angling them upwards so they would fall like steel-tipped rain. Across the way, thousands of arrows and spears plummeted into the valley, glinting in the crimson glow of the moon.

A moment passed where all was still, where the Lost Hills were peaceful and silent. Then came the screams.

Dayne nocked another. Draw. Loose.

His hands fell into a rhythm. Nock. Draw. Loose. Nock. Draw. Loose. He lost himself in the repetition, his arrows vanishing amidst the swarm of steel and wood that fell upon the Thebalans.

He gave two more sharp whistles, one after another, signalling for the warriors on the flanks to pull their shields from the ground and fall into position on both sides of the Thebalans, blocking off any escape, trapping them in the valley of mud and death.

As more arrows and spears fell, Belina touched Dayne's arm. "If we press them now, they'll surrender. They're broken."

Dayne laid his bow in the grass, then slid his arm through the strap in his shield and ripped it from the earth. He snatched his valyna from beside the quivers. "Surrender is not an option for them, Belina. They turned their backs on us twice already. We can't give them a third opportunity. Today they die."

He gave one more sharp whistle to halt the barrage of projectiles, then let out a roar and charged down the hillside.

Vibrations jarred Dayne's legs, his steps heavy as he sprinted downhill. The footfalls behind him thundered, warriors bellowing war cries. The Thebalan forces ahead were shattered. Arrow shafts and thick spears jutted from the broken bodies that littered the valley floor. Torches burned in the mud, their light glimmering in the pools of water. The groans of the dying and the wails of horses were like a nightsong, sad and slow. And those who yet lived were exhausted.

As Dayne reached the bottom of the hill, a group of Thebalans emerged from behind an arrow-studded cart, one of the horses squealing in the mud, a spear pinning a man to its side.

Dayne dropped his left shoulder, allowing a thrown spear to glide past and lodge into the earth. He swung himself back, hefting his valyna and launching it. The weapon caught a charging Thebalan in the chest, punching through his cuirass and knocking him off his feet.

Ripping his sword from its scabbard, Dayne hurled himself forwards. He twisted, deflecting a spear with his shield, then drove his blade up through the woman's neck. Her eyes rolled, blood sluicing down the steel. Dayne pulled the blade free and in the same motion swung his shield arm and rammed the steel rim into a man's mouth, teeth snapping like brittle wood.

Three more times he swung his blade, and three more times blood sprayed. His own forces fell in around him, the Andurii holding tight to his flanks, moving as a solid unit despite the saturated earth.

A sharp whistle sounded to Dayne's left and a glint of steel punched through a Thebalan's neck, bloodmist pluming as the man fell into the mud. Two more flashes of steel, two more Thebalans fell. Dayne knew Belina's throwing knives anywhere.

"Sorry I'm late," Belina called, weaving through the Valtaran spears around her, her footsteps somehow light even in the mud. She had a mud-smeared ordo strapped to her left arm, a valyna in the same fist. She grabbed the spear with her other hand, freeing her left to hold the ordo's grip properly, then nodded towards the shield. "I changed my mind about the shield. These things are fucking heavy."

Dayne only grunted in response, taking a moment to survey the carnage. The waterlogged valley was nothing but blood and death. Clutches of Thebalans fought tooth and nail, backing against broken carts and stacks of bodies. They wouldn't last long. It was a massacre, but that was precisely what Dayne wanted. He needed Loren Koraklon and the other traitors to know the cost of their choices. He needed to put fear in their bellies.

"Andurios!"

Dayne twisted at the call, seeing three mounted lances charging from the left.

Dinekes surged forwards, hurling his valyna through the chest of the first rider, then hefting his shield across his body as several Andurii swarmed around him, spears levied. The horses were cumbersome in the dense mud, their hooves sticking and sucking, then sliding as they tried desperately to find traction. Dayne grimaced as the beautiful creatures slammed into the wall of Andurii spears, steel punching through flesh. The horses and their riders fell, blood flowing into the puddles.

The battle, if it could truly be called that, didn't last much longer. The Thebalans who tried to flee were caught by the spears at both ends of the passage or shredded by Mera's Wyndarii, who wrought death from above.

Those who fought to the bitter end were given that end.

"The battle is won, Andurios. They never stood a chance. Stories will be told of this night." Barak was covered from head to toe in mud, a number of gashes along his left shoulder. Dayne felt guilt at whatever Thebalans had stared down the beast of a man in this voidpit. "I've sent detachments to round up the surviving horses and recover any gear that can be salvaged."

Dayne nodded to Barak before yanking a valyna free of a Thebalan corpse, blood pumping from the open wound. He turned and drove the spear down through a twitching body. The woman cried out, reaching for her sword as she lay dying in the mud. Dayne twisted the spear and pushed it deeper. She went limp. He turned to Barak and the other captains who stood about him, calling out. "Make sure the dead stay dead. We will burn the bodies and let them enter Achyron's halls, but they will not walk from this place."

Dayne turned and picked his way through the blood-sodden battlefield, driving his spear through anything that moved.

"Dayne." Sweat and mud slicked Belina's face. She grasped his shoulder, moving her head to meet his gaze. She didn't need to speak. He knew the question her eyes asked.

"It must be this way," he said, pulling his spear free from the body at his feet. "The lines have been drawn, Belina."

"When I said 'who are we killing now' and you said 'all of them', I didn't know you actually meant *all* of them."

"This is it. This is where the future of Valtara is decided. I want Loren and every soul under his command to see me in their nightmares. I want them to fear us like they feared the night as children. I am ready to be their demon."

CHAPTER TEN

FOR THOSE WE HAVE LOST, WE MOURN

6th Day of the Blood Moon

Aravell – Winter, Year 3081 After Doom

Dann fidgeted with the top button of his tunic as he walked. It was too tight, and it rubbed against his neck. But Therin had gifted it to him for the ceremony, and Lyrei had nearly taken his hand off when he'd tried to undo the top button. Apparently, it was against tradition and would have done Therin a great dishonour. Even then, as they made their way through the city, thousands walking around them, Lyrei glared at him, her eyes sharp as his mother's words.

He stared back at her, moving his hand closer to the button, then pulling it further away, trying his best to make her laugh.

A flicker of a smile touched her lips but vanished as quickly as it had appeared, and she stared off into the distance.

Dann let out a subdued sigh, reaching back and pressing his fingers into the muscles along the nape of his neck. Lyrei had barely spoken since the battle – since Alea's death – and Dann had no idea what to say without making everything worse.

He wished he had Calen's knack of always seeming to know how to say the right thing at the right time. Calen had been born with it. He would never admit it, but he had been. Those speeches Therin would tell tales of, the ones given by ancient heroes on the eve of legendary battles, Calen had been born to give them.

Dann, on the other hand, had not. Words came easy to him, true enough, but rarely the right ones and never at the right time. All he wanted was to take Lyrei's pain away. He hated seeing others in pain. There was nothing worse. Well, except maybe the cockrot - as it had been so beautifully named.

Ahead, elves marched in the red and gold that Dann had come to associate with the kingdom of Lunithír. They loved their gold.

The elves marched in step, as though all their minds were connected by an invisible string. The single-minded discipline was otherworldly. Each of them was garbed in the finest of clothes. Thick crimson trousers embroidered with gold. Polished black boots that came up past their shins. Stiff, high-collared white tunics – not dissimilar to Dann's – with golden cloaks draped over their shoulders and swords strapped to their hips.

He looked over his shoulder at the column that marched behind him. It stretched off into the distance, winding through the streets of Aravell. Three thousand three hundred, a blend of elves and humans. Each of them had pledged to fight at Calen's side in the war to come.

The elves among them all wore the same stiff tunics and thick trousers, but none displayed the colours of any kingdom. In fact, when Dann looked closer, he saw that a number wore ribbons of white and purple tacked to their trousers. Colours that had fast become tied to Calen.

In contrast to the elves, the men and women who had come from across Epheria could not have looked more disorganised and incoherent. They were a confused assortment of random colours and garments; some in fine linen shirts, others in battered cottons, and others still in all varieties of garb from sleeveless tunics to roughspun woollen jerkins. Many of them had come to Aravell with nothing but the clothes on their backs. But still they walked with their heads held high, moving with a rhythm that Haem and the other knights had drilled into them.

Despite the disparity between the elves and humans, between the armies of Aravell and those who stood behind Calen, there was something common between them, something shared: pain.

Dann had felt it from the moment they'd stepped out into the streets. It clung to the air, made its home in the stone, and pierced the heart of every soul that walked towards the ceremony.

Three thousand three hundred. That number had been near five thousand three days before. Almost the entire population of the villages around The Glade – dead. Thousands more had died from the three elven kingdoms that called Aravell home, and the number of dead went up every day as the Healers struggled to keep the injured alive.

Friends, mothers, fathers, sons, daughters, brothers, sisters. The scale of the death had been so vast that no soul had gone untouched. It was a horrible thing to share – loss. But in a way, there was nothing else in the world that bound people together more closely.

Dann's throat tightened as he walked, and his thoughts wandered. Alea and Baldon's faces floated in the back of his mind, the realisation settling in that he would never hear the sound of their voices again. He would never see the gold of Alea's eyes or Baldon's toothy amused grin. They were gone, and he was less for it. Before he'd left The Glade, Dann had barely seen death. Now it seemed to follow him like a wicked shadow.

"You all right?" Erik appeared at Dann's left, his blond hair tucked back behind his ears, his eyes focused on Dann. Around them, elves and humans alike shuffled their way forwards, the slap of feet and the murmurs of quiet chatter drifting through the city. But the man had a way about him, a kind of intensity that made it feel like his attention was always singular.

"Me?" Dann asked, raising an eyebrow. He sucked in his cheeks and shook his head. "Never better. If only I could undo this damn top button."

Erik gave Dann a half-smile that held more sadness than he'd anticipated. The man forced a laugh and touched the high collar of his own shirt, identical to Dann's but for its deep yellow hue in place of white. "It's customary," he said, trailing his finger along the rim of the collar. "A bit uncomfortable, but still. Therin gifted you that one, did he not? It would—"

"It would be a great dishonour to him if I were to undo the top button. I've been told." Dann inclined his head towards Lyrei. "*Many* times. Where I'm from, a great dishonour would be taking a shit on someone's doorstop, not undoing the top button of a shirt."

Erik choked out a laugh, turning as Tarmon Hoard patted him on the back and stepped between him and Dann, Vaeril following close behind.

"Correct me if I'm mistaken," Vaeril said, lifting his index finger in the air, "but I do believe Therin would also find great dishonour in you shitting on his doorstep."

"I think you might be right," Dann answered. "When did you develop a sense of humour?"

"We're not so different, elves and humans."

"I wouldn't go that far."

The smile that spread across Vaeril's face made Dann think back to the first time he'd met the elf, the same time he'd met Alea and Lyrei. Every one of the five elves that had accompanied them from the Darkwood to Belduar had been stony-faced and rigid. For a time, Dann had actually thought elves couldn't feel emotions at all. How wrong he'd been.

A silence passed amongst Dann and the others. He didn't like silence – it left him alone with his own thoughts – so he filled it.

"Do we have much further to walk?" he asked nobody in particular, stretching onto his toes to see over the column of elves that marched ahead. "If I'd known this ceremony was taking place on the other side of the continent, I'd have brought food."

"It is not far," Vaeril answered, looking ahead. "With King Silmiryn falling in battle – Heraya embrace him – King Galdra and Queen Uthrían had the Craftsmages construct a new section of the city for the ceremony as a memorial."

Tarmon shook his head, casting his gaze about at some of the white stone towers that jutted up towards the sky. "You would think there would have been better uses of the Craftsmages' time, given half the city is still in ruin."

"To my people, there is little that is more important than remembering those we have lost."

"Well," Tarmon said with a tilt of his head, "if we don't repair the gaps in the walls, we'll be joining the lost once the Uraks reach the city."

"Delightfully morbid, Tarmon," Dann said, shaking his head.

Tarmon shrugged. "Just realistic."

After a short while, the street sloped downwards, broadening into a large courtyard.

"Well, fuck." Dann stopped in his tracks.

Before him, on the other side of the courtyard, stood an enormous archway where the city backed against a sheer cliff that rose a couple hundred feet. Two dragon statues framed the arch, both carved from the rock itself. They stood a measure with the arch, wings folded at their sides. Glowing veins of erinian stone traced along the pattern of the scales. It was, quite simply put, the most beautiful thing he'd ever seen, even in the crimson light of the moon.

The elves ahead of them continued their march, passing through the archway without a second look at the statues. Dann hoped he'd never grow so accustomed to beauty that he failed to notice its presence.

Erik tapped Dann on the shoulder, then nodded behind them to where the column of over three thousand had ground to a halt.

"Why did they all stop?"

Erik looked at him as though he were an idiot. "Because you stopped."

Dann paused a moment, narrowing his eyes at Erik before looking back at the others. The five captains Haem had selected – Ingvat, Surin, Narthil, Allinín, and Sylehna – all looked to him, backs straight, shoulders squared.

"Does anybody realise how bad an idea it is to put me in charge of anything?" Dann whispered to Tarmon.

"You're not in charge," Tarmon whispered back as he turned towards the column of warriors, many of whom were still gawking at the statue. He raised his voice. "Captains, ensure the silence is kept during the ceremony. Onwards."

Tarmon straightened his back and rolled his shoulders, bringing a closed fist to his chest. The five captains mimicked the gesture, lifting their chins.

It was in that brief moment that Dann remembered Tarmon Hoard had once been Lord Captain of the Belduaran Kingsguard, if for a short time.

"He's in charge." Erik inclined his head at Tarmon as they started off once more, a shit-eating grin on his face.

Dann mouthed the words back at Erik, twisting his face in a mock impression. To his surprise, he found Lyrei laughing. He didn't care that it was him she was laughing at. He was just happy she was laughing.

Lyrei held Dann's gaze for a second, her laughter fading, her golden eyes seeming to stare into his soul. She gave him a soft smile before turning and following Tarmon.

The sound of thousands of boots clipping against stone echoed through the passage beneath the arch, the crashing of water at its back.

"Blessed be Hafaesir," Tarmon said as they marched into the enormous basin on the other side of the archway. The basin was cut from the rock itself, flowing outwards in a series of perfectly smooth circular terraces. Thousands upon thousands of elves made their way up ornately carved staircases of hewn rock, cloaks of gold, silver, and green adding colour to the grey. Dann had heard of the great stadiums in Ardan where tens of thousands gathered to watch warriors fight for glory and coin; this seemed grander than any tale he had heard.

Five waterfalls cascaded over the ledge at the top of the basin, flowing into streams that fed a circular moat surrounding a central island at the heart of the 'stadium'.

Four bridges of white stone traversed the moat, providing access to the island. Upon the island itself stood five massive statues about half as tall as the two dragons by the arch.

Each of the statues was built from grey rock, not a seam or crack in sight. One stood taller than the others, its body comprised of thick slabs of muscle, its face smooth and angular, its hair tied in a single braid: a giant – a Jotnar.

The other four were those of an elf, a human, a Dvalin Angan, and a Fenryr Angan. The statues all faced out towards the terraces, their hands clasped at their fronts.

"Well," Dann said, staring upwards, his eyes tracing the stone antlers of the Dvalin Angan. "I can see why the Craftsmages were busy."

Elves in white robes directed Dann and the others up a staircase to the left that led to one of the many terraces.

Elven Highguard in their gleaming silver plate occupied the central island below. The armoured warriors stood at either ends of the bridges and around the island's perimeter, with what looked to be an enormous pit nestled in the island's centre.

"Excuse me."

Dann looked up to see Therin approaching, Aruni and Valdrin at his side.

Valdrin wore the same stiff white tunic as Dann, but, as per usual, he was covered in dirt, soot, and grease. Dann couldn't hold back his laugh at the sight of black fingerprints all along the collar of Valdrin's tunic. *Well, at least I'm not the only one who doesn't like the top button.*

"I was beginning to think you weren't going to make it," Dann said, inclining his head to Therin.

"You try getting Valdrin to leave the forge while he's working," Therin said as he took a spot beside Dann.

Lyrei inclined her head to the elf, stepping aside so Valdrin and Aruni could find space.

"There is a lot of armour to craft and little time to do so." Valdrin pulled at his collar again, leaving fresh black fingerprints. "And everything's slower when you have to tell others what to do. I don't like it."

Aruni frowned at Valdrin, then stepped into line beside Therin, smiling at Dann. "It is good to see you well, Dann Pimm."

"And you." Dann had only met Aruni once or twice. She had the same motherly demeanour as Elia Havel, but Dann couldn't help but feel unsettled around her. Whenever she looked at him with those red-ringed black eyes, it sent a shiver down his spine. It wasn't her eyes themselves that unsettled him, but more the idea of what must have been done to her. The night Valdrin had given them their armour, it had been raining, and the damp had caused Aruni's dress to cling to her skin. Dann had seen the scarred rune markings carved into her chest.

He drew a breath, pushing the image from his mind, and leaned into Therin while looking out over the thousands of gathering elves. "Have you seen Calen? He said he was to arrive with Aeson and the others, but I saw them down near the island and he and Valerys weren't there."

"He'll be here." After a moment, Therin leaned in, lowering his voice to a whisper. "Dann…"

"Please don't." Dann shook his head, a knot twisting in his stomach. He knew what Therin was going to say. And he wasn't quite sure why, but the sincerity in the elf's voice had somehow cut straight through him.

"Baldon thought very highly of you, Dann."

"Therin, I said please."

Therin nodded gently, letting out a soft sigh.

After a while, the flow of souls into the basin waned and ceased. Tens of thousands occupied the terraces, the sounds of their low chatter and shuffling feet echoing in the natural acoustics. Those sounds dropped to nothing though when a voice thundered through the gathering.

"My people." The voice was so loud it sounded as though it boomed from the mouth of a god. Dann had seen the trick many a time from Calen and others. "Din närvarvin gryr haydria t'il valana."

Dann didn't understand the elf tongue – or the 'Old Tongue', as Calen was fond of correcting him – but he had recognised the word 'valana'. *Lost.*

"Your presence brings honour to the lost," Therin whispered.

Dann looked down at the central island to see a group arranged near the pit at the island's centre. Two figures stood ahead of the group, likely Queen Uthrían and King Galdra. Dann would be surprised if the others weren't the elven Ephorí – the sycophants who trailed after the monarchs wherever they went. The voice that spoke was that of Uthrían.

"We have come here today to mourn the loss of those we loved and to mark their passing in history. I…" The queen trailed off, whispers and murmurs spreading through the crowd, rising to a din.

"What's going on?" Aruni asked.

"There." Lyrei pointed towards the ridge that overlooked the basin.

It took a moment for Dann to realise what she was pointing at, but then he saw the light of the Blood Moon glistening off Valerys's white scales as the dragon spread his wings. Dann could just about make out Calen's outline standing to Valerys's left, his hand resting on the dragon's side.

Dann gave a downturn of his lip. "He's certainly gotten good at making entrances."

"He's showing them who he is."

"Who?" Dann asked.

"The Inari – Uthrían and Galdra." The smile that spread across Therin's lips looked almost out of place on the usually stern-faced elf. "He's learning."

As Therin spoke, another murmuring wave spread through the crowd.

Two more shapes emerged on the ridge, so large they cast shadows that covered half the basin.

"Varthear and Sardakes." The tone in Therin's voice completely changed into what Dann could only describe as reverence. The elf looked down towards the bridges where Aeson and the other Rakina stood.

The larger of the two dragons – Sardakes – spread his wings wide, blocking out the light of the moon, and unleashed a mighty roar. The creature's black scales stood stark against the striking blue of his wings.

Valerys and the third dragon both followed suit, their roars carrying through the basin, slowly fading until only silence remained and the three dragons stared down over the gathered crowd. Many still whispered when Queen Uthrían spoke again.

"The light of the Enkara shines upon us," Uthrían's voice echoed, amplified by magic. "And the fire of the dragons returns to our side. Du gryr haydria til ourín elwynar, Velikír Ayara."

"You bring honour to our hearts, Great Ones," Therin whispered again.

"I got the gist of it," Dann whispered back.

Therin frowned.

"The Eleswea un'il Valana is not simply a ceremony to mourn those we've lost," Uthrían called, her voice lingering unnaturally in the air. "It is a waypoint in history. It is a monument upon which our descendants can look back and say, 'this is the day something changed in the fabric of the world'."

To Dann's surprise, a raucous cheer erupted from the gathered elves. They'd never seemed the cheering type. They barely ever seemed the smiling type, if he was being honest, more like frowning happily.

A second voice rang out – King Galdra of Lunithír. "For hundreds of years, we have taken shelter within the Aravell. The Nithrandír have guarded our borders, the glamour has kept our existence a secret, and the rangers have stifled the Lorian ability to move from north to south. Yes, this day is a marker of remembrance for those we've lost. But it is also a marker of the return of our people to Epheria and the rebirth of old alliances. We once again stand with a Draleid watching over us, the Rakina at his back. It was not only elves who stood in the defence of Aravell. It was humans, Jotnar, Angan, dragons. This is a day that will echo in the annals of our continent. This is the day the elves of Lunithír, of Vaelen, and of Ardurän stopped hiding. This is the day we joined the fight. *This*," Galdra said, holding his breath for just a second, "is the day the empire first began to crumble."

"And so," Uthrían continued, "we mark the dead and this point in time by remembering who stood here."

As Uthrían spoke the last word, brilliant white lights burst into existence at the base of the statues, illuminating every groove and line in the immense stonework, making each one look alive. Dann had seen Calen and the others make their baldír before, but he'd never seen baldír like this before. It was like the light of the sun had been casked and controlled on command.

"As you all know," Uthrían said, "we lost many unique souls in the battle for Aravell. One of those such souls was my dear friend and the beloved king of Vaelen – Silmiryn Vaelen, the Silver Hawk. As King Silmiryn left behind no heirs, we waited until the succession was decided before we held this day. And as such, today is both a mourning and a celebration. A lament and a triumph. For today, I present to you the niece of King Silmiryn, and the new queen of Vaelen – Queen Tessara Vaelen Alumír!"

The cheers that broke did so amidst subdued murmurs as over a hundred Highguard poured from somewhere down near the island, creating a framed pathway over the eastern bridge. A figure made its way onto the island, too far for Dann to make out any features.

"Not everyone seems pleased," Erik said.

Therin pressed his fingers into his chin, scratching. "Tessara is… divisive."

Once Galdra and Uthrían had placed the crown on Tessara's head, the applause and murmurs quietened and the new queen stepped forwards. She allowed the silence to hold for a few moments more before speaking. "For over four hundred years, my uncle guided the people of Vaelen. Through our darkest hours, our darkest centuries, he was our beacon. And I will not let his light be lost. Now, I would ask Asius, son of Thalm, and Thacia, daughter of Ulin, to join me in commencing the Eleswea un'il Valana."

Tessara gestured towards the same bridge she had crossed. Two hulking shapes stepped onto the bridge, their bluish skin and Thacia's blood-red hair striking against the grey stone.

"The Jotnar are the oldest and dearest friends of our people. Once, we were sworn enemies. For hundreds of years, the Blodvar filled the soil with the bodies of our ancestors, but after the Doom at Haedr, we set our differences aside and grew ever stronger for it. Today, their numbers are few, for they did not succumb to Fane Mortem's influence. They fought to the last. And during the battle for our city, one more gave her life. Senas, daughter of Iliria. The Eleswea un'il Valana is one of our oldest traditions, taught to us by the Jotnar as an offering of peace – a shared unity over the cost of war. So it is fitting today, of all days, the day we reforge the alliances of old, that our people perform this ceremony side by side—" Tessara turned her gaze upwards "—with the dragons watching over us, as they always have."

On the ledge above, the dragons shifted, watching, Calen by Valerys's side.

Therin leaned closer to Dann. "I know we don't always see eye to eye."

"That's because you're taller than I am," Dann whispered back.

"Dann, please, shut up for just a second."

"Harsh, but continue."

Therin stared at Dann for a moment, then shook his head. "I need you to be serious for a moment. Can you do that?"

Dann clenched his jaw, then nodded.

"Good. What you're about to witness hasn't been seen since before The Fall. Even I have seen it but once. In the days of old, the Jotnar would sing entire forests into existence. Watch. For the likelihood is you will never again see what you are about to witness. I think it is something that will stay with you."

Dann looked back at Therin, then inclined his head. "Thank you, Therin."

"You've come a long way, Dann Sureheart."

That name cut straight through Dann. Just as they had many times since the battle, Baldon's words repeated themselves in his mind. *It is the name you have earned. As Therin Eiltris is Silverfang, Aeson Virandr is Broken One, you are Sureheart.*

Dann swallowed, his throat growing dry. A hand rested on his shoulder, and he turned to see Tarmon behind him. The mountain of a man gave him a simple nod and returned to watching the ceremony, but his hand remained where it lay.

Below, columns of elves marched over the four bridges and onto the central island, setting themselves around the edges of the pit in the middle. More again lined the moat that separated the island from the terraces.

"What's inside the pit?" Dann asked, leaning closer to Therin, though he had a feeling he already knew the answer.

Therin drew a long breath in through his nose. "The bodies of all those who fell during the battle. Washed, cared for, and wrapped in linen."

"Baldon and Alea are in there?" Dann's words held a tremble. "But—"

"Watch, Dann."

Dann looked down at the pit and the elves that ringed it – Asius and Thacia standing at the foot of the Jotnar statue – but saw nothing.

"Listen."

He hadn't noticed, but the entire basin had grown silent as a winter's night in The Glade. It should not have been possible. Tens of thousands of people gathered in one place. The mere breath of so many should have pushed through the silence in a rocky basin like this. But, impossible or not, silence held the entire ceremony in its grasp.

Then, just as the absence of sound became so deafening Dann began to hear the beating of his heart, a slow, melodic hum reached his ears. It started as faint as the buzzing of a wasp's wings, rising steadily.

Words followed the melody, but they were not in any language Dann understood. With each passing second, the song grew louder, the words echoing amongst the gathered crowd. The air seemed to shift and sparkle, catching the light of the lanterns and the crimson glow of the moon overhead.

Dann's chest fluttered. A sensation swept over him as though someone were running their hand across the hairs on his arms.

"Therin, what's happening?" Dann's breaths were quick and short as he spoke, a slight panic setting into him. He turned to Therin to see the elf staring down at the pit, entranced. The elf's lips were moving, the words of the song flowing from his mouth.

Before Dann could say anything else, the terrace shook beneath him and he grabbed hold of the low wall. He looked back at Tarmon, whose face conveyed the same sense of fear and uncertainty that twisted Dann's gut.

Dann stumbled as another tremor shook the entire basin, a rumble echoing like a clap of thunder.

And then he saw it.

Roots burst from the ground between the statues and the pit, twisting and turning over each other in patterns that, at the same time, seemed completely random and impossibly complex. It was as though Dann was watching an artist weave a tapestry of earth and root.

The roots spread over the pit, covering it entirely. They climbed, coiling around each other, growing thicker and thicker, melding into a solid form. As the twisted roots merged and rose, so too did they spread until they formed what looked like the stump of a tree.

Dann stared on with a visceral sense of awe. The song had grown louder and louder, every other sound in the world yielding to its melody. It was then Dann realised his lips were moving, the words flowing through him. He hadn't even noticed he'd begun singing. And as he looked left and right, he saw he wasn't the only one. Every soul in the basin sang.

Erik stood with one hand to his chest, his eyes fixed on the climbing roots. Tarmon's hand gripped Dann's shoulder, his lips moving in perfect time.

A hand touched Dann's, grasping it so tightly he thought his fingers might break. Tears rolled slowly down Lyrei's cheeks as she squeezed, her golden eyes glistening. Dann tensed the muscles in his hand and allowed Lyrei to squeeze.

He turned his gaze back towards the winding roots to see they now took the shape of a tree trunk, as wide as the entire pit. The trunk spread up and out, forming dense branches that stretched over the statues and covered the central island, casting shadows over the entire basin. Small green buds sprouted from all along the branches, growing and peeling open. Thousands of long, thin vines burst from the buds, tumbling down towards the ground. And from the vines bloomed masses of white flowers tipped with purple that hung in clusters. The flowers swept across the vines, like butterflies bursting from their chrysalises until a canopy of purple and white blotted out the sky.

Then, as the song reached a crescendo, Dann's breath caught in his lungs and the petals of every flower illuminated with a purple light.

CHAPTER ELEVEN

BLOOD OF THE LION

6th Day of the Blood Moon

*The Dead Tower, north of the Burnt Lands – Winter,
Year 3081 After Doom*

ist sat in the dirt, his knees pulled to his chest, his gaze lost in the firepit's flames. A cup of wine rested beside him, untouched, a dead fly floating on the surface. Extra casks had been sent around once they'd made camp near the edges of the Burnt Lands. Garramon had said it was a token of celebration, but Rist wasn't quite sure what they could be celebrating. The Chosen had crossed, true enough. From what Rist had seen, from the power they wielded, these beings could only have been sent by a god. But how many had died to bring them into this world? How many lives was a single Chosen worth? And the most pertinent question of all: could the gods be trusted? Could Efialtír be trusted?

Rist had always liked numbers. They were certain and true, with no muddled grey, only black and white. Numbers were simple and honest, and there was a beauty in that. But something about these numbers made him feel nauseous. He'd not heard a count of the dead yet, but they'd entered Ilnaen with eighty thousand souls and left with far fewer. No more than sixty Battlemages remained in the First Army. Three-fifths of their initial number. If the rest of the armies had suffered such casualties, that would mean over thirty thousand had died. Just by a glance, Rist could see that wasn't the case, but he would not have been surprised if the number sat around fifteen or twenty thousand. That number of dead was near inconceivable. Just the thought of it caused his chest to tighten and his stomach to twist.

He sucked in his cheeks, then grabbed the cup of wine and downed it in a single draught. He only remembered the fly when something a little too solid caught in his throat.

He let out a long sigh, placing the cup back in the dirt. The night was still and silent, nothing but the sound of crunching footsteps, the breeze, and the occasional shout in the distance to fill the emptiness. They'd been there for two days and two nights, waiting on Fane's orders to march for Berona. Most of the other armies had already been sent onwards to reinforce Elkenrim, Merchant's Reach, Greenhills, and Catagan against the elves and Uraks, but the Fourth, First, Eighteenth, and Seventh armies had remained with Fane and the Chosen.

Only a handful of mages from the First Army sat about the fire, scattered and listless. Rist knew their faces and probably should have known their names, but many of them were new recruits after the Battle of the Three Sisters – now the Two Sisters, as Magnus kept reminding him. He found it difficult to try to learn the names of people who would likely not live to see the turn of the new year.

Rist grimaced at that morbid thought and cast it from his mind, making himself a promise to learn the names of every mage in the First Army. Like numbers, names had power. A name let someone know you cared. At least, that's how Rist felt anytime someone said his name. It meant they had taken the time to learn it and to associate small pieces of information with him: his name, his eyes, his hair, his sense of humour, his choice in books. There was no greater act of decency than giving someone your time. Time was precious and the only resource in the world that was truly finite. He cherished it.

His breath misted before him as he looked out at the night, the crimson light of the Blood Moon illuminating the clouds in a pink glow.

Rist reached into his shirt and produced the pendant that hung from his neck, the gold chain clinking. The wire-wrapped gemstone pulsed with a soft red light. He remembered what Garramon had said the first time he'd shown Rist the vessel. "Through the gift of Essence, Efialtír allows something to come from death. He allows the act of creation to be born from destruction. With the wielding of Essence, no death is in vain."

The morality of it all was something Rist still struggled with. A part of him demanded he cast the pendant into the flames and never touch it again. That was what his father would have told him to do, and Calen and Dann, no doubt. But Fane and Garramon had been right in that it was his own preconceptions of Efialtír and Blood Magic that drove that part of him. Preconceptions built on stories and hearsay rather than facts or evidence.

Blood Magic or no Blood Magic, thousands would have died at Ilnaen either way. At least with the vessels, every death, every drop of blood spilled, had not been wasted entirely. At least something could come from death. In fact, much of the Essence collected that night had already been drawn upon by the Healers to keep the injured from Achyron's halls – or 'Efialtír's embrace', as they said in the North, though that was something else he was still trying to get used to.

He ran his fingers over the glowing stone, feeling the power calling to him. With any luck, the Essence within the gemstone could one day save a life.

With a last long sigh, Rist stood and made his way from the fire to the tent where the mages slept. Neera had gone to rest hours earlier around the same time Garramon had left to see Fane. Rist would have followed her had he not wanted to hold the dreams at bay for a little longer. He had always been afraid of many things, but one thing he never even contemplated fearing was sleep. It was a fear he didn't much care for. He liked sleep, at least he used to, but sleep brought him little solace of late, for his dreams seemed intent on reliving the carnage of Ilnaen the instant his eyes shut.

That was an appropriate word: carnage. The violent killing of a large number. The great and bloody slaughter of many.

As he thought on it, he could see the Uraks ripping men and women to pieces, see the steam wafting from spilt intestines, smell the stench of shit and burning skin. The Bloodmarked tearing through flesh and bone, the knights in green plate carving soldiers in half with single swipes of their glowing green blades. Níthrals, Rist was sure they were called. He'd never seen one before, but they matched the descriptions in *A Study of Control,* by Andelar Touran. He made a mental note to ask Garramon more about them. If Garramon's answers didn't suffice, he would ask Gault for a reading list. The old man was the single most well-read individual Rist had ever known, possibly even more so than Fane.

Rist allowed himself a sorrow-touched laugh as he felt his brain picking through the pages of *A Study of Control,* trying desperately to avoid seeing the images of the níthral carving through Anila, of the look of shock on her face, her innards spilling into the sand, the wails of Magnus's grief. He'd not heard that sound before: pure, unfettered grief. He hoped he never heard it again.

In The Glade, some of the elders had talked about the Varsund War and how seeing so much death was something that stayed with a person, something that altered souls. He had never quite understood what they'd meant. Of course, any event in life can alter how a person perceives things, but how could something change who a person was? How could something rearrange the core of a soul?

He understood now.

There were things in life that once seen could not be unseen. Things that allowed a person to understand the darkness in the world that they had once thought impossible.

Seeing that darkness, seeing the depths to which living beings would go, seeing the carnage and death and abject horror that was war... Seeing all that had changed the way Rist looked at the world, which in turn had changed the things he was willing to do to save it. Even the thought of that darkness touching The Glade cut cold fear through him. He would *never* let that happen. He would die before he did.

As Rist walked through the camp, he lifted his gaze to the sky, admiring the pink hue that tinged the blackness, scattered stars shimmering.

"You're still awake, lad?"

Magnus was perched at the top of a boulder to Rist's right that rose higher than the tents around it. The man was shirtless, revealing the scars that covered his chest and shoulders – likely from his 'education' in the Circle. The stump of his left arm, however, held no scarring, only clean, rounded flesh where the Healers had knitted the skin back together. He held a bulging waterskin in his right hand that Rist was absolutely sure did not contain water.

"Couldn't sleep." Rist walked towards the foot of the boulder.

Magnus nodded towards a flat space beside him. "Get your skinny arse up here."

Rist's muscles groaned as he climbed up the rock and settled himself to Magnus's left.

Magnus handed him the waterskin. Rist's suspicions were confirmed when he pulled the stopper from the top and burned his nostrils from the fumes.

Magnus only laughed, the sharp smell of spirits wafting from his breath. "Whiskey from Drifaien. Wine is for celebrating. Whiskey… whiskey is for everything else. Let it sit on your tongue before swallowing."

Rist took a swig, forcing himself not to swallow the harsh spirit. To his surprise, the taste mellowed, becoming almost sweet.

"Couldn't sleep or didn't want to?" Magnus asked as he took the skin back and poured the whiskey, as though it were water, into his open mouth.

Rist stared off into the distance. "Didn't want to."

"It'll get easier."

"Will it?"

"No." Magnus handed the skin back to Rist. "Whiskey helps though."

"Are you not cold?"

Magnus gave Rist a toothless smile that held no joy. "The whiskey is my blanket tonight, lad. Sometimes the cold reminds me I'm not dead. Though, that might have been an easier path." Magnus snorted, letting out a gruff laugh. "Typical Anila, always taking the easy road."

Rist looked back at him for a moment, then turned his gaze towards the ground below.

"How are you holding up, besides the nightmares?"

Rist nodded, sipping from the skin. "Fine. I just… can't wrap my head around everything that happened."

"I'd be more worried if you could. I've seen a lot in my years, but I've never seen anything like that. We watched Efialtír's Chosen cross through the veil between worlds. We watched a god reach his hand into our world and save us. It was a thing of beauty, but beautiful things are often the most terrifying."

That wasn't quite how Rist remembered it, but he said nothing.

"I would have preferred if he'd arrived in time to save my arm, though." Magnus looked down at the stump of his left arm, which extended only about six inches from his shoulder. "I can still feel it, you know. Still feel my elbow bending, my fingers moving. It's the strangest thing. At least it was my left."

"I couldn't even imagine having to learn to use a sword with my other hand."

Rist stretched his off hand in front of himself, trying to imagine the weight of a blade, the pull of the leather. "It took long enough to learn with my good hand."

"Hah." Magnus choked on a laugh after swigging from the waterskin. "Sure, sword. That's what I meant."

They sat there in silence for a while, passing the skin back and forth, Rist trying to work out what Magnus had meant.

"I've lived over five centuries, lad, and only recently did I learn a very important lesson." Magnus stared up at the Blood Moon as it emerged from behind a dark cloud, his eyes glassy. "Even though you didn't ask, which is strange because usually I can't shut you the fuck up for all the questions, I'm gonna tell you anyway because whiskey is the world's best lubricant."

The man shifted where he sat so that he stared into Rist's eyes. Beads of whiskey dripped from his thick black beard.

"When you care for someone, tell them. There are things in this world we always assume don't need to be said because they are understood." Magnus shook his head, leaning one arm on his knee. "But we're always wrong. I loved Anila. Not in the sappy, mushy, spread my heart on her face kind of way, but I loved her. She was good." Magnus nodded to himself, frowning. "Better than most anyone I know. She was kind, too. I know she came off as a bit of a bitch from time to time. But that was just her way. That woman's heart was golden. She was like a hedgehog – prickly on the outside, soft on the inside."

Magnus spluttered laughing, spraying whiskey into the air. "If she knew I'd compared her to a hedgehog…"

"She'd give you one of those stares."

"Too right. Or she'd stab me."

"Stab you?"

"Oh, she's done it before. Now, we were both drunk and she swore her hand slipped, but I'm not so sure."

Both Magnus and Rist laughed, and the man passed Rist the skin.

"That was about three hundred years ago in a little tavern just north of Fearsall. Shithole of a place… She took a shine to you, lad. Might not seem like it, but she liked you. I can see why."

The smile that touched Rist's lips was one born of nothing but sadness, and the laughter in his throat was cut from the same cloth.

"It's not that funny." Magnus looked at Rist as though he'd grown a second head. "I tell a lot of fucking fantastic jokes and you barely ever laugh. And now you laugh at our dead friend?"

"No," Rist said, still laughing. "I'm thinking of what she said to me the day I got my robes."

"She threw a stick at me that day," Magnus mumbled. "Fucking hurt. What'd she say?"

"Not much."

"She never said much. But what?"

Rist put on his best Anila impression. "*'The robes suit you, Brother Havel.'*" He hesitated for a moment, feeling the tears suddenly welling in his eyes. He took another swig of the whiskey, hearing it slosh in the skin. "The way she said 'Brother'…" He gave a fake smile, clenching his jaw. He had no idea why he was telling this to Magnus of all people, but something about the man felt like home. "The way…"

"It's all right, lad. Take your time. She's dead now. She's got all the time in the world."

Rist choked, caught off guard by Magnus's candour. He took a moment to gather himself. "Why do you do that?"

"Do what?"

"Make a joke out of everything?"

Magnus reached across and snatched the whiskey from Rist, draining the dregs of the skin in one go. "Sometimes, Rist, if you don't laugh, you'll cry. And I fucking hate crying. Always gives me a damn headache. Anila…" The man looked up at the stars. "I would have burned the world for her. She was family, and I'm going to feel her absence every moment I live. It's a strange thing. You can go without laying eyes on someone for years and think little on it, but when you know you'll never see them again, everything is different…" He ran his tongue across his lips. "I heard her, that day. I heard what she said – what I should have said. I tend to talk too much until it's time to say something important, and then I go mute as a dead fish. Anila, on the other hand, had a way of saying a lot with very few words. She had a way of making people feel good about themselves. That's a rare quality. Even rarer now."

Magnus tossed the waterskin to the ground at the foot of the boulder, then reached into his pocket and produced a small flask, taking a swig.

He offered the flask to Rist, and Rist stared at him in disbelief. "You didn't remember a shirt, but you remembered more whiskey?"

Magnus shrugged, pulling his lips into a dopey smile that seemed strange on the enormous man. "Whiskey is more important than shirts, Rist. If I teach you nothing, I'll teach you that." He leaned back, resting his hands on the boulder and looking at the campfires and tents spread around them. "Garramon made a good choice with you. You're a little strange, but all the good ones are. Gods know I'm at least five points short of a star." He drew in a long breath, patted Rist on the shoulder, and stared into his eyes, nodding. "I'm pretty sure I'm going to puke."

Before Rist could even begin to process what the man had said, Magnus slid from the boulder with surprising grace for a man with more whiskey in his veins than blood.

Once on the ground, Magnus spread his shoulders, drew in an enormous lungful of air, and emptied the contents of his stomach into the dirt.

⤤⤦

Garramon folded his arms, the scent of peppermint wafting from the mug of tea in his right hand as he looked down over the map pinned to the table before him. He stood in Fane's tent, which, although large, was sparse to the point of being austere. His old friend had never been one for luxuries.

Fane sat cross-legged on the ground, leaning back against the edge of his cot, a book in his hand. He'd been there for hours, barely a word passing between him and Garramon. That had often been the way of their friendship, a quiet comfort that seldom needed more than company.

He took a sip of his tea, just hot enough to provide him with the faint satisfaction of almost burning his lips but not quite. He let out a sigh, looking around him at the scattered marble markers and icons strewn on the cotton floor. They had been like that since before he'd arrived in the tent, with the table flipped on its side. He'd lifted the table back into place but refused to do the same with the markers. He wasn't Fane's mother. That lovely woman had died many centuries ago.

With one last look at the map, his gaze moving from Ilnaen to Steeple, Garramon dropped himself into the foldout chair across from Fane, crossing his right leg over his left. He cupped the mug with both hands, allowing the tea's warmth to spread through him. The sooner spring came, the better. He hated winter.

Fane lifted his gaze from the book before letting out a sigh. He slid a thin red steel bookmark from his trouser pocket, marked his place, then set the book down on the ground. He sat there wordlessly for another moment, drawing his knees to his chest.

Fane pursed his lips, leaning his head back against the cot. He seemed more frustrated than upset.

"We allowed the Chosen to cross." Garramon shifted in his seat, resting the base of the mug on his leg. "That was our goal. Champions of Efialtír himself walk this very camp. They stand guard at your door, sentinels of The Saviour. Without them we would not have survived Achyron's knights. We lost many, but this can only be seen as a victory. We are one step closer to ending all of this."

Even as he spoke, Garramon doubted his own words. It wasn't that he'd lost faith. He still believed in The Saviour. But he had started to weigh the cost, placing the bodies of the dead on the scales in his mind.

Fane lifted his head, nodding slowly. "You speak true, old friend, as you so often do. But no, Ilnaen proceeded precisely as I'd expected it would. Plans must be laid within plans to counterbalance the inevitable failure of all plans. Achyron's knights would never have allowed us to draw Efialtír through the void that night, but now, if we take each step carefully, we will be in a position where there is nothing they can do to stop us. First, however, we must find this damn Heart of Blood."

Garramon switched his legs so his left leg sat atop his right, relieving the pain that had set into the side of his knee. He glanced over at the icons and markers that dotted the floor. Something had ignited Fane's fury. If it had not been Ilnaen, then what? He pushed the thought to the back of his mind. "What is our path forward then?"

The faint beginnings of a smile touched his friend's lips, the corners of his eyes creasing. "I will find who took the Heart, and I will tear their head from their shoulders."

"A fine plan." Garramon lifted his mug mockingly as though saluting Fane's genius. "Maybe lacking in the nuance I've come to expect, but fine nonetheless."

"I have my suspicions, old friend." The smile vanished from Fane's face, and he took on an altogether more serious tone. "I'm moving the pieces, setting the lures. We just have to see who bites. And in the meantime, I have what I need to move forward."

Fane held Garramon's stare for an altogether too long moment.

Garramon inclined his head. He knew there was no point in pursuing the conversation further. For every word that left Fane's lips, there was always one left unspoken. The man wove plans like a spider wove webs. Garramon would know what he needed to know when he needed to know it. That wasn't the way with all things, but at times like this, he knew what to expect.

Fane let out a puff of air, running his hand through his dark hair. He looked back towards the table where the map was pinned, the markers and icons scattered about the ground. "I received a hawk this morning," he said, changing the subject. "From the South. Argona is nothing but ash and dust. It was necessary. The signs of a full rebellion in the South have been multiplying over the last year. With the elves advancing across the western cities and the Uraks flooding from the mountains, we don't have time for a gentle hand. One slip, one mistake and everything burns. Argona sends a firm message – any and all rebellion will be crushed. Valtara must be dealt with similarly, as must the brewing insurgency here in Loria. I'll have it arranged. I wish these kinds of messages didn't need to be sent. If we can bring Efialtír back to this world, if we can aid in his crossing, we can end all this. Death is a part of life, but I'd prefer if we weren't so well acquainted with it."

Fane pushed himself to his feet, snatching up the book as he did.

The sensation of the Spark tickled the back of Garramon's neck as Fane wove threads of Air through the tent, lifting the hundreds of icons and markers from the floor and placing them back atop the map. Marble counters, hewn lion heads, and small dragon carvings spun about the air like debris in a hurricane before settling in their places. Fane sauntered through the storm, laying the book on the table's edge. It was bound in black leather and looked as though it had been dragged along behind a cart.

Kiralla Holflower's research papers. The last Garramon had seen of those, Brother Pirnil had been scribbling away on them after the crossing at Ilnaen.

Fane reached down and picked up the counters from beside the lion heads set in the Darkwood. "The armies sent into the Darkwood were routed, but the remnants are regrouping at Kingspass and Argona's Ruins. They'll march for Valtara." He tossed almost half the counters into a wooden box on the floor, then proceeded to lift two of the dragon carvings from the table with threads of Air, shattering them into a thousand shards. "Ilkya and Jormun are dead, as are their dragons."

"Surely that can't be true." Garramon snapped his neck around so fast he heard a *click*. He walked to Fane, wide-eyed. It had been a damn long time since a dragon had been killed in combat, and the outcome of the attack on Aravell had felt like a foregone conclusion. This explained Fane's anger. "We sent eighty thousand men into the Darkwood. And Ilkya, and Voranur, and Jormun…" Garramon stared at the map, his face scrunched in thought. "What am I missing? This new Draleid could not possibly be powerful enough to overcome any one of the Dragonguard, never mind three at a time."

Fane drew in a long breath, folding his arms. "You're right. The report states that no fewer than four dragons flew alongside the Draleid." Fane looked into Garramon's eyes, a laugh catching in his throat. The man smiled as though a child had just beaten him in a game of Tarkat. "It seems that Aeson Virandr and his rebels have been better at hiding their secrets than we gave them credit for. That or the gods play with us, old friend. They sense we are close. They see their reckoning on the horizon." The man's eyes seemed to gleam as he lifted his head to stare at Garramon. "Did you ever think, when you were a child, that one day you would draw the attention of the gods themselves?"

Garramon stared down at the dust on the floor that had once been marble dragon carvings. "Did the dragons have Draleid?"

Fane shrugged. "From the report, Voranur barely escaped with his life and has likely flown further north to Eltoar and Lyina. We won't know more until I speak with Eltoar. I've sent a herald."

Garramon pressed his tongue against the back of his top teeth, staring at the map. Over just a few months, everything had shifted. A new Draleid had arisen, six Dragonguard had been reduced to four, and the empire was now under siege on all sides.

"You look worried, old friend." Fane stood with his arms still folded, a smile spread across his lips.

"And you look distinctly the opposite."

Fane let out a laugh. "Our course was never going to be an easy one. Our will would always be tested, as it has been many times over." Fane moved around the table and clasped Garramon's shoulder, looking into his eyes. "Whatever stands in our way, we will face it and we will roll over it like a storm. We have come too far, sacrificed too much, to allow it to be any other way. Besides, the path remains the same."

A shiver spread through Garramon as Fane's eyes glowed with a red light. The sight caused Garramon to straighten. There was no surer sign that Efialtír himself watched over them.

"Let the elves bring their dragons. Let the Uraks come. Let Achyron's knights crash against us. We will rip the dragons from the sky, we will grind the Uraks into the earth, and we will shear the knights' souls from this world." The light in Fane's eyes dissipated, and he stared back at Garramon, a hint of sadness in his voice. "Hundreds of thousands of our people have died, but we will avenge them. I give you my word. This will be the last war, my friend. The last time we must kill for peace. And when we are done, the gods themselves will know the meaning of fear. On that note, brother, I have something I wish to discuss with you in regard to your young apprentice."

Before Garramon could answer, the rustle of the wind flowed into the tent from behind him, followed by heavy footsteps.

The voice that spoke was harsh and rough. It was as though two voices spoke over each other, perfectly in sync and in utter discordance. "Harbinger. It is time."

Garramon turned to see two of the Chosen standing before them. The first was a woman almost a head taller than he, only her head visible, ridged silver plate flowing over her body. Red runes marked her breastplate and arms. The other was a man who still hadn't seen his twentieth summer, his face bearing all the signs of youth. So many of the candidates for the ritual had been little more than children.

Garramon inclined his head, pulling a closed fist to his chest. "The Saviour's light upon you, Chosen Ones."

The woman fixed her gaze on Garramon, her eyes as black and cavernous as a herald's. Something about her stare set a cold knot in Garramon's stomach, his pulse quickening.

She dipped her head, returning Garramon's gesture. "Our god has spoken to me of you, Brother Garramon. Your service has not gone unnoticed. Please, call me by the name Enaril."

"I live to serve," Garramon said, bowing. He looked to the young man. "And yours?"

Garramon narrowed his gaze at the sight of the swirling blue tattoos snaking up from the collar of the Chosen's armour and winding around his neck. The skin about the markings was red and raw, blood spotting at the edges. *No, it couldn't possibly be.*

The young man followed Garramon's gaze, tucking his chin in to look at his own spiral tattoos. "There is a story behind them." The voice was young and bright, yet also dark and grating. Two voices speaking in tandem, one over the other. "I must tell you some day. This armour doesn't make for markings, but the skin is surprisingly pliable."

"How is this possible? Herald Azrim?"

The young man inclined his head, giving a mocking bow as he did.

"But you are a herald… How could you be one of our god's Chosen?" Garramon thought back to the last time he had seen Azrim. The herald had taken Artim Valdock as a host and had been part of the force marching to the Darkwood.

"You humans always define things so rigidly. It is one of many weaknesses. I am a Vitharnmír – your *Chosen*. But unlike many of my kin, I find this realm more… amusing. And so I elected to exist here in a diminished form. At least now," he said, spreading his arms and looking down over the suit of silver plate, "I am not so weak. I have, as you humans say, 'a score to settle'."

CHAPTER TWELVE

FULL CIRCLE

6th Day of the Blood Moon

Elkenrim – Winter, Year 3081 After Doom

Claps of thunder rolled across the sky, flashes of lightning striking down over the mountains of Mar Dorul in the distance while Eltoar stood at the top of the hill overlooking Elkenrim.

A vivid hue of pink painted the skies above the city, the Blood Moon hidden behind a dense black cloud. Hundreds of lanterns marked the two walls that enclosed the inner sections of the city, and hundreds more spread through the homes and buildings that sprawled outwards. But those flickering flames paled in comparison to the ocean of lights that stretched across the landscape to the east and south.

Over the weeks, almost fifty thousand soldiers had amassed in Elkenrim's surrounding areas, pulled from the west. Another twenty thousand held back at Merchant's Reach, and fifty more at Catagan. Eltoar would have preferred all one hundred and twenty thousand be garrisoned at Elkenrim, but feeding that many mouths in one place was all but impossible, particularly amid the raging chaos that had consumed the continent. The Uraks had burned the fields and granaries south of Greenhills, and with the western cities razed by the elves, food was in short supply.

In truth, the empire was in tatters. Shipments from the South had stopped, merchants and traders dared not travel the roads, and without the iron from Dead Rock's Hold, the armies would soon be fighting with sticks.

Worse, the elves knew precisely what was happening. After burning Steeple and Holm, they had halted their forward momentum, hiding in that wall of fog.

It was precisely what Eltoar himself would have done. The longer the Lorian armies were forced to remain encamped, the thinner the supplies would run, the deeper the fear would set. If it was left to a waiting game, the empire would crumble and wither while the elves walked over the ashes. The only saving grace was that elves were not known for their patience. They would not sit on their hands while honour and glory awaited them. It was not in their blood.

Eltoar drew a long breath of cold air into his lungs, looking up towards the Blood Moon that was now partially exposed through a gap in the cloud cover. Four hundred years had passed since he'd seen that moon, since the night he'd sacrificed everything.

The sound of soft footsteps drew Eltoar's attention. Voranur approached, his blue and black robes flapping behind him. He inclined his head. "Eltoar."

"Brother." Eltoar looked to Voranur, but the elf strode past him and stopped only to stare out over the horizon. "Sleep evades you?"

"I evade *it*," he said, clasping his hands behind his back.

"May I ask a question of the heart, old friend?" With Lyina and Pellenor – Heraya embrace him – Eltoar had grown accustomed to the human ways, but with Voranur he held to elven tradition.

Voranur nodded, the muscles in his neck tensing.

Eltoar took his place beside Voranur, both looking out over Elkenrim, the sea of lanterns, and the distant horizon. "How are you and Seleraine dealing with the loss of Jormun and Ilkya? Of Hrothmundar and Eríthan?"

"Not well." A fleeting smile touched Voranur's lips, as though he were trying to muster some semblance of joy, only to watch it melt away. "We had flown together for so long, to me they seemed as immutable as time itself. Their absence..."

"Is like missing a piece of yourself."

Voranur nodded, turning his head just enough for Eltoar to see the light of the Blood Moon in his eyes. "I want to rip them apart, Eltoar."

Eltoar didn't have to ask to know Voranur spoke of Calen Bryer and Tivar. "Voranur—"

"I want to tear them limb from limb." He took a step closer. "Come with me. With Helios and Karakes beside Seleraine, we can set the whole Darkwood alight. We can burn them all."

"If we leave, brother, the elves swallow this place whole. There are two hundred thousand souls within Elkenrim—"

"Let them die!" Voranur shouted, veins bulging in his neck. A roar erupted in the sky, Seleraine mirroring her soulkin's fury. The dragon burst from a bank of clouds overhead, blue scales glittering purple in the light of the moon. A heartbeat, and Helios emerged behind Seleraine, blotting out the moon's light. The two dragons circled as Voranur's chest heaved.

Voranur gestured down at the city below the hill. "Who are they? I don't know them, don't know their names or their faces, don't know their hearts. Look at us, Eltoar. We are elves," he grabbed at the tapered point of his left ear. "If we were not Draleid, these people would have slaughtered us centuries ago."

"But we *are* Draleid, Voranur." Eltoar grasped the collar of Voranur's tunic, wrapping his fingers in the cotton. "And we made a vow to protect the people down there. To protect the people who need us."

"You sound like the council." Voranur sneered at Eltoar, lightning flashing in the sky behind him. "Like Alvira."

Eltoar clenched his jaw, his fingers tightening around Voranur's collar. The earth shook as Helios landed behind him, a deep rumble resonating in the dragon's throat. Helios lowered his neck, looming over Eltoar, forelimbs pressing into the soil.

Seleraine dropped behind Voranur on the downward slope of the hill, talons holding her in place. She was half Helios's size, but still an immense creature in her own right. The horns that framed her face were thick and sleek, the colour of deep ice, and angled outwards like the spikes of a morning star. Her muscles were lean and powerful, as quick as she was strong.

The two dragons towered over their soulkin, thunder rolling in the skies above. Eltoar could feel the rage smouldering in Helios's chest, the dragon's protective instincts taking hold. His fury would make the flames of Argona look like a campfire.

After a moment, Voranur rested his hand atop Eltoar's – which still had hold of the elf's collar – and shook his head. The tone of his voice was no less than a lament. "Uvrín mír, akar. Myia saleere tanathil mír."

Forgive me, brother. My pain devours me.

The words rang in Eltoar's ears, and he stared into Voranur's eyes. Over the centuries, he had watched the elf grow darker, pull into himself.

Eltoar let go of Voranur's collar and clasped his temples, pulling their heads together, then wrapped his arms around his kin. The two had never been close. Before The Fall, they had known each other only in passing, and since then, they had been bound by little more than their choices. But at that moment, Eltoar squeezed Voranur as though the elf was the dearest friend he had ever known. Eltoar squeezed him as though he were Alvira, as though he were Pellenor, as though he were everyone Eltoar had ever lost. There were so few of them left now, all they truly had was each other.

Voranur pulled away and turned back towards the city, Seleraine bowing her head and pressing the tip of her snout against his chest.

A crack of thunder opened the skies, and rain sheeted down over them, cold against Eltoar's skin. He leaned back his head, letting the droplets crash against his face and soak into his clothes. A shadow spread across the ground before Eltoar, the rain abating as Helios's wings unfurled to form a canopy. Helios stretched forward and nuzzled his head into Seleraine's jaw, a low whine escaping his throat.

Eltoar brushed the wet hair from his face and made his way to Voranur, who dropped himself to the ground and looked out through the downpour.

Eltoar sighed and sat beside Voranur, the already sodden grass squelching beneath him.

They sat there in silence, the rain drumming against the two dragons' scales and wings, thunder cracking overhead, lightning flashing across the horizon.

"I know what they became," Voranur said, finally. "Jormun and Ilkya. I watched the darkness take them. But they were everything I had."

"I know." Eltoar leaned forwards, wrapping his arms around his knees, cold rain trickling down his cheeks. He understood Voranur's pain. Losing Pellenor had set him in a dark place, but this wasn't about him.

"I don't regret what we did all those years ago." Voranur sucked in his cheeks and shook his head. "The Order had run its course. It was rotten. But I do regret that we couldn't show more of our brothers and sisters the light. I remember every face, the roar of every dragon. They haunt my sleep." He wiped water from his eyes. "I wanted to create something better, something worth fighting for."

The short laugh that Voranur choked out held as much joy as a funeral pyre. "Tell me, brother." He turned his head from the horizon of sheeting rain and locked his gaze with Eltoar's. "What is the point of tearing something down if what we build in its place is no better?"

Eltoar wished he had an answer, but the question was one he had wrestled with for a long time.

As they sat there, the words Tivar had spoken to him in the temple at Dracaldryr drifted thorough his mind. *"I will not put another of our kind in the ground. I will not tear another soul in half. Not on the word of that monster you call a friend. That demon you brand an emperor."*

At first, when Voranur had told Eltoar and Lyina that Tivar had betrayed them, Eltoar had been furious. A rage had burned in him like little else he'd ever felt. She was the closest thing he had to a sister. Even after his brother had fallen, Eltoar had still loved her like family. She *was* family, if not by blood, then by bond. Her betrayal was a knife in his heart.

But slowly, the rage had faded to sorrow and eventually to understanding. Tivar had not betrayed him. She had simply done what her heart required of her. Calen Bryer and his soulkin were the only thing that stood between their kind and extinction. She had always been a protector, always been driven by the need to help others. That was her way.

"Eltoar! Voranur!" Lyina's voice broke the monotony of the rainfall.

Both Voranur and Eltoar glanced at each other, then rose.

Lyina marched towards them in her full white plate, dark blonde hair tacked to her face, rain rolling over her skin.

"This was in the tent when I returned from patrol." Lyina lifted a sheet of parchment as she stepped beneath the canopy of Helios's wings. Her eyes were dark, brow furrowed, rage etched into the lines of her face. She shoved the parchment into Eltoar's hand.

"They want to meet," she said through gritted teeth. "By the old temple on the hill to the east."

"The temple to Elyara?" Voranur leaned across Eltoar, reading the letter.

Eltoar,

It is time we talked. Meet us by the temple of The Maiden atop Darnírin's Hill.

We will wait.

Salara

"Salara Ithan…" Eltoar stared at the name, his finger brushing over the ink. That was not a name Eltoar had expected to see. "It can't be. She wasn't at the Three Sisters. She…"

"Whether it's her or not, we need to go." Rage simmered in Lyina's voice.

Eltoar swallowed, a knot forming in his throat.

"Lyina is right. We must go." Voranur crossed his arms, staring down at the letter in Eltoar's hands. "Whatever the outcome, they are the last of us."

Eltoar nodded, lifting his gaze at the sound of wingbeats. Karakes soared over the treeline behind the command tent at the bottom of the hill, alighting behind Helios, rain splashing off his scales.

"We will go." Eltoar folded the paper, keeping it in his hand. "Voranur and I."

"What?" Lyina rounded on Eltoar, her stare hard and cold.

"Sister." Eltoar made to rest his hands on her shoulder, but she swatted them away.

"Don't treat me like a child, Eltoar. I don't have the patience for it."

He took a breath, then looked to Voranur and back. He would give her honesty, as he always had. "You are not ready, Lyina."

"Not ready?"

"The elven Draleid killed Pellenor." Eltoar's stomach turned as he spoke. But still, he pressed onwards. He found no joy in twisting the knife in Lyina's heart, but he did what he needed to do. "They ripped Meranta's wing from her body, tore out her chest, and snapped her neck."

Lyina's eyes widened, her mouth opening. She staggered backward as though Eltoar had punched her in the gut.

"They took him," she whispered. "He was good." She clenched her jaw, muscles twitching "And they took him."

"They did, and you would kill them all if you had the chance."

"You wouldn't?" Lyina stepped closer to Eltoar, tilting her head as she stared into his eyes. The next words were not a question. "You wouldn't."

Eltoar shook his head.

"He was our brother, Eltoar. He was better than me and he was certainly better than you." Tears mixed with rain on Lyina's cheeks. She shoved Eltoar, her gauntleted hand slamming into his chest. "Did you not love him? Do you not feel his absence like I do? Am I mad, or are you cold and heartless?" She shoved him again. "Answer me!"

"Of course I loved him," Eltoar said calmly. "But he is gone."

"And they took him from us."

"And we took more from them. How many of their loved ones did we kill that night? And in the years following 'The Fall'? If you ask them, I'd wager they think the scales are far from balanced." Eltoar shoved the folded letter into his wet pocket, then pushed Lyina's hands aside and cupped her cheeks. "I will feel Pellenor's absence until the day Heraya takes me from the world. He was my brother, and I loved him. But hearts grieve differently. Yours needs to bleed, needs to rage and weep so it can heal. Mine needs to push forward, lest it will break."

As Eltoar spoke the words, Helios's mind brushed against his, warmth flooding from the dragon's soul. Their hearts broke together, their wounds both doubled and shared.

Lyina held Eltoar's gaze, then brought her left hand up to rest it atop his. She didn't speak; words would have held no meaning.

"Vir væra vëna aier andin," Eltoar whispered. "Nur anis, aiar alura."

We will see them again. For now, they rest.

Lyina nodded softly. "You and Voranur go. You're right. I would kill them before they opened their mouths." She brought Eltoar's hands down and pulled away. "What if it's a trap? What if they're trying to draw you out?"

"I wish luck to anyone trying to trap him." Voranur looked up at the towering figure of Helios.

The great dragon shifted, and the rain broke through, drumming the ground and splattering against Eltoar's face as he looked up at his soulkin.

Helios stood over them all. The endless rain drummed against enormous wings, crimson moonlight glinting off the ocean of black scales that flowed over his body. He craned his head down so Eltoar could rest a hand against his snout. "Let them try."

The rain fell heavier as Eltoar and Voranur flew towards the old temple that stood atop Darnírin's Hill, some fifty miles east of Elkenrim. So heavy in fact, and Helios moving with such speed, that Eltoar had pressed himself against the dragon's scales, closing his eyes and allowing his mind to drift into Helios's.

There was no greater existence. They were one. Soul, heart, blood, eyes, scales, limbs. Eltoar was nothing more than an extension of his soulkin, and Helios the same. Thunder rolled across the skies, a flash of lightning igniting behind a bank of dark clouds to Eltoar's left. To his right, Voranur sat at the nape of Seleraine's neck, white plate armour pressed against scales of deep blue.

It wasn't long before the ruins of the old temple came into view a few miles ahead. But it wasn't the ruins Helios focused on. It was the gargantuan shape beside them. The dragon stood twice as tall as the destroyed temple, easily larger than Karakes, with a thick neck and powerful wings.

Even from that distance Helios's keen eyes could pick out the stunning red of the scales that covered the creature's back and wings, along with the deep gold across his chest and speckled along his snout. Both Eltoar and Helios would have known that dragon anywhere, though he was far larger than when Eltoar had last laid eyes on him.

Vyrmír.

An elf stood at the dragon's feet, golden armour and red cloth matching Vyrmír's colouring.

Without a word, both Helios and Seleraine angled their wings and swept downwards, riding a gust of wind.

Screeches and roars rippled through the night, breaking the monotony of the wingbeats and rainfall. Through Helios's eyes, dark shapes moved in the clouds, flashes of lightning illuminating winged shadows.

How many dragons had survived and stayed hidden within the bounds of Lynalion? Eltoar had pondered this in the years following the elves' retreat into the woodland. But when decades passed and turned to centuries, he'd all but dismissed the thought. The fighting had been so thick in those last years, so many dragons and Draleid cut from the world. For so long he'd believed the Dragonguard were the last of The Bound.

Helios folded his enormous wings and plummeted towards the earth, wind crashing over his scales with the force of a broken dam. Had Eltoar not been pressed against the dragon's neck, scales moulded to his body, he would have been ripped from dragonback. As it was, he drew a deep breath through his nostrils, filling them with the scents of turned mud and fresh rain as Helios alighted on the ground, his talons sinking into the earth beneath his weight.

It was in that moment, as Eltoar opened his eyes and lifted himself upright, that the eerie silence of the rainfall settled into him. Heavy rain had a strangeness about it, a way of evoking a sense of calm and stillness that pure silence could not emulate.

He took a moment, staring up at the cloud-blanketed sky, the rain cold against his face. Whatever happened next, he would be glad of that moment.

With one last long breath, Eltoar wove threads of Air around himself and slid from Helios's back, boots sinking into the sodden grass.

Seleraine alighted beside Helios, a crack of her great wings sending the rain swirling in spirals.

Voranur dismounted. "You saw the skies?"

Eltoar nodded.

"I counted seven." Voranur looked to the clouds, then over towards the waiting Vyrmír and Salara. The dragon loomed over his Draleid, head lowered, eyes fixed on the new arrivals. "Eight. Are you ready for this?"

"No."

"If it goes sideways?"

"Then we kill them."

Eltoar turned and made his way across the grass towards Salara and Vyrmír, Helios following, Voranur and Seleraine at their side.

"It's been a long time, Master." Salara's voice rang out, piercing the rainfall. She stepped forwards, her left hand resting on the pommel of the sword at her hip. She wore no helmet, her long black hair flattened against her head by the rain.

It was beyond strange to see her in the red and gold of Lunithír. When she had first come to Dracaldryr and held Vyrmír's egg in the Cradle of Fire, she had been a fisherman's daughter of no more than fourteen summers. From then on, the only armour she'd worn had been the white plate of the Draleid.

"It's been even longer since you've called me by that title."

"I've called you many things since then."

The drum of rainfall filled the emptiness between them as Salara stared at Eltoar, the rise and fall of her chest slow and steady. She advanced until she stood only ten feet away, her hand never leaving her sword's pommel. Vyrmír tensed, lowering his head, the red and gold frills on his neck standing on end, his monstrous teeth showing.

The dragon's eyes were like those of a wolf, ever shifting molten gold. When he had first hatched for Salara, talk had spread through the entire Order that the most beautiful dragon the world had ever seen had just been given life. Now, seeing him fully grown, Eltoar knew that statement to be true.

"I would have thought you'd have more to say, Master." She lingered on the word 'master'. Salara tilted her head, her stare never leaving Eltoar's. "It's been a very long time, and when last we spoke, you tried to convince me to turn on my kin. You had a lot to say then."

"I thought you were dead, Salara. If I'd known—"

"You'd have come to kill me yourself?"

"No, I…"

"Stop with these games and get on with why you asked us here." Voranur took a step closer but stumbled backwards as Vyrmír moved over Salara, threw his head forward, and unleashed a monstrous roar.

Both Helios and Seleraine shifted, lips curled back, teeth bared. If the three dragons fought, this entire valley would be nothing but dust and ash.

Eltoar made to speak, but before he could, roars blended with wingbeats and dragons burst through the dark storm clouds overhead. He counted seven, just as Voranur had. They swirled through the air, twisting and turning through the rain before crashing to the ground around Eltoar and the others, tearing up chunks of earth and clay as they landed.

He recognised a number from the Battle of the Three Sisters: the crimson-scaled dragon with scars along his wings where Helios had ripped him open, along with the three others with scales of purple, black, and blue.

Eltoar scanned the remaining dragons who had not fought at the Three Sisters. The first, he did not recognise. The second, larger than the first by some distance and covered by deep green scales accented with cream, was Dravír with his soulkin Irulaian. The third, with pale pink wings and dull yellow scales, was Andrax, soulkin of Lomari. Eltoar knew them well.

All seven of the surrounding dragons closed in, deep rumbles resonating from their chests, their soulkin sitting at the napes of their necks in golden plate.

Helios lunged forwards, the talons of his forelimbs digging deep into the ground on either side of Eltoar. The great dragon swung his neck side to side, unleashing a visceral roar, his rage flowing over Eltoar's body.

The air shook and the earth trembled at the mighty dragon's fury.

A flicker of hesitation swept through the others. None were a match for Helios in size or strength, not even close. If it came to it, with Seleraine at Helios's side, the likelihood was that no soul would leave this place.

The only dragon to stand their ground was Vyrmír. The dragon leaned further over Salara, frills raising higher, lips pulled back, chest puffed out. At two-thirds Helios's size, Vyrmír was the largest elven dragon. His muscles were thick and dense, his shoulders broad, his eyes fierce and unyielding.

Salara drew a breath, then moved to within arm's reach of Eltoar, Vyrmír's head moving with her, his eyes never leaving Helios.

"I didn't bring you here to talk of the past. Let me make things clear for you." She leaned closer, staring into Eltoar's gaze. "You burned my world. You slaughtered those I held dear. You murdered my master and put a demon in his place. You are not Eltoar Daethana, though you may wear his skin. You are a pale imitation, a shadow, an empty shell. There is not a word you can say, not a thing you can do. Forgiveness is not within your reach." Salara clenched her jaw. Even through the rain, Eltoar saw a tear fall, and what was left of his black heart broke. "I will kill you." She shook her head, pressing her tongue against the inside of her bottom lip. "For everyone you turned your back on. For those you swore to protect. I *will* kill you, and I will bring our people into the light again."

The rain fell harder, splashing in the puddles at Salara's feet and rolling down her face.

"But not today, for I still hold to the honour that you cast aside. No, I will kill you in the skies on Helios's back, with a sword in your hand. And I will look into your eyes when I do it. I will give you the death you did not give our brothers and sisters. Not because of who you are, but because of who I am."

Eltoar stared back at Salara, at the elf he had known since she'd been but a child, the elf who had been like a daughter to him. When she had refused to fight by his side, he had bound both her and Vyrmír and left them on Driftstone so they would not fall on that first night and so that she might come to her senses. But when he had returned, they were both gone. He had heard reports of them after that but never again laid eyes on them. From the reports, they had died in the Battle of Andillar Hill.

As he looked upon her now, standing tall in her gleaming golden plate, the fierce lines of her face and fire in her voice, he held no anger at her words. Eltoar had not earned the right to anger. No, he was instead flush with pride. For it was every master's dream that their pupil would one day be their better.

But with the pride came the shame. "Ask me what you called me here for."

The tears in Salara's eyes were gone, replaced by hardness. For a moment, Eltoar thought she would rethink everything she had said, but then she let out a breath and spoke. "We have heard word of a hatchling. Of a white dragon born to a human. Is it true?"

"It is."

Salara's eyes widened and she leaned forwards. "You're sure?"

"I did not see the egg hatch myself, but—"

"Then you're *not* sure."

"I fought them." Voranur moved closer to Eltoar and Salara. "The dragon is too small to not have been hatched recently."

Salara raised an eyebrow. With anyone else Eltoar would have thought the curl on her lips was a touch of amusement, but with Salara he knew it was fury bit back. She shifted her focus to Voranur. "So you bring our entire race to the edge of extinction, and then you to try to kill the first of us bound in four hundred years?" She narrowed her eyes. "You said you fought them, but you didn't say you killed them. Did they kill any of you?"

Voranur's jaw clenched.

"They did." She gave a slight nod. "Good. Less work for us."

"How dare you." Voranur marched forwards, reaching for his blade. Eltoar cried out to him, but Voranur's rage drowned out his words.

In the span of a second, everything shifted.

Seleraine roared and launched herself over Voranur at Salara. But the dragon never reached her target. In a display of speed and strength that would have been rare even in the old days, Vyrmír surged forwards and slammed into Seleraine's chest. The earth shook as the dragon crashed to the ground in a writhing tumble and then again as Vyrmír landed atop her.

The red and gold dragon sank his talons into her chest and legs, scales cracking. As he made to wrap his jaws around Seleraine's neck and rip out her throat, Helios spun, his tail slamming into Vyrmír with such force that the large dragon was knocked free of Seleraine and sent sprawling through the mud, the ground quaking.

Voranur howled and ran to his soulkin.

Pure, untempered fury surged through Eltoar from Helios, and the dragon hammered into Vyrmír, sending him careening back even further, wings tangling in themselves.

Three of the other elven dragons alighted beside Vyrmír, snapping and screeching at Helios, while the others lifted themselves into the air and circled.

Eltoar's soulkin stood over Seleraine and unleashed a roar that shook through the earth, his crimson frills standing on end. Even outnumbering him four to one, the others hesitated. They were nothing but hatchlings in his shadow.

Eltoar rounded on Salara, who stood calmly with her hand resting on her sword pommel. "What happened to your *honour*?"

"I think you'll find he attacked me first, *Master*." Again, she emphasised the word, seeming to find joy in repeating it. "It is not my fault if your traitors cannot control their tempers."

Salara stared over at Voranur, a look of disgust on her face. He had dropped to the ground beside Seleraine, hands crimson with the blood flowing through the broken scales as he tried to offer comfort. From where Eltoar stood, Seleraine would live, but the wound was deep.

"I can put her out of her misery," Salara said, motioning to draw her blade as Vyrmír rose behind her, shaking off mud and rain.

Eltoar opened himself to the Spark, pulling threads of all five elemental strands into his body, and summoned his níthral. Tendrils of piercing blue light burst from his hand, coiling around each other until the light-wrought greatsword was fully formed.

Vyrmír unleashed a mighty roar over Salara's head, his frills shaking, his wings spreading wide.

Eltoar didn't allow his gaze to shift from Salara even for a second. "Take another step, and your soul will wander the void until time breaks. Do not test me."

Salara waved her blade at Eltoar in much the way a mother might wag a finger at a child. As she did, the three circling dragons dropped to the ground behind Helios, each roaring. The Spark thrummed in the air around the Draleid that sat astride the dragons. "Choose your next move carefully, Master. You might strike me down, but even the great Helios, the Black Sun, cannot stand against eight of his kin. I meant what I said. Today is not the day I kill you, not unless you force my hand."

She turned her gaze from Voranur to Eltoar. "Do you know how hard it was for us to remain in Lynalion's depths while you hunted your own kind like animals? Every passing day was agony. We are Draleid. It is not in our blood to stand by and do nothing, to let the world burn, to let the rivers run red. Each night I closed my eyes and lay there knowing that while I slept, you hunted my kin. We couldn't take more of us in. Too many and you would have come looking. We needed you to think us dead. I hated myself for centuries while we waited and waited. If we emerged from Lynalion too early, it all would have been for nothing."

"This isn't the way, Salara." Eltoar released his Soulblade, reaching out an open palm. "There are so few of us left."

"Because of you!" Salara raised her sword at Eltoar, all semblance of calm vanishing. Vyrmír moved forwards, spittle flying as he roared like thunder, mirroring Salara's movements. "I loved you. I *worshipped* you." Her voice trembled, hand shaking as she held her blade. "And you brought us to this. You broke us. Why? Was it worth it? Did you get what you wanted?"

Eltoar once again found himself lost for words.

"I told myself I wouldn't let you in. Told myself you would hold no sway over me, that I would be steel. But even after all this time, you still make me feel like a child." She drew a breath, a steadiness returning to her voice. "It's time you leave. From this day on, you will know what it is like to be hunted. I will kill you all, one by one, and I will burn your empire to the ground."

Eltoar touched his hand to his breastplate, sensing the gemstone that hung around his neck beneath the steel. It had been a lifetime since he had tapped into Essence, since he had felt its power coursing through his veins. If he called on that power now, he could end everything there and then. None of them would leave this place alive. But as he stared at Salara, Tivar's words from the temple at Dracaldryr spoke to him.

"He manipulates us, Eltoar. Can you not see it? Can you not feel how that stone twists and turns you? How it seeps into your mind."

Eltoar *had* felt it… felt Efialtír's touch stoking his fury, feeding his blood lust.

He looked around, seeing the elven dragons surround Helios, their frills raised, muscles tensed.

He rested his palm against the cold white steel of his breastplate, feeling the Essence pulse. All power came with a price, and Essence was no different.

"Do it." Salara's voice cut through the haze of Eltoar's focus. "Call on your Blood Magic, just as you did back then. Your god's moon hangs in the sky." She gestured towards the crimson circle that had found a gap in the dark clouds. "But if you do, neither you nor your soulkin will leave this place. This earth will be your tomb, that much I promise you."

Eltoar looked from Voranur to Seleraine and back to Salara. He could kill her, of that he had no doubt. But if he did, the others would fall on Helios and Seleraine in a heartbeat. They would never survive such an onslaught.

His mind flickered to Lyina, who waited at the camp near Elkenrim, her heart already broken from Pellenor. He could not leave her alone to face this storm. And then, there was the new Draleid: Calen Bryer. With his soulkin's hatching, there was once again hope for the future, hope Eltoar had thought he'd all but destroyed… hope that needed to be protected.

Slowly, Eltoar pulled his hand from his breastplate and allowed the power of the Essence to fade from his mind. He took a step towards Salara, his gaze never leaving hers.

She didn't move.

"You will know the pain soon." Salara slid her blade into its scabbard, her stare unwavering. "Go, fly back to Lyina. Lick your wounds. And when I kill her and this traitor—" she gestured to Voranur, who was now coaxing Seleraine to her feet "—I will give you the courtesy you never gave me. I will let you mourn, let you weep. And then I will destroy this world you have stitched together from the carcass of the one you ripped apart. I will burn it to the ground, and I will kill everything and everyone your black heart still cares for."

Eltoar stared into Salara's eyes, then turned and walked towards Helios, the rain falling around him. Salara didn't call after him, and neither did he speak. All the words worth saying had been spoken. She was right. Forgiveness was not within his reach. He didn't deserve it, nor did he crave it. He had earned every word. He had made his choices, and he would face the consequences as he always had.

But that did not mean he would simply bend and break. Everything he had done had been to create a better world.

Maybe the world they had built was no better than what they had destroyed, but what was done was done. The old world was gone. But the elves had razed every city from Easterlock to Steeple. Half a million dead. Whether this world was better or not, he would not allow them to continue ripping it to pieces.

CHAPTER THIRTEEN

RECLAMATION

6th Day of the Blood Moon

*Elven encampment, east of Elkenrim – Winter,
Year 3081 After Doom*

Salara didn't speak as she marched through the silent camp, lanterns atop posts illuminating the night. Red tents were pitched all about her, banners emblazoned with the golden stag flapping in the breeze. The sigil of the dead kingdom of Lunithír, reborn as the mark of Numillíon – of all free elves.

Every elf she passed bowed at the hip, placing a hand across their chest as they did, whispering the word, "Draleid."

She returned their greetings with a nod, never stopping, never lingering. On the surface she was calm and still, her expression stoic. She knew this because she had spent centuries perfecting it. She was a Draleid, the beacon of hope her people looked to. In an ever-shifting world, she was their constant. It was tiring but necessary.

Contrary to the stillness she outwardly portrayed, her mind was chaos. She could feel Vyrmír's heart beating, his lungs swelling with air, his talons slicing into the soft earth beneath him.

The dragon lay curled on the edge of the camp with Baerys and Nymaxes, but his mind was with her. Warmth flooded through the bond as he tried desperately to ease her pain, but she pushed him away. Seeing Eltoar alive after all these years, hearing his voice, feeling the weight of his stare… It had taken far more from her than she had ever expected.

Two guards stood to attention at the entrance to her personal tent. Both were armoured in gold and crimson, fingers wrapped around the shafts of long glaives.

They protested when she waved them away, but acquiesced.

The tent itself was rectangular in shape, wider than it was long, with enough space for three or four inhabitants. A small oil lantern sat by the side of her cot at the tent's rear and two more on the small table to her right.

As soon as the flap closed behind her, Salara stumbled, her legs fumbling beneath her, her chest feeling as though it had been hollowed out and filled with stones.

She dropped to her knees on the rug by the entrance and ran her hands through her sopping wet hair, shaking. Gods curse him for doing this to her. She had been preparing herself for the day she would once again lay eyes on her old master, the things she would say, the things she would *do*. But how naive she had been to think that anything could have prepared her. There are some wounds so deep that nothing could fill them.

Queen Vandrien's voice sounded behind Salara. "Narvír."

Commander.

Salara hauled herself to her feet, wiping her eyes with the cold steel of her gauntlet. She straightened her back and brought a closed fist to her chest. "Myia'nari. Laël sanyin—"

"There is no need for apologies, Salara." Queen Vandrien Lunithír stood at the tent's entrance, a flowing crimson dress threaded with gold reaching just past her knees. Vandrien was everything an elf should be. She was grace and beauty, hard as steel and strong as diamonds. Her arms were lean and muscled, her hair white as snow.

Vandrien raised her hand, looking into Salara's eyes. She walked around Salara, her dress swaying as she moved, and stopped at the table. She raised an eyebrow at the glass bottle beside the candle.

Vandrien had gifted that bottle to Salara after they had destroyed the human city of Easterlock and finally begun the Reclamation. The grapes had been harvested from the vines in western Numillíon, the only such vines that could trace their lineage back to the soil of Caelduin. Under the dense canopy of Lynalion, grapes were not easily grown. That one bottle of wine was a rarity, a treasure, a taste of what had once been.

"I was waiting," Salara said, inclining her head towards the bottle, pulling her gauntlet off and rubbing at her eye with the heel of her hand. "Until we have won the war. Until we have taken back what was stolen from us."

"We have waited for four hundred years, Salara." Vandrien pulled on the Spark, sliding thin threads of Air around the bottle's cork and lifting it free. "I do think that is long enough. Don't you?"

The queen pulled two wooden cups across the table, poured the wine, then passed one to Salara.

Vandrien swirled the wine in the cup gently, lifting her nose as she drew a long breath. She shook her head, a smile curling her lips, then sipped the wine.

The queen let out a long, happy sigh. "It seems strange that something so..." She pondered, looking towards the tent's ceiling, then continued, "frivolous can remind you of what you're fighting for." She stared into the glass. "Though, I suppose wine is not frivolous. It is history and culture. It is time and hardship. Our ancestors in Caelduin worked the vineyards tirelessly, refusing to use the Spark, keeping to the old ways. This wine is their legacy, our heritage preserved in glass... In essence, it is everything we fight for. Our past, our way of life..." Vandrien lifted her gaze, a nod letting Salara know the queen wished for her to drink. "Forgive me, I'm wandering."

Salara did as instructed, swirling the wine and inhaling the scents. Some said they could pick individual scents from wine – cherries, peaches, chestnut, oak. Salara figured they were full of shit. She smelled wine. It was sweet, fruity, pleasant. But not much else. The taste, however, was a different world altogether. She might not have known the individual notes, might not appreciate the subtleties, but that wine reminded her of home. It was full, and rich, and warm.

"We must allow ourselves these small things, Salara." Vandrien gestured towards the cup in her hand. "We are at war now. We will never know when Heraya will choose to call us into her embrace. Don't hold these things in hope for what might be. Embrace them, let them fill you with longing. Let them fuel you. We cannot wait for our destinies to unfold. We must forge them ourselves." Vandrien moved back towards the table, looking down over the map that Salara had tacked there, red ink marking the land Numillíon had already reclaimed. Ice crept into the queen's voice. "You went to meet with Eltoar Daethana."

It wasn't a question.

"I did, Myia'nari."

"I'm assuming there was a good reason you did this without speaking to me first?" Vandrien looked from the map to Salara, studying her. "The young dragon and their Draleid. What did Eltoar say?"

"He confirmed the reports. A new dragon has hatched. We must..."

Salara allowed her words to fade as Vandrien raised a hand.

"We must follow the plan, Salara. I promise you, on my honour, that I will do everything I can to find out more about this, but we must hold fast."

"Du haryn myia vrai, Myia'nari." *You have my thanks, my queen.*

Vandrien nodded, sipping her wine. "May I ask a question of the heart?"

Salara nodded. A queen did not need to ask. Vandrien gave Salara more honour than she was due.

"How was it, seeing him again? How is your heart?"

Salara took a long draught of her wine, breathing in through her nose as she did. "Torn," she said, exhaling. She folded her arms, staring off at an empty patch of red canvas on the tent's wall. "I can't reconcile the Eltoar I knew with the monster that ripped us apart. Seeing him only made that worse because he doesn't look like a monster." Salara turned to Vandrien, not bothering to hide her emotions. "He doesn't, Vandrien. He looks like my master, like my friend. He looks like the elf who taught me everything, who taught me what honour truly meant, what it was to be a Draleid. He taught me who I am."

"We are, each of us, capable of things we could never imagine." Vandrien moved beside Salara, following her gaze. "No soul is incorruptible. Good and evil are words created so that our minds might grasp, in its most simplistic form, the concept of what is right and what is wrong. But the words themselves serve no purpose. For boiling down right and wrong into such basic forms is not possible in the living world, only in theory."

Vandrien placed her cup on the table and filled it once more, doing the same with Salara's. "Eltoar Daethana is not evil. He is not a monster, nor a demon, nor a god. He is an elf, a Draleid. Nothing more. He is capable of both good and evil, right and wrong. But it is through his actions and the actions of those who followed him that so many of our people died. He is your former master, but he is also the butcher of everything you loved. He betrayed us, betrayed you. He hunted and slaughtered more Draleid than we could ever hope to count." The queen gave a soft sigh. "Come. I have something you need to see."

Salara followed Vandrien from the tent, the queen's Sunguard taking up positions on either side as they made their way back through the camp. There were six in total, never any more, never any less. Each guard wore a suit of smooth plate forged from Antherin steel and brushed gold. Charging stags adorned the tops of their articulated pauldrons, while their breastplates were marked with depictions of the sun. Unlike the rest of the army, the cloth that decorated their armour was not crimson but white trimmed in gold.

They were, each of them, the greatest warriors in Numillíon, masters of the blade, artists of the Spark. Even Salara herself would be hard pressed to fight her way through their steel.

"Alaith anar, Draleid." Their commander, Olmaír Moridain, inclined his head to Salara. He was a tall, lithe elf with long, wiry arms and sharp eyes and had seen a hundred battles by the time Salara had drawn her first breath. A living legend.

Salara returned the gesture, bowing slightly. There were few for whom she held as much respect as she did for Moridain. Her father had raised her on stories of the elf.

As they walked, there were no bows from the elves they passed along the way. A bow was not sufficient for the one who would lead them from the darkness. Instead, each elf dropped one knee, leaving it to hover just short of the ground, resting their sword hands atop their pommels. It was something they had taken to doing when Vandrien had commanded them not to kneel, a sign they were always ready to fight for her.

After a while, they came to a section of the camp where the canopies switched from crimson and gold to a plain cream, marking where the elves who had been freed from the human iron mines were housed. She had not visited in the days since the mine's sack, for which guilt still wracked her. She simply could not bring herself to look upon what the humans had turned her kin into.

The guards who stood about wore no armour and held no weapons. Crimson tunics adorned their shoulders, linen trousers falling over sandalled feet. Vandrien stopped and spoke with one of them, then gestured to Moridain. "Wait here."

"Myia'nari." Moridain and the Sunguard spread out in a line.

"Leave your sword with Olmaír," Vandrien said to Salara, moving forward and gesturing for her to follow.

Salara did as commanded.

"You have the blood of Achyron in your veins, Salara," Vandrien said when Salara caught her up. The smile that sat upon the queen's lips was one of sorrow and sympathy. "You are a warrior through and through. But you still bleed like any other, still feel the crush of heartache."

Salara looked at the ground as she walked, as much to avoid Vandrien's gaze as to mind her step.

"Feel your grief," Vandrien continued. "Let it flow through you. But so too feel your *anger*." Vandrien's voice rose, a growl forming in her throat. "Feel the rage at what was done to our people. Feel the fury at what *Eltoar Daethana* did to our people, *his* people. Feel the fire."

Vandrien rested a hand on Salara's pauldron, her voice gentle. "Lift your gaze, Salara. Do not look away."

Before them, the tents had parted into an enormous opening with hundreds of baldír lined along the edges, their white glow dim. Now that she focused, she could feel the thrum of the Spark in the air, see the threads of Spirit, Air, and Fire swirling about the mages who sat with their legs folded.

After a moment, her gaze moved to what Vandrien had brought her here for.

"So long have they been surrounded by rock on all sides that they refuse to sleep in the tents for fear of being trapped." Vandrien clasped her hands behind her back, worry in the creases of her eyes, anger in the tremble of her voice. "The baldír give them comfort, shelter from the darkness."

Everywhere Salara looked, elves lay in the dirt or sat huddled in groups. They were packed so tightly it was like looking upon a colony of ants. Each was garbed in the finest spider-silk woven in Eselthyr – beautiful, vibrant garments of blues, yellows, greens, and reds. They had been bathed in warm waters, their hair brushed, skin scrubbed. They had received treatment fit for royalty, and yet they huddled in the dirt, looking as though they feared their own shadows would come for them.

Rage smouldered in Salara's chest, her jaw clenching.

"They have known little else besides the mines, besides the darkness and the walls, the hopelessness and the pain. They were born into a life of chains and bonds. Brought to the surface only so that they would know the light – know what they would never have." As Vandrien spoke, Salara felt her draw from the Spark, threads of Earth and Spirit. "Generations of our people born into subservience, born to believe they were worth nothing more than the dirt in the ground." The cup of wine that Vandrien had carried from the tent cracked and splintered, shattering, wine spilling like blood. Her hand shook, still holding the cup's remnants. The queen's dress flapped and lifted, threads of Air swirling around her. Waves of power surged from her, pulsing like a beating heart. She looked to Salara. "Warmarshal Luilin leads their integration. He is having the bralgír tell them stories of times passed, showing them our customs and culture, teaching them of honour and how to hold a weapon, educating them on the choosing of a valúr and what it means. But sometimes these things are not enough."

Vandrien let out a long sigh, then rested her hand on Salara's cheek, staring into her eyes.

"I know how much I have asked of you. I know it is not fair. But I also know that I would not have asked it of you if I did not think you capable of it."

"On my honour, my queen, I am yours. Ask of me what you will, and I will see it done."

Vandrien smiled softly, brushing her thumb across Salara's cheek before turning back to look at the hundreds of elves huddled together in the open camp. "Show them they are safe. Give them a reason to believe, as you have done for us all. But most of all, show them that the darkness cast upon them will not go unpunished. Eltoar Daethana is not the master you once knew. That elf is dead. He is what remains. I need to know you will do what must be done."

Salara looked out at the rescued elves, pity swirling with rage in her heart. She dropped so that her right knee hovered just off the ground. "Eia væra cuaran i sanvîr. Ur myia haydria."

He will pay in blood. On my honour.

"Rise." Vandrien pulled at Salara's arm and lifted her upright. "Although the gesture is appreciated, I wish you to teach these elves how to stand, not how to kneel." She pulled a long breath through her nose, then exhaled slowly. "The Lorians will strike at us soon. Once they see we are waiting for Efialtír's moon to wane."

"How can you be sure?"

"Because it is what I would do, and Fane Mortem is many things, but he is no fool. The moon gives his mages an advantage over ours, an advantage that fades when the Blood Moon sets. In fact, I am quite curious as to why they haven't attacked already."

"Our scouts report large numbers of Lorian soldiers joining the ranks at Elkenrim, many of them travelling from the Svidar'Cia. Perhaps they are mustering."

Vandrien's eyes widened at that. She gave a sombre nod. "So he returned to where all of this began. Have our scouts push harder. Intercept messages, eliminate patrols. Take as many alive as you can. I want to know where the Lorians sleep, where they empty their bowels, what songs they sing. I want to know what Fane Mortem eats to break the fast. Knowledge wins wars, Salara."

"I will pass the command on to the generals. What of this attack? How should we prepare?"

Vandrien traced her finger along the map. "Have you ever read *The Art of War*, by Sumara Tuzan?"

Salara shook her head.

"She was a human tactician, from the Age of War. A brilliant mind for warcraft. If humans know anything, it is destruction and death." Vandrien folded her arms. "Sumara posed that the simplest way to win a war is to destroy your opponent's capacity to wage it. We began that by taking the mines near the Sea of Stone, and now we must continue on that path."

"What would you have us do?"

"With the mines, we took their iron. Next, we must take their food, their gold, and their ability to communicate. We will use their advantage against them. Cut off the blood, and the limb will die. Cut off enough limbs, and the body will die."

CHAPTER FOURTEEN

FROM THE ASHES

6th Day of the Blood Moon

Three hundred miles west of Greenhills, Loria – Winter,
Year 3081 After Doom

The icy embrace of the Rift pulled itself from Kallinvar's bones as he stepped through, the hard, dry earth cracking beneath his boots.

The rest of The Second waited a few feet ahead, tall trees rising about them, dim pink light drifting through the canopy. Sylven remained in the temple, her wounds not yet healed. Even Heraya's Well could not so easily mend the pain of a lost limb.

The Rift rippled behind him, and Sister-Captain Emalia stepped through, her entire chapter at her side. The Tenth was the only chapter still yet to suffer a loss, which was a testament to Emalia herself.

Emalia inclined her head to Kallinvar, bowing deeper than she ever had before. That was the case with many of the knights after Kallinvar had told them of Achyron's voice. It had not been the response he'd expected but one that had eased the chaos in his mind.

Kallinvar looked about the dark woodland. The place would have seemed innocuous enough to mortal eyes, but to Kallinvar, the rot of the Taint clung to the air and oozed across the forest floor like a dark sludge. More importantly, drifting just below the surface, he felt a heart beating apart from his own, faint but alive.

A new Sigil Bearer.

He was still getting used to the sensation ever since Achyron had pulled him into the Godsrealm. Even as he stood there in the woodland, the dying voices of other potential Sigil Bearers whispered in his mind as they gave their last breaths to the wind. It was a dark thing to know that for any Sigil Bearer he chose to offer knighthood to, ten more would die, alone and helpless. Ten more who may well have been just as worthy, just as willing to fight for the world they loved. Another weight on already weary shoulders.

To think this was another burden Verathin had lived through alone. He had spoken to Kallinvar in the years past about hearing the heartbeats of the new bearers, hearing their whispers. Kallinvar himself had been given the honour of anointing no fewer than eleven bearers himself. But Verathin had never explained that in order to save one, so many others must be left to die. As it turned out, there was a lot Verathin had never said.

"Stay tight." Kallinvar left the thoughts to float in his mind. "The Traitor's hand is strong here. Have your knights move in pairs. Never alone."

"You don't think the Heart is here, do you?" There was earnestness in Emalia's voice. "Should we summon the others?"

"I don't believe so." Kallinvar shook his head. "But stay vigilant. Sister-Captain Arlena and The First are waiting if we need them."

Kallinvar didn't have the faintest idea if the Heart was there or not. Hundreds of pulses of the Taint were scattered all across the continent since the Chosen had crossed, and he didn't even truly know what to look for. But of all the voices he'd heard calling to him, all the heartbeats, this one had felt the most dire, the most urgent. And it emanated from the same location as a deep well of the Taint. As Verathin had so often said, the situation killed two birds with one stone.

Kallinvar approached Ildris, who stood like a hound with his head tilted to the wind. The man had always been more attuned to Efialtír's touch than others, like a sixth sense. "What do you feel?"

"Nothing you don't already know," Ildris answered. He gestured north. "The Taint should not be so strong out here. We are hundreds of miles from any Lorian encampments or Urak holds. We will find nothing here but death."

Kallinvar grasped Ildris's pauldron. "Then let's go say hello to an old friend."

Twigs snapped beneath Kallinvar's weight as he and the knights pushed through the wood, half-frosted leaves crunching. Above, old branches groaned in the shrieking wind, clacking against each other. Apart from the occasional flapping wings, there was little sign of life.

With each step, the corruption of the Taint grew stronger, pulsing outward from a centre point like a rippling wave. But so too did the heartbeat in the back of Kallinvar's mind.

There was something different about this place, something that pulled at Kallinvar, clawed at him. It was as though Efialtír's hand scraped the ground and his breath tarnished the air. He'd felt something similar at Ilnaen, but its presence here was unsettling.

Could the Heart truly be in this place, hundreds of miles from anywhere the scholars had considered? A place he had come with no intention of finding it, and so soon? If that were true, he was either the luckiest or most unfortunate soul in all the known world.

It mattered little. They were here now, and they would find what they would find. If the Heart resided in this place, he would summon every knight alive and they would do what they'd been saved to do. They would fight.

After a while, a lantern flickered in the distance, followed by several more, their warm light glowing through the trees.

"A fort," Lyrin called in a hushed tone as he and Arden emerged from the shadows ahead. "Large enough for a few hundred. It bears no markings, but it's certainly not Bloodspawn-built."

"Lorians," Ildris whispered, the air changing between the knights. None ever questioned killing Bloodspawn. The creatures were born of The Shadow, gifted life by Efialtír's power. They were monsters who would destroy everything. But to kill men and women, to kill humans, was never a task any of the knights yearned for, imperial or no. But they would do their duty.

"Servants of Efialtír," Kallinvar corrected. The knights drew closer as he spoke. He straightened, bringing his tone firm and level. "Black and white do not exist."

"We live in a world of ever-shifting grey," Ruon finished the words.

Kallinvar nodded, allowing his gaze to linger on her for a second longer. "There will be men and women inside that fort who do not deserve our blade. They are nothing more than spokes in a wheel. But wheels break. Spare who you can, but do what you must. Steel first. Soulblades for anything that touches Essence. Above all else, do not hesitate. This place reeks of the Taint."

A chorus of 'Grandmaster' ringed the group.

"It reeks of something else as well." Lyrin pinched his nostrils between a thumb and forefinger. "What in the fuck is that?"

Barely a moment after Lyrin had spoken, the same stench flowed into Kallinvar's nostrils. He covered his nose and mouth and made to speak, but Emalia got there first.

"Burning flesh." Sister-Captain Emalia clenched her jaws.

"What's the plan?" Ruon asked, drawing closer. "Do we know where the Sigil Bearer is?"

Kallinvar shook his head in answer. That pulse tapped away in the periphery of his thoughts, muffled by the oily sickness of the Taint spilling from within the fort's walls. "I need to get closer. The heartbeat is faint."

"Through the front gate it is then," Lyrin said with a shrug, rolling his shoulders. "It's always courteous to knock. That's what my mother always said."

As the young knight spoke, a bird shrieked overhead, its dark shape visible against the moonlight as it soared over the fort.

"I'm sure your mother was a good woman, Brother Lyrin," Kallinvar said, summoning the Rift behind him, "but I believe I may have a simpler option."

KALLINVAR'S PULSE THUMPED SLOW AND steady, the blood in his veins cold, the familiar blackness surrounding him. Then he was falling, the Rift washing over him. The world burst to life, warmth wrapping around his bones even in the winter cold.

Torch lights flickered below, the roars of battle rising upwards. Five heartbeats, and he collided with the ground, a tremor sweeping through him, cracks spreading beneath his feet.

"Grandmaster!"

Kallinvar barely had a second to react to Arden's call. In one motion, he pulled his sword from its scabbard, stepped back, and swung.

Steel met leather. Leather failed. Flesh parted.

The Lorian soldier collapsed on the ground in a heap, blood flowing from his opened chest. All about Kallinvar, Lorians charged from log buildings, some in full leathers and armoured plates, others in little more than their smallclothes. They threw themselves at the knights who descended from the sky.

The Taint was so strong in this place that even allowing himself a second to stop and think almost turned Kallinvar's stomach, the oily tendrils probing at his mind. What in the gods was happening here?

A flash of motion signalled in his periphery, and he swung his free hand, catching the head of a warhammer in his grasp. Even through the soldier's helm, Kallinvar could see the shock in her eyes. He lifted his foot and planted it into her chest. The strength given to him by the Sentinel armour ripped the hammer free from her grasp and sent her careening through a nearby log wall. Her spine snapped on a support beam, cutting her screams short.

More movement sounded to his left. He released the hammer's head, tossed it into the air, snatched its shaft in his grasp, and swung. The hammer crashed into a man's chest with enough force to collapse his breastplate inwards with a series of sharp snaps. He hit the ground, his screams drowned out by the sounds of him choking on his own blood. Kallinvar swung the hammer back down and ended the man's misery, crushing his skull like a rotten melon.

Emalia and two knights of The Tenth surged past him and crashed into a clutch of Lorian soldiers, scything them down. These soldiers were like children next to knights in Sentinel armour.

Just as the guilt touched Kallinvar's heart, a well of the Taint pulsed behind him, and he turned to see two Fades emerging from the shadows, their pale skin taking on a pink hue beneath the moon's light.

"*Urithnilim.*" Achyron's voice was a hushed whisper in Kallinvar's mind. "*There are more here, my child. This place hides something. Send their souls to the void.*"

"With pleasure," Kallinvar whispered. He sheathed his sword and charged at the Fades, calling out to his Sigil.

Green light burst from his closed fist, illuminating the night. By the time he brought his arm across his body, his Soulblade had taken shape in his right hand, the warhammer still gripped in his left.

The Fades lunged at him as one, black-fire Soulblades bared. He blocked a strike from the left, green light bursting as the two blades collided, then swung his blade back across and caught the arc of the second Fade's blade inches from his helmet. The creature smiled at him, its lips a pale blue, its light-drinking eyes gaping.

Kallinvar rammed the head of the warhammer into the Fade's gut, bones *cracking*. As the Fade howled and staggered backwards, Kallinvar swung the hammer behind him, hoping to catch the other creature off guard. Instead, the second Fade twisted unnaturally, the heavy steel head gliding past its face. It stretched out its hand, and a surge of the Taint erupted from its palm. Kallinvar barely had a second to think before he was sent hurtling through the air.

He smashed through something wooden, hitting the ground hard. He dragged himself to one knee, gasping for air.

Another surge of the Taint pulsed, and Kallinvar was lifted from the ground and hauled into the air, helpless as a newborn babe, his arms pinned to his sides.

"The arrogance of your god…" the Fade hissed as it pulled Kallinvar closer. "You reek of it."

The second Fade stepped into Kallinvar's vision, that same eerie smile still pasted on its face, its head tilted sideways. Cracked bones twisted from broken flesh where Kallinvar had hit it with the warhammer, but the creature showed no signs of pain. "I've always wanted to see what you look like on the inside of that armour. Are you human?" His black eyes scanned Kallinvar. "Like a… what do the humans call them? Crabs? Hard shells on the outside. Tender meat within."

"Yes," the other responded. "Crabs."

Shouts and screams drew Kallinvar's gaze to the wall. Arden surged along the battlements, knocking soldiers from the walls through his sheer momentum. The young man leapt from the parapet, raising his hands in the air, his Soulblade forming in a burst of green light. The Fade who held Kallinvar in its unseen grasp turned, but not fast enough.

Arden's Soulblade cleaved the creature clean in half from crown to groin, the weight of his landing lifting a plume of dust into the air. The Fade's two halves remained standing for a heartbeat as though they might knit themselves back together, but then they wavered and folded to the ground, bloodless and forsaken.

The bonds of Blood Magic that held Kallinvar in place faded, and he dropped to the ground, recalling his Soulblade in the same motion and taking the second Fade's head from its shoulders as it turned.

"You talk too much," Kallinvar said as he stared down at the creature's severed head, its mouth agape, empty black eyes staring at nothing.

Ruon appeared at Kallinvar's shoulder, her helm removed, a crack spreading down the side of her armour. She followed Kallinvar's gaze. "A Battlemage. Took three of us to take her down. Under the moon's light they are savage," she said with a shrug. "You all right?"

Kallinvar grunted, giving the crack in her plate one last look before gesturing to Arden, who had risen and released his Soulblade. "Thanks to Brother Arden."

Kallinvar looked about the courtyard that fronted the fort's gate. Bodies were strewn through the dirt, the dry ground absorbing the blood like a thirsty sponge. Horses neighed in the stable as Brother Yorik of The Tenth dragged his blade from a man's chest and let the body slump to the ground.

In the silence that followed, Kallinvar heard the Sigil Bearer's heartbeat slowing in his mind. And then Kallinvar's own Sigil burned with a roaring fury and Ruon's eyes widened as they both felt Sister Rialis's soul leave the world.

"Where's Emalia?" Kallinvar scanned the yard frantically. All of The Second remained, but he could only see three knights of The Tenth walking amidst the Lorian fallen. He searched for the pulse of Emalia's Sigil, his eyes drawn to an archway in a wooden gatehouse that led through to another yard. Agony and fury flowed from Emalia at the loss of her knight, seeping into Kallinvar.

I will not lose another. He charged towards the gatehouse. "With me!"

Shouts rang out as Kallinvar and the knights surged towards the arch. Chain rattled and a thick iron portcullis dropped into place as arrows rained down from soldiers who'd scrambled to the battlements over the passage. Pulses of the Taint erupted from the parapet and arcs of purple lightning tore strips from the earth. A bolt caught Lyrin in the chest, and the knight hurtled through the door of a building, ripping it from its frame. Panic flared in Kallinvar, only easing when he felt Lyrin's racing heart through the Sigil.

"Arden, Ildris, Varlin!" As Kallinvar charged, he summoned the Rift to his right, his Sigil burning, ice sweeping over his skin. Two green orbs burst into life, one at his side, the other in the air above the ramparts, spreading into the familiar black, green-rimmed portals. The world rippled as Arden, Ildris, and Varlin sprinted into the black waters of the Rift and emerged through the other side within the span of a breath, dropping onto the shrieking soldiers and mages above.

All the while, Kallinvar continued his charge, his long strides eating the ground beneath him. He drew a solid breath into his lungs and reached out through his Sigil.

Give me the strength I need.

"You already have it, my child. Break them."

Kallinvar drove his feet into the ground and launched himself through the air. He closed his eyes and collided with the portcullis, the sound of crashing metal ringing in his helmet, the force shaking him to his bones. For a moment, the world froze, and then the portcullis bent inwards and ripped free of the gatehouse in a chorus of snaps and cracks.

Kallinvar crashed down and tumbled, the clang of iron and the *thump* of the portcullis slamming into the ground ringing in his head. His bones aching, Kallinvar staggered forwards on his hands and knees, snatching up the warhammer from atop the remnants of the portcullis.

"Get up." Ruon grabbed Kallinvar in the pit of his arm and hauled him to his feet. He didn't have to ask what had put the tone in her voice.

The Taint surged throughout the second courtyard in waves as knights of The Tenth raged against a score of Lorian Battlemages. Arcs of purple lightning shattered earth and stone, plumes of black fire ignited the air, shards of stone battered against Sentinel armour, and the green light of the knights' Soulblades illuminated it all.

At the centre, Emalia twisted and weaved between two figures in smooth steel plate, a match for her in height. Red light shimmered through runes all about their silver armour, crimson Soulblades gripped in their fists.

"Vitharnmír," Achyron hissed in Kallinvar's mind. *"Rip their souls from this world."*

Emalia's Soulblade was a blur as she fought the two creatures, Rialis's broken body at her feet.

Kallinvar's legs were moving before he'd had another second to think. Emalia stood alone. She needed him.

Sparks of purple lightning flickered to Kallinvar's left as a Lorian Battlemage charged into his path. Kallinvar swung the warhammer across his chest and launched it forwards with every ounce of his strength. The weapon smashed the mage's shoulder to pieces in an explosion of bone and gore, ripping his arm free and sending him, shrieking, backwards.

A second mage roared to his right. The roar turned to a scream as Ruon carved him in two across the belly with her Soulblade, her stride never faltering.

Ildris, Arden, and Varlin leapt into the fray from atop the gatehouse, Lyrin following close behind. But Kallinvar was focused on one thing and one thing alone: Emalia.

He lunged forwards, throwing himself between his sister-knight and the Vitharnmír on her right, his Soulblade bursting to life just in time to stop the creature's downward swing from cleaving Emalia's arm at the elbow. The two Soulblades collided in a burst of light, and for a brief moment, Kallinvar stared into the Vitharnmír's glowing red eyes set in a silver helm moulded like a mask to its face.

Kallinvar pushed forwards, forcing the Vitharnmír onto the back foot, then spun, his back rolling across Emalia's as they traded places. He swung for the second Vitharnmír's head, finding resistance in the form of its Soulblade. He brought his blade back across the creature's body, slicing down at its knee, only for the blow to be blocked once again. Twice more he struck, and twice more the Vitharnmír matched him blow for blow before ramming a steel-covered fist into his side.

The strike knocked the air from Kallinvar's lungs, and he felt a crack spreading through his Sentinel armour. He staggered sideways, gasping, regaining his composure just in time to watch Emalia's Soulblade carve through the Vitharnmír's elbow as it moved to tear his soul from the mortal world. The howl that left the creature's throat was a visceral, blood-chilling thing, two voices layered over each other, one a high-pitched shriek, the other a primal growl.

"Now would be the time to summon Arlena," Emalia shouted, dropping to one knee to avoid the swing of the second Vitharnmír's Soulblade, then rising to ram her shoulder into its gut.

Kallinvar lifted his gaze to see Arden and Varlin weaving through three Fades, Soulblades glowing. More mages flooded into the yard as though materialising from the shadows themselves, Fades moving amongst them. Some wore the black of the Battlemages, while others had the red cloaks of the Inquisition knotted at their shoulders.

What in the gods are so many mages doing in a fort in the middle of fucking nowhere?

Kallinvar reached out to Arlena through the Sigil, then summoned the Rift, his veins igniting.

The Rift had been open no more than a breath when Arlena and The First charged through, Soulblades already ignited.

A flicker of movement drew Kallinvar's attention, and he threw himself sideways to avoid being sliced open by the now one-armed Vitharnmír, who had shifted its Soulblade to its remaining hand. The creature rained down a maelstrom of ferocious strikes, each one shaking Kallinvar's bones even through his Sentinel armour.

A brief respite from the barrage came as Ildris slammed into the creature's back and it staggered forwards. Kallinvar took advantage of the Vitharnmír's lost footing by dropping low and carving his Soulblade through its knee.

The Vitharnmír collapsed on its back, thrashing and hissing, its dual-tone voice sending shivers through Kallinvar, the runes in its armour blazing.

"For Rialis." Kallinvar grasped the hilt of his Soulblade with both hands and drove it down between the Vitharnmír's eyes.

Even with the blade lodged in its face, the creature writhed, arms and legs flailing, black smoke billowing from the runes carved into its silver armour. The runes erupted in a burst of light as the Vitharnmír's soul was shorn from the world, then faded to nothing as the creature was sent to wander the void.

The silver armour that covered its body shivered and twisted, turning to liquid. It rolled over the Vitharnmír, receding into the many runes carved into the pale flesh and revealing the face of a woman of adolescent years, the light of his Soulblade shimmering in her open black eyes.

Kallinvar pulled the blade free, a coil of regret twisting in him. One constant had always remained throughout his many lifetimes: the young had always paid the price for mistakes made long before their time – and the price was always blood.

As he stood staring down at the twisted corpse, the Lorian mages rallied around the remaining Vitharnmír, fighting with void-wrought fury. Some held nithrals of varying colours in their fists, others spewed black fire from their palms, the world twisting around them. It was like that night in Ilnaen four hundred years ago all over again.

The knights closed around them, fighting in pairs as commanded, the added numbers of The First proving the difference. With every swing of his Soulblade, the dying pulse of the chosen Sigil Bearer grew weaker, fading in Kallinvar's mind. This needed to end now, or it would all be in vain.

"Emalia, Arden, Varlin – with me!" Kallinvar surged into the thick of the fighting, his Soulblade carving a path of blood and bone. If the Vitharnmír died, the mages would break.

He swung his Soulblade in an upward arc across his body, slicing through a mage's forearm and cleaving his face from chin to brow before swinging back across and taking another's head from her shoulders.

The sickly oil of the Taint surged in pulses as the Lorian mages tried to keep the knights at bay. But in these close quarters, even the power of Efialtír's moon couldn't save them.

Tendrils of Essence wrapped around Kallinvar's feet, holding him in place as the Vitharnmír charged through the swell of the bodies and swung its crimson

Soulblade. The weapon came within a handspan of Kallinvar's neck before Arden crashed into the creature's side and the pair tumbled to the ground.

Kallinvar staggered forwards, the bonds of Essence that held him in place evaporating as Varlin swept past and took the head of the mage responsible.

Within seconds, both Arden and the Vitharnmír were back on their feet, their Soulblades a blur of light. Kallinvar charged into the fray, Emalia and Varlin at his side.

He swung at the creature's flank, only for it to turn and send a shockwave of Blood Magic slamming into his chest from its open palm. He careened backwards, the air fleeing his lungs as he hit the ground.

Kallinvar rose, struggling to breathe, staggering, when his Sigil ignited with aching loss. He lifted his gaze to see the Vitharnmír standing over Sister Uriban's body, the breastplate of her Sentinel armour collapsed inwards under the creature's weight.

The roar that filled the yard was one born of anguish and loss. Sister-Captain Arlena hurled herself at the creature bound in its twisted Sentinel armour. The Vitharnmír turned to meet the charge, its foot pressing into Sister Uriban's chest, blood spraying.

The two Soulblades crashed together again, and again, and again, until the Vitharnmír carved a gouge across the breast of Arlena's armour.

For a moment, Kallinvar's heart stopped, his breath catching. But Arden, Emalia, and Varlin charged in, and the Vitharnmír stood no chance.

First Arden took its left arm, then Varlin drove her Soulblade through its thigh, tore it along the creature's leg, and ripped it out at the knee. Emalia plunged her blade into its heart, and Arlena took its head. The Vitharnmír may have been born of godsblood, but even gods could bleed.

As the silver armour slithered over the demon's skin, the surviving Lorians threw down their arms, steel ringing out through the yard.

In the silence that ensued, a slow heartbeat drummed in the back of Kallinvar's mind, weak, fading.

Dum dum. Dum dum. Dum dum.

Kallinvar looked to Arlena and gestured towards the surrendering Lorians. "Bind them. Knights of The Second, with me."

Kallinvar led the way across the yard and into a tall wooden structure that sat at its northern edge, two storeys tall, thick, and broad. He could hear Ildris and Ruon speaking, but their words were muffled, drowned out by the dying heartbeat.

Dum dum. Dum dum.

He pushed open the wooden structure's doors and stepped into a large open hallway, barren except for an empty table against the right wall and a row of hooks beside it with three dangling coats. The place had been built purely for function.

That same putrid smell of burning flesh from outside clung to the air, thick and heavy. It pressed on the back of Kallinvar's throat and pushed into his nostrils.

Kallinvar followed the thumping of the heartbeat through the arch on the opposite end of the hall, stepping into a room illuminated purely by candlelight.

Fifty cots stretched the length of the room, split evenly on either side.

"In the name of all that is sacred," Ruon whispered from behind Kallinvar.

He didn't look to see what it was that brought such horror to her voice. Instead, he focused on the mages who were scrambling about, grabbing scrolls and notes and stuffing them into sacks.

Kallinvar marched down the central path between the rows of cots as a mage stood in shock, staring. He was a Scholar by the grey of his robes.

"I..." The mage staggered backwards, looking up at Kallinvar with eyes that held nothing but fear. "I didn't... I..."

"You didn't what?" Kallinvar grabbed the man by the throat and lifted him to dangle off the ground. Ruon and the knights subdued the other mages in his periphery.

As Kallinvar held the man in the air, he looked about the room, his gaze falling on what had caused Ruon so much disgust. Every cot was occupied, but none of the occupants were moving. Each was stripped naked, raw, angry wounds carved into their flesh in the shape of runes. Limbs were twisted and snapped in preternatural directions, skin blackened and cracked. Other victims had knotted masses of flesh where their eyes had been. Each looked to have died a death of uniquely excruciating pain.

Kallinvar tightened his armoured fingers around the mage's throat, feeling a groan from within. Snapping his neck would have been as easy as breaking a twig.

"They... they're volunteers. At least, they were... I swear it."

"It's a shame none are alive to make the same oath." He squeezed a little tighter. "Convenient, that."

"I swear on The Saviour himself."

"Oh, your god isn't listening." Kallinvar pressed his tongue against his palette, his rage sour in his mouth. The faces of those on the cots were just as young as the girl who had played host to the Vitharnmír, just as vulnerable. "The duty of the strong is to protect the weak, mage. These are just children. *Children.* You should have protected them, but instead you preyed on them, mutilated them... Is this the god you worship? The god that feeds on the young?"

"They..." The man trembled, his voice barely a whisper. "They were volunteers. They—"

"Look at them!" Kallinvar roared, turning to hold the mage over one of the cots, twisting his neck so he couldn't look away. "They are children!"

Anger was an emotion Kallinvar knew intimately but one he had long since believed under his control. He now accepted that belief to be false.

Kallinvar threw the man to the ground, looming over him. The mage leaned back on his elbows, shaking, staring back up at Kallinvar with terror in his eyes.

Never allowing his gaze to leave the mage's, Kallinvar's helm receded into the collar of his Sentinel armour. "Stay here. I'll deal with you after."

"I just—Argh!" The mage unleashed a high-pitched shriek as Kallinvar stomped on his shin, snapping the bone clean, blood splattering the stone. The scream died out after a few seconds, the mage losing hold of his consciousness.

Kallinvar stepped over the man, following the weak heartbeat that thumped in his head.

Dum... dum.

He found a small passage at the far end of the room that led to a rock-enclosed opening within the forest's bounds.

It was here he discovered the source of the smell. An enormous pit had been dug at the centre of the opening, and within it were bodies, black and burnt. Smoke still drifted from the charred corpses, the vile stench of burning flesh and clothes clutching the air.

Ruon and Arden stepped through the passage and out into the clearing. Silence held them, but Kallinvar could feel the all-consuming sorrow that radiated from their Sigils.

Dum... dum.

A grunt sounded to Kallinvar's left, followed by deep, rasping breaths.

Armoured in ruby plate, a man was slumped against a post, a spear driven through his abdomen, just below the ribs. The weapon appeared to be the only thing holding him upright, pinning him to the wood at his back. The front of his armour was slick with blood, a pool seeping into the grass at his feet.

The potential Sigil Bearer was an Inquisition Praetorian.

Kallinvar stepped closer and lifted the man's chin, staring into his eyes.

The Praetorian grunted again, returning Kallinvar's gaze. "Make it quick." He coughed and spluttered, choking on his own blood. "At least quicker than this."

Kallinvar rested a hand on the man's drooped shoulder, gripping tight. "This will hurt."

He yanked the spear free with an almighty pull, and the Praetorian collapsed forwards into Kallinvar's arms, blood pumping from the now open wound.

"You will be dead within minutes. Or we can offer you a second chance in this life. A chance to protect the things you love. But it comes at a cost."

The man stared back at him, straining hard to maintain his consciousness. "I'm pretty sure... I'm past saving."

"The duty of the strong is to protect the weak," Kallinvar said, ignoring him. "Do you agree?"

"Can I not just die in peace?" He choked, spots of blood painting his bottom lip, then swallowed and answered the question. "Always."

Kallinvar glanced at the pit of burning bodies, his anger getting the better of him. "Is this what you call protecting the weak?"

"Why do you think—" The Praetorian coughed up more blood, his eyes rolling to the back of his head. He drew a breath, grimacing. "Why do you think you found me on the pointy end of a spear?"

"Hmm. No decision is straightforward. Black and white do not exist. We live in a world of ever-shifting grey. Do you agree?"

"More than you know." The Praetorian's breathing grew shallow, but no sign of panic or fear hid in his eyes. He was not afraid of death.

"If we save you – if we grant you the Sigil of Achyron – are you willing to leave behind everything that you were? To forget every piece of the man you are now and become something more?"

"What in the fuck is the Sigil of Achyron?" The man licked the blood from his lips, then coughed up a laugh. "Fuck it. I would give everything to forget.

I thought we were on the right side. It all made sense, until it didn't. Though I suppose that's always the way." He stared at Kallinvar. "Yes."

"If you take the Sigil of Achyron, you are bound to him. Should you betray his creed, your life will be ripped from you and you will know pain the likes of which you never thought possible. I must be clear. You will live, but there will be nothing easy about your life."

"There never has been. But I'm afraid, if you don't hurry up, I'm going to be dead pretty soon anyway."

"I need you to understand the gravity of what it is to bear Achyron's Sigil."

"And I need to know…" The man grunted, then lifted his head and nodded towards the pit of smoking bodies. "Will Achyron stop that? Will he end all this madness?"

"Or die in the trying," Kallinvar said, inclining his head.

"I'm dead already, am I not? I'll take his Sigil, as long as he understands that his is not a name I've ever prayed to."

"He doesn't need your prayers. He needs your blade."

"He will have it."

Kallinvar nodded. "Sister Ruon, the Sigil."

Ruon removed the metallic green Sigil from the pouch at her hip, and Kallinvar took it as though it were made of glass.

He traced his fingers along the sword that ran through the centre of the Sigil. "This belonged to a great man."

"I'll wear thick socks."

Kallinvar laughed at that. "This will hurt more than the spear."

The man closed his eyes and gritted his teeth, then nodded.

Kallinvar rested the Sigil over the Praetorian's breastplate. The Sigil shimmered, brilliant light radiating from its surface. Unlike the previous times he had anointed new Sigil Bearers, Kallinvar could *feel* the power flowing through him and into the Praetorian, the Sigil acting as a conduit. In the span of a fleeting second, the Praetorian's memories flashed across Kallinvar's eyes. Not all of them, not every moment of his life, but the defining ones. The moments that shaped and moulded the man before him now.

Three brothers, all lost before the age of twelve in the great fires of Khergan, along with both parents. Saldan – that was the Praetorian's name – had spent nearly two days trapped beneath ash and rubble until he'd finally been pulled free by an Imperial Praetorian.

Five years later, at the age of fourteen, he killed a man over fish at Khergan's port. He'd been starving and alone, and yet even still to this day the memory haunted him.

At sixteen, he was accepted into the Praetorian Order and finally found the family he had yearned for, the family that had been taken from him.

Many moments across many years flickered through Kallinvar's mind. Saldan was not a perfect man, but he was one who always tried to be decent. He had taken many lives but never without questioning why.

The last memory was of that day. He'd been posted at the fort earlier that morning. The sight of the young men and women lying on the cots had stopped his heart. He'd gone into a rage when the rune markings had started to kill the hosts, twisting their bodies and snapping their bones. The others had subdued him and strapped him to the post in the clearing. When they'd carried the bodies to the pit, he broke his bonds and charged his own. They skewered him and left him to die.

The memories faded from Kallinvar's vision and before him the Sigil shimmered one last time before waves of heat radiated from its surface, the steel of the Praetorian's breastplate melting like butter.

Saldan's eyes snapped open, bulging, but he didn't scream. He shook, jaw clenched tight, hands tearing tufts from the grass.

"Pain is the path to strength, brother."

Smoke drifted upwards, the smell of burning flesh reaching Kallinvar's nostrils.

Saldan convulsed, mouth open, breaths short. And still, he didn't scream. Kallinvar had screamed. He'd screamed like a newborn babe, and he'd wept rivers. The pain of taking the Sigil was unnatural. Nothing in all his years had ever come close. It was the first test of knighthood. Feeling pain, screaming, weeping, that was not the test. The test was whether the knight persevered.

In Kallinvar's mind, perseverance was the single greatest attribute a human soul could possess. It was the one and only thing that was always within your control. Talent could be wasted, luck could run out, charm faded. But a soul that could persevere despite all odds could overcome anything.

After a few moments the power that coursed from Kallinvar into the Praetorian ebbed and faded, and the man stopped convulsing. A shiver set in, and Saldan's teeth chattered, as was normal.

The centre of the ruby steel plate that had covered his chest had melted away, hardening in streaks along both flanks and in small pools on the ground. Through the gap in the armour, Saldan's bare chest was exposed, dripping with sweat, his skin raw and pink. A tattoo in the shape of Achyron's Sigil ornamented his skin, metallic green, glinting in the light of the moon.

"Rise," Kallinvar said, grasping the man's forearm. "Brother Kevan."

CHAPTER FIFTEEN

JUDGEMENT

6th Day of the Blood Moon

The Eyrie, Aravell – Winter, Year 3081 After Doom

Aeson had not visited Aravell often over the centuries since The Fall, but he had never before seen the Eyrie empty. Valerys, Sardakes, and Varthear were still making their way back from the Eleswea un'il Valana with Calen and the others, but they were all that was left. The last remnants of the world he remembered.

Ithrax, Thurial, Onymia, and Aradanil had all perished in the battle for the city. In a sense, he was happy they would finally be with their soulkin again, that they would finally be allowed the rest they so readily deserved. But that didn't stop the pain in his chest.

He walked through the Eyrie and towards the passage in the western rock face that led to the cells and the old courtyard. The opening rose over a hundred feet into the rock, spreading one and a half times that left and right.

Two guards stood at the entrance, the symbol of a white dragon adorning their steel breastplates. They placed their hands on the pommels of their swords and dipped their heads.

Aeson inclined his head and passed through the entrance into a long corridor of hewn rock large enough for a dragon to pass. It felt strange to think of this place as a prison. At one point, it had housed over forty Rakina who had wished to stay closer to the dragons, but it had been empty for almost three hundred years. It seemed as good a place as any to hold Farda and the others, but it still felt strange.

A low rumble echoed down the corridor, reverberating against the stone.

Aeson pushed onwards. He didn't have long; the others would be there shortly. His steps grew slower as he approached the archway at the end of the corridor. He knew what he would find, but even still, when he finally reached the arch and looked out into the courtyard, his heart cracked.

Avandeer lay curled on the paved stone, enormous rune-marked shackles around her ankles and a collar about her neck, chains tethering her to the ground. Scars of fused scales raked her body, and her breathing clearly laboured with each rise and fall of her chest. After seeing Avandeer and Tivar defend the city, the elves had taken enough pity on them to heal the major wounds, but healing dragons took time and energy.

Even before The Fall, Avandeer had been amongst the most breathtakingly beautiful creatures in the world. The purple and white pattern of her scales had captured the hearts of many artists across the continent. To see her trapped, to see her light diminished, her spirit shattered, sliced into Aeson's already tattered soul. In the back of his mind, he thought he could feel Lyara, like the fragment of a shadow lingering in the light, begging him to comfort Avandeer.

As he stepped through the arch, the dragon stirred, chains clinking, talons clicking against stone. She lifted her head, turning to face Aeson, her lids peeling back to reveal eyes the colour of marigold.

He moved closer, Avandeer staring at him. The dragon's jaws were unchained. She could have bathed him in fire if she so wished, but she held no fury or wrath in her eyes, only apathy and loss. After all these years, Avandeer and Tivar had turned and fought against those who had betrayed The Order, and as soon as they did, they were wounded, separated, and shackled. Aeson had never had the displeasure of wearing rune-marked shackles while Lyara still drew breath, but from what he'd heard, it was as close to being Rakina as the soul could come.

The dragon shifted once more as Aeson came within arm's reach, a low rumble emanating from her throat. Avandeer's upper lip pulled back into a snarl, the smell of embers and ash floating from her half-open jaws.

"Laël sanyin," Aeson whispered as he lifted his palm, ignoring the dragon's snarl. *I am sorry.*

His breaths shallow, he rested his hand on the dragon's warm scales. Two parts of his mind warred as his finger traced over the edge of a jagged groove just below Avandeer's eye. Sorrow consumed half of him, rage the other. The Dragonguard had taken everything from him. They were meant to be his brothers, his sisters, his kin. But they had betrayed their oaths and destroyed all that he had held dear. And yet, now that he looked upon Avandeer, he found no joy in the dragon's darkness, no solace in her pain.

Aeson wanted to speak, to say something – anything – but the words were as elusive as the wind. What could he say? Judgement would be passed soon – life or death – and that was when his words would matter.

He allowed himself a few moments before pulling his hand away. There was a question he needed to ask before the others arrived, and now he had given himself little time to do so.

Avandeer stared at him for a moment longer, then rested her enormous head on the stone once more, the rumble fading from her throat as though Aeson no longer existed.

"This is not how it should be," Aeson whispered to himself before turning and walking back through the archway.

Aeson made his way along the candlelit corridor until he came to a stop outside an iron-banded wooden door with old Jotnar runes carved into the wood. Dumar, son of Rahlin, had once called this room home. Aeson remembered the day he'd found the letter, the day Dumar had joined his soulkin. Dumar had been the first among the surviving Rakina in Aravell to make that choice, though not the last.

Drawing a slow breath, Aeson opened himself to the Spark. He could see the elemental strands pulsating in the dark of his mind, their light flickering, fading.

Not now.

He closed his eyes, reaching for the translucent strand of Air. He clamped his teeth down, the muscles in his jaw twitching as he tried to pull a thin thread from the strand.

It had taken Aeson many years to find the symbolism in what Lyara had taken from him when she died. He could go weeks without difficulty when drawing from the Spark, only for it to abandon him for moments, or hours, or days at a time without warning. It held no rhythm nor rhyme, no beat nor cadence.

It mirrored his grief. Months could pass without Lyara touching his mind, without thoughts of Naia crushing his half-soul, without the memories of those he had loved rending his heart. But then, once he had allowed himself to breathe, to sleep, to rest, it would come rushing back to remind him he was no longer whole. For grief is not a constant thing. It is a monster that does not kill its prey but plays with it, torments it. Grief is not an obstacle to be overcome. It is an injury that must be accommodated. It never leaves, only waits.

Aeson let out a gasp as the Spark flooded into him, the thread of Air whirling around his body. With a sigh of relief, he pushed the thread into the door before him, where the outside lock had been fused shut.

A *click* sounded, and the door creaked open.

Aeson pushed the door open slowly, the candlelight behind him carving a path through the darkness of the room within. His footsteps echoed in the sparse room of hewn rock, each clip of his boot like a hammer drop.

"I was wondering when you'd come."

Aeson looked down on the man who sat with his back against the far wall, steel manacles clamped around his wrists. Chains connected the manacles to a bolt in the floor, the blue light of the runes illuminating the scars on the man's face.

"Farda."

"It's my time then?" Farda Kyrana lifted his gaze to meet Aeson's. Four claw marks ran along his left cheek where Ella Bryer had raked her nails across his face.

The Healers hadn't given Farda the same attention they had Avandeer. The wounds were scabbed and red, dried blood mingling with crusted dirt.

"Not yet."

"And yet here you are."

"Here I am." Aeson sucked in his cheeks, biting down. He walked to the left side of the room and lowered himself into the seat against the wall.

"Four hundred years." Chains clinked as Farda shifted himself, pushing his back further up the wall. "This is the longest we've spent in the same room without trying to kill each other."

Aeson leaned forwards and rested his elbows on his knees. "Not for lack of desire."

"No…" A silence passed for a moment. "You took Shinyara from me." Farda pulled in a long, hard breath. "I can never forgive you for that."

"Forgive me?" Aeson glared at Farda, meeting the man's cold gaze. "I would sooner open my veins than ask your forgiveness for anything. You deserved to feel the pain, the loss. What you did… You were not worthy of the bond."

"What *I* did?" Farda scoffed. "You're all the same. I know what I did. I know the darkness in my choices. But it appears, after all these years, arrogance and ignorance are still your closest friends. Why are you here, Aeson? I'm tired."

"I want to know why."

"Is it not a little late for that?"

"No, I want to know why you came here. Why you turned your back on the empire after all this time."

"What does it matter?"

"It matters."

"Ella…"

"Calen's sister?"

"Mmm." Farda nodded, his fingers clenching and unclenching.

"What of her?"

"Just go, Aeson. We're past this. Soon my head will be on a spike and I'll be done with this world, and we'll all be the better for it."

Aeson leaned forwards a little further. "Answer the question, Farda. What of Ella Bryer? After everything you've done, what in the gods turned your mind?"

Once more, silence filled the dark room, the light of the candles in the corridor and the runes on Farda's shackles casting shadows across the walls. Farda let out an exhausted sigh. "Something changed in me when I met her, something that reminded me of why…" Farda looked up towards the ceiling and shook his head. "Why I fought in the first place."

Aeson pressed his tongue against the roof of his mouth, then looked to Farda. To his surprise, the man's eyes glistened from welling tears. He'd needed to know. Before the judgement was passed, he'd needed to know *why* Farda had turned on the Lorians.

"Aeson, I want you to know I think about that night every time I close my eyes. I…"

Farda's voice trailed off as Aeson lifted himself from the chair and turned towards the door.

"I trusted you." Aeson rested his hand on the open door, the iron band cold against his skin. He didn't look back. He couldn't. So many years had passed that he'd wished he could have had this conversation, and now that it was here, he had no time for it. "You were my brother and I trusted you. *Alvira* trusted you."

"She let them die, Aeson. I could have saved them. She let them die."

Without looking back, Aeson stepped from the room and closed the door behind him, the lock *clicking* back into place.

CALEN STOOD WITH HIS HAND on Valerys's flank, staring out over the edge of the plateau, the sound of crashing water drifting up from below.

Valerys rumbled in the back of his mind, and through the dragon's eyes Calen saw Tarmon, Erik, Lyrei, and Vaeril emerging from the passageway in the rock on the western edge of the Eyrie. Ten warriors bearing the mark of the white dragon on their breastplates followed, flanking four figures who marched between them, chains clinking.

Aeson, Chora, Thacia, Atara, and Harken all stood waiting at the edge of the Eyrie's main plateau, the other Rakina spread about, stares fixed on the procession. The two dragons, Varthear and Sardakes, were curled up near the Eyrie's entrance, their backs pushing against the lowest branches of a nearby tree.

Calen drew the cold air into his lungs and turned, observing the scene with his own eyes. His pulse picked up as he caught sight of Farda walking at the head of the prisoners. Four angry gashes ran across the left side of his face. Beside Calen, Valerys pushed himself upright with his forelimbs, a growl reverberating in his chest. Calen had to physically slow his breathing, trying to calm the rage that burned in Valerys at the sight of the man, a rage that shifted between them.

A hand rested on Calen's shoulder, pulling him from his mind.

"Are you all right?" Dann asked, his gaze not leaving Calen's.

Calen shook his head, clamping his jaw down. He lowered his voice to a whisper. "I want to cut his heart out, Dann."

"I don't think you're the only one." Dann tilted his head, gesturing at those gathered. All twenty-six of the Rakina who resided in Aravell, along with Therin and Dann, stood about the plateau. All twenty-six stared unblinking at Farda and the others.

"He killed her," Calen whispered, to himself as much as to Dann. "He set her on fire... he..."

Calen's hands shook, the memory replaying in his mind. The look on Farda's face, the flames, his mother's screams.

By force of habit, Calen reached down to rub his thumb and forefinger between the silk of the scarf that had long been tied to his belt loops. All his fingers found was the rough touch of leather. He had given the scarf to Haem. He could see it in his mind's eye, the autumn red, the vines of cream and gold, but it wasn't the same as feeling its calming touch against his fingertips. The scarf's absence only served to amplify that of Haem's. Moments like this were when he needed his brother, his sister.

Dann's hand squeezed tighter on Calen's shoulder.

The *clink* of chains echoed through the passage, accompanied by the sound of talons on stone and the drum of footfalls.

Valerys moved forwards, the force of his anxiety causing Calen to stagger with him.

Eight elven mages, each bearing the white dragon, marched through the enlarged passageway, trepidation on their faces as they wove threads of Spirit, Air, and Fire about themselves. Behind them walked eight more elves, fists gripped around long chains connected to the neck and legs of a dragon twice Valerys's size, purple scales tipped with white, eyes of brilliant yellow.

"Avandeer…"

Calen's gaze fell on the blue light that shimmered from the runes marked into shackles on Avandeer's legs and the collar around her neck. His heart stopped, his breath catching. Calen had not seen Tivar and Avandeer since the fighting, but he knew those bindings, knew the pain and emptiness they caused. He looked to Tivar at the end of the four prisoners. She had stopped and now stared back at Avandeer, pulling at her chains. He knew that agony, that hopelessness, felt it still in his bones.

His jaw twitched, memories flitting through his mind of the cell in Drifaien, of Artim Valdock, of the apathy, the loss… An insuppressible fury ignited within Valerys, pouring into Calen, flooding his veins and burning his mind; he tried to push it back, to soothe it as he had been learning, but it was too raw. The sight of Tivar and Avandeer suffering as Calen and Valerys had suffered was too much.

"Get those manacles off them." Calen strode across the plateau, ignoring the staring Rakina, his arm shaking as he pointed from Tivar to Avandeer.

The rage that flowed over him burned cold, ice in his veins, frost on his skin.

"Calen, take a moment. Breathe." Aeson moved to stand in Calen's way, his arms open.

"Take the manacles off, Aeson." Calen clenched his jaw, trembling. The purple light of his eyes reflected in Aeson's as he once more pointed at Avandeer. He tried to hold back the rage within, tried to calm himself, tried to calm Valerys. The dragon had no heart for calm. Calen steadied his voice as best he could. "Take them off."

"Calen, I—"

"Take them off!" Calen's roar scratched at his throat, and he could feel the veins in his neck bulging. A surge of power swept through him as he and Valerys's minds collided.

Aeson stepped back, his expression shifting. He raised his open palms, his gaze lifting upwards.

Calen didn't have to look to know Valerys loomed over him, purple light misting from the dragon's eyes, teeth bared, a vicious rumble in his throat. They had moved as one, completely and entirely. Calen could feel each pump of their heart, blood coursing through their veins.

As though in response to Calen and Valerys, Varthear and Sardakes rose in the southern section of the Eyrie, their eyes fixed on Aeson, their frills raised, lips pulled back.

The entire eyrie stood on a knife edge. The elves who held Avandeer's chains looked from Calen to the other Rakina, dumbfounded expressions on their faces.

Calen stared into Aeson's unwavering gaze. Once more, he lowered his voice and attempted to calm himself, though the rage he and Valerys felt would not be quelled. "Do you know what those bindings do, Aeson?"

"Calen, if you could just—"

"Do. You. Know?" Calen spoke each word slow and steady, staring into Aeson's ice-blue eyes. "It is a simple question."

"Yes."

Calen took a step closer. "And yet you still put them on?"

Chora wheeled towards Aeson and Calen, looking up at Calen. "It's the only way to hold them safely."

"Is it? Or is it simply the easiest?" Calen turned, looking for Thacia. He found the blood-haired Jotnar standing to his right. "Do you have the key?"

The Jotnar stared back at him, curiosity in her eyes, but she didn't speak.

"You?" Calen asked, looking to Aelmar, one of the other Jotnar Rakina.

Aelmar returned Calen's gaze, but he, too, remained silent.

Calen looked from Thacia, to Aelmar, to Moras, his fury rising with each breath. "Who has the key?"

"I do." Harken Holdark stepped forwards, his long hair falling over his shoulders, the dense muscle on his arms tensing as he folded them.

"Give it to me, Harken."

Harken glanced to Aeson, who, to Calen's surprise, gave a short nod. The man reached into the pocket of his coat and produced a thin metal cylinder with glowing runes carved along its length.

Calen snatched the key from Harken's hands, then marched towards the elven mages. They straightened, each of them pulling a fist to their chest as he approached and uttering a stifled, "Draleid."

"Can you contain her? Contain her fire?" There were eight of them. That should be enough.

"Yes, Draleid... but..." the elf closest to Calen stuttered, but she quickly regained her composure. "But if she—"

"Do it." Calen looked to Therin. "Can you ward Tivar?"

A look of understanding flashed across Therin's face, and he gave a sharp nod. "With aid, yes."

As the air ignited with the thrum of the Spark, and Therin and the mages warded Tivar and Avandeer, Calen moved to the dragon's side and tapped the key against the shackles around her legs. Both shackles gave a *click*, then clanged to the stone.

He moved to Avandeer's head, then rested one hand on her snout and looked into her eye. "I'm sorry. Laël sanyin." He lowered his voice and leaned closer, the warmth of Avandeer's scales brushing against his skin. "When I take this off, I need you to stay calm. Can you do that?"

The dragon let out a puff of warm air from her nostrils, her scales vibrating as a rumble of acknowledgement escaped her throat. She leaned her head into Calen, bone-white horns pressing against his leg and shoulder.

"It'll be all right," Calen whispered, touching the key against the collar around Avandeer's neck. "Go to her."

A *click* sounded.

Avandeer shook her head, the collar crashing to the ground, and she unleashed an almighty roar. The plateau shook as the enormous dragon sprang forward, leveraging her forelimbs and spreading her wings to clear the distance between her and Tivar in a heartbeat.

The warriors who had been holding Tivar and the others' chains backed away and scrambled for their swords. But Avandeer stood over her soulkin, her frills standing on end. She threw her head back, then leaned forwards and roared once more, spittle flying, the warriors stumbling backwards.

Calen followed Avandeer, Valerys behind him. The other Rakina stared at him as he walked, but none moved to stop him. Even Aeson and Chora remained silent.

Avandeer lowered her head as Calen approached, a rumble in her throat. The dragon stretched out her forelimbs and dipped her back, as though bowing.

Tivar lifted her gaze. Her face was dark and bruised, and marks streaked the dirt on her cheeks where tears had flowed. She leaned heavily on her left leg, and scabbed cuts ringed her wrists where the shackles bound her. Her breaths trembled as Calen approached.

"I'm sorry I couldn't come sooner," Calen said, his chest tightening. "You stood by me. When you had no cause to, you stood by me, and I owe you my life… sister."

"We were meant to be guardians," Tivar whispered, her dark eyes locking with Calen's. Calen saw his own agony reflected in her gaze, the memories of his time in the cell overwhelming him.

Calen reached forwards and took Tivar's trembling hands into his own, then touched the runekey against her shackles.

As the shackles fell, the elf dropped to her knees, shivering, her eyes closing and lips spreading in relief. Avandeer craned her neck forwards and nuzzled her snout into Valerys's jaw.

Calen drew a deep breath, his gaze meeting Farda's for a brief moment. Just a flick of Calen's wrist, just one thread of the Spark, and the deed would be done. Calen's fingers tapped on the coin pommel of his sword. He glared at the man for a moment longer, then turned back to face the other Rakina.

Chora, Aeson, Harken, Atara, and Thacia all stood before him, the others in a tight semi-circle.

"You know what it feels like to be broken," Calen said, staring at the five in front of him. "And yet you would inflict that pain on another? Did that make you feel strong? Did it make you feel powerful? Do you know how twisted that is?"

"She deserved to feel it." One of the other Rakina, a woman with short black hair, stepped forwards. Calen had not spoken to her, but he knew her as Imala.

The rage in her eyes was something he knew well. "She deserved to know. Her pain is nothing next to the breaking of the bond. She made her choices a long time ago."

"Pellenor Dambren is the reason I escaped Berona. When I asked him why he helped me, he answered that 'time doesn't move backwards', that he couldn't change the things he'd done, but that it would never be too late to recognize the mistakes he'd made." Calen moved closer to Imala. "When the empire captured me in Drifaien, they clamped those manacles around my wrists. They locked me in a cell, beat me, tortured me. But above all else, not being able to feel Valerys all but tore me in half. When Artim Valdock wrapped his fingers around my throat, I leaned in. I wanted to die." Calen shook his head and scoffed, staring at Aeson. "You dragged me across the continent. You convinced me of this war, convinced me that this was worth fighting for. Yet here you are, doing the exact same thing the empire did to me – the same thing they did to every one of you. Explain that, Aeson. Explain how we are any better than they are. Explain to me why we're even fighting this war in the first place. Explain how we can do this to one of our own."

"She is not one of our own," Imala snarled, her body stiffening, her tone flashing cold. "And you speak of things of which you do not know, things you could not possibly comprehend. I've been bound by those shackles before. It was horrible. I couldn't feel Amaros's mind, his soul. I couldn't feel his heart."

"Then why—"

"But it was *nothing*—" Imala cut Calen short "—compared to the agony that ripped through my soul when one of these traitors dragged me into the dirt and drove a spear through his head while he looked into my eyes."

A shiver swept through Calen at Imala's words.

"Until you watch your soulkin die, until you feel, and I mean *feel,* your soul shatter, you have no place speaking of what it is to be Rakina."

Calen's heart broke as he watched the tears roll down Imala's cheeks, Valerys pulling their minds together.

"Calen is right." Aeson stepped forwards and moved to Imala, who looked at him, her anger turning to dejection. He placed his hands on her shoulders and held her gaze. "We were betrayed by those we held close, and that betrayal cost us things that cannot be communicated in words. Things that... can never be recovered. But sometimes our pain blinds us. What happened to Amaros, there is no justice for that. But Tivar's pain will not ease yours, sister. The only justice we will find is in the righting of wrongs, not in the doing of more. In the years since losing Lyara, I have learned that a thousand times over. What's left of my soul is tarnished. We cannot simply claim to be better than Eltoar and the others, we must *be* better."

Imala nodded slowly, wiping the tears from her eyes, her shoulders drooped and trembling, her fury consumed by sorrow.

Aeson inclined his head to Calen.

Calen returned the gesture, the rage in his and Valerys's shared soul ebbing.

"With that," Aeson continued, "the continent is changing before our eyes, and decisions must still be made. Before we continue, I must ask that all those who are not Draleid or Rakina leave the Eyrie. We have already denied Queen Uthrían, King Galdra, and Queen Tessara's presence here. This is for our kind and our kind alone." Aeson looked to Therin and the elven mages. "You may stay and maintain the wards, but your voices will not be heard."

Therin responded with a soft nod, while each of the elven mages pressed a fist to their chest and bowed.

Dann, Tarmon, Erik, Lyrei, and Vaeril all looked to Calen. He gave them a reluctant nod. He would rather have them by his side, but he knew this was something the others would not be swayed on.

Once they had taken their leave, each of the Rakina drew closer, circling around Tivar, Farda, and the two other prisoners – the dark-skinned elf and the white-haired woman whose hand was curled into a twisted fist.

Without chains binding Avandeer, the dragon could easily have torn through many of those gathered, but Calen knew she would not put Tivar in that danger. What he did fear, however, was what Avandeer might do if the others decided death was Tivar's sentence.

With silence again settling in the Eyrie, Aeson stepped into the centre of the circle, his gaze passing along the prisoners. "Farda Kyrana, Ilyain Altair, Hala Nôri, and Tivar Savinír. You are all here today to be judged for what you have done. It would take a hundred lifetimes to list your crimes, so I will state but a few. You betrayed your brothers and sisters. You butchered your own kind. You plunged all Epheria into war. You were instrumental in the near-eradication of the entire Jotnar race."

"Quite the list," the white-haired woman, who Calen assumed was Hala, muttered.

One of the Rakina, Willam, spat on the stone, his eyes burning holes into Hala.

"Do you have anything to say for yourselves before judgement is passed?"

To Calen's surprise, Tivar lifted herself from her knees and stepped forwards. She held her chin high. Slowly, she passed her gaze around the circle, her stare hard and unyielding. "I deny nothing. I did what I did because I believed it to be right. I loved The Order, and I will *always* love my brothers and sisters. But what we had become was not what we were meant to be. I will not make excuses for my actions, and not a day has passed that I don't wish I could take it all back, but I can't. I betrayed you all." She lifted her gaze to Avandeer, who stood over her. "*We* betrayed you all. I swear, we believed we were doing what was right, but by the time we saw the truth, it was too late. I ask of you only two things."

"You have arrogance to ask for anything," Chora spat.

Tivar gave Chora a brittle smile, tears once more welling in her eyes. "And yet, these are two things I must ask. The first is that you do not make the same mistakes The Order did. Do not allow our people to become instruments of war sent at the behest of kings and queens who care little for the blood-cost of their greed."

"And the second?" Aeson asked.

Tivar drew a long breath in through her nose, rolling her shoulders and straightening her back. "It is a simple thing. Take Avandeer's life first, quickly and as painlessly as you can. I would not have her live a single moment where she does not know the touch of my mind. That pain is mine to hold, no matter how brief. I would save her from it if I could."

Tivar's words carved a hollow in Calen's chest. Valerys's mind pulled his closer, wrapping around him. He could see by the dumbfounded expression on Aeson's face that he, too, had not expected that request.

"Tivar… I…"

Tivar jerked forwards, her chains pulling at her. "Aeson, I need you to promise me on your honour. If I could go back, I would, but I *can't*. Please, let me take her pain. Do me that kindness. I know I don't deserve it, but she does."

"This is madness." Calen looked around at those gathered, incredulous. "How many of us are left in the world? How many dragons?"

"There have to be consequences, Calen," Chora said.

"This continent has been at war for four hundred years." Calen opened his arms wide, pleading. "All our legends, all our histories are of death and blood and darkness. After The Fall, the empire almost wiped us from existence. You all know that better than I, and yet here we are talking of taking one more dragon from the world." He slowed his voice. "We are doing their work for them. We are murdering each other. Tivar and Avandeer saved us. They risked their lives to protect ours. What good to the world is one more dead dragon, one more dead Draleid? One more of our kind in the ground?"

"What would you have us do, Calen?" Aeson turned to face Calen. There was no anger or fury or hatred in his eyes, only agony. For the first time, Calen saw the true struggle in Aeson, the conflict. "What is your solution?"

Calen looked to Tivar, his decision made. "Would you fight by my side?"

"What?" Disbelief painted Harken's voice. "You cannot be serious."

"Would you fight by my side?" Calen repeated to Tivar, ignoring the others' stares.

"I…"

"It was you who told me we should be guardians. You who made me understand *why* I am here, made me understand what I am. You do not deserve forgiveness for what you did, but that does not unburden you of your obligation to your brothers and your sisters and to every soul you shattered and every life you destroyed." As Calen spoke, he looked around at the others. "Death is the easy way out. Death is not a consequence. It is an escape." Calen looked back to Tivar. "I would not have you die, Tivar Savinír. I would have you wake every day and look your brothers and sisters in the eyes, knowing what you did, bearing that weight. I would have you face the results of your treachery with every sunrise. And I would have you give every drop of blood in your veins to bring the empire to its knees. So I ask you, will you fight by my side? Will you swear to protect your brothers and sisters, by the light of Varyn? Will you stand against the darkness you helped forge? On your honour, on your very soul, do you swear it?"

A moment passed where Calen thought he might hear objections from those around him, but none came.

Tivar dropped to one knee with a *thump* and brought a hand to her chest. Above her, Avandeer dropped low, bowing her head.

"I swear by The Father to give my life protecting the kin I betrayed. I swear by The Mother that I will walk openly into her embrace to save the lives of others. I swear by The Warrior to stand by your side no matter the odds. I swear by The Maiden to be both your shield and your sword. I swear by The Sailor to be your anchor in the darkest seas. And I swear by The Smith to forge you into the greatest Draleid that ever walked this earth." Tivar held Calen's gaze for a moment, then looked around at the others. Tears rolled from dark and bloodshot eyes. "I swear these things so long as your heart remains true. If you want me dead, I will stretch my neck out for you. But if you allow me to fight, I will bring fire and fury on Fane Mortem the likes of which he has never known. Please, let me give you my dying breath. It is the only thing I have left worth giving."

For a moment, nobody spoke, until one of the Rakina, an elf by the name of Danveer shook his head. "She deserves a noose. I say no."

"As do I." Chora rested her hands on her lap, using threads of Air to move the wheels of her chair until she was next to Calen, eyes level with Tivar's. "I cannot forgive what you did. I wish I was better, but I'm not. My vote is death."

"I say life." The sound of Aeson's voice speaking those words took Calen by surprise. The man dropped to one knee before Tivar, drawing more than a few looks from the others.

Aeson cupped Tivar's cheeks in his hands and stared into her eyes. "You turned your back on us when we needed you most, and it cost us everything." A tremble set into his voice. "I can never forgive you. I need you to know that. But I can allow you to spend the rest of your days trying to earn a semblance of your honour back and to die knowing that in the end you did something worthwhile."

Tivar nodded softly, the muscles in her jaw clenching.

"If you even think of betraying us a second time, I will drive the blade into your heart myself." Aeson rose and moved to stand beside Calen.

"Thank you," Calen whispered.

"I did it because you were right, we can't keep killing each other. A line must be drawn, and we must be the ones to draw it."

One by one, the other Rakina stepped forwards until all had cast their vote. Of the twenty-six who resided in Aravell, fourteen had chosen death, twelve life. With Aeson and Calen's votes, that left fourteen a piece.

Atara and Thacia were amongst those who had chosen life, while Harken stood to Chora's left, guilt etched into his face.

"There are two more," Harken said, folding his arms. "Coren Valmar and Farwen Ethylion."

"So there are." Aeson let out a long sigh, staring down at Tivar, who still knelt before him. "What say you, Chora?"

The woman stayed silent for a few moments, her stare unblinking. "This is the first major decision our people have made together in a very long time. We should send for Coren and Farwen. Their roles in our survival have been as vital as yours, young Virandr."

"I agree."

"It is settled then. We will send for Coren and Farwen. They will be needed either way. If we are to stand together as one, a new Archon should be raised, and that cannot be done without all our say. The journey should only take them a few weeks. Until then," Chora continued, "the final decision will be suspended and the prisoners will remain here under guard. They will not be permitted to leave this eyrie under any circumstances. If they do so, they will be killed on sight."

"Prisoners?" Calen rounded on Chora. "What about Farda?"

"What about him?" Chora raised an eyebrow, the touch of amusement in her voice only irritating Calen further.

"He murdered my mother. He has—"

"He has done no more than Tivar." The woman looked at Calen as though he were an idiot. "If you wish to pardon her, that same grace extends to him and the others. You cannot pick and choose who lives or dies based on your own grievances. All four of them betrayed The Order. All four of them have slaughtered and burned and destroyed." Chora wheeled herself closer to Calen, looking into his eyes. "I don't have enough fingers to count the number of people I loved that were killed at Tivar and Avandeer's hands. What makes your loss greater than mine?"

"I..."

"You have much to learn about the world, Calen Bryer. So much to learn."

HOURS AFTER THE ALTERCATION AT the Eyrie, Aeson stood on the ledge of one of the many cliffs in one of the many valleys that snaked through the Aravell. The rain had started only moments after Farda and the others had been escorted back to their quarters, and it fell like the skies themselves had opened. It was poetry, in a sense.

His clothes clung to his skin, and his hair matted his face. He had stood on that ledge for what must have been an hour. The rain calmed him. It stilled his mind, and he had much to think on.

Aeson lifted an eyebrow, turning his head at the sound of rocks crunching beneath wheels.

"You were hard on him," he whispered, just loud enough for his voice to rise above the rain.

"The world is hard." Chora stopped her chair beside Aeson, her blonde hair tacked to her face. "There will be much more difficult choices ahead. He needs to learn, and we don't have the time for him to learn slowly. You and I both know I would have been happier to take Farda's head, but he is more useful this way." Chora stared out into the valleys. "Seeing the others, seeing them so close I could touch them... so close I could break their necks. It was... It unsettled me."

"As it did us all." Aeson wiped the water from his eyes and folded his arms. "Tivar can never be forgiven, but she and Avandeer could be the difference in this war. She truly has regret in her heart. She could be what keeps Calen alive. She could be what he needs."

"If Coren and Farwen vote to spare her, I will honour that decision."

Aeson let the rain fall for a moment. "You didn't allow them to roam free in the Eyrie out of kindness."

Chora choked back a harsh, dark laugh. "No. Let young Bryer see his mother's killer wander around the Eyrie. Let him see the pain he puts us through by forcing us to keep Tivar's head on her shoulders... The arrogance of youth."

Aeson let out an exasperated sigh. "The longer you and the others spend in Aravell, the more like the elves you become. Games and tricks and schemes."

"It was always that way, Aeson. You just never saw it. You were never willing to look."

The drumming of the rain against the stone grew louder as the pair stood in silence.

"We are to meet the Triarchy in Mythníril tomorrow," Chora said. "The steps forward must be decided. With the Blood Moon in the sky and the empire distracted in the North, now is the time to solidify our allegiances in the South. We must move swiftly and crush every foothold they have here. With Jormun and Ilkya gone, Calen can fly more freely. The Warden of Varyn. That is a title we can use. I suggest we secure Illyanara then push for Valtara and Drifaien. Our support in those regions seems strong by your reports."

"It's good to see a fire in you once more."

Chora stared out at the open valley. "It is good to feel somewhat warm again. If I can do one thing before I see Daiseer, it will be to rip Eltoar Daethana's beating heart from his chest."

"Agreed. We will talk on it tomorrow." With that, Aeson turned and began to walk away but stopped after only a few feet. "They believe in him, Chora."

The woman scoffed as she pushed one wheel and turned her chair. "Who believes in whom? And why must you always be so vague and dramatic?"

"My son, the elven rangers, the rebels from the North. They followed Calen across the Burnt Lands because they believed in him. Not because of who he is as a Draleid, but because of who he is as a man. Even Atara and Thacia and Harken – I see it in their eyes. He has given them hope." Aeson paused a moment. "He will do what must be done, I am certain of it. He was right about Tivar, and he had the strength to stand for it. He has been bound for barely a breath, and he held no fear in his heart at standing for what he believed in. We should never have put her in those shackles. We knew the pain it caused. We didn't do it to stop her from touching the Spark. We did it to make her know the agony of not feeling Avandeer's soul. We are broken, you and I, and we will never be whole. But he is different. I have watched him grow, watched him turn from a naïve boy into a warrior who refuses to lie down. He is becoming what we have let slip away. Give him time."

As Aeson stood there, the rain pelting down around him, he remembered Calen's words when the Aravell burned. *"There's no point in living if we don't fight for what we love. We're meant to be Draleid. We're meant to be guardians, not survivors."*

"It sounds like you're starting to believe in him too, young Virandr."

"Hmm." Aeson let out a half-laugh and turned back towards the trail that led to the city.

Calen sat by Ella's bed with a towel around his neck, his hair dripping onto Faenir, who lay curled up between the chair and the bed. He'd come to Ella first thing from the Eyrie, but Elia had practically marched Calen to his room to change the moment she'd found him sitting beside Ella's bed, his clothes saturated from boots to shirt.

"You'll catch your death sitting in wet clothes," Elia had said as she'd grabbed him by the shirt and shoved him from the room. "Your mother will torment my dreams for allowing it. Go change. I'll fetch you some more of that lamb. Men – less sense than a pig's arse."

Calen laughed, running his hand through his soaked hair. Aneera still sat in the corner of the room, legs folded, arms resting on her knees. From what Tanner had told him, she'd barely eaten all day. He'd found the other Fenryr Angan who'd arrived in the city not long before the attack – Diango – prowling around the plateau as he'd arrived. The Angan had greeted him with a bow and a short 'Son of the Chainbreaker' before continuing on like a sworn guard.

A knock sounded at the door, and Calen knew it was Elia by the way she didn't wait for him to answer before coming in.

"Here." She handed him a bowl and a knife, the smell of rosemary and slow-cooked lamb mingling with the lavender that already tinged the air. The woman's head twitched left, and her eyes glazed over for a moment. "If you're still hungry, there's more downstairs. You have a visitor."

As Elia left, Therin moved to stand beside Calen.

The warmth of the braised lamb spread from the bowl and into Calen's hands as the silence settled.

"A fork would have been more useful." Therin's expression didn't change as he spoke, staring down at Ella.

Calen lifted the knife from the bowl, looking down at the lamb, roasted potatoes, carrots, and some green root he'd never seen before. "She's only given me knives ever since she's come back to herself. I don't ask why. Easier just to eat." Calen swallowed, his mouth growing dry. The pair had not truly spoken since Therin had lied to him about Ella's survival. "I trusted you, Therin."

"I know."

"If anything had happened to Ella…"

"*I know.*"

"You took my choice from me."

"I know, Calen," Therin whispered.

Therin walked to the other side of the room and dragged a chair across, setting it beside Calen and dropping into it. "I've watched you grow since the day you were born. You, Ella, Haem. I've loved you like you were my own, but I've never been able to say it. That was your father's choice, and I respected it." Therin shook his head. "He was one of my closest friends, and yet I had to watch from a distance as an Inquisitor who wasn't fit to lick his boots held him with threads of Air and ran a sword through his chest."

Therin reached out and brushed a strand of Ella's hair from her face.

"I made a promise to him that day that I would protect you with my life, you and Ella both. I'm not proud of keeping Ella's survival from you, but if I hadn't, you would have flown north to find her. Of that I have no doubt, because it's exactly what your father would have done, and you two are cut from the same cloth in almost every way. And it's likely you and your sister would both be dead, and with that, every soul in Aravell would have burned alive without you."

Therin shifted in his seat, hands resting on his knees. He tilted his head to look into Calen's eyes. "I swear to you that I will never keep a secret from your ears so long as you swear to me that you will heed my counsel in return. I don't ask that you do everything I advise, only that you listen. If you give me your word, I will give you mine."

Calen gritted his teeth and reached down to scratch Faenir's back, once again looking to Ella, who lay motionless in the bed, her chest rising and falling steadily. He nodded. "You have my word."

"And you have mine."

"What happened in the Eyrie..." Therin leaned back in the chair.

"Hmmm." Calen kept his gaze on Ella, watching as her lungs filled and she let out a slow breath.

"Chora is testing you."

"Let her test me. I don't care."

"Calen, it's not that simple. What happens when you see Farda sitting on the grass in the Eyrie? What will you do then?"

"I'll open his throat."

"And all Aravell will turn against you for breaking your word. And even if they don't, Chora will use it as an excuse to kill Tivar and Avandeer."

"I don't want to talk about it."

"Calen, you—"

"I don't want to talk about it." Calen snapped his head around, his anger creeping up on him. "Please. I'm sorry. I just need a break. Can we talk about something else? Tell me about him. My dad. Not the stories, but about what he was like."

"You know what he was like, Calen."

"Do I? Do I really? I feel like I didn't know him at all."

"That's as idiotic a thing as you've ever said. Your father hid things from you for a reason, but he was always the same man who raised you. He was stubborn, pig-headed, and always seemed to do things the hard way. He held grudges and spent more time worrying about the people he cared for than could possibly be healthy. Sound familiar?"

Calen let out a laugh, sitting back in his chair.

"He was also kind," Therin continued. "And loyal to a fault, and passionate, and honourable. Everything he did, he did for others. Your father was not a perfect man, not by a distance. He was flawed, and he made mistakes – many of them –

but he was the best man I ever knew, and I see him in you every day. Please, forgive him for the things he never said. All he ever wanted was to keep you, your brother, and your sister safe. He and your mother would have given everything for that."

"If we'd known…"

"Nothing would have changed. Be wary of that path, Calen. The past is set in stone. It is immutable. Look forwards."

Another knock sounded at the door, and the wood creaked as Elia Havel pushed her way inside once more, handing both Calen and Therin mugs of piping hot Arlen Root tea.

Before Calen could open his mouth, Elia raised one finger in the air. "Ah." She nodded towards the mug in Calen's hand. "Drink."

Elia's expression softened, and she gently pinched Calen's cheek before making her way from the room.

Both Therin and Calen sat in silence for a while before Therin let out a short laugh. "This tea always reminds me of your mother. I don't think there was ever a time I saw her and she wasn't brewing a new batch."

Calen pulled a long breath through his nostrils, the deep, loamy smell of the tea filling him. He lifted the mug and took a sip, trying his best not to grimace. "At least she didn't force it down your throat."

"There is that." Therin lifted the mug, staring into the depths of the dark liquid. "I'm going to have to drink it now, aren't I?"

Calen nodded, giving Therin an expectant smile.

The elf sniffed, recoiling and puffing out his cheeks. "Are you sure we can't honour your mother a different way?"

"Drink," Calen said, mimicking Elia.

To the elf's credit, he took a deep draught of the tea, then produced a gurgling sound as he choked it down. "Gods."

"Even they can't save you from the tea." Calen took another sip, enjoying the contortions of Therin's face as the elf experienced the tea's aftertaste. "Thank you."

"Hmm?"

"For talking. There's so much I don't know about him…"

"Sometimes you can know a person without knowing their past, Calen. Your father wasn't a Draleid. He wasn't a mage or a king or a lord. But he was someone who always tried to do what he knew to be right. He cared deeply about the ones he loved, and he fought fiercely to protect them. In all honesty, after everything I'd seen, he showed me there was still good left in the world." Therin shook his head, brushing the back of his hand against his eye and sitting up. "Despite all the death I've seen, I still can't believe he's truly gone. There are some people, Calen, who just leave an indelible mark on the lives they touch. In that, you are most definitely your father's son."

A third knock rapped on the door.

"Elia, please." Calen twisted in his seat. "We don't… Haem."

Calen's brother stood in the open doorway, steam wafting from a mug in his hand. He held himself like a man who hadn't slept in days, shoulders drooped, eyes sunken. "Little brother."

Haem nodded at Therin, moving across the room and squeezing Calen's shoulder. He leaned over and scratched the top of Faenir's head, the wolfpine nuzzling into Haem's palm.

Haem pulled himself back to his full height, letting out a soft sigh as he looked down at Ella, who lay still in the bed. "How is she?"

CHAPTER SIXTEEN

THE OLD WARS

6th Day of the Blood Moon

Níthianelle – Winter, Year 3081 After Doom

The songs of the ethereal forest drifted on the wind as Ella marched through the undergrowth, wisps of white smoke rising with each footstep that pressed into the earth. The woodland was as alive here as it was in the waking world. And it was all so much clearer than it had ever been before. Now she felt as though she could truly see, and in seeing, she found herself enamoured with the trails of white mist that drifted in the wake of the birds that weaved through the trees. The same mist wafted from everything, but there was something about the way the birds moved that was singularly beautiful.

She had awoken from her slumber an hour or so previous. Though, slumber felt a strange word. She had been asleep, but no dreams had filled her mind, no nightmares had haunted her. It had simply been darkness and then light. And yet she was rejuvenated, as though she'd had the single best sleep of her life. She'd thought about waiting in that spot for Tamzin to return, but she'd never liked standing around twiddling her thumbs and waiting on others to give her direction. Besides, she had no idea how long she'd been asleep. Time was immeasurable in this place. How long did she wait for Tamzin? What if the druid never came back? What if this was Ella's fate? To walk endlessly through the Sea of Spirits, never quite alive, never quite dead.

The thought sent a shiver through her.

No, she would not sit around and wait. She'd seen her father's maps many times as a child. If she kept the Marin Mountains on her left, then moved north with the Argonan Marshes on her right, she would eventually reach the Darkwood. Tamzin had found her the first time. She would find her again. Besides, the woman had said it herself that it was best to keep moving.

As Ella walked, her mind wandered, sensing the souls that filled the world around her, hearing the multitude of tiny wingbeats, the scampering of small creatures through the undergrowth, the thumping of hundreds of hearts.

After a while, time slipped away, the ground ceding to her stride, the world blurring around her. But as soon as she noticed the shift, everything refocused and she doubled over, pulling ragged breaths into her lungs. Her head spun, and her stomach lurched. Fighting the urge to retch, Ella stood straight, clasping her hands at the back of her head and drawing long, deep breaths as her father had taught her when practicing with the sword all those years ago.

The memory twisted in her like a knife. She would never hear his voice again, never see his face, never feel the warmth of his embrace. If only she'd known what would happen, she would've said goodbye properly before she'd left. In fact, she never would have left at all and Rhett would still be alive…

Ella pushed the thoughts aside. They would do her no good here. She needed to focus. She needed to get back to Calen and Haem and Faenir – to those who needed her.

"Wait, that can't be possible," she muttered as she took in her surroundings. When she had started walking, the Marin Mountains had run like an endless wall to her left, their peaks shrouded in cloud. Now they were at her back, the sky clear. How long had she been walking? How far had she journeyed?

Just the thought alone summoned aches in her muscles and lethargy in her bones.

"I told you," a familiar voice called. "Distances are different here. As is time. I do not understand it, not truly. And nor do I ever hope to. But some things are as they are, with or without our understanding."

Tamzin walked past Ella, white mist trailing behind her. The woman's eyes were once again a deep ocean blue, her pupils like those of a kat's.

Ella kept her hands at the back of her head, slowly filling her lungs and exhaling controlled breaths. She met Tamzin's gaze, unflinching. She still didn't trust the woman. There was too much Tamzin wasn't saying. But for now, she was the only thing that gave Ella any hope of getting back to the waking world – any hope of seeing her brothers and Faenir again. So she would play along.

"You covered an impressive distance. I've not seen one so untested move so quickly here. I thought I told you to wait for me?"

"Actually, all you told me was that you would return and that if anything came for me, I was to run. You never said anything about waiting."

Tamzin rolled her eyes. "Spoken like a true wolfchild."

"Well, first you told me how dangerous this place was, how many people or wraiths would come to kill me… and then you left me alone in this oh so dangerous place."

"And you decided to wander into the unknown, with nothing but your head, your heart, and the wolf in your blood." Tamzin shook her head and laughed. "Definitely a wolfchild. Come. As much ground as you made, there is still more to go. It's best we don't stay still any longer than we have to."

The forest gave way to open plains as Tamzin marched Ella forward at a relentless pace, the Marin Mountains shrinking into the distance. They moved far quicker than they had the first day, the world seeming to shift and churn beneath Ella's feet. It was the strangest sensation, as though time was moving faster than was natural. Whenever she lost focus, the feeling intensified, seconds and minutes slipping past her before she'd even noticed.

"How did you find me?" Ella asked when they stopped for a moment.

"What do you mean?"

"Well, I've been thinking about it. When we walk here, our bodies in the living world stay where they are. So when you left me, you would have returned there. Correct?"

"Correct."

"Then how did you make it back to me so quickly? If we have to walk all the way to the Darkwood, surely you had to walk all the way to me."

Tamzin stopped in her tracks and turned fully to look at Ella. Her bottom lip was upturned, her eyes back to a kat-like shimmering blue. "I had a feeling you were quick of mind. We'll make a Blooddancer out of you yet." The woman continued walking, talking over her shoulder as she went. "As I said before, this place holds many secrets. There are other ways to travel, paths known as Warrens that traverse this place. There are few left alive who know how to travel the Warrens. Which makes me a very lucky woman."

"I'm going to assume there's a reason we're not using one right now then, and it's not that you just like long walks."

"Fragments can't walk the Warrens."

"Why not?"

"I don't know. But they can't. Don't test the truth of that statement." Something in Tamzin's voice changed, the scent of her shifting with it. She was… sad, perhaps. No, melancholy was a better word. Ella decided not to press the matter.

"I have more questions." Ella tried not to smile as she spoke, the pair of them carrying on walking. She knew when a memory hurt, and she could see that hurt in Tamzin now.

"I'm sure you do," Tamzin said with a laugh, giving Ella the response she'd hoped for. "It's a long walk, but if you have half the number of questions I had when Amatkai found me, it might not be long enough. Ask, and I will try to answer."

"Before you left, you spoke of someone called Kerith. Who are they?"

"What Kerith is has many names amongst our people. My sentinel, my guardian, my reflection… But Amatkai refers to her as my keeper. All Aldruids create a tether to a keeper. We give them strength, intelligence, companionship, and in turn they watch over us. We are a pair. When Aldruids walk in Níthianelle, we are exposed in the mortal plane. There are some whose blood is strong enough that they can move in both worlds at the same time. I am gifted as such. But even then, our mind is never truly in one place. It is our keepers who guard our bodies while our souls wander. You will find your keeper one day…" Tamzin gave Ella a curious look. "If you haven't already?"

A realisation struck Ella. "Faenir."

"A wolf, I assume?"

"Wolfpine," Ella corrected.

"Is there a difference?"

Ella let out a long, exasperated sigh. It was like walking with Farda. A smile curled her lips, but then her mood soured as her memories flooded back from before the battle. If this all worked and Ella found a way back to her body, she prayed Farda had survived the fighting, if only so she could kill him herself. "Yes. There's a difference."

Tamzin raised her open palms. "Well, I'm going to leave that one firmly alone. You've noticed changes in Faenir since your blood made itself known? Stronger, larger, quicker?"

Ella nodded, thinking back to when she'd first noticed the changes. "I can feel him, his heartbeat, his fear, his anger. I can tell when he's hungry… He's always hungry."

"Well, Ella Bryer, it looks like you found your keeper."

The thought warmed Ella's heart. It was a fitting name for what Faenir was to Ella: her keeper. It was he who had been there when Rhett died, he who had saved her, and he who had never left her side from that day on. Even then, as she focused on that thought, she swore she could feel the wolfpine watching her, protecting her body in the waking world. She could feel his coarse fur brushing against her skin, feel the warmth of his touch.

"You say we are Blooddancers. Are there others? Or are all our kind like us?" Ella had heard stories of the old druids, but those were from a time even more ancient than The Order. They were more myth than legend.

"There are others. Many of the Gifts have been lost with time." That same melancholy returned to Tamzin's scent, her voice a requiem. "Once, long before we set foot in Epheria, our people could perform all sorts of wonders. There were some with the Gift to make crops grow at twice the usual rate, influence flowers to change their colours. They would sing, and the trees would bend their trunks so as to better hear. Others could walk the dreams of the sleeping, chasing nightmares from their heads. Moonwalkers could bend the light around them, vanishing from plain sight. Listeners could hear the vibrations of rare ore buried deep in rocks, find water wherever they roamed, tell the species of a bird by only the beating of its wings." Both Tamzin's voice and scent continued to change as she spoke, a warm joy seeping in. "Amatkai even tells of those who could heal wounds with the touch of their hands and those who had such a connection to the animals of the world they could create new life, new species…"

"And now?"

Tamzin scratched at the back of her neck, her clawed fingernails leaving bright red marks. Ella noticed she did that anytime she seemed uncomfortable. "There are but four druidic Gifts we know to have survived the purge of our kind.

Those of the Blooddancers, the Stormcallers, the Pathfinders, and the Starchasers. Though, those are names from the time of the first landing. Alternate names were given by those who hunted us. The Blooddancers are Aldruids. The Stormcallers are Skydruids. The Pathfinders and Starchasers are Seerdruids and Aetherdruids. Far lesser titles if you ask me."

After a while, when Tamzin stopped near a slow-moving stream and ran her hand over something on the ground, Ella built up the courage to ask the question that had been circling in her head. "Have you heard anything about the battle in the Darkwood? Who won? Who survived?"

Tamzin had said that if Ella were still alive, that meant there was someone tending to her body in the waking world. But that didn't mean that someone was Calen or Haem. It didn't mean the battle had been won.

When Tamzin didn't answer, Ella repeated herself. But before she could finish the sentence, Tamzin was on her feet, her hand clapping around Ella's mouth, blue kat-like eyes staring into hers. Tamzin's face was so close Ella could feel the warmth of the woman's breath.

Ella tried to push Tamzin back, but then a scent touched her nostrils, clean and fresh like wet grass and squashed berries. She'd smelled it for a while, but it had blended with the world around her, so she'd thought nothing of it. Now though, it was more prominent, more distinct. And with that scent came another that wafted from Tamzin: fear.

Tamzin slowly lifted her hand from Ella's mouth, grabbing her forearm and leading her into the flowing stream. Ella didn't say a word as Tamzin walked deeper into the rushing water until only their heads remained above the surface. Ella widened her stance, trying desperately to stay on her feet against the current, her heart racing.

Tamzin pressed her fingers to her lips as she pulled Ella around a large rock that jutted from the stream, the current breaking around it. She nodded upstream over Ella's shoulder.

It was all Ella could do to hold in the gasp at the sight of a bear so large bards would have told stories of it. The creature must have stood at least ten feet tall on all fours, its shoulders broader than a wagon. Smoke as black as its fur drifted from its body, twirling and shifting with the breeze.

The bear moved strangely, with a careful grace, its steps slow and purposeful. It was looking for something, and it was drawing closer.

Tamzin pulled Ella back behind the rock. She once again pressed her finger to her lips and shook her head. The bear's scent grew stronger in Ella's nostrils, the deep, sonorous thump of its heart steadily rising.

Tamzin gestured down at the water, then mouthed: *three, two, one.*

Ella drew a deep breath on 'one' and submerged herself in the stream. The cold water rushed over her, and her pulse quickened even more, panic setting into her veins. She closed her eyes and tried to settle herself, one hand leveraging against the rock to keep her under. A slow burn ached in her lungs, her throat growing tighter and tighter. She'd never had a fear of water, but drowning was another story.

Tamzin's fingers closed around hers, and the woman pressed Ella's hand against her chest. In the chaos of the rushing current and the panic, it took Ella a moment to understand. Then she felt Tamzin's heartbeat. Slow, controlled, calm.

Ella's pulse settled, Tamzin's heartbeat steadying her. She lost her sense of time. Seconds could have been minutes, minutes seconds. The burning in her chest turned to a searing pain, her lungs begging her for air. All the while, the cold water rushed around her, drowning out all sounds.

Tamzin pushed under Ella's armpit, signalling her to rise, but kept Ella's hand pressed over her heart.

When Ella broke the water, her body urged her to gasp and drag in a lungful of air. She resisted, drawing her breath in slowly through her nostrils, only allowing her head to emerge so as to check her surroundings.

The bear was gone. Or at least, she couldn't see it.

Tamzin tapped her on the shoulder, and Ella turned to find the woman's head and neck free of the water's surface, one finger pressed to her lips, her other hand wrapped around the shaft of an axe. She mouthed the words 'stay here', then left the cover of the rock and moved out of Ella's sight, white mist drifting up from the river's surface.

Ella pressed her back up against the rock, savouring the sweet taste of air, the sense of panic slowly ebbing. She drew a long, burning breath, then turned about the rock, moving against the current. She wasn't going to sit around like some lamb waiting to be slaughtered. If that bear was still there, Tamzin would be an idiot to face it alone.

She almost leapt from her skin when she found herself staring directly into Tamzin's eyes.

"This time I definitely told you to stay where you were."

"You did."

The woman stared at her, the edges of her mouth giving the slightest of turns. "It's gone. For now. We should follow the river east for a while. It will mask our scent."

Tamzin turned and started off towards the far bank. She climbed from the river, then pulled Ella back to dry land.

"What was that thing?" Ella asked, kneeling on the bank, water dripping from her hair and nose.

"We need to keep moving. It won't be far." Tamzin helped Ella to her feet and started off east along the riverbank. She continued, "It was an Angan of Clan Bjorna."

"The Angan can travel here?"

"The Angan can do many things. They are the first children of our gods, carved from pieces of their flesh. Níthianelle is how they communicate so quickly. They travel the Warrens, sending messages from one to another, spanning great distances in short times. More than that, we may have power here, power we can learn to wield and mould and shape, but the Angan are as much part of Níthianelle as they are of the waking world. They move between both like shadows. In this world, there is no greater predator."

"It was hunting us."

"It was."

"But why?"

"The Angan are bound to our gods. They are as branches to a trunk or fingers to a hand. They do not question the will of the gods nor, I believe, do they have the capacity to. The children of Bjorna, those that are left, are zealots left over from a war that died out long before our time because there weren't enough bodies to fight it. A war in which gods killed gods, a war in which the blood of our people fed the land in rivers. There were once many more gods than there are now and with them many more of our kind. They didn't all get along. The Bjorna still live that war, still hunt the remnants of what is left. It is their purpose to kill all gods but their own."

"But there are so few of us now…" Ella trailed off, her mind lingering on the word 'us'. She had said it without thinking. *Us.* "How can they keep fighting a war with their own kind with so few of us still breathing? Or are the stories all wrong? Is there a nation of us hiding somewhere, just like the elves?"

"Oh, if only the world were that simple," Tamzin said. "No, the stories are not wrong. Exaggerated, but not wrong. I would wager there are a few hundred of us across the continent in one form or another. Maybe fewer, but not more. Many stick to the old clans, following their gods. Others have formed more *colourful* groups, like ours. But the majority simply do not even know what they are and wander alone. But you see, Ella, if there was only one piece of shit in the world, people would kill each other to possess it. To live is to want, to want is to need, to need is to take. That is the unbreakable cycle this world finds itself in. By the time we all realise we're just killing each other, most of us will likely be dead."

"Well, that's cheery."

"It's the truth. Take it or leave it." Tamzin looked over her shoulder at Ella. Her eyes were a deep chestnut brown now, her pupils more human-like. "The only thing we can control is what we choose to do about it."

"And what have you chosen to do? Besides finding helpless women who have somehow managed to what? Separate their soul from their body?"

Tamzin laughed at that. "You are far from helpless. Of that I am sure."

Ella's throat tightened. All she could see in her mind's eyes were images of Rhett lying in the dirt, blood pooling, her own screams echoing. She knew what it was to be helpless. If Faenir hadn't found her that day, her body would have lain next to Rhett's – likely in a ditch somewhere.

"What I've chosen to do," Tamzin said, noticing Ella's silence, "is not lie down and die. I've chosen to fight. To live. To carry on with the hope that some day, all of this killing will mean something. When Amatkai found me, he promised me one thing – that I wouldn't have to be scared of who I am for a moment longer. And since that day, I haven't been."

"Amatkai. You've said that name before. Who is he?"

"You will meet him. While we travel here, he makes his way to your body in the mortal plane. It is he who can help guide you through the veil."

Ella started to answer but stopped herself when a cold breath brushed the hairs on the back of her neck. She snapped her head around and leaned back towards

Tamzin. Her skin goosefleshed from head to toe, and a terror like nothing she had ever known wrapped around her heart as she stared at the face of a woman long dead.

The woman stood barely half a foot from her, dark, saturated hair clinging to her milk-pale skin. She stared at Ella with eyes of deathly grey ringed with black, the whites laced with veins of blood-red. Her dead, black lips were twisted into an unnatural grin, the corners of her mouth seemingly pinned in place.

A heartbeat passed, and Ella stood frozen like a deer, her limbs unresponsive as she stared into the woman's eyes. She could hear Tamzin shouting something, but the woman tilted her head slowly to the right, those terrifying eyes holding Ella's gaze, and then she let out a shrieking wail and lurched forwards.

Before Ella could think, fingers were wrapped around her throat, squeezing as she thrashed, the woman's wail scratching at her mind. Ella's feet went from under her, and she was falling, slipping from the riverbank. The icy water swallowed her whole, the woman's fingers squeezing tighter, that horrific grin contorting cold flesh.

Ella screamed, air fleeing her lungs, water flooding in, the wolf howling inside her.

Memories flooded her mind, memories that were not her own. She was fleeing, her heart racing, sweat streaking her skin. Only fear held her as she sprinted through tall grass, moonlight overhead. Pain flared in her stomach. She looked down to see a barbed arrowhead protruding from just below her belly button, a little to the right. She staggered, her knee scraping the stones on the ground. Something slammed into her back and sent her sprawling, a *snap* signalling the breaking of the arrow shaft.

A man stood over her, his eyes orange as a sunset, lips black as coals, a dark bow in his hand. A massive hawk alighted on his shoulders, one taloned foot either side of his head.

"It's always more fun when you try to run." The man drew another arrow from the quiver at his hip and nocked it. "Goodnight, Wolfchild. Sleep well."

The man drew back the bowstring, and Ella reached outwards with her mind, panic and terror consuming her entirely. The memories flitted through her, seconds becoming minutes, becoming hours, days, weeks, years, centuries…

And then Ella was back in her own mind and being hauled from the water. She coughed and spluttered, choking on every breath, grasping at her throat. It felt as though a noose had been wrapped around her neck and she'd been dragged behind a horse.

As she shivered, soaked to the bone, gasping for air, Tamzin appeared over her, out of breath and soaked.

"Look at me," she snapped, the tone in her voice sharp and panicked. She placed her hands gently atop Ella's. "Breathe. Breathe. Are you all right?"

"I… I don't…" Ella continued to pull in panicked breaths, her hands clutching her aching throat.

She turned her head to the side to see a pale, wet, headless body lying in the dirt, white blood spilling. The woman's head sat a foot away, those cold eyes still open, mouth ajar. Ella snapped her stare back to Tamzin. "What the fuck was that? What happened? What… I saw her. I felt her fear…" Without warning, a feeling of skin-crawling dread and terror overwhelmed her and Ella burst into tears. She stared into Tamzin's eyes. "She fragmented… She was trapped here for centuries, Tamzin. *Centuries.* Alone. All she saw was darkness. I felt her lose her mind. I felt every piece of her break, sliver by sliver. I… I…"

"Breathe, Ella. You're safe." Tamzin took one last deep breath, then dropped to the ground beside Ella.

Ella stared into the cold dead eyes of the woman's decapitated head. "Is that what I'll become? A wraith? I can't become that. I can't."

"You won't. I won't let you." Tamzin pulled herself to her feet and reached a hand to Ella. "But we need to move. There's not a soul in this place that didn't hear that. The Bjorna won't be the only thing hunting us."

Ella took Tamzin's hand and rose. And as she followed the woman, she stopped and looked back at the body and severed head that lay in a pool of white blood by the riverbank.

"Ella." Tamzin tugged at Ella's sleeve.

"Her name was Laurel Hardin." Ella's jaw twitched involuntarily. "She was seventeen when she fragmented. She was terrified."

"We need to go."

"I'll remember you," Ella whispered. "I promise."

CHAPTER SEVENTEEN

THE SPARK IS LIT, THE FIRE BURNS

7ᵗʰ Day of the Blood Moon

Aravell – Winter, Year 3081 After Doom

Aeson stood with his hands clasped behind his back, the bronze doors that guarded the central chamber of Mythníril behind him. He stared upwards at the white-stone branches and leaves that twisted and weaved across the chamber's sweeping ceiling, dropping into the tree-like stone columns that framed the chamber's many arched windows. A forest canopy frozen in time.

"I can see why this new queen is divisive," Dann whispered to Calen, the both of them standing on Aeson's left.

Calen stood with his arms folded, his eyes fixed on the stone map carved into the enormous table before them. Erik, Therin, and the others were at his side, fraying patience visible on all their faces – except for Vaeril. That elf rarely let his emotions slip.

"Quiet," Therin snapped in a hushed voice.

"What? If I was this late, you'd hang me by my ankles."

Aeson truly wished he had Dann's ability to laugh in these situations, but there was too much at stake. Too many pieces moving at the same time, too many lives hanging in the balance. This moment was the culmination of centuries of patience and sacrifice. The decisions made in this chamber would shape the world moving forwards.

And yet, they'd been waiting for at least an hour, Queen Uthrían and King Galdra unwilling to allow them to proceed until this new queen of Vaelen arrived: Tessara. Aeson had heard her name mentioned more than once in his brief time in Aravell. He had not known Silmiryn particularly well and this niece of his even less so. But from what he'd heard, she'd made almost as many enemies as he had. Which perhaps meant she was doing something right.

"This is becoming ridiculous." Chora wheeled herself forwards from where she had waited on the right of the table. Both Thacia and Harken frowned but made no move to stop her.

King Galdra, who had been staring out one of the arches at the valleys beyond, turned to show Chora a raised eyebrow. "We will wait for Queen Tessara, just as we would wait for you, Chora Sarn. Patience is a virtue."

Seemingly sensing Chora's frustration, Harken rested a hand on the woman's shoulder, but Chora swatted it away. "Don't speak to me like a child, Galdra. I remember when you still sucked at your mother's tit. Do not think yourself my elder. I have lost more patience than you have ever known."

For as long as Aeson had lived, he had known the elven rulers to be masters at games and wordplay. Even before The Fall, there was always something churning in the background, always a game, or a test, or a scheme. Which was why Aeson was surprised at the outward look of shock on Galdra's face.

Chora smiled, revelling in the reaction she had goaded from the king. The woman's fire had returned ever since the battle for the city.

"You are speaking to a king," Thurivîr, one of the Lunithíran Ephorí, snapped. The elf's crimson and gold robes trailed along the floor as he rounded the table and moved between Chora and Galdra. He stood tall and broad, looming over Chora in her wheelchair, his black hair pulled back with a golden circlet.

Chora met Thurivír's gaze without flinching. "I have spoken to many kings, young Ephorí. I have outlived them all."

"Was that a threat?" Thurivîr gave Chora an amused smile, regaining his lost composure in an instant. It was his eyes that betrayed him; they spoke of fury and wrath.

"I don't make threats."

The enormous bronze doors creaked open, and the new queen, Tessara Vaelen Alumír strode in, black and silver robes flowing elegantly behind her. The elf moved with an almost arrogant grace, her two Ephorí, Dumelian and Ithilin, following in her wake.

Dumelian, as he always did, marched with his chin in the air, silver jewellery adorning his fingers and neck, the beginnings of a grin on his lips. No doubt he had been relishing this entrance for the better part of the last hour.

In contrast, Ithilin had a scowl like a stormhead, her gaze trailing the ground. The older elf had always had little time for the games the others played and, as Aeson knew well, had a particular proclivity for punctuality.

"This is going to be interesting," Tarmon Hoard whispered, leaning closer to Erik.

Tessara glided across the floor, taking up a position on the opposite side of the table beside Galdra and Uthrían. She inclined her head towards both, bowing at the waist as she greeted the matriarch of the Dvalin Angan, Varthon, who stood to the left of the stone table.

King Galdra returned Tessara's gesture, his features carved into a dark stare.

Uthrían ignored her completely, which showed a very different side to their relationship than the one on display at the Eleswea un'il Valana. They were behind closed doors now, and the queen of Ardurän clearly had patience that was wearing thin.

Observing the reactions to the new queen, Aeson had the feeling Tessara played a different type of game than the others. Whereas her predecessor, Silmiryn, had been subtle and cautious in his manoeuvrings, often sycophantic to those that might aid him, Tessara seemed as though she might be far more blunt an instrument. Aeson was yet to decide whether that was a good thing, but time would tell.

The new queen of Vaelen moved closer to the table, clasping her hands before her and staring down over the stonework map of Epheria, pretending to be blissfully unaware of the many frowns and scowls that filled the room around her.

One look at Chora told Aeson that the woman wanted to tear a hole through Tessara there and then.

"Apologies for my lateness," Tessara said finally, her voice lacking even a drop of sincerity. She lifted her gaze, casting it about the room, her stare resting on Calen for a moment before moving to Chora and Thurivîr, who were still only a few paces from each other. "I hope we're all getting along?"

"Are they always this dramatic?" Dann whispered. "I think I'll come to these more often."

"If you don't shut up, Dann, I'm going to skin you alive," Therin whispered back.

Aeson turned to glare at Dann, only to see Tarmon clip him on the back of the head.

"I'm going to piss in your boots," Dann whispered before shuffling forwards just enough so that Tarmon couldn't reach him without making it obvious.

"Well," Chora said, holding her stare on Thurivír long enough for even the elf to seem uncomfortable. "Now that we are all here, I believe it is time we set out the path forward."

"Please," Uthrían said, breaking her self-imposed silence.

Aeson looked to Chora and the others, who nodded for him to proceed. He was about to take a step forward when he turned to Calen and met the young man's gaze.

Calen had emerged from the Burnt Lands an entirely different person from the boy Aeson had found in the western villages almost two years prior. He was harder, colder, and more sure of his own strength. But he'd also still shown the marks of captivity and torture, the weariness of travel and war. His eyes and cheeks had been sunken, his skin dry and cracked, and his frame had a frailty to it.

The man who stared back at Aeson now held that same sense of iron, even more so. He walked with his shoulders back, chin proud, gaze up. But his body had healed. The months of training and hearty meals had filled out his shoulders and hardened his muscles. He still looked tired, but not weary.

As Calen looked at Aeson, the purple hue of his eyes shifting with the light, he inclined his head, gesturing for Aeson to lead the talks, the petulance of youth gone. It was at that moment that Aeson was absolutely sure of one thing: the boy had become a man, and the man had become a warrior.

"The time for waiting is over," Aeson said as those gathered moved closer to the table. "The Blood Moon may taint the sky, but the empire is exposed. It is a wounded animal, attacked from all sides. The imperial mages are stronger under the moon's light, but so too are the Uraks."

Aeson leaned over the table.

"Urak hordes sweep across Illyanara, from the western villages to Falstide and Baylomon. They have laid waste to Stonehelm and Cardend in Arkalen, currently besiege Camylin, and have ravaged the villages near the base of the Marin Mountains. But crucially, their warpath in the South pales in comparison to the sheer destruction they wreak in the North. Between them and the elves of Lynalion, the bulk of the Lorian forces are hemmed in on the northern half of the continent. Which means now is the time to finally cut the cancer of the Lorian Empire from Southern Epheria."

"Hear, hear." Tarmon said, folding his arms and nodding as he moved his gaze across the table with pursed lips. There was a cold fervour in the man's eyes. The empire had destroyed his home, and Tarmon had been powerless to stop it. Aeson knew that feeling well.

"What, then, is your proposal, Rakina?" Galdra clasped his hands behind his back, looking down over the map with a raised chin, his silver-white hair resting on his shoulder, straight as needles. Aeson could tell by Galdra's tone that the elf wasn't going to be as cooperative as he had promised at the Eleswea un'il Valana. He'd expected no less.

"We have finally received word from Alina Ateres in Valtara. The Valtaran rebellion has pushed High Lord Loren and the imperial loyalists back to Achyron's Keep and are holding position. Loren's forces number over fifty thousand to Alina's thirty, and they boast a contingent of imperial mages. Loren holds back because unless they are resupplied, the Valtarans can only keep their position until the next moon. An imperial force blockades the Hot Gates, and, from our reports, the armies garrisoned near Argona, along with the remnants of those who attacked Aravell, are moving to quell the rebellion. The Valtarans will soon be vastly outnumbered. They can win this war, but they will need our help."

"It is unfortunate then that there is nothing that can be done," Galdra said with an upturn of his lip. "We cannot simply empty Aravell of its warriors. Not with the Uraks pushing inwards from the Lodhar Mountains. We must deal with the threat to our home first. And even if that were not the case, we would never reach Valtara in time to be of aid. The distance is too great with the lands in between swarmed by Uraks."

"Hmm." Galdra had said precisely what Aeson had expected him to. Uthrían and Tessara, however, remained silent, watching. "What was it you said at the Eleswea un'il Valana, Galdra?" Aeson rolled back his shoulders and added as much pomposity to his voice as he could muster. "'This is the day the elves of Lunithír, of Vaelen, and of Ardurän stopped hiding. This is the day we joined the fight.' Powerful words."

"Do not goad me, Aeson. This war will be won by making choices with our heads, not our hearts. We simply cannot mobilise enough warriors and cross the continent in that time. You know this to be true. We will arrive too late, Valtara will be ashes, and Aravell will be defenceless."

"I do. Which is why I propose that Calen flies me to the Stormwood by dragonback."

"What?" The look on Calen's face matched the surprise in his voice.

"We have allies gathered there. An Arcarian by the name of Verma Tallisair, along with some four thousand seasoned warriors led by a contingent of former Arkalen Stormguard. It would take weeks to travel by horseback. But Valerys can make that journey in days."

"And how do you then propose to get these four thousand from Arkalen to Valtara before the next moon?" Uthrían's tone was curt, but Aeson could tell by the look in her eyes that she was intrigued.

"I have not spent these past centuries idle, as you well know. And the time has finally come for all the threads to be pulled. When Valerys hatched, I sent letters across Epheria and beyond, preparing for today. One of those letters was opened by Kayala Latrak, fourth in line to the Royal House of Latrak in Narvona. It was her vessel that carried me to Valacia and brought back Valerys's egg." Aeson gave Calen a soft smile, seeing the understanding in the young man's eyes. "It was also her vessel that was set afire off Epheria's western coast by the imperial navy. As we speak, she sails two hundred ships across the Narvonan sea, manned by some twenty thousand strong. Several of those ships are already docked near Land's End to carry me and our forces in Arkalen along the coast to Valtara. With some luck, and Neron's blessing, we can avoid any Lorian ships and arrive well before the next moon."

"Your plan, Aeson, if I understand correctly, is to bring a foreign army to these shores?" Galdra raised an eyebrow, his arms still clasped behind his back. "And what will they want in return, I wonder?"

"Do you have a better plan, Your Highness? I'm all ears. Please, do tell." Aeson knew it was a dangerous game, trading words with Galdra. The elf had a long memory and an easily slighted honour. But Aeson's sufferance had worn out long ago. "Unless you suggest it is simply better to watch the Valtarans burn? And once their nation is in ruins, the Lorians will gather. The Varsundi will fall in line, as they always do, and Carvahon will be the empire's next target. Our allies will crumble one by one, and we will be left alone, weakened and ripe for the slaughter."

Aeson took Galdra's silence as acquiescence.

"Kayala has many reasons to despise the empire. She yearns to see it crumble. I have known her family for many generations. If she wants lands to settle when this is all done, so be it. We will carve her a piece of the North for the blood she has given. Most importantly, she has honour. I trust her."

"You trusted Eltoar Daethana once." Venom laced Galdra's words, but his expression softened, his gaze dropping. "So did I."

"Why not have Calen fly you to Valtara itself?" Tarmon Hoard asked, allowing Galdra's comment to fade before it could be answered. He tilted his head as he surveyed the map, opening his right palm. "Send a message through the Angan. Have the ships leave Arkalen immediately. It would cut days of travel."

"Because if Calen goes to Valtara, he will be dragged into the battles there, and he is needed elsewhere. Valtara is just one piece of an infinitely larger puzzle. We have not heard from Castor Kai since the razing of Argona. He was due here days ago. In his stead, Aryana Torval is already en route. As is Tukul Unger of the Red Suns, who commands just short of seven thousand near the Baylomon Mountains. And even more besides that pair. All the faction leaders across Illyanara will be here in a matter of days. Calen must be here when they arrive. They must see him, see that he is flesh and blood, see that Valerys is not some whispered tale but a dragon of legend. Illyanara is the largest province in the South; we need its strength behind us. And if we do not bind these factions now, they will scatter to the wind and rip each other to pieces for control of the province."

"And then what? What do I say when Aryana Torval and these other leaders arrive? You built this rebellion, not me." There was no anger in Calen's voice, which was a welcome change, but Aeson sensed he wasn't far from it. "I don't know these people. I don't know what they want." He pressed his tongue against his teeth, hesitating. "I need you here."

"I may have built this rebellion, but you set it alight." Aeson turned to face him. "Your legend is building, and there are many who would attach themselves to it. Therin will stay here with you, as will Chora. You will be well counselled."

Calen shook his head, his right hand clenching into a fist around his sword pommel. "Valerys and I shouldn't be sitting around drinking wine and talking while others fight our battles."

"This is not about your pride, Calen, nor your courage, which none who have seen it can doubt. This is about wisdom. The wisdom to know when to charge and when to hold. If Castor Kai is dead, then his banners will flock to either Torval or Unger. We need them at our back if we are to succeed, and you are our greatest hope at that." Aeson let out a sigh. "With those forces behind you, we can push into Drifaien and give Alleron Helmund the edge he needs to replace his father. We can convince High Lord Talian Kalas to declare Carvahon under our banner. And we can push the Uraks back from the western villages. There will be many battles ahead, don't worry."

Calen's jaw twitched at those last words.

"I have not heard word from my contact in Argona since the city's destruction. But the Angan that Baldon – may his soul rest – sent to Salme has reached out. Dahlen reports that Salme's defences are holding, but they won't for long. The Uraks attack in greater numbers with each passing night. He requests immediate aid."

"Then we go." Calen didn't hesitate for even a heartbeat. "We have almost five thousand who follow my banner..." Calen stared off into the distance for a second, hesitating at his own words, then pushed on. "I'll fly with Valerys. We'll break the siege and drive the Uraks back into Lodhar."

"I need you to fly me to Arkalen, and five thousand will not be enough to route the Uraks. We need to have patience. Trust Dahlen. Once you persuade Aryana and Tukul to join our cause, we can march west."

"It is my home, Aeson." Calen's eyes shimmered with a purple light, wisps of pale mist drifting outwards. "I cannot leave it to die. I *will* not."

"And it is *my* son." Aeson stared back at Calen. He had known this would be the most difficult part. He looked to Asius, who stood a few feet from the table with his hands clasped behind his back, observing quietly. The Jotnar stood head and shoulders above all others bar Thacia, his bluish skin tinted a shade of purple by the Blood Moon's light spraying in from the arched windows. "Asius?"

The Jotnar raised an eyebrow.

"What word from Larion? Are your people gathered? Could they give aid?"

Asius returned Aeson's stare for a moment, then unclasped his hands and moved closer to the table, Dann and Tarmon stepping aside to give him space. "For the first time in centuries, the Jotnar are one. Those Larion has gathered march for Aravell as we speak. The last message I received, they had left their encampment where the Aonan Wood meets the mountains. When they pass the Arythn Plain, Larion will send another hawk. I can have a letter left by the waypoint in the Marin Mountains, but until then, I will not be able to contact them."

Aeson nodded sombrely.

"Do you see? Patience is our friend, Aeson." The smug upturn of Galdra's bottom lip caused Aeson to physically bite his own tongue. "We must wait and be careful. In war, losses are inevitable. Haste born from fear or desire will lead to nothing but greater death."

Aeson clenched his jaw, and he thought he could hear an echo of Lyara's roar in the back of his mind, setting his hairs on end.

If I left every decision to you – you self-righteous piece of shit – we would sit and wait until every shred of this continent bar the Aravell was aflame before we left this place. They were the words Aeson wanted to say. But instead, he let out a breath and gave the elf a half-smile. "Hesitation born from fear or desire walks the same path, Your Majesty. But at least with haste we make our own choices instead of having choices made for us."

"Take another five thousand from Vaelen and march on the western villages." Queen Tessara stood straight, one hand resting over the other at her waist, her face expressionless. "I can have them outfitted and ready by first breath of morning."

Both Uthrían and Galdra stared at the new queen but said nothing.

Tessara raised an eyebrow at the silence that followed. She looked to Calen. "I do not know you, Draleid. And I dare say you do not know me. So let us learn each other quickly and have our words match our secret hearts. You protected my home, and you were willing to give your life for my people. And so I will do the same in return, with hope that this is but the beginning of such exchanges. Vaelen commands some nine thousand warriors. I will leave four here in defence of Aravell, and I will personally march with the other five. Add your forces to mine and place them under the command of your most trusted. We will defend your home while you do what must be done. On my honour."

Slowly, the purple light ebbed from Calen's eyes. He nodded slowly. "Du haryn myia vrai, Inarí. La'værakanra glinmahíl denír."

Thank you, Queen. I will not forget this.

Tessara inclined her head. "Vrail mír nåir denír er beskír."

Thank me when this is all over.

"I will add another two thousand." Queen Uthrían drew a sharp breath, her gaze locking with Calen's. "I cannot spare any more, not with Aravell still under threat. We cannot put out fires in the homes of others while leaving our own to burn. But we can help."

Calen dipped his head in thanks.

Aeson held back the smirk that attempted to find its way to his lips as he looked at Galdra.

The king glared at both Uthrían and Tessara. They had forced his hand. "I, too, can offer two thousand, but no more."

"It is settled then," Aeson said, leaning on the table, his palms laid flat. "Calen will fly me to the Stormwood, where I will sail to aid the Valtaran rebellion. Tessara will march to Salme with nine thousand Triarchy warriors and five thousand sworn to the rebellion while Calen and Valerys will return here and secure the fealty of Aryana Torval, Tukul Unger, and as many of the smaller factions as possible." He looked to Calen. "Once that has been secured, you can fly to join the army before they reach Salme. And we can commit forces to Drifaien and Arkalen. Carvahon will fall under our banners with little encouragement. Then we can turn our eyes to Varsund. With the gold from Aonar and the imperial garrison already stationed there, Varsund will require the most blood."

"What of the North?" Asius asked.

Aeson knew precisely what Asius's true question was: what of Coren Valmar? What of the woman apprenticed by Kollna, daughter of Luan – his mother?

"Our forces in the North are hemmed in on all sides. For the moment, many of them remain relatively safe in the outpost in the Firnin Mountains, but we don't know how long that will last. I've asked Coren and Farwen to travel here on Draleid business. To save time, they will cross the Svidar'Cia. It may take some time as the imperial forces are at heightened alert, but the Fenryr Angan are aiding in the coordination."

"Surely not." Uthrían narrowed her gaze. "That is suicide, Aeson. Calen and the others crossed, but to my knowledge they are the first in four hundred years. Their crossing does not increase the likelihood of success for others."

"We'd heard rumours that after the Blood Moon rose, the madness in the Svidar'Cia faded. Reports of refugees forced into the wasteland by the Uraks. Most died from hunger, thirst... blood loss. But reports from our ears in Kingspass are that some made it through, their minds untouched by the madness." Aeson gestured towards Calen's brother, Arden, who stood at the back with his arms folded. "The Knights of Achyron confirmed this to be true."

Arden stepped forwards, unfazed by the many eyes upon him. The mountain of a man inclined his head towards Aeson. "It is true. On the night the Blood Moon rose, Fane Mortem opened a rift in the veil. One of my brothers sacrificed himself to close it. Ever since, we have not felt the Taint in the Burnt Lands as we previously had. Efialtír's hand no longer holds the waste in its grasp."

"You can... feel it?" Galdra asked.

"Much like you can feel the moisture in the air on a humid day or the smoke at the back of your throat when something burns. It is like a sickly oil that stains everything it touches. To know it is part of the burden we carry, part of Achyron's gift."

"It does not sound like a gift." A genuine twinge of sadness touched Galdra's face, only for a fleeting moment. "Perhaps it is a mercy Achyron has never chosen one from our people."

Arden glanced at Calen, then returned his gaze to Galdra. "I was given a second chance to protect the people I love. There is no burden I would not bear for such a gift."

A sombre silence fell over the chamber until all that could be heard was the rushing wind through the arches and the drum of the rain that had begun to fall outside and onto the stone table through the oculus.

"Arden, Kallinvar requested an audience with regard to a matter of urgent need," Aeson said. "Now that these matters are tended to, he may come."

The knight bowed his head, then closed his eyes.

Barely a minute had passed before a green orb materialised behind Arden, its light battling the crimson glow of the Blood Moon and washing the stone in an odd, muted brown. Within seconds, the orb had spread to a disc over ten feet tall and wide. The centre of the disk rippled like water, its surface black as molten onyx.

A man in green and gold plate stepped through, followed by two knights.

Kallinvar rested his hand briefly on Arden's shoulder as he passed and moved to the table's rightmost edge, his helmet turning to liquid metal and receding into his collar as he did.

"Thank you for granting me an audience with this council," Kallinvar said, bowing slightly towards the elven Triarchy and those gathered. "When I last stood here, I made a vow to fight at your side in the war to come. I intend to keep that vow. But now I am here to ask for your help."

"Speak, Grandmaster Kallinvar." Uthrían bowed her head. "If we can help, we will."

The relationship between the elves and the knights had always been a strained one, and although likely unnoticed by many, Uthrían's gesture was one Aeson was glad to see.

Kallinvar smiled, touching his open hand against his breastplate in acknowledgement. The man looked to Aeson before lifting his head and staring up at the oculus in the centre of the ceiling, the crimson light sparkling in the rain that fell through. He then proceeded to tell all those gathered about the battle that took place in Ilnaen the same night as the battle for Aravell – of Fane Mortem, of the Uraks, of Efialtír's Chosen crossing into the world, and of the losses the knights suffered.

The silence that followed held the room in such firm a grasp it had an almost tangible presence. Even the new queen, Tessara, stared at Kallinvar, wide-eyed.

When nobody else spoke, Kallinvar continued, resting his gauntleted palms on the chamber's stone table. "The Blood Moon is in its seventh day. It will not wane for some time, and while we wait, Efialtír's hand grows ever stronger in this world." He lowered his gaze, looking around the room before settling on Aeson. "You do not need to take my word for it. All you must do is look across the continent. The Bloodspawn pour from the mountains like a raging tide. Towns and cities across Epheria, north and south alike, lie empty, smoke and fire pluming from their bowels. And with Efialtír's Chosen at their side, the empire's armies are more powerful now than they've ever been. We cannot stop what is to come on our own."

"What is it you need?"

All heads turned as Calen spoke, more than a few looks of scorn on the faces of the elven Ephorí. Draleid or no, he was young, and despite their bows and carefully chosen words, many of the elves still saw him as a child – a thing to be used.

Kallinvar sucked in his cheeks, then spoke. "For four hundred years, we have waited for the Blood Moon to rise again. And now that it is here, I can tell you that it is not our greatest threat. There is a war coming, a war like nothing you've ever seen."

"I don't know if you've looked, old friend," Aeson said, gesturing to the map. "But war is already here."

"Next to what comes, this is nothing. The Godwar looms."

Aeson stared at Kallinvar open-mouthed. "This is everything," he said, incredulous. "I care little for what the gods do to each other. Four hundred years I've waited to lift the empire's iron boot and take back everything that was stolen. How can you say this is nothing? I was there in Ilnaen all those years ago. I watched your brothers and sisters die at Eltoar's hands. I watched your knighthood crumble just as my order did. I watched Fane Mortem and his empire hunt the Jotnar into near extinction. What did the gods do then?"

Aeson's right hand clenched into a fist, the muscles in his jaw tensing.

Kallinvar's sombre expression didn't change. He held his gaze on Aeson. "You misunderstand me, old friend. Winning this war does not matter if Efialtír crosses into this world. Everything you save will die anyway."

"What do you mean?" Therin's voice rang clear in the chamber as the elf took a step from beside Asius. It was the first time Therin had spoken a single word within the chamber's walls.

"You have no voice here, Therin Eiltris." King Galdra looked to Therin with fire in his eyes. "You saw to that many years ago. Know your place, Astyrlína."

Therin bowed his head, nodding slightly, but Galdra did not stop.

"It is insolence enough that you dared return here." The king's eyes narrowed as he walked slowly around the table. "But for you to speak in these chambers… Your arrogance knows no bounds. We suffer your presence out of respect for the Draleid and Rakina, but make no mistake, your honour is forfeit. Your own daughter has shed your name, so deep is your betrayal. Speak again, and I will send you to Achyron's halls."

Out of the corner of his eye, Aeson saw purple light misting from Calen's eyes. He placed his hand on Calen's chest and shook his head. As he did, he laughed.

"What about this amuses you, Rakina?" Galdra's anger still laced his voice.

"You, Galdra." For so many centuries, Aeson had stood by and said nothing. The elven ways were the elven ways. So it had always been, so it always would be. But he'd had enough. "The traitor god is at our gates. Epheria burns. This city, burns!" he roared, a fury he had not felt in a very long time rising. "And still you cling to your grudge like a child."

Thurivîr stepped across Aeson. "How dare you speak to—"

"Speak again, Thurivîr—" Aeson lowered his voice, levelling his gaze at the Lunithíran Ephorí "—and I will bury you so deep your own mother would give up digging."

Thurîvir's hand hovered over his sword pommel, his usually calm demeanour shattered, the veins in his neck bulging. Aeson could feel the ripples of the Spark flowing from the elf.

"You all talk of honour—" Aeson cast his gaze across the Triarchy and the Ephorí, holding it a half-second longer on Thurivîr and Galdra "—and yet you prance around this city as though the world outside is not in flames. You call Therin faithless, strip him of his honour, and treat him as though he is not worth the shit on your boot, when, in truth, he is your better in every way."

"Careful, Aeson." Galdra walked slowly around the table, all the rage gone from his eyes. He spoke with calm, but his voice was laced with violence. "You are drawing a line that cannot be undone. You are not a fool. Do not act one."

Aeson moved square to Galdra. "You asked Therin to choose sides in a war between his people. A war he did not believe in. He chose exile instead of creating more division and for that you claim he is without honour. Yet while you hid in this woodland, pretending you were making a difference, Therin *continued* to fight. When his own people turned his back on him, he continued to fight. Líra built this city to keep you safe, and you cast her Ayar Elwyn from its walls and poisoned their daughter against him. The problem with honour, King Galdra, is that it lies in the eye of the beholder, and in my eyes, yours is lacking while Therin's is unquestionable." Aeson looked to Therin, who stood in shock, his mouth ajar. "All these years, I have stood by and said nothing, and for that I failed you. Laël sanyin, myia yíar. Uvrín mír."

I am sorry, my friend. Forgive me.

"Du é uvrínil."

You are forgiven.

A palpable sense of relief clung to Therin's voice, the most fragile of smiles adorning his lips.

"As beautiful and moving as this all is," Chora said, her arms folded as she sat in her chair. She gestured towards Kallinvar. "I believe it best we settle our grievances later."

King Galdra looked to Chora and, after a moment of silence, inclined his head. "Well spoken, Rakina." He turned his gaze to Aeson. "We will settle this another time. But we *will* settle it."

The king moved back to the far side of the table and nodded to Kallinvar.

"The Blood Moon is only the beginning," Kallinvar continued. "Efaltír seeks to cross the veil himself and take form in this world."

"Is that even possible?" Aeson asked.

"There is a vessel known as the Heart of Blood that we believe, if used by The Traitor's Chosen, possesses the ability to tear a rift in the veil large enough for such a thing."

"And where is this 'Heart of Blood'?" Uthrían clasped her right wrist with her left hand.

"We do not know. That is why we need your help. What we do know is that Fane does not hold it. If he did, we would not be having this conversation. The Watchers in our temple have been consulting the old texts and have surmised a number of locations where they believe the Heart may reside."

Kallinvar walked around the stone table, tapping spots with his finger: Mar Dorul, Kolmir, Mount Helmund, Ilnaen, Wolfpine Ridge, the Marin Mountains.

"Those are not places you can simply walk into." Harken Holdark folded his arms as he moved to the table's edge. "They are also not places easily searched."

"They are mountain ranges and a wasteland," Chora remarked. "It would not be searching for a needle in a haystack. It would be searching for a needle in a field of burning corn with wool over your eyes."

"There is no choice." Kallinvar leaned against the table. "We cannot allow Fane to find the Heart before we do. If he does, everything you know and love will perish. This war will mean nothing because there will be nobody left to fight it and nothing left to fight for."

Queen Uthrían opened her hands wide. "What if the Blood Moon sets and nobody finds this Heart? We are better off fighting the war of steel and flesh and blood than chasing the ghost of something that might never be found. If we ignore the Lorians, they *will* kill us. If we leave this *Heart of Blood,* it may simply be lost forever and our task will be complete without a wasted second."

"Kallinvar, we vowed to fight together. To stand by each other's side in this war." Aeson gestured towards the table. "But we cannot simply abandon everything to go searching for something that may not even exist. We don't have the numbers. Not yet. There are contacts I have in Al'Nasla, Berona, and Catagan who are well placed. I will send word that they are to hunt down any traces of this 'Heart of Blood'. If the empire finds it, we will know. And as soon as we know, we will rain down fire and fury. I promise you."

"Empty promises and empty words." Kallinvar let out a long sigh, then shook his head. "I should have known better."

"On my honour, I swear it." Calen reached out and offered his hand to Kallinvar, and every elf in the room – particularly Therin – stared at him with open mouths. Were it anyone else, Aeson wouldn't have thought much of it, but Calen knew what it was to swear on his honour in an elven realm. "My father always taught me that a man's vow is a sacred thing and that I should not give it unless I intend to answer when called to fulfil it."

Kallinvar grasped Calen's forearm. "Your father was a wise man."

"He casts a large shadow." Calen gave a sharp nod. "If you find this thing you're looking for, or if Fane does, call us and we will come."

In the valley beyond a roar rose to rival thunder.

CHAPTER EIGHTEEN

OUR CHOICES DEFINE US

7th Day of the Blood Moon

Berona – Winter, Year 3081 After Doom

Trusil whinnied as Rist ran the hard brush over the horse's flank. Trusil had been well cared for at the imperial stables while Rist had journeyed to the Burnt Lands, but the guilt of leaving him still gnawed at Rist a little. He'd never considered himself a lover of animals, but the horse was changing that. Rist had amassed a total of six brushes and combs for the horse, which was, as he thought about it, more variations of the same thing than anything else he'd owned in his life.

One of the books he'd brought with him from Berona, after they'd last stopped there before the Burnt Lands, had been *Of Horses and Men, and Why the Former is Better Than the Latter,* by Olga Unimi. The title was a bit long-winded so he abbreviated it in his mind to '*Of Horses and Men*'.

The book had spoken at length of the importance of keeping a horse well maintained and cared for and had outlined the specific needs for each brush. It might have seemed excessive to some, but Rist enjoyed the specificity of it. Each tool had a purpose and a place, each uniquely crafted to fulfil that purpose. Not only that, but he enjoyed the routine, the methodical repetition. And the fact that Trusil's hair was soft as silk only added to that enjoyment.

"Shhh," he whispered, running the thumb of his free hand across the horse's cheek as he brushed. "I've heard we're being given leave to spend the day and night in the city before marching east. I'll bring you back apples."

The horse nickered, shaking his head side to side and stamping his front foot.

"And carrots too, yes." Rist rubbed Trusil's cheek again with his spare hand as he brushed a particularly stubborn piece of caked mud from the horse's shoulder.

"I don't like carrots. Bring me pastries and cheese." The voice came from behind, high-pitched and mocking.

Rist smiled, turning his head just a little to see Neera approaching, Lena at her side. He doubted that if horses could speak, they would produce a tone and pitch even remotely similar to that voice, but he'd learned enough to say nothing.

"If Trusil doesn't want the pastries, I'll have them. And the cheese." Neera brushed Rist's shoulder with her hand before scratching at Trusil's muzzle affectionately. "If we work together, we can get pastries *and* apples. Viara will share them with you. Fair deal?"

Rist stepped back, watching with a smile on his face. Tharn Pimm had once told him that how a person treats an animal is a fine judge of their heart. Even those who are scared of animals could still be tender.

"Do the horses ever answer you when you talk?" Lena folded her arms, green robes falling just short of her ankles. She'd not been in Ilnaen during the fighting. Her, Brother Halmak, and the other consuls had remained at a rear camp some ten miles north, along with many of the Healers, infirmerers, and apprentices.

"Only if you speak horse," Rist said with a smile.

"Was that a joke, Rist? You're getting better at those. Tommin will..." Her voice trailed off. "Tommin *would* have liked that one."

Rist gave Lena an awkward smile. He had a feeling that even if he knew what words to say, they wouldn't have helped. Words were pretty but often ineffectual when it came to loss.

An elbow prodded him in the ribs and he looked to see Neera standing beside him and inclining her head towards Lena, who had grown silent and was now staring off towards the city.

He'd lost his focus again.

"Tommin *would* have liked it." Neera linked arms with Lena, then stroked Trusil's muzzle. "In fact, I think Trusil bears a striking resemblance to Tommin."

Lena let out a soft laugh, squeezing Neera's arm closer to her ribs, then scratched under Trusil's cheek.

"Why the long face?" she whispered, and both her and Neera burst out in hysterics.

"Don't try and understand it, lad." Rist hadn't heard Magnus approach. "Women are a different species. They're smarter, stronger, and they feed off our confusion like mosquitoes do blood. If anyone tells you any different, they're lying."

Rist looked up to see Garramon and Magnus, the latter attempting to fold his arm across his chest, only to frown when he realised the other arm wasn't there to leverage against.

Magnus looked at Rist then shrugged. "Like I said, still feels like it's there. Anyway, you lot, gather what you need and piss off into the city. You've been given relief for the night, along with the Fourth Army. The Eighteenth and the

Seventh will hold watch before they march east in the morning." A look of visible irritation crept onto his face. "Taya Tambrel has instructed the First and the Fourth to remain at Berona for a while longer."

As Neera and Lena made for the tents, Garramon grabbed Rist's arm. "Not you. We have other plans."

Dilapidated tents and hastily constructed wooden shanties sprawled outside Berona's white walls, creeping for miles like tendrils of fog. Dark smoke pumped upwards from shoddy chimneys and a discordant din of hacking coughs, stamping feet, and clashing voices filled the air.

The people who occupied this makeshift city outside a city – and there must have been tens of thousands – looked as beaten and bruised as the soldiers who'd fought at Ilnaen. Some of them wouldn't have been out of place in the triage tents.

A child no older than ten passed with bloodied bandages wrapped around the stump of his right leg, a crutch made of tree branches keeping him upright. A woman stumbled across the street from one tent, her entire face scarred and blistered, her eyes nothing but knotted flesh, and what looked to be her two daughters guiding her path.

Rist could have gone on listing the injuries in his mind, but he would have stood there for months. It would have been quicker for him to list those who appeared unharmed. Whatever state they were in, whatever limbs remained, every last one of them looked to be firmly in exhaustion's grasp, their skin caked with dirt, their eyes sunken.

Imperial soldiers and cavalry marched through the wide main street in groups of eight, swords belted at their hips, the crowd parting before them. At first, Rist had thought the show of force too much, but the more he watched, the more he understood: Berona was a tinderbox ready to ignite.

These people had lost everything and most had marched hundreds or thousands of miles. They were tired, broken, hungry, and in pain. He counted at least six brawls within the space of two hundred feet. One man had thrown a rock at a mounted rider, resulting in him vanishing beneath a swarm of black and red leather.

"If you're ever wondering why we fight," Garramon said, leaning in, "this would go some way towards explaining it. It's been months since the elves destroyed the cities on the eastern coast, and still the refugees pour in, their lives razed to the ground, their loved ones left to burn in piles."

A man bumped into Rist's shoulder, apologising profusely, his hand covering his mouth with a cloth. The man's eyes were bloodshot and weeping, yellow crusts forming along his lids. Dark lesions cracked outwards from behind the cloth.

Rist had read about illness and squalor in *The Art of War*. There were entire chapters dedicated to the collapse of cities without the swing of a single blade. The logic had been sound. If you forced enough of your enemies into a single place where the infrastructure could no longer contain them, collapse would ensue. Space would vanish, food would be consumed faster than it could be produced, and illness would spread. When you finally marched your armies through the gates, the city would already be crumbling, more akin to a tomb than a fortress.

The way Sumara Tuzan had written it, it had seemed almost poetic. Intellect over brute force. A masterful method of taking a city without losing a soul. But this was not poetic or masterful; this was brutal, and cruel, and horrid.

Two men passed, dragging a woman in a barrow lined with straw. Both men stared at the ground, their hands bloody and cracked around the wooden handles.

The woman was dead. Her legs had been shattered from the knees down, bandages and splints failing to hold the broken bones together. Had Rist not seen battle, he wouldn't have known she was dead just by looking. But he knew what dead bodies looked like now. Her skin was too pale, her chest had no rise or fall, and she was far too still.

"If the Uraks or elves attack, all of these people will be slaughtered…"

Garramon didn't answer. It hadn't been a question. There was no other outcome. If the city's gates were already closed, then Berona was close to bursting. If the guards opened the gates and let these people in, their fate would be sealed. Sure, they would avoid a quick death beneath Urak or elven steel, but disease would spread like wildfire, starvation would kill within weeks, and then the corpses would pile.

Rist did not envy the man or woman who would be forced to make that choice. Open the gates and invite a slow death to all within, or leave the gates closed and watch these people die at the walls.

"Is this what it's like in the South?" Rist stared at a motionless man who lay on the ground by a tent as a blend of sunlight and pink-hued moonlight crept in through the gaps in the shanties. His hands, feet, eyes, and mouth were marred by deep black stains. *Consumption.*

"From what I hear, no," Garramon answered. "Though some places are faring worse than others, the Uraks seemed to have focused a large portion of their efforts in the North." Garramon looked to Rist, slowly understanding the true meaning behind his question. His mouth formed a grim line, and he hesitated before continuing. "I've not heard word from The Glade or the other villages. No new letters, no new reports."

Rist stared back at Garramon before shifting his gaze to the faces that peered from shanty doorways, dirty and disheveled.

His heart hurt.

After Ilnaen, he would have given anything just to hear his mam's over-enthusiastic voice or have his dad spend hours explaining how the pollen of different flowers affected the taste of honey and, in turn, mead.

"There are several armies stationed in western Illyanara," Garramon continued. "I'm sure your parents are fine. Between the Uraks and the elves, news from the South has grown scarce. The best we can do is keep fighting here and trust our forces in the South to do the same."

"I wouldn't be allowed to go back even if I wanted to, would I?" Rist knew the answer, but he wanted to hear it spoken aloud. He needed to hear it from Garramon's lips.

Garramon hesitated, then shook his head. "Not unless you were instructed to do so. You would be branded a deserter."

Deserters were killed. He knew this from Orduro Alanta's *The Forging of an Empire*, but *The Art of War* had also recommended the execution of any deserters from a standing army. He understood the principle: if soldiers could abandon their duty with no repercussions, an army would quickly crumble and wither at the first sight of hardship. The overarching threat of repercussion was what kept society from collapse. It was practiced by mothers and fathers to keep children on the correct path. And it was often the only deterrent from theft or murder – which was a sobering thought in itself. It was a sound principle for the moral framework of a society. But just because he understood it didn't mean he liked it.

It was something he was finding to be true more often than not recently: the written word had a distance from the reality of things. A way of focusing on cold, hard logic with no allowance for the humanity of an act. Logic had always been something Rist cherished. It was essential and inarguable. But his recent experiences were tarnishing his love of logic.

"Rist?" Garramon leaned forwards, meeting Rist's gaze.

Rist gave him a weak smile, nodding. He didn't want to talk on it any further.

Over a hundred spearmen were arranged in two blocks on either side of Berona's main gates, their backs stiff, eyes watching. A number of Varsundi Blackthorns stood at the ready, towering over any refugee who dared approach the gates. Above, archers lined the parapets.

Soldiers of the First and Fourth armies marched through the assembled guard and into the city, the spikes of the iron portcullis looming overhead.

"Where are we going?" Rist asked as they pushed through the crowded streets. The stench of piss blended noxiously with what should have been the sweet aroma of fresh-baked bread, the acrid sting of vomit dulling the scents of lavender and rosemary that Rist was sure would have been beautiful in a time before the war.

"You're asking that now?"

"I wanted to change the subject." Rist hadn't asked the question when he and Garramon had first set off from the camp. It hadn't seemed important. Wherever Garramon was taking him, he wouldn't have had much choice in the matter either way. He may have earned his colours, but Garramon was still an Exarch and he was still Rist's mentor. Besides, he trusted the man.

Garramon laughed at that, shaking his head. His expression sobered. "You'll see soon enough. Come, we're late."

As GARRAMON LED RIST THROUGH the Beronan streets and past the enormous keep at the city's centre, it didn't take Rist long to realise where he was being brought.

A tower rose in the northeast of the city. Carved from white stone, it stood three times the height of all else around it, a low cloud obscuring its peak. Sweeping bridges and broad walkways sprawled from its base as though the tower was the centre point of all life within Berona's walls. Not even Al'Nasla's palace pulled the breath from Rist's lungs the way the High Tower did. It was easily hundreds of feet wide with markings and symbols etched into the stone, red and black banners flapping in the wind. Balconies and plateaus stretched outwards from arched openings, overlooking the city from impossible heights.

But more than what he could see with his eyes, the closer he drew to the tower the fiercer the air rippled with the energy of the Spark. In Al'Nasla, Emperor Mortem had spoken of how Berona – like the capital – was one of few cities where the very fabric of the world resonated with the Spark's power for those who could feel it.

Rist had spent so long in Al'Nasla that the sensation had become little more than background noise in his mind, like the burbling of a river or the chatter in an inn. It had been the same when he'd first stepped through Berona's gates, but with each step towards the tower, that thrum rose and deepened until it became a tangible thing, a sound rushing in his ears, a sensation burning in his blood. Al'Nasla was a trickle, a meagre drip, in comparison.

He stopped and pressed his fingertips into his temple. The sensation had grown to the point that it roared in his ears and clouded his thoughts.

"It will balance out." Garramon rested a hand on Rist's back, guiding him past two women arguing over a loaf of mouldy bread.

"How can anyone function…" He squeezed the bridge of his nose to the point he thought the bone might snap. "It's… deafening."

"Not all Spark wielders can feel it as viscerally as you and I, and the vast majority barely feel it at all. You're more sensitive to the Spark than others. As your strength grows, so too does that sensitivity. It takes time to filter it. Give yourself a distraction. Focus on your breathing. Slow in, slow out. Feel your lungs and chest expand."

Rist did as he was instructed, focusing on the air as he pulled it in through his nostrils. He closed his eyes for a moment, continuing to walk forwards with Garramon's hand on his back.

People knocked into him, bumping his shoulder or clipping his leg. He heard dull voices, admonishing shouts. He ignored them. He had no choice. The thrum had grown so intense it had consumed all else, a storm raging in his mind.

"*Druids, a Magic Lost,*" Garramon whispered in his ear. "Page two hundred and eleven."

"What?" Rist grunted, moving his hand back to his temple and pressing in his fingers.

"Read it to me. Tell me the first line."

"I…" Rist made to argue, but all logical thought abandoned him. His mind was chaos. He pictured the book, flicked through the pages, and settled on page two hundred and eleven. "*From the collected research of Angmiran Skarsden, Katja Landira, Indinam Muhdeeb, and other admittedly less reliable sources, I have composed a list of over one hundred and twenty-nine druidic gods. Some older texts suggest there may even have been more, but much of the pages are worn and frail, the ink blurred beyond legibility. Some have been transcribed, but I trust their accuracy as much as I do that of a blind goat. It appears that the druidic bloodlines began to dwindle somewhere around the year four hundred After Doom, taking many of their gods with them. By the year one thousand After Doom, the number of recorded gods had plummeted to no more than fifteen, and by the end of the Age of Honour, accounts of druidic histories had all but vanished. The only mention of the druidic gods are of Dvalin, the Stag; Bjorna, the bear; Vethnir, the hawk; Fenryr, the wolf; and Kaygan, the kat."*

Rist paused, realising he had just spoken three full paragraphs aloud. But the sound had dulled to the edges of his mind, the thrum of the Spark ebbing, his pulse slowing. He opened his eyes to people flooding past him and Garramon smiling.

"Better?"

"Much." Rist drew in a calming breath. His mind still thumped with a dull ache and a thin whistle sounded in the back of his head, but he could think. "Thank you. I've never felt anything like that… Even in Al'Nasla."

"That's because Al'Nasla doesn't have the High Tower and all the mages within. The first time I came to Berona, I curled up in a ball near The Leaping Salmon in the western quadrant of the city," Garramon said as they carried on through the street ahead, which was full of hawkers peddling everything under the sun. "I lay in that alley for hours, people stepping over me like I was a diseased rat. Some of the initiates taken in at the same time barely felt a pin prick in the air, others could feel it tickling their skin. Most felt nothing at all. Once you get used to it, it changes… transforms. If you had felt the power at Ilnaen before it fell, by the gods, the air in that city was like breathing lightning. It was something special, something beautiful."

A few moments passed as Rist weighed his next question, mulling it over in his head. "I've sat through Brother Pirnil's lectures, and I've read eight different books on the liberation – though that still feels like a strange word – but if I'm honest, it all feels… curated. It's too simple, too black and white. I enjoy black and white. I enjoy numbers and rules. But if the past year or so has taught me anything, it's that human nature is as grey as stone and murky as mud. Why did *you* make the choice you did? What actually happened?"

It was a question Rist had wanted to ask for a long time. He had hoped to find more honest answers in Orduro Alanta's *The Forging of an Empire*, but it seemed to him that the original volume had clearly been destroyed after the man had been sent to work the mines at Dead Rock's Hold, an edited account left in its place. There were only three people Rist would have trusted to tell him the truth. Anila was dead, and Magnus had a tendency to exaggerate far past the point of believability. That left Garramon.

Garramon's step faltered and he turned his shoulder, unable to avoid crashing into a giant of a man with a thick beard, the chest of an ox, and a bloated, hanging gut. Garramon held up an open palm, apologising as the man rolled back his shoulder and made himself seem as large as possible.

It was only when the man gave Garramon a second look and glanced at Rist, his eyes falling to the lionhead pommel of the sword at Rist's hip, that he stood back and carried on his way.

"Subtlety will never be something you master, will it?" Garramon said as he patted himself down. He gestured for Rist to follow him as they drew closer to the tower. "That's a conversation that would take a lot more time than we have, but one I think you deserve. For now, I will say that I came to a crossroads where I could no longer reconcile The Order I had joined with what it had become."

In the time it took Rist and Garramon to walk from the main gates of Berona to the walls that surrounded the base of the High Tower, Rist was certain he could have walked most of the way from The Glade to Milltown. The thrum of the Spark slowly bubbled in the back of Rist's mind, constantly threatening to overwhelm him. He moved through the pages of *Druids, a Magic Lost* in his mind's eye, focusing himself.

Rist and Garramon moved through the gates in the wall, entering a sprawling courtyard that looked as though it ran around the entire base of the tower. The symbol of the Circle was inlaid in jet into the white stone ground at the yard's entrance, black and white banners with the Circle's insignia hanging from golden poles.

Many buildings lined the inside of the walls, with hundreds of mages, porters, guards, and tower staff moving between them. Mages of all ranks and affinities occupied the yard, from Consuls in their green robes and Lectors in their grey, to Exarchs and Master Craftsmages in robes trimmed with silver. Apprentices, acolytes, and initiates moved in groups, the brown of their cloaks mingling with the colours of their various affinities.

The crowds made Rist realise just how unique his own experience had been in Al'Nasla.

Garramon led Rist across the courtyard, greeting several other mages as he did. They passed through an arched doorway in the tower's base that rose higher than The Gilded Dragon's roof, two enormous golden doors framing it.

The tower's antechamber opened into a vast hall that held as much life as a bustling village. The ceiling stood hundreds of feet above, ornamented with delicately carved panels depicting the faces of people Rist had no knowledge of.

Beautiful red carpets threaded with gold sat atop white stone, while all manner of tapestries, paintings, and mosaics adorned the walls. He paused for a moment to examine a truly gargantuan depiction of a battle, worked entirely from gold, that was set into the curved inner wall on his right. The piece stretched for at least fifty feet, dragons soaring through the air, armoured warriors doing battle on the ground, Uraks tearing through everything that moved.

Never in his life had he seen such opulence, not even in the imperial palace.

Rist stared open-mouthed as he followed Garramon through the antechamber and up a winding set of stairs on the northeastern side. Ten-foot-tall alcoves lined the right-hand wall of the staircase. Within each recess stood statues hewn from bronze, gold, marble, and all manner of other materials. Rist even spotted two carved from solid obsidian, dark as night and shimmering as the light moved.

They spent what felt like the better part of an hour traipsing through winding corridors and climbing steps. Every floor was as busy and grandiose as the last, mages hustling from room to room, gilded red carpets lining the floor, artwork and ornaments adorning the walls. Even the door handles were made from solid gold.

Garramon stopped before a large gilded door with the symbol of the Circle worked into its front. In any other place, that door would have marked the entrance to the grandest chamber in the wealthiest of houses, but there, in the High Tower, it was as unassuming as any other – simplistic, almost.

The room on the other side was dimly lit, the curtains drawn across windows, tallow candles casting soft light on the stone.

Two men stood at the chamber's heart, deep in conversation. Even before Rist could see their faces, he could tell by the gold and red trims on their black cloaks and by the undulating waves of power that rippled from them that they were none other than Andelar Touran and Fane Mortem.

It seemed such a ridiculous thing that he would be standing in this place, in the same room as these two men. Rist Havel, son of Lasch and Elia Havel, standing in the High Tower of the Circle of Magii with the Primarch of the Imperial Battlemages and the emperor of Loria. It felt as unbelievable as one of Dann's stories.

"Ah, Garramon. Right on time." Fane Mortem exuded that same insouciant charisma he'd had the first time Rist had met him. He held that same focused look in his eyes, that same intensity. "Wine?"

Garramon shook his head, greeting Fane and the Primarch. "Primarch Touran, this is Rist Havel, Brother of the Imperial Battlemages."

The older man took a step closer, the soft light of the candles illuminating the deep wrinkles in his skin. Such visible aging meant the Primarch was nearing the end of his time – but how long had that time been? He'd heard some say Touran had witnessed over nine hundred summers. From what Rist had read in multiple accounts, how long a mage lived was as varied as how long any soul lived. Some saw four hundred summers, others eight hundred. But there are some instances of mages surviving over a thousand. Rist couldn't quite grasp the concept of watching that much time pass him by.

In the chamber by the Well of Arnen during Rist's Trial of Will, he hadn't realised quite how tall Andelar Touran was. The man's frame was thin and bony, but he was taller than Rist by several inches.

Andelar stared at Rist, examining him. The Primarch's cold expression gave away nothing.

"I remember you," he croaked, his voice sounding far less indomitable now that it wasn't amplified by threads of Air and Spirit. "Your Trial of Will was interesting."

Rist couldn't help but wonder why the man had said that, why he had chosen the word 'interesting'. There was a subtlety in the word that was not lost on Rist, a subtlety that confirmed something he had long wondered: the Primarch had seen what Rist had seen.

"Emperor Mortem has told me of your exploits." Andelar looked to Fane, who held a cup of wine in his right hand, his arms crossed. "He believes you have a unique potential. As does Exarch Garramon. I am yet to be convinced."

Fane let out a short laugh and grabbed a second cup of wine from the table beside him. "Always so serious, Andelar. Even when I was only a child, you were the same, back in your... 'youth'." He offered the cup to Rist. "Wine, Brother Havel? I fear you might need it."

"Ehm... Yes." Rist looked to Garramon, who raised a curious eyebrow. "I mean, no. Thank you." He hesitated for another moment, then took the cup. "Yes."

Rist wasn't sure what was about to happen, but he'd grown quite fond of wine and thought of what Magnus would say if Rist told him he'd refused a cup from the emperor of Loria.

"Brother Havel." Fane gestured to a set of three black leather couches surrounding a low table a few feet away, then dropped himself languidly onto a cushion. He leaned back and crossed one leg over the other, draping his right elbow over the armrest. "Do you remember our conversation in Al'Nasla's library?"

Rist and Garramon both took a seat on the couch opposite Fane while the Primarch occupied the third.

"I do, Emperor Mortem."

"Please, call me Fane. You're a full Brother now, the youngest in the history of the Circle, if I am correct? Taking the record from me."

Rist stared back awkwardly, which drew a grin from the emperor.

"You remember, Rist, how we spoke of that thrum in the air, that rhythmic vibration? And how you said you had felt it in Al'Nasla? Did you feel it here?"

Just the mention of the thrum brought it back to the fore of Rist's mind, overwhelming his senses. A low buzz rang in his ears, the hairs on his arms pricking. He stopped himself from closing his eyes and pressing his fingers into his temple. As he looked at the others about him, he realised he could almost 'see' the power pulsing from all three men, like the ripples that undulate across water when a rock is dropped. Focusing, he could see that although power flowed from Andelar Touran, the old Primarch was nothing in comparison to Garramon or Fane. If Touran was a stone dropped in a lake, Garramon and Fane were boulders.

Rist once again opened the pages of a book in his mind and settled himself with the words, the thrum fading.

"Your reaction answers my question," Fane said, sipping his wine. "I'm sure Garramon told you of his first time in Berona. Well, some years after that, I walked through the main gates, fresh as a spring flower, and do you know what I did?"

Rist shook his head.

"I emptied my guts onto the stone after about five minutes. Then I passed out in my own vomit. I was six." The emperor laughed, shifting back into the hard cushion behind him and taking another drink. "I don't tell many people that story for obvious reasons. But most people can't relate to it, can't understand. You can, can't you?"

Rist took a deep mouthful of the wine he hadn't touched until that moment. He recognised the taste immediately. It was the same wine he'd been given before the Battle of the Three Sisters: the wine from Etrus. Garramon had said Fane kept some of the casks for himself. "It's like I can't think," he said, scratching at his arm. Thinking of the sensation sent an anxiety through him. "...or breathe, or hear, or feel. It just... it takes over."

"You've obviously found something that focuses you, judging by your current state – far quicker than I did, might I add. What is it?"

"Books."

"Books?" Andelar Touran's voice was equal parts curiosity and scepticism.

"Books," Rist confirmed. "Your books are some of them. *A Study of Control* and *The Spark: A Study of Infinite Possibilities.* When the feeling gets too strong, I read the pages in my mind. It calms me, allows me to focus."

"Interesting." The Primarch shifted forwards, swirling his wine in his cup. "You've read my works then?"

"I have, three times each."

"Your thoughts?"

"Page one hundred and twelve of *A Study of Control* saved my life at Ilnaen."

Beside Rist, Garramon leaned back, smiling.

"May I ask why I'm here?" Rist pursed his lips as the words left his mouth. Here he was sitting with the Primarch, the emperor, and the Arbiter. Each one of them could have torn him to shreds before he'd even have the time to react. He was not supposed to be the one asking the questions, and that was something he was very aware of. But he'd never been good at not asking questions.

"As I said before, I can appreciate someone who speaks their mind. I had asked Garramon not to tell you until you were here." The emperor nodded slowly, gesturing towards Andelar Touran.

The old Primarch sipped at his cup, then set it on the low table. "Have you heard of the Arcarians, Brother Havel?"

Rist scanned through his memories, flipping pages, reading lines. He stopped on page two hundred and seventy-nine of… *Druids, a Magic Lost* – surprisingly. "The Arcarians were a sect of elite Battlemages formed in the year three hundred and seven After Doom. Each possessed power far beyond that of their peers, and their abilities often spread throughout all affinities of The Order's magii. By key historical accounts, there were nine founding members. They…"

Rist stopped when he realised Andelar Touran was staring at him open-mouthed. He glanced right to see Garramon smiling ear-to-ear.

Emperor Mortem just laughed, finishing the last of his wine. He laid the cup on the table and refilled it from a decanter. "You consume information like you do air. How many books have you read since being granted access to the library?"

"One hundred and twenty-seven."

"Pages?"

"Forty-nine thousand and fifty-one."

"How many statues are in the yard at the base of this tower?"

"Thirteen."

"How many steps did you climb on the way here?"

"In total? Or divided by staircase?"

"Enough of this nonsense." Andelar shook his head. "You have an impressive memory. But that won't keep your head on your shoulders. On the field of battle, it is power that triumphs. It will do you no good to remember every place steel has pierced your hide." He sat straight. "The Arcarians are legend. They are the most powerful mages to have ever walked the known world. Before the liberation, they numbered twelve. Now, only three still draw breath. A woman by the name of Verma Tallissair, may Efialtír burn her soul. Emperor Fane Mortem, the youngest to have ever been inducted. And lastly, Arbiter Garramon Kalinim."

Now it was Rist's turn to stare open-mouthed. Garramon looked back at him without expression.

"To be an Arcarian, Rist, is to control the very nature of the Spark, to be one with it, to understand how it flows and shifts. Arcarians are not forged, they are born. Just as a man can build his strength for a lifetime and never be capable of shifting a mountain, a mage born without the raw power necessary can never become an Arcarian." Fane leaned forwards. "In the library in Al'Nasla, I told you that Garramon was insistent that you had the power to become a hero of legend, a mage who is written about for centuries to come – an Arcarian. Now, with the elves pushing deeper into our land and the rebels causing chaos across Epheria, it is time to find the truth in that claim. It is time to find out who you are."

Rist opened his mouth to speak, but no words came out. He moved his gaze from Fane to Garramon and over to Andelar.

"If you choose to walk this path," Fane continued, "I will have you know that it will be the most difficult thing you have ever done in your short life. You will feel pain the likes of which you could never have dreamt. You will work day and night. You will push yourself to the limits of your soul and then past them. Your bones will ache, and your very soul will feel as though it has been set on fire. This is not a decision to be made lightly. You must know that very few who walk this path become Arcarians. I can feel the strength within you, but in all cases this kind of power is like the roots of a tree. We do not know how deep it runs until we uncover it."

"What happens to those who don't succeed?"

"Many burn themselves out, some die… painfully." Garramon sat straight. His expression darkened, his gaze cold and hard. "Listen to me. You do not need to do this, Rist. You have nothing to prove."

Much like with Neera, Rist had grown to understand Garramon's mannerisms and tone. Genuine fear saturated the man's voice.

"If it is worth anything," Andelar Touran said, languidly running his finger along the rim of his wine cup, "I do not believe you will survive. The testing alone kills the vast majority of candidates. That is why so few are selected…"

"What happens when I succeed?" Rist turned his gaze to Fane Mortem.

The man gave Rist a broad smile. "You will become one of the most powerful Spark wielders to have ever existed."

CHAPTER NINETEEN

DEPTH OF WORDS

7ᵗʰ Day of the Blood Moon

Berona – Winter, Year 3081 After Doom

From the southern edge of Lake Berona, under the blended light of the Blood Moon and the morning sun, the city was at its most beautiful. Eltoar clasped his hands behind his back, his bare feet resting against the cool surface of the rock beneath him. The waves blew south-westerly with the wind, glittering in the same light as the city.

The silence was almost as beautiful as Berona itself, even more so for it was a much rarer thing. He drew a long breath, closing his eyes and listening as the air swelled in his lungs. The gentle waves lapped at the rocks, the spray splashing his feet and rising to tickle his face.

"A question of the heart, old friend?" Fane hadn't spoken since Eltoar had told him everything that had happened, both from Voranur's report of the battle in the Darkwood and of their encounter with Salara. The only piece of information he withheld was of Tivar's defection – if she was even still alive. Fane was a friend, one of very few, but Eltoar was not naive enough to think that would stop the man from taking action if he thought the Dragonguard were defecting.

Eltoar opened his eyes and grunted at Fane, who stood to his left in nothing but a loose black tunic and white trousers despite the frigid air.

"That is three of your kin lost within months of each other."

"That's not a question."

"No," Fane said. "It's not. I would know your mind. What is it thinking?"

Eltoar let out a deep sigh. He spread his fingers, the cold morning breeze slipping through the gaps and rolling over his skin. "I lost Jormun and Ilkya a long time ago. They were my kin, and I mourn them. They were among the last of my kind, and I will mourn that also. But they were not the souls I once knew."

"And Pellenor?"

"He deserved better."

"That he did. When this is all over, we will build a monument where he and Meranta fell. You have my word."

"Will this ever be over?" Eltoar turned to look at Fane, searching the man's eyes for the truth. "I mean truly?"

Fane's smile was fleeting as he clasped his hands behind his back and stepped up to a rock closer to Eltoar. "Yes." A moment of silence passed between them, the waves swashing. "I promised you much all those years ago, and I would like to think I have followed through on many of those promises. In these last two hundred years, northern Epheria has seen more unbroken peace than in the previous two thousand. The people are fed, and they want for little. If it were not for the southern rebels, that peace would extend across the continent. But I am acutely aware that there are also many promises upon which I have not followed through. But I have never, nor will I ever, stop trying to fulfil them. All great things require sacrifice. You know this more than most. One last push and we can bring this war to an end."

A shadow engulfed them both, sweeping from left to right, sapping what little heat was given by the morning sun. That same shadow spread across the lake, and a gust of wind blew Eltoar's hair to the side, his coat following suit.

"If there is any chance of bringing life back to the eggs," Fane said as Helios soared across the sky, "it lies with Efialtír."

Eltoar folded his arms, watching Helios. Fane always knew which cog to turn, which wound to prod and poke.

"I know you have never been as strong a believer as I. You didn't choose your path based on faith. But faith is all you have now. Four centuries and not one of them has hatched."

"One has."

Fane drew a long breath. "True. But have you seen signs of any others? In the Üvrian un'Aldryr or in Venira? Or in those you keep in the Sea?"

Eltoar glanced at Fane out of the corner of his eye. The eggs Eltoar kept in the Sea of Stone were not a secret, but nor had he openly spoken of them to Fane. This was Fane's way of letting Eltoar know that he knew.

"No."

"Well, that doesn't mean none will be found. Perhaps this is a new dawn. And we can only pray that it is. But it is always better to assume the worst and act accordingly. Say the word, and I will arrange two thousand attendants to be split between Üvrian un'Aldryr and Venira and your retreat in the Sea, if you so wish. I will reinstate the Dracárdare, and we will begin testing for the Calling and warming the eggs. But even still, we must not stop our course. The Uraks call Efialtír the Lifebringer for a reason. We *must* recover the Heart of Blood. It is the only way. With the power contained in that vessel, there is little we couldn't do, Eltoar."

Eltoar lurched forwards, a sudden rush of sorrow bleeding from Helios's mind to his. The thought of all those eggs, all that life, dead, brought the dragon's memories rushing to the fore. Helios unleashed a roar that ached in Eltoar's chest.

There was nothing they wouldn't do to see another egg hatch. And perhaps Fane was right. If Varyn and the other gods had stripped the life from the eggs in punishment for what Eltoar and the others had done, then perhaps Efialtír could give that life back. If that was the last thing Eltoar did before leaving this world, he would die with a smile on his lips. But the thought of the Heart put caution in his veins. That vessel was a thing of power the likes of which Eltoar had never felt. He remembered feeling it as he had stood atop the Star Tower the night Ilnaen fell. He remembered the sky as it filled with lightning and the fire as it swept across the land like the world had cracked open.

Another roar sounded overhead, and Helios dropped into a dive. The dragon spread his wings and pulled himself parallel to the lake with such force that he sent a ten-foot wave surging across the surface.

Helios dropped his head and opened his jaws into the water, his claws trailing, his tail whipping back and forth. The dragon snapped his jaws shut and opened them again and again, blood and water spilling through his teeth.

"They are preternatural creatures, are they not?" Fane stared at Helios as the rent bodies of fish fell from the dragon's open maw. "Predators with no equal in the known world, capable of incomprehensible destruction. It is no wonder Varyn sought to take their fire. If they did not need us, we would all be ash, all as helpless as fish in a pond. Bones and blood."

Fane continued to stare as the wave from Helios's earlier manoeuvre surged towards them, growing as it moved, fish and eels writhing within. Without turning his head, the man pulled on threads of Water and Air and the wave lifted, crashing against an invisible shield that surrounded Eltoar and Fane.

Fish, both alive and dead, some little more than snapped bone and torn flesh, were trapped within the twisting water, spiralling helplessly. A burst of power pulsed from Fane, and the water furled and unfurled like strips of linen in a gentle breeze, rejoining the lake seamlessly.

All the while, Fane stood with his hands clasped behind his back, watching as Helios rose into the morning sky. Not a bead of sweat adorned the man's brow. Not a single marker of lethargy touched him. Fane talked of dragons, of how they were not of this world, of how their power was unnatural. And yet there the man stood with a grasp of the Spark unlike any Eltoar had ever known. Fane was himself a dragon, one unhindered by the gods.

Helios's mind pressed against Eltoar's, and he pulled them together, the world sharpening around him, the lapping waves like claps of thunder, the water's reflection like glaring fire. Through the dragon's eyes, he saw two riders rushing from the city gates, dust trailing in their wake. The horses were Blackthorns, the riders garbed in the same shade of night as their mounts. The message must have been urgent if Taya Tambrel was sending her Blackwatch to deliver it.

When the riders skirted the lake and reached the rocks where Eltoar and Fane waited, one dismounted and dropped his plated knee to the ground.

"Emperor, I come with urgent word."

Fane's gaze lingered on Helios, his attention totally and fully captured. After leaving the man kneeling for what must have been a full minute, Fane turned and gestured for him to stand. "Speak, Captain. If it's urgent, we don't have all day."

"The elven fog, Emperor. It has started moving again. Towards Elkenrim. And a dragon has laid waste to almost half the fleet of fishing vessels off Antiquar's coast."

"The dragon," Eltoar said before Fane could speak. "Do we have a description?"

"Green scales, Draleid. Big as a house."

"Insightful," Fane said, rolling his eyes.

"It's Irulaian and Dravír."

Fane nodded, scrunching his lips in contemplation. "Captain, please thank Supreme Commander Tambrel for the swift dispatch. Inform her that I will require both her and her generals assembled within the hour."

The Blackwatch captain inclined his head and mounted his steed, then set off for the gates with his companion.

"The wait is over," Fane said a few moments after the two riders were in the distance. He pursed his lips.

"Vandrien is no fool. If she moves before the Blood Moon has fallen, there is a reason for it."

"I agree."

"Our response?"

"We play the game. She has moved first, which means her position is the weaker. Irulaian and Dravír, what say you?"

"They are bait. They burn the fishing fleet to draw our dragons away from Elkenrim."

"Hmmm. And how would you respond?"

"I would send Lyina. Bait or not, we can't allow them to burn our ships unchecked. Without the fish from Antiquar, we'll have more hungry mouths than a tree has leaves."

"Agreed. You would not go yourself?"

"Lyina is the better choice. I would rather be at Elkenrim, and I don't entirely trust her emotions around the elves at the moment. She and Karakes are more than a match for Irulaian and Dravír."

"See that it is done. I will have reinforcements sent from Merchant's Reach and Catagan."

As Eltoar made to leave, Fane grabbed him by the wrist and stared into his eyes. "Where is your heart on this, Eltoar?"

Eltoar didn't need to ask what the man meant. "I will do what needs to be done, as I always have and I always will." He hesitated for a moment, then grasped Fane's shoulder and pulled him close. "Viel akara. I denír viël ar altinua."

We are brothers. In this life and always.

Fane let go of Eltoar's forearm and grabbed the back of his skull, pressing their foreheads together. "Uthikar, yíar'ydil, vir væra faelrin denír valirdín, nakil det eram. Silvrím il fahír er norîl, il nära er vantihír. Vi matív uil sarvinis."

Together, old friend, we will change this world, make it better. Even though the night is dark, the light is waiting. We must only persevere.

CHAPTER TWENTY

THROUGH BLOOD AND SACRIFICE

9th Day of the Blood Moon

West of Achyron's Keep – Winter, Year 3081 After Doom

Dayne and Mera walked through the camp in silence, Dinekes and Lavarn – one of Mera's Wyndarii – walking close behind. They had returned from the Lost Hills no longer than an hour before a messenger had arrived from Alina.

"Dayne…" Mera brushed her hand against Dayne's, but he pulled his fingers away. They'd not spoken about the massacre in the valley, but he knew she wanted to.

"Leave it be, Mera. It needed to be done." Dayne stared off into the camp, focusing on nothing in particular.

"It did."

Dayne raised an eyebrow, turning his head to find Mera looking into his eyes.

"It needed to be done," Mera repeated. "They had already betrayed us and would do so again if given the chance. We can't win a war with enemies outside our gates and within. I don't judge you for what you did, but I want to make sure you don't either."

Dayne shook his head, turning his gaze to where a flickering torch cast dancing shadows across a tent canopy. "I'm not the man you remember, Mera. I've done things… spilled more blood than any man has a right to. I'm cold –

numb – and I hate it. But it's who I am now. At least now every life I take brings Valtara closer to freedom. That is something."

Mera once again brushed her hand against Dayne's, wrapping her fingers in his. "I've known many men and women with an apathy towards death. Worse, I've known those who revelled in it, took pride in the killing. Loren Koraklon threw celebrations while your mother and father hung in the plaza. He'd come down day after day and watch the bodies swing with a smile on his face. Do you take that kind of pride in it, Dayne? Do you seek out the next heart to stop, just to feel that rush in your veins?"

Mera stared at Dayne with an unsettling intensity, her eyes gleaming in the light of the torches.

"In the heat of battle, with your blood hot, there's a thrill that most do not admit to. It can be intoxicating…" Mera kept her gaze locked on Dayne's. A lump caught in his throat, words unable to escape. "When the blood stops flowing and the spears are put away, that thrill fades. It is in that moment a soul can be judged, not before. Do you feel guilt? Remorse? Or do you crave that heat in your blood? Do you hunger for that thrill?"

"Of course I don't!" Two soldiers in the armoured skirts of Herak stared at Dayne as he raised his voice. "Of course I don't," he said again, quieter. "I hate it. I hate that I feel it. I hate the power it has over me."

"You're not numb, Dayne. I see the weight of every life on your shoulders. I feel the pain in your heart. Hold on to that pain. I'll help you carry it if you help me carry mine."

"Always."

Mera smiled, then squeezed Dayne's hand once more before releasing it.

They followed the path through the camp, past an endless sea of tents dyed in the colours of the various Houses. The burnt orange of House Ateres, the deep red of House Herak, the green and gold of House Deringal, the black of House Vakira, and a scattering of those from Houses Koraklon and Thebal who had chosen to abandon their colours after The Night of Broken Oaths, which is what the warriors had taken to calling the night Miron Thebal and the others had slaughtered so many.

Alongside the Major Houses, Dayne spotted tents bearing the colours and sigils of hundreds of the Minor Houses. No matter how this all ended, bringing this many Valtarans together behind a single cause was a marker for the annals. Even before the fall of The Order it had not been done.

The sound of clacking wood rang in the air as they came to two sets of banners on either side of the path – one a brilliant white emblazoned with the wyvern of House Ateres in orange, the other a deep orange, bearing two black wyverns coiled around a white spear.

The guards who stood by the banners stepped back, the wooden shafts of their valynas clicking against their bronze cuirasses as they greeted Dayne and the others, allowing them to pass.

"Andurios," one of the guards said, bowing her head. She was young, twenty summers perhaps.

Dayne searched his memory. "Iola of House Kallisti, daughter of Iphis and Maruk. I hope your watch has been short and uneventful."

Iola straightened, her eyes widening. "… ehm… yes, Andurios. You honour me."

"You earned that honour when you stood by my House. And you earn it again every day when you place that armour on your shoulders. By blade and by blood, Ordite."

Iola nodded sharply, her knuckles whitening around the shaft of her valyna at Dayne's use of the old Valtaran word for warrior. The title of Ordite could not be bought or given. It was earned through acts of valour and strength.

Dayne gestured to Dinekes. "My forces fought hard in the Lost Hills and have marched double for days to return to our queen. Would you be so kind as to escort my captain to the stewards so that food and wine can be arranged?"

"At once, Andurios." Iola spoke to the other guards, then led Dinekes back the way they had come as Dayne, Mera, and Lavarn pressed onwards.

"You have a way with them," Mera whispered.

"With who?"

"People. No matter what House they hail from, they respect you, Dayne."

"I do not have *a way* with anything."

"Yes, you do."

"People are simple, Mera," Dayne said as he nodded to two passing guards. "Show them they matter to you, and you will matter to them. Show them you will bleed for them, and they will bleed for you."

"Yes," Mera said, letting a long puff of air out her nose. "Simple."

Ahead, the path widened to an area of loose dirt dotted with large rocks that rose a few feet over Dayne's head, tents scattered around the perimeter.

At the centre of the opening, in a rough-marked circle, Alina sparred with two of her newly formed Royal Guard: Alcon of House Arnen – Tyr Arnen's son – and Glaukos of House Nerok. Glaukos was taller than Dayne and broader by a distance, while Alcon was leaner and just a little shorter. They both bore full markings of the spear and blade and moved like kats.

Dayne had hand-picked both men, as he had her entire guard.

After The Night of Broken Oaths, Alina – at Dayne's insistence – had allowed the formation of a ten-strong Royal Guard. It was a large enough number to keep her safe and a small enough number to ensure their loyalty. She had given Dayne the task of selecting each member.

As he looked around the makeshift sparring pit, he could see the other seven members standing at attention, fully armoured with valynas and ordos in hand, swords at their hips. On the far side of the pit, the new commander of the guard, Olivian Arnon, nodded to Dayne, her gaze leaving Alina only momentarily.

Mera inclined her head towards where her wing-sisters – Amari and Lukira – leaned against one of the large rocks, watching Alina spar. Lukira pursed her lips as Alina whirled beneath an arcing swing of Glaukos's staff, then spun sideways over a sweeping strike from Alcon.

Dayne could do nothing to hide the smile that crept across his face as his sister danced between the two warriors. A blue bruise marked her left eye, and fresh blood trickled from her lip and from a thin gash on her forearm, but both men bore wounds of their own.

"How long have they been at it?" he asked when Amari nodded to them in greeting.

"Hours now." Lukira gave Dayne no more than a glance, her head weaving and bobbing with Alina's movements.

"She broke only to send for you." Amari folded her arms and leaned back against the rock, giving Dayne her attention, her lips curled in that ever present half-smile. "Where is your sharp-tongued friend?"

"Belina? Last I saw she was getting some Vakirans drunk and stealing their coin at dice."

"Go to her," Lukira said to Amari, a wry smile on her lips as she pulled her gaze from the sparring.

Amari glared at her wing-sister, a touch of rose on her cheeks. She pulled herself forwards from the rock and turned towards the pit. "We received word from High Commander Joros yesterday."

Dayne raised a curious eyebrow. They'd spent days marching after the ambush at the Lost Hills and had heard nothing in that time.

"Myrefall is ours once more. As soon as Joros waved our banners, the citizens turned on the small garrison and opened the gates in Queen Alina's name."

Dayne drew a lungful of air, then tilted his head back and watched his breath rise, a knot untwisting in his chest. "Thank the gods." He narrowed his gaze at Amari. Her face was devoid of any sense of victory. "What is it?"

"A Hand assassin waited in Myrefall's keep. She killed both of Joros's sons, his wife, and his two daughters, along with a slew of his captains while they all slept. The High Commander was still drunk from the celebrations and stumbled upon the woman standing over his daughter's body."

"... Joros?"

"Alive. He took her head from her shoulders and mounted it on a valyna in the city's plaza. Then he executed every member of the Thebalan garrison to the last, setting their heads alongside the first."

Dayne nodded, looking to Mera, then over at Alina in the sparring pit. His family. "I'd have done the same."

"I'd have done worse," Lukira said without turning her head.

Mera rested her hand on the small of Dayne's back, the warmth of her skin seeping through his thin linen shirt.

He folded his arms and watched the sparring, unable to force more words from his lips. Joros's world had just been ripped from under him. The man had been loyal to Dayne's family for decades, and now it had cost him everything. That was a pattern that seemed to repeat itself across all those loyal to House Ateres. A pattern he would stop.

Alina glanced in Dayne's direction, giving him an almost imperceptible nod as she sidestepped a thrust of Glaukos's staff, then cracked him on the inside of his knee with her own. She twisted, swinging her staff upwards into Alcon's chin, then shifted her weight and allowed the two men to crash into each other.

As Glaukos recovered, Alina raked her staff along the ground and lifted loose dirt into his eyes. The big man fell, Alina's staff resting against the back of his head before his knees hit the dirt.

She tapped his skull to let him know he was dead, then swung her staff backwards ferociously, bringing it to a sharp halt as Alcon's staff pressed into her stomach.

She stood there like that for a moment, heaving breaths, sweat rolling down her forehead, her sodden tunic clinging to her body. Then she laughed.

Alina spat a glob of blood and saliva into the dirt, then grasped Alcon's forearm and inclined her head in acknowledgment of his win before they both moved to check on Glaukos.

"They spar a little heavy," Dayne remarked as he watched Alina and Alcon brush the dirt from Glaukos's eyes. All three of them were bloodied and bruised.

"She needs to be ready if the empire comes for her again," Lukira said. "She needs to train like her life depends on it. So do they."

"Hmm." Dayne nodded slowly as Alina and her guards approached.

Alina handed her staff to Alcon, whose arm was wrapped around Glaukos's back, then embraced Dayne.

"Alina, I…" Dayne stared down at his sister, allowing his words to fade. She'd not shown him open affection like that since she'd first laid eyes on him upon his return to Skyfell. And she'd smacked him across the face not long after that. This display caught him off guard, and yet over the years, he'd done little but dream of moments like this, so he reached his arms around her back and hugged her in close.

After a few moments, she pulled away and stared into Dayne's eyes. It took him only half a second to see that what had happened to Joros had shaken her.

"It's good to see you in the flesh." Alina touched her fingers against Dayne's cheek, her lips curling in a smile. She nodded, then released him. "You succeeded then?"

Dayne had sent some of Mera's Wyndarii ahead to carry news of the victory at the Lost Hills – if it could be called that. "We did. Seven thousand fewer spears pointed at us from within Achyron's Keep. No prisoners. Almost two thousand horses, along with a string of wagons and plenty of weapons and armour to add to our stocks."

Alina nodded. She had known Dayne's plan to leave no survivors. She had agreed to it, begrudgingly. That was something he admired in her. It was the reason why Alina would make a fine queen: even those who turned their backs on her, she did not turn hers on them. But she also knew when to make the hard choices, or at least she was learning.

It was the empire that had wrought chaos, darkness, and loss in Valtara, but it was not blackened imperial bones that sizzled and smoked in the Lost Hills. Seven thousand Valtarans lay dead. Seven thousand of Dayne's own people. In another life, they might have been fighting at his side instead of dying on his spear.

Alina gave Dayne an awkward smile, gesturing towards the sparring ring. "First to three?"

Dayne snorted, pushing the sombre thoughts to the back of his mind. "I think not."

"Five coppers she puts him on his arse inside a minute," Lukira said.

"I'll take that." Mera shrugged at Dayne's glare.

"I'm not sparring you."

"And why not?"

"Because I'd prefer to keep my dignity intact."

"Good answer."

"I'm assuming you didn't send for me just to check I was alive with your own eyes?"

"No." Alina's jaw clenched, and she swallowed. She gestured towards a low rock set into the ground just past the sparring ring. "Sit with me?"

Dayne looked to Mera. She inclined her head towards Alina, who was already walking towards the rock. Whatever Alina was about to say, Dayne was absolutely sure Mera already knew what it was.

Alina grimaced as she dropped herself into the dirt beside the rock, leaning back against it. "Glaukos caught me hard in the leg. That's going to hurt for a few days."

"You moved well out there." Dayne sat beside his sister, pulling his legs in and resting his arms atop his knees.

"Not well enough. I need to be quicker." Alina rubbed the bruise beside her eye. As she leaned forwards, Dayne caught a glimpse of the sunburst tattoo on the back of her neck – the mark of a mother. The tattoo brought his mind to Baren and to the son that had been taken from Alina. His nephew. Another he had not been there to protect.

Alina rested her palms on her knees and looked up towards the crimson-hued sky, the Blood Moon hanging behind a dark stormhead in the distance. "I'm sorry, Dayne." She turned her gaze to him. "I should have said it sooner, but I'm sorry."

"Alina, you don't have to—"

"I want to." She ran her tongue across her lips, then pulled her legs to her chest, mimicking Dayne's posture. "Ever since you returned, I've treated you like—"

"Shit."

Alina snorted, a smile spreading from ear to ear. She hung her head between her knees. "Yes. Like shit." A few seconds passed, and the mirth drained. "I had been so angry at you for so long… Angry at you for dying and leaving me and Baren to rot here, leaving me to live in a world without you. I know it wasn't your fault, but it was easier to be angry with you. And then when you came back, all I could think was why hadn't you come back sooner?" Alina stared off at the sky. "Why had it taken Aeson's letter – the man who left our parents to die – for you to finally come home? Did we mean *that* little to you?"

Dayne started to speak but thought better of it.

Alina lifted her head, meeting his gaze. "I fought every day of my life after our parents died. I lost my love, my child, my family. Baren treated me like a thing to be traded. Had it not been for Rynvar hatching and for the rebellion… I don't know. Every morning I woke plotting vengeance, and every night I went to sleep with blood on my hands. Everyone looked at me as though I was forever the little girl who sobbed in the plaza while her parents' bodies swung. I *earned* their loyalty, their respect. I earned it in blood and sacrifice. It took years. And then you come back, and I saw everything I'd built slip away in my mind. The eldest child of Arkin and Ilya Ateres, returned from the dead. By birthright, House Ateres is yours. You don't have to earn it, or kill for it, or sacrifice for it. It is simply… yours."

"Alina, I would never…"

Alina's glare caused Dayne to cut himself short. "It's taken me this long to say all this. Are you going to let me finish?"

Dayne smiled and flicked his hand upwards for Alina to continue.

"You could have taken it with ease. Turik would have handed it to you on a silver platter. Gods' know there were enough who would have supported your claim, especially after the way you fought at Lostwren and Myrefall. You weren't just a returned son of House Ateres, you were a hero – their champion. You could have taken it all… but you didn't. When you killed Turik, my anger was born of you keeping me in the dark, nothing more. I've spent years with everyone lying to me, everyone trying to play me for a fool, and then you didn't trust me enough to tell me what you were planning."

"I trust you with my life."

"I know…" Alina nodded absently. "Over the years, I've learned to think the worst of people. That way none of them can surprise me. It's something that's kept me alive. So when you came back, talking of Aeson and rebellion, I just…" She took a breath, settling herself. "I didn't know what to do. For the first time in a long time, I felt like that little girl again: helpless and scared. All you have done is stand by my side, and I'm sorry for not standing by yours. I'm sorry, Dayne. And I promise to be better."

"Apology accepted."

"That's all you're going to say?"

"Well, a wise woman once told me 'Actions. Not words.'"

She sniffled, but no tears fell as a soft smile brightened her face. "I deserved that."

"You did." Dayne reached over and rested his hand atop his sister's, squeezing for just a moment. "What brought all this on? Mera made you say it, didn't she?"

Alina pulled her hand away from Dayne's, then stood, her gaze passing over the flickering torches of the camp.

Dayne stood with her. "Alina?"

"With Myrefall back under our control, all that's left is Achyron's Keep. At last count, Loren's forces were fifty thousand strong. We have just over half that number, and our mages are Alamants – nothing compared to the imperials. I'd wait them out, but they're better stocked than we are. They hold the Hot Gates and bring supplies through from Varsund. With so many of our farms and stores damaged in the fighting, they can keep their forces fed a lot longer than we can. If we want a free Valtara, then we have to hit them with everything we have. We must burn out the Lorian roots and raze Achyron's Keep to the ground. I didn't want all this hanging over us. I didn't want to die without…"

"Alina… I know what you're going to say, but we don't have to do this alone. Just reach out to Aeson. Please, I beg of you. Just talk to him. With him by our side, we can take the keep. We can free our home."

"I already have. I sent word to Aeson while you were marching from the Lost Hills. You were right. You've always been right. I let my pride and my anger blind me. But no more. After Marlin's death… I… He was like a father to me all these years. He begged me to listen to you, and I shut him out. And if I learn nothing from his death, then what am I? I won't do that again. I won't. But Dayne, if Aeson abandons us like he did our parents, I will let Rynvar rip him to pieces."

"He won't."

"You're always so sure… I wish I could be."

Footsteps sounded behind Dayne, and both he and Alina turned to see the towering figure of Olivian marching towards them, the Angan, Crokus, at her side. True to its word, the creature had remained with the camp since the day it had brought Aeson's message.

The Angan moved with a loping grace, its long legs matching Olivian stride for stride, its fur-covered chest and arms dense with muscle. It was the face that unsettled Dayne: both human and wolf, its teeth sharp, its nose flat and black, its eyes the colour of molten gold.

"My queen." Olivian bowed at the waist, her right hand gripping the shaft of her valyna, her left hand resting on the pommel of the short sword at her hip. "Crokus of the Fenryr Angan."

"Thank you, Olivian. You may leave us."

The woman's eyes widened, and she looked as though she were going to object, but instead she bowed more deeply. "As you wish, my queen."

"Well met, Crokus." Alina inclined her head, showing the Angan far more respect than she had the first time they'd spoken. "Aeson has sent an answer?"

Crokus returned Alina's gesture, resting a clawed hand on its chest as it did. "Blessings of Fenryr upon you, Queen Alina of House Ateres. Aeson Virandr wishes you to know that he will honour the vow he swore to your family. He will fight with you, and he will not come alone."

The hairs on Dayne's arms stood on end.

"This is good news, Crokus. How soon will he be here?"

"Before the next moon. With the red moon in the sky, the Uraks ravage the lands from here to the eastern shores. The journey will not be an easy one."

Alina visibly tensed. She tucked her thumb into her fist, her knuckles going pale. She nodded. "Thank you. Will you deliver one more message for me?"

"Of course, Queen Alina."

"Will you tell Aeson that if he is not here by the next moon, he should not come at all. I can only feed my army for so long before my options are taken from me."

"It will be done." The creature's golden eyes shimmered in the crimson moonlight as it once more inclined its head and strode back towards the camp.

"How long can we wait?" The sense of relief that had come over Dayne was as fleeting as most of the happiness he'd experienced through his life. In its place, a coiling knot tightened. If Alina could not keep her army fed, it would soon scatter to the wind. "Can we last until the next moon?"

"I don't know." Alina clasped her hands behind her back. "Joros will have a better answer when he returns." She let out a long breath, then turned to Dayne with a fire in her eyes, her lips curled with a touch of sadness. "I will not let everything we have built crumble on empty stomachs, Dayne. I will find a way to feed our forces until the next moon, but if Aeson doesn't hold true, we *will* raze Achyron's Keep to the ground ourselves. There will be no siege. We will fill the sky with wyverns, we will blot out the sun, we will…" Alina heaved in breaths, her jaw clenching. "This ends by the next moon, no matter what."

Dayne clasped Alina's shoulders. "If Aeson doesn't hold true, I will be the first over the walls. I've not been able to choose much in my life, but if I'm to choose how I die, it will be fighting for my people. No matter the path, I will follow… my queen. But I do not believe we should simply sit around and wait for Aeson to come to our rescue. Loren and the imperials have many camps scattered between Ironcreek, Myrefall, and Achyron's Keep. They harass our caravans, raid our villages, and disrupt our supply lines. What's more, the port of Ankar is their only access by sea and lies a hundred miles from the Keep."

"What are you suggesting?"

"I'm suggesting that while we wait to tear down those walls, we teach them to fear us. Teach them to piss themselves at the whispers of our names, make them think that every one of our spears is worth twenty of theirs. Steel kills men, sister, but fear wins battles."

DAYNE RAN HIS HANDS THROUGH his hair as he stepped into his tent, letting out a heavy sigh. Two oil lamps, one on a small table, the other on the ground beside his cot, flickered shadows across the canopy.

He narrowed his eyes at the sight of a wax-sealed letter sitting by the lantern on the table.

"You knew what she was going to say." Dayne glanced back at Mera, who stepped into the tent behind him, then made his way over to the table. The letter was sealed in black wax and bore no sigil. It had not been there when he'd left the tent to see Alina.

"Of course I did." Mera dropped herself onto the cot, leaning back on her elbows and blowing out a sigh. Gods, she was gorgeous. He allowed himself to drink her in before looking back to the letter.

"You could have warned me," he said as he tapped on the seal before picking the letter up. It could have been sent by any number of people, but the marks on the parchment let him know the original seal had been peeled off with a hot knife and replaced. Old Girda who ran The Orange Tree inn was notorious for doing such.

"I told you I'm done being in the middle of you two. Besides, it was Alina's apology to give." In Dayne's periphery, Mera leaned forwards, sitting upright on the cot. "What is that?"

"A letter," Dayne said, cracking open the black seal.

"Helpful." Sarcasm oozed from Mera's voice. The iron frame of the cot creaked as she rose and moved to his side, looking over his shoulder. "From who?"

"Baren."

Mera rested her hand on Dayne's shoulder. He'd told her about the letter he'd found at the farmhouse in Myrefall, told her everything.

"Are you going to read it or just admire the paper?"

Dayne let out a short sigh, nodding to himself.

Dayne,

I'm hoping Girda got this to you, wherever you are. Girda, if you're reading this, stop reading this.

I know I said I'd send the reports to Girda in case anything happened, but I asked her to get this one into your hands as soon as she could. I found him, Dayne. I found Alina's boy. He's in Berona.

I'm leaving Catagan by nightfall. With any luck I'll reach the city by the time you get this. The North is chaos. Elves have swarmed from Lynalion. I'm hearing they wiped out everything along the Lightning Coast. There are trails of refugees stretching back for miles. Between the elves and the Uraks, the empire is on the brink of crumbling. You were right. This is the time. This is the chance for our people to be free.

I'll send word when I get to Berona.

I know Alina won't forgive me, but I'm going to bring him home, Dayne.

I love you, brother. I'm just sorry it took me so long to say it.

Baren

Dayne swallowed hard, placing the letter on the tabletop. He traced his fingers over the last line. "Please come home safe."

"He'll be all right." Mera pressed her fingers into the back of Dayne's neck. "He knows how to look after himself."

Dayne nodded. "But he's desperate, and desperate men make stupid decisions."

"Men make stupid decisions in general."

Dayne placed a kiss on her forehead. "So many years lost. So many years…"

"Look forward, Dayne, not back."

A rustling sounded at the tent's entrance and one of Dayne's Andurii stepped inside, a man by the name of Lycas of House Vohar.

Dayne raised an eyebrow.

"There's a man here, Andurios. Said you'd know him. Said you'd want to see him."

"What's his name?"

"Savrin Vander, my lord."

Dayne took a step closer to Lycas, his pulse quickening. He must have heard the man wrong. "Savrin Vander? That's the name he spoke? You're sure?"

"Yes, Andurios. Quite sure."

Dayne pressed the fingers of his right hand into his cheeks. "That cannot be. You are *absolutely certain* that was the name he gave you?"

Lycas nodded.

"Send him in." The hairs on Dayne's arms pricked, his pulse quickening.

The Andurii bowed at the waist and left.

Dayne looked to Mera, who stared back without a word. Her eyes said what Dayne was thinking: surely it couldn't be. Marlin had said none of his father's Andurii had survived. Or had he? Dayne couldn't quite remember the words Marlin had used. Alina had said Savrin had helped Marlin cut down Ilya and Arkin's bodies. So the man had at least survived until that point. But Dayne had heard nothing of him since retuning.

More shuffling sounded outside the tent, followed by footsteps.

A lump formed in Dayne's throat, each second seeming to stretch until Lycas returned with Ileeri at his side and another man between them. Dayne's breath caught in his lungs.

Dayne's captain stepped forwards. "Savrin Vander, Andurios."

The man stared down at the dirt, walking as though he were a child awaiting punishment. Full markings of spearmaster and blademaster adorned his forearms, various other inkings swirling about his body.

He was lean and all muscle, his face freshly shaved. His hair had greyed since last Dayne had set eyes upon him, but then the man had seen thirty summers, now more than forty. The skin on his face was leathered beyond what the years should have done, his fingertips cracked and bleeding, his lips dry. But despite the marks of time's passage, when the man lifted his head and Dayne looked into his dark, sunken eyes, Dayne knew him.

Savrin Vander. The Champion of House Ateres. The greatest blademaster to have graced Valtara in five centuries. The Golden Spear of the Andurii. He looked tired, worn, and weary, but very much alive.

A long moment passed where the two men stared at each other in silence, until Dayne finally spoke. "I thought you were dead."

"I was." Savrin's voice was harsh and gravelly, more so than Dayne remembered. "The day your father died, I died with him. Or at least, I should have."

The man drew in slow breaths, letting them out with a rasp, his gaze constantly flitting between Dayne and the dirt. Dayne knew guilt when he saw it, knew its venomous touch.

"Where have you been? Why did you not come sooner?"

Savrin shrugged like a man tired of making excuses. "I spent nearly a decade at the bottom of a bottle. Not proud of it."

"And now?"

"Marlin pulled me from a puddle of my own piss not too long ago. Told me you were alive, told me Arkin's son had returned and he needed me, but that I had no place by your side until I pulled myself together."

"Have you?"

Savrin pursed his lips. "I'm trying. I've not touched a drop in weeks."

Dayne stared back at Savrin. He had spent countless hours as a child watching in awe whenever Savrin sparred, watching in reverence. The man moved like someone who could see the future. He'd been a legend, a living, breathing bard's tale.

He looked a shadow of that legend now.

"Speak plainly. Why are you here?"

"To the point." A smile graced Savrin's face, then yielded to a deep sadness. "Just like your father."

The man dropped to a knee before Dayne, placing a closed fist against his chest. He kept his head bowed, his eyes down. "Your father was the closest thing I had to a brother, and I failed him. He died, and I wasn't there to die with him. Your sister is the closest thing I had to a niece, and I failed her too. I stood by as her child was ripped from her breast. Your brother? I saw what he was becoming, and I did nothing. I wallowed and looked inwards. This House is the only home I've ever known, and I let it burn. I ask only that you grant me the honour of wearing the Andurii crest once more. An honour I don't deserve. I ask that you let me stand at the front of every charge, that you let me fight where the battle is bloodiest, and that you give me the chance to do right by your father's name. Let me protect his son in this war."

Dayne looked down at the man who knelt before him. "You're old."

"Put a spear in my hand. I'll show you how old I am."

"You're tired."

"I'll rest when I'm dead."

Dayne reached down his hand, palm open.

Savrin looked up at Dayne, then grabbed Dayne's forearm and lifted himself to his feet.

"By the next moon, we march on Achyron's Keep. We will climb tooth and nail over that wall if we have to."

"I'll be the first over."

"Loren's forces number over fifty thousand, ours barely thirty."

"The odds are in our favour then." The words were in jest, but the tone in Savrin's voice quickly sobered. "We all live, and we all die. It is how we do both that matters. I'm ashamed of the last thirteen years. I'd like a death to be proud of."

"I can't let you wear the Andurii crest, Savrin." In that moment, Dayne thought he saw Savrin's heart break. "Your time as an Andurii is over. I have my captains now and—"

"I do not ask to be a captain, my lord—"

"I have my captains now," Dayne continued, cutting Savrin short, "but Alina's Royal Guard could use one more spear. I would ask not that you protect my father's son, but his daughter. Would you pledge your life to Alina's? Give every drop of blood in your veins to protect your queen? Would you keep my sister safe, Savrin? Give your blood for hers? Your life?"

Savrin once again dropped to a knee, pressing his hand to his chest and bowing his head. "It would be the greatest honour of my life. To protect this House, to protect Valtara, that is all I ask. I, Savrin Vander, pledge all that I am to Queen Alina Ateres. My life, my blood, my honour. Death before failure, I swear it."

"Rise."

Savrin stood slowly, his eyes wet, his breaths trembling.

Above all else, Dayne needed people he could trust at Alina's back. And there had been none who bore the wyvern of House Ateres with as much pride as Savrin Vander. Whatever his failings, the man was as loyal as they came. He had taken a spear three times over for Dayne's father. He had dedicated his life to the Andurii. And above all else, Dayne considered himself a good judge of a man's character and he could see by the look in Savrin's eyes that the man would give anything and everything to protect Alina, give anything to right his wrongs. Dayne knew that pain, that ravaging guilt. "Savrin Vander, I hereby name you to the Royal Guard to Queen Alina Ateres."

Savrin let out a gasp of relief. "By The Warrior and The Sailor."

"By blade and by blood."

CHAPTER TWENTY-ONE

THE WEIGHT OF IT ALL

9th Day of the Blood Moon

Temple of Achyron – Winter, Year 3081 After Doom

It seemed to Kallinvar that he spent every waking moment standing at the edge of the war table, staring down at that stone map. He blinked, his eyes raw and tired.

Hundreds of pulses of red light – convergences of the Taint – covered the continent, Efialtír's bloody hand tearing into the world. More than the knights could ever hold back. But the blanket of red that had previously consumed the Burnt Lands had shattered and splintered into small flecks, dotted throughout the desert waste. When Tarron had charged the tear in the veil, he truly had closed it and broken the tether between the worlds.

If you had done nothing else, brother, that act alone was worthy of a bard's tale. Kallinvar drew a long breath. *Wherever you are, I will find you. I swear it.*

Small green dots were scattered through the red – the Knights spread across the continent. And around many of these dots were tiny pulsing sparks of white: the beating hearts of potential Sigil Bearers. With the entire continent at war, new hearts called out every hour, thumping in Kallinvar's mind. Some lasted hours, others minutes, and many no more than seconds. It never ended. Even then, the thumping of a hundred hearts in his mind drowned out the chattering voices in the chamber about him. As one faded and Kallinvar felt the death of a weeping soul, two more burst into life, followed by four dying and one more emerging. It was a relentless cycle, one that left most of his nights sleepless.

He had searched through Verathin's journal entries earlier that morning and found that his old friend's experience with the new Sigil Bearers had been dramatically different to his own. The journal sat open to Kallinvar's right, resting over the stone depiction of the Stormwood. He'd marked the page with a silver ribbon.

9th moon – Year 2943 After Doom

I have not felt the beating of a new heart in over forty years. Not since Sister Vimia. There are twenty-four Sigils left. Twenty-four Sigils until the knighthood is once more at full strength.

Two hundred and sixty-one summers have come and gone since that night, and still it haunts my dreams. When I think back, I can feel the moment that each one of my brothers and sisters died. I can hear their last words, feel the fear in their hearts.

In one night, eighty-three of their souls were ripped from the world. That's all it took. Just one night. And now, almost three centuries later, we still have not recovered. Are there so few worthy of the Sigil? Is there any purpose to it all? Am I saving these souls, training them, all just to be slaughtered at the rise of the next moon? Is that the cycle we have fallen into now that we have failed? Are we destined to be the wardens of the breaking of time? Has the end already been sealed?

I look back, and I see the entries of the Grandmasters before me. None bear these worries, or at least none dare to bring them into inked existence. Perhaps I am simply the most honest, or the weakest. Not that it matters. I will do my duty either way. Achyron granted me this Sigil so that I may stand against the coming Shadow, not yield to it.

The duty of the strong is to protect the weak. Pain is the path to strength. Though, I have felt much pain and feel no stronger for it. The others look to me as though I am something more. Even Kallinvar. He is twice the man I am, and he does not see it. The truth is that my knights died because I was not strong enough to protect them. Not strong enough in body, nor in mind, nor in heart. I failed them thrice over.

We are flawed, all of us, but I suppose it is not the existence of flaws that destroys us but our willingness to bow to them.

Kallinvar tapped his middle finger against the paper, clenching his jaw. Reading Verathin's journals was like once more sitting with his old friend. Every word left his heart bleeding to the point that he often ignored them, preferring to read those of Telemanus, Uvrilin, and the other Grandmasters. Though none had ever served as long as Verathin. Most grew weary after a century or so and willingly passed on.

Kallinvar read back again.

And now, almost three centuries later, we still have not recovered. Are there so few worthy of the Sigil?

Why did he feel so many heartbeats now when Verathin had felt so few?

In that moment, he felt another heartbeat falter and die. Another soul lost. Another potential knight stricken from the world. Within a span of seconds, three more sounded in the back of his mind.

He wanted desperately to silence them, to give his mind even just a few minutes' respite, but all he could do was clench his hands into fists and draw slow, calming breaths.

These are dying heartbeats of worthy souls. The least I can do is listen to them as they fade.

Valerian, Darmerian, Armites, Airdaine, and Olyria were all currently granting Sigils to potential bearers. Five granted the gift of Achyron's strength while a hundred others faded into Heraya's embrace. At the very least, of the Sigils granted since Brother Kevan had joined them, none had cost the life of a knight. Their number stood at eighty-six now. Had he more knights to grant Sigils, he would do so. But even if they had their full hundred, there would not be enough knights to do what needed to be done.

The Bloodspawn poured from every shadow, slithered from every crack and crevice in the world, and set fire to Epheria. Every village from Copperstille to Holm was gone. Nothing but ash, broken wood, and shattered bones remained. The same could be said of every settlement along the foothills of Lodhar and Kolmir. And with each passing day, the Bloodspawns' attacks probed further and further from their holds.

There were only so many places he could send his knights at one time, only so thin he could spread them before they were overwhelmed. And amidst it all, they needed to find the Heart of Blood.

"What am I meant to do?" he whispered, looking down at the stone map. With every decision he made, thousands died regardless. The entire knighthood had stormed a large convergence north of Aonar not one day past. They'd emerged from the Rift into some form of Bloodspawn temple. The Heart had not been there, but hundreds of Bloodspawn had been, Bloodmarked and two shamans amongst them.

The knights had killed every last one of the creatures but lost five of their own. And while that battle had raged, more villages and towns had burned and more heartbeats had died in Kallinvar's mind.

He had tried. He had done what no Grandmaster had done before: he had called out to all those across the continent, to all the new factions across the land, to Aeson and his new Draleid, to the elves… and for what? They all preferred to war amongst each other, to scrape and grab for every shred of power and land dropped amidst the chaos.

Aeson was so consumed with his rebellion that he couldn't see how pointless it would all be if Efialtír crossed. What did freedom matter if it would be taken back in a heartbeat?

He had called out and nobody had answered. And with that he had come to the grimmest of realisations: the others would not fight until it was too late. They would not turn their gazes from crowns and vengeance until Efialtír stood before them and forced them to do so with his presence. And then, there would be nothing to be done except stand and watch the world burn.

"That is why you are here, my child." Achyron's voice sent a shiver through Kallinvar.

"And what do you want me to do?" he whispered in reply to the god, his right hand clenching into a fist. "You have sent me searching for a blade of grass in a field, a drop of rain in a storm. How am I meant to find this Heart before Fane or the Bloodspawn? With not even a hundred knights. And even then, how?" The rage built within him, his closed fist tapping on the stone. "We are stretched thin as ice. With every day that passes, we let countless die no matter what we do. And with every knight I send in search of the Heart, we have one fewer to hold back the tide. We cannot protect them all. We simply cannot."

Kallinvar's heart thumped like a galloping horse, his skin itched, and a pressure built within him as though he were about to shatter and break. A hundred heartbeats thumped in his head, growing louder and louder, each beating to a different rhythm. He scraped his nails against the stone table, the crimson light of the convergences growing brighter.

"I can't save them…" His breaths grew ragged. "I can't save them."

"Breathe." Ruon's voice whispered gently in Kallinvar's ear, a hand resting on his arm. He had not heard her approach. "Slow and steady."

Kallinvar closed his eyes for a moment and reached his left hand up, resting it atop Ruon's. He squeezed.

Ruon drew a long breath in through her nose, then released it slowly, continuing to do so until Kallinvar followed suit.

"You cannot," Achyron's voice whispered, Kallinvar's heart quickening once more. *"But you were never meant to."*

"You need to rest." Ruon pulled her hand from Kallinvar's, then moved around him, grabbing him by the shoulders.

He opened his eyes to stare into her pools of emerald green. Her emotions drifted from her Sigil to Kallinvar's: worry and concern, so deep and strong it almost overwhelmed him.

He pulled away, instantly cutting the cord that connected her heart to his mind, the concern and worry vanishing. He despised being able to feel the emotions that ran through her. It was a violation.

Even though he could no longer feel the working of Ruon's heart, Kallinvar could clearly see the hurt in her eyes.

"I'm sorry." He cupped her cheek, then became astutely aware of the presence of the Watchers who occupied the Heart Chamber going about their tasks and pulled his hand back. "I… My mind is not my own."

Ruon's expression softened. "It's all right. The weight of it all is too much for any one person to bear."

"You must call the knights back from the cities and towns," Achyron's voice echoed. *"Their time is wasted there. You cannot protect them all, and for every moment that you try, your chance of finding the Heart grows slimmer."*

"You would have me abandon them?" Kallinvar snapped.

"Abandon who?" Ruon looked into Kallinvar's eyes as though he were mad. "Kallinvar?"

He stared back, realising she could not hear Achyron's voice. "I…"

"I would have you do what must be done."

"The duty of the strong is to protect the weak," Kallinvar said, incredulous.

"It is." Ruon reached down to the table and once more rested her hand atop his. "Kallinvar, come. You *need* rest. It's been two days since you've slept."

"No." Kallinvar snapped his hand away from hers and shook his head, turning back to look over the war table. Watcher Adriahn came to a halt on the other side of the table, only for a brief moment, then carried on. "I'm fine, Ruon. Just leave me be."

"The duty of the strong is to protect the weak, Kallinvar. But how many of the weak will die if you fail? If we fail? How many of those you are trying to protect will be cut down by your own inability to do what you must? This is a world of ever-shifting grey. You must look past the morality of an individual moment and instead look to what this world needs of you. Every second wasted is a life lost."

"If I leave them, they will all die."

"And if you don't, the world will die."

"I can't just leave you be." Ruon grabbed the sides of Kallinvar's head and pulled him close, staring into his eyes. "Your mind is not right. You *need* to rest. Or so help me Achyron, I will put you to sleep myself."

Kallinvar grabbed Ruon's hands and tore them from his face. "Ruon. Leave me."

"Kallinvar—"

"*Grandmaster* Kallinvar."

Kallinvar snatched Verathin's journal from the table and strode from the Heart Chamber, not looking back for even an instant. His footsteps echoed in the temple's massive halls, like Hafaesir's hammer pounding against the stone, only matched by the beating of his heart.

"I can't just let them die," he whispered, throwing a sideways glance at the young porters who passed and eyed him askance.

"You can, and you will, lest everything we have done is for nothing. You will save more of them by finding the Heart."

"I can't… I just… No!"

"Grandmaster?" Brother Sangwen of The First stepped through a door to Kallinvar's right, his eyes narrowed in concern. Uncertainty and a touch of fear drifted from the man's Sigil. Kallinvar slashed at the feelings in his mind, shearing them from his thoughts.

"I'm fine, Brother Sangwen," Kallinvar said without stopping.

Sangwen called out something in response, but Kallinvar couldn't hear him over the sound of the beating hearts in his mind. The Sigil Bearers. At that very moment, he felt Olyria pressing the Sigil that had once belonged to Brother Tursen into the chest of a new bearer. The wave of emotion swept through him with such force he stumbled, catching himself against the foot of one of many enormous statues that lined the hallway.

A passing priest tried to aid him, but Kallinvar pushed the woman away and carried on, his hand twitching relentlessly at his side.

"You cannot ignore this, Kallinvar."

Kallinvar moved through the corridors of the temple, Achyron's voice booming in his mind, the heartbeats of the potential Sigil Bearers never stopping, his own heart feeling as though it were going to tear itself from his chest.

He swung open the door to Verathin's study, barely hearing it smash against the wood and slam shut. He clasped his two fists against the sides of his head and screamed. "Get out of my fucking head!"

"You cannot run from this, my child. There are no choices from here on out that will be easy. I know you can make them. I know your heart."

Kallinvar slammed his fist's down onto the stone desk and swept his hands across it, sending pens, inkwells, journals, and all manner of trinkets smashing against the stone bookcase set into the wall.

"No..." He pulled two scrolls free of their alcove, trying desperately to wipe off the ink that had splashed from the shattered inkwell. Those scrolls had been Verathin's. They were not his to destroy.

Achyron's voice continued to speak in his mind as he dropped to the ground and rested his back against the stone desk, tossing the ruined scrolls into the shifting puddle of ink on the ground. He ran his fingers through his hair and pressed the tips into his scalp.

"Why did you leave me?" he whispered, staring up at the ceiling with his hands clasped behind his head. In his mind's eye, he could see Verathin before him, that all-knowing smile on his old friend's face. "You had no right to leave... We were meant to stand side by side when the time came... meant to enter his halls together."

His memories returned to the battle at Kingspass. To charging as Verathin stood alone. To crashing into the ground when Verathin needed him. To not being strong enough. Not being quick enough. Not being good enough. And finally, to seeing the Fade plunge its black-fire blade into Verathin's heart.

Verathin had died because Kallinvar hadn't been strong enough to stand at his side.

Kallinvar pressed his fingers into the creases of his eyes, then ran them along his scalp from front to back, tears rolling down his cheeks.

His father – a man he had not seen in over seven hundred years – had taught him that men didn't cry, and they most certainly didn't weep. Men were forged by Hafaesir, they were wrought iron given life. Their duty was to be strong and fierce for the ones they loved. To be the immovable, immutable anchor. That was what his father had tried to be after Kallinvar's mother had died. And to his credit, Yor Thrace had not shed a single tear that Kallinvar had witnessed. Not one. Not a red eye or a cracked voice. And for as long as Yor had not wept, he had not spoken his dead wife's name. It was as though Kallinvar's mother had taken every shred of his father's heart with her when she'd died. Every drop of his joy and every sliver of his love.

After her death, he was exactly as he had said a man should be: iron. Cold and unyielding. Hard and silent.

The night Amendel had burned, Kallinvar had brought the man his moon's pay to ensure the family had food to eat. Yor had simply looked at him, nodded, then left for his day's work in the fields, leaving the coin purse on the table.

That was the last time Kallinvar ever saw his father, or his brothers. They all died in the fires that night while Kallinvar bled in the fields outside the walls. After taking the Sigil, he'd wept for days on end and spent every moment feeling ashamed of his tears – of his weakness. He had failed in life and then continued to do so in death.

"Even iron is tempered before it can become stronger," Verathin had said when he'd come to Kallinvar on the fifth day. *"We quench our weapons in water and our hearts in tears. Those who weep are those who wish to become stronger. This is the way of things, brother."*

Verathin had taught Kallinvar more about being a man in five days than his own father had in thirty-five years. And he didn't think a day would pass in which he'd draw breath and not miss the man who had been a friend, a teacher, a mentor, a father.

"I could use some of your wisdom now…" Kallinvar looked around at the hundreds of compartments in both the chamber's right and left walls. Each one was filled with scrolls and texts spilling out past their edges. He'd had a thought to tidy them, but he'd not been able to find the heart. Not all the scrolls and texts and notes had been written by Verathin, but most had. The others were things Verathin had collected across the years: notes, letters, poems, and texts he had considered worth reading. Perhaps if Kallinvar left all in its place, untouched, a small piece of Verathin would linger in the living world.

Kallinvar closed his eyes for a moment and pulled his knees closer to his chest. He sat there for a while, unmoving, until the door creaked open. He could feel Ruon's Sigil in the darkness.

"Grandmaster?" The title left Ruon's lips with the appropriate amount of venom. He should not have snapped at her.

"I don't have the patience for a chastisement." Kallinvar kept his eyes closed, his fingers tangled in the hair at the back of his head.

Ruon sat beside him, resting her back against the stone, her arm pressing against his.

They stayed like that, without a word, for minutes, not a sound but the patter of footsteps from the hallway outside and the occasional crackle of candles.

After a while, Kallinvar opened his eyes. Ruon sat staring at the ground, her gaze following an ant that marched across the stone. She drew a breath. "Do we mean that little to each other that you would suffer alone?"

"That's not it at all, Ruon. None of this is about you."

"No, it isn't," she said, shaking her head. "It's about you." She turned to face him. "And there is no me without you. We are intertwined, you and I. Seeing you in pain hurts more than a blade. I should know. I've felt the bite of many."

Kallinvar swallowed hard, wiping at the long-dried tears, his eyes stinging, a headache slowly thumping. "They all look to me. The same way they looked at him. But I'm not him. And no matter how hard I try to be, I never will be. I don't know what I'm doing, Ruon."

"You are obsessed with being what he was."

"Because he was better."

Ruon shook her head. "Verathin was exceptional. The wisest soul I've ever known. But you are incapable of seeing his flaws – of which there were many. We are, all of us, flawed. Verathin was too cautious and took little counsel. For all his centuries, he could not wield a blade like you. Not even close. But most of all, he wasn't a leader of men like you are. He inspired with his mind and with his heart. But you… These knights – *your* knights – would do anything you ask of them. They would place their naked hands in a raging fire if you promised them it wouldn't burn."

"What are my flaws then?"

"Would you like me to start alphabetically?" Ruon smiled ear to ear.

Kallinvar couldn't help but laugh. "Verathin built our knighthood back from the precipice of eradication. And then, with everything he had done, he was taken before the moon rose, and I was left in his place. I led our brothers and sisters to their deaths in Ilnaen, and for what? Tell me that, for what? Tarron is gone. Illarin is dead. Mirken, Daynin, Rivick, Lumikes. So many others. Dead."

"And you think Verathin would have fared any better?"

"Of course he would have."

"Verathin had four hundred years to prepare. Four hundred years. You know I loved him, Kallinvar, but what did he do with it? How did he leave us in a better place than we were before The Fall? He didn't. He did absolutely nothing. He sat, and he read, and he learned, and he rebuilt, but he didn't have the courage to reach out like you did. He didn't—"

"And what good did that do, Ruon? Where are our hundreds of thousands of allies? After I went against the wishes of so many captains. I would love for you to tell me, because I can't see them."

"You've had less than a year, in a time when the entire continent is at war, every soul grasping at whatever they can. If you'd had four centuries, don't you think it would have been a little different?" Ruon leaned back into the desk and stared at the door of the study. "I understand you miss him. I do. But you can't keep wallowing like this."

"I'm not wallowing, Ruon—"

"Yes. You are." Ruon shifted onto her knees and stared at Kallinvar. "I need you back. Tarron is gone. Ildris has barely spoken in days. And you spend every moment lost in your own head talking to a fucking god. I need you back, Kallinvar. I can't keep doing this alone."

Kallinvar didn't dare pull his gaze from Ruon's. "He wants me to abandon them."

"Who wants you to abandon who?"

"Achyron. He wants me to abandon the villages and the towns and the cities.

He wants me to leave them to fight the Bloodspawn alone, leave them to die, so that we can focus on searching for the Heart."

In that moment, Kallinvar realised he'd not heard Achyron's voice in some time. He could still hear the beating hearts of the Sigil Bearers, but it was a faint noise in the background, like the burbling of a river. It was the most peace he'd found in days.

"And what do you think?" Ruon asked calmly.

Kallinvar's jaw trembled, his hand tapping against his side, his skin crawling. He told the truth. "I think if we keep going the way we're going, then we will all die and Efialtír will cross and everything will have been for nothing."

"Then you know what needs to be done."

"We can't just leave them, Ruon. They will be like lambs. Thousands will die, hundreds of thousands."

"But millions will live. Achyron has given us our task, Kallinvar. We must find the Heart before Fane or the Bloodspawn. What good is saving those lives, only to let them die?"

Ruon sat back against the table's base and pulled her knees to her chest like Kallinvar had.

A silence descended between them, and after a time, Ruon shifted in her place, letting out a short, sharp breath. "You..." She drew another breath and shook her head, pinching the bridge of her nose. "You... Fuck."

"What?"

When Ruon looked at him, her eyes welled with tears. "Almost six hundred and fifty years I have known you. There are mountains that have lived shorter lives. We have passed through almost everything there is in life. And yet, now, we stand at the end..." She tilted her head up and swallowed, her lips curling in a half-smile as she choked back a laugh. "Why are things like this so hard?"

"Things like what?"

"You're such a fucking idiot," she said, laughing again. "Kallinvar, you are my counterpoint in this world. You are the thing around which everything flows. It has been that way since as long as I can remember. Your company, your conversation, your heart. That heart that does nothing but care for others. I would have given the moon and the stars to have met you before all this. To have found you and held you..."

"Ruon—"

"No, shut up. It's taken me over six hundred years to speak these words. I was always so afraid of destroying what we had. But if everything might end, I refuse to go quietly into Achyron's halls." She swallowed hard. "I love you in a way that physically hurts. I feel it clenching in my chest. I feel it in the way my heart aches every time yours does. And now, as I sit here, finally saying these words out loud, I realise how many nights we've lost because I've been too much of a coward to speak my mind. How many nights we've both spent cold and alone that could have been warm and together. I like to think there's a world out there in which we did meet, and we had children, and they had children, and we died old, me first so I wouldn't have to spend a moment without you. But that world isn't this world, and so I'll settle for every second I can get. I'm not scared anymore. I know you love me. I know you would stand by my side through anything in this life. That you would give the air in your lungs so that I could breathe. That you would walk through fire to keep me safe. I know because you would do that same thing for a man you'd never met, and that is why I love you. Because you are the single greatest soul I have ever known in this horrible, bloody, godsforsaken world. You sit around and wallow and think that the best of us died with Verathin, but you are wrong. Even he knew it. You are everything this knighthood is meant to be. You—"

"Ruon."

"What?"

Kallinvar reached across and rested his hand against her chin, brushing the tears from her cheek with his thumb. "Stop talking."

He looked into her eyes. Those beautiful, vivid green eyes he had looked into a thousand times over – those eyes that searched his soul – and pressed his lips against hers, his heart seeming to swell in his chest.

In that moment, he felt calmer and safer than at any other point in his life. His lips pulled away from hers for just a second, their foreheads pressing together, their noses touching. "I have loved you for the better half of a thousand years."

"I know." Ruon kissed him once more, her fingers tangling through the hair at the back of his head. "You are never alone, Kallinvar. Never. We will do what must be done, and we will do it together. And if we die in the trying, then we will see each other again in Achyron's halls. I just need you to promise me one thing."

Kallinvar stroked the sides of Ruon's head with his thumbs. "Name it."

"I need you to promise you won't die before me."

Kallinvar shook his head gently. "You know I can't do that."

"I know," she said, smiling softly. "I just had to ask."

Ruon pulled away and stood. She walked to the door and reached out her hand. "Are you coming?"

"Where?"

"To bed, Kallinvar. And then we will sleep, because two suns have set since the last time you did. And then we will make the hard choice, and we will do our duty."

CHAPTER TWENTY-TWO

DEEP IN THE BELLY

10th Day of the Blood Moon

*Somewhere in the Dwarven Freehold of Lodhar – Winter,
Year 3081 After Doom*

Silence and darkness were all Kira knew. Echoes drifted down the corridor outside, the creak of metal, the occasional drum of footsteps, the sounds of the groaning mountain.

She lay on her back, partly unwilling to move, partly unable. It had been days since she'd found the strip of red cloth. Days since that ray of hope had faded. How naive had she been to think anyone was coming for her? Hoffnar was meticulous. He always had been. The reality was that every member of her guard had likely returned to the stone and that the Belduarans were dead, their blood feeding the mountain. The king toyed with her, twisting her mind.

She still held the strip of linen in her right hand, the fabric soft against her cracked skin.

Kira grunted as she tried to lift herself upright, the air catching in her throat, pain flaring. They'd fed her that morning. Stale bread and dried goat. But afterwards, they'd kicked her so hard in the ribs she'd spewed most of it up in the middle of the cell.

That was one positive: she'd spent long enough in this place that the smell of her own vomit, shit, and piss was barely noticeable.

Eventually, she gave up trying to move and just let her head rest on the hard stone, her eyes closing to the same darkness as when they were open. She gave a deep sigh, her lungs and throat groaning as she did. Perhaps Hafaesir had abandoned her, or perhaps he had never watched over her at all. Either way, she was alone now and she would die alone. But she would not die quietly. When they came for her, she would fight. And she would return herself to the stone rather than let Hoffnar do it for her.

Kira jolted awake at the creaking sound of the door bolts sliding open. She tried to move, but her body fought back, weak and broken. Her eyes were all but stuck shut, blinding blue-green light burning through her lids. Where the cell had been dark and silent, it was now bright as the sun and filled with thunder, the sudden shift overwhelming her senses.

Hands grabbed at her torn tunic and slipped beneath her armpits, hauling her upright. She heard voices but couldn't distinguish the words amidst the chaos of shouts and metal boots clanging against stone. She tightened her fist, the strip of red linen still tangled between her fingers.

"Get your... hands... off..." It had been days since a word had left Kira's lips, and she barely had the energy to stay awake.

Her bare feet dragged along the ground, her eyes flickering between open and closed. The stone walls of a long corridor flashed past, the blue-green light blinding. They hadn't taken her from the cell since the day they'd thrown her in. This was it, this was the day Hoffnar would parade her through the streets, humiliate her, and make a spectacle of taking her head from her shoulders.

There was a piece of Kira that wanted it, that wanted everything to finally be over. But she pushed that part of herself deep down, burying it where she could no longer hear its poison whispers. She turned her head and forced her eyes open, her vision blurry. An armoured hand was tucked beneath her left pit, the black and yellow cloak of Volkur draped from broad shoulders.

Cries rang out, and suddenly she was falling. The ground rose to meet her, and a hoarse scream escaped her as she slammed into the stone. Before she could understand what was happening, hands looped beneath her once more, hoisting her up and dragging her forwards. Her vision was clearing, her eyes adapting to the light. Groggily she turned her head side to side and saw two dwarves in heavy plate and black and yellow cloaks.

"Take her," a voice said.

Kira's stomach turned as she was hefted up, her feet lifting clear of the ground. Arms slipped beneath her legs and around her back. She bounced and rocked in a dwarf's arms, looking up to see a face obscured by a sharp-cut helmet. She clenched her jaw and readied herself to jab her fingers through the slits in the dwarf's helm. Just as she'd summoned the strength to do so, a dark blur flashed across her vision and a bolt slammed into the dwarf's neck, shattering the mail that covered his throat.

The dwarf staggered, then collapsed forwards, sending Kira sprawling. She slammed against the floor and rolled, her head cracking against the wall, body aching.

New hands grabbed her and hauled her up, the sound of colliding steel ringing through the corridor.

"This way!"

Whoever was carrying her stopped and shifted in the direction of the voice.

Time blurred and sped past, Kira's bones jarring with each step as her captor jostled her in their arms. Wherever they moved, shouts and crashing steel followed. The corridor turned to an open chamber, followed by another corridor and another chamber. Volkuran banners adorned the walls, mosaics decorating each ceiling.

Where in Hafaesir's name were they taking her?

"There!" a voice called. "Through there, go!"

A sharp whistle *whooshed* past them, followed by an explosion. Stone dust filled the air, and Kira hacked a cough, her lungs burning with the thick dust. Her captor stumbled to a knee, then pulled themself upright and charged onwards. A door slammed behind them, and they stepped into a dimly lit chamber, the stone dust still occluding Kira's sight.

"Quick, get her up!"

Kira drew a sharp breath of clean air, then made a choice. If she were to die, it would be here, fighting. She would not kneel at a headsman's block or hang from a rope or be paraded through a street. She would die like a warrior, not a coward. She would make Hafaesir proud.

As the dwarf shuffled her in his hands, Kira struck upwards, slamming a closed fist into the chainmail that protected their neck. She howled, the steel ripping the infected scabs on her knuckles. But the blow had the intended effect.

The dwarf dropped her, clasping both hands over his throat.

Kira ignored the roaring pain as she hit the floor. She staggered to her feet. Her legs wobbled beneath her, threatening to give way entirely. If she could just get to the door.

Hands grabbed her shoulders and spun her, slamming her against the wall.

She struck out, flailing with her hands and snapping with her teeth. She would not let them put her in another cell or drag her through the streets of her home. She would not die like an animal. Tears flowed as she roared and slammed her hands into the helmet of the dwarf who held her.

"Kira!" The dwarf grabbed Kira's arms and held them down with the ease of a Jotnar subduing a child. "Stop. Stop."

Kira trembled, her hands shaking, her eyes blurring with tears. "I'm not going back. I'm not going back!" she roared. "Kill me now!"

"Listen to the rock," the dwarf said, her voice calm and familiar. "Silence is the sound of our home. Listen to the wind, for it breathes life into the soul of the mountain. See by the light of the Ward. Heraya watches us always. The beating of the hammer is Hafaesir's heart. It guides us in the darkest days."

Kira stared into the dwarf's eyes through the slits in her helmet. She knew those words, remembered them as though they were still spoken in her mother's voice. 'The Soul of the Mountain', by Igmar Olik. Kira stopped struggling. "Erani?"

The dwarf removed her helmet, revealing a face that Kira had not seen in over two years. "You didn't think I would leave you there, did you?"

Kira tried to speak, but her throat closed, nothing but sharp breaths leaving her lips.

"It's all right." Her sister lifted her to her feet and slipped an arm around her shoulder. "We need to get you out of here. They'll not be long in finding us."

A look around the room told Kira they were in an access chamber, one of many that connected to the great tunnels. The dwarf she had struck in the throat stood beside a virtuk-drawn wagon, two more dwarves at his side. Another stood to the left, a human with dark hair and steel plate. Kira recognised her as Lumeera Arian, the captain of Oleg Marylin's guard.

"Help me lift her up," Erani said to the dwarf who was still rubbing his throat.

Kira's back had barely rested against the frame of the narrow wagon before the virtuk launched into motion and the entire wagon lurched.

"How did you…" Kira tried to gather her thoughts. The last time she'd seen her sister, Erani was taking an emissary party south to the dwarves of the Rolling Mountains. It had been after their mother's death. They had both argued to the point that Kira had told her never to come back, never to show her face in Durakdur again. She had regretted those words from the moment she'd spoken them, but she'd been too stubborn to take them back – too weak.

"Don't speak." Erani grabbed the sideboard, balancing herself as the wagon rocked. "Drink." She pressed a waterskin to Kira's lips.

"Slower," Erani said as Kira almost choked herself on the water.

"I received word via the navigators the day after you were taken." Erani dropped back and rested her head against the opposite sideboard. "I came as soon as I could, but Hoffnar has most of the Freehold locked down." She gestured towards two of the other dwarves. "Some of his own defected. That's how we got you out."

"It's also the only reason any of my people are alive," Lumeera said. "We were warned just before the attack happened, and many got out in time… Most of us didn't. Your Queensguard stormed the Heart but were outnumbered five to one. Afterwards, Hoffnar branded you a traitor. Said you butchered Elenya and Lakar and tried to kill him as well, used your dead guards as proof of your attempted coup."

"Durakdur is under his control, as are Azmar and Volkur," Erani said. "It is only Ozryn that remains apart, but even they will not help us openly. I believe they will open their tunnels soon and accept Hoffnar as their king. He spins a web as well as any spider. And with you in chains and the others dead, he offers them a new dawn for the dwarves, spinning tales of heroism and glory. But there are many who see him for what he is and are waiting for your word. Hoffnar knows this. Other splinter groups have already attempted to break you free, but clearly they failed. Our sources told us that he had originally planned on keeping you alive, but after the latest attempt only yesterday, he changed his mind. He was to execute you today in the central plaza of the Heart of Durakdur. We had no choice but to make our move."

"Oleg?" Kira coughed.

"He is alive," Lumeera answered.

"Where are we going?"

"One of the old mining outposts in the far north," Erani said. "Turim Arlan and the Wind Runners Guild pulled out of the cities and evacuated many. They stand by you, Kira. Probably the only piece of good news we have."

"What of Hoffnar?" Kira pushed herself back against the sideboard, her heartbeat finally slowing. "What do we know?"

"Our spies tell us he's holding some of the navigators against their will and forcing them to run Wind Runners down the old tunnels. They've been digging non-stop, pushing the tunnels deeper, driving them further. Some say he's searching for Vindakur or the old Portal Hearts, but I think there's more to it than that."

Kira nodded, her head lolling as the vibrations of the wagon drummed through her. She tried her best to keep her eyes open, pushing sleep away. But she was exhausted, more so than she had ever been.

"Sleep, sister. Soon we'll plan how to break Hoffnar's neck."

CHAPTER TWENTY-THREE

FEAR

10th Day of the Blood Moon

*Salme, western villages of Illyanara – Winter,
Year 3081 After Doom*

ahlen ran his hand along the length of splintered wood that, only hours before, had been part of Salme's palisade wall. Now it jutted from the mud, shattered and broken, dried blood staining its surface.

Another night, another assault, another stay of execution earned through sheer desperation and unwillingness to die.

The wind snapped, and he pulled his coat tighter. His fingers trailed the wood, brushing over the splintered end as he watched two men pulling a broken body from beneath a dead horse.

The body – if he could truly call it that given its current state – belonged to a man who had seen no more summers than Dahlen had. Dahlen had seen him trudging through the gates that morning, tired and hungry, one of the refugees from a farming settlement on the other side of Ölm Forest. That afternoon, they'd filled his belly and given him a place to bathe in warm water. That evening, they'd found him a cot and blankets. That night, they had put a spear in one hand and a shield in the other. And now they dragged his lifeless corpse across the mud, legs so broken that one pointed west and the other east.

More people flooded into Salme every day, but by each following morning, the population had grown by only a handful. The Angan his father had promised had arrived a few nights prior, and he'd sent a call for aid but heard nothing back. At any other time, he would be drowning in the not knowing if his father and Erik were all right. But all he could do was push that thought to the back of his mind and pray to Heraya that she hadn't taken them into her arms. He needed them to be all right. In part because the thought of a world without them was one that threatened to consume him, but also because he himself would be dining in Achyron's halls within a fortnight if aid didn't come.

The sound of squelching footfall drew Dahlen's attention away from the two men tossing the young man's body into the back of an already brimming cart. Thick black smoke rose up over the walls, the smell of burning flesh filling the air as the Urak bodies were set aflame.

"Lord Captain." Thannon inclined his head, resting his hand on the pommel of his sword, his silver plate dripping with freshly shed blood.

Dahlen frowned but returned the greeting. Ever since the council had put him in charge of Salme's defences, the Belduarans had given him that title. It hadn't been long before the people of the villages had taken to the moniker also. Even some of the Lorian soldiers used it. He didn't dislike the title. In truth, hearing it gave him a certain warmth. But it was hard to take pride in something so frivolous when men and women were dying by the score each night.

"The Alamant has started work on the northern section of the wall."

"Good." Dahlen let out a long sigh. "When he's finished, have him do what he can here. I'll arrange a warm meal and some mead for him."

"Understood, Lord Captain."

The Alamant – Oaken Polik – had arrived a few days back, half-starved and barely clothed. His power in the Spark was limited and he tired easily, but without him Salme's walls would have been nothing but splinters and mud. Gods know the Lorian mages wouldn't lift a finger for something so far beneath them. Dahlen had only met a few Alamants in his life, and most could barely light a candle, so Oaken was a very welcome sight.

Just as Dahlen made to return to surveying the damages caused by the night's Urak assault, Nimara's voice rang out. "Dahlen!"

He turned to see Nimara sprinting towards him, the many rings in her hair glinting with fresh blood. "Fuck. Again?"

When Dahlen, Nimara, and Thannon reached the northern section of the wall, the place was a tinderbox waiting to ignite. At the centre of it all was Erdhardt Fellhammer.

The mountain of a man stood with a muddied sword in his hand, the tip of the blade pressed to Exarch Dorman's neck. Erdhardt's hammer rested in the mud beside him.

The other two surviving mages and a number of the infantry stood at the mage's back, weapons gripped in their fists. Everything about the language of their bodies told Dahlen they were more than ready to spill blood.

A number of Illyanarans – along with some of those from Belduar – were positioned behind Erdhardt, the same tension in their bodies.

"Do it." The Lorian Battlemage leaned forwards, pressing his neck against the steel. "Do it and see how this ends for you. I can guarantee it won't end the way you think."

Dahlen stormed through the gathered crowd. He shoved the first few men and women out of the way, the others parting before him, Nimara and Thannon moving at his back.

"Stand down!" he roared.

Exarch Dorman turned his head, but Erdhardt kept his eyes forward, staring at the man's neck, the muscles in his jaw tensing.

Dahlen stepped between the two, slapping Erdhardt's blade down with one hand and pushing him backwards with the other. The man barely moved an inch, his stance so strong it was like he'd grown roots.

To Dahlen's right, Dorman took a step forward. But Dahlen dropped his hand, snatched a knife from his belt in reverse grip, and pressed the steel to the man's throat. "Take another fucking step and I promise you this will end *exactly* how you think it will."

The mage glared at him, tensing, but stepped back. To his left, Erdhardt leaned forwards, pressing into Dahlen's palm.

"That goes for you too," he said to Erdhardt.

The stare Fellhammer gave him was calm and cold. He grunted and leaned back, tossing the sword into the mud.

All the while, Dahlen's heart pounded like a blacksmith's hammer. Dorman could end his life with a thought, and Erdhardt could likely snap him in two with little effort. Dahlen was sure he could take either of them with him to Achyron's halls, but then he'd still be dead. And dying didn't sound particularly appealing.

"Speak." Dahlen lowered the knife, gesturing to Dorman. He could feel Erdhardt's gaze weighing on him as he allowed the Lorian to speak first.

"They left us to die." Exarch Dorman made to move closer to Erdhardt again, but one flick of the knife in Dahlen's fist made him think better of it.

Dahlen narrowed his eyes, looking to Erdhardt and then back to Dorman.

Dorman continued. "We executed the agreed upon plan. But just as the Bloodmarked began their charge, this fucking prick pulled his forces out to the right and left us completely exposed. Six good men are dead. Six good men that should still be breathing. Six good men that will never see their children grow old." His voice lowered to resemble a growl. "I will not stand for it."

"The flank was collapsing." Erdhardt gestured towards the section of wall that had been destroyed by the Uraks, dead bodies still pressed into the mud. "If I'd not called for the move, it would have fallen apart entirely. I wasn't going to let my people die."

"But you'll let mine?"

"With a smile on my fucking face."

Both men lunged for each other.

Dahlen held his ground, his feet squelching in the mud as he shoved Erdhardt and Dorman back. Both were taller than him by a head and broader, but they were off balance as they moved.

"What is wrong with you?" he roared, opening his body and turning, addressing the crowd as much as the two men. "We are limping. Every night, we lose more lives. Every night, we come closer to collapse. The Uraks don't give a fuck. They don't care if you are an Imperial Exarch or a fucking farmer." He stared at Dorman, emphasising every word. "They. Do." Dahlen switched his gaze to Erdhardt. "Not. Care. And if they get past us, if they get past these walls and into the homes beyond, it will be the children they will tear limb from limb. The elderly whose skin they'll peel from their bones. The sick and the weak whose throats will be ripped open. I don't care about anything else, but I will not let that happen."

Dahlen stood in between Dorman and Erdhardt, casting his gaze around the crowd, studying the blank stares and open mouths.

"Whatever shit there is between you, bury it. We are not Lorian or Illyanaran here, we are just people trying to survive. We are the only thing that stands between Salme and ashes. When this is all done, tear each other to pieces for all I care, rip each other apart. But here, now, you pull your fucking shit together, and you stop acting like children. And if you can't, we can give you enough food and water for two days and you can try your luck on the road east, because you're nothing but a liability to every other soul defending these walls."

He made a point of looking to Erdhardt as he said those last words.

"What will it be?"

Erdhardt grunted, then grabbed the shaft of his hammer, swung it up onto his shoulder, and marched off towards Tharn Pimm and another man Dahlen didn't recognise.

"And you?" he said, turning to Dorman.

The Battlemage clenched his jaw, but Dahlen could see the fury ebbing from his gaze. He moved closer to Dahlen. "I appreciate what you're saying, 'Lord Captain'. So I will do as you ask, for now. But I need you to understand I will not stand around and watch the men and women under my command be left to slaughter. If he pulls another stunt like that, I will personally snap his neck."

"Hmm."

"You should've left Fellhammer to it," Thannon whispered as Dorman left and the crowd dispersed. "One less Lorian in the world is never a bad thing. Six less is even better."

"Have some respect for the dead." Dahlen looked around at the bodies still left to be collected. In his mind's eye, the world shifted back and forth between the calm of now and the chaos of the hours before. The soft whistle of the wind and the screams and roars as steel carved through flesh and shattered bone.

Thannon tensed. "Yes, Lord Captain."

Thannon had as much right to hate the Lorians as anyone – more so than most. They had destroyed his home, slaughtered his people. Dahlen understood that, he understood the hatred. But they couldn't afford to hate anything or anyone but the Uraks.

"Thannon, fetch Camwyn and the others, and watch over Oaken while he makes the repairs to the wall. I'll ask Kara Thain and her spears to watch the other section."

"As you say, Lord Captain." Thannon dipped his head and turned to leave.

Dahlen grabbed Thannon's shoulder. "We do what we must to keep those we love alive. Do you understand what I'm saying?"

"We do what we must," Thannon repeated, his expression softening.

"You handled that well," Nimara said, moving to Dahlen's side.

"We're just one wrong word away from doing the Uraks' work for them. One mistake, one fuck up, and we'll all be food for the crows. And every Lorian left defending the walls is a Lorian who can take a spear to the heart in place of one of my warriors."

Nimara nodded sombrely. She drew a short breath. "One day at a time. That's all we can do. That and pray to Hafaesir that your father gets here in time."

"He will." Dahlen folded his arms, staring out into nothingness. He and his father had their problems – many of them – but there was one thing Dahlen believed without question: Aeson would give his life for Erik and Dahlen in a heartbeat. His father would not leave him to die.

Beside him, Nimara nodded to herself, the rings in her hair glinting in the crimson moonlight overhead. Even through the blood and dirt caked into her hair and dried onto her cheeks and neck, Dahlen couldn't help but take in the dwarf's beauty. Not just her beauty, but her strength. She was ferocious on the field of battle, uncompromising. And in the aftermath, she was a rock, anchoring him in the present.

"Enjoying yourself?" Nimara didn't turn her head to look at him, but the corner of her lip turned up in a smile.

Since arriving in Salme, Dahlen and Nimara had shared a bed more than once. He couldn't understand how a woman who had seen him in nothing but his bare skin could cause his cheeks to redden with just a few words. But she could.

"I've got a few more hours on watch," Nimara said, turning to face him. The dwarf looked up into Dahlen's eyes, holding his gaze for a few short moments. "This place and all the people in it would be dead if not for you. Don't dwell on what we've lost, dwell on what we haven't."

She gave his hand a brief squeeze and set off towards the eastern wall.

Dahlen watched Nimara walk away, his gaze lingering until she vanished behind the wall of a stout log home.

He turned his attention to the breach in the wall that Oaken was repairing with his magic, shattered lengths of wood lifting into the air, fibres mending and twisting. What Dahlen would have given to have such control over the world.

The Spark terrified him to his core. No matter who wielded it, friend or foe, the simple notion that someone could snap his neck from ten feet away and there was nothing he could do about it... That chilled his bones.

He could practice the sword for hours a day, every day for the rest of his life, and even the weakest of mages could snuff him out like a spent wick if he wasn't careful.

Dahlen watched Oaken work for a few moments more, then turned and made his way towards the small hut that was his home in this place. He would welcome sleep with open arms.

SODDEN EARTH SQUELCHED BENEATH THE weight of Dahlen's boots as he walked through the streets of Salme towards his hut, the occasional howls of wolfpines echoing in the distance.

The town had grown into the beginnings of a city since he'd arrived. Refugees from the other villages had swelled the population, erecting makeshift homes left and right. The sheer speed at which the town had grown, along with the heavy rain, had turned the streets to nothing but churned mud.

He marvelled at how the people of Salme had taken in the refugees from the other villages. There had never been a question about it, never a hesitation. Sure, the elders squabbled and spat, but the people of these villages looked after each other. Even the Belduarans had been welcomed with open arms. It was a type of kindness, a type of community, Dahlen had never known, and one he thought he could get used to.

He nodded as two men passed him in patched leather jerkins, gloved hands wrapped around spear shafts.

"Lord Captain," they said in sync, carrying on their way.

As though from nowhere, Anya Gritten appeared before him, white apron smeared with a mixture of wet and dry blood. Somehow, despite the dirt and blood, the woman still managed to smell of fresh flowers.

"Lord Captain," she said, dipping her head ever so slightly. "May I walk with you?"

Dahlen gave her a half-smile, then gestured for her to join him as he carried on. "How are the injured?"

Anya rubbed her hands in a linen cloth she pulled from the pouch of her apron, the blood turning the white fabric a dull pink. "Better than they were the night before." Her expression didn't shift, and she kept her eyes on the muddy ground. "Though I fear there are three who won't make it through the night. I'll make them as comfortable as I can. I'd heard tales of Lorian mages who could heal as though they had the hands of gods. But either none of the three present have the ability or they simply refuse to."

Dahlen nodded slowly. "Do what you can. We can't ask any more than that."

They walked a while, silence hanging between them.

"What can I do for you, Anya? I'm assuming you didn't seek me out for my riveting conversation. Is it about Erdhardt?"

"No," she said, a half-smile flickered on her lips. "And I didn't come for Erdhardt. From what Tharn told me, you dealt with that as best you could. Erdhardt has lost a lot… He's trying his best to look after us."

"I know." There was nothing more Dahlen could say. He could see the pain in Erdhardt. The man did nothing to hide it. But Erdhardt was also a behemoth on the battlefield, and Salme's defenders looked to him with nothing short of reverence. Dahlen respected him, but he also couldn't allow the man's rage to undermine everything they were fighting for.

"I actually came to ask you about Calen." Anya continued to rub her hands with the linen cloth despite having already scrubbed the blood from her skin. "Tharn and Erdhardt told me what you told them… He is the Draleid? The one all the bards and merchants have been speaking of?"

"He is." Dahlen clenched his jaw.

"Is he all right?" Anya looked up at Dahlen, just for a moment, as though she didn't want to see an answer in his eyes.

Dahlen wasn't sure how to answer that. "In truth, I've not seen him in a long time. But from what my father has said, he is well. Both him and Valerys. They've been through a lot, but they're well."

"Valerys…" Anya whispered the name. She stared at the ground for a moment, then gave Dahlen a weak smile. "Thank you."

"It's what he was born for." The words left Dahlen's lips without much thought. And in a way, they brought a sense of relief with them, something uncoiling in the depths of his mind.

Anya gave him a curious look.

"Calen. He's a good man…" Dahlen swallowed. "Having spent time here, I can see why he is the way he is. He's also stubborn as a mule."

"That sounds like him all right." For the first time since Dahlen had met the woman, the laugh she gave felt genuine.

As they walked, Dahlen caught sight of a shadow shifting in the alley between two of the older log homes. He stopped, his hand dropping to the knife at his belt.

"What is it?" Anya whispered.

Dahlen pressed his finger to his lips, then stalked towards the alley, carefully weighing each step as the mud sloshed beneath him. The pink moonlight drifted into the alley, diffused by the clouds above, painting a small silhouette against the wall.

He slipped the knife from his belt.

A hand rested on his shoulder.

"Put that away." Anya pushed his knife hand down, her fingers brushing against the flat of the blade as she moved past Dahlen and into the shadowed alley.

"Anya," he hissed before relenting and following.

With his eyes adjusting to the dark of the alley, he found the woman on her haunches with both hands cupped around the cheeks of a young man. He looked as though he'd scarcely seen sixteen summers, golden hair caked with mud and gore.

"Is he all right?" Dahlen dropped a knee into the mud, looking over the boy's face.

"Where hurts?" Anya lowered herself to her knees, lifting the boy's head and checking him for wounds.

"I'm… I'm…" The boy's voice trembled, his hands shaking as Anya lifted them.

That was when Dahlen realised who it was. "Conal? Is that you? What happened?"

The boy had been a porter in Belduar and had come with them when they'd left Lodhar. He was a good lad, strong and sharp.

Conal looked up, blinking mud from his eyes. "Lord Virandr… I…"

"Look at me," Anya said, pulling Conal's gaze towards her. "I need you to focus. Where are you hurt?"

Conal shook his head, swallowing hard. "It's not my blood."

"What happened, Conal?"

"The Uraks." Conal turned his gaze to his hands, his palms open. "I know I wasn't meant to be out there, but I couldn't just stay behind. I couldn't. I'm old enough… I can hold a spear…"

"Fuck," Dahlen whispered, moving closer. "I ordered you to stay back for a reason, Conal. You could have died out there. What about the others?"

Almost forty children had come with them from Belduar, some as young as six and seven, and there were many more besides from across the villages.

"Only myself and Tora went. We got spears from the armoury, and… We thought we could help. We…" Conal shook, his hands trembling. "I'm so sorry… I'm so sorry…"

"Tora…" Dahlen breathed, realising what had happened.

"I couldn't save her. That thing, that big Urak… It just… it just picked her up, and… she was everywhere… bits of her." Conal looked up at Dahlen, tears streaming from his eyes. "She screamed for me to help, but I couldn't. I can still see her."

Dahlen set himself down into the mud beside Conal, resting his back against the house's log wall. His gaze met Anya's, her eyes wide with sympathy. She, too, had seen firsthand what kind of damage the Bloodmarked could do to a human body.

"There's nothing you could have done." Dahlen pulled his knees towards his chest and rested his forearms on them, letting out a sigh. "Take it from me. If you'd tried to save her, you'd only have joined her."

Looking down at Conal beside him, Dahlen couldn't help but remember his father comforting him the first time he'd taken a life. The first time he'd seen the light dim in someone's eyes. It had been an imperial guard in Holm, a man of about twenty summers. Dahlen had been a bit younger than Conal. His father had told him to honour the man's life by never forgetting his death. He had told him to *feel* the guilt and that if he ever stopped feeling it, to put the sword down and never take it back up again. This wasn't quite the same, but guilt was guilt.

"I just can't stop seeing it in my head." Conal put his face in his hands, weeping, his shoulders trembling.

Dahlen understood viscerally. He couldn't remember the last time he'd slept peacefully without memories of Belduar and Durakdur plaguing his dreams. Even then, as he sat in the mud, images of the battle that night flowed through his head like a moving picture. "It's all right to be afraid. Fear reminds us what we have to lose. It forces us to think, to question our choices. What's important is that we embrace our fear, but never let it control us. Do you understand?"

Conal nodded slowly. "I think so."

"Will you do something for me? Will you promise to never forget this night? Promise to never let Tora be forgotten? Promise to think of her whenever you're not sure why we're fighting?"

Conal's expression grew harder. "I promise."

"Good." Dahlen reached behind Conal's head and ruffled his hair. "Nothing about battle or war or killing should give you joy, Conal. Most days, it gives us nothing but darkness, and on the best days, all we can hope for is a sense of relief. We do it because we have to. We do it because of what would happen if we didn't."

Conal nodded, sniffling.

Dahlen pulled himself to his feet, then reached his hand down and lifted Conal after him. "Meet me tomorrow after I've done my rounds. I don't want you on the front lines, but everyone should know how to protect themselves."

"Are you going to teach me how to use a sword?"

"Even if we had enough to go around, wielding a sword is something that takes endless practice. We'll start with the spear."

The boy looked a little deflated at that.

"Come." Anya rested her hand on Conal's back, motioning him towards the main street. "There are some hot baths running. Let's get you cleaned and rested."

She turned to Dahlen. "You should do the same. Exhaustion is as likely to kill you as a blade."

"Not quite."

Anya gave Dahlen the same unimpressed look his mother had often given him.

"I'll sleep. But first I need to tell Tora's father. He lost his wife in the attack five nights ago. I want him to hear this from me."

The look on Anya's face melted away, and she let out a mournful sigh, her eyes closing. She nodded. "You made a difference with him," she said, gesturing towards Conal, who stood at the end of the alley waiting for Anya. "He looks up to you."

"I had a good teacher."

DAHLEN STILL LAY AWAKE BY the time Nimara slid into the room, her steps tired but careful.

"Let me help," he said at the sound of her struggling to remove her armour in silence. He grunted as he dragged himself from the bed and helped her remove her breastplate.

"What are you doing awake?" Nimara let out a sigh of relief as the plate came free. She removed her gauntlets, then pulled her gloves from her hands and pressed her fingertips to his cheeks. "Nightmares again?"

He shook his head, then gave her a broken smile.

"Two of the older children took spears and went to fight at the walls." He cupped her hands in his.

"Shit."

"One of them lives, but he watched a Bloodmarked tear the other one apart. She was only fourteen."

"Dahlen..." Nimara gripped the back of his neck and pressed her head into his chest.

"Her father just broke when I told him." Tears wet Dahlen's eyes as he thought of Tora's father, one of the Belduaran Kingsguard, wrapping his arms around

Dahlen, shaking and sobbing. Dahlen pulled away and leaned his head back so he stared at the wooden ceiling. He squeezed his eyes shut.

"You need to sleep." Nimara brushed her thumb across his cheek.

He pressed his fingers into the creases of his eyes.

"Come." She took Dahlen by the hand and put him to bed before undressing and climbing over him to lie at his back.

"My brother and my father are off somewhere fighting a war I should be fighting, and I have no idea if they're dead or alive." He stared across the dimly lit room as he spoke, curtains drawn to keep out the morning sun. "When my mother was dying, I promised her I'd look after Erik. Swore it to her as she lay there all broken, her skin all covered in those black marks. She didn't cry. She just smiled at me..." He shook his head, a tear rolling over the bridge of his nose to drip onto the sheets. "I'm sorry. I don't know why I'm telling you this."

Nimara didn't say anything, but she wrapped her arms around him and pressed herself against his back.

"I don't know what I'd do if I lost them." For as long as Dahlen could remember, he and Erik had fought beside their father all across the continent. From Vaerleon to Cardend, to Arginwatch, Khergan, and Antiquar. And for that entire time, they had felt invulnerable. Aeson Virandr was a living, breathing legend. He was a Draleid of old, one of the greatest warriors to have ever lived. And he was their father. What harm could come to them with a father like that? A father who had trained them to wield a blade with his own hands.

Somewhere along the way, that fantasy faded. His father *was* a warrior of legend, a master of the blade, a hero... but he was mortal. And mortal men could die.

"It's all right." Nimara pulled Dahlen tighter, her breath warm against the back of his neck.

"No, it's not," he whispered. "I wanted so desperately to prove that I could be what he had always trained me to be. That I wasn't a failure. I wanted it so badly that I left him to find Erik on his own. Then I marched halfway across Epheria... If they die because I'm not there..."

A sharp pain flared in Dahlen's left ear and he spun around in the bed, glaring at Nimara. "What the fuck was that?"

"I flicked your ear."

"Why?"

"Because you were being an idiot."

Dahlen turned back around and shuffled into the mattress, letting out a frustrated sigh.

A few minutes of silence passed before Nimara spoke again. "The people of Salme are alive because you are *here*," she whispered. "You have nothing to prove to anyone. The men and women of this place would lay down their lives for you in a heartbeat because of who you are... So would I."

Dahlen didn't answer, but he intertwined his fingers with Nimara's where her hand rested over his chest, and for the first time in two days, he slept.

CHAPTER TWENTY-FOUR

HIDDEN MEANINGS

10ᵗʰ Day of the Blood Moon

The Eyrie, Aravell – Winter, Year 3081 After Doom

alen twisted at the hips, swinging his blade in a wide arc and dropping into Waiting Dark. He moved upwards into Howling Wolf, sweat slicking his palms.

"Good." Gaeleron stood before him, his right hand gripping his left wrist behind his back. Over the months since returning to Aravell, the elf had regained some of the strength he'd lost and was slowly starting to look like the warrior he had once been. His cheeks were no longer gaunt and hollow, his eyes no longer sunken. A layer of muscle now sat between the skin and bones he had been left with after his torture. He still carried his walking stick with him, but he rarely had need of it. "Mind your footwork. You're overextending, and your base is too narrow."

Gaeleron pushed Calen's shoulder, and Calen stumbled to the right but stabilised himself quickly. He nodded, then pulled his lead foot back and stood wider.

"Your elbow is out too wide," Gaeleron continued, pressing his finger against the flat of Calen's blade and pushing. "You must be stronger. Continue."

Calen did as instructed, moving from form to form, emptying his mind of all else, which, after the meeting in Mythníril, was something he sorely needed.

To his left Vaeril and Atara matched his every movement, not so much as a bead of sweat on their skin. They flowed through the sword forms as though practicing a dance, fluid and smooth. If there was any soul that did not need instruction in the way of the blade, it was Atara Anthalin, and yet she listened to every word that left Gaeleron's lips.

"The valathír is a movement that focuses on power and decisiveness. It centres on swift and efficient strikes, overwhelming an opponent. But it will put you in positions of vulnerability. True masters of this movement have learned to limit those vulnerabilities, learned to twist them into temptations for their opponents. Lure your attacker into striking at a weakness, then pivot and take their head from their shoulders."

"It looks exhausting," Dann called out from where he sat by the stream, slathering a piece of crusty bread with fresh butter and blueberry jam.

Lyrei threw Dann a glare from where she stood behind him, one hand on Drunir's flank, her cheek resting against his side as she brushed his coat. She'd not said much since the Eleswea un'il Valana, but somehow she seemed… lighter.

Valdrin sat cross-legged on a rock to Dann's left. An inkwell balanced on the elf's knee while he watched Calen practice and scribbled notes in a leatherbound journal. They had passed the young smith on their way from Mythníril to Alura, and when he'd learned Calen was about to practice sword forms with Gaeleron, Valdrin had sprinted off mumbling incoherently. Not long after, he'd come scrambling into the Eyrie, dripping sweat and covered in soot and grease, then perched himself on the rock.

Calen couldn't help but smile at the sight of Valdrin talking to himself as he wrote, blissfully uncaring about anything else around him. The elf reminded him of Rist.

"Focus." Gaeleron cracked Calen in the side of the knee with his walking stick.

Calen's leg gave way, his knee dropping into the soft grass. For a moment, his anger bubbled, and he could feel Valerys watching from where he lay on the other side of the Eyrie with Sardakes and Varthear. But then he looked up to see Gaeleron standing over him with an implacable look in his eyes, his expression cold and harsh, and the anger faded.

Calen nodded, rising. "Laël sanyin, Sainör."

I am sorry, teacher. The word 'Sainör' was one Vaeril had taught him. Loosely translated it meant 'teacher', but the elf had explained that it was only ever used by a person who held their mentor in such high esteem as to think their honour unquestionable. It was a title Gaeleron fully deserved.

Calen still remembered the first words the elf had said to him after they'd broken him free from Berona.

"I didn't break…"

Gaeleron stared back a moment at Calen, then inclined his head. "Back to the valathír."

By the time Tarmon and Erik approached from the archway through to Alura, even Vaeril was sweating – if only a drop.

Erik held a finger to his lips as he stalked around to the right, slipping past Lyrei and Drunir and approaching Dann from behind. He moved with exaggerated strides, the burbling of the stream drowning out his steps.

"Why thank you," he said as he swooped down over Dann and snatched a freshly slathered chunk of bread from Dann's hand.

"I swear to the gods." Dann leapt to his feet, but as he did Erik shoved the entire chunk of bread into his mouth and extended his leg behind him.

Dann being Dann was too focused on the bread to see Erik's foot and sent himself tumbling.

Erik swallowed the last of the bread and licked the blueberry jam from around his mouth. "Have a nice trip?"

Dann glared at Erik. "When I'm done with you, Virandr, your own father won't recognise you from a potato."

"I'm… I'm not really sure what that means," Erik said with a shrug. He raised his hands, clenching them into fists in a mock fighting stance. "But come on, Pimm. Let's see what you've got."

Dann charged and threw his shoulder into Erik's chest, sending them both tumbling.

Tarmon slowed as he approached Calen, both eyebrows raised at the sight of Erik and Dann wrestling in the grass.

After a few moments, even Valdrin lifted his gaze from his journal. He looked from the pair to Calen, then to Tarmon. "Should we—"

"No," Tarmon said, raising a hand and cutting Valdrin short. "If we play this right, we might get a bit of silence." He looked to Calen. "Do you remember silence? It's such a sweet sound."

Out of the corner of his eye, Calen noticed Lyrei smiling at Dann and Erik. He'd not seen her smile since Alea's death. Though in truth, he'd not seen much happiness at all since that night.

"We have to allow ourselves the small things," Calen whispered to himself.

"That we do." Tarmon rested his hand on Calen's shoulder, smiling softly.

A thump of wings echoed through the Eyrie, and all of them looked up to see Valerys soaring though the air, white scales glistening in the perpetual crimson twilight. The ground shook as the dragon alighted beside Erik and Dann, towering over them. He stretched his neck down and shoved the wrestling pair with his snout, knocking them free and dropping them onto their arses.

"Calen…" Dann stretched his neck back, swallowing. "Tell him I'm not food."

Erik burst out laughing as he pulled himself to his feet. "Valerys is only a pup," he said, brushing his hand across Valerys's snout, the dragon giving a soft rumble as he leaned into Erik's hand.

Dann shifted backwards on his elbows, then patted himself down as he stood. "What pup do you know that's the size of a house, has teeth larger than my hopes and dreams, and survives exclusively on a diet of raw meat?"

Valerys spread his wings and pulled his lips back, exposing rows of alabaster teeth.

"Don't listen to him," Erik said mockingly as he scratched at one of Valerys's scales. Again, Valerys pressed his snout into Erik's palm, almost knocking him backwards. The dragon's head alone was larger than Erik's entire body.

Dann glared at Erik before walking back towards Lyrei and Drunir. "Only a fucking pup…" he muttered. "A pup with shits the size of your head… and it's not a small head."

"Children." Tarmon shook his head, letting out an exasperated sigh. He turned to Calen. "How are you getting on?"

Calen sheathed his sword and wiped the cold sweat from his brow. "Fine. Just needed to clear my head." He reached up and pressed his fingers into his forehead. "I just hate the idea of sitting here while I send others to fight for my home."

"I understand. But Aeson is right. Having you here when Aryana Torval and the others arrive is important. They need to see you, need to know you are not just a tale whispered into the wind. Their numbers could be the difference down the road." Tarmon squeezed Calen's shoulder. "There are fourteen thousand souls marching to Salme, Calen. You can't do everything yourself. You just can't."

"I know. Doesn't make it any easier though."

"No."

It was only then, at the sight of the forced smile on Tarmon's face, that Calen realised Tarmon had been in much the same situation after the Wind Runner crash in the evacuation of Belduar. He'd sworn to protect his home – to protect Daymon. And instead, he'd been following Calen across the continent. "Tarmon, I didn't mean—"

"It's all right. I know. That's all life is, Calen – decisions and consequences. I made my decisions. And as much pain as they might have brought me, I'd make them again." He looked off into the valley beyond the edge of the Eyrie, then back to Calen. "On that note. Those souls start their march to Salme tomorrow. I've arranged for some casks of wine and enough food to fill their bellies twice over. Your brother and Lyrin are there, and Aeson and Therin are going through the supply inventory now. The elven smiths are doing their last check of the new armour. In fact," he said, looking to Valdrin, who scribbled away in his journal like an elf possessed, "he's meant to be leading the checks."

Calen only laughed as Tarmon shook his head. Valdrin was well known for his wandering mind, but his brilliance superseded any shortcomings in that area.

Tarmon looked back to Calen. "Erik and I thought you'd like to join the soldiers for a drink before they go. I know it might not seem like much to you, but it would make all the difference to them. You're the reason they're here. They didn't come here because of Aeson's words or promises, they came because of you. And they're marching to war in your name."

Those last words were like a gut punch. It didn't seem real. How had it come to this? How had it come to people marching to war in Calen's name? The last thing he ever wanted was war. But the reality was that it didn't matter how or why. War was here. That was an inescapable fact.

"It would be my honour."

❦

ARDEN LOWERED THE WOODEN CASK to the stone, the wine sloshing as he laid it down beside one of Calen's captains – Ingvat.

The woman nodded her thanks, instructing three men to shimmy the cask over closer to a cluster of others. Her head barely reached the crest on the breastplate of

Arden's Sentinel armour, but she had an air of authority around her not dissimilar to his mother. Even Erdhardt Hammersmith had listened when Freis Bryer had talked, whether he wanted to or not.

The thought caused Arden to reach down to his hip where the scarf Calen had given him was tied between his belt loops. He recalled the armour from around his hand, feeling it roll back over his skin as his fingers brushed the soft silk.

Arden drew a long breath through his nose, then looked about.

Rows and rows of wagons lined the courtyard's edges, stocked to the brim with salted meats, hard cheeses, bread, fruit, and everything else a marching army required. It was there that Aeson, Therin, Harken, and another of Calen's captains – Narthil – double and triple checked the supplies. This, Arden decided, was a key difference between a battle and a war.

There was an inherent chaos to a battle, a madness within which all reason became lost. Battles were won and lost on the stroke of a sword.

War was the exact opposite. It was meticulous and slow and purposeful. Wars were won and lost on empty stomachs, exhaustion, thirst. And somehow that difference set a much sharper fear in his belly.

"Well." Lyrin's voice cracked through Arden's thoughts, and the man appeared at his side with a cask of wine over his shoulder. "How do you think Achyron feels about our Sentinel armour being used to move wine? You reckon the big guy has a sense of humour?"

"Shut up, Lyrin." Arden wiped the sweat from his brow.

"I've barely seen you in days, and this is how you talk to me?" Arden didn't answer, but Lyrin carried on. "The way I see it, if pain is the path to strength, then a morning after drinking your bodyweight in wine should make us strong as an ox."

"I should have appreciated the silence more." Arden held a straight face as long as he could before allowing a laugh to break through.

"You're an arsehole, you know that?"

"I've been told."

Lyrin frowned. "He'll be fine, Arden. He'll be resting nice and snug within the city walls. We can't lie around and watch over him like a babe. Not now. There are not enough of us."

Arden didn't have to ask to know Lyrin was talking about Calen. Was he that easy to read?

Shouts rang out across the courtyard, followed by deep, thumping wingbeats. The enormous figure of Valerys rose over the canopy of the trees that encircled the yard. The dragon soared upwards, blotting out the Blood Moon, then swerved back around, casting a shadow large enough to cover twenty wagons.

"Speaking of your brother." Lyrin gave a downturn of his lip, looking up and following Valerys's flight.

The dragon's white scales glinted pink as he twisted in the air and caught the moonlight. In a way, it was beautiful, but at the same time, the sight reminded him that the world outside these walls was on fire.

Images flashed in his mind of the battle at Ilnaen, of Efialtír's Chosen cutting through his brothers and sisters, Fane's black-fire nithral plunging into Illarin's chest.

The thought caused his jaw to clench, his breath catching.

Again, memories flooded his mind, this time of the battle at Elmnest. Screams and wails filled his ears. Bodies lay everywhere, limbs scattered like snapped twigs after a storm. He remembered carrying Sylven through the fighting, Ruon, Lyrin, Varlin, and Ildris holding back the Bloodspawn while the city burned.

He heard the screams on the nights he tried to sleep. That battle had been different to all the others. Those screams had been different. They weren't screams born from the thick of the fighting. They were screams that echoed through the valley as the Bloodspawn fell back to the city and slaughtered thousands. They were the screams of the people Arden couldn't save. The people he had failed.

"Arden?" Lyrin stepped in front of Arden, staring into his eyes. "You all right? Let's go get your brother a drink before he gets trampled."

Arden nodded. Sweat dampened his palms, his breath came short, and the slightest of trembles had set into his hands. He looked up to see Valerys had alighted near the centre of the courtyard and those gathered had quickly swarmed in around him.

CALEN TOOK A LONG DRAUGHT of wine from his cup, then breathed in the cold night air. Men, women, and elves alike – thousands of them – huddled around fires all across the courtyard, the discordance of songs, shouts, and chatter carrying through the open air.

Not far from him, over to the left, two elves sang and played lutes for some three hundred onlookers who clapped and cheered, wine sloshing in cups.

In the distance, by the supply wagons, a number of Dvalin Angan had gathered close to a group of rebels Calen had recently learned had travelled all the way from Varsund. One of the men was a bard. Calen could see his arms flailing dramatically as he wove some tale of time past. In the absence of horses in Aravell – with the exception of Drunir – the Dvalin had offered themselves to pull the wagons to Salme.

Calen had hoped to hear from the dwarves of Lodhar, but no news had left the mountains in weeks. From what he knew, the civil war that had ended in the deaths of both Pulroan and Hoffnar would take quite a while to resolve. If for no other reason than their prowess in battle, Calen hoped they would come to a resolution sooner rather than later.

"It's a special thing," Tarmon said, following Calen's gaze across the yard.

"What is?"

"Being here." Tarmon took a sip of wine. "The only elf I'd ever met before you came to Belduar was Therin. Now here we are about to march to war, standing shoulder to shoulder with them. You know what's even stranger?"

Calen raised a curious eyebrow.

"Marching to war alongside Lorians." Tarmon gestured towards where Ingvat, Surin, Kiko, and Loura sat with the rebels who had crossed the Burnt Lands. "They're good people."

"They are," Calen agreed. "We're lucky they're here."

"I wonder what Falmin would say?" Erik appeared to Calen's right, a cup of wine in each hand.

The mention of the navigator's name pulled at Calen's heart. Loss was a cruel kind of pain. He'd not thought of Falmin since the battle for Aravell. But all of a sudden there was an ache in his chest.

"Fuckers," Tarmon said, putting on his best impression of Falmin. "Wouldn't trust 'em as far as I'd throw 'em. What? They've got whiskey? Maybe they ain't that bad."

"That was one of the worst Falmin impressions I've ever heard." Erik stared at Tarmon in disbelief, a broad smile on his face. He rolled his shoulders back and cracked his neck. "I reckon at night we steal their shoes and wear 'em the next day. See how long it takes 'em to notice." Erik shrugged. "That or he'd knife them while they slept. He was a bit unpredictable like that."

"I think it'd take him a while, but he'd be sitting there with them. Telling jokes that might start fights, and drinking more than any man should," Calen said. "He had a way of seeing the good in people."

"That he did," Tarmon said, tipping his cup off Calen's and Erik's.

"There are a lot of people who should be here but aren't." Erik let out a soft sigh, taking a drink from each cup. "Korik and Lopir. Those two dwarves were solid… Alea."

"They're here." Tarmon folded his arms, pressing a closed fist over his heart. "Carry them with you. They'll make you fight harder."

"I see why you write poetry," Erik whispered, just loud enough for both Tarmon and Calen to hear.

"Fuck off," Tarmon said with a laugh.

All three of them tipped their cups together at that, and a silent moment passed between them.

"Speaking of Alea," Erik said, looking about. "Where are Dann and Lyrei?"

"I'm not sure." Calen looked to where the pair had been sitting near Valerys on the other side of the nearest fire. Haem, Lyrin, Gaeleron, Vaeril, Aeson, Chora and the others sat about, drinking and talking – but no Dann and Lyrei. Even Valdrin was there, still scribbling away in his journal. When the young elf had first arrived in the courtyard, he'd spent the better part of an hour chastising two of the Vaelen smiths for not properly polishing a batch of the new armour. Then he'd just sat and scribbled.

"What do you reckon?" Erik asked Calen, an expectant look on his face.

"What do I reckon about what?"

"Lyrei and Dann? I bet the two of them snuck off and—"

"What about us?" Dann's voice sounded from behind Calen, and Erik looked as though his soul had left his body.

Calen turned to see Dann and Lyrei standing there with Lasch and Elia Havel, along with Tanner Fjorn.

Both Tanner and Dann held the long handles of a large hand-drawn cart filled with iron-banded wooden casks.

"Hmmm?" Dann looked at Erik with a grin that said he knew exactly what Erik had been suggesting. "Can't find your words now?" His eyes narrowed. "Is that my wine?"

Erik looked down at the two cups in his hands and gave Dann a fake smile. "Maybe?"

"Maybe?"

"Well, it *was* your wine."

"Give it to me." Dann lifted one hand off the cart's handle and tried to snatch the cup from Erik's hands.

Erik pulled the cup into his chest. "Say please."

"I'm going to knife you in your sleep."

"He's just like Falmin," Erik said with a mocking shake of his head.

"Who's Falmin?"

And just like that, Calen's heart ached again. He'd never realised that Dann had never met Falmin. Their paths had simply never crossed. That was a strange thought.

"It doesn't matter," Dann said before anyone could answer his question. "I'm going to be nice. You can keep the wine."

Erik gave Dann a sceptical look. "Did you piss in the wine?" He looked down into the cup. "I knew it tasted off."

Dann turned to Lasch, who had simply stood there with an eager expression on his face. "I've just got something better."

Calen stared past Lasch at the casks piled high in the cart. "Wait... It can't be."

"It is." A satisfied grin spread across Dann's face. "Lasch Havel's mead. *Real* mead. Not that elvish shit." He looked to Lyrei. "No offence."

The elf just stared back at him, pressing her fingers into her forehead like an exasperated mother.

"You look tired." Elia Havel stepped past Dann and cupped Calen's face in her hands, her thumbs warm on his cheeks. "Have you been sleeping? Eating enough? When's the last time you bathed?"

"I'm fine, I'm fine." Calen brushed Elia's hands aside, careful not to be too rough. In truth, he liked that she coddled him; it meant she was regaining the pieces of who she was. He'd give just about anything to go back to the time where Elia's overbearing exuberance had been his biggest concern.

"Help us unload the casks." Dann climbed up onto the side of the cart and started shimmying one of the casks into place, Tarmon and Erik moving to lift it down.

"Where's Yana?" Calen asked Tanner as he helped the man lift a cask of mead from the cart.

"She's watching over Ella." Tanner rested a hand on Calen's shoulder. "Don't worry. She told me to tell you to enjoy the mead. She's got Faenir keeping her company. Honestly, I think she's starting to prefer that wolfpine's company to mine."

When all the casks were unloaded, Dann and the others proceeded to roll them towards the fire where Aeson and Vaeril sat.

Before helping, Calen turned to Lasch. "How... When?"

"Over the last month or so," Lasch said with a shrug. "I thought you and Dann needed a bit of home. Dann thought it would be a nice surprise. It's not aged as long as I'd like, but I'm sure it will still taste good—"

Lasch grunted as Calen pulled him into as tight an embrace as he thought the man could endure.

"Thank you," Calen whispered.

Lasch pulled away and clasped the sides of Calen's head. "We're of The Glade, Calen. We stick together. Always. Now come on, before Dann drinks every drop. We know what he gets like after five, and from my reckoning he's already had at least four."

LAUGHTER ERUPTED FROM ALL AROUND as Dann swung his arms, mead sloshing in his cup, the light from the fire dancing across his face. "I've never seen so many feathers in my life!" he roared, turning to face a group of elves and humans who sat behind him, all of them in hysterics. "It was mayhem. The chickens were jumping from the windows where the mesh had come loose, they leapt from the roof, squawking and flapping, and they ran about like… well, like headless chickens…" Dann stopped for a moment, scratching at his chin in exaggerated thought. "But with heads. There was shit everywhere. Now I don't know how much you all know about chickens, but there isn't a single creature that shits more than a chicken. So use that to paint the picture."

Haem sat to Calen's left beside Elia and Lasch, a mix of men and women from Carvahon, Arkalen, and Illyanara around him. His hand was pressed against his stomach, his smile pulled wide as though he had hooks in either side of his mouth. Haem hadn't been there the time Faenir had stormed into Tharn Pimm's chicken coop. He'd died the year before.

"Now I know you all see Calen as 'The Draleid'," Dann said in as dramatic a voice as he could before taking a deep draught of mead. "But back then he was just Calen, and the three of us hid behind a stack of crates while my dad screamed and roared, chickens swarming him as an enormous wolfpine squeezed his way through the coop's door – which he had no right to fit through. And Calen will probably argue…" Dann gestured towards Calen, receiving a raucous applause. "But I'd say the entire thing was more or less his fault."

Calen frowned at that, shaking his head but holding up his cup of mead in mock salute to Dann.

"Ah, great idea." Dann lifted his cup in the air and hundreds more followed from those who sat around listening. Hundreds that Calen could see at least. As the revelry had gone on, more and more of the warriors had huddled closer around the fire where Calen and Valerys sat. The dragon currently lay curled up a few feet behind Calen, his snout resting on his tail. Calen wouldn't have been surprised if someone had told him over a thousand pairs of ears listened to Dann at that precise moment.

"I propose a toast," Dann bellowed. "To Calen Bryer, the Butcher of Chicken's Coop!"

Again, the crowd erupted in laughter. Many voices hollered, "The Butcher of Chicken's Coop!"

Haem was laughing so hard his face had gone red and mead spilled over his lips.

A hand rested on Calen's shoulder, and he turned to see Tarmon with a cup in his hand, shaking his head at Dann. Erik, Vaeril, and Gaeleron were a few paces behind, pushing their way through the crowd.

"Well, he's certainly helping to build your legend. Just maybe not the legend we'd been hoping to build." He rolled his eyes, then tipped his cup against Calen's as he sat. "To the Butcher of Chicken's Coop."

"To the Butcher of Chicken's Coop," Calen repeated with a laugh, drinking deeply.

After soaking in the applause, Dann dropped himself in front of Calen, grinning ear to ear.

"You're a fucking arsehole." Calen tried to stop himself from smiling but failed horrendously.

"I think I was quite good," Dann said with a shrug. "Perhaps I should talk to Therin. Maybe being a bard is my true valúr."

"Not another one." Erik dropped his head into his hands. "For the love of the gods, please not another one." He looked to Vaeril. "This madness needs to stop."

Even the elf laughed before taking a sip of his mead. He opened his arms as if to say 'leave me out of it'.

"Fine, fine, fine. I'll stick to the poetry for now."

Erik looked at the ground for a moment, then tilted his head sideways.

"What's wrong?" Calen asked.

"Well…" Erik puffed out his upper lip. "I'm actually not sure who won that argument."

Dann leaned over, keeping his face as serious as he could. "I'm going to write a poem about you."

"I definitely didn't win that one." Erik pressed his fingers into his cheeks, then took a deep mouthful of mead.

As the night pressed on and the singing and dancing grew louder, Dann sipped slowly at the mead, just allowing himself to drink in the joy around him. Though he tried not to think too much on what came after. Every soul in this army was marching to war. Many of them might not live to once again see a sky without a crimson moon tainting its hue.

Dann pushed the thought to the back of his mind. He wet his lips with Lasch Havel's mead, allowing the sweetness to sit on his tongue. If home had a taste, it was Lasch's mead. Even just the look on Calen's face had been worth the innumerable bee stings Dann had suffered when trying to help Lasch collect the honey. What it said about Calen that he'd never noticed the red dots all over Dann's legs was another story.

After a moment, he found his gaze wandering to Lyrei, who sat on the other side of the fire, talking with Sylehna, Narthil, and some of the other elves. Neither of them had said anything about the Eleswea un'il Valana. About how she'd grabbed his hand, about how she'd squeezed it.

Dann shook his head, laughing at himself. Those around him were drinking and dancing and singing, readying themselves to march to war, and there he was overthinking the squeeze of a hand. He wasn't even marching to war. He was staying with Calen.

As he laughed to himself, he found his gaze meeting Lyrei's, the flames causing her golden eyes to shimmer. His heart stopped, the air catching in his lungs, and then she smiled.

"Dann," Calen said.

"Hmmm?" Dann stared into Lyrei's eyes, returning her smile.

"I want you to go with the army tomorrow to Salme."

"Sorry, you what?" Dann snapped his head around in disbelief. "I thought I was staying here with you? Tarmon is leading the army. I couldn't lead a fish to water."

"He is." Calen leaned forwards and inclined his head to Tarmon, who returned the gesture. "But I want you to go as well. It's our home, Dann. And what's more, your mam and dad are there. With any luck I'll be able to join you before you reach Salme, but if I can't, you should be there."

"Mam and Dad…" A realisation set in along with a pang of guilt. All he'd thought about was staying with Calen. Any other choice had seemed pointless. Dann had all but given up on seeing home again anytime soon. He wanted to see his parents. He wanted to hear his mother's voice, wanted to see his father's eyes, wanted to let them both know he was all right. But he couldn't leave Calen alone. Calen already carried so much weight. Dann could see it night and day. He was always tired, always bore dark rings beneath his eyes and resignation in his voice. "I don't know, Calen. I want to go home, but not without you."

A weak smile touched Calen's lips. "I'll be fine, Dann. Gaeleron will stay with me. As soon as we've met with the faction leaders, Valerys and I will fly to join you. But in the meantime, I want you, Erik, and Lyrei to join Tarmon."

Dann looked over towards Erik, but the man was lying on his back, staring up at the stars, lost in thought.

"Tarmon will be in command," Calen continued. "But he's going to need you with him." He paused as though trying to find the words. "These people," he said, looking at the men, women, and elves dancing and drinking around them. "They came here from all across Epheria. They came to fight for a reason. As much as it pains me to admit it, Aeson is right. I need to be here for when Aryana Torval and the other leaders arrive. They need to see me and see Valerys. But that doesn't mean I don't hate the idea of sending the army off to fight for our home while I sit here and play these games. They look to you, and Tarmon, and Erik, and Vaeril, and Lyrei. Whether you see it yourself or not, to them you are a hero. You charged down a Fade with nothing but your bow. Gods, you killed it. Without a dragon at your side, without the Spark."

"Well, it did sort of have me by the throat before you showed up."

"Dann."

Dann drew a long breath. "I'll go."

"Thank you." Calen leaned across and tipped his cup against Dann's. "I want you to take Elia and Lasch back with you. This isn't their home. It's not fair to keep them here."

"Ah-hem."

Both Calen and Dann looked over to where Elia and Lasch sat beside Haem.

"Do we get a say in the matter?" Lasch raised an eyebrow.

"Of course. I..." Calen stammered. "I just thought you'd been here so long you'd want to go home. You're both stronger now. You..."

Calen stopped talking as Lasch raised a hand in the air.

"There is no home, Calen. The Glade is gone."

"But the others, they're in Salme. The Glade might be gone, but the people aren't."

Elia's head twitched, her shoulders clenching. After a moment, she looked past Calen into the night. "Our Rist isn't there, Calen. You're not there. Dann isn't there. Ella and Haem aren't there. If something had happened to us, we'd have always hoped that Vars and Freis would care for our boy. All we'd be going back to is a place we care nothing for when the people we care everything about are here. Rist is alive. I know, I know." She held up an open palm as though cutting Calen off when he hadn't even opened his mouth. "It sounds crazy, but I can just *feel* it. A mother knows... a mother knows. And if we ever have a hope of finding him again, it will be here, with you. So if you don't mind, we'd like to stay."

Calen looked from Lasch to Elia. Both stared at him unwaveringly. Something in him cracked just a little bit, just enough for a tear to fall. "I'd like that."

"Oh, come here." Elia leaned across on her knees and pulled Calen in tight, wrapping her arms around him and burying her head into his neck. "Let nobody ever say you're not your father's son – all steel on the outside, soft as mud within."

Aeson leaned back, his elbows resting on a twice-folded blanket, a cup of Lasch Havel's mead in his right hand. After all Calen and Dann had said about Lasch's mead, he'd had high expectations, expectations that were exceeded.

Campfires roared all about the courtyard, humans, elves, Jotnar, and Angan alike all talking, dancing, and singing. Across the way, Erik, Calen, Dann, and the others drank and laughed, the enormous silhouette of Valerys visible behind them only by the glints of reflected firelight.

Four hundred years he'd waited. And finally, the time had come. All his plans, all his promises, all his hopes had finally come to a head. When he awoke the next day, Calen and Valerys would fly him to Arkalen, and from there he would finally fulfil his promise to Arkin and Ilya Ateres. Valtara would be free.

And with the army marching to the western villages and Calen securing the loyalty of the Illyanaran leaders, the rebellion would be in a position to completely sever the empire's hold on the South. And from there, they would take the fight north.

He'd expected to feel… something. But his heart would not allow such a thing. It was not done until it was done. And not until then would he feel any kind of peace.

In truth, his heart was torn. One half wanted to fly to Arkalen and hold to his promise, but the other demanded he ride with Erik to Salme. Dahlen was there. Aeson hadn't seen his son in months. It was the longest they'd been apart since the moment Dahlen had taken his first breath. Deep down, Aeson knew Dahlen needed that space, that freedom to be his own man, but that didn't make it any easier. He couldn't protect his son if he wasn't there. And if something were to happen…

He pushed the thought from his head. The decision was made. Dahlen was strong, stronger than Aeson could have ever hoped. And soon Erik would be with him, and the two of them together were a force of nature.

Aeson pulled himself from his own head, turning to look at Therin, who sat cross-legged beside him. The elf stared into the heart of the fire, his sketchbook on his right knee, a tin of charcoal sticks on his left. It didn't take Aeson long to realise why Therin was lost in the flames: the left page of the sketchbook held a life-perfect image of his daughter, Faelen, in charcoal, the right page given to Líra.

Therin had not been himself since the confrontation in Mythníril. All Aeson had wanted to do was stand by his friend, but perhaps he had crossed a line. The honour of elves was a precarious thing, and anytime Aeson thought he understood it, he was proven very much wrong.

"It's not you," Therin said without turning his head. Shadows danced across his face, welling in the bags beneath his eyes. He turned his head to look at Aeson and gave him a weak smile. "What you did… what you said to Galdra and Thurivîr… I will remember it until my dying day. I fear it will come with a cost, but still, I will never find words to explain what it meant to me."

Aeson shook his head with a sigh, taking a deep draught of his mead. "I should have said something long ago."

"No." Therin turned his head back towards the fire. "It was my choice to make, my battle to fight. I just… I can't help but think…"

"Think what?" Aeson pulled himself upright, wrapping one hand around his knee. "Therin, talk to me."

"That maybe I made the wrong choices, Aeson."

"We could both spend a lifetime questioning our choices, old friend, and not a second of it would do us any good."

Therin let a short breath out through his nostrils, vapor rising in the cold night air.

"Is that all that's on your mind?"

Therin nodded. He folded over his sketchbook and placed the lid on his charcoal tin before sliding them both into a satchel at his feet. "I need to walk."

As Therin made to rise, Aeson leaned over and grasped his wrist. "There is more. I can see it in you."

Therin allowed the most insincere of smiles to adorn his lips, then pulled away and left, pushing through the crowd.

Aeson stared after him a moment before setting his cup down and hauling himself to his feet.

"Where are you going?"

Aeson turned around to see Chora sitting there in her wheelchair, one eyebrow raised.

"I need to find someone."

Calen watched from across the fire as Therin and Aeson stood and left, both moving in different directions through the crowd. Therin had been out of sorts since Mythníril. Calen had chosen not to say anything, thinking it best to leave him be. But the look on Therin's face as he left had Calen questioning that decision.

"Heart of Blood!" Erik bolted upright, his eyes wide and everyone staring at him.

Erik had spent the past hour or so gazing up at the stars, lost in thought. He'd been so quiet Calen had actually forgotten he was there.

"How many drinks have you had?" Dann asked.

"Shut up." Erik waved Dann away, then stared into Calen's eyes, his gaze so intense Calen wasn't sure what to make of it. One hand hovered between them, aimless at first until it sharpened into a finger jabbing towards Calen's chest. "The riddle."

"What riddle?"

"The one the old seer told you. What was his name? Rokka?"

"What about it?"

"How did it go?" Erik rolled his hand. "I think I have it right, but I need to be sure."

"Ehm... I can't remember. He wrote it down. 'A city once lost'..."

"'Found it needs to be'," Dann continued. "'A gem, a jewel, a trinket of sorts, but truly more a key. Not a door that it unlocks, a secret to be revealed. A trick, a mask, a painting over truth, thought forever sealed.'"

"Yes." Erik nodded frantically. "That's it, that's it! Wait, you weren't even there. How do you remember it?"

"Because you've been muttering it for days. You're worse than I am."

Tarmon rolled his eyes at them both. "'There is a stone, a heart of—'"

"A heart of blood!" Erik shouted, excited now, his hand waving frantically. "That's what Kallinvar said! 'There is a stone, a heart of blood, cast into the sea. The essence of life, drawn from birth, stolen, taken, seized. The moon of blood, of death and life, linked the two may be. For connections made will rise once more when the moon you can see.' Right?"

"Right." Tarmon shifted so he faced Erik face on. "What is it?"

Erik folded his legs beneath himself and then opened his hands wide. "I've not stopped thinking about this since the old man said it. But something was missing. There's no way it's a coincidence that what Kallinvar is looking for is called the 'Heart of Blood' and then that's the same thing as in the riddle."

"Well..." Vaeril shrugged, pulling a face that Calen knew meant he disagreed.

"All right, yes, it's possible, but bear with me."

Vaeril inclined his head.

"Let's *assume* it's not a coincidence."

"You know what they say about assuming," Dann chimed in.

"Dann." Erik gave Dann a flat stare. "If you don't shut the fuck up, I'm going to kill you – slowly, with a spoon."

Dann closed his mouth, turning his lips inwards and leaning back.

"Good. Now, can everyone please stop interrupting me?" Erik waited a moment before continuing. "I think I've figured it out – well, most of it. Like I said before, 'A city once lost, found it needs to be' must be either Vindakur or Ilnaen. One lost in time, the other lost both in battle and perhaps lost in a moral sense. So with that, we have a place we need to go. Either Vindakur or Ilnaen."

"There were a lot of cities lost by those means during The Fall," Vaeril noted.

"Vaeril, stop killing my ideas."

"I'm not going anywhere near those fucking stone spiders from now until the day Heraya takes me." Tarmon folded his arms. "Not a fucking chance. I would rather drag my stones across a mile of broken glass."

"Nor me." Vaeril rubbed at his calf where the kerathlin claw had torn through the flesh.

"What did I miss?" Dann asked.

"Honestly?" Erik said. "You don't want to know. And with that, let's just hope the riddle means Ilnaen and not Vindakur. I think the focus on the Blood Moon leans heavily towards Ilnaen anyway. 'For connections made will rise once more when the moon you can see.' It *has* to be Ilnaen. 'There is a stone, a heart of blood, cast into the sea'," Erik repeated. "What if the sea is not a sea?"

"You're going to have to explain that one," Calen said.

"What did we call the Burnt Lands? We said it was like an ocean of sand... or perhaps a *sea* of sand?"

Calen's jaw wasn't the only one that opened wide.

"Ilnaen is a city once lost, connected to the Blood Moon, and set in a *sea* of sand."

"That actually makes sense." Dann looked a little irritated. "You're not as stupid as you look."

Erik glared at Dann.

"Don't mind him," Tarmon said, patting Erik on the back. "I think you're just as stupid as you look."

Calen ignored them and leaned forwards. He grabbed Erik by the shoulders. "I think I know the last part."

THE DOOR TO CALEN'S CHAMBERS smacked against the wall with a resounding *crack*. He rushed into the room, searching frantically for his satchel, tossing aside sheets and old clothes.

"By Elyara," Dann said as he walked into the room behind Calen. "You haven't cleaned in a while then?"

Calen just ignored him, tossing aside a pile of linen towels that had been sitting there for far too long.

Rushed footsteps sounded as Erik, Vaeril, and Tarmon stumbled into the room behind him.

"Here." Calen snatched up the satchel from beneath a pile of clothes and upended the contents on his bed.

The metal disc Rokka had given him sank into the mess of sheets, the pendant he'd found in Vindakur falling next to it, followed by Alvira's letter.

"What is all this?" Dann picked up the metal disc, turning it over in his hand.

"I don't have a clue what that is." Calen held out the letter. "But this is a letter written by Alvira Serris that we found in Vindakur beneath the Lodhar Mountains."

Dann was about to ask more questions, but Calen started reading.

My dearest Eluna,

I have left more. The pendant is the key.

Always remember, even in the shadow of what was lost, we can find light anew.

Your Archon, and your friend.

Alvira Serris

"The pendant is the key…" Erik whispered.

"The pendant is the *key*." Calen grabbed the pendant from the bed, its brass back cool against his palm. The symbol of The Order was marked in white against the obsidian glass.

"All right." Dann held out his hands. "I'm completely fucking lost."

"The riddle," Erik said, taking the pendant from Calen and staring at the black glass front. "'A gem, a jewel, a trinket of sorts, but truly more a *key*.'" He looked up at Calen, a broad smile on his lips, more excitement seeping into his voice with each word. "'Not a door that it unlocks, a secret to be revealed. A trick, a mask, a painting over truth, thought forever sealed.' Calen, you're a genius."

"I'm… I'm still completely lost."

"It's a glamour key." Vaeril's eyes opened wide, his jaw slackening. "How did I not realise it before?" Vaeril took the pendant from Erik, who handed it over reluctantly, then explained to Dann, "Do you remember when we brought you to Belduar?"

Dann nodded, his mouth scrunched in thought. "The passage in the rock – the glamour. The old magic Therin talked about, the same thing that kept Aravell hidden."

"Precisely. This isn't a key to a door. It's the key to unlocking secrets, unlocking truth…" Vaeril's expression shifted, and he gestured for Calen to hand him Alvira's letter. He held the pendant over the page. "The pendant is the key."

Calen felt Vaeril drawing from the Spark, pulling threads of each element into himself and weaving them through the pendant. His threads of Spirit were the thickest, but he probed with thin slivers of Fire, Earth, and Water, as though trying to pick a lock. Barely a few heartbeats had passed when the obsidian glass glowed, veins of white light rippling through. The symbol of The Order pulsed – once, twice, three times – and then the words on the letter faded, slowly replaced by blurry black ink that reformed into new letters and words.

Vaeril handed the letter to Calen.

My dearest Eluna,

I apologise for the secrecy, but it is needed. I sense what we have feared may come to pass. Fane grows bolder. He has followers within The Order's ranks. I do not know how many, but it's only a matter of time.

I have moved everything to the place where we first met. The pendant remains the key. Kollna knows. She cast the runes. Trust nobody else. Eltoar struggles enough already. I would not burden him further.

With hope, this will all be for nothing.

Alvira

Only the sound of breathing broke the silence as Calen read the last word.

"We need to show to this to Aeson… and to Haem."

CHAPTER TWENTY-FIVE

OLD WOUNDS

10th Day of the Blood Moon

Tahír un Ilyienë, Aravell – Winter, Year 3081 After Doom

Thunder rolled across the sky, the rain falling so heavy that the basin's waterfalls flowed like broken dams over the top of the ledge. Therin drew a long breath, his tunic and trousers clinging to his body, droplets streaming down his face.

The twisting branches of the Ilyienë tree sprawled above him, sheltering him from the worst of the rain while the glow from its purple flowers illuminated the dark night. He'd always thought the name to be as fitting as it was beautiful: Ilyienë – *remembrance*. There had once been over twenty of the sacred trees across Epheria.

The empire burned them all.

He took a few more moments to gaze up at the shimmering lights that hung in clusters, then walked forwards, traversing the closest bridge that crossed the moat.

The five statues that framed the central island from which the Ilyienë tree grew stood proud and tall. Each was easily a hundred feet tall, though the tree dwarfed them all.

Despite the statues' obvious beauty, Therin couldn't help but notice their flaws – or lack thereof. Líra had always told him that beauty in art was often mistaken for the objective meaning of the word. That true art was not something that simply existed in perfection, but something that came alive because of the flaws that made it unique.

Each statue was beautiful, crafted to perfection. The Jotnar was stoic and wise, the human strong and proud, the elf noble and graceful, and both the Dvalin and Fenryr Angan portrayed an air of ancient power.

But none of them felt *alive*. They had each been crafted from necessity, without love, without feeling. Perhaps that wasn't fair on the Craftsmages who'd created them, but it was true. Líra had often taken him across Epheria to show him the meaning of art and creation. He remembered when she had walked him through the Wood of the Lost near Jukara, where Jotnar had sung trees into the shapes of their loved ones. And he remembered their visit to the renowned gallery in Caelduin, where each painting and tapestry had been created by hand over months and years. When visiting these places, she always enjoyed weaving stories from the art, trying to imagine who that person had once been, whom they had loved, why they had died.

As he looked up at these statues, he felt nothing of their past, of their love, of their life.

Therin lowered himself to his knees, running his hand through his soaking hair.

"I'm tired," he whispered, closing his eyes. A drop of rain rolled from his hair, down his forehead, and over the bridge of his nose, eventually dripping onto the stone. "I'm so tired."

The basin was mostly empty, but in the distance, footfalls echoed from the terraces as people came to pay their respects. He wasn't sure how long he knelt there before the sound of boots drew closer, crossing the bridge behind him and stopping a few paces short of where he knelt.

Whoever had approached didn't come any closer, nor did Therin turn. What did it matter who it was?

If it was Calen come to talk about his father, a man who had given Therin so much and whose life had been snuffed out with such little reason? If it was Aeson come to tell him that their fight was finally here, a fight that had cost Therin everything?

It did not matter.

What had happened in the chamber in Mythníril still pulled at his heart. For centuries, Galdra and the others had simply treated him as though he didn't exist, as though he were a ghost. And so in some way, the simple fact that the elf who Therin had once called a friend had finally spoken to him had lifted a weight from his shoulders. Perhaps there was some small, minute chance that old wounds could be mended. Perhaps.

But with that, the mention of Líra and Faelen had taken him off guard. He saw Líra everywhere he looked in Aravell. She was in the sweeping arches, the broad plateaus, the open valleys. She was in every vein of erinian stone that gave the city life. Every piece of beauty was by her hand. Without her, Aravell would not have existed. And without her, Therin was hollow. And no matter what stories he wove or how many battles he survived, he could not bring her back. Sometimes Aeson forgot that although Therin did not know what it was to be Rakina, that didn't mean he did not know loss enough to crack his soul in two.

After a time of silence, a voice sounded behind Therin.

"You never came."

Therin's heart lurched at the sound, twisting in his chest. He opened his eyes, droplets of rain rippling the small puddles that had formed before him. "Faelen."

Slowly, Therin rose, his legs like reeds beneath him. He stood like that, with his back to his daughter, his gaze fixed on the Ilyienë tree, finding himself unable to turn.

"Can you not even look at me?"

"Of course I can." Therin turned, tears mingling with rain the instant he saw his daughter's face. She looked so much like Líra with her dark hair matted to her face by the rain, her eyes a deep gold.

"You never came," she repeated.

"You made it clear the last time we spoke that I wasn't welcome." Therin forced himself to hold Faelen's unwavering gaze.

"I was angry… and then you were gone. And then when I saw you again in the forest after the Uraks…" Faelen drew a sharp breath, steadying herself. Her lips curled into a half-smile at her own emotions – something her mother had always done. "When I saw you again, I…"

"It's all right. Myia ilise amar."

My sweet child.

Therin took a step towards Faelen and reached out his hand, but she moved back, clutching her hands to her chest.

Therin swallowed, trying to hide his pain. "How did you know I would be here?"

Faelen looked at the ground, then back to Therin. "Aeson came to me. He told me you needed me, so I came."

Therin nodded slowly, feeling the rain tickle the back of his neck. "Sit with me?"

Faelen inclined her head. She followed him to the base of the Ilyienë tree, where the roots were thicker than his torso and stretched out many feet past the trunk.

Therin sat himself on the stone, leaning back against a root. He patted his hand on the ground beside him. Faelen moved slowly but eventually sat at his side.

"I'm sorry I didn't come. The last time you spoke, you were so angry and I didn't know what to do. I'd already caused you enough pain. You already hated me. I wanted to give you peace. I owed you that."

"I never hated you." Tears welled in the corners of Faelen's eyes as she looked up at the drooping clusters of luminescent purple flowers. Welled but didn't fall – another trait she shared with her mother. "I was furious at you for not standing by our side. For choosing exile over condemning the Astyrlína."

"The elves of Lynalion are our people too, Faelen. Before The Fall, many were my friends. Your mother's sister—"

"Do not speak her name." Faelen straightened her back and once again turned her gaze to the glowing canopy above. "You think that I called your honour forfeit because you refused to declare your support for Aravell over those who withdrew to Lynalion. I didn't. I can see the honour in that, I can see the honour in standing by your people, in trying to do everything you can to stop us tearing each other apart."

"Then why?" Therin twisted where he sat, staring at Faelen, who continued to look upwards.

"Why?" Faelen shook her head. "Because you chose your honour over your family – over me. You refused to declare for Aravell, knowing full well they would cast you out. Knowing full well it would mean leaving me and Mother alone. You knew she was sick. You knew, and you went anyway because you would never have it said that Therin Eiltris was without his honour. And then she died, and I needed you, and you weren't here."

"Faelen…"

"She asked for you. When Heraya was taking her, she asked for you. And you weren't there. No, you chose not to be there because it was your duty and your honour to not choose a side between your people even though you *knew* the Astyrlína were wrong. Even though you knew they stood against everything you loved."

"Why didn't you tell me all of this? When I came back during the Valtaran Rebellion, or the Varsund War, and again with Aruni and Valdrin, you never said anything."

Faelen looked at him in disbelief. "It took you three hundred years to come back, and when you did, it wasn't to make amends, it was to ask for aid in another peoples' war. That was all you cared about."

"That's not true." Therin leaned back against the root, his chest feeling moments from caving in. Faelen was right. He could see it now, see everything he had done. A realisation set in, and tears flowed over his cheeks. "Do you know why I came here to the Ilyienë?"

Faelen sucked in her cheeks and shook her head.

"Because I don't know where your mother was returned to the earth. I don't know. I never had the heart to ask because I didn't feel as though I had a right to." Therin rested his palm on the rough bark of the root to his left, his fingers pressing into the wood. "I came here in the hope that through the Ilyienë she might hear me and I might feel her again."

"Father, can I ask a question of the heart?"

Therin could do nothing to stop himself from laughing. It started in his belly, then rose to his chest, taking over until he leaned forwards and pressed his fingers into the creases of his eyes.

"Why are you laughing?"

"Because," he said, "you are meant to ask before you crack my heart open, not after." He shook his head, still laughing. "You may ask anything. I denír viël ar altinua, sond'ayar. Laël diar."

In this life and always, dear one. I am yours.

"Are you all right?" Faelen finally turned to meet Therin's gaze, her golden eyes glistening with tears. "When Aeson came to my door talking of you, I wanted to throw him out the window."

"He has that effect on people," Therin said, his laughter returning.

Faelen's own laughter caused her tears to fall. "But he told me that he was worried about you. Worried about what being here was doing to you. You hold everything deep inside and lock it away. It's how you've always been. It's how you were when the Healers could do nothing for Mother's illness. You walk around as though nothing breaches your walls. I don't know how to help, but I want you to know that I'm here. I'm still angry, but I'm here."

Therin nodded, finding himself short of words. "I just really wish your mother was here right now."

"Me too."

As Faelen whispered those two words, something happened that broke Therin completely: she hugged him. His daughter wrapped her arm around his shoulder and buried her face in his neck, squeezing him tight, and for a moment it was like she was a child again.

After a time that could never have been long enough, Faelen pulled away, wiped the tears from her cheeks, and stood.

"Where are you going?"

Faelen reached out her hand and pulled Therin to his feet. "We're going to where she was returned to the earth. I don't forgive you. Not yet. But I can."

CHAPTER TWENTY-SIX

FOUND FIRE

10th Day of the Blood Moon

Aravell – Winter, Year 3081 After Doom

Aeson read the letter for the fifth time. A piece of his soul ignited at the sight of Alvira's name, at the smooth ink of her script. She had written this letter, of that he had no doubt. And yet, his heart broke a little more knowing he would never again lay eyes on her, knowing that even before The Fall she had realized something had been wrong and she had not told him. She had not trusted him.

He reached his hand up and slicked back his rain-soaked hair.

Along with Calen, Erik, and the others, Chora, Harken, Thacia, Atara, Arden, and Asius were all crowded around the table in the common room of Aeson's house on the plateau in Alura. The room's white stone ceilings were so high even the Jotnar did not need to bow their heads.

"It's just what Kallinvar said." Calen rested his hands on the table, looking to Aeson. "The Heart of Blood. Rokka's Riddle. Ilnaen. Alvira. It all makes sense."

"And this riddle." Chora placed one hand atop the other on her lap. "Where did you hear it again?"

Aeson gave her a sideways glance. She was well aware of the riddle's origin.

"We already told you," Calen answered. "From—"

"Yes, from an old man in a hut north of Kingspass. Not the most reliable of sources. Why is your confidence in him so high? There are many old men in this world, and I'd wager you would not march to Ilnaen so willingly on their word alone. What makes this… Rokka, any different?"

"Because it makes sense," Erik said. "Even if we didn't trust him. The riddle matches with everything. The pendant was a key, a glamour. Alvira said 'in the shadow of what was lost, we can find light anew.' Ilnaen. It cannot be a coincidence."

"Coincidences are more common than you would—"

"He's a druid," Calen interjected. "A Seerdruid."

"Ahhh, so now he's not just an old man. He's a crazy old man who thinks he can see the future. Much better."

"I believe they're right." Aeson placed the letter on the table. "This letter is in Alvira's hand. You know Eluna Faviril, Chora. She and Alvira were inseparable, until they were not."

"Yes," Harken agreed. "Some years before The Fall, Eluna left Ilnaen. I'd heard she'd had a row with Alvira, but it never made sense. She took up a position as The Order's emissary to Vindakur – a position far below her station. I thought it strange at the time but never questioned Alvira on it."

"Precisely." Aeson tapped on the letter. "Kollna, Coren's master. Why would Alvira mention her name? But what's more. I know where Alvira and Eluna met – at the base of Ilnaen's western hatchery tower. There is too much here to be coincidence, Chora, even for you."

Before Chora could respond, a green orb appeared behind Arden. The knights' Rift appeared, and Kallinvar stepped through.

Aeson's old friend looked a behemoth in his gold-trimmed armour, the slits in his helmet shimmering with green light. Kallinvar's helmet liquified and rolled back over his skin, vanishing into the armour's collar. There was a tiredness about the man, a weariness that had set into his eyes and the language of his body.

Kallinvar rested his gauntleted hand on Arden's shoulder. He gave Aeson a cold stare. "You've changed your mind?"

Calen stood straight, inclining his head to Kallinvar. "We believe we might have an idea where this Heart of Blood is."

Calen went on to explain Alvira's letter, the old druid's riddle, and the pendant he'd found in Vindakur.

Kallinvar folded his arms, his expression growing sombre. "That city haunts my dreams and plagues my waking hours. I can't help but feel that it will continue to call me back until it takes my very soul."

"Valerys and I are going with you." Calen stood with his palms pressed against the table, his gaze fixed on the letter and the pendant beside it.

Chora snapped her head around. "To the void you are. Your place is here, Calen. There is too much at stake—"

"It wasn't a request, Chora. I'm going. We promised Kallinvar we would stand by his side as he stood by ours. Not only that, but this is Ilnaen, this is where The Order fell. That letter is written in Alvira Serris's hand. What else do you think might be there? What if it's something to do with the eggs?"

"*If*, Calen."

"Everything is an if. Look around. There is no certainty in anything we do. Even *if* there is the slightest chance Alvira left something for us to find or if what she left was this Heart of Blood, then I need to go. Besides, only someone capable of touching the Spark can activate a key. The knights can't use it on their own, and it would take weeks for anyone else to reach Ilnaen. I will be here to meet with Aryana Torval and the others, but I will not sit here on my arse while everyone else does their part. I will do what you ask of me, but I am *going* to Ilnaen."

"We'll go with you." Erik stood straight, nodding to Calen. "Queen Tessara can lead the army west."

"No. We don't have the time, and you'll only slow me down. Valerys can make it there in days. Tomorrow, you, Tarmon, Vaeril, Dann, and Lyrei will march with the army. Gaeleron will stay here with Lasch, Elia, Tanner, and Yana to watch over Ella, and I'll take your father to Arkalen on dragonback as planned. From there Valerys and I will fly to Ilnaen. All going well, we'll be back in Aravell before the faction leaders arrive, and we might even reach Salme before you do – gods be good."

"I hold worry in my heart, Calen Bryer, son of Vars Bryer." Asius had not spoken until that point. The Jotnar fixed his stare on Calen, worry marked in his usually expressionless face. "You do not know Ilnaen. The city holds darkness and demons of old. It is a place of death, a place of deep agony. To go alone... I fear you do not know the darkness of this place."

"He won't be alone." Arden crossed his arms, looking to Kallinvar.

"No," Kallinvar said. "I will send all surviving knights of The First and The Second. I cannot recall the others as they are needed to continue the search elsewhere, but if you are right, if the Heart of Blood truly is at Ilnaen, I will bring the full force of the knighthood to bear. You will not be alone, Draleid. On my word."

"It's settled then." Calen tapped a closed fist against the tabletop, nodding sharply.

"I still don't think it's wise," Chora said. "Enough Draleid call that wasteland their tomb. Calen, I say what I say not to control you but to keep you safe. We must take risks, but this feels a risk too far. Wait. Fly Aeson to Arkalen, let the army march west, meet with the Illyanarans. If they pledge to our cause, ask them to journey with you to Ilnaen. None would dream of denying you. The chance to stand as honour guard to the first free Draleid in four centuries as he travels to the ancient home of The Order? They would climb over a mountain of corpses to be a part of that tale. We will go with you." She gestured around at Atara, Thacia, Asius, and Harken. "And more still. It will take time, but it is the plan that makes the most sense."

Calen studied Chora for a few moments, then nodded slightly. "Or you could allow Tivar and Avandeer to fly with me. They would not slow me down, and with them by my side, we could stand against whatever comes."

An awkward silence followed Calen's words, but he did not break eye contact. Calen had known precisely what Chora's response to that request would have been. He was learning how to play the games.

When the silence had finally grown too long, Calen spoke again. "Grandmaster Kallinvar. What happens if this Heart of Blood is truly in Ilnaen and we drag our feet and the Lorians or the Uraks find it first?"

"They will use its power to bring Efialtír into this world. And then we will not just be faced with the Lorian armies, and the Bloodspawn, and the Fades, and the Chosen, but the traitor god himself made flesh."

Calen drew a long, slow breath through his nostrils. "Chora, I will not sit and hide while those who are sworn to me march to war. I will fly with Valerys over Illyanara, over Arkalen. I will show the people of this continent that we are not afraid, that the empire's hold here is dead. And then we will go to Ilnaen and we will find where this letter leads. And then to Salme, and to Valtara, and to wherever else needs my blade. There is much I fear in this world, many things that would keep me from doing what is needed. But a wise man once told me that 'everything you seek lies on the other side of fear.'" He turned to Aeson. "Be ready to leave by dawn."

Aeson inclined his head, a smile touching his lips.

Atara, who hadn't spoken a word up to that point, came a step closer to the table. She didn't look to Aeson or Chora, but to Calen. The elf pressed her hand across her heart and bowed. "I would like to accompany the army west."

Harken mimicked Atara's gesture but did not speak.

Aeson watched closely, examining Chora's expression. The simple fact that Atara had asked Calen's permission meant everything.

Hesitation flashed across Calen's eyes, but it was gone as swiftly as it had appeared. He reached out and grasped Atara's free forearm. "Anta mentahl. La maeri du aldryr ar orimyn, Narvír."

Then go. I wish you fire and fury, Commander.

The look in Atara's eyes was one Aeson had not seen in hundreds of years. Atara Anthalin, the Blade of Anadín, once again had found a fire in her heart, and it was Calen who had set it alight.

CHAPTER TWENTY-SEVEN

HUNTING THE HUNTERS

10ᵗʰ Day of the Blood Moon

Níthianelle – Winter, Year 3081 After Doom

The snapping of twigs and rustle of leaves woke Ella. She shifted in place, white mist drifting from the thick branch beneath her. Strands of gossamer light passed through the canopy overhead, pale and sickly. There was no day or night in Níthianelle, only this eternal ghostly twilight.

Another snapping sound caused her to lean over the edge of the branch upon which she was perched, twenty or so feet up the trunk of the tree.

Below, the branches and leaves of the brush moved back and forth lazily in the wind, leaving trails of white mist behind them. A squirrel, leaking the same ethereal glow, scampered through the foliage, bounding over fallen branches and rocks. Ella leaned back, closing her eyes for a moment. Assuming sleep worked in Níthianelle as it did in the waking world, it had been five days since Tamzin had found her. They were almost to the Darkwood.

Since coming across the Bjorna Angan and that wraith, Tamzin had pushed them both to an exhausting pace. They'd not come across another of the Bjorna, but now Ella saw the wraiths everywhere. The vast majority were not like the one that had attacked her. They were not 'hungry', as Tamzin had put it. They were simply lost, wandering endlessly, their minds gone. There was something sadder about that.

A short time passed with more rustling below, creatures shifting in the undergrowth, birds flapping their wings and chorusing their songs, until voices broke the serenity.

"Anything?" The voice belonged to a man – young and tired. He was twenty feet away, maybe thirty. His heart galloped like a rabbit's and his sweat smelled stale and sharp. That was something new Ella had learned about this place: people still sweated. At first, the sound of the man's heart unsettled her. Then she felt the wolf prowling in the back of her mind, a low rumble in its throat.

"The trail is hard to read. But they passed through here." The second voice was much closer, only a few feet away. It was older, harder. His pulse was slow despite his heavy breaths. The wolf within her was wary of this one.

"Who do you think found the Fragment?"

"It matters little. It was not our people."

"But what if it was the Bjorna? What if—"

"Calm yourself, eyas. Watch and listen. Attune your senses."

The younger voice didn't speak, but Ella could sense the change in his smell. He reeked of anger, of frustration. The wolf in her blood stood tall, hackles rising. It urged her to leap from the branch, to take the elder first, then stalk the cub. They were hunting her. She needed to hunt them back.

No. Tamzin told her to run if something came for her. There were too many things she didn't know about this place. Too many ways something could go wrong. If she stayed where she was and didn't make a sound, they would pass, she was sure of it. She leaned back and pushed her foot into the branch, trying to press herself tighter against the trunk. The branch gave the slightest groan in response, a near inaudible rustle of its leaves.

"You see, eyas. Patience is a virtue."

Ella's hackles stood on end, and she leaned over the branch to see a grey-haired man staring up at her from the base of a nearby tree.

She snapped back, pressing herself against the tree's trunk, her pulse pounding.

Wingbeats thumped on the wind. A hawk perched on the branch across from her, its head tilting side to side, its eyes fixed on Ella. The bird's crest was a rusty orange, its wings striped black and white. It stared at her for a moment, then unleashed a sharp shriek that rose and fell.

Ella pushed herself back as far as she could without falling, but the creature leapt from its branch and swooped towards her, its talons extended, white light streaming in its wake.

The wolf within her took over, and Ella swung her hand. Her fingernails lengthened and hardened, claws ripping through the hawk's wing and into its chest, hollow bones cracking.

The strike tore the hawk apart and it smacked against a branch, limp, then fell like a stone, feathers floating in its wake. A howl came from below.

But as the hawk fell, Ella lost her balance and slipped from her perch. She scrambled, her claws raking furrows in the branch's bark. For a moment, she thought it would hold, but then her claws ripped through and she was falling.

A thick branch knocked the air from her lungs. She spun, bright light and shadows swirling across her vision. She slammed into another branch, then hit the ground. Hard.

Ella's head spun, stars flitting across her eyes as she lay on her back, gasping for air. Her lungs burned, and her entire body throbbed. She could barely move, but the wolf within howled, demanding she rise.

She hauled herself upright, ignoring her body's screams. Voices floated, dull and faint.

"Kadal, no!"

Something slammed into Ella's chest and sent her bouncing back off the hard-packed ground. Fingers wrapped around her shirt, pulling tight, then someone knelt over her.

"You killed him." Ella's vision was still blurred, but the face above her was all angles, sharp and sleek. Vibrant amber eyes shone through the haze. "I will make this slow."

Ella let the wolf loose. The familiar red mist tinted her vision, and before she could think, her claws were buried in the neck of the man who knelt over her.

She could feel the vibrations of his attempted scream, but all that came out was a gurgle, luminous white blood spitting from his lips. She dragged him closer, claws tearing skin, then opened her jaws and ripped out his throat, spitting a hunk of flesh into the dirt.

The man dropped in a heap at Ella's side, white blood spilling from the wound.

She looked again into the man's eyes, her head no longer spinning. It was the younger of the two. More a child than a man. Fourteen summers at most. Her stomach lurched but she held herself together. She didn't have the time to dwell. She could feel the older man's heart, the pulse steadily rising, growing louder.

Ella crawled backwards, shaking the stars from her eyes. The older man just stood there, staring at the boy's body. He didn't speak, didn't move an inch, but Ella could smell the bitter blend of sorrow and rage wafting from him.

She stumbled to her feet, grabbing purchase on a rough tree trunk. Her head spun again at her sudden change in orientation, her stomach turning. With each passing moment, more aches and pains set into her bones as the rush from her fall faded.

Something shifted in the air, a change in the smell.

The older man's eyes snapped to Ella, his pupils widening, head cocking to the side. Ella's hackles stood on end and signalled only one instinct: *run*.

Ella bolted through the brush, half-sprinting, half-staggering, her legs disobeying like petulant children, still shaken from the fall. She clambered over fallen trees and tore through dense foliage, never looking down, her instincts carrying her.

The wolf was in control.

She didn't have to look back to know the man was in chase. She could hear his every movement, *feel* his fury. At any other time, she would have turned and fought, but the wolf refused. Whoever this man was, he had seen Ella tear that boy to pieces and still chased her like a predator would a fleeing doe. Something about his smell told her he was far more dangerous than she was.

A shriek erupted to Ella's left. She twisted just in time to avoid the hawk that swooped past her, talons readied. The creature spun in the air and whirled off between two trees. Before Ella could collect herself, the hawk dropped from above, screeching.

She wasn't quick enough. The bird's talons wrapped around her forearm and sank into flesh. She screamed and went tumbling, bouncing off the earth and rolling to a stop with a *crack*.

The hawk's talons squeezed, sharp as razors, and Ella screamed again. The creature tore through Ella's shirt with its beak, ripping a strip of flesh from her shoulder. Ella lashed out with her free arm, sinking her claws into the bird and squeezing with every drop of strength she had. Bones snapped, but the bird's talons continued to carve into her arm.

The red mist consumed Ella, and she slammed the hawk against a tree trunk, her claws crushing its hollow frame, ghostly white mist streaming into the air. Again and again, she smashed until the bird was nothing more than shattered bone and white-bloodied feathers.

Ella rolled onto her back, her entire body throbbing, silvery-white blood flowing from the wounds in her forearm and shoulder. She crawled backwards on her elbows, but the older man was atop her in seconds.

He loomed over her, his head cocked to the side, three more hawks perched on branches above him. The man's hair was long and grey, his body lean, his skin marked by time. His eyes were an unnatural yellow, his pupils huge and black as coals. Sweat dripped from the tip of his nose as he let out a slow breath. "Fenryr then... You dogs never seem to die easy."

"Who..." Ella swallowed, trying to get some spit in her dry mouth. "Who are you?"

"Doesn't matter, girl. Dead people have no use for knowledge."

"I don't understand." Ella grimaced, wrapping her fingers around the pumping wound. "Why?"

The man snorted, a bead of sweat dripping from his nose and onto Ella's neck. He lifted his foot, then stomped on Ella's leg. She cried out, her flesh tearing open as though sliced by knives.

Ella lunged forwards desperately. She would not just lie down and wait for death. She swung her right hand at the man's leg, but he crunched his fist into her face and her head bounced backwards, her vision blurring and eyelids drooping.

"Why do we do anything, girl?" The man spoke with a calm, level tone as though this were just another day, just another life he would snuff.

Ella's head flopped to the left in a daze, and she saw he wore no shoes. The skin on his bare feet blended from human flesh to wrinkled and leathered, taking on a yellowish hue. His toes were bent and curled, long black talons sinking into the earth.

"For what it's worth, I don't take any pleasure in this." Through drooping lids, her head ringing, Ella saw the man bend over and lift a large rock into his arms. "War is war."

"Please," Ella managed to mutter, the taste of blood on her tongue. "You don't have to."

"I do…" The man's tone shifted, rising higher. His pulse quickened, the slightest tinge of fear in his scent.

Ella flinched at the sound of the rock hitting the ground a few feet away. It was then she noticed the other scent in the air, heard the other heartbeat.

Something about the smell was familiar, yet she couldn't put her finger on it.

A low growl was followed by snapping branches, rustling leaves, and thumping feet. Then there was silence as Ella slipped in and out of consciousness, her head spinning.

She didn't know how long she lay there in the dirt before she could drag herself over to a tree trunk. White blood still oozed from the deep gashes on her left arm, her leg much the same. The strip the hawk had torn from her shoulder throbbed, her head thumped, and her nose felt as though it had been broken for a third time. It would have been easier for her to list which parts of her body weren't in pain than the other way around.

She grunted, straightening her back against the tree trunk and lifting herself more upright, then proceeded to tear strips from her shirt with a claw to bandage her wounds. There were too many questions to which she had no answers: could wounds become infected in Níthianelle? Would blood loss kill here? Were the plants and flowers here the same as the living world? Did they have the same healing properties? Would her wounds in this world take shape in the other?

The thought of that last one sent a shiver down her spine. She pushed it into a dark corner of her mind and sealed it off. Thinking on it would do her no good. Her mam had always taught her to focus on the things she could control instead of dwelling on the things she couldn't.

"Stop the bleeding. Fix the wounds you can. Deal with everything else as it comes." Ella remembered her mother saying those words after Joran Brock had fallen from a horse and broken his femur. Everyone had said it was a miracle Joran had even survived, let alone that he'd walked again. *"If you're too busy worrying about something that might happen, you're more likely to miss something that is happening. Fear and panic, Ella, those are the real killers."*

Ella grunted as she pulled a strip of linen tight around the wounds on her arm, white blood flowing.

She sat there for what felt like an hour, but which could have been either half or double that time, until a familiar scent touched the air, followed by a familiar voice.

"I told you to run." Tamzin stepped from the shadow-obscured forest, her vibrant blue eyes glistening in the white light, her pupils thinned to slits.

"I did run. It didn't work."

"Well, you're alive." Tamzin knelt before Ella, examining her make-shift bandages.

"No thanks to you."

"You're a big girl. You don't need me here to hold your hand. Can you walk?"

"I'm not sure."

"Let's find out." Tamzin wrapped an arm around Ella's back and hauled her to her feet, receiving many a grunt and groan for her efforts.

A pain jolted through Ella's calf when she put weight on her left foot.

"That'll do," Tamzin said, standing back and watching Ella. "Wounds heal faster here, so long as they aren't mortal. If we start moving now, you'll be right in a few hours."

"Infection?"

Tamzin shook her head. She turned around, leaving Ella to lean against a nearby tree. The woman knelt by talon marks in the ground, noting the white blood clinging to the soil. She lifted her head. "The other one?"

"I'm not sure. I couldn't see... I thought he was going to kill me, but then something else came and chased him off, I think. How did you know there were two?"

"Well," Tamzin said, rubbing the earth, "besides the imprint of talons in the soil, the one I found in a pool of his own blood back there was too young. Vethnir would never send an eyas out on a hunt alone. Particularly not on a hunt for a Fragment. They'd have known there'd be others prowling."

"An eyas? The older man said that. What does it mean?"

Tamzin rose. "It's what Clan Vethnir names their young. The unfledged nestlings."

"Vethnir," Ella repeated. "The hawk."

"Hmm."

"Why try to kill me? They don't even know who I am. What would that gain for them?"

"It's not what they would gain but what others would lose. Like I said, our people are broken into many factions. Some are simply fighting to survive, others cling to the old ways, and some seek a better future. The likelihood is they were searching to see if you were a child of Vethnir. When they saw you weren't, well..."

"But we're not the same bloodline and you haven't tried to kill me. Why?"

"Doesn't mean I haven't wanted to." Tamzin smiled. "Amatkai wants to build a future where we stand together. Vethnir does not." Tamzin rested a hand on Ella's shoulder. "Don't dwell on the boy. Far younger souls have died in this war, and younger still will continue to do so. Vethnir hunters are no easy prey no matter their age. Come. We must make good pace today. There are not many things that would scare away a Vethnir hunter, and I didn't find any bodies on my way here. Which means the hunter and whatever scared him off are likely both still out here."

CHAPTER TWENTY-EIGHT

THE PATH WE HAVE CHOSEN

12ᵗʰ Day of the Blood Moon

Berona – Winter, Year 3081 After Doom

Rist collapsed, his lungs heaving, sweat pumping from every inch of skin on his body. He knelt on all fours, his palms flat against the stone. His stomach lurched and his mouth salivated. *Don't throw up.* He swallowed hard, holding his breath and tensing. *Don't. Throw. Up.*

"Better." All Rist could see were Garramon's feet, bare except for a pair of sandals. The man placed a wooden plate before Rist, laden with slabs of fresh cooked beef dripping in gravy and a pile of buttered mashed potatoes bigger than a horse's turd.

Rist dry heaved, pushing the vomit down.

"If you puke on the food, you're still eating it."

That was it. That was what broke him. Rist lurched to his side and retched, the familiar metallic taste sliding up his throat. His puke was orange, made so by the carrots he'd forced down only hours before. Chunks of chewed meat decorated the spew, lying amongst other – completely unidentifiable – remnants of partially digested vegetables.

Above him, Garramon sighed. "Whatever you puke up, we'll have to replace."

"I know." Rist wiped the vomit from the corner of his mouth, then reached his hand up.

Garramon hauled Rist to his feet.

"You're going to have to learn to keep it down."

Rist nodded, leaning his head back, cold sweat dripping down his torso. "Water?"

"Can you keep it down?"

"Water, please."

Garramon handed Rist a waterskin, which he drained in its entirety, savouring the cold as it flowed down his throat. A few seconds later, he immediately regretted that decision as he spewed up a flow of clear liquid.

"Eat," Garramon said, shaking his head. "And then we will channel."

Rist dropped to the floor and folded his legs, staring at the slabs of beef as though they were poison.

"You agreed to this, Rist. I warned you."

"This isn't quite what I had in mind."

"Your mind is strong. Your grasp of the Spark already far exceeds that of any with your summers. But mind and body work in tandem, and your body, quite simply, is not up to the task. If you push yourself past your limits now, you *will* die. And I for one would prefer that not happen."

"That would be my preference also." Rist swallowed hard, then let out a heavy sigh as he bit into a slab of beef. He was absolutely sure it would have been one of the best tasting pieces of meat he'd ever eaten if his mouth hadn't already been coated with the acrid taste of vomit.

"You will only get one chance at the testing. You need to be ready before that day comes."

Rist knew what that meant. It had already been made clear to him. Those who failed the test had a high likelihood of dying. The more powerful a mage became, the greater the risks. The larger the flame, the bigger the fire. Young, untested mages were more likely to burn the Spark from their veins, but more powerful ones risked far more than that. "If you and Fane are the last two Arcarians, why not simply admit me?"

"Because an Arcarian by name is nothing at all. That name means something, Rist. For Fane to even consider you is an honour itself."

"You still haven't told me what the testing entails." Rist choked down another piece of meat, raising a closed fist to his mouth as he forced the beef down. "And you're not going to, are you?"

Garramon shook his head. "Finish that, and come with me. There's something I want to show you before we spar."

"Before we spar?" Rist's pulse quickened at the thought of standing up, never mind sparring. "Can I not just… read and sleep? I would love to read and sleep."

GARRAMON CLASPED HIS HANDS BEHIND his back, filling his lungs with winter air as he gazed out at Berona. The sun was nearing the end of its cycle, hanging above the mountains to the west, but it was not alone. The Blood Moon was carved into the sky just above it. He could feel the moon's pull, feel the power that seeped from its light. A part of him was furious that he and the First Army hadn't marched east with the others. With the Blood Moon at their backs and Efialtír's Chosen at their side, now was the time to strike with their full might. Not for another four hundred years would they have this strength. But Fane had chosen patience.

Whatever the reason, Garramon knew there was logic behind it. Fane never did anything without a reason. He was meticulous, precise, and always weaving plans within plans. Garramon had learned to simply trust his old friend. Fane had never let him down, not truly. But that didn't mean he liked being in the dark.

The sound of huffing and puffing echoed from the arch behind him.

"You made it."

"Why…" Rist paused, sucking in air. A series of clinks signified Rist dropping the sacks of iron rings to the floor. "Why did you make me climb more stairs?"

"To push past your limits, you must first reach them."

"That's poetic…" Rist's stumbling footsteps sounded across the balcony upon which Garramon stood, and the young man stopped beside him and doubled over, heaving. Hundreds of thin scars decorated his back – Brother Pirnil's work. "But I don't like poetry. It takes too long to get to the point."

Garramon laughed. "Did you keep your food down?"

"Hmmm." Rist stood slowly, stretching out his back. "But I can't promise anything for the way back down."

The young man was a different creature entirely from the one Garramon had met that first day in Al'Nasla. He had been a wisp of a boy, barely capable of holding a sword, never mind wielding one.

The biggest change however was not in his appearance, but in the way he held his chin higher, in the confidence with which he spoke, and in the way he was no longer over-awed by every little thing like a sheltered farm boy. His ascension to full Brother may have been accelerated by necessity and circumstance, but it had also been earned. And yet, Garramon feared what might happen if Rist took the test of the Arcarians. He was strong, but was he strong enough? Garramon would have rather waited, but Fane was insistent.

"I could have taken you to the top," Garramon said, resting his hand on the crenellation that topped the balcony's low wall.

"Please, gods no." Rist pulled a long breath, stretching his hands behind his head.

From the balcony where they stood, they could see the entire western section of the city sprawling outwards, the Lodhar Mountains in the distance, Lake Berona on their left glittering a blend of orange and red.

"You asked me a question when we entered the city almost a week past."

Rist straightened, but he didn't say anything.

"What happened all those years ago? Why did I make the choice I made? It's a fair question. One most people would have the respect not to ask."

"Fear can often be mistaken for respect." The words left Rist's lips so plainly it caused the corners of Garramon's mouth to curl. The man's candour was a refreshing thing.

"True enough." Garramon leaned forwards, looking out at the light glinting off the rooves of the buildings below. "When I first pledged my life to The Order, I was younger than you were. Ten summers had passed me by when my mother and father sent me to be tested in the elven city of Baraduílin. I cried, a lot. I'd never been away from home. My parents loved me, of that I never doubted, but I was the second son. Tharahír was to inherit my father's farm, and I had four brothers and three sisters. The Order paid good gold for any initiates who were accepted. The harvest had been bad for three years, and we had many mouths to feed. They tested me first for the Calling. I'd always dreamt of becoming a Draleid, of a dragon egg hatching, of soaring through the skies. As you can see, that didn't happen. But I could touch the Spark. I was to be a mage of The Order. There were few greater honours in all Epheria. And so The Order became my life."

Garramon pulled away from the wall and folded his arms, gazing out at the horizon. It had been some time since he'd talked about those years.

"For over a century, everything was as I had imagined. We stopped a Karvosi invasion on the Andean coast – now Arkalen – two from the Ardanians, fought a bloody war along the Lightning Coast with three Urak clans... Gods, there was so much more. But I felt like we were doing good. I felt like a hero in a bard's tale. After sixty years, I was inducted into the Arcarians. I met Fulya, had a son – a beautiful boy, so full of life, so kind."

"What changed?" Rist's stare was as intense as ever, his attention unwavering.

"Everything." Garramon let out a long sigh. "As you've already pointed out, the world is not black and white, no matter how much we will it to be. All we can ever do is what we believe to be right. There wasn't one event or one moment in time. As it often is, the change was slow and subtle, like a disease or a rot spreading from the heart, creeping through The Order's lifeblood. We began to be involved in wars we had no place in. Brutal, bloody, and savage. And unlike the past, there wasn't always a clear reason why – at least not to me. You see, Rist, our purpose wasn't to become embroiled in every conflict that plagued the continent. Our purpose was to protect those who were caught in the middle, to stand against any one power seizing control of another, to push back any armies that threatened our shores. The warriors of The Order were warriors of the people. We belonged to all Epherians. Somewhere along the way, that was lost."

"And so you burned it to the ground? Turned on the people you called friends?"

Garramon snapped his head around, his jaw clenching, fingers twitching on the stone. "Watch your tongue."

"Am I wrong?"

"Without context, no." Sometimes Garramon forgot how plain the young man was, how simply he thought of the world. Rist was one of the most intelligent souls he had ever met, but he had a habit of thinking only in straight lines. A strength at times, but a weakness at others. "Context is what grants comprehension of any fact, Rist. If a tree is tall, what makes it tall?"

"Its height."

"No. If a tree stands twenty feet, it is simply that. It is neither tall nor small. Tall is a relative term. One thing can only be tall in context. A twenty-foot tree is tall amongst a forest of trees no taller than ten feet. But if it sits amidst a thicket of hundred-foot titans, it is not simply small, it is tiny. Right and wrong, good and evil, these things are relative also."

"It is always right to save a life," Rist countered, his expression unshifting.

"Even if that life goes on to take another? Or ten? Or a hundred? Or a thousand? What if that life rode a two-hundred foot-dragon and was willing to burn an entire city alive to fill a coin chest?"

Rist pondered that a while, giving that same blank stare he always had when he was thinking.

"Over time, more gold flowed into The Order's coffers than I'd ever seen in my life. People I'd known for a hundred years began to wear the finest silks and gorge on the most decadent of feasts. They built homes that were better called palaces. They stopped caring about the people they were meant to protect, looked down on them. It all became about power and who wielded it."

Rist opened his mouth to speak but visibly stopped himself, waiting for Garramon to continue. The man never made the same mistake twice.

"Alone, these are not things that justify a rebellion. But everything requires context. The gold, the opulence, the greed, it twisted them. It changed *why* they fought. Everything was steered by trying to retain what they had. Wars were fought for gold and favour. Souls burned in the North because a king in the South willed it. We became nothing more than enforcers and cutthroats, just in finer silks. And those who weren't dreamt of wearing the crowns themselves. In ten years, more Epherians died by The Order's hand than in the previous two hundred. There was always a reason, always a story woven by the most silver of tongues. You see, Rist, the desire for *more* is as human a thing as any. But when a person wields the power of the Spark, or that of a dragon, they must be held to a higher standard. When a person possesses the power to snuff out hundreds of lives in a heartbeat… that changes everything. I could tell you stories of the tens of thousands of bodies I watched twitch and crackle in the fires that razed the city of Unmire because their king refused to pay a debt. Or I could tell you of the cries for help ignored because a member of the 'esteemed council' held a grudge against another man who had been chosen by a woman he desired. Or of the executions that took place again, and again, and again for those who crossed the wrong people. But if I did, we would be here all night and all day. The simple fact is, we became tyrants, our presence actively darkening this world. The people we were meant to protect were the ones who suffered the weight of our failure."

Garramon looked to Rist, seeing the young man deep in thought. It was then he realised the simplest way to convey information to Rist was in terms of something he understood. "You've read the memoirs of Edmire Burkiln. I've seen you with it."

"I have."

"All that is required for evil to triumph is for good men to do nothing."

"Those are not actually his words." Rist pursed his lips. "They are those of Jon Stilvar Milner, a philosopher from the old kingdom of Endiral, though Burkiln adopted them as his own. 'Let not any soul stay their conscience by the delusion that they do no harm if they take no part. The darkness of this world needs nothing more to triumph than good souls looking on and doing nothing.'"

"Well," Garramon said with laugh. "The point remains the same. When Fane came to me, he gave me a choice – stand by and watch while The Order I gave my life to slowly rotted and turned against everything we stood for, or fight. I chose to fight. I chose to not allow darkness to triumph by my apathy."

"And now?"

"I would do it all again." Garramon nodded slowly as he spoke. Not a word of a lie left his lips. He *would* do it all again. "You weren't alive in the days before the fall of The Order, or 'the Liberation' – what a fucking stupid name. What we did wasn't a liberation. It was a war. I am not naive enough to think any different. We waged a war, and we won, and Epheria is better for it."

"Is it?"

"Yes. In your lifetime, how many wars have you seen? How much family have you lost by the blade? Have you wanted for food? Yes, there are taxes, just as there were before. There are rebellions, just as there were before. But the peace this continent has known in the last three hundred years is unprecedented. Rebellions like the one burning in the South prey on short memories and fickle hearts."

"What about the Valtarans? Or the Kolmiri dwarves? Or any of the other rebellions the empire has crushed?"

"Your reading is even more extensive than I'd thought. But do you think The Order would have dealt with them any differently? Alvira would have argued, like she always did. She was good, but she was weak. All the council had to do was prey on her honour and her code, and they could twist her any way they wanted. She didn't understand their manipulations." Garramon sighed, closing his eyes for a moment. He could feel the anger rising within him, feel it burning his cheeks and clenching his fists. It wasn't an anger at Rist but at the memories of the past, of the decisions he had been forced to make. "You remind me a lot of my son, Malyn. Never stop questioning things, Rist. Never stop questioning me, or Fane, or Primarch Touran, or anyone."

"What happened to him, your son?"

"He died a long time ago." Garramon didn't have the heart to discuss what had happened to Malyn, how his son had betrayed them, how he'd watched Malyn kneel at the headsman's block, and how Garramon had put him there by letting Solman Tuk wrap his venomous hands around Malyn's mind. Garramon had died a little that day. "Come, it is time to spar before the sun sets completely. And I'd advise you to put on a shirt."

Rist let out a long puff of air, running his hand down his sweat-soaked chest. "It's a lot colder up here than it is down there. My nipples could cut glass."

"Some things, Rist, are better left unsaid."

⌒⌒

LATER THAT NIGHT, RIST TRUDGED through Berona's streets, the lanterns fading, the pink shimmer of the moonlight cascading across the stone. Each step felt like it would be his last, hips groaning, feet stinging, legs aching. Bruises had formed within bruises, deep black atop blue and yellow.

He was one swift strike of a staff away from breaking, and yet, he had never felt stronger – or fuller. Just the thought caused his stomach to rumble, and he rested a palm across it, puffing out his cheeks. Garramon had him eating like a horse, or probably more aptly a bear. He had learned three days ago that a human can sweat simply from consuming too much meat at one time. It was an entirely useless piece of information, but it was something Rist had never known before. It was also something that burned him with guilt. There were people outside the walls surviving off rations, and there he was eating enough for three.

The city was strangely quiet at night. Aside from the occasional drunk and more than a few shady figures here and there, the only people Rist passed were guard patrols. A dour atmosphere had settled over the place. Berona would see bloodshed. Between the Uraks and the elves, something was coming. It was not a matter of if but when. And to make everything worse the Lorian rebels were not only attacking and looting along all roads in and out of the city, they were actively raiding within its walls as well. That was why the Fourth and First armies had remained and been given barracks within the city limits.

With his slow, plodding footsteps for company, Rist made his way through the city and towards the barracks assigned to the First Army, praying to Varyn his legs wouldn't give way. Unlike at Al'Nalsa, where the barracks were situated in camps outside the city, a number of barracks had been purpose-built within Berona's walls as the city itself lay at the outer reaches of Loria and far closer to Urak territory.

Each was a small fort of its own, walled even within the city limits, with towers at all four corners and battlements manned night and day. Similar layouts had been applied to the eastern cities along the Lightning Coast. Not that it had mattered when the elves had rained dragonfire upon them.

Rist nodded to the guards at the barracks gate, then stepped through and into the courtyard lined by stables ahead and baths to his right. The barracks consisted of twelve enormous halls, a stable, baths, its own storehouse and granary, latrines, several cookhouses, and a headquarters. Ten of the twelve halls were two storeys high and capable of housing up to five hundred soldiers bunked in tiers of three. The two remaining halls were broken into individual chambers for the one hundred and thirty mages of the First Army. Taya Tambrel and her generals took residence in the headquarters at the northern end, along with the Blackwatch.

As Rist stumbled through the barracks, his legs sensing he was close to bed, three mages of the First Army rounded the corner of the baths with towels around their waists and steam wafting off their bodies.

"Brother Havel." One of the mages inclined his head.

"Exarch Gurney." Rist reciprocated the gesture, greeting the other two mages in kind before they continued on to their chambers in the other hall.

Rist stood a little taller, rolling his shoulders back. It still felt strange to have the others, even the Exarchs, treat him as one of their own, treat him as a Brother. It felt stranger still to find pride in that recognition considering none of the High Mages had bothered to even glance in his direction previously. But his steps were lighter the rest of the way to his chambers in the far hall.

He twisted the handle and pushed open the door with his shoulder, grunting as he did. The room was small and sparse, just how he preferred it.

He pulled on thin threads of fire and lit the wicks of the candles on the desk and on the shelf above the straw-stuffed mattress set against the far wall. Books were piled high on the desk, some he'd brought with him into the Burnt Lands, others he'd sequestered from the Circle's library. *Druids, a Magic Lost* sat on top of *A History of Magii* – the book he'd acquired in the Milltown markets almost two years ago – and beneath *A Study of Control* and *The Spark: A Study of Infinite Possibilities*.

He glanced at the wardrobe by the end of the bed that held his armour, clothes, and gear. He truly didn't have the energy to remove his clothes, fold them, and set them back in the wardrobe. All he wanted to do was sleep. But that wasn't how his mind worked. This room was his space. If it was cluttered, so too was he. The last time he'd tried to leave clothes lying on the floor, he'd lain awake for hours until finally forcing himself to rise and put everything back in its proper place.

As he stared at the wardrobe, unmoving, his shoulders slumped, a moment of genius struck him. If he didn't remove his clothes, then he didn't have to fold them or put them away.

And with that thought, the aches and pains dulled and Rist flopped onto the bed like a dead fish and let sleep take him.

RIST AWOKE TO SOMEONE TUGGING gently at his boot. He didn't have the energy to roll onto his back, so he just grunted.

Another heave and his boot popped off.

"Really?" Even had he not recognised her voice, the sheer exasperation would have told him it was Neera pulling his boots from his feet.

"What?" Rist lay face down on the mattress, his eyes closed.

"Well, you're fully clothed for starters, and you left the candles burning. You could have set the whole place on fire."

"Is it on fire?"

"No—"

"Well, then let me sleep."

"Stop being a puckered arsehole." The mattress shifted as Neera sat down. She pulled his other boot off and removed his socks. "I need to remember this night. I don't like feet. They're like… hands on the end of your legs. And yet here I am holding your sweaty sock."

Something soft and a little damp landed on the back of Rist's head. The smell told him it was his sock.

"Come on, you lug, roll over, and we'll get these trousers off. You can't sleep like this."

"I beg to differ," Rist answered, his voice muffled by the mattress.

"Roll over, you goat." Hands wrapped around his waist, fingers tucked into his belt, and then Neera hauled him onto his back. She started laughing as she undid his belt and stripped him down. "You're honestly such a pain."

The mattress shifted again, and Rist opened his eyes to see Neera standing with his trousers in her hand. She folded them once, then twice, and started to place them into the wardrobe until she caught his eye. "What is it?"

He wanted to tell her she'd folded them wrong and that they needed to be hung, but he could hear Dann in the back of his mind. *"Don't you fucking dare. Don't you fucking dare."*

"Thank you," he said instead.

"Hmm."

Neera finished putting away Rist's clothes, then removed her armour, blew out the candles, and climbed into the bed.

"How are you feeling?" she asked as she traced her finger along the welts on his right shoulder.

"I've been better. How was your watch?"

"Quiet and boring. Just what I'd hoped for." She turned Rist over so he faced the other wall, then wrapped her arms around him. She traced her hand down the black and yellow skin of his arm. "He's going to kill you if he keeps this up."

"One less thing for you to worry about."

Neera slapped Rist's bruise just hard enough to elicit a sharp 'tssk'.

"You shut that stupid mouth of yours." She slid her arm under his, pressing her palm against his chest. A moment of silence passed. "Don't say things like that."

Rist rested his hand over Neera's, slipping his fingers into the gaps between hers. "Sorry."

She let out a sigh, nuzzling into the crook in his neck. "It's fine... It's just this place. Everyone's on edge. Uraks attacked one of the scouting parties this evening, just before sunset. Ripped them all to pieces. Then rebels set fire to one of the granaries in the garrison barracks. Do they not understand the city watch will just rebuild it and replenish it from the city's stores? They're setting fire to food while we're anticipating a siege. What do they think will happen if the Uraks or the elves breach the walls? Who do they think will suffer the most?"

Rist did all he could not to let out a sigh. All he wanted to do was sleep, but he could hear the worry in Neera's voice. "They're not thinking. They're just fighting."

He could tell by how Neera tensed that was the wrong thing to say.

"Fighting *us*. Two women died in that granary fire. Two women who would have stood on those walls and protected this city. Two women who weren't expecting to be burned alive by their own people. And you're saying that's all right?"

"That's not what I'm saying." Rist drew a calming breath, exhaling through his nostrils.

"Then what *are* you saying?"

"I'm saying that it's not always so simple."

"It's as simple as you make it." Neera pulled her arms free from around Rist and turned the other way, placing her back against his.

"Wait... What just happened?" Rist twisted in the bed, the back of Neera's head visible in the dim moonlight that drifted through the window. "How... Ah, fuck it."

He turned back around, shuffled his pillow, and closed his eyes. He was too tired for this.

CHAPTER TWENTY-NINE

ALL GREAT THINGS

12th Day of the Blood Moon

Elkenrim – Winter, Year 3081 After Doom

The fog spread for miles in all directions, swallowing hills and trees and streams, like a great beast of the gods. It moved with an unnatural creep, tendrils of grey snaking across the ground. Eltoar had never seen anything of its like until the Battle of the Three Sisters. It rose hundreds of feet from the ground, crashing against an invisible ceiling as though hemmed in by a sheet of glass.

In the days since his return to Elkenrim, he and Voranur had tracked the fog's movement from dragonback while the armies had dispatched scouts along the adjacent hillsides to watch for any advance elven forces. Lyina had not been happy to hear she would be kept from the fight to come, but her mood had shifted when she'd realised she was being sent to intercept Irulaian and Dravír off the Antiquar coast. Neither Draleid nor dragon had been present at the Three Sisters when Pellenor and Meranta had fallen, but that mattered little to Lyina. Vengeance was vengeance, and she would have hers. But she was unpredictable at present, and Eltoar needed predictable in the defence of Elkenrim.

Rise.

At Eltoar's thought, Helios angled his wings, and the great dragon swept upwards, the force pulling at Eltoar's shoulders, the wind whistling through the slits in his helmet.

The sun was already half-sunken over the mountains in the west as Helios ascended, the light of the Blood Moon tinting the landscape in a deep red. The soft glow of hundreds of lanterns spread across Elkenrim's twin walls, and more again illuminated the staked trench that had been dug around the city's perimeter.

The elven army would be at the gates by the time night had fully taken hold. But what Eltoar still couldn't understand was why. Something didn't sit right with him. Honour and glory were one thing, but neither Vandrien nor Salara were fools. The Lorian armies gathered at Elkenrim contained two and a half thousand Battlemages between them, augmented by the Blood Moon. That force was bolstered by another hundred thousand trained soldiers if the garrison and the reinforcements from Catagan and Merchant's Reach were included. Even with their dragons, any elven victory would be a pyrrhic one.

The thought led Eltoar to only two possible conclusions. Either Vandrien and Salara had lost their minds, or there was something he didn't know. The latter was far more likely.

He had known the force shown at the Three Sisters was but a fraction of the elven power. But how large truly was their host? A hundred thousand? Two? Three? If that were the case, Elkenrim's defenders would need the blessings of every god to prevail.

There was always the possibility that the eight dragons he'd counted at Darnírin's Hill were not the entirety of those kept hidden all these years. Though that was less likely. If that number were much larger, the elves would not be hiding in the fog.

Eltoar filled his lungs as Helios banked left and swerved towards the city, Seleraine swooping from above to hold level at Helios's right wing.

"What do you think?" Voranur called from his soulkin's back, threads of Air carrying his voice.

"That there is something we are missing."

"Agreed."

"Make for the city."

Night had descended by the time the wall of fog stopped moving a hundred or so feet beyond the trench that ringed Elkenrim's outer wall. Even the light from the many lanterns at the trench's edge failed to pierce the opaque grey.

Eltoar clasped his hands behind his back, looking on from the battlements as a number of elves in gold and red stepped from the fog and marched to the trench. One drove a banner into the ground. The golden stag of Lunithír, illuminated by lanternlight, rippled in the night's breeze.

"I don't see Vandrien." Voranur rested his hand on the pommel of his sword.

"Nor Salara," Eltoar responded.

"How can you see that far?" Argil Ford was the commander of Elkenrim's city guard, a short man with a wiry frame and hair brown as bark. He was a dour and cantankerous man.

As though answering Argil's question, Helios unleashed an enormous roar, matched by Seleraine as both dragons dropped low over the city and swept a gust in their wake, leaving cloaks and banners flapping and dust spiralling.

Cheers and roars erupted, and all along the walls grew a cacophony of sound as the city's defenders threw their fists in the air, clapped their gauntlets against their breastplates, and knocked wood against stone. All one hundred thousand were within the walls. Just short of eight thousand manned the outer wall, six thousand more at the inner. The rest stood by for replenishment or were arranged across chokepoints throughout the city. Plans had already been put in place for if, and when, the elves broke through the various sections of Elkenrim's defences.

With Helios's roar, Eltoar felt no need to answer Argil's question. Instead, he continued to observe through the dragon's eyes.

Eight elves stood before the trench, unmoving, their gazes fixed on the city as the golden stag banner flapped before them. Even with Helios's sight, it was impossible to make out their faces through their helms. But he would have known Vandrien or Salara anywhere. They were either not at Elkenrim at all, or they lingered within the fog. Neither option made sense.

Another roar thundered in the night, followed by a second and a third. The fog whirled and twisted, bursting outwards as three enormous shapes erupted from within its bounds.

The cheering on the walls stopped.

All three dragons bolted upwards like streaks of lightning, twisting about each other and weaving through the low bank of clouds that had drifted in. One had scales of deep crimson – the dragon from the Three Sisters. The second was Andrax, yellow scales and pale pink wings marking him. But it was the third creature that held Eltoar's attention.

The Blood Moon's light glinted on the golden scales that adorned Vyrmír's chest and snout. The dragon was almost twice as large as the others, his powerful wings blotting out the moon's light.

"So you *are* here," Eltoar whispered to himself. In the back of his mind, he could feel Helios soaring on a current of air, twisting as he tried to get a better look at the three dragons and their Draleid.

Three rows of armoured elves with long glaives stepped from the fog, moving in perfect time. They stopped with a snap of their boots and drove the butts of their glaives into the ground, still as statues.

"Commander Ford. Assemble a guard of ten and send word to the commanders of the armies. It is time."

"So be it." Argil turned but then hesitated a moment. "What are the chances we live to see tomorrow?"

Eltoar looked back at the man, then at the faces of those around him. The mood was dark, their expressions grim. He could feel the fear in their hearts. These men and women were good soldiers, but they had never faced elves on the field of battle. That might have been a good thing, if they had not heard tales of the devastation along the Lightning Coast or of the Battle of the Three Sisters.

He'd heard the stories spreading through the ranks. As far as many of the Lorians were concerned, the elven army was a host of demons sent from the void to rip the living world to pieces. Eltoar felt no need to correct them. That was how war functioned. Or at least, that was how a soul survived war. You turned your enemy into monsters. Monsters were easier to kill – not in the physical sense but in the sense of the soul. Fewer sleepless nights were born from the deaths of monsters. But it was Eltoar's intention to show these men and women that monsters could bleed.

"Focus on today, Commander. I'll see what I can do about tomorrow."

THE PORTCULLIS SQUEAKED AND GROANED as it opened, aged iron that was long past needing oiling. Soldiers marched, carrying a large wooden bridge on their shoulders, their backs straight and expressions sombre.

Eltoar, Voranur, and the army commanders followed in the bridge's wake. Not one of them spoke. There was nothing to be said. Eltoar had already explained the elven tradition of Narvírinín – 'the meeting of commanders' – before a battle. He had explained Alvadrû, and he had explained that there would be no slow, long siege. Elves did not lay siege in that way. There was no honour in watching your enemies starve and wither. Battle was meant to be quick and savage, not slow and fumbling.

The men lowered their bridge, setting it in place across the trench, then bowed their heads as Eltoar and the others passed.

The crunch of dirt beneath Eltoar's boots was all he could hear after he stepped from the bridge, his gaze fixed on the flapping banner of the golden stag, the banner of his home.

Had he never heard the Calling, never been bound to Helios, he may well have been standing on the other side of this battle, garbed in the same gilded plate his mother had once worn. That was lifetimes ago though, and the choices had been entirely out of his control.

He remembered what Alvira had once told him long ago, after his sister had fallen in the war between Lunithír and Kavathíl, and he had not been there to die by her side. *"Every soul has a thousand lives not lived, born of a thousand choices not made and a thousand paths not walked, Eltoar. We must not dwell on those other lives. They are ghosts, and if we let them, they will haunt us. Look forward. There are more choices to make, more paths to walk, more life to live."*

Eltoar's jaw clenched reflexively at the memory, a wave of sorrow and regret bleeding into his mind from Helios's.

If only we'd walked the same path. I miss you.

Eltoar stopped within ten feet of the banner and the eight elves who stood about it. For a brief moment, the wind was the only voice that spoke, crimson cloaks and tabards flapping. The rows of elves behind the banner stood still and rigid.

"Eltoar Daethana." One of the elves by the banner stepped forwards, pauldrons ornamented with charging stags, a blazing sun on his breastplate. The cloth on his armour was white as opposed to the usual crimson of Lunithír. "I had hoped it would be you."

"I'm afraid I do not know you as well as you do me."

The elf removed his helmet and held it into the crook of his arm. "Better?"

"Olmaír Moridain…" So many faces Eltoar thought were lost had resurfaced these past months. And of them all, Olmaír's was the least welcome. Eltoar dipped his head, bowed at the waist, and pressed a fist to his breastplate. "Alaith anar, Aeldral."

Well met, Elderblade.

"Stand straight, traitor. And take the sound of Enkaran from your lips. Speak the tongue of your chosen people, for you have lost the right to ours."

Eltoar straightened, clutching his pommel so tightly he could feel the steel pressing into the bones of his hand.

"Bloodshed cannot be avoided this night, nor any night until the empire is ash. I offer you the right of Alvadrû. Should you accept, I will see that a shard of your broken honour will be reclaimed as you die. The people of this city will be spared, but they will be chained and collared as ours were in the northern mines."

"And if it is your blood that feeds the earth when our blades part?"

"Then my army will lay down its steel and you can stand by and watch as more of your kind are placed in chains. I'm sure that would delight you."

"You should reject the offer, my lord." Denmar Roy, commander of the Twenty-Third Army, leaned into Eltoar. His breath smelled of garlic and onions. "Let them beat themselves against our walls. There is no need to risk your life when the advantage is ours."

Voranur stepped forwards before Eltoar could speak. "I will accept the right of Alvadrû."

A smirk crept onto Olmaír Moridain's lips. "It was not offered to you."

"That is not our way," Voranur said.

Olmaír's smirk widened, and he tilted his head as he stepped closer. "*Our* way? You are not one of us, Voranur. You are a stain on the Evalien. You are without honour. By rights I need not offer Alvadrû at all. And if you speak again, I will cut you from groin to navel and your dragon will weep over your corpse."

"How dare you." Voranur made to close to the distance between them, but Eltoar rested a hand on his shoulder.

Eltoar shook his head, then looked to Olmaír. "Tell me, where is your queen? Does she not have the honour to face me herself?"

"Honour? Queen Vandrien takes shits with more honour than you. She need not waste her time on your blood. Enough talk. Eltoar Daethana, I offer you the right of Alvadrû. Do you accept?"

Eltoar pulled his and Helios's minds together. Fear and fury pushed to the fore. Memories flowed from the dragon's mind to Eltoar's. Memories of watching Olmaír spar, of watching him carve through Uraks, elves, humans, Jotnar, and dwarves alike. Olmaír the Bloody. Olmaír the Undying. The Dread Reaper of Caelduin.

I must show them that monsters bleed.

In the sky above, Helios roared in defiance.

Have you no faith in me? Eltoar thought the words with a smile on his face. And Helios sent him memories of the day the obsidian black egg had hatched and the tiny dragon had crawled free. He had been so small he'd fit in Eltoar's palm. One of the smallest hatchlings Eltoar had ever seen. Along with the memory came feelings of trust, honour, love. But all the while, the fear permeated everything, accompanied by a sense of helplessness.

I do not sense this is the day I die. But if it is, we have lived a long life, my friend.

Eltoar stepped forwards. "I accept."

Olmaír inclined his head, then replaced his helmet. "There is some honour left in those bones then."

Voranur grasped Eltoar's forearm. "Makri alaith, akar. Draleid n'aldryr."

Fight well, brother. Dragonbound by fire.

"Rakina nai dauva," Eltoar whispered back. He looked to Argil Ford. "Commander, return to the city. If I die here, the armies are to yield. There will be no bloodshed. You've heard what happened to the eastern cities, and I would rather Elkenrim not be added to that list. But if the vows of the Alvadrû are broken, there will be no mercy. And if I should emerge victorious, we will need a place to hold our captives."

The man's tongue twisted in his mouth, and he turned his bottom lip inward. "How do we know they will hold to their end of the bargain?"

"Do as you are instructed, Commander."

Eltoar held Argil's gaze until the man finally gave a short nod and turned, ordering his ten guardsmen with him.

The elves spread in a large semi-circle, Olmaír Moridain taking position at its centre.

Voranur instructed the commanders to do the same, and Eltoar stepped out to meet Olmaír. He slid his sword from its scabbard, the rasp ringing out.

He loosened and tightened his grip on the hilt, subconsciously feeling the weapon's weight. Of course he'd owned the blade for centuries. He knew its weight intimately, knew its balance and curve. Eltoar let out a short laugh.

"It is good you find humour at the end, Oathbreaker." Olmaír flourished his blade, the steel catching the pale pink light of the moon. All elves of Lunithír knew the name of that blade: Galbarak. *Vengeance.* It was a weapon of the Second Age – the Age of Honour – passed down through the blood of Moridain for over a thousand years. That sword had crowned kings, ended bloodlines, and finished wars. It was a legend unto itself. "I will not make this quick."

In truth, Eltoar had laughed because for the first time in a long time, he was nervous. Had this moment come fifty years earlier, that might not have been the case. But now... There was a new hatchling and too many things left unfinished, too many questions left unanswered. He was needed in this world, or, if he was being honest, he needed to be in this world.

That was not the only reason for his apprehension. To say Eltoar and Olmaír had not always seen eye-to-eye would be a grave understatement. And yet, to slay one of his people's greatest legends was not something Eltoar desired. If he lost, he would be dead and Helios would be alone. If he won, he would be despised by every elf beneath the Lunithíran banner until the breaking of time – more so than he already was. Neither was a particularly desirable outcome, but he knew which one he preferred.

Eltoar focused on his breathing, feeling his lungs swell. He glanced towards the city, where the lanterns lit the walls like stars in the sky. Above, he felt Helios soaring lower, staying as close as he could. Lastly, Eltoar looked towards the elves arranged around him and those who stood in the rows before the fog. Once, they had cheered his name, and now they would cheer his death. The thought was a sobering one.

Every soul has a thousand lives unlived.

Olmaír took the first step, holding his blade low, the tip hovering just above the dirt. He moved around Eltoar, tilting his head, watching.

Eltoar did the same, and the pair circled each other slowly. After a few moments, Olmaír stopped and shifted his stance into Howling Wolf. The elf was a master of many forms, but it was upon svidarya that his legend was built.

"Dauva alaith." Eltoar pressed the guard of his sword against his breastplate, bowing slightly.

Die well.

He set his feet, gripped his blade, and sank into Swooping Hawk.

Olmaír stared back at him. "Dauva irilka."

Die slow.

The elf surged forwards, twisting right, then left, adjusting his blade with every movement.

Eltoar fell into Tenp i'il Uê. *Stone in the Water.* A movement of his own making.

Olmaír's first strike came in hard and fast to Eltoar's right hip. Eltoar dropped and took the blow on the edge of his blade, the steel ringing out. He twisted at the hip, then swept Olmaír's sword upwards, swinging his left hand onto the pommel and stabbing at Olmaír's head as though he held a spear.

The elf snapped his neck back, avoiding the steel by a finger's width. He came at Eltoar with four quick strikes, one to the right hip, then to the left, a third to the right shin, and then a fourth that scraped upwards along his breastplate through the black flame emblazoned on the white steel.

Eltoar staggered back, his heart punching his ribs.

Olmaír came at him again. Every step the elf took was purposeful, each twist of his wrist and bend of his knee existing with perfect reason. For every blow he blocked or parried or turned aside, he struck two more. Were it not for Eltoar's plate, he would have been opened four times already.

A flicker of worry bled into him from Helios, but he pushed it away. *I need your rage, not your fear.*

A roar thundered overhead, and for an instant Eltoar saw with both Helios's eyes and his own as the dragon plummeted towards the ground. Two of the elven dragons followed, unleashing sharp screeches, but Helios ignored them as an eagle would a fly and alighted over the trench, the ground shaking beneath his weight.

All those in the circle, elves and humans alike, staggered as the enormous dragon loomed over them, the smell of burning embers wafting from his jaws.

The two elven dragons were not far behind. They landed on the other side of the ring, deep growls in their throats. Their frills were standing on end, Draleid seated at the napes of their necks.

"Enough games," Olmaír said, looking from Helios back to Eltoar. The elf charged once more with a flurry of strikes, each quick as lightning, each strong as a hammer.

Eltoar took the last strike at his head, redirected it with a swift snap of his wrists, then slammed his pommel into the cheek of Olmaír's helmet. Blood sprayed, and the elf staggered backwards. Eltoar pressed, swinging for Olmaír's neck, but even stunned the elf turned away three successive blows. The fourth strike, a stab through Olmaír's guard, sliced open the golden mail that protected the outside of his knee, biting into flesh. Olmaír dropped, letting out a grunt, but lunged forwards as soon as his knee touched the dirt.

He crashed into Eltoar, sending them both toppling to the ground. Eltoar scrambled for purchase, then hauled himself upright, watching as Olmaír did the same.

His instinct was to reach for the Spark, to pull on threads of Air and drag the breath from Olmaír's lungs. But there would be no honour in that, and the elves would not obey the agreement that had been made. The Spark could never be used in Alvadrû.

Olmaír reached up and touched the dent on the right cheek of his helmet, then undid the strap and tossed the helmet to the ground. He drew slow, steady breaths as he stared at Eltoar, beads of sweat rolling down his skin.

With his free hand, Eltoar did the same, dropping his helmet at his feet. He rolled his neck around and was rewarded by a series of *cracks*.

Olmaír spat a mixture of saliva and blood into the dirt, shifted into Striking Dragon, then lunged.

The first swing came in high to Eltoar's left. Steel crashed against steel, and Eltoar was spinning past, blocking a second strike to his hip.

He saw an opening and lunged, shifting the tide of the duel and sending Olmaír on the defensive. Olmaír deflected Eltoar's stab, but Eltoar pushed forwards through the elf's guard. He grabbed Olmaír's sword arm with his free hand, then hooked his sword hand behind the elf's head and dragged it down onto his rising knee. A *crunch* sounded, and blood spurted over the dirt as Olmaír staggered backwards.

Eltoar swung his blade in a downward arc, angling to split Olmaír's skull through his temple and cheek, but the elf launched himself forwards, crashing into Eltoar's chest and sending them both to the ground once more. Eltoar gasped, the impact hammering into his back and knocking the air from his lungs.

A fist slammed into his face and his head bounced off the dirt, a blinding light bursting across his eyes. A second fist crashed into his cheek from the other side.

Blood coated Eltoar's tongue as Olmaír's steel gauntlets smashed into his face again and again. With each blow, Eltoar's consciousness flickered, his vision blurring.

In the back of his mind, he felt Helios roaring, felt the dragon's rage burning like the sun.

No. Even as Eltoar thought the word, another punch bounced his head against the earth with a crunch that let him know a bone had broken.

Helios roared back in defiance, and through his blurred vision Eltoar could see his soulkin and the other two dragons looming over him and Olmaír. Helios would burn every elf in Epheria alive before he'd let Eltoar die.

Another fist rained down, but this time, Eltoar twisted his neck to the right and Olmaír's armoured hand collided with the earth. Eltoar reached up, wrapped his two hands around Olmaír's neck, then pulled the elf's face into his pauldron with every drop of strength he had.

Blood sprayed over Eltoar's cheek as the steel crushed Olmaír's nose and burst his lip. The elf didn't let go however, and the pair grappled in the dirt, smashing pieces from each other. Bloody and sweat-soaked, they knelt in the dirt, staring into each other's eyes, both dragging in ragged breaths.

Without taking his gaze from Eltoar, Olmaír slowly lifted himself to his feet and allowed Eltoar to do the same. The elf nodded toward Eltoar's blade, which lay on a small patch of grass to Eltoar's right, then moved to snatch up his own.

Eltoar grunted as he picked up his sword, tasting blood in his mouth, his nose broken and blocked. He turned to face Olmaír.

The Dread Reaper of Caelduin smiled back at Eltoar, blood trickling from his torn lips and rolling over his chin, his left eye already black and bruised. He dropped into Howling Wolf, *Vengeance* gripped in his fists. The elf spat blood into the dirt, then cracked his neck. This had gone on long enough. The next time their blades clashed, one of them would lie dead in the dirt. "Heraya tael du ia'sine ael, Eltoar Daethana. Du katiran val haydria."

Heraya take you into her arms, Eltoar Daethana. You fought with honour.

"Ar du, Aeldral."

And you, Elderblade.

With one last long breath between them, Eltoar and Olmaír collided in a flurry of steel.

Eltoar turned a strike left with his blade and grabbed Olmaír's left hand, pulling it away from the hilt of his sword, then smashed his forehead into the elf's already-broken nose.

Olmaír staggered backwards, and Eltoar twisted, flipped his sword into reverse, grabbed the hilt with both hands, and drove the blade back. Even exhausted, Olmaír managed to palm the steel away and swing with a single-handed strike of *Vengeance* that skittered off Eltoar's pauldron.

Eltoar pressed forwards, attempting to catch Olmaír off balance, but the elf caught Eltoar's swing with his vambrace, and a searing, sharp pain erupted just below Eltoar's ribs.

The world stood still, and Eltoar's breaths slowed. He looked down to see the hilt of Olmaír's sword protruding from below his breastplate, its tip having torn through the mail. He pulled in a breath but found it catching in his chest.

His gaze locked with Olmaír's, whose breaths were just as heavy as Eltoar's, sweat, blood, and dirt coating his face.

Olmaír placed his second hand on the hilt of his blade and tried to pull it free from Eltoar's body, but Eltoar wrapped his left hand around the hilt and held it in place.

The elf opened his mouth to speak, and Eltoar threw back his right shoulder and thrust the tip of his sword into Olmaír's open mouth. Steel cracked teeth and sliced through flesh, then burst out the back of Olmaír's skull, blood flowing down the blade.

Eltoar yanked his sword free, bringing chips of tooth and bone with it. Olmaír collapsed, blood pooling around him, and Eltoar stood in the open plain before the city of Elkenrim, ringed by both humans and elves, one sword gripped in his fist, the other jutting from his torso.

Fighting the urge to collapse in the dirt beside Olmaír, Eltoar pulled on threads of Air and Water, using them to contain the blood flow as he wrapped his left hand around the hilt of Olmaír's sword and pulled it free of his body. It was only then that he allowed himself to drop to his knees beside the ruined body of a warrior who was legend even when Eltoar was but a child.

"Can you stand?" Voranur said, grasping Eltoar's arm. "We need to get you to the Healers."

"Help me up."

Eltoar slid his own sword into its scabbard, then grunted as Voranur stuck his hand beneath Eltoar's arms and lifted him to his feet. The other elves who had stepped through the fog with Olmaír hadn't moved an inch. They all still stood in a semi-circle, their stares fixed on the corpse of Olmaír the Undying.

Eltoar limped towards the nearest, who bore the same sigil of the sun on his chest as Olmaír. "By the rights of Alvadrû, you are defeated this day. Lay down your weapons and submit or your honour be forfeit."

A long silence was Eltoar's answer. But then the elf before him lifted her helmet and held it under the crook of her arm as she knelt, bowing her head. "By the rights of Alvadrû, I yield this day to you, Eltoar Daethana, the Unworthy, the Black of Heart. We are yours. We trust in what is left of your honour to uphold the ways of war."

The other six elves followed suit, each removing their helmets as they knelt, and behind them, the rows of elven warriors did the same.

"Your trust will be honoured. And I shall return Olmaír Moridain's body to you, so that it may be properly cared for in the ways of the Evalien."

The elf before him lifted her gaze, blue eyes staring into his. "That is truly how you see us then? Are we no longer your people? Are you no longer one of the Evalien?"

Eltoar tried to speak, but the wound in his abdomen flared, burning with pain, a blinding light flashing in his vision. In his weakened state, the drain sapped at him, the threads of Air and Water that stopped him from bleeding out waning. If he wasn't tended to soon, he would be joining Olmaír in Heraya's embrace.

Before he could answer, a warning from Helios flashed in his mind, and through the dragon's eyes he watched Vyrmír burst from the wall of fog behind the elves, rising ever upwards. The dragon did not fly towards Helios and Seleraine, but instead he moved eastward, back towards Steeple. The two other dragons lifted into the air and fell into formation at Vyrmír's wings.

"What is the meaning of this?" Eltoar snapped, Helios's rage seeping into him as he glared at the kneeling elf.

"The great dragons were never participants in this battle. They observed only, with no intention of joining, and therefore are not bound by the laws of Alvadrû."

Helios tore through the sky after Vyrmír, but the dragon was already too far gone. Through Helios's eyes, Eltoar saw that it was not Salara who sat at the nape of the dragon's neck. It was a human woman with dark hair, a rune-marked collar binding her neck.

"What in the gods is happening?" Eltoar whispered.

As Vyrmír faded into the clouds, the wall of fog dissipated, spreading over the ground and thinning. Eltoar stepped past the seven elves kneeling before him and stared out at the empty field of grass where the fog had been.

There was no army. Not even a trace.

"What games do you play?" Voranur roared, dragging the elven captain to her feet, his fingers wrapped around the arm loops in her breastplate.

A smile spread across her face, and she turned away from Voranur to stare at Eltoar. "All great things require sacrifice. Is this not true, Eltoar Daethana?"

CHAPTER THIRTY

THE SPIDER AND THE FLY

12ᵗʰ Day of the Blood Moon

Catagan – Winter, Year 3081 After Doom

Salara stared at the stars, watching her breath twist lazily upwards. Olmaír was dead.

The ache in her chest, born from the sorrow that flooded into her from Vyrmír, told her as much. Her old master had taken yet another great soul from this world. She had wanted to go in Olmaír's place, to be the one to drive the steel through Eltoar's heart, but Vandrien had forbidden it.

"You and Vyrmír are too important to risk in this," she had said. *"If there is any among us who can best Eltoar with the blade, it is Olmaír. If he falls, he does so with honour and his sacrifice will move our people forwards. If he succeeds, this war will be over swiftly. There will not be a better opportunity to take Eltoar Daethana and Helios from this world."*

Salara drew a breath, holding her gaze on the sparkling broken-glass sky. "Na daui nai din siel væ'ryn von myia haydria, Aeldral. Din imadrû værakanra i'lanír."

To die by your side would have been my honour, Elderblade. Your sacrifice will not be in vain.

"Ah-hem."

Salara lowered her gaze to stare across at the two humans who stood before her. Two rows of Lorian cavalry were arranged behind them, the lantern-lit city of Catagan at their backs. Salara sensed four mages amidst the cavalry already filling themselves with the Spark.

"This offer of yours," the smaller of the two men said, gesturing towards the man at his side. "We accept. Keval here will be our champion. If you kill him, we will cede the city to you as you ask. If he kills you, though, your army will lay down its weapons and submit."

"This is the way." Salara glanced at the taller man as she spoke, the crimson light of Efialtír's moon shining on his polished head. He was at least a foot taller than she, and he looked as though he were raised sucking at a Jotnar's tit. He didn't concern her.

"And how do we know your people will obey the rules if you die?"

"Honour demands it," Salara said, turning away from the man and facing Vandrien and the five captains who stood at her side. Behind them, thousands of golden-armoured warriors of Numillíon were spread across the plain, crimson and gold banners flapping.

While Salara's soulkin had flown to Elkenrim alongside Barathûr and Andrax, accompanying Olmaír Moridain and the others, Vandrien had led fifty thousand souls behind Lorian lines through the Elkenwood. They had encountered Lorian sentries spread throughout the woodland, but not one had seen their death coming. The humans had grown arrogant across the centuries.

The hope had been that the threat of an attack on Elkenrim would draw forces from the other cities, and the presence of the dragons there – alongside Dravír on the eastern coast – would keep the Dragonguard occupied. In this, everything had proceeded flawlessly. But the cost had been great, and it had been Olmaír and his party who had paid it. They had always known there would be a slim chance of returning from Elkenrim. They had volunteered.

Salara took a deep breath, then pulled her sword from its scabbard. She unclipped her belt and handed it to Captain Undrír, who took it with a bow.

She gestured for Taran and Indivar.

"Go to your soulkin," she said in a half-whisper. "This will not take long, and I have as much faith in these humans' honour as I do in that of a snake. This night will not know the sound of peace."

"And yet you offer them Alvadrû?" Indivar was a few inches shorter than Salara, with a leaner build and dark hair tied into knots so intricate it hardly seemed worth the time.

"When the outcome is certain, is it truly an offer?"

"Hmmm. And yet, it is more than they deserve."

"This has nothing to do with them," Salara replied, looking into Indivar's eyes. "History will speak of this war. It will speak of us. I will not allow it to say that we did not always strive for the path of least destruction. We will not be what they were. We will not be demons in the shadows, quiet blades on the throats of the sleeping. We will be warriors, and whether we live or die, history will remember us as such."

"History is written by the victors," Indivar replied. "It will say whatever we tell it. The humans wrote their own history after they butchered our kin."

"And as I said, we are not them."

Indivar made to speak again, but Taran laid a three-fingered hand on her shoulder and shook his head. He looked to Salara. "It will be done, Narvír. We will await your call."

Indivar stiffened but acquiesced, inclining her head before she and Taran set off towards their soulkin, who waited behind a rise in the land some distance away.

Both Taran and Indivar had been young at the time of the Cuendyar. *The Sundering.* The night their own brothers and sisters turned against them, the night the humans waged a holy war in Efialtír's name. That youth still shone through.

"Salara." Salara turned to see Queen Vandrien gesturing towards the rows of elves that stood apart from the bulk of the force, just over Vandrien's right shoulder. Each wore newly forged golden armour with blue bands of cloth tied around their arms and waist.

Volunteers from those saved at the mines in the north. Those who felt strong enough, those who wanted to fight. Il'Onarakina – The Unbroken. It was a name given to them by Warmarshal Luilin, and it was a name Salara was inclined to agree with. Had she suffered what they'd suffered, there wasn't a doubt in her mind she would have been shattered into a thousand pieces.

None of them truly held the strength in their bodies to wage war, nor did they have the skill with the blade. But their lives were their own and if they wished to fight, Salara would be honoured to stand by their side. Along with Luilin, she had handpicked two hundred of Numillíon's finest to stand within their ranks with the sole purpose of keeping them alive long enough to feel the sweetness of vengeance.

Vandrien grabbed Salara's pauldron. "Show them what it means to be Evalien. Show them how we stand with our heads high and our shoulders back, how we will never kneel again." She lowered her voice. "Show them what we do to those who hurt our blood. And Salara, show them the power of a dragon's fury."

Salara inclined her head. "Myia'nari."

"With this victory, we cut the Lorians in half. We threaten the heart of their empire. And if Visenn and Falisín are successful, we will come ever closer to bringing Fane to his knees."

Salara's mind shifted to Visenn and Falisín, who at that moment were flying with their soulkin somewhere along Epheria's southern coast towards Aonar. The fourth prong in the plan.

"Cut off the blood, and the limb will die. Cut off enough limbs, and the body will die." Queen Vandrien's words rang in Salara's head. At that moment, a realisation hit her and she forced herself to look into the queen's eyes. "Olmaír has gone to Achyron's halls."

The twist of pain was only visible on the queen's face for a fraction of a second, but Salara saw it. She saw Vandrien's jaw slacken, saw her breath catch and her heart skip a beat. Then the queen was iron once more. "Then we must ensure his sacrifice holds purpose. Go."

"Are you certain you wish this honour to be mine?"

The queen pulled away and drew a short breath, smiling back at Salara. "I'ldryr viel asatar, Salara."

In fire we are forged, Salara.

"I sanvîr viel baralun," Salara answered.

In blood we are tempered.

Salara inclined her head to the queen one last time, then turned to face the human who awaited her. He stood alone now, the smaller man having returned to his horse some ten feet back where the other riders waited.

A thick breastplate guarded the man's torso, a coat of mail beneath, while more slabs of plate were strapped to his shins, forearms, and thighs, augmented by thick leather. In his arrogance, he wore no helmet, not even a mail cap. The sight brought a laugh to Salara's throat.

He gripped a wicked looking morningstar in his right fist, almost eight feet long with a thick steel-banded shaft and a spherical head studded with brutal spikes. A singular spike sat at the top of the head, as long as Salara's middle finger and thick as the weapon's shaft.

She glanced down at her own weapon, the red light glinting off the smooth steel, the blade curving slightly, the leather handle decorated with delicate ornamentation. The contrast between the two weapons seemed a fitting thing.

One was brutal and harsh, designed to break and snap, to puncture and dominate. The other was sleek and elegant, polished and refined, created with a single purpose: to kill.

"I am Salara Ithan, soulkin to Vyrmír. I would know your full name," Salara said, offering him more respect than he was due.

"What's it to you?" The man rolled his shoulders, glaring down at her. "Won't matter much when your brains are sliding out your mouth. Less talking, more dying, bitch."

"So be it." Salara pressed the guard of her sword against her chest, steel clinking. "Det er en aldin går til dauv. Må Achyron inwê du ia'sonei unatair."

It is a good day to die. May Achyron accept you into his halls.

The man shook his head and laughed before swinging his morningstar into a two-handed grip and marching towards Salara.

She felt Vyrmír roar in her mind, his will flowing through her, his power flooding her. The dragon flew towards the encampment on the other side of the Elkenwood, Boud strapped to his back. He had despised the idea of allowing Salara to go to battle without him but trusted her to know what was needed. If Vyrmír flew to Catagan, so too might Eltoar and Helios. That could not be risked. If it was, then Olmaír's sacrifice would have been for nothing.

We will be together again shortly, my light. I will not leave you alone in this world.

Salara lifted her blade and settled into valathír – the Frozen Soul - as the human drew within striking distance.

The man let out a roar, then swung the monstrous morningstar at her head.

She watched the weapon's flight, then jerked her neck back, the tip of a steel spike sweeping past her chin close enough to sting.

The Lorian swung again, an almighty blow that would have caved in Salara's breastplate, but she sidestepped, letting the man stagger from his unmet momentum. He was strong but slow, his armour heavy and thick. He moved like a milk-drunk child.

"Slippery fucker," he growled, veins bulging in his neck and forehead. He lunged a third time.

Salara watched his feet and hips, his steps cumbersome, his turns slow.

"En aldin går til dauv," she whispered. *A good day to die.*

Her opponent roared once more and swung his monstrous bone crusher. One blow and her skull would be mush or her ribs shattered. But the blow needed to land.

The swing came from the left. Salara stepped back. The second swing came from the right. She ducked beneath it, then levelled her blade across her body and swept it along the man's hip where the leather connected the plates. The elven steel sliced through the thick hide and bit into the flesh beneath, causing the man to stumble, crying out as blood flowed.

She twisted, snapping her blade back around and running it just below the plate on his back, slicing through more flesh.

The man dropped to one knee but hauled himself upright with surprising speed, using the shaft of his morningstar for leverage. But as he turned, Salara swung her blade from right to left, carving through his face. The skin, muscle, and tendons parted on the right side, giving way to the steel. The blade smashed into his teeth on the left side of his mouth with a chilling *snap*.

The man's knees crashed into the dirt, and he stared at her in disbelief, eyes wide, jaw hanging loose, cheeks split, two shattered teeth hanging on by stringy bits of flesh. She'd seen it before, seen how the body and the mind took long moments to comprehend true trauma. And just like that his eyes bulged, his body shook, and he gave a horrible, muffled, spluttering scream. Blood spilled from his severed tongue as he fingered the remnants of his mouth, convulsing.

Salara stepped forwards and swung, hacking through the thick muscle of his neck. She took his hand with his head, both appendages hitting the ground moments before the body did.

A pang of pity attempted to rise in her heart, but she squashed it. When an animal was in its death throes, the kinder thing was to put it out of its misery. Only a savage let it suffer.

Shouts erupted behind her, and she turned, allowing herself a half-smile at the sight of the Lorian cavalry charging back towards the city, kicking up a cloud of dust in their wake.

Three shapes formed amidst the cloud, rushing in the opposite direction as the others: directly towards her. Hooves lifted chunks of earth into the air, cloaks flapping. All three riders were mages, and Salara could feel the Spark flowing from them.

She didn't move an inch. They had not yet broken their vows, not yet breached the sanctity of Alvadrû. And she would not be the first to do so.

She pulled in a lungful of air, holding it as she touched her fingers to her chin to feel the thin scratch where the morningstar had grazed her. No matter how skilled or how powerful someone was, life and death were only ever a hair's breadth apart, a half-second, a hesitation. But she had burned that hesitation from herself long ago.

A tingling sensation ran down her spine. She released the air in her lungs as arcs of blue and purple lightning streaked from the hands of the three riders, tearing through the earth, lifting clay, and setting fire to the dead leaves strewn about the ground.

"Predictable," Salara whispered as she pulled threads of Fire, Spirit, and Air into herself and slammed them down through the path of the lightning, splitting it and sending it skittering harmlessly around her.

She looked back towards Vandrien and the other commanders and arced her sword through the air, calling, "Ilvar!"

Spear.

In the same breath, Vandrien's sister, Cala, snatched Salara's sword and tossed her a thick-shafted throwing spear in return. Salara judged the flight of the weapon, glanced at the riders, then snatched and launched the spear in a single fluid motion.

The spear caught the leftmost rider in the face, tearing open their cheek and mouth before punching through their skull in a cloud of gore and bone. The force of the blow, combined with the horse's forward motion, sent the rider soaring from the horse's back. They crashed to the ground while the horse scampered away to the left, letting out a high-pitched scream.

Poor creatures. The humans loved using them as fodder. Their souls were too beautiful for such savagery.

Both surviving riders paid their fallen companion the briefest of glances before urging their horses on faster. One attempted to weave threads of Earth beneath Salara's feet while the other drew the heat from the air around her with threads of Fire. Both manoeuvres were snuffed out by threads that came from behind Salara – Vandrien and the others.

Salara glanced back and Vandrien gestured for her to continue, giving an acknowledging nod. The humans had broken the rights of Alvadrû and the city would burn for it, but these deaths belonged to Salara.

The two riders drew their swords, glowing red light emanating from beneath their breastplates. They were only a few feet away.

She pulled threads of Air through her, then launched them at the charging Lorians. She split the threads, thinning them and slamming them into the riders' chests. The two men let out violent howls as they were ripped from their saddles.

It would have been simpler to burn them, but the horses did not deserve that fate. And she could have pulled the air from their lungs or crushed their chests, but these men had ridden away from the city with the sole intent of ending her life. They had deemed her death worthy of theirs, and so she would look into their eyes as she pulled the light from their souls.

The men scrambled to their feet as their horses scattered. A moment of hesitation flitted between them: stand and fight, or run. One plucked his sword from the ground, and they moved towards Salara.

Fight it is.

The two men closed on her, one moving left, the other right. The man on the left walked with a limp, likely sustained from the fall off his horse. The one on the right had a steady hand, and a number of knives glinted on the baldric across his chest. He would die first.

She caught a glimmer of a smile on the knife-wielder's face at the sight of her empty hands. She'd left her sword with Cala and her spear in the chest of the dead mage.

The two men circled until they stood at the periphery of her vision. A moment of wind and silence passed, then they launched themselves at her, wheeling threads of Fire, Spirit, and Air about them.

Salara pulled threads of Spirit through her, sharpening them like knives as she sliced the Lorians' threads. Both men swung their steel, one at her head, the other at her shin. She took the higher blow on her vambrace, catching the steel and redirecting it, while lifting her left boot and slamming it down, pinning the second sword to the ground and snapping it free from her attacker's hand. They moved with the speed and strength of souls augmented with Blood Magic, but they lacked the skill to make it matter.

The man on her left staggered, his injured leg unable to support him. Salara rammed her armoured knee up into his face, the crunch of bone audible. As he flailed to the ground, Salara twisted, narrowly avoiding the swing of the second mage's blade, its tip almost scraping her breastplate.

Tendrils of something unseen wrapped around her, serpents wrought of Efialtír's darkness binding her. The coils of Blood Magic pulled her arms to her side and tightened. It had been centuries since she'd last felt the tainted touch of that dark power. She pushed threads of Earth outwards and into the two mages' breastplates, pushing the metal inwards. She wasn't sure which of the two held her in their grasp. Better to be certain. Within a heartbeat, the unseen bonds holding her evaporated as both men scrambled to cut through her threads of Earth before their armour caved in.

Salara launched herself towards the closest mage, and as he swung his blade, she pulled on a thin thread of Air, ripped one of his throwing knives from his baldric, and sent it plunging into the wrist of his sword arm.

He released the blade with a howl. Salara caught the weapon mid-air with her left hand and opened his throat in a single motion. As he stumbled forwards, blood pouring through his hands, Salara wrapped her fingers around his opened throat.

"Din haydria er fyrir," she whispered as the man choked on his own blood. *Your honour is forfeit.* She plunged the Lorian blade into his belly, then tossed his lifeless body to the ground.

The mage with the limp stood behind her, having regained his blade and risen, his hand shaking around the hilt.

"You call yourselves Battlemages," Salara said in the human's Common Tongue, taking slow steps towards him. She looked into his eyes, shaking her head. "You are but shadows of what came before you."

The man limped backwards, his eyes fixed on her, his sword extended outwards in an entirely useless position. "Stay back."

A glowing red gemstone pendant had come loose from its nook under his breastplate. He reached for it, but Salara wrapped the pendant in threads of Air and snapped it free, pulling it into her own hand.

It was then she saw it in the man's eyes: he was nothing more than a child. Perhaps twenty summers, and he'd not known the feel of a blade in his hand for many of those. He was but a fawn staring into the eyes of a starving wolf. The Lorians were growing desperate, sending half-trained children into a war they could not comprehend.

She looked down at the glowing stone, staring into its depths. Something within called to her, urging her to open herself, to welcome its power into her blood.

She pushed threads of Earth and Spirit into her hand, then clenched her fist around the stone. Wisps of red light burst from the gaps in her fingers as the gemstone cracked and shattered, a shiver running through her. She turned her hand sideways and poured the crushed remnants of the stone into the dirt.

"Such a waste of life," Salara said aloud, sighing as she moved towards the young man.

His eyes widened, and he made to draw from the Spark, but Salara encased him in a ward of Spirit before it answered him.

The fear that had made its home in his eyes now visibly spread through his body, and he turned to flee.

Salara pushed a thin thread of Earth into the ground and formed a small lump at his feet. The man's boot connected, and he hit the ground like a sack of stones, his face taking the brunt of the impact.

He scrambled onto his back, his eyes flitting between Salara and the ground around him as he searched desperately for the sword he had dropped as he'd fallen. She could feel the fear in him as he tried frantically to push through her ward of Spirit.

"Please…" His voice trembled.

"Please what?" Salara asked, genuinely curious.

A voice called from behind her – Vandrien's – and Salara lifted her gaze momentarily to see a curtain of arrows stretching across the sky.

"I am sorry," she said to the young Lorian mage, whose jaw slackened at the sight of the arrows loosed from his own walls. "There is no honour in this death."

The man's hands shook and his breaths grew rapid. "For the…" he stammered. "For the empire. Efialtír will take you with me."

"No," Salara replied. "He won't."

Salara raised her hand and pulled in threads of Air, forming a wedge before her while holding her ward over the Lorian mage. She gave him a tender smile and inclined her head. "Mā du alura i'il rhyním un Heraya."

May you rest in the embrace of Heraya.

As the words left Salara's lips, the arrows fell, slamming into the ground like steel rain. The hail split around her wedge of Air, leaving a patch of untouched earth where she stood. The young Lorian mage was not so lucky. He thrashed as arrows plunged into his flesh, piercing his legs and arms, ripping into his torso, and turning his face to ribbons.

When it was all done, Salara stood unharmed, a touch of sorrow in her heart at the sight of the body that now comprised more steel and wood than flesh and bone.

An eerie silence followed, holding until dirt crunched beneath footsteps.

Queen Vandrien and her sister, Cala, stopped at Salara's side, ten members of the Sunguard spread about them, along with High Paladin Thryn Erimal and Warmarshal Luilin.

The queen cast her gaze over the two dead bodies, both studded with arrows, the earth looking like the back of a spined anditar. "They sought glory," she said, her gaze lingering on the younger mage. "But it was death who came to meet them." She looked to Salara. "Begin."

Salara pinched her thumb and forefinger together and whistled, augmenting the sound with threads of Air and Spirit.

Two roars answered her call.

Moments later, the thump of wingbeats carried on the wind and shadows fell over Salara and the others as Nymaxes and Baerys soared overhead. The pair were two of the smallest surviving dragons from the Cuendyar, but even the smallest dragons were enormous creatures in their own right. They swirled around each other, their movements intimate, black scales blending with blue, dark green wings striking against pale cream.

Another hail of arrows loosed from Catagan's walls, but the two dragons simply rose above the rain of steel and wood, the arrows falling harmlessly to the ground.

Beside Salara, High Paladin Thryn lifted his horn to his lips and blew.

More horns answered, followed by the thunder of footfalls as the army began its march. The dragons descended on the walls, rivers of fire pouring from their jaws.

Less than two hours later, Salara stood at the centre of a wide street beyond Catagan's second wall, her blade buried in the gut of a woman who had died well, her foot resting on the neck of a man who had not.

Shadows danced across the white stone walls, cast by the flames that consumed the city, accompanied by the screams and shouts of those who prepared to enter Achyron's halls.

Salara slid her sword from the woman's gut and let the body slump to the cobblestones, her gaze fixed on the blood-stained white walls. This city had once been home to the Evalien kingdom of Quelyin. She remembered their story well. They had survived longer than most after the Cuendyar, won many battles, sent many Dragonguard into The Traitor's arms. But like all those before them, they eventually fell, barely a handful surviving to find shelter within Lynalion's limits. And now she stood in their legacy: a burning husk of a city awash with Lorian blood.

She turned her gaze from the walls to the fighting around her. Though, in truth, 'killing' was a more appropriate word. The Lorian soldiers that remained in this area of the city were stragglers left behind by those retreating to the keep, and the Onarakina were brutal and savage in their dealing of death.

All about her, the armoured elves with bands of blue cloth at their arms and waists tore into Lorian soldiers like starved wolves. They hacked limbs and stabbed corpses until nothing but a mush of diced organs and skin remained.

For generations, these elves had been forced to work the northern mines until their bodies gave way or their minds broke. Now they had been given a chance to unleash all that rage, all that agony and despair. And though Salara understood their pain, respected it, she found the sight difficult to witness.

The thump of armoured boots sounded behind her.

A column of Numillíon warriors marched through the street behind Salara, their burnished golden armour marred by still-wet blood. They moved in step, crisp and precise, only stopping to drive a sword or spear through the belly of a moving body on the ground.

The column ground to a halt before Salara.

"Draleid." Captain Undrír stepped from the ranks and removed his helmet. Dried blood flecked the skin around his eyes where the helmet did not cover, and his sweat-soaked hair clung to his face. Another elf moved with him, the ornamentation of golden tree roots on her armour marking her as a galdrín.

Undrír gave a short bow, grimacing at the sight of the Onarakina tearing the remnants of the Lorians apart.

"Sankyar," Salara replied with a nod. *Captain.* "What news?"

"The queen wishes you to move on the keep. She has taken the western sector of the city with minimal losses."

"It appears the majority of the city's mages were sent to reinforce Elkenrim, Draleid." The galdrín mimicked Undrír's welcoming gesture. "We have moved through the city with little resistance. The plan has worked even more smoothly than we had hoped."

"Hmmm." Salara nodded her head slowly as she looked at the butchery around her. "It appears so."

With The Traitor's moon overhead, the Lorian mages had a distinct advantage over those of the Elven galdrín. Their Blood Magic was the strongest it had been since the night of the Cuendyar. When Vandrien had proposed the four-pronged strike, she had theorised the Lorians would send perhaps a third of their mages and warriors to reinforce Elkenrim. But from what Salara had encountered, they had sent all but a fraction. The city's walls had fallen in minutes, the garrison routed into the streets. And through all the bloodshed, Salara had encountered but three mages where she had expected a hundred. Something wasn't right. The city had fallen too easily.

"You seem displeased, Draleid." Captain Undrír tilted his head, trying to catch Salara's gaze. "Is this not the victory we had hoped for?"

"It is not a victory yet, Sankyar. There is still much death to come."

Undrír straightened, lifting his chin. "Yes, Draleid. Forgive me." The elf swallowed. "Queen Vandrien offers you the honour of reclaiming the city alongside her."

"She offers too much."

"Respectfully, Draleid, I do not believe so." Undrír gave a slight bow at the waist, pressing a closed fist against his breastplate. "She asks that you send word to Draleid Taran and Indivar. No more fire is to be cast on the city, and she wishes them to be there when you take the keep."

Salara released a short breath through her nostrils, then nodded. "It will be done. First, I would have fifty of your warriors escort the Onarakina away from the fighting."

She cast her gaze around the street. Many of the Onarakina sat on the ground, their backs resting against broken walls or piles of shattered bodies, blood dripping from their hair, their faces, and their hands. They were the living dead. Only a handful still stood, and one knelt over a body, slowly dragging a knife from the flesh before lurching forwards and driving it back in.

"They have seen enough of this day."

"As you command, Draleid."

As Undrír turned and called out to his warriors, Salara cautiously approached the Onarakina who knelt atop the savaged corpse, his blade buried to the hilt in its ribs.

"Akar," she whispered.

Brother.

The word drifted on the wind. The elf remained where he knelt, slumped over the corpse, one hand on its chest, the other on the pommel of the knife.

"Akar," she whispered again, dropping to one knee and resting her hand on his back.

The elf roared and lunged at her, a frenzy in his eyes, a rabid hunger.

Salara caught both his wrists mid-flight and twisted left, dragging him from atop the body and slamming him against the stone.

When she looked down, she saw tired, rage-filled eyes staring from a gaunt face marked by scars and lines born of a life in servitude, in slavery. The elf's hands shook in Salara's grasp, his breaths trembling.

"Alura, myia'kar. Alura. Du é varno. Inyen væra sâre du anis."

Rest, my brother. Rest. You are safe. Nobody will hurt you now.

The elf stared back at her wordlessly.

"Of course," Salara whispered, bringing the elf's hands lower, one to his side, one against her breastplate. "I am sorry, brother. They took our language from you, our heritage, our history... You are safe. You are loved. You are Evalien."

She let go of the elf's wrist, slowly, holding his gaze the entire time. "What is your name?"

"Tu..." He hesitated a moment. "Tualin, Draleid."

"Stand with me, Tualin."

Salara lifted herself back onto her haunches and took Tualin's hand into her own as she rose. With as much care as she might use to pluck a flower, Salara removed Tualin's helmet and dropped it to the ground.

His dark hair was soaked in sweat, and streaks of it ran through the blood on his face. He could not have witnessed more than twenty-five summers, but his cheekbones almost pierced his skin, his lips cracked... and his eyes... She had never seen such turmoil, such fear and uncertainty, in another soul's eyes.

What did they do to you?

She had seen the Onarakina when they had been freed from the mines. Seen their withered bodies, their scarred and scabbed flesh, their dark, listless eyes.

And so too had she watched them receive the finest silks and heartiest meals and everything any soul could want. Queen Vandrien had ensured it. And in her naivety, Salara had thought them on the path towards healing, that the clothes and the food and the luxuries would close their wounds, both of body and spirit. She could see now that naivety was too meagre a word. Idiocy, absurdity… ignorance. Yes, ignorance was the word.

What was done to these elves would never heal, never scab over or fall away. It was a torture of the soul and the mind, a torture of the blood.

Salara gave a soft sigh, then gently rested her gauntleted hands on Tualin's cheeks. "I cannot give you back any of what was taken. I cannot give you solace, or peace, or serenity. And so I will not make that promise. But I can give you vengeance. I can hone you. I can teach you to take that rage in your heart, that darkness, and give it a place in this world, give it a way to earn a different life for our kind. What do you say to that?"

Tualin's stare hardened, his lips pressing together, his nostrils flaring. He gave a sharp nod. "Ah… Avis."

Yes.

A smile broke out across Salara's face at the sound of the Old Tongue – of Enkaran – leaving Tualin's lips. It was such a simple thing, such a small and insignificant thing, at least on the surface. But language was culture, it was heritage, it was history. Language was the path that connected a soul to their ancestors. "Go," she said, gesturing towards the elves who were helping the other Onarakina to their feet. "You have done all you can here. Sleep, eat, rest. What remains is up to us."

Salara handed Tualin over to one of the warriors Undrír had selected to escort the Onarakina back to the camp. Once more, she whistled, three sharp bursts, augmented by Air and Spirit – the signal for Taran and Indivar to halt their assault and join her.

A pair of monstrous roars answered her call.

"Sankyar Undrír," she called, finding Undrír helping an injured Onarakina to her feet, blood seeping from an arrow embedded in her shoulder. "When they are all seen to, we march for the keep. Kill whatever stands in our way. The time for mercy is long past."

CHAPTER THIRTY-ONE

WARS ARE NOT WON

12ᵗʰ Day of the Blood Moon

Aravell – Winter, Year 3081 After Doom

Calen sat by Ella's bedside, his hand resting over hers. Faenir lay on the ground at his feet, the crest of the wolfpine's back reaching past Calen's knees.

"I have to go." He pressed his forehead against the back of his sister's hand. "I'll be back as soon as I can. If you want to wake up in the meantime, I won't argue." He lifted his chin so it rested on her knuckles, then let out a sigh. "Lasch and Elia are staying, as are Tanner and Yana. They'll watch over you."

Calen sat there a while longer before he drew a breath and rose. Aeson would be waiting for him, and he still had one more thing to do. He moved past Faenir and leaned over Ella. He brushed her hair aside and placed a tender kiss on her forehead.

"Don't give up," he said, stroking her cheek with his thumb.

He hunkered beside Faenir, resting a hand on either side of the wolfpine's head. Faenir pressed his head left, then right as Calen scratched, a low rumble in his throat. "Keep her safe."

The wolfpine lifted his head and met Calen's gaze, his golden eyes full of understanding. He pressed the flat of his snout against Calen's forehead, giving a high-pitched whine.

Faenir climbed onto the bed, the frame creaking and groaning beneath his weight. He squeezed himself between Ella and the wall and rested his chin on her shoulder. There was no soul in the world that would protect Ella more fiercely.

Calen picked his gauntlets up from the ground and slid them into place, then grabbed his helmet from beside the chair and slung his satchel over his shoulder.

When he made his way downstairs, he found Elia Havel standing over a pot of boiling water, two mugs on the counter beside her. "Oh, Calen. You're leaving already? The water's only just boiled. I was about to bring you up a mug of Arlen Root tea."

"Not today, Elia. I fly for Arkalen soon with Aeson. I need to be on my way."

"Are you sure?" she said, offering him a mug. "Your mother would want you to."

Calen shook his head. "When I get back."

The front door creaked open, and Lasch stepped in. "I'll have fresh mead ready for when you get back, my boy. The tea can wait."

The man strode across the room, folding his arms as he shook his head and let out a long sigh. "I'll never get over seeing you in that armour." He laughed to himself. "I suppose this is where I say something deep and meaningful? I've not got much left to say. Your father was always better with words than I was." Lasch cupped his hand on the sides of Calen's head. "We'll watch over Ella. All we need you to do is come home, you hear?"

Calen nodded. "Are you certain you don't want to go with Dann and the army? To go home?"

Lasch gave Calen a warm smile accompanied by a sigh. "Home is where you make it, my boy. Were you not listening? Our home is with you and Ella and Dann, and Rist… when he returns."

Calen's throat tightened at that.

"Go." Lasch patted Calen on the cheek. "But before you do, could you tell me how to get Gaeleron to come inside and drink some mead? The damn elf just stands outside the door like a statue."

"He does that."

"No advice?"

"If you figure anything out, let me know."

Calen shook his head as he stepped through the door, the crimson twilight washing over the basin of Alura. It was the twelfth day of the Blood Moon. Calen would not be sad to see the red wound gone from the sky.

From the reports that had started coming in again from Aeson's contacts, all Epheria was on fire. Refugees flowed from city to city in both the North and the South. The Uraks laid siege to Camylin, Elmnest was gone, and Carvahon was in chaos. The worst of it was that this was only the beginning.

Vaeril stood to Calen's left with his arms crossed, leaning against the doorframe, Gaeleron beside him.

"I'm assuming you heard Lasch then?" Calen asked Gaeleron.

"I did."

"Will you drink with him?"

"That depends how much mead he offers." Gaeleron attempted to keep a straight face, but a smile flashed across his lips. The elf had come a long way since they'd first met in the Darkwood.

Calen laughed, then grasped Gaeleron's forearm. "Thank you for watching over them."

Gaeleron inclined his head. "It is my honour, Draleid."

Calen did the same, then gestured for Vaeril to follow him as he made his way across the plateau.

The pair made their way across Alura and into the Eyrie, talking of the war to come. In truth, from the moment they'd been attacked in Camylin, it had felt like a war to Calen. But now, talking of armies marching and cities burning, Calen understood what made war so different to everything else: the cost and the consequence.

It was no longer just his life but the lives of thousands, hundreds of thousands. The consequence of failure was no longer his alone to bear. And no matter the outcome, a cost would be paid in blood. From this day on, Epheria would never be the same. No matter what he did or what choices he made, thousands would die and cities would burn. Wars were not won, they were ended.

Calen cast his gaze around the basin as he stepped onto the Eyrie's main plateau. Sardakes lay by the stream that ran off the main plateau's edge, his head resting on the grass, his chest rising and falling methodically. The other plateaus were empty, save for a number of Dracårdare who tended the grass and the trees, ensuring all was properly kept.

The Prime Keeper – Undiör in the Old Tongue – Yanîr, approached, bowing as he did. "Draleid."

"Undiör." Calen returned the gesture. "Where is Varthear?"

"Flying, Draleid." Yanîr inclined his head towards the open valley at the other side of the plateau. "Since before the morning woke."

Calen thanked the elf, then set off towards the old quarters where the Rakina had once held residence but where the prisoners were now kept. After the judgement, Chora had allowed the prisoners to roam free within the old quarters and within the Eyrie itself. Calen was well aware that she allowed it simply to get under his skin, but none of the prisoners – Tivar included – had chosen to set foot in the Eyrie.

Sardakes lifted his head. A low rumble of acknowledgement left the great dragon's throat, his deep blue eyes finding Calen's. Though still prone to listlessness, it had become more and more clear that both Varthear and Sardakes had been changed since the battle at Aravell. Even the simple fact that Varthear had taken to the air, that she soared the valleys, meant something had shifted within her.

From what Calen had seen in his vision – if that was what he could call it – when he had touched Varthear, he understood what it was that had changed: purpose. A reason to live. A need to protect.

As they walked, wingbeats sounded from the open valley that connected to the Eyrie, and both Calen and Vaeril turned to see Varthear rise above the precipice of the plateau, her enormous vermillion wings spread wide, blue scales glistening. A gust of wind followed in the dragon's wake, cold against Calen's skin.

Varthear soared around the basin, a tremor running through the plateau as she alighted on the white stone.

Calen stared into her eyes, molten fire rolling about black slits, the dragon's warm breath sweeping over him and abating the chill that had set into his skin.

Vaeril approached on Calen's right, bowing deeply at the waist. "Alaith anar, Velikír Ayar."

Well met, Great One.

Varthear gave an almost imperceptible inclination of her head, a low rumble in her throat. The simple act was enough to send a smile to Vaeril's lips.

The dragon lowered her neck and pressed her snout into Calen's body. Her lower jaw scraped the ground at Calen's feet, her nostrils rising past Calen's head. Varthear was so large Calen could have walked into her open jaws without a need to crouch. She was twice Valerys's size and radiated power. But even while Calen stared at her in awe, a knot coiled within him at the thought of how large Helios must be. Legends were told of Eltoar and his soulkin Helios, The Black Sun, The Shadow of Death. It was said that no dragon in living memory had ever come close to matching Helios in size.

He placed his right hand over a scar of fused scales that ran just under Varthear's right nostril, warmth spreading through his skin. The wound felt like rough stone beneath Calen's fingertips.

Varthear held herself there a moment, the smell of ash and char wafting from her jaws, then lifted her head and made her way towards where Sardakes lay by the stream.

Calen and Vaeril continued on to the passage on the western edge of the Eyrie.

The two guards pressed closed fists to the white dragon emblazoned on their chests and bowed deeply. Calen had seen neither of them before. He inclined his head, pressing his hand to his heart. "Your names?"

The first, an elf, straightened, her fingers tightening around the pommel of the sword at her hip. "Aneir, Draleid."

"Tordan." The other guard's voice was deep and rough. Through the gaps in his helm, Calen could see the marks of many summers on his skin, along with blue eyes that had seen their fair share of pain and loss.

"Well met, Aneir and Tordan. I am Calen and this is Vaeril." He gestured toward Vaeril. Calen looked to Tordan. "Where have you come from?"

"Kingspass, my lord. I was part of the garrison the night the Uraks breached the walls. When word came in through the network that you were mustering forces, I made for the next ship to Falstide and marched from there. Better not to make it obvious." Tordan stood straighter, raising his chin. "I saw what you did at Kingspass. It's an honour to wear the white dragon."

Tordan looked down at the sigil emblazoned across his breastplate. Valdrin and his veritable army of smiths had not sacrificed quality of work in their haste to produce so many pieces.

The man glanced to Aneir. The elf nodded and inclined his head towards Calen.

"I'ldryr viel asatar." It was clear by the way he stumbled over the words that Tordan was not familiar with the Old Tongue. But his attempt was certainly better than Calen's first. *In fire we are forged.* Calen thought he had heard the phrase before, but he couldn't quite remember where.

"I sanvîr viel baralun," Vaeril replied, a broad smile stretching his mouth. *In blood we are tempered.* "You speak the Old Tongue well, Tordan…"

"Tordan Falmor, Narvír."

If it were possible, Vaeril's smile grew even wider. "You speak the Old Tongue well, Tordan Falmor. Du grýr haydria til ourín elwynar."

The man's eyes widened and he glanced at Aneir, who stifled a laugh.

"You bring honour to our hearts," Calen translated, allowing the slightest of smiles to touch his lips as he looked to Vaeril. "Forgive Vaeril. He often gets carried away when it comes to the Old Tongue. He is honoured by your effort."

A look of pride brightened Tordan's face and he gave a sharp nod.

"As you were," Calen said, stepping past the two guards and into the long passageway carved into the rock. He would never stop being astounded at the sheer scale of everything the elves built. The ceiling must have been a hundred feet high, higher even, and the passage itself maybe a hundred and fifty across. It seemed everything was built with dragons in mind.

"What was that back at the entrance?" Calen asked Vaeril. "In fire we are forged? In blood we are tempered?"

"It's an old saying of the first elves bound to dragons, long before The Order. At least, that's what I was told as a child. It's become somewhat of a motto amongst Dracurïn."

"The what?"

"The Dracurïn. The White Dragons. Tarmon and I thought it would be wise to give them a name, something to bond them. We asked the elves to teach the humans some of the Old Tongue and the humans to teach their songs and stories in return. If they are to fight together, they need to learn to see each other as worth dying for."

Calen shook his head. "I've been absent."

"You've been with Ella," Vaeril corrected. "And dealing with politics, as a Draleid must. You can't do everything, as hard as you try."

Calen nodded, giving Vaeril a half-smile.

It wasn't long before they reached an arch at the end of the corridor that led out into a central courtyard.

Avandeer lay curled in the yard's centre, soft light spilling in through the opening above. The dragon lifted her head and peered at Calen and Vaeril, her deep yellow eyes striking against the white and purple scales that decorated her face. A series of clicks resonated in her throat, accompanied by a low rumble.

She pressed her snout into Calen's chest, blowing warm air over him. Calen ran a hand across her scales. He could feel the tension within her, feel the rage simmering. She and Tivar might not be chained, but they were still prisoners and Tivar was kept under constant guard. Avandeer did not agree with the current state of affairs. The dragon was not locked in this courtyard and yet she had not left, not flown since the judgement. Calen was unsure if it was a form of silent protest or simply an unwillingness to leave her soulkin.

As Calen stood there, Valerys pulled their minds together from where he waited with Aeson and the others. The world around him shift as the dragon's senses blended with his own.

A deep protective instinct echoed in Valerys's mind – their shared mind – as images of Tivar and Avandeer flowed between them. Tivar and Avandeer were their own, their kin. And Valerys would not allow harm to come to them.

In the stories of old, the dragons were legendary creatures capable of levelling entire cities and turning wars on their heads. They were beasts of unequalled power. Every tale told of their fury and their rage, told of their power and their capacity for endless destruction.

But few ever spoke of the great creatures' compassion and loyalty, of their pain and suffering, of their undying will to protect what they loved. Those were stories Calen wished he had heard, stories he hoped he'd one day have the chance to tell himself.

"It won't be much longer," Calen whispered, running his hand along Avandeer's scales.

The noise that came from the dragon's throat was akin to a purr accompanied by a series of clicks before she settled her head back on the white tiles.

Calen released a frustrated sigh, then gestured for Vaeril to walk with him towards the cells. They stepped from the open courtyard into a long candlelit corridor that Calen had grown familiar with over the past days.

"Aeson says Coren and Farwen should be here by the time I return from the Burnt Lands." Calen had never met the two Rakina, but the other Rakina spoke of them in the same breath as Aeson. From the stories Therin had told him, they were two of the fiercest warriors in all Epheria.

"Indeed," Vaeril said. "But their journey will not be an easy one."

"How kind of you to grace us with your presence." The voice was not one Calen recognised, but he knew to whom it belonged.

He turned to his left to see the woman with white hair and the dark-skinned elf standing in the connecting corridor. Hala and Ilyain. Four guards bearing the white dragon on their chests walked alongside the pair, threads of Spirit encasing them in a ward.

Hala raised a curious eyebrow and moved closer, the fingers of her left hand clenched into a fist. "What brings you here?"

"Take another step and it will be your last." Calen turned so he was square on with Hala, anger flaring within him, Valerys growling in the back of his mind.

Hala grinned, revealing teeth as white as her hair. She tilted her head to the side, her gaze moving from Calen's head to his feet, then back again. "So confident, so arrogant. You even stand like him."

Hala took another step closer and before her foot had even touched the stone, the tip of Vaeril's blade pressed into her chest.

"La'værakanra mahavír, Varíen Nahar." Vaeril tilted his wrist upwards and pressed so the sword point created a crease in Hala's tunic. *I will not hesitate, Kin Killer.*

Hala's grin faltered at the title.

Ilyain stepped past Hala, keeping his hands firmly behind his back, two of the guards moving with him. Threads of Fire joined the threads of Spirit as they watched his every move. The elf's face was raked with thin scars, his eyes a milky white.

"You are him, then." Ilyain stared at Calen as though he could see him. A tense silence held where Ilyain drew a long, rasping breath through his nostrils, then pressed an open palm across his breast. "I am so deeply sorry for the world we have left you. And for the burden we place on your shoulders as we ask you to fix it."

Those words were not the ones Calen had expected to leave the elf's lips. Even Valerys's rage ebbed in the back of his mind.

Hala dropped her gaze to the ground, her shoulders slumping, the tip of Vaeril's blade still pressed into her chest. Calen knew the look on her face: shame.

Calen made to speak, but then he saw him.

Farda stood some forty feet down the corridor behind Ilyain and Hala, three guards with him, the blended light of the moon and sun drifting over him through an arched window. The man stood still as a statue, his gaze fixed on Calen. The scars on his face were healed somewhat, though the flesh was pale and pink.

The fingers on Calen's right hand tensed reflexively as he stared into the eyes of the man who had killed his mam. The man who had burned her alive. All Calen had to do was reach out and snap his neck. A life for a life. Surely the gods would find that fair.

Valerys's fury bled into his own. Calen's thumping heart rose over all other sounds, his vision seeming to dim and narrow until all he saw was Farda.

"My lord?" The guard closest to Calen stepped forwards tentatively. "My lord, are you all right?"

A hand rested on Calen's shoulder – Vaeril's. The elf shook his head, and Calen noticed the purple glow of his eyes reflecting in the guards' armour.

Calen pulled a long breath into his lungs, exhaling sharply. "Carry on."

He pressed his tongue to the roof of his mouth and turned to leave, but Ilyain grabbed his arm with a grip that seemed made of iron.

The guards ripped their swords from their scabbards, steel rasping through the corridor. Vaeril's blade slid across Ilyain's throat, drawing a thin trickle of blood. Only Calen's raised hand kept Ilyain's heart beating.

"Move a hair and I will open your throat." Vaeril glared at the Rakina, his sword holding true and steady.

Ilyain leaned into the blade, quickening the flow of blood. His pale, milky eyes stared at Calen. "Vengeance does not bring peace. Trust me, I know. The things we do in anger are a rot within us." He drew a slow breath. "A dragon's fury is a Draleid's greatest strength and deepest weakness both. You must temper it before you can wield it, lest it will consume you."

"If I wanted your advice," Calen said, leaning in, "I would have asked for it."

"We cannot ask for the things we do not know we need. Paspå varno, akar. Du é orin talos du vidim."

Stay safe, brother. You are more than you know.

Calen stared back into Ilyain's vacant eyes, searching. He cast one last glance down the corridor at Farda – who still stared back, unmoving – then turned and strode away, his heart still hammering, his veins on fire, Valerys roaring in the back of his mind.

"Still your fire," Calen whispered as he walked, the clang of his boots echoing.

After a moment, Vaeril appeared at his side. They walked in silence until they stopped before an iron-banded door marked with Jotnar runes. An elf garbed in long dark robes over a breastplate bearing the white dragon stood to the left of the door. Amaril, along with four others, had been assigned to maintain the ward of Spirit around Tivar so as to keep her from the Spark. It was a small price to ensure those runemarked shackles stayed off her wrists.

Amaril inclined her head in greeting to Calen and Vaeril.

Calen gestured at the door. "She is inside?"

"She is, Draleid."

"Thank you for watching over her."

"Of course, Draleid. Det er myia haydria."

It is my honour.

"I'll just be a moment," Calen said to Vaeril. He drew a quick breath, then pushed the door open and stepped into the cell.

An oil lantern hung on the leftmost wall, bathing the stone in soft orange light.

Tivar sat with her legs folded beneath her at the back of the room. She lifted her head as he entered, her dark eyes fixing on him.

"Alaith anar, akar." She smiled weakly, inclining her head. *Well met, brother.*

"Alaith anar."

She gave a downturn of her lip. "The armour looks well." She leaned forwards. "Antherin steel… of a sort. The smith who forged it is skilled. Antherin steel is not easy to work with, and Jotnar rune work is even more difficult still. I assume you did not come so I could compliment your armour?"

"No."

"Have Farwen and Coren arrived to put this waiting to an end?"

Calen shook his head. "I am to leave."

"When?"

"Now. I'm taking Aeson to Arkalen, and then I fly with Valerys to Ilnaen."

The sound that left Tivar's lips was akin to a hiss. "That place… that place holds nothing but poison."

Calen let out a soft sigh, sitting on the bench that rested against the wall beside the door, his armour clinking as he did. "Farwen and Coren are due here soon. I promise, no matter what happens, I will not let you be executed."

Tivar sighed and met Calen's gaze. "You will do no such thing. You will allow Coren and Farwen to pass their judgement, and you will accept what is chosen."

"I will not." Calen sat forwards, his jaw clenching. "Where do we draw the line, Tivar? If we execute you and Avandeer, take another Draleid and dragon from the world, then what? I'm left alone to fight Eltoar and Helios and the other Dragonguard? That's a death sentence in itself. And what of the elves from Lynalion? What if they turn their sights on us? How many dragons do they have?"

Tivar drew a long, slow breath. She stared at the ceiling with an almost sympathetic smile on her lips. "You are not wrong, Calen. But you speak with a simplicity born of youth. I know you don't want to see it, but I am guilty of everything they say. I turned my back on my brothers and sisters. I burned, and I killed, and…" She stopped, clenching the muscles in her jaw. "I see the faces in my nightmares, hear the last screams of the Draleid whose bonds I shattered. I can give you excuses, I can tell you the reasons why I followed Eltoar, why I believed what we were doing was right. I can tell you how Efialtír twisted my mind… But when all is said and done, it was my hands that held the blade, my heart that yielded to the rage, my soul that let weakness in."

"Tivar—"

"You don't know me, Calen."

"I know that when I needed you, you came. I know that you taught me what I am, what I needed to be."

She shook her head, her eyes sunken. "I deserve death for what I did. I do not blame Chora and the others, the same way I do not blame a house for burning when it is set on fire."

"No." Calen rose and walked to where Tivar sat, dropping to a knee before her. He stared into her eyes, taking in her pale skin and the cleft in her lip. "That's not enough."

Tivar stared back at him curiously.

"You're right. I don't know your past and I don't know you. But I know that you knelt before me and pledged to give your dying breath to this cause. Dying is not enough. When Fane Mortem is dead and the empire is nothing but dust, then, and only then, may you die. Until that day, I need you to fight. I need you to be the guardian you were meant to be. Do you understand? I will not accept anything less."

Tivar held Calen's gaze for what felt like an eternity. "You are like her second coming. I just hope you are stronger." She looked as though she were going to say more, but she simply nodded. "I understand."

"I hope you do, because you will help end this or I will swing the blade myself." Calen stood and made for the door.

"Anataier aldryr ar orimyn," Tivar said as Calen pulled the door open. *Give them fire and fury.*

"I will see you free from this place. I'm sorry I didn't come sooner."

She shook her head. "You were angry."

"I was scared. Scared of who I am, of what I might do."

"Fear exists for the sole purpose of being overcome."

Calen stared at Tivar a moment longer, nodded softly, then stepped back through the door and closed it behind him. He drew a sharp breath, felt it tremble in his chest, and did his best to stop his hands from shaking at his sides. He hated this. Tivar had saved his life, saved Valerys's life, and likely all lives within Aravell's walls. But so too had she been a part of the slaughter of The Order. Chora and the others had as much right to want her dead as he did Farda.

Ilyain's words repeated themselves in his head. *"I am so deeply sorry for the world we have left you. And for the burden we place on your shoulders as we ask you to fix it."*

Collecting himself, Calen thanked Amaril and set off back through the corridor with Vaeril.

His hands shaking, Calen stopped in the middle of the corridor, candlelight flickering shadows on the ground.

Vaeril raised an eyebrow.

"I don't know what I'm doing here, Vaeril. Gods, I don't know what I'm doing at all. I'm the son of a blacksmith and a healer," he said, shaking his head. "Two years ago, I didn't know anything but The Glade. And now there are thousands of men and elves readying to march across the continent in my name, bearing a sigil of Valerys's likeness on their breasts. They're marching to *war*, Vaeril – in *my name*. The man who murdered my mother walks these corridors freely, and all I want to do is tear his heart from his chest, and I can't. I can't touch him, but I can send a thousand men to die. Explain that to me. None of it makes sense. This should have been Erik or Dahlen, or you or Tarmon, or anyone but me."

Calen's chest heaved, his pulse racing. All the while, Vaeril stared back at him, watching.

The elf looked towards the ceiling as though searching for an answer in the white stone. "There are some who have picked up your banner because of what you are – more than some," the elf said with a shrug. "They wish to be part of a saga tale, part of the legend of the first free Draleid in four hundred years. They don't care who you are, just what you are. I was one of them. But I'm not anymore. At Belduar, you risked your life to buy the Kingsguard time, men and women you didn't know, people to whom you owed little loyalty. In Vindakur, you were the last one through the Portal Heart. You saved every life you could. No exceptions. In Kingspass, you were willing to die to protect the people of a nation that had taken everything from you. You were so unwilling to give up on Rist that you crossed the Burnt Lands, a thing that had never been done. Above this very city, you and Valerys risked your lives to buy precious moments for my people. There are many who might feel they deserve what you have, who feel they have a right to it, who feel they are your better. But none of them would be half of what you are if they stood in your place. There is a difference between you and Aeson Virandr. He would watch the world burn if it meant the empire lay in the ashes. He cares about tearing down what stands, but you care about what will be left when it's all done."

Vaeril grasped Calen's forearm and stared into his eyes. "I am with you. Heart and soul. We are Vandasera. I will follow you into the void if that's where you lead. And so would every soul wearing that sigil. Not just because of what you are, but because of who you are. That army isn't marching to die in your name, Calen. It's marching because someone finally showed them they can stand and fight, because someone finally showed them that there is something greater to fight for."

AESON PULLED A LONG BREATH in through his nostrils, the cold flowing through him, his lungs swelling. Calls and shouts echoed across the yard as the army went about its final checks. Queen Tessara had come good on the promise of her five thousand, as had Uthrían and Galdra, and along with those who bore the white dragon, just short of fourteen thousand strong filled the courtyard to capacity.

Wagon axles squeaked and groaned, armoured boots drummed against stone, and the constant hum of chatter floated on the air.

All this lay at Aeson's back, filling his ears with a calming buzz. This was what he had waited for, what he had fought for: the rebellion was well and truly under way, and the empire was burning. Thousands marched in the name of something new, something better. In truth, it was a sight he wasn't sure he'd ever see. Everything he had done, every sacrifice he had made, had come to this. And yet, all he could focus on was the dragon that stood before him.

Valerys, scales gleaming as though freshly polished, had to be seventy feet long. His neck was thick and muscular, his chest deep. Just like the other dragons in Valacia, he radiated a sense of power and grace.

Aeson had seen many dragons in his lifetime, and he had watched Valerys grow from a hatchling that could fit in Calen's lap to the great beast he was now.

But this was different.

For the first time since Lyara had been taken from him – ripped from him – he would once again sit at the nape of a dragon's neck, feel the power beneath him, the air crashing against his skin.

To ride a dragon, to feel that shared trust, that freedom, was among the most intimate of things. It should have filled him with joy, but instead the thought carried with it fear, sorrow, anxiety, and a numbness in his chest. It made him all the more conscious of the shattered pieces of his soul.

Lyara had been his, and he had been hers. Until the oceans dried and time broke. But she was gone, and he was alone.

As though sensing the pain in Aeson's heart, Valerys twisted his neck and lowered himself, his forelimbs bending, his jaw scraping the stone. As the dragon's eyes fixed on Aeson, a chill swept over him, his heart suddenly racing.

Valerys craned his neck forward, a low thrum in his throat.

Aeson reached out, the din of the preparing army rising to a crescendo in his ears. He could *feel* Valerys's soul. It wrapped around him like a shroud, flowing over him and through him, just as Cukulkan's had in Valacia.

Valerys pressed his snout into Aeson's outstretched hand. Aeson gasped, warmth spreading from his fingertips, through his hand, and into his bones. Myriad emotions flooded him, each tied to a moment in time as memories rushed through his mind. Images of Erik and Dahlen, then Valerys's egg, images of Cukulkan, of Aeson, of Calen.

Each breath trembled as Aeson drew it, his stare lost in the lavender of Valerys's eyes.

In all the lifetimes he had lived, Aeson had felt nothing akin to this.

All fear, all anguish and darkness fled him. Valerys did not need words for Aeson to understand him.

Aeson's jaw tensed as more of his own memories came to the fore: Lyara hatching. She had been so tiny. On that first night, she had slept with her belly on his forearm, those thin blue wings wrapping around his wrist.

Again and again, memories flashed through his mind; some his own, some Valerys's. In each the story held through: Aeson and Calen watching over Lyara and Valerys. And in the last, the roar of two dragons filled him and he knew what Valerys was trying to tell him. Valerys was not Lyara, but he would protect Aeson as though he was. Just as Aeson had protected Valerys's egg, just as he protected Calen.

In that moment, the memories stopped and everything shifted. A portentous, swirling rage flowed from the dragon into Aeson as a deep, boneshaking rumble sounded in his ears.

The black slits in Valerys's eyes sharpened, his lips peeling back, enormous, jagged teeth bared.

"If I hurt him," Aeson whispered, brushing his fingers across Valerys's warm scales, "you'll burn me alive."

The aroma of burning wood accompanied the warm breath that left Valerys's open jaws, that deep growl unceasing.

A hush rose at Aeson's back, and he suddenly became aware that the clamour of the preparing army had stopped. One last time, he stared into Valerys's eyes, brushed the dragon's scales with his thumb. "I will protect him always."

Aeson turned. Thousands of warriors filled the yard, organised into blocks of fifty, burnished plate glinting in the combination of the sun and the Blood Moon. Enormous purple banners flapped in the wind, the white dragon adorning the centres. No doubt those were a 'gift' from the Triarchy. Others rippled also, some in the black and silver of Vaelen with a seven-pointed star at their centre, and others in the deep green of the Triarchy with three white trees painted across their fronts.

Across the eastern and western edges of the yard, hundreds of Dvalin Angan stood by a horde of wagons, waiting to act as beasts of burden.

Aeson's gaze settled on the yard's northern edge, where the stillness was heaviest. Blocks of warriors had pushed back, leaving a wide path to the plateau where Aeson stood with Valerys.

Calen walked the centre of that path, every eye upon him.

Tarmon stood at the base of the plateau near the courtyard's rear. His left hand rested on the pommel of the sword at his hip, his right thumb tucked into a loop on his belt. On the outside he was sure he looked the picture of calm, his armour polished to a mirror finish, his hair combed and tidy, his face clean-shaven.

The inside, however, was another story. Tarmon had never had children – he'd never had the joy. But he imagined the pride he felt at watching Calen march through the blocks of warriors, the runes in his armour glowing with a deep purple light, was the pride of a father. The only stain on that feeling was the guilt that he was the one there to feel it and Vars Bryer was not.

Even Dann, with his white wood bow strapped to his back, looked the part. And if Tarmon was being honest, after the way the young man had acquitted himself in the battle for Aravell, he could certainly play the part too.

On Tarmon's right, Erik pulled in a long breath and let it out slowly, clasping his hands behind his back. "This is it then. We march today."

"Nervous?"

"A little."

Tarmon looked out over the blocks of warriors, all lined up in perfect formation, all standing to attention as Calen made his way to Valerys.

Thousands of purple cloaks stood stark against polished steel, the banners rippling above their heads. The colours reminded him of Belduar, and he couldn't help but think that, in some way, his home lived on. It was a strange comfort.

It wasn't long before Calen reached the plateau, Vaeril marching at his side.

Calen held his helmet in the crook of his arm and grasped Tarmon's forearm. He stopped and looked back over the courtyard. "They look…"

"Like an army." Tarmon folded his arms. "Soon we'll see if they fight like one."

Calen's expression shifted to one of visible discomfort at Tarmon's words.

"Long before you were born, this day was coming."

"I know." He looked to Dann, his expression softening a little. "Are you ready, Commander Pimm?"

Dann puffed out his bottom lip, giving a slight shrug. "Has a ring to it, doesn't it?"

Calen laughed, the hardness in his eyes cracking. "With any luck, I'll catch up with you long before you reach Salme. If I don't…"

"Then we'll push through," Erik said.

Calen drew a long breath through his nostrils, nodding slowly. As he made to speak, footsteps sounded to the right.

Queen Tessara of Vaelen approached with a column of Highguard flanking her, long glaives in their fists.

The queen wore a full suit of smooth, black elven steel, the star of Vaelen worked delicately into the breastplate, a curved sword strapped to her hip.

"Queen Tessara." Calen pressed a hand to his heart, inclining his head towards the queen, the others following suit. "Din närvarvin gryr haydria til myia elwyn."

Tarmon spoke as little of the Old Tongue as he did Narvonan – none – and so he stayed quiet, keeping his head slightly bowed. The elves were a strange folk, and he'd already had a few brushes with their 'honour' system. It was best to let Calen and Vaeril do the talking.

"Ar diar, myialí, Draleid." The new queen of Vaelen allowed a smile to grace her lips. She was the image of beauty, her voice soft, her eyes bright. But Tarmon was under no illusions that this elf's blade was as sharp as her tongue.

"Your command of the Old Tongue is impressive, Calen Bryer. I can hear the Vaelen in your pronunciation." She gestured towards Vaeril, who stood by Calen's side. Vaeril seemed even more rigid than usual, his back stiff, his chin raised. "You are a pride to your people, Vaeril Ilyin."

"Myia'nari…" Vaeril's eyes widened, his jaw slackening. It was as though he had been given the praise of a god. "Du haryn myia vrai, myia'nari. Laël haydrir."

"And my thanks are yours." She flicked her wrist, and a Highguard brought forward an ornate wooden box, stained black with silver decorating its edges.

The Highguard clicked two silver latches open and lifted the lid. A gently curved sword sat within. It gleamed in the light, delicate engravings swirling from the guard up through the blade. The grip was black leather, the pommel the likeness of a silver star. In its design the weapon was similar to Calen's, if more intricate in its embellishments.

"Myia'nari?" For the first time since meeting the elf, Tarmon heard an uncertainty in Vaeril's tone. Whatever this weapon was, it was more than a simple gift.

"This blade is Ünviril – Dawnbringer. It is a sword of the First Age. The Age of War. It comes from a time when our people were at their most divided. It once belonged to Elyin Shadvír, the first champion to the High House of Vaelen. It was Elyin who first fought beside humans and not against them. He was a warrior who found legend in the wielding of this blade but found eternity in the sheathing of it.

"I offer this weapon to show you that your accomplishments have not gone unnoticed by your people. You have brought great honour upon the kingdom of Vaelen. Not only have you protected the Draleid, protected our hope, but you have shown him the ways of our people and named him a friend of the Evalien. You fought at the Battle of Aravell, led our people forwards, and never turned back. In a time where elven heroes are few and far between, your star guides us."

Tessara lifted the blade from the box, resting the flat steel against her palm and holding the hilt with her other hand. She proffered the weapon to Vaeril.

"Vaeril Ilyin, I offer you Ünviril. Will you accept my offering and in turn take on the mantle of Champion of Vaelen? Will you lead our forces, and those of the Draleid, in this, the Last War?"

Vaeril stared openly at the blade, his mouth ajar. The elf had always been a quiet one, but he had never been as short of words as he was now.

"I..." Vaeril stuttered. "It would be my endless honour. An honour I do not deserve."

"You are blind, child of Vaelen, for there are none more deserving beneath our banner. You are the first elf of Vaelen in hundreds of years to fight beside a Draleid, the first to slay a Bloodmarked. You crossed the Burnt Lands. The only true shame is that King Silmiryn did not bestow this honour upon you sooner."

Tentatively, Vaeril reached forwards and wrapped a hand around the hilt of the sword, gauging its weight and balance. As he did, another Highguard stepped forwards with a black leather scabbard.

Calen put out a hand to stop the Highguard. He rested a hand on Vaeril's shoulder, then unbuckled the elf's scabbard and sword, leaving the new scabbard in their place.

For as long as Tarmon could remember, Calen had walked with a weight over his head. Even in moments of joy, the young man's eyes had betrayed him. But now there was nothing but pride on his face.

Vaeril thanked him, then drew a long breath and sheathed Dawnbringer, dropping to one knee as he did. "I accept, Myia'nari."

CHAPTER THIRTY-TWO

THE HEART OF WHO YOU ARE

12th Day of the Blood Moon

Aravell – Winter, Year 3081 After Doom

Farda held his breath, his eyes closed, the water cold around him. His fingers gripped tight at the edges of the rock pool, holding him in place. The sound of the small waterfall drummed in his ears as though horses trampled on his head, and yet somehow it was comforting.

In his mind's eye, he saw the boy, now a man, standing in the corridor. Even in that suit of pristine plate, still and calm as a statue, Calen Bryer's eyes had betrayed him. They were the eyes of a man who could not keep fury and sorrow from intertwining. Staring into them had settled another emotion on Farda that had not touched his soul in a long time: shame. Gut-wrenching, heart-swallowing shame.

Strangely, the feeling was almost a relief, as though a signal to let him know he was still human, still alive, that his heart had not completely withered, that his soul – what was left of it – wasn't all black and empty. The shame wasn't born of killing Calen's mother. Though the act had not been without its own burden, the shame came from never giving it a second thought.

That loss had so clearly consumed Calen Bryer's every waking moment, and yet Farda had genuinely forgotten about it until the night the young man had reminded him. Even in Ella's presence, it had barely surfaced in his waking mind.

"He killed Mam." Calen's words sounded again and again in Farda's head, his lungs burning as he kept a fresh breath from them, submerged in the pool. *"He set her on fire…"*

Spoken so plainly, the words had sliced into the soft black flesh of Farda's heart. *"He set her on fire…"*

In the moment, almost two years ago, Farda had barely thought of the act. He hadn't been happy about it, but he'd had little choice. Calen had attempted to kill an Imperial Inquisitor, and when Farda had stepped in, Calen's mother had intervened. Examples needed to be made. Actions had consequences. That was simply the way of things.

Freis Bryer was not the first mother to die in war. She would not be the last. Her death was a consequence of the rebellion.

Now, though, as Farda held himself beneath the water's surface, his heart did not feel the same way. He was not the same man he had been two years ago. Something within him had shifted. He had Ella to thank for that. Ella, the other child of the woman he had killed, the woman he had murdered in the empire's name – one of countless. She hated him now, to her very core, and that hate had been borne entirely from his own actions.

After Shinyara's death, after his soul had been shattered, his joy stolen, his bones filled with nothing but apathy, Farda had been lost. Truly and completely. He had been a shell that had continued to move through habit alone.

But that moment in the Eyrie, when Ella had looked at him, the way her eyes had turned to molten gold, the way the sound in her voice had been nothing but hatred… that moment had led him to a realisation that had been hundreds of years in the making.

A realisation that he had always known but in truth had cared little for.

He had become the monster he had sought to destroy. He had become worse. His hands were bloodier than any others. The weight of a hundred thousand souls bore down upon him. He was death, he was loss and murder. He was darkness incarnate.

The burn in Farda's lungs rose, searing through his chest and up his throat. His hands gripped the edges of the rock pool tighter, forcing him to stay below the surface.

Ella had given him back his purpose, given him back something to fight for, something to live for. She had allowed him to feel – something he had never thought possible. Every time he looked upon her, he saw Hana and Valyianne. He had failed them, and now he had failed her too. History repeating itself, a cycle unbroken.

Farda's hands shook, his throat closing, his lungs begging him for a breath.

He had lived a long life. A long life with far too little joy. A life of failure, and loss, and poor choices. By the gods, choices so poor he could hardly understand them now. He should have pushed harder when Alvira had told him no, when the council had refused him. He should have torn the whole place down… but he hadn't. He had done as he'd been told. He might not have killed Hana and Valyianne and all those others in Orinhale, but they were dead by his inaction, and that was the same thing.

That choice had cost him everything. If he had been stronger, if he had been better, the world would be different.

After staring at the darkness in Calen's eyes, Farda was sure of only one thing: this world would be a better place without him in it. There was no place left for him. He had nothing left to give.

The shaking in his hands settled and the burn in his lungs spread, his vision blurring. He pushed himself back so a jutting rock held him in place.

And then, for a moment, a sense of calm washed over him and the burning in his lungs seemed to fade as a warmth flooded his veins.

A roar sounded in the back of his mind, a touch he had not felt in centuries, a wholeness that had been ripped from him.

For all the gods in the world, he swore that in that moment Shinyara's heart touched his once more, her broken half of their shared soul enveloped him, and the world faded. His head lolled. His heartbeat slowed.

He was ready.

But then, just as peace embraced him, Shinyara's roar grew louder. It thundered, defiant and furious. Every memory that had ever touched his mind cycled through him. Every battle he had fought, every life he had saved or taken. All the good, all the bad, all the sweet and sour, and Shinyara roared again. And again, and again. Rage consumed him, a dragon's rage.

Hands grabbed at Farda and hauled him upwards. The water broke around him, the sounds of the world crashing into his ears. He coughed and spluttered, collapsing forwards, gasping for air, shaking. Everything about him was still dark and blurred, lights sparking at the edges of his vision. The same hands that had heaved him from the water now dragged him over the edge of the rock pool and slammed him onto the ground.

A sharp slap struck his right cheek and his vision came flaring back, his mind focusing. Another slap and he covered his face with his hands.

"What in the gods were you doing?" Farda knew the voice; he knew it well.

He slowly lowered his hands to find Tivar standing over him, her face and hair soaked, her eyes raw and red, her chest heaving. Several guards stood around her, none moving to help, none caring.

"What were you doing, Farda?" Her voice shook, as did her hands as she grabbed his wrists. "What were you doing?"

An hour or so later, Farda sat on a low ledge near the edge of a cliff. The area had clearly been carved with the Spark as a viewpoint over the valleys for whomever had once lived in the place that was now his prison. He leaned forwards, resting his forearms on the tops of his knees, the cold wind nipping at his bare chest and back.

"She wouldn't let me do it," he whispered, staring up at the red moon that tainted the sky.

"Who?"

He and Tivar had sat in silence for quite some time, but the anger radiating from her had said enough.

Farda swallowed hard and ran his tongue around his top teeth. He knew what she'd say. "Shinyara."

Tivar snapped her head around, disbelief in her eyes.

"I know what it sounds like," Farda said before she had a chance to speak. "But she was there. There was a point where I could feel the other side and Shinyara waited there for me. She was so close."

Tivar sat in silence, turning her gaze to her feet.

"She refused to let me cross."

"Why?" Tivar asked, looking back at Farda once more.

"I don't know… She just—"

"No." Tivar shook her head. "*Why?*"

Farda drew a long breath and once more looked up at the Blood Moon. "There is nothing left for me here, Tivar. My time in this world is through. I have lived long enough to become the monster I fought to kill. And it should never have taken me this long to realise that."

"And that's it? You face what you've become and just accept it?"

"What choice do I have? I can never take back the things I've done. I can never right the wrongs… I'm tired and she waits for me."

"What about me?"

"What about you?"

"Do you think you are the only one who has done terrible things?" Tivar shifted, turning her body towards Farda. "Do you know how many Draleid I've killed? Thirty-seven. Thirty-seven who should have been like brothers and sisters to me." Her jaw clenched, the muscles in her throat tightening. "And I didn't have an excuse like yours. My soulkin's heart still beats. Shinyara took your love and your joy and your empathy… She took everything with her. If I'd lost Avandeer, I don't know what I'd have done. But I wouldn't have done that."

Farda knew she meant what he'd intended to do in the pool. "What is it to you what I do with my life? What claim do you have to force me to stay here? I turned my back on my friends, on my kin. I betrayed everything I'd ever fought for to try and break what The Order had become. I gave *everything*. My blood, my honour, my worth. I gave half my soul. Everything I've ever loved is gone. What have I left here?"

"There was a time," Tivar said, letting out a soft breath, "a time when you and Eltoar were both the brothers I'd never had. And then you lost Hana and Valyianne, and I would say if anything we grew closer. What would they say now?"

"They would despise me for all the things I've done, for what I've become—"

"A coward?"

Farda narrowed his eyes. "You think what I tried to do was cowardice?"

"No." Tivar shook her head, answering swiftly. "Not at all. That is not a cowardly act. It is the act of someone who is tired, someone who sees no path forward and can carry the weight no longer, but it is not cowardly. Your cowardice lies not in that choice but in your unwillingness to stand now, to make a choice not because you will be lauded for it or because others will look upon you differently, but because you know it is right. You taught me that." Tears glistened in Tivar's eyes. "When I was only an apprentice. Do you remember?"

"I remember."

"I can never right the wrongs I've done. I will never wipe the stain from my soul. I will never be the hero I always dreamt of being. But I can be something." Tivar stood, looking out over the ledge. "It is never too late to make the right choice. Never. When Coren and Farwen reach this city, they will pass judgement. And if they judge that I am to live, I will give every drop of blood in my veins to fight the darkness we created. Because it is the right thing to do. I will give my life for the people of Epheria. Not those who sit on thrones or stand on the parapets of the highest castles, but those who want only life and peace and love. Because that is all I've ever tried to do, all I've ever wanted to do. And I will guide Calen Bryer and teach him to not make the same mistakes I did, because he has greatness in him. He has a hero's heart. I know because he stirred mine. And if they sentence me to die for what I have done, I will accept that too. Because what is right comes before my desires."

Tivar stepped away from the cliff edge and walked slowly towards the opening in the rock that led back to the main chambers. "Your eyes are open now, Farda. Your cowardice lies in your refusal to face the things you've done and stand anyway. The man I knew would never see what is coming and leave the rest of us alone to face it without him. I know you're in pain, and if you face everything that you are and decide that in your heart you think it is the right time to join Shinyara, I will stand beside you and I will help you pass. But if instead you choose to stand and be counted, to once again fight for the right reasons, then I will stand beside you in that as well. You will not be redeemed, nor will I. That is not possible. But you can still do good in this world. That is why Shinyara would not allow you to cross. Because she knows you are a better man than to leave us alone in this. She knows that the man who taught me what kindness was deserves better than to leave the world this way. Whatever your choice, do not make it alone. I will always be here."

Tivar's footsteps echoed through the passage as she left, and then Farda sat in silence.

Those were the first words to pass between them since they'd been taken prisoner. She'd left her chambers to sleep next to Avandeer and little else.

Farda leaned forwards and stood. He walked to the edge of the cliff and looked down. The drop looked to be over a thousand feet, nothing but trees visible below, illuminated by the shared light of the Blood Moon and the evening sun.

The wind howled, whipping at him as he stared down.

He reached into his pocket and produced the thick gold coin he'd carried for hundreds of years. He ran his thumb across the worn crown face and nicks in the metal before turning it over and doing the same to the other side.

To live or die. To finally rest or to stand one last time.

Farda drew a long breath, then flicked the coin into the air.

He watched its flight, watched it glint in the yellow and red. And then, as the coin started its downward arc, he turned and walked away.

He never heard it land. It would have taken a while to hit the bottom.

As he walked, a part of him swore that he once again heard Shinyara roar in the back of his mind, his heart skipping a beat, his hairs standing on end.

One last fight, my love. If they let me. I promise you.

CHAPTER THIRTY-THREE

SUREHEART

12th Day of the Blood Moon

Aravell – Winter, Year 3081 After Doom

The forest air smelled of ash and burnt leather. Charred twigs and brittle blackened grass snapped beneath the weight of Dann's boots, the sound drowned out by the ceaseless rhythm of thousands ahead and behind.

The army marched down the wide channel the Dragonguard had torched through the Darkwood. Most of the bodies had been cleared or 'taken' by the forest, as Lyrei had put it. Images of the Aldithmar flashed across his mind: the long, bark-covered limbs, the black smoke that drifted from their broken bodies, the pulsing white eyes.

He stared into the dark-obscured forest on his left, the blended rays of the sun and moon pushing only a few feet inwards before being swallowed by the shadows. Shapes moved in the dark, subtle shifts of light and space. More than once, Dann caught a glimpse of misting white eyes staring back. He wasn't sure if he preferred it this way or not. Having an illuminated path through the woodland was definitely better than trekking through the darkness by baldírlight. But at least the last time he'd come through the Darkwood he'd only had a feeling he was being watched. Now he knew, and he knew what watched him.

His heart stopped for a fleeting second as a pair of glowing white eyes appeared at the edge of the trees, staring at him. More eyes flickered into existence. They didn't move, just watched. They wanted him to know they were there. After a moment, the eyes vanished, dissipating into nothingness.

He gave an involuntary shiver, and beside him Drunir snorted, shaking his head.

"What are you snorting at?" Dann glared at the horse, patting his muzzle. "You barely even saw them the last time. You galloped off like a chicken shit and left me behind."

The horse snorted again.

If Dann didn't know any better, he'd think Drunir was laughing at him.

A particularly sharp snap sounded beneath his feet, and he looked down to see his armoured boot had cracked straight through the blackened shin bone of a charred corpse. His gaze instantly shifted to the corpse's head. Torn flesh dangled from a half-blackened skull where animals and birds had feasted on the burnt remains. He yanked his foot free and staggered backwards, his heart beating like a hammer.

"This place is a graveyard." Tarmon appeared at Dann's side, staring down at the charred corpse.

Dann looked around the clearing. Human and elven remains were scattered amidst pools of melted steel and the husks of burnt-out trees. Memories of that night raced through his mind. The battle had been fierce and bloody, but when the dragonfire had poured through the canopy, the world had turned to nothing but chaos. The screams rang in his ears: the howls and shrieks of the souls being burned alive. He watched in his mind's eye as the Fade's black fire washed over Alea, as its sword punched into Baldon's chest.

Dann drew his breaths in slow, trying to stop the panic from slithering from his mind into his veins. In through his nose, out through his mouth. Nice and slow.

"That dragonfire killed as much of their own as it did ours." Tarmon pressed his boot into an empty breastplate, brushing off the soot to reveal the sigil of a roaring black lion.

Dann nodded sombrely, patting Drunir on the side as they continued. "How long will it take us to reach Salme?"

"Depends how hard we march. A few weeks, maybe a bit less if we march every hour the gods give."

"Then that's what we'll do. It took us a lot longer to get from The Glade, but we didn't exactly take the quick route."

Dann looked over his shoulder. Hundreds of banners rippled in the wind, many bearing Calen's white dragon sigil, others in the varying colours of the elven kingdoms. Valdrin had been hard at work since the battle for the city, commanding an army of smiths and craftsmen to churn out new armour, and banners, and tabards, and all manner of things that could bear Calen's sigil. The strange elf had taken it upon himself to ensure that any soul who set eyes on the army saw that white dragon.

As he watched the banners flap in the wind, Dann still couldn't quite understand how he of all people had ended up in this position. Two years ago, he'd been drinking himself silly and throwing axes in The Two Barges, and now... well, now he didn't really know what he was doing at all. He wore the suit of polished armour and mail that Valdrin had crafted for him. He had a glistening white cloak knotted at his shoulders – which was a nightmare to keep clean – and a white wood bow strapped to his back. That morning, was even been assigned his own attendant – Nala – who looked after his gear and followed him around like a puppy. He should have felt like a hero of legend, but instead he was more like a fish dragged from water and told to fly.

He was not a leader. He never had been and never would be. In fact, he'd go as far as to say that anyone with half a brain would do well to do the exact opposite of everything Dann said.

Drunir dipped his head and pushed his muzzle into Dann's temple.

"Oi! Stop that."

The horse snorted again, this time flapping his lips and spraying spittle over Dann's face.

"I'll turn you into a nice coat if you keep that up."

Drunir let out a puff of air, peeling back his lips to show long teeth and thick gums.

"I was joking, lighten up." Dann turned his head to see Tarmon staring at him with a bemused look on his face. "What?"

"You're talking to a horse."

"And?"

"I suppose you've done stranger things."

"This doesn't even come close. Did I ever tell you about the time I saw a horse with a horn growing from its head? And not like a little lump, but a proper horn, right from the crown. Calen and Rist never believed me, but I swear to Varyn that thing was real."

"How drunk were you?"

"I'd had enough meads to feel warm but not so much I couldn't piss standing up. I—ah, shit!" Dann leapt to the side at the sensation of something jabbing into his leg. He looked down to see a stout bird the size of a pup. It had a rotund torso, with a stumpy neck that bobbed like a chicken's when it walked. Its beak was long and sharp, its feathers dark brown and black.

The bird scuttled away as Dann tried to kick it, rounding a fallen tree then bounding atop the trunk with surprising grace for something so short and fat. It stood there and stared at him, its chest puffed out, watching.

"What in the fuck is that thing?"

"It's a weka," Vaeril said, calling out from the other side of Drunir. The elf joined Dann and Tarmon, Lyrei beside him. "They're native to the Aravell woodland, though they tend to stay closer to the outskirts. Be careful."

Dann eyed the bird with suspicion. "Why? How dangerous is it?"

"It's harmless."

"Then why be careful?"

"Because it's smarter than you are and will steal anything you don't chain up."

"Smarter than us?"

"No," Vaeril corrected, a grin spreading across his face. "Just you."

Dann was about to argue until Lyrei burst out laughing. Instead, he just shoved Vaeril to the side, letting the elf have his victory. Lyrei deserved to laugh more. He shook his head at Vaeril. "I liked you more when you had no sense of humour."

The elf wrapped an arm around Dann's shoulder, the shit-eating grin stuck to his face.

As they marched, the weka kept pace with them, disappearing into the forest, then reappearing a few feet later, always lurking. Dann had never seen a creature in his life that looked more naturally born for mischief.

After a while, the elves that marched ahead came to a stop, their black banners flapping in the wind. Queen Tessara and the Vaelen army had taken the lead in the march through the wood, with the forces from Ardurän and Lunithír holding the rear.

Tarmon nodded to Dann, Erik, Vaeril, and Lyrei, and they pushed their way through the stopped elves, leaving Ingvat in command.

An enormous, hulking mass of steel and shattered branches lay on the ground, blocking the path: one of the Nithrandír. Dann hadn't even considered it possible that those enormous monstrosities could be killed. He'd never seen anything like them in his life. Then again, if he had a silver mark for every time that thought had come up recently, he'd be a rich man. He'd lived in The Glade his whole life – he'd never really seen anything.

"Heraya tael du ia'sine ael, ydilír ayar," both Lyrei and Vaeril whispered as they approached, bowing their heads.

Queen Tessara stood beside the fallen Nithrandír, her palm pressed against the inch-thick pauldron that could have been mounted onto the side of a house.

Dann had never been good at knowing when to be quiet, but he'd been learning. This seemed like one of those moments.

The queen stared down at the remnants of the Nithrandír. To Dann's surprise it was not sadness he saw in her eyes but relief, a soft smile resting on her lips.

Several of the robed elves that walked with the queen stepped forwards, and the ground beneath Dann's feet shook with enough power to cause him to stagger.

The Nithrandír's armour moved and jostled as roots and vines that had once formed the creature's body shifted and slithered over each other, plunging into the charred earth. More, smaller roots broke through the soil and snaked up over the armour, joining together until a sapling sprouted at the top of a newly formed mound.

"Du vyin alura anis, mavaeri maviríl. Du haryn tiunil din vandasír."

The queen looked back to Dann and the others, giving the slightest of bows before calling out and setting off along the path once more.

"She seemed… happy," Dann said as he approached the root-covered remnants of the Nithrandír.

"It is a thing to find joy in." Vaeril ran his finger along one of the roots, then whispered something in the Old Tongue.

"What was that?"

"Du vyin alura anis. Du haryn tiunil din vandasír. It means 'You can rest now. You have fulfilled your oath.'" Vaeril stared at the mound of roots and steel, his fingers tracing along a piece of protruding armour. "When my people first came to Aravell, broken, shattered… lost… a number of our eldest warriors and those who had been injured past the point of healing made the greatest of sacrifices.

Through the aid of Jotnar runecraft, they bound their souls to these bodies of earth and steel, forgoing their entry into Achyron's halls so that they might continue to protect the ones they loved in this life, beyond what a mere mortal body could." He gestured towards the fallen Nithrandír. "This is a joyous thing because this soul's watch has finally come to an end. They protected their people, they fought until the end and then even still. And now, finally, they may rest. They may enter Achyron's halls knowing that their oath has been fulfilled and their honour is without question."

Baldon had told Dann of how the Nithrandír were the souls of old elves who had given themselves to protect their people, but now that explanation felt lacking. It was more than just simple sacrifice. These elves had given everything. They had waited in those shells of steel and root for centuries. "That entire time… were they conscious? Could they see and hear?"

"Every second of every day," Vaeril answered, a twinge of sadness in his voice. "Always watching, always protecting. It was their oath."

The thought set the hairs on Dann's neck on end. To stand there for hundreds of years, not being able to move, to speak… being trapped inside a shell. He couldn't think of a worse fate.

Dann stepped closer and rested his palm on a winding root. "Du vyin…" He looked to Vaeril. "How do you say it?"

"Du vyin alura anis. Du haryn tiunil din vandasír." Lyrei placed her hand next to Dann's as she spoke, a blend of sorrow and joy in her voice.

"Du vyin alura anis, Alea." Dann repeated, brushing his finger against the side of Lyrei's hand. "Du vyin alura anis, Baldon."

You can rest now.

Tarmon rolled his shoulder, stretching out the muscle before swinging his mallet and driving the stake into the soft earth, cold sweat rolling down his brow.

A strike of wood-on-wood sounded to his right.

"That's the last of 'em, High Commander." The young squire drew heavy breaths, his hair soaked from the earlier rain. Over four hundred souls that had not yet seen sixteen summers marched with the army, hauling armour and weapons, helping to pitch tents, tending to horses. Many were humans from Loria and the southern provinces, but quite a few young elves had joined as well. There was no better way to learn than by doing. And an army needed squires.

Tarmon gave the young lad a smile. "Good work, Mikal. Unload my armour and cot into the tent, then go see if Surin, Ingvat, or the captains have need of more hands. The sooner we're camped, the sooner we eat."

Leaving the boy to go about his work, Tarmon patrolled the camp. The breeze bit at his exposed skin, his loose linen shirt flapping. Moving through the Darkwood was a far quicker endeavour with the path carved by the Lorian forces before the attack, which allowed them to reach just outside the bounds of the Darkwood before stopping to set up camp for the night. Tarmon had been hoping that would be the case. Even with the Dvalin Angan with them, he had dreaded the idea of sleeping within the woodland's reach. During the battle for the city, he had seen more than a handful of men and elves stray too far and be ripped to pieces by those twisted spirits – the Aldithmar. He shivered at the thought.

He walked past a group of men and women – Carvahonan by their accents – struggling to pitch their tents. They stopped roaring at each other as he passed, bowing their heads sharply before scrambling to stop the tent from collapsing behind them.

Tarmon shook his head and moved on. The sight was a common one that night. Over the months in Aravell, and under the direction of himself and the Knights of Achyron, the mishmash of elven volunteers and the rebels from across the continent had slowly begun to resemble something that looked vaguely like an army. Their drilling had become tighter, their movements more fluid, and their discipline was growing. On the battlefield, they would do well. Of that, he was sure. They weren't fighting in the name of some king they'd never met or for a cause they didn't believe in. They were fighting for their homes, their loved ones, their future.

But there was more to being an army than battle. It seemed a strange thing to say, but anyone who had been part of a larger whole understood. Battle was the last step in each movement. It was the culmination of all other acts. And even the greatest could lose the battle if each step leading to that moment wasn't taken with care.

Learning how to march, how to make and break camp as efficiently and quickly as possible, how to ration, how to hunt and live off the land, how to work together as a cohesive unit at all times – each one of those things came before battle. A well drilled force could march and set up camp with their eyes closed. They kept their armour clean and oiled. They marched in file and held their discipline in the deepest moments of fear.

The Belduaran Kingsguard had been one such force, and even they were gone now after Daymon's death. Though from the letters Dahlen Virandr had sent, many still remained as Oleg Marylin's guard while some of them manned the garrison at Salme.

At first it was strange to think of Oleg as Belduar's leader, and yet there was no one better suited. Oleg was a kind man with a keen sense of purpose. He cared for the people. He was also sharp as a blade and quick as a whip, though he often pretended that wasn't the case.

"High Commander Hoard." The two Rakina who had accompanied the army – Atara Anthalin and Harken Holdark – strode towards Tarmon. It was the elf, Atara, who had called to him. She pressed a closed fist to her leather jerkin, a coat of mail clinking beneath. "Harken and I will scout the area while the first watch gets in place. We would take fifty bodies with us, if it pleases."

"Of course, Rakina. Take as many as you need. Talk to Ingvat. She's on the western edge of the camp. She'll assign you scouts."

"I would take some of the Dvalin also. They move quicker."

Tarmon nodded. The Dvalin Angan were not his to command, but Matriarch Varthon had said they would do what was needed.

Atara gave her thanks and she and Harken set off towards the camp's western edge.

Harken looked as though he had been bred from a bear. Even Tarmon had to lift his chin a little to meet the man's gaze. During the Battle of Aravell, Tarmon had watched him snap a soldier's leg in half with a single kick and lift a man clean off his feet with the throw of a spear. And yet, it was Atara who Tarmon was most thankful to have marching with them, a living legend long before the fall of The Order. The Blade of Anadín, Therin had called her. And after seeing her fight with his own eyes, Tarmon could understand why. She was singular with a blade in her hand. He would go as far as to say the things he'd seen her do should not have been possible. Even in sparring she had taken down Tarmon, Erik, Calen, and Vaeril at the same time without a single blow landing against her. She moved like a bird and struck like a hammer.

When Tarmon had been appointed Lord Captain of the Belduaran Kingsguard, it had been the proudest day of his life. He'd only wished that same appointment hadn't required Baria Hawe's death in the First Battle for Belduar. Now, he stood at the head of an army with figures quite literally pulled from the annals deferring to him. He let out a long breath, the fading winter air turning it to steam. He whispered to himself, "I need a drink."

Tarmon found Vaeril, Lyrei, Erik, and Dann sitting by a copse of fir trees near the centre of camp. Drunir was tethered to a post with his muzzle buried in a bucket of water, Dann's squire, Nala, brushing the horse's coat. Like Tarmon, that horse had come all the way from Belduar. Even if he hadn't already known, the grey-dappled black coat would have given it away. It was an Albireenan, a rare breed that could trace its lineage back to Terroncia, though the few hundred that remained were reared only in Belduar. That Therin had arranged for one to be given to Dann said a lot about what the elf thought of the young man. A strange thought crossed Tarmon's mind that Drunir may in fact be the last Albireenan in the known world.

"Ah, there he is." Erik, seated cross-legged on a rock, inclined his head at Tarmon. "We thought you'd gotten stuck helping pitch the tents. I hope they're faster at taking down than they were at setting up."

"Just doing a last round." Tarmon nudged Erik in the back with his knee as he passed, sending Erik sliding to the dirt. "As you should have been doing."

"Bastard." Erik brushed the soil from his knees, returning to his rocky perch. "I was busy making sure that damn bird didn't kill Dann."

"Don't talk about that fucking bird." Dann knelt by a pile of dried logs, twigs, and leaves, sparking quenched steel with flint.

Tarmon leaned into Erik, then sat beside him. "Did you bring that bottle of Raven's Ichor Kiko gave you?"

"I thought you'd never ask." Erik grabbed Tarmon's shoulder for leverage, heaved himself upright, and vanished into the tent behind him.

"What did the bird do?" Tarmon asked.

Both Vaeril and Lyrei broke out in the kind of fierce, rumbling laughter that felt strange to hear from elves.

Dann shook his head as the two continued chuckling.

"Anyone going to tell me?" Tarmon asked, genuinely curious now.

A hand rested on his shoulder, and Erik shoved a clear glass bottle of black liquid into his hand.

"Well," Erik said while setting himself down beside Tarmon, "it appears that weka took quite a liking to Dann, followed him the whole way here."

Tarmon pulled the stopper from the bottle and breathed in the sweet and spicy anise scent. He took a swig, grimacing as the burn spread from his throat and through his body, wrapping him in a warm blanket.

He handed the bottle back to Erik. "Do I want to ask what happened?"

"The little shit stole one of my shirts while I was pitching the tent." Sparks flew from the quenched steel, and the branches and twigs caught fire. Dann dropped back onto his arse, setting down the flint and steel and exhaling into the night. "I liked that shirt."

Behind Dann, Drunir snorted, stomping a foot.

Dann threw his hands in the air. "Even the damn horse is laughing at me."

Everyone around the fire erupted in laughter. Even Dann cracked a smile.

"What news of the path to Salme?" Vaeril asked once the laughter subsided.

"Reports have Uraks swarming the Illyanara plains. The smaller groups will likely stay clear of us for the most part, but we're bound to find trouble sooner or later. Atara and Harken have gone to scout for tonight, but I may need you to take some bodies and move ahead of the column tomorrow."

"Done." The elf looked as though he were about to speak again before his eyes narrowed and he looked at something near Dann.

Tarmon followed Vaeril's gaze. The weka had returned and was now stalking around Dann's tent, its head bobbing back and forth.

"Dann." Tarmon pursed his lips.

"What?" Dann raised a curious eyebrow.

"You might want to…" Tarmon nodded over Dann's shoulder towards the weka that was now nudging aside the flap to Dann's tent with its long beak, peering inside.

Dann turned, leapt to his feet, and charged the bird. "Little shit! Get away!"

The weka cocked its head to the side and scuttled away, rounding Dann with surprising speed and darting back towards Tarmon and the others. The bird stopped just short of the fire and stared at the flint and quenched steel Dann had left in the grass.

"Don't you fucking dare!" Dann leapt, but the bird was too quick. The weka snatched the piece of flint into its beak and bolted off into the night like a man who'd just been caught with someone else's wife.

Dann stopped for a moment, his gaze flickering from the group to the escaping weka. He dashed into his tent, then emerged a few seconds later with a quiver strapped to his hip and his white wood bow in his hands.

"We're breaking the fast with weka tomorrow," he called as he charged off after the bird.

Erik stared after Dann, then handed the bottle of Raven's Ichor back to Tarmon. "One copper says the bird steals something else from him before he makes it back."

DANN WIPED THE COLD SWEAT from his brow as he trudged back into the camp. That damn bird was faster than it looked, and it was almost impossible to see in the night.

"I'll get the bastard," he whispered to himself, his bow hanging loose in his left hand. He grimaced as he stepped into a particularly waterlogged patch of grass, mud squelching, the water seeping into his sock.

"Catch it?" Erik asked when Dann made it back to the campfire. Three of the captains – Surin, Narthil, and Sylehna – had joined the others, but Lyrei was missing. "Did it... wait, Dann, where's your shoe?"

"Don't ask." Dann dropped himself in front of the fire, pulling off his remaining shoe and both socks and letting the flames warm his feet. He set his bow down beside him, shifting the quiver at his hip as he stared into the flames and laid out his next plan in his mind.

He would catch that bird, no matter the cost. Well, perhaps that was a little dramatic. He would catch that bird as long as the costs were minimal.

Tarmon sat upright with an amused grin on his lips, his eyebrows raised curiously. "Dann, did the bird steal your shoe?"

"No."

"Then where's your shoe?"

"I didn't need it anymore," Dann said with a shrug.

"The bird stole your shoe."

Dann clicked his tongue off the roof of his mouth. "It didn't *steal* the shoe. It borrowed the shoe... without asking... and with no intention to return it."

"That's stealing, Dann."

"You know what, Tarmon?" Dann stood, snatching up his bow, socks, and remaining shoe. "You better watch out, because I'm going to steal *your* fucking shoe."

The group erupted in laughter, and Vaeril called as Dann made to leave. "Dann?"

"What?" Dann called back, allowing the exasperation to seep into his voice.

"Did you bring spare shoes?"

Once again, they all burst out in fits of laughter. Erik laughed so hard he started coughing and fell on his side.

"If you keep chasing that bird," he said through watering eyes, "you're going to be naked by the time we reach Salme."

"Ah, fuck off!" More laughter rang out as Dann stormed off to his tent, glancing at Nala, who was still brushing Drunir's mane.

He pushed through the flap in the tent and tossed his shoe and socks to the ground, letting out a string of curses as they squelched against each other. He laid his bow down on his cot, then snatched the skin beside his bed and popped the stopper. He let out a sigh of relief after taking a deep draught of the cold mead within – the taste of home.

"Commander Sureheart?" a squeaky voice called from the tent's entrance.

"What?" Dann felt a twinge of guilt at the irritation in his voice when he turned to see young Nala standing there, her hands clasped before her.

The girl had barely seen fifteen summers, and she had the soft accent of Carvahon. For a moment, it looked as though she would bolt from the tent in tears, but she stood firm.

"I'm sorry, Nala. It's been a long day." Dann stoppered the skin and tossed it onto his cot, giving Nala his full attention. "What is it?"

Nala swallowed hard and lifted her chin. "Drunir has been fed and watered. I also heated some water over the fire for you." She gestured towards two wooden buckets, steam wafting from within, that sat in the corner of the tent. "There are towels by your pillow."

Dann let out a sigh, feeling like an idiot. "Thank you, Nala. Do I smell that bad?"

"No, my lord, I didn't mean—"

"It was a joke," Dann said, smiling. "Thank you. Please, blanket Drunir, make sure he's comfortable, and then get some sleep. We march early."

"Yes, Commander Sureheart."

"Nala," Dann called as the girl made to leave. "Where did you hear that name?"

"Commander Ilyin, my lord."

Vaeril. Dann nodded. "Good night, Nala."

"Night, my lord."

Dann let out a long sigh and dropped himself to his haunches beside the nearest bucket of steaming water. He removed his shirt and splashed his face and body, running his hands through his hair. He was used to being called 'strange', 'arsehole', 'idiot', and whatever other name a person could conjure, but 'my lord' was a new one.

He scrubbed the dirt from his face and hands, then dropped to his knees and cleaned his feet, sighing in relief as the hot water chased the cold from his bones.

The girl – Nala – was sweet and far too young to be marching with the army. Though as soon as the thought crossed his mind, he realised that he had only seen about five summers more than she. So much had happened in the last couple of years. He was barely the same person he had been.

As he knelt there, Dann ran the pads of his fingers over the knotted scar that covered his left shoulder and collarbone. He had acquired myriad other scars in all shapes and sizes since then, marking his arms, chest, back, and legs with pale, smooth skin. But the mark the Fade had left on him in the great hall of Belduar would be the one that stayed with him forever.

His mind drifted to the Fade in the Aravell. The monster that had killed Alea and Baldon. The words it had spoken when it held him by the throat. *"Ahh... I thought it might be you. I never forget a face – or a mark."*

Dann had pondered those words constantly since that night. He didn't know how it was possible, but he was absolutely certain it was the same Fade that had almost killed him in Belduar. It wore a different face, spoke with a different voice, but it had been the same one.

He shook his head and splashed more warm water on his face.

Footsteps sounded behind him, accompanied by a draught sweeping in through the open tent flap.

"What is it, Nala?" Dann rose, drying his face with the towel. When the girl didn't answer, he turned. "Lyrei? What... Is that my shoe? And my shirt?"

Lyrei stood in the tent's entrance, a shirt draped over her shoulder and Dann's missing shoe in her hand. She wore a white tunic trimmed with purple and a pair of tan trousers. Her blonde hair, now far longer than it had been when he'd first met her, was loose over her shoulders.

She set the shoe and shirt on the edge of Dann's cot. "I didn't want you getting yourself killed trying to find the shirt... I wasn't expecting to find a shoe."

"Damn bird. It's smarter than it looks." Dann laughed, drying his hair with the towel. "You didn't find my flint?"

Lyrei rummaged through her pocket and produced the piece of flint and placed it down beside the shirt. "They always store the things they take. If you follow them, you can find their nests. Though they don't usually stray this far from the Aravell. I think it likes you."

"It has a strange way of showing it." Dann picked up the skin full of mead and offered it to Lyrei.

She took it without question, popped the stopper, and drained a mouthful, wiping her lips with the sleeve of her tunic.

"It's Lasch's mead," Dann said, watching her drink. "He said it will only keep for a few days, so I guess we'd be fools not to finish it."

To Dann's surprise, Lyrei stepped towards him and reached out with her free hand, gently brushing her fingers over the twisted scar across his shoulder.

Dann made to speak, but no words came forth.

Lyrei's touch was warm against his skin. "This was from Belduar?"

"Mmh." Dann relaxed his shoulders, looking down at the pale flesh that marked him. "The Fade's lightning."

"The one that killed Elissar..." Lyrei looked up, her golden eyes staring into his. She turned and sat on the ground, pulling her knees to her chest, her back pressing against the side of the cot.

Dann joined her as she took another mouthful of mead.

"When I said we'd be fools not to finish it," he said, snatching the skin from Lyrei, "I did mean *we*, not just you."

They sat there, drinking and saying very little until the skin was empty and Lyrei had fallen asleep, her head resting on Dann's shoulder. He could feel the rise and fall of her chest with each breath, her cheek nuzzling into him. He was so worried about waking her that he didn't move for what must have been the better part of an hour. If there had been a competition for best impersonation of a statue, he would have won. But then, eventually, as his back started to ache and the muscles in his side cramped, he shifted gently and scooped her up in his arms. She was heavier than she looked.

As Dann stood, one arm under Lyrei's back, the other under her knees, he cradled her head to his chest. His heartbeat quickened. For some reason, holding Lyrei in his arms was more nerve-inducing than charging down a Fade.

He drew slow breaths, being careful not to wake her as he lay her down on the cot and pulled the blanket up over her shoulders.

For a moment, just a fraction of a second, as he looked down at Lyrei, the mead dulling his senses, he saw Alea. A lump caught in his throat. Dann had spent so long with the two sisters, he'd almost forgotten they were twins. To him they had never been difficult to tell apart, not even in the slightest.

Dann brushed a strand of hair from Lyrei's face.

"I would have taken her place if I could have," he whispered. And he would have. In a heartbeat. "I'm so sorry."

Dann scanned the tent, spotting a pile of blankets stacked in the corner behind a candle. He'd have to let Nala ride Drunir for a while the next day.

He spread one of the blankets out on the ground and rolled a second up as a pillow, then lay down and pulled the third up over himself. He didn't mind sleeping on the ground; he'd done it a hundred times, and the mead would dull the discomfort anyway.

Drawing a long breath into his lungs, Dann glanced at Lyrei. The elf let out a soft groan, shifting in place and pulling the blanket tighter over herself. She was the most beautiful thing he'd ever seen in his life.

He rolled fully onto his back, clasped his hands behind his head, and stared up at the tent's canopy for a moment before closing his eyes. He knew what he'd dream of that night: catching that damn bird.

CHAPTER THIRTY-FOUR

FORWARD, BROTHER

12th Day of the Blood Moon

Fifty miles west of Narrith – Winter, Year 3081 After Doom

The wind ripped at Aeson, crashing against him as he sat behind Calen with one arm around the man's waist and the other gripped firmly around a horn protruding from Valerys's neck. The dragon's warmth seeped from his scales into Aeson's body, but even still Aeson wove threads of Fire through his extremities to keep them from freezing. Threads of Air swirled around him, holding the worst of the wind at bay while his entire body shook and his eyes watered any time he lifted his head from Calen's back.

Aeson had never flown with any dragon but Lyara. He had always had the bond to protect him, always had her scales moulding to his shape. Flying with Valerys still had that same sense of wonder, but it also gave him a new appreciation for the sheer power of the creature beneath him. Every beat of Valerys's wings sent vibrations through Aeson's bones, and he could feel the dragon's muscles rippling against him.

A weightlessness set into his stomach as Valerys lurched upwards, angling his wings and catching a vicious current of air. Aeson drew deeper from the Spark, holding himself firm to Valerys's back while holding on to Calen for dear life. He lifted his head to see the dark sky for only a moment before the clouds enveloped them.

Roaring wind filled his ears, and dark clouds obscured his vision, the air damp and heavy. And then, in a burst of motion, Valerys shot upwards and the world erupted in a deep crimson light.

The Blood Moon hung in the sky, clearer and more vivid than Aeson had ever seen. Dark patches marred its surface, and a faint crimson mist fell towards the world as though the night itself were bleeding.

For a moment, the dragon hung in the air, the world seeming almost peaceful, and then he angled his wings and swooped down. Valerys soared parallel to the luminescent ocean of dark pink clouds that stretched into the distance, illumined by the light of the Blood Moon as though a fire raged beneath them.

They soared over the sea of burning pink, Valerys's enormous wings spread wide, black veins streaking through snow white. The dragon truly was a powerful creature, particularly for one so young. In all his years, Aeson had never seen a dragon grow at such a pace. Valerys was already the size Lyara had been in her eighth summer, his chest deeper, his muscles denser.

Perhaps Valacian dragons grew more quickly than those native to Epheria. Or perhaps the druidic bloodline affected the bond. He'd only spoken briefly to Calen about what had happened when the young man had first met Queen Uthrían. Aeson knew little of druids, but there were no doubts in his mind that Ella was of the blood. And judging by the way the Angan treated her, Calen, and Haem – they all were. He'd never heard of a druid being bound before, not even in the old stories. How that might affect the bond, he wasn't sure.

As Aeson pondered, Valerys plunged through the clouds, and Aeson leaned forwards, bracing himself against Calen. The young man shifted and moved with the dragon as though they had been bonded for decades.

"We'll set down here," Calen called out, his voice muffled on the wind as they broke through the clouds, rolling hills and thick forests taking shape beneath them. "Valerys needs to rest."

The dragon swooped down over the landscape, the tips of tall pine trees brushing against his feet, before alighting near a sheer cliff nestled within the woodland.

Once dismounted, Calen and Aeson unloaded the bags of armour and food that had been strapped to Valerys's chest, allowing the dragon to take flight again as soon as he was unburdened, setting off to hunt.

Aeson pulled some bread, cheese, cured rabbit meat, some apples, and a block of butter from the food satchel. Since the journey was only a day or so, it made sense not to light a fire and risk unnecessary attention.

"Thank you," Aeson said while placing the food on a cloth and unfurling his blanket roll. He and Calen hadn't spoken much since the battle, at least not in private and not about anything of substance. There were bridges that needed mending.

"What for?" Calen didn't lift his gaze as he shook out his blanket roll, grabbed an apple, and lay down.

"For agreeing to take me to Land's End. For understanding the need for patience." Aeson sat with his legs folded, and he gestured towards the bread, butter, cheese, and meat to see if Calen wanted any.

"Please."

"I know it isn't easy leaving Tarmon, Erik, and the others to march for Salme without you," Aeson said as he broke the loaf in half and ripped it lengthways, spreading a thick layer of butter across the inside with his knife. "No decision from this point on will be easy. And if one seems easy, question it."

He layered the hard cheese and cured rabbit on top of the butter and passed it to Calen, who sat up and nodded his thanks but said nothing. It was the quietest he'd ever seen the young man.

"Sometimes, learning when not to act, when not to charge forwards, is just as important as knowing when to knock down the gates with a battering ram. If we can break the Valtarans free from imperial control, they will be one of our greatest allies in this war. There are few men finer than Dayne Ateres and few warriors more skilled than the Valtaran blademasters. Not to mention, a few hundred wyvern riders is nothing to sniff at. And with any luck, Aryana and the others will reach Aravell in a matter of days. If we can convince them to stand behind your banners, we will finally have the numbers to truly push the empire back. Once that's done, you'll be able to join the army marching towards Salme long before any battle."

"Hmm." Calen bit off a mouthful of the bread, staring off into the night as he ate.

"I don't think I've seen you this quiet since the day I met you."

Calen stared at Aeson, those lavender eyes fixing on him. The hardness in his stare broke. "I'm just tired." Calen laid his food down on the blanket roll. "Everywhere I turn, people are trying to tie strings around me. Everyone knows what I *should* do, and they're not afraid to tell me. I can see it clear as day. Chora, Galdra, Uthrían... you. It's exhausting."

"That's not true, Calen."

"Don't lie. I will do what I need to do to protect the people of Epheria. But I've no patience for the lies anymore. Speak to me plain, speak to me honestly, and I will do the same."

Aeson stared back at Calen, their gazes locked. He nodded. "You've earned that much." Aeson allowed a moment of silence to settle between them. "I am sorry for what I kept from you. I understand why you hate me for it. I wanted to tell you Ella was alive, but ever since The Fall, all I've done is survive, keep fighting, keep believing that one day, *one day*, it would all be worth it. I learned to weigh the odds, to weigh what I wanted to do against what needed to be done. Which is something I see you learning too. This very moment is proof of that."

When Calen didn't answer, Aeson let out a long sigh and set his bread down. "You are right." He clenched his jaw. "When you first heard the Calling, when Valerys hatched for you, all I cared about was that a dragon had entered the world and a Draleid had been bound. I couldn't have given a single fuck who you were, or what you wanted, or what pain and loss you would go through on this path. I would have dragged you across a thousand miles of hot coals or through the void itself if it meant turning the Lorian Empire to dust. I had spent four hundred years in pain, why should I spare you any? What was your pain next to the things I've seen?"

Calen stared back at Aeson, disbelief in his eyes.

"You want honesty and I'm giving it to you. In my eyes, your pain, your loss, your suffering was nothing compared to that of the millions who perished in the great wars after The Fall. I had seen the hearts cut from a hundred dragons. I had seen mothers, fathers, sons, and daughters butchered in front of the ones they loved. I had waded through literal rivers of blood. I had grown cold and apathetic towards everything but seeing the empire burn, seeing Fane dead, and seeing a new world for Erik and Dahlen." He shrugged. "You and Valerys meant hope. That was all I cared about. When a person…" Aeson's throat tightened as he thought of Lyara, as he thought of the shattering of the best pieces of him. "When a person becomes Rakina, the apathy just consumes you. And the only way to keep going is by finding a purpose so singular and powerful in itself that you cling to it and it pulls you forward. This rebellion was my only purpose for a long time. Then along came Naia and Dahlen and Erik, and for a time I felt almost whole again… until she, too, was taken from me."

Aeson allowed a tear to fall, feeling its cold path as it rolled down his cheek. He would not hide it from Calen.

"When I met you, my soul had been shattered and my heart had been ripped from my chest. Dahlen and Erik were everything. They still are. In truth, you were an inconvenience. Half of me only cared that the egg had hatched, but the other half of me loathed that it had hatched for you – one who cared little for the war we were fighting, one so young with so much to learn. One who cared for nothing but his own tiny little world. A selfish child."

Ever since Aeson had first met Calen, the young man had been dominated by his rage, consumed by his loss. But now, as he stared into those lavender eyes, he saw no anger, only understanding.

The thump of Valerys's wings echoed in the night. Calen kept his gaze fixed on Aeson as the dragon emerged over the treetops and alighted behind him, the body of an elk in his jaws. Valerys dropped the carcass, blood and innards slopping against the ground.

"You proved me wrong," Aeson said as Valerys's talons pressed into the soft earth on either side of Calen. "You have become everything that I should have been, Calen. Everything that I was meant to be before The Fall took that life from me. That is the reason I kept Ella's survival from you. Because if I'd told you, then you would have gone to her, and you would have been right to do so. Because that is what a Draleid does. They protect the ones they love. They protect those who need them. Before you and Valerys rose to challenge Jormun and the others, you said, 'We're meant to be guardians, not survivors.' And you were right. I've not been a guardian in a very long time." Aeson paused for a moment, pressing his tongue against the roof of his mouth to keep himself centred. "The truth is – hard as it is to admit – my presence matters little. My name carries weight amongst those who know it. But it means nothing to the common people or to the factions that are rising. My words will not convince them to stand together and fight as one, to throw down the temptation of consolidating dropped power while the world is in flux. But you… Calen, you are a leader. I've seen it. People are drawn towards you. Even Erik would die for you, die beside you. My son believes in you. That is why I want you to stay and talk with Aryana Torval and the others. Whether you want it or not, your will alone can change the hearts of those around you, and with Valerys at your side you are the light they will look to."

"You think too much of me," Calen said, letting out a sigh. "Which is not something I ever thought I'd say."

"I've never spoken to you of the journey to find Valerys's egg in Valacia. But when I was given the egg, do you know what I learned? Valacian dragons don't require the bond to hatch or to keep their fire. Varyn never took it from them. Some lie dormant for hundreds or thousands of years, hatching for reasons entirely unknown. The man who gave me Valerys's egg said that it came from the most ancient of Valacian lines. Valerys had slept for over eight hundred years. Until he found you."

Those words seemed to visibly shake Calen. He stared back at Aeson for a moment before looking up at Valerys, who had moved to stand over him. The dragon stared down at Calen, a dim purple light glowing in his eyes.

"I don't know what will happen tomorrow, or in a year," Aeson said. "We may not live to see the next moon. Our heads might be on spikes. Fane Mortem might raze the continent, or Efialtír himself might burn this entire world to the ground. But in your own words, 'there's no point in living if we don't fight for what we love.' No matter the outcome, I can say with my hand on my heart that you are not a puppet or an instrument or a tool to be used – not anymore. And if any try, it will be my blade they'll find pressed to their necks. Du é myia'kar. Du é myia'ríen. Ar na daui nai din siel væra myia haydria."

You are my brother. You are my kin. And to die by your side would be my honour.

Calen let out a long breath, Aeson's words lingering between them. "Akar…" he whispered. *Brother.* He lifted his gaze and gave a soft nod, then leaned forwards and offered Aeson his hand. "Il tavu er tavu. Vir ketat imbahír, akar. Draleid n'aldryr."

The past is the past. We move forwards, brother. Dragonbound by fire.

Aeson grasped Calen's forearm. "Rakina nai dauva. Imbahír," he agreed. "Altinua imbahír."

Broken by death. Forwards. Always forwards.

Calen held his gaze on Aeson for a moment before releasing his arm and snatching the bread, meat, and cheese and taking a hungry mouthful. "It's good," he said, giving Aeson the slightest of smiles. "Now that we have time, tell me of these people in Arkalen, these allies. Who are they?"

"Most are people who've been a part of the rebellion their entire lives. Many are old friends. Were it not for them, we never would have made it back to Epheria with Valerys's egg. They've been waiting in the province for this exact moment, garnering support, building strength."

"They were with you?" Calen's interest piqued. "When you went to Valacia?"

"They were. Verma, Pylvír and his daughters, Ildur, Fearn… Malari, må Heraya beskír sine."

May Heraya watch over her.

"We lost near a hundred and barely made it out with our lives."

"Before, after Milltown, you said you were there for three days and three nights. You never said anything about losing so many."

"I didn't know you. I didn't trust you."

Calen shifted in place so he was facing Aeson. "You've never talked about it since then. About how you got the egg – how you really got the egg."

"And you've never asked."

Calen set his food down once more and gave Aeson his full attention. "I'm asking now."

They sat there for more than an hour as Aeson told Calen of the journey to the icelands of Valacia, of the Dakar and of Cukulkan and the Valacian dragons, and of the journey back. He told him of Amatkai and the others. His instinct was to omit the fact that they were druids, Amatkai's words sounding in his skull.

"If you tell a soul what I, Boud, or Tamzin are, I will personally pull the knife across your sons' throats."

But Aeson was not the kind of man to learn nothing from his mistakes. If he hid this from Calen and the young man were to find out, there would be no reconciliation. Honesty was the only way forward.

When Aeson had finally finished weaving the tale, a short silence fell upon them as Calen sat wordlessly with his legs crossed.

"I need you to promise me that you will not tell a soul what I have just told you. It is a story I promised not to tell, and in telling you I have broken that vow. The Dakar and Cukulkan gifted us Valerys's egg in the hope that the blood of dragons would not die here. All they wish is to be left alone. Do you understand?"

"I do."

CHAPTER THIRTY-FIVE

LEGACY

14th Day of the Blood Moon

Land's End – Winter, Year 3081 After Doom

Calen leaned tight against Valerys's scales, the wind whipping past on either side of him. The dragon's warmth seeped into his bones as he closed his eyes and pulled their minds together. Rolling thunder roared through the skies, bolts of lightning tearing across the night, rain sheeting down as though the Godsrealm had opened.

It had taken two days of almost non-stop flying to reach the southern tip of Arkalen, hundreds of miles a day, stopping only to eat and sleep. Had Valerys been at his fullest, the journey may not have been so arduous, but as it stood, he still was not fully recovered from the battle at Aravell.

Through the dragon's eyes, Calen watched as the deluge obscured the night, an ocean of dark forest sweeping past below. He could see the warmth radiating from the birds that braved the raging storm and the creatures sheltering in the trees, smell the char of burning where lightning had struck wood, hear the rain drumming like a thousand hammers.

The dragon cracked his mighty wings and rolled to the right, sweeping into a dive, then catching a current of air that carried them forwards. With each twist and turn, Aeson pulled tighter on Calen's belt, pressing against his back. Had it been anyone else flying with him, they would have fallen to their death hundreds of miles back. Even with Valerys's scales moulded to him, even with the bond,

Calen often struggled to stay in place when his soulkin manoeuvred at such speeds. The simple fact that Aeson still clung on was a testament to the man – his kin.

Ahead, the forest opened to a plain of hills and craggy, moss-covered rocks. Hundreds of feet below the enormous, jagged cliffs, dark waves raged against the rock face, harsh and brutal. Flashes of lightning illuminated the night, pink moonlight diffusing through heavy charcoal clouds that made the sky seem starless.

A few miles from the edge of the plain, a formation of serrated rock nestled within an enormous basin fed by seven streams jutted from the unforgiving landscape. Flickering lights decorated the rock as the stars might decorate the sky, hundreds of golden specks – windows.

"That's it," Calen whispered to himself, the wind swallowing his words. Aeson had told him what to look for, but he hadn't quite expected something so monstrous. The fortress was not built from or on the rock, but into it. As Calen looked closer through Valerys's eyes, he saw towers, their peaks twisting with the rock. Staircases and walkways wound around the formation, blending seamlessly.

A single gargantuan bridge carved from stone as black as night traversed the dark waters of the basin, connecting the fortress to the mainland. If Calen listened with Valerys's ears, he could hear the flags flapping angrily in the wind.

The fortress itself may as well have been an island at sea. The place seemed nigh-on impregnable.

"There's a plateau on the southern face of the fort!" Aeson's voice sounded in Calen's ears, amplified by threads of Air and Spirit.

Valerys swooped lower as they approached, the rain battering off his scales. He skirted the rim of the basin, angling his right wing towards the water. For a moment, Calen pulled his mind apart from Valerys's, seeing through his own eyes as the dragon's reflection stared back at him, the white stark against the dark waters.

Calen could feel the roar building before it erupted from the dragon's jaws, so loud it may as well have been a slap of Hafaesir's hammer. The roar resonated through the basin, resounding off the stone and crashing against the waves. If the fortress's garrison hadn't known they were there, they did now.

Valerys dropped lower, the spearhead tip of his tail slicing through the water's surface. Waves crashed against the rocks, the spray tickling Calen's exposed skin. Valerys surged upwards as he reached the southern face of the fortress, the shift in momentum pulling Calen backwards, Aeson's arm wrapping around his waist.

The plateau was rimmed by a high wall carved straight from the rock, large enough to hold Valerys twice over. A group of armoured guards stood at the far side, arranged in a semi-circle before a set of iron-banded gates, torches flickering in their hands.

Valerys dove, spreading his wings wide and cracking them against the air as he alighted on the stone.

VERMA TALLISAIR LOWERED HER HOOD, the raging storm saturating her hair in seconds. A thunderclap erupted in the distance, the wind howling. She stared through the deluge, her gaze fixed on the white-scaled dragon that tore across the sky, its wings veined with black.

The creature was enormous for one so young. Some of the horns around its jaw and face were easily as long as her arm, its wingspan well over a hundred feet. The sight of the creature brought back memories of old.

"Al'il nära un Varyn," Pylvír whispered as he, too, lowered his hood and stared up at the sky. *By the light of Varyn.* The look in the elf's eyes was both awe and wonder. "He has grown like a seed planted by Heraya's own hand."

Pylvír's daughter, Andira, stood at his side, over a head taller than her father. In the near two years they had been at Fort Saldar, not a day had passed where the elf hadn't spent every waking hour training and preparing for Aeson's call. And now that he was here and the time had come, she stood silently, staring into the storm.

"It's nice to see one of those things and not worry it's going to set me on fire – or eat me." Ildur folded his arms. The old Stormguard watched the dragon with grey eyes as it swept upwards across the basin's rock face.

Aurelian Animar, High Mantle of the Arkalen Stormguard and leader of the newly formed Free Nation of Olmiron, folded his arms to Ildur's left. The man was rock personified. Verma hadn't seen much of him, but from what she had seen, he was harsh, cold, honest, and honourable. A man with those traits and the wrong ideals was more often called a tyrant, but Aurelian seemed a decent man and one who wished for his nation to be free of Lorian control. He had arrived from Seaside three days prior to ensure he would be there for Aeson and the Draleid's arrival, leaving his generals to carry on the war with Syrene Linas.

A chorus of gasps sounded as the dragon plummeted towards them, its massive wings spreading so wide the shadow consumed the entire plateau.

"Keep your heads," Ildur called to the dozen Stormguard spread out around them. Verma could feel the tension in the air. None of these guardsmen had ever laid eyes on a dragon that wasn't intent on slaughtering everything they knew. Over half of them rested their hands on their swords' pommels. The sight caused Verma to laugh to herself. What good was a sword against a dragon? If this creature wanted them dead, their places would be laid in Achyron's halls. Better to jump from Saldar's walls than to charge that beast with a sword.

A vicious crack of the dragon's wings set a gust in the air and a spiral in the sheeting rain. The plateau trembled as the dragon alighted, its legs touching the stone first, followed by its winged forelimbs. The creature shook its head like a hound trying to loose the rain from its fur. Black and white frills stood on end, a deep rumble coming from the dragon's throat.

The clink of metal on stone sounded to Verma's left as one of the Stormguard staggered backwards, steel rasping as he reflexively pulled at his sword.

The dragon's head snapped to focus at the sound, its cold lavender eyes fixing on the guardsman. It shifted in place, lips pulling back to bare alabaster teeth the size of daggers. It threw its head forwards and unleashed a roar so visceral that Verma could see the rain shake.

"I said keep your head!" Ildur roared. He grabbed the guard by the pauldron and used his free hand to shove the sword back into its scabbard.

The dragon glared at the man, its breath heavy, its lips curling back. It had only been two years, but Verma had almost forgotten just how terrifyingly monstrous dragons were. They were creatures totally outside the natural order of things, capable of destruction beyond all measure. The size of the largest ships, capable of melting steel with a breath, and covered from head to tail in scale armour.

By all measures, the creature was magnificent. But the sheer power it radiated set the hairs on her neck on end.

After a few moments, the dragon bowed, extending out its right forelimb. The sensation of the Spark tickled the back of Verma's neck, and two figures dropped from the dragon's back, their landings cushioned by threads of Air.

"Move," Ildur called to the waiting guards as he strode towards the two figures.

"To attention." Aurelian followed Ildur, the guards spreading out on either side of them, framing a path, the flames of their torches whipping wildly in the wind.

"Ildur," Aeson called out, his cloak flapping behind him, water dripping from his hair and nose. He opened his arms wide, pulling Ildur into a bearhug. "It's good to see that hair isn't all grey just yet."

"Aeson Virandr." Ildur returned the embrace. "You've still not aged a day, you bastard."

Aeson clapped Ildur on the cheek. "My day will come, old friend. My day will come."

He greeted Pylvír with just as much enthusiasm, then turned to the elf's daughter.

"Andira, you look even stronger than before." He clasped her shoulders, a broad grin on his face, then her temples, touching their foreheads together. "What have they been feeding you here?"

"Nadíl," she replied affectionately. *Uncle.* "Det er aldin na vëna dir. É dir mære?"
It is good to see you. Are you well?

"I am, thank you. Your mother?"

"She's in the stores with Fearn, sorting shipments."

"Is she still mad?"

"Does the grass ever stop being green?"

Aeson laughed at that, finally turning his attention to Verma. "Vésani."
Sister.

"Akar." *Brother.*

Verma grasped Aeson's forearm, staring into his eyes. They were even more blue than she remembered.

Aeson turned to Aurelian and inclined his head. "It's good to see you well. I'm sorry for what happened at Yarrin."

The High Mantle nodded absently. "There was nothing anyone could have done. The Uraks washed over the city like a tidal wave. We were lucky to escape with our lives. It's an honour to have you here."

Aeson rested one hand on Aurelian's shoulder. "It is an honour to be welcome here. And with that, may I introduce you to Calen Bryer, soulkin to Valerys and the first free Draleid in four centuries. Calen, this is Aurelian Animar, High Mantle of the Arkalen Stormguard and leader of the rebellion in Arkalen."

Aeson gestured for his companion to draw closer. The man was young, twenty or so summers perhaps. Tall and lean-muscled, hair dark, eyes the same piercing shade of purple as the dragon's. She'd never seen purple eyes. But even all the way down in Land's End she'd heard the stories of the battles further north. Of how the young man had earned the name 'Warden of Varyn'. He carried himself like a veteran of a hundred battles, his gaze measuring and assessing each of the plateau's occupants. His shoulders were squared, his hand never straying too far from the coin pommel of the sword at his hip – an elven blade, old by the working of the guard and the detailing on the steel. The power of the Spark pulsed from him. Draleid always had a far deeper well to draw from than most mages, but this young man was unique, he was… *more* than most.

"Fort Saldar is yours, Draleid." Aurelian pressed a closed fist to his chest and bowed his head.

"And we are yours." The Draleid mimicked Aurelian's gesture, the show of mutual respect clearly pleasing the High Mantle.

"Calen." Aeson gestured towards Verma. "This is Verma Talissair, one of the last Arcarians and one of my oldest friends."

Verma grasped the young man's forearm in greeting, but as she did, his eyes flashed a milky white and the world around her plunged into darkness before exploding with all manner of colours and light. Memories flitted across her vision, battles long fought and lost, friends dead for an age, tender moments of vulnerability kept hidden.

And then she was back on the plateau, the rain cold against her skin, the storm raging overhead, her hand trembling.

Somehow it felt like both hours and only fractions of a second had passed at the same time.

Calen Bryer stared back at her, his eyes returning to their lavender hue. His fingers squeezed her forearm, and she noticed an almost imperceptible shift in his stance, as though he had only just about stopped himself from collapsing to the ground. Behind him, the dragon moved forwards, its head tilted sideways, the rain splattering against its scales.

None of the others seemed to have noticed anything at all.

Calen gave the slightest nod, his gaze staying fixed on Verma. Had he seen the memories she'd seen? How could that even be possible?

Her heart pounded against her ribs, her mouth going dry.

"Alaith anar." *Well met.* Calen's stare never left hers as he spoke.

"Ar du, Draleid." *And you, Draleid.* Verma gripped the man's forearm tighter and pulled him close. Those memories had been her darkest, the ones she'd locked away and buried the key. She whispered, "Those moments were not yours to see."

Before the Draleid could respond, Aeson pulled him away and introduced him to the others one by one.

"Come," Ildur shouted over the storm. "Let's get you inside before the rain seeps into your bones. The fire is roaring, and there's some warm food to fill your bellies."

He ordered a handful of the guards to fetch the bags and sacks strapped to the dragon's chest. The looks on the faces of the men and women saddled with that task were ones of utter shock, which in truth was the exact response Verma herself would have given if she had been asked to fetch a bag from a dragon.

The Draleid lifted an open palm, signalling the guards to stay where they were, then walked to the dragon and pulled off two sacks and a satchel, swinging them over his shoulder. He handed them to Aeson, then turned to address Aurelian. "I'll stay for food, Lord Animar, but not the night. Valerys and I must be back in the air."

"The storm is too fierce, Calen." Aeson rested a hand on Calen's shoulder. "And Valerys is tired. We'll have food brought to him. Let him rest, and leave at dawn."

The Draleid looked back at Aeson for a few moments before nodding and heading back for the rest of the bags.

AFTER SUPPER HAD BEEN SERVED, Verma and the others stood about the fireplace in one of Fort Saldar's many drawing rooms. Cups of wine had been poured and poured again, and the fire's warmth sank into Verma's bones.

Aeson sat on a long couch, conversing with Pylvír, Andira, and Pylvír's Ayar Elwyn, Elara. Fearn had joined them, along with Ithaca, and they both sat in armchairs on the far side of the room, fresh cups of wine in their hands. It had taken the better part of a year for Verma to trust the Ardanian sellsword after what had happened on the journey back from Valacia. But Ithaca had worked hard and helped recruit more than a few souls to the rebellion.

Ildur, Heraya bless his ageing heart, was passed out in a leather chair by the fire, his wine cup still gripped firmly in his fingers. The man was nearing his sixtieth summer. He could still cut his way through a battle like he had barely seen thirty, but time was slowly creeping up on him. He deserved a rest.

Across the way, near a long table with clay vases of wine and empty bowls of beef stew, the Draleid pulled himself away from a conversation with a handful of the Stormguard captains, letting out a puff of air as he walked towards the fireplace.

"Enjoying yourself?" Verma asked, sarcasm dripping from her voice as the man stopped in front of the fire and stared into the flames. The Stormguard captains had all but chained him to the table, launching question after question at him. She didn't blame them. He was a Draleid. To them, he was a thing of legend, a symbol, a hero. To her, he looked like a young man who had been forced to become something he'd never asked to be and had lost a great deal because of it. She could see it in the way his eyes always glanced towards the floor after he spoke, in the way his smiles faded and cracked, and in the rigid and practiced nature of his posture. It was a strange irony that the greatest of hopes always landed on the youngest of shoulders.

"Hmm." He glanced her way, that smile forming then breaking. "It's a nice respite from only having Aeson for conversation."

Verma snorted, sipping at her wine. "I feel that pain."

"I apologise for earlier." Calen's tone grew sombre in a heartbeat. "It's not something I can control. And it's not happened in a while… I don't…" He trailed off, staring back into the fire. "I'm sorry."

Verma had lived long enough to know a truth from a lie. The young man's words were genuine. Over the course of the supper, she had trawled through her memories, trying to remember where she'd seen that kind of power before. At last, she'd landed on the works of old Duran Linold. *Druids, a Magic Lost.* It had been five centuries since she'd read that book.

"What did you see?"

Calen bit down on his lip, folding his arms. "Death…" His voice cracked a little. "So much death. And other things… things I had no right to see."

"No, you didn't. But what is done is done." She tapped the rim of her cup against her lips. "Do you know what you are?"

The Draleid turned his gaze from the fire, his peculiar eyes locking with hers.

"You do then. I've never met a druid before, not in the flesh." The Draleid flinched at the word. "Does Aeson know? I suspect he does. There's not much gets past him."

Before Calen could answer, Aurelian stepped between the two, his hands clasped behind his back, the fireplace's flames casting a warm glow on his skin. The man wore a grey tunic with the emblem of the Stormguard – a shield with twin bolts of lightning – on its breast. He greeted both Calen and Verma with a nod.

Aurelian picked a piece of meat from between his teeth with his tongue, staring into the flames with the same intensity the Draleid had. "Your chambers have been prepared, Draleid," he said without lifting his gaze. "Aeson Virandr informs me you are to make for the Darkwood come daybreak. I will not be offended if you retire early."

Another broken, placating smile. "Thank you, Lord Animar."

"No lord, Draleid. Just a man."

"Thank you, nonetheless. Aeson told me this was an old Stormguard fort," he said, looking around the room. "But this place is far more than that. An army of thousands couldn't take it. How, may I ask, did it end up in the hands of rebels?"

Animar gave a short laugh. "Fort Saldar was built some fourteen hundred years ago, back when the five kingdoms warred for Arkalen. It was the heart of the Sakarnan Kingdom, an impregnable fortress that could see for miles in all directions, garrisoned by the legendary Sakarnan Stormguard. It was a wonder of the age. But when the Sakarnans refused to submit after The Fall, the Lorians torched the land in all directions and the mages poisoned the soil. The fortress was all but abandoned some two hundred years ago. There's nothing out here save for storms and rocks. An impregnable fortress is little use to anyone if it's in the arse end of nowhere. A skeleton garrison was left to keep it operational should it be needed. High Lord Syrene Linas and myself don't quite see eye to eye, to put it delicately. She couldn't remove me as the High Mantle of the Stormguard, not while I had the loyalty of my brothers and sisters. But she could exile me here to waste away on this 'worthless rock', as she put it." Aurelian let out a long sigh, staring into the flames. "I'm afraid I didn't get to converse with you over supper. May I be candid?"

"I'd prefer it."

"I don't know you."

"Nor I, you."

Aurelian Animar gave the man a half-smile. "I do not fight this war for Aeson Virandr. I do it because I want my people to be free of imperial bonds, to be free of a tyrant like Syrene Linas, who holds no loyalty but to those that fill her coffers. She treats the Stormguard like her personal handmaids, and she would take food from a child's mouth even if her belly were full. I fight not because I have no food at my table but because there are others who go without."

"Very noble of you." The Draleid winced after he spoke. "Apologies. It was a long journey."

Aurelian waved him away, laughing. "You truly do prefer to do away with the pleasantries."

"I've spent a lot of time with elves," Calen said, shaking his head absently. "Have you ever met an elf?"

"My experience has been somewhat limited. Why do you ask?"

"I owe my life to more elves than I could begin to count. But amongst their rulers, the politicking and the games and the wordplay... it's endless."

Aurelian gave a gruff laugh and warmed his hands by the fire. "You are still young then."

The Draleid raised a curious eyebrow.

"That is not elves, Draleid. That is all who seek power. Very well, I will be straight as a razor. I consider myself a man of honour. A man of principles and logic. A man of duty. Duty to my people, duty to my brothers and sisters of the Stormguard, duty to Arkalen. I align myself with Aeson Virandr and Verma here because their cause aids my duty, which is to Arkalen, not to Epheria. I couldn't care less if Valtara burns or if Drifaien is drowned in snow. Their plight is their own. Ildur and his followers sail for Valtara in the morning, some four thousand and a handful of former Stormguard. Ildur is a good man, keeps his word. There are another three thousand Stormguard in Fort Saldar who have come from across the province to fight for Arkalen. I cannot spare many, but I would send some with Ildur and Aeson if I had a reason. Do I have one? Why would I send my warriors to fight in your name for some foreign land?"

The Draleid's lip curled, forming a flicker of a smile. "Don't."

"What?" Aurelian was genuinely surprised at that.

"Don't send your warriors to fight in my name." Calen drew a long breath, clasping his hands behind his back. He let it out slowly. "I may be young, High Mantle, but I've watched a lot of people die. I've heard the names they call as the blood pours from their veins, seen the light fade from their eyes as they die hundreds of miles from everywhere they know and everything they love. I don't want people dying in my name. If you're going to fight or die, do it for something you believe in. On that, I must wish you goodnight. It's a long way back. I appreciate the chambers, but I will sleep on the plateau with Valerys."

The Draleid inclined his head and made to leave.

"You can't be serious?" Aurelian looked at the Draleid as though the man had ten heads. "There's a storm out there."

"There is." The Draleid met Aurelian's gaze, and for the first time since Verma had met the young man, his smile was no longer cracked or brittle. He turned again to leave, then stopped. "Fight the battles you think worth fighting, Lord Animar. Just remember that if we call and you don't answer, there might not be anyone there to hear your screams when the Lorians bring the dragonfire."

Without waiting to hear a response, the Draleid ambled across the room, stopping to talk with Aeson for a moment before the two of them left through the main doors.

Aurelian stared after Calen Bryer, one hand hovering, his index finger extended as though he were about to make a counterpoint. If looks could kill, the scowl on Aurelian's face would have decapitated a horse. To Verma's surprise, the man clenched his hand into a fist and snorted. "I like him."

"I do too…" Verma answered in a whisper, staring at the doorway Calen Bryer and Aeson had just walked through. Only two years past she had left Aeson Virandr at Milltown's port with a dragon egg that had been paid for in blood. It seemed that it had been blood well spent. "I do too."

CHAPTER THIRTY-SIX

DEATH BECOMES YOU

14th Day of the Blood Moon

Salme – Winter, Year 3081 After Doom

Erdhardt sat forwards on the steps of his porch, stretching out his chest and pulling his head back. His spine and neck cracked, the muscles in his back spasming. He grimaced and held himself in that position until the spasms petered out and faded to a dull ache, his muscles loosening once more.

He let out a long, exhausted sigh, then dipped the rag in his right hand back into the bucket at his side and continued to clean the blood from his hammer. His original warhammer had been crushed by a Bloodmarked some time ago, and one of Salme's weaponsmiths had crafted him the weapon that currently lay across his lap. The head bore a hammer on one side, spread into nine points like a butcher's meat pounder, with a hefty spike occupying the other side. It was nothing fancy, but it killed Uraks, and that was all he needed it to do. Some of the children had taken to calling the weapon 'Bonebreaker', but Erdhardt cared little for the name. Naming a weapon was a pointless thing.

He squinted as he looked up at the morning sun, picking a strip of grey flesh from the hammer's teeth. That night's Urak attack had been the bloodiest in a while, and he'd not yet slept. Not that he slept much anyway. The beasts had been quieter the past few days, but he was under no illusions. All that meant was that they were busy either killing more travellers along the roads or adding their numbers to the siege of Camylin. And once that city fell, Salme would be next.

He set his hammer down beside him, grabbed a clean rag, dipped it in the water, and wiped the dried blood and dirt from his face and neck. Keeping himself clean was a task in and of itself. He couldn't bathe every day, that simply wasn't feasible, and yet every night he painted himself in fresh Urak blood. A wet rag was the best way for him to keep from looking as though he'd crawled from a pile of corpses.

As he wiped a piece of gore from behind his ear, young Lina Styr and her mam, Mara, appeared around the corner. Lina carried an armful of baskets so high they rose above her head while Mara held a massive iron pot.

"You're meant to be sleeping." Mara frowned at Erdhardt, shaking her head. "And you could do with a hot bath."

"I could do with a great many things, Mara."

The woman's frown turned to a sympathetic gaze. She'd lost her husband four summers gone in the same battle that had taken Haem Bryer and many others. She understood Erdhardt's loss. He softened, giving Mara a half-smile and looking to young Lina. "And what do you have there, young lady?"

A small blonde head appeared from behind the tower of baskets, with bright green eyes and a smile that seemed far too genuine for the current state of the world. "We brought you food, Master Hammersmith." She puffed out her chest a little, raising her chin. "I made the carrot cake myself. Swear I did. And the bread. It's got seeds and walnuts!"

"Is that right?" Even a grumpy old man like Erdhardt couldn't keep a smile from his face at the pride in Lina's voice. He hauled himself to his feet, his knees arguing, his back aching. "And is all this for me?"

"No," she said, laughing.

"I think it is." Erdhardt pretended to take the entire stack of baskets from her.

"No, it's not." Lina giggled, twisting to keep the baskets from him. "Just one!"

"Oh, all right then. But what happens if I eat the whole cake in one sitting? Will you make me another?"

"You couldn't eat the whole cake! Not on your own!"

"That's a challenge I'm willing to accept." He ruffled Lina's hair gently, then turned to Mara. "Thank you. You didn't have to."

The woman shook her head. "Nonsense, Erdhardt. We all have our parts to play. I'm no good with a spear, but I can keep you fed. Gods know you're no good at that yourself. Here."

Mara handed him the iron pot, which was far heavier than she'd made it look.

"Lamb stew. It will stay fresh enough for a few days if left sealed in the cold. But I don't suspect it will last that long." She grabbed the top basket from Lina's tower and placed it on the step beside Erdhardt. "Bread, sweet carrot cake, blackberry jam, and scones."

"Mara—" Erdhardt made to protest but was cut off by a sharp 'tssk'. They'd done this dance many times in the months since arriving in Salme.

"I have other people to feed, Erdhardt. And I don't have all day to stand here and argue with you over blackberry jam."

"You're a good soul, Mara Styr."

"You look too far from yourself, Erdhardt." The woman gave a slight bow, then carried on with Lina in tow.

Erdhardt slung his hammer through the loop on his back, grabbed the basket, and brought it, along with the pot, into the squat wooden house he called his own, and laid them both down on the table. There was little else inside. A bed, a chest, a table, a wardrobe, and a chair, with a fireplace set into the eastern wall. He'd no need of much else and rarely spent time within the four walls unless he was sleeping.

This place was not his home. He would never have a home again. That had died with Aela. She'd been his safe place, his warmth, his comfort. His only task now was to protect the people of The Glade, to watch over them as The Father would. After that, he would find his wife in Achyron's halls.

It was a simple plan, but it was a good plan.

The thought of Aela made him lift his right hand and stroke the obsidian earring, carved into the shape of a feather, that hung from a still-healing hole in his right ear. He had been wearing it since the night she'd died.

A knock sounded at the door.

"You've not slept either then?" Anya Gritten stood in the wide-open doorway, blood and dirt mashed into her leathers, her face much the same, her red hair brown as bark.

Erdhardt grabbed a clean rag from the counter and tossed it to her. "There's a bucket on the steps."

As Anya cleaned her face and hands, Erdhardt pulled Lina Styr's sweet carrot cake from the basket and cut two slices. He stepped out onto the porch and offered one to Anya.

The young woman refused, but he set it into her hands anyway. She was as bad as him for refusing kindness.

"No fork?" she asked, setting herself on the steps.

"No fork means no cleaning." Erdhardt sat beside Anya, giving her a weak smile.

"Spoken like a man."

"Spoken like a *wise* man." Erdhardt bit into the carrot cake, letting out an involuntary sigh. Lina Styr made a damn good cake. "Many injured?"

Anya nodded, her mouth full of cake. "More than I'd hoped. Some that are far beyond my ability. Parlim Sten's legs were both broken, shattered like glass. I stayed with him for hours, tried to keep him with us. But in the end, all I could do was give him Altweid Blood and hope it eased his journey."

"I'm not sure how you do it, Anya. Your mother would have been proud. It's far easier to take a life than to save one." Images of Verna Gritten's broken and twisted body flashed across Erdhardt's mind. He'd known the woman his entire life, and now she was simply gone.

Anya smiled softly, a smile that faded within seconds. She shoved the remainder of her cake into her mouth, almost inhaling it. "On that, I'm exhausted and need to sleep. Shall we?"

Erdhardt and Anya walked the streets of Salme, nodding to those who passed while going about their morning. He remembered what Salme had looked like only a year or so prior. No more than a village, with stout log homes not much different to The Glade and a population of no more than a few hundred.

Now the place was a city by any definition, home to thousands who had flocked from across western Illyanara. The homes that had been erected to house new citizens were a mishmash of stone, log, and mudbrick with rooves of thatch and shingle.

Erdhardt and Anya stopped at a patch of land at the western edge of the city, far enough from the water that the soil was moist but not sodden. It was there they had planted the ash seeds.

It had been Tharn Pimm's idea. In The Glade, they had taken locks of hair from every body they'd buried and planted each with its own seed. When humans had first come to Epheria, the ash tree had been sacred to their gods – the tree of life and death. The teachings and worship of those old gods was all but gone and dead, but the knowledge of the ash tree remained.

Erdhardt knelt before Aela's sapling, which was less than half a foot tall. He laid his palm flat against the soil. "I miss you again today, my love. Just as I will tomorrow. Just as I did yesterday. Why didn't you just run?"

He'd been angry at her for quite a while. Furious, even. But then he'd realised that at least this way, he could bear the pain of a world without her. A pain she would never have to know in return.

He knelt there, unmoving, his hand pressed into the soil, until Anya finally broke the silence.

"It's time I slept." Anya stood over the sapling that was her mother's, her eyes raw, tears dripping from her chin. "And you. You're no good if you're too tired to swing that hammer."

"I will see you again tomorrow," Erdhardt whispered to Aela. He placed his fingers to his lips and kissed, pressing his hand into the soil before standing. "Sleep doesn't call me yet."

He turned to Anya and held out his arms, offering a hug. The young woman wrapped her arms around him and pressed her head into his chest, sobbing gently.

"Two peas in a pod we are." He rubbed his hand on her back.

"Except I'm a lot younger and I smell better." Anya sniffled and laughed, smiling as she pulled away.

"You watch your tongue. I'm still an elder of The Glade." Erdhardt squeezed Anya's shoulders softly, sighing and brushing a tear from her cheek. Anya Gritten had saved him. Not physically but mentally and emotionally. Of all the people in The Glade, it had been she who had refused to let him wallow in his cups, to let him lose himself. And for that, he owed her an unpayable debt. "Go get some rest."

With Anya gone, Erdhardt placed one last kiss on Aela's sapling and went to do his round of the city before retiring himself. It was a routine he had fallen into, and thank the gods for it. More than once he'd found a broken section of wall unattended, an injured man or woman left lying in a ditch, or any other manner of issues, of which there seemed to be no end.

Many of those problems had grown fewer and fewer since Dahlen Virandr had taken over as the commander of Salme's defences – or the Lord Captain, as many of the others had taken to calling him. He was an impressive young man, clearly bred for war. Were it not for him, the Belduarans, and the dwarves – and he supposed the Lorians if he was being truthful – Salme would have been nothing but rubble months ago, every soul within dead.

As he walked, he passed one of the many squares built into the city. There he found near a hundred youths with spears in their hands, all standing tall and paying close attention to three of the Belduarans, who were instructing them on the proper way to stand and move in formation. Dahlen had introduced these training sessions. The young – sixteen or younger – didn't fight on the walls. At least not yet. And so they were drilled in the morning with the second rotation.

Once past the square, Erdhardt ascended a set of stairs that led to ramparts along the city's palisade wall, which had grown thicker and taller. The Uraks had only attacked during the day three times. But twice out of those three, Salme's defenders had been caught with their trousers around their ankles. It wouldn't happen again.

He marched along the ramparts, ensuring each and every guard stood at their post.

They knew him. They all did. 'Fellhammer' they called him. It seemed as silly as naming a sword. Perhaps heroes of legend deserved names. And even then, the true legends never needed one – the great Cassian Tal, Alvira Serris, Ruarc Oden. Erdhardt had never gone to fight for the Illyanaran army like Vars and the others. The most battle he'd seen had been during his time in the town guard of The Glade in his younger years, where his hammer had crushed many an Urak chest. But even then, that had been nothing on the scale of the war that now burned Epheria. Still, he would abide the name so long as it put courage in their hearts to think him worthy of it.

As he made his way around the rampart and closer to the gates, he found Lanan Halfhand, one of Salme's elders, looking out at the land on the other side. She stood with her arms folded, head tilted to the side.

She glanced at Erdhardt as he approached.

"Hammersmith. You should be resting." Her eyes were dark and sunken, and flecks of blood on the back of her neck and behind her ears had clearly been missed when she had cleaned herself after the fighting.

"I've heard that a lot this morning, though only from hypocrites."

Lanan snorted at that as Erdhardt took his place beside her. She had been watching the workers toil before the walls, digging the dry moats that Dahlen had ordered. One was already finished, and at that very moment, men and women were pulling impaled Urak corpses from the stakes set into its base.

While the bodies from the night before were removed, another group worked on a second moat, some ten feet further from the walls than the first. They dug the trench with shovels, piling the dirt high on the other side, before setting long wooden stakes in place. It was hard, gruelling work, and even in the cold winter air, many of the workers were shirtless and sweating.

"I never thanked you, Hammersmith," Lanan said.

"For?"

"Beating Benem bloody. He's been much easier to deal with ever since."

"My pleasure." Erdhardt folded his arms. "Though men like that never let things lie. He will come for me, whether it's a spear in the back during the fighting or some kind of poison in my drink, or perhaps one night I might simply fall from the wall. I reckon I can keep him in check. But I'd advise you to exercise the same caution."

"I'm not new to these games, Hammersmith. As you well know. It just so happens that Benem's food of late carries a bit more sweetness than it usually would."

"What did you do?"

"Me?" Lanan pursed her lips, raising an open hand with only two fingers and a thumb. "I would never do anything. But when Freis Bryer last visited Salme at my request, she planted many Fanril flowers near the main hall – a natural remedy for constipation, if I remember correctly. And I could have sworn I saw one of the cooks from Pirn picking them accidentally. It's very easy to confuse Fanril with blooming Barntip."

"Lanan, you're going to kill the man by making him shit himself to death."

"As I've already said, Erdhardt. I've done nothing. I'm simply a casual observer. And my observation is that Benem has been too occupied drinking his bodyweight in water and emptying his bowels to cause me any concern. I'm simply speculating that perhaps the cook picked the wrong flower."

Across the years, Erdhardt had always known Lanan as a sharp woman, quick of wit and more than capable in a fight. But at that moment he made a personal note in his mind to never make her an enemy. All men died, and there were many ways to do so. But shitting himself to death was one he hoped to avoid.

"Well, the moats seem effective." He gestured down at three men struggling to haul the body of an Urak from a set of four stakes through its leg, chest, and neck.

"Very much so. Simple, crude, and viciously potent. And that is another thing I must thank you for. Suggesting Dahlen Virandr lead the defence was an inspired choice. Though I dare say he sleeps less than even you and I."

Erdhardt followed Lanan's gaze to see Dahlen Virandr on his hands and knees in the second trench, dragging an enormous stone free so the trench could be deepened. "By The Father, the man never stops."

So much blood and dirt were mixed and mashed into Dahlen's face and skin he looked closer to a corpse than a living man. Since the Uraks had attacked that first night, Dahlen had always been where the fighting was thickest, he, the Belduarans, and those three dwarves that never left his side. And that had also been true only hours ago when Dahlen had manned the ramparts over the gates from sunset to sunrise. The young man had even leapt from the walls after one of the Belduarans had been knocked from the battlements. The woman had broken her leg in multiple places, but because of Dahlen and the others who followed the madman, she yet lived. Erdhardt himself had carried her back through the gates whilst the fighting had been dying down.

Erdhardt was not surprised to see the man still awake, as that had been the case most mornings, but to see him digging the trench was unexpected indeed.

"How long do you think we can last?" Lanan broke the silence, still looking down at Dahlen Virandr and the others.

"That depends entirely on how hard they come at us. They've eased off these last few nights. The mood's been better. But I don't doubt for a second they're going to come back twice as hard. If Camylin falls, we're next. And they'll come with much larger numbers."

"Unless they make for Midhaven."

"There's that. But I'd rather prepare for the worst and pray to Varyn for the best. Much will depend on if the forces sent by Dahlen's father and Calen arrive in time." Even as he spoke the words, Erdhardt couldn't quite believe them. It hadn't been two summers since Calen had passed The Proving. Erdhardt could remember the young lad's face after he'd emerged from Ölm. How had it come to this? How, by all divine will, was he standing on the walls of Salme, awaiting relief from an army sent by Calen Bryer? It wasn't even stuff of bards' tales. It sounded more akin to one of Dann Pimm's drunken stories, like that time the boy had sworn he'd laid eyes on a horse with a horn growing from its head. "All we can do is fight as hard as we can as long as we can. There is nothing else. Live for tomorrow."

Lanan gave a half-smile and nodded to herself. "Ylinda Pimm is a good leader. Not as considered as Verna Gritten was, but still, a good leader. But are you sure—"

"I'm sure, Lanan." They'd had this conversation already. "My days sitting on councils died with my wife. Someone making decisions about the future of a place and its people should have a will to be around to see that future. As things stand, I'll settle for doing my best to make sure we see tomorrow."

"Where are you going?" Lanan asked as Erdhardt turned and started towards the nearest set of stairs.

"To let a man get some sleep."

Erdhardt descended the stairs, nodding to the guards who stood at the gate in a variety of torn leathers, hastily-constructed gambesons, and old shirts. At least all four of them gripped solid steel-tipped spears in their fists now instead of pitchforks and scythes and clubs.

There wasn't much trade to be found, not with the Uraks roaming across the continent. Even ships were few and far between. But there was one trader who hailed from Skyfell in Valtara who had begun to frequent the sea route between the two cities. It was from him that fresh steel, iron, leather, and fruit had flowed into the city. Though Salme's coffers would soon be dry, and they would have little left to trade.

He passed through the gates and over the two planks laid across the first trench, which bowed precariously under his weight.

Erdhardt found Dahlen standing in the second moat, shirtless, blood trickling from near fifty tiny cuts across his body, some fresh, some broken scabs, and some which had clearly once been sutured. Sweat rolled down the man's shoulders and back, and he breathed as heavily as a panting dog. The dwarven captain, Nimara, stood by his side, as did some of the Belduarans and the young lad who had taken to following Dahlen around like a shadow – Conal.

"You need sleep." Erdhardt stood at the top of the trench, looking down at the young man.

Dahlen drove his shovel into the earth, then rolled his head around, his neck cracking. After a few moments, he looked back, raising his hand to shield his eyes from the sun. "You still alive, old man?"

"It's up for debate."

Dahlen gave a laugh, wiping the sweat from his brow. "All good?"

"A few new scars to call my own." Erdhardt pursed his lips and twisted his arm to show a long gash that ran from his elbow to his shoulder. He'd actually not thought about it until that moment, and that was when it began to sting. "Not as many as you though. You're getting slow."

Dahlen wiped his hand across his back, smearing blood with the sweat. "Fuck."

"I told you I could suture them." Nimara shrugged, sunlight glinting off the innumerable rings laced through her blonde hair. She looked as worse for wear as Dahlen, a piece of her left earlobe missing, a sloppily sewn chunk taken from her right shoulder. In fact, it was clear to see who among them had still not slept from the night before based on the amount of blood and dirt mashed into them.

"You use a needle like you use an axe."

"And you bleed like a little bitch."

Erdhardt let out a heavy sigh, pulled his hammer from his back, dropped it to the ground, and climbed into the trench.

"What are you doing?" Dahlen eyed him askance.

"Go and get those wounds taken care of. Anya is sleeping, but the man from Ölm should be in the bloodhouse. See him, then get some rest." Unlike his usual opinions on naming things, Erdhardt had quite liked the name given to the converted inn where the majority of the injured were treated. So much blood had dripped onto the floorboards it had begun to look like paint.

"I'm fine." Dahlen made to grab the shovel he'd lodged in the ground, but Erdhardt wrapped his fingers around the wooden shaft and ripped it from the earth.

"I didn't ask if you were fine." He thought back to a time when he had been an elder of the Glade, when he had spoken and others had listened – when he had been whole – and he brought that man forward. "In fact, I don't remember asking you anything. Go and get your wounds seen to, then rest. These people need a leader, not a martyr. You'll do nobody any good if those wounds get infected or if you're too exhausted to swing a sword."

"What about you? You've slept as little as I have, and those bones are a lot older."

"These bones have lived through more pain than you could understand. They can take a bit more." He rested a hand on Dahlen's shoulder and lowered his voice. "A shouldered burden breaks a lonely man. You might be willing to die for them, but that's not what they need. I'll take over from here. We're both off rotation tonight. Sleep. I'll do the same once more wake to take my place, and I'll see you for a drink in The Rusty Shell. Gods know we need one." Erdhardt raised his voice. "The same goes for all of you who fought last night. Get seen to, and get some rest."

"They don't need you to die for them either, Erdhardt."

Erdhardt patted Dahlen on the shoulder, then looked around him. "I already did. I'm just lingering a little longer."

CHAPTER THIRTY-SEVEN

FEAR THE NIGHT

14th Day of the Blood Moon

Port of Ankar, southeast of Achyron's Keep – Winter,
Year 3081 After Doom

Dayne stood atop the westernmost cliff that curled around Ankar's port, dense black clouds blotting out the moon, the wind battering at his cloak and roaring in his ears. Below, the bay that provided the port safety from the harsh waves that plagued the rest of the coastline was filled with at least fifty ships. When they'd heard Loren was gathering a fleet, they'd had no choice but to act. They could have mobilised their own fleet from Skyfell or Lostwren, but this was quicker and, if done right, would make the Lorians and the traitors fear every shadow that moved in Achyron's Keep.

"It's time." Alina approached from over Dayne's left shoulder, Mera walking at her side. Both Rynvar and Audin moved behind their riders, dark talons clicking against rock, blue and gold eyes seeming to glow in the moonlight. Dayne was still in awe of the creatures. He'd never expected to lay eyes on a wyvern again for as long as he lived.

Mera ran her hand along Dayne's right cheek, pulled her fingers into the back of his neck, and planted a kiss on his lips, then moved on to stand at the edge and look down at the ships below.

Dayne nodded to his sister – his queen – as she came to stand at his side.

Even as he looked at her then, the sunstone crown atop her head, her body covered in dark leather armour, the tattooed markings of a Wyndarii on her fingers and hands, Dayne couldn't help but see the little girl he'd left behind all those years ago.

He could hear her voice so clearly. *"That'll be me one day. I'll be a wyvern rider. Just like mother."*

"What are you thinking?" Alina asked, lifting her gaze from the water below.

"Just remembering." He allowed his thoughts to linger on that memory for a moment longer, savouring it. That time was long gone, and there was no getting it back, but it didn't mean he would ever let it go. "I know your answer already, but can I ask you one last time to reconsider? You're the queen now, Alina. This rebellion holds fast because you are at its head. If anything were to happen…"

To Dayne's surprise, Alina didn't snap back at him. She simply shook her head softly. "I've spent a lot of time thinking on what type of leader I want to be. And the answer I always come back to is that I want to be like our mother. I will never be the queen who sits on a throne while she sends others to die. Queen or no, I am the daughter of Ilya Ateres and I'm a Wyndarii. Fighting is in my blood." The smile that followed was soft, and she gave Dayne a nudge. "Besides, I will not have the bards say that Dayne Ateres haunted the Lorians' dreams while his sister sat back and reaped the rewards."

"We shall haunt them together then." Dayne allowed himself a half-smile. He wanted to tell her how proud he was, how she was already everything their mother had been: strong, fierce, loyal, compassionate. But words spoken too often meant little, and now was not the time. "Have either of you seen Belina? She should have been here by now."

"Perfect night for it."

Dayne gave a start, then let out a sigh at the sight of Belina standing by the cliff's edge a few feet away, her arms folded, bottom lip turned up. Over a decade together, and he still had absolutely no idea how the woman always managed to sneak up on him. "Were you waiting there for when I asked?"

She gave him a smile that said that had been precisely what she'd been doing and that she was delighted about it. She sauntered over to stand between him and Alina, tilting her head upwards and watching Rynvar with a cautious eye.

Rynvar's nostrils flared, and he lifted himself taller, winged forelimbs spreading around Alina protectively. In the dark, the creature's black and orange scales made him look almost unnatural, sections of his body blending with the night.

"He's a very big dog," Belina said as she handed Dayne a satchel that he slung over his shoulder. She looked down over the cliff once more. "You sure you still have it in you?"

"Try to keep up." Dayne looked to Mera and Alina. "Ready?"

Both nodded in response.

"Don't do anything stupid." Mera kissed him once more, then mounted Audin, clipping her straps into place on the saddle while the wyvern rolled his shoulders and let out a quiet, high-pitched, vibrating rumble.

Alina grasped his forearm. "By blade and by blood, brother. It means everything to have you by my side."

"By blade and by blood. Stay safe. Leave the mages to me."

"You two are adorable," Belina said. "But it's fucking freezing up here, and the wyverns are looking at me like I'm supper. I mean, who could blame them? Look at me."

A deep growl and a series of high-pitched pulses escaped Rynvar's throat as the wyvern stretched his neck forwards and curled his lips, the frills on his neck shaking.

"Good boy. Gooood boy." Belina lifted a hand. "I'm not as tasty as I look. Lini, a little help?"

Alina held up an open palm and Rynvar purred, brushing the scales of his jaw against her fingers.

"My queen." Belina gave a bow too deep to be believable and winked at Alina, who both glared and blushed at the same time.

Belina turned her bow in the wyvern's direction, seeming to enjoy the hiss Rynvar aimed at her before he continued to allow Alina to scratch his jaw.

"Belina." Dayne did little to hide the irritation in his voice. The woman was perhaps the only soul in the world with stones big enough to antagonise a wyvern.

"What? I'm just trying to be nice. What more do you want from me?"

"Silence would be appreciated every now and again."

"You don't mean that."

Dayne moved closer to Belina and grabbed both of her forearms. "Oh, but I do."

Belina's eyes widened when she realised what he was about to do. "No, please, not again. You didn't tell me that was how we were getting down. No," she repeated. "I'll climb. Just start without me, and I'll catch up."

Dayne's smile stretched from ear to ear. It wasn't often that he had Belina squirming instead of the other way around. It was a sweet thing.

"Give us some time to get to the ships. We'll move on your mark," he said to his sister before looking back to Belina. "Don't scream. The cliffs will carry the sound, and they'll hear us coming."

"I'm going to fucking bite you the whole way down. I'm going to fucking bite you, and I'm going to draw blood."

Dayne's smile didn't falter. "Deep breath."

With that, he wrapped his arms around Belina and hauled her off the edge of the cliff.

Alina shifted forwards and pressed herself close to the scales of Rynvar's neck, gripping the saddle's handles as tight as she could. The wyvern's body snaked, and he surged upwards, the buckles clinking as the thick leather straps that held Alina in place pulled taut. She loved the feeling when Rynvar climbed, the pressure of the world pulling at her shoulders, trying to rip her free and failing.

Once the wyvern levelled out, Alina signalled for the others to hold formation. Amari and Lukira flew at her left, their wyverns – Syndel and Urin – blending with the night. Mera sat astride Audin on Alina's right, ten other Wyndarii at her back.

They flew just below the black clouds that covered the sky, faint pink light piercing through. Below, the Lorian ships swayed in the dark water, the crashing of the waves echoing up the cliff. Dayne and Belina would be in position now, somewhere to the right of the fleet. The woman irritated her to no end. She had no sense of etiquette, and every thought that drifted into her snake pit of a brain seemed to flow between her lips. But Dayne cared for her in a way he cared for few. That was something Alina had seen from the first moment Belina had walked into the tent.

And what's more, she fought with a cold efficiency that Alina could only respect. Between her, Dayne, and the Andurii, countless Lorian and Koraklon caravans lay burning in the dirt and almost five hundred heads were mounted on spikes along the main road leading to Achyron's Keep.

It had been Belina and Dayne's idea to only attack at night, to rip apart any and all raiding parties without mercy, to destroy every caravan, every camp, and every outpost they could find. To use the Wyndarii to harass the supply lines from Varsund along the Hot Gates. They could not attack the Keep without the reinforcements Aeson had promised – not without risking a horrible defeat. But they could teach the Lorians and the traitors to fear the dark.

The plan had worked perfectly. The raids on Valtaran villages near the keep had slowed to almost nothing, and some of the villagers had taken to calling Dayne and the others the 'Demons of the Pass', referring to the section of Valtara that connected to Achyron's Keep.

The most irritating part about the woman though was that Amari was infatuated with her. But that was a problem for another day.

Alina took a deep breath, holding it as Rynvar dropped to catch a current of air that broke below them. Just a little longer, to ensure Dayne and Belina were in place. Savrin, Olivian, Glaukos, and some fifty of the Andurii would already be situated by the port's gates, ready to hunt down any stragglers, letting only a handful through. Scouts had reported that some fifteen hundred spears guarded the port, along with several Lorian Battlemages. Alina had insisted they attack with greater numbers, but Dayne had been adamant they keep the party small. She trusted him, just as she trusted his judgement on naming Savrin to her Queensguard.

A hand signal to Alina's right drew her attention: now. Attack. Question.

Mera wore a white glove on her left hand, as did Alina and the others, to make signals more visible at night.

Alina answered, then touched her spread palm to her chest: by blade and by blood.

Mera reciprocated the gesture, and Alina pressed a hand to Rynvar's neck and shouted over the wind. "Dive."

Dayne treaded water, keeping his head just above the surface, the spray of the waves lapping at his face. He wove thin threads of Water around the satchel that bobbed in front of him, preventing the contents from flooding. In his years with Belina, he'd found that most mages couldn't sense the use of the Spark if the threads were thin enough and the distance great enough. Few useful functions could be performed with threads that thin, but this was one of them.

"I've still not forgiven you." Belina floated in the water beside him, ceaselessly shaking her head.

"Shut up," he whispered, watching the sky, his shoulder stinging from where she'd bitten him.

"You know I hate jumping from cliffs like that. You remember Karvos? I thought I was dead. Not all of us can do your little la-dee-dah magic tricks. Besides, do you have any idea how long it takes my hair to dry? Hair doesn't look this fabulous on its own."

Dayne curled a thin thread of Water around himself and used it to splash Belina in the face.

"I know that was you."

"No idea what you're talking about," he said, purposefully not looking at her. The closest ship sat in the water no more than fifty feet away. A handful of Lorians occupied the deck, garbed in red and black leathers. They called to each other, their shouts echoing.

The port itself was a different story. Patrols of both Lorians and Valtaran traitors moved in groups of twenty across the dock, lanterns illuminating their path.

Mera's scouts had reported numbers of over a thousand in the garrison, set behind a freshly erected palisade wall and augmented with several Lorian mages. The Lorians should have sent more spears.

Something moved in the sky at the edges of Dayne's vision. A flash and then it was gone. A low whistling noise touched his ears, followed by a series of crashes and shouts as Alina and the Wyndarii swooped low and launched the Godfire down onto the decks.

The substance was a concoction used for naval warfare. Its makings were guarded ferociously by the Narvonan Pyroclast Guild, and the secret of its creation was one of few things all the kingdoms agreed on. But if a person had the right connections, it could be obtained in small quantities. Belina had first introduced him to it almost seven years ago during the burning of the fifth fleet in the Bay of Light. He had no idea what comprised it, but as soon as it was lit, the liquid burned with the ferocity of dragonfire. Even water couldn't quench its flames. And when launched in small clay vessels, there was nothing that could sink a ship faster. Thankfully, Belina knew more smugglers than a bird does trees.

"Time to move," Belina whispered, swimming towards the closest ship.

"What in the fuck was that?" a voice called out from the deck above.

"There's bits of it everywhere," another voice called back.

"Smells kind of nice," another answered.

Dayne pressed his finger to his lips, holding his position a few feet from the ship's hull, the waves lifting him up and down.

Belina mimicked his gesture, mocking him.

From the satchel that floated around his neck, he produced a tin with flint and quenched steel along with two clay jars plugged with waxed stoppers and handed them to her. Without a word, she twisted onto her back, stuck the tin between her teeth, held the jars above the water, and swam past the ship's bow.

More crashing sounds signalled the wyverns' second run, the vessels of Godfire smashing onto the decks of the ships.

Dayne moved himself to the bow. He could just about make out Belina fifty or so feet away, her dark hair bobbing in the water.

He removed the waxed stopper from the first jar, the horrid stench of the rags soaked in rendered fat wafting from within. One thin thread of Fire later and flames burst from the small jar. Dayne launched the jar up and over the ship's rail.

A heartbeat passed, followed by a smash, and then the ship's deck erupted with raging fire, the flames burning like a signal fire in the dark. Soldiers shouted and boots slapped on wood, and before long, the sails and rigging were ablaze as well.

A moment later, another ship erupted in flames as Belina did her part.

While the fires raged, Dayne swam to the next-closest ship and tossed his second jar. Smash. Flames.

Dayne ducked below the water and swam as hard as he could towards the eastern edge of the port, rising only for air. By the time he reached the docks, three more ships had caught fire, the wind fanning the flames. There truly was nothing like Godfire. All it took was the whisper of flames, an ember on the breeze, and another ship exploded in a blazing inferno. Before long, the entire fleet would be nothing but smoke and ash.

Bells rang out, men and women shouted, and feet pounded against wood as the entire port descended into pandemonium.

Dayne grabbed the dock and lifted himself from the water as the guards scrambled to kill the flames.

He drew his breaths in slow through his nose, settling himself, clenching his jaw tight so his teeth wouldn't chatter. The winter air was bitter and he was soaked to the bones, but he needed to move quickly. He crossed the wooden planks, dipping into the shadows between two buildings that overlooked the docks. Soldiers rushed past in the streets, carrying buckets, screaming and shouting.

"The flames won't die!" a voice called.

It didn't take long for Dayne to feel the tingle of the Spark running down his spine. He moved so he could get a clear look at the jetties to which the ships were moored. Six Lorian mages stood amidst the chaos, black cloaks draped over their shoulders, threads of Fire, Water, and Air weaving about them.

Just as planned.

A screech sounded overhead, echoed by another, and another, and then the wyverns swooped through the raging flames, the Wyndarii on their backs dropping the last of the Godfire over the docks after having drawn the mages in.

Dayne held his breath for half a second, watching as a piece of burning sail drifted downwards, slowly, twisting and turning. It landed, and the flames caught the Godfire and swept over the docks like a blazing wave. Men and women screamed as they jumped from the jetties, the shrieks growing louder when they rose from beneath the surface to find the water itself had caught fire.

The Battlemages had not been so easily swept aside. From where Dayne stood, he saw one lying in a burning heap, but the other five had shielded themselves with the Spark and shifted to face the attacking Wyndarii.

An arc of lightning streaked from a mage's palm and caught a wyvern in the side. The creature dropped without a scream or a howl, smoke billowing as it crashed into the port town.

Dayne drew a knife from his belt and charged from the side street, keeping his heart still. He'd told them not to fly low. The wyvern's scales had been dark blue. Not Audin or Rynvar.

As Dayne stepped from cover, a soldier shouted to his left and lunged, only to go limp mid-run and collapse into the dirt. Dayne threw a glance upwards and spotted Belina leaping from roof to roof, staying low, steel glinting in her hands.

Two more soldiers spotted him in the chaos. The first never got his sword from its scabbard. Dayne leapt towards him, flipped the knife in his right hand, then drove it down into the man's neck, blood gushing as he pulled it free.

The second soldier thrust a spear at Dayne's head as his companion fell. Dayne twisted, grabbed the shaft, and yanked the soldier in close. The man stumbled off balance, and Dayne leaned in, ramming the knife through his right eye, the hilt clicking against bone. Abandoning the knife lodged in the man's socket, he tossed the spear into his right hand and launched it.

Before the spear connected with its target, Dayne was running, slipping a new knife from his belt. The spear punched into the back of the closest Battlemage's head, bursting out through his face in a cloud of shattered bone, blood, and brain, the force dropping the body forward.

For all a Battlemage's strength and power, their greatest weakness was their unbridled arrogance. They believed nothing could stand in their way, that the Spark was theirs to command and theirs alone. Centuries of little opposition emboldened this belief. They never expected to be hunted, never for a second imagined there might be bigger predators in the world. And that made them easy prey.

Four left.

A woman bearing the yellow skirts of House Thebal, a bucket in one hand, spotted him out of the corner of her eye and lunged. She threw the bucket and drew her sword.

Dayne planted his front foot, stopping dead, the bucket soaring past him. He twisted at the waist and closed the distance between himself and the Thebalan in a heartbeat.

He grabbed the wrist of her sword hand mid-swing, then drove his knife into her belly. One, two, three times, then once into her throat. Blood flowed free as she slumped to the wood.

Dayne kept moving, leaping over a still-burning corpse. The remaining mages hadn't spotted him yet. They continued to weave threads of Fire, Air, and Spirit about themselves, looking towards the sky for wyverns. One had even resumed attempting to quench the fires blazing on the ships. They were lions believing they stalked deer, stumbling their way into a wyvern's Rest.

Dayne slipped past a group of soldiers dragging their companions from the flames, the Godfire clinging to everything it touched.

He stepped up behind the first of the remaining four mages, wrapped his hand around her mouth, and slit her throat. The mage to his right twisted, calling to his companion, eyes widening as he saw Dayne striding through the flames while she choked on her own blood.

The mage pulled on threads of Fire and Spirit, whirling them around himself and funnelling them into his right hand, a red glow emanating from the pendant that hung from his neck.

Dayne opened himself to the Spark and drove a whip of Air into the side of the man's knee, bones snapping. The mage screamed, his eyes wide with shock. Those eyes were still wide when Dayne reached down his throat with that same thread and pulled the air from his lungs. That was always the same with the Battlemages. So sure in their own power they rarely ever thought to defend themselves.

Dayne walked through the flames, his attention fixed on the two surviving Battlemages – one launching arcs of lightning into the sky, the other pulling the air from around the ship fires.

As he moved, he pulled on threads of each element, weaving them through his hand, the power of the Spark burning in his veins. Light streaked from his hand, his níthral taking the shape of a gleaming white spear that trailed along the wooden dock.

The first mage noticed him in her periphery and stared in disbelief as she fumbled to free her sword from its scabbard while unleashing a column of black fire from her hand, drawing on the power of the Blood Moon. Dayne split the flames with threads of Air and Spirit, stepping through and driving his níthral into her chest. She twitched for a moment, her gaze meeting his, then fell back and off the edge of the dock, the water taking her.

When the last mage finally realised that all her companions were dead, she looked at Dayne, mouth agape. "Who… what are you?"

Dayne wove threads of Spirit around the woman in a latticed web, encasing her, feeling a thrum when the final thread clicked into place, cutting her off from the Spark.

She let out a gasp but immediately reached for something beneath her breastplate. The red gemstone she produced had already begun to glow when Dayne snatched it from her grasp with a thread of Air and pulled it into his hand.

He didn't even have to hold the mage in place with the Spark. She simply stood there like a stunned deer, unmoving while Dayne looked down at the glowing red gemstone in his hand, his níthral casting a white light across the dock.

Lorian soldiers and Valtarans in the colours of Koraklon and Thebal circled around him but dared not come closer. They'd seen what he had done to the mages – what he was currently doing.

One man dared take a step forward, only to drop like a sack of stones when Belina put a knife in the back of his head from atop a nearby roof, vanishing again before the others could spot her.

Dayne looked down at the glowing gemstone. He'd held one before but had never allowed himself to draw from its strength. But something about it felt different that night beneath the Blood Moon. It called to him, whispered in his ear, yearning for him to tap into the strength it offered. And for a brief moment, Dayne considered it. He'd seen what the Lorian mages could do with the power their Essence offered. And in his hands, in the hands of someone who understood death, it could be used to free Valtara.

But he had also seen what Blood Magic did to the mind over time. He had sent enough warped mages into Heraya's embrace. And so Dayne lifted his gaze to meet that of the last surviving Battlemage, pushed threads of Earth and Spirit into his hand, and crushed the gemstone to dust. Crimson light sprayed through his fingers, bright as a star, then died in a wisp of red mist.

"Do you have any last words, mage?" Dayne asked as he tilted his hand and let the dust fall onto the docks. He could feel the woman probing at the ward in which she was encased, desperately trying to break through.

"You don't have to do this," she called back. Dayne could hear the fear in her voice. He knew it well. When a person lived with the Spark at their fingertips, it became engrained in everything they did. And when it was taken away, they were helpless as a newborn babe suckling at their mother's tit. "You don't," she repeated. "We will surrender the port without further bloodshed. I promise it."

Dayne believed her. "Unfortunately, it's your blood I need. Not your surrender. I truly wish that were not the case. But it is. May Heraya embrace you."

Dayne released his níthral and at the same time wrapped a thread of Air about the mage's waist and another around a sword on the dock behind him.

He pulled.

The woman careened through the air, screaming. He grabbed her by the throat just as his fingers wrapped around the hilt of the dropped sword, then drove the steel through her gut.

"In another life," he whispered as the light went out in the mage's eyes.

He could have dealt with them all quickly, but that night wasn't about efficiency, or haste, or even death. It was about terror. It was about the traitors and the Lorian soldiers watching their mages be ripped apart one by one. Watching the shadows hunt them. It was about making them fear the dark.

Dayne released the woman's throat and let her body drop. He wove threads of Spirit and Air into his voice, looking about at the soldiers around him, the light of the burning ships drawing shadows across the docks.

"I am Dayne Ateres. This is my home, and you are no longer welcome." He cast his gaze over the Lorians and Valtarans who stood about him, their weapons drawn. "Those of you who survive tonight, tell them what happened here. Tell them that the wyvern of House Ateres flies again and that it yearns for blood. Leave Valtara and never come back. If you do this, you may yet live to grow old and grey."

Dayne opened himself fully to the Spark, feeling it pull at him, feeling it burn in his veins and crackle over his skin. He found the elemental strand of Air in his mind and plucked, its smooth, cool touch rolling over his skin.

"Now, I say to you but one last thing – run."

He drew a deep breath, then cast threads throughout the port town, spreading them over the burning ships and every lick of flame he could find: the candles, the lanterns, the firepits.

In a single breath, he quenched them all, and with the black clouds above blocking the moon's light, Ankar descended into darkness.

⁂

Petrick Leoth ran with such haste he could hear nothing but the sound of his own heart and the scrambling of feet and shouts around him.

He'd never seen a night so dark. He could barely make out the ground before him.

A sudden burst of white light illuminated the street, revealing the mass of men and women around him, Lorian and Valtaran both. That shimmer of white gifted him a momentary sense of relief, only for his eyes to fall on the dark silhouette of the man who had called himself Dayne Ateres, a coruscating spear in his grip. He swung the weapon in a wide arc, ripping through three soldiers. And then the spear was gone and, with it, the light.

"What the fuck is he?" someone shouted to his left. "He's like some kind of—"

Whoever had been speaking never finished the sentence. A sharp *thunk* was followed by the sound of a body hitting the ground.

That was when wingbeats thrummed above, accompanied by those sharp, pulsing screeches.

"Petrick!" A hand grabbed Petrick's shoulder. The voice belonged to Mikhail. "This way!"

Petrick hesitated. The gates were forward. The voice was not.

The white light burst into life once more, and Petrick watched Dayne Ateres drive his white spear through a man's chest, arcs of lightning streaking from his palm and tearing a group of Thebalan loyalists to pieces.

A second hand pulled him in the opposite direction – Gwinton Jon. Sweat-streaked ash covered Gwinton's face, his eyes wide, veins in his neck bulging. "What are you doing? Move, move!"

Petrick made to answer, but then something crashed into Gwinton from above, slamming him to the ground. Deep red scales and savage horns. The wyvern opened its jaws and ripped chunks of flesh from Gwinton's shoulder and neck, its rider sitting calmly on its back. The creature lifted its head, and bright golden eyes looked into Petrick's.

The wyvern tilted its head to the right, strips of flesh dangling from its teeth, blood dripping. A moment of calm passed as he stared into the creature's eyes, and then the wyvern opened its jaws and shrieked, the frills on its neck and back shaking. The light vanished once more, leaving Petrick's pulse scrambling.

Mikhail grabbed him and yanked him backwards into what must have been an alley.

He dropped to the ground, panting like an exhausted dog, his back pressed against the wooden wall, his hands clasped behind his head. "What is happening? What is happening? What is happening?"

"Petrick." Mikhail grabbed him and shook him. "Petrick, shut the fuck up."

Bloodchilling screams and howls filled the air, wingbeats and wyvern screeches answering.

"We're dead." His hands trembled furiously as he pulled them away from his head. He tried to stop them shaking, but he had no control.

"No, we're not. We're going to make it out of here. I just need you to stay quiet and stand up."

"No," a third voice said, a touch of sadness to it. "Your friend's right. You're going to die here."

Mikhail jumped backwards, and Petrick jerked away from the voice, fingers digging in the dirt, feet pushing.

A woman stepped from the dark, close enough for Petrick to make out her face. He saw dark skin and long, braided hair. Narvonan. She moved like a lion stalking its prey.

Mikhail took a step towards her. "Who… who are you?"

Her lips curled into a sad smile. "On any given day? A woman trying to finally do something worthwhile. But tonight? Tonight, I am death. So very sorry to meet you."

Petrick didn't see what happened next. There was a flash of movement, and then Mikhail was holding his neck. His friend looked back at him, a vacant expression on his face, and when he pulled his hand away, blood spurted.

Petrick pushed himself back in the dirt as Mikhail reached for him, stumbling, blood spurting from the wound in his neck.

Mikhail crashed to his knees, and the woman stepped over his body. She eyed Petrick, a soft sigh escaping her. "Wrong place, wrong time."

Petrick scrambled backwards and hauled himself to his feet, springing from the alley and back into Ankar's main thoroughfare.

He crashed into someone, scrambling to stay on his feet. Wingbeats sounded, a screech, then a gust of wind swept across his face and the person he had bumped into was gone.

The sky was a bit brighter now, his eyes adjusting to the dark. Those scaled beasts soared over the town, swooping only to tear people apart.

The gates weren't far. He could make it.

He pulled his gaze from the sky and made to run, footsteps sounding all around him.

That same white light burst into life once more, and there stood Dayne Ateres in the street before him, looking like a demon that had crawled from the void itself. The man – if that's what he truly was – swung his spear of light and smashed it into a fleeing soldier's head. Petrick assumed the pieces that exploded outwards were bone and brain.

As the man walked towards him, Petrick tripped over a body, feeling a *crack* as his elbow slammed hard into stone. He tried to haul himself to his feet, but something held him down. Something he couldn't see or touch. He'd been around mages long enough to know it was the Spark, to know there was nothing he could do.

This was where he would die. Thousands of miles from home, in a place for which he cared little, surrounded by the dead bodies of men and women he had once called friends. Worse, even as Dayne Ateres stood over him, that white spear pulsing light, Petrick still wasn't quite sure what he was meant to be fighting for.

If he'd been the given choice, he would have died fat and drunk in the arms of a woman who loved him. And a dog, he would have loved to have a dog.

Petrick squinted at the bright light of the white spear.

"I take no pleasure in this," Dayne Ateres said, standing over him, shadows welling in the hollows of his face. "But nor will I shy away from it. Heraya embrace you."

He raised the spear and then thrust it down into Petrick's heart. The pain lasted for but half a second. Then the world went cold and black, and a strange sense of panic and unease consumed him. He screamed, but no sound came.

CHAPTER THIRTY-EIGHT

NEITHER BENT NOR BROKEN

14ᵗʰ Day of the Blood Moon

Lodhar Mountains – Winter, Year 3081 After Doom

Kira grunted, pain shooting up her legs and through her lower back with every step she forced herself to take, moving towards the end of the short corridor. The healer had urged her to stay in bed, but Kira had already spent too long doing nothing. It had been days since Erani and the others had broken her free, and she'd slept far more of that time than she'd been awake. And even then, her memory was thick and opaque. She remembered eating, devouring anything that was handed to her, savage and insatiable. She also remembered Erani's face, her sister's calm voice.

No. She could rest when she was dead. The world was shifting beneath her, and she knew if she lay down too long, she would arise to find it unrecognisable.

She hobbled towards the door and pushed through. A deep yellow-gold light filled her eyes where she had expected the blue-green of Heraya's Ward. The lanterns beside her bed had been the Ward she knew. She'd only heard of Ward this colour in the stories her mother used to tell her, of Vindakur and the Portal Hearts. Surely that's not where she stood now, in the lost city?

One look around as her eyes adjusted to the light told her no, she most definitely was not in the lost city of Vindakur.

The buildings around her were all smooth stone and little else, old and battered from centuries of use and abuse. A tall cavern stood about them, small patches of the golden Heraya's Ward sprouting from cracks in the rock. She remembered now Erani had said they were taking her to an abandoned mining outpost in the far north. Many of those outposts had been abandoned even before Vindakur was lost, stripped of all valuable minerals and ores.

Her mind still slow and foggy, Kira turned her attention to the movement around her, dwarves and humans carrying crates of grain and root, virtuk wagons hauling thick lengths of wood and strips of iron and steel.

"My queen."

It was only then Kira realised that two dwarves in the crimson cloaks of Durakdur knelt on either side of the door from which she had just emerged. She recognised them both: Ahktar and Kalik. They had been by her side since her ascension to the throne.

"May your fires never be extinguished and your blades never dull." She bowed her head to them both, clenching her jaw in pain as she did. "I cannot explain how much happiness it gives me to see your faces."

Ahktar rose first. "We did everything we could, my queen. I swear it by Hafaesir's hammer, I swear it by my place in the rock. I will die before I let them lay a finger on you again."

Kalik opened his mouth to add to Kalik's words but said nothing at the sight of Kira raising her hand.

"Swear to me only one thing." Kira stumbled, and Ahktar lowered his shoulder so she could steady herself.

"Name it, my queen." Ahktar pressed a hand to his breastplate.

"Swear that you will stand by my side when I take Hoffnar's head from his shoulders."

"I will stand at your side until Heraya takes me, and when she does, my axe will be wet with the traitor's blood."

"As will mine," Kalik added.

Even in her state, Kira could tell the two dwarves did not speak from hurt pride alone. Erani and Lumeera had said her Queensguard had stormed the Heart to protect her. She did not know what number had survived, but judging by the wrath in Kalik and Ahktar's eyes, the price had been high. "Please, take me to my sister."

Kira clenched her jaw and forced herself not to wince with every step as the two Queensguard led her through the outpost. Both Kalik and Ahktar offered her their shoulders to lean on, but she refused them. Not because she was too proud to take their help, but because she wanted the other dwarves and humans to see that she still walked with her head high. That she was neither bent nor broken, but defiant and hungry.

And with each hobbled step she took, more dwarves stopped in the streets of the outpost and emerged from within the old buildings to stare at her.

Were it not for the two Queensguard in crimson cloaks flanking her, she didn't think any of them would have recognised who she was. But they did.

Whispers of 'my queen' and 'by Hafaesir's grace' sounded all about her, and one by one, dwarves either bowed deeply or dropped to one knee. More than a few wide eyes couldn't look away from her shaved head, she had no doubt.

Many of the Belduarans stopped to see what the fuss was but only watched with curiosity as she passed. Every few feet, a warrior stepped from the gathering crowd with a crimson cloak knotted at their shoulders, knelt before her, then moved to stand at her side. She recognised every face, and each one warmed her heart.

There were more survivors than she'd dared hope. By the time Ahktar and Kalik stopped before the doors of a squat stone structure, forty-eight Queensguard marched slowly in formation around her, keeping her pace, and a crowd of dwarves and humans both had gathered around them.

The bulk of the Queensguard remained at the entrance while Kalik and Ahktar escorted her inside.

Kira found her sister in a large rectangular room, leaning over a stone table covered in maps and letters, with several familiar faces gathered around her.

Erani looked up from the table and frowned, the rings in her dark hair catching in the golden flower light that shone through the window behind her. "You should not be out of bed."

"I should be dead." Kira grunted as she hobbled towards the table.

She nodded to Lumeera Arian, who stood at Erani's side. The Belduaran captain returned the gesture, raising an eyebrow as a figure beside her shuffled out of place and around the table.

Oleg Marylin wiped sweat from his brow with his hand, placed that same hand over his heart, and bowed. "Your Majesty, may your fire never be extinguished and your blade never dull. I cannot express my happiness to see you up and about."

Oleg's shirt was torn and filthy, his dark trousers much the same. His bald head was coated with dust from the mine, and the tip of his right ear was missing, a roaring red scab in its place. All in all, the man looked like he'd been through the void and back. Though Kira hadn't seen herself in a mirror, she'd no doubt she looked much worse.

She limped towards Oleg, gratefully taking the shoulder that Ahktar offered. A strong front was not needed for those in this room. "Oleg Marylin, Keeper of the Mountain. May your fire never be extinguished and your blade never dull. You have my thanks. I don't remember much from my time in the bed, but I do remember my sister telling me that I wouldn't be standing here were it not for you and the warriors of Belduar."

"And I wouldn't be standing here if not for you, Your Majesty. It seems we owe a debt to each other."

Kira smiled at that and gave the man a soft nod before looking about at the other faces who crowded the table.

Six Belduarans stood near Lumeera. All of them looked hard as iron; former Kingsguard no doubt. Kira could learn their names later.

The only other human in the room was Turim Arlan, Guildmaster of the Wind Runners. Tall, lean, and chisel-jawed, with stone-grey hair. Even then, standing about a makeshift war table, he still wore his padded navigator glasses with their thick black lenses and copper blinders. She'd known the man since she'd been a child, long before she'd had any notions of becoming a queen. Two navigators framed him on either side, both elves.

He lifted a hand as though grasping the brim of a hat that didn't exist, then inclined his head, a warm smile on his lips. "Good to see you breathing, young one."

"And you." There was more in the smile she gave him than simple happiness. There was thanks, respect, and deep pride. There would be a time to express that with words, but he knew her well enough to understand the gesture.

A number of dwarves bearing sigils of Azmar, Ozryn, and Volkur crowded about the table. She greeted them much the same. If they were there, they had stood by her in her darkest hours and they had seen through Hoffnar's deceptions. They would be forever welcome around her table.

Several of her own Queensguard and warriors of Durakdur made up the last of the count, including Vikmar, who had been Mirlak's second. His was a face she was glad to see. She would call them all to council later. They deserved her time.

Once they were all settled, Kira leaned against the table, using it as leverage to keep herself upright. By all accounts she had not been in the cell more than two weeks, and yet her strength had withered like a dying flower, her stomach still twisting in pain, her broken ribs and fingers constantly throbbing. "Don't stop on my account," she said, holding back a grunt. "What are we looking at?"

"A lot has happened while you were resting," Erani said. Kira bristled at the word 'resting', as though she was relaxing while the others fought. Erani pulled over a map etched in charcoal depicting what looked to be an intricate system of tunnels. "Hoffnar is building new tunnels branching off from Volkur." She traced her finger from a large node of charcoal along a series of black lines that stretched to the edge of the page. "We're not sure where they lead just yet, but we have some ideas."

Kira gestured for her sister to continue, which earned her a glare. Erani had never been good at taking orders. She was the eldest. It had been Erani their mother had groomed for leadership, but she had shunned it at every turn. She didn't want to be a leader but despised being led.

"Hoffnar has not been shy since butchering Queen Elenya and King Lakar and throwing you in that cell. He has given many public addresses and sent emissaries the length and breadth of the Freehold. He is proclaiming a new dawn for the dwarven people. He is offering them the sun, promising to lead them from the mountain, and announcing the time is now and may never come again, that the Lorian Empire is weak and ripe to reap what they have sown. It does not take much to connect his rhetoric to an attack on the Lorians, though we can't be sure of his target. That information is being kept tight. And Hoffnar's own personal guard, along with a small contingent of three mages he appears to have brought into his service, are hunting down any and all who hold loyalty to you – and they're not being quiet about it. There are many who rally behind him, many who share in the dream he is promising."

Kira nodded slowly, trying to absorb what she had just been told. Everything she had ever known was being dismantled piece by piece. Her head pounded like a forge hammer, and her stomach felt as though it would soon eat her liver for want of food.

The sound of a door slamming against a wall thumped through the corridor outside the chamber, followed by footfalls.

Four dwarves in sharp, thick plate marched into the chamber, the hammer of Durakdur worked into their breastplates, axes mounted on their backs.

"Blessed be the mountain and the fires within. Kira." The lead dwarf removed his helmet to reveal a line-marked face half-covered by a thick blond beard so laden with rings of silver and gold it looked wrought from metal. The dwarf's blue eyes were soft, lines creasing at the sides from smiling.

He strode forwards and pulled Kira into a tight embrace, causing pain to flare through her ribs.

"Uncle." Kira squeezed Alrick with all the strength her body could muster. "I had hoped, but I didn't know if… Erani didn't tell me you survived."

Alrick pulled away and stared into Kira's eyes as though he hadn't seen her in a hundred years. "You look like shit, little one."

"And you look worse."

"Pity they didn't cut out that tongue. Would have been an improvement."

Kira yanked her uncle back in close, squeezing him once more before letting him go and greeting the other three dwarves who marched with him. Lomak, Kandzal, and Okra. Alrick's two sons and his daughter. Her cousins.

"I thought it best to wait until their return before promising you their lives." Erani gave Kira a sympathetic smile.

Alrick approached the stone table, then swung a satchel from his shoulder and produced a severed head from within. He let it drop with a thump.

"Gods," Oleg chirped, his eyes widening.

"Yarzik Olnak. High Captain of King Hoffnar's Kingsguard." Alrick twisted his fingers in the head's bloody, ring-laden hair, pulling so he could stare into its eyes. "Put up a good fight. Died screaming, though." He spat onto the dead dwarf's face. "May he burn in the fires of the void. We've secured the harvest from Ozryn's northwest tuber fields. Enough to see us through for a while."

"Uncle." Erani frowned. "As pleased as I am to hear that, would you mind removing the severed head from the table? It's dripping onto the maps."

Alrick lifted the head by the hair and brushed two tunnel maps out of the way before repositioning it.

"I didn't mean…" Erani trailed off as Alrick turned and pulled a second head from a satchel around his daughter's waist, dropping it beside the first.

The face was sleeker and smoother, clean shaven with long, dark hair; faded eyes; and ears that tapered to a point.

"An elf?"

Turim Arlan's two navigators whispered something in the Old Tongue, their faces sombre.

"More than just an elf." Alrick gestured to his son, who handed him what looked to be a crimson rag. He smoothed the fabric on the table. "An elf bearing the sigil of the golden stag."

"Lunithír…"

Alrick nodded.

The Kingdom of Lunithír had long been dead, but the Freehold had caught word of the elven attacks on the Lorian coast.

"Yarzik wasn't protecting a tuber field. We came across him on the return journey, meeting with this pretty little bastard."

"The enemy of my enemy is my friend," Oleg Marylin whispered, folding his arms and scratching at his chin. "Until our enemy is dead and we argue over the corpse."

"What did Yarzik say? What were they planning?" Kira had known Yarzik for over two decades. She'd drunk with him, sparred with him, played dice till her eyelids folded. She hated this. She hated all of this. Dwarves should not be killing dwarves.

"We didn't do a lot of talking," Alrick said with a shrug. "Tried to take him alive, but he lost his head."

Kira gave her uncle an unamused stare.

"They left your tongue intact and took your sense of humour instead then?"

"Uncle." Erani's tone was firm.

"Hmm. No, we didn't glean anything from them. But I don't think it takes a mage to know Hoffnar is working with the elves of Lynalion. I'd bet the stones between my legs their end goal is to catch the Lorians in a pincer. Crush them from both sides while their lines are thinned. I can't say I'm not happy about it. With any luck we'll crush two roaches with one stone and they'll all butcher each other."

Kira nodded sombrely. Her uncle was a clever man and a ruthless warrior, but he had a tendency of seeing things plainly. If only the world were as simple as he saw it.

She lifted her hands and pressed her fingers into the creases of her eyes, exhaustion kicking at her, thoughts swirling. As much as she was loath to admit it, she would need sleep again shortly. She looked to Erani. "What about communication? Can we get word out? Aeson Virandr? The Draleid? Nimara and those sent with Dahlen Virandr? The Rolling Mountains? The Marin Mountains?"

One of the dwarves with the sigil of Volkur marked into his pauldron shook his head, gesturing at the map. "Hoffnar has locked down all of Lodhar. We've tried for the Southern Fold Gate and every pass we know of, even the ventilation shafts. Every attempt has ended in bloodshed. Any Wind Tunnel that comes anywhere close to the surface is guarded, the Wind Runners stationed there dismantled."

"We've lost six navigators trying to send out messages." Turim Arlan pressed his fingers into his cheeks, his green eyes meeting Kira's gaze for only a fleeting moment. The man had always seen his navigators like his children, always taken such pride in each and every one of them. Kira could hear the loss in his voice.

"What about you, Erani?"

"What about me?"

"You entered the Freehold from the Rolling Mountains. Can we not send word out the same way you came in?"

Erani shook her head. The entire conversation seemed to be Erani shaking her head. "The guard was tripled after I slipped through, and with your escape that has since been doubled. Nothing leaves or enters this mountain without Hoffnar's say."

Kira closed her eyes for a moment, not bothering to guard the long sigh that left her throat. "Is there any good news? Anything at all?"

"We found Vindakur."

"You what?"

"Would you like me to repeat myself, sister?"

Erani smiled at Kira's scowl.

"Our scouts found an entrance two days ago just east of this outpost." She gestured out the window to the flowers that jutted from cracks in the rock, emitting that yellow-gold light. "The Heraya's Ward seems to shift colour in proximity to the city. "We're currently working to unearth what appears to be a Portal Heart buried beneath the rubble. It's delicate work. We have to be careful not to damage anything, but so far, we've exhumed two rings, one intact, one broken beyond repair."

"Why didn't you lead with this? If it truly is a Portal Heart, we may have found our access to the world outside."

"Because it's not that simple, dear sister. Hoffnar's patrols are spreading wider since we broke you free. We must take every precaution not to lead them to the city. Besides, we still don't know if the Portal Heart is operational. The chamber had collapsed in on itself. We found bodies amongst the rubble. Both dwarves and humans bearing the colours of Belduar, along with hundreds of kerathlin. By the looks of it, the city had become a nest. At least we now know what happened."

Kira drew a long breath. She had seen dwarves torn to pieces by kerathlin in her earlier years, heard that *click-clack* reverberating through the tunnels, watched those black claws tear through flesh. It was a horrible way to die. "What of the nest now? Surely, you're not recovering the Portal Heart with a swarm of kerathlin around you?"

"We're not sure why, but every one of those horrid little bastards is gone. It's almost as though something scared them away."

"Or called them," one of the Ozryn dwarves added. "There's been rumblings of strange kerathlin movements throughout the Freehold. Outposts overrun, Wind Tunnels swarmed. It's Hoffnar. The forge fires in Volkur are running day and night, and it's not weapons or armour they're producing. It's giant bells – of a sort – built onto movable platforms."

"Bells?" Kira did all she could to keep the scepticism from her voice, but it was a difficult thing to mask. "May I ask your name?"

"Drekker, Your Majesty. And I understand what it sounds like. But the kerathlin, as you know, are sensitive to sound. It's how they move in the dark. It can't be a coincidence. Hoffnar is scheming. And we would do well to know his plans."

"On that we most certainly agree, Drekker. If he is breathing, he is scheming. Erani?"

Kira's sister nodded in agreement. "I can send word to our eyes and ears. But there is another thing that requires our attention also."

Kira raised a curious eyebrow.

"It's been centuries since any dwarf alive has laid eyes on Vindakur – or on a Portal Heart, for that matter. Even if we can unearth the remainder of the rings, we need someone who understands it. There is an old engineer we've tracked down. A scholar of Hafaesir. Without him we may never get the portals operational, or we may walk through them blindly without any understanding of what we are facing."

"Then bring him here."

"Wonderful idea, sister. Truly. I understand why you wear the crown... Actually, we're going to have to get you a new crown – a task for another day. Unfortunately, as nothing in this life is ever simple or straightforward, the scholar in question – Rikber Lars – is Volkuran and resides deep within the city. I am already arranging his extraction, but much like that of the Portal Heart, it is a delicate matter. With any luck, once we place him in front of a genuine Portal Heart, his love for his scholarly endeavours will outweigh his allegiance to Hoffnar."

"Hafaesir willing," Kira replied.

After that, Erani and the others continued marking the maps, counting losses, and plotting raids. Kira stayed as long as her body would allow, but eventually sleep called to her.

When she finally awoke, she did so to find Oleg Marylin waiting outside her door.

The man sat atop a foldable chair with a journal in his hand, deep in thought, muttering to himself as his pen flitted across the paper. Two guards stood behind him, the purple cloaks of Belduar knotted at their shoulders.

Oleg almost leapt from his skin as Kira cleared her throat, pulling her deep crimson cloak tight around her shoulders. The man started, knocking his inkwell from the armrest and onto the ground, ink spilling across the stone.

"Gods." He patted something invisible from his stained shirt, rising from the chair in a fluster. "I, ehm... I'll have that cleaned. Ink comes out of stone, doesn't it? I'm sure it does. It has to."

The man was completely lost in his thoughts when Kira waved a hand. "There are slightly more pressing matters, Keeper Marylin."

Oleg straightened himself at that, pulling his shoulders back, a flash of pride in the smile that touched his lips. "Quite right, Your Majesty. Quite right."

The man had a way about him, a warmth. His smiles were always genuine. That was partly why he had been the perfect candidate to lead Belduar. He had something that Daymon had lacked: compassion over self-interest. Specifically, compassion for those he served.

Kira's mother had been a harsh teacher, but she had always said a ruler needed three things: compassion, strength, and wisdom. Everything else could be gathered. But without compassion, a ruler was nothing more than a tyrant. Without strength, a head would soon become unacquainted with the neck. And without wisdom, strength and compassion were wasted.

By Kira's measure, Oleg possessed all three, though he played a good part in hiding it, further showing his wisdom. "Kalik tells me you've been sitting out here for the better part of three hours."

Oleg raised his eyebrows, then pulled a small timekeeper from beneath his shirt, brass chain jingling. He clicked open the face guard. "By Elyara, I suppose I have. None the matter, I've had much to do. No time wasted."

"What was it you wanted to talk about?"

"Well…" Oleg held up a finger, then looked back at his guard and nodded towards the chair and spilt ink. "Please, Captain Harnett, I'd be much obliged." As the captain set about folding the chair, Oleg gestured towards the building given over to Kira's use. "We can sit and talk, if it please. I'm sure your body is still recovering."

"On the contrary, I've spent far too much time sitting within four walls. Walk with me. A little pain lets me know I'm alive."

They walked in silence for a while around the outpost, both dismissing their guards.

"The journal," Kira asked, inclining her head towards the black leather journal Oleg still clutched in his right hand.

"A record of those of us who are left…" He looked down at the journal, his expression growing sombre. "Nine thousand three hundred and forty-six in full health – mostly. Two thousand one hundred and eleven children in that number. Another three thousand two hundred and seventy-one injured, maimed, or ill. There are more alive, I'm sure, somewhere within the mountain. Some spies have given word that Hoffnar has prisoners, but the majority were executed. The early warning saved many of us… but far from all."

"Oleg…" Kira didn't have words. Before the Lorians had attacked Belduar, the city had been home to over two hundred thousand souls. Almost three quarters of that number had been evacuated to the Freehold. Near enough a hundred and twenty thousand. Hoffnar wasn't fighting a war, he was committing genocide. Kira couldn't help but think if she had done things differently, perhaps all of this could have been avoided. If she'd agreed to help retake Belduar… perhaps all those lives would not have been lost for nothing. Perhaps Elenya would still draw breath.

A sad smile that seemed more habit than anything else settled onto Oleg's features. He shook his head. "I know what you're thinking. Don't. We've all made the mess that we're floundering in. But what's done is done, and we can only look forward as we flounder together." Oleg tapped his thumb off the black leather. "You've always been clear and honest with me, my queen, and so I will be the same. Your sister has told me what the Portal Hearts can do. When we repair it – if we *can* repair it – I wish to send my people through. They've had enough hardship. Lost their homes, their loved ones… everything. I do not wish this mountain to become their tomb. Before you say anything, I will remain behind with Lumeera and half our fighting number. Near enough three thousand. Four hundred former Kingsguard. When Pulroan had us by the throat, you came. I would not have it said that we didn't do the same. But I need to send the others through with the children, elderly, and infirm. They won't survive otherwise. I'll send them to Salme to rejoin with Dahlen and the others. I know it's not what you would want, and by rights as your vassal, I should be asking rather than telling, but…"

"You're doing what a strong leader should do. You're looking after your people." Kira stopped. Her legs begged for rest, but that was not why she stopped.

"Oleg, there is no peace in what happens next. This mountain will run red. I cannot simply walk away after what has happened. I just can't." She licked her bottom lip, trying to decide how honest she wanted to be. "I don't know if we can win... If you take every Belduaran through that Portal, I will hold no ill will. This mountain is my home. It's all I know. If I die here, I die in the arms of my ancestors. If you die here, you're just another corpse."

Oleg had been the Belduaran emissary to the Freehold for almost twenty years. In that time, he'd always been polite, accommodating, and what her mother had described as 'a little goofy'. Ankora had always had a soft spot for Oleg. And she didn't have many soft spots. But the word 'goofy' had never seemed further from apt than that moment right then. The look in Oleg's eyes was steel.

"Durakdur and Belduar have been allies since before my father's time," Oleg said, "and his before him, and so on, and so on. I will not be the one to break that bond. I've spoken to Lumeera, and she has spoken to the guard. Many of them have no family left. Mothers, fathers, brothers, sisters, sons, daughters – all dead. Their closest friends – those not already dead – are the men and women at their sides. And all of them, every single one, lay the blame at Hoffnar's feet. They want blood. They want vengeance. It's all they have left." Oleg twisted his mouth and for a second, Kira thought the man's eyes would water. "I never married – as you and everyone else well knows. Not many women's ideal man is one with a bald head, a patchy beard, too much bread around the waist, an attention span as fleeting as good luck, and a fixation on dwarves and everything dwarven. But when my brother's heart gave out five years ago and his wife was taken by Heraya in the last famine, I took in my two nephews. Fourteen days ago, they were decapitated in Durakdur's central plaza, taken prisoner while they played with my friend's daughter. She wasn't spared either, neither was her father. A hundred thousand Belduaran bones rest beneath this mountain. If I die here, I will die in the arms of my ancestors as well."

THAT NIGHT, AS KIRA LAY in her bed, footsteps echoed along the corridor and her sister entered the chamber, a glowing lantern of Heraya's Ward in her hand.

Kira pushed herself upright in the bed, resting her back against the cool stone behind her. She gestured towards the chair by the wall. "Sit."

"I'm fine standing."

"If I told you to breathe, you'd suffocate yourself, wouldn't you?"

"Likely. But if you asked nicely, I'd only suffocate you."

Kira laughed, coughing as she did. Erani leaned against the wall, resting her lantern on the chair.

"The last few days are a blur. I'm not sure what I've said, but thank you... for coming for me."

Erani stared at Kira in disbelief. "Do you honestly think I ever would have left you there? You're my sister. You're an arrogant, self-important kerathlin-fucker, and you said things you're going to spend a long time apologising for, but you are my sister. My blood."

"I don't want a fight, Erani."

"Well too fucking bad." The gold and silver rings in Erani's hair gleamed green and blue in the flowerlight as she pushed herself from the wall. For a moment, she looked as though she were about to launch into a tirade fit for the bards' tales, but instead, she sat on the edge of the bed, resting a hand on Kira's knee. "My little sister. My only kin."

"Well, there is uncle. And our three cousins."

"Stop interrupting. I left. I stand by my leaving. I made strong allies in the Rolling Mountains. And after mother died, I just couldn't look at Durakdur anymore. But I should have written, should have come back sooner. And for that I'm sorry." Erani turned so she faced Kira fully. "But don't ever even dream of a world in which I wouldn't have come for you. If anyone is going to kill you, it's me." She paused for a moment then gave a dramatic head bow. "*My queen.*"

"Understood."

"Now, to what do I owe this summons?"

"There is a house in the western section of Durakdur."

"There are many houses there, sister. This is not news."

Kira glared at Erani but continued. "I need you to take me there."

"Take you there? In this state? The pair of us just stroll through the streets of Durakdur while Hoffnar hunts our blood? I can ask Vikmar to send someone. What is it you need that's so important?"

"No." Kira pushed herself further up the bed and pulled her legs from beneath the sheets. "I'm not some broken doll." She pressed her hands against the wall and stood. Her legs trembled beneath her as she rose, but that was more from exhaustion than anything else. "This must be you and I. Only us. It is too important to place our trust in any other."

Erani stood slowly, searching Kira's eyes. "What is it? What other secret have you kept from me?"

"Rockblood."

"Virtukshit. That was all burned eight hundred years ago as part of the accords…" Her jaw slackened, head tilting to the right. "Wasn't it?"

"King Baldrik was not a trusting dwarf. And the prominence of the bersekeer blood in our lines grew that distrust tenfold. We had the most to lose. He assumed the other kingdoms would betray the accords eventually, and so he kept a patch of Rockblood for when that day occurred. This knowledge is passed only from ruler to ruler through the rites of passage."

Erani turned her head, shaking it as she stared over at the lantern of Heraya's Ward. "Kira, the Rockblood almost destroyed us. It is known for generations."

"And so you see now why it must be you and I. I will task Uncle with the testing of bersekeer blood. It runs in his veins as it does ours." Kira rested her hands on her sister's shoulders. "Without this, Erani, we die. Our people die. I don't want to fight just to reclaim my power. Who do you think Hoffnar will send in the vanguard of his war against the humans? It will be warriors of Durakdur, offered a chance at redeeming the honour that I blackened by butchering Elenya and Lakar. You know it to be true. I never wanted the crown. But now that I have it, I know I was meant for it. Because I will do anything to protect my people. I will give my life, my blood, my honour. I will not let him do this."

"Are you sure this is the path you want to walk?"

Kira pushed her tongue against the roof of her mouth and nodded.

Erani pressed her forehead against Kira's, hands clasping the sides of Kira's head. "Then we will walk it together. Let me see what can be arranged."

CHAPTER THIRTY-NINE

WAKING THE LION

15th Day of the Blood Moon

Berona – Winter, Year 3081 After Doom

One unforeseen benefit of the Blood Moon was that it was far brighter than its pale, cold counterpart. Which meant that even after the sun had set, on a clear night like this one, Rist could sit and read without any need for a candle. He'd spent the day channelling the Spark with Garramon, and all he wanted to do now was sit in the nook near the top of the barracks' western watchtower and lose himself in a book.

The book in question was one he had recently procured from the dark depths of the Circle's Library. *The Origins of Runecraft*, by Ursula Klimmon. Runes fascinated Rist. Their capabilities, their limitations, and the fact that they were both entirely separate and infinitely capable of symbiotic use with the Spark.

Though it felt strange to him to be reading a book on Jotnar runecraft not written by a Jotnar. But censorship, he had found, was commonplace within the imperial libraries. And he did not suspect any books written by a Jotnar hand would have survived to adorn the shelves. Though, he had a sneaking suspicion that some scholars rewrote certain books in their own words, passing off the work as their own before burning the original. It was a sad thing, but it meant that if Rist was lucky, the information on the pages might actually be useful.

He sat there, unmoving, perched on the window ledge, his back against the stone, reading of glamours and keys, and bindings, and augmentations, and all manner of applications for runecraft. But after a while, one thing became painfully obvious: the book had not been stolen and transcribed. It was Ursula Klimmon's original work. And that would have been a good thing if Ursula Klimmon had even the slightest understanding of how Jotnar runes actually functioned. As it was, the woman just rambled and rambled for pages, discussing the different applications of runecraft without actually diving into any tangible information on how or why runes functioned.

Disappointed, Rist tossed the book on the ground beside his satchel, frowning at the *thump* it made. He loved books. And no, love was not an exaggeration. Books were a thing of insurmountable beauty and power. Be they immense repositories of knowledge, transcendent works of philosophical quandaries, or transportational tales, they were a thing to be cherished and adored. But there were some that were a waste of the precious paper on which they were printed. Some that would have been better off as trees. And a common factor amongst those particular books, he found, was a lack of passion and a lack of purpose. Sometimes one, often both.

The Origins of Runecraft, by Ursula Klimmon, was both.

As he sat there, distraught at his disappointment, he pulled out a folded letter from his pocket, opened it, and placed it down on the sill before him.

He'd not received word from his parents in quite a while. Months. He'd sent one before first reaching Berona and had received no response. Garramon could tell him nothing except that reports from the South had been few and far between.

Rist had considered slipping away in the night. He could take Trusil and ride to Antiquar. From there he was reasonably sure he could talk his way onto a ship heading south. His robes would likely be enough. He was a full Brother now, and he'd seen the power Battlemages had over other men. If all went to plan, it would take him just over a month, perhaps a bit longer, to reach The Glade.

But even then, he could hear his dad whispering in his ear, warning him of the folly in relying on everything going to plan.

Up to this point, the thought of leaving had not really been one worth entertaining. He would never have survived the journey across Loria, never have been able to afford passage on a ship from North to South, and likely would have been caught in the act either way. And even if those things hadn't been as they were, he would have been too weak to protect his parents or anyone else for that matter. But he was stronger now, harder. He was a Battlemage. He'd fought elves and Uraks, seen dragons, watched thousands burn alive. He still had so much to learn, but he wasn't that frail, helpless boy he remembered. Not anymore.

Rist leaned back and watched his breath steam in the cold air. If he was to leave, he would need to expect failed plans and plan for those failures in turn.

He lowered his head and read over the letter he'd written the night before last.

Mam and Dad,

It's been a while. I wrote you some months back, and again more recently, but have heard nothing. I hope those letters were lost along the way, that they never found home, or that the same could be said of your reply.

I hope you're all right. I hope you're reading this. We all know I've never been one for the gods, but I hope Varyn is watching over you.

An ink stain marked the page just below that line, where a tear had dropped while Rist had been writing. As he looked at it, he realised he'd used the word 'hope' far too frequently.

I met someone. A woman. Her name is Neera. She's as sarcastic as Dann but much prettier. You'd like her, Mam. She's kind, though she hides it sometimes. She watches over me, and I her. I'll bring her with me when I come home.

I am coming home. No matter what it takes, I'm coming home. I promise.

Please stay safe.

Your son,

Rist

Reading that letter over caused Rist's throat to tighten and his stomach to feel like a tight ball of lead. What if they were dead? What if his mam and dad were already gone?

The thought terrified him to his core. He had never known the world without them. They had always been his compass, his map, his stars. How was he to find his way in the world without his stars to guide him?

They couldn't be dead. Because if they were dead… if they were dead, then he no longer understood the world. People like Lasch and Elia Havel were meant to die old and fat in their beds. Their hair was meant to turn grey, their faces lined from laughter, while Rist brought them dinner and passed them their grandchildren to hold. That was how it was meant to be. Good people were rewarded with a happy life and an old death. Because if that wasn't true, then what in the void was the point of everything?

He refolded the letter and returned it to his pocket, staring out over the city. He could feel the tears welling in his eyes, but he held them back.

His thoughts moved to Calen. Vars and Freis had been good people, some of the kindest and most loving Rist had ever known. They had not died fat and old. They had died in the street, murdered.

Murdered by soldiers of the same empire Rist now fought to protect. The thought was not one that avoided him. But he'd reasoned out the logic. If an entire group of people should be condemned for the actions of a few, then all of Pirn should have been slaughtered after Jonas Urn killed Iain Timbal of Erith over two cows. And even more directly, The Glade should have been burned after Calen and Dann killed those soldiers outside The Two Barges.

The soldiers who'd killed Calen's parents were nothing like those Rist had met. They were not Magnus, or Anila, or Neera, or Garramon. He was under no illusion that there were no evil souls within the armies of the Lorian Empire, but the same was true in every corner of the world. At least where he was, he had the power to make a difference. If he'd never left The Glade, never learned what it was to touch the Spark, what would he even be? Nothing. He'd be pouring mead behind the bar of The Gilded Dragon, reading and eating until he grew fat and old. Which, if he was being honest with himself, didn't sound half bad. But he would still have been weak and helpless in the face of Uraks.

Even still, he'd spent no insignificant amount of time pondering Ella's words after she'd attacked him in the tent after Steeple.

"How could you fight for them? You're meant to be his closest friend. How could you turn on him, Rist?"

At first, he'd thought she'd been referring to what had happened to Vars and Freis. That would have made sense.

But that wasn't it.

Ella had not been there when Vars and Freis had been killed. But more so, she had specifically said 'how could you turn on *him*'. On Calen, not her.

Rist pinched the bridge of his nose, trying to stop his mind from racing, from cycling through every possible permutation of every situation. He tried the trick Garramon had taught him to focus when the thrum of the Spark grew too overwhelming, reading pages of *A Study of Control* in his mind, the words settling him.

"Thought I might find you up here."

Rist started at the sound of Magnus's voice, almost falling from the window ledge. That would not have been a pleasant way to die. He shivered at the thought.

"Catch." Magnus threw the waterskin before the words had left his lips. It soared through the air, past Rist's face, and out the window. Three heartbeats were followed by a wet *splat* and the roars of an irate guard.

Magnus gave Rist a look of sheer and utter disappointment. His lips moved, but no sound came. He just stood there and stared.

"You threw it at my head? How was I meant to catch that?"

"With your fucking hands, lad." He pressed his palm to his face. "I only have one, and I'd have caught that. Has anyone ever told you that you have the coordination of a drunk Varsundi donkey with one eye?"

"They've not been that specific, no."

Magnus let out a long sigh, swinging a satchel around to his front and pulling another skin from within.

"You're lucky I always come prepared," he said, making to hand the skin to Rist but drawing it back at the last moment. "You sure you've got it?"

"I'm sure."

"Want me to warn you before I pass it to you? Count back from three?"

"What is it?" Rist snatched the skin from Magnus's hand, examining the cork stopper before pulling it free. The sweet scent of honey mead drifted to his nostrils.

"I thought you could use a taste of home. It's mead you said your father brews?"

And just like that, Rist was warm again, memories of home flooding him. "It is."

"I'm sure it's not as good as your father's, but I'd wager the second mouthful will taste better than the first."

"Thank you." When Rist had first met Magnus at the camp outside of Al'Nasla, the last thing he'd expected from the bearded mountain of a man was the kindness of an old friend. But Magnus had continued to prove that assumption wrong time and time again.

"Don't thank me till you've tried it. Berona's known for many things, lad. Good mead's not one of them. Come to think of it, I've not seen bees in quite some time. It might not even be mead."

Rist took another sniff over the mouth of the skin. It did smell a bit sharper than his dad's mead, the scent of honey a bit more pungent. He took a deep draught.

That was a mistake.

The first taste on Rist's lips was an overly sweet slap of honey, followed by a sour burn the likes of which Rist had never experienced. He spluttered, spraying the mead in all directions.

Magnus jerked backwards to avoid the mist of spit and mead, sweeping his arms out of the way. "Ah, for fuck's sake, lad. Do you need a fucking bib?"

"Sorry," Rist choked, pressing his hand with the skin to his stomach and holding the other over his mouth. "I wasn't expecting that. That's like honeyed spirit." He puffed out his cheeks, relieved the shock was slowly ebbing from his body. "Shit. Magnus, are you trying to kill me?"

"Don't tempt me." Magnus made a motion to push Rist from the ledge. He was joking, of course, but something about Magnus made Rist think the man was only ever one intrusive thought away from following through with something stupid. "Now, come on. You're joining me on patrol."

"Ah, leave me be. I'm happy here with my book and my... mead?" He held up the skin tentatively. "It's not my night anyway, and Garramon's not let me breathe all day."

Magnus leaned against the wall on the opposite side of the window. "Rist, when I say patrol, I mean walk about the city getting drunk. I'm not asking Brother Havel, Imperial Battlemage. I'm asking Rist, uncoordinated, one-eyed Varsundi donkey."

"You know, when you want something, you're supposed to be nice to the person you want it from."

"Agree to disagree. Now, put that book away and let's see how quickly this piss gets us walking like a one-legged tree."

Rist didn't bother to point out that trees didn't have legs, one or otherwise. He gave Magnus the benefit of the doubt that the man already knew that. But it still took all his self-control not to do so.

RIST DISCOVERED THAT THE ANSWER to Magnus's question of how quickly the mead would have them walking like one-legged trees was just less than an hour.

"You know," Magnus said, snatching the skin from Rist – the second one he had produced from his satchel. Third if they were counting the skin he'd thrown out the window, which Rist wasn't. "This shit isn't that bad."

He took a swig from the skin and shrugged. "I mean, I've had a lot worse. Did you ever taste Anila's ale? The one she tried brewing in a big wooden barrel? By The Saviour, that genuinely tasted of cat piss – and don't ask how I know what cat piss tastes like."

Rist took back the skin. "When did she do that? When did she even find the time?"

"Agh." Magnus threw his arms in the air in what Rist supposed was meant to pass for another shrug. "I can't remember the specif… spicefic… spocifisipic…" He stopped in his tracks, taking a long, exaggerated breath. "Specific. Damn, I hate that word. Always trips me up. Although, might also be the mead. I can't remember the *specific* time, but it was just before the Valtaran rebellion. The first one, I'm pretty sure."

"Magnus, the first Valtaran Rebellion ended eighty-five years ago."

"Well done, Rist. I always knew you could count."

Rist pursed his lips, taking another sip from the skin. It didn't burn anymore. "Magnus. I wasn't born then."

"And?"

"How could I have tasted Anila's ale if it was brewed sixty-five years before I was born?"

"Ah… I suppose you couldn't. Didn't quite think of that." He pursed his lips and scrunched his nose, snatching the skin back from Rist. "I forget you're only a toddler."

Rist shook his head, looking at the stars that were tinged pink by the light of the moon. "In Ilnaen, Emperor Mortem said that Efialtír wished to walk among us."

"If we are so lucky, lad. If we are so lucky."

"How would that even be possible?"

"Fuck if I know. That's why Fane's Fane and I'm me." Magnus grabbed Rist by the shoulder, pulling his attention down from the stars. "We've already discussed your coordination being similar to a donkey's – and now you're drunk. It's probably for the best if you walk with your head facing what's in front of you. As funny as I think it'd be to see you fall down a set of steps, I don't much fancy having to carry you back up them."

They walked for a while, drinking and talking – mostly nonsense, but it was nice. It was probably the first time in a long time Rist's mind had just drifted to nowhere in particular, and he felt at ease. That was, of course, until he realised he was at ease and his mind promptly refocused on whether or not his parents were dead.

Even with the sun below the horizon, the streets were far from empty. Men and women pushed past, finishing out their day as the pedlars and hawkers on the side streets set down their stalls and patrols marched past. Groups huddled around the doors of taverns and inns, clouds of tabbac shrouding them, the sounds of music drifting from within.

"You would think there wasn't a war," Rist said as they passed a couple kissing against a wall, both still holding a cup in one hand.

"Life doesn't stop, Rist. What do you want them to do? Sit in their homes and weep?"

"No… I just… I guess I don't know what I'm trying to say."

"That's part of the dichotomy of war – and before you say it, yes, that is a fancy word, and no, I didn't read it in a book. Anila liked to use it. I always find I use fancier words when I'm drunk anyway. Where was I? Yes. That's part of the *dichotomy* of war. While we're out there dying, they're in here drinking. Because that's what we're fighting for – their freedom to get drunk and smoke tabbac while fondling each other against the wall of a butcher shop."

Rist snorted laughing, then choked as mead spurted from his nostrils. "I don't think we're fighting for that specifically."

"I am," Magnus said with yet another shrug.

Rist pulled Magnus to the side of the street as a cart rolled past, bouncing on the cobbles, drawn by a single black horse. Somewhere off in the city, a dog barked, answered by another, and then another, until it sounded as though all Berona was singing.

"Garramon's been working you pretty hard then?"

Rist nodded, his shoulders and legs still aching from earlier that day, his body enduringly weary from the drain of drawing so heavily on the Spark. "We've been channelling."

"Ah, that shit hurts. Pulling as much of the Spark into your body as you can without tearing yourself to pieces – all just for what? To see how much you can hold? To make yourself that little bit stronger? No. Seems impractical to me. I gather he's testing to see if you could be an Arcarian?"

Rist stopped dead. "How did you know?"

"The Arcarians aren't a secret, lad. Most of them are just dead, killed each other in the war – the Great War. Garramon went through the same training when he was preparing. I contemplated it but never bothered in the end. Risk killing myself or burning the Spark from my veins just so I have the right to get an obnoxiously large tattoo on my back and call myself an Arcarian like some twat? Sorry, you're not a twat – much. And Garramon's back and forth depending on the day. But no, thank you, I'm happy where I am. I'm an Exarch of the Imperial Battlemages. I defend my people, I drink what I want, I eat what I want, and there's only a handful of people in this world who can tell me what to do. Honestly, I don't know what they were thinking giving me so much freedom. Actually, hold on." Magnus rooted through his satchel and produced a half loaf of bread, split in the middle and stuffed with thick cheese and chunks of ham. "Garramon asked me to give this to you. Told me to make sure you eat it. Makes sense why now."

Rist's stomach turned a little at the thought of more food. But then something occurred to him. "Did he give you half a loaf or a full loaf?"

"Full loaf." Magnus gave a broad smile, teeth visible through his thick black beard. He knew full well what Rist was asking.

Rist narrowed his eyes.

"Taxes, lad, they'll be death of us all."

It wasn't the joke that made Rist laugh, it was how straight Magnus kept his face while telling it. He took the bread from Magnus, shaking his head, then stuffed it into his mouth and took a bite worthy of a bear. "That's not bad at all, actually," he said, choking the mouthful down. "A bit dry but—"

An enormous explosion cut Rist short, booming like a clap of thunder, and the night erupted in an orange blaze.

The light receded and was followed by shrieks and screams and the ringing of bells.

"What the fuck was that?" Magnus looked up at the sky, where a column of smoke billowed.

Before Rist could answer, a second explosion sounded, closer than the first. Rist could tell by the tremble in the ground beneath his feet and the shiver of the Spark that ran down his spine.

"Did you feel that?" Rist stared off in the direction of the second explosion, still feeling the lingering touch of the Spark.

"Feel what? The shaking?" Magnus turned and grabbed a sprinting soldier by the chest. "What's happened?"

The man looked as though he were going to launch Magnus to the ground until his eyes fell on the silver trim of Magnus's black cloak, widening in realisation. "Exarch," he said, visibly standing straighter and trying to control his panting. "I don't know. I was patrolling the plaza when I heard the explosion. The southeast wall is on fire. So too the southwest and—"

A third explosion roared, further away, the sky now tinged with blazing oranges and reds.

"We're under attack," the soldier stammered.

"No fucking shit." Magnus released him, shaking his head in disbelief. "Unless you've any further useless insights, get to the fucking wall."

The man sprinted away, looking more than relieved to escape the situation.

"We need to get to the barracks." Magnus stuffed the skin back into his satchel, then snatched the bread from Rist and stowed it. "We might be hungry later."

"Who do you think it is?"

"Maybe the elves weren't satisfied with just Catagan."

A fourth explosion sounded, and Rist's heart stopped. "That was the north wall."

Magnus looked into Rist's eyes with a raised eyebrow, signalling for him to elaborate.

"Neera is on watch tonight. She's stationed on the north wall."

By the time Rist and Magnus were anywhere near the north wall, the city was in absolute pandemonium, bells and horns sounding endlessly. Screams rang out all about the city, and the harsh ring of colliding steel drifted down the occasional alley.

They didn't stop.

A man vaulted from a side street, almost knocking Rist to the ground.

"Sorry," he said, holding his palms up for a moment, frantic, a wrap of dark cloth covering his face. "I didn't mean to..." His expression shifted, and he must have realised who Rist and Magnus were because a flicker of steel flashed low, and it was only by luck that Rist caught the man's forearm before the blade was firmly lodged in his side.

Rist lifted his gaze from the knife to the man's eyes that stared back at him, more fear than hatred or anger. He held that gaze for a fraction of a second before Magnus slammed his fist into the side of the man's head with a *crunch*.

The man dropped to the ground, motionless.

Rist stood there, still a bit in shock, the mead slowing his mind, while Magnus dropped on top of the limp man.

Magnus pulled the cloth from around the man's face, grabbing his cheeks and turning his head left and right.

"Not elves, lad. Rebels," he growled, rooting through the man's pockets for anything that might be of use. The man grunted and twisted beneath Magnus. The Exarch grabbed the knife that now lay on the ground and rammed it into the man's neck without a second's hesitation, pulling it free in the same motion and getting to his feet.

Rist stared down at the body.

"What?" Magnus gave Rist a pointed look. "He was literally about to do the same thing to you. Come on, we don't know how many of these bastards are out tonight or what else they've got planned."

Rist could see the flames through the buildings, bright and raging. But it was only when they drew closer and emerged into the open street that fronted the base of the walls that he realised the full extent of the attack.

The northern gatehouse was entirely consumed by a raging inferno. The flames spread for at least a hundred feet across the walls in both directions, devouring two watch towers that lay in their path. Sections of the stone had been completely broken free from the gatehouse and towers, jutting into the ground through the cobbled stone and cultivated patches of grass.

Everywhere Rist looked, people were dragging bodies from the rubble and flames, soldiers and citizens alike; it mattered little.

Even more bodies were scattered across the street, broken and twisted in unnatural ways, bones protruding from torn flesh, blood and gore splattered across the stone. Some had died from the impact after being blown from the walls, others had been crushed beneath debris. Quite a number still burned, black and crackling in the flames.

"She's all right, lad. Women are like cats, nine lives the lot of them."

Magnus's reassurance had little effect on Rist. Neera had been stationed here. He had no way of knowing whether she'd been in the gatehouse, on the walls, or on the towers. Logic dictated that she was likely dead. Rist cared little for logic at that specific moment in time.

Without much thought, he rushed forwards, leaving Magnus to chase after him. Rist turned over every body he could find, flames burning around him. His heart beat like a charging bull, stopping for a brief moment just before he turned over each body, relief flooding him when he saw a face he didn't recognise. Some were burned or mangled beyond all realms of recognition. But none wore Neera's armour.

Rist glanced over his shoulder to see Magnus following suit without question, dropping to one knee and holding the stump of his left hand to his chest while he flipped over bodies.

A woman screamed as Rist turned her over, her hair incinerated down to her scalp, the right side of her face bloody and smoking, flesh slopping. She wore no armour, only a tunic and a pair of charred trousers. Not a soldier, just someone walking the wrong street at the wrong time.

"It's all right," he said, swallowing, his breaths quick and sharp. He rubbed at her unburnt shoulder, trying to calm her – failing. She shrieked and groaned, turning to convulsions. Rist cried out. "Healer! We need a Healer!"

The only answers were more cries of the same. People screaming, others calling for help.

"Is it her?" Magnus dropped to the ground beside Rist, manoeuvring to get a look at the woman.

Rist shook his head. "No… but she needs help. She's—"

"She's dead, Rist. She's gone. We need to keep looking."

Rist hadn't noticed the woman go still in his arms. He laid her back down gently, closing her too-still eyes. With screams, shouts, and crackling fire still sounding all around him, he whispered, "Heraya watch over you."

"And The Saviour take you into his light," Magnus added, his voice softer than Rist had ever heard. That softness dissipated as he got to his feet, the light of the fires burning in his eyes. "This isn't rebellion. This is butchery. Most of these people were just trying to get home."

"Rist!"

Rist's heart fluttered at the sound of Neera's voice, and he turned to see her marching towards him through the flames, four soldiers at her back in red and black leathers. He pulled her into his arms. "You're alive."

"I was checking on a disturbance when the gatehouse exploded," she said, pulling away, her hands lingering on his shoulders. "Came back to find it like this. We've been trying to pull the bodies from the rubble. There are just so many… They were Alamants, Rist."

"What do you mean? Who were Alamants?" Magnus moved closer.

"The explosion. It was Alamants who caused it. I was close enough to feel the Spark. It was weak, but there was a group of them, a hundred at least, linked together. We caught some of them and other rebels trying to escape."

"Alive?"

"Not anymore."

"Bastards." The muscles in Magnus's face twitched, his fingers clenching into a fist. "Fane grants them amnesty, lets them roam unchecked, and this is what they do? They burn their own people? Set fire to the walls that keep their city safe? Void take the lot of them."

Footfalls sounded as more soldiers flooded into the streets, mages with them. Healers scrambled to the injured, Craftsmages rushing to the crumbling sections of wall, the thrum of the Spark crackling in the air. The Battlemages sprinted to Magnus, who sent them scouring the streets for the rebels and Alamants.

"Kill them on sight," he said, staring into the eyes of the Battlemage closest to him. "If you see them in a group, don't think, act. Alone they are weak as children, but if they link…" He gestured towards the blazing walls. "Don't let that happen again. The people of this city are ours to protect. Do you understand?"

"Yeh… yes, Exarch."

"Supreme Commander Tambrel, have you seen her?"

"She took a contingent to the southeast wall, Exarch Offa."

Magnus nodded, dismissing the man. As more soldiers arrived, he sent them to the walls to help pull the injured free and clear the bodies.

"What is the point of this?" Magnus muttered to himself, taking in the chaos.

"Does there need to be a point?" Neera asked. "These rebels just kill and burn. There's nothing noble in what they do."

"There's always a point, Sister." Magnus squinted through the flames, watching. "Always. I've seen enough rebellions to know. Their resources are limited. They won't waste them for no reason. There is a 'why' here somewhere, we've just not seen it yet."

The thrum of the Spark intensified, rippling in the air, power building. Rist looked about, searching for whatever had caused that surge. The Healers and Craftsmages were weaving threads over threads, pulling on each elemental strand, but they were not the source. Their power was steady and constant; this was shifting and building, clouded by the threads of the other mages.

"What is it?" Magnus grasped Rist's shoulder, looking into his eyes. "Rist. You feel something. What is it?"

It was then Rist realised what was happening. He could see the threads of Fire, Spirit, and Air swirling about each other, growing dense, thick, welling into a sphere near the base of the gatehouse – where the mages worked and people were still pulling the injured from the rubble.

"No!" He leapt forwards, dragging threads of Spirit through him and launching them. But he was too late. A ripple of power swept through the air, followed by the crackle of lightning and then an explosion of Fire and Air.

The sound consumed everything, flames sweeping outwards like a tidal wave, debris crashing down everywhere.

Rist ignored it all and opened his mind as Garramon had been teaching him, feeling the power of the elemental strands. He grasped the strands of Fire, Air, and Spirit, unravelling them, channelling them through his body and into the world. He pulled so deep his own blood felt like fire in his veins, his skin like ice. He pushed the pain down and swirled the threads around himself, Neera, Magnus, and anyone within reach.

The sweeping flames poured over the shield – over the Sparkward – like waves crashing over a glass dome. Rist slammed his eyes shut as the fire turned the world to nothing but a bright burning light. The drain pulled at him the moment the flames hit, dragging the power from his bones to hold the ward in place. He could feel chunks of stone slamming against the barrier, shattering to a thousand pieces, sending tremors through his body.

As the flames faded and the pressure bearing down on Rist's soul ebbed, the roar of the fire was replaced with an eerie silence, broken only by the sound of crackling and agonising groans.

Rist opened his eyes and drew weighted breaths, his brow slick with sweat. His arms hung heavy, shoulders slumped, but he still felt strong, far stronger than he would have if he'd tried that a few months ago.

The first thing Rist looked for was Neera. He found her at his right side, staring back at him, one hand resting on the pommel of her sword, the other on his shoulder. The briefest of smiles graced her lips before vanishing at the sight of what stood before them.

Everything was on fire. Corpses littered the ground, blazing, flesh and cloth crackling as it burned. The injured and the people who were pulling them free, the Healers, the Craftsmages, and everyone else who had come to aid: all dead. Here and there a survivor crawled beneath blocks of shattered stone that had shielded them from the flames. But those were few and far between. They'd never stood a chance.

"That would have been us," Magnus said, nodding to Rist. "I wasn't quick enough. There's an Arcarian in there somewhere, lad."

Shouts sounded from all directions as people rushed from nearby buildings, sharp steel in their fists. The Spark pulsed from several of them, weak but still there.

"Aaagh. Come to clean up the stragglers." A wicked smile stretched Magnus's lips. The Spark surging from him as strands of red light ignited into life in his hand and took the form of a glowing blade. "Come to Magnus, you fucking rats."

The Exarch surged forwards, crashing into the rebels with no heed for self-preservation. Magnus dodged the swing of the first attacker's axe, then carved through the man's forearm before hacking off his jaw and leaving him to slump to the ground. The next rebel fared no better, Magnus's níthral cleaving his leg at the knee before plunging upwards through his throat and out the back of his skull. Magnus was a man possessed. Anything that came near him fell in a heartbeat, his red blade carving open chests and severing limbs.

Rist, Neera, and the soldiers turned to face a group charging them from the rear, steel ringing as they collided.

A man wielding a massive black axe careened towards Rist, the weapon carving through the air in a devastating swing. Rist reached for his sword – a sword that wasn't there. It was back in the barracks.

Without thought, Rist snared the axe and held it in place with a thread of Air. The man stood there, frozen, tugging at his axe to no avail. The rage in his eyes faded to fear, and suddenly Rist felt a pang of sympathy for the helplessness before him. Against the power of the Spark, this man was nothing.

A tingle ran down his spine, and Rist shifted to dodge a shard of rock that had been launched at his head by an Alamant rushing towards him. He pivoted and hurled a sphere of air into the Alamant's chest, sending her hurtling into the flames at her back. A roar sounded to his right, and he pulled on threads of Earth, dragging a section of stone from the ground and launching it upwards.

When the Alamant had attacked, Rist had released the threads of Air holding the axe-wielder in place. The man now hung suspended from a stone spike that impaled him through the chest. The rebel coughed, blood spluttering from his open mouth. He took one last rasping breath, then the life left his body, limbs slumping, head lolling forward.

Rist pressed his hand to his chest, feeling the gemstone pendant hanging beneath his tunic. A voice in the back of his mind told him to harness the life Essence that flowed from the man's body, but he couldn't. Something about this particular death felt so pointless. And yet, to let the Essence drift away, to let it fade to nothing... How was that any better?

The shifting of dirt beneath boots sounded behind him and he twisted to avoid a spear thrust. The steel tip sliced through the belly of his tunic but missed his flesh. Rist whipped a thread of Air into his attacker's side and heard bones crunch as the woman was lifted from her feet and bounced across the stones, her spear skittering away. She lay there, twitching and coughing up blood.

A pulse of the Spark rippled to his left, and before he could react, threads of Air wrapped around him, coiling and twisting. The first thought that flared in his mind was panic, but that quickly died when he realised how weak the threads were.

He slid thin threads of Spirit down through the threads of Air that held him, watching them melt away. When he turned, he found himself looking into the eyes of a man who'd seen at least ten summers more than he.

The man stared at Rist blankly, eyes wide, mouth ajar. He was twice Rist's size, thick-muscled with a black beard dense as a bush. He held a short axe in his left hand, but instead of charging, he sent threads of Spirit, Fire, and Water into Rist. The threads pushed through Rist's tunic, through his skin, and into his bones. He could feel them flooding him, feel his soul quiver at their touch.

The man was trying to burn him out.

Rist's natural instinct was to push back, and so he did. There was no struggle, no moment of panic where either man wondered who was stronger. Nothing like that. Rist overwhelmed the Alamant completely and utterly.

A piercing white light burst from the man's eyes as he collapsed to his knees, screaming and writhing. Rist tried to pull back, tried to stop, but it was far too late. The skin around the Alamant's eyes bubbled and smoked, burning to black as the white light seared forth.

The shrieks that clawed their way from his throat sent a chill down Rist's spine. And then they ceased, and the Alamant fell onto his side, arms splayed, tongue hanging from his open mouth, eyes burned from his sockets. Rist felt the pendant calling him once more, heard that little voice telling him to draw the life Essence, to save it. But again, he let it drift away.

To his right, Neera pulled her sword from a woman's belly, flames pouring from her hand and washing over another man who charged towards her. A rebel hurled himself forwards and caught Neera in the side with the swing of a hammer. Neera stumbled sideways, and the man struck her again, this time in the chest. She tripped over a body and hit the ground hard. Rist could feel threads of Fire whirling around her, but he was already there, charging, his feet moving before he even had the time to think.

A woman came hurtling at him from the right with a battered sword. Without breaking stride, he caught the blade mid-swing with a thread of Air, wrenched it from her hand, spun it, and rammed it back down through her neck and out her back.

Rist wrapped threads of Air around the throat of the man with the hammer, hauling him across the ground. The man's feet hovered over the stone and burning bodies, his hands clasping at his throat.

Rist pulled the rebel through the air until his fingers were wrapped firmly around the man's throat. Dark eyes stared back at him as fists slammed down on his arm. But Rist tapped into the gemstone around his neck, the feeling of ice shooting through his veins, the world growing quiet and dim before bursting to life. He let the Essence flow through him, and the man's slamming fists became nothing more than a nuisance.

Neera leapt past Rist and took a rebel's head from their shoulders as they made to run him through with a spear.

"We give our lives to keep you safe." Rist tilted his head to the side, trying to glean some sort of answers from the man's eyes. He closed his hand tighter, the cords of the man's neck tense beneath his fingers, only the slightest of gasps dragging air past Rist's grip. "She stood on that wall, watching over this city while it slept, and you tried to steal the life from her veins."

"You..." the man choked out through ragged breaths. "You..."

Rist loosened his grip.

"You're fucking scum." He glared at Rist, eyes wide with bitter rage. "You and your bitch will burn. Your whole fucking empire will burn."

The Essence in Rist's blood flared, and he squeezed, feeling a *snap*. The man's body went limp, and Rist drew the fading Essence into the gemstone around his neck, a red glow pulsing beneath his tunic.

As soon as Rist realised what he had done, he released his grip and let the lifeless corpse crumple to the ground, nestled between a burning body and a lump of broken stone. He stared down at the body, feeling the Essence surge through him, feeling as though he could tear a hole through a stone wall with his bare hands.

Soldiers rushed in around him, shouting, swords drawn, swarming over the remaining rebels who had charged from the buildings. Several of the Battlemages who had been sent to scour the streets followed only moments after, the air crackling with the power of the Spark.

Neera grabbed Rist and turned him to face her.

He let go of the Essence, feeling its absence as it faded from his veins, and cupped her cheeks, his hands trembling. "Are you all right?"

She grunted and looked down at where the hammer swings had dented her armour. "I don't think anything's broken. Are you... all right? I saw—"

"I'm fine," Rist lied. He hated lying in any capacity. But lying to Neera was worse somehow. He had omitted things to her before, like when Garramon had given him the Essence vessel and he'd not told her, but he'd never outright lied. He wasn't fine. The smell of the Alamant's burning eyes still lingered in his nostrils, the image of the man impaled on the stone clung to his mind's eye, and the sound of the snapping neck *cracked* over and over in his ears.

With all the death he'd seen in the last two years, all the blood, and loss, and darkness, he'd only taken two human lives. The two Lorian soldiers he'd killed when trying to flee Camylin. And even then he'd not known what he'd been doing, he'd been terrified, scrambling for his life, barely able to move. This was different though. The ease with which he had killed these people shook him. They were not Uraks or Bloodmarked or ferocious monstrosities trying to tear him limb from limb. They were people, people fighting for their home. People who were nothing but fodder to the Spark. Even the Alamants. Rist had forever been curious as to just what an Alamant could do, how weak their grasp on the Spark truly was. Now he knew. Together, in groups, they could cause mayhem. But alone, they were akin to children running with knives, just as likely to kill themselves as others.

And then he remembered what they had done, the lives they had destroyed so mindlessly, the innocent people they had targeted, and his sympathy withered.

Magnus approached from the street, covered in blood head to toe, flames still blazing at his back. Behind him, the last of the rebels were being cut down as they ran. There would be no prisoners that night, of that Rist was sure.

"You two all right?" Magnus's chest rose and fell as he drew heavy breaths. He wiped at the blood on his face, only succeeding in smearing it further.

Rist gave him a sharp nod, pulling away from Neera.

"I still can't figure out why." Magnus scanned the bodies around Rist and Neera, his gaze lingering on the Alamant with burnt-out eyes. He raised an eyebrow at Rist, asking a wordless question, to which Rist responded with another nod.

"There must have been hundreds of Alamants together," he said, looking back at the destruction in the street and the walls, the raging flames and charred, broken corpses. "I've never seen them cause this kind of damage."

As Magnus spoke, a shiver ran down Rist's spine and he inhaled sharply.

Both Magnus and Neera snapped their gazes to him.

"Fuck." Magnus sighed. "What is it now—"

A shockwave of the Spark swept through the air, tangled with Essence, followed swiftly by the sound of an enormous explosion. Rist watched in horror as the ground shook and clouds of fire burst from the walls of the High Tower, chunks of stone soaring through the air to crash down into the city. Another explosion and a section of bridges and walkways near the base erupted in flames.

"They drew us out," Magnus said, his jaw slack and eyes wide. "They fucking drew us out." He pushed Rist forward, then Neera, turning and roaring, "To the tower! To the tower!"

As Rist, Neera, and Magnus sprinted towards the tower, the thrum of the Spark in the air grew so powerful it felt only moments away from stopping his heart. It was like entering the city for the first time all over again, but somehow this was even greater, like the air itself was alive.

Magnus and Neera could feel it too, he could see it in their eyes. With each step, each vibration through his legs, that sensation grew and grew. He had felt the power of the Alamants by the walls. There was no way in the gods this was them. Even if there were thousands, they couldn't wield raw power like this.

Flames raged across the tower, black smoke billowing into a cloudless sky, horns roaring. The tower's base came into view as Rist and the others turned onto the main thoroughfare. The gates were already open, a host of Praetorians standing in the street outside.

"Why haven't they gone in?" Neera shouted, panting.

Garramon and a clutch of other Battlemages emerged from a side street, their hands and faces marred with blood and soot. He grabbed Rist by the shoulder, his voice wracked with worry. "You're all right?"

Rist nodded sharply, words escaping him.

"Garramon, the tower." Magnus tilted his head towards the flaming tower and broke into a run once more.

Rist, Neera, and Garramon followed, along with the other Battlemages.

As Rist ran, he could hear nothing but the roar of the Spark, the edges of his vision blurring to a dull haze, every hair on his body standing on end. He flicked through the pages of *Druids, a Magic Lost*, whispering the words as quickly as his lips would allow, trying to find calm within the chaos. But when he stepped through the gates, everything faded into a sudden stillness amidst the storm.

The air was crisp and sharp, each breath like taking ice into his lungs. And for some reason, there was no sound, not even the whistle of the wind. Just silence.

Before him, Fane Mortem stood in the central courtyard at the foot of the tower, his black and red robes billowing as though he stood amidst hurricane winds. Five of the Chosen in their gleaming silver plate, crimson níthrals in their fists, stood about him in a circle. Threads of each element swirled around the emperor, pulsing, power sweeping from him in waves. Fane's eyes were closed, and bodies were piled about him. Screams echoed in the night as Fane's threads of Air pulled rebels from the tower's windows, their bodies bursting into clouds of bone and gore as they hit the stone.

Alamants charged from the archways in the tower's base, their eyes igniting with white light as soon as they set foot in the courtyard, threads of Spirit searing their veins.

Fragments of debris and shards of shattered bone whirred, slicing through anything that moved, threads of Fire setting flesh alight. Hundreds of threads layered over each other, twisting and turning, coiling like snakes. It was a symphony of death, a horrific, terrible work of art Rist hoped would never be painted again. Awe inspiring and gut churning, both.

The sheer display of raw power just didn't seem real. How could any one soul wield such immense power?

As the bodies piled around him, bone and blood painting the stone, smoke drifting from burnt-out eye sockets, the emperor stood at the centre of it all with his eyes closed, hands outstretched, expression unchanging.

Whichever rebels were fortunate enough to evade the emperor's power were cut down in a heartbeat by the Chosen, crimson blades cleaving bone as an axe would a branch.

When the final bodies hit the stone and the thrum of the Spark settled, sound once again returned to Rist's ears, but there was nothing more than snapping flames and hushed whispers, bells and horns fading into the night.

Fane Mortem opened his eyes and strolled through the canvas of corpses, a frown on his face as he surveyed the yard, the High Tower still burning and smoking behind him. He stopped barely two feet in front of Garramon, shaking his head as he looked back. The emperor inhaled slowly through his nose, then sighed and turned his attention to those before him.

"We're fighting too many wars at once, old friend," he said to Garramon. "It's time to burn the rats from the hole."

CHAPTER FORTY

IN THE BLOOD

15ᵗʰ Day of the Blood Moon

Níthianelle – Winter, Year 3081 After Doom

The world around Ella drifted in clouds of white, ever-shifting. Shapes appeared before her in shades of grey: a fence, a door, a house. But every time she reached out and touched them, they dissipated as though made of smoke.

This place was not Níthianelle. It was a world of dreams, one she had visited a number of times since finding herself in the Sea of Spirits. Not every night, but some. It was different to dreaming in the waking world, a dream within a dream, both real and ethereal. And just as she had each time she had walked this place, she heard her mother's voice calling to her.

"Ella." Freis's voice echoed as though she called through a long tunnel. *"Could you fetch me a wooden spoon?"*

The world swirled and spun, smoke twisting and filling with colour. Within seconds, Ella stood in a room composed of stout logs, the fireplace roaring behind her. It was her home. She knew it like she knew the lines of Rhett's face, like she knew the amber flecks of Faenir's eyes. This was her home as sure as the grass was green and the sky was blue.

"A wooden spoon?" The words left Ella's mouth without her consent, her lips moving of their own volition. They were the words she'd spoken that night, some five years ago. The night her dad had come back from The Gilded Dragon with a wound in his side. It was a memory she'd long forgotten, one she'd pushed to the back of her mind, one with more questions than answers.

"To beat your father around the head with," Freis answered. Ella could hear her mam's voice but couldn't see her. She was alone in the home that no longer was.

The house around her evaporated into plumes of smoke, spiralling then reforming.

"Can you tell us the story of Cassian Tal?" A young Calen ladled stew into a bowl and rushed past her. He was so innocent then, so pure. He'd needed her.

Ella's heart stopped as the smoky figure of her dad took shape, his arm tucked tight to his side, his breaths far steadier than they should have been, as though he were trying too hard to keep them that way.

That night flooded back. Vars had said he'd slipped on the way back from The Gilded Dragon, but he'd lied. She'd always known when he'd been lying.

Once more the world shifted, smoke twisting around her as though blowing in a storm. When the smoke resettled, she was once again in her home, but not the kitchen. She stood outside her parents' room, candlelight glowing from within, the door open just a crack.

Her mam and dad both sat on the bed, but Vars wore no shirt and a vicious gash adorned his side, blood trickling down his ribs. The wound was not anything that could have been sustained by a fall, and it had been sewn with all the skill of a five-year-old donkey. The sharp scent of Brimlock sap clung to the air. She'd smelled it the moment her dad had walked in the door and kissed her on the head, she'd just not pieced it together at first.

She watched as her mam removed the catgut and re-sewed the wound with a delicate hand, applying a thick salve. The entire time, her dad didn't so much as flinch. He just watched Freis, his hand resting on her knee, his breathing steady. Even when the needle pierced the skin, he gave not so much as a hiss or a twitch. She had always seen her dad as a tough man, a man hardened by work in the forge, a man of iron and steel. But that night, as she watched from behind the door, as her mam sewed the wound in his side, she saw a man she barely knew. He was still her dad, still had that same caring look in his eyes, but he was also someone else entirely, someone colder. She knew there was more they weren't telling her and her brothers. She just never knew what it was.

"Ella!" Freis's voice thundered, shaking the air, and the world blurred and warped.

Ella's skin goosefleshed, and she snapped her gaze to her mam. Freis no longer sat on the bed. Now she stood before Ella, her eyes pure white from edge to edge. Her body was no longer smoke. It was solid, real, but her eyes glowed with a white light.

Freis extended her hand and opened her fingers. "My girl."

Ella reached out, her hand shaking, every hair on her body on end. Her jaw trembled, teeth chattering. And then her hand touched her mother's, warmth spreading from fingertips to fingertips, and the air fled Ella's lungs. "It's… it's you… you're not…"

Freis leaned forwards and brushed Ella's cheek, and Ella all but melted into her.

"I thought I'd lost you," she said between sobs.

"My girl," her mam said again, running her hand through Ella's hair. "I'm so sorry."

Ella leaned back, tears blurring her eyes. "For what?"

"For keeping everything from you." Freis brushed the tears from Ella's cheek. "For not telling you who you are. We were trying to protect you, to keep you from the darkness. We thought we had more time." Her voice caught in her throat and she repeated herself, whispering and pulling Ella close. "We thought we had more time. She saved me, but—"

A third voice erupted from all around, so loud the world shook and broke into smoke once more. "Ella!"

Ella panicked, grabbing her mam's wrist with all her strength. "Don't you dare leave me."

The voice boomed again. "Ella!"

"Trust in the blood." Freis rested her free hand atop Ella's. "Blood is all you can trust."

"What?" Ella felt hands gripping her shoulders, shaking her, fingers pressing in so hard it hurt. "Mam, what do you mean?"

Freis simply smiled. "Trust in the blood, Ella. I was wrong. Find me again. I will listen for your voice."

"*Ella!*" the voice roared, and the world of smoke swirled around her like a tempest, then smashed.

Ella lurched upright, her eyes opening. Tamzin stood over her, hands grasping Ella's shoulders.

"What did you do?" Ella roared and shoved Tamzin off her, then leapt to her feet. She extended a clawed hand, visibly shaking. "What. Did. You. Do?"

Tamzin stepped backwards, white mist rising from beneath her feet. She raised both hands in the air. "Ella, I need you to breathe."

"What did you do to me?" The wolf prowled in the back of Ella's mind, teeth bared. "Why did you make me see that?"

"See what? Ella, I have no idea what you're talking about."

"Then why did you wake me?" Ella made no attempt to hold back her fury. "*Why?*"

"Because we needed to keep moving." Tamzin's fingernails grew, curling and sharpening, her fingers growing thicker, fangs protruding below her upper lip. "If you don't back down now, I'll put you down. That is your only warning."

Ella clenched her jaw but held herself in place. She drew a long breath through her nose, letting it out slowly.

"I woke you because we are less than a day from the Darkwood and we need to move. When I tried, you were limp as a doll. I panicked. People can lose themselves in this place."

Ella recoiled as the woman made to rest a hand on her shoulder, but Tamzin moved closer, placing both her palms flat on Ella's forearms and meeting her gaze. "What did you see?"

"My mam. I think she's alive."

Tanner Fjorn stood on the edge of the plateau that overlooked Alura, a warm mug of Arlen Root tea cupped in his hands. The tea was one of the worst things he'd ever tasted, but Elia Havel had brewed a batch every day since she'd begun to recover. After a while, Yana had started to do the same. That meant a lot of tea was going to waste. He didn't like waste. And most tastes could be acquired with a little perseverance.

His breath misted and rose into the morning sky, glinting in the pale red light of the Blood Moon. That damn moon had sat there, carved into the sky, for just over two weeks now, making every day too dark and every night too bright.

In a sense, he had been a little underwhelmed. The last time the Blood Moon had risen, the entire continent had run red – or so the legends told. And now there he was, sipping a mug of tea to the sound of birdsong. The tea tasted like shit, but the sentiment remained. He was under no illusions though. There in Aravell – surrounded by walls and mountains and a forest that had a nasty tendency to kill anything that moved – he was sheltered from the chaos. The reports from elsewhere in Epheria were very different. Entire cities had been wiped from existence, burned to ash, tens of thousands slaughtered – hundreds of thousands.

The world was on fire. The idea of Tanner sitting around sipping tea while so many fought and died clawed at him. He had never been a man to sit back and wait. It was not his way. A glass of brandy by the fire after a long day, that was something that warmed his heart, but this was different. Farwen and Coren and the others, they were still there, still in the heart of the war. He had made the choice to leave, to go with Ella, but that didn't mean he was free of the guilt at leaving the others behind.

He took a sip of the tea, grimacing as the aftertaste of dirt hit his tongue.

Once Ella woke – and she would – the sitting around would be over. They would join the fight once again. That girl was a fighter, a warrior in her heart. She had a will of wrought iron. She would come back to them. She had to. If she didn't, Tanner wasn't entirely sure that it wouldn't break Yana forever.

Women were strange creatures. He'd found that they were slow to love, slow to trust, but when they did, they bound themselves to that love with all their strength. And that was the way it should be as far as he was concerned. Love should be hard won and defended with every shred of a person's soul.

Tanner sipped at the tea again, watching as Alura started to awaken and the soft sound of chatter drifted through the basin. Without Ella's brother and the others, the place felt empty, quiet. Thousands had become a handful. Most of the Rakina remained, along with the sick and injured, a number of guards left behind from the Draleid's army, and the elves who tended the dragons – Dracárdare, he believed they were called. At that time, only a handful of souls wandered the paths and tended the plateaus, mostly elves who had been assigned to keep everything in order.

Tanner turned and ambled across the plateau, nodding to two men in half-plate with the white dragon emblazoned across their chests. He stepped through the doorway to the familiar, earthy scent of Arlen Root and Elia Havel in the same place he'd left her: stirring a pot of steeping tea, her neck tilted to the side, her eyes fixed on something that wasn't there.

The woman may have recovered physically from her time in the Beronan dungeons, but the horrors she'd experienced there were very much still with her. At times he thought two minds lived within her skull. One a woman so sweet and chirpy as to almost cause him a headache, the other a crippled soul who saw demons lurking in every shadow.

"Elia." Tanner approached slowly, holding his empty mug in his left hand. She didn't answer. "Elia."

Elia continued stirring the large pot, her head twitching.

"Elia, are you all right?"

Tanner rested his hand on Elia's shoulder, and she jerked away, catching the pot with her arm and knocking it, the scalding tea pouring over the floor.

"No!" Elia snatched up the pot and set it on the counter. She grabbed a pile of neatly folded cloths and dumped them on the steaming tea that was slowly spreading across the stone. "No, no, no." With every passing second, she grew more frantic, eventually wrapping her arms around herself and clutching her shoulders as she sat on her haunches. "I'm sorry, I'm sorry. Please," she pleaded, terror in her eyes. "Please don't hurt me, I'm sorry. I'm so sorry. I'll tell you anything you want. He always reads, he… he…"

"Elia." Tanner lowered himself to meet Elia's gaze, sitting back on his heels. He didn't touch her – he'd learned from that mistake – but moved his head until she looked into his eyes. "Elia, it's only tea."

She stared back at him blankly, her shoulders trembling, her fingers pressing creases into her tunic.

"You're safe now," he repeated. He touched his hand to his chest, resting it over his heart. "You're safe. Nobody will hurt you here."

Her stare softened at those words, and she nodded softly, her teeth chattering.

"Come on, let's get you to your feet." Tanner gestured for her to stand, trying his best to give her a warm smile. He rose slowly and offered his hand, not forcing it. She would take it if she wanted.

It took a moment, but Elia eventually grasped his outstretched hand and stood upright but kept her gaze fixed on the mess of cloths and the liquid creeping across the ground. She was tiny, at least a foot shorter than he was, her frame dainty, fragile. The woman had been through the void.

"Are you all right? You didn't hurt yourself?" Tanner asked.

She shook her head, still not lifting her gaze from the ground.

"Why don't you go and see if Lasch needs any help with the bees? It's getting warmer outside. Earlywinter is creeping in. The fresh air might be nice."

Elia glanced at him without speaking, then looked back to the pot on the counter and the mess on the floor.

"I'll clean it up and get a new pot started. You go."

Elia nodded. That seemed to be her preferred method of communication whenever these episodes struck. She made to walk past him and stopped, opening her mouth as though to speak, then closing it. She lifted a hand and held it up tentatively before resting it on his arm. "Thank… thank you." Her eyes softened. "I'm sorry for…" She looked back at the mess. "I'm sorry."

"Don't ever be sorry." Tanner shook his head. "Not for this. Not ever. Go. I'll look after everything here."

As Elia grabbed a coat and stepped from the house, Tanner mopped up the spilt tea with the cloths, then tossed them into a bucket beside the counter.

Once he was sure the place was in a tidy enough state that Elia wouldn't start cleaning when she came back, he climbed the stairs and walked the corridor down to Ella's room.

The sweet scent of lavender touched his nose as he opened the door, released by a fresh whorl of the purple flowers set in the vase beside the door. A soft whimper sounded to his right, a wet nose pressing into his hand.

"Food?" Tanner asked rhetorically, running his hand along Faenir's snout and scratching the side of the wolfpine's head. The wolfpine always needed food.

The crest of Faenir's head reached Tanner's chest, golden eyes looking at him with a keen sense of understanding. Faenir nuzzled Tanner's hand, letting out a low grumble in response to his question.

"All right. I'll fetch something for you soon. Where's she gone?" Tanner gestured over to the corner of the room where the Angan, Aneera, usually sat cross-legged. From the day Ella had collapsed, the Angan had barely eaten or slept. She'd spent almost every waking hour with her legs folded and her eyes closed, doing whatever it was that Angan did. Aeson had explained to Tanner about the creatures' ability to communicate across long distances, but he still didn't quite understand it.

"Actually." Tanner frowned, looking from the empty spot where Aneera usually sat, then back to the door. "Where've they all gone?"

It was only then Tanner realised not only was Aneera not in the room, he'd seen none of the Angan on the plateau either. There were usually three or four of them prowling about, never moving too far from the house. At first, it had only been Diango, who'd arrived just before the battle almost two weeks past, but the others had dripped in as the days had passed.

The wolfpine gave a low growl, his hackles rising, lips pulling back in a momentary snarl before he padded across the room to where Yana was slumped in a chair. The wolfpine dropped himself to the ground with a sigh, nuzzling his head against Yana's leg. The creature was so massive that even lying down, his back came up as high as the flat of the chair.

A smile broke out across Tanner's face at the sight of Yana passed out in the chair, her hand resting atop Ella's. He moved behind the chair and leaned over, resting his chin on Yana's shoulder and cupping his hands across her stomach. "I think a bed might be a good idea."

Yana grumbled, shifting slightly but not opening her eyes.

"Mmph… Get off me, you big oaf." She pressed her cheek into Tanner's arm, planting a kiss just below the elbow, then wrapped an arm around his. "Carry me."

"Carry you?"

"Carry me. If you really loved—"

Tanner swung around the chair, tucked one arm under Yana's legs and the other around her back, then scooped her into his arms. He bent his knees slightly in a mock bow, staring down at the woman who looked back up at him groggily, a smile on her lips. "At once, my queen."

"You're such an idiot," she said, laughing as she nuzzled into his chest.

"And you need to lay off those elven cakes." Tanner lurched forwards, dropping his arms and pretending to struggle before pulling Yana back up.

Yana slapped Tanner's arm, her expression turning sharp and serious. "Careful, boy."

Tanner just laughed, carrying her from the room and down the hall before laying her atop the bed they shared.

"Get some rest." Tanner placed a kiss on Yana's forehead as she pulled back the sheets and crawled into the bed. "I'll watch over her. Did you see where Aneera went?"

Yana nodded, her eyelids already drooping.

Tanner laughed to himself, then made his way back to Ella's room. Faenir had repositioned himself at the foot of Ella's bed. The wolfpine looked like a mound of fur coats, the bed frame straining under his weight.

Faenir lifted his head at the sound of Tanner's entry, promptly resetting it back atop his paws.

Tanner moved about the room, scratching Faenir on the neck, picking up Yana's half-empty mug of cold Arlen Root tea, and pulling the ruffled bed sheet up over Ella's collarbone.

He rested the back of his free hand against Ella's forehead, checking her temperature. She was far warmer than she should have been, but that was the way she had been from the first night.

The young woman's eyes moved back and forth behind her lids as though she were roaming through a whole other world in her mind.

He thought back to the night he and Yana had helped the woman escape from Berona, how she had barged into his office wearing nothing but a night dress covered in blood, a sword gripped in her fist and the wolfpine at her side. *It's not my blood.* Tanner shook his head, holding back a laugh. The situation had been anything but funny, but there were not many young women who would find themselves in that position and think so little of it. She was a fighter at her core, and Tanner understood completely how his nephew had been so madly in love with her.

Leaving Faenir to watch over Ella, Tanner brought Yana's empty mug back down the stairs, set another pot of water over the fire to boil, and cut himself a slice of bread with a wedge of cheese. With a second thought, he cut another slice of cheese for Faenir and slipped it into his pocket. That wolfpine loved cheese.

When the water had boiled, he poured it over the tea-soaked rags he'd left in the bucket, steam pluming upwards. He'd leave them to soak a while, then wash them out with some soap. Tanner refilled the pot and set it back over the fire, tossing in chunks of Arlen Root. Elia tended to chop the root into small pieces, but he had neither the inclination nor the energy.

He splashed some water on his face, then fetched a whetstone, a small jar of oil, and his sword from where it sat by the door. It was a routine he had grown accustomed to over the last week or so. He wasn't the kind of man who took easily to sitting in the same place for hours on end with nothing to do but twiddle his thumbs. So instead, he sharpened his sword and his knives, preparing for the inevitable moment he would once again need to use them. Of course, sharpening the same weapons day after day was as pointless as lips on a chicken. Which was why every sword within walking distance now had a blade sharp enough to cut leather like cheese.

Tanner ascended the stairs, pushing open the door to Ella's chambers with his shoulder. He had barely set a foot across the threshold when he realised he hadn't left it ajar.

A man stood by Ella's bed, grey-streaked hair falling short of his shoulders, brown robes tumbling to his ankles.

Tanner dropped the whetstone and oil, the jar smashing as it hit the floor. In the same motion he pulled his sword from his scabbard, turning so he stood across the doorway. "Step away from her."

The man raised a bony finger. "I would rather like not to kill you this time."

This time?

Tanner moved further into the room, never lowering his sword. Something about the man wasn't right. "I feel the same way. Step away from her, sit in that chair, and we can talk."

"My bones are sore anyway." The man dropped himself into the chair in which Tanner had spent many a night watching over Ella. It was only as he did that Tanner noticed Faenir still lying at the foot of Ella's bed. The wolfpine was awake, his eyes open. But he simply lay there, his chin resting on his paws, his gaze fixed on the man.

"What did you do to him?" Tanner tightened his grip on the sword's hilt, setting his feet. The man looked as though he had seen twice Tanner's summers, his skin wrinkled and pulling tight around his bones, but he sat straight and held his chin high, the smile on his face that of a much younger man.

"I simply told him to obey." The man crossed one leg over the other, resting his hands in his lap, his blue-grey eyes shifting from Tanner to Faenir. "Isn't that right?"

Faenir didn't move, but his pupils sharpened. Something else was happening here. Something of which Tanner had no understanding – which seemed to be a common occurrence of late.

"Who are you, and why are you here?" Tanner shifted his sword into his left hand, skirting the man in the chair and brushing his free hand through the coarse fur on Faenir's crown. The wolfpine didn't so much as flinch or grumble.

The man stared at Ella, his expression unshifting. "You may call me Amatkai. I am a… friend, come to check on our dear Ella – and also to wait on another friend, as fate may have it. Many friends for you. He should be here soon, though I wouldn't serve him that tea."

"Tea? You're mad." Tanner gestured towards the door with his sword. "Stand up. Get out. I've changed my mind. We can talk about why you're here outside."

Unperturbed, Amatkai tilted his head to the side and gave Tanner a toothy grin.

Tanner stumbled backwards a step at the sight of two long fangs protruding from both Amatkai's upper and lower jaws. The old man ran his tongue along one of the sharp teeth, his smile widening. He waved a hand, and Tanner howled in pain, his fingers peeling from the handle of his sword against his will, the bone in his pinky snapping as he tried to hold it in place.

"Apologies." The man opened his hands out. "I see a path where that was not necessary – but on this path it was. The finger will heal."

Amatkai rose from the chair, sweeping back his robes as he did.

Tanner lunged, aiming to smash the man to the floor. But before he could reach his target, his entire body froze, suspended in time as though caught in a web unseen. Panic slithered through him, his limbs refusing to respond to his commands.

Amatkai leaned over Ella and brushed a strand of hair from her face. "The paths we walk," he said absently, "they are ever winding, ever twisting, ever turning. It can often be so difficult to see which path is the one I need, which path is the one that leads to…" He tilted his head to the side, listening. "Ahhh, finally." He stood upright, and the invisible bonds holding Tanner dissipated.

Tanner crashed to the ground, pain burning in his finger.

Amatkai hunkered beside him, resting his elbows on his knees with the spryness of a teenager. "Don't worry, you live on all variations of this path. As does she, but she will have a headache. I tried to avoid this."

Tanner lifted his head to see Yana storming into the room, a knife gripped in each fist. She howled and launched herself at Amatkai. The man just flicked his wrist, and Yana flew across the room and crashed into the wall, steel clattering, her body twisting into a heap.

"Yana!" Tanner tried to haul himself up, but those same invisible bonds held him in place. He looked from Yana to Amatkai. "Release me! Now!"

Amatkai wagged a finger. "Sometimes it's like herding children. Stay down. This will all be over soon. I promise you, this was the only path without bloodshed."

Another voice sounded from the hallway, one Tanner didn't recognise. Deep and calm. "Why am I not surprised to find you here?"

"Because you're smarter than you look." Amatkai stood, leaving Tanner pinned to the floor by whatever magic the man possessed.

Tanner stared across the room at Yana. She grunted, her chest rising and falling slowly. He tried to twist so he could look at the newcomer's face, but it was as though a collar bound him in place.

"I brought your child home," Amatkai said. "She will be here shortly."

"Am I to thank you?" Irritation slipped into the stranger's voice.

"It would be a welcome change."

The stranger laughed, a harsh, insincere laugh. "Your blood killed three of mine to bring her here. Do you think me so blind I cannot see the work of your hand? You did not bring her here for me. You simply couldn't find the path to keep me from her."

"I did what I needed to do. Do you blame me?"

"You wouldn't have made these mistakes in past lives." A pair of dark leather boots came into Tanner's view, travel-worn, a mix of dry and wet dirt on the soles.

"I simply play the game differently than I used to."

"That is your problem. You've always seen this as a game."

"And your problem is that you have not." Amatkai's voice grew sharper, more deliberate. "You have never seen the pieces, never understood the board. Heart over mind."

"Loyalty over all."

More footsteps sounded. Tanner recognised these. He could hear claws clicking against the stone – Aneera and the other Angan. He continued to try and lift his head, to push himself from the floor, but the unseen bonds around him had not weakened in the slightest.

"What will it be then?" Amatkai asked. "Blood or patience?"

"You already know the answer, or you wouldn't be here," the stranger said, his boots marking the floor as he moved around Amatkai, closer to Ella. "Now remove your hold on the Blessed One, and leave before I change my mind."

Claws tapped against the stone, and Tanner could see three pairs of fur-covered feet moving through the room, low growls rumbling.

"Ah, a Blessed One… That explains it. I thought I was losing my touch. Of course."

Almost instantly, Faenir howled and lunged from where he sat on Ella's bed, his weight sending a vibration through the stone. The wolfpine's head dropped so low his chin scraped the ground, and Tanner could see his lips pull back, exposing vicious white teeth. The guttural sound that came from the wolfpine's throat set even Tanner's hairs on end. It was a thing of fury and death.

And yet, Faenir didn't attack. The wolfpine stayed low to the ground, snarling and snapping, but drew no closer to Amatkai.

"You've earned an enemy today," the stranger said, moving closer to Faenir.

"A fang in the light is easier to see than a fang in the dark." Amatkai walked towards the door. "That is something I'd hoped you'd learned by now. Your Fragment should be here shortly. Her blood is strong. But she is lucky Tamzin found her when she did. I would remind you of that. Our time is coming again. Thanks to my hand, the pieces in this game you so despise are coming together. If we walk the right path, the shadows will be our home no longer."

THE TOWERING TREES OF THE Darkwood loomed over Ella, white mist blowing as the wind swept through their branches. The woodland stretched into the distance on either side, no end in sight. Within its depths, Ella could feel the thumping of innumerable hearts, the beat almost deafening.

In the twilight of Níthianelle, the woodland didn't seem as ominous, and yet there was something in the air that set her off-kilter, a heaviness, a pain.

"What is that?" Ella stared into the woodland as she asked the question, her gaze searching its depths as though the answer lay just out of reach.

"This place is… it holds memories." Tamzin moved so she stood beside Ella. "There are creatures here older than the trees and rivers and rocks, creatures that exist both in this world and the mortal plane but belong in neither."

"The Aldithmar."

"I do not know that name, but if you have seen these creatures, you will know them. I have only ever encountered them in this world, never in the mortal plane." After a moment of silence, Tamzin spoke again. "This is as far as I take you."

Ella pulled her gaze from the woodland and stared at Tamzin. The woman's eyes were brown again, her pupils human. "What do you mean this as far as you take me? I have no idea what to do once I find my body." A flash of panic set into Ella. "I don't even know how to find my body. I don't know… I don't know anything. What's the point in bringing me this far and then leaving me?"

"It's not really a choice." Tamzin gestured towards five figures emerging from the woodland. Two took the shapes of enormous stags, white and gold smoke swirling around them as they moved, their antlers black as jet. Two more were the largest wolves Ella had ever seen – larger even than Faenir – golden eyes swirling and sparkling as though filled with the molten metal.

The last walked on two feet, its body covered in dark grey fur, its limbs moving in long, willowy sweeps.

"Aneera…" Relief filled every fibre of Ella's being, her legs shaking beneath her, chest fluttering. The Angan's face, her golden eyes. For the first time since finding herself in this place, Ella felt the tiniest sliver of safety brighten in the depths of her mind. She truly had made it back – *they* had made it back.

"I am not welcome here." Tamzin folded her arms, looking from the approaching Angan to Ella. "That was made clear while you were sleeping."

"While I was sleeping?"

"Amatkai will no longer be the one guiding you through the veil." The half-smile that touched Tamzin's lips was one born of frustration. "There is another now." Tamzin drew a heavy breath, then pulled Ella into a hug she wasn't expecting. "This will not be the last time we meet. I promise you that. Our kind are at the edge of a precipice, Ella. Fall, and we will become extinct. Fly, and we may yet be born anew." The woman stepped back and inclined her head. "It has been a pleasure, sister. I hope you are standing at our side when it comes time to fly."

Tamzin made to leave, but Ella grabbed her wrist. "I never thanked you for saving my life… for saving me."

"No, you didn't." Tamzin gave Ella a wry smile.

"Thank you. I would never have made it here without you."

"No," Tamzin said again. "You wouldn't. I will see you soon, Ella Bryer. Take care of yourself, and hold your keeper close. There are many hands at work here, many wars raging, many egos. And when it comes down to it, those who move the pieces on the board care little about whether you survive to see the new dawn. Remember that, and remember our journey. We are not enemies, I swear this to you."

Tamzin turned and set off in the direction they had come. Ella watched her for a moment, then turned back to the approaching Angan. As the creatures reached her, the two stags, whom she knew to be Angan of the Clan Dvalin, circled around her while Aneera and the other Fenryr Angan stopped before her.

"Daughter of the Chainbreaker." Aneera dropped to one knee, turning her gaze downward. "We never ceased searching."

The two enormous wolves moved one paw forward and bowed their heads.

"Aneera." Ella lifted Aneera from her kneeling position and wrapped her arms around the Angan, unable to keep her hands from trembling. It was all Ella could do to stop her knees from buckling and the tears from flowing. She hadn't known Aneera long, but there was a part of her that had believed she would never make it back, that she would wander Níthianelle until her body withered and her soul was left to wander the Sea of Spirits. That she would become a wraith.

The Angan staggered back a step, caught off guard. But after a moment, Aneera returned Ella's embrace. "It lightens my heart to see your soul safe."

Ella pulled steadying breaths into her lungs as she released Aneera. "I would very much like to return to my body now."

"Of course. He waits for you. Please follow us."

THE JOURNEY THROUGH THE DARKWOOD was the longest walk of Ella's life. Where earlier she had felt relief at the sight of Aneera, doubt had crept in with each step. What if it didn't work? What if she couldn't 'retether' herself? What if this was it – this was the end?

She pushed the thoughts down, instead focusing on the world around her. It wasn't a hard thing to do. In this world, the Darkwood was a living, breathing thing. It was almost overwhelming. A thousand scents clung to the air, and a wall of sound washed over her: heartbeats, rustling leaves, snapping branches, flapping wings. She did as Tamzin had been teaching her, honing in on her own racing heart, her own breaths, so as to filter out the chaos around her.

Slowly, she let more in, allowing the thumping hearts of the five Angan around her to hammer in her ears, allowing their scents to flow through her.

The exercise calmed her. That was, until she felt something else in the air, something that raised her hackles, something that caused the wolf to rise in her blood.

She stopped in her tracks, the Angan following suit. No more than twenty feet to her right, a number of tall figures had taken shape. They weren't the seven-foot monstrosities wrought from shattered bark that Ella knew as the Aldithmar from the battle, but it *was* them; she could feel it. They looked almost human, their eyes sharper, more angled, with pupils of vibrant orange. Their skin was a pale grey, ridges of bone adorning their brows and cheeks, flowing backwards into something that looked part hair, part horns. Their hands held only four fingers, long and slender, with pointed claws at the end. Black smoke shrouded them, drifting in all directions. The Aldithmar had no heartbeats, no smell. They were both hollow and yet full of pain and suffering. It wasn't the look on their alien faces or something in their eyes that told her this, it was something more visceral, something more primal. These creatures weren't just in pain, they *were* pain.

"They will not approach," Aneera said, following Ella's gaze.

"What are they?"

At Ella's question, one of the Dvalin Angan burst into a spiralling cloud of smoke, tendrils twisting around each other, and reshaped into its more human form, hooved feet pressing into the soft earth. She bowed her head, as though greeting Ella for the first time. "They have existed in this form since long before your people, and ours, reached these shores. The story of their own telling is that they were once a race of people that inhabited these lands before even the Blodvar of old, when the elves and Jotnar crossed blades on dragonback. A great catastrophe struck their people, one of which they will not speak. They are bound to this place, bound between worlds, unable to rest, unable to live, unable to die. Millenia ago, Blessed Dvalin struck a deal with their kind. We would protect this woodland, their home, and in turn they would grant us refuge from those who hunted us. Many of our Gifted perished before the oath could be made, but today more Dvalin Angan survive than any other clan. We owe them much."

"Why would they grant you such a deal?" Ella could still feel the wolf prowling in the back of her mind, wary under the Aldithmars' gaze.

"It is postulated amongst my clan that if Aravell is destroyed, the 'Aldithmar', as you call them, will be severed from both this world and the mortal plane, left to drift in the void. Given how fiercely they protect the land, I believe this to be true, for I cannot see another consequence."

"Daughter of the Chainbreaker," Aneera said before Ella could respond, "we must keep moving. Time is always of the essence when a mind has been fragmented."

"You've seen this before?"

The Angan nodded.

"Many times?"

"Yes."

"How often do they survive?" The question was one that had floated in Ella's mind for quite a while, but until then she had refused to put it into words.

Aneera stared back at her for a moment, then spoke. "Time is of the essence."

CHAPTER FORTY-ONE

CALL OF THE WOLF

15th Day of the Blood Moon

Nithianelle – Winter, Year 3081 After Doom

Ella's heart beat so wildly she thought it would come through her chest. With each step she took, the thumping in her veins grew louder. Around her, the city of Aravell was cold and empty, the ethereal light of Nithianelle draining it of all vibrancy or life.

Thousands of small heartbeats thrummed, birds soaring overhead, mice scurrying in the depths, all manner of creatures moving through the woodland around the city. And yet, not a single human or elf. That was something she had noticed in her time in Nithianelle: she could feel and see the souls of animals, but not of elves or Jotnar or humans. When she thought back, the same had been true of when she had travelled there in the Lorian camp and during the battle for Aravell.

A thought came to her, and she stopped in her tracks, staring up at a white tower that rose for a hundred feet, topping off in a plateau.

Aneera and the other Angan stopped beside her.

"What is wrong, Daughter of the Chainbreaker?" Aneera looked from Ella to the tower.

"That tower was destroyed during the battle, but here it stands. How?"

"Nithianelle is a mirror of the mortal plane," Aneera said, looking up at the tower. "But the reflections take time and do not always behave in the way you would expect."

Ella thought back to when she had been walking through the Darkwood itself. She had seen no trace of dragonfire, no burnt trees or charred earth. This place seemed governed by no rules she could understand, and it terrified her.

"We are almost there," Aneera said.

The Angan led her across the bridge between the city and the place the others had called Alura. The lanterns set along the parapets burned with a pale light, the waterfalls pouring over the cliff edges on either side and crashing into the enormous chasm below.

Two more Fenryr Angan stood on the white plateau at the other end of the bridge where it sloped downwards, the pathway of arching trees behind them. The creatures dropped to one knee, grey and white smoke wisping from their bodies. They, too, joined the procession, and the group carried on through the pathway of trees and again through the arch cut into the rock at the end of the path.

She stepped out into the enormous basin of Alura. Even in Níthianelle, with the strange twilight draining most of the colour from the world, Alura took her breath away, just as it had the first time. Beautiful structures of white stone, smooth as bone, woven through the rock face as though part of it, pathways of grass connecting building to building. Below, she saw the courtyard where she had discovered that Farda had killed her mam. It felt strange to her for that to be how she remembered this place, but it was. That spot would forever be engrained in her memory.

"This way." Aneera gestured towards a path on the left, bowing slightly at the waist.

More Angan awaited them on the path, all of them of Clan Dvalin, their fur white as snow, black antlers wrapping around their heads. They each bowed in turn, then joined, forming a guard of sorts.

Ella wasn't sure the precise moment she became aware of it, but a strange sensation prickled at the back of her neck. The same feeling spread down through her body, creeping over her arms and legs. Her lips went dry, and her breaths grew short.

At the end of the path was a plateau with eight of the white stone buildings sitting atop it. By the time they reached the plateau, her hands were shaking, a ringing noise had set into her head, and she had become acutely aware of the beats of her heart. Her true heart.

"In there," she said, gesturing towards one of the white buildings set with its back to the rock face. It called to her, the air shimmering and rippling around it, and as she focused her gaze, the sounds of the world drowned out and her beating heart was all she could hear. That place was her counterpoint in the waking world; she was sure of it. Inside that building was her one and only chance of returning to Calen, Haem, and Faenir.

"Yes," Aneera answered. "We are almost there, Daughter of the Chainbreaker."

Drawing in a short breath, Ella turned her head to Aneera. "Why do you call me that? 'Daughter of the Chainbreaker'? What is that? You and Baldon both called me that from the moment I arrived in Aravell."

Aneera's expression softened at the mention of Baldon. "It is not my place to tell, but you will learn the answer very shortly."

Ella followed the path to the plateau and crossed it until she stood before the door of the house, her pulse clapping like thunder in her veins.

Aneera followed her through the door, but the others remained outside. The common room was plain, a fire and cookpot set into the far wall, an island counter in the centre, and a long table to the right. It would have been as calm and simple as the homes back in The Glade if not for the eerie silence and the strange shimmer of the light that passed through the windows.

Aneera led her up the stairs to a long landing, where two more Fenryr Angan stood on either side of a door at the end of the hallway. Both stood half a foot taller than even Aneera, the crowns of their heads almost scraping the ceiling. Their shoulders were just short of rivalling Haem's, and the thick fur on their bodies covered dense muscle.

Both Angan stared at Ella, golden eyes peering through a shroud of smoke that drifted around their ethereal shapes. The pair dropped to a knee, their gazes never leaving hers.

"Daughter of the Chainbreaker." The voices that left the Angans' throats were rough and harsh. When Ella had first heard Aneera and Baldon speak, she had thought their voices the strangest things in the world, but these Angan spoke as though the Common Tongue had never touched their lips.

Aneera stared into Ella's eyes, flecks of gold swirling in her irises. "You are a Blooddancer of the warrior blood of Fenryr, Ella Bryer. Do not fear. You are strong. And he will never leave you. Not while there is air in his lungs. To the blood of Fenryr, loyalty is all."

"Thank you for taking me this far, Aneera." She gripped Aneera's forearm, much to the Angan's surprise. "I'll see you on the other side."

Ella stepped past the two Angan who still knelt by the door, their heads now dipped. The doorknob was cold to the touch, a chill spreading from her fingertips up through her arm and into her body. Once more she became aware of how loud her heart was beating, its thumps pounding in her blood. She could hear the air swelling in her lungs with each breath.

Swallowing hard, Ella turned the knob and stepped through.

Darkness washed over her. The world on the other side of the door was an ocean of emptiness without end.

She snapped back around. The door was gone.

Panic set in.

"No, no, no..." Ella spun, searching the darkness for something, anything. Her breaths trembled as she tried to settle the dread crawling through her veins. "Breathe..." she whispered, pulling a long breath through her nose. "Breathe."

"You are never alone." Freis Bryer's voice drifted in the nothingness. "Open your eyes, Ella. Open your mind and trust in the blood."

The wolf growled in the back of Ella's mind, an answer to Freis's call.

"Mam? Is that you?" Ella clenched her jaw, her eyes watering. "Am I just losing my mind? Please tell me I'm not losing my mind."

"Trust in the blood, Ella. Let it guide you."

"Mam, please..." Ella looked about frantically, staring into the abyss.

"Let it guide you, Ella. I'm sorry I kept you from it. I was wrong. We were wrong. We only wanted to keep you safe."

Ella closed her eyes and clenched her jaw.

I need you. Oh, Mam. I need you.

In the darkness of her mind, two amber eyes opened, white fangs materialising.

The wolf lowered its head, lips pulled back in a snarl, a low rumble in its throat, its enormous frame taking shape in the dark. A howl thundered through the caverns of Ella's mind, her eyes never leaving the wolf's.

The creature stalked her, circling, one massive paw following the other. Its back was arched, its hackles raised, saliva dripping from its fangs.

"This is who you are," a voice called, sounding all around her. No longer her mother's voice, this one was much deeper and resolute. She had never heard it before, and yet she knew it intimately. "To retether yourself, you must embrace the blood in your veins. You must become more than you were. You conquer the wolf by becoming it. You kill the fear by letting it in. You find your path by allowing nothing to stand in your way."

As the voice spoke, the growl in the wolf's throat deepened, lowering to its chest.

"Become what you are meant to be, young one."

Ella bent her knees and opened her hands, watching her fingers twist and crack, lengthening as her nails yielded to dark claws. In her mouth, her teeth shifted, fangs pressing into her lips, the iron tinge of blood on her tongue.

She matched the wolf stride for stride, her heartbeat slowing.

Thump. Thump.

In the reflection of the wolf's molten eyes, she saw her pain, her loss, her anger, and her fear. The night she found out Haem would never come back. The day she watched Rhett die. The moment she realised her mam and dad were dead and what was left of her heart had cracked. The instant she discovered Farda had killed her mam… Each of those moments had changed something in her, broken her, and rebuilt her.

You conquer the wolf by becoming it.

A growl built in Ella's chest and rose to her throat as she continued to circle the wolf, never allowing its gaze to leave her own, staring into those memories.

You kill the fear by letting it in.

Those memories cycled through Ella's mind. Again and again, she forced herself to relive them. They were part of her.

You find your path by allowing nothing to stand in your way.

The reflections in the wolf's eyes changed as it pulled its lips back, snapping. Ella could see herself lying in a bed, arms by her side, motionless.

Without a moment's more hesitation, she charged.

The wolf launched itself through the air, swiping for Ella's head with an enormous claw.

Ella twisted, raking her claws along the ground and swinging her free hand at the creature's side. She found flesh, soft and yielding.

The wolf howled, blood dripping from a fresh wound, and then it came at her once more, jaws snapping. She tried to sidestep it, but the creature caught her with a paw and the pair tumbled to the ground.

Ella thrashed, ramming her claws into the wolf's side again and again, its weight crushing her. It clamped massive jaws around her shoulder and ripped its head side to side.

White hot pain caused her to shriek, warm blood pumping. The shriek turned to a howl, and she sank her teeth into the wolf's neck, biting down as hard as she could, fangs tearing through skin and muscle, scraping against bone. She had lost all feeling in her left arm but continued to plunge the claws of her right into the beast's side while blood filled her mouth. Strike after strike, flesh yielded to claw. And with each strike the wolf continued to rip her shoulder to pieces.

Ella released her bite on the wolf's neck, grabbed ahold of its shoulder, and tensed her core, lifting her knees. She raked her clawed feet down the beast's belly, then swung her leg to the side and kicked like a demon.

The wolf released her, howling in pain and collapsing on its side as Ella's clawed foot slipped from the wound in its belly.

She hauled herself up to one knee, her left arm dangling at her side. The flesh was torn to ribbons, snapped bone protruding, blood flowing freely. The agony was so intense her lungs struggled to take in a breath and she staggered sideways as she tried to rise, pain redoubling.

The wolf dragged itself to its feet, white blood streaming from its neck, side, and belly. In its golden eyes, the only reflection Ella saw was herself.

"Come on then!" she roared, her throat scratching, eyes watering. "Kill me!"

A half-second passed, and the wolf lunged.

Ella didn't run or twist or dive out of the way. She charged forwards, unleashed a guttural howl, and swung her clawed hand into the creature's jaw. White blood sprayed, the wolf's momentum carrying it forwards and smashing Ella into the ground. The pain from her shoulder was blinding, lights flashing across her eyes and her stomach turning. She ignored it all and slashed at the wolf atop her, chunks of fur and flesh coming loose in her hand. She rolled, pushing the beast off her, then leaping on top of it.

The creature stared up at her from its back, eyelids drooping lazily over golden irises. The sound in its throat alternated between a whimper and growl, its fangs bared.

Ella looked down at the enormous creature, her pain numbing, her consciousness fading. And in that moment, she let out a visceral howl, tilting her head upwards, trails of white blood running down her chin.

The wolf in her blood answered her howl, and the familiar red mist descended over her vision.

Ella shot upright, shaking and screaming. She scrambled backwards, her vision blurred, a howl shrieking in her head.

Dull voices rumbled in the back of her mind.

Something reached for her, and she swiped it away, feeling something hard against her back. She snapped and snarled like a trapped animal, feeling her fangs lengthening, the wolf alive in her blood like never before.

Slowly her vision began to clear, blocky forms taking shape, light seeping in.

"Ella, it's all right." The voice was still muffled but sounded familiar.

Another hand, or claw, or something, snatched at her.

"Get away from me!" she roared, her throat dry as sand, her own voice sounding foreign, strange. Her hands shook uncontrollably, and her stomach felt as though it would turn itself inside out. "Don't touch me!"

A feeling of pure joy hit her like a rampaging bull, and then a weight crashed into her chest, pushing past her arms and bearing down over her. Thick fur pressed against her fingers and palms, a wet tongue lashing her face. Sharp whimpers and whines sounded in her ear.

"Faenir?" Ella's heart stopped. She moved her hands, feeling the shape of the wolfpine's snout, her fingertips brushing over his wet nose as he tried desperately to lick the soul from her body. Her vision was still blurred, but she snapped her eyes shut and wrapped her arms around Faenir's neck, squeezing him as tightly as she dared.

The wolfpine nuzzled into her, continuing to whine as he pressed the flat of his head into her neck. Sweet relief and pure joy radiated from him, and the massive wolfpine wiggled his hips like a newborn pup.

"I'm here, boy," Ella whispered, pressing her face into Faenir's muzzle. "I'm here."

"Ella."

The voice was Tanner Fjorn's. Ella recognised it now, the howl fading from her ears. She peeled open her eyes, the light in the room causing her to wince. Shapes formed around her, dark blotches blocking out the light. "Tanner?"

"By the gods, girl..." His voice trembled with a worry that sounded strange on his tongue. His scent was the same: all fear and concern. "We weren't sure if you'd ever come back to us."

A hand settled on Ella's arm, a second brushing her cheek. Ella recognised Yana's voice before the woman's face came into focus, her dark eyes staring into Ella's. "You took your time."

Ella's lips broke into a smile, and she rested her hand over Yana's, pressing it to her cheek. "Just trying to teach you patience," she said, coughing, her throat dry as cotton. "I thought you'd like the peace and quiet."

"You're a piece of work," Yana said with a laugh.

"Is there any water?" Ella pushed herself back, looking down to see she sat in a bed. Faenir still pressed himself to her, letting out low whimpers, his snout now nuzzled beneath her left arm – which she was happy to see was still attached. She swallowed hard, trying to get some spit into her mouth. "I feel like I've been drinking sand."

"Here." The third voice belonged to a face Ella was overjoyed to see: Lasch Havel. She'd only briefly crossed paths with him and Elia before the battle for the city, but seeing faces from home set a warmth in her. Lasch popped the stopper from a waterskin and handed it to Ella. "Elia's brewing a new batch of tea. She'll be up in a minute."

Ella gave him a soft smile, nodding her thanks, then took the skin and drank deeply. She coughed and spluttered, the water spraying over her lips and onto Faenir's head. The wolfpine jerked back with a yelp, then licked the moisture from his muzzle and lay down across Ella, dropping his chin over the blanket covering her knees.

"Drink slow, child. You found your path, but your body has been idle for some time."

Every hair on Ella's body pricked, her breath catching in her lungs. The wolf within her bowed its head, and she felt a compulsion to do the same. Faenir flattened his chin against his paws, his eyes fixed on the corner of the room.

Both Tanner and Lasch stepped aside as a man rose from a stout wooden chair beside the wall. Aneera and another Fenryr Angan walked at his side.

The man was almost as tall as Tanner but leaner and less densely muscled. His hair was golden with flecks of black and brown, a thick beard covering his face.

Instinctively, Ella made to rise, but the man lifted an open hand. "No." His voice was deep and calm, his eyes fixed on her. "You must rest, child."

Yana stood as the man approached. When he reached the bed, he dropped to one knee and rested a hand on Faenir's head. "You did well, as I knew you would. Thank you for keeping her safe."

The wolfpine gave a low grumble and nuzzled his head up into the man's palm, closing his eyes.

With his other hand, the man reached across and gently gripped Ella's forearm. She wasn't sure why she didn't pull away. She didn't know him, but something within her told her she was safe.

"Decades ago, your father risked everything for me, for my children. It is a debt that cannot be repaid. You are also of your mother's blood, of *my* blood, and so you are pack. It is a pleasure to finally meet you, Ella Bryer."

"You..." Ella's voice trailed off as she stared into the man's swirling golden eyes. She knew him now, knew him in his entirety. "You are Fenryr."

"I am. And you are Ella Bryer, daughter of Vars and Freis Bryer. Daughter of the Chainbreaker and born of the oldest sept of my blood. And I swear to you, neither you nor your brothers will be alone in what is to come."

Ella had no idea what to say, but every impulse in her body told her she could trust this man... this god.

As she met Fenryr's stare, the door behind him swung open and Elia Havel half-walked, half-ran into the room, carrying a tray with a teapot and a number of mugs. The smile on her face stretched from one ear to the other, her eyes wide. "Ella Bryer. Every day I prayed Heraya would keep you safe."

"Heraya did nothing," Fenryr whispered, a sharp tooth biting at his bottom lip. "She only watches as we die."

Elia didn't hear him. She pushed Tanner and Lasch aside and laid the tray on a small table by Ella's bed. Ella could already smell the earthy aroma of Arlen Root tea. In fact, she had smelled it from the moment she'd woken, but it had sat in the back of her mind, muddled by the haze.

"Here." Elia poured the tea into a clay mug and made to pass it to Ella before Fenryr placed his hand in the way.

The man – no, the god – raised a finger and gave Elia a gentle smile. "May I?"

Elia stared at him curiously for a moment, then handed him the mug, her eyes remaining narrowed. Despite Fenryr's pleasant demeanour, the atmosphere in the room darkened. Both Lasch and Tanner moved a little closer, Aneera and the other Angan taking a position behind the still-kneeling Fenryr.

Fenryr held the mug in one hand, his palm on the base, his fingers snaking up the sides. He stared down into the murky liquid. "Do you know the history of Arlen Root, Ella Bryer?"

"The history? It's the root of the Arlen Odus, a flowering perennial with dull orange petals and long leaves. It's native to western Illyanara. My mother used to pick it fresh all the time."

Fenryr gave a soft laugh. The smile that touched his face was one of pain. Ella could... *smell* him. He smelled of anguish, and the wolf in her blood mirrored that same grief. "The Arlen Odus plant is native to Terroncia. We'd thought we'd burned every shred of it we could find. Thought we'd left it behind us when we sailed to these lands. We were wrong."

"I don't understand."

"This plant, this root, is poison. It is the reason my children, my people... *our* people are on the edge of extinction. We were betrayed three thousand years ago when some of our own smuggled it onto the ships. They thought to use it to gain power in this new land. But all it brought them was death. When ingested, Arlen Root poisons the blood of the Tuatha – the children of gods, the Gifted. It blocks your Gifts, making you weaker and dulling your senses. It is how the Ungifted – the Itharín – controlled your kind, how they kept them sedate and corralled them like cattle for the slaughter. They put it in the food where the taste could be hidden, then put you in chains. This root was the slow death of tens of thousands."

"But my mam... she—"

"She made her choices. She did what she needed to do to protect her pack."

"She was a druid?"

Fenryr nodded slowly. He stood, taking a seat on the edge of the bed, Faenir shifting without complaint. "When you are recovered, I will answer any and all questions you have. I will show you the paths once walked. For now, I will tell you that your mother was of the Pathfinder blood of my veins. She was, as you are, a descendant of one of the oldest and greatest septs to bear my name – Sept Eridain. By the time of her father's father, the imperials were using collared Tuatha to hunt and track their own kind. Freis made a choice to use the root against them – and against my counsel. She used it to block her Gifts, and yours after you were born, so the trackers could not follow the scent of the wolf in your blood."

Fenryr extended the mug towards Ella. That same earthy scent that only moments before had reminded her of home now turned her stomach. All these years, her mother had poured that tea down her throat, had fed her poison – had lied to her.

"But now," Fenryr said, twisting on the edge of the bed so that he could look into her eyes, "I feel it is only right that you know the truth and that you are given the opportunity to make your own choice. The landscape of this continent is shifting, and I think we've spent enough time in the dark. Gods are not all knowing, or all seeing, or all powerful – not even the Enkara. Decades ago, your father risked his life for mine many times over. He had no cause to do so. He was not aware of his blood, and he had nothing tangible to gain. He freed me from the chains my complacency had bound me in. And I will be complacent no more. What say you, Wolfchild?"

Ella stared back at Fenryr, into the golden eyes of a god. Taking a breath in through her nose, she took the mug from Fenryr, allowing the deep earthy smell to fill her nostrils. The wolf within her stood on all fours, a rage swelling. That same red mist that had once blinded her now wrapped around her like a blanket. It warmed her and filled the cracks in her brokenness. Her fingers closed around the mug, nails darkening and extending to claws. She closed her grip, and the mug shattered in her hand, tea spilling over the floor, shards of clay bouncing on the stone.

"Gods. What a mess." Elia Havel looked completely flustered, her gaze darting around the pieces of broken mug on the floor, her hands moving frantically. "Let me get that for you."

Lasch rested his hands on her shoulders and shook his head gently, then pulled her closer.

Ella stared at the remnants of the mug, her hand in a tight fist, blood trickling through the seams, deep and crimson.

CHAPTER FORTY-TWO

A CITY ONCE LOST

17th Day of the Blood Moon

The Argonan Marshes – Winter, Year 3081 After Doom

Calen had heard tales of the Argonan Marshes, of how thousands of corpses lay beneath the water's surface from after The Fall, how dragon bones jutted from its depths and ghosts and demons prowled the vast expanse of sodden earth.

Now that he stood there, staring out at the fog-blanketed wetland with his own eyes, he couldn't say he saw anything of the sort. The place held that same sense of otherworldliness as Ölm Forest and had the same ability to make his skin crawl. But that likely had more to do with the old stories roaming in the back of his mind than with the place itself.

The marshes were unnaturally quiet, which meant that every tiny sound that broke the stillness was as sharp as a blade. The occasional bird call rang out, echoing endlessly, but it was the splashing that kept Calen from his sleep. Every time he got close to his dreams, a splash would sound somewhere around him and jolt him awake. Awake to the vast emptiness, the quiet, the dark.

Which was why he now stood with his hands behind his back and his breath misting into the air as he stared into the night.

Much like the dunes of the Burnt Lands, the marshes seemed to stretch into eternity. Sodden strips of earth, laden with dense, squelching vegetation, traced through the wetlands like lengths of dropped string. Tufts of grass that rose as high as Calen's chin rustled gently in the wind. The light of the moon tinted thick layers of fog in a deep red as they drifted over the thousands of pools of murky marsh water pockmarked into the land.

He'd not particularly liked the idea of spending the night in the marshes. But they were to fly for Ilnaen the next morning, and the marshes were the safest place to rest with just the two of them. The only sign of life Valerys had spotted for miles were small rats, rabbits, snakes, and birds. The dragon had seen some deer with strange backwards antlers near a larger patch of earth a few miles back, but for the most part, the marsh's occupants would leave Calen and Valerys alone as long as they did the same.

Calen drew a cold breath of air through his nostrils, closing his eyes and leaning his head back. He let the breath out slowly.

Alone.

The word had once terrified him. But at that moment it gave him peace.

This was the first time he and Valerys had been truly alone in months. The marshes stretched for hundreds of miles, and not a single soul within its bounds wanted anything from them. They were not being pulled in all directions, not being told how and when to act, not having people look at them like they were some saviours or heroes of old.

Calen dreamt of climbing onto Valerys's back and flying away. Just leaving. They could rest in the Varsundi mountains, fly south to Narvona, where the cities were built from marble and gold, or to Ardan, where the land stretched endlessly to the horizon. He allowed himself a few moments of that dream before setting it on fire.

Calen opened his eyes without lowering his head. The stars shone bright above, that same pink hue tarnishing their light. He turned his gaze to the source of the poisoning glow.

The Blood Moon was at its fullest. It waxed and waned like any moon, or so he had been told. Though the Order had fallen on the twenty-eighth day of the last Blood Moon, which told Calen that the waxing and waning meant little.

Sheltered within the walls of Aravell, his only experience with the Blood Moon's effects had been during battle for the city and in scouring the remnants of the Lorian forces afterwards. The Uraks that had set upon them in the woodland had been different creatures to the ones Calen knew. Stronger, more vicious – if that could even be possible. But still, from the reports he'd heard, the moon's effects on the rest of the continent were far greater. Entire cities were gone, razed to the ground, tens of thousands, hundreds of thousands of souls snuffed out.

And all the while, he and Valerys had just sat in Aravell, licking their wounds, twisting words with the elves. The thought was infuriating. At least now they were doing something. At least now they could make a difference. First, they would see what awaited them in Ilnaen. Then, they would do as asked and win Aryana and Tukul Unger's oaths. After that, they would go and protect their home.

As the word 'home' lingered in Calen's mind, Valerys alighted behind him, the damp ground absorbing the shock of his landing.

The dragon dropped the body of a half-eaten deer into the grass, blood painting his scales and dripping from his maw.

"Home," Calen whispered as he approached Valerys, who nudged the deer carcass before ripping a leg free with a snap of tendon and bone.

The dragon eyed Calen sideways and nuzzled into his outstretched palm, continuing to crunch on his meal. Images of The Glade passed from Calen to Valerys, images of the home Calen had grown up in, of The Gilded Dragon, of Vars's forge, of the Moon Market.

The smile that graced Calen's lips vanished as quickly as it had appeared. That home was gone. Burned to ash and dust by the same Uraks that now laid waste to the continent.

Up until learning the truth from Haem, he had at least been able to believe that no matter what, no matter where he travelled or what things he'd seen, he could always go home. His parents might not be there to greet him, but his home would always be his home. That fact had been immutable, except it was not.

The Glade was gone. His parents were dead, Rist likely with them. And now Ella lay unconscious on a bed in Aravell, and Calen had absolutely no idea if she'd ever wake. It felt as though the threads that tethered him to the world were slowly coming loose. Dann, Haem, Elia, Lasch, and Faenir – and he supposed Therin, in a way – were all that remained from the life he'd left behind.

Valerys stopped chewing and let out a warm breath of air that smelled of ash and fresh blood. He nudged his cheek into Calen's shoulder, a low rumble in his throat.

Warmth flooded across the bond, allowing Calen a soft sigh as the cold fled his fingers and toes. But with the warmth came faces that drifted through Calen's mind: Jorvill Ehrnin, Ferrin Kolm, Aela and Erdhardt, Tharn and Ylinda… Anya Gritten.

Even without words, it was clear to him what Valerys was trying to say: the home may be gone – the wood, and the stone, and the glass – but the people remained.

He remembered his mother's words when he'd asked her why she'd never wanted to go home. Home in her case had been a village somewhere in southern Illyanara. Karikloan, she'd once told him it was called. Calen had never been there; he'd barely left The Glade before meeting Erik and the others.

"Home isn't a place, it's a feeling," she'd said. *"Home is knowing you're safe and loved. Home is knowing that you are where you need to be. My home is here with you,"* she'd said, brushing his cheek with her thumb. *"With you and Haem and Ella and your dad. Home is where your heart goes when you let it wander."*

Calen sighed softly, resting his forehead against Valerys's scales, the warmth bringing relief from the frigid air. A pressure built behind his eyes, and his throat grew tight. He would never hear his mother's voice again, never get the chance to tell her how much comfort all those words of wisdom had given him.

The sorrow turned to anger at the thought of Farda walking free in the Eyrie. At the thought of the man who'd murdered his mother still drawing breath while she lay in Heraya's embrace.

He butted his head against Valerys's side, running his hands over the small horns that jutted from the dragon's forelimb. Those thoughts led to dark places.

After Valerys had consumed every shred of muscle, bone, and cartilage, Calen laid out his blanketroll at the dragon's side and stared up as Valerys closed his wings around him.

That night he dreamt vivid dreams. The dreams that felt real. If Ella did wake up – no, *when* Ella woke up, he would ask her if she dreamt those same dreams. He would sit down and talk to his sister until the sun set and rose again and set once more. He would never again take the sound of her voice for granted.

The next day, Calen and Valerys flew for hundreds of miles without a break, clearing the marshlands and leaving the thick fog and eerie silence behind.

They stayed high, soaring between the clouds and blending with the sky so that nothing below could mark their flight. But through the dragon's eyes, they could see the comings and goings of the land from above. Caravans of people journeyed eastward, towards the marshes and the coastal cities. No doubt they were coming from Argona. Calen had never laid eyes on Illyanara's capital, and now he never would. He'd heard it had been enormous, that The Glade itself would have fit inside its walls a hundred times over – a thousand, even, if the bards and travelling merchants were to be believed. Though, now that Calen had seen more of the world, he understood that all stories were both exaggerated and diminished.

Apart from the weary travellers trudging along the roads, large groups moved about bearing all sorts of colours, sigils, and banners. Some numbered no more than fifty, while others were in their hundreds. It was precisely as Therin had said. As the empire's hold on Illyanara faltered, others were beginning to grab at any shred of power they could find.

In the death of an animal, nature went to war over the rotting carcass. Wolves, foxes, kats, wolfpines, bears, even the birds and insects, all called by blood. This felt much the same to Calen. The lion was wounded and bleeding, and so the factions circled, too scared to face it while it limped and died, but ready to tear it to pieces once it hit the ground. What would happen if they finally brought the empire to its knees? What came after? Would this war simply lead to more war?

The thought had plagued Calen's mind on more than a few nights. He'd not admit it to Aeson or Chora, but that was why he understood the need to bring the factions in Illyanara behind him. The more structure they had in place before, the less chaos would follow after.

He pondered those thoughts as the Darkwood passed below. The fires had stopped now, no more black smoke billowing into the air. The path the Dragonguard had burned through the woodland was like a scorched wound in the forest's flesh, carving through the wood from its very edge to the southern gates of Aravell. More blackened patches were scattered about the main path as a result of the fighting and the dragonfire.

It was strange to see the city of Aravell from so far above and without the glamour to keep it hidden. The basin within which the city sat was enormous, the valleys around it sharp and deep, the rock rising high to meet the walls. It didn't look like a creation made of mortal hands, more like something akin to the brushstrokes of a god. If he squinted, every bridge, tower, and sweeping platform blended seamlessly with the nature around it.

Calen dared not fly too close, lest he be tempted to stop. He hated leaving Ella there alone, particularly as vulnerable as she was. Though 'alone' was unfair to those who watched over her. She wasn't alone. He just hated not being there.

After a while, dark storm clouds rolled in, and the rain fell in sheets, followed by rolling thunder. Valerys brought them higher, angling upwards with such force that Calen grabbed the ridge of a scale at the base of the dragon's neck, leaning forwards and pressing himself down. He pulled their minds together and lost himself in the bond.

The higher they rose, the more vicious the cold became, biting and slashing, but the warmth of their blood held it at bay. A blinding light filled their vision as they broke through the head of clouds, the sky above clear and blue. This place, this open sky, the wind washing over them, this was where happiness was found, and both Calen and Valerys could have soared for hours without a thought or a care.

But eventually the dark clouds faded, and the trees of the Darkwood yielded to cracked earth and rocky hills.

They dove, folding their wings tight against their side. The wind crashed over them, rolling across scales and skin. An untethered wildness flared in their blood at the sensation of freefall. It was the purest feeling in the world. To completely let go, to have absolutely no control of the world around you and yet to hold no fear in your heart.

They opened their wings to their fullest a few hundred feet from the ground, curving forward with such speed the force of the world dragged against them.

Calen pulled his mind back as they approached the edge of the Burnt Lands. The knights had told him the barrier around the waste was dead and gone, but still trepidation crept into his heart with each beat of Valerys's wings. He would know as soon as they crossed the threshold.

Below, the brittle earth and dried rivers faded into sand, the dunes stretching on, and on, and on. With the sun dipping low, capitulating to the crimson moon, and the wind whipping the sand into the air, a warm orange-red light sparkled across the dunes. Despite himself, the scene took Calen's breath from his lungs.

Staring out at the landscape, he couldn't help but think of the words Falmin had spoken in the tunnels below Lodhar. *"There is nothing more important in the darkness than a ray of light."*

In that moment, those words struck a chord within Calen. The Burnt Lands had seen more death and horror and abject darkness than any place on the continent. The Blood Moon was the harbinger of Efialtír himself, a portent of unspeakable slaughter and bloodshed. And yet, amidst the blending of these two dark things, a moment of unparalleled beauty could be found.

Falmin would have appreciated the view.

Reluctantly, Calen closed his eyes. Ilnaen lay northwest, and in the endless desert, to become lost was an easy thing. But he knew that would not be his fate. He waited patiently, seeing through Valerys's eyes as the dragon soared, the night slowly encroaching, shadows creeping over the mountains in the distance.

And then, in the quiet moment, he heard it.

Thump.

That same pulse he'd felt when he'd first entered the wastes called to him once more. It thrummed in his bones and rang in his mind.

Thump.

Just as he had then, he knew what it was that called to him now.

The beating heart of Ilnaen.

He'd spent many a dream wandering the burning streets, watching as dragons fell from the sky and crashed through buildings of white stone. He'd stood and watched as rivers of blood flowed through the grooves of paved streets and listened in horror at the screams of the thousands who burned alive. That same heartbeat, that same feeling of familiarity had permeated those dreams.

Thump.

Ilnaen called to him. The last time he had crossed the waste, he'd ignored it, but now he would answer the call. He would go to Ilnaen. Where The Order had fallen. Where the world had changed. Where the ghosts of the dead had been left to linger.

CHAPTER FORTY-THREE

EVEN IN THE SHADOW

18th Day of the Blood Moon

The Burnt Lands – Winter, Year 3081 After Doom

Arden knelt with his hand on the N'aka's rib cage, his blade slick with blood. They were the strangest creatures he'd ever laid eyes on. Recesses where ears should have been, dark grey skin tight as a drum, hind legs all thickly bunched muscle. The third set of limbs that protruded from the sides of their deep chests seemed entirely unnatural, with dark scythe-like talons stretching half the length of his arm. If there had been no other evidence of Efialtír's effect on this place, these creatures would have been enough.

He wiped the blood from his blade on the creature's hide, then slid it back into its scabbard as he stood. Fifty of the N'aka lay dead in the sand around him, knights of The First and The Second standing amidst the bodies. They'd been prowling in the dunes since not long after the knights had arrived, far braver than they had been when the sun had been up the last time Arden had crossed the wasteland. Though they had still waited for the sun to sink behind the mountains before attacking.

Calen had said he would reach the city by sunset on the fifth day. That was some hours past. Arden would have worried if Calen hadn't been late to just about everything in his life, including his own birth.

"I hate this place," Lyrin whispered as he approached, staring over Arden's shoulder. Sweat rolled down the man's nose and streaked his brow. Even in winter's grasp, the Burnt Lands were a furnace. "The Taint coats every grain of sand and covers every rock and stone. Just being here makes my skin crawl."

Arden turned to face the city.

Browned and broken walls rose in patches, sand stretching in paths through gaps the size of houses in the stonework. The highest points were at least two hundred feet, crenellated battlements mounted at the top. Some sections of wall stood like islands, surrounded by sand and half-buried rubble. It was clear that at some point, monstrous towers had intersected the walls at set intervals, but now only a handful remained. Enormous platforms sat at the towers' tops, large enough for dragons, the remnants of mighty support beams bracing the bottoms. Through the openings in the wall and above the parapet, ruined towers and buildings climbed towards the sky, broken and battered.

Ahead, Kallinvar, Ruon, Ildris, and Sister-Captain Arlena stood about a jagged rock that protruded from the sand, their gazes all fixed on the city. The decision had been made not to enter until Calen arrived. None wanted to spend a second longer within the broken walls than they had to, which Arden understood. He hadn't been there the night the Blood Moon had risen. He hadn't watched his brothers and sisters be cut down, their souls torn from the world – but he had felt it. He had felt each and every one of them die.

They had scouted the outskirts around the walls and found signs of Bloodspawn and Lorians alike, but with the sand and the heat, it was difficult to tell how long ago anything or anyone had passed through.

"How does the armour feel?" Varlin approached from the left, her helm receding into her armour, white cloak fluttering at her back. Valtaran tattoos ran down the shaved sides of her head, the hair from the top pulled into a long plait. She looked past Arden to Brother Kevan, who stood behind him.

"Strange." Brother Kevan looked down at the dark green armour that covered his body. As he did, the metal melted and pulled back over his fingers, exposing hard, calloused hands. The man was midway between his thirtieth and fortieth summer, his long black hair streaked with grey. "It weighs nothing, like a second skin... and yet..." He allowed the metal to flow back over his fingers, flexing them as he did. "I've never felt so strong in my life."

"It takes a while to get used to." Varlin gave Kevan a half-smile. "It all does. Though I'd argue the Rift takes the longest."

"Well," Lyrin interrupted. "Coming back from the claws of death and gaining eternal life in the service of a god was the difficult part for me, but we all have our things."

Varlin glanced at Lyrin, then back to Kevan, giving an upturn of her lip. "If a squirrel could talk, Brother Kevan, its name would be Lyrin."

"And if a sword had a sense of humour, it would be funnier than Sister Varlin."

"Kevan..." the newly anointed knight whispered, shaking his head softly.

"It gets easier," Arden said to Kevan as Lyrin and Varlin mocked each other back and forth. "All of it does."

Kevan gave Arden a placating smile that faded faster than it had appeared.

"I was two years in the knighthood before I stepped back through the Rift after taking the Sigil. You've had to do it in only a span of weeks. It can be overwhelming."

Kevan shook his head, staring off at the shattered walls of Ilnaen. "That's a word all right." He paused, letting out a short sigh. "The city of Ilnaen," he whispered, just loud enough for Arden to hear. "Not in a hundred years would I have believed you if you'd told me I'd lay eyes on Ilnaen's walls. Not in a thousand. You're a Southerner?"

"Mmm." The use of the word 'Southerner' chafed at Arden.

"Where I was raised, we were taught this place was the root of all evil. This city was the seat of The Order's power. It was from here that they burned and slaughtered at their whim. From here they orchestrated wars and wove lies. The death of this place was the beginning of peace." Kevan gave a laugh, catching the look on Arden's face. "Don't look so shocked. I was raised smarter than to believe tales woven by the victors of war."

"And yet you joined the Inquisition."

"We live in a world of ever-shifting grey," Kevan said, quoting the words of his vow.

Arden grunted.

"The beauty of living today, *Brother Arden*, is we can look on the past with knowledge we never had. Just because something isn't the right decision now doesn't mean it wasn't the right decision then. We do what we can with what we have. I made my choices, and if not for you and this knighthood, I would have died for them, and that would have been a fair enough death."

Before Arden could answer, Lyrin turned his head towards the sky, prompting Arden to do the same.

High above, in the perpetual twilight that was the Burnt Lands, Valerys soared, white scales stark against the night.

VALERYS LEVELLED OUT, SPREADING HIS wings wide and riding a current. Calen's hands rested on the leather straps tied around Valerys's neck and over his chest to carry the supplies. He pulled his breaths in slow, a contrast to the beating of his heart, which thumped like a galloping horse.

The horizon bled crimson, the red moon bright in the dark sky. The city of Ilnaen lay before him.

Calen had lost count of the number of times he'd seen a place so much larger than The Glade he'd scarcely believed it. The first time he'd seen Camylin, Calen had been but a boy. The sheer size of it had left him silent for almost an hour. The white walls and gargantuan towers of Midhaven had taken his breath away. But even they had paled in comparison to the legendary cities of Belduar and Durakdur, to which even the bards' tales had failed to do justice. Arisfall, Berona, and Aravell had all held their own wonders, their own awe.

But even in ruins, broken and shattered, Ilnaen surpassed them all. It had to have been three times the size of Berona, perhaps more. Past the sundered remnants of the old walls – sections of which still stood higher than Midhaven's tallest towers – the ruins of old structures spread into the distance as far as the eye could see. Their damage was too great, and too much time had passed to tell what most of the buildings had one day been.

Thump.

The heartbeat of the lost city resounded in Calen's mind, and the familiar ringing noise filled his ears, low but rising. His vision flicked, blurring, colours shifting. He didn't fight it this time, he leaned into it. If he truly was a druid, if he truly could see glimpses of the past, maybe, just maybe he could see something that might help the present.

The sound of the rushing wind dulled until all Calen could hear was the low, rising noise and the beating of three hearts: his own, Valerys's, and that of the city itself.

Thump.

Thump.

Thump.

On the third beat, the light of the world blinked and darkness consumed him. A moment of panic flared in Calen's heart. He exhaled slowly, calming himself.

The ringing stopped.

Light spilled from the edges of Calen's vision, pure and golden. It rolled over the mountains to the east, flowing like a river across the land, illuminating the world itself.

The city of Ilnaen was whole. Its white walls stood tall as mountains, glistening as though polished. Towers broke the walls at regular intervals, each almost fifty feet wide and topped with platforms large enough for even Avandeer to land. Enormous banners hung just below the battlements, white-backed with the symbol of The Order displayed in black and ornamented with elaborate patterns of gold that wound into roaring dragon heads.

Four towers in the city stood above all. One at the northern edge, one to the east, one to the west, and one near its centre, attached by a bridge to a fortified keep that was larger than Belduar's entire Inner Circle. He allowed his gaze to linger a little longer on the western tower. That must have been the tower Aeson spoke of: the western hatchery. The place where Alvira had first met Eluna.

The outer towers stood at least four hundred feet tall, maybe taller. But the tower at the city's centre rose higher again, with a domed golden roof that sparkled like glass in the sun. The Tower of Faith, the tower where Alvira and the council had died. Therin had spoken of it often in his teachings. And Calen remembered viscerally the dream in which he'd seen through Vyldrar's eyes. He could still feel the dragon's fear as Helios tore him from the side of the tower, the fear of not being able to protect her, of leaving her alone in the world. And he remembered the moment the dragon had died, the moment his soul had shattered. That moment would stay with him for the rest of his life.

The land around the city was lush and vibrant, rivers flowing through dense vegetation and woodland, wide-open plains of grass crawling towards the mountains.

A roar sounded above Calen, followed by a dragon twice Valerys's size with scales of polished silver flecked with ruby. The creature's wings were a pale red, its horns the colour of sun-bleached bone.

The dragon soared past Calen and Valerys, sweeping a gust in its wake. Three more roars sounded, each belonging to another dragon that streaked past Valerys on the right and left. The dragons varied in size and colour, one not much larger than Valerys himself with ochre-brown scales, black wings, and long spindly limbs. The four dragons twisted and turned in the air, weaving about each other with abandon.

Something about the way the dragons moved spoke of pure joy. As he watched, he began to notice that even more dragons flew above the city and in the sky beyond. And just as many lazed about atop the platforms, deep in sleep. So many. Maybe a hundred, maybe more. The sight of such a number in one place sent a feeling of elation through the bond, so strong that Calen wasn't sure if it originated in himself or Valerys.

A blood-chilling, earth-rending scream erupted, followed by another, and another, and another. The world flashed and shifted before his eyes. The sky bled red light, rain sheeted, and arcs of lightning tore through dark clouds and crashed into the buildings below. Columns of fire plumed across the night, crashing over scales and melting steel. Below, the city burned, flames consuming everything.

A crack sounded, and a tower fell, collapsing inwards and sinking into the flames.

Calen's heart stopped as a shriek rang out and an enormous grey dragon buried its claws into another less than half its size and ripped its neck clean from its body, blood spraying. While the two halves of the smaller creature fell towards the city, the grey dragon rained fire over a stretch of wall.

Everywhere Calen looked, dragons ripped each other apart, fire and lightning flashing.

And then, for a moment, it all stopped. The Blood Moon was gone, the golden sun returned. The roars and shrieks quieted, the wails of the dying fading. The city was as it had been minutes before: pristine, peaceful, and full of wonder. The banners flapped in the wind, and dragons soared on the breeze.

Calen's heart had just enough time to find hope when the world shifted and the city was ablaze once more. Four dragons ripped through the air, tearing strips from each other, rending scales and slashing wings. Jaws wrapped around necks, legs, and tails. Talons sliced into bellies. All the while, the Draleid who sat on the dragons' backs wove tapestries of the Spark, whips of Air and Fire, arcs of lightning, shards of rain frozen into missiles.

A rush of wind gusted past Calen's face, and he looked down to see the same beautiful silver-scaled dragon he'd seen earlier. The creature thrashed and shrieked as three others fell upon it with tooth and talon. Its pale red wings flapped helplessly, wet with blood, the membrane shredded. The other dragons tore at its belly, slicing the wondrous creature open, innards spilling into the sky.

It unleashed a blood-chilling screech as another tore its wing from its body and buried a talon in the wound.

Calen pulled his gaze away, unable to watch, his stomach turning.

Once more the world blinked, and the red sky turned to warm marigold, birdsong replacing dying shrieks, the soft glow of lanterns supplanting the blazing flames.

A dragon soared past, scales and wings like a painting of the night sky, savage horns dark as stone. The scales along its snout and chest were lighter in colour, pale as the bellflowers in Verna Gritten's garden. The creature was equal parts power and beauty, devastating and regal. When it angled its wings and swooped back around, Calen finally saw the face of the Draleid on its back.

Aeson Virandr.

The man couldn't have seen much more than his twentieth summer, his skin smooth and unmarked by time, not a trace of grey in his hair. He wore the white plate of The Order, twin swords with ball pommels on his back.

A sudden realisation touched Calen that the dragon upon which Aeson rode was Lyara. The sight of her twisted in Calen's chest. She was beautiful, truly beautiful.

Again, the world snapped and turned to blood and fire, continuously shifting and changing as Calen followed Aeson and Lyara through the raging battlefield in the sky. Nothing could have prepared Calen for the carnage that ensued.

Aeson and Lyara only flew where the fighting was thickest. They threw themselves into the heart of everything. One after another, they tore traitors from the sky. They were relentless, savage, brutal. But for every foe they slew, they watched two of their kin die.

And then something changed in the air, in the light, in the very fabric of everything. He could *feel* it. A flash of blinding light consumed Calen's vision.

Screams followed. Screams, and shrieks, and wails, and roars.

As the light dimmed, Calen watched Lyara climb towards the sky, tearing upwards with every drop of strength in her body, flames licking at her tail, lightning flashing in the night. Across the city, hundreds of winged shapes did the same. Friend and foe were forgotten as the flames rolled over the city like a tidal wave, growing with every second, taller and wider. Everything in its path died. Every man, woman, elf, Jotnar, Urak, dragon – everything.

Any dragon who did not rise quick enough was devoured, vanishing into nothing, their dying screams swallowed whole.

Calen trembled, his heart breaking, tears streaming down his face as he watched what he had always known as 'The Fall'. He knew now how utterly and completely inadequate that name was.

This was not a fall. It was not even a battle. It was slaughter and carnage, destruction and death on a scale incomprehensible to both heart and mind. This was everything dark and hopeless about the world.

The flames rose higher and spread relentlessly to the east and west, the light filling Calen's eyes. Everything shifted one final time, and Calen found himself once more staring out over the ruins of the city he had just watched burn, sand glittering pink in the wind.

He slumped forwards, pressing his chest against Valerys's warm scales, chest heaving, his brow slick with cold sweat. The dragon's mind pulled at him, their pain shared, their agony bleeding from both hearts. Valerys had seen it too, seen the butchery – or at least he had felt it through Calen.

"I'm here," Calen whispered.

Calen looked out over the city before them, overlaying the beauty of what he had seen atop the rubble of what remained. All four of the great towers were shattered. Of them all, the eastern tower retained the most of its original height but was still a shadow of what it had once been. The keep at the centre was now a mound of brown rock, with worn slits for windows and sand spilling from every crack. Its splendour was gone, its memory reduced to nothing. And the Blood Moon looked down over it all, mocking with its red light.

With a heavy sigh, Calen lifted himself so he sat upright. Everywhere he looked he saw echoes of the vision. He supposed that's what they were – visions. Visions of the past.

Valerys banked left, the air shifting around Calen, the wind blustering against his face and through his hair. They were to meet Haem and the knights by the walls near the western hatchery tower.

Alvira's second letter to Eluna had said she'd left 'everything' – whatever 'everything' was – at the place where they'd first met. And according to Aeson, that was the western hatchery tower. Though it was now nothing but rocks and rubble.

They found the knights precisely where they'd said they'd be, a host of fourteen, each garbed in that strange green armour.

Sand whipped in spirals as Valerys alighted at the foot of a dune, talons sinking. With the sun set, the air held the same chill as it had in the clouds, Calen's breath pluming before him. He'd forgotten how swiftly the heat fled the Burnt Lands as the night rose.

Valerys leaned forwards, extending his winged forelimb, and Calen slid from his place at the nape of the dragon's neck. He landed with a thump, his pulse still racing.

"Brother." Haem marched towards Calen, his armour turning to liquid as he walked, flowing over his body and vanishing into his chest. He grasped Calen's forearm, then pulled him in close, squeezing him in a tight bearhug. Haem let out a relieved sigh. "You had me worried."

Calen savoured the embrace before answering. After the events of the last two years, he'd learned to savour the moments with the ones he loved. "The storm at Land's End was unrelenting, and Valerys was still weak after Aravell. We spent the night in Fort Saldar."

Haem pulled back and stared into Calen's eyes, a soft smile on his lips. "You're here now."

The rest of the knights gathered round as Valerys lowered his head and nudged his snout into Haem's chest, a soft rumble resonating in his throat.

Grandmaster Kallinvar greeted Calen with a grim expression, Ruon and the other knights of Haem's chapter at his side. N'aka bodies decorated the sand, fifty or more at least.

"Any sign of the Uraks or the Lorians?" Calen asked.

Kallinvar shook his head. "But that doesn't mean they're not here. And even with the tear mended, the Taint still clings to this city like a parasite. We will not be alone here." He gestured towards the packs strapped to Valerys's chest. "I hope your armour is in there."

THE ABSOLUTE SILENCE OF ILNAEN made Arden aware of every breath he drew, every step he took, every rasp and clink of steel as he moved. Sounds echoed in the city, bouncing off the sand-stained rock and along the exposed paved path where the winds had cleared the cracked stone. If Bloodspawn or Lorians did await them within the city's depths, they would have heard them coming the moment they'd passed the walls.

Arden eyed the rooftops and the vacant windows, looking for shifting shadows or any signs of movement.

A *whoosh* sounded as Valerys swept overhead, whipping up sand in his wake, his massive white wings glinting like rubies in the moon's light.

It had been agreed that the dragon would scout overhead while Calen and the knights searched the ruins of the western tower. At the least, if something came for them, they would have warning.

"He seems different," Lyrin whispered, gesturing to Calen, who walked ahead, the purple glow of the runes in his armour washing over the sand.

Lyrin was right. Calen did seem different. Colder, harsher, more distant. He'd not spoken a word more than he'd had to before entering the city, and now he walked in silence, entirely focused on the western tower.

It seemed every time Arden laid eyes on his brother, the young man had changed and grown. He was barely recognisable from the boy of sixteen summers Arden had left in The Glade. That boy had been sweet and gentle, if a little headstrong. He'd looked to Arden for everything, never straying too far.

Arden remembered on his fifteenth summer, Calen had helped their mam make him an apple and blackberry tart, but Calen had mistaken salt for sugar. Calen had only been eleven at the time, and he'd stared up at Arden, expectation in his young eyes, a beaming smile spread across his face, the last of his baby teeth having been knocked out when he fell from a tree the week prior.

The image of Calen's gap tooth smile caused Arden to laugh. He'd eaten three slices of that tart while Calen had watched and refused to take a slice for himself because the tart wasn't for him. It was only when Freis had tasted a piece and her eyes had bulged that she'd asked Calen to help her with the washing and gestured for Arden to get rid of the tart's remains.

Arden had vomited not fifty feet from the house, right into Tach Edwin's roses. He'd not had the heart to tell Calen.

Calen was a man now, and that broad toothy smile was rarer than gold. He was a man weighed down by the things boys did not have to know. There came a point, Arden had realised, where all children discovered the darkness in people, where they saw what living things were willing to do to each other. That point was the death of innocence. He'd hoped to keep Calen ignorant for a little longer, to shield him, but the gods had other plans. He'd tried to do the same for Ella, but she'd always been too sharp, always noticed things more quickly than others. She'd understood the world long before Arden had hoped she would.

That sweet boy still existed somewhere in his brother, he was sure of it. But it was somewhere deep, somewhere in the darkness.

EVEN IN RUINS, THE WESTERN hatchery tower still rose some two hundred feet, deep gouges raked all through the stone. After the centuries, the sand had stained the white walls a pale brown, scorch marks still visible where the lightning had struck. The top was shattered and broken, while the courtyard surrounding its base was a mix of rubble, sand, and bones.

Slabs of stone twice the size of Calen jutted from the ground, skeletons and armour peeking through the sand that cradled them.

A massive skull, five times as high as Calen was tall, rested near the tower's base, a crack splitting the bone around the right eye. The body was nowhere in sight. Here and there enormous ribcages and a variety of enormous bones lay strewn about, discoloured by the many centuries in the sand.

A wave of sorrow flooded him, pushing from Valerys's mind to his. The dragon circled overhead but saw the devastation through Calen's eyes.

Calen took a few steps forward and brushed his boot across the sand, exposing a small piece of The Order's sigil that had been inlaid in black stone. The centre of the sigil was no more. A crater, half-filled with sand, sat in its place.

Thump.

Calen's vision blurred, and that same sound – the beating heart of Ilnaen – hammered in his mind.

The world shifted again, and Calen was staring down at the same sigil, but this time it gleamed with orange-red light, blood smeared across its polished surface. Calen lifted his gaze to see fires blazing around him as Uraks, humans, elves, and Jotnar hacked each other to pieces.

Everywhere he looked, steel sliced through flesh and blood sprayed. The roar of the flames and the clang of clashing steel dulled the screams and howls. Calen had seen battle, many times now, and he always thought it was chaos. But he'd been wrong. *This* was chaos. There was no rhyme nor reason to the killing, no purpose, just slaughter.

Elves in golden armour butchered each other without prejudice while Uraks drove black steel through anything that moved. Even warriors in the white plate that Calen recognised as The Order Highguard carved each other apart. On the left side of the yard, two Jotnar fought back to back against a clutch of Battlemages with glowing red gemstones hanging around their necks.

A shriek rang out above as a bolt of lightning slammed into a dragon's flank in a brilliant flash. The creature tumbled through the sky, one wing streaking flames, trying in vain to recover its flight. The air shivered with a scream, and a large dragon with dull purple scales slammed into the other and smashed it into the side of the tower.

Chunks of stone came loose, crashing into the ground around Calen, crushing bodies in bursts of gore and bone.

The larger dragon ripped the other away from the tower's wall, talons sinking into its soft underbelly as jaws wrapped around its neck. The two dragons spiralled downwards, scales cracking and shattering, blood raining down over the fighting below.

A terrible cracking sound was followed by a roar, and the larger dragon ripped its foe's head clean from its neck, leaving both parts to crash to the ground at the base of the tower. Even then, the larger dragon had taken too many wounds and was falling too fast. It twisted and splayed its wings, then smashed into the side of a tall white structure at the edge of the yard. The creature crushed three score beneath it. Sixty lives snuffed out in an instant.

Calen looked back towards the base of the tower, finding himself staring into the open red eye of the smaller dragon's severed head. The left eye stared straight at Calen, lifeless and empty. The right eye was a gaping wound of blood and gore. The creature's tongue lolled out through its jagged teeth, blood dripping from the end.

As he stared slack-jawed into the creature's only remaining eye, the red iris flecked with gold, the world blinked.

The flames were gone. The fighting ceased. The screaming silenced. He was back in the sand-covered yard at the foot of the tower, staring into the empty sockets of the dragon skull.

"What did you see?" Haem stood to Calen's left, his helmet gone, nothing but concern in his eyes. Before Ella had arrived at Aravell, Calen had told his brother of the visions. He'd not quite explained everything – mostly because he didn't understand everything himself – but he'd told Haem of the things he'd seen. Told him of Vyldrar and of what he'd seen when he'd grasped Queen Uthrían's arm. He'd even told him of how he'd relived that night in The Glade, when Kallinvar had granted Haem the Sigil.

"The same thing I've seen since the moment I set eyes on this place." Calen tilted his head sideways, staring at the dragon skull, seeing the lifeless red eye, the pale pink scales, and the blood flowing over the stone. "I saw death. Pointless death."

Calen crossed the yard, navigating the field of bones and rocks, his gaze combing the sand.

"Do you have any idea what it is we might be looking for?" Kallinvar asked, matching Calen step for step, his gaze searching the yard.

Calen shook his head. "All I know is what's in Alvira's letter. This is the place Alvira and Eluna first met. Whatever she hid, she hid it here."

Kallinvar gave a short nod, then gestured to Ruon and Arlena, issuing commands. In Calen's periphery, the knights spread across the yard, turning over everything they could find, their polished green plate stark against the brown sand.

"Sister-Captain Arlena and The First will start in the yard," Kallinvar said. "They'll look for anything that seems out of place, anything that stands out. They'll move outwards in closed sections until Arlena deems they've strayed too far from the tower. I and my knights will stay at your side."

Calen nodded his thanks, glad for Kallinvar's aid. Now that he was here, he had no idea what the next step should be.

"The pendant is still the key," he whispered, repeating Alvira's words as he reached beneath his breastplate and produced the brass-backed pendant he'd found with her letter in Vindakur. Calen turned the pendant over, looking down at the white symbol of The Order set into the black obsidian.

He opened himself to the Spark and pulled on threads of each element. He mimicked what he'd seen Vaeril do back in Aravell, probing through the pendant with threads as though it were a lock to pick. He pushed and pulled, winding the threads over each other and trying every conceivable combination he could think of. For a moment, he thought he saw a light flicker within the black glass, but if it did, it'd only been for a fraction of a second.

He sighed. He should have known it would never be that simple. Alvira hadn't been leaving clues for Eluna to find something. She had been leaving clues for Eluna to open whatever she had hidden. Eluna already knew where it was.

Calen drew one last long breath and looked from the top of the tower – at least, what was left of it – to the bottom, his gaze settling on the arched opening that looked as though it had once held a door. Now, it was more a gaping hole in the stone, blocks at the side ripped away as though the hinges had been torn free.

Calen started for the arch, but Haem caught his arm. "That thing looks like it's ready to collapse."

"Let's hope it doesn't," Calen said, stepping through the arch. The doors that had been torn from the archway lay ten feet inside the tower's antechamber. The wooden frames were charred and splintered, the steel twisted. Large golden plates that had clearly once been affixed to the door's front were scattered on the ground, depictions of dragons and scaled eggs worked into the metal.

The ground floor of the tower was enormous, large enough to fit a few hundred souls with ease. The chamber was flooded with sand and armoured bones. Staircases, some broken, some intact, led to the upper levels. Corridors spouted off in all directions, moving deeper into the tower.

Calen dropped to one knee beside a bleached skeleton covered in the white plate of the Draleid. Four enormous holes punctured the steel from the right breast down to the navel. The Order's sigil was set into the breast in now-shattered obsidian, glinting in the light that flowed through the arch. Calen brushed his gauntleted hand against the shards of black glass.

Once more, the visions flooded over him.

Screams reverberated through the antechamber, high-pitched and wailing. Uraks charged through the doors, monstrous Bloodmarked rampaging amidst the swarm.

Calen looked down to see the shimmering black sigil of The Order on his chest. About him, his brothers and sisters of the Draleid fought like demons, carving paths through the Uraks with blade and Spark, some wielding nithrals of brilliant light. Elven Praetorians and Order Highguard fought alongside the Draleid. And they fought valiantly, as mighty as the stories had named them, but the Uraks kept coming, hacking with black steel, tearing flesh with tooth and claw. The Bloodmarked ripped through the Praetorians and the Highguard like wolves would sheep.

Calen found the largest of the beasts with his gaze, then charged. He cut down two Uraks as he moved, taking a head with a mighty sweep, then cleaving a jaw with the backswing. No matter the cost, he could not let them get to the eggs. He would not.

He opened himself to the Spark and pulled on threads of Earth and Fire, weaving them through the stone at the Bloodmarked's feet.

The creature spotted him. It slammed its two hands together, unleashing a shockwave of fire and air that tore through two elves in a burst of gore, their innards spraying in clouds. Calen pulled threads of Air and Fire into a wedge before him, breaking the shockwave in two as he leapt forwards. He hit the ground and rolled, keeping his sword tight. As he rose, he carved through the Bloodmarked's knee in a single swipe. The creature collapsed, and Calen pulled on those threads of Earth and Fire he'd woven into the stone. The ground beneath the Bloodmarked rippled, the stone turning to liquid then surging upwards into a polished spike that burst through the falling Urak's neck. The creature's runes ignited in a blaze of crimson light, black smoke billowing. And then it went still, the runelight dying.

A shriek sounded, and a fledgling flew overhead. The dragon couldn't have been more than a month old, no larger than a dog. Its golden scales shimmered in the light of the lanterns. The tiny creature shrieked and wailed, swooping onto an Urak's back and ripping out the side of its throat.

Calen's heart broke as he watched the small golden dragon. Judging by the agony and rage, the creature's soulkin had died. To see one so young feel a pain of that measure… It wasn't right. The thought alone made Calen reach out to his own soulkin, feeling her as she soared over the courtyard outside, raining fire on the Uraks.

Stay strong. This day will not be our last.

A warmth spread from Antala to Calen, filling him. But with the warmth came a rage, an unyielding fury that burned in his bones. Their brothers and sisters had betrayed them this night, slaughtered their own in their sleep. So many dragons dead. So many Draleid… and for what?

Only the chilling shriek of the fledgling pulled Calen's attention back to the fighting, the rage still simmering in him.

"No…" Calen watched in horror as a Bloodmarked snatched the fledgling from the air and crushed it in an iron grip, snapped bones bursting through scales, blood pouring over leathered fingers.

The beast bit down on the dragon's tiny skull and crushed it in its jaws. The shrieks of the young fledgling cracked shards from Calen's heart. About him, his brothers and sisters were falling, the tide of Uraks too strong.

He pulled his and Antala's minds together, wrapping them tight around each other. He could feel the strength of her wings, the power of her heart, the fury in her flames.

"Draleid n'aldryr, myia'niassa Na solian nai din siel harys von myia thranuk ilumel. Ayar elwyn. Ayar nithír." Calen raised his blade and set himself for the svidarya, pulling deeper from the Spark. "Uthikar."

Dragonbound by fire, my love. To live by your side has been my greatest privilege. One heart. One soul. Together.

He charged, carving through the Uraks like a god unleashed, threads of each elemental strand whipping about him. Lightning streaked from the tip of his blade, and fire poured from his open palm. With threads of Earth, he crushed Uraks in their own armour, bones snapping like brittle twigs. With Air and Spirit, he pulled the breath from their lungs and the hope from their hearts.

With every swing of his steel, he felt Antala's claws slice through leathery flesh in the yard, felt her flames devour and her jaws destroy.

If these voidspawn would destroy everything Calen loved, he would take them with him into the darkness. He set his sights on the Bloodmarked that had killed the fledgling and wrought a path of death and blood.

One of the beasts stepped before him and roared, a black-steel axe in its fist. Calen didn't stop or slow. He grabbed the Urak's neck with a thread of Air as he moved and snapped it, charging over the body as it fell, his gaze set on the Bloodmarked.

The creature was pulling its claws from an elven belly when Calen fell upon it. First, he took its leg at the knee with a swing of steel. Then he raked the blade across the creature's back, flesh parting and runes blazing.

The creature fell forwards, thrashing and howling, its claws tearing through the calf of a nearby Highguard.

Calen planted a boot on its shoulder and kicked it onto its back before angling his blade and driving it into the Bloodmarked's gut, pushing up into its chest until the hilt pressed against the bottom of its ribcage.

The Bloodmarked made to grab him with its clawed hand, but he twisted the sword in its gut and it howled.

Calen placed his hand on the creature's rune-marked chest. He drew as deeply from the Spark as he could, then pulled on thick threads of Fire, Spirit, and Earth.

He looked down into the creature's red eyes. The Bloodmarked stared back at him, its breath dragging through bloodied lips, black pupils dilating.

"May the pain follow you through the void." Calen pushed the threads of Earth into the creature's bones, crumbling them from the inside out. He wove the threads of Spirit and Fire together, driving them through the Bloodmarked's failing bones, setting them alight. He stared into the creature's eyes as its bones ignited, its blood boiled, and the flames consumed it from the inside.

The creature shook and thrashed, the howl that left its throat unnatural in its pain. The runes carved into its flesh burned with a crimson light so bright Calen winced. But he didn't stop. He pushed harder, funnelling the threads through the Bloodmarked's bones and into its blood. If this creature's death was the last drop of joy in his life, that would be enough.

The red of the Bloodspawn's eyes grew brighter, turning a shade of orange, then yellow, until they eventually erupted in a plume of white flames. It thrashed for a moment longer, then went limp, its arms slumping by its side, its eyes nothing more than blistered sockets.

Calen dragged his blade from the corpse, then let Antala's rage flow freely through him. He hacked and slashed at everything that moved, the Spark flooding him.

A black spear glanced off his breastplate, just below the ribs, and he took both of its holder's arms in a single flowing downswing. He pushed forwards and drove his steel through the Urak's chest, driving it deep until his face was close enough to smell its breath.

He pushed off, leaving the blade embedded in the creature's chest as it staggered backwards. Turning, Calen pulled on threads of each elemental strand, weaving them together into his fist. The power of the Spark surged through him, lightning in his veins, and bright yellow light burst from his right fist. The light twisted in strands, coiling around each other like warring snakes until they finally took the shape of a glowing yellow longsword. His níthral. His Soulblade.

About him, few of his kin remained, though they stood like bastions in the dark night, the Highguard and Praetorians rallying around them. A flare of panic signalled in his mind as Antala watched through his eyes.

We must protect the eggs. No matter the cost. Their fire has not yet been lit. Help will come. We just need to hold them off as long as we can.

Calen thought the words, but both he and Antala knew the hollowness of them. There was little chance either of them would survive this night. All that mattered was that their death held meaning. And so he felt Antala roar, heard it with his own ears from within the tower's walls. He felt the pressure building in the back of his mind as she laid waste to a clutch of Uraks battling in the yard, her flames stealing their life.

Calen fell back beside his kin and the other survivors, regrouping in a tight formation, forcing the Uraks back closer to the destroyed door. Something crunched beneath his feet, and he dared not look down for fear of being relieved of his head. Friend or foe, the corpse no longer drew breath, and it had no need for its bones.

The line held for a few minutes, a brief flare of hope igniting in his chest. Then three Bloodmarked came charging through the thick of Urak bodies, their shoulders clear above the heads of the lesser beasts. The creatures slammed into the surviving defenders with the force of a hurricane, a storm of claws slashing, a tempest of fire burning everything it touched. And then the chaos resumed.

Calen hurled himself into the middle of the melee, his Soulblade cutting through Uraks like a scythe through grass. Where the yellow light shone, blood spilled. He moved through the forms of svidarya, from Howling Wolf to Crouching Dragon, his Soulblade guiding him as much as he did it. In the skies above the tower, he felt Antala's every movement as she weaved between tooth and talon, protecting a contingent of Highguard from the rear. She had been forced to take the lives of six of her kin and the blood weighed on her heart. This was not how it was supposed to be. They were her brothers and sisters, her family.

That did not mean she would not do her duty though. She would guard the eggs until her dying breath.

Calen lost himself in the killing, his mind fading to a blur. A sword sliced along the side of his neck, and a spear split the links of his chain below his breastplate. The pain was nothing but an old friend, emboldening him. He had fought and killed these beasts for three hundred years. He would not stop now.

A heavy blow took his helm from his head, ringing his ears and sending stars across his vision. He pushed on, hacking, slashing, carving his way through the seemingly endless sea of Uraks. Movement flashed in his periphery, and he shifted his feet, twisting at the hips as he swung.

A flash of light erupted, and he found his níthral levelled against another – a spear wrought of white light.

His heart slammed against his ribs as he looked up at the mighty frame of Kollna, daughter of Luan. The Jotnar had clearly been sleeping when the attack had come. She wore no armour, and her clothes were in tatters, her body laced with bloody wounds. The left side of her face and neck were covered in burns that trailed down over her shoulder, the fabric scorched away.

As Calen stared into her dark eyes, he also looked through Antala's to see Kollna's mighty soulkin Tinua swoop around the northern face of the tower and rip a traitor's wing free with his monstrous jaws.

"Kollna…" Calen's mouth was dry, his every breath ragged. He pulled his Soulblade away. "It's good to see you still draw breath. Coren, is she safe?"

"None of us are safe, Tarast. But she was alive when I left her. With Farwen and Dylain."

"The Archon? Eltoar? The council?"

She shook her head. "The city will fall, old friend. The Archon has set me a task. I need three of your warriors."

Calen looked about him. The Dracårdare had come charging down the stairwells with sharp steel in hand, reinforcing the lines, and yet their numbers were still far too thin. "You will have them," he said, steeling himself. He grabbed three of the Highguard closest to him and ordered them to go with Kollna. He straightened, reading the sombre lines of Kollna's face. "Aldryr ar orimyn, vésani. Det harys von atil haydria."

Fire and fury, sister. It has been an honour.

Kollna gave him a knowing look. "This is not the end, Tarast. Only our end."

And with that Kollna and the three Highguard were gone. He did not ask to where they went. It mattered little. His place was there, at the base of the hatchery. If the Uraks wanted to get to the eggs, he would make them pay a price of blood so high as to put fear in the hearts of their ancestors.

He turned and rejoined the fray.

The world flickered and blurred, and Calen was once more kneeling in the sand-filled antechamber, his gauntleted fingers trembling against the obsidian symbol of The Order on the dead Draleid's chest.

"What's wrong?" Haem's hand rested on Calen's shoulder, concern in his voice.

Calen stared into the sockets of the skeleton before him. Into the eyes of the man whose last moments he had just witnessed. Tarast, soulkin of Antala. He rested his palm on the shards of obsidian that adorned the man's breastplate, broken by whatever had stolen his last breath. Calen had never met the man, never exchanged a word or a passing glance. He'd died hundreds of years before Calen had even been born, and yet Calen felt as though he knew him intimately. He whispered, "Alura anis, akar. Du dauvin val haydria."

Rest now, brother. You died with honour.

When Calen stood, he took in details that he had first missed. The snapped fragile bones of what must have been baby dragons – fledglings Tarast had called them. The breastplate that bore the flaming dragon egg insignia of the Dracârdare – the dragonkeepers, those responsible for the care and protection of the eggs and the young. He brushed his foot across the sand, finding more bones beneath, dense and large. Urak bones. The entire antechamber must have been covered in the remnants of the battle, concealed by the sand.

"Kollna was here," Calen said to Haem, still examining the mass grave upon which they stood.

"The one mentioned in the letter?"

Calen nodded. His hand still trembled, his pulse quick. "I saw her."

Haem narrowed his eyes and stared into Calen's, his expression asking a wordless question: 'Are you all right?'

"I've never had so many of these... visions." Calen shook his head, the world flickering back and forth around him between sand and bones to blood and carnage. "There's just... just so much. I can't control it. This place... It's full of ghosts."

"Take it slow."

Kallinvar and the other knights appeared at Haem's shoulder, expectant. To Calen, hours had passed since he'd last looked upon the Grandmaster, but it seemed mere moments had expired.

"Anything of use?" the Grandmaster asked. His gaze softened as he looked about the antechamber, the lines around his eyes creasing, his bottom lip drooping. Haem had told Calen of Kallinvar, about how the man had fought in the battle at Ilnaen all those years ago. Calen had seen only fragments of the slaughter, only slivers of time through the eyes of others, and even still his heart was heavy as iron. He dared not think of the pain behind Kallinvar's eyes.

Calen gestured towards the corridor at the other side of the chamber, which he'd seen Kollna and the Highguard vanish down. "This way."

No light touched the corridor's depths save for a trickle of pink moonlight that shone over Calen's shoulders, revealing nothing but bones, rubble, and sand. He pulled on threads of Fire, Spirit, and Air, a baldír forming before him, pale white light illuminating the path.

The corridor was wide enough for four men, the ceiling tall enough for a Jotnar. Glass oil lanterns were set into the alcoves in the walls, some shattered, some whole – all long dead. Patches of carpet peeked through the sand and bones. The colour was faded, but Calen could make out depictions of dragons worked into the fabric.

His vision flickered. For a moment, the sounds of battle raged at his back and the oil lanterns were in full flame. He marched down the corridor, a fellow Highguard to his left, the Jotnar Draleid on his right. It pained him to keep walking while his brothers and sisters in arms fought and died to hold the antechamber. But he would do what the Archon commanded. He would do as he had vowed, even on this night, his last night. He would not falter.

Everything shifted once more, blending into coloured blotches and mixing until a new picture was formed.

He walked down the same corridor, but the sounds of battle were gone and the lanterns burned lower, drawing near their end.

"Who else knows?" The words that left Calen's lips were not his own. He knew by the voice on his tongue and the bluish hue to his skin that they were the words of Kollna.

He looked down to see a woman at his side, half his height. She didn't return his stare, instead looking forward. She was lean with dark hair falling past her shoulders. She wore a long white dress threaded with gold, The Order's insignia woven into the right breast, a sword belted at her hip. A pendant hung from her neck, that same insignia in white, marked into black glass, the very pendant that now hung around Calen's neck.

Alvira Serris.

"No other soul but Eluna."

He and Alvira turned left at the corridor's end, then right, reaching a stairwell.

Alvira stopped and turned to look at Calen, her eyes dark, her stare unyielding. The way the woman held herself, Calen felt as though she could carve through armies. There was power in every breath that left her lips. "I hope to the gods that I am wrong, that I am all paranoia and mistrust. But I am the Archon. It is my duty to safeguard our people and our future, and so this is what I must do."

"I am always at your service, Archon. Speak, and it shall be done. But why do we keep the circle so small?"

"We do not know how far or how deep the seeds of Fane's words go, and still we may be seeing shadows. There are rumblings amongst the mages, whispers in the dark, but nothing more. My web of spiders grows quieter with each passing month, as though vanishing. Fane gathers support, and with each moon, his words grow harsher, his intentions more muddled. It would be easier to guess which way the wind will blow on this day next year. I may be seeing shadows, Kollna, but I must fear what lurks in those shadows. The Draleid cannot be the ones to make the first move. Power is a precarious thing. If we use ours to destroy something that does not yet exist, history will name us worse than that which we seek to destroy. Fane has eyes and ears in the wind. We cannot risk an overheard whisper or a wandering eye. This is the future of our kind."

Calen and Alvira continued on, moving through a series of corridors, everything blurred, the colours dancing, the light moving in a haze around him.

When everything settled, he was once again seeing through his own eyes, both Haem and Kallinvar staring back at him, voices dull and distant in his ears.

"Calen." Haem shook him, hands clasped at his shoulders. "Calen. Wake up. Wake up."

"What are you doing?" Calen stepped back, pushing Haem's arms at the elbows to release his brother's grip. "What..." He looked about himself. He no longer stood in the corridors. A chamber rose around him, illuminated by the baldír at his side. The walls climbed into a vaulted ceiling, carvings of dragon scales and wings marked into the white stone. At the centre, shards of sapphires, emeralds, amethysts, and a dozen other coloured gems comprised a mosaic of a dragon egg. A swirl of rubies and topaz flowed about the egg, mimicking the movement of flames.

The chamber had only two entrances, one behind him and one ahead of him. He looked back at Haem, who was staring into his eyes.

"You just kept walking," he said, unblinking as he watched Calen. "We called to you, but you didn't stop. Your eyes... they were like Ella's, white as clouds."

The knights all studied Calen, some curious, others uncertain. They didn't know what he was... though, in truth, neither did Calen himself.

Kallinvar met Calen's gaze. The man didn't speak, but the look on his face told Calen that he expected an answer.

"I can... see... things. The past. In glimpses. I've no control over it, and I've not experienced it like this before. At first, it was only when I slept, in dreams."

"When you say you see glimpses, what do you see?"

Calen explained what he'd seen outside the tower, in the antechamber, and again in the corridors. Speaking the words aloud somehow made even Calen sceptical.

"Very well." Kallinvar nodded slowly, staring past Calen as he did. "Carry on. You lead, we will follow."

"You believe me?"

"I knew Tarast. Met him and his soulkin many years ago in Amendel before I joined the knighthood. Laid eyes on his níthral at the Battle of Ulthar's Helm. I cannot see a way you would know his name, and that of Antala's, let alone know the light of his níthral. I don't know the workings of druids. I've never laid eyes on one. Maybe you are, maybe you aren't. But if you can lead us to the Heart, I can sacrifice understanding for faith."

Calen drew a long breath, letting the knight's words sink in. He looked between the two doorways. "Which way did we enter?"

Haem gestured to the one behind Calen.

"This way then," Calen said, marching in the other direction.

The doorway led to a long stairwell that sank into a dark abyss. Calen hesitated a moment, Valerys rumbling in the back of his mind. The dragon soared in the sky above Ilnaen, watching for any signs of movement. He'd spotted some N'aka and a few drifting shadows, but nothing that set his frills on edge. And yet, the idea of Calen moving deeper into the ground, where Valerys couldn't get to him if needed, was one the dragon vehemently opposed.

They should never be apart. Dark things happened when they were separated. Memories flooded his mind. Memories of Drifaien, of the agony, of the emptiness.

Haem will be by my side. He would never let harm come to me.

The dragon snorted his disapproval. Haem was family, but he had not been able to protect Ella. He had not been there when Calen had needed him. He was strong, but he was not Valerys, and in the protection of Calen's life Valerys trusted no-one but himself.

There are no choices here. I must go. If you trust no-one else, trust me.

The dragon gave a reluctant rumble of acquiescence in the back of Calen's mind and wheeled off to watch over three of Sister-Captain Arlena's knights, who searched the rubble to the tower's south.

Calen stared down into the stairwell's shrouded depths for a moment, then adjusted his baldír and descended.

CHAPTER FORTY-FOUR

FORGED IN FIRE

18th Day of the Blood Moon

South of Midhaven – Winter, Year 3081 After Doom

Tarmon walked with his hands clasped behind his back, his warm breath misting in the winter air. Campfires crackled, and chatter floated on the wind. Three elven guards bearing Calen's white dragon on their breastplates inclined their heads as they passed.

The mood in the camp was a strange one, but one Tarmon recognised well: bittersweet triumph.

In the week they had spent traversing Illyanara, marching every second they were gifted, they had fought four battles. One against Uraks, two against Lorian forces, and another against some emerging warlord who bit off more than he could chew. Such was their numbers advantage that they were never truly in danger of losing even once out of the four.

The second battle with the Lorians had been the most evenly matched. It had been a full Lorian army, some five thousand. Atara and her scouts had found them camped at the foot of a valley, headed south towards Valtara. But between the cover of night, the sheer number of elven mages, and Dann somehow managing to steal away with just over four hundred of the Lorian horses with nothing but a bow and a skin of Raven's Ichor, the battle had been quicker work than it had any right to be. Dann had taken a minor wound to his leg in the midst of it all, though he acted as though he'd need an amputation.

Still, over the course of those days, they had lost about three hundred souls. Some human, some elves; mostly human. With an army this young, these battles were key to forging them into a single cohesive force that could withstand far greater tests, but it was a delicate balance. Many had travelled far and wide when Aeson had sent out the call, but they were not warriors. They were farmers, fishermen, blacksmiths, pedlars. The vast majority had not even held steel before arriving at the outskirts of the Darkwood. They had suffered, and they knew grief and pain, but death was not as familiar an acquaintance to them as it was to Tarmon. And watching someone die was not the same as killing them. Caught up in stories of the first free Draleid in four hundred years, of rebellion, of heroism and great deeds, they were only now learning the truth of war.

Tarmon paused for a moment, watching as a group of Dracurïn shared stories around a fire, elves and humans both. It was good to see smiles on faces. He allowed himself a moment to linger before setting off towards Dann's tent.

"SHIT, FUCKING, DONKEYDICK MOTHERFUCKER." DANN stuck a leather strap into his mouth and bit down hard. He closed his eyes tight and pursed his lips, exhaling.

After a moment, he opened his left eye to see Lyrei staring at him in pure shock, a needle and catgut in one hand, her other hand pinching the flesh of his upper thigh.

"What?" he asked, still grimacing, both hands bunched into fists.

"Elven children complain less than you." She shook her head, then passed the needle back through his skin without warning, eliciting a grunt. "It was you who insisted on having your wounds sewn by hand. One of the Healers could have seen to you if you were not such an infant."

Dann ran his tongue across the front of his top teeth, biting back his words. "There are worse injured. I'm fine."

"You're fine?" As though making a point, Lyrei squeezed at the wound in Dann's leg.

"Sweet fucking Elyara's toes." He slapped at Lyrei's hand. "Really?"

"Small pleasures are hard to come by." Lyrei gave Dann a mocking smile and carried on.

Dann leaned back on the bed with both his hands, looking up at the tent's roof. "You enjoy my pain."

"On the contrary…"

Dann tilted his head back down, and for a moment he found himself lost in the shifting gold of Lyrei's eyes. Then the tent flap opened, and Nala shuffled in.

"Commander Sureheart… sir… my lord." Her cheeks were flushed red, and she looked from Dann and Lyrei back to the tent's opening. "I…"

Dann realised he sat on the edge of the bed in nothing but his smallclothes, raw, stitched wounds on his legs, neck, and arms. "What is it, Nala?"

Before the young porter could answer, Tarmon strode in, his armour replaced with a linen tunic, thick trousers, and a long coat. No matter what the man wore, he just looked like a tree with mountains for shoulders. Or a mountain with trees for shoulders. Dann couldn't quite decide.

Tarmon looked to Nala and bowed at the waist. "Thank you, Nala."

The young attendant stiffened and returned the bow, nodding repeatedly as though something had broken in her head.

"How is he?" Tarmon moved to stand by Lyrei's side, staring down at the half-stitched gash that ran from close to Dann's groin down to just above his knee. The armour Valdrin had crafted was a fine thing, and if he'd not been wearing it, his chest would have resembled a fishing net from all the holes.

"*He* is right here," Dann snapped, narrowing his eyes.

"As irritating as usual," Lyrei said, driving the needle back through Dann's skin so he couldn't respond.

"To be expected." Tarmon folded his arms, looking down at Dann like a disgruntled uncle might a nephew. "He'll live?"

"Unfortunately."

"Keep it up," Dann said. "I swear to the gods." He hissed as Lyrei ran the catgut through again. "If you ever want to see that shoe of yours again, I'd start being a lot nicer to me."

"Keep it," Tarmon said with a shrug. "Unlike you, I brought spares."

"I know." Dann tried his best to give Tarmon as menacing a look as possible. "Mikal told me."

He'd made good friends with Tarmon's attendant – or squire, as Tarmon had called him. And Mikal looked after all of Tarmon's gear, including his boots and shoes.

For a second, Tarmon looked as though he were going to snap, but he collected himself and gave a downturn of his bottom lip. "The bird is back."

"Fucking bird." Dann pushed himself upright, face contorting as Lyrei drove the needle in again. "What did it take?"

"Well, it was last seen fleeing your tent with a pair of smallclothes in its beak."

Dann flashed a look at Nala, who still stood by the tent flap. The young attendant lifted her gaze from the ground to meet Dann's. Her cheeks went bright red, and she snapped her head back to staring at the tent floor.

"What do you want, Tarmon?"

"One of the farmers gave us twenty cows, hung and dried on their way to market in Midhaven, after we drove the Lorians off their land. It's beef stew tonight. I was coming to see if you'd join us. Your stunt with the horses is making the rounds."

"Mmh." Dann grunted. "Once she's done turning me into a human pin cushion."

"Lyrei?" Tarmon raised an eyebrow.

Despite the promise of fresh beef, Lyrei took every slow second she could to finish the sewing on Dann's leg, seeming to savour each pierce of the needle. As soon as she was finished, she wrapped it in a bandage, Dann threw on some clothes, and they made to leave.

Dann stopped at the tent flap, resting a hand on Nala's shoulder.

"I'm sorry, my lord."

"For what?"

"I wasn't watching the cart when we were setting up camp. The bird, I should have stopped it."

Dann let out a laugh. "Go find Ingvat. She won't be drinking. She'll likely be at the guard post with Surin or Narthil on the northern edge of the camp. Tell her I've asked for her to procure you a bow, quiver, arrows, belts, some good boots, and a warm coat."

"Yes, my lord… but, why, my lord?"

"Less of the 'my lord', Nala."

"Yes, my lord."

Dann pressed his hand to his face and squeezed his thumb and forefinger into the creases of his eyes, shaking his head. "We'll work on that. You want to know why, Nala? Because we're going to hunt that fucking bird."

As Tarmon emerged from the tent, three young squires and four soldiers led a column of enormous black horses past a clutch of tents on the right. Those animals would be a welcome addition to the army. The elves had a strange aversion to horses, but Tarmon had no such qualms. A strong cavalry charge could turn the tide of any battle.

"Whoever rescued those beautiful creatures should be worshipped until his dying day," Dann said as he emerged from the tent with Lyrei and Nala. He gave Tarmon a grin wide enough for a cart to pass through, then folded his arms and raised his eyebrows. "Well?"

"What?" Tarmon narrowed his eyes.

"We both know you didn't make a trip out to my tent just to make sure I wouldn't miss the beef. You would have sent Mikal – or just eaten my share yourself. What is it really?"

Tarmon suppressed a laugh and started walking. Dann had a higher capacity for idiocy than most anyone he knew, but the lad was far from stupid. "Queen Tessara asked us to join her for supper tonight. Vaeril asked me to get you, and I figured I'd better do it myself before you set off after that damn bird again."

For a second, Dann looked as though he was going to argue, but a shrug followed. "Probably a good choice."

"What else has it stolen from you now?"

"I don't wanna talk about it." Dann looked off into the night, muttering to himself. The only words Tarmon caught were "Damn fucking bird."

"I'm going to need you to be on your best behaviour when we eat with the queen."

"Me? I'm always on my best behaviour."

"Dann…"

"What?"

Dann looked left to Lyrei, who walked at his side, her head tilted and eyebrows raised.

"*What?*"

"You loosed an arrow past Ingvat's head two nights ago while we were eating."

"Yes, but—"

"Then jumped through the fire shouting 'I got the fucker.'"

"The… the bird. I almost got him. He was just…" Dann's voice trailed off as Tarmon raised his eyebrows. "I see your point."

"Good." Tarmon stopped and let out a long sigh, resting his hand on Dann's shoulder. For a moment, Tarmon thought about reminding Dann of his position. Dann was a commander in the rebellion now. Everything he did, every word that left his lips, reflected not only on himself, but also on Calen. But Dann knew. Behind all the jokes and all the humour, he knew.

VAERIL SAT IN THE DIRT with his legs crossed, a bowl of stew in one hand and a cup of wine balanced on his knee. The fire's warmth drove the cold from his bones. Even at that moment, Ünviril sat on the ground before him.

Dawnbringer.

He'd never wanted to be so far from any one single thing, and yet that one thing spent most of his waking hours strapped to his body. It seemed a cruel joke.

Not two feet from him, Queen Tessara Vaelen Alumír sat just as he did: legs crossed, a bowl of stew in one hand. At first glance, her clothes were simple. A long-sleeved tunic, trousers, boots, and a mantle clipped together by a silver broach in the shape of a star. All black with silver embellishments. Cut gems of jet were set into the polished silver circlet atop her head, a silver star at its fore. She wanted to appear as a queen of the people, sitting in the dirt with those not of royal blood, eating food from her lap, drinking wine from a wooden cup. And yet, every single item she wore was carefully chosen to signal who she was and the power she wielded. To make others feel grateful she deigned to honour them with her presence. There were layers in everything.

Vaeril knew little of Queen Tessara. But she was Vaelen, and she played the games well, as was becoming of any ruler of Vaelen.

Her Ephorí, Dumelian, sat at her side. Though, judging by the way he kept shifting uncomfortably and pulling faces at the dirt, he would have been far more comfortable at a table with a silver plate.

Many others sat about the fire at the queen's invitation also.

King Galdra had sent his Ephorí, Thurivîr, to act as commander of the elves pledged by Lunithír, while Queen Uthrían had sent Baralas. Both elves sat across the fire, eating quietly, their personal guards arranged around them.

Thurivîr was a stark contrast to Queen Tessara, all blazing gold where she was shrouded in black. His golden silk shirt – ornamented with rubies – was paired with stiff maroon trousers, and his dark hair was swept back from his temples and tied with gold string. Opulence was a weapon the kingdom of Lunithír had long wielded. Gold and crimson were their colours, the mighty stag their crest.

Baralas was garbed as though he were a ranger of Aravell. A thick brown leather cuirass covered his chest, while a deep green cloak hung about his shoulders, his sword still belted at his hip. His part in this theatre of politicking was that of a warrior who fought alongside the common elf. Though, if Vaeril was being fair, Baralas had not shied away from the battles. He had thrown himself into the thick and bore a new scar along the right side of his chin for it, along with bruises that ran all about his neck. His leathers were neither polished nor pristine. They bore the marks and wear of well-used armour. And they fit him well, which meant they were likely his own. Vaeril respected him, even if he didn't like him very much.

The young smith, Valdrin, had travelled with them also. Both Calen and Therin had attempted to convince him otherwise, but he had been quite insistent that he see how his armour performed in the field. He sat alone, his wine untouched, his entire focus on the journal in his lap as he sketched new designs for not just armour, but livery, banners, weapons, and all manner of things.

Besides Tessara and the Ephorí, Atara and Harken ate to Vaeril's right, while Dann, Tarmon, Lyrei, and Erik sat on his left. He was not sure how to express it, but having them there, having his Vandasera by his side, meant a great deal to him. It brought him honour, but also comfort.

The only ones missing were Gaeleron and Calen – and Alea. Calen, the one who bound them all together. Since crossing paths with Calen Bryer, Vaeril had barely been apart from the man. Even chained in Arisfall, they had not been this far from one another.

It was a strange thing. Once, Calen had been his oath. Now, the man was his brother. No longer a responsibility, now a privilege. And now Calen and Valerys were alone, flying from Arkalen to Ilnaen, and there was nothing Vaeril could do to keep them safe. He was honoured to be leading this army alongside the others, to protect Calen's home as Calen had protected his, but he'd be lying if he said he wouldn't rather be at Calen's side.

Besides, he hated being a piece in the game of kings and queens. And around this fire, that's all he was.

Queen Tessara caught Vaeril's eye, a cup of wine in her hand, her bowl of stew finished and already being carried away by a young attendant. "You fought well today," she said. "You brought much honour to Vaelen."

"The honour is mine, Myia'nari."

"Seeing you wield Ünviril against the same souls who destroyed our world… It was a special thing. An elf of our kingdom, wielding the new dawn and bearing the sigil of the first free Draleid in centuries. The bralgír will tell stories of you, Vaeril Ilyin."

Vaeril cast a furtive glance at the silver star pommel of the sword at his hip. He took a last mouthful of the flavourful stew, then placed the bowl on the ground. "The bralgír will have many stories to tell from this age, Myia'nari. I do not believe there will be time to tell mine."

Before the queen could respond, an excessively long and wet slurping noise cut through the campfire. Vaeril turned to see Dann holding his bowl of stew to his lips, glistening beads of grease clinging to the stubble that surrounded his mouth.

Dann's eyes widened, the bowl still pressed to his lips, as he realised everyone was staring at him. He carried on.

"Thank you for having us around your fire tonight." Tarmon gestured towards Queen Tessara, a flash of irritation on his face at Dann.

Vaeril held back a smile.

"You are most welcome." It was not Queen Tessara who spoke, but Thurivîr. The queen didn't say anything, but her eyes betrayed her. "If we are to fight in the same wars, we should 'break the same bread', so to speak. The stew you eat is an old Lunithíran recipe from when my people held sway over everything they could touch from Ilnaen to the foothills of Mar Dorul in northern Lynalion, back when we had the land to raise cattle. It's been almost three hundred and fifty years since I last tasted beef. Nowadays the stew is typically made with venison or boar, but this—" he gestured down at the drained bowl of stew in his hands "—there is nothing quite like beef in a good Milaríse. I only wish my son and daughter were here to taste it." For a fraction of a second, Thurivîr's unreadable expression cracked. "They were born after The Fall."

"Where are they now?"

Vaeril clenched his jaw at Tarmon's question. He knew Tarmon was only trying to find common ground, but he also knew the Ephorí never gave information freely unless it was for a purpose.

"Iyana passed into Heraya's embrace long ago, taken by the Astyrlína." Thurivîr sucked in the sides of his cheeks, staring into the flames before him. "My son, Thronil, fell during the battle for the city. Dragonfire."

"My apologies, Thurivîr… I didn't mean to…"

Tarmon stopped speaking as Thurivîr held up an open hand and shook his head. "You have lost family, Tarmon Hoard. I can see it in everything you do. And neither you nor I are alone in that. Loss is what binds us. A common grief, a common enemy."

The candour with which Thurivîr spoke surprised Vaeril, but Vaeril still didn't trust the tenor of his voice. There was something searching in it, something pointed.

Tarmon raised his cup of wine, the fire casting a warm orange glow on his face. "To those we've lost."

"To those we've lost," chorused the others, mimicking Tarmon's gesture and drinking from their cups.

Out of the corner of his eye, Vaeril saw the tips of Queen Tessara's fingers go white as she gripped her cup. That was it then. That was the game they were playing. Who could ingratiate themselves more with Calen's highest commander. There was always a game, always an advantage being sought.

Baralas had been quiet up until that point, but he lifted his cup once more. "Nur temen vie'ryn valana. Din dauva værakanra i'lanír. Din viël værakanra glinmatar." The Ephorí held his cup in the air, allowing the silence to settle. "In the Common Tongue, 'for those we have lost. Your death will not be in vain. Your life will not be forgotten.'"

Vaeril lifted his cup along with the others and repeated Baralas's words. Baralas's voice held none of the practiced theatrics that Thurivîr's did. The sorrow was genuine, the words not just another carefully chosen sentiment. A rare vulnerability amongst those in the higher echelons. Though, Baralas was an

Ephorí of Ardurän and so had been instructed in the art of politicking while still in his mother's womb, so Vaeril could have been mistaken. But he didn't feel as though he was.

"There is another matter that must be discussed," Queen Tessara said after a few minutes of silence. "Dumelian informs me that our scouts report word that the human city of Camylin remains under heavy Urak siege. The city is blockaded, and the Uraks have set fortified encampments. The siege has lasted since before the Blood Moon rose, and food will soon be short."

"With respect, Inari." Thurivîr inclined his head, barely, the smooth gold silk of his shirt glowing in the firelight. "We knew Camylin was under siege before we left. This is not new information. Our course remains unchanged. We must skirt the blockade, keeping our distance, and fight our way through to this city of Salme."

"To hear that a child starves on the other side of the world is a terrible thing, is it not?" Queen Tessara asked, raising an eyebrow.

Thurivîr returned the queen's gaze, a hint of caution in his eyes. "Of course."

Tessara's expression remained unchanged. "If you heard a child was starving, would it move you to cross two thousand miles to place food in their belly?"

Vaeril saw where the queen was going, but he wasn't sure Thurivîr did. He cast a glance at Erik, Tarmon, Dann, and Lyrei. None of the four had said a word, but they all watched. Even Valdrin had stopped his sketching.

"Of course not," Thurivîr answered. "The child would be dead before I arrived. What is your point?"

Tarmon shifted in his place, crossing his arms and drawing in a long breath. "Her point is that to hear of something and to witness something are two separate things. You would not cross two thousand miles to feed a starving child you have never met. But if you watch that same child starve before your eyes, you would give them your last morsel. We already knew of the siege, but now we are about to march past the starving child."

A broad smile stretched Tessara's lips, and she bowed her head deeply to Tarmon.

"Mmh…" Thurivîr shrugged, opening his palms out. "It matters little. Pretty metaphors aside, there is nothing we can do. If we throw our forces against the Uraks at Camylin, we will not have the numbers to relieve Salme. And even if we did, Camylin's garrison is Lorian. Would we give our blood to save soldiers who would put us to the spear?"

"The garrison might be Lorian, but the people are Illyanaran," Dann said, joining the conversation. As soon as the words had left his lips, Dann looked unsure of himself.

"And what would you have us do, Commander Pimm?" Thurivîr emphasised Dann's name and his rank, amusement in his voice.

"I don't know. But we can't just leave them to die…"

"So you would have us die in their stead?"

"No… that's not what I meant. I… no."

"Come now, surely with your vast experience leading warriors into battle you have a plan? You have seen death like I have, have you not? You understand the weight of sending souls to die? Or I suppose not. One so young." He smiled and raised his hands with a false smile on his lips. "With a head full of ideals."

Erik shifted in place, jaw clenching. The man glared at Thurivîr.

"Nothing to say, Commander Pimm?" Thurivîr continued. "Usually, you are so full of words."

"Watch your tongue," Erik snapped, leaning forwards, his stare fixed on the Ephorí.

"There feels like a threat in those words, Commander Virandr. Are you prepared to—"

"Enough." Vaeril had never seen Tarmon angry, truly angry. Until now. Perhaps to others there was little more than a stiffness in his voice. But Vaeril had grown to know the man. He could see the twitch in Tarmon's jaw, his pale knuckles as he squeezed his cup, and the way he refused to look at Thurivîr. Tarmon glanced at Queen Tessara. "We cannot spare the time nor the lives to break Camylin's siege. We do not know how long Salme's defences will hold, and Salme is our priority." He pondered for a moment, his jaw relaxing, the anger seeming to fade. "We are now in possession of some four hundred horses, with no small thanks to Commander Pimm. I will arrange for outriders to harass the Urak lines as we pass. A hundred well organised riders can cause havoc and may just buy Camylin the time it needs. Once Salme is safe and Calen has rejoined us, we can reassess. I do not wish to leave the men and women in that city to die, but war is nothing more than a series of impossible choices, and we do what we must."

Tarmon drew a long, deep breath, then pulled himself to his feet. He gestured to Vaeril and the others before bowing slightly in Tessara's direction. "We thank you for the food, and the wine, and the conversation. But it is late and we have many injured, and we rise with the sun. I fear sleep calls us."

The queen bowed her head in return, then gestured to Dumelian. "We have Healers we can spare. Please show Dumelian to your wounded. He will make the arrangements."

There seemed to be a hint of satisfaction in her voice. Vaeril was still learning the subtleties of his new queen, but she appeared to favour a direct approach.

"Du haryn myia vrai, Inari."

You have my thanks, Queen.

Vaeril smiled as the words left Tarmon's lips. As soon as the army had left Aravell, Tarmon had asked Vaeril to school him in the Old Tongue. It didn't come as naturally to the man as it did to Calen, but Tarmon had practiced night and day since they'd set out, and his pronunciation had improved tenfold. The man's determination was admirable.

"Din vrai é atuya sin'vala, Harindavír. Ata'é din ordis."

Your thanks are welcome here, High Commander. As are your words.

Vaeril's smile widened further at the queen's response. Not because her words brought him joy, but because he knew Tarmon didn't understand most of them judging by the falter in his stare.

The man inclined his head in response, then made to leave, but stopped. He looked back for half a second as though pondering something, then turned, his stare falling on Thurivîr.

The Ephorí raised an amused eyebrow, his lips still curled in a laugh.

"Our cultures are different, Thurivîr. I respect that." He walked slowly past the fire until he reached Thurivîr, coming to a halt barely a foot away. The seated elf had to crane his neck to look up at Tarmon's looming bulk. "But I need you to understand something. Where I was born, we do not talk in twisted riddles and half-truths, not to those we would call friend. We talk plainly and simply. If you have a problem, you say it outright. You don't cover it in sugar and lace it with venom."

He tilted his head to the side, then dropped to his haunches before the Ephorí. Thurivîr's guards shifted, but the elf gestured them back.

Tarmon glanced at each guard in turn, then looked back to Thurivîr and held his stare for a long moment. At last, he drew in a breath through his nose and exhaled slowly. "So let me speak simple and plain. If you dare mock one of my commanders like that again, disrespect them in any way, I will stick my boot so far up your arse we will see if your shit is as gold as your shirt."

"So, is sleep truly calling us?" The silence as they'd walked through the camp had driven Dann insane. Thoughts were not things to be left alone with. They were dangerous little bastards that deserved all the caution in the world.

"No." Tarmon shook his head but didn't stop. "We're going to get piss drunk and pass out under the stars."

"Tarmon Hoard, why do you always say such beautiful things?"

Tarmon only grunted in response.

Erik grabbed Dann by the shoulder. He shook his head in disbelief as though staring at a three-headed goat. "What is wrong with you?"

"How long do you have? My father always said it was easier to say what wasn't wrong with me. I think I hit my head when I was a baby. That or my mam dropped me."

"Stop. Stop fucking around. This isn't the time for it, Dann. We're at war. We've lost hundreds just in the days it's taken us to get this far. Can you comprehend that? People in this army have lost friends, brothers, sisters. And you prance around acting like the world is nothing but sunshine and flowers."

"Which is why it's *precisely* the time for it." The others had stopped and were now watching, along with a number of guards wearing Calen's sigil. Tarmon motioned them on. "What's wrong, Erik? What did I do to make you this angry?"

"No…" Erik glanced at his hand, realising how tightly he had been gripping Dann's shoulder. Releasing him, Erik stepped back and ran his hands through his hair. "I'm sorry… I'm not angry at *you*. I just… How are you not furious? How can you make light of *everything*, *all* the time? We all saw what Thurivîr was doing. Poking you, prodding you, mocking you."

Dann shrugged. "True. But I think Tarmon dealt with that, did he not? 'We will see if your shit is as gold as your shirt.' Gods, I wish it was me who'd said that. That was beautiful. The man is a mountain with a poet's heart."

"Dann." Erik twisted his tongue in his mouth, the frustration visible on his face.

Dann let out a sigh, staring off at a row of tents to his right, torch flames blowing in the wind. "What good would it have done to be furious, Erik? Thurivîr *wanted* me to get angry. He wanted me to lose my senses so he could mock me even more. So he could laugh at the 'emotional human'. At the young man who doesn't deserve his place. Why? I don't know, for his own amusement perhaps. Elves think they speak in riddles, but they overestimate themselves." Dann gestured to Vaeril, who stood only a few feet away. "No offence intended, Vaeril."

"A little taken."

Dann continued. "I refused to give him what he wanted. And then Tarmon called him out plain, and now he looks like a fool in front of the others. I don't know about you, but I'd call that a victory. The elven kings and queens and their Ephorí like to play their little games. They like to twist their words – and yours – and make you squirm, make you feel weak and helpless. But their flaw is that they always think they are the only ones who can do it, the only ones smart enough to play their games. If Thurivîr thinks I'm an idiot, so be it. I like it that way. Now, can we stop talking about that gold-covered shit stain and go get pissed?"

TARMON STOOD WITH HIS ARMS folded, an almost-empty cup of wine in his left hand, watching the men, women, and elves dancing around the fire as a pair of elves sang while playing the lute and violin.

He lifted the cup to his nose and breathed deeply. All his life he'd only ever drunk Belduaran wine. Trade was a crucial part of Belduar's survival, and imported wine was low on the list of essential goods. That wine had been light and fruity, sweet almost. The wine he held in his hand was an entirely different beast. It was deep, dark, and bold. It left his mouth dry, and the flavours seemed to change and shift as the liquid sat on his tongue. He turned to Vaeril, who stood beside him with his own cup. Vaeril had not offered the bottle to anyone else, and Tarmon had a feeling it was slightly more special than the elf was letting on. "Where did you say this was from?"

"A vineyard in the western section of Aravell. Though the grapes come from a place long dead. It was a gift from Queen Tessara." Vaeril watched the others dance and sing, his head tilted slightly to the side. Something that wasn't quite a smile brought warmth to his features as he watched Lyrei, Dann, and Erik twirling about with the others. He looked back at Tarmon. "Thurivîr will neither forget nor forgive what you said earlier."

"Good. I meant it. We're all on the same side of this war. Elves of all three kingdoms are pledged to Calen, wear his sigil, fight in his name. I don't care who that snot-nosed golden prick is, but I've not time for his shit."

Vaeril gave a half-smile, touching the rim of the wooden cup to his lips and laughing.

"What?"

"I've just never heard one of the Ephorí referred to as a 'snot-nosed golden prick'."

Tarmon laughed at that himself. "Fuck."

Vaeril raised an eyebrow.

"I think Dann's rubbing off on me."

They both guffawed at that, but Vaeril's laughter quickly died as a group of five elves approached and bowed deeply. They spoke words in the Old Tongue, bowed again, then moved on to join the drinking and dancing.

Vaeril's mood soured after that.

"May I ask a question of the heart?" Tarmon wasn't sure if he'd said the words correctly, particularly given the surprise on Vaeril's face.

The elf allowed himself a smile once more, one that broke into a soft laugh. "You're learning quickly."

Tarmon shook his head. "I've had a good teacher."

Vaeril laughed softly, sipping at his wine. "Ask your question."

"Ever since Tessara gifted you that sword—" Tarmon gestured at the star-pommelled sword strapped to Vaeril's hip "—you've been different. Darker. Why?"

Vaeril looked down at the sword, his lips thinning. He drained his cup, then refilled it from the glass bottle resting on the satchel at his feet. "As you've seen, my people love to play games. To twist and manipulate. To work with strings in the shadows. This sword is nothing more than another string, another piece on their board. On the surface, it is the highest of honours, but in truth, it is a chain around my neck. A chain that ties me to Tessara and her to Calen through me."

Vaeril set his wine cup down and unbuckled his belt, then handed the sword and scabbard to Tarmon.

The scabbard alone was a work of art. The body was black leather marked with stars and coiling tree branches. Both the locket and the chape were worked from polished silver. The pommel was shaped into a silver star and looked as though it would smash through a skull with little effort.

"This blade, Ünviril, is the most legendary weapon in my people's history. I am as deserving of it as I am of a crown. Not two years past I had barely been raised to full ranger, and now I am the Champion of Vaelen? Do you know what Elyin Shadvír did with this blade to earn that title? He forged Vaelen from a High House into a kingdom. He single-handedly turned the tide of a war. He altered the relationship between our peoples beyond measure. He was not simply a hero, he was a true legend, almost a myth. I was told stories of his deeds when I was but a child. I am not fit to bear Ünviril, never mind wield it, and I'm not the only one who knows it. It's a two-edged blade, honour and shame both. And I'm trapped between the two. Every elf that sees me wear this weapon at my hip knows that it was given to me solely because of my connection to Calen, that I do not deserve it."

"It's a funny thing about legends," Tarmon said as he ran his finger along the silver pommel. "They're only legends after the fact. At the time, they're nothing more than people."

He handed the sword back to Vaeril, who took it hesitantly.

"Wield that blade beside these warriors in battle. Guard their lives with it, carve the path forward with it. You'll soon find yourself worthy. Legends aren't passed down, Vaeril. They're forged. Nobody is worthy until they are."

Vaeril strapped the scabbard back around his hip, then picked up his cup and tapped it against Tarmon's.

"We've come a long way, you and I." Tarmon sipped at his wine, thinking back.

"I'd never even left Aravell before meeting Calen."

"I'd not even have survived Belduar if not for you." Tarmon subconsciously fingered at the scar on his stomach. "First you pulled the arrow from my stomach, then you dragged me from the wreckage of the Wind Runner. You kept your calm in the tunnels, guided us down the side of Mount Helmund. Were it not for you, the N'aka would be picking our corpses clean in the Burnt Lands. Void, I figure we'd all be dead a dozen times over if you'd not been there. Whatever that sword means, whether you think you deserve it or not, I'm proud to call you brother."

Vaeril returned Tarmon's stare, then once again tapped his cup against Tarmon's. "Vandasera, akar."

Tarmon knew those words. *Oathsworn, brother.* He repeated them, then drank deeply.

After a while, Dann came twirling from the song and dance, releasing Lyrei, who spun away and grabbed Erik's arm and carried on.

Dann doubled over, resting his hands on his knees and panting like a dying dog. He lifted his head, sweat streaming down his face and dripping off his chin. "Wine?"

Vaeril snorted with laughter, then poured a cup from his bottle and handed it to Dann.

Dann grunted and lifted himself into a more upright position before taking a deep mouthful. "Shit, that's good. I love wine, did I ever tell you that? I'd not tasted it before Belduar... You know, when all this is over, I think I'll settle down in the villages and plant vines, spend my years sipping wine and watching sunsets." When neither Tarmon nor Vaeril spoke, Dann let out a long breath, then moved to stand between them. He shook his head as he watched the dancing and singing. "Not going to join?"

"We march with the rising sun. I can either have a sore head or be tired, I can't do both. I choose the sore head." Tarmon took a deep drink of his wine to emphasise his point.

"Spoken like an old man."

"Spoken like a man who's responsible for the lives of almost five thousand souls. Besides, you're dancing enough for all of us."

"We're alive," Dann said with a shrug, taking a draught of the wine. "Not everyone who woke this morning can say that. You never know which dance will be your last."

"Between what you said to Erik earlier and that, one would almost think you've become wise, Dann Pimm."

"Almost? I'm a veritable sage. Honestly, what I said earlier were just things Therin taught me. I figure if I repeat everything he says word for word, someone's bound to think I'm the one who came up with it. I actually miss having the old walking chastisement around. He's not as crusty as he lets on. Well, not as crusty as you anyway."

"Dann?"

"Shut up?"

"Shut up."

"See, you're even talking like Therin now." He looked back at Tarmon, all mirth leaving his voice. "What you said to Thurivîr. Thank you."

"You're a fuckwad, Dann. But you're our fuckwad."

"Tarmon, what in the gods is a fuckwad?"

Before Tarmon could conjure an answer, Dann leaned forwards and narrowed his eyes, staring at something to the left of the fire.

Tarmon followed Dann's gaze to see the stumpy little bird that had been harassing the man weaving and bobbing through a group of dancing soldiers. The thing moved with surprising nimbleness. Then Tarmon realised what it held in its beak: a sock.

"That feather-covered little shitsmear."

"Dann, it's just a bird."

"That's no bird," Dann said, draining the remainder of his wine and setting his cup down, never taking his eyes off the bird. "That's a demon covered in feathers. Its sole purpose is destruction and terror… and it has my sock. This is where I leave you both. We all have our destinies. This is mine."

As Dann tiptoed off, Lyrei came swinging out of the crowd and grabbed him by the shoulders, shaking her head. "No."

"It's got my sock. This needs to end, Lyrei. There isn't room enough for both of us in this world."

Lyrei cupped her hands on either side of Dann's face, staring into his eyes. "*No.*"

"But…"

She shook her head again.

Dann looked from Lyrei to the bird, who was slowly slipping away. With a sigh, he acquiesced and followed the elf back into the dancing, continuously casting his gaze back over his shoulder.

"Do you think he's had enough wine?" Tarmon asked.

"Calen once told me that with each drink Dann becomes a new person. From what I remember, this sounds like nine drink Dann."

"Well…" Tarmon held out his cup. "If it please, I'd like to become six drink Tarmon."

CHAPTER FORTY-FIVE

THE RUSTY SHELL

18th Day of the Blood Moon

Salme – Winter, Year 3081 After Doom

By the time night fell, Erdhardt was already awake again. He'd never needed much sleep. Always retired long after Aela and woke when she did. Her voice had been his morning bells, her warmth his sliver of the rising sun. Now he woke quiet and cold.

He grunted as he slipped on a shirt and trousers, the sutures along a cut on his back splitting, the blood seeping into the fabric. Anya had been sleeping when he'd gone to see her. The man from Ölm had done what he could, but his hand was half as deft as Anya's and there were more injured than he knew what to do with. There were others who helped at the bloodhouse, but most were more used to tending pigs or sheep, not people. There were few things he wouldn't have given to have Freis Bryer living and breathing. That woman had no equal when it came to the art of healing.

He ran his finger down the thick catgut stitching along his right arm before slipping on a long coat and boots. He slid his arms through the straps of his weapons belt and dropped his hammer into the loop on his back.

Erdhardt left his cabin and strode through the city, lanterns hanging on the ramparts, guards moving back and forth. With input from Erdhardt and the others, Dahlen had established watch and combat rotations to allow the city's defenders to get some rest. Though Dahlen himself often ignored his nights of rest. Erdhardt couldn't tell the man off as he was much the same. He couldn't remember the last time he'd slept so little.

Two sharp horn bursts would let the defenders know the Uraks were charging the walls. Three called for the resting rotation to be woken. In theory it was a sound plan, but few men or women could return to sleep knowing that Uraks attacked the walls and a battle was raging. So as soon as two horns blew, the city was awake.

Before long, Erdhardt found his way to The Rusty Shell. The place was older than The Gilded Dragon had been, built some two hundred years ago. And those added years in the world were clear in the rotting wood that plagued some of the floorboards and the grime built up on the stone – though Erdhardt doubted Lasch would ever have allowed The Gilded Dragon to suffer the same way. The roof had been leaking profusely when they'd first arrived, but a few weeks back, a thatcher who had travelled from Camylin had patched it up for a few tankards of ale.

Erdhardt found Tharn Pimm and Jorvill Ehrnin at the bar, nattering like old hens, Jorvill's wife on the other side of the counter serving out ale and stew. The tavern's proprietor, Shola Holten, had found herself bitterly outmanned when the refugees from across the western villages had flooded through the doors in search of something to ease their pain. And with the loss of The Glade – and her son – Paloma Ehrnin had been keen to find a task for her hands and mind.

Jorvill and Tharn slapped Erdhardt on the back in greeting, immediately dragging him into some conversation about the best wood to use for arrow shafts. A conversation for which he could not have had less interest.

"Ale?" Paloma Ehrnin gave him a sympathetic smile, drying her hands on a rag that she tossed over her shoulder.

"I'd love to say mead."

She nodded in agreement, a sad soft nod. "If only."

Both Lasch and Elia Havel had vanished from The Glade around the same time the Lorian soldiers had left. At first he'd thought they'd gone after Rist, but Lasch would never have gone without a word. The soldiers had taken them, that was a certainty in Erdhardt's mind. But by the time he'd realised, it had been far too late. The one question that plagued him, though, was *why*. They'd not taken Tharn or Ylinda Pimm. It was a question he didn't expect to ever be answered. And one that would plague him until Heraya finally let him rest.

Paloma dropped a full tankard of ale on the counter and waved away the coppers he offered, as she did every night he stepped through the door. *"Keep those Uraks away from my tavern,"* Shola Holten had said, *"and you'll not ever worry about a coin purse in here."*

It took all of ten seconds of Tharn Pimm talking about the merits of turkey feathers versus goose feathers when it came to fletching for Erdhardt to slowly extract himself from the conversation and pull away from the bar.

A hand stuck up amidst the swell of bodies.

Dahlen Virandr sat near the middle of the tavern, Nimara, Yoring, Thannon, and a number of others sitting at his side at a long rectangular table. The others who usually marched around with Dahlen must have been on watch.

"Feeling better now, old man?"

"Vibrant as a spring chicken." Erdhardt bit down against a sharp pain in his knee as he took a seat on the bench across from Dahlen, Yoring shifting over to create space.

"Fellhammer." Yoring tapped his tankard against Erdhardt's, ale sloshing from one to the other. Erdhardt had fought side by side with Yoring and Almer on many nights, hard as iron the pair of them. Never in his days had he expected to meet a dwarf. They had retreated into the mountains since long before he was born, and now there he was drinking and fighting beside them. "May your fires never be extinguished and your blade never dull."

"Nor yours, Master Dwarf."

"Nobody's ever called me master except for you, Fellhammer."

"It's a sign of respect in the villages."

"Well, Master Fellhammer it is. Knees still aching?" He nodded to where Erdhardt was subconsciously rubbing the side of his knee.

Erdhardt nodded, squeezing. "Only when I stop moving. As long as I'm warm, it's fine."

"I know the feeling." Yoring pulled the trouser of his left leg up past the knee to reveal a twisted patch of hairless flesh as big as a coin. "Arrow during the Burning of Belduar. Right through and out the back. Hurt like a kerathlin-fucker." He lifted his tankard and pointed it at Dahlen. "Were it not for this son-of-a-goat I'd be nothing but another body on the city's second wall."

Erdhardt watched Dahlen as Yoring told the tale of how Almer and the young man had dragged him through the city and onto the Wind Runner while the Lorian forces flooded over the second wall. It was a strange thing, amidst a sea of strange things, to sit around a table with a group of warriors who had fought at the fall of Belduar, at the burning of the great city of legend. Even Erdhardt had been told stories of Belduar as a child, of the last bastion of mankind that remained entirely free of Lorian control.

Dahlen Virandr had an uncomfortable smile on his face the entire time, both hands cupping his tankard, which he never seemed to drink from.

"No taste for the ale?" Erdhardt whispered, leaning across the table while Yoring went on with his story. He nodded down at Dahlen's ale. "You've barely had a thimbleful."

Dahlen raised an eyebrow, then looked down at the dark liquid in the tankard, gave a half-smile, and took a short draught.

"Do you ever stop?"

"Stop what?" Dahlen watched Yoring, who had stood up from the bench and was now making axe swinging motions with his hands.

"Waiting. For the next attack, for the next moment you have to spill blood. There's more to this life than sleeping and killing."

"No. There's not. Not now, not while the Uraks could come flooding over those walls any night. If my father were here, he'd probably sleep on the wall itself, cradling his swords. He'd likely never sleep."

"But he's not, and you're not him. Nobody can be anything but what they are."

Erdhardt let out a long sigh, stroking his beard. "You're a young man, Dahlen. How many summers have you seen? Twenty? Twenty-two?"

"This will be my twenty-fourth." He took a reluctant sip of his ale.

"Even the strongest steel breaks beneath enough weight. Let yourself breathe. Let yourself rest. You deserve one night."

Dahlen nodded slowly, then straightened his back and looked around the inn. "So many of these men and women have never even held a sword," he said, leaning closer to Erdhardt once more. "And now they face Uraks? Now they must stand on a wall, or in the dirt and mud, and watch their friends be run through, maimed, disembowelled, beheaded. I'm not good at many things, Erdhardt. I can't sing, can't cook anything that won't end up burnt or tasting like shit, I can't dance, can't brew, or forge, or any number of things. I can survive. Hunt and forage, sew a wound or clothes, track, fish. But there is one thing above all else – I can fight. I can wield a blade better than anyone in this city, and I know that for a fact because my father taught me how and my father is the greatest swordsman I've ever seen in my life, the greatest warrior. My brother, Erik, is coming with an army, and all I have to do is keep Salme alive until he gets here. And if me standing on that wall, night after night, day after day, gives these people the courage to do the same, then that's what I'll do. Because I can do very little else."

"Well, you won't do it alone." Erdhardt tapped his tankard against Dahlen's and gave him a short nod. The young man spoke with the heart of someone who had seen twice his summers and the head of someone who had seen twice Erdhardt's.

Erdhardt had always taken pride in the young men and women of The Glade, in how they were raised. He'd always thought that the people they became reflected not only on the village but on himself. As an Elder it had been his task to guide them, to teach them the things that mattered in life. And as such, he very much looked forward to the day he met Aeson Virandr. Because any man who raised a son with that kind of integrity was a man Erdhardt wanted to meet.

An hour or so passed. Erdhardt drank three more tankards, Dahlen drank one, and they watched the inn fill to bursting.

A short man with a balding head and grey-black beard shouldered through the crowd, his stare fixed on Dahlen.

Erdhardt tensed, watching the man push past a group of Lorian soldiers in their black and red leathers drinking around a circular table. He shifted in his seat, lifting one leg from across the bench so he could stand if needed.

"Dahlen Virandr." The man opened his arms as he stepped by a serving girl wearing a long brown dress and apron.

Dahlen looked up from the conversation he was having with Nimara and Thannon about constructing a tower by the gates. It took a moment, but then his jaw slackened and he tilted his head as he rose to his feet. "Darda? Darda Vastion?"

It was only then Erdhardt recognised the man. He'd run a shipping operation from Milltown, sending goods north. He'd carried a bit more weight the last time Erdhardt had seen him.

Darda stuck out his hand. "I've not been called anything else. It's good to see you, my boy."

Dahlen grasped the man's forearm and pulled him close, clapping him on the back. "And you. How long have you been in the city?"

"A while now. But I twisted my foot fleeing Milltown from the beasts, not been right since. Your father, brother?"

"Well – alive." Dahlen turned to Erdhardt, gesturing at Darda. "Erdhardt Hammersmith, Darda Vastion. Darda 'exported' weapons and supplies for our... 'friends' in the North. My father's known him since before I was born. Erdhardt is—"

"Ah, I know Erdhardt Hammersmith." Darda nodded at Erdhardt. "Known him for many a year. It's a pleasure to see you well. Aela?"

Erdhardt shook his head.

Darda nodded and let out a sigh. He reached out and grasped Erdhardt's forearm. "She was a good woman."

"She was a great woman," Erdhardt corrected. He gestured for Darda to join them at the table, eager to move on. "You used to smuggle for the rebels?"

"That I did. Sent them up north to a spot nestled between the island of Antiquar and the Lodhar Mountains. Weapons from Vars Bryer, along with whatever else was needed."

"Vars Bryer?" Dahlen narrowed his eyes, looking from Darda to Erdhardt. "Calen Bryer's father?"

"You know Calen? He's a good lad." Darda broke into a smile. "He brought me the last shipment of weapons I ever sent. You remember, Erdhardt. It was right after The Proving. Calen and the others – what were their names again? Stan Pinn? And Havel... Lasch's boy?"

"Dann and Rist."

"They're the ones. Victors of the Hunt. Brought back an Urak head! Never seen the likes of it."

Dahlen started laughing. He downed his tankard, draining it to the last drop, then ran his hands through his hair, the rumbles of the laugh still clinging to his throat.

"What's so funny?"

"Nothing." He shook his head. "It's just a very small world. Calen's father..."

"Vars was a damn good friend." Erdhardt clenched his jaw, memories of Vars swelling in his heart. They'd been close ever since they'd been children, and he missed his friend dearly. He missed a lot of people dearly.

"Aye." Darda clacked his tankard off the table in agreement. "And a damn good man to boot. Finer than me, and finer than any of you, that's for sure!" He laughed at that, sipping at his ale. "That was until those Lorian bastards killed him in cold blood." Darda hocked and spat on the floor, true anger in his eyes. The Darda Vastion Erdhardt knew was cool and calm, very reserved. This was almost an entirely different man. "When I heard what happened... Fuck them. Fuck them all to the void. Lorian fucking scum."

"You got something to say?" A man in red and black leathers stood behind Darda, his chest puffed out, the look of drink in his eyes.

"Fuck," Dahlen whispered.

"Lorian scum," Darda said again.

"Stand up like a man and say that to my face."

Within a split-second, Darda was on his feet, nose to nose with the Lorian. And in the same span of time, six more men and women in red and black had emerged from the throng of people like hungry dogs.

"Shit for brains. Ugly as fuck. Would look better on fire. Lorian. Scum." Darda made sure to emphasise every syllable. "You killed my friend. Killed him in the streets of his home, killed his wife, his daughter."

"And they probably fucking deserved it."

Dahlen leapt to his feet, placing a hand on both men, pushing them apart. "Not the time for it. You go back to your drinks, we'll go back to ours. Ale is our friend and enemy both."

"Like fuck we will." Darda slapped at Dahlen's hand, but the young man held him firm and pushed him back, glaring into his eyes. Thannon rose beside Dahlen, jaw clenched.

Erdhardt got to his feet, fighting the urge to sling his hammer from his back.

"We come down here to these southlands and bleed for you fuckers. And this is what you do? We don't wanna be here. We're stuck here with you ungrateful shitsacks." The man shoved Dahlen in the chest, the other Lorians moving closer.

"Don't do that again."

"Or what? You're that one they all call 'Lord Captain', aren't you?" The Lorian scoffed, grinning and shaking his head. "I've got boots older than you. Why the fuck does Exarch Dorman listen to a word you say?"

The man pushed Dahlen in the chest again, but this time Dahlen remained rooted to the ground, his stare fixed.

"You're drunk. And we lose enough warriors to the Uraks. Turn around and walk away, and we'll all laugh about this in the morning."

"You talk like a real man, you know that? I heard you. Heard you all. Smuggling weapons to the rebels in the North. I should go to Exarch Dorman and have you strung up for treason."

Something in Dahlen shifted, something in the way his gaze hardened. Nimara and Almer lifted themselves from the bench, hands resting on the axes that hung from their hips. The other dwarves and Belduarans at the table did the same. Dahlen leaned forwards. "You don't seem to understand your place here, Lorian. Say one more word."

Erdhardt made to rest his hand on Dahlen's shoulder, but then the Lorian shoved the young man one last time and the whole void broke loose.

Dahlen grabbed the man's fingers and snapped them back, bone breaking through flesh. The Lorian had a fraction of a second to scream before Dahlen reached his right hand forward, grabbed the back of the man's head, and slammed his face into the table with enough force that a pair of tankards tipped over. He slumped to the floor like a sack of potatoes.

A second Lorian piled in after the first, but again Dahlen dropped the man in a heartbeat. A swift punch to the throat followed by an elbow to the face that made Erdhardt wince.

Nimara tackled the third before he got anywhere near Dahlen, while Thannon, Yoring, and Darda Vastion smashed into a group of the others.

Erdhardt contemplated joining in but found it much more entertaining to just watch. The only man Erdhardt had ever seen who could match Dahlen with a sword was Vars Bryer, but the young man was just as efficient with his fists.

The crowd spread wide, forming a circle as more Lorians charged in, drunk and howling.

One man threw a punch at Dahlen's head, only for Dahlen to turn so the man was at his back and the arm slid over his shoulder. Dahlen wrapped both hands around the Lorian's wrist and pulled downward. A horrible *snap* accompanied the inhuman way the man's arm shattered.

The problem, Erdhardt realised, was the Lorians were having a drunken brawl. But Dahlen wasn't trained to brawl. There was no wasted energy. Every movement was as clean and efficient as it was brutal and devastating. The man was trained to kill.

Another fist soared towards the side of Dahlen's head, and he twisted, leaned back, and clasped his hands at the side of the woman's face as she stumbled off balance. He pushed forwards and rammed her face into an approaching fist. Erdhardt couldn't tell if the resulting spray of blood had come from knuckles breaking teeth or teeth tearing into the man's hand.

Everything stopped when a horn blared. Once, then a second time. The entire tavern silenced in an instant. Chests heaved and sweat rolled until finally a third horn bellowed.

Dahlen spun and roared orders. He grabbed the Lorian who had begun the fight and hauled him to his feet.

The man's fingers looked like a tree branch with shoots going in all directions, and blood streamed down his wrist.

"Get your soldiers to the wall." The man's head lolled, but Dahlen lifted it. "If I hear word of a single man or woman among your number not fighting, I will personally put their head on a block come the rising sun. And I *will* be the one who swings the blade. Do you understand?"

The man nodded, his good hand holding the wrist of his shattered one.

Dahlen gripped Erdhardt's shoulder. "You ready to give this place one more day?"

CHAPTER FORTY-SIX

BLOOD OF THE BERSEKEER

18th Day of the Blood Moon

Durakdur – Winter, Year 3081 After Doom

Kira stepped out from the dark alley and onto one of the many walkways that overlooked the great waterfall of Durakdur. She moved through the crowd of dwarves and rested her hand on the parapet, allowing herself just a moment to admire the beauty as the droplets refracted the blue-green light of the Heraya's Ward lanterns. Above, a whoosh sounded as a Wind Runner shot from one tunnel to the next. The Wind Runners Guild had sided with Kira and abandoned the Freehold cities after Hoffnar took power, but reports said Hoffnar had recruited Alamants in an effort to keep the Wind Runners operational. Many had already died in the resulting crashes, but some of the Alamants were slowly learning their way.

"I don't like this." Vikmar moved to stand beside Kira, pretending to look out over the city. She had recently appointed him as the new High Commander of her Queensguard in Mirlak's place, and he had vehemently opposed the notion of Kira entering Durakdur whatsoever.

"I don't require you to like it. I require you to keep me alive."

"And you're not making that easy."

"If it were easy, anyone could do it." Kira gave the dwarf a smile, receiving a blank stare in return. Vikmar had always been a serious dwarf with very little room for a sense of humour, but he was a fine warrior and over the years he had grown very close to Mirlak.

Mirlak had been more than the commander of Kira's Queensguard. He had been her friend, and she missed him dearly. She supposed having Vikmar close meant Mirlak wasn't entirely gone.

"May the fires of Hafaesir's forge keep you warm, old friend. I may join you shortly," she whispered. Kira spotted Erani and Ahktar stepping from an alley on the opposite side of the street. She met her sister's gaze only for a moment, and then Erani moved on.

Kira inclined her head, and she and Vikmar followed Erani and Ahktar, staying thirty or so paces behind. She pulled her hood tighter, keeping her head down. Kira hated the idea of wearing a hood when trying to keep attention from herself. People only wore hoods when they wished to conceal their identities; it was much more practical to hide in plain sight. But the sight of her shaved head would draw more attention than any hood.

Ahead, Erani stopped by a staircase that led to a higher level, two statues framing the bottom step.

"Why has she stopped?" Vikmar whispered.

It only took a moment for Kira to understand why. A dwarf in crimson and gold robes stood atop a podium opposite the staircase, arms wide, preaching to a throng of dwarves gathered around him. "The time is now, brothers and sisters of Hafaesir. The Smith has forged our path in blood and steel. He calls us to be his hammer, to be his vengeance! Too long have we been forced to hide from the sun's light. This mountain is our home, and so it will forever be, but so too are we destined for more. No longer will the dwarves of Lodhar stand idly by while the powers of this continent brandish their will as they please. Look to the dwarves of Kolmir, slaughtered by the Lorians upon their ascension. The dwarves of Mount Helmund, butchered in the War of Flowers. Our kin who settled in the Wolfpine Ridge, burned alive by the elves during the Blodvar for aiding the Jotnar. Our kind are always the casualties in the wars of other races. No longer. This time we will stake a claim ourselves, and we will show Epheria what it means to be dwarven!"

The crowd erupted in a chorus of cheers, and even many of those walking past stopped to add a voice.

"He's convincing." Kira would have liked nothing more than to climb up onto that podium and pull the dwarf's intestines out through his mouth, but that might have caused a scene.

For some reason, hearing the preacher made everything so much worse. No longer could she imagine that those dwarves of Durakdur who followed Hoffnar did so because they were honourless traitors. They did so because Hoffnar was offering them something Kira herself might have been swayed by if she were a decade younger and a decade less wise.

"It's best not to linger any longer than we have to." Kira could tell that Vikmar had to actively stop himself from adding the words 'my queen'. Kira nodded.

Vikmar followed her through the crowd as the preacher continued, the roar of the waterfall drowning him out once she got far enough away.

Kira led Vikmar along the walkway and down a set of staircases that led to the lower levels, Erani and Ahktar following close behind in the crowd. The lower levels of Durakdur were just as cramped as those closer to the centre and near the Heart. Much of the lower section was residential with a mix of taverns and shops, with tunnels leading deeper into the mountain. Quedahar they called it, and the dwarves who lived in this quarter of the city were often those who worked the mines, the refineries, and the forges that lay even deeper still. They were the backbone of the dwarven world, the cogs that kept everything turning. There was no greater call than that of the stone and all that lay within it.

"Not far," Kira said, gesturing to an alley up ahead. "What do you think of what the preacher said?"

"I am yours, from this moment until my last moment. If there was only one certainty in this life, that would be it."

"I do not question you. I want to know, what do you think?"

"I think any words that stir a fire in your belly are words worth thinking on. Our people have suffered in the wars of the elves, the Jotnar, the humans... That cannot be denied. And the idea of ensuring that, when a new world is formed from the ashes of this one, our voices will be heard? That is something that stirs a fire in my belly." Vikmar paused, considering. "But another thing worth thinking on is the soul who speaks the words. Hoffnar speaks of unification, of honour and glory, and yet he is a traitor to our kind. Eight hundred years had passed since dwarves had gone to war with dwarves. And he shattered that peace. He slaughtered my brothers and sisters of the Queensguard, slaughtered Mirlak. He has consolidated his power with the blood of honourable dwarves. To me, that sounds like someone who wishes to be remembered. And I have found that there are two kinds of leaders – those who wish to be remembered, and those who refuse to be forgotten. He is the former. You are the latter."

"That's the most I've ever heard you speak."

"I don't speak unless I have something worth saying. There are enough people who do the opposite."

Kira smiled at that, drawing her hood tighter and dropping her head as they passed a group of miners singing and drinking outside a tavern.

"Good evening," one of the dwarves called out as Kira and Vikmar tried to pass. He was older than Kira by a few years, his beard thick and red and laced with gold, silver, and copper rings. There were few in the dwarven kingdoms with more experience fighting kerathlin than miners. "Drink with us, friends! The ale is cheap, and the night is long."

"Another night maybe," Vikmar said as Kira lowered her head beside him.

"Ahh, friend, come!"

"I am not your friend." Vikmar's voice was sharper this time, and he tried to push past, but the dwarf stepped into his path.

"Round here we speak to people with more respect."

Kira moved to place a hand on Vikmar's shoulder before the situation got out of hand, but something bumped into her shoulder and caught her off balance. She stumbled a step, her hood slipping back just a fraction.

Vikmar was across faster than Kira's eyes could follow. He grabbed the throat of the dwarf who had bumped her and slammed him against the wall.

"It was an accident," the dwarf stammered.

The other dwarf, who Vikmar had been speaking to, narrowed his eyes and looked at Kira. "My queen?"

Vikmar spun and at the same time slipped a small, polished axe from a belt beneath his cloak, which he brandished at the dwarf who had spoken. "Whoever you think you saw here this night, you are mistaken. I expect you to choose your next words very, very carefully."

The dwarf looked past Vikmar, staring instead at Kira. "My queen, I sought council with you once. When the mine shafts at the Ungbad outpost needed repairs. You granted my request in the same time it took for me to take a breath. I'd not forget your face, even at a glance."

"You would want to learn to forget it. Or I will have to carve it from your memory." Vikmar moved a step closer. As he did, Erani and Ahktar caught up, drawing their axes.

"Watch them." Erani pointed an axe at the other miners, Ahktar stepping between them and Kira. "What is happening?"

"Stop." Kira pulled back her hood, eliciting gasps. "Let him be, Vikmar."

Vikmar gave an acknowledging grunt but didn't lower his axe.

"My queen, your hair..." The red-haired dwarf came a step closer to Kira, pain in his eyes and shock in his voice. Vikmar pressed a palm to his chest. "Your rings... King Hoffnar did this to you?"

Kira nodded slowly. "He did."

"Hafaesir crush him." The dwarf rested his hand on Vikmar's arm, shaking his head. "That is not necessary, my friend."

"I am still not your friend, but if you press me, I will be the one who prays to Hafaesir when you are returned to the stone."

"Easy. We are the queen's." The dwarf dropped to a knee. "We never believed a single word, my queen. Never."

The other dwarves followed suit.

"Get on your feet," Erani hissed, dragging the red-haired dwarf upright by his armpit. She turned to Kira. "And you, pull your hood up."

"The people of Quedahar belong to Queen Kira of Durakdur," one of the other dwarves said. "You will not find traitors here."

"You will find traitors everywhere," Erani snapped. "Kira, we need to keep moving. This was risky enough before you started pulling down your hood."

"They need to see I am alive."

"No," she corrected. "They need you to *be* alive. Which you will not be if we stay here. You are my queen, but I need you to start listening to me."

"You cannot fight for something you think is gone." She grasped her sister's arm. "I will listen to you, but I am right in this. Trust goes both ways."

Erani bit at her cheeks but nodded.

"My queen." The red-haired dwarf pressed his hand over his heart. "May your fires never be extinguished and your blade never dull. We will fight for you. Just say the word. Tell us where to go, and we will be there. By Hafaesir's hammer, I swear it."

"For now, do nothing," Kira answered. "Wait. I will not be idle. And when the time comes to rip the usurper's heart from his chest, I will have need of your steel."

"You will have it, from now until we are returned to the stone."

As Kira and the others pressed on, Erani insisted on doubling back on themselves multiple times and forging false paths, twisting and turning to the point that Kira almost lost all sense of where she was.

"It's your fault," her sister said as they turned a corner. "That was stupid. I don't care what you say."

"Watch your words." Vikmar glared at Erani, his stare cold and hard. "You speak to your queen."

"I speak to my sister, whose naked arse I helped wash as a babe. I will speak to her how I please."

Vikmar made to argue, but Kira waved him away. There was no sense in it. Erani was as stubborn as a rock at the best of times. There was truth in her words – which would only make her more stubborn – but Kira also believed in what she said. Her people needed to know she lived.

"It's here," Kira said after what had felt like an eternity of wandering alley after alley. She stopped in front of a metal door that looked no different to the other six hundred or so metal doors they had already walked past. But she knew it. She had been there several times across her years as queen. Always alone. And even before then, she had seen it in the memories of the past rulers. This would be the first time in hundreds of years that any soul except for the ruler of Durakdur would set eyes on what this house contained.

Vikmar and Ahktar took up positions on either side of the door while Kira produced the key from her pocket and turned it in the lock.

"Light?" She held out a hand to Vikmar.

The dwarf reached into his pack and produced a small brass lantern with a hand loop. He pulled the cover from the circular opening, blue-green light spraying outward from the handful of Heraya's Ward within.

Once the others had stepped over the threshold, Kira locked the door behind them and led them through the antechamber and into the main room.

The home was decorated with the finest of furniture: hand-carved stone tables with rubies set around the rim, reliefs worked into a ceiling twice as tall as it needed to be, and busts on pedestals that displayed the depictions of kings and queens of old. On the eastern wall there was even a clock crafted entirely from arisenim – a crimson gemstone, deeper in colour than ruby, that could be mined in deposits as large as twenty feet wide. That clock would have been worth twenty times its weight in gold. And yet, for all the opulence, thick layers of dust had gathered on every surface.

"This place is like a tomb. Are you sure you're not lost, sister?"

"I had the key, Erani."

"Hmmm..." Erani ran her finger over the top of a stone counter, drawing a line through the dust. "Then perhaps you've simply lost your mind? Because there's nothing I see in here except an abandoned home of an old king."

"That's the point." Kira stepped past her sister and over to the back wall. She pulled a knife from her belt and ran the blade over her left forearm, drawing a thin stream of blood. She brushed her right hand through the blood and then placed it onto the stone.

"Are you sure you've not lost your mind?"

"Patience, Erani. Something you've always lacked."

A moment passed, then a *whoosh* sounded and dark lines formed in the stone, air rushing out around them. The creak of cogs and wheels echoed in the wall, and the door pulled back and receded into the wall.

"The blood of the ruler leads the way," Kira said, repeating a passage spoken to her when she first took the Rites of Leadership after King Turak had returned to the stone and passed into Hafaesir's forge.

"Well, that's certainly one way of hiding something." Erani stepped past Kira into the corridor beyond, staring at the doorway from the other side – likely trying to decipher its mechanisms, as she had a habit of doing. When they were younger, Erani was forever in trouble for dismantling and reassembling anything she could get her hands on.

"Come, sister. There is much more to see."

Erani traced her fingers over the seam in the wall into which the door had receded, trying to see within. "Are they theruvan crystals? They couldn't be, could they? How else could they have recognised your blood?" It had not really been a question. At least not one for which Erani awaited the answer. She had a tendency to ask questions of herself out loud. "I've never seen one with my own eyes. The books say they were all destroyed in the great wars. All except the three in the mountains of Marin."

"Erani."

"What?" Erani was feeling the grooves in the stone with her fingers.

"Leave the door." Kira turned towards the long corridor, pulling the light of the lantern with her. The ray of blue-green carved through the near-complete darkness, illuminating a second door in the solid wall at the far end of the chamber.

Once more, Kira placed her bloody hand on the stone, and the door revealed itself with a rush of air.

"More theruvan crystals?" Erani stepped up beside Kira with a face that spoke more anger than awe. "Kira, these... In the name of Hafaesir and all the gods."

As the door pulled back and receded into the wall, golden light spilled from the chamber, accompanied by a low hum.

The chamber was circular in shape and over a hundred feet across, the walls rising ten times Kira's height. An enormous column of hewn stone occupied the room's centre, stretching from floor to ceiling. Rows and rows of glass vials lined the column, each filled with a pearlescent black liquid veined with glowing gold. Plants with thick black leaves grew from the chamber's walls, completely covering the rock. Glowing veins of gold ran through the leaves.

Two long desks stood on either side of the column stacked with various apparatus for grinding, mixing, and extracting the blood of the plants.

"With my own eyes." Vikmar walked behind Kira as they entered the chamber. "I did not doubt you, my queen, but never in my wildest dreams could I have imagined this."

Vikmar stared up towards the ceiling, turning to look around.

"This has been here all this time?" Erani stood by the door, her jaw slackened.

"Ever since the accords after the Great Wars. King Baldrik had it built in secret and then killed each and every dwarf who had laid eyes on its construction with his own hand. He knew it was folly to destroy our greatest weapon, a weapon the dwarven people might one day need. The elves and humans have their magic and their dragons. The Uraks feast on Efialtír's strength. Hafaesir forged the blood of the bersekeers into our people so that we may have the strength to wield his hammer." Kira walked towards the column and pulled a vial from its place, holding it up in the air. The pearlescent black liquid swished and swirled within, the veins of gold shimmering. "And in the eight hundred years since the accords were struck, every ruler of Durakdur has stayed faithful to Baldrik's wishes. The Rockblood has been harvested but never wielded. Waiting patiently until a time when it is our people's only hope, when the Kingdom of Durakdur is so threatened that Hafaesir will offer his hammer once more."

Erani moved so she stood beside Kira. She reached for the vial, and Kira relinquished it.

"Once this is done, it cannot be taken back." Erani held the vial in the air, examining the shimmering light.

"It is not the blade's fault for the blood it spills, but the hands holding it." Vikmar knelt, resting both hands on his knee. "The bersekeer blood runs in my veins, my queen. I volunteer to be the first."

"You've heard the stories, Vikmar?" Erani raised an eyebrow, holding the vial out in front of her.

"I have."

"And yet you are so quick to volunteer yourself? You must know that even among those with bersekeer blood, many who drink the Rockblood are dead within the hour. And from the histories I've read, the death is not a quiet one. Bones twist and snap, organs turn to rock within their bodies, blood runs hot as molten steel."

"Less than half." Kira let out a long, laboured sigh. "Less than half survive, even with bersekeer blood. Without, it is lethal as Nightfire. None survive."

"Half," Vikmar repeated. "If we do not stop Hoffnar, how many of our people will die in his name as he launches a crusade on the continent? More than half, I reckon. Ours will be the first. He'll send the axes of Durakdur in the van. Besides, we all die eventually."

Kira grasped Vikmar's forearm and pulled him to his feet. "With any luck, the Rockblood can remain dormant still. But if it is needed, you will not be the first. I will."

CHAPTER FORTY-SEVEN

WHAT WAS LOST

18ᵗʰ Day of the Blood Moon

Ilnaen – Winter, Year 3081 After Doom

Footsteps and heavy breaths filled every passing moment as Calen and the knights descended into the tower's depths. Each step seemed to grow steeper and steeper, moving ever downward. Calen walked with his right hand trailing the wall, his left out in front for balance. One misstep and he would go tumbling. He quickened his pace. Forward and only forward. Down and only down.

As he moved, his vision flickered to that of Kollna treading the same path, her head scraping the arched ceiling, her hands trailing the wall as Calen's did, her steps slow and steady. Ahead of her, Alvira descended with purpose, her stride clean and unflinching, her hands at her sides.

He shook his head, trying to loose the images from his eyes. It was a disorienting thing, to have his mind drift between centuries, between the sight of the world in front of him and the sight of things that had long since passed. If he'd had even the slightest of control over the visions, it wouldn't have disoriented him so much. But he was helpless, a feeling he knew too well, a feeling he despised.

By the time the white light of the baldír illuminated a smooth floor some thirty steps below, Calen had almost given in to the thought that the stairwell descended into the pits of the void itself.

The floor belonged to some sort of antechamber with more long-dead lanterns occupying nooks in the walls. Armoured skeletons lay strewn about, steel rent and bones snapped. The fighting had raged even there in the depths of the city.

It looked as though a massive door had once been built into the wall at the far side of the chamber. All that remained was a gaping hole in shattered rock that stared into an endless abyss.

Calen's steps echoed as he crossed the chamber, the baldírlight illuminating the dead. Most were clearly Uraks, but many were Highguard or Draleid or elves or Jotnar. They had died here in this dark desolate place, and here they had remained for four hundred years. He wondered if anyone had ever searched for them, if anyone had waited for them to come home.

"What is this place?" Lyrin asked. He, Haem, and Ruon walked beside Calen as they approached the opening in the wall.

Calen's vision shifted between the world in which he stood and the world that had already ended. Through Kollna's eyes, he saw Alvira standing where he stood. Before them was an enormous circular door of hewn white stone, the symbol of The Order inlaid in black glass at its centre.

The door flickered before him, solid one moment, in ruins the next.

Alvira pressed her hand against the black-glass symbol of The Order's insignia. At her touch, a white light spread through the glass, runes glowing. A *click* sounded, and a low vibration thrummed through the stone beneath Calen's feet. The door split into spiral segments and receded into the wall, warm light spilling through.

The world shifted again, and the door was gone. Calen once more stood before the gaping hole, darkness before him, his hand stretched out, palm open as Alvira's had been.

Ildris now stood a few feet in front of him, Soulblade gripped in his fist, its green light illuminating a plateau strewn with rubble, bones, and black glass, a parapet-framed walkway stretching into the darkness.

Before Calen could speak, the world again shifted before his eyes, the shadows fleeing the warmth of a hundred lanterns.

Beyond the door was a cavern that reminded Calen of the wonder and awe he'd experienced when he'd first laid eyes on Durakdur. The walkway connected the circular door to a central platform that ran for hundreds of feet and from which countless other walkways sprouted.

On the outside of the parapet, the ground fell away, dropping into a chasm that seemingly held no bottom. Massive plateaus of hewn stone rose from the chasm between the walkways. Each held a white stone carving of a dragon egg at its centre, as wide as Calen was tall and double that in height. Four braziers blazed at the corners of each plateau.

Rows of pillars on the central platform supported another platform above it, and another above that, and so on for five storeys. The walkways that moved outward from each of the central platforms connected to open corridors that looked out into the cavern, doors and stairwells lining their walls.

Everything was smooth stone and sharp angles, not an inch of bare rock in sight. The entire place had been cut with the Spark, carved with purpose and intent.

Once more Calen knew he looked through Kollna's eyes. He knew this place, knew it well. It was a vault. The only one of its like in Ilnaen. A place where only the Draleid and the Dracárdare were welcome. Elves, humans, and Jotnar moved along the walkways and the platforms, the flaming egg of the Dracárdare embroidered into their tunics and robes.

A Jotnar approached, shorter than Kollna, with long white hair and dark eyes. Black robes hung from his shoulders, white trim along the edges and the Dracárdare insignia on the left breast. Calen knew him – or rather, Kollna knew him. He was Umildan, son of Indara – Prime Keeper.

The Jotnar bowed deeply. "Archon Alvira Serris," he said, each word slow and steady. "Daughter of Tamira Serris." He turned his attention to Calen. "Draleid Kollna, daughter of Luan. It is an honour to welcome you both to this sacred place. I am told you wish to inspect the eggs and pay your respects."

Calen's vision blurred again, the lights of the lanterns and braziers growing bright before dimming and vanishing, leaving only the pale light of his baldír and that of Ildris's Soulblade to hold the shadows at bay.

Calen squinted, traces of the lanternlight flashing in his eyes, playing tricks on his mind. "Whatever Alvira hid, she hid it in here."

"You're sure?" Kallinvar asked.

Calen didn't answer. Instead, he pulled deeper from the Spark, pushing more energy into the baldír as he summoned it to rise and float above their heads. The pale light illuminated the vault, casting the walkways, platforms, and stone dragon eggs in dark shadows.

"By Achyron," Ildris gasped, staring up at the open corridors to the right, his gaze lowering to fix on one of the many carved egg statues.

Calen moved onto the plateau and past Ildris and onwards to the walkway that connected to the central platform. Just like the rest of the city, skeletons adorned the walkway, many missing limbs, faces shattered, bones snapped. It felt almost wrong to Calen to be walking there, to be walking across their resting place. And yet another part of him thought it fitting that a Draleid be there to bear witness, to remember the cost of what had come before, to remember those who had fallen.

His vision flickered again, the skeletons vanishing to be replaced by Dracárdare moving across the walkways. Their robes flowed behind them in a way that made it look as though they were hovering, the lanternlight casting shadows around them. Some carried food and wine, others pulled small carts of wood and kindling or moved in pairs carrying chests between them, chests Calen knew contained dragon eggs.

A few moments and the lights and colours muddled once more, the chamber returning to the dark tomb it had become.

Calen wondered how many souls had found their final rest in Ilnaen. How many souls were simply never seen again, their corpses left to rot or the skin and flesh burned from their bones in the fires that had consumed all the Svidar'Cia.

A sigh touched his lips, warmth wrapping around his bones as Valerys pulled their minds together. The past could not be changed. It was stone and steel and iron, and it was set and cast. The dragon urged Calen onwards. They had come here for a purpose. And despite all the loss and death, that purpose must not be forgotten.

"I had no knowledge of this place." Kallinvar's voice carried in the open chamber as he caught up with Calen.

"I believe that was the intent," Calen said, looking along the platform at the many walkways.

"Which way?"

Calen knelt by the Jotnar remains, faded and time-decayed robes still draped around the fleshless bones. He pressed his hand over the brittle fabric, hoping for... *something*. Expecting it. But nothing came. The world didn't shift or blur, the colours didn't muddle, and the lights didn't flicker. And so he stared into the hollow caverns where the Jotnar's eyes had once been, then rose, feeling sightless for the first time since coming to Ilnaen. "I don't know."

"I thought you said you could see the paths they walked?" Frustration crept into the Grandmaster's voice, his stare hardening. "Thought you could see where Alvira hid what she hid?"

"I have no control over it." The admission grated at Calen. What good were these visions if he could not call on them when he needed them? This place was enormous, and it rose for five storeys, and even if they searched every shadowed corner and shard of split stone, there was no guarantee they would find any trace of what they were looking for.

A realisation dawned on him. What if whatever Alvira had hidden was already gone? What if Eluna had come here centuries ago and brought the pendant back to Vindakur?

He pushed those thoughts down. They would do him no good. "There are nine of us," he said, rising and looking around at the knights. "If we break into groups, we can cover ground quicker. I may yet see something as we search, but there is no sense in us standing here arguing."

Kallinvar stared into Calen's eyes for a long moment, then nodded. "Agreed. Though there are more than nine of us."

A light flickered behind the Grandmaster, and the portal Haem had called the Rift appeared, its green light sharp against the pale stone of the platform. One by one, Sister-Captain Arlena and her five knights stepped through the Rift.

"What are we looking for?" Kallinvar asked once the Rift had closed.

Calen read through Alvira's letter in his head, thinking. "Alvira said that Kollna cast the runes. So wherever this hiding place is, there will be Jotnar runes nearby." He fingered the pendant that hung around his neck. The key. He held it up. "And anything that looks similar in shape and size to this pendant. A slot, or a symbol, or anything at all."

"That's a start," Haem agreed, Ildris nodding at his side.

Once broken into groups, Calen and the knights set about searching the vault-turned-tomb. Only he could cast a baldír, but the knights' green Soulblades acted as lanterns well enough and allowed him to spot their movements across the walkways.

Calen, Haem, and Lyrin crossed to the open corridor on the left side of the cavern and ascended a stairwell to the second storey. To Calen's left, doors and openings were set into the stone all along the wall and off into the shadow-obscured distance. On the right, a parapet rose as high as Calen's navel. Arched openings ran along the ceiling and connected to the low wall, providing a clear view of the open chamber.

Calen placed a hand on the parapet and stared out into the darkness, the glow of the knights' Soulblades moving across the walkways and along the opposite corridors. The world flickered again as he stared, the sound of footfalls and conversation echoing all around him, the lanternlight warm against the stone, the walkways alive once more.

Then it was gone, and the vault returned to being pale, and cold, and silent, and dead.

"Best to work away from one end to the other," Haem said, eyeing Calen curiously. "We could be a while."

Calen nodded, then pulled his hand from the parapet, allowing his gaze to linger on the open chamber just a moment longer.

The closest door was nothing but splinters and twisted steel, the stone shattered where the hinges had been torn away. Calen drew a long breath and prepared himself for what he feared he would find inside.

The light of his baldír crept across the stone floor, the shadows seeming reluctant to retreat at its touch. Bones and steel were the first things he saw, black bloodstains marring the white stone. Calen loosened his threads of Spirit within the baldír, allowing more light to shine through. They stood in an antechamber as wide as The Gilded Dragon but only half as long. Five braziers of black iron lined both the left and the right walls, evenly spaced. Ornate golden boxes sat between each brazier, the symbol of the Dracárdare worked into their sides, each stuffed to the brim with coal.

Lyrin ran his gauntlet-clad finger over the iron of a brazier, brushing the dust away. He looked from his finger to the skeleton draped over another brazier a few feet away, a prong of iron sticking through its ribs, its skull and arms black as night from the flames.

Calen looked to the second door at the opposite end of the room. That, too, had been smashed from its hinges, gouges clawed into the stone.

Bloodmarked. Calen had faced the creatures enough now to know their work.

Haem must have seen the look on his face, must have known what Calen had expected to find inside, for his brother shook his head. "I'll go."

"I need to see it." Calen's voice was just short of a whisper, and he felt Valerys in the back of his mind, the dragon's heart beating quickly as he soared over the city.

Calen moved past Haem and stepped through the doorway. In the shadowed depths of the room, beneath dust and stone, fragments of broken dragon eggs shone in the white baldírlight.

A wave of sorrow washed over him from Valerys, and memories of Vindakur, of the broken eggs in Eluna's office, flashed between them. Seeing through Kollna's eyes, he had known what he would find in this place. But knowing and seeing were two entirely different things.

Calen moved further into the room, the ache in his heart growing deeper with each new shattered shell that met his gaze. The eggs in Vindakur had been but a grain of sand.

The room stretched onwards for almost fifty feet before the baldírlight revealed a wall at the end, and the ceiling rose twice as high, ladders connecting to the top sections.

There must have been thousands of shards of broken dragon eggs, the pale light reflecting a sea of colours as it hit the scales. So much beauty in such a horrific thing. So much colour in such a dark, lonely place.

More bones lay amongst the shattered eggs and the rubble. A pair of legs was half-buried on Calen's right, a severed spine jutting from between crumpled stone. To Calen's left, a skeleton sat headless against the collapsed shelves, the remnants of two eggs still clutched in its arms.

"Gods…" Lyrin's hushed voice echoed softly, drifting over Calen's shoulder. "This has all just been sitting here for four hundred years…"

Calen knelt, letting out an exhausted grunt as his knee hit the stone. He touched the gleaming sapphire scales of the egg clutched against the skeleton's right breast.

The baldírlight dimmed to black and the world blurred around Calen before the sounds of pure chaos crashed against his ears.

He stood in the thirteenth egg chamber, in the vault beneath Ilnaen's western hatchery tower. The same place he had been standing when the shouts and screams had rung through the chamber.

"What do we do?" Frincisca asked frantically, her hands shaking. She'd been that way since they'd rushed out to the corridor and seen the Uraks swarming into the chamber below, slaughtering everything that moved. "Mirk?"

It had seemed a pretty reasonable reaction to him, but strangely it was not how he himself had reacted. No. He had stood in the chamber, staring about at the eggs without a word leaving his lips.

Frincisca grabbed his shoulders, her short brown hair hanging down over her bloodshot, tear-filled eyes. "Mirk… what do we do? What… where do we even…" She stared into his eyes, her grip growing tighter, then loosening all of a sudden. "We're going to die here, aren't we?" Her breaths quickened, slicing through her words. "We're… go-going to die in this place… Who will tell Olban? If I don't come home… he'll… my children… Tua still needs milk… She's not seen a summer… Olban told me I needed to step down, but I couldn't. I…"

Calen didn't have the heart to tell her that if the Uraks had come this deep below Ilnaen, Olban and her children were likely dead, dying, or close. If they were this deep, in those numbers, then the whole city was likely dead. He didn't know how it had happened, or why, but those two questions mattered little in the face of the fact that it *was* happening.

He rushed to the door and slammed both bolts across, pressing the flat of his back against the wood. Sweat rolled down his forehead, screams and shouts echoing up from the lower levels.

Frincisca still stood in the middle of the vault, muttering to herself, shivering.

Calen's throat was dry as dust, and he couldn't for the life of him seem to find even the slightest dribble of spit. He'd never been in a fight before, much less a battle. He'd joined the Dracàrdare when he'd seen but ten summers. He wasn't a fighter, but he'd always wanted to be a part of The Order, be a part of something greater than himself. And to care for dragons? *Dragons?* What man wouldn't jump at a chance like that. An idiot, that's who.

He drew slow breaths, trying to think. There had to be something he could do. There just had to be. Even if the city had fallen, The Order had a hundred strongholds across the continent. Ilnaen was only one place. They just needed to stay calm, take as many eggs as they could, and get free of the vault. If they could do that, the Draleid would see them safe to Caelduin, or Anadine, or Thurinsil. There was nothing in this world that could stand against Draleid.

With one last long breath, Calen pulled himself from the door and sprinted to where the leather sacks lay in a heap by the wall. They used the sacks for moving tools and books and all sorts of whatever they needed. They never used them for eggs. The eggs were always carried by hand or mounted in golden chests. But there was a first time for everything.

He snatched an egg off the nearest shelf – orange scales and spots of blue – and shoved it into the bag with such haste the Prime Keeper would have slapped him back into the Age of War had he witnessed it.

"What... what are you doing?" Frincisca stared at him, seeming to have regained some semblance of composure.

He stuffed another egg into the sack – muddled brown, dark at the roots, light along the scale edges.

"Something," Calen muttered as he tried and failed to shove a third egg in with the other two. The damned sack was too small. He pushed the sack into Frincisca's arms. "Take it. Keep them safe."

"Mirk. What are you doing?" she repeated, incredulous, looking down at the worn leather in her hands.

"I'm doing *something*," he snapped. He regretted that the minute he'd done it. She was a kind soul, if a little dull. He slowed for a moment. "I'm doing something, Frinny. Anything. These eggs are ours to protect. We can't protect them all. But if we can take some and climb to the upper levels, then maybe we can escape through the ventilation tunnels. There has to be a way. I'm not just going to stand here and die. I'm not. I am a Dracàrdare, and I have a duty – *we* have a duty. Now either you help me or get out of my way."

Calen stuffed two more eggs into a second satchel that he then laid at his feet. He made to fill a third when he realised he'd only grabbed two.

He plucked an egg, ruby-red, from the shelf, then turned back to Frincisca, who was still staring at him in bemusement. "Well? What'll it be?"

"I'm not... I... Mirk. Mirk, I'm scared."

Calen sighed softly. He often forgot the woman had seen but twenty-six summers to his forty. "I'm scared too, Frinny. I'm so terrified that if something catches me by surprise, I'm afraid I might shit myself. And I wore my white trousers today. Not ideal."

That broke her, a laugh escaping her throat, a smile cracking her lips. Neither lasted long, but she'd calmed a little. Jokes always calmed her.

Calen placed a hand on her shoulder. "I'll not lie to you. We might die this night. But if we have any chance, we need to take these eggs and get out of here *now*. Are you with me?"

Frincisca sniffled as she nodded, clutching the leather sack close to her chest.

"Say it."

"I'm with you."

"Good." Calen brushed a tear from her cheek with his thumb. "Tua and Rin need their mother."

Calen turned back to the shelf and took one last egg – sapphire streaked with deep crimson. He would have given a hundred gold to see the beauty of the creature that would hatch from that egg. "All right. Let's—"

A clap of thunder boomed through the vault, accompanied by a light so bright it blinded him. Calen slammed back against the shelves, his head ringing, shrieks and screams and wails flooding into his ears. A pain shot through his spine as though he'd been trampled by a horse.

"Frinny?" He clambered upright and peeled his eyes open but saw only rays of lanternlight piercing a cloud of dust. The ringing noise still echoed in his ears, unceasing. He dragged in a sharp breath, hacking a cough as the dust filled his lungs.

"No Frinny," a harsh voice answered, cold and deep.

Calen lifted his arm, his right eye stinging as he brushed the dust away with his shoulder. At first, all he could see were sprays of red and orange light, but after a second or two, shapes took form.

His blood froze in his veins. Two Bloodmarked stood in the vault, massive and hulking, their runes burning a red glow into the air. A third creature waited between them, its skin white, lips cold, eyes black – a Fade. He'd never seen a Fade in the flesh before, but he'd read enough to know one.

The Fade ambled through the vault as though savouring the scents of a flower garden in spring. But all Calen could smell was coal, fire, and dust, the taste of blood on his tongue.

Calen clutched the two eggs closer to his chest, stumbling backwards, pain shooting through his left leg. There was no other way out.

"Frinny," he called again, panicking, his stare fixed on the Fade.

The creature's thin lips cracked into a broken grin, its black eyes drinking in the light.

Calen swallowed hard, then pulled his gaze away from the Fade.

A sinking feeling set into his stomach. Two feet stuck up at odd angles, blood pooling on the stone. It took all the courage he could muster to lift his head a little further and see Frincisca's shattered spine protruding from the lump of torn flesh and bone that had once been her hips, innards slumped in a pool of blood.

The top half of Frincisca's torso lay almost ten feet back, her right arm crushed between the stone and the door that had been launched off its hinges. Bits of her were everywhere.

"No…" Calen turned back towards the Fade, his chest numb, his jaw quivering.

The Fade tilted its head to the side. "Oh, to be so insignificant." It narrowed its deep black eyes. "How does it feel? Nobody will ever find you. Nobody will even remember that you were flesh and bone. That is what you creatures crave, is it not? To be remembered?"

Every instinct in Calen's body screamed at him to run, to fight, to do something. Instead, he froze, his limbs ignoring his command, his pulse deafening him.

The Fade stretched out an open hand towards the ground. Black fire moved over his palm in a slow, unnatural roll until it formed a sword, black flames dancing along its edge.

Calen took another step back, his legs finally responding. He pulled the two eggs closer, his fingers pressing tight into the scales. "Heraya embrace me," he whispered. "Varyn protect me. Achyron guide my hand. Heraya—"

"You pray to gods who abandoned you long ago." The Fade's black eyes stared deep into Calen's. "When you pray and a god does not answer, why do you keep praying?"

Calen stared back wordlessly, his mouth ajar, his mind still processing the question.

"No matter." The creature moved in a flash, the black-fire blade slicing through the air.

Pain burned, and the world erupted in a flash of light.

Calen fell backwards, his arms jarring as he braced himself against the stone. He snapped his head around, reaching for The Spark as he did, but found himself staring back at Lyrin and Haem, concern in their eyes.

"It's all right."

Haem's voice was steady as he reached out a hand, but Calen recoiled, his vision flashing between his brother and the Fade.

"It's me," Haem said, taking a step closer to Calen. "I'm here."

Calen looked about at the shattered eggshells and rubble, his breaths deep and ragged. He could still feel Mirk's fear in his heart, in his bones. His heart felt as though it were about to leap from his chest.

"What did you see?" Lyrin asked.

Calen slowed his breathing as he recounted the vision to them, his eyes never leaving Mirk's bones.

He pulled himself to his feet and pressed his fingers into the creases of his eyes, hoping to rid himself of the images that clung to his mind. He, Lyrin, and Haem searched the rest of the vault and found nothing – no runes and nothing that looked related to the pendant.

They moved along the corridor, searching every room and passageway. Some lead deeper into the earth, some were no larger than the room Calen had slept in back home. There were more vaults, chambers for sleeping, privies, baths, kitchens.

But in them all, one thing remained consistent: death.

As Calen stepped through the next doorway, a chill crept up his spine and the back of his neck, a shadow shifting somewhere down the corridor.

Haem raised an eyebrow.

"I..." Calen narrowed his eyes, staring down the corridor. Had he imagined it? It was almost impossible to tell. He could barely trust his own eyes. More than once the world had shifted and turned skeletons to fresh bodies, blood leaking, screams ringing out. "Nothing."

He allowed his gaze to linger on the shadows before stepping into the room. All he found inside were bones, shattered eggs, and sorrow. Just like all the others.

"This is pointless," Lyrin said as they searched the next room, which appeared to be another antechamber, bare except bones, armour, and old sconces on the walls. "There are hundreds of these rooms in here. By the time we find what we're looking for, the war will be over. That's if there's even anything here."

Again, the hairs on Calen's arms and neck stood on end, a chill creeping over him. For a second, he could have sworn the light from the baldír dimmed.

He rubbed at his eyes, the steel of his gauntlet cold against his skin. A shout echoed from the main chamber. All three men glanced at each other before darting back into the corridor.

"Here!" another shout bellowed. The green light of a Soulblade waved back and forth from the fifth storey.

When Calen and the others reached the top level, they found Sister Ruon kneeling by a pile of rubble, Sylven and Kevan at her side.

"What did you find?" Kallinvar, Varlin, and Ildris arrived only moments after Calen.

"This…" Ruon stood, touching her palm against a section of exposed wall where rubble had been removed.

"Ruon…" Lyrin took a step closer, tilting his head to the side and biting his lip. "I don't mean to alarm you, but that's a wall."

"Well observed, Brother Lyrin. Is there anything else your genius mind has discerned?"

"There are a lot of walls in here."

"There's something missing," Haem interrupted, staring at the section of wall upon which Ruon's hand rested.

"Precisely." A soft smile touched Ruon's lips, stretching to a smirk as she looked at Lyrin.

"The chambers and passageways are all evenly spaced along the corridor." Haem looked up and down along the corridor, his gaze lingering a few moments as though counting something. He tapped his fist against the stone. "There should be a door here, an arch… something."

As the others debated, Calen pulled the pendant from around his neck. He remembered what Pellenor had called the glamour in the dungeons below Berona: a touch glamour.

Just as he had then, Calen pictured the lock in the chest that had sat below his bed back in The Glade. As he did, he pushed six threads of Spirit through the pendant in his hand and onwards into the wall before him. With the threads in place, he opened the lock in his mind.

The rubble piled against the wall tumbled as the ground shook beneath Calen's feet, drawing shouts from the knights.

"A little warning next time?" Lyrin pushed himself upright against the wall.

Calen didn't answer. The wall was gone, vanished as though it had never been.

In its place was a corridor with three sconces set into the walls on each side and a tall metal door at the end.

Six Urak skeletons were strewn about, along with seven smaller sets of bones, their deaths marked by long gouges in the stone and shreds of time-withered carpet.

Calen studied the skeletons as he approached the door, the knights following in his wake. Clean holes had been punched into two of the Urak sternums and one skull, while the others were missing heads and limbs. The other bones appeared to be humans or elves.

Calen knelt beside the skeleton that lay slumped against the wall near the door, the battered plate of the Highguard resting on its bones. He placed his hand against the symbol of The Order worked into the plate. As he did, he cast his gaze at another of the remains and the worn, hooded cloak around its shoulders. The fabric tore at the slightest touch of his finger, time having wreaked havoc on its constitution. Calen could feel something odd about the cloak, something… *wrong*.

"Fades," Kallinvar hissed. "Even now the stain of their souls inks this place."

Calen snatched his hand back, then rose and turned towards the door.

In sharp contrast to everything else in the vault, the door was simple and plain and built entirely from what looked to be solid steel. Calen had not seen anything of its like. Where he'd expected to find a keyhole instead was a small circular alcove containing a spiral pattern.

Calen flipped his pendant over and looked at the brass back. The pattern on the back matched that of the alcove in the door. Rokka's riddle sounded in his mind.

A City once lost, found it needs to be.

Ilnaen.

A gem, a jewel, a trinket of sorts, but truly more a key.

The pendant.

Not a door that it unlocks, a secret to be revealed. A trick, a mask, a painting over truth, thought forever sealed.

The glamour.

In that brief moment, Calen had a realisation that he might not want to find out what lay on the other side of the door. Whatever it was, Rokka had led him there. The man had not told Calen that riddle out of the goodness of his heart. And Calen couldn't shake the feeling that one more soul was trying to tie strings around him, and yet there was nothing he could do. He could not simply tell Kallinvar and the knights that he wouldn't open the door because he had a 'feeling' or because he hated the idea that he was doing another man's bidding.

He reached forwards and pressed the pendant into the alcove.

It snapped perfectly into place.

When nothing happened, he noticed that the symbol of The Order was upside down. He turned the pendant to the right. It resisted slightly but moved, turning in place. A click sounded when the symbol was right way up.

The sounds of metal sliding and cogs turning rumbled from within the door. With one final click, the door moved, less than an inch, and silence followed. Calen looked to Haem, who gave him a short nod.

He pushed open the door.

CHAPTER FORTY-EIGHT

THE LAST OF US

18th Day of the Blood Moon

Aravell – Winter, Year 3081 After Doom

Ella walked with her hands in her pockets, the sound of crashing waterfalls like music in her ears. The warm light of the midday sun formed deep shadows in the crevices of the two dragon statues that framed the archway before her. There was a time when the two carved dragons atop the balustrades of The Gilded Dragon had been the greatest work of craftsmanship Ella had ever laid eyes on. And now they were mere trinkets compared to the statues before her that looked almost alive, the erinian stone glowing with an otherworldly light.

But no matter the beauty before her eyes, her mind would not shift from thoughts of her mam. She had lain awake each night, going over everything Fenryr had said again and again. All those years, her mam had been a druid. Her mam had lied to her, poured poison down her throat. The woman she had trusted with every fibre of her soul had lied to her from the day she'd been born.

Faenir gave a low rumble, his shoulder pressing against Ella's arm. The wolfpine had been her shadow ever since she'd woken, never letting her out of his sight. Even then his hackles rose at every elf who came within a few feet.

Three Fenryr Angan stalked the shadows behind her, keeping their distance but never letting her stray too far. That had been the way in the days since waking.

"These are dangerous times, young one," Fenryr had said.

As she passed beneath the arch, Ella looked up to see a sprawling relief carved into the stone, impossibly delicate and beautiful with a level of detail she would only have thought possible with charcoal or a brush.

She carried on, stepping into the basin that the elves called Tahír un Ilyienë – the Garden of Remembrance. She preferred the name in the Old Tongue. The word 'garden' could not have been less suited to the place in which Ella now stood.

Five waterfalls flowed over the edge of the basin, cutting through circular stone terraces that looked down over an enormous central yard. The waterfalls fed into streams and onwards into a moat that surrounded a stone island in the basin's centre, where five statues stood at least ten times as tall as Ella.

At the centre of it all was the tallest and largest tree Ella had ever seen in her life. Its thick trunk climbed upwards from the middle of the island, branches coiling about one another like snakes, sprawling outwards. Vines dangled, blooming with flowers of white and luminescent purple. The great tree's canopy covered two thirds of the sky, strands of warm orange and pale pink piercing through.

Many elves sat in the terraces, their legs folded beneath them, eyes closed. Some walked about the base of the tree, others sat with their feet in the streams.

She crossed the white stone bridge nearest to her, walking between the statues of the human and the elf. She stopped before the base of the tree and looked up at the glowing purple canopy. She could *feel* something emanating from the tree, like a heartbeat or a soul. She wasn't sure if *she* or the wolf within her could feel it, but it was there nonetheless. This tree had a connection to the Sea of Spirits. It calmed her. As she stared up at the tree's canopy, Ella could have sworn she could hear her mother's voice echoing.

"You are Ella Bryer." The voice that spoke was soft and delicate.

Ella lowered her gaze to find an elf in a light blue dress standing a few feet to her left. Ella gasped as her stare found its way to the elf's eyes. Her irises were black as jet, surrounded by a ring of pale red. "I'm sorry. I didn't mean to—"

"It's all right. You're not the first, and you won't be the last." She gave Ella a weak smile that held a deep sadness. "My name is Aruni Enathrea. It is a pleasure to finally meet you."

"You know who I am?"

"Ah, apologies. Your brothers, they spoke of you often, particularly Calen. He's a lovely boy." Aruni reached up and brushed a strand of blonde hair from her face, her sleeve pulling back to reveal raw wounds on the elf's wrists, scabs old and new forming a ring around her forearm. "My Valdrin admires him quite a bit."

Ella had been heartbroken to find that both Haem and Calen were not in the city when she had woken. Though the others insisted they would be back, it did little to quell the anger within her at Calen for leaving so soon after she'd finally found him. But Haem... She would have given the moon and the stars to have Haem beside her at that moment.

She couldn't help but feel as though she'd imagined him. He'd been dead for years, and then he'd just been standing there before her, alive. How could it have been possible? Surely it had been some sort of trick? Her big brother was alive.

"What brings you to the Ilyienë?" Aruni looked up at the godlike tree that stood over them.

"I needed a place to think." Ella had spent the days since waking doing exactly that, saying very little to anyone. There had been so much to think on, so much to process. It had been clear that all Tanner and Yana had wanted to do was ask her a thousand questions, but both had left her be, something for which she was very thankful. "I heard of what this place is, what this tree is. Is it true that the bodies of those killed in the battle lie in the ground beneath it?"

Aruni nodded softly.

"So much death…"

"Life and death are part of the same circle. We return our dead to the earth so that they may bring life. The Ilyienë is a sacred thing to my people. It is said that each flower is a soul that touches the tree, attempting to call home. The greater the loss, the larger the tree. This place is a conduit that bridges this world and the others. A place where we can be closer to everything we've lost."

"Is that why you've come here?"

"In a way." Aruni ran her fingers over her chest, tracing something beneath her dress. "I was born in a woodland to the far north, along the Lightning Coast. My people were few, and so we lived in peace for many centuries after The Fall. But some years ago, the Lorians found us. They slaughtered many and took the rest of us captive. I…" Aruni's hand trembled, and she picked at the scabs on her wrist, blood trickling. "The things that were done in that place… I do not know if the ones I loved ever found Heraya's embrace. At least here, I feel like I can, in some way, be close to them again. And with Valdrin gone, it's nice to feel close."

"I understand that."

"Did you lose someone?"

Ella nodded softly. "My Ayar Elwyn… my mam and dad. I never got a chance to say goodbye…"

"It is not an easy thing," Aruni said, "to lose the ones you always turned to for safety. It sets the world out of balance."

Ella paused a moment. "Your son, would you ever lie to him?"

Ella regretted the question the moment it left her lips. She didn't know this elf. She had no right to push her sorrow onto Aruni.

Aruni turned her black eyes from the tree and stared into Ella's. This time Ella didn't gasp or flinch. She found sorrow and loss and loneliness in Aruni's eyes. "Valdrin is not my son."

"I'm sorry," Ella said, suddenly feeling ashamed. "I just… The way you said his name, I just…"

Aruni shook her head. "He is not my son by blood, but he is mine. We are bonded." Aruni let out a soft sigh. "Lies are a strange thing. What they are changes with what we need. They are necessary. They are evil. They are white. They are black. A lie is what we are willing to accept. Would I lie to Valdrin in order to keep him safe? Yes, I think I would. Because I am willing to become the thing he hates as long as it means I have kept him safe and warm and loved. That is my task as a mother. I hope he loves me. I hope he thinks the world of me, because if he didn't, it would break my heart. And yet, as a mother, I'm willing for my heart to be broken to ensure his is whole."

Ella pressed her tongue against the back of her bottom teeth and stared up at the glowing flowers that dangled on the vines. Part of her wanted to stop the conversation there, but the grief within her took over. "Would you lie to him his whole life? Would you lie about who he was? About who you are? About everything?"

A hand rested on Ella's shoulder, and Aruni's soft voice sounded once again. "Did your mother love you?"

"I don't know anymore. Did she? How am I meant to know if she is willing to lie to me about everything?"

"You hold your mother to such high standards, and yet you lie to me with ease."

"I didn't lie."

"And you lie to yourself, too. If you didn't know your mother loved you, you wouldn't be so angry. She loved you dearly, that's why it hurts."

That cracked Ella, cracked her heart, cracked her soul. The wolf within her whimpered. "I don't even know why I'm telling you all this. I don't even know you."

"Sometimes opening our hearts to strangers is far easier than doing so with the people who know us. There is no risk. We are free to be honest where we may not always be. That and I have a way with people." Aruni reached over and scratched Faenir's chin with her right hand, stroking his head with her left.

The wolfpine moved forwards and licked her face from chin to forehead, unapologetically.

"Oh, gods. He's wonderful."

Faenir had gotten so large that Aruni barely had to bend over to look into his eyes. A deep, protective instinct drifted from Faenir to Ella. He leaned forwards and nuzzled the side of Aruni's cheek.

"He's not normally this trusting of strangers."

"Those who have suffered have a way of finding each other." Aruni scratched at Faenir's ear, then stood back to her full height. "Ella, I would sincerely like if you joined me for some tea. Not now, but whenever you are ready. Therin can bring you. I'll ask him. That is, if you would like to?"

"I would. Not Arlen Root tea, no?"

Aruni shook her head. She placed her hand on the trunk of the tree. "I've been drinking a lot of Tarveenan Starlet tea these past weeks. It was a favourite of a friend of mine. I think you'll like it." She turned back to Ella. "It was a pleasure to meet you, Ella Bryer. And please know this – to be a mother is a difficult thing. Balancing the scales of protecting the ones you love and allowing them the room to grow will always be a precarious task, so do not judge too harshly."

Aruni gave Ella a soft smile, then left.

Ella watched the woman leave before returning to the reason she had come here in the first place. She turned to the tree and rested her hand on the trunk, closing her eyes. As soon as she did, a growl resonated beside her.

She opened her eyes to find Faenir glaring at her with hackles raised and snout crinkled.

"What?"

The wolfpine continued to growl, lowering his head.

"I need to know." Ella closed her eyes once more. She called to the wolf within her, howling. For a moment there was silence, until the wolf howled back and the world shifted.

Unlike the previous times she had entered Níthianelle, the world was not a vast empty darkness. She stood in the Tahír un Ilyienë, the sound of the waterfalls crashing around her. The elves were gone, as was Faenir, but the three Angan who had followed her remained, their bodies wisping grey and black smoke. Two of the creatures stared at her, while the other folded itself to the ground to sit.

Ella turned away from the Angan and stared up at the Ilyienë tree. In the Sea of Spirits, the tree's leaves glowed in a multitude of colours: purples, reds, greens, blues, yellows. It was a rainbow of pulsating colour in a world dominated by cold ethereal light.

She lifted her hand and placed it on the trunk, white mist trailing. "Mam?"

Branches and flowers rustled overhead, Ella's heart beating in her ears.

"Mam, please. I know you can hear me. I know you're there."

Silence.

Anger bubbled within her. "Please… please, just answer me."

For a brief moment, Ella thought she heard a voice, a whisper on the wind, and the wolf in her blood snapped its jaws, growling.

"You idiot child!"

Ella's heart stopped at the sound of Fenryr's voice, deep and rasping.

A hulking shape shrouded in black and gold smoke marched across the stone island and grabbed her by the collar. Fenryr yanked her away from the tree, his golden eyes bright and gleaming.

"Leave this place!"

Fenryr shoved Ella backwards. The world exploded in a swirl of mist and smoke, colours spiralling. Everything collapsed inwards, and Ella hit the ground, the light of the waking world flooding back into her eyes. She sat on the ground before the Ilyienë, Faenir at her side with his hackles raised and teeth bared.

Fenryr stood over her, golden eyes glaring.

Ella's heart raced, her stare moving from Fenryr to the three Angan, who now stood around her, and to the elves who had gathered on the island and the bridges connected to it.

"Silence." Fenryr raised a finger to the snarling wolfpine, and Faenir whimpered.

The god stepped past Faenir and lifted Ella to her feet as he might a feather. She didn't argue as Fenryr placed a hand on her back and guided her from the Tahír un Ilyienë, leaving the elves watching.

He spoke only once he'd led her up through a winding path to an empty plateau that overlooked a section of the city. "What did you think you were doing?"

"I needed to know… I…"

"After what you have already been through, how can you be so senseless? You know nothing of Níthianelle. When you told me you needed time, young one, I respected it. But this? Are you really so arrogant and naive both?" Fenryr turned away, shaking his head.

"I needed to know if my mother is alive. I heard her… in Níthianelle. I heard her voice. I…"

Fenryr tilted his head back and exhaled slowly. "Your mother no longer walks the mortal plane. That I can assure you. But when you call out in the Sea of Spirits, there are other things that might answer. You must be more careful, lest you betray us all."

A hole formed in Ella's chest where her heart had been. "I heard her… I heard her voice."

Fenryr's eyes softened, the tension leaving him. "There is so much you do not know, my child. A world you have not seen. I will show it to you, and I will explain everything. But I need you to promise me that you will not attempt to cross back into Níthianelle without my guidance. You were Fragmented, and the tether between your body and soul is weak. It needs time to mend. I need you to have patience. Can you do that?"

Ella wanted to argue, wanted to roar and scream and tell him to go and fuck himself. But she didn't. This was a god, a true god, formed in flesh and blood before her. And every moment she was around him she was forced to fight the compulsion to kneel.

"Yes."

Fenryr let out a sigh. "There are those who would twist and chain us, those who would open our throats and drink our blood as it spilled. We must not make it easy for them. Go and rest. Diango, Aneera, Nuada, and Sennik will escort you."

The three Angan who had followed Ella stood on the far side of the plateau. They were joined by a man with wavy black hair down to his shoulders and a long green cloak. An Aldruid, a Blooddancer. Just like Ella. He had introduced himself the day Ella had awoken, he and four others. All Aldruids – the last Aldruids of Fenryr's blood. An enormous black wolf lay on the ground beside him. Sennik's keeper, Balmyras. The creature was larger than even Faenir, with deep golden eyes.

"I don't need an escort."

"I will not force them on you if you do not wish. But you are their family, and they worry for you, whether you believe it or not."

Ella glanced over at the Angan, who now knelt with their heads bowed. Sennik stood with his hands behind his back, his stare fixed on something in the city. His keeper, though, watched Ella intensely, ears pricked.

"Fine."

Sennik, Balmyras, and the three Angan walked with Ella and Faenir through the streets of Aravell and back towards Alura. They drew more than a few eyes as they went, but Ella was used to it. They were staring at Faenir – and now Balmyras. She, too, would stare if she saw a wolfpine that rivalled a small horse for size.

"How are you feeling?" The words were the first Sennik had spoken to her since their introduction. The silence, though, had mostly been Ella's doing.

"Bright as a sunflower." Ella kept her gaze ahead as she spoke, watching two elves wheel a cart full of terracotta vases down the street, smiling at each other like children.

"My favourite colour is blue."

"What?" Ella shook her head and stared at Sennik.

"There are eighteen of us alive who have Fenryr's blood in our veins, and two of those are my sisters. I would like to know you, and if you insist on being as abrasive as a whetstone, then it is up to me to bridge the gap. So, my favourite colour is blue. My mother used to dress in blue all the time before she died. I think that's why. I can't remember her face, no matter how hard I try. I was only four when the Vethnir hunters took her."

Ella frowned at the man but eventually yielded. "Mine is purple. My mam used to grow lavender outside our home. The smell always reminds me of her."

"Lavender, you say? Of course."

"Why 'of course'?"

"Lavender is particularly calming to our kind, and it masks our scent. We keep lavender in all the dens around the continent. It makes life difficult for the Vethnir hunters and the Bjorna. It's not from Epheria, you know? It comes from Terroncia, specially grown by the Woodhearts – a Gift long lost. It blends with the scent of the Fenryr and creates something only our kind can smell. Your mother was a smart woman."

"That she was. She was many things."

"Aren't we all, Ella Bryer. Aren't we all."

CHAPTER FORTY-NINE

HOPE ANEW

18th Day of the Blood Moon

Ilnaen – Winter, Year 3081 After Doom

The chamber behind the door was circular in shape, with walls that rose into a domed ceiling plated in gold with The Order's symbol at its centre. The baldírlight glistened against that gold, illuminating the chamber to its fullest.

A soft blue light radiated from Jotnar runes carved into the ground around a raised stone platform in the middle of the chamber. A skeleton – much too large to be human – rested against the base of that platform, legs folded, arms hanging by its side, tattered clothes draped from fleshless bones. The sight dragged a sorrow-filled sigh from Calen's lungs. It was Kollna. He knew it as well as he knew the sky was blue and the grass was green.

Calen closed his eyes for a second, clamping his teeth together and clenching his jaw. And as he opened them, his gaze fell on what was perched atop the platform: nine dragon eggs.

Settled dust had muted the sheen of the scales, but the eggs were unmistakable, easily the size of his head, scales overlapping from top to bottom.

Calen took a step, his heart pounding, and the world spun once more. Colours muddled and turned to blotches as they shifted around him, smearing like paint. When everything settled, he stood on the central platform of the vault's first level. Lanterns burned, frantic chatter filled the air, and people darted all about him. Three Highguard stood at his side with satchels of eggs strapped to their backs.

A vicious crack sounded from the vault's door, followed by a roaring explosion. Shards of stone and black glass ripped through the air, dust pluming.

Beside him, a sliver of obsidian as long as his forearm blurred past and lodged itself in a Dracárdare's throat, blood sluicing as the woman thrashed on the ground, twitching in her death throes.

Screams of agony echoed in the massive cavern, rocks still tumbling, the clink of black glass against stone dancing on the air like music. The crimson runes of Bloodmarked glowed through the settling dust, and the Uraks poured forth, black steel and claws tearing flesh and bone.

"Draleid Kollna." One of the Highguard looked from Calen to the charging horde. "We must stand. Without us they—"

"No." The word was like acid on Calen's tongue. The Dracárdare were not warriors. They would die like babes to the Urak steel. And yet, he had no choice but to leave them. The eggs were more important. They were everything.

The world shifted, and Calen was charging up a stairwell, pushing past anyone in his way. Below, the Uraks swarmed through the vault, Fades and Bloodmarked among them.

A flash and Calen stood in the hidden chamber, torches blazing. He set the six eggs onto the platform beside the three already there. Eluna had never come for them. For a moment he feared what might have happened to her, but that thought died quickly. Eluna's life meant little now. At least she had brought others to safety, wherever that may have been. With the runes set, these eggs would be safe here.

A call rang out from the corridor, and Calen turned to see the three Highguard fighting and dying as Uraks and a pair of Fades charged. Calen drew on all five elemental strands, a spear of white light forming in his hand.

The world blurred and twisted, and Calen found himself on the floor, his back resting against the stone platform, blood pouring from the two holes the Fades had poked in his side.

The door was closed. He had closed it. Beyond that, the glamour was set once more. The runes marked into the floor were ignited. He had done all he could, given all he had to give. Even if the Uraks destroyed every other egg in the city, these nine would be safe.

That was all he could do. That was everything. Instinctively, he reached for the touch of his soulkin's mind. The feeling of emptiness cut into him. He had felt Tinua die, felt his soul break and shatter. The dragon had faced his end with as much courage as he had faced everything in life, protecting a clutch of fledglings as they fled the city. Protecting those who needed him. There was no greater cause.

"An honourable death," Calen whispered, coughing, tasting blood in his mouth. The words were in Kollna's voice. "I will be with you again soon, my heart of hearts." In his last moments, Calen's thoughts went to his young apprentice. He hoped Coren and Aldryn still drew breath. "Daughter of the sea. You are ready. Fly."

The world shifted, and Calen found himself kneeling on the stone floor, once more seeing through his own eyes. Tears rolled down his cheeks. Staring at Kollna's remains, he reached out to Valerys and pulled their minds so tightly together he could not tell where the dragon stopped and he began. Wind rolled over their scales and tears flowed from their eyes. They saw both Kollna and the broken city. Their heart bled as they stared at the ruins of everything that had been lost. At the blood that had been spilled, the lives taken, the bonds destroyed.

"Alura anis, Tinua ar Kollna, davitir un Luan," Calen whispered. "Draleid n'aldryr, Rakina nai dauva. Du é alanín til ata ilynír abur er kerta."

Rest now, Tinua and Kollna, daughter of Luan. Dragonbound by fire, Broken by death. You are called to make whole what is half.

As Calen stood, the knights waited silently, not a word passing between them. Both Kallinvar and Haem watched him, but the others turned their gazes elsewhere in the chamber.

Calen wiped the tears from his cheeks with the back of his gauntlet. "She gave her life to bring these eggs here," he whispered, explaining. "Gave her life to protect them."

Calen stepped forwards and brushed the dust from the closest egg to reveal buttercream scales with streaks of green.

"Why?" Kallinvar moved to the other side of the platform, examining the eggs, his stare harsh and sceptical. "Why *these* eggs? And why *here*? There were thousands of eggs in the city."

Calen shook his head. "Not *these* eggs. Just any eggs she could save, any eggs she could carry. They would be safe here, hidden from the Uraks."

"These must be the runes you spoke of in the letter." Ruon knelt beside a glowing rune carved into the stone. "What are they for?"

"I don't know runecraft." Calen proceeded to brush the dust from a second egg, the light glinting a deep orange from the scales. "They were to protect this place – to protect the eggs."

"There has to be more," Kallinvar cut across, his tone sharp.

Calen looked up to see the man marching about the chamber. Kallinvar swept his hands across a desk Calen hadn't even realised was there. Once Calen had seen Kollna and the eggs, he'd not looked about for anything more.

"Heart of Blood," Kallinvar muttered, whipping through the pages of a journal that had rested on the desk. When Calen had met Kallinvar before, the man had seemed strong as iron, unshakable. But the man before him now was something else, erratic and frayed. He turned and gestured at the other knights. "Search everything."

It was only then that Calen took the time to look about the rest of the room. Two swords hung on the far wall, sitting on either side of a suit of armour atop a polished wooden stand. The desk at which Kallinvar stood was one of two. Both were stacked with sticks of wax, journals, scrolls, and piles of parchment. Chests sat beneath the desks, heavy and wooden, inlaid with gold. The more he looked, the more he saw. This must have been where Alvira had kept everything of value to her... perhaps even the Archons before her.

"We take all of it with us. Nothing remains. Gildrick and the Watchers can sort through it. If the Heart of Blood is here, we will find it."

"That's not for you to decide." Calen didn't allow even a hint of hesitation in his voice. He needed to be firm here, needed to be strong. "These are the possessions of Alvira Serris. The last Archon of the Draleid. By rights, they belong to her people. You can't just—"

"With respect." Kallinvar's voice held no malice or venom. It was simply cold and steady. "Alvira is dead. She has no need for anything here."

"That does not mean you can claim it as your own."

"I wasn't asking, Draleid."

Calen took a step closer to Kallinvar, fighting his natural instinct to open himself to the Spark. "Neither was I."

"We made a deal, Calen Bryer. We came here for the Heart of Blood, on your word. I will not leave empty handed."

"And I left an army of souls to march in defence of my home while I honoured my promise and stood by you here."

Kallinvar's stare broke. He turned his head inwards towards his shoulder, eyes watching the floor. Quick as a snake, his head snapped back up. But he no longer looked at Calen. Instead, his gaze was fixed on the eggs. There was a hardness in the man's eyes. He didn't look himself. "What of the eggs?"

Kallinvar's voice was barely a whisper.

"What of them?" Calen glanced at Haem. His brother stood with his back straight, body tense.

"What if they are the Heart of Blood? What if it is with those eggs that Fane brings Efialtír into the world?"

"No egg has hatched in four hundred years."

"And yet everything has brought us here." Kallinvar kept his gaze on the eggs as he moved closer, the light of the baldír gleaming in his eyes. "These runes are not marked for no reason. Perhaps they are a shield, but from what?"

Calen opened himself to the Spark, the purple glow of his eyes shimmering off the egg scales and the green plate of Kallinvar's armour. "There is a line, Grandmaster. And you are close to crossing it."

Calen stopped himself from unsheathing his sword. Even if he did believe he could best the man blade to blade – which he didn't – the rest of the knights would see to it that he never left that chamber alive. He glanced at Haem again, seeing the hesitation in his brother's eyes. What would Haem do, Calen wondered, if forced to make that choice?

"Is there truly a line, Draleid, when it comes to stopping Efialtír crossing into this world? Stopping the Shadow from consuming everything? From devouring? From obliterating?" Kallinvar looked to Calen. "Where is the line you draw to protect this world?"

Calen could hear Tarmon in the back of his mind, urging him to stay patient, to think with his head and not his heart. But so too could he feel Valerys's fire raging. They could not allow any harm to come to the eggs. They *would* not. Whether the eggs would hatch or not.

"Thousands of broken eggs fill this city." Calen didn't raise his voice, didn't shout or take a step closer to the Grandmaster, but he fed on the cold fire in Valerys's veins. "I will not allow you to add any more. There is always a line. Always. The Fall itself was a line crossed with the best of intentions. Understand this – if you want these eggs, you will have to take them over my cold, dead body. But it will be one of your knights doing the taking, because you will be lying right next to me. I swear this by the bond."

A brief silence passed in which Kallinvar stared back at Calen, none of the other knights speaking a word. Sister-Captain Arlena and the others had reached the chamber now, and Calen stood fourteen to one. It mattered little. He would do all he could to protect these eggs, and he would take as many with him as the gods allowed.

The light from his eyes and the runes of his armour burned bright, Valerys rumbling in the back of his mind. The dragon had alighted on what remained of the roof of a ruined building by the tower, his rage an unrelenting blaze. If Valerys were in Calen's place, every knight would burn, their ashes would burn, their souls would burn.

Calen looked at Haem. His brother had come a step closer, positioning himself only a few feet away.

"Take everything else," Calen said, his hands trembling as he tried to still the fury that raged within Valerys. "The notes, the chests, the journals, the armour. Everything. Take them. Have your Watchers go through everything piece by piece. Just return them when you're done. Do that, Grandmaster Kallinvar, and we will all walk out of here with our heads. But the eggs go with me. That is the hill I will die on, and so will you."

In the ruined city above, Valerys unleashed a defiant roar. Kallinvar had threatened the eggs, and he had meant it. Those were not words that would be easily struck from the dragon's mind.

Kallinvar sucked in his cheeks and stared directly into Calen's eyes for what felt like minutes. The other knights didn't move an inch. Haem's stare never left the Grandmaster.

"Very well." Kallinvar held his gaze on Calen long after the words had left his lips.

The tension held as the man opened the Rift right there in the chamber and the knights carried through everything that wasn't bolted down. Everything except for the eggs.

Haem just stood there in silence, watching. Every time his gaze met Calen's, he looked away. But Calen didn't.

When Calen began to place the eggs in the satchels he'd found beside Kollna's body, Haem joined him, silently.

A sharp warning flared in the back of Calen's mind from Valerys, and every hair on his body stood like needles.

"What?" Haem paused, a dust-covered egg in his hand, his eyes narrowing.

Calen stuffed the remaining eggs into the last satchel, caring little for delicacy. "Uraks," he said, slinging the satchel over his shoulder. "They're here."

"In the city?" Kallinvar strode from across the room, urgency in his voice.

"In the tower." The creatures must have moved through the city while Valerys was distracted by the eggs. But now the dragon could see them clear as day from the sky, hundreds pouring through the tower's door.

"How did they—"

"It doesn't matter. They were waiting for us. There are too many, and we don't have time." Calen grabbed the last satchel from Haem and threw it around his neck with the other two. The weight pulled against him, pressing his armour down into his shoulders.

"There's only one way in and out of here. You can't travel through the Rift…" As Haem spoke, Calen could hear the realisation in his voice.

"There are ventilation tunnels somewhere on this level." Calen remembered the tunnels from his vision through Mirk's eyes. "Down the northern end. If I can get there, I can get to the surface."

Kallinvar looked back at the Rift that floated behind him. For a moment, Calen thought the man would leave him for dead. "Go," Kallinvar said, cracking his neck side to side. "We'll hold them back while you get to the tunnels."

"There are too many."

"More for us to send to the void."

Through Valerys's eyes, Calen watched as the dragon folded his wings and dropped, the air whipping over his scales as a pressure built within him. With the rage of a burning sun, Valerys spewed fire from his jaws. Fire that turned sand to glass and melted steel and bone. Fire that ignited the air and incinerated everything it touched.

And when the flames cleared, the Uraks charged over the glass and ash.

Bolts of purple lightning tore upwards, and Valerys rolled, the light flashing past his eyes.

"There are mages."

"Shamans or Fades." Kallinvar gave a sharp nod. "Nothing we can't handle. Go, now."

As Calen made to leave, Kallinvar pressed his hand against Calen's breastplate.

"When next I call, remember today." He drew a sharp breath through his nostrils. "We want the same thing, Draleid."

"Do we?"

"We want the ones we love to still be breathing when the next summer dawns. Thank you for trusting me."

CALEN SPRINTED DOWN THE CORRIDOR, his legs burning, the weight of the eggs and the armour taking their toll. He glanced over the low parapet to his left. Far below, on the first platform, green Soulblades flashed back and forth as Kallinvar, Haem, and the knights fought to keep the Uraks at bay – to buy Calen time. They would have to fall back through the Rift soon. Even they could not stand against such a tide.

As he moved, the light from the baldír seemed to dim for a moment before flickering back to life.

"Come on, come on…" He scanned the ceiling and walls, praying to Elyara he would find something that signalled the ventilation tunnels. His memories of Mirk's vision were blurry.

There had to be an easier way of finding these tunnels. He stopped, shifting the satchels in their place and rolling his shoulders, muscles bunching and joints cracking. And then, just like that, Falmin's voice whispered in his ear. *"We call it the drift."*

Even in death Falmin was his ray of light in the darkness. And Calen was absolutely sure that if he ever met the man in Achyron's halls, Falmin would remind Calen of that fact a thousand times over – and Calen would welcome it.

Calen pulled on threads of Air and Spirit. The world thundered around him, the roars and clash of steel below as crashing stars in his ears. He closed his eyes and twisted his threads, thinning and spreading them, allowing them to drift on the air. One by one he filtered out the other sounds, fading them into his periphery. Then he heard it: the low whistle of the wind, the gentle push of the current as it flowed into the vault from the city above. There were multiple sources. He chose the closest and ran.

In the city above, Valerys rained fire and fury down on the Uraks who remained outside the tower. He laid waste to anything that moved while arcs of lightning tore past him.

Two of the beasts leapt from the roof of a building. Valerys twisted and snatched one in his jaws, the other falling, the ground taking it. Valerys tossed the Urak upwards, then beat his wings, rose, and ripped the creature in half with a single bite, blood and innards spraying into the wind.

Don't stop moving, Calen urged the dragon. He'd seen what the Fade's lightning had done in Kingspass. Valerys roared back in defiance, his rage aimed not just at the Uraks but also at Calen. It was Calen's choices that had once again separated them, once again left Valerys unable to protect his soulkin.

Calen reached a point in the corridor where the whistle of the wind split. One path led left along the open corridor, the other led right through an arched passage. He didn't have time for decisions. He turned right.

He followed the passage for about fifty feet and found himself in a circular chamber with a statue of an elven woman at its centre. She wore smooth plate armour, her hands resting on the pommel of a sword that pressed into the stone at her feet.

Sand had piled up against the wall behind the statue, and spread across the floor. Above the sand, two enormous rectangular iron grates were set into the wall. Each was at least ten feet across and five feet high: the ventilation tunnels.

He moved past the statue and wove threads of Fire into the iron grate on the right, pulling the heat from the metal. He may never have been anything but a shadow of the blacksmith his father was, but Vars would have looked down on Calen in shame if he'd not remembered that cold forced metal to shrink. After this many centuries, he was sure the grates would be more than stiff.

He pulled two latches out of lock with the threads of Air, then sent the grate dropping into the sand with a *thump.* With a quick check of the eggs, Calen waded into the sand.

He gripped the ledge of the tunnel and started to pull himself up when a shiver crawled up his spine. Half a heartbeat later, the light from Calen's baldír dimmed to a dying flame.

"Warden of Varyn." The Fade's voice was like rusted nails drawn across iron. "It was not you we expected to find in this place."

Calen turned slowly, the Spark burning in his veins. The creature's hair was white as bone, draped across a pale face with thin blue lips and eyes that pulled the courage from Calen's bones. He couldn't see past the Fade's face, all light seeming to bend around it.

The creature must have been following them from the moment they'd entered the city. They'd led it straight to the eggs.

"Though it was only a matter of time. Your kind always comes back to the heart of your pain. All we ever need do is wait." Its eyes flickered towards the satchels of eggs. "Interesting… I had thought we'd killed them all. That will have to be corrected."

Calen slid the satchels from his shoulders, rested them in the sand, and drew his sword. There was no choice. He would have to fight. He let Valerys's rage swallow his fear.

Black flames snaked from the Fade's palm and took the shape of a long, two-handed greatsword. A níthral.

Calen dropped into Striking Dragon and surged forwards. Flickers of light-drinking black swirled outwards as the blades collided. Calen swung high, then twisted his neck back to avoid the creature's counter, the heat from the black fire burning at his chin.

The Fade hissed as it swung, but Calen turned the blow left into the statue, the níthral digging into the stone. The black-fire blade dissipated in a wisp of smoke, and the Fade slammed into Calen, sending him sprawling backwards. The next strike must have been Blood Magic because before Calen could think, he was hurtling into the wall, the breath stampeding from his lungs and leaving him choking for air.

Gasping and staggering forwards, Calen pulled on threads of Earth and Air, pushing them into the Fade, picturing the creature's bones snapping like twigs. But the Fade sliced through Calen's threads with its own, a harsh laugh entering its throat. "I thought you'd be stronger." The reformed black-fire blade trailed along the ground, smoke rising. "Pity."

Valerys roared in the back of Calen's mind as he tore through a Bloodmarked with his talons. The dragon pulled their minds together, settling Calen's heart.

End this. Calen could feel Valerys's intent in his blood. *End it now.*

Calen pulled Valerys's mind into his, unleashed the dragon's fury in his blood, and surged forwards. He flowed through the forms of svidarya, losing himself in the movements, steel colliding against black fire. As he did, he pulled on threads of Earth and Air and slammed them into the statue. An explosion of stone and dust plumed outwards, the statue shattering. The Fade tilted its head back, hissing.

The distraction was enough.

Calen brought his blade down and cleaved the creature's arm just below the elbow, then opened the Fade's belly with his backswing. Intestines tumbled out, dry and ragged, but not a drop of blood spilled.

Before the Fade could react, Calen drew on threads of Fire and Spirit, Valerys roaring in the back of his mind as he unleashed a pillar of fire. He dropped his sword, and the flames poured from his hand like a raging river, the Spark burning in his veins. He let out a roar that matched Valerys's, threads of each elemental strand swirling around him, urging him to draw from them.

But even as the raging fire crashed down over the Fade, the flames parted, split by a force Calen could not see. Blood Magic.

"Warden of Varyn," the creature hissed. "*Tssk, tssk, tssk.*"

Threads of Fire and Spirit swirled about the creature, and it pushed back, black fire spewing from its hand.

The two pillars of fire crashed against one another, shadow and light battling. The Fade stared at him through the flames, those black, light-drinking eyes glaring into his soul.

The black fire pushed harder, and Calen's body shook, the Spark searing within him, the drain sapping at his bones. In the city above, Valerys ripped Uraks to pieces, his rage swelling. The dragon roared, unyielding, defiant.

His soulkin would not be taken from him.

Valerys's fury swallowed Calen whole, their shared soul igniting. And Calen did just as he had done in the Burnt Lands: he let go. The flames that poured from his hand redoubled, pure energy rippling through him, Valerys roaring. Threads of each elemental strand wrapped about him, pulling through his blood and his bones and his soul. They wove together, coiling and twisting, burning like a hundred suns.

Just as Tarast and Antala, just as Kollna and Tinua, they were one, completely and entirely. They were soulkin, and their fire would not be quelled.

The Fade staggered backwards, its black fire barely able to hold Calen in place. The fire that poured from Calen's hand flickered, changing at its core. Orange-red flames yielded to those of a purple hue until the fire shone with the same light as Calen's eyes.

The Spark burned in him like never before, strands of Air, Fire, Earth, Water, and Spirit forged into a single entity that burned with the rage of a dragon.

Calen roared, clenching his fingers into a fist by nothing more than instinct alone. The flames died, and in Calen's hand was a sword wrought from purple light that rippled like fire. It was not simply a weapon, but a physical manifestation of his shared soul.

For a brief moment, the Fade looked at him with its mouth ajar. Then it lunged, black-fire blade forming in its fist. Calen met the swing in a burst of purple light and stared unflinchingly into the creature's bottomless eyes. And there, in the depths of darkness, he saw something he'd least expected: fear.

Valerys roared in Calen's mind, and Calen pushed forwards with all his strength, threads of Air and Spirit whirling around him. He caught the Fade's black-fire blade twice more, and on the third he wrapped the fingers of his left hand around the creature's wrist and drove his níthral through its already savaged gut.

The shriek that left the Fade's throat was an otherworldly, blood chilling thing that threatened to rip Calen's skin from his bones. Calen pulled his níthral free, and the Fade's body hit the stone. The shadows retreated and the light of the baldír bloomed once again.

Calen stood there, panting, sweat dripping from his nose and brow. He stared down at the pulsing purple light of the sword in his fist. A níthral. A Soulblade. Therin had told him briefly of the legendary weapons, but Calen had only ever seen them in the hands of the Fades and the knights – and in his visions.

He stared at the monster's pale, bloodless, face.

He'd just killed a Fade. Alone.

Valerys roared in his mind again, and the purple blade flickered from his palm.

Calen grabbed his sword from the ground, slid it into his scabbard, slung the egg satchels over his shoulder, and climbed into the ventilation tunnel.

CHAPTER FIFTY

DEATH OF WHAT WAS

18th Day of the Blood Moon

Aravell – Winter, Year 3081 After Doom

Ella walked without saying a word, the wolf prowling in the back of her mind. When they reached Alura, she dismissed Sennik and the Angan and was almost across the basin when Gaeleron called to her.

The elf wore a smooth suit of steel armour, decorated with gold leaves along the edges of the breastplate, the emblem of a white dragon on the front. Both his pauldrons were wrought from white steel, and tassets composed of small white scales protected his groin and hips. Ella's dad would have marvelled at the craftsmanship.

"I would walk with you, if you'll have me?" The elf gave Ella an overly formal bow, his hand resting on the pommel of his sword.

Ella would have preferred to walk alone, particularly to where she was going, but there was something about Gaeleron that put her at ease. The elf had been there from the moment she'd woken. He was forthright, and Ella knew she could trust him. She could… *smell* the loyalty in his blood.

"I'm assuming you didn't seek me out just for the pleasure of my company?"

"I would do as well seeking out a rose bush if that were the case."

Ella burst out laughing as she ran her hand across the side of her head, feeling the long-healed scars left by the Urak. The elf had a dry sense of humour that she appreciated.

Gaeleron returned her smile and continued. "I sought you out because both Queen Uthrían and King Galdra sent emissaries directly to me, enquiring as to your availability. It appears they have sent multiple already who were refused at your door."

"Where I come from, that would be understood as a lack of desire to speak."

"Unfortunately, they are quite insistent."

"I'm sure they are."

Ella lifted her gaze as they walked along the path that connected Alura to the Eyrie. When she had first arrived in Aravell, before the battle, the path had simply been a long section of white stone with two sheer walls of rock on either side. But after she'd woken, she'd found Craftsmages working on the rock walls for hours at a time. She'd not seen the fruits of their labour until that moment.

Enormous statues of dragons now lined the walls on either side of the path. Where the statues that fronted the archway into the Tahír un Ilyienë were noble and stoic, these were fierce and proud. Each dragon was unique in its appearance, but they all stood facing forwards, roaring, forelimbs pressed into the ground, the frills on their backs raised. As she walked, Ella realised she recognised some of them, knew their hearts, their souls.

One was larger than all the others, her shoulders broad, the horns around her jaw long and slender. Though all the statues were a pale grey, Ella could see Ithrax's green scales in her mind, hear her mighty roar. How she knew the dragon's name Ella had no idea, just as she had no idea how she knew Ithrax had once been bound to an elf by the name of Athír, and how, when Ithrax was barely a few years old, they once rode the length and breadth of all Epheria. She knew it as though the memories were a piece of her.

The statue opposite Ithrax was of Onymia. Her scales had truly been as pale and grey as the rock, her horns black as night, her eyes the blue of a distant sky. Onymia had been eight hundred years old when the lightning tore open her chest in the valleys of Aravell and ripped her from the world.

Thurial and Aradanil stood next to their kin, fierce and defiant. In her mind, Ella painted the soft pink of Thurial's scales and the vibrant red of his wings. She shuddered as she remembered his head being ripped free, images flashing in her mind. Aradanil had been mighty and majestic, scales the colour of marigold, eyes green as emeralds. His belly had been sliced open in the sky.

Ella shuddered with each and every one she passed, these dragons who had allowed her to share their hearts, to share their bodies. She remembered that moment viscerally. The moment where those noble creatures had agreed to make one last stand, one last sacrifice, a sacrifice she would carry with her forever.

She passed more statues of dragons she did not know, dragons, she thought, who had made similar sacrifices.

As she stepped past the statues, wingbeats sounded overhead, and she looked up to see Varthear alight on the grass before Ella, spreading her ruby wings, the blended light of the sun and the moon shimmering through. The dragon dipped her head, eyes of liquid fire fixing on Ella.

Varthear was like something pulled from one of the oil paintings she'd seen in Berona. Scales of sapphire and horns of onyx. Not even the thick scars that ran along Varthear's scales diminished her beauty.

Beside her, Gaeleron bowed his head and pressed an armoured fist to his breastplate while Faenir stood tall on Ella's right. The wolfpine didn't growl and his hackles stayed low, but neither did he back down.

Varthear blew a warm breath over Ella, and the smell of ash and the sweet scent of fresh blood filled her nostrils.

Just as she had done every time she had entered the Eyrie since waking, Ella placed her hand on the scales of Varthear's snout.

The dragon pushed her snout forwards and pressed it into Ella's palm, a deep rumble resonating in her throat.

"It's good to see you, too." Ella ran her fingers along a fused ridge where a talon had torn the dragon's lip open. "You look stronger each day."

A deep rumble resonated from across the Eyrie, and a black mound in the corner of Ella's vision rose, pale blue wings shaking as though trying to loose a settled layer of snow. Sardakes was an altogether different beast than Varthear. Where Varthear was lean and sleek, Sardakes was dense and powerful, his horns thick, his shoulders almost a third again wider and more muscled than the other dragon's.

The obsidian dragon nuzzled his snout into the base of Varthear's jaw, a purr in his throat. There was something pure in watching creatures capable of such destruction show such deep affection.

Sardakes twisted his neck to look towards Ella and blew a warm breath over her before leaning down and nudging Faenir's side with his snout. The wolfpine bowed, paws spreading, his tail whipping back and forth.

As Faenir played with a creature that could eat him for supper, Ella turned to Gaeleron, who was busy staring in awe and reverence at the two dragons.

"Why do Queen Uthrían and King Galdra wish to speak to me?"

"To thank you for what you did during the battle."

"Why do Queen Uthrían and King Galdra wish to speak to me?" Ella repeated.

Gaeleron frowned. "Likely to influence you before Calen returns. The Triarchy have been in a constant, silent war since long before I was born. Not a war of blood and steel, but of words and power. You are the Draleid's blood."

Ella nodded. The candour was refreshing. "I will see them on one condition."

Gaeleron raised an eyebrow.

"I need you to take me in there." Ella gestured towards the enormous passageway in the rock on the western edge of the Eyrie. "They've refused me three times."

"I know why you wish to go in."

"It is your choice. Either you bring me inside and I will take an audience with both king and queen, or you don't and I won't." Ella didn't like playing these games, especially not with Gaeleron, but she would play them if she needed to.

Gaeleron shook his head. "I will do as you ask, but I will go in with you. That is not negotiable."

Ella pursed her lips and agreed. She followed Gaeleron across the platform. Across the way, near the stream that tumbled off the edge, three of the Dracárdare

– the Dragonkeepers – cleaned the remnants of what looked to have been the dragons' most recent meal. They scrubbed blood from the rocks and picked strips of skin and fur from the grass. And as Varthear lifted into the air and alighted in the stream, water spraying, all three of the elves knelt and pressed four fingers to their foreheads.

"Their lives have been dedicated to the dragons since before they had seen their twentieth summer," Gaeleron said. "Andinarí, the elf on the far right, has now seen one hundred and twenty-one summers pass him by. And in all that time both Varthear and Sardakes had been listless and unmoving. Seeing the dragons like this is akin to Varyn himself extending his hand into the world."

Ella watched Varthear dip her head into the stream as the elf Gaeleron had pointed to scrubbed at one of her teeth. "Do you spend a lot of time here?"

Gaeleron shook his head. "I'd never been here before Calen brought me. Very few of my people ever have. No. Andinarí is my uncle."

Four guards stood by the enormous opening in the rock, all bearing Calen's sigil. But one thing Ella had learned since finding her way back was that Calen's sigil didn't always mean Calen was the one giving the orders.

"Narvír." One of the elves stepped forwards and bowed his head to Gaeleron. The guard glanced at Ella and Faenir, his gaze lingering on the massive wolfpine.

"This is Ella Bryer." Gaeleron inclined his head towards Ella. "She is the Draleid's kin. I am to escort her within the walls of the holding quarters to conduct an interrogation of the traitor Farda Kyrana. By order of the Draleid himself."

The guard licked his lips, glancing back at the others. "Nobody is to pass, Narvír. Not until the Draleid returns, by order of Chora Sarn. The prisoners may venture into the Eyrie, but they are to be sheltered within the rock – for their own protection."

"Is it Chora Sarn's sigil you wear on your chest or Calen Bryer's?"

"I…"

"It is a simple question."

"Calen Bryer's."

"Good. And so I command you to step aside, lest your honour be called into question."

The guard straightened at that, his eyes widening. "That won't be necessary, Narvír."

"Your honour will be noted. Du haryn myia vrai." Gaeleron inclined his head towards the passage, gesturing for Ella to follow him.

"Din vrai é atuya sin'vala. Aiar gryr haydria til myia elwyn."

"What did he say?" Ella whispered, following Gaeleron past the other guards, who watched closely.

"I thanked him, and he appreciated the thanks. I do not like lying, Ella Bryer."

"And yet you did it anyway."

Gaeleron only grunted. He led Ella through a long stone corridor illuminated by thick beeswax candles in sconces. She would have known that faint, sweet scent anywhere. To travellers passing through The Glade, Lasch Havel's beeswax candles smelled of nothing, which in and of itself was a special thing when set next to tallow candles. But Ella had lived around those candles all her life, and they had been her light on many a dark night.

Gaeleron stopped at the end of the corridor, where it intersected another that moved in both directions in a circular pattern, arched windows looking into an enormous courtyard.

A dragon lay curled in the central yard, the light of the sun and the moon spilling in through the open roof and glinting off its scales. The only word Ella could use to describe the creature was 'beautiful'. Its body was a work of art, like a living flower, scales of purple and white that reminded her of the Gloxinia flowers that grew along the road from The Glade to Milltown.

An elf with pale skin and dark hair leaned against the dragon's hind leg, unconscious, her chest rising and falling slowly.

Memories of the battle flickered on her mind.

"Why are they kept here?" Ella whispered. "They saved Calen, risked their lives. I saw them."

"She is of the Dragonguard." Gaeleron tilted his head to the right, watching the sleeping woman. "Tivar Savinír. She was once of my people, the elves of Lunithír. But she and Avandeer betrayed The Order."

"And then she came back."

"If only the world were that simple."

"If only." Ella allowed her gaze to linger on Tivar and Avandeer for a moment longer. Whatever they were, she had them to thank for Calen still drawing breath. "Where is he?"

Gaeleron's expression grew grim, and he gestured for Ella to follow.

"Ella Bryer. Something told me we would cross paths again."

Ella spun on her heels at the sound of Ilyain's voice. The elf stood beneath the arch of a passageway in the rock, his usually shaved scalp now showing short black stubble. Even staring into those milky eyes, Ella had always found it hard to think Ilyain was blind. Nothing ever got past him.

Ella darted across the corridor and, much to Ilyain's surprise, wrapped her arms around him.

The elf simply rested a hand on Ella's back, gentle and reassuring. "It is pleasing to see you well. I had heard what happened and feared for the worst."

Ella pulled away, scrunching her fingers against her palms. "I'm sorry. I'm not sure what came over me."

"Do not apologise, Ella. The simple comfort of a warm embrace is not something I have come by often these past centuries. And depending on the outcome of this place, it may be the last time."

Ella hugged Ilyain again, receiving a startled 'oomph' for her troubles. "It won't be."

She had grown fond of the elf over their journey from the North to Aravell. It had been Ilyain's openness to discuss his Ayar Elwyn's life that had saved Ella's, his teachings of Níthianelle and of everything Andras had told him of the druids that had kept her grounded when she would have panicked. Ilyain may not have known it, but he had saved her life.

"You are here for Farda."

It wasn't a question.

"You will find him in his quarters."

Ella nodded and turned to leave. Just the mention of Farda's name had conjured a rage within her, the wolf snapping and snarling in her blood.

"You wish him dead." Another non-question.

"Should I not?" Ella snapped, rounding on Ilyain. She hadn't wanted to unleash her anger on him, but it was uncasked now, and it would burn whichever way it desired. The wolf was part of her, and she it. "Should I forgive him? Should I stroke his fragile ego, mend his broken heart? Should I wash my mam's blood from his hands?"

Faenir snarled at Ella's side, a deep growl in his throat.

"No. But I suggest you talk to him. And maybe don't kill him quite yet, even if he asks you to."

Ella could smell the sorrow in Ilyain's smile.

She glared at him, finding herself increasingly frustrated at the realisation that the elf couldn't see her face. She turned and stormed off down the corridor.

"Which room?" Ella pushed at each door as she walked, finding them locked. She twisted to face Gaeleron, who followed her with Faenir at his side. She roared, "Which room?"

Gaeleron looked at the floor for a moment, then lifted his gaze, lips pursed, and inclined his head towards another corridor. Ella turned the corner and found two elves in steel plate stood on either side of an iron-banded door.

She stopped at the door, her blood pounding in her veins, the wolf baring its teeth. She was equal parts rage and fear. One she understood, the other she didn't.

"Stay out here," she said to Gaeleron through gritted teeth. "Faenir. Come."

The guards attempted to stop her, but she snarled, her fangs long and sharp, then slammed her palm against the door, which swung inwards and crashed against the wall. The warm glow of those same beeswax candles illuminated the room.

A wooden bed sat in the far right corner, a small desk and chair on the left, an arched window at the back.

Farda sat on the ground with his back to the far wall, his knees pulled up, his arms hooked around them. He looked at the ground, unflinching at the slamming door.

Ella stared down at the man, her hands shaking at her side, the wolf within her yearning for blood. Her teeth lengthened into fangs and pricked at her lips, the nails on her hands darkening and forming into claws.

She'd never felt a rage like this. So all-consuming, so raw in its power. She could smell the sweetness of his blood, hear the slow beating of his heart.

All she wanted to do was walk across the stone and drive her claws into Farda's belly, rip him open, and leave him there to die in his innards. But she fought that desire, fought that lust for death. She had made that promise to herself long ago, before the battle at the Three Sisters.

I am in control.

The wolf howled back in answer, and Fenryr's words echoed in her head. "*You conquer the wolf by becoming it.*"

The words set a growl in Ella's throat. She was the wolf. She was of the blood of Fenryr. The voice that left her lips was cold and calm. "Has your courage deserted you? Will you not look at me?"

"Do you want me to?"

"Look at me!"

Farda lifted his head. Four pale scars ran from the man's ear across his cheek and jaw. His skin and hair were clean and washed, and he looked far better than he should have.

"The wounds healed well." Ella squeezed the fingers of her right hand into a fist, her claws pricking at her palm, blood trickling. She held the wolf at bay, feeling it loom over her like a spectre.

"I'd have left them to rot and fester, but they insisted." He traced his fingertips along the scars, his gaze never leaving hers. "It's good to see you well. Truly."

Ella ignored him and walked further into the room and over towards the desk. A journal, a glass inkwell, and a pen sat beside a half-burnt candle. She peeled open the journal to find empty pages. As she did, Faenir padded over to Farda and pulled his lips back in a snarl, hackles raised. "And they insisted you bathe as well? You're very well looked after for a traitor, a coward, and a liar."

"That was Hala who insisted. Said I smelled like 'twice-excreted shit', if I remember correctly. Can't argue with her."

Ella tapped her claw against the journal, then grabbed the inkwell and smashed it against the opposite wall. Faenir snapped and growled, his body rigid. The fury came in waves, ebbs and flows, the wolf breaking through, then Ella, then the wolf.

"I trusted you," Ella whispered, her voice trembling. "Everything in me told me not to. But I did."

"I know."

"You lied to me... All that time, you looked me in the eyes and you lied to me. And I let you worm your way into my head. What was it you said? 'When you're near, I don't feel so fucking broken'? Well, you are fucking broken! You're a monster. There is something evil in your heart, something dark and empty."

The wolf broke free from Ella's hold, but the anger that burned through her was a cold one. A sharp, icy, calm fury. She settled her breathing, then lowered to one knee before Farda.

The man stared into Faenir's eyes, unblinking.

"Don't look at him." Ella leaned closer. "Look at me."

Farda stared at Faenir a second longer, then turned his gaze to Ella, and she felt those deep green eyes pierce her soul.

"You killed my mam."

"I did. And for the little it's worth, I am sorry."

"I didn't ask you to speak." Ella grabbed Farda by the throat, slamming his head against the wall, her fingers tightening. He didn't fight her or push her away or beg her to stop. She clenched her jaw as she squeezed tighter. "You burned her alive. Burned the flesh from her bones. Did you feel anything as she screamed? Can that black heart feel at all? She was the kindest woman I ever knew. Everything she did, she did for others. She was a healer, did you know that? Of course you fucking didn't. When I was little, she would put me on her back and carry me everywhere, show me everything she did, and talk to me like I was a woman grown. When I was sick, she would sit by my bedside with cups of tea and bowls of soup and stew, holding a damp cloth to my head. She was the greatest mother anyone ever had." Ella loosened her grip on Farda's throat, not much, but just enough to allow him to breathe. She lowered her voice to a whisper, Faenir's growl matching it. "And you took her from me."

The wolf within her begged for Farda's blood, begged to feel his still-beating heart in its jaws.

Ella growled and released Farda's throat, turning away and rising. "Is there anything else? Any other lies you've held? Any other people you've slaughtered?"

"I sent the men."

"You what?" Ella turned back and looked to Farda, who stared into her eyes. For the first time since she'd entered the room, Ella smelled fear wafting from the man.

"I sent the men who found you on the merchant's road to Gisa. I didn't just cross your path in the city. I sent soldiers to track you down."

"You…" Ella's heart skipped a beat, and her lungs struggled to drag in air. "You sent…" Her mind replayed the memories of that day. The memories of Rhett holding his hands to his belly. The feeling of Rhett's thumb brushing her cheek. The blood. Her own screams resounded in her mind. "You killed him, too?"

Ella didn't roar or howl. She didn't cry, didn't tremble or shake. She just stood there. The calm that swept over her was something numb and devoid of all feeling. "You took everything from me…" It was a simple statement of fact. "You… took everything."

"I'm sorry."

"Sorry? Do you think that word holds any meaning on your lips? Your 'sorry' is worth less than a dead man's promise. You are darkness. You are every evil deed done in this world. And you want me to forgive you? To grant you redemption?"

"I seek no such thing," Farda said plainly. He rose slowly, Faenir snarling in his face. "Some are beyond redemption, and I count myself in that number. You're right. I am darkness. I am a monster, and I know what I've become. I ask you no forgiveness, for I am not, nor will I ever be, deserving of it. I just wish you to know that I regret what I did."

Faenir shifted so he stood at Ella's side, teeth bared, saliva dripping.

"What would your precious Shinyara think of you now, Farda? What would she think of the man who slaughters innocent women, the man who has spent hundreds of years butchering and murdering in the name of a monster?" Ella's hands shook at her side, claws extended. "If I have my say, you will die slowly over many years, cold and alone. You will pray to your god for death, but it will not come. There is no pain that could be enough, no agony fitting. And so I would do the only thing I know could harm you. I would keep you from death, keep you from the only thing you love in this world. Just as you have taken so much of what I love from me."

Farda swallowed, and Ella thought she saw pain in his eyes.

Good. He deserves pain.

Ella walked from the room without saying another word. She stormed past Gaeleron, back along the corridor, and out into the Eyrie, through the passageway adorned with dragon statues, along the paths of Alura, and made her way up to the high plateau upon which eight houses of white bone stood.

Several Fenryr Angan prowled the plateau, along with men and women bearing Calen's sigil, standing guard with sharp steel in their hands.

The Angan all bowed to Ella and Faenir as they walked, and she inclined her head in return but didn't speak.

When she finally reached the white home backed against the cliff wall, the one in which she slept each night – the one that would never be home – and opened the door, a plethora of scents and sounds washed over her.

Fresh baked bread, seared venison, roasted potatoes and rosemary, garlic, tomatoes, onions. She could smell each aroma, each piece of a whole, the wolf picking between them. And amidst it all, the fresh and sharp scent of lavender brought itself to the fore. Pots clanged, and something boiled, popping and bubbling. The roar of the hearth fire soothed her, the warmth brushing her skin.

"Are you just going to stand there, my dear?" Elia popped up from behind the central counter, a massive pot in one hand. She removed the pot's lid, and the pungent earthy aroma of freshly diced Arlen Root pierced the other scents. Even after what Fenryr had said, Elia had continued to bring Ella Arlen Root tea every morning, noon, and night, no matter how many times she refused. Ella had given up trying to explain to the woman after her sixth attempt. Something within Elia was broken. Whatever had been done to her in the dungeons below Berona was beyond comprehension. Lasch was better. He seemed weaker than before, smaller somehow, but his mind was still there, and he still had the same heart.

"Well, come in." Elia beckoned her forwards. "And close the door behind you. You're letting the heat out."

Ella did as instructed, ushering Faenir past her. She stood in the middle of the room, just watching as Elia stirred a pot by the fire and wafted the steam towards her nose.

"I've given up on trying to master your mam's braised lamb. The woman should have been sent to the Circle for practicing magic. I'll never work out how she got that flavour. Don't worry though, Gaeleron brought me enough venison this morning to feed a horse… or a wolfpine." Elia flashed a smile at Faenir, who bounded over and nuzzled her shoulder.

Footsteps sounded, and Lasch descended the stairs. He pressed his fingers to his lips as he crept up behind Elia, who was lost in stirring the pot. Lasch wrapped his arms around his wife from behind and planted a kiss on her cheek.

"Smells incredible." He inhaled sharply through his nose, then looked to the pot of tea Elia had left on the counter and gave Ella a sympathetic smile. "How was your day, Ella?" Lasch tilted his head to the side and narrowed his eyes. "Ella? What's wrong?"

Ella hadn't realised she was crying. It was only when Lasch spoke that she felt the tears rolling down her cheeks, softly dripping from her chin.

Lasch stepped around the counter and brought his embrace to her. And as soon as he did, the trickle of tears became a waterfall, her gut churning, chest heaving.

"I just miss them so much." Everything came crashing down on her. Every drop of loss and loneliness and sorrow she had pushed down and sealed tight. "I miss them."

"I know." Lasch wrapped one hand around the back of Ella's head, and she wept into his chest. "I know, sweet girl. I miss them too."

FARDA FOUND HIMSELF STANDING AT that ledge once more, the day slowly yielding to the night. He was barefoot, his toes curling over the edge, dirt and small rocks tumbling.

He drew slow breaths, tracing his finger over the scars on his face.

Ella's voice sounded in his head. *"You took everything from me…"*

"We're back here?"

Farda shook his head softly, turning to look at Tivar as she approached. Hala and Ilyain walked with her. "It has not been a good day."

"Have you had *any* good days recently?" Hala asked.

"Define recently?"

"Within the last four hundred years." Hala moved so she stood at his side, her white hair falling loose, a broken smile on her lips.

"Two or three."

"More than I, so." Tivar looked out at the valley beyond. "What did she say?"

"Truth."

"Where is your head, brother?" Ilyain folded his arms and turned to look at Farda with those milky-white eyes.

"Firmly attached to my body." Farda sighed when Ilyain continued to stare. "I'm all right."

They stood there in silence for what must have been hours, teetering on the cliff's edge, the wind nipping at them. There was a peace in it.

"Before I die, I want to be what I was before," Farda said finally. "I want to be who I was."

"I'm not sure you can be." Tivar drew a sharp breath in, then exhaled. "I'm not sure any of us can. But being better than we are now is a good place to start."

"They're probably going to kill us anyway," Hala said with a shrug. "I'd kill us."

Ilyain frowned.

"I follow where you both go," Hala said, sighing through her nostrils. "I trust Ilyain's heart a lot more than I do my own."

Farda nodded slowly. He touched at his pocket reflexively, feeling for the coin that should have sat there. He pulled his hand away as soon as he realised what he was doing. "Are you three going to watch over me forever?"

"Only until I think you won't try to hurl yourself off the edge or drown yourself in a pool," Tivar answered. She had never been one to shy away from things.

"I won't."

"What changed?"

Farda gave a half-smile, then looked down over the edge. "Little... but you were right."

"And what was I right about?"

"A great many things," Farda said, mustering as genuine a smile as he could for his old friend while Ella's pain-filled eyes floated in his mind. "It is never too late to make the right choice," he said, repeating Tivar's words from the night she had pulled him from the rock pool. "The last few centuries of my life have been pointless. They have been dark and empty, and I let myself become the thing that I hated. I would prefer if my death meant something. If I could, in some small way, ease the suffering I've caused. Then, at least, I can find Shinyara again with a heart that holds a little light in it. I would like to be worthy of her again."

CHAPTER FIFTY-ONE

DEEDS OF GODS

18th Day of the Blood Moon

Ilnaen – Winter, Year 3081 After Doom

The moon's light signalled the end of the ventilation tunnel ahead, cold air rushing down and tumbling over Calen's face. He pulled Valerys's mind into his and fed from the dragon's fury before sending a sphere of Air crashing into the grate that separated him from the city outside. Iron creaked, and stone rumbled, and the grate ripped free from its hinges.

Calen hauled himself from the tunnel mouth and dropped onto what appeared to be the roof of a ruined building. The dark of night still held the city in its grasp, the light of the Blood Moon glittering in the sand that swirled in the air.

More sand covered the stone beneath Calen's feet, and behind him the two shafts of the ventilation tunnels jutted from the roof at an angle. Thousands of rooftops spread in every direction, broken towers jutting from their midsts.

A roar sounded to his left, and he twisted to see Valerys swoop low and bathe a street of Uraks in dragonfire. The dragon whirled upwards at the touch of Calen's mind, wisps of fire swirling from the street and coiling about his wings as he rose.

Calen checked the satchels one last time, a hand lingering on the buttercream scales of the first egg he'd found.

Valerys swooped low and dropped to alight on the roof when arcs of purple lightning crashed into the side of the building. Shards of shattered stone dinged Calen's armour and sliced into his cheeks and brow, a cloud of dust pluming into the air. Valerys wheeled upwards, screeching, smoke drifting from his hind leg where the lightning had caught him.

Calen turned at the sound of stone crunching, only for something to collide with his chest and send him careening across the rooftop. By instinct alone, he pulled the Spark into himself and shielded the eggs with threads of Air as he hit the stone with a *crack*, the back plate of his armour grinding on the sand as he slid. The low parapet that framed the rooftop stopped him from tumbling over the edge.

His head rang like a bell and his vision was blurred, and still only half his mind was focused on himself. Valerys's pain seared in him as the dragon wheeled away.

Calen stared through the dust and sand thrown into the air, searching for Valerys through haze-filled eyes. Just as he caught sight of the white dragon in the night sky, a cold, armour-clad hand wrapped around his throat and lifted him into the air with the ease of a man lifting a newborn.

He found himself looking into two glowing red eyes set into slits in a silver helm. The warrior held Calen with his arm at full stretch, Calen's feet dangling over the rooftop. His captor must have been ten feet tall.

Lungs burning, Calen slammed his fists down onto the outstretched arm as the fingers tightened. His vision blurred, limbs growing heavy, the pressure clamping down on his throat. Desperate, Calen reached for the Spark, but the man gave him a choking laugh and tossed him from the roof.

Any breath that had been left in Calen's lungs fled as he dropped like a rock into a mountain of sand. He gasped for air, dragging himself to his feet, reflexively feeling for the eggs in the satchels. Relief flooded him when he felt them intact, their armoured shells withstanding the drop.

Above, the warrior that had held him stood on the roof's parapet. The man was clad in a full plate of silver steel that reminded Calen of the strange armour the knights wore, smooth and flowing as though poured into place. Though this armour was covered in glowing red runes. This was one of the warriors Haem had spoken of: one of Efialtír's Chosen.

A heartbeat passed, and the Chosen launched himself from the roof.

Calen threw himself forwards as the Chosen crashed down in a cloud of sand where Calen had been lying.

Calen drew his sword, his breaths ragged. Looking at the Chosen's armour, he had no idea where he would strike. There were no weak points, no vulnerabilities. That thing wasn't a man, it was a mountain of steel.

Before he could think, the warrior strode forwards, a níthral wrought of bright red light forming in its fist. It grabbed the hilt with two hands and swung in a vicious downward arc.

Calen sidestepped, then swung his blade into the man's hip, a vibration jarring his arms as his blow skittered away harmlessly. The weight of the eggs in the satchels threw him off balance, and he stumbled to the right.

The warrior twisted and swung down with his níthral. Calen lurched backwards.

A roar sounded, and Valerys soared overhead. Too large to land, the dragon snatched at the Chosen with his talons. The Chosen swung wildly with his níthral, missing Valerys's left leg by a hair. But he didn't see the dragon's spear-tip tail until it slammed into his chest and sent him careening down the sand and further into the street below. When he rose, a thin crack spread across the front of his breastplate.

"So," Calen whispered, his eyes tracing the crack in the armour, "there is a way in."

Calen pulled threads of Air, Spirit, and Earth into his body and charged down the sand, only stopping when Valerys roared, the dragon demanding he run. They needed to get the eggs to safety. That was what mattered.

He stared down at the Chosen, whose crimson níthral had now reformed. A piece of him wanted to charge, wanted to drive his blade through the cracks in that monstrosity's armour just to prove it could be killed. But the knights were fighting, risking their lives, to give him a chance to escape. Calen drew a sharp breath, then turned and sprinted up the hill of sand towards a nearby roof. He slipped and scrambled upright, dragging himself forwards. All he needed to do was mount Valerys and take to the skies.

Calen dug his hands into the sand and hauled himself forwards, his feet sinking as he climbed. Something wrapped around his waist and slung him backwards. The world spun, and his stomach turned, the eggs swinging about him in their satchels. He hit the ground with a *thump*. He gasped, trying to drag the breath back into his lungs.

A hand reached down and hauled him into the air, metal fingers wrapping around his throat once more. This time, he didn't stare through the slits of a helm. The face of an Urak, crimson runes carved into its leathery grey skin, stared back at him. Its eyes were black as a Fade's, like bottomless wells.

A crimson light began to form in the creature's free hand. Overhead Valerys roared, dropped from the sky, and lifted his head back, a pressure building within him.

Calen pulled their minds together and channelled Valerys's rage through him, feeling the dragon's fury in his blood. He slammed a ball of Air into the Chosen's chest. The force of the blow sent the creature crashing into the wall of the building behind it.

The moment the Chosen hit the stone, Valerys unleashed a river of dragonfire. The flames crashed down over the creature and its gleaming silver plate, and for a second Calen allowed himself a flicker of hope. Until the dragonfire parted around the Chosen's outstretched hand.

Calen didn't hesitate. He pulled on threads of Fire, Earth, and Air, weaving them through the sand around him. With Earth and Fire, he pulled the grains of sand together and bound them into shards of glass with the heat of a dragon's fury, then hurled them through the air.

The shards crashed into the Chosen like a raging storm, smashing into its armour and slicing through the grey flesh of its face before molten steel flowed from its collar and its helm reformed. Taking advantage of the moment, Calen dropped the satchels into the sand and charged.

He swung at the creature's side but changed his course when the red light of a crimson níthral ignited in the corner of his vision. Calen twisted and caught the blow head-on with his sword, the impact jarring his arms.

A second Chosen stared down at him, crimson light misting in the slits of its helm. The pressure faded in the back of his mind as Valerys's fire ebbed. A glance over his shoulder told him the first Chosen moved towards him.

Calen drew a sharp breath, opened himself to the Spark, and unleashed a shockwave of air, knocking both the monstrosities backwards. In that same breath, he sheathed his sword and pulled Valerys's mind into his. Ayar viël. Ayar elwyn. Ayar nithír.

One life. One heart. One soul.

With the dragon's power surging through him, Calen pulled on each elemental strand and felt a wash of relief as the purple flames burst from his fist, raging and thrashing before settling into the shape of a light-wrought sword.

The two Chosen fell upon him, crimson níthrals hacking and slashing. Calen fell into the movements of the fellensír, bursts of light igniting around him as the blades collided.

The Chosen to his right swung its blade downward in an attempt to cleave Calen in half. But Calen twisted, avoiding the strike by the breadth of a hair. Valerys's rage swirling within him, he funnelled threads of Earth and Spirit into his left hand, then rammed the fist into the creature's side. The impact jarred Calen's arm, but it also spread a crack through the Chosen's armour.

Before Calen could take advantage of the blow, the second creature sprang forwards and slammed something unseen into Calen's chest. The force of the Blood Magic sent Calen tumbling backwards before he rammed a gauntleted hand into the sand and steadied himself.

Above, Valerys attempted to swoop down once more, but Uraks leapt from the rooves and grabbed at his feet and wings, trying to carve him open. The dragon split one from groin to throat with a swing of his tail and crushed another with his jaws, but the beasts kept coming.

Fly higher! Calen lifted himself to his feet. The dragon roared back in his mind, tearing the Uraks apart as he landed on the roof above, refusing to leave Calen. Calen was his soulkin, not his master.

The two Chosen charged again and a memory flashed through Calen's mind, a memory that was not his own, a memory of Tarast, Soulkin of Antala, the world shifting around him. The light of his níthral flickered from purple to yellow, and it was as though Tarast moved through him. He drifted through the movements of a form he did not know, turning away strike after strike before he dropped to one knee in the sand, then spinning as a níthral soared over his head. He swung his blade as he spun and carved through the silver armour that protected one of the Chosen's bellies. It was like slicing through parchment. Blood poured from the opening, but the creature kicked out and slammed its boot into Calen's chest.

Calen lay on the flat of his back in the sand as the Chosen lifted its glowing blade and moved for the killing strike.

A roar erupted, and Valerys crashed down into the street, folding his wings in tight. The tip of the dragon's tail burst though the Chosen's chest in a spray of blood. With the talons of his winged forelimbs clinging to the stone around him, Valerys lifted the Chosen up, snapped his jaws around the creature's body, and ripped it in half with a terrible wrench of his neck.

As the severed torso dropped to the sand, purple lightning streaked upwards and crashed into Valerys's chest. The dragon shrieked, tearing chunks of stone from the buildings on either side, smoke pluming.

The surviving Chosen stepped forwards, the runes in its armour pulsing with a vibrant red light. Something coiled around Calen, an unseen rope constricting his limbs, crushing him and lifting him off his feet.

The Chosen's helm receded once more, black eyes staring into Calen's, rune-marked grey skin stretched tight across thick bone. The hairs on Calen's neck stood on end as a voice like no other left the Chosen's throat. Harsh, guttural, and deep, almost like its throat was bleeding. "Why did you return here? Did your god send you for the Heart?" The invisible bonds clenched around Calen's throat, and he screamed. The Chosen roared, two voices shouting at once. "Answer me! Where is the Heart?"

Calen tried to reach out to the Spark, but it was all he could do to hold on to consciousness as the threads of Blood Magic tightened around him, Valerys roaring, trying desperately to get to Calen as more Uraks leapt from the rooves above. And then, all of a sudden, he hit the sand, and the Chosen was gone.

Calen gasped for air, looking over to see the giant beast in silver steel plate pulling itself from its knees some twenty feet away along the sand.

A knight in dark green armour stood over Calen. In a flash of green light, a Soulblade ignited in his fist, the green glow sparkling in the sand. Then Calen heard his brother's voice.

"If you want him, demon, come and get him."

CHAPTER FIFTY-TWO

PROTECT THE ONES YOU LOVE

18th Day of the Blood Moon

Ilnaen – Winter, Year 3081 After Doom

Arden stood between Calen and the Chosen, his Soulblade ignited in his fist. The others had said they'd seen rune-marked Uraks the night the Blood Moon had risen, seen them become hosts for the Chosen. The thing was a monster, a head and shoulders above even him in his Sentinel armour.

"Go." Arden didn't dare take his eyes from the Chosen, but he felt the sand shifting beneath his feet as Calen rose.

"I'm not leaving you." Calen stepped up beside Arden, a purple níthral bursting to life in his hand. When had that happened? "We do this together."

"I'll be right behind you, little brother. But I will not let you die here."

"Haem—"

"Go!" Arden roared, his gaze still fixed on the Chosen, who now marched across the sand. He looked to the satchels of eggs Calen had dropped in the sand. "Get those eggs out of here, Calen. Valerys is injured. You need to leave while you still can."

Blood streaked from Calen's lip, his jaws clenched. The mention of Valerys's name softened his stare. For a moment it looked as though he was going to argue, but he nodded. "Thank you."

"Always," Arden whispered as Calen sprinted up the sand towards the rooftop, scrambling to throw the satchels over his shoulders as he did.

The Urak Chosen moved forwards, a snarl on his scarred lip as he stared after Calen.

"Ah, ah," Arden said, shaking his head. "You can have him. But you'll have to go through me first."

The creature snarled, then spat a mixture of saliva and blood into the sand. Liquid metal flowed from the collar of its armour, and its helm reformed as it charged, crimson Soulblade levelled.

The first strike came at Arden's head. He blocked it in a burst of light, tightening his grip on the hilt of his Soulblade. Three more times the creature tried with blunt force to take Arden's head from his shoulders. Grace and poise it had none, but the thing hit like a rampaging bull.

Arden glanced over his shoulder to see that Calen had vanished over the parapet of the building's roof behind him.

Don't look back. Arden reached out to Kallinvar through the Sigil, letting the Grandmaster know he was ready.

"Come, demon," he said, circling the silver beast. "Let us see whose god stands taller."

Arden charged. He swung his Soulblade at the creature's thigh, then its shoulder, then ribs. Quick and hard. The Chosen blocked all three but shifted backwards with each, feet sinking into the sand.

It swung its crimson blade in a wide arc meant to cleave Arden at the waist. Arden dropped to one knee, spinning, switching his blade into his left hand. He was half a second from slicing through the Chosen's shin when a pulse of the Taint erupted from the creature and sent him crashing into the wall of the building behind him.

A striking pain ignited in his lower back, punching the air from his lungs. He recovered just in time to throw himself to his right as the Chosen's crimson blade slammed into the stone where his neck had been.

Arden hit the sand and rolled. He sprang to his feet and drove his Soulblade at the creature's back only for something heavy to fall on him from above. He staggered backwards and collapsed into the sand, an Urak kneeling over him, howling as it swung its blade above its head.

Arden released his Soulblade, pressed his fist against the creature's side, and summoned the ancient weapon once again. Green light burst from his hand and ripped through the creature's torso. Blood poured out around the light-wrought blade, and Arden shoved the lifeless creature to the side, rising. Six more Bloodspawn now stood in the sand-filled street, the Chosen warrior at the centre.

He didn't like those odds. Arden sent another pulse through the Sigil to Kallinvar, more urgent this time.

"My god, warrior of Achyron, seeks to cross into this world, seeks to fight for the things he loves. What does your god do? Cowers while you die. Where is he? I do not see him." The Chosen's voice sent a shiver down Arden's spine, two voices overlapped, both harsh and preternatural. "You fight well. A worthy soul for my blade."

"And you talk too much." Without giving the Bloodspawn time to react, Arden rushed towards the one closest to him. He sidestepped the thrust of the creature's spear, hacked through its arm, then split its face from the bottom of its jaw up through its skull. The body stood for half a moment before slumping into the sand as Arden leapt over it.

He made for the roof. Fighting the creatures in the street would have been easier, but he would die either way. He needed to put distance between him and them. He needed to give Kallinvar time.

Lyrin's voice rang out as Arden reached the top of the sand slope and crested the roof's parapet. "Down!"

Arden dropped to the ground, Lyrin's Soulblade slinging past his head and removing that of a Bloodspawn who had leapt through the air after Arden.

The head hit the stone in front of Arden, red eyes wide and staring, blood seeping from its severed neck.

"Where's Kallinvar?" Arden pulled himself to his feet, then he and Lyrin moved backwards in tandem, holding their guard as the Chosen and more Bloodspawn charged towards them.

Lyrin tilted his head towards a set of rooftops nearer the tower where green and crimson Soulblades clashed. "He's a little tied up." Lyrin dropped his shoulder and rammed the first Bloodspawn over the parapet, sending it soaring down, then spun to parry the swing of a blackened steel blade, splitting its wielder's stomach open. "Where's that brother of yours?"

"Safe." Arden swept past Lyrin and sent three Bloodspawn to wander the void as they leapt over the parapet, his Soulblade carving through flesh and bone.

The Bloodspawn kept coming, more and more flowing over the parapet, pushing Arden and Lyrin back across the roof. The silver armour of the Chosen rose clear above them all, gleaming ruby in the moonlight. Smoke drifted from the runes set into the creature's armour. Three more of the creatures had joined it, and now moved at its side.

"There are too many." A touch of fear painted Lyrin's voice. He grabbed a Bloodspawn by the back of the neck and slammed his helmeted head into the bridge of its nose, blood bursting, then drove his Soulblade into its belly before ripping the blade free and opening another beast's throat. He glanced over the rooftops to where it looked like Kallinvar and the others were still fighting.

"I'm sorry." Arden didn't have to explain further. Lyrin knew why he was sorry. He'd charged off when he'd seen Valerys whirling towards a different roof. He'd separated from the others to help Calen, and in doing so, he'd left himself isolated. And now Lyrin was isolated with him.

"Not really the time for apologies," Lyrin called back as he pulled his Soulblade from a Bloodspawn's chest. "Later." He opened an Urak navel to groin. "When it's quieter." He stomped down into a shin, bones splintering and blood flowing free. "Less blood."

The Bloodspawn continued to flow over the parapet until Lyrin and Arden were back to back and surrounded on all sides. More than once his Sentinel armour saved him from a blow that would have killed any other man.

The four Chosen strode with slow purpose, a sense of inevitability about them.

Another Bloodspawn walked at their side, shorter but still bigger than the others – a Shaman. A glowing red gemstone topped the staff in its right hand, and a mixture of metal plates and stiff leather armoured its body, grey robes draped over its shoulders. But there was something else, something Arden had never seen before: barbed horns coiled around the Shaman's head like some kind of bone-hewn crown.

A gust of wind swirled, and before Arden could react, a river of fire poured down over the rooftop, sweeping from right to left, illuminating the night in a blaze of light. The stone shook and parts of the roof collapsed, cracks creeping outwards, Bloodspawn shrieking and howling.

He looked up to see Valerys tear through the sky overhead, spreading his wings and turning back for a second pass. The wounds on the dragon's chest were blackened and raw, the scales scarred around them.

"I told you to go," Arden hissed. He blocked a swing from an Urak blade, then carved open the beast's chest.

Amidst the flames and chaos, the Shaman raised its staff and unleashed a maelstrom of black fire laced with lightning into the air, forcing Valerys to twist and turn before swooping behind the remnants of an old tower.

The four Chosen broke into a charge, the firelight glowing incandescent on their silver plate.

"Lyrin!" Arden gestured at the charging Chosen with his Soulblade before whipping it back across his body to deflect the swipe of a Bloodspawn sword, then back again to carve into its cheeks and the bridge of its nose, and once more to sever the creature's head. Half the creatures had been caught in the dragonfire, but the other half had only been shaken and were now regaining themselves around Arden and Lyrin.

"I see them!" Lyrin howled back.

With a pulse of the Taint, one of the Chosen leapt over a collapsed section of roof, its legs carrying it further than should have been possible.

The creature swung its níthral for Arden's head as two Bloodspawn lunged from the left and right. Arden swept his Soulblade around, parrying two strikes while planting his right foot in the third attacker's chest and sending it screaming through one of the newly-made holes in the roof.

The Chosen caught Arden in the helmet with a monstrous backhand that sent him reeling, then followed up with a downward swing of its Soulblade. The strike would have carved Arden open from the gut down had Lyrin not launched himself into its chest. The creature grabbed Lyrin by the back of the helmet and made to run him through with its crimson blade, but Lyrin released and reignited his own Soulblade in quick succession, the green light bursting through the Chosen's forearm and ripping it free as Lyrin fell away.

The Chosen unleashed a feral howl, pulses of the Taint flowing from it in waves.

A roar gave a second's warning before Valerys appeared in Arden's periphery and dropped atop the Chosen. The dragon lifted the creature into the air, one talon wrapped around its leg, the other around its arm. He held it there for a moment before slamming it down a few feet to the left, the roof shaking once more, Bloodspawn scrambling to make way.

Valerys's tail whipped back and knocked a clutch of Bloodspawn from the roof while arcs of blue lightning streaked from Calen's palms at the nape of the dragon's neck.

Valerys lifted his head, rolled his neck, then unleashed a torrent of white-hot fire down over the Bloodspawn Chosen. The creature's legs thrashed for a moment, then went still, the Bloodspawn around it shrieking as their flesh and leather burst into flames.

A surge of power rippled through Arden's Sigil, and the Rift opened behind him, but still he found himself staring into the raging dragonfire. And when the flames ceased, only ash remained.

"Go!" Calen roared from Valerys's back, pointing towards the Rift. The dragon tore a Bloodspawn to pieces with a swipe of its forelimb, then unleashed another pillar of fire across the rooftop. "Haem, go!"

Through the flames, the Shaman stood tall, its gaze moving from Haem to Calen and Valerys, and behind it more Chosen leapt from the other rooves, the runes in their silver armour glowing.

Lyrin grabbed Arden by the shoulders and threw him backwards towards the Rift as more Bloodspawn closed around them. One last look over Arden's shoulder saw Valerys lifting into the air, and then Arden fell through the Rift.

Ice washed over him and flowed through his veins, time standing still, the world becoming nothing but blackness.

He emerged from the Rift's embrace into the Heart Chamber, dropping to his knees, his heart thumping.

Watchers swarmed around him, the candlelight sending their shadows in all directions. They were shouting. Why were they shouting?

The Watchers and priests didn't stop at Arden, they rushed around him, their voices dull in his ears.

Slowly, he stood and turned. His mouth went dry, his throat tight.

Lyrin lay on the ground behind him, a black blade jutting from his chest, the handle of a staff sticking from his back, sheared where the Rift had sliced it.

"It's all right, brother." Arden pushed the others out of the way and pulled Lyrin into his arms. "I'll get you to Heraya's Well." Arden rushed across the Heart Chamber, shoving aside anyone in his way. "Move! Move!"

"Didn't see it coming," Lyin choked, his helmet receding into his armour. He puffed out his cheeks. "Fucking hurts."

"Stop talking." Arden kicked open the door and charged down the hall, his steps echoing, people stopping and staring.

"Never." Lyrin coughed.

"Lyrin, stop fucking talking." Arden twisted as he stepped between two priests. "Get out of the way!"

Lyrin grunted. "I'm just happy I got to see a dragon." He coughed, blood sprinkling his lips. "Fucking gods. Why does nobody tell you how much dying hurts?"

"You're not dying. Now shut your mouth."

"I'm pretty sure I'm dying."

"If you don't shut up, I'll kill you."

Lyrin coughed a bloody laugh, his lips curling into a weak smile. "Don't look so sad, big guy. At least you'll not have to put up with any more jokes." His breathing grew heavy and laboured, his face twisting in pain. "It was an honour."

"Just hold on." Arden charged through the temple's corridors and burst into the Tranquil Garden. He could see the glowing waters of Heraya's Well ahead. "We're here, we're…"

Arden looked down, and there, in that moment, Lyrin was gone, his eyes empty, his head lolling.

A wave of loss pulsed from Arden's Sigil and swept through him. Lyrin's Sentinel armour turned to liquid and flowed back over his body, returning to the Sigil in his chest.

Arden stood in the garden with his friend's body in his arms, the black blade protruding from a bloody tunic.

Watchers, and priests, and porters crowded around him, flooding into the garden.

Heraya's Well was so close… They had almost made it.

"Why didn't you shut your mouth?" Arden whispered.

"Brother Arden," Gildrick called, grasping Arden's arm, panic in his voice. "You must hurry, he doesn't…"

Arden shook his head, and Gildrick's voice faded. He clenched his jaw so tight he thought his teeth might snap, and then he pulled Lyrin's body closer.

CHAPTER FIFTY-THREE

STONE BY STONE

18th Day of the Blood Moon

Cuinviel, formerly Catagan – Winter, Year 3081 After Doom

"I am you, and you are me." Salara closed her eyes as she pressed her forehead to Vyrmír's scales, pulling their minds together and looking out over the world with his eyes. The landscape sharpened, and every scent grew more pungent and crisper. She could feel Vyrmír's mighty heart beating – their heart – their blood hot as molten steel.

"Aer vailír, myia'nära."

Be free, my light.

The dragon didn't need another word. He dropped past the treeline and swept over the ground with the speed of a shooting star. He banked right as he came to a herd of deer being stalked by a pride of black lions. The same lions from which the Lorians had taken their sigil.

Vyrmír twisted sharply and swooped onto the largest of the animals, with a mane thick as a dark cloud and a body that rippled with muscle. It was a fierce thing, a powerful thing. But to Vyrmír it may as well have been a sheep. He snatched the lion in his talons and ripped the creature in half, carving clean through the flesh and bone alike.

When the Lorian Kingdom had first been born, the old Lorians had taken the black lion as their sigil for its ferocity and beauty both. The black lions were twice the size of those found in the South, powerful predators with territories that ranged for hundreds of miles. Salara had spent many hours on dragonback admiring them in her youth, which was why she wished she did not hate the sight of them so. Another – if smaller – thing the Lorians had taken from her.

Vyrmír tossed one half of the lion carcass into the air, then snatched it in his jaws and choked it down, blood sprinkling the wind. He kept the upper half of the body in his left talon as they flew.

Salara saw the city through Vyrmír's eyes from miles away: Catagan, or Cuinviel as it had once been known and now was again. Much had already been rebuilt by the Craftsmages, though not in the image of what the Lorians had turned it into. The sight almost reminded her of before the Cuendyar.

Five winged shapes dotted the sky, with a sixth nestled not far from the white walls. The sight was a bittersweet one. To see dragons fly openly over a reclaimed Lunithíran city of old was a thing of beauty, a thing she had never thought she would see and a sight she was now sure she would never forget.

But there was one missing. Dravír and Irulaian had fallen on the eastern coast, slain by the traitors Lyina and Karakes, their remains dashed against the cliffs and lost to the waters of the Antigan Ocean.

The thought drove Salara's mind deeper into Vyrmír's as they shared in the grief. All of them had known the risks of flying to war. They had known them and been willing to take them ten times over. But that didn't diminish the sense of loss that cut at her heart. The loss that had set her mind in stone. Never again would she allow one of her Draleid to fly these skies alone. Risks needed to be taken, but flying alone left them far too vulnerable. The Dragonguard had not survived so long, through so much bloodshed, by dumb luck. They were fierce and merciless.

As Vyrmír approached the city, he pulled upwards, spreading his brilliant crimson wings. Shouts rose from below, the Craftsmages and workers pausing their toil to cheer, steel clattering and hands clapping together.

The dragon soared over the walls and swirled around the newly erected tower that rose twice as high as any within the city.

Nymaxes and Baerys took positions on either side of Vyrmír, Taran and Indivar at the napes of their necks. The three dragons rose sharply, diving and darting about each other, chirping and shrieking. Both were far smaller than Vyrmír, but they were fierce warriors and a bonded pair. Though their eggs – like all others – had not hatched.

The three soared over the city, and Salara admired the flapping banners of the golden stag that hung from every tower. This city was theirs now. The Reclamation was no longer a dream.

Nymaxes and Baerys pulled away as Vyrmír alighted on the flat top of the central tower at the rear of the keep. A hundred and fifty feet wide with no battlements, just open smooth stone at the top. It was just as the old hatchery towers had once been, purpose-built for dragons.

Before Vyrmír's talons even hit the stone, the Dracàrdare were moving across the tower's top with buckets of water and baskets of cloths and mops. They sat themselves down not ten feet from the dragon as he dropped the severed carcass of the black lion to the ground and began tearing it to pieces. Vyrmír had made a habit of taking his meals to that particular tower over the past few days, and the Dracârdare had not been long in learning.

They greeted Salara as she slid from the dragon's back and walked across the stone, and she inclined her head in return. She was met by Ithandel of Vandrien's Sunguard, who led her down the stairs and through the tower's corridors, stopping at a door that appeared to have been spark-carved from solid gold. An enormous depiction of a dragon egg dominated the doors, split through the middle, dragons swirling about it. There was no elf alive that she knew of who could have carved it by hand in that time.

Salara removed her helmet as the guard pushed open the twin doors, and a rush of air swept her hair across her face. The chamber on the other side was enormous, adorned with swooping arches of white stone and golden eggs atop polished pedestals. Hundreds of alcoves were set into the walls, lantern flames flickering all about.

"Beautiful, is it not?" Princess Ervian Lunithír, Vandrien's youngest sister, strolled through the newly built hatchery, a broad, beaming smile gracing her lips. She was everything that beauty should be: elegant, soft, graceful, awe-inspiring. Her hair was as golden as Vyrmír's scales, her eyes the same.

"It is." Salara stared straight at Ervian as she spoke, and the princess gave a wry smile.

Ervian cupped Salara's cheek with one hand and placed the other over Salara's heart. "I promised you the hatchery would be one of the first things built, did I not?"

"You did." Salara savoured Ervian's touch. She had not felt it often of late.

"Enough nests to hold four hundred eggs in just this one chamber. As large as any at Ilnaen." Ervian pulled away and gestured about at the alcoves in the walls, each of which lay empty.

"And yet, they may as well be used to hold rocks."

Ervian narrowed her eyes and glared.

"I'm sorry." Salara pressed her fingers into her forehead. "I'm sorry."

"Don't apologise, Salara." Ervian once more cupped Salara's cheek, setting her heart fluttering.

"You are always so full of hope. I don't mean to cut you down. It's just hard…" She lifted her gaze to survey the hatchery. "It's beautiful. All of it. Not even before the Cuendyar has a more beautiful hatchery existed." Salara could physically feel her heart darkening in her chest, feel the weight of it bearing down upon her. "And yet, it will never know a hatchling's cry. Never echo with the beats of tiny wings or the cracking of shells."

"Stop it." Ervian pressed a finger over Salara's lips, golden eyes staring into hers. "We focus on what we can control and leave what we can't to the gods."

"I trusted the gods before, Ervian…"

"*Salara*." Ervian's voice dropped into that tone it took when she had reached the end of her patience.

They'd had this argument many times over. Despite everything, Ervian still believed in the gods. Still trusted them. Still prayed to them. Salara could do no such thing. She still believed they existed. Their marks were everywhere; they were undeniable. But she could not bring herself to think they were anything other than malevolent or, at best, uncaring. No god that was good would have allowed The Fall to happen… would have taken the life from the dragons. She sighed. Some arguments weren't worth having.

"Focus on what we can control," Salara repeated.

"You lead our people on the field of battle, fill their hearts with courage, watch over them. And I will build our home anew, stronger than it ever was before."

A third voice sounded, echoing in the open chamber. "Salara."

Queen Vandrien stood on the far side of the hatchery, her hands resting on the low parapet of an open arch set into the wall. She had her back to the chamber, looking out over the city.

Ervian smiled once more and squeezed the sides of Salara's head before planting a tender kiss on her forehead. "Be patient, my Ayar Elwyn."

"Am I not always?"

"As much as the sun is cold." She ran her thumb across Salara's cheek. "Patience," she whispered as she ushered Salara towards Vandrien.

Salara stepped up beside the queen, drawing in a slow breath and exhaling as she watched the sunlight spill over the city. They stood there in silence for a time until Salara spoke. "I assume, judging by how firmly Ervian cautioned me towards patience, that we are to remain here for some time longer?"

"Wheels are in motion, Salara. This war will not be won in a day. Nor a week, nor a month, nor a year. The first phase of our plan succeeded. We have reclaimed Cuinviel, and Visenn and Falisín set fire to Aonar and its ports. The mines still stand, but the Lorian's gold will not be moving any time soon."

"All at great cost." Salara's thoughts drifted to Irulaian and Dravír, and to Olmaír Moridain.

"At immeasurable cost," Vandrien agreed. "Do not think I weigh those lives lightly, Salara."

"I know you do not… I know."

"Our plan to take the city was a success. But I am more than certain we will not find the same success twice. We are in the heart of Loria now. The only thing that keeps Fane, Eltoar, and the Uraks from burning this place to the ground are you and the dragons. Each step we take from here must be careful and planned. There is no room for error anymore. No forgiveness for mistakes. We must be patient."

"I've sat on my hands for the better part of four hundred years… I had thought now was finally the time for action. We have them on their heels. The Uraks press them from all sides, and the South is in full rebellion. Now is the time to pull the blade across their throat, Vandrien, not step back and let them fortify their position."

Vandrien looked to Salara, an unreadable expression on her face. She held the silence for a few moments. "Did I say you must sit on your hands?" A grin stretched her lips. "I said there is no room for error. That we must be patient. Not that we must do nothing."

"My queen?"

"A Lorian force marches east from Berona."

Salara straightened. "What would you have us do?"

The queen raised an eyebrow.

"Patience," Salara whispered.

"Patience." Vandrien looked back out the arched window at the city beyond. "We wish to build a nation that stands for millennia. And so what is a few days? I told you we would have vengeance and that you would be the tip of our spear. Have I spoken a word of a lie?"

"You have not."

"We will let the Lorians march, wait until they reveal their desires. And then we will act accordingly. The time will soon come where you will face Eltoar Daethana and Helios in the sky. The stars demand it. And when that day comes, Salara, you will emerge victorious, and dragon will fight dragon for the last time. Perhaps your presence will draw him from Elkenrim. And if it does, the city will be ripe for the taking, as will Berona. I have sent word to our forces in the east to be ready. And the seeds we have planted have both grown and flowered. King Hoffnar of the Lodhar dwarves proceeds as planned. Patience, Salara, is an attribute all predators share. Soon the black lion will die on its back, the jaws of a dragon around its throat."

"I am yours, Myia'nari. I should not have questioned."

"Always question, Salara, lest my pride swallow me whole. Luilin asked that you pay a visit to the Onarakina on your return. They struggle. I wish you to ease that struggle while your patience thins."

"As you command, my queen."

"I do not command it. But I ask."

Salara smiled as she inclined her head. She dropped so that her right knee hovered just off the ground. "Myia'nari."

CHAPTER FIFTY-FOUR

PURPOSE

18th Day of the Blood Moon

Cuinviel, formerly Catagan – Winter, Year 3081 After Doom

yrmír alighted in the centre of a massive yard at the city's western edge, Baerys and Nymaxes beside him. It was here that Warmarshal Luilin trained the Onarakina in warcraft and other matters.

At the sight of the three dragons, every soul in the yard ceased whatever they were doing and stared in awe. The Onarakina in particular watched slack-jawed and wide eyed, pressing their hands to their hearts in reverence.

As Salara slid from Vyrmír's back and landed with the aid of thin threads of Air, Luilin and Captain Undrír approached while the other elves tried and failed to persuade the Onarakina to return to their previous tasks. Instruments were scattered about the yard among sheafs of paper, inkwells, paint palettes, hammers, chisels, and all manner of things.

Luilin was attempting to teach them of the valúr.

"Draleid." Both Luilin and Undrír bowed – the latter more deeply than the former.

"How are they?" Salara asked, Taran and Indivar moving to stand on either side of her.

"A difficult question to answer, I'm afraid. It is like trying to rebuild a house while it is still burning. They drill well with swords and spears in their hands." Luilin folded his arms and released a long sigh. "The training focuses them, gives them an outlet, something tangible to hold on to. Though it will take years to bring them to any kind of true skill. For now, what they lack in technique they make up for in rage and savagery – as you saw."

"We are not teaching them to be warriors," Salara said, barely more than a whisper. She watched as an elf who looked little more than a child dragged a brush with bristles coated in blue paint over a canvas stretched across the stone and weighted with rocks. "We are teaching them to be Evalien. Something the humans took from them."

"Of that I am aware, Draleid."

Salara and Luilin were not friends. Nor were they enemies. Salara had not been the easiest to get along with in the centuries within Lynalion. The Warmarshal had been born after the Cuendyar and had seen no more than two hundred summers. In that time Salara had been cold and distant, caring little for the nurturing of new friendships. "And what part do I play in this, Warmarshal? The queen says you asked for me."

"I did. Though weaponscraft focuses them, their learnings do the opposite. What does an elf who has spent their life in the darkness of a mine care for the history of a people they never knew? They push against the concept of a valúr, impatient to move forwards. After the taking of this city, they have a taste for battle, a taste for the blood of their former captors. Everything else is an obstacle. I believe, as I expressed at the time, we blooded them too early. They were not ready."

"Perhaps." Salara clasped her hands behind her back and watched a group of the Onarakina who still stared at Vyrmír, Baerys, and Nymaxes, awestruck. "Or perhaps the path they have been set upon without their own choosing is a complex and painful one, and our task is to guide them along it no matter the difficulty. If I had been born into slavery and then denied my right to fight against those who put me in it, I don't think I would have taken too kindly to that."

"We are already bending our ways by teaching them the art of war alongside the valúr instead of after." A flare of anger simmered in Luilin's voice. "They *must* come to heel."

"To heel, Warmarshal?" Salara asked disappointedly.

Luilin opened his mouth, nothing but a short grunt escaping his lips as he pondered whether Salara's words were a dent in his honour. Whether they saw eye-to-eye or not, she was a Draleid and her words carried weight, and she knew that. "Yes," he stammered. "To heel, Draleid. Like we all once did."

"Would you train a dragon the same way you'd train a wolf?"

"I'd rather not train either, if I'm being honest."

Salara frowned. "My point, Warmarshal, is that our ways apply to those who have been raised *our* way. These elves have been slaves since the day they took their first breaths. The Lorians beat and bent them into submission like raw iron. Doing so again will not yield the results you wish. You must give them a reason, give them a purpose. The hammer will not work here. You must instead be the guiding hand."

The Warmarshal turned to the side and opened his body to Salara, gesturing towards the Onarakina. "We do not always agree, Draleid. But I am always willing to be wrong if I can learn how to be right. Either way, the Onarakina look to you like they might look to a herald of the gods. They heed your words where they do not heed mine. That is why I asked for you. Pride exists to be swallowed."

Salara inclined her head graciously. She decided in that moment that a friendship with Luilin might be worth nurturing. She looked out over the yard. Most of the Onarakina still stood, staring at her and the others, backs rigid. But some had returned to their various valúrs, frustration evident in the language of their bodies. That same young elf had covered her painting in furious red strokes and snapped her brush in two, which was a slightly easier form of frustration to identify.

Salara looked back at Vyrmír and pressed their minds together. The dragon responded by unleashing a visceral roar that drowned all other sounds and echoed off the high walls that surrounded the yard.

Every elf in the yard ceased what they were doing and looked to the great golden dragon, his crimson frills shaking as he roared.

When silence finally settled, Salara stepped forwards into the crowd of elves and spoke as loud and as clear as she could, her voice carrying through the yard. "You are, each and every one of you, at a juncture in this life. A point where you must make a choice. Face the darkness and the injustice that was done to you, bind it to your will and overcome it… or let it swallow you whole. Let the humans win."

An elf, almost a head taller than Salara but reed-thin, stepped forwards and bowed, his fingers white as snow as he clenched his hand into a fist at his chest. "Draleid…" He licked his lips, his voice trembling a little. "Respectfully… I… You don't know what they did to us… It is not as easy… You don't know." He shook his head fervently, and others around him agreed, whispers of 'no' and 'they don't know' spreading through the crowd.

The elf looked over both shoulders, flustered still, but heartened by the number of voices that joined his. "We are grateful for everything you have done for us. So grateful that I could not find the words to thank you if I lived a hundred lifetimes. My children…" He gestured towards four smaller elves behind him, none looking as though they'd seen more than fifteen summers. "They will not know the darkness like I did. They will live a full life. A *free* life. And that is because of you."

"That is because of Queen Vandrien and because of all the evalien of Numillíon, not just myself and my kin. We are *one* people. All of us."

The elf bowed his head, smiling softly, his confidence growing. "And we will forever be in your debt. But how can you ask us to care about these pointless tasks when those who are responsible for our torment await us? Teach me how to use a spear like you do. Teach me to move like a warrior, teach me to defend my people so that we may never be placed in chains again. Do not ask me to care about these songmakers."

The elf gestured to a harp and a flute that lay on the ground, and it settled in Salara's mind that the elf had never seen an instrument before.

"My father died in those mines. He was born there, and he died there. He saw thousands upon thousands of candles. He was broken from the moment I met him. I will not spend another moment of my life unable to protect my family as he was."

A brief silence passed where all eyes seemed to be focused on Salara and the tall elf before her.

Salara looked into his eyes. "What was done to you can never be undone. But you will not gain vengeance at the tip of a sword, nor your freedom. Surely, that is part of it. We *will* burn the Lorian Empire to the ground. But you will never truly be free until you allow yourself to be. Even now, you allow your every thought to be consumed by them. Every dream, every nightmare, every waking moment belongs to them. Your mind and your heart are theirs. They hold you in chains still."

A murmur spread through the crowd, a few angered shouts.

"Whether you want to kill them or serve them, you are still allowing them to rule your thoughts. Is not your every decision predicated on how you might claim vengeance? I want you to fight. It would bring me great honour to stand by your side in the battles to come. But more than that, I want you to live. I want you to spit in the faces of those who would have kept you in chains until Heraya embraced you. And you do that by becoming what they tried to keep from you. You do that by becoming Evalien. Our ancient elders devised the valúr as a way to teach our young the beauty and value of this life, before we teach them how to wield a weapon. To teach creation before destruction so that we know the cost of the latter. A common flaw is to think a valúr is nothing more than an obstacle, nothing more than a task to be completed. But the true value of a valúr is not in the learning, but in the finding of passion. In the finding of something that sets your heart alight so that you may understand the joy this life can bring."

Salara turned as she spoke, staring out at the hundreds of Onarakina, who had all drawn closer. The silence was so complete she could have heard a pin drop.

"I remember where I was the moment I felt my heart ignite. I was but a child, many years ago, struggling – as you all struggle – to find my valúr. I heard an elf with the voice of a god sing 'The Lament of Gods and Ashes'. Her name was Líra Alunea."

As Salara shifted in place, she spotted Ervian, Cara, and Vandrien all watching from a low balcony that overlooked the yard. The druid, Boud, stood at their side. "It is a song written during the Age of War, and it found new meaning after the Cuendyar. It speaks of loss, and death, and darkness. But also of hope, and heart, and finding strength within ourselves and in those around us."

Salara closed her eyes and thought back to that night in the city of Mynivír, in the great auditorium where the legendary Craftsmage Líra Alunea had sung the song that had changed Salara's life. Her mother had taken her while her father had been serving as an emissary to Caelduin. It had been a long, trying day, and her mother had bribed Salara with promises of sweet cakes and pastries. Simpler times.

"Hearing that song, hearing Líra sing it as though she were bleeding her heart into every word… it changed me. And as I look back on my life, I realise it played a large part in forging me into the elf I am today. And that is why I ask that you pursue your valúr with the same vigour and relentless determination that you do weaponscraft. Because it is our culture, our history, our language – and our pride in all three – that make us Evalien. Whether your valúr is song, or storytelling, or crafting, or sculpture, or anything in the world, wear it with the same pride you would a gilded suit of armour." Salara slammed her fist against her breastplate. "Because you *are* Evalien. You are proud. You are strong. And no matter what they try to take from you, you are no longer alone. Your valúr is yours. Your passion is yours. And you are home. I denír viël ar altinua!" she roared, a burning passion rising within her, the flames ignited by Vyrmír, who lent his voice to hers, Baerys and Nymaxes joining. "Du é evalien!"

Feet stamped, and beside her Undrír and Taran began to clap their hands to their chests.

"In this life and always. You are elves!"

A low hum, rising and falling to the melody of 'The Lament of Gods and Ashes', touched her ears, and she glanced over to see Taran humming the tune.

"When the Lorians face you on the field of battle, let them face Evalien who would die for what they are. Let them know that, after all this time, they still could not strip your heart from you, that you found your people!"

The long, sweet strokes of a violin sounded, followed by the delicate plucking of a harp. Two of the elves charged with instructing the Onarakina had taken up the instruments and accompanied Taran's humming.

Salara looked back at the elf who had spoken. "A valúr is yours. It is part of who you are and where you are from. It is your blood, and your bones, and your soul."

She turned to where Warmarshal Luilin stood with Captain Undrír. She clasped Luilin's shoulder and met his gaze. "These elves were stripped of everything that made them elves. They were collared and chained and forced to work until their bodies gave way." She turned back to the crowd of Onarakina, who were now clapping their hands to their chests along with the beat of an elf who had taken up a drum. The smile that stretched Salara's lips was a precious sliver of joy in a dark world. "They have never heard the sound of instruments. Never seen a summer's twilight or a winter's dawn. They do not need to be brought to heel. What they need is someone to give them back their pride. To give them purpose... Give them that, Warmarshal, and you will have them forever."

Salara walked back through the crowd to Vyrmír. The dragon bowed his head to her, gold and crimson scales gleaming, a soft purr in his throat. Pride and honour and defiance flooded from his mind to hers. The Onarakina represented everything they were fighting for. And Salara and Vyrmír would protect them with their lives.

As she climbed onto the dragon's back, Taran's voice rose above the hum, singing the words of 'The Lament of Gods and Ashes' clear and true. She patted Vyrmír's scales and urged him upwards, adding her voice as the dragon ascended.

> *"In ashes of a burning world, I kneel before you now*
> *My voice is torn, my body broke, the flames are growing higher.*
> *My tears could never quench the fire, my cries are never heard.*
> *Do you listen anymore? Have you ever done?"*

Having left Vyrmír to rest in the eyrie he had claimed for himself in the cave of a nearby hill, Salara sat alone at a long table in one of the many halls of Cuinviel's newly-erected keep. Moments alone were rare and precious. And the silence was even more so.

Before her was a cup, a bottle of deep-red wine, and a plate piled high with roast pheasant, slices of duck breast, half the flesh from a leg of lamb, carrots, tubers, glazed onions, and a plethora of other multi-coloured vegetables that made the plate look like a painting. All of that, along with a basket of bread fit for three people and a pitcher of lamb gravy that would act as a pond for every morsel of food to pass her lips. Food in Lynalion had never been scarce, but neither had it been as opulent or as varied.

In a war such as the one being waged, Salara never knew which day might be her last, and so she felt not a drop of guilt as she devoured the contents of the laden plate.

She was washing down a mouthful when footsteps sounded through the doorway that led to the hall. She motioned to wave away the porter before realising it was not a porter that approached.

Boud held an empty cup in one hand and an enamelled plate as full as Salara's in the other. Six guards followed the druid into the hall, two holding position at the doors, the other four framing her as she walked.

"Mind if I sit?" The woman had already set her plate down before asking the question, but Salara nodded. She was not destined for silence or a moment alone, it seemed.

Boud gestured to the bottle of wine, and Salara grunted in response.

"My thanks." She filled her cup to the point of spilling, then set the bottle back in its place.

The sounds of eating and drinking echoed in the empty hall, not a single other soul bar the guards in a place fit for hundreds. It would have been such a glorious silence.

"That was a rousing speech you gave in the yard." Boud stripped the meat from a small chicken leg, the skin crackling as she tore with her teeth. She washed it down with a mouthful of wine. "I watched from your queen's side on the balcony. Very impressive."

"Hmm." Salara glanced up at the woman while sipping at her own cup.

"Truly. I was stirred." Boud gave the falsest of smiles. Vandrien didn't allow the druid to roam the city at will but gave her certain freedoms within the keep. She wanted to keep Boud close. Though, in all the time since they'd captured her, Boud had never tried to escape. And for some reason, that didn't sit well with Salara.

"I did have one problem, though. If you're taking critique."

Salara raised an eyebrow at that as she crunched on a particularly robust tuber.

"Well," Boud continued when Salara didn't respond, "it was a touch hypocritical, don't you think?"

Salara swallowed, setting her hands down against the wooden table. "Careful, druid."

That same false smile. Boud dropped her head and continued eating, then drained the remnants of her wine.

"Go on then." Salara couldn't help herself. Boud had been with them quite a while, ever since they'd found her wandering the depths of Lynalion. She had always been far too arrogant for a prisoner and had done little to shield her wit. And when she chose to speak, there was always a point to it. Salara had learned to listen.

Boud reached across the table, grabbed the bottle, and poured herself more wine. She didn't ask this time. "Well," she said with an exaggerated sigh, "you spoke of chains and collars and of what the Lorians took from these former slaves – the Onarakina you call them, no?" She didn't wait for an answer. "You revile the Lorians for what they did to those elves, and rightly so, slavery, binding living souls in iron, is not a pleasant thing. And yet… I am a little perplexed by your revulsion."

Boud fingered the rune-marked collar around her neck. "Apparently, it's only a dark and horrible deed when someone else does it. Seeing as my collar doesn't affect you so."

"Yours is necessary."

This time the smile was genuine, breaking into a stifled laugh. "You really believe that, don't you? The arrogance."

"Watch your tongue. I won't warn you again."

"Or what, you'll take it from me? What then? Do you think I will do what you ask after you've taken my tongue?"

"There's plenty left to take after that."

"Have you ever stopped and listened to the words that leave your lips, Salara Ithan? You talk to those elves as though what was done to them is the darkest of all horrors. You tell them how they will have their vengeance, tell them how things will be made right. All the while, you keep a collar around my neck and threaten to cut out my tongue and more pieces of me besides."

"You do not look like a slave," Salara said, tilting her head towards the plate of food before Boud and the full cup of wine in her hand. "And you do not act like a slave."

"Is that what you tell yourself?" Boud drank deeply from her cup. She shook her head and continued eating without speaking another word.

Salara stared at her, clenching one hand into a fist beneath the table, unable to look away as the woman devoured her food.

Once the plate was emptied, Boud picked it up in two hands and licked it clean, fully aware that Salara was staring at her. When she was done, she placed the plate down carefully and let out a long, satisfied sigh, leaning back on the bench, her two hands bracing against the wood. After a moment, she rose from her seat, then leaned across the table and stared into Salara's eyes. "I'm not sure whether it's arrogance or wilful ignorance, but it is for a certainty interesting that you do not see how you are no different from the empire you wish to destroy. An endless cycle."

Salara jolted upright, pushing the bench back, Vyrmír's rage stirring within her. She did not temper it. She leaned forwards so her face was only inches from Boud's. "I would kill you right here and leave your blood to drain into the stone."

"And what would your queen say about that? About you killing her prized little pet?"

"You think yourself more than you are. You are a boon, not a necessity. We will win this war with or without you. You would do well to remember that."

The false smile crept onto Boud's lips once more. "I guess we will see."

CHAPTER FIFTY-FIVE

CHOICES

18th Day of the Blood Moon

Berona – Winter, Year 3081 After Doom

"This depicts the first ever taming of black lions by Thrandon Firehand, before Loria was even a kingdom – four hundred and nine After Doom, I believe." Fane stood with his hands clasped behind his back, fingers interlocked. The wall before him was adorned with a tapestry woven in fine threads of gold, crimson, and black, accented by thin embellishments of pure white.

Eltoar was silent at Fane's left shoulder. The elf had taken the loss of Catagan as a personal failure. Near enough a hundred thousand had died. Almost every living soul within the city. Some reports said the city's garrison had surrendered and the elves had slaughtered them anyway, while others insisted the garrison had fought till the end, refusing to yield the city to the foreign invaders. Fane found it unlikely that the elves had refused the garrison's surrender, but it was not a rumour he was going to stop.

"As it moves on," Fane said, pointing from the left side of the tapestry and then across its length, "it traces the Lorian history from the first king, Orden Ubbein, all the way to now. Every thread of it was woven by hand. One of the largest of its kind created without the Spark. A true testament to human craftsmanship and dedication. I wouldn't have the patience for it."

"Is there a point to this?"

Fane raised an eyebrow and examined his old friend. The frustration was precisely what he had hoped for. "Understanding our past, understanding where we came from, is important, do you not think?"

"This is not where I came from." Eltoar matched Fane in clasping his hands behind his back.

"But it is where you are now."

"I will take Helios to wing and recall Lyina," Eltoar said, ignoring Fane. "The elven dragons haven't left Catagan since the city was taken. I will set sentries on watch with signal fires in a perimeter around Catagan. They will not catch us off guard again. Voranur can go to muster more spears, men and women across the lakelands who have been displaced from their homes. Once they see him waving the banner, they will flock. Salara and her Draleid will be reluctant to face all three of us in the open sky. If we force it, storm the city with everything we have, we can end this—"

"We are losing this war, Eltoar." Fane's words echoed in the silent chamber. "We are losing it, and if something drastic does not change, everything we have built, everything we have sacrificed, will have been for nothing. All that was lost at Ilnaen and in the years that followed."

The mere mention of Ilnaen had a tendency to leave Eltoar speechless. That was a wound Fane chose to prod with the utmost caution. It was a useful trigger when called upon, but a delicate one. A single candle could light a room but, if left unattended, could burn that same room to the ground. "We could never have planned for this, old friend. Even if we take the city. Even if we rip every last one of their dragons from the sky, put their soldiers to the sword, and burn Queen Vandrien alive, our losses would be incalculable. And all three of our Draleid would not leave the field of battle. We would succeed only in wiping the elves from the conflict, and ourselves in turn. With the burning of Aonar added to our injuries, we are now short on gold as well as iron and food. The Uraks would obliterate what was left of us while the rebels feast on the carcass. We are a wounded animal, and the blood is drawing everything that thinks it has a chance."

Eltoar turned to face Fane. "And I'm sure what comes next is the plan you have devised, as you always do."

Fane snorted through his nostrils, giving a half-smile. "I have always prided myself on my understanding of the world and the people within it. On my ability to navigate whatever the traitor gods could throw against me. But I fear, in this, my friend, I have failed. I cannot see a path forward from this place where all Epheria is not on fire. Everything we have done was to create a stronger, better world. A world we were promised by The Order… But we stand at a juncture now. Our Draleid are whittled to just three, our armies wounded, our cities burning, our coffers and stores at the end of their lives. We face too many foes on too many sides. Our defeat at Catagan was unequivocal, and now the elves are in the heart of our lands with a fervour in their blood. The rebels attacked the High Tower itself – the beating heart of the Circle. The Uraks feed off the Blood Moon as we do. And so we lose ground with each day. With the Heart of Blood, I could bring Efialtír through the veil between worlds, end this war… perhaps even bring life back to the dormant eggs. But without it, I fear all may be lost."

"Bring life back to the eggs…" Eltoar's stare grew hard as steel. "You keep saying this, but is it possible? Truly? Or are you simply dangling hope before my eyes?"

Fane nodded slowly. "It is possible, I swear it by the blood in my veins. If there is any hope of it, we must find the Heart, and we must do it before the Blood Moon sets." He shook his head. "If we don't, the world will have seen the last of the dragons and the last of the Lorian Empire."

Eltoar's expression remained unshifting, but Fane could see the loss in his eyes. He could see it in the way Eltoar's shoulders slumped just a fraction, in the way that the most powerful individual Fane had ever known refused to make eye contact.

Guilt, shame, regret. Fane could feel all three wafting from the Draleid. "It is I who am to blame, old friend. I and I alone." Fane shook his head and turned to pick up the goblet of Etrusian wine he'd left on a nearby table. He folded his arms and sipped at the beautiful liquid, savouring the taste. "I should have guarded the Heart more carefully. Shouldn't have been so careless, so trusting."

Fane studied Eltoar's face as he spoke the words. He was almost precisely where Fane needed him to be. "We sacrificed so much, and now, due to my hubris and my complacency, we risk it all. How different everything would be if I'd not allowed it to be taken from beneath my nose. Perhaps our skies would be full and our lands peaceful."

Eltoar brought his hands around to his front and reclasped them, then let out a long, weighty sigh. "We succeed together, and we fail together, my friend. I am sorry for my dour mood." He shook his head. "Salara was my apprentice. I should have seen her ploy coming. I, too, have grown complacent, and we suffered for it. My pride does not take that wound well. And if I am honest, the thought of facing her in battle does not sit well with me either."

"No matter what she has done in the past four centuries, Salara is no match for you and Helios."

"It is not my death I fear. It is hers. Enough of my kind have died at my hand. It does not sit weightless upon me."

Something moved within Fane. Before The Fall, he had grown to consider Eltoar a true friend. And in the years that followed, that had only strengthened as they'd fought side by side. But when the dust had settled, when the war was all but won, when dragon bones littered the lands and rivers ran red with blood, Eltoar had withdrawn into himself. They had spoken often, and their friendship had never waned, but Eltoar was not the same. He had never spoken of his regrets, never said a word. He was a warrior, and he pushed forwards. This… this admission was something Fane could use. "You did what you needed to do. Nothing more. Nothing less."

Eltoar gave a short sigh through his nostrils. "All great things require sacrifice?"

"Indeed."

"But where is the line we draw?" Eltoar lifted his head and stared into Fane's eyes. "Where is the point in which we realise we have sacrificed too much and gained too little?"

"What brings this on?" Fane gestured to a second goblet, offering Eltoar wine. It wouldn't take much more.

The Draleid stared at the goblet for a few seconds before allowing Fane to pour. "Think not of it," he said as he took the goblet and drained half in a single mouthful. "My mind wanders of late. Losing Pellenor, seeing Salara, the word of an egg hatching, I… My apologies. I shouldn't trouble you with this." He shook his head again and drained the goblet, making to leave. "These are my wounds to bear. My mistakes. My burdens."

Fane placed his goblet on the table and grabbed Eltoar by the arm. "Brothers in battle are brothers in life, Eltoar. Sit. I will have more wine brought. We will talk into the night if we have to. I would not see your heart bear the weight of this all."

"No. I have no desires to drown my sorrows. There is too much to be done to wallow." Eltoar held Fane's gaze. Something shifted in the Draleid's eyes, a change, a thought. "We *will* win this war. I will not allow everything we have done to be for nothing. I *cannot* allow it. Do you understand me? I cannot."

"I have heralds and Chosen and hundreds of mages scouring the continent in search of the Heart." Fane held on to Eltoar's arm as he spoke. "If we can find it before the Blood Moon sets, we may yet save the lives of millions and change the face of Epheria forever."

Eltoar turned to leave.

"Where are you going?" Fane asked, the answer already confirmed in his mind. He knew by the look in Eltoar's eyes that he had found his thief.

"To win this war."

Eltoar walked through Berona's northern gates and out into the motley collection of hastily constructed shelters that many of the refugees had taken to building after the city had reached its limit. In the dark of night, the trodden paths of mud and dirt were empty save for a few souls who huddled around fires. The sight of it cut into Eltoar. This was everything he'd been trying to stop. The wars, the death, the suffering. It was always the common people who paid the heaviest price. Always.

By Alvira's time, The Order had waged wars for no reason other than building favour and filling their coffers. And while the gold and silver piled high, the council members and those too ignorant or blind to see the truth revelled in their power. But Eltoar saw the truth. He saw the fields of charred corpses. He watched mothers and fathers weep as they held the bodies of their children. He heard the cries of the mutilated and the maimed. Eltoar had walked through the aftermath of every battle, forced himself to look and to listen, forced himself to understand the cost. Alvira had too, and she had wept and drowned her misery in wine. And though she would protest, voice her dissent, she would always, inevitably, obey. She was a truly good soul, but she was blind, and her heart was weak.

Images of her headless body circled in Eltoar's mind. Killing Alvira was the darkest of all his memories. Fane had insisted upon it. Alvira needed to die for The

Order to fall. And Eltoar needed to be able to sacrifice the things he loved to forge a better world for the people he wished to protect. And he did sacrifice, because when everything was said and done, his purpose as a Draleid was nothing more than to keep the people of Epheria safe. At his core, that was all he was meant to do.

And now, there he was, four hundred years later, the same crimson moon in the sky, everything he'd ever loved dead, and those same people were still the casualties of someone else's war. He could not allow all that sacrifice to be for nothing. He could not allow Alvira's death to be for nothing.

The black mountain that was Helios shifted as Eltoar reached the outskirts of the dwellings, his back rising higher than the city walls, his wings blocking out all light. The crimson in the dragon's wings glistened in the pale pink light of the Blood Moon, seeming to almost shimmer. Shocked voices rose in the night as the dragon shifted, the ground trembling beneath his weight, a low rumble resonating in his throat.

Rain began to sprinkle from the grey clouds as though roused by the great dragon, moonlight shimmering in the droplets.

Torches shifted on the walls, soldiers moving about to get a better look as Helios lowered his head to greet Eltoar. Helios let out a puff, and a gust of warm air washed over Eltoar's entire body.

Eltoar didn't speak. He simply pressed his forehead against the scales of the dragon's lower jaw and ran his hand along a horn longer than his leg. They did not need words. He closed his eyes and pulled their minds together. Everything blended into one. The world did not exist beyond the pair of them.

Memories flashed through their shared mind. Hundreds of dragons and Draleid dying. Killed. Murdered. Slaughtered. All at their hands. The images were blood and fire. Together they had burned cities to the ground and laid waste to armies of thousands.

Pain. Loss. Anguish. Misery.

All done for a reason, for a purpose. To create a better world. A world where Draleid and dragons were not used like pieces on a board by kings and queens who cared little for anything or anyone but themselves. People who sat on thrones or in ornate chairs of marble and gold they refused to call thrones.

Eltoar and Helios had done things they both knew were terrible, monstrous even. Because they had been willing to sacrifice their own honour to protect the people of Epheria. If history called them monsters, so be it. But they had sworn to be guardians of those not strong enough to stand for themselves, they had given their solemn vow… just as the rest of The Order had.

Images of the soldiers burning at the Battle of the Three Sisters flowed from Helios to Eltoar, and he answered with thoughts of Catagan and of all the eastern cities, burned to ash.

If they did not do what needed to be done, then every sacrifice they had made would be in vain. The people they had tried to protect would be ground to dust.

"It's time, old friend."

A high-pitched sound pulsed from the dragon's throat, followed by a low rumble. A blurred image of a white dragon held in Helios's mind.

"We will protect them. I promise you."

More images followed of Vyrmír and Salara and the other dragons and Draleid loyal to the elves of Lynalion.

There were two wars raging. The war for Epheria. And the war for the survival of dragons and Draleid as a species.

"We will cross that bridge when we come to it. For now, we must make haste. Every hour counts."

Once Eltoar had mounted Helios, the dragon took a few steps from the city, cracked his mighty wings, and took flight.

Leaves and twigs swirled in the air, thin trees bending and bowing in the dragon's wake.

They flew for hours, north, over the Kolmir Mountains. They passed the rubble of what had once been Fort Harken, torn down by the Urak hordes, its inhabitants harvested for their Essence. Reaching the river Talinik, they headed northeast.

Even through Helios's eyes, the city of Catagan was nothing but a speck in the distance. Reports had already come in that the elves were reconstructing the city. Some had claimed that as many as fifty dragons soared through the skies over the city. Eltoar doubted that number. If the elves had that kind of advantage, they would have pressed it, Blood Moon or no.

Even so, he dared not fly closer, instead pulling Helios higher through the clouds, emerging on the other side to an endless canopy of grey and white tinged pink with the moon's light.

The air was thinner that high, breaths shorter. But the sight itself was worth it a thousand times over. It was a different world altogether. A world without war, without death and loss.

It was peace. Peace and solitude, those were two things Eltoar and Helios had little of in their lives.

After a time, and with much regret, they dipped back below the clouds, the darkness of night lifting. By the time the discordant peaks of the Sea of Stone came into view, the warm light of the rising sun was spilling over the horizon. The mountainscape was the largest in all Epheria by a great margin, stretching north as far as even Helios could see, hundreds upon hundreds of miles in all directions.

When he was nothing but a young apprentice, his master had taught him that the Sea of Stone was created during the great wars before even the Blodvar. Master Ochra had said that the mountains were formed in the wake of a dying god, the world reclaiming the god's bones and blood for its own.

There were, of course, a thousand theories as to how the Sea of Stone came to be, but Eltoar had always preferred his master's. The thought that the mountains had come from the body of a dead god was a comforting one. It meant that gods could die.

They dropped lower as the mountains swallowed the ground beneath them. The peaks were so high and wide that even Helios could become lost in the spaces between.

Helios spread his wings as wide as he could, over five hundred feet from tip to tip, and even still could not span the valley between the rock faces.

The dragon alighted in an arid basin, where two thin streams trickled from within the mountain.

Eltoar slid from Helios's back before the dragon's talons had touched the ground, allowing himself to drift in freefall before whipping threads of Air about himself and landing as gently as a feather.

Helios lowered his head and pressed his snout into Eltoar. The dragon's lower jaw alone was larger than Eltoar was tall.

"We must be completely aligned," Eltoar said as he pressed his head into Helios's scales. He clenched his hands into fists and rested them on either side of his head. He could sense Helios's uncertainty.

"For four hundred years, we have held it and we have watched. What would you have us do?" he whispered.

Helios let out a low whine, the vibration thrumming through Eltoar. The sound spoke of regret, of sorrow, but also of acceptance.

"If you think it is the wrong choice, I will stand by you with all my heart."

The dragon shook his head, a rumble in his chest.

Eltoar drew a slow breath in and held it in his lungs, looking up into his soulkin's ruby eyes. "Myia nithír til diar. We can only do what we think is right. I will speak to the others first."

Leaving Helios in the basin, Eltoar walked across the dried and cracked ground to where a single small shrub with red flowers was nestled against the rock face of the rising cliff. He had planted that same shrub there a long time ago.

He reached into the satchel around his shoulder and produced a small green stone veined with black and white. Opening himself to the Spark, Eltoar funnelled threads of Spirit and Fire into the keystone. The white veins illuminated with a bright light, seeming to shift and flow like small streams within the stone.

In the span of a heartbeat, a passageway appeared in the rock, twice as wide as Eltoar was tall. The passageway stretched off into the mountain, smooth as glass on all sides. Fane knew of the eyrie Eltoar had carved into a peak in the Sea of Stone fifty or so miles west, where Eltoar had moved hundreds of eggs over the centuries, but he didn't know of this place. This place had been created for a single, specific purpose.

I will not be long.

Helios rumbled in the back of Eltoar's mind.

CHAPTER FIFTY-SIX

MONSTERS, MEN, AND BROKEN THINGS

19th Day of the Blood Moon

Northeast of Berona – Winter, Year 3081 After Doom

With Trusil's hooves squelching in the mud, Rist leaned back, closed his eyes, and let the cool rain splatter against his face, his hands resting on the soaked hair of the horse's neck.

The First and Fourth armies had left Berona four days ago, marching hard from sunrise to sunset, and in that time the rain had been unrelenting. And still, Taya Tambrel had forced a pace of almost twenty-five miles each day. Even mounted, Rist was exhausted, his muscles aching and his thighs chafing from the rain and constant friction. He didn't dare try to imagine the state the infantry were in.

After the attack on Berona and the High Tower, both armies had been replenished to their full complements of five thousand four hundred – along with Taya Tambrel's Blackwatch. The armies were also bolstered by some ten thousand auxiliaries – volunteers drawn from those within the city and the refugees who had flooded into Berona and the burgeoning town that had formed outside Berona's walls. Many had lost friends or family in the attack, and a marching army also meant food. When the call for volunteers had gone out, the response had been overwhelming. The people wanted vengeance; they wanted blood. The limit had not been the number of souls willing to join and fight, but the capacity to feed and armour them. And now, together, they marched for the rebel stronghold in the Firnin Mountains. From what Magnus had said, the Seventh and Eighteenth armies were marching from Elkenrim, along with ten thousand more from Merchant's Reach. Over forty thousand souls.

According to Garramon, the empire had known of the stronghold for quite some time but had held off on launching a strike due to the emergence of the Uraks and the elves from Lynalion. They were an irritation that could be ignored.

The attack had changed that.

Rist opened his eyes to the strange hue of pink from the light sparkling in the heavy rain, falling diamonds forged from blood.

Looking up at the crimson moon dragged his thoughts to the gemstone around his neck and the Essence that filled it. The Essence collected from a man Rist had killed with his bare hands. The Essence that called to him even at that very moment.

He barely remembered doing it. Just anger, rage, and then *snap*. It had almost seemed as though he were floating above himself, watching his body break the man's neck. But he did remember the whispers in the back of his mind, his own voice, his own thoughts, urging him to take the man's life. To break his neck for even daring to harm Neera. And he had done just that. He had let his rage control him.

"Your arse sore?"

Rist lurched forwards as Magnus clapped him across the back, almost falling from his own saddle in the process.

The big man rode on a beautiful buckskin gelding that rivalled the Varsundi Blackthorns for size – and almost looked like one with the amount of mud darkening its coat. "Whoa now, ya big bastard. Steady as she goes. I don't like you, and you don't like me. We have an understanding. But if you throw me off, you better believe it's horse for supper."

The horse snorted and shook its head but carried on walking.

Magnus held up the stump of his left arm, gripping the reins once more with his right, the rain splattering against his cloak. "Still forget it's gone. Anyway, how's your arse?"

Rist raised his eyebrows, glancing at Garramon and Neera, who rode to his right.

"Your arse, lad. It's on the other side of your prick."

"Magnus," Garramon called. "May I suggest you elaborate?"

"Ah, you filthy dogs. I meant from the saddle. Mine's raw as a slab of beef. Fucking hate riding horses."

"Then why are you riding one?" Neera asked.

"Because I'm lazy," he said in a way that implied the question need not have been asked, almost sending himself from the saddle a second time as he scratched at his thick black beard. "And I don't fancy trudging through this shit heap like those poor bastards."

Magnus gestured to the ranks of the soldiers who marched around them. The Exarch had ensured there were enough mounts for all the mages. Taya Tambrel, her Blackwatch, and the light cavalry were also mounted, but the some twenty thousand infantry and auxiliaries trekked on foot through the unceasing downpour, hauling stuck wagons free of the mud, sliding and slopping, never finding a minute's respite.

As Rist looked out over the marching infantry though, his gaze moved to something entirely different.

The emperor did not accompany them for the assault on the stronghold, which surprised Rist, though he didn't presume to understand the mind of a man like Fane Mortem. According to Garramon, the emperor had remained in Berona in case of attack by the elves or Uraks. Although the emperor was not there himself, he had sent ten of the Chosen in his place, along with Primarch Andelar Touran and his own personal retinue of Exarch Battlemages.

The Primarch rode at the head of the army in a sheltered wagon, while the Chosen were scattered amongst the army, each marching in isolation, never seeming to say a word or show a shred of interest in anything at all. Though, since the first day the army had set off, there seemed to be one of the Chosen within Rist's eyeline at all times.

At that moment, one marched not ten feet to his left. It stood a measure in height with Rist, with short brown hair and the face of a man who had seen perhaps five or six more summers than he. It wore nothing but black trousers, thick leather boots, and a light crimson tunic so saturated it clung to the skin, revealing the rune markings carved into its flesh. It didn't even carry a sword.

The men and women who walked at its side gave it a wide berth, but not from fear or uncertainty, as Rist would have expected, but from reverence and awe, as though Efialtír himself walked among them. Several priests of Efialtír had marched with the army simply to stay close to the Chosen – a hundred in total, ten for each.

At that moment, ten priests, garbed in crimson robes with white circles marked on each breast, moved in a wide circle around the Chosen. Each of them held a golden thurible on the end of a chain wrought from gold links, and incense wafted into the air in thick plumes. It seemed a strange thing to Rist, to dedicate your entire life to a thing you've never seen and to creatures of which you knew nothing more than stories you were fed by those who knew as much as you did. It was a cyclical thing, myth and legend becoming fact over time through the perpetuation of stories told across millennia. Yes, Rist had seen enough evidence to believe that the gods truly did exist, but he had yet to see anything tangible that spoke to the intentions of any one of them.

Rist had seen the Chosen throughout Berona and within the High Tower, but he'd never had a chance to look at them up close. And as he examined this one, he found himself wondering if the correct term was 'it' or 'he'. Was the man that walked before him more human or spirit? More flesh and bone or servant of a god?

The question joined a hundred thousand others in the cavern that was Rist's mind. And like all others, Rist was determined to have it answered.

His breath caught in his chest as the thing turned its head and its dark black eyes stared into his. The Chosen continued to walk forwards, stride unbroken as it held Rist's gaze. Something about it was mesmerising, as though the creature was staring into the very core of his soul.

Heavy hoofbeats drummed in the back of Rist's mind, faint and foggy. And it was only when a bay horse, travelling from the front of the column, stopped before Garramon and Magnus that Rist forced himself to look away from the Chosen and the priests.

The young scout exchanged words with the two Exarchs, then galloped back towards the front, hooves tearing up chunks of sodden earth.

"What is it?" Rist asked, pulling Trusil up beside Garramon.

"The path ahead is…" Garramon hesitated a moment. "The path ahead is covered in corpses. Looks like a caravan of refugees fleeing from the villages around Greenhills, soldiers with them. Uraks tore them apart… There were a lot of children. The scouts say it's not pretty. Taya is ordering us to take the longer route around, but we will have to up the pace to make sure we don't lose time."

"That doesn't seem practical," Rist said without a second thought. And it wasn't practical. The army had already been marching double, slogging through mud and rain and cold and wind. And when they did finally arrive at the Firnin Mountains, they would have to face a force of rebels of which they had no known number. Not to mention the obvious risk of Urak attack. Marching further and harder, and adding to the exhaustion that already plagued the army, was not only impractical, it was careless. But he settled for the word 'practical'. He was learning, and he didn't think the word 'careless' would be taken too well.

"You've not seen many dead children, have you, lad?" Magnus asked.

Rist didn't quite understand the relevance of the question. "No, I don't suppose I have, but I *have* seen many dead bodies. And I'm sure I will see many more. These are no different. I wish they were alive, but walking around them won't change that. The exhaustion of marching harder in this weather, however, might add us to their number when we finally reach the Firnin Mountains."

"You would have us march this army through a field of dismembered corpses?" A Healer who rode nearby, silver-trimmed white robes draped over his shoulders, pulled his horse closer. Rist knew his face: High Ardent Solman Tuk. He had joined the army at Berona, and Garramon's mood had soured immediately. The man stared at him with that same strange look Rist had seen many times across the years.

"I would have us take the shortest and safest route from here to the mountains. That is all."

Solman shook his head in disgust. "Is there a sliver of humanity in those cold eyes, Brother Havel? Do you see death as such a worthless thing that the mutilated bodies of your people mean nothing to you? It seems you truly did find the correct affinity. Did you feel the same way about your friend Tommin? He was a member of my affinity. Apprenticed to Sister Danwar. Would you march over his bloated corpse as well? Would that not bother you?"

Rist stared back at the man, unable to find words that could adequately convey the sorrow in his heart at the thought of Tommin. Beside him, Neera grew stiff, her fingers pale as she clutched the reins. Rist looked to her, but she didn't meet his gaze.

"Hold your tongue, Brother Tuk. Or I will cut it from your mouth." The Spark pulsed from Garramon as he rounded on the High Ardent. "Your grievances with our affinity are your own."

"With a Sponsor like you, Arbiter Kalinim, I'm not surprised this one is the way he is. You Battlemages care little for the devastation you leave in your wake. Monsters the lot of you." He looked from Rist to Garramon. "You have a knack for mentoring the young. Do you think this one will fare any better?"

"Speak one more word, and then never again. I promise you, that is not a threat, it is a certainty."

The two men glared at each other for a long moment until Brother Tuk snapped at his reins and drove his horse forwards, the other Healers moving with him.

Horse hooves squelched and rain drummed, but otherwise silence held sway as the army marched on. Garramon didn't turn to Rist or speak another word. He seemed to vanish into his own thoughts.

Magnus pulled his horse alongside Rist's. "Solman and Garramon have history, lad – a bitter one. And the Healers tend to look at us as monsters anyway. I get it. They pledge their existence to saving lives, and we pledge ours to ending them. Don't take it personally. He's a bitter twat with a small prick, trying to use you to get to Garramon. He knows the places to prod."

"He's not wrong though, is he? How could he be when I still don't understand. We're at war. I saw more corpses at the Three Sisters than I've known people in my life. Hundreds died in the attack on Berona. And when we reach the Firnin Mountains, what do we plan to do other than create more corpses? Why then do we march around instead of through? It's nothing we haven't seen and won't see again. I don't want to kill the rebels, but I understand the necessity of it. I saw what they did in Berona."

Magnus gave Rist a soft smile. One similar to those his mother would give him when he didn't understand what was apparently obvious to everyone else – which happened often. "If we all thought like you, Rist, the world would be a much simpler place. But we don't. And when it comes to leading an army, you aren't just managing their bodies, and their armour, and their training. You're managing their fear, their desire, their fervour – you're managing their hearts and minds. Logic is all well and good, but it evaporates when it comes into contact with the human heart." Magnus tapped his stump against his chest. "The men and women in this army have seen endless death this past year. They've lost loved ones, brothers and sisters. Some have lost their homes. And I can tell you one thing with a certainty born from centuries of fighting wars. If we march an exhausted army through a waterlogged field full of bloated corpses, we will have deserters by sunrise. And when we finally reach the Firnin Mountains, we will have an army ready to break and route. Steel cuts and kills, but when a battle teeters on the edge of the precipice, when two armies are tooth and nail, it is fear and desire that decide the day – morale. It is a fickle thing and must be tended with care." Magnus angled his head down to catch Rist's eye. "You're a little strange, Rist, but I'm batshit crazy too. There's not a person here who isn't."

Some hours later, Rist stood by the front of the command tent, staring up at the Blood Moon, the rain tapping against his skin, cold and rhythmic. He'd been there for a while, the others keeping dry inside. Something about the drumming of the rain calmed him, allowed his mind to wander. It rained a lot in The Glade.

"Rist?" Neera stepped from the tent and out into the rain, wrapping her arms around him from behind. She rested her hooded head against his back. "You'll catch your death. Get back inside."

"It's only rain." He placed his hands on top of hers, his fingers slipping into the gaps. "I like rain."

"Do you not have the Drowned Fever in the South?" She hugged him tighter, pressing her face into his saturated cloak.

"We do. Mara Styr's first daughter died of it when she was barely old enough to walk."

"Well then come inside and change out of these clothes and stop being an idiot. I'll not sit by your bedside, tending you like your mother."

"I miss my mother..." Rist glanced over his shoulder. "Neera?"

"What? And don't ask me something that'll make me think. I just want to sleep."

"Am I a monster?"

Neera loosened her grip a little and shifted so she could see into Rist's eyes. She shook her head, smiling softly. "What about 'don't ask something that'll make me think' do you not understand, Rist Havel?"

"Probably everything, if I'm being honest. What's the point of questions that don't make you think?"

She laughed at that. "You're not a monster, Rist. It's that High Ardent who's got you thinking like this, isn't it? Don't let him into your head. You are a Battlemage. You vowed to fight for our people, to protect them. And these rebels," she scoffed, pure hatred tinging her voice, "they violated that. They burned their own people alive. The Healers never understand who we are because they live safe behind walls that *we* protect. That Solman Tuk is nothing but a—"

"I didn't mean it literally," Rist said, cutting Neera short.

Neera pulled her head back and narrowed her gaze. "You always mean *everything* literally. Always."

Rist looked away, back up at the star-dusted sky.

"Rist, what's wrong?" Neera grasped his elbows, moving around him and trying to meet his gaze, but he refused to look down. "Talk to me."

"I'm not like everyone else," he said, his heart skipping every second beat, then quickening. "I know that. I've never been like everyone else, no matter how hard I've tried. Never been like Calen or Dann, never knew what to say, always had trouble seeing things they thought were obvious. I can't count the number of times I've said something wrong or done something wrong and everyone's looked at me like I was... Everyone but Calen and Dann, and you, and Garramon and Magnus... and Anila. I don't... With the bodies earlier, I... Is Brother Tuk right?"

Neera lifted a hand and pressed it against Rist's cheek, forcing him to look at her. To look at the rain dripping from the hood of her cloak, rolling over her soft skin, strands of hair saturated. Her eyes stared into his with a gaze that refused to let him look away. "Rist, you don't see things the same way, and I'd never want you to. You are kind, and thoughtful, and selfless, and brave, and strong... You spend hours – or even days – thinking on things that others forget in an instant. You put so much thought and care into everything you do. You are entirely yourself and nothing else, and I love that about you."

"But I just…" He didn't know how to take the words in his mind and place them onto his lips. His tongue kept tying itself in knots even trying to do so.

"Look at me." She placed her other hand on his opposite cheek, pulling him a little closer. "Do you understand why we walked around the corpses?"

He nodded. "Not at first, but I do now. It took a lot of thinking. The rain helped. Rain always helps me to think. I'm still not sure I agree, but I understand."

"So you didn't know, but you learned and now you do?"

"Yes."

"Would you chastise me for not knowing something that was plain as day to you? Think of me as less?"

"Well—"

"You wouldn't," she said, cutting him off. "I know you wouldn't because you never have. So why do you do it to yourself? Should you be held to a higher standard than I am? Am I not capable?"

"No, that's not it at all."

Neera wiped the rain from her eyes with her shoulder. "Rist, Brother Tuk is a self-righteous prick who thinks he is anointed by The Saviour himself. You are a better man than him by a distance that cannot be measured. You understand that there are things you do not know, and you are always willing to learn. I love you, both because of who you are *and* who you are not. I love how you lose yourself in the tiniest of details and how you seem to develop a new obsession every other day, or every other hour – like that goat in Al'Nasla."

"I actually discovered the answer to that not long after Ilnaen," Rist said with a touch of pride.

"The answer to what?"

"How the goat had gotten to the top of the crates in Al'Nasla. Did you know that goats are incredible climbers? In Maru Katir's book, *Wardens of the Mountain,* there are drawings of whole herds of goats pressed to the sides of sheer cliffs, seemingly standing on thin air. It was truly fascinating. I actually asked Marien, the librarian, to keep the book safe for me so I could show you when we're back. She's not as thorough as Gault but… Wait, did you say you love me?"

Neera pressed her forehead against Rist's sodden shirt and moved her hands down to grasp his cloak.

What had he said wrong?

After a moment, she laughed. "Only you, Rist Havel."

"Only me what?"

"Only you would have an entire monologue on the climbing ability of goats before realising what I said." She pulled her forehead from his chest and looked up. "Yes, I do love you." Her expression grew stern. "But if you tell anyone, I'll kill you."

Rist smiled, brushing his hand against her cheek.

"No, seriously. If you tell anyone, I'll push you off a cliff."

A brief moment passed where Rist couldn't quite tell if she was serious or not. Neera had never been one to openly display affection – unlike Rist's mam, who was the exact opposite – but Rist quite liked that. He was much the same as Neera. At night, her comfort warmed his heart, but in general, just her presence was enough for him. Just knowing that she cared for him and that he cared for her.

"I'm joking, Rist. Kind of."

"I think I love you too."

As often happened, Rist realised he'd chosen the wrong words just after they'd left his mouth. Though he wasn't quite sure why those were the wrong words, he could just tell by the opened-mouthed and narrow-eyed expression on Neera's face. "You *think*?"

"Well, I—"

"You better have a damn good explanation for this one."

Rist searched his head for the right words, trying to run through the scenarios in his mind as to how many different ways he could say the same thing wrong. "I don't know how it feels to love someone. I do know that my dad is a man of few words, not quite as few as me, but still few. He could go through the day without speaking barely more than three sentences, just keeping the bees, checking the mead, baking bread. I always found him harder to read than most, and I never found anyone easy. He doesn't smile a lot, doesn't frown a lot either, so that didn't help. Smiles and frowns are the easiest. Smile, happy. Frown, sad – or angry. Sighs are really difficult. There are so many reasons to sigh."

"Rist, this better have a point."

"It does, sorry. No matter how long the day was or how quiet he'd been, my dad would always smile when he saw my mam. She's everything he isn't. Excitable – almost too excitable – bubbly, enthusiastic even in the mornings, and she never stops talking. But when he sees her, it's like everything melts away and all the words he hadn't said throughout the day come pouring from his mouth. He laughs and smiles and becomes almost a different person. It's like he only becomes himself around her. And I think that's love, because if that's not love, I'm really not sure what is. And that's what you do to me. So I think I love you, but that's all dependent on the definition of the word. So if my dad loves my mam, then I love you."

Neera stared back up at Rist, her eyes glistening, lips pressed softly together. He didn't think he'd ever seen her silent for so long.

"Did I say something wrong?"

"No." She shook her head, just slightly, her lips curling at the corners of her mouth. She leaned up and kissed him, pressing her fingers through the hair at the back of his head. "That was… that was a very good explanation."

"Are they tears or rain?" he asked, brushing droplets from just below her eyes.

"Tears, you idiot."

"I didn't mean to make you sad."

"I'm not sad," she said with a laugh. "Fuck, Rist." She rested her hands on his cheeks once more. "You're the furthest thing from a monster this world has ever had."

GARRAMON WATCHED RIST AND NEERA through the open flap in the command tent. He'd never have placed the two together, but she filled the cracks in him and he in her. The same was true of Garramon and Fulya all those years ago, until he drove her away, until he made a choice that defined him. A choice he regretted to that day.

"Brother Garramon." Two voices in one spoke at the same time, layered atop one another. Azrim approached him, the leg of a rabbit in his right hand, little meat – or bone – left upon it.

"The Saviour's light upon you, Azrim."

"And upon you." Azrim leaned to the left and looked out at Neera and Rist. "Strange, isn't it, how this world of yours works? It was not long ago I brought him to your door." The Chosen looked from Rist to Garramon. Azrim had always been different from the other heralds, always more intrigued by the mortal plane, always curious. "You're attached to him."

Garramon glanced at the Chosen, staring into his black, bottomless eyes, then back at Rist and Neera. "He will always be my apprentice."

Azrim smiled – if it could be called a smile, his lips struggling to hold the gesture. "Your sentimentality is a curious thing also. I wish to know more of it."

"Forgive me if this is too direct a question, but why have you come back?"

"I adore questions in all their forms, Brother Garramon. Answers do not exist without questions, and I so crave answers. And that is what leads me here. Yes, Efialtír commands it of me, but my curiosity about this world remains unsated. And now, I can explore it in a body more fit for its purpose, a body moulded for my soul."

Azrim held out his arms, admiring the scarred rune markings and swirling blue tattoos that adorned his skin. The Chosen had not bothered to change his clothes for dry ones.

"Do not worry," Azrim said, stripping the rabbit leg of the last of its flesh and tossing the remnants of the bone on the tent's floor. "I will keep him safe as the harbinger requests."

Azrim strolled from the tent and out into the rain, spreading his arms wide and tilting his head towards the sky. Rist and Neera were gone, back to their cots most likely.

Garramon watched as Azrim vanished into the night. What had the Chosen meant? Had Fane asked Azrim to watch over Rist? Why? Rist's preparation for testing had been more than promising, but to have one of Efiatltír's Chosen watching over him was a strange thing. His old friend had always worked within the confines of his own mind, but Garramon had noted it even more so of late.

Garramon had been surprised when Fane had chosen not to accompany the army himself. With ten thousand infantry, a full contingent of Battlemages, Taya Tambrel's Blackwatch, Primarch Touran, ten of Efialtír's Chosen, and the reinforcements from Elkenrim and Merchant's Reach, it did not matter what awaited them in the rebel stronghold. But he'd seen the fury in his old friend's eyes, the fervour of long past battles. Fane should have been there with them, but as always, Fane had plans within plans, layered and twisting. And Garramon was absolutely sure that Brother Pirnil played a central role in those plans. Fane had never had any particular liking for the man, but now Pirnil was never far from Fane's side. When Garramon returned to the city, he would find the truth of it all. He'd spent too long trusting blindly and too long suffering for it.

With Azrim gone, Garramon joined the others by the fire. The conversation centred mostly around the remaining days of the march, provisions, fatigue, and the plan of action when the Firnin Mountains were reached. Garramon contributed little, instead sipping slowly on a cup of wine and watching Brother Tuk.

The man saw him watching, but Garramon didn't look away. Solman had said something earlier that day, something that had lingered in his mind. *"You have a knack for mentoring the young. Do you think this one will fare any better?"*

There was something in the way he'd said it that pricked the hairs on Garramon's neck. Something he couldn't let go.

Once the conversation petered out and faded to frivolous matters, Garramon said his farewells, leaving Taya, Brother Halmak, and a number of generals about the fire, and stepped out into the rain, pulling up his hood.

The mud sucked at his boots, puddles forming in the hollows where too many footprints had overlapped. It had been quite some time since he'd seen rainfall of this magnitude, and of course it had come just when the army had set out from Berona.

He ambled through the deluge, passing dying campfires and soldiers running about holding sheets and cloaks above their heads. He knew where he was heading but was in no rush to get there. He had time.

As he walked, the sounds of slapping feet and sharp breaths touched his ears. It was not soldiers clambering about in the rain. The sounds were too controlled, too measured and repetitive. And within a few heartbeats, he knew precisely what it was he was hearing.

He let out a sigh, shaking his head as he walked towards the sounds. And sure enough, turning the corner around a tent that could not possibly have been pitched any worse, he saw Rist standing in the rain, his feet shoulder-width apart, set low in the first stance of form two, movement three.

The rain pummelled down on the young mage, bouncing off his cloak and the steel in his hands as he flowed through the movements, completely unaware of everything around him. Never in Garramon's life, perhaps with Fane as the only exception, had he seen an individual with such unwavering dedication. When Rist committed himself to something, the young man became iron itself. And much like with Fane, Rist's dedication was rewarded with a rate of improvement unreachable by the fickle of heart.

Garramon stood with his hands clasped behind his back and watched. Rist moved through all fourteen forms, again and again.

"I thought you went to find sleep." Garramon stepped out into the open, raising an eyebrow at Rist.

The young man finished his movement, ending with his blade fully extended in a killing strike. The steel didn't so much as quiver.

"I practice every night before I sleep."

It was a statement of fact. The rain was not even a consideration.

"I know." It felt a strange thing to have such pride in a young man that wasn't of his own blood, and yet, that's precisely what Garramon had. "I admire your dedication, Rist. But you'll catch your death out here in the rain. Exhaustion and cold bones don't mix."

"So Neera told me." Rist pulled his sword arm in and straightened. "I'm sorry for earlier. I spoke out of turn and I—"

"You have nothing to apologise for." Garramon held up an open palm. "You questioned a command that deserved questioning. Nothing more, nothing less. For what it's worth, I think the men and women of this army would have found strength in the sight. They just watched rebels attack Berona, kill innocent citizens, kill their brothers and sisters who watched over the city. I think the sight of refugees slaughtered while fleeing to a place they thought to be safe may have only added fuel to their fire. But it is Taya's command, and I trust her. I will hear no more of it, understood?"

"Yes, Exarch."

"And Rist, get back to the tent, get out of those clothes, dry yourself off, and get some rest. The heart of your argument earlier was to do with exhaustion. It's a bit hypocritical to then run yourself into the ground." Garramon didn't think it necessary to have to tell someone to remove their wet clothes and dry themselves before climbing between the sheets. But sometimes Rist took things a bit too literally, and Garramon had learned to be explicit with his instruction. "And dry the sword, lest it rust."

Rist stared at Garramon for a moment, then inclined his head, droplets of rain streaming from his hair and down his face.

"I will see you at dawn before we march to continue your channelling."

The young man inclined his head once more before heading back to his tent.

With that, Garramon set off towards the tent that had always been his destination. It wasn't long before he found it. Two guards with the roaring lion on their breastplates stood at the entrance, candlelight coming from within. Good, the man was still awake.

The two guards straightened as Garramon approached, pressing closed fists to their chests. "Exarch."

"Your watch has ended."

"Excuse me, sir?"

"Your watch has ended, soldier. Brother Tuk says he no longer requires your presence. You may retire for the night. I have left a cask of Etrusian wine along with fresh cuts of lamb and clean blankets in the cook tent – a thank you for your understanding. Tell Omelda that Exarch Garramon Kalinim sent you. You will be well looked after."

The two men exchanged an unsure glance, which was slowly replaced by one of realisation.

"If the High Ardent requires it," one of the guards said, inclining his head.

"He does."

The guards left Garramon alone before the tent's entrance, the scent of burning sage drifting from within.

Candles puddled in small iron bowls about the tent, two atop a long wooden desk to the right next to a third in a bowl that wafted white smoke.

High Ardent Solman Tuk stood with his arms crossed, a cup of wine in his hand and red stains on his lips. He looked down at an open ledger on a table, his brow furrowed. It took a moment for Tuk to notice Garramon, but when he did, his expression shifted to one of surprise, then caution. "Garramon, what are you doing here? Where are my guards?"

"They have the same taste for wine as you, I'm afraid." Garramon took slow, measured steps, scanning the tent. No fewer than three finely woven rugs adorned the ground, spun with vibrant reds, golds, silvers, and blacks. Two heavy chests worked with gold rested at the foot of the wooden-framed bed, and at least six thick blankets lay across a feather mattress. It appeared the High Ardent never travelled without his luxuries, and Garramon would do well to inform Taya that there might be some inefficient use of her wagon space.

"What do you want, Garramon? It's late."

"It is."

"Is this about earlier?" Tuk let out an irritated sigh, shaking his head.

Garramon nodded, slowing his steps as he drew closer to the High Ardent.

"There's nothing to talk about, Garramon. You're all the same. Cold and apathetic. That boy is no different. You Battlemages attract the type. I will not apologise."

"I didn't much come here to talk, nor to seek an apology."

Tuk's eyes widened at that, and he unfolded his arms, his back stiffening.

"If you ever speak to any of my Brothers or Sisters like you did today, I *will* pin you to the floor and remove your tongue with a blunt spoon. And I will call one of your companions to stop the bleeding only because death is too quick for a weasel like you."

"Your threats don't scare me. I answer to the Grand Ardent and the emperor, not you. You hold no power over me, Garramon. You are not the Arbiter anymore, and even when you were…" Tuk shrugged.

There it was again, that tone in his voice, that smug look of pomposity in his eyes. There was something Tuk felt as though he had gotten away with, a battle he thought he had won – a battle he thought he was now safe from. He was wrong.

"Oh, but I do have power over you." Garramon opened himself to the Spark and pulled on threads of Air, wrapping them around Tuk's throat.

The man dropped his cup, wine spilling across the intricately woven rug, hands slapping at his neck, veins popping, skin turning red.

"Don't worry," Garramon said. "I won't kill you like this. A child could overpower you with the Spark."

Garramon released the High Ardent, who fell to the ground, choking. Tuk lifted himself to his feet, eyes filled with rage.

"That's it, Brother Tuk, feel the anger. Breathe it in."

Tuk clenched his jaw, teeth grinding, hands twisted into fists, white robes stained from the spilt wine. "You arrogant piece of shit. I will report this to the Grand Ardent, and he to the emperor."

"Let it out."

"You always thought you were better than me, always thought my affinity worth nothing but the dirt beneath your feet. Were it not for your tongue being so far up Fane's arse, you would be nothing."

"Is that right?"

Tuk's lip curled in a grin, red-marked teeth flashing. "Who won in the end, Garramon?"

"I'm sorry, Brother Tuk, but I don't understand. What did you win?"

The High Ardent's eyes widened when he realised he had said too much, the wine making him too bold.

"Don't worry. I already knew." Garramon took another step closer. "I just needed to be sure... to be completely sure."

"I didn't... I don't... I don't know what you're talking about."

"Oh, come now, Brother. You insult yourself. You know exactly what I mean. It was you who whispered in my son's ear, you who gave him the letter to pass to rebels, and you who told of his betrayal."

"I did no such thing." Tuk's voice was strong and steady, but his body gave him away. He swallowed. Took a step back, hands shaking, gaze darting for an escape. "Your son did what he did, Garramon. Accept it."

"Yes, you did, Tuk."

"You have no proof." His tone grew sharper, his face red.

"I don't need proof," Garramon said with a shrug. "Back then I did. You held too high of a position for me to simply slit your throat. I needed evidence to bring to Fane. But I'll give you one thing, Tuk, you're a smart man. You covered your tracks well. The young man you hired to turn Malyn over betrayed you but didn't live long enough for his words to reach any ears but my own." He tapped a finger on the long desk, still moving forwards. "I thought I had you. But then I began to question myself. Was I obsessing? Was I wrong? Did the man just give me the first name that came to his head to save his own hide? Everything in my bones told me it was you, but every time I thought I found something to prove that theory right, it vanished into thin air. I wouldn't have been able to live with myself if I'd killed an innocent man. So all these years I've wondered but stayed my hand... until tonight. You slipped, Brother Tuk. It's not your fault. It's time's fault. Time makes us grow complacent, makes us feel safe."

"You found no proof because it's not true, Garramon." Tuk moved tentatively back towards the table, rubbing at his throat. "I would never."

Garramon gave him a smile, then looked down at the burning sage in the bowl. "You know, I remember, back before the liberation, when we had an argument. Do you remember?"

"We've had a lot of arguments. But that's always been the way. Battlemages and Healers, two sides of a coin."

Garramon wagged his finger, stepping ever closer. "No, no, this one was different. We were drunk, you more than I, much like you are now. You wanted the prisoners from the Lyonin campaign turned over to the Healers. Do you remember now?"

"I don't think... No, it doesn't ring any bells."

"You came before the council arguing that if the prisoners could be used as specimens for study, then the Healers' understanding of the living body could rise to new heights." Garramon ran his finger across the edge of the table, rubbing away ash from the burning sage. "I was in the chamber myself at the time, providing reports on the rising Urak threat near Caelduin. Alvira called you a monster and – if I remember correctly – told you to rot in the void. And when Folan asked for further opinions, I gave mine. You didn't much like it. You confronted me in the Grand Hall during the feast that night. Threw a cup of wine over me. And then you told me that I would regret what I said, that I would 'rue the day'. Rather dramatic. You had this look in your eyes, this…" Garramon rolled his hand in the air as though trying to find the thought. "This arrogance mixed with superiority. The same look you had today when you spoke to Rist. And then when I walked into this tent and spoke of my son, I saw that same look."

Garramon moved so he was within arm's reach of Brother Tuk. To the man's credit, he held his ground, though judging by the way his hand tapped against his hip, it was taking all of Tuk's resolve to do so.

Again the man swallowed hard.

"I know it was you. After all these years, I know. And I will not let you do the same thing to Rist that you did to Malyn. I will not let you get inside his head. Twist him, and break him, and make him think that he is less, that he needs your approval. You are a self-important worm who clings to any side he thinks will win. You sit and you judge others, but Alvira was right – it is you who is the monster."

Garramon held Tuk's gaze, waiting, watching. A trapped animal always snapped, and Garramon needed to be sure. He would not kill an innocent man.

"Garramon. Come to your senses. None of this is—" Tuk broke off and reached for the Spark, slamming threads of Air into Garramon's chest, then tried to break into a run.

The threads knocked Garramon back a step but did little else. He rammed his fist into Brother Tuk's gut.

The man doubled over, coughing and grabbing his stomach. Garramon took him by the scruff of the neck and threw him to the ground.

"Where did you think you were running to? There's nowhere you could hide from me. I am the Arbiter after all. Get up."

Tuk twisted and threw open the lid to the chest nearest him, producing a long golden dagger, an Essence vessel set into its hilt. He leapt to his feet and swiped at Garramon's arm, neck, then chest.

Each time, Garramon shifted in place, allowing the man to stumble around like a hapless idiot. And when he felt Tuk tapping into the gemstone, Garramon grabbed the man's wrist and snapped it back, catching the dagger with his other hand.

He turned the blade over, admiring it. "There is something ironic about a Healer pulling a dagger on a Battlemage. Then again, you always were a snake."

Garramon smashed his forehead into the bridge of Tuk's nose, earning a beautiful *snap*, blood spurting as the man staggered backwards into the foot of the bed.

"Up. I'll give you one last swing at this."

The man grunted and stumbled forwards, pinching his bloody nose. "You won't get away with this, Kalinim. You won't."

"It's been four hundred years since the war ended, Solman. I could slit your throat and bury you beneath this tent, and this army will march on without asking a single question. Come on, it's just me standing between you and leaving this tent."

Tuk squeezed his nose one last time before lunging at Garramon. He snatched an iron bowl off the table and hurled it through the air.

The bowl bounced off Garramon's raised arm, hot wax splashing over his face and shirt. The pain was nothing compared to the fire in his veins. He sidestepped a punch from Tuk, then jabbed him in his already-broken nose. As the man howled, Garramon grabbed the back of his neck and slammed his face down into the bowl of burning sage on the desk.

Tuk screamed and reeled backwards, swatting the hot ash from his skin.

Garramon threw a fist into the man's ribs, and as Tuk doubled over, he clasped the back of Tuk's head and dragged it down into his rising knee.

Tuk slumped to the ground, rolling onto his back. He gasped for air as Garramon rested his knee into the man's gut.

"If you ever so much as look at Rist Havel..." Garramon wrapped his fingers around Tuk's robes and lifted the man's head and chest from the floor. "I will burn out your eyes."

Garramon slammed his fist into Tuk's face, knocking the man's head back to the floor, a fresh cut bursting open just below his eye.

He wrapped his fingers tighter and pulled the man back up. "If you speak to him, I will break your legs and leave you in the Burnt Lands."

Garramon drove his fist into Tuk's broken nose as hard as he could, the skin on his knuckles cracking with the impact.

"The only reason I'm not going to kill you is because death is too swift." Garramon snatched Tuk's dagger from the floor. He let his anger rise, let it burn in his voice. "You twisted my son, fed him lies, then betrayed him, all for what? To hurt me?"

"To *break* you," Tuk spat, his head lolling, face covered in blood. "To teach you what it is to lose something."

"There it is..." Garramon's jaw trembled, and his fingers tightened around the dagger's hilt. Where Garramon thought he would find blind rage within himself, he suddenly instead found a sense of relief, of calm. He had been right all these years. He had been right. "So you admit it?"

"Of course I do. You already knew. You knew then, and you know now."

"You took my son from me."

The High Ardent shook his head, coughing blood. "No... No. *You* killed your son. You had a choice, and you made it. All I did was tempt him. He was the one who took the bait, and you were the one who swung the sword. You killed him, Garramon. Not me."

"I did. I made the wrong choice, and I will never make that mistake again. I will not. But my guilt does not absolve yours, and I'm the one with the knife. I won't kill you, Tuk."

"Thank you… Brother Garramon." A fake smile danced on Tuk's lips. "A life for a life and we'd all be dead. I'm sorry for what I did, truly. I'm sorry."

Garramon nodded and returned the man's smile. "You're right, a life for a life serves no purpose. But you took my son from me, and now I must take something in return."

"What?" Tuk lifted his head from the floor, eyes wide.

Garramon pressed his knee down harder into the man's stomach and wrapped his hand around Tuk's throat. "This will hurt more than anything you can imagine."

Garramon opened himself to the Spark, thick threads of each elemental strand flowing through him. He held them, savoured them, then pushed every drop of power in his veins into the High Ardent.

Tuk screamed, but Garramon's hand around his throat silenced him. The High Ardent tried to push back, but his strength was a trickling stream next to Garramon's. He jerked upwards, veins bulging in his head and neck. And then Garramon felt it – felt the man's connection to the Spark shatter. Tuk convulsed, his fingers snapping and cracking as he twisted and jerked. A white light shone from his eyes, growing brighter and brighter until the smell of burnt flesh filled the air and Tuk's eye sockets were nothing but blackened husks. The man stopped kicking and screaming.

Garramon took no pleasure in what he did. He knew it was monstrous. But he cared little. Solman Tuk had wormed his way into Malyn's head, convinced him to turn on his family and his friends, only to tear him apart. There was no pain in the world Garramon would not inflict on this man for what he had done to Malyn. And Garramon would not let the same thing happen to Rist. Rist, whose mind was already more fragile, already more vulnerable than Malyn's had ever been.

Garramon's hands were just as dirty as Tuk's, just as bloody. He knew that. There was no redemption for the things he'd done. But he would use those bloody hands to keep Rist safe. He would not fail him like he had failed his son.

Cold rain dropped on Garramon's face as he stepped from the tent, the smell of burning flesh still clinging to him.

As he turned and made for his own cot, Magnus emerged from the shadows between two tents opposite the High Ardent's.

"I was planning on paying our friend Solman a visit." Magnus glanced down at the red droplets falling from Garramon's hands. "Have you seen him?"

"It appears he burned himself out, attempting to draw more power than he was capable of."

"Awful. How is he?"

"I was just on my way to fetch a Healer. Wouldn't want to leave him in that state."

"You're such a considerate man, Garramon Kalinim."

Garramon stared into the night, then looked into Magnus's dark eyes. He allowed the pain in his heart to seep into his voice. "He killed Malyn, Magnus… He admitted it. It was him who betrayed my son."

Magnus only nodded, the rain dripping from his black beard. He let out a long sigh. "Some wounds don't heal, we just have to let them bleed. Come. I've got some Drifaienin whiskey. Then you need some rest. We'll fetch a Healer on the way."

CHAPTER FIFTY-SEVEN

PATIENCE

19th Day of the Blood Moon

Berona – Winter, Year 3081 After Doom

Fane stood on the balcony of the chambers he had taken as his study in the High Tower of Berona. He leaned forwards, looking over the city, his arms resting on the low stone parapet.

The dark skies had cleared, the rain following Garramon and the First Army northeast towards the mountains. And with the stormhead gone, the Blood Moon's light washed down over the white city, painting the buildings pink, just as it had in Ilnaen all those years ago.

The sections of the wall destroyed during the attack were still under repair, with many of Berona's Craftsmages sent to Elkenrim and Greenhills, along with Al'Nasla, to strengthen the cities' defences.

Slowly, everything was falling into place. He'd had centuries to prepare for these moments, and he had done so meticulously. There were always variables that could not be accounted for – the new Draleid, Eltoar's fluctuating conscience, the elven onslaught – but Fane relished creating opportunity from the unexpected and deciphering the hearts and minds of others. And if those hearts and minds continued to behave the way he expected them to, the Heart of Blood would soon be his.

He took no joy in twisting the knife in Eltoar's heart or keeping Garramon in the dark, but he would do what needed to be done. All great things required sacrifice. That was something Fane believed utterly. Everything he had done, all the choices he had made and all the losses he had accepted, had been for a reason, for a cause. And he would not falter now, not so close to the end.

The proverb 'patience is a virtue' was oft spouted sarcastically and in a mocking tone. Fane had found that those who spoke the proverb were frequently the same people who lacked the necessary patience when it mattered. The world was a spider's web, millions of threads interwoven, everything connected. A man who knew which thread to pull – and possessed the patience to know when to pull it – was a man who could achieve anything. The threads had been pulled, the pieces placed, and now all he needed to do was wait. But patience and waiting were two separate things. He had the former but was never good at the latter.

Drawing a deep breath of the winter air, Fane stepped back inside his chambers, moving to the two black leatherbound books that rested on the desk he'd had brought to the room.

Kiralla Holflower's research – with invaluable input from Brother Pirnil. The Scholar had proved himself a surprisingly valuable asset, picking up where Kiralla had left off with voracious rapacity. He had a keen mind and an unquestionable devotion to Efialtír – which had only strengthened since the Chosen had crossed. Even then, with the sun long set, the man worked tirelessly on the new tasks he had been given.

Brother Pirnil had a twisted and black heart. Fane had seen that from the moment he'd met the man. But at the very least, Pirnil was obsessed with the consumption of knowledge, and as long as that obsession remained focused on blood runes, Fane could look past the other details.

As Fane touched the black leather that covered Holflower and Pirnil's research, a knock sounded at the door, followed by the creaking of wood at Fane's admittance.

"Emperor." Brother Drakus Pirnil bowed deeply. His eyes were sunken and ringed purple, his clothes stained and creased. Obsession had indeed been the correct word. Fane knew that feeling all too well. There were many times in his youth when he'd gone for days on little or no sleep, neither bathing nor changing for fear of losing even a moment. Though as Fane felt the sweet taste of Essence radiating from the man, it was clear this was not simple exhaustion. Pirnil had been consuming Essence at far too high a rate. Subtle veins of red snaked through the whites of his eyes, and his skin had grown ghostly pale. Fane needed to ensure that Pirnil finished his work before he succumbed.

"Brother Pirnil, I was only just thinking of you." Fane tapped his index finger against the black leather book. "What do you need?"

"I've done it, Your Majesty." The man swallowed, his head twitching slightly, the thumb and forefinger of his right hand rubbing back and forth over each other.

"I'm going to need you to elaborate, Brother Pirnil, and perhaps take a second to slow your mind."

The Lector's hands shook as he held them in the air. He spoke so quickly Fane could hardly understand him. "The runes, the runes of the Bloodmarked. I understand them. They are not just carved, there is more to it. I was right, you see. A blade is not used. No. Not a blade. Also, intent. You need intent. Runes require a purpose. A purpose, yes. They are pieces of your soul."

"Brother Pirnil." Fane raised his voice, firm and deep.

The man snapped his gaze back to Fane, eyebrows twitching and lips curling. "Apologies, Your Majesty. I've not slept. Barely eaten, if I'm honest. But I was right. The runes are carved with Essence itself. Essence worked directly into the flesh, infused within the wounds. It's wondrous. A tether to the force of life joined with the flesh of the living. It's no wonder the Bloodmarked can bear such power – with the correct runesets, of course. What you asked. We can do it now. I'm sure of it. Absolutely sure. We need to bind the Essence to the Spark. Give the runes purpose. I'm sure of it."

"I'm happy you're sure, Brother Pirnil. But given the state some of the previous rune recipients have been left in, I do feel it prudent that your theory be tested prior to application. We will only have one chance at this, and I would prefer the candidate not end up like the others."

"Oh. Yes. Of course. I will… I will need more. We've run out of the current stock."

The word 'stock' didn't sit right with Fane. He understood the need for sacrifice, the need to look past the flawed perception of morality that was so commonplace. He understood that more than any living soul. But life was still a precious thing. At the core of it all, that was what mattered. He could allow a hundred to die to save a million or a million to die to save everything. But that didn't mean those sacrificed should not be remembered with respect and dignity. It was a precarious balance, life and death. And at the end of everything, at the breaking of time and the sundering of worlds, perhaps Fane would look back on his life and find himself the truest of all monsters. Perhaps everything he had done and everything he would do was wrong. And perhaps he would shroud the world in darkness instead of bathing it in light. But he knew that the world would burn if he did nothing, and so even the slightest chance that his actions would save it was all he required. He would be the monster. He would make that sacrifice. And he didn't care how his name was remembered so long as he knew within his heart that he had done all he could.

Fane plucked himself from his own thoughts, realising that he had become lost in their gravity. Brother Pirnil simply stood there, staring at him vacantly and scratching at a rash on his neck. The man would lose himself soon.

Fane let out a sigh. "There are rebels we captured after the attack. I will have them sent to you."

Brother Pirnil bowed even deeper than before. "You have my endless thanks, Your Majesty."

Fane inclined his head, thoughts wandering again to what Brother Pirnil's discovery might bring. This had been the missing piece. The one obstacle standing in the way. If Pirnil's theory could be proven and replicated, then the perfect path could be walked. Everything would be worth it.

"You are welcome, my Brother. Now, as much as I am eager to see your work continue, it would do neither of us any good if you were to die of hunger or deprivation of sleep. Go to the baths. Wash. Visit the kitchens and eat your bodyweight. Then sleep. In the morning, we will see if the power of the gods can truly be harnessed."

With Brother Pirnil gone, Fane left the High Tower and walked through the streets of Berona, the pale pink light of the moon shimmering in puddles left from the rainfall.

He didn't bother to wear a hood or cover his face. Most of Berona's citizens had never laid eyes on him up close. And even the ones who had weren't likely to recognise him as he wandered the city at night. Even in Al'Nasla, roaming the streets had been something he took great pleasure in. For hundreds of years, the people of Loria had been safe in these cities, safe from Uraks, and elves, and the ambitions of the over-entitled. That was a safety he had created, wrought with his own will. And there were days when he needed reminding of it – or nights. Nights like that night. Nights when doubts crept into the depths of his mind.

The streets were quieter since the attack, but many inns were still full, the sounds of song and dance drifting from within. He had half a mind to stop and join, to just sit in the corner of a dark tavern and drink ale while the bards sang and the people danced. It was something he'd missed in his younger days, his nose buried in books, his mind refusing to sit still. But for the same reason he had not partaken then, he walked on now: there were greater things on the horizon, and all great things required sacrifice. He repeated the mantra in his head.

He carried on, walking the streets until he came to a squat house with red shingles on the roof in the southern quadrant, framed on either side by tall white structures.

On first glance, the door to the house looked like any other, except for the small fact that it lacked a keyhole.

Fane pushed thin threads of Air into the door, working them just below the handle and sliding them through the locking mechanism built into the wood. He received a sharp *click* for his troubles, and the door swung out an inch or so. He stepped inside and reconnected the locking mechanism behind him.

The lock wouldn't stop someone from breaking in if they truly wanted to, nor did Fane consider it ingenious. No, the reason for it was much more mundane: Fane always lost his keys, and he hated carrying things in his pockets. This solved both problems.

He moved through the dark house, not bothering to light any candles. With a flick of his wrist, threads of Air shifted the solid wood dining table a few feet backwards, legs scraping against the floor.

He produced a small green stone from his pocket – precisely the reason there hadn't been room for a key. One thing in his pocket was bad enough.

Fane funnelled threads of each elemental strand into the keystone, admiring the filaments of light that came to life at their touch, swirling within the stone. The art of Jotnar runecraft and glamour construction was something that had fascinated Fane from a young age, something he had become obsessed with. And in his experience, when obsession was mixed with dedication and perseverance, the end result was often mastery. The Bloodmarked runes had been the missing piece he needed.

Before him, a section of the floor was now gone as though it had evaporated into thin air, and in its place was a staircase that sank into the ground. Fane created a baldír as he descended, the pale light guiding the way.

The stairwell led to a small antechamber Fane had carved with the Spark. The antechamber was grey and austere with only a single door. And just as the door at the front of the house held no keyhole, this was the same. It was black and wooden, and a blend of blue and red light creeped around its frame.

Fane opened the door with the Spark.

The room on the other side was four times larger but similarly sparse.

He laid Kiralla Holflower and Brother Pirnil's research on the desk to the right, next to an array of Essence vessels that glowed a deep red. And then he turned to face the true reason he had created this chamber in the first place.

There, kneeling on the far side of the room, was one of the Chosen – a Vitharnmír – stripped bare, arms outstretched, rune-marked manacles closed around each wrist. Chains forged from repurposed Antherin steel connected the manacles to bolts of the same metal fused with the ground.

More runes were inscribed into the stone ground, marked into a circle that bound the Vitharnmír at its centre. The alternation of blood runes and Jotnar runes was one of Fane's own discoveries, augmented by Brother Pirnil. It cut the connection between the Vitharnmír and Efialtír, severing their connection to both the Spark and Essence while also binding them in place. Even without the manacles, the creature would not have been able to cross the circle, but Fane was cautious by nature.

The creature knelt with its eyes closed, its chest rising and falling steadily.

"The arrogance of your kind knows no bounds." The voice of the Vitharnmír layered over that of the man who had volunteered to be its host. Even for Fane, someone who had seen more than his fair share of the world's horrors, that voice set his hairs on end. "What do you think will happen to you when our god discovers what you have done?"

Fane approached the kneeling Vitharnmír and sat on the ground before it, folding his legs beneath him and staring into its black eyes. "If I were you, I would be more concerned about my own fate."

CHAPTER FIFTY-EIGHT

BLOOD OF MY BLOOD

19th Day of the Blood Moon

*North of Aravell, where the Darkwood meets
the Burnt Lands – Winter, Year 3081 After Doom*

Calen drifted in and out of sleep, the vibrations of Valerys's wingbeats thrumming in his bones. They had flown through the night and into the next day and so on even when the sun sank once more, Valerys ignoring the pain in his hind leg. Calen had done his best to hold sleep at bay, but his eyelids refused him, exhaustion firmly rooted in his bones.

Whether awake or asleep, Ilnaen plagued his mind. He'd experienced those visions before, but they had been few and far between, seconds at a time, splashes of emotion and shifting images. He had no idea if Ilnaen itself had been the cause of the shift or if the strange power in his blood was pushing itself forwards. But no matter the cause, he needed to find a way to control it.

The visions he had experienced at Ilnaen had deeper roots than any he'd seen before, ones that felt as though they clung to him still, as though they were a part of him now. Tarast and Kollna were a part of him, their defiance, their refusal to be anything other than guardians. They had lived as Draleid, and they had died as Draleid, protecting those who could not protect themselves.

And if he was not thinking of Ilnaen, worry for Haem plagued him. He could only hope the knights had all made it through the Rift.

Valerys swooped low across the Burnt Lands, dropping from the clouds, that familiar weightless feeling twisting in Calen's stomach. The dragon tracked a group of N'aka across the dunes, following the heat of their bodies as they moved.

He spread his wings wide and rode the air currents, staying as silent as he could – one of the tricks he had learned when hunting N'aka the first time they had crossed the wasteland. The creatures had astoundingly keen hearing, vanishing into the sand at the beat of Valerys's wings. As the dragon gradually dropped lower, Calen pulled their minds together, allowing the thrill of the hunt to take him.

Even in the sky, they could smell the surprisingly sweet scent of the N'aka's fur against the dry earthy aroma of the dunes. Fifteen heartbeats thumped in almost perfect unison.

They angled their wings and dropped quicker, watching the warmth of the N'aka's bodies flit back and forth, tracing their heartbeats.

One deep breath, filling their lungs, and they swooped, the air crashing against their scales and rushing over their skin. They dropped and snapped their jaws around the largest of the creatures before it had any idea what was happening. Blood filled their mouth, bones snapping.

Two of the N'aka leapt into the air, lunging for Valerys's throat. The dragon threw the dying catch from his mouth and snatched it into his right talon. In the same motion, he twisted and whipped his tail across the two leaping N'aka. The spearhead tip sliced open the belly of the first creature, then collided with the second, hurling it up through the air.

While the N'aka careened upwards, a pressure swept through Calen and Valerys's joint body, and the dragon unleashed a pillar of fire that consumed the soaring creature. Valerys snatched the smoking carcass from the air, his jaws wrapping around the charred flesh, then lifted and flew upwards, away from the reach of the other N'aka.

Calen pulled back, just a touch, drawing a cold breath into his lungs, the hairs on his arms and neck standing on end, his heart racing, a feeling of euphoria permeating his shared soul.

The thrill of the hunt was something unique and singular. Something that Valerys relished.

The dragon threw his head forwards and launched the charred N'aka corpse into the air, toying with it, then snatched it back into his jaws and devoured it in a crunch of bone and blackened flesh.

He kept the second kill clutched in his talon as they flew towards the edge of the Burnt Lands. It was close enough to see now – the place where the sand gave way to the cracked and dried rocks that would eventually yield to the dark green canopy of the Aravell.

They soared, the wind carrying them, allowing Valerys's wings the break they so desperately deserved. And as they did, Calen reached back to the satchels that still hung from his shoulders, pulling at him. He'd thought to have Valerys land and to load the eggs into the packs strapped to the dragon's chest. But aside from not wanting to stop, Calen felt a deep urge to keep the eggs as close as possible, to feel them near him.

A warning flashed from Valerys's mind to Calen's, and Calen jolted upright, the force of the wind dragging at him. He looked through the dragon's eyes, searching.

Miles ahead, where the dunes yielded to the ridge of broken rock, four figures stood atop a flat, still as statues. Three on two legs, one on four.

A familiar scent touched Valerys's nostrils. He couldn't quite place it, but he knew it.

Calen pressed himself to Valerys's scales as the dragon cracked his wings and ripped across the sky. They swept over the ridge, turning and alighting on a patch of rock behind the four figures, who turned to face them.

Three were human – or at least they looked to be – while the fourth was some kind of monstrous kat, at least the size of Faenir, its fur white as snow over a body of dense muscle. Black glass-like scales jutted from the creature's chest and neck, as well as patches along its side, legs, and back. It hugged tight to the figure on the left – a short woman with two axes at her belt.

Valerys's leaned forwards and lowered his head, a hissing rattle escaping his throat, his frills standing on end. Calen sat up straight, holding the Spark just out of reach.

"My my, how you've grown." The figure in the middle stepped forwards, lowering his hood.

Calen stiffened. "Rokka?"

The old druid smiled, the lines around his face and eyes creasing even further. He looked somehow taller than the last time Calen had seen him in his hut between Kingspass and the Burnt Lands, his shoulders a little broader, his back a little straighter. "Calen Bryer. You walk the path I had hoped, though even that path leads many ways."

Valerys leaned lower, and Calen slid from his back, softening his landing with threads of Air. The dragon moved so his head hovered over Calen protectively. Valerys had little trust for the druid.

Calen stared at Rokka without speaking a word, studying his two companions and the kat-like creature. He was not as naive as he had been the last time he and Rokka had crossed paths. This man was all riddles and clever words, all games and secrets. Whatever path Rokka wished for Calen to walk, it was to Rokka's benefit, not Calen's. Calen needed to take care with his words.

"Ah." Rokka snapped his fingers. "Where are my manners? On a different path most like." He gestured to the two women who stood beside him. "These are my kin, blood of my blood. As they are yours."

"Mine?"

"Come now, Calen. Let us not play games. I've seen the paths, and so, I believe, have you."

Calen made to speak but stopped himself. This man was always a step ahead of him, always knew what he would say.

"Hmm." Rokka narrowed his eyes a little, his smile faltering. He gestured to the woman on his left, blue eyes staring through strands of blonde hair. "This is Una. To our people she is what is known as a Starchaser. A druid of the aether."

Una pulled back her hood, revealing a face not much older than Calen's. She gave a slight incline of her head. "Greetings, Wolfchild."

The other woman took a step forwards, her eyes flitting between Calen and Valerys. She settled her gaze on the dragon. "You are beautiful."

Her eyes turned a milky white, and a shiver swept over Calen's body, something probing at his mind – at Valerys's. His sword was free of its scabbard in a heartbeat, and Valerys unleashed a roar that sent the woman stumbling back, pressing her hand to her head, and then the probing feeling was gone. She staggered back another step, whispering to herself as the kat-like creature lunged forwards and snarled, its eyes fixed on Valerys.

"Stay out of our heads or lose yours." Calen glared at the woman.

"Tamzin here, whose etiquette might need a little re-education, is a Blooddancer, or an Aldruid as some now say, like your sister."

A flicker of rage rose in Calen, seeping over from Valerys as the dragon leaned forwards at the mention of Ella, but Calen pulled their minds together and calmed the dragon. "What do you know of my sister?"

"Maybe this is not the path I thought it was." Rokka turned down his bottom lip, tilting his head side to side as he studied Calen. "It appears the dragon is not the only one who has grown. How many did you save? The eggs? Nine or five?"

"How…" Calen looked down at the satchels slung across his back. "No. No, you're answering me. What do you know of my sister?"

If this man was indeed a druid, then perhaps he knew what afflicted Ella – perhaps he could save her. But Calen didn't want to give away too much.

"There is plenty of time to talk of your sister. But there are other things more pressing. You—"

Calen slid his sword back into its scabbard and moved so he stood within a foot of Rokka. "We will talk about her now, or we have nothing to talk about."

Calen stared at Rokka for a few moments, and when the man remained silent, Calen turned and Valerys lowered his head and stretched out a wing for him to remount. He was sick and tired of people wasting his time, thinking him nothing more than a tool for their own devices. He would carve his own path now, not walk the one others had laid for him.

"Ella is awake."

Calen stopped in his tracks at Tamzin's words. The hairs on his arms pricked, his breath catching in his chest. "What do you mean she's awake? How do you…" He stopped, turning slowly to face Tamzin. He searched the woman's eyes. "If you're lying, I swear by the gods I'll take your head. That is not a lie I will abide."

The kat-like creature stepped across Tamzin, hackles raised, enormous obsidian fangs bared. It snapped at Calen, hissing.

In a heartbeat, Valerys was over him, a deep rumble in his chest. Valerys could have ripped the creature in half with a single bite, and yet it didn't back down.

Rokka flashed a glare at Tamzin, one that evaporated in moments. A glare that had shown Calen more about the man than anything else: Tamzin had said something she was not meant to say. Calen now knew for a certainty that Rokka played the same games as the elves, and Aeson, and all the others.

"Did you know what we'd find at Ilnaen?"

"Did you find what you needed?" Rokka asked.

Calen shook his head and laughed. "More twisted words. Good luck on your paths."

Calen turned to mount Valerys, but the old druid leapt forwards and grabbed his arm. Ice flooded Calen's veins, and the world turned to an oily black.

He spun in circles, breaths heavy, heart pounding. He looked down to see upon what ground he stood but instead found nothing but blackness. Panic flared within him at the sight of his limbs shimmering with a white light, mist trailing with every movement.

"Where am I? What did you do?"

"Níthianelle," a voice echoed as though calling through a tall valley. "The world between worlds. The Sea of Spirits."

Calen spun to see Rokka standing behind him. Though the man who stood before him was nothing like the ancient druid Calen knew. Not a line or mark of age touched his skin. His hair was dark as chestnut, his body lean and muscular. This was a man barely five summers older than Calen. And yet, Calen knew it to be Rokka. Unlike Calen, his body was wrought from flesh and solid things, but white mist still trailed after him.

"What have you done to me? What are you?"

"So many questions, young one, and yet you were just about to leave. Such is the world we live in. We all desire so much, but few of us have the patience to seize it." Rokka opened his arms and gestured towards the empty blackness. "This is the ancestral plane of our people. It is here our souls linger before passing into the eternal cycle. But it is much, much more than that."

"It is nothing." Calen looked about at the endless dark.

"Only because you do not yet see. But now is not the time to open your eyes."

"Then why am I here?" Calen lunged towards Rokka, but the man evaded him with ease, moving quicker than should have been possible.

"Because you do not have the patience in the mortal plane. There are things you must know, things you must understand so the correct path may be walked."

"What if I don't want to walk your path?"

Rokka smiled, his youthful face still unsettling Calen. "Does the leaf wish to blow across the valley? Or does it do so because the wind wills it?"

"Why should I trust a word that leaves your mouth? You're worse than the elves. I should have seen it in the hut. You were always playing these games, weren't you?"

"Did I ever say otherwise?" He shrugged. "From the beginning, I told you what I was. I told you I could see the paths, and I told you there was one I wished to follow. My only desire was to find the path where our people are not obliterated, where we can walk free once again. I have been nothing but honest with you. Though, I'll admit, my honesty is convoluted by necessity. Such is the burden of the Pathfinders. The truth is still the truth if it is given in drops, is it not?"

"Then answer me something, 'Pathfinder'. Am I a druid?"

"Yes, but you already knew that. Your sister, now... She is something else, something truly unique."

"Why didn't you tell me all of this when we first met in the hut?"

"The same reason I have not told you many things. Because that would have sent you on the wrong path. I am not opaque because I enjoy the games. I am so because the seeing of paths is a delicate affair. Every moment is connected, every word, every thought, every emotion, and every preconception. What you know affects what you do. If I tell you something before you're meant to know it, I change the path you walk. Our people have been on the brink of extinction for over a thousand years. Hunted for a thousand more. Betrayed by those we trusted, fractured by wars of old, wars amongst ourselves. You walk on ice so paper thin you don't even know it exists. There are so many things you do not understand, so many threads long woven, so many traps long set."

"Then tell me!" Rage bubbled in Calen's blood, fuelled by Valerys. He could not see the dragon, but he could feel him, feel his beating heart, his tethered soul. And every moment the druid held them in this place was a moment they could not be by Ella's side. "Tell me why you brought me here or let me go."

"Ah, if only things were that simple."

"I'm growing very tired of this." Calen rounded on Rokka.

"I've been tired for a thousand years and not much better for the thousand before that."

Calen let Rokka's words sound again in his mind. "You've lived to see two thousand summers?"

"I saw your ancestors step from boats onto the shores of this continent. My feet were among the first to feel the sand."

"That's not possible…"

"After everything you've seen, my longevity is where you draw the line?" Rokka chuckled. "You are just like your father. Arrogance, ignorance, honour, and strength, all in equal measure. That can be a dangerous combination, Calen. Particularly for one burned by the rage of a dragon."

"You knew my father?"

Rokka nodded, puckering his lips. "Quite well. Though, I suppose he never truly knew me." Rokka let out a long sigh, then took a step towards Calen, locking their gazes. "You are a druid, bloodborn from Fenryr. You are a Pathfinder of paths once walked. Watch, listen, learn. Do not waste a second. The past is a precious thing. It tells us why the present is as it is and how the future must be forged."

"How do I control it? How do I… How do I see what I need to see?"

"You are the leaf, Calen. Not the wind." Rokka kept his gaze fixed on Calen. "Moments and places of powerful emotion, of extreme loss or joy, they hold sway over one who sees the paths once walked. They call to you, pull you in. The Gifts of the Pathfinders are those of little control. Do not fight the wind. Embrace it, use it to take you where you need to go. If it shows you something, there is a reason."

"Do you say anything that isn't a riddle?"

Rokka only smiled at that. "I cannot hold you here forever, so I will speak plainly this once. Fenryr is at your sister's side. He has an honourable heart but a fool's mind. Approach him with as much caution as you do me. I ask you nothing more." Rokka licked his lips and folded one arm across his chest, the other hand stroking his chin. "We would need many sunsets for me to explain the history of our people. And perhaps we will get the chance to walk that path, or perhaps he will show you. It will be quicker if he shows you. This continent is shifting. The entire world will feel it. A hundred factions rise, a hundred causes, a hundred notions of what Epheria should look like when the dust settles. It is a time of opportunity, not just for our kind, but for anyone willing to seize it. Hands will tug at you from all directions, but knives will come from even more. There are things I want from you, things that would give our people the chance they need. But for now, what you need to know is that a time of gods is coming, a time of flesh and bone. Efialtír seeks to cross the veil to this world, and if he does, then all sides lose. I see paths beyond his manifestation. The empire must become dust, and Fane Mortem must be bled dry. All of us are aligned in this one thing. Do you understand me?"

Calen's head spun, but he found his way to a question. "The riddle you spoke, back at the cabin. What is the Heart of Blood? Is it real, or is it just some web you spun so the Knights of Achyron would think what they sought was in Ilnaen? The knights say that it is what Fane seeks, the missing piece that will allow him to bring Efialtír into the world. Do you know where it is?"

"Perhaps it is real, perhaps it is not, but as I said then, I do not know what the words meant, only that I must speak them."

"Gods dammit! Why are you here? What is the point? You bring me to this place only to speak words that make no sense, talking in circles like a drunken fool."

"A drunken fool often speaks the truth, even to those they wish to hide it from. If I could answer your questions, I would. Come, it is time we leave, but first let me show you what it is to walk the paths."

Rokka reached out and cupped his hands on either side of Calen's face, and the world twisted and turned, the misting white light blending with the blackness before everything snapped into place and a wave of sound rolled over him: screams, wails, crackling fire, crashing steel, falling rocks.

Calen stood in a field of corpses, no end in sight. Some were blackened and charred, others mutilated beyond the realms of understanding, some simply still and lifeless.

Enormous shapes lay amidst the bodies, still and cold, their fires extinguished. Calen counted thirteen dragons, all dead, horrendous wounds gouged through their scales, limbs severed, blood flowing like rivers. One dragon with orange scales and golden wings lay slumped over the body of another, a hole the size of a wagon in its side.

Everywhere he looked he saw faces he knew: Ella, Haem, Tarmon, Vaeril, Erik, Dann, Rist...

Calen's eyes fell on the corpse of a white dragon, its belly opened from navel to throat, smoke billowing from scorched wounds in its side. The creature was far bigger than Valerys, but he would know his soulkin anywhere, in any time, in any world.

As his heart broke and he reached out with his mind, the world spun once more, and he now stood at the centre of the battle. Two enormous figures marched through the corpses, one clad in green armour with sunbursts for pauldrons, the other wore black leather, the light seeming to shrink around him.

The two figures charged at one another, swinging blades of pure light as large as Calen was tall. Each time the weapons collided, a shockwave swept across the ground, sending corpses careening through the air.

A creature with leathery wings swooped and was sliced clean in half by the glowing green blade, its two sections slopping to the ground, innards spilling.

These were gods, of that Calen had little doubt. Everywhere they moved, the dead were crushed beneath them, the living faring little better. Each motion was death and destruction.

"One path in a million." Rokka appeared at Calen's side, his face sharp and youthful, his eyes a gleaming blue-grey with black slits.

The world shifted and blurred before it all took shape once more and Calen was perched atop a hill, a battle raging at its base. Wolves and stags the size of horses crashed through a sea of black and red leather while giant hawks swooped and tore into the flesh of anything that moved.

Banners rippled across the battlefield: the golden stag of Lunithír, the silver star of Vaelen, the green tree of Ardurän, the black lion of Loria, a red gryphon in a white sky. Hundreds more banners jutted into the air above the carnage. Some Calen recognised, many he didn't. One stood out in his mind: the white dragon on a purple field, golden leaves blowing about the edges. His banner. It was spread all across the carnage, only matched in number by the black lion.

The world continued to shift and change at a pace that turned Calen's stomach. Battle after battle with the slightest of variations, dragons falling from the sky, flesh and bone torn asunder with the Spark, rivers of black fire consuming everything.

A thousand times he watched himself and Valerys die. A thousand times he watched Dann, and Rist, and Ella, and Tarmon, and Erik, and Vaeril, and everyone he loved burn or take an arrow to the heart, an axe to the neck, a talon to the chest.

Again, and again, and again, until eventually Calen found himself kneeling on the broken rock at the edge of the Burnt Lands, Valerys standing over him, Rokka before him, and the other druids at Rokka's back.

"Why... what..." Calen's mind was a storm, the images flashing over and again, blood spraying, people screaming. He swallowed hard, his hands resting on his lap, sweat slicking his face. "What was that? Why did you..."

"I once told you that the path you were on would bring death beyond your wildest dreams. You are the leaf, Calen, not the wind. Death is coming and you cannot change that, no matter what you do. I want you to be ready, to be steel unbending in the face of what is to come. You are an anchor to which others bind, a point at which paths cross. Without you, this world always burns. Without you and your sister."

"Ella..." Calen stood, his chest heaving. He wiped the sweat from his brow with the back of his gauntlet.

"Go to her. We will not be far behind."

Calen flinched as Rokka laid his hands on Calen's pauldrons and stared into his eyes. But this time the world didn't shift or change. "Together, we can save them all. With the Gifts of our people, we stand a chance. You are a druid, Calen. One of few. Do not forget your blood."

Calen nodded as he walked backwards, his mind still racing. He looked to the druid with the two axes hanging from her belt – Tamzin. "She is all right?"

"She is. I delivered her myself."

Calen nodded again, feeling incapable of anything else. He climbed up Valerys's outstretched wing and took his place at the nape of the dragon's neck.

He gave one last look down at the three druids and the kat-like creature, then Valerys launched into the sky. With every beat of the dragon's wings, a new image of death burned in Calen's mind. He urged Valerys on faster.

CHAPTER FIFTY-NINE

FAMILY

19th Day of the Blood Moon

West of Achyron's Keep – Winter, Year 3081 After Doom

Alina rested her head against Rynvar's snout, her eyes closed. She drew a long, calming breath through her nostrils, rubbing her hands along the scales that armoured the ridges below his eyes.

"Not much longer," she whispered, her fingers trailing over a long wound that stretched from just above the wyvern's mouth and back to his jaw. A new scar to go with the old. "I promise."

Not a night had passed in which they hadn't flown out and torn into Lorian forward camps or ripped a supply caravan to pieces.

Dayne and Joros had used the horses their forces had captured in the Lost Hills to chase down any supply caravans or wagons that moved during the day. But they left no survivors.

The night attacks always left survivors. 'To spread the fear', Dayne had said. Her brother liked to think he didn't understand the logistics and semantics of war. But to him it was second nature. Dayne understood the ways of the human mind to a depth that almost unsettled Alina. He knew how to drive terror into human hearts, knew how to break them.

She exhaled, then leaned back and opened her eyes.

Two pools of sapphire blue stared back at her, deep and vibrant. There was understanding in those eyes. Wyverns may not have been able to speak, but they were still creatures of immense intelligence. Rynvar understood her, felt her pain, saw into her heart, just as she did his.

A soft, clicking purr left Rynvar's throat, and the wyvern nuzzled his head into Alina's chest. He continued to purr as he moved around Alina and curled into himself, his tail trailing about her legs, his head resting on a rock.

She drew another breath and stroked his head. When he was tired, he was more like a pup than a wyvern, always seeking out her hand, always curling up in the first place he found warmth.

"Rest," she whispered, running a hand along the black and orange scales of Rynvar's snout. "You've earned it. You did your part, and now I must do mine."

Alina checked the poultice mashed into a wound on the wyvern's flank, held in place by straps and cloth, before stepping from the shallow cave he had dug in the side of the rock face.

A small ledge jutted from the cave, and a cool wind greeted her as she stepped to meet it. She allowed herself to stand there a moment before descending the ladder that had been pegged in place.

In the wild, wyverns always built their Rests in the highest possible place, ensuring that predators on the land couldn't butcher them in their sleep or ravage their eggs while they hunted. When traveling, those wyverns who had been claimed by riders could delay that natural inclination to create a Rest, but in a case like this, where they had been encamped for weeks on end, there hadn't been a choice.

The entire rock face of the cliff that overlooked the camp was now cratered with shallow Rests, hundreds of wyverns creating homes away from home. And from each Rest dropped ladders of thick rope and short planks, some descending over two hundred feet to the ground.

Even Alina, who was well used to heights, had to stop for a moment when a gust of wind pulled a peg from the rock and the ladder swayed. She paused as the wind died down and looked out over the camp.

Thirty thousand strong, gathered from all the Major and Minor Houses in Valtara, along with hundreds of wyverns and Wyndarii. Never in Valtara's history had such a force been brought together in a single place with a single cause. Pride swelled within her at that thought, but she curbed it. It was not time for pride. Valtara was not free. And if Aeson Virandr didn't fulfil his vow and arrive by the new moon, the army she had assembled would either starve or crash against the walls of Achyron's Keep. And even if he did arrive, it might still be too late.

Besides, there was little pride to be taken in what needed to be done next.

Five of her Royal Guard stood waiting at the bottom of the ladder, the wyvern of House Ateres worked into their new golden cuirasses, capes of burnt orange clasped to their shoulders.

"My queen, this way." Savrin Vander pressed his hand to the wyvern on his chest. He gestured towards a path through the camp, bowing his head. Savrin had said little to her since Dayne had appointed him, but he had always been a man of few words. In truth, until Dayne had brought him to her, Alina had not known Savrin was still alive. The man had lost himself to drink years ago. She wasn't sure if she could trust him again, at least not so soon. But she trusted Dayne, and that was enough.

"Rynvar is well after the battle, my queen?" The commander of her guard, Olivian of House Arnon, stood a head and a half taller than Alina. Her face was soft and kind, but beneath the surface the woman was wrought iron. "I can arrange to have food brought to him if he is too weak to fly. And two new Alamant Healers arrived with Captain Kiron's ship last night."

"He needs rest, but he will be fine. That would be kind of you, Olivian." Alina looked back over her shoulder at Rynvar's Rest nestled into the rock face almost two hundred feet up. "But—"

"I will bring the food myself, Your Grace. I spent my childhood climbing the Abaddian cliffs, watching the wyverns soar over the ocean. It would be my pleasure."

Alina nodded softly in thanks.

Her guards led her through the camp, walking in a square about her, Olivian at her side. They eyed everything askance as though the evening shadows themselves might come alive and strike her down. Two Hand assassins had snuck into the camp the night before, killing twelve guards and injuring three. Had Alina not decided to spend the night in Rynvar's Rest, she may well have been dining in Achyron's halls come dawn. As it stood, the pair found the end of Savrin's blade. That, combined with the battle earlier that day, had set the whole camp's hackles on edge.

They walked past a set of House Ateres banners on the camp's western edge and up a dirt track that curved around to a sheltered flat.

There Alina found her brother along with three of his Andurii captains, Belina Louna, Mera, Luka, Amari, Joros, and the heads of each Major House with the exception of Hakari Herak, who remained in Ironcreek to protect their flank.

The group circled around four women who knelt in the centre, their hands bound. Two of Alina's Royal Guard stood behind them, Ravan and Evrian, valynas gripped in their hands.

The others greeted Alina as she moved closer, tilting her head to the side, a rage swelling in her belly. Black ink tattoos covered each woman's fingers, lines tracing down towards their hands. Wyndarii they had captured in the battle that morning. Traitors who had sided with Loren.

Not a word was spoken as Alina stood there in silence. Even Tula Vakira, who always seemed to have something to say, held her tongue, her son Oben at her side.

Alina took another step closer, Olivian matching her, never straying further than an armspan. "Why?"

The wind whistled through the flat, rasping against the rocks around them.

"Why?" Alina roared this time, allowing the fury to fuel her. "After everything we have been through, fought for, died for… Why do you turn to Loren and the empire? You are Wyndarii …"

The woman closest to Alina lifted her head and stared back, green eyes looking into Alina's. She had looked into those same green eyes in the sky above the battle only hours ago at the River Makeer, right before Rynvar tore the woman's wyvern to pieces.

"Because you will set Valtara on fire." The woman stared back at her.

"On fire? We are nearly free."

"You are either naive or stupid, Alina Ateres. You—"

Amari strode forwards and struck the woman across the face with a vicious backhand. "You are talking to your queen. Alina of House Ateres, First of the Wyndarii."

"Not my queen." Blood trickled down her lip, a bruise already showing across her cheek. She collapsed on her side, Amari's second strike making the first look like a warm hug.

Amari made to draw her sword, but Alina shook her head. "What is your name?"

"Hanal of House Okur." Hanal shifted her weight and lifted herself back to a seated position, her hands tied behind her back. "I was the rider to Tryaer before you left his body in a river."

"You flew against me. That was your choice, and so the weight of his death lies with you."

"Look what you've done." Hanal gestured at the other Wyndarii beside her and those who stood watching. "You have split us in two. Valtarans killing Valtarans while Loria watches. Do you think I want to stand by the empire's side? There is an army of forty thousand marching from Aonar. They will be here within two weeks. A fleet of a hundred ships sails from Aerilon, another two hundred from Antiquar. Valtara will be blockaded from north and south. What happened the last time Valtara declared open rebellion? My son was ripped from my breast, my firstborn, my love. What do you think they will do this time, Alina Ateres, Queen of Valtara, and First of the Wyndarii? What does a lion do to the lamb that keeps stepping on its paw? It crushes it. They will not let us live this time, *my queen.* If you have your way, Valtara will be erased from the annals. I followed you once, but I was naive. I was angry, hurt, lost."

"And what are you now? Found?" Alina shook her head. "I would rather die trying to free my home than spend a lifetime in fear and darkness. Than live in a world where they take our firstborn, where they hold a boot on our neck because they fear what would happen if they didn't. And do you know what, Hanal? They are right to fear. We will raze Achyron's Keep, and we will turn the Hot Gates into a fortress. And we will honour our oaths and march with this new Draleid. We will burn the Lorian Empire to ashes, and their banner will never fly in Valtara again."

"And what will you do when the dragons come? When they pour fire over everything you love?"

"I will fight. And I will die if needs be. But never again will I be their pet."

Any arrogance faded from Hanal's expression, her eyes holding only grief. "Hera was right then. You will die, and you will take all Valtara with you."

"Hera was a coward and a traitor who cost hundreds of Valtaran lives when she led the assault on Lostwren – against my orders. She didn't give a single fuck about your life or any Valtaran lives that day. All she cared for was her own gain, her own honour and glory. And when she learned the size of the force Loren had amassed at Achyron's Keep, she turned coward again."

Alina stood over Hanal, allowing her heart to calm. "Hanal of House Okur, for treason against the crown of Valtara and its people, I, Queen Alina Ateres, sentence you to death. Do you have any last words?"

"I pray to The Sailor and The Warrior that you are right and I am wrong."

Alina inclined her head. She drew her sword, but Olivian approached with her hand on the pommel of her own.

"Allow me, my Queen."

Alina gestured for Olivian to step back and sheath her sword. "What am I, Olivian, if I can cast the sentence but not swing the blade? I am exactly what Hera said I was. Exactly what this Wyndarii thinks I am."

Alina moved so she stood at Hanal's side and gripped the pommel of her sword with both hands. "By The Warrior and The Sailor, by blade and by blood."

Hanal didn't squirm or weep or thrash about. She simply leaned forwards and stretched out her neck. "If you do me one kindness, Queen Ateres, make it clean."

Alina hoped that in such a position, she would have the same dignity and control. And in that thinking she couldn't help but know pain at the thought of killing the woman. Valtara needed warriors with that kind of courage, that kind of strength. And yet, Hanal had betrayed them, and that betrayal had led to the deaths of hundreds. It had led to the death of Marlin Arkon.

Alina tightened her grip on the hilt, then swung. Her strike was clean, and Hanal's head came free in one swing, dropping to roll in the dirt. Her body stayed upright for a few seconds before collapsing on its side.

Alina lifted her gaze and looked to Dayne, who stared right back at her. He gave her a sharp, approving nod.

Blood dripping from the tip of her blade, Alina moved to stand before the next Wyndarii. "What is your name?"

EVEN IN THE COLD OF winter, Alina dripped sweat as she moved around the sparring pit, a long wooden staff gripped in her fists.

Alcon, Glaukos, and Savrin stood before her, each with their own staff, each bleeding and sweat-soaked. Both Olivian and Saralis of House Toth observed from the sides while the rest of her Royal Guard watched over the entranceways.

The three men circled her, trapping her between them. On a different day, she would have held her patience and waited for one of them to strike first. Men were bigger and stronger, and they knew it. In battle, whether they realised it or not, that simple fact informed everything they did when they fought a woman. It made them sloppy, careless. And that was a weakness she could take advantage of.

But it was not a different day, and Alina wasn't standing in that sparring yard to practice or to learn. She was there for release.

She bounded forwards, ducked beneath Glaukos's strike, and slammed her staff into the back of his knee as he pivoted. She twisted, leveraging her back swing and ramming the other end of her staff into the man's now-exposed belly. He reeled backwards.

Alina made to go for the killing strike but was forced to turn away a swing from Savrin's staff and then Alcon's in quick succession. The two men came at her together, not allowing her a moment to breathe as she parried their strikes one after another, twisting and turning, her muscles screaming, the rage within her blazing.

She lunged, catching them both off balance and dropping past their guard. Alina rammed the butt of her staff into Alcon's gut and then snapped it upwards into his chin. She whipped the other end towards Savrin's leg, only for him to ram his own staff into the sand and block the strike.

Alina smashed her shoulder into Savrin's chest, knocking him backwards and following up with a flurry of powerful swings. Savrin blocked each with ease but never struck back. She pushed harder, exposing herself. She cracked her staff into his left hip, then back across his jaw, into his chest, and hard as a hammer against his shoulder.

"Fight back," she growled through gritted teeth. She doubled down, driving Savrin harder, her staff a blur as she rained blow after blow after blow. Marks of black, blue, and yellow already bloomed on the man's flesh, and yet he didn't stop or yield. He let her unleash her fury with abandon and that only angered her more. She lunged forwards and shoved Savrin in the chest, knocking him back a few paces. "Hit me!"

The man simply stared back at her, blood trickling from his nose and lip. "You did what needed to be done, Alina. Your mother would have made the same choice."

Alina clenched her jaw, swallowing. She lunged again. Savrin blocked her first three strikes, then redirected her fourth, sending her stumbling off balance. She dug her foot in the sand and twisted, hammering her staff into the side of his shin.

Alina let out heavy breaths, Savrin's staff levelled against the side of her head, just resting gently against her temple.

"Emotions are only useful on the field of battle if you can control them, my queen," he said calmly.

"Savrin, if you will not spar with me, I will have to strip you from my guard. It is your responsibility not only to protect me but to ensure I am prepared to protect myself. How can I be prepared if you refuse to fight me to the fullest? Do you understand?"

"I understand, my queen."

"Then fight back!" Alina smacked Savrin's staff away with her own and bounded to her feet. She struck hard to his right leg, finding his staff instead, then again to his left arm with the same result. Twice more she hurled herself at him with all the rage and fury she could summon, but on that second strike, he blocked, then countered.

Savrin's staff collided with Alina's ribs on the left side of her body, then slammed into her jaw on the right with the force of a horse's kick.

She hit the ground like a sack of stones, blood filling her mouth, her head ringing. She spat saliva and blood into the sand, then lifted her head to see Savrin extending his hand.

Alina gripped the man's forearm and pulled herself upright, stumbling as her head spun.

"You asked me to hit you." The slightest semblance of a smile flickered on the man's lips, his shoulders twitching in an even slighter shrug.

"That I did." Alina pressed her tongue against a tooth on the right side of her mouth, overjoyed to find it wasn't loose. She stared down at the bloody pool of spit at her feet and then at Glaukos and Alcon, who had pulled back and were now watching. Olivian and Saralis were both a few steps closer, their stares hard.

"I'm sorry." Alina licked the blood from her teeth.

"There will not come a day when your need for apology outweighs my own, Your Grace. But what is given is accepted. If I may?"

Alina nodded.

"Today I watched a queen with the strength to make the hard choices and the heart to feel the consequences. In my experience, those are two qualities rarely found in the same soul. And when they are, one is often burned away by the other. I would counsel, if you care to hear it, that you not allow either side to die. This was only the first hard choice of many. A true queen does not rule over her people, she serves them. She makes the hard choice and bears the weight and the cost so they do not have to."

"STOP WRIGGLING." DAYNE UNDID THE buckles of Mera's cuirass. He peeled the armour away from her skin, the blood dried and tacky.

Mera hissed, slapping at his hand. And as she did, Audin rose from where he lay against the rock wall of the Rest, a trembling rumble resonating from his throat.

"I'm not the one who sliced her open." Dayne turned to glare at the wyvern, regretting his decision as soon as his gaze fell on the maw of savage teeth that stared back at him.

The wyvern blew a puff of warm air from his nostrils, the smell of blood and fresh meat blowing over Dayne.

"And you," he said, turning back to Mera, who was pulling her blood-soaked undershirt free. "Do you remember back in Stormshold, when you sewed my shin? This is going to be sweet revenge."

Mera frowned at him, peeling the undershirt from her body, strings of part-dried blood pulling tight and snapping. The wound ran along her right side, just below her arm and along her ribs. Long and angry. A nasty piece of work, given to her by one of the treacherous Wyndarii's javelins that morning.

"Sit." He gestured to the rickety wooden chair he'd hoisted up to the Rest only two days prior. The sight of her truly hurt cut all the mirth from his heart. He didn't know what he would do if he lost her. The thought didn't bear considering. She was a Wyndarii, just as his mother had been. It was her purpose to fight for Valtara, just as it was his. And as much as he wanted to keep her safe, he would never take her purpose from her. That was a hard thing for him to accept, but he understood it. She was a warrior, just as he was.

Dayne snatched the satchel of dressing and catgut from atop the blanket rolls near the wall. He produced a small tin of brimlock sap and a cloth from within. He puffed out his cheeks at the sharp, pungent stench of the sap but drew a deep breath and proceeded to kneel beside Mera and clean the wound.

He wasn't quite as deft a hand as Mera when it came to stitching a wound, but he took his time, ensuring the catgut pulled tight and the wound was neatly closed. In truth, he was more used to working on his own wounds than somebody else's.

"Try to be more careful next time." Dayne brushed Mera's naked shoulder gently before grabbing a clean tunic from atop the blanket rolls in the corner and tossing it to her. "It's easier on my heart when it's you stitching me back together instead of the other way around."

"I'll make sure to keep that in mind." Mera slid her arms into the tunic, grunting as she pulled it over her head. "Do you have any other sensibilities you'd like me to pander to, oh mighty Dayne Ateres?"

Audin pressed his snout into Mera's shoulder, a soft purr vibrating in his chest. It was such a strange thing to see a creature so powerful and vicious behave so gently.

"I'm fine." Mera rested a hand on either side of the wyvern's jaws, fingers brushing across his deep red scales. She pressed her forehead against the tip of his snout, exhaling softly. "You're like a mother hen. Go and eat. I'll be fine."

The wyvern gave Mera a deep growl in response, his lips curling, nostrils flaring. Mera growled back, pressing her head harder against his.

"Go," she repeated.

Audin's breath blew Mera's hair back over her shoulders. He pressed his snout into her once more, then turned and leapt from the edge of the Rest, dropping like a stone before swooping back into view and soaring over the camp.

"He's a little needy, isn't he?" Dayne said.

Mera snapped herself around and stared at Dayne as though he were an idiot of the highest order.

"What?"

"Did you really just say that out loud without realising the irony in it?" She moved closer to Dayne and cupped his hands in hers. "You know, there was a point years ago when I believed you had died and your spirit had found me again through Audin. That you held on and found a way to watch over me. He is stubborn, courageous, gentle, protective... irritating at times. You are one and the same."

Dayne brushed a strand of bloody hair from Mera's face. He could have looked into her eyes until time broke, and he'd die happy.

"What are you staring at?" She narrowed her gaze in mock suspicion.

Dayne let go of Mera's hand and cupped her cheeks. "The one thing that keeps my heart warm."

He turned and walked towards the back of the Rest, his gaze trailing along the scratch marks in the rock that Audin had carved. He tilted his head back and fixed his gaze on a spot on the back wall.

"Dayne. What's wrong?"

"Nothing's wrong." He let out a long sigh, then reached into his pocket, feeling the dulled edges of the hard wooden box. Even in the flames of battle, his heart never beat as furiously as it did in that moment. His throat constricted, breaths fluttering.

"There is clearly something wrong, Dayne. Talk to me."

Dayne shook his head, still looking at the back wall. "When I was gone all those years, not a day passed that I didn't think of you, that I didn't think of coming home."

"Dayne, I know. You don't have to—"

"I would replay the night I left again, and again, and again. I made the right choice. I know I did because we both stand here now. But that doesn't mean it didn't cut me so deep I still bleed."

"We've already spoken about this, Dayne. Where is this coming from? I don't care that you left. I only care that you came back."

Dayne turned, staring into Mera's eyes, his own brimming with tears.

"Why are you crying?" Genuine worry bled into Mera's voice.

He looked at the ground, his hand trembling in his pocket. "You are the fire that kept my heart warm on the coldest of nights. You are the reason I want to be a better man. I wasted so many of our years. Twelve long years that I could have felt the warmth of your skin, heard the sound of your voice, built a family... So many years gone."

Mera leaned forwards and wiped the tears from Dayne's cheeks. "I'm here, Dayne. And I'm not going anywhere. We can't take back time lost. We can only look forward."

Dayne pressed his forehead to Mera's, then stepped back. "Mera Vardas, you are everything that is good about me. You are warm when I am cold, you are right when I am so very wrong, you are strong when I am only ever a moment from breaking. You are the light that keeps my ship from crashing against the rocks, the star that guides me home. I have wasted so much of my life not looking into your eyes. And I refuse to waste another second."

Dayne dropped to one knee and pulled the small wooden box from his pocket, prying it open. Inside, on a bed of orange silk, was a gleaming gold ring, wyverns etched into its curves, small gleaming sunstones set into their eyes. "I will never deserve your heart, but I vow to do everything I can to earn your love from this day until my last day. Would you please make the mistake of taking me as your husband?"

Mera stared down at Dayne, her mouth ajar, eyes wide, hands shaking. "Dayne Ateres, get off your knees."

She leaned down and hoisted him up by his arms, kissing him deeply.

"Is that a yes?"

"I've waited for you to ask that question for over twelve years. Of course it's a yes. It has always been a yes. You are mine, and I am yours. Now give me my ring."

Tears welled in Dayne's eyes as he laughed and slid the golden ring onto Mera's hand. He could not remember another time in his life when he'd cried from happiness.

"It's beautiful."

"I asked Senya to have it made by the same jeweller who made Alina's crown. She gave it to me the day she died."

"I will cherish it forever and pass it on to our own son."

Dayne stared at Mera.

She took his hand and placed it on her belly. "I am with child, Dayne."

For the second time that night, and only the second time in his life, Dayne cried tears of joy. He wrapped his arms around Mera and pulled her close, his fingers tangling in her hair, his tears dripping onto the crown of her head. "Are you… are you sure?"

Mera slapped him on the shoulder. "Of course I'm sure, you idiot."

"You say such sweet things." Dayne pulled away, then planted a kiss on Mera's forehead. Then another one, and another one, continuing until she pushed him away, laughing.

"I'm going to be a father?"

"You're going to be a father."

"A son?"

"Would it matter?"

Dayne shook his head. "A son, a daughter… None of it matters. My child. I love them already. Is that even possible?"

Mera nodded, tears rolling down her soft cheeks.

"How long have you known?"

"I've not bled for two moons now. And I can feel the changes. I was thinking Ilya if it's a girl, Arkin if it's a boy."

"I would love that."

"Thought you might."

Dayne pulled his hands away from Mera, fighting the urge to scratch his skin.

"Dayne, what's wrong?"

"I just…" Images of the night attack on Ankar flashed in Dayne's mind. The blood. The carnage. He had done what he'd needed to do, had become what he had needed to become to ensure Valtara's freedom, but that didn't absolve him, it didn't clean the blood from his hands. And Ankar had just been one of many… One thousand four hundred and sixty-three. That was how many men and women had died at Dayne's hands. What kind of man was he to think he could raise a child?

"I'm not interrupting, am I? It feels like I'm interrupting."

Dayne let out a long sigh and ran his hands through his hair. He looked past Mera to see Belina standing at the mouth of the Rest, shrouded in darkness, her face lit only by the setting sun that drifted in behind her and bounced off the rock.

"What is it, Belina?"

"Well, that's not a very nice way to greet a friend who might have just saved your life." Belina shrugged as she always did.

"Belina, I'm not in the mood. What is it…" Dayne brushed his hand against Mera's shoulder and squinted. "Belina… is that a hand… in your hand?"

CHAPTER SIXTY

A MESSAGE

19th Day of the Blood Moon

West of Achyron's Keep – Winter, Year 3081 After Doom

"I found him following you after the executions." Belina stood with her arms folded, a man kneeling at her feet with a rope tied around his throat and tethered to the trunk of a thin tree. He was awake, but barely, his head lolling. "Waited a while, watched him. Had a little conversation."

Dayne looked down at the man, arms cleaved at the wrists, the wounds cauterised, red and raw. "Why does he have no hands?"

"I cut off one when he reached for his knife. And then… well, have you ever tried to put manacles on a one-handed man? Not easy. Impossible some might say."

"That doesn't explain the second hand."

"If you think about it…"

"I'm thinking about it."

"Well, if I left the other hand, he could have just untied himself. I had no choice."

Dayne pinched the bridge of his nose. "There were so many choices."

"Look. You weren't there. I made a decision, and I stand by it. None of that is important right now." Belina knelt beside the man and patted his cheek. "Tell him why you were following him."

The man grunted. "I was… I… I was sent by High Lord Loren."

"For what purpose? To kill me while I slept?"

"No." The man leaned his head back. "He wants you to meet him. He says if you're not at the bank of the River Makeer tomorrow, by sunset, he will kill your brother."

"Baren?" Dayne looked from Mera to Belina. "He's lying. Baren is in the North. He's in Berona."

"No." The man pushed himself backwards and up against the tree. "He's not."

"How can you expect—"

"He's not lying, Dayne." Belina stared into Dayne's eyes in a way she rarely did, and Dayne's heart sank. She swung a small cloth sack around from her side and reached in to produce what looked to be something akin to a thick piece of parchment, its edges rough and jagged. "When I found him, he was carrying this."

Belina reached out her hand, letting the parchment catch the moonlight. The sigil of House Ateres was marked in black ink across the centre. It was only when Dayne reached out to touch it that he realised what the parchment truly was: a patch of flesh carved from Baren's chest where the sigil had been tattooed over his heart.

Dayne took the piece of carved flesh into his hands, the blood long dried. He drew in slow breaths, then knelt before the handless messenger. "Is my brother alive?"

The man nodded. "I only saw him the once, right before I left. That was three days ago. He was alive then."

Dayne swallowed hard. "And Loren wants me to meet him at the River Makeer?"

"By the old fort on the east bank. Alone."

Dayne nodded slowly. "Is this how you thought this night would go? Did you think you could just walk into this camp carrying flesh from my brother's chest, wave it in my face, and walk away?"

"I'm just a messenger. You can't—"

"I can't what? You are no messenger. A messenger comes with words. You come with a piece of my younger brother and a tongue painted with threats. No." Dayne stood, turned to Belina, grabbed a knife from her belt, then dropped back down and drove the blade into the man's stomach. The man gasped and grabbed at the blade with his arms, the blood flowing around the steel. "You will die here, slowly. You will feel the pain my brother felt as this sigil was carved from his chest. I have no mercy for the likes of you."

As Dayne stood once more, Mera grabbed him by the shoulders. "You're not going."

"He's my brother, Mera. I won't leave him there."

"It's a trap. Loren is just going to kill you on sight."

"Of course it's a trap. But no." Dayne shook his head. "Loren gains nothing from that. If he kills me, this army will march on Achyron's Keep. Thousands will die. Loren, for all that he is, doesn't want more Valtarans dead. He wants control. That's what he's always wanted. He knows I will come for Baren. He will keep me alive to use me, to force Alina to stand down."

"Then why would you do *exactly* what he wants? Dayne, this is madness."

"Because Loren thinks he's smarter than he is. He thinks he knows me, and he doesn't. He has no idea what I am."

"Dayne—"

"No." Dayne rested one hand on Mera's shoulder, the other on her belly. "I will *never* leave my family again. Never. And I refuse to allow my child to live a life like we did. It's all different now, Mera. There is no more room for mercy, no more room for mistakes." Dayne moved in closer and stared into Mera's eyes. "Do you trust me?"

"With my life."

ALINA LEANED ON THE TABLE at the back of the command tent, her thumbs tucked inside her fists. Her jaw trembled. Savrin and Olivian stood at her side, while Mera and Belina were on the opposite side of the table.

"And you just let him go?" She drew a sharp breath through her nose, slowly out through her mouth. "Just let him walk away…"

"His mind was set, Alina. You know what Dayne is like."

"How could you let him go?" Alina hadn't felt this way since she was a girl, since she'd realised Dayne was gone and wasn't coming back. She hated it to her core.

"Alina—"

"Loren destroyed my family! He hung my parents' bodies on hooks until the birds picked the bones clean. And now he will take Dayne too?"

Alina roared, unleashing the fury within her heart. She slammed her fists into the table, cracking the wood, then swept her hands across the surface, knocking everything to the ground, paper flapping in the air, stone markers thumping into the dirt. And when it all settled, she just stood there, her throat tight, each breath shaking. "He is my brother, Mera. I cannot lose him again. I only just got him back. *We* only just got him back. And you let him walk right into Loren's hands like the fucking idiot he is? For what? For Baren? No. I will not allow it. That monster cannot have any more of the people I love."

"Alina, where are you going?" Mera grabbed Alina's arm as she made to storm from the tent.

"I'm taking Rynvar to the skies, and I'm going to stop my brother before he gets himself killed. If we're going to die, we're going to do it side by side, fighting." She held Mera's gaze. "I will not let him die alone with Loren standing over him. He's spent too long alone. I will not allow it."

Alina turned back to towards the tent flap, finding Belina Louna standing between her and the exit.

"You will not lose him," the woman said, her stare unflinching.

"And what do you know? *Belina Louna.* You are not Valtaran. You are not of this House. Why are you even here?" As soon as the words had left her lips, Alina regretted them. Her anger was not at this woman, or at Dayne, but at the world, at the gods and whatever unseen powers deigned to rip away everything and everyone she loved.

Belina remained silent for a few heartbeats, then spoke with as soft a voice as Alina had ever heard. "I know that there is nothing in this world that means more to Dayne than his family – than you and Mera and Baren. You and I do not know each other well, but I know that when you're angry, you tuck your thumbs into your fists."

Alina looked down at her hands and yanked her thumbs free.

"I know that your favourite smell is that of freshly peeled orange. I know that when you were a child, you wore a sapphire pendant around your neck that your mother gave you. I know that you used to climb the trees at the farm in Myrefall and then realise you couldn't climb back down, and your father would send Dayne to get you. I know that you had seen twelve summers when your mother and father were killed."

Belina stepped past her, bent down, and collected the loose sheets of parchment and a small map from the floor, laying them on the table.

"I know all these things because Dayne never stopped talking about you. For twelve years, all I heard was 'Alina, Mera, Baren. Alina, Mera, Baren.' He loves you with a ferocity I've never seen in my life. He loves you in a way I had always wished my family would have loved me. And that love is what made me love him. Now, seeing as I know so much about you, let me tell you a little bit about me.

"I was brought here from Narvona as a child by my father. My father who murdered my mother. My father who trained me to kill from the moment I could hold a knife. He abused me, he beat me, he tortured me, all to make me 'stronger'. He sold my life to the Hand when I was twelve. I was raised in blood, to kill without question, to not be human, but to be a tool, a weapon. Dayne broke me free of that, and he showed me a kindness I didn't deserve. And I would kill the gods themselves if it meant protecting him. I believe all three of us have that in common."

Alina held her tears at bay, clenched her jaw, and shook her head softly. "All this and you let him walk to his death?"

"That man never does anything without a plan."

"And what is this plan of his, as he walks right into Loren's jaws?"

"Us." Belina looked from Mera to Alina. "The three of us. The three people who would give anything and everything to keep him alive. He wants you to assault the keep."

"Oh, that's all. And how do we go about doing that? Because last I checked, we were still outnumbered by nearly twenty thousand and Aeson is yet to arrive with his promised reinforcements."

"It will take Dayne at least a day to reach the river and another two for him to make the journey to Achyron's Keep. Loren will attempt to use Dayne as leverage to force your surrender. Once he does, we can drag out negotiations to buy time. With any luck, Aeson will arrive before we have need to attack."

"Luck is neither something we have much of nor something I wish to rely on. We are now in the same situation we have been for weeks, but without Dayne at our side."

"No, we are not. Now we have Dayne on the inside and the warriors in your army have something very real to fight for. I'm not sure if you've noticed or not, but your people love him."

Alina closed her eyes, stood back, and put her face into her hands. "Why does he do this to me?"

It wasn't Belina who spoke next, but Mera. "Because he is Dayne Ateres. Because, for better or worse, there is no world in which he would leave his brother in the hands of the man who killed your parents. And no matter what you say, no matter how much anger you feel in your veins, neither would you. Do you think I wanted to let him go? You're not the only one who waited all those years for him to come home, thinking he was dead, thinking… He has a thousand flaws, but he is my world, Alina. *My whole world.* The father of my child, the love of my life. I would give every drop of blood in my veins just to hear his voice one last time. Now are you going to help me knock down the walls of Achyron's Keep, or will I have to take the Wyndarii and do it myself?"

Alina's breath caught in her throat. "Father of your child?"

Mera's expression softened, and she held up her left hand. For a moment Alina had no idea what the woman was trying to show her, until she saw the sparkle of an orange gemstone on her finger.

"Mera…" Alina took Mera's hand into her own. A beautiful, ornate golden ring sat on her finger, with engravings of wyverns twisting about it. "It's beautiful."

"It is. Now, can we please go and get my idiot husband before he gets himself killed?"

Alina nodded slowly. "If it were any of us in there, Dayne would sack the keep on his own. It was always going to come to this." She drew a long breath and exhaled sharply. "Let's burn it down. Let's burn the whole thing to the ground."

"Good. I was hoping you'd say that." Belina turned and made to slip out the door.

"Where are you going?"

"Me? I'm going with Dayne."

"What?"

"It will take you time to break camp and get the army marching. If I leave now, I can catch up with him."

"And what do you intend to do?"

"Kill anyone or anything that tries to harm him. And with any luck, we can open the gates from the inside. That might make the siege a little easier. It's all part of the plan."

"And how will we know when you're in position?"

"Oh, you'll know."

"No, we're not playing that game. How will we know?"

"Fuck. I'll set something on fire. Something big."

CHAPTER SIXTY-ONE

TICKING CLOCK

20th Day of the Blood Moon

Southeast of Camylin – Winter, Year 3081 After Doom

The thunder of Drunir's hooves rippled through Dann as the horse galloped at full stretch. He hovered over the saddle, the horse's body moving in free flow beneath him, his white wood bow in his left hand, his right hand on the reins. Ahead, the columns of smoke rose above the hill, screams piercing the still morning.

Dann risked a quick glance over his shoulder. The fifty scouts who rode with him were quite a distance behind, Erik among them. Their horses were no match for Drunir in the open plains. Even the six Dvalin Angan in the forms of giant white stags couldn't keep pace, each galloping with an elf on their back, Vaeril at their head, Lyrei just behind him. Dann's head told him to slow and let them catch up, but his heart told him that every second wasted would be a life lost on the other side of that hill.

They'd been scouting ahead of the main army, attempting to gauge the siege at Camylin, when they'd spotted the smoke and heard the screams.

"Faster," Dann shouted. As though the horse had been holding back, Drunir lunged forwards, his stride opening, his hooves tearing the ground apart.

The village on the other side of the hill was in flames. Men and women fought Uraks with whatever they had been able to find: pitchforks, axes, knives, staffs. A handful were armoured in leather and gambeson, but most wore nothing but tunics and trousers. The Uraks ripped them apart.

As Drunir galloped down the hill, two of those monstrous Bloodmarked came into view amidst the flames, their dark claws tearing through flesh and bone.

Dann drew a sharp breath and brought his bow to bear. He slipped an arrow from the quiver he'd strapped to Drunir's saddle, took a half-second to pick a target, and loosed.

The arrow punched into the side of an Urak's head in the middle of the creature's downswing. The beast stumbled sideways, then dropped.

Drunir responded to every shift in Dann's weight, moving as though his body were an extension of Dann's own. They swerved to the right, bounding over two bodies in the dirt.

Dann nocked, drew, and loosed twice in quick succession. Two more beasts fell, and the five men who had been fighting them turned to look at Dann, their expressions painted in surprise and shock.

He looked ahead to see the thick of the fighting lay in the village's centre. Drunir wouldn't be able to manoeuvre in there. He swung his leg over the saddle and dismounted, grabbing Drunir by the reins. "Go."

The horse nickered, flapping its muzzle at him.

"Those things will tear you apart if you can't move around them. Go." Dann slapped the horse in the flank, then turned and loosed another arrow into an Urak's heart, but the beast continued to charge, two more joining it.

Dann turned to the group of men who now stood at his side. "Go for the heart or the head. If you can't, cut their legs from under them. Bring them down, then kill them on the ground."

"Who are you?" An older man with grey-black hair and thin wiry arms stared at Dann's armour, his gaze fixing on the emblem of the white dragon on his breast.

"A man with a bow." Dann broke into a run, the men following after. It was at that point he realised he'd left his quiver strapped to Drunir's saddle and decided that was something he would never tell Tarmon or Erik.

Hooves sounded over his left shoulder, and he turned to see Drunir galloping towards him, white-and-grey-dappled coat glistening in the light of the burning buildings.

"I thought I told you to run?" Dann snatched five arrows from the quiver without stopping, and Drunir charged onwards.

Dann's heart stopped for a moment as a massive Urak with pale brown skin and a black spear in its hand came hurtling from the thick of the fighting and launched itself at the horse.

Drunir reared onto his hind legs and smashed a front hoof clean into the Urak's face. The beast dropped backwards like a stone, a gaping wound of shattered bone and blood where the horse's hoof had caved in its cheek.

As two more of the creatures charged towards Drunir, Dann howled, "Forward!"

He drove four of the arrows into the ground before him, then nocked the fifth, drawing and loosing in a fluid motion. He caught an Urak in the eye. The creature howled and stumbled backwards, only for Drunir to kick out with his back feet. The horse kicked the Urak with such power that the beast was lifted from its feet, and once it hit the ground, it didn't get back up.

Emboldened, the five men charged past Dann, axes, pitchforks, and spears raised. He snatched a second arrow from the ground and loosed it into the second Urak's throat. The men fell upon the beast, hacking and stabbing until it went limp.

As Dann leaned down to retrieve his third arrow, the thundering of hooves rose over the din of the battle. Lyrei, Erik, and Vaeril rode at the head of the cavalry as the horses and Angan flooded into the village and tore through the Uraks.

Vaeril leapt from the back of a white stag with all the grace of a kat, hit the ground, and rolled. He lifted his hands, and the earth cracked around him, spikes of solid rock rising and streaking through the air, finding a home in the chest of a Bloodmarked. The elf pulled that shimmering silver sword from its scabbard and drove it deep into the Bloodmarked's gut, smoke pluming from the runes in the creature's chest.

Lyrei planted an arrow in the Bloodmarked's skull before three more skewered its neck, and the light of its runes died.

Erik led the rest of the cavalry through the centre. He swung his blade through an Urak's face, opening the creature's jaw from left to right, then drove the steel down through the eye of a second, dragging it free in a spray of blood.

Dann nocked his third arrow and loosed it into the temple of the Urak closest to Erik.

But even as the missile plunged into the beast's skull, the second Bloodmarked ripped apart two villagers and slammed its shoulder into Erik's horse. The horse screamed as it flopped on its side, unable to keep upright.

Erik leapt from his mount's back before it hit the ground. He crashed down into the dirt, rolling and pulling himself to his feet.

Dann charged, snatching up and nocking his fourth arrow as he went. An Urak lunged at him from the right, taking a woman's head from her shoulders with a sweep of its black steel sword without breaking stride.

Dann twisted and drew back his bowstring, only for an arrow to lodge itself in the centre of the Urak's skull. He turned to see Lyrei nod at him from atop a white stag.

The Bloodmarked sent a shockwave of fire and earth through the street, everything in its path bursting into blazing flames, the ground cracking. Four of Dann's scouts were caught in the fire, their screams echoing.

Erik, Vaeril, and several others hurled themselves at the Bloodmarked, carving open its thick hide, black smoke pluming from its runes. One swipe of the creature's obsidian claws opened two chests and a second turned a woman's face to nothing but mangled bone and blood.

Arcs of lightning streaked from Vaeril's fingertips, but the Bloodmarked took the strike head-on, strips of flesh tearing free. The runes carved into its skin burned with a bright crimson light, and the beast unleashed a guttural roar. It drove its claws through a soldier's chest, then sent a plume of fire washing over three more.

Dann sprinted forwards and loosed his arrow into the Bloodmarked's throat, but it barely flinched, as though the arrow was nothing more than a fly.

As Dann reached for the quiver at his hip – the one that was not there – something crashed into his back, and he slammed into the ground, his head cracking off something solid. Blood streamed into Dann's eyes and over his lips. He shook his head and wiped his face as he pushed himself up. He'd lost his grip on his bow. He rolled over onto his back just in time to watch the Urak standing over him drive its spear down.

Dann clasped his hands on the weapon, the blade slicing along his palms. He howled in pain, twisting and turning the blade left, forcing it into his shoulder instead of his chest. He swore he could feel the steel scraping bone, peeling open his skin and carving through muscle.

A neigh more akin to a roar rang out, and Drunir slammed into the Urak's side.

The Urak hit the ground hard, and the horse leapt over Dann, trampling the creature, hooves smashing down over and over. Drunir pulverised the Urak's chest, splattering Dann's face with blood and bits of bone.

"Need a hand?" Erik appeared over Dann.

Dann bit back a grunt, the steel tip of the spear pinning him in place. His shoulder screamed in pain, but he didn't want to give Erik the satisfaction. "Actually, I was thinking of staying here a while," he said through gritted teeth. "It's quite comfortable."

"Hmm." Erik wrapped his hands around the spear shaft and pulled it free.

"Gah!" Dann lurched upwards, the steel slicing him open for a second time, scraping his armour. He took Erik's hand and pulled himself to his feet. "Could you not have been a little gentler?"

"I can put it back in if you like?"

Drunir leaned forwards and nickered, pressing his muzzle into Dann's cheek.

"You should have listened to me." Dann pulled his injured arm close, blood flowing out over the steel of his spaulder, the gashes on his hands flaring in pain.

The horse blew a long breath of warm air over Dann's face, flapping his lips.

"Fine. Thank you. I don't know how I'd survive without you."

A group of the villagers approached, battered and bruised, many limping, others burnt or bleeding. Perhaps fifty in total, three hounds walking between them and eyeing the Angan askance.

A short woman in a torn, blood-stained dress decorated with a spear in her left hand stepped from their number. She didn't look much older than Dann. Her gaze moved from Dann to one of the elves who rode a Dvalin Angan.

"Thank you." She planted the butt of her spear into the earth.

"It is our honour. Though I wish we had come sooner." Dann looked about at the burning village, the slaughtered horses in the street, the butchered sheep in pens. Everything these people had called home was now dead. "The bulk of our army marches behind us. If you wish it, we will escort you west. There is a settlement there on the coast. It is where we are headed."

"This is all we've ever known." The woman glanced back at the rest of the villagers, her gaze lingering.

"You need not make your choice now," Vaeril said. "We ride northwest to

Camylin, but I will stay and tend to your wounds. When the rest of our forces arrive, you may choose then."

"You ride to Camylin?" An older man with a thick grey beard moved forwards.

"Aye." Erik raised a curious eyebrow. "What have you heard?"

"Trader passed through last night, said Camylin had fallen with the setting sun. And that the Uraks move west."

"West?" Dann's heart quickened. "You're sure?"

"Sure as I am the grass is green."

Dann turned to Vaeril and showed him his sliced palms. "Can you do something about these and my shoulder? I'll send a messenger back to Tarmon and the others, tell them to quicken their pace, then ride for Camylin."

By the time Dann dismounted on the plains before Camylin, the sun was at its peak in the sky, its light blending with that of the crimson moon. The first time he had laid eyes on the city, he'd marvelled at the red slate rooves, the enormous walls, and the massive cylindrical towers. It was the first city he'd ever seen, the only time he'd ever gone further than Ölm.

Now those red rooves were shattered and broken, smoke billowing into the sky. Whole sections of the walls had collapsed, and only three towers still stood. It was a ruin.

Dry grass crunched beneath Erik's feet as he moved to stand by Dann's side, Lyrei with him. "Heraya embrace them."

"Camylin held tens of thousands of people." Dann stared at the smoke rising from the destroyed city, the ruins of the central keep still towering above all else. "Surely some of them made it out alive."

"Perhaps," Erik said. He let out a long sigh. "But they were surrounded on all sides, under siege for months…" He looked to Dann. "If the Uraks that did this are marching west…"

"Then we must march faster. We're a day behind." Dann rolled his neck, pressing his fingers against the puncture in his spaulder. Vaeril had knitted the wound and mended the bone, but the stiffness remained, an ache in his muscles. At least now he would have a scar to match the other shoulder.

Dann turned and swung himself into Drunir's saddle. "All this is for nothing if Salme is already gone by the time we reach it."

Erik climbed into his own mount's saddle, his gaze still fixed on the smoking city. "I'd hoped Calen might have been with us by now."

"You and I both."

CHAPTER SIXTY-TWO

PAST AND PRESENT

20th Day of the Blood Moon
Aravell – Winter, Year 3081 After Doom

Ella clasped her hands behind her back while Faenir sat alert at her side, ears pricked. She stood on one of the many plateaus of white stone that overlooked the city of Aravell. Now that she actually had the time to stop and look, the place was like something out of a dream, and even then she didn't think her dreams had the ability to conjure something of such beauty. Endless valleys and streams and waterfalls, all blending seamlessly with the city that looked as though it had been grown rather than built. The dense forest of the Darkwood bore down on the city's limits on all sides, looming like a spectre, the shadow that surrounded the light.

Staring out over the tranquillity, it was difficult to imagine that the world outside this place was at war. But it was. She had seen it with her own eyes. She had seen the battle at the Three Sisters, seen the elves in their golden armour, seen the Uraks tear Farrenmill apart. She had seen more death since leaving The Glade than she'd ever thought possible. And now, resting in the sky, the moon was as red and ominous as it had been the night of the battle for Aravell.

The Blood Moon. The thing the bards had told wicked tales of for as long as she could remember. Perhaps the tale of this Age would be told a thousand years in the future. She wondered what they would call it.

To Ella's left, Chora Sarn tapped on the wheel of her chair. The woman let out a long, frustrated sigh.

Ella glanced towards Chora out of the corner of her eye but said nothing. They had already exchanged more than a few sharp words over the past few days as the leaders of the varying factions throughout Illyanara had started to arrive at Aravell. Queen Uthrían and King Galdra had asked Ella to join the welcoming party in Calen's stead. At first she had been unsure what reason they had for such a request. The obvious answer was that she was his kin, or perhaps they thought her strong or capable or even just necessary.

But upon the arrival of the first faction leader, it had become clear that they had done so in an attempt to weaken Chora's position. As a Rakina, she clearly saw herself as Calen's natural second in this situation, something that Ella's presence alone refuted. Ella had no taste for being used, but if she could help Calen, she would.

"Chora." Therin looked out over the city as he spoke, not turning to look at the woman, who continued to tap on the wheel.

"What?"

Therin frowned.

"Calen should be here." Chora bit at her cheek, continuing to tap away at her wheel.

"We must deal with the situation as it is. He will be here when he is here," Therin said. Ella looked past Chora to the elf. Therin Eiltris, the legendary bard. It felt as though barely a few months had passed since she'd last heard him weave a story in The Gilded Dragon. The story of The Order and The Fall, and of Fane Mortem. It was the strangest thing to find the elf here, of all places, entangled in everything that was happening. None of it made sense, and she'd not had a chance to ask him.

"He should never have left in the first place."

"What's done is done, Chora."

"And what if his broken corpse lies in Ilnaen as we speak? What if his blood runs into the same sands that drank that of my brothers and sisters? What then, Therin?"

"Quiet, the both of you," Ella snapped. Faenir turned his head, a low rumble in his throat. He pressed himself to Ella's side.

Chora turned her chair to face Ella. "I've had headaches that have lasted longer than you've been alive. You may be Calen's sister, but that means little here. Watch your tongue."

Ella pressed her tongue into the back of her bottom teeth. She lowered her voice to a whisper. "I cannot express how little I care for what you think. I don't know you. But you speak of my brother like he is your property. As though his death is the end of your plans and that is all it is. So for what little I know, I like you even less. But more importantly, *they* are listening. So *be* quiet."

Ella flickered her gaze towards the three elven Ephori who also occupied the platform, along with the other three Rakina who had accompanied Chora. Ella had learned quite quickly that she would do well to mind her words in Aravell. And after meeting with Queen Uthrían and King Galdra, it was clear that beneath all the fine words and pleasantries, they would do anything to get what they wanted.

Chora followed Ella's stare, then gave a soft nod. The muscles in her jaw twitched, and she looked out over the edge of the plateau for a moment. "I do not think of him as my property," Chora whispered so that only Ella could hear. "I care for him, believe it or not. I don't want to see him added to the bodies at Ilnaen. But he also has a responsibility that comes with the power he possesses."

"Hmmm." There was something in Chora's voice that told Ella the woman wasn't lying, but Ella wasn't in the mood to admit that.

"You remind me of your mother." Therin had walked around and now stood at Ella's right shoulder.

"What did you know of my mother?"

"That will require a little more time than we have here. We can talk on it tonight. There is a lot you don't know."

"So everyone keeps telling me, but then they rarely tell me the things I don't know."

Therin chuckled, stroking at his chin. "You have that same fire in you."

"What do we know of this Aryana Torval?" Chora interrupted, eying Ella askance as she spoke. Ella got the feeling the woman wasn't used to being on the other end of a chastisement.

"Very little, I'm afraid," Therin answered. "From the reports she's fierce, forthright, and brazen. She leads from the front, and she's already won her fair share of victories. Against Lorians, Uraks, and other factions. She and Castor Kai together command as many swords as the other factions combined, followed by Tukul Unger. And there is no love lost between them."

The High Lord of Illyanara had arrived the night before last, along with an escort of some fifty riders. From what Ella had gathered, the man had been presumed dead following the razing of Argona. His irritation at travelling so far only to find Calen absent had been clear, which had set Chora off on her tirade.

Footsteps slapped against stone, and Ella peered over the plateau's parapet to see a young man in a dark purple tunic with the sigil of the white dragon stitched into the left breast come bounding up the path. He stopped at the entrance to the plateau, exchanging words with the Highguard stationed there, then sprinted through to face Ella and the others.

The young man dragged in long breaths, sweat glistening on his brow. He looked from Chora to Therin and then to Ella, clearly unsure who to address.

"Out with it then." Chora rolled her hand in the air, gesturing for the young man to speak.

"Commander Gaeleron approaches with Aryana Torval and her retinue, my lords." The young man couldn't have seen any more than fifteen summers, his face bright and innocent, his eyes panicked. When Ella was fifteen, she'd spent her time helping her mother pick berries and herbs and whatever else was needed. She'd drunk mead in The Gilded Dragon and danced until the moon and the sun traded places. She'd been happy, and life had been simple. She pitied him.

"Very good." Chora smiled and nodded, her earlier irritation seeming to vanish in an instant. "You did well, Joen. Please wait over there in case you are needed. There'll be extra sweetcakes waiting for you at supper."

"Yes… Rakina." Joen nodded, his mind still clearly mulling over as to whether he had used the correct honorific or not. The word 'Rakina' only ever reminded Ella of Farda… of how he had described what it was to lose his dragon, Shinyara. *"Everything lost meaning after Shinyara died… and with her she took my pain, my love, and my happiness…"*

She hated how those words pulled at her heart. He had no right to her sadness, no right to her pity.

Not long after, a procession marched up the long path around the plateau, banners raised and flapping. Ten warriors in bright steel plate with Calen's sigil on their chests and purple cloaks on their backs marched at the front and fanned out to the left and right.

Those were followed by twice that number of Aravell Highguard with long glaives in their fists, armoured in silver plate with green cloaks emblazoned with three white trees.

Next came Gaeleron and the city's steward, Halmír.

A woman walked at their side, five men behind her in dark leathers with what looked to be some kind of four-legged eagle painted in white and red across their chests. Was that what a gryphon looked like? Ella had never seen one of the creatures, but she'd heard a few stories.

The woman, who Ella assumed was Aryana Torval, was far younger than Ella had anticipated. Perhaps a similar age to Ella herself. Two long scars ran horizontally across her neck – claw marks by the looks of them – and her nose was just as broken as Ella's.

Halmír stepped forwards and delivered the same over the top introduction he had given upon the arrival of each faction leader, but one that paled in comparison to what she knew the Ephorí would give once Aryana was introduced to Uthrían and Galdra.

"May I also introduce you to Chora Sarn, representative of the Rakina present here in Aravell. Ella Bryer, kin of the Draleid, Calen Bryer, and his representative in his stead."

Halmír once again refrained from even mentioning Therin's existence. There was a noticeable coldness between Therin and essentially every other elf in the city with few exceptions. She supposed she would add the 'why' of that to the list of questions she would ask him that night.

When Halmír was finished spewing excessive pleasantries, one of the men bearing the white gryphon emblem began to introduce Aryana, but the woman raised a hand and took a step towards Therin.

"And who, may I ask, are you?" Her voice was soft as silk. "It seems you are the only one here without a name, and so I will make an exchange. Mine for yours."

Therin smiled at that. "A fine deal. I am Therin Eiltris, bard."

"Bard? You must be the most skilled bard in all Epheria to be standing here." Aryana laughed, shaking her head. In those brief seconds, Aryana Torval had impressed Ella to no end. The woman had an aura about her, and she seemed entirely unfazed by her surroundings. Likely she'd grown up much as Ella had, and now she stood in the city of Aravell, surrounded by elves and warriors quite literally plucked from legend, and she spoke to them as though they all stood in the common room of The Gilded Dragon.

"I know some stories," Therin said, placing one arm across his stomach and bowing.

"I'm sure you do. Well, Therin Eiltris, bard, my name is Aryana Torval." She looked over to Halmír and the Ephorí. "I am the daughter of a dead man and a fearless woman. My people trust me to lead, and so I do. I am here because I was invited by Aeson Virandr to discuss terms on how we might work together to rid the South of the Lorians once and for all. I was also told that the Draleid we have all heard so many tales of flies in support of Aeson's rebellion. And yet, now that I am here, I see neither of their faces. Or do they hide amongst you?" She raised an eyebrow at Therin. "Another pair with no names?"

Ara, the Ephorí of Lunithír, stepped forwards, her crimson and gold robes flowing elegantly after her. The elf was possibly the most beautiful living creature Ella had ever laid eyes on. "Aeson Virandr has sailed for Valtara to aid the rebellion there. Calen Bryer's return is expected shortly. But now, we would escort you to meet with King Galdra, the Golden Stag, ruler of the elven kingdom of Lunithír. Even now our forces march alongside those of the Draleid to aid the villages of western Illyanara. A new dawn emerges, Aryana Torval, and we would like to witness it side by side."

The Ephorí of Ardurän threw a sideways glance at Ara, barely a flash of an instant, before also stepping forwards and spinning tails of gold and silver about Queen Uthrían. These were their usual theatrics, the only variance being which one spoke first.

On all other occasions, Ithilin, the Ephorí for Vaelen, had stayed reasonably quiet. With Queen Tessara marching with Calen's army, Ithilin's ability to boast and brag was severely diminished – or so Ella had thought. But this day, Ithilin followed the other Ephorí. The elder Ephorí stood in silence for a moment before inclining her head to Aryana. "In the time before the Blodvar ended, my kind had a saying. 'I'ldryr viel asatar. I sanvîr viel baralun.'"

"In fire we are forged. In blood we are tempered."

Ella wasn't the only one surprised when Aryana translated the words. Therin gave an impressed downturn of his lips, his eyes widening, while Chora laughed.

Both Ara and the Ardurän Ephorí, Liritháin, gave only blank stares, but Ithilin smiled. "You speak the Old Tongue?"

Aryana shook her head. "Fragments. Passed down from my father's father and so on. That's a saying my family has lived by. You never know who you are until you've been tested and you've come out the other side."

"And who are you, Aryana Torval?" Ithilin stared into the woman's eyes, suddenly seeming younger and taller.

"Someone who is done with living under the boot of another. Someone who is done hiding."

"We have much in common then. My queen, Tessara Vaelen Alumír, will not be in the hall to welcome you. For she too is tired of hiding, and as we speak, she marches with the Draleid's commanders along with five thousand of Vaelen's finest warriors. There is a human saying my mother passed down to me. We have a similar saying in the Old Tongue that doesn't quite capture the simplicity as well as yours. 'Actions speak louder than words.'"

The glance that Ithilin threw in the direction of the other two Ephorí was a subtle one, but one that Ella didn't miss.

The plateau emptied, and the procession marched towards the enormous white structure know as Mythníril. Ella had been inside its walls many times over the past few days, and yet she still could not comprehend how such a place had ever been built. As they walked, the Ephorí took their turns regaling Aryana with tales of their history and that of the various buildings that jutted up across the city.

At one point, as Ara and Liritháin argued over something for which Ella had absolutely no concern whatsoever, she turned to find Aryana Torval walking beside her, gaze fixed on Faenir.

"Kin of the Draleid." She puffed out her bottom lip then lifted her gaze. "Surely you are more than that?"

"We can't control what we are in the eyes of others," Ella responded with a shrug. The truth was she didn't have two fucks to rub together when it came to how the Ephorí described her.

"Too true. Your mother or your father?"

Ella raised a curious eyebrow.

"Who taught you that? I don't doubt your wisdom, but that's too profound a sentence to not have been passed down."

"My mother. She wasn't the kind to care what others thought."

"A woman after my own heart. So, your brother rides a dragon? I'm assuming it's not your son. Definitely not your father, given how young I've heard he is."

"Brother."

"Well, sister of the Draleid, I'm about to go into a room where people who think they're better than me are going to tell me whatever they think I need to hear in the hopes that I will commit the lives of my people, and my own, to their cause. I am well aware that I mean very little to them outside of any military advantage I might grant them or as a trophy for their shelves, judging by how they argue now over the outcome of a battle that happened over five hundred years ago. So tell me, before anyone else does, what is your brother like, and why should I fight for him instead of securing my own lands and keeping to myself?"

Ella couldn't help but choke back a laugh. Whoever had delivered the report on Aryana deserved a bag full of gold and a higher position. "Would you believe a word I said?"

"I'm not sure yet. It depends on what your eyes tell me."

"Calen was a sweet boy growing up. A handful and a pain, but he was sweet. He always gave me the first bowl at supper, always teased me but at the same time would leave the last slice of bread in case I was hungry. He sang a lot when he thought nobody was listening. The last few years have bled the sweetness from him. He's not that boy anymore. But I'm damn proud of the man he's become. He's not like these fools." She inclined her head towards Liritháin and Ara, who still argued up ahead. "I could stand here and tell you a hundred different things, but the honest truth is I'd be lying. I've not seen much of Calen since I left our home, since the empire slaughtered our parents. But when Lorian armies marched on this city, Calen fought in the thick of it. And when the Dragonguard tried to burn this place to the ground, he and Valerys refused to let that happen. There were three of them. Each twice as large as Valerys." Ella laughed, shaking her head at her brother's stupidity. "The pair of them just flew straight at them. They didn't care what happened to themselves as long as they could buy time for those of us fighting in the city. So I don't know what that says, but one thing I can guarantee you is if you fight for Calen – and even if you don't – he will die for you, because that's just who he is."

"Sounds like quite a man."

"He is." *And I miss him.* Ella clenched her jaw as the words echoed in her mind. Beside her, Faenir stopped. The wolfpine raised his head, ears and tail pricking. He heard something.

The crack of wings sounded in the sky, followed by a shrieking roar.

The procession stopped halfway across a white stone bridge, the many murmurs only half-swallowed by the waterfalls cascading over the edge of a cliff to the left. Aryana Torval's men gasped, hands pointing towards the sky. For a second, Ella's heart stopped beating as she waited for Valerys to drop through the clouds and sweep overhead.

But instead, Varthear emerged from the blanket of white above, brilliant blue scales gleaming. The mighty dragon wrapped her wings close and dropped like a stone, looking as though she might collide with the bridge, until she unfurled those massive red sails and tore forwards with impossible speed.

As the dragon whipped past overhead, many stumbled in the force of the gust that followed, two of Aryana's men hitting the stone.

"Fuck me…" Aryana held an arm out to keep her balance, her gaze fixed on the sky, watching as Varthear twisted and turned, all beauty and grace. The earlier composure in the woman's voice cracked. "That's a dragon – a *real* dragon."

"Did you think we were lying?"

"No, I…" Aryana stood to her full height, still staring after Varthear. "I just never really thought I'd see one." The woman stepped past Ella. "There are two?"

"Two?" It took Ella a moment to process Aryana's words, but then images of two dragons swirling in the sky pushed themselves in from Faenir's mind. One blue, one white.

Gooseflesh swept over her skin. She spun and stared slack-jawed at the white dragon that had emerged from the clouds and now wound through the sky with Varthear. "Calen…"

"So, he has returned," Aryana said, following Ella's gaze.

Ella looked to Gaeleron, who had paused just behind her. "Take Aryana and her retinue to Mythníril."

"Where are you going?"

Ella had broken into a sprint before the elf had even spoken the words.

CHAPTER SIXTY-THREE

GHOSTS OF A TIME LONG DEAD

20th Day of the Blood Moon

*River Makeer, west of Achyron's Keep – Winter,
Year 3081 After Doom*

"Easy, girl." Dayne ran his hand along the neck of the bay mare he'd taken from the camp. The magnificent creature had carried him through the night and into the morning with little complaint. Ahead, the light of the rising sun sprayed over the Rolling Mountains, glistening in the mist of Dayne's breath, winter still holding its grasp on the world.

The horse came to a stop in the middle of an open glade, snorting, the river ahead. Dayne laid his spear across his lap and patted the creature's neck. He gave a tap with his heels, and the horse walked forwards.

The River Makeer had three points of crossing where the water was shallow enough. Dayne stood before the southernmost crossing. The old fort sat about a mile back from the far bank, nestled against a thicket of trees.

Fort Lukaris, named after the great Valtaran general Alexin Lukaris. It was here that Alexin fought the Battle of the Bleeding River against the Karvosi invasion back in the Age of Honour, around the year one-four-three-six After Doom. It was said that the Karvosi casualties were so high it had taken months to clear the bodies and the river had run red all the way to Myrefall.

Dayne's mother had told him the story a thousand times when he was a boy.

Alexin was known as the greatest military leader in the history of Valtara. A man who'd never lost a battle. Not a single one. The skulls of three Great Horns were still mounted on the walls of Macidea, the ancestral home of House Lukaris, just south of Skyfell. Dayne had never seen one of the creatures alive, but the skulls were easily as long as he was tall, the enormous horns the same length.

Staring out at the river, Dayne found himself longing for those days when his mother let him and Baren stay up long past the setting sun and into the early hours, the fire roaring, her strong voice spinning stories of all the ancient battles and generals of Valtara. His mother had always had a love of history and the blood spilled to accomplish the present. Knowing your past allowed you to appreciate the gifts you'd been given, or so his mother had always said.

The Battle of the Bleeding River, the Broken Isles, the Weeping Wood, The Battle of the Shattered Spears, The Burning of a Thousand Ships. All some of Dayne's favourites.

That was all before he'd fought a battle himself. Before he'd truly known the stomach-turning sound of snapping bones, or the way skin crackled as it burned, or the particular scream of a man being eaten alive.

He still appreciated the genius of minds like Alexin, even more so than he once had. But now he knew well enough not to yearn for the glory of battle. Death would find him anyway, wherever he went, as it always did. But there was nothing noble about watching a man shit himself with a spear buried in his gut. Nothing righteous about walking waist-deep through a river turned red with blood and floating corpses.

He was already too far gone. There was no good deed in the world that would clean his hands. But he would end as many lives as he needed to if it would keep his child's hands from bearing the same stains.

His child. Such a strange notion. In his arrogance, he had thought he'd understood the grief Alina had gone through when her son was taken from her. But as soon as Mera had told him of the child growing in her womb, he knew how wrong he'd been. That child was barely formed, a shell not yet ready to protect the soul within, and yet he would die for it. He would crawl across a field of shattered glass, let the flesh be burned from his bones, blacken his soul to the point that even the void would turn him away – all this he would do to protect that child. A child who had not yet taken a breath, a child who, if taken, he would bathe himself in blood to find.

Dayne took a moment, allowing the sounds of the river to drift to the back of his mind – a brief peace – then signalled the horse to cross. The water at the crossing point barely came up past the horse's knees, in contrast to the deeper sections where the river would have swallowed the animal whole.

He led the horse on a slow walk towards the fort, which now lay in disrepair. The remains of the limestone walls were dank, grey, and webbed with vines. Cylindrical towers intersected the wall at each bend, topped with crenelated battlements. The keep rose about a hundred feet into the sky, sections of stone missing where they had been chipped away across the centuries. As Dayne rode closer, he could see the temples to Neron and Achyron through the gaps in the walls. Once, those temples had been finished in the finest Valtaran marble mined near Ironcreek. But that had long been stripped by House Koraklon and repurposed in the temples at Achyron's Keep. That thought alone caused Dayne to grate his teeth. Temples were sacred things, and for a great Valtaran House to defile them as such was – to Dayne – an unforgivable thing. But the gods, as of yet, had not seen fit to punish House Koraklon. He would be happy to do it for them.

If this war ever ended, he would ensure Fort Lukaris was brought back to what it had once been, the temples restored, the walls rebuilt.

Dayne dismounted and led the horse through a gap in the wall, climbing over chunks of moss-covered stone that had long since become part of the earth. He walked through the ruined fort and stopped at the base of Neron's temple. The statue of the god was one of few things mostly intact. The Sailor's left arm was missing, a chip taken from his cheek.

Dayne tethered the horse to a stone post, then knelt at the base of the statue, placing his spear on the ground, his eyes closed.

"Neron," he whispered, "I kneel before you as a man who has no right to ask anything of anyone, let alone a god. And yet here I am. I do not kneel at Achyron's feet, for it is not strength I need. It is guidance. You have watched over Valtara for millennia, guided us to safe shores when the storms threatened to swallow us whole, kept us from oblivion when greater powers crumbled. And now I come to ask of you a smaller deed, one far below you. I ask that you keep my family safe, that you show them a safe path through this storm. I will pay whatever price you seek. Just keep them safe, I beg of you."

When Dayne was finished, he pulled a long, aching breath into his lungs and exhaled slowly, dragging himself to his feet. The gods seldom dealt with the minor happenings of men. But on the off chance The Sailor was listening, Dayne had thought it worth speaking.

He left the horse tethered where it was grazing on tufts of grass that sprouted from the cracks in the stone, and climbed to the top of the closest tower he thought wouldn't collapse on him. Once there, he perched atop a merlon, folded his legs beneath him, and rested his spear across his lap.

Dayne slid his hand into his pocket, allowing his fingers to rest on the smooth stone within. Power radiated from it even then, calling to him, demanding he open himself to it. Dayne closed his eyes and drew his breaths slowly, listening to his beating heart. He needed to show himself that he had the will to resist, that he was strong enough to do what needed to be done. He would not abandon Baren.

He stayed like that for quite some time, the gemstone whispering in the back of his mind, until he eventually pulled his fingers away and opened his eyes.

Hours passed, shadows bending and shifting as the sun moved across the sky. Midday had just passed when Dayne spotted the cloud of dust ripping towards him in the distance.

Ten riders approached the fort from the east, slowing as they drew closer. Seven wore the pale blue skirts of House Koraklon, the Oranak squid worked into their silver cuirasses. Loren was easy to spot with his head of short white hair, his armour gilded, his mount covered in blue and gold barding. The other three wore the black cloaks and markings of the Lorian Battlemages, and the power of the Spark pulsed from them.

Dayne smiled at that. His tactics had been working if Lorian Battlemages wouldn't even approach him without the Spark firmly held in their grasps.

The riders came to a halt near the base of the fort's walls. Shouts rang out, and four of those in armoured skirts galloped towards the river, spreading out along the banks. Dayne watched for a while, taking a small pleasure in knowing that he could snuff out Loren's life in a heartbeat if he so wished. But that death would have been too quick. And if Loren died now, Dayne was absolutely certain that all he would find of his brother would be a corpse.

It seemed a fitting thing to him. All those years ago, Dayne had been forced to run to save his family, and now he was forced to do precisely the opposite. He had tried running, and all it had brought his House was ruin. He would not run again.

"I could snap your neck right now," Dayne called down.

Even before the heads turned, the Spark rippled from the Battlemages. All three of the mages turned their horses about, eyes fixing on Dayne. So too did Loren's guard, but Loren himself kept his mount steady.

"Dayne Ateres. It's been a very long time. You might snap my neck, but you won't live to draw another breath if you do. And your brother will have the skin peeled from his bones. And your sister? Well, I'll make sure that crown is melted and poured over her head. Why don't you come down here and we'll talk face to face?"

"Why don't you come up here? It's a lovely day. You can see for miles in all directions."

When silence answered, Dayne climbed down from his perch and descended the tower. The horse waited for him where he'd left it, still munching on tufts of grass. It snorted as he approached, lifting its head and pressing its muzzle into his chest.

"Good girl." He ran his hand along the far side of the horse's neck and rested his head against her soft coat for a moment. Then, giving two short *clicks* with his tongue, he led the animal back through the ruined fort and out to where Loren had now dismounted along with his guard, the three Battlemages remaining on horseback.

Well into his fifth decade, Loren was still densely muscled, his frame broad and lean. Full markings of the spear adorned his right forearm, four black rings on his left.

"You've been busy." Loren stood with his hand resting on the pommel of his sword. "The whispers in the keep call you voidspawn, a demon sent to tear us limb from limb in the night. But I am familiar with your work, Dayne. I have not sat by blindly all these years. I heard of what you did to Harsted Arnim. Setting a man on fire is a harsh kind of vengeance, don't you think? For someone of the noble House Ateres. I thought you were the honourable sort?"

"I've never claimed such a thing. Though Harsted didn't scream nearly as much as the thousands you let burn at Stormwatch."

Loren's lips curled downwards before he gave Dayne a fleeting smile. "I've no idea what you did with that Draleid – Sylvan Anura. She just vanished. The dragon's corpse was found south of Catagan with a spear formed entirely of stone jutting from its right eye. That was you, I presume? I've watched and listened through the eyes and ears of others for the past decade or so. You leave patterns, you know? Markers. A trail to follow. And what a trail you've left in your wake, you and that companion of yours – the Narvonan."

Dayne tightened his grip on his spear.

"Did you think I would be so naive as to think you would never come back here? You are your father's blood. All arrogance and pride. You would never let the honourable House Ateres collapse, no matter how many need die. Once I heard of Harsted's death, I knew. And now here you are. I'll give it to you, Dayne. You came close. You did more than your mother and father ever did, and even those before them. But how many Valtarans have died for your words of freedom? Tens of thousands. At Myrefall, and Skyfell, and let's not forget the Lost Hills. There is not a soul beneath the banners of House Thebal who would follow you after that act of butchery."

"You talk a lot, Loren. When I kill you, it's your tongue I'll take first."

Loren smiled. "And when I melt that crown over your sister's severed head after she is executed for treason, I'll hang her body next to yours in Skyfell's plaza, right where they hung. It would be poetic, don't you think?"

Loren walked closer until Dayne could smell the scent of oranges on his breath. "I bet you've dreamt of this. Of being so close you could drive a dagger into my heart. How does it feel now, knowing that if you do, if you take the vengeance you seek, it will cost not only your life, but that of your brother and your sister..." He leaned closer. "And your sister's child."

Dayne froze, almost dropping the spear from his grasp, his stomach sinking.

"I thought that might get your attention. How do you think I came by your brother?"

"Every word that leaves your mouth is a lie."

"When have I ever told you a lie, Dayne? Not once. I admit, I can be short tempered, stubborn, unforgiving, and at times cruel if there is a need for it. But I am not a liar." He turned and gestured to his guard. "Whether you believe me or not is irrelevant. You will see soon. You have come this far, Dayne. Won't you come a little further?"

The guard stepped forwards with a pair of iron shackles. As he did, Dayne felt the mages pulling on threads of Spirit, preparing to ward him.

This was the point of no return. He could kill them all right then and there, peel the flesh from Loren's bones and cut out his heart. The cost would be Baren's life and that of his nephew – if Loren truly wasn't lying. And even then, the war would still not be over. The Lorians would still hold Achyron's Keep, and reinforcements would likely arrive through the Hot Gates. Loren would be dead, but Valtara would still bleed. The only victory to be had would be a personal one.

No, patience would be his friend. There was a path on which he could keep his family whole and lessen the cost of freeing Valtara. That path required shackles.

"I assume it's easier if I get on the horse first?"

"I'd prefer watching you climb up with your hands bound, but if you insist."

Dayne mounted the bay mare, then allowed Loren's guard to place the shackles around his wrists. The hardest part was doing nothing as the Lorian mages erected a ward of Spirit around him and the Spark was pulled beyond his reach.

As they rode along the dirt track that led towards Achyron's Keep, Dayne spotted Belina sitting above him in the branch of a densely-leaved tree, balancing like a kat. She smiled at him as they passed.

The Warrior and The Sailor. By blade and by blood. I will end the line of House Koraklon. I will see Valtara free.

CHAPTER SIXTY-FOUR

SWEET BOY

20th Day of the Blood Moon

Aravell – Winter, Year 3081 After Doom

By the time Ella had charged through the passage that led to Mythníril, Faenir bounding beside her, Valerys was already visible across on the eastern side of the basin.

The sight of the white dragon standing on the plateau above drove her to sprint even harder, her lungs burning. Two guards who walked along the grass path jerked out of the way as Ella charged between them without breaking stride.

As she reached the plateau, Valerys shifted and turned his head to face her and Faenir. The dragon bowed slightly, but Ella flitted past, the door of the house ahead opening.

Calen emerged in his full suit of armour, runes glowing purple, cloak trailing behind him. Ella collided with her brother so hard it knocked the wind from her lungs. She jumped onto his chest, wrapping her legs around his waist and her arms around his neck, pressing the side of her head against his.

He stumbled backwards, catching himself on his back foot, then wrapped his arms around her, pulling her in tight.

"I thought I'd lost you," he whispered, his hand pulling her head in closer. "I thought you were gone."

"I'm here." Ella leaned back and looked into her brother's eyes, the lavender hue of his irises still catching her off guard. She cupped her hands to his cheeks. "I'm here."

Ella pressed herself in close once more, her arms still around her brother's neck. They stayed like that for quite a while, neither wanting to let go. When Calen finally put her down, Elia, Lasch, Tanner, and Yana all stood behind him.

He lowered her to the ground, seeming almost as tall as Haem in his plate.

"You saved my life." Calen rested his gauntlet-clad hand on Ella's right cheek. "I know what you did. And if you hadn't, both Valerys and I would be dead and this city nothing but embers. You saved everyone."

"You're my little brother. Watching over you is my duty. Mam would kill me otherwise."

Faenir bolted past Ella and slammed into Calen's chest with all the weight and force of a battering ram.

And in that moment, as Calen floundered to the ground, the clang of his armour drowned only by the laughter on his lips, Ella saw the boy within the man. That sweet boy. That sweet boy who had been forced to grow older before his time. That sweet boy who had lost his brother, his father, his mother… his sister. That sweet boy who had become what was needed. She would do anything to protect that piece of him.

Something nudged Ella's shoulder. She turned around just in time to receive a puff of warm air rolling over her face.

Valerys's head hovered over the ground before her, his lavender eyes staring intently. In one sense, the dragon felt like a part of Calen, like family. And in another, it was a monstrous beast that could rip her in half with little effort.

The dragon leaned forwards and pressed the warm scales of his snout into her cheek, hot air wafting over her neck and shoulders. A rumble resonated in his throat, soft enough to be a purr.

"Faenir, for the love of the gods, get off me." Calen was trying to add a serious tone to his voice, but he failed in between Faenir's onslaught of licks. "I've not been gone that long!"

For the first time since before Rhett's death, Ella felt a warm fullness in her heart. Faenir's love, his loyalty, his dedication… all of it flowed through her. All the wolfpine needed in this world was a full belly, a good night's sleep, and his family – his pack.

"You've gotten far too big to keep doing that." Calen knelt on one knee, scratching both sides of Faenir's head. He stopped for a moment and ran his hands back over the wolfpine's ears, pressing his nose to Faenir's snout. "It's good to see you back to yourself. You did a good job watching over her."

Something moved in the corner of Ella's vision, and Aneera stepped forwards. She inclined her head to Ella and placed her palm against her forehead. "You move swift as the wind."

Ella returned the Angan's gesture.

Aneera repeated the greeting to Calen. "Son of the Chainbreaker."

"You brought her back to us." Calen pressed his palm to his forehead and reached out his hand. "That is a debt I can never repay."

Aneera stared down at Calen's hand as though it were a red-hot poker. But after a few moments, she wrapped a clawed hand around his forearm, and he did the same with hers.

"I did not do it alone." Aneera looked over Calen's shoulder, first to the right, then the left, then all about. Fenryr Angan stalked from the shadows around the white homes on the plateau. Fifteen in total.

"Another wolfchild returns." The voice was deep and measured, and Ella knew it instantly.

Fenryr walked up the path behind Ella, Sennik and the four other druids at his back, their keepers strolling beside them. The god walked slowly, a black tunic clinging tight to his body.

Calen rose to his feet, eyes narrowing at Fenryr. He didn't speak, but Ella knew the feeling she could see in his eyes, his mouth slightly ajar, lips searching for words. Calen could *feel* Fenryr's presence in the same way she could.

Fenryr pressed his hand to his forehead as he passed Ella. He reached out to place his hands on Calen's shoulders, but Calen stepped backwards and lifted a hand.

In the span of a heartbeat, everything shifted. Valerys let out a screech of sorts, a clicking sound coming from his throat, and the dragon moved to stand over Calen, lips pulling back in a snarl. Valerys's spearhead tail whipped back and forth in the air before going rigid.

"Who are you, and how are you in my head?" Calen held his left hand between himself and the god, his right hovering near his sword.

"Do not fear, young one. There is much—"

"There is much I don't know. Yes, I'm aware. But one thing I will know is your name." Calen's eyes shimmered with a faint purple light, and his stare grew hard.

Fenryr nodded. "There is not a doubt in this world of the wolf in your blood. I would have it no other way. I am Fenryr."

Calen stared back, wordless, as rigid and wary as Valerys.

"I can feel your doubt, feel it creeping through your blood – *my* blood. *Wolf* blood. You are of the Pathfinders, seeker of the paths once walked. A rare Gift, particularly in these times. Your mother was Gifted as such. Though she saw the paths yet to be walked, the paths that may yet be or may fade from the light. The last of my blood with such a Gift."

"My mother?"

"As I tried to say, there is much you do not know, but nothing I will keep from you."

Calen continued to stare into Fenryr's eyes, his chest rising and falling slowly. "The things I've seen… the visions… are they real?"

"Seeing the paths is not straight forward, young one. Though the paths once walked are more so than those yet to be. The events are real, for a certainty. But they are coloured by the lenses you look through. I will let you settle, but tonight I will answer every question you ask of me. At least those that are within my capacity to answer."

"Tonight." Calen nodded. "But first I would eat with my sister and drink," he said, looking to Ella. "If Lasch still has mead?"

"Well, you and Dann haven't been around to drink it all."

Calen smiled, turning back to Ella. "Have you seen Haem?"

Ella shook her head. None of the knights had been to Aravell since she'd woken. She'd hoped that when Calen returned, he'd do so with their brother at his side.

The smile evaporated from Calen's lips, supplanted by a sombre line.

Footfalls echoed through the basin from the archway that led back to the city. Images of Therin, Gaeleron, Chora, and several Dracurïn marching along the path drifted from Faenir's mind.

The Dracurïn lined up in two rows of five, pressing their hands to their breastplates, their backs straight and stiff, their chins raised. They all stared at Calen like some hero of old.

Gaeleron walked to Calen and pressed his fist to his chest before grasping Calen's forearm. "Draleid. It is good to see you return."

"And it's good to see you not walking around with that stick. Valdrin must have finished your armour before he left then?" A warm smile adorned her brother's lips, his gaze moving from Gaeleron's smooth, gleaming boots to his pristine white cloak ornamented with golden leaves. She hadn't noticed it before, but now that she looked closely, she realised she'd never seen even a speck of dirt on Gaeleron's armour, never so much as a stain or a mark on his cloak. The steel was always so polished she could have used it as a mirror.

"He did," Gaeleron answered. "Det er myia haydria ar myia thranuk til bære denír amiar. Ilån denír går indil myia sidir."

"It is my honour and my privilege to wear this crest. From this day until my last," Therin whispered in Ella's ear. She had heard the elf approach but was too focused on Gaeleron to turn and meet his gaze.

"It is mine to see you wear it." Calen grasped Gaeleron's pauldron. "Du gryr haydria til myia elwyn, myia yíar."

Chora wheeled herself forwards. "It's good to see you, Calen."

Calen held Gaeleron's gaze for a few long moments before turning to meet Chora's. When he did look at her, Ella saw something cold in his eyes, and she thought sharp words weren't far from his tongue. But then something shifted within him. "We found something."

He didn't wait for Chora to reply. Instead, he walked back to the doorway of the house and pulled something from a satchel left there. When he walked back to face Chora, he held a scaled egg larger than his head, cream with streaks of emerald running through it like lightning.

"There were nine." Calen placed the egg into Chora's hands, a smile beaming on his lips. "Kollna hid them in a chamber below the western tower."

Chora took the egg and nestled it on her lap. She gave a soft smile, but the scents of sorrow and loss wafted from the woman, filling Ella's nostrils, the wolf within her whining. "You did well, Calen. You did well."

"What's wrong?"

"Nothing." She drew a long breath in through her nose, exhaling in a deep sigh. "The Epherian eggs do not hatch." Genuine sympathy entered the woman's voice, a thing Ella hadn't thought Chora capable of. "I fear your hopes are far too high. We will have the Dracârdare begin warming them and testing them for the Calling. What of Kallinvar and the knights? Did they find this 'Heart of Blood' they were looking for?"

Calen looked genuinely dejected by Chora's change of topic, his gaze fixed on the egg, his lips forming unspoken words. "I... No." He shook his head. "No, they didn't. At least, I don't think so. The chamber contained many of Alvira's possessions – weapons, armour, journals, chests. The knights took them to have their Watchers search through everything for a clue or a hint or something. Anything that might set them on the right path."

"You just let them take everything?"

"It was that or the eggs."

"You let them take Alvira's journals, her chests, her... you... for eggs? We *have* eggs, Calen. Hundreds. There are thousands of eggs across Epheria. Eggs that haven't hatched in four hundred years. You have no idea what might have been in those journals, in those chests."

"They will return everything once they are done."

"And what if they choose to keep something? We'll never know what might be missing."

Valerys craned his neck over Calen, baring his teeth, a deep growl in his chest.

"Oh, fucking eat me then!" Chora roared up at the dragon, her eyes wild. She clasped her hand to her forehead. "Fuck."

Ella watched the dejection in Calen's eyes shift to rage, then fade away to something far colder. Her brother stood straight. "Unlike you, I have not lost my ability to trust. I did what I thought was right. I'd do it again. Master Kollna died for those eggs. She bled out on the floor before them. It was the last thing she did, and I chose to honour that." Without waiting for Chora to respond, Calen took the egg from her lap. He turned to Gaeleron. "Send word to Yanîr and his Dracârdare. Tell him that we have new eggs that are to be warmed immediately, and that any soul brought to test the Calling is to be brought to those eggs first."

A soft whisper sounded behind Ella, so soft even the wolf in her blood barely heard it.

"Mother..." Ella looked over her shoulder to see the giant, Asius, standing at the edge of the plateau, watching from a distance. He smelled of sadness.

"At once, Draleid." Gaeleron signalled to two of the Dracurïn, issued their commands, and sent them off back down the path that led to the plateau, heading for the Eyrie.

"Was there something else you needed, Chora?" Calen asked, the cold anger still radiating from him.

The look on Chora's face shifted from one of shock to one of uncertainty and eventually settled on something Ella thought was – strangely – pride. "The leaders of the varying factions across Illyanara have arrived, bar two or three. Some are rather impatient to meet you. And I use the word 'impatient' lightly."

"It's been a long journey, Chora. Valerys and I are exhausted. He has injuries that need to be seen to. We will meet them come the morning in Mythníril."

"Calen." Therin raised an open hand. "Castor Kai is among them."

"He's alive?"

"He is. He left Argona before the Dragonguard burned it. But he has taken these past weeks to rally his forces. He arrived barely two days after you left."

Calen pursed his lips. Purple light misted from his eyes, and above him Valerys let out a deep growl.

How did Calen know the High Lord of Illyanara?

"How many warriors do we have within Aravell?" Calen said, turning to Gaeleron.

"Two hundred and twenty-four, armoured and trained. One hundred and forty-seven fresh recruits who have arrived since you left for Arkalen – though they are not fit and ready."

Calen nodded. "Go to King Galdra and Queen Uthrían. Tell them that I have requested two thousand warriors from each of them – armoured and ready – to take part in welcoming these leaders properly. I'm sure they'll jump at the opportunity. Have the leaders escorted to the southern gates, and make sure our warriors are in formation and ready. Get banners, sigils, whatever we have. It's time we give them the welcome they've been waiting for."

Chora frowned. "Calen, we can do this tomorrow. It's all right. I didn't mean—"

"No. We do this now."

AN HOUR LATER, ELLA STOOD on the stone of the courtyard that fronted the southern gates of Aravell. The white stone was smooth and clean, veins of the glowing erinian rippling through it. Several watchtowers now stood about the courtyard's perimeter, each capped with a domed top, swooping arches open to each cardinal direction.

Faenir waited at her side, along with all fifteen of the Fenryr Angan, the other druids and their keepers, and Fenryr himself. The god was now clad in a mix of impossibly burnished steel plate and black leather. The pauldrons were worked in the shape of snarling wolf heads, their eyes set with obsidian. The other druids wore similar armour, silver steel and black leather, depictions of wolves on gorgets and breastplates.

Ella herself was garbed in the same tunic and trousers she'd worn all day. She'd lost the leather armour Coren had gifted her when she'd been captured by the Lorians, something she regretted deeply. The woman had pushed Ella to breaking, but the things she had taught her had kept her alive. She truly hoped she would see Coren again, and Farwen, and even Varik.

Beside her, Faenir let out a high-pitched whine, which was echoed by the wolves who sat beside their druids. All five of the creatures were far larger than any wolf had a right to be, but smaller than Faenir by some distance – with the exception of Sennik's keeper, Balmyras.

Ella turned her attention away and back to the open courtyard before her. The speed at which Gaeleron had assembled the mass of armoured humans and elves was rather impressive.

Two formations stood before her, split by a direct line from the open gates.

Thousands of elves stood on each side of the path closest to the gates, various banners rippling above them.

The green banners of the Triarchy emblazoned with three white trees flew closest to the gates, hundreds of Highguard beneath them.

The star of Vaelen was next, the number of elves in black cloaks barely more than the Highguard as Queen Tessara had taken most of their numbers west. The green tree of Ardurän and the golden stag of Lunithír followed, on banners of brown and red respectively. Both King Galdra and Queen Uthrían had mustered far more than the two thousand each Calen had requested. If Ella was to hazard a guess, the monarchs had arranged five thousand at least, two and a half on each side of the path, all standing in perfect rank, armour gleaming.

Calen's Dracurïn stood furthest from the gates – and closest to Ella – a hundred and twenty or so on each side. Above them purple banners with golden leaves fluttered in the breeze, the white dragon at their centre.

Both Galdra and Uthrían had insisted on being present and now stood to Ella's left, at the very centre of the courtyard at the end of the path created by the two formations.

Chora and the other Rakina, along with Varthon, the matriarch of the Dvalin Angan, and the giant, Asius, all waited on the opposite side to Ella.

"Quite a sight," Therin whispered. The elf clasped his hands behind his back, a soft smile on his lips. A younger elf stood beside him, leather armour across her chest, arms, and legs, a green cloak at her back. Her hair was dark where his was silver, but her face held many of the same features. A daughter maybe? It seemed strange to think of Therin as having a daughter.

As Ella stared at the elf, trumpets bellowed, the rhythmic thumping of drums joining. Images of the procession reached her mind through Faenir's eyes before she turned her head.

Even more elves marched at the procession's head, led by ranks of Highguard with Triarchy banners flapping over their heads, followed by soldiers of each kingdom aligned side by side in columns of two.

The elves certainly had a flare for the dramatic – something Calen had apparently taken to heart. All of this, simply to make an impression on the leaders of the various factions, who now walked with their retinues just behind the marching elves. Some groups were almost a hundred in number and held banners high, their armour donned, the colours all matching. The six black stars of Illyanara on a yellow sky and Aryana Torval's white gryphon against red stuck out above them all, along with that of a black bull on dark green cloth. Other groups numbered no more than five or six, with nothing but the clothes on their backs.

The elves fanned out to the sides as they reached the end of the long path. Halmír and a group of elves in white robes directed the leaders and their parties to Galdra and Uthrían, performing their typically long-winded and over-elaborate greetings.

Once they were done, Castor Kai stepped forwards. The man was as tall as Haem, if a little narrower in the shoulder, and despite having likely seen his sixtieth summer come and go, his black hair wasn't marred by even a single strand of grey.

But for all that, his armour didn't have so much as a scratch, and it had been polished to within an inch of its life, the six stars of Illyanara set into the breast in gold.

"Great *Inari*." Castor bowed deeply, bringing one hand across his belly. It was clear by the way he over emphasised the word 'Inari' that he had spent many hours stumbling over its pronunciation. 'Ruler', Gaeleron had explained it meant.

The man continued. "You honour us with this procession, as you have done with your hospitality from the day my soldiers and I arrived. But my army waits some hundred miles south, entrenched in the Argonan Marshes, awaiting my return. And yet I have been here for days as my enemies crowd in around me." He glanced at Aryana Torval and the other leaders. "And now I have been told that this *Draleid* has finally arrived after leaving us waiting, and he is nowhere to be seen. I'm assuming there is an explanation for this? I travelled a long way at your request while my city was burned to ash."

"Your presence brings honour to our hearts, High Lord Castor Kai." Queen Uthrían took a few steps closer, her brown and green robes trailing on the stone, her guards moving with her. "It has long been our hope for our two peoples to one day fight alongside each other on the field of battle. Your hardship must have been severe across the years, waiting so close to the lion's den for your chance to finally strike. Surely your bravery is without equal."

Ella couldn't help but smirk at that.

The sound of heavy wingbeats reached Ella's ears before they did most at the gathering, the wolf's hackles raised in her blood. And before the High Lord could answer, a murmur swept through the crowd. Hands lifted from the leaders' retinues, pointing towards the sky.

A low clicking shriek echoed, and the silhouettes of two shapes moved through a bank of clouds above. The murmurs slowly faded to an unerring silence as the two shapes drifted from sight, anticipation holding the crowd in its grasp.

Fenryr turned his head, following something even Ella couldn't see. "Not once since our people landed on these shores has a soul of druidic blood joined with a dragon. It is a beautiful sight."

A roar erupted from Ella's left, drawing gasps and panicked shouts. It had not come from the sky, nor the city, but from the mouth of the valley to the east, where the trees had all been burned by dragonfire. Minutes passed, heavy thumps drumming the ground, a deep rumble resonating.

Sardakes emerged from the valley, his neck craned low, his head hovering just above the ground like a prowling wolf. The dragon's tail rose high in the air, the spearhead tip shaking. The talons of his winged forelimbs sank into the earth as he stalked forwards, a trembling click in his throat. Even hunched over, the creature's back reached over half the height of the towers, his sapphire frills standing on end. This seemed like an entirely different beast to the one Ella knew. This Sardakes set fear in her veins.

As all eyes turned to the black dragon, two more roars thundered overhead, followed by a high-pitched shriek.

Both Valerys and Varthear broke through the clouds, rays of sunlight spraying behind them. The two dragons soared forwards, their massive wings casting shadows across the yard. As one, they dropped and hurtled towards the ground at such a rapid pace that even Ella took a step backwards.

The only ones who didn't look terrified were the Rakina. Each of them had a broad smile on their lips, eyes wide. Even Chora, who seemed to have a permanent scowl etched into her face, appeared completely awestruck.

Both King Galdra and Queen Uthrían, along with their guards, were sent scattering as Valerys cracked his mighty wings and alighted upon the stone precisely where the elven Inari had been standing.

Varthear landed to Valerys's left with a crack of her vermillion wings, her long, slender neck shaking as she let out a series of sharp shrieks.

Just as the elven rulers and the leaders of the Illyanaran factions regathered themselves, the sound of steel on stone rang out as every one of the Dracurïn slammed an armoured boot against the stone, then pivoted on the spot in near-perfect unison and began a slow march towards Calen.

Even Ella would be hard-pressed not to admit she was impressed at the sight of both columns of Dracurïn marching as though a hidden tether connected them all, their cloaks driven behind them, banners rippling in the wind.

The two columns stopped once they stood in line with Calen, pivoted again, and marched inwards. All the while, Calen sat at the nape of Valerys's neck in his white steel armour, purple runes shimmering.

The ranks of Dracurïn formed up on either side of Valerys and Varthear, and turned to face outwards. As they did, Valerys lowered his belly to the ground and bowed, allowing Calen to slide from his neck.

Calen inclined his head towards the Rakina, bowing at the waist. He walked to where Castor Kai and the other leaders stood, his stare unyielding as he surveyed those before him. His gaze settled on the High Lord of Illyanara, a cold look in his eyes.

Valerys puffed out his chest and spread his wings before lifting his head and unleashing a roar that rattled the entire courtyard. Both Sardakes and Varthear added their voices, sending rolling thunder out across Aravell. When the roars finally faded, a pin could have been heard dropping on the stone.

Ella could tell by the mix of fear and awe on the faces of Castor Kai, Aryana Torval, and the other visitors that the display had elicited the desired result. That was when Ella realised how much the world had changed since the day she'd left The Glade. Three dragons, monstrous creatures with horns as big as her legs, teeth that could tear through her in seconds, and breath that could melt the skin from her bones, stood over her – and still her heartbeat remained slow and steady, her mind calm.

She had watched her love die, felt the shattered soul of a dragon, wandered the vast expanse of Níthianelle, and stared into the eyes of a god. The world had changed but so had she.

Calen stepped away from Valerys, the dragon still looming over him, and bowed at the waist, his hand pressed to his chest.

A still silence spread through the courtyard, and even the birds in the woodland seemed to quieten so as to better hear the words that would be spoken.

"I know each of you has travelled a long way at my request, and I am honoured that you chose to come." Calen's voice reverberated in the air, sweeping all around the courtyard as though he stood in an empty hall, and Ella's skin goosefleshed, the wolf within her feeling a shift in the air. "I apologise for leaving you to wait. War rages across Epheria and Valerys and I were needed. As I speak, our army marches to the western villages without me. It marches to defend my home, and I am not there because I am here. I was born and raised in Illyanara, far to the west in a place called The Glade, a small village at the edge of Ölm Forest. My father fought in the Varsund War. A part of him died there." Calen's gaze once more fixed on Castor Kai as those words left his lips. "My blood is your blood. Illyanara is my home, and I will give everything I am to see it free. Tomorrow, when the sun rises over the Veloran Ocean, I will ask you to make a choice that will define your entire lives. The choice to stand alone while the Lorians and the Uraks burn our home to the ground, to fight amongst each other for the ashes of what is left – *if* there is anything left. Or the choice to stand together."

Ella's hackles rose, the wolf within her sensing another shift around Calen – much more powerful. She could almost *see* a ripple about him, as though the air itself were swirling water.

Calen raised his right arm, and a purple light burst from his hand, slowly forming into the shape of a sword that flickered with wisps of purples flames. A murmur spread through crowd, whispers of 'Warden of Varyn' and 'by the gods'. Beside her, Fenryr's smile spread from ear to ear, sharp fangs showing.

"This war is greater than all of us," Calen called, holding that glowing sword in the air, Valerys looming over him like a mountain. "It is a war of gods, and demons, and darkness, and if we do not, each of us, stand and fight for what we love, there will be nothing left. I promise you one thing – I will fight until my last breath, until I have given all the blood I have to give. And if we fail, if the sky falls, I will stand beneath it and hold it up for as long as I can."

Calen lowered the glowing sword and looked about him at Varthear and Sardakes, then Valerys above him. "Nur temen vie'ryn valana, ar nur temen vi maklar til valahír. Vir væra anataier aldryr ar orimyn!" Calen waited a moment, then translated, "For those we have lost, and for those we refuse to lose. We will give them fire and fury!"

The dragons roared, and the crowd answered with clattering steel and fervorous shouts.

CHAPTER SIXTY-FIVE

BIND TO ME

20th Day of the Blood Moon

Berona – Winter, Year 3081 After Doom

Fane drew deep slow breaths as he sliced through the skin of his forearm with threads of Spirit. He tapped into the gemstone clutched in his fist and bound the threads with a weave of Essence. Power surged through every fibre of his being, each heartbeat sounding like the thump of a drum, each breath like a roaring storm.

He watched closely as the interwoven threads of Spirit and Essence delicately parted the flesh, carving in the rune of binding. Blood flowed, dripping onto the stone. A moment passed. The rune glowed with a bright red light, veins of pearlescent white striped throughout it. And as the light poured from the rune, the strength emptied from his bones like a cut wineskin. He dropped to his knees, holding himself upright by gripping the edge of the table at his side.

His eyes drooped, heartbeat slowing. He squeezed the edge of the stone table, feeling the blood flow over his arm. There was no other way to test these runes, and without them, everything was for nothing. Fane had always found that to be the way of things. There was always a weak link in the strongest of chains, the most elaborate of plans hinging on the most fragile of things, the greatest of deeds requiring the unlikeliest of occurrences. Everything he had done, every life he had taken, every line he had sworn he'd never cross… It had all hinged on what happened next. It would all have been for nothing if the workings of these runes had not been deciphered. Kiralla Holflower and Drakus Pirnil, two of the most inconsequential mages to cross his path, and yet the necessary links in his chain. In their command of the Spark they had been entirely unremarkable. And yet, their research would save the world.

"There is nothing you can do." No matter how many times he heard it, the Vitharnmír's voice made Fane's skin crawl. It was not a natural thing. "There is nowhere you can hide from him now. Your fate is sealed, traitor."

Fane looked down at the runelight that shone through the blood on his arm, then hauled himself upright using the table edge for leverage.

"I am not hiding," he said as he turned to the kneeling creature before him, glowing red runes inscribed across its body.

The Vitharnmír gave a cruel laugh, hands tugging against the chains that bound it in place. "Then release me."

"I am not stupid either." Fane shook his head at the creature and paused for a moment. He tapped a finger against the black leather of Kiralla Holflower's research notes, which sat atop the two volumes of Brother Pirnil's. The Scholar had been hard at work.

Fane faced the Vitharnmír. "How does it feel?"

The creature stared at him with those dark empty wells that had once been eyes.

"You are a Vitharnmír, one of Efialtír's Chosen. The greatest of his champions. You have fought wars in the Godsrealm for millennia beyond counting. You have seen this world in all its iterations. You are a higher form of existence." Fane walked forwards until his toes were a fingernail from the circle of runes set into the ground around the Vitharnmír. "And yet, now you are nothing. You are mine." He dropped to his haunches so as to stare into the creature's bottomless eyes. "Your soul will shatter in this tiny room, your light will die, and no eyes will watch it fade but mine. Your god will not hear you, he will not see you or feel you, he will know nothing of you but your absence. And there is not a thing you can do to prevent that fate. For all your power – all your hubris and arrogance – you are as helpless as the people upon which you feed. How does it feel?"

The Vitharnmír's expression didn't shift. "He will carve you apart for eternity. He will flay your body and burn your soul every second of every hour until the breaking of time. You will know pain eternal, and I will smile and listen to your screams as the music that they are."

"Perhaps," Fane said with a shrug. "You are likely correct. If I fail, he will not show me mercy. And the odds are ever skewed towards failure. But I have a chance, and that is all I need. And it is more than you have, for you were wrong on more than one account. You will not smile, and you will not listen to my screams. You will be shorn from the aether. And everything that you are will be mine."

Fane stepped inside the circle, and the Vitharnmír lunged, snarling, its chains snapping tight. With the Spark flowing through him, Fane bound the creature in threads of Air and slammed its knees back down to the stone, twisting its head so it could do nothing but stare at the bloody rune carved into Fane's now outstretched arm.

"Did you know that it was Jotnar who first created blood runes?" Fane asked.

The Vitharnmír strained against the threads of Air, the veins on its neck bulging, its muscles twitching, but Fane held it in place. He wanted this creature to know exactly what its fate would be.

"I didn't. Not until recently. They created them during the Blodvar, when the elves had pushed them to the edge. They carved runes into their own flesh and infused them with the Essence of life, bound their bodies to Efialtír in exchange for the power to defeat their enemies. An immortal sacrifice. But this," he said, gesturing to the rune on his arm, "this is a thing of my own creation. One of which I am very proud."

Fane moved so he stood over the Vitharnmír. He manipulated the threads to angle the creature's head upwards.

"I will cleave your soul from this body you have stolen, and before it is lost to the void, I will snatch it and bind it to my bones. You will become my flesh and my blood. Your strength will become mine, and your soul will be trapped, screaming and helpless, awake and aware, but numb and cold. You will know pain eternal. I will ensure it."

The Spark pulsed through Fane, and he pulled on each elemental strand. His níthral took form in his fist, blue light washing over the stone. It was a strange thing to look upon a níthral formed from his own soul after all these years. The chamber severed his connection to Efialtír, just as it did the Vitharnmír.

The creature pulled backwards, chains holding it in place, its limbs visibly stiff. Fane could feel the fear in the creature, true, genuine terror.

"Now you understand," Fane said. He pulled a slow breath into his lungs, savouring the moment, savouring the fear. The Vitharnmír were the closest things to the Enkara that walked the earth. If this creature feared what Fane would do, then he was on the right path.

Fane stepped forwards, clasped his left hand on the Vitharnmír's shoulder, and drove his níthral through its chest. As it shrieked, he leaned closer. "The gods were not always gods, and so they may not always be." He paused for a moment, then recited the Jotnar binding. "Ikol ukir olan mitik, Gothandur. Tur brekka ku, binthe ehn mite, ruhnl mite, iklan mite."

Your soul is mine, Vitharnmír. I command you, bind to me, obey me, become me.

Blue light burst from the Vitharnmír's bottomless eyes and swirled through the air, twisting and turning like a trail of luminescent mist. For a moment, it hung there, weightless, before surging into the furrows of the rune carved into Fane's flesh.

Fane snapped his head back and let out a gasp. His body burned as though his blood were molten steel and his bones living fire, and for a moment he feared that he had pushed too far, that he had overstepped. That was until the burning ebbed and was replaced by a strength that set lightning in his veins.

Before him, the Vitharnmír collapsed, its body reduced to little more than skin and bone, a lifeless husk.

Fane reached down and grabbed the creature's skull, turning it so that he could look into its eyes. Those deep, black pits stared back at him, empty and devoid of all life. If he focused, he could feel the creature's soul within him, feel it thrumming in his bones. The rune on his arm glowed dimly, the light shifting from blue to white.

He drew in a long breath and squeezed. The Vitharnmír's skull shattered in his hand, blood, gore, and bone splattering the floor.

CHAPTER SIXTY-SIX

PERMANENCE

20th Day of the Blood Moon

West of the Firnin Mountains – Winter, Year 3081 After Doom

ist sat in a crater almost a hundred feet in diameter, its centre about six feet into the ground. Judging by the moss and small patches of vegetation that sprouted from every crack, the crater was far older than Rist himself. He had no idea what had created it, but whatever it was, it was large.

"Focus, Rist." Garramon sat before him, legs folded, arms resting on his knees. The Spark thrummed in the air as both mages held themselves open, threads weaving about them.

Channelling was the act of intentionally drawing as much of the Spark into your body as you were capable of and holding it there while continuously drawing on more. Pushing yourself to your limits, and then past them. It was not a particularly safe thing to do. Neither was it safe for anything within a stone's throw – which was why they sat in the crater.

"Your mind is elsewhere."

"I'm trying to decide what formed this crater. Do you know?"

"Rist, I need you to focus. Vastly more people die trying to earn the title of Arcarian than those who do not. If you don't channel, if you don't push yourself and learn your strength, you will die in your trial. And if you push yourself now without focus, you will burn the Spark from your veins."

"Apologies, Brother." Rist shifted, his arse numb from sitting on the rock. He ran his tongue across his teeth. "What is the point?"

Garramon rolled his eyes and sighed. "Of what?"

His voice held that tone he used when he'd run out of patience.

"I see the point in channelling. In carefully testing your limits in a controlled environment—"

"The Spark cannot be controlled, Rist. We are conduits, wielders. But the Spark is raw, untamed power. We do not control it, we direct it. This environment is not safe and controlled. With the kind of power you are calling upon, one slip of the mind could lead to death. You need to respect the Spark."

Rist pursed his lips, nodding. The truth was, he had been distracted since Neera had said she loved him. That moment was a uniquely singular thing in his life. And as soon as he'd had a second to think – for his thoughts to percolate and his mind to settle – all he'd wanted to do was tell Calen and Dann. He had so much to tell them. So much… Throughout his life, nothing had ever felt *real* until he'd told Dann and Calen. He sighed. "I see the point in pushing my limits. But why would I duel an Arcarian and risk death, simply to earn a title?"

"You do not have to, though now I do not believe Fane would be too pleased if you refused." Garramon let out a sigh to match Rist's. "You have a strength within you, Rist. I have known it since the moment I first laid eyes on you. How deep that strength goes, we will soon find out. But the title of Arcarian is a thing written in legend. To even offer you the opportunity to bear its weight, Fane does you a great honour. You ask why you should risk death to earn a simple title?"

Rist shrugged. "It seems unnecessary."

Garramon smiled at that. "I cannot tell you why *you* should do it. That is a choice you must make yourself. But I can tell you why *I* did it. I did it to become something greater than what I am. It was part ambition, part hubris, part longing. I did it to be remembered long after my body has withered. To be named amongst the most powerful mages to have ever lived. To have the name Garramon Kalinim entered into the Book of Arcaria. To tell you anything otherwise would be a lie. Whether we admit it or not, all living things seek permanence in one way or another, a way to leave our mark on the world before we die. For me, becoming an Arcarian was part of that. I am part of something that has stood for thousands of years. And I'm not going to lie to you and say it wouldn't give me great pride to watch you do the same. As difficult as it is for you to believe, there are things that transcend logic. Things deep within our hearts that demand to be answered. The question you must ask yourself, Rist, is what is *your* permanence? What is the mark you wish to leave on this world?"

Rist only stared back. It was not a question he had ever asked himself.

"Close your eyes and listen to my voice."

Rist did as instructed, the Spark flowing through him.

"Take a deep breath in, and let the darkness flood around you. See the elemental strands in your mind."

Rist sat in complete darkness, the black emptiness of his mind washing over him like the liquid from the Well of Arnen. But in that darkness, light burst into existence.

The elemental strand of Fire was the first to come to life in his mind, pulsing with a deep red light, twisting and coiling in the blackness like a snake. Spirit followed, pulsing with a faint white light that reminded Rist of dawn clouds illuminated by the rays of the rising sun. As the two strands coiled around one another, Water and Earth came to life like kindling catching ablaze. The strand of Water was a bright blue, while Earth shifted from brown to green, in constant motion. Air was the last to take form. It held no light, but the space around it rippled, the light of the other strands seeming to warp in its presence.

"Call to them." Garramon's voice echoed in Rist's mind as though in a bottomless cavern.

Just as Rist had done every other time Garramon had brought him to channel, he pulled on threads of each strand, each no thicker than a grain of rice, and pulled them through his body.

The threads moved like meandering streams, whirling through the emptiness, the light gleaming in bends and turns. In the darkness of his mind, the threads wove a tapestry around him.

"Now take more."

Rist did as instructed and pulled deeper from the Spark, allowing each thread to thicken, the energy pulsing in his veins.

"I will tell you when to stop."

Rist drew a long breath and continued to pull harder. The drain itched at the back of his mind as the Spark burned in his veins.

His jaw began to tremble, and he clenched his hands into fists so tight his nails pressed into the skin of his palms.

"Good, Rist. Slowly."

Rist could feel Garramon probing at the edges of his consciousness with threads of Spirit.

"More."

Rist drew a sharp breath, and with it a surge of power swept along the threads and burned in his veins. The crackle of lightning swept over his skin.

"Hold," Garramon whispered.

"No, I can go deeper."

"Rist, *hold*."

Garramon's voice faded, drowned out by the thrum of the Spark. Rist felt as though his blood itself was on fire, but it was tantalising, intoxicating. The Spark *wanted* him to draw deeper, to pull harder. It called to him, and he answered.

Garramon's words had awakened something in him.

"What is your permanence? What is the mark you wish to leave on this world?"

Rist had never been good at anything in particular. He loved reading, but was that a skill? He didn't think so. Not compared to the way Dann could hunt and use a bow, or the way nothing scared him, the way he was fearless. Not compared to how Calen wielded a blade, the way he always chose the right words, or the way he could just *do* anything. Besides the bow, anything Calen set his mind to he excelled at. Rist had actually found that quite frustrating as they'd grown up. Rist had never been like either of them. But with the Spark, he had found that thing, that one thing in which he truly excelled.

This was his.

The Spark was his permanence, his mark on the world. If he could draw on enough of it, he could make a true difference in this war. He could become an Arcarian. He could be remembered for something worthwhile. But most of all, he could matter. He wanted to matter.

Rist continued to open himself and draw harder and harder until the threads that spun around him were thick as his forearms, the air itself seeming to ripple and burn. He lost sense of his body, his mind pulling away and losing itself in the Spark.

The threads continued to spin in the darkness until they were as thick as the elemental strands themselves, creating a sphere of variegated light that whipped about him like the winds of a storm. The pain slowly ebbed and was replaced by an almost euphoric burning that swept through him. He felt as though he could shape the world itself with his will alone.

And then, in an instant, everything was gone, and he snapped his eyes open while his lungs chased after air. He slumped forwards, deep aches setting into his bones and joints. He shivered, the warmth pulled from his body. He'd never felt so weak in his life.

Garramon sat before him, just as he had been, frowning.

Rist's vision blurred, and the world went dark.

When Rist awoke, he was wrapped in a thick woollen blanket and the sun was setting, red-hued golden light spilling over the Lodhar Mountains in the west.

Garramon sat opposite him, drinking from a small metal flask, a book in one hand: *The Essence of Life and Death*, by Mona Shikart. Rist knew the title. It was a book he'd seen in the emperor's chamber. But this one was new, recently copied and bound.

Rist propped himself up on his elbows, still weak, a slight shiver still holding his bones. "What… what did you do? How long have I been asleep?"

"I warded you before you killed us both." Garramon flicked his gaze up from the book, his mouth a thin line as he examined Rist. He slid a strip of black steel into the book's pages, closed it over, then leaned forwards and offered Rist the flask. "You've been out a few hours. The march has been long, and I didn't fancy carrying you back to camp. You've put on quite a bit of muscle since we first met."

Rist grunted as he accepted the offer and slumped onto his left elbow. One sniff and he knew the liquid within was whiskey. He'd never forget that smell. Rist took a swig, the warmth washing through him almost immediately, then handed the flask back.

"You were reckless and more than a little stupid," Garramon said, pursing his lips. "Do that when I'm not here to stop you, and you *will* die."

Rist narrowed his eyes at Garramon, then noticed the black char marks across the broken earth at the man's back. All about the crater, new gashes had been carved into the rock.

The Exarch took a swig of the whiskey and leaned closer to the fire. "You must walk slowly in this. The Spark is like a drug. It is intoxicating and euphoric and, if left unchecked, viciously corrupting, because *all* power corrupts. I know what it feels like the first time you truly reach beyond what you thought possible, the first time the Spark *truly* floods your veins. Once you reach that point, it is a more potent show of strength to resist the temptation than to lean into it. The Spark craves to be used. It will consume you and everything in its path to be so. Do you understand?"

It took all the strength Rist could muster to pull himself into a seated position. He tucked the blanket tighter around himself, welcoming the warmth from the fire. He stared into the flames. "It was like nothing I've ever felt... like my veins were on fire and my very soul burned... and yet, I felt like a god."

"You wouldn't have felt much like a god when your eyes burned out of their sockets. And when drawing as deeply as you were, The Saviour likely would have welcomed you home."

Rist pulled in a long, drawn-out breath, sighing as the flames flickered before him. At any other time, the idea of dying would have shaken him to his core, but at that moment his mind was all haze and fog. "At least it would be quick."

Garramon laughed. "If you kill yourself drawing this deeply from the Spark, I can promise you two things. One, it will be the most painful, horrendous experience of your life. Two, it will not be quick."

Rist lifted his gaze from the fire, and Garramon sat forwards, pulling his knees to his chest.

"In all the centuries I've seen, I've watched thirty-seven mages kill themselves by drawing too heavily from the Spark when attempting to control power like you are. Twenty-four of those mages did so while channelling in preparation for the trial of an Arcarian."

"The others?"

Garramon glanced at the flames. "The others did so as a last resort, attempting to turn the tides of battles already lost. The years following the fall of The Order were the darkest years since the Blodvar." He continued to stare into the fire for a while longer before looking back at Rist. "When the Spark kills, it boils your blood from the inside. Your skin cooks, blistering and crackling, before sloughing off your bones. Some mages die within minutes, but I've seen others live for hours... I cannot imagine a worse death."

Every hair on Rist's body pricked at the horror of a death like that.

"You need to understand the depth of the risk you take when you push yourself to the limits you are currently trying to reach."

Rist nodded slowly.

"That said, I'm proud of you. The kind of power you drew... very few people can hold power like that." He paused a moment and gave Rist a soft, acknowledging smile. "It's about time we head back. Supper will be ready, and Taya will want to go through the plan."

They left the fire burn and climbed from the crater. Some three hundred feet down the side of the rocky slope of the crater's southern edge, crimson banners bearing the black lion flapped in the winter breeze, tent canopies spreading in all directions. And there, looming over everything, were the broad peaks of the Firnin Mountains. By the reports, the rebels had forged their stronghold within.

That word - 'rebels' – still felt strange in his mind. Rist held no desire to kill a single man or woman within that mountain. Those he'd killed in Berona still haunted his sleep.

"What will you do if the next order is to march south?" a voice whispered in his mind. *"What will you do then?"*

There was nothing in the world that would make Rist draw a blade against his home. Nothing.

"But what will you do?" the voice whispered.

COREN VALMAR STOOD AT THE edge of the cliff, the light of the bleeding moon tainting everything it touched. She drew a long breath in through her nose as she looked down at the hundreds of lanterns below. She had always known the Lorians would come eventually. But she had not expected them so soon, not while the Uraks and the elves threatened their cities.

"The attack in Berona." Farwen clasped her hands behind her back, staring out into the night. "They believe it was us."

"Mmh." Ever since they'd heard of the attack on Berona, Coren and the others had done everything they could to discover who had been behind it. But none of their networks had heard a thing. Whoever had carried it out had gone to pains to place the blame at their feet. And that alone was a reason to find out who it had been.

But first, they had an army to deal with.

"Forty thousand," Farwen said. "The scouts indicate that Primarch Andelar Touran himself has travelled with the army, along with the Lorian Supreme Commander and the Blackwatch."

Those were not good odds on any night.

Farwen turned to Coren and stared into her eyes. The elf didn't need to speak aloud. Coren knew the question she asked with the stare. "Have we received reports of the Dragonguard?"

Farwen shook her head. "Last we've heard is that Lyina and Karakes laid waste to an Urak force near Harken's Ride. Voranur and Seleraine have watched over Elkenrim since the Elves of Lynalion took Catagan. Helios was last spotted flying north, but that was two days ago. With the delays in reports, it's difficult to pin a location on him."

"Have the Angan reach out to Aeson in Aravell. Tell him that we need the Draleid, and that we need him now. We have a day or so. Even with their advantage, Taya Tambrel will take her time and scout the mountains. She is not the type to rush where no rush is needed. If we can break this Lorian army here, we will have a clear path to the Burnt Lands and to Aravell. But we can't do it alone."

"I will see it done." The elf made to leave but hesitated for just a moment. Their gazes met, but nothing further was said, and at last Farwen went in search of the Angan.

Alone, Coren let out a long sigh. Aeson had asked her and Farwen to travel to Aravell almost two weeks past. They had intended to do so, but there had been too much chaos with the elves and the Uraks running rampant. Coren and Farwen were the heart of the rebellion in the North. They couldn't simply leave every soul in Tarhelm and beyond to fend for themselves. That was not the way of the Draleid.

"Never forget, to be a Draleid is not simply a privilege. You must always rise, so that others rise with you. You must be the beacon they look to."

Her master's last words had been the creed Coren had lived by for centuries. These people had given everything to the rebellion, given their homes, their lives, their futures. They had placed their trust in Coren, and she could not abandon them when they needed her most, when they looked to her for guidance. Especially not for the sentencing of traitors. Their resolution was not worth the lives of men and women who had given everything.

Coren stared up at the crimson moon. The same moon that had marred the sky the night her world had died. The last time she had ever laid eyes on her old master.

A rumble sounded in the back of her mind.

Soon. I promise.

CHAPTER SIXTY-SEVEN

A MOMENT OF PEACE

20th Day of the Blood Moon

Aravell – Winter, Year 3081 After Doom

The sound of chatter and crackling fire reached Calen as soon as he opened the door and descended the stairs, the warm scents of lamb and rosemary filling his nose. The dirt was washed from his skin, his armour exchanged for a soft tunic and trousers Elia had laid out on his bed.

Faenir sat impatiently at the bottom of the stairs, his ears pricked, his bum wiggling, ever the pup.

Calen dropped to his haunches on the bottom step, scratching the side of Faenir's neck. The wolfpine whined and leaned into Calen's hand. He stared into Faenir's golden eyes, the wolfpine's tongue hanging from the left side of his mouth. Faenir had been like a different animal when Ella was asleep, as though Calen were a stranger to him, but now Faenir was back to being that same pup that had fallen asleep in Calen's lap a hundred times over.

"As long as you keep her safe." Calen scratched Faenir's snout and rose.

Tanner nodded to him. The man stirred a giant pot with a wooden spoon while Elia Havel watched him like a mother wolf. The woman was in her element, that same smile Calen had grown up with adorning her lips. She half-walked, half-skipped across the kitchen, stirring pots, licking spoons, and adding seasoning at her leisure. It was good to see her smile again.

By the far wall, Lasch was filling tankards of mead from casks and passing them to Yana, who was setting them on the table beside Gaeleron and Ella. The pair were deep in conversation while helping themselves to chunks of fresh baked bread dipped in oil and vinegar.

"You look clean."

Calen almost leapt from his skin at the sound of Elia's chirpy voice beside him. He looked down to see her staring back up at him, her head twitching. "I… ehm… thank you?"

She pinched his cheek. "You look good. Like he did when he was younger. Except your eyes. They must come from your mother's side."

Elia was gone as suddenly as she had appeared, turning to slap Tanner's hand as the man attempted to taste the stew.

Calen walked up behind Ella and wrapped his arms around her, resting his chin on her head.

Ella looked up, let out a soft sigh, then squeezed Calen's arms and pressed her chin into the back of his hand. "You do look a lot better without all the blood and the dirt crusted in your hair. If you'd asked my advice, I would have said to give that rousing speech *after* you'd bathed."

"Watch it," Calen said with a laugh.

Lasch offered him a fresh tankard of mead. "You look like you need it, my boy."

"Do I look that bad?"

Lasch raised both palms. "You look tired. Nothing some good food, great mead, fantastic company, and a world of sleep won't fix. Now sit down."

"I'll raise a drink to that."

Calen took a seat beside Ella and inclined his head to Gaeleron. "You've been busy since I've been gone. Thank you for watching over her," he said, tilting his head sideways towards his sister. "And for keeping everything level here. I'm sorry I left you alone."

"It's been an honour, Draleid. But I wasn't alone. Therin Eiltris rarely left my side. And Chora and the other Rakina aided in the training of every new recruit who arrived."

"You'll never just call me Calen, will you?"

"No, Draleid." Gaeleron smiled, then raised the stump of his left hand to his forehead in a mock salute.

Calen took a long, thirsty draught of his mead. It wasn't quite the same as the one Lasch served at The Gilded Dragon, but it still tasted of home.

The door opened behind him, and he turned to see Therin shuffling in, Aruni and another elf at his side.

Calen lifted himself from the bench, and as Therin made to greet him, Calen pulled the elf into an embrace. He wasn't entirely sure why. A part of him was still angry at Therin, still mad the elf had lied to him. But Therin had been there at every turn, and perhaps it had taken everything Calen had seen in the visions at Ilnaen to realise that. Seeing how much others had lost had reminded him to hold on to what he still had.

"It's good to see you too, Calen." Therin pulled back and gestured to the other elf behind him. "This is Faelen. My daughter."

"Daughter…" Calen traced the lines of Faelen's face, her cheekbones high and sharp like Therin's, her eyes soft. Calen realised this was not the first time he'd laid eyes on the elf. "I've met you before."

"You have, Draleid." Faelen bowed her head. "In the outer reaches of the Aravell."

"You were one of the rangers who came to our aid."

"Sankyar Alunea." Gaeleron now stood by Calen's side with one hand pressed to his chest, a droplet of mead rolling down his chin. "Din närvarvin gryr haydria til myia elwyn."

Captain Alunea. Your presence brings honour to my heart.

"Ar diar, myialí, Narvír Athis."

And yours, mine, Commander Athis.

Gaeleron straightened his back and lifted his chin at Faelen's words.

As they all piled in, Calen greeted Aruni with the same warmth he had Therin. And to his surprise, so too did Ella. The pair exchanged a quiet whisper, and Aruni squeezed Ella's shoulder gently.

Once they were all seated around the table, Elia carefully supervised Lasch and Tanner placing the giant pot of stew directly in the table's centre atop a stone tray. The two men strained, their faces red and hands shaking as she forced them to hold the pot over the table while she adjusted the tray, trying to position it just right. When she finally deemed the tray's position acceptable and the two men were allowed to lower the pot, she proceeded to lay even more plates of bread, roasted vegetables, sauces, potatoes mashed with goat's milk and hard cheese, strips of seared lamb and venison… the list went on and on. The last time Calen had seen so much food had been in Arthur's halls in Belduar. The thought was a sombre one. The last time Calen had stood in those halls, Arthur sat dead on his throne with his heart ripped from his chest.

"One night of peace," Calen whispered, pushing the thoughts from his head. "Just one night."

Lasch stood and moved to the top of the table, his tankard in his hand. "Before we eat, I'd like to say something." A moment of silence passed, all at the table looking up at Lasch. He took a deep draught of his mead. "Liquid courage," he said with a laugh. "I wanted to thank you all. Not only for how you have cared for and welcomed both Elia and me, but for how you have looked after Calen and Ella – and Dann, the little toe-rag. Where we come from, family, and your people, mean everything. Their blood is your blood, their pain is your pain. Freis and Vars Bryer were two of our closest friends. I grew up with Vars, knew him since we were little shits no taller than my knee. And so that makes Calen and Ella our children in a sense. It's only a shame our own son isn't here with us…"

Lasch stared off at something on the other side of the room for a moment, and as he did, Calen's heart bled. He would have given almost anything to have Rist there with them. He had tried, he'd done everything, and still it didn't feel like enough.

"Apologies." Lasch swallowed hard, staring down into his mead. Elia reached up and grabbed his hand, her fingers intertwining with his. "What I was trying to say is thank you for making this place our second home and for making our family a little bigger."

Lasch raised his tankard, and so did the others. Calen bit at the inside of his cheek, then mirrored the gesture. Ella was the last. She glanced at Calen, then gave him the falsest of smiles and raised her tankard.

"There is a prayer we say in the villages. A prayer for those we love and for those we wish to keep safe. May The Mother embrace you, and The Father protect you. May The Warrior guide your hand, and The Maiden guide your mind. May The Smith keep your blade sharp, and The Sailor see you to safe shores. To family, together and apart."

"To family," they all chorused.

As Lasch returned to his seat and the others filled their plates, Calen leaned in to Ella. "What's wrong?"

"Nothing," she said, repeating that same false smile.

"Ella, I've known you my whole life. I know when you're lying."

She bit at her lip and tapped her fingers against the table in the way she did when she was debating something in her head. "After. Can we take a walk when the meal is done?"

Calen nodded and Ella took a bowl of stew passed over by Tanner, her lips curling in a broad smile of thanks. He continued to stare at her, wondering what it was that had his sister in such a strange mood.

She placed her hands over his. "Eat, Calen. And for the love of the gods, drink."

And so, he did as his sister asked. He sat and he drank and he ate, and he listened to Lasch and Tanner tell stories about Vars and about Rhett and about a hundred other things. And the entire time, Valerys's mind drifted with his from where the dragon lay with Avandeer and the others in the Eyrie. And he was warm.

Later, when Elia had fallen asleep in a chair by the fire and Lasch, Tanner, Yana, and Faelen were enthralled by one of Therin's stories, Ella tapped Calen on the shoulder and the two made to creep out the door.

"Draleid," Gaeleron whispered, standing from his chair quietly so as not to interrupt the story. "I will go with you."

"No." Calen clasped the elf's shoulder, shaking his head. "Ella and I need some time alone."

"With respect, Draleid. Now that you have returned, a personal guard should be arranged. Even in Aravell."

"If it will make you rest easier, Gaeleron, we will arrange one first thing in the morning. Five handpicked by you."

"It will, Draleid."

"But give me tonight. And give it to yourself as well. Sit, drink, eat. There's plenty of stew left. And between Therin, Lasch, and Tanner, I'm sure there'll be stories told until the early hours. Enjoy the small moments."

Gaeleron nodded, turning his gaze to the floor.

Calen leaned his head down to look into the elf's eyes. "You of all people have earned this, Gaeleron. I will never forget who and what you are. Sit. Drink too much. Sleep in my bed if you can't walk," he said with a smile. "I'll sleep in the Eyrie tonight with Valerys."

With that, Ella and Calen slipped from the house and strolled along the grass paths of Alura towards the Eyrie, Faenir trailing at their heels.

They walked in silence for a few feet, the nightsong of birds and the burbling of Alura's streams in the background.

"I was worried you'd never come back." Calen swallowed, looking down at the grass path before him. In an instant, the warmth from earlier faded to ice and was swallowed by fear and worry and loss. "There was nothing I could do... just stand there and watch as you slipped away."

"I'm here now." She wrapped an arm around his shoulder and planted a kiss on the side of his head.

Calen slowed his pace as they walked through the passageway to Alura, allowing himself a few extra moments to admire the statues of the dragons that had been added since he'd left, the crimson moonlight drifting down from above. No matter how much of the Spark he saw, he would never be able to comprehend the sheer beauty of what some people could do with it. Not if he lived for a thousand years would he be capable of creating anything even close to the likes of these statues. Calen had only ever seen the Spark as a weapon, a thing to be wielded and used for violence. And yet the Craftsmages used it as a tool for creation, Healers to pull souls from the jaws of death. He'd never put much thought into it, but perhaps that was why The Order had created the separate affinities. Different minds used the Spark in different ways.

"Chora had them crafted." Ella placed a hand on the stone talon of a dragon that Calen was absolutely sure was Ithrax. "I swear, some days I want to strangle the air from her lungs and others I can't help but be impressed by her."

Calen stared up at the statue of Ithrax, memories of the night the great dragon had died flashing in his mind. "It is a hard thing to explain," Calen said, tracing the lines of the carved scales with his gaze. "To be Rakina. Chora has lost a piece of herself. More than that..."

Calen thought back to the vision he had seen of Varthear's past, of her soulkin's – Ilmirín's – death. And the emptiness he had felt through Kollna when she had reached out to her soulkin and felt nothing.

"When one half of the bond dies, the other withers, severed, burnt, and broken. Without your soulkin, the world holds no joy, no warmth. You are half of what you were before – less, even. It's not grief or sadness or loneliness. It's deeper. It's like your bones have been hollowed and your veins left open to bleed. Like the world itself has no purpose, like breathing is not worth the effort it takes, like you are treading water in a dark ocean and the level keeps rising and you're swallowing and you're sinking and the easier thing to do would be to let go. To grant yourself relief from the endless pain. The elven translation for 'Rakina' differs from the direct translation. Literally, it means 'one who is broken', but they interpret it as 'one who survived'. Chora can be harsh and cold because the broken pieces of her soul have left her jagged, Daiseer's loss robbing her of the very warmth in her veins. She is broken, but she is *here*. She has survived where so many others have not. I don't think I'd survive, Ella. I'm not strong enough. And so, I don't always agree with her, but I respect her and I admire her."

"I didn't know…" Ella touched Calen's cheek and turned his head towards hers. "You talk like you've felt these things, like you know them."

"I have… in a sense." Calen placed his hand over Ella's. "I've seen them in my visions – the paths once walked, Fenryr called them. Do you see things like that?"

Ella shook her head. "Our Gifts are not the same." As she spoke, her eyes shimmered golden, reflecting the moon's light.

Calen only nodded and walked on, Ella following. There was so much he didn't know, so many things he had missed over the past two years. Where did they even start?

When they stepped into the Eyrie, Valerys lifted his head from where he lay on a plateau a hundred or so feet up on the right, his white scales stark against the mounds of blue, black, and purple nestled in beside him. That was the first time Calen had seen Avandeer resting in the Eyrie. He would go to Tivar when the sun rose and tell her everything that had happened in Ilnaen.

Valerys shifted and began to rise.

Rest.

The dragon pushed back. He could feel the ache in Calen's heart, the touch of his mind easing the sorrow.

I'm all right. Just a little sad.

Valerys lowered his head, but those lavender eyes remained open, watching intently.

Calen dropped himself to the grass where the stream tumbled off the edge of the plateau, his feet dangling. He looked out at the sprawling valley beyond, illuminated only by the stars and the pink light of the moon.

Ella sat beside him to his right, letting out a long sigh. Faenir nuzzled between them.

Feathery wings flapped and echoed up the edge of the cliff, two dark shapes alighting in a nest cradled in a cranny on a cliff to the left.

"When I left," Ella said, breaking the silence, "I never thought it would be the last time I'd see them again. I always kind of thought they'd just…"

"Live forever?" Calen turned his attention from the nest and looked to Ella, who was staring out into the darkness of the valley.

Ella nodded softly.

"Me too." They'd not spoken of their parents. That was a wound he didn't ever think would heal. One he perhaps didn't want to heal. The pain reminded him of how much love he'd been lucky enough to know.

"It's hard to imagine a world without them. They were always just… there."

Calen tilted his head upwards, drawing a long breath and letting it out slowly in an attempt to hold back the tears he knew would spring forth if he didn't stop them. "Why did you leave? You and Rhett."

Ella let out a long sigh. "How long do you have?"

"However long you need." Calen knew it was a joke, but the answer wasn't. It had been nearly two years since he'd seen his sister. Two years since he'd thought her dead. The longer they could sit there on that ledge, the better, because he knew once they stood and left, the world would drag them forwards.

And so they sat for hours, talking of everything from Rhett, to Haem, to their parents, to Calen's visions, and all that had happened since they'd last seen each other. Never in his life had he spent so long sitting with Ella and just talking. There had always seemed to be more important things, like drinking with Rist and Dann, practicing sword forms, working in the forge. In truth, everything had seemed more important than just sitting and talking with his sister. But at that moment, there was nothing in the world he wanted to do more.

After silence had settled on them for a while, Ella spoke again. "Calen, earlier, when you asked me what was wrong..."

"What is it?" Calen had never known Ella to dance around something so much in her life. She was usually as blunt as a hammer. It worried him. "Are you all right?"

"No, I'm fine." Ella shook her head.

"Ella, talk to me." A touch of panic settled in, and Valerys rumbled in the back of his mind.

She leaned forwards, ran her hands through her hair, and whispered to herself, then turned back to face him. "Rist is alive."

"That's not funny, Ella. It's not—"

"He's alive, Calen. I saw him with my own eyes."

Calen stared back at his sister, his pulse quickening. He stared into her eyes, searching. On the plateau above, Valerys lifted his head, his frills standing on end. "He can't... I went to Berona... He wasn't there... He—"

"With my own eyes, Calen." Ella clenched her jaw, and Faenir growled beside her. His head lay on his paws, his snout creasing as he bared his teeth and stared into the night. "He's a mage. He fights for the Lorian Empire."

"No," Calen argued, shaking his head. "No. That's not possible. He would *never* fight for them. They took so much. They killed our parents." A rage twisted in Calen, coiling in the pit of his stomach. "They killed Mam and Dad. Rist knows what they did. He would never..."

"Ask Farda. He was there."

"And why would I believe a word out of the mouth of the man who burned our mother alive?"

"Because for some reason you don't seem to believe *me*," Ella snapped.

Calen looked back out towards the valley, his hands shaking at his sides. How could it be true? None of it made sense. How could Rist be alive? How could he be fighting for the same people who had imprisoned and tortured his parents, murdered Calen's, and destroyed everything? "He wouldn't..."

"I told you that when I was captured after the Battle of the Three Sisters that Farda broke me free. Probably the only decent thing he's ever done. But there was a part I left out. Rist was there too. He'd come earlier that day with other mages. I recognised him, and he recognised me. He came back that night to rescue me."

"Then why isn't he here?"

"It was all chaos. I was exhausted and angry. I wasn't in my right mind, and we needed to get out of there."

"You left him?"

"I wasn't in a position to leave or take anybody." Ella twisted her tongue in her mouth. She always did that when she was trying to stop herself from getting angry. "I didn't leave him, Calen. He stayed. There is a difference. He never asked to come with us."

Calen pressed his hands into his face, then ran them through his hair. "None of this makes any sense. Why? I just… I don't understand. If he was alive, why did he not come back to us? He fought at the Three Sisters? He fought for the Lorians?"

"I don't know, but I think so."

The rage that swelled in Calen was a tangible thing. It rose from his stomach, burning in his blood and twisting in his chest, his hands clenching into fists. His mind melded with Valerys's, and the dragon's fury burned with his.

"I didn't want to say anything earlier. I wanted to talk to you first. I don't know what to say to Lasch and Elia… if anything."

"We need to tell them." Calen drew in slow breaths, attempting in vain to calm the fury that swelled within him. "They need to know he's alive. Whatever else comes with that will be dealt with. But I know what it's like to think someone you love is dead, only to find out you've been lied to. Even hard truths must be swallowed."

He looked to his sister, but in an instant, Ella's eyes shifted to pools of gold, her pupils dilating.

Every hair on Calen's body pricked, and he leapt to his feet, opening himself to the Spark. On the plateau above, Valerys rose, the rumble in his chest echoing through the Eyrie, Varthear, Sardakes, and Avandeer grumbling in return.

"Calm yourself, Wolfchild." A pair of golden eyes shimmered in the darkness, gleaming. "You asked me to come to you tonight, and so here I am."

CHAPTER SIXTY-EIGHT

PATH OF THE WOLF

20th Day of the Blood Moon

The Eyrie, Aravell – Winter, Year 3081 After Doom

The wolf god folded his legs beneath him and sat facing Calen and Ella, who turned away from the valley. Power seeped from every breath Fenryr took, every word he spoke. The very air around him seemed to shift and ripple at his movements. Calen had encountered many strange and powerful souls in the past two years, but this was different. This was a god. Calen could feel a pull in his mind every time Fenryr was near.

"My blood runs in your veins, young one." Fenryr tilted his head to stare into Calen's eyes. "You are cut from me, and we are intertwined." The god pulled a long breath through his nostrils. "I can smell the uncertainty in you, hear the hesitation in the beating of your heart. You are fierce, but you are yet a pup."

The soft, welcoming smile that spread across Fenryr's lips exposed a sharp white fang that pinched into his bottom lip.

As Calen stared at the god, other shapes formed in the night: Angan prowling. Four of them; two in the forms of giant wolves, the others in their more human shape, gangly limbs flowing smoothly as they moved. He recognised one immediately: Aneera.

Fenryr looked over his shoulder as Aneera imitated his seated position a few feet to his right.

"You did not think I would let you wander this place unguarded, did you? Calen, Aneera and Nuada will be your sworn protectors. Diango and Luteir will be Ella's. They will go wherever you go, they will watch and listen where your eyes and ears cannot. They will protect you with their lives."

"Why?" Calen leaned a little closer. "What are we to you? Therin has told me of what my father was, why you call him the Chainbreaker. But you have repaid your debt. You brought Ella back. You have other druids. Why are they not guarded as we are?"

Calen had learned to be wary of those who offered much and asked for little. Everybody wanted something. Some were just better at hiding it than others.

Fenryr stared a long while, then exhaled and shifted in place. "There is not one answer to that question, but many. The first is something you have always known. In the core of my blood, in the beating heart of what Clan Fenryr is, loyalty is all. To a wolf, there is nothing more sacred than the pack. Your father pulled me from chains, and when his entire world was threatened, still he refused to hand me over to those who would do me harm. He did not simply rescue *me* that day, but all the Angan carved from my flesh. And he did so with nothing to gain – without a notion of his blood. I swore to him I would protect you, that I would answer his call and that of his descendants whenever I was needed. I will not break that vow. And yet, that is only a small part of what you are."

The god reached out both his hands, extending one to Calen and one to Ella. "Take my hand, the both of you. The histories of our people stretch back for thousands of years, since long before we set foot in these lands. There is so much to tell, and the night is only so long. This is a thing that is easier shown than told. It is time you know the blood of your ancestors."

Both Calen and Ella exchanged a glance, and Faenir lifted his head from where it lay on his paws, his stare fixed on the wolf god.

Calen reached out to grab Ella's hand. "Together and only together."

Ella interlocked her fingers with his, and his sister gave him a sharp nod. They both lifted their free hands and grabbed Fenryr's open palms.

Just as had happened every other time Calen had experienced a vision of the past, the world around him turned and changed, shifting into smoke and streaks of colour.

Fenryr's voice boomed in the sky. "Thousands of years ago, our people called Terroncia home."

The shifting colours and smoke settled, and Calen stood atop an enormous cliff, thousands of feet high, jagged and carved from red rock. Ella stood only a few feet away, Fenryr between them.

A landscape of lush green spread out below, the sun blazing in the sky. Rivers carved winding paths through the trees, waterfalls crashing from great heights.

"The gods you know, the Enkara, were the ones who forged this world, brought it into existence, gave it life and purpose. This is what you know."

Calen nodded, staring at the sky in wonder as a flock of birds the size of horses whipped past his head, the air cool on his skin, his hair tussling in the wind.

He let out a long, mournful sigh. "It is a lie deepened by the passing of time.

The Enkara did not create the world – we do not know who did – and the Enkara were not always as they are now. They were the mortal plane's first inhabitants – the precursors to all life. They did not create the world, but they shaped everything in it with a primordial magic long since lost, and there are far more than those you know. Hundreds. They ascended from this plane before time itself came into existence. Some continued to meddle in the pit from which they crawled, others never looked back. The gods you know, and the gods you don't."

"Are you not a god?" Calen asked.

"The word god has different meanings to different people. To you, I am a god. To the Enkara, I am but a child. My people call ourselves the Danuan. But you would call us Lesser Gods, gods of flesh and bone, gods who have never ascended."

The world around Calen collapsed inwards and he was pulled forwards by a force unseen, wind crashing against him as though he were caught in the heart of a hurricane.

Beside him, Ella cried out, her eyes wide and golden. He grabbed her hand, holding on for dear life as they hurtled through the darkness. A second later, hard rock formed beneath their feet. The sky above shattered repeatedly, broken by lightning in shades of purple and blue.

"Fifty Enkara claimed Terroncia as their own. Carved its rivers and sculpted its mountains."

Thunderous cracks ripped through the air, and the ground shook. Deep fissures tore the rock apart as mountains rose and basins fell. Trees sprang from the earth, and water filled hollows the size of Camylin. Everywhere Calen looked, the world shifted and changed. Flowers in all the colours of a rainbow ripped across an entire field while chunks of clay pulled free of the earth and rose, drifting like clouds, trails of water misting from their edges.

"They gave it life, filled it. Amongst their creations were a race of people both savage and brilliant, beautiful and monstrous, capable of the greatest love and the darkest horrors. The Cealtaí – 'humans' in what is now the Common Tongue."

The world shifted, and brushstrokes of blue, green, and brown swirled around Calen. And when it all settled, he stood in a city the likes of which put even Aravell to shame. Buildings and towers hewn from cream stone rose for hundreds of feet all around. Rooves of domed sapphire glinted in the sun, shimmering with accents of silver and gold. Calen turned about in awe, his eyes following the rise of a statue that dwarfed even the towers. It looked human, its hand outstretched, an orb of pure light in its palm.

Sounds burst into existence, and the streets were thronged with people in robes of snow white, gold jewellery hanging from their necks and snaking around their arms.

"For thousands of years, there was peace of a sort as the Enkara walked the mortal plane. And then came the Fracturing. The Great War. The Enkara battled amongst each other, and the continent bled."

The world shook beneath Calen's feet, and screams filled the air. The towers and structures of the otherworldly city burst into flames, cracking and collapsing. The ground itself opened and fire spewed forth, burning flesh and bone alike. In the midst of the chaos, the beautiful robes of the people in the streets dissipated into clouds of smoke and reformed into glistening plates of armour, swords and spears of fire-red steel in their fists. They ripped each other to pieces in that beautiful armour with those beautiful weapons.

"It is not known why the war occurred – at least not to anyone but the Enkara themselves – but Terroncia didn't suffer alone. All across the known world, the Enkara waged war and the mortal plane itself cracked open. There were once fourteen continents. Seven were swallowed whole, completely obliterated as the gods turned this plane into their battlefield. And at some point in the wanton destruction, a peace was brokered. A peace that saved the very existence of life itself. The Enkara – those who survived – left the mortal plane and ascended to what we call the Arathír, the Godsrealm. Horrified by the cost of their war, they vowed to never again set foot in the mortal plane, to never again allow their creations to pay in blood for the Enkara's own hubris. That was when the fourteen surviving Enkara of Terroncia forged us, the Danuan. We were created to act in their place, to guide and shepherd the Cealtaí. We carved the Angan from our own flesh, to be our eyes and ears, extensions of ourselves. And each of us gifted a chosen number of the Cealtaí with our blood, to be our voices in the world, our heralds – the Tuatha. Our strength weakened, diluted by the Gifts we granted the Tuatha, but few became many and the sacrifice was necessary. In the four thousand years that followed, Terroncia faced periods of brutal war and glorious peace as many of the Danuan and our clans proved we were no better than what came before. But at least our powers were not capable of breaking the mortal realm itself."

Thousands of years flitted before Calen's eyes. Houses became villages, became towns, became cities, and were then burned to the ground, the cycle beginning anew. Armies crashed together, feeding the earth their blood, forests sprouting where the corpses were given to the soil. Mountains spewed molten fire, the earth cracked open like a brittle egg, and waves the size of a dragon's wings crashed against the coast.

Fenryr turned in place, watching the centuries streak past. Where Calen's visions had been chaos, Fenryr's command of the path was complete and utter. Where the world had moved around Calen, Fenryr walked through *it*, controlling every shift and every passing second. Where Calen was the leaf, Fenryr was the wind.

"That was," Fenryr said, a deep and pure sorrow in his eyes, "until one of our own found a way through the veil between worlds in search of an advantage in the wars and unleashed the horrors of the void into the heart of Terroncia."

Calen squeezed Ella's hand harder as the skies darkened and bled, lightning crashing down and carving strips from the earth. A dark tear ripped through the fabric of the world and terrifying creatures poured forth. Great, winged monstrosities tore armies limb from limb, horns twisting from their skulls, bones protruding through their chests, claws larger than even those of the Bloodmarked. Demons with the faces of men tore out throats and drank blood while creatures whose flesh seemed nothing but burning rock and molten fire razed cities to the ground. And along with all the death and destruction, Calen watched as men and women collapsed, their skin bubbling and melting. Others grew blisters of vibrant green that burst and spewed, the liquid within burning flesh and melting bone. One man collapsed before him, clawing at his own flesh, nails carving furrows of blood while slender worm-like creatures wriggled beneath his skin. The sight twisted Calen's stomach in knots.

Fenryr knelt beside the man, his hand hovering just above the writhing flesh. "The demons that surged through the tear between worlds swarmed over the continent like flood waters unleashed, and like hounds at their heels, so too came plagues and diseases that ripped through our flock in a way that steel and claw never could. The war waged for almost two hundred years, our arrogance leading us to believe we could triumph, until eventually that same arrogance was drowned in the blood of those we had sought to protect. That was when the exodus began and we fled to Epherian shores, leaving Terroncia to sink into the oceans."

Calen's vision blurred and turned to nothing but smears of muddled colour, and when everything reshaped, he stared out at a vast ocean of white sails that stretched to the horizon in all directions.

"Some of my brothers and sisters crossed the oceans for Narvona, Ardan, Karvos, Valacia, Tathos… but the vast majority settled in Epheria. That choice, perhaps, was our greatest folly. For from that moment onwards, we have not known a day of peace. We warred amongst each other for land and power and safety. Tore each other to pieces. And then the Urak wars broke out. And the elven wars. Endless war. And in those wars, we faced creatures as powerful as the demons that laid waste to our home, creatures large as the ships that bore us across the oceans, armoured from snout to tail, with breath that could melt steel."

"Dragons." As Calen spoke, more centuries flitted past his eyes, the world shifting and changing, armies clashing, skies of dragons setting entire battlefields alight.

Fenryr nodded. "We more than stood our ground in those wars," he said, pride in his voice. "Our people were mighty. Our Stormcallers struck the dragons from the sky with lightning. Our Blooddancers battled them through the eyes of wyverns and gryphons. My kin and I fought tooth and claw alongside our children. But those wars were bloody and brutal. There were no victors. Enough bodies were set into the earth in those years to build mountains, enough funeral pyres to light the sky. In the end, it wasn't the wars that killed us. It was greed and arrogance. Even our Pathfinders could not foresee our own downfall, so sure were they that those paths would not be walked. We tore ourselves apart, piece by piece."

The lights of the world flickered a hundred colours, then dimmed to black. Fenryr stood before Ella and Calen with his gaze fixed on the black ground. "As the centuries passed, many of our people lost who they were. In their search for power, they betrayed their own. Many of the Cealtaí turned on the Tuatha. Either from jealousy or from sheer greed, or a thousand other reasons. Even the Tuatha turned on each other, the wars between clans taking on new forms. My brothers and sisters were hunted, enslaved, murdered. Even gods can die. Eventually, hundreds of Danuan were dwindled to the five that survive to this day – Kaygan, Bjorna, Vethnir, Dvalin, and the one who stands before you."

Fenryr lifted his head, his golden eyes seeming to stare straight into Calen's soul.

"I show you all this, Calen and Ella Bryer, because in my heart there is nothing more important than the preservation of who and what you are. You are the children of my blood, the Tuatha. And our history, our saga tale, our lessons, our missteps and wrong turns cannot be forgotten. And there are too few of my Tuatha left – too few of any Tuatha. So upon your shoulders, and the shoulders of all those who bear my blood, is the weight of remembering, the weight of knowing, and the weight of ensuring that past mistakes are not repeated. The question you asked was what you are to me. Why you are guarded when the other Tuatha are not. There are three reasons. The first is my vow to your father." Fenryr pressed his palm to his forehead. "May his soul find its way in the blood of time. The second is a deeper thing. I told you that your mother was Gifted, as you are," he said, looking to Calen. "You are Pathfinders. You see the paths once walked, and she saw those not yet taken."

"And she fed us poison to keep our Gifts from manifesting." That wound was still fresh. Even after Ella had said it aloud, he still couldn't quite take it in. Their mam had lied to them for so long – just as their dad had. None of it made any sense. And yet… Calen wasn't angry. He wanted to be furious, to be consumed by rage. But all he felt was loss. There wasn't a doubt in his mind that there was a reason for everything, that his parents had done what they had thought was right. Because that's what they had always done. That was who they were. Even with the lies, he trusted them entirely.

"You are here, you are safe, and you draw breath." Fenryr clasped his hands together and gave Calen a sympathetic smile. "That was all your mother ever cared for." He stopped for a moment, then let out a long sigh. "I want you to understand your blood. To understand why you are the way you are. You feel it, don't you? Not just now, but always, you feel the wolf inside you. A willingness to die for those around you, a devotion beyond all measure to the ones you love. A deep fury in your heart, a savage rage that burns for your enemies. That is Fenryr blood. *My* blood. The Tuatha of the clans are broken into septs – families. Your mother is a descendant of the Great Sept of Eridain, an old and proud sept of my blood. Since before we set foot in Epheria, Sept Eridain were the greatest of my children. Generations upon generations of kings and queens. Our most powerful Pathfinders, Stormcallers, and Heartseekers. But the name Bryer holds its own legend."

"Bryer?"

"But our dad wasn't a druid." Ella looked from Calen to Fenryr. "He's wasn't – was he?"

"No." Fenryr stood in the darkness, his golden eyes gleaming. "But the blood of the wolf ran in his veins. Though he did not know it, your father was of the Tuatha blood. But he was what our people call a Truan lan Volas. Without Light – Lightless." A touch of sadness crept into Fenryr's voice. "It is a name given to those born without Gifts, those who are not true Tuatha. There have always been Volas in the druidic peoples. In the early days, one in every ten was born without a Gift. Their blood was still my blood, they still bore the hearts of wolves, the loyalty, the strength, the rage, but the Gifts had not reached them. As our people were hunted and our bloodlines grew weaker, the number of Volas increased. And now, new Gifted pups are rare as red moons. When our people first made landfall in Epheria, my clan was not counted amongst the Great Clans. We had lost many in the wars against the demons and in the unceasing battles within our own. By the time we reached Epherian shores, we numbered no more than a few hundred Tuatha, a similar number Angan, and two thousand Cealtaí who followed me. But within that, Sept Bryer played a major part in bringing about a new dawn for Clan Fenryr." Fenryr's fangs bit into his bottom lip as he smiled. "Sept Bryer is a sept famed for their Blooddancers. Bold and proud, an old sept who bled for their clan. A sept that rose to become the greatest of my champions. In the centuries and millennia that followed, I thought Sept Bryer dead and lost. They were of that ilk – the kind to die rather than yield. The name carried on, but the blood withered, blending with that of the Cealtaí. And as Ages came and went and my Tuatha and Angan were hunted, many of the Great Septs were lost. It wasn't until Baldon Stormseeker found your father and I felt the wolf in his blood that I knew the sept of Bryer still lived. That he and your mother had found each other in this dark world is something beautiful beyond measure. To see the two bloodlines meet... It brought warmth to my long-cold heart. You are not simply Tuatha, or druids, or whatever name you choose. Your blood is that of the wolf, it is the blood of my greatest champions, my wisest kings, and my most powerful Tuatha."

As Fenryr's words echoed in the darkness, the world shifted, and Calen found himself once more sitting in Alura's Eyrie, his right hand clasped in Ella's, his left hand gripping Fenryr's.

His hands trembled as he pulled them back. He should have had a thousand questions in his mind, yearned for a thousand answers. But instead, he was consumed by a hollow feeling and emptiness where something should have been. Tears welled in his eyes but didn't fall.

Ella's hand rested on his knee. "I know."

Calen clenched his jaw at his sister's words, clutching her hand. So many things his parents hadn't told him, so many lies kept. He wanted to be angry, to feel that rage he knew so well. But the only images in his head were of his dad's lifeless body and the flames that had taken his mam from him. If they had only told him, maybe everything would have been different. He could have helped. He could have been stronger.

Ella squeezed his hand, and a high-pitched whine rang out from the plateau above, Valerys's mind wrapping around his. The dragon's warmth filled the cracks in Calen's heart but didn't mend them.

"Why?" Ella asked, her hand still squeezing Calen's, Faenir whining beside her. "All of this, why did they keep it from us?"

"To keep you safe. From the moment your mother was born, she was forced to hide and run. Clan Vethnir, loyal to Fane and his empire, hunted us to the edge of extinction, while Bjorna's Angan slaughtered any they could find. Both of my brothers command Tuatha and Angan in far greater numbers than I. One by one, your mother watched her brothers and sisters torn from this world, watched her own mother's throat ripped out by a Vethnir hunter. When she had seen only sixteen summers, her father died protecting her. Freis fled to western Illyanara, where she found your father. Years later, your father found me, and I, in turn, found Freis. I told Vars of his heritage, but he cared little for it. Your mother was with child, and both of them wanted that child to never live the lives they knew. She had chosen to dull her Gifts and to ward against yours to keep the hunters from her door. She chose to protect her pack, and I honoured that. And your father chose to do the same. I left Faenir as a guardian to watch over them, blessed with my blood."

Calen shook his head, his throat tightening.

Valerys cracked his wings and lifted himself into the air, then soared down to the central plateau upon which Calen and the others sat. The dragon alighted behind Fenryr, the ground shaking beneath his weight. He craned his neck down and pressed his snout into the side of Calen's head.

Calen brushed his hand along Valerys's jaw and pushed his forehead into the hard, warm scales.

"What is the third reason?" Ella asked, lifting her hand from Calen's knee and leaning forwards. "You said there were three. What is the third?"

Calen stared at his sister. Where tears had formed in his eyes, hers were hard and cold, her blue irises now a glittering gold, her nails turned to dark claws, fangs pressing into her lips.

Fenryr drew a long breath and let out a heavy sigh. "Enough lies have been whispered in your ears and enough promises to fill an ocean, I'd wager. So I will speak plain. The third reason is a selfish one – I need you. Our clan is at the brink of death. Our people as a whole are not far away." Fenryr tilted his head back and looked up at the dragon looming over him. "Astride Valerys, Calen is the most powerful weapon we have. One of your blood has never been bound to a dragon. Pathfinders do not have keepers as Blooddancers do. In this, Calen and Valerys are unique and their bond has created something singular. I want for Calen's power – and yours, Ella."

"Mine?"

"Your father's bloodline is that of my greatest warriors. And you are the last of that line, a Blooddancer of Sept Bryer. You are far from seeing even your thirtieth summer and yet what you did – shifting with the souls of dragons – has never been done. Not once. That alone shows me the power you hold." Fenryr laughed, a deep choking laugh as he muttered to himself, "Of course, the blood of Darand and Alannah's line would emerge precisely when it was needed."

"I fragmented." Ella shook her head, and Calen could see her twisting her tongue in her mouth as their mother had taught them to do when biting back anger. "If not for Tamzin, my soul would be drifting through Níthianelle until the breaking of time. What about that speaks of power to you?"

"You're alive, young one." The laughter had gone from Fenryr's voice, the mention of the name Tamzin seeming to sour his mood. Calen recognised the name. It was the druid he had met at the edge of the Burnt Lands alongside Rokka, the one who had told him Ella had awoken. "Our Blooddancers attempted to shift with dragons from the emergence of the very first wars after we made landfall. Tuatha who had fought a hundred battles, who had waged war against the voidspawn. Tuatha who had shed more blood than you have seen water. If we had been able to do so, those wars would have been shorter than a breath. I felt their minds shatter and burn. Felt their souls bleed. Dragons are beasts unlike any other. The fact that your mind still holds itself together says more than a thousand words ever could. And so I say again, my motives are not entirely pure. I came here to guide you back to the mortal plane, but I stay because I wish to use your strength to forge a second dawn for the children of my blood, to forge a new world."

"There is already a war raging," Calen said.

"I am aware." The god turned his eyes on Calen, and a shiver ran through him, the very blood in his veins growing cold. "They are the same war. If Efialtír crosses into this world, we will all pay the price. The Enkara left the mortal plane for a reason. All I ask is that I and Clan Fenryr be welcomed to stand at your side and, when the blood has been spilled, the fires have died, and the living crawl from the ashes of what is left, that our people have a place in the new world."

Calen held Fenryr's gaze, something deep within him refusing to look away. This was a god that sat before him. Not Aeson or Chora or the Triarchy. A god. Of all those who had sought to use him and twist him, Fenryr was the one who truly had the power to do so, and he had chosen not to.

As though reading Calen's mind, the god spoke again. "I would fight at your side, not on your back with chains in my hands. I have felt the pull of chains around my neck. It was your father who freed me from them. And it is not something I would inflict on another."

"What of the other gods?" Calen glanced at Ella, who was staring back at him, Faenir now sitting upright at her side. "You spoke of Bjorna, and Kaygan, and Vethnir, and Dvalin. Where are they in all of this?"

"Dvalin resides within this very woodland. Though I am not surprised she has yet to reveal herself. She has always been a cautious one. Though, I do not believe it will be long before she shows herself. As for the others…" Fenryr flicked his tongue off the tip of his right fang. "Bjorna wants for nothing but blood – my blood and that of the others. He does not care for the wars of this land. He is fighting the same war he has been fighting since Terroncia. He would be the last of us. We will find no friend there. Kaygan I'm sure we will be seeing shortly. That kat is many steps ahead of us all. The moment you think you know his will is two moments after the knife is buried in your gut. He will require caution. As for Vethnir…" The name turned to a growl on Fenryr's lips, and he spat on the stone. All about the plateau, the other Angan snarled.

"Bjorna wants us dead. But he and his clan fight like warriors. They fight for their own will. That I respect. Vethnir betrayed us all. He was the first of the Danuan to hunt his own kind and sell his captives to the Cealtaí, the elves, the Jotnar. Even now, he has been aligned with Fane Mortem since The Order fell, buying his safety with the heads of his kin. I would rip out his throat and feel his blood run down my chin."

"I would do the same." The voice echoed in the vast open space of the Eyrie. Faenir snapped upright, the Angan following suit as Valerys spun, frills vibrating, wings spreading wide.

Calen and Ella were both on their feet in a heartbeat, Ella's claws extended, the Spark flowing in Calen's veins. Only Fenryr moved slowly, letting out a sigh as he pulled himself upright.

Two women and a man stood at the edge of the Eyrie, along with that same kat-like creature Calen had seen on the edge of the Burnt Lands, scales of black glass glimmering on its body. Calen recognised each of them.

"Tamzin…" Ella took a step forwards, her stare softening as she looked to the short, dark-haired woman.

Tamzin smiled softly and bowed her head. "It is good to see you well."

Fenryr stepped past Ella as Aneera and the other Angan drew closer. For a moment Calen thought the Eyrie might run red with blood, but instead, Fenryr gave the slightest of bows towards Tamzin and pressed his palm to his forehead. "I am told it is by your grace that my child has returned to this plane. You have my thanks and my boon. If you find yourself in need, ask what you will of me. If it is within reason, I will fulfil it."

Tamzin mimicked the gesture, bowing far deeper. "You honour me, Danuan. I would not have seen her taken by the Vethnir or slain by the Bjorna. She is my kin. Your thanks is more than I require."

Fenryr inclined his head.

Rokka pressed his hand to his forehead and moved closer, only flinching when Valerys lowered his head and pulled his lips back in a snarl. The old man looked up at the dragon, a smile cracking his hesitant expression. "Don't."

Valerys leaned closer, the rumble in his throat rising. But after a moment, he pulled back, the rumble never truly dissipating.

"My most sincere thanks." Rokka bowed deeply to the dragon, deep enough for it to seem almost theatrical. He looked to Calen and smiled. "Being burned alive is not as fun as it sounds." He turned his attention to Fenryr. "It is good to see you, brother."

"Is it? I see you still hide behind smoke and dead faces."

The pair exchanged greetings, but all the while, the words that had left Rokka's lips spun in Calen's mind. He took a step forwards, eyes narrowing on Rokka. "Brother?"

Fenryr let out a long sigh, pursing his lips. "You have encountered him then? Which name did he give you? Which guise did he wear?"

"Rokka… He said his name was Rokka."

The wolf god shook his head, laughing almost in disbelief. "You stand before Kaygan the kat. The god of many faces. The prowler of the paths unwalked. The Trickster and collector of strays. Show yourself, brother. I'm weary of all this."

Rokka opened his arms wide as though caught in an act, and as he did his face shifted. The man's skin tightened, the deep wrinkles vanishing, the grey in his hair turning to deep brown. He stood a little straighter and held his head a little higher. The only thing that didn't change were his eyes. They retained that same vibrancy, that same ever-changing blue-grey. "You do me a great honour bestowing upon me all these titles, brother. Truly, I am nothing more than what I am. And what I am is here to broker an alliance."

"A proposition you've made before – many times."

"Ah yes, but there are only five of us now. Bjorna has lost his mind, Vethnir has the moral fortitude of a flea-riddled weasel, and Dvalin would happily play this game of hide and seek until time itself breaks. You would seem like the logical choice."

"You're a god…" The words left Calen's lips of their own volition.

"I am," Kaygan replied, giving Calen a toothy grin before turning back to Fenryr. "We are opposites, you and I, but we need each other."

"Do we now?" Fenryr growled.

"I've seen this conversation a thousand times, brother. And you know we do. I have a Starchaser and a Stormcaller, and I can see the paths not yet walked. You can see the paths that have already come, you have more Angan than I, you have a dragon, and—"

"*He* does not have a dragon." Calen pushed all his doubts and questions to the dark corners of his mind. *No more strings. No more chains.* He pulled the Spark through him as he marched towards Kaygan. The druids, Tamzin and Una, moved to block Calen's path but drew up short as Valerys loomed over him, teeth bared and eyes misting purple light. The dragon let out a roar, his head shifting from Tamzin to Una, spittle wetting their faces.

Calen stared at them both until they glanced back at Kaygan, who gestured for them to step aside.

"Neither I nor Valerys belong to anyone." Calen stood so his face was barely a few inches from Kaygan's, Valerys's warm breath rolling over the back of his head and rustling the god's no longer grey hair.

Kaygan curled his lips downward as though impressed by something. "Hmm." He looked Calen over. "This is not the path I thought we were walking. It will do though."

The way the god looked at Calen, the way he spoke as though Calen weren't even there, called forth a fury within both himself and Valerys. A fury that burned cold and slow. "If you talk of your 'paths' once more, I will cut out your tongue and feed it to you, god or no."

Tamzin stepped forwards, her eyes shifting to bright blue with kat-like black slits for pupils. The druid's fingernails extended and sliced through the tips of her fingers, curling into massive claws. "Try it."

The kat-like monstrosity beside her let out a deep growl, baring its fangs and arching its back.

Ella was between Calen and Tamzin in a heartbeat, Faenir at her side. The wolfpine stood level with the kat, hackles raised. Ella shook her head at Tamzin. "Not a step closer."

Valerys lowered his head over both Calen and Ella, the pressure building within him, the fire calling.

"Easy – Tamzin, Kerith." Kaygan pressed a clawed hand against Tamzin's chest and gently pushed her back, the armoured kat, Kerith, moving in step with her. "That is not a path we wish to…" He glanced to Calen and stifled a laugh. "Apologies, old habits." Kaygan drew a long breath in and studied Calen. "I have seen many of your ilk across the millennia. They all have one thing in common."

"And what is that?"

"They are dead, and I am not."

"That can be changed."

A low shriek reverberated in Valerys's throat, and the dragon lifted his neck and opened his jaws. The heat of the fire within Valerys warmed the back of Calen's head.

"It would take more than dragonfire to kill a god, Wolfchild."

Calen leaned forwards, staring into Kaygan's eyes, his voice level and calm. "Then why do you look so scared?"

Wing beats echoed through the Eyrie, and both Varthear and Avandeer soared overhead, alighting behind the god. The vermillion frills on Varthear's neck stood on end, while smoke drifted from Avandeer's nostrils.

Una made to step closer to Kaygan, but Varthear snapped at her, a hiss forming in the great dragon's throat.

Vibrations swept through the Eyrie as Sardakes descended on foot from the same plateau, his sapphire eyes standing stark against his black scales in the darkness.

"So it is this path then," the god said before turning down his bottom lip. He looked to Calen and inclined his head. "You are full of surprises, Calen Bryer. I am yet to decide whether that is to your benefit."

"I don't have time for you or your riddles." Calen sucked in his cheeks and calmed himself with a breath. Though not a shred of that calm touched Valerys. Kaygan's words had only stoked the fire within the dragon, and he wished to test the claim that dragonfire couldn't kill a god. Valerys had his doubts.

Kaygan only smiled back. "Oh, you'll make the time, I'm sure." Those blue-grey kat eyes searched Calen's, Kaygan's smile growing wider. "When you need us, we'll be in the empty barracks in the city. Not the one by the fruit tree – that one needed a clean – the third on the right. For now, if you'll excuse us, we are late to meet a friend. You won't need us for a day or so. But you *will* need us."

With that, Kaygan signalled to his two druids, turned, and left, strolling right between Sardakes, Avandeer, and Varthear without a glance at any of them.

"He has been precisely that infuriating for thousands of years." Fenryr moved to stand beside Calen, his gaze fixed on the passage that led back to Alura.

"How did they get in here? The gates are guarded every hour of every day. The Dracur'in patrol Alura ceaselessly."

"One of the Tuatha with him is a Starchaser. A druid of the aether. Their Gift allows them to open gateways between one place and another so long as they have set eyes on their destination."

"She's been here before?" Calen's chest tightened. How deeply were these druids of Kaygan embedded within Aravell? And what friend were they meeting? The uncertainty unsettled him.

"Perhaps," Fenryr said. "Or Kaygan guided her. He was here the day I guided Ella back to the mortal plane."

The wolf god clasped both Ella's and Calen's shoulders. "You are your father's and mother's children both. I see their fire in you, their passion. Let Kaygan drift to the back of your mind. His plans will unfurl as they were meant to. I have spent millennia learning as such. You have enough to think on. More Angan will arrive by the day. But I have kept many dispersed through the continent. Clan Fenryr will be counted in the battles to come."

Fenryr and the Angan started to leave, but the god turned back. He stood there for a moment before approaching Calen once more, golden eyes locking with his. "There is nothing in this world heavier than the weight of a crown. Those not fit to wear one break from the strain of their own failures. And those who are must struggle not beneath the weight of the metal from which it was forged, but that of all the souls who hang in the balance of every decision made. Whether born from honour or desperation, that weight leads kings and queens to make dark choices. When the empire killed The Order, it also killed the weight of a hundred crowns. But as the empire dies, hands will come from the shadows, clawing at the crowns of dead kings and queens. Be careful, young one, even of those who call themselves 'friend'. The only way to truly test that word is to put yourself between a person and the thing they desire most in the world. Your neck will ache from the weight of it."

"I have no crown," Calen answered. "Nor do I want one."

"We seldom get what we want." Fenryr gave Calen a weak smile, then turned and left.

CHAPTER SIXTY-NINE

THREADS EVER WINDING

20th Day of the Blood Moon

Cuinviel, formerly Catagan – Winter, Year 3081 After Doom

Salara awoke to a hand over her mouth and gleaming blue eyes staring back at her. Cold steel pressed into her neck. She reached for the Spark but felt nothing, her heart racing at the realisation that a ward surrounded her. Vyrmír roared in the back of her mind, and so too could she hear the dragon's roar echo in the distance as he lifted himself from the cave he'd claimed as his eyrie and ripped through the sky towards the city.

"Even think about moving, and I will open your throat, Draleid." The woman's voice was firm and level, and she pressed the blade harder against Salara's throat to emphasise her point.

"How did you—"

"I'm asking the questions. You were looking after a friend of ours, and now we'd like her back. Where is the key to her collar?"

"What are you talking… Boud."

"Speed it along, Tamzin. The dragon won't be long getting here." Boud's voice sounded from somewhere within the chamber, but Salara couldn't lift her head to see where.

"And how's that thing going to get in here?" The woman's stare never broke from Salara's as she spoke, her lip curling to reveal long, sharp fangs. "That's the problem with these beasts. Sometimes size isn't everything. Isn't that right, Kerith?"

A low grumble sounded to the left of Salara's head. A large shape slowly emerged from the darkness at the edge of her vision. It was some kind of animal, though like nothing she'd ever seen. It had the face of a lioness or a frostkat, but larger still, with a flat nose and arched brow, two enormous fangs protruding from its upper jaw. Pale moonlight that shone through the window glistened against obsidian-like scales that armoured its chest and neck, smaller shards studded into its face.

"Now that you and Kerith have been introduced… Where is the key to the collar?"

"What collar?"

Salara grunted as Tamzin pressed the blade harder, drawing blood. Another roar sounded in the skies outside, and Vyrmír's fury flowed through her like a raging river.

"Please, time is not something worth wasting," a third voice whispered, deep and considered. A shape moved from the shadows on Salara's left – a man. A pale, sharp face formed in the darkness over Salara. The man reached out a hand, his fingernail slicing through the flesh and forming a dark claw, which he pressed to her cheek. "Answer our questions, and there will be no pain. You are required on this path, but not all of your limbs are." It was this man who warded her. Everything about the language of his body spoke of power and control. He turned his head. "Boud?"

The druid stepped from the shadows and rested a hand atop Salara's. The woman seemed taller now, her shoulders broader. "Despite your ignorance, I do like you, Draleid. And I would prefer if we didn't have to cut pieces from you, despite your threats to do so to me." She knelt beside the bed so that her eyes were level with Salara's. "You see, your character is not measured by what you do when you're fighting for your freedom, or your lost home, or your honour, or whatever cause you choose. Your character is measured by what you do when you *have* the power. And right now, that power is mine. You can refuse to tell us where the key is, but the end result will not be one you wish for. We will find it. I know it's not far, and Kerith has a good nose. But I'm afraid you will be missing things you're fond of. Which, I say again, is not something I want to do but am willing to do."

Once Boud had spoken, the man dragged his claw along Salara's cheek, the skin parting as though opened by a diamond blade. She grunted and clenched her jaw but refused to give him the satisfaction of her pain.

Vyrmír roared again in response. He was not far. If she delayed them, the dragon would come crashing through the side of the keep. But there was also no telling how many others might die if that were to come to pass – herself included. There were hundreds who chambered in the tower, and hundreds more below. Boud's life was not worth theirs.

"It's in the chest at the back of the room, hidden beneath clothes." Vandrien had given the key to Salara for safekeeping two weeks ago. Clearly, Boud had discovered as much. Either the woman would escape that night or she would die in the trying. Whichever happened, she would no longer be of use to the Evalien. And so Salara chose the path of least resistance.

"Well," Tamzin said, not removing the blade from Salara's throat. "That was a lot easier than I thought it would be. Una."

The sound of shuffling feet came from the back of the room as a fourth person moved to find the chest.

"I would suggest you take it and go quickly before Vyrmír tears open that wall behind you. Though I'm not sure how you're getting out now that his roar has woken the keep." Shouts already echoed from the yard below, and footsteps and clanging steel reverberated in the stone corridors. The Evalien of Numillíon knew a dragon's warning.

"We'll be just fine." Tamzin's lips spread into a wide grin.

A loud *clang* rang out. The sound of Boud's collar hitting the stone floor.

A moment later, Boud leaned over Salara, her head beside Tamzin's. She looked over Salara's face and down at the steel pressed to her throat. She sighed. "It would be so easy… but no. Threats aside, you did not mistreat me. And so I will do unto you as you did unto me. It's funny to think this entire time you saw me as a tool… when it was you being used. Ironic. Think on that. The world is not always as we see it."

With that, Boud was gone and Tamzin pulled the blade from Salara's neck and leapt backwards off the bed. Within a heartbeat, Salara was on her feet, a knife slipped from its place beneath her pillow.

But before her, a white light illuminated what she could only describe as a tear in the world, like a spear had torn through a breastplate. On the other side of the tear was dense woodland, flames flickering in the distance.

Tamzin and the other woman – Una – had already stepped through to the woodland on the other side. But Boud and the man still stood in the room, only a pace from the gateway.

She let out a gasp as the ward around her vanished, the Spark suddenly within reach, calling to her. The man stared back, his head tilted to the side, watching.

One whip of Air and Boud would have been strapped to the ground. A prisoner once more. And if she moved fast enough, she could ward the man and drive the knife through his heart. But something in that thought gave Salara pause. Who was she if she trapped this woman in chains and placed a collar around her neck once more, just as the Lorians had done to the Onarakina?

"Good choice," the man said, nodding. "There are many paths ahead, Salara Ithan. You have your part to play. But your fate is not yet decided. It is in your own hands. What do you want to be? A hero or a monster?"

Salara could hear the beating of Vyrmír's wings, feel the rushing blood in his veins.

Boud glanced at her and gave a soft nod before stepping through the gateway, but the man came a step closer. The coldness of his stare crept under her skin. "In two days, look to the Firnin Mountains. The path you wish to walk lies there. Vengeance and opportunity."

His gaze lingered for another moment, then he stepped through the gateway and it collapsed behind him, the white light evaporating into thin air.

Salara dropped the knife and reached out to Vyrmír, who was now careening towards the tower. *I'm all right, my light. I'm all right.*

The roar that left the dragon's jaws shook the stone, and his fury burned through Salara. He was not as understanding as she was. Images of Vyrmír ripping Boud in half flashed from the dragon's mind to Salara's.

I'm safe. That is what matters.

The dragon twisted and tore upwards, scanning the city and the lands beyond for any sign of the intruders.

A moment later, three guards burst into the room, torches and swords in their hands.

"Draleid! Are you hurt?" Captain Undrír stormed across the floor and snatched the knife from where Salara had dropped it, then took a blanket and draped it over her naked shoulders.

"We heard Vyrmír's roar. Something felt wrong." Undrír looked about the room for any signs of struggle or an intruder, his mouth scrunching in confusion when he saw none.

"The druid is gone. Taken by more of her kind. Bring me to Vandrien."

CHAPTER SEVENTY

THE BELLY OF THE BEAST

20th Day of the Blood Moon

Marin Mountains – Winter, Year 3081 After Doom

Arden ripped his Soulblade from the Urak's chest, letting the beast drop. He twisted and caught another creature in mid-jump, his armoured fingers wrapping around its throat. Twice he drove his Soulblade into its gut before tossing it aside and unleashing a primal roar.

Shouts rose, hands pointing towards a tunnel on the other side of the cavern. The words were muffled in Arden's ears. He charged forwards into a group of Bloodspawn. All he saw in his mind's eye was Lyrin's face, and the only sound that echoed was his fallen brother-knight's voice.

He blocked the downswing of a massive black sword, green light bursting from the collision, then planted his boot in the wielder's chest and sent the creature careening into an open chasm in the ground. He swung back his elbow, feeling a *crunch* as the plate of his Sentinel armour shattered bone. One backstep, one swing, and the creature was opened from shoulder to hip.

Arden twisted as a black spear thrust at his abdomen. He released his Soulblade and grasped the Urak's head with both hands and rammed his helmet into its skull. As the creature staggered, Arden slammed his boot into the side of its knee, blood spraying as bone splintered. He ripped the spear from its arms, spun it, then drove it into the howling Urak's neck, blood spurting around the shaft.

He left the weapon in its place. He pivoted and summoned his Soulblade in the same motion as he cleaved another beast in half, innards slopping onto the stone, blood glistening in the green light.

Arden heaved in laboured breaths, his blood on fire. Lyrin had died because of his choices. He had died because Arden had separated from the others. He would not allow that to happen again.

The sound of crunching rock caused Arden to spin. He released his Soulblade and caught a falling sword with his open palm, the steel clanging against his Sentinel armour.

The Urak before him roared, blood-red eyes wide, spittle flying. Arden grabbed its throat with his free hand and roared back. He jerked his right hand, twisting the beast's wrist so that it lost its grip on the sword. Drawing all his strength, he drove his right fist into the Urak's gut, the power of his Sentinel armour snapping bones, and still he roared. The beast clawed at him, howling.

"Is that all?" he screamed. In his mind, memories flitted from Ilnaen to the ambush in Ölm Forest to the battle of The Glade. These creatures had been at the heart of his darkest days. They had taken his closest friends, one after another.

He would not wallow in what he had lost, but neither would he forget them. He would use their memories as fuel. He would tear these beasts apart, and he would paint his vengeance in blood.

Arden placed a closed fist against the Urak's skull and summoned his Soulblade. The creature went limp in a burst of green light.

He turned just as a monstrous weight slammed into his chest and sent him hurtling across the ground. His head rang from the impact, and it was by pure instinct that he threw himself to the side as a clawed foot crashed down where he had lain.

Arden dragged himself to one knee, a Bloodmarked staring down at him, the runes in its flesh billowing black smoke.

A green Soulblade burst through its chest from the back while a second cleaved its arm at the elbow. When the beast fell, Brother Kevan and Sister-Captain Ruon stood in its place.

Ruon offered Arden an arm and hauled him to his feet. "Not the time for it. Focus."

She needed no more words. They had spoken at length in the Tranquil Garden. She knew his burdens, knew his loss.

"Yes, Sister-Captain."

"I need you to lead, Brother Arden. There are many new souls within our ranks this night. You are now a veteran of our number."

"Yes, Sister-Captain," Arden said again.

"Forward!" Kallinvar's voice echoed like thunder, and Arden turned to see the man charging through three Bloodmarked, a score of knights around him.

The other knights moved about through the enormous cavern, their Soulblades blending with the light of the hundreds of gemstones set in iron sconces fixed to rock. The entire knighthood bore down on the Urak hold – a decision Kallinvar had made after Ilnaen.

So many brother and sister knights had fallen since the Blood Moon had risen. He'd lost count. As one fell, their Sigil was granted to another, and so on, and so on. Brother Galvar and Brother Turilin of The Third fell to a Shaman the same night they had lost Lyrin in Ilnaen. And Brother-Captain Darmerian of The Fifth as well. They were stronger together, fighting as one.

Many of the knights Arden fought beside now were faces he had not known a month before, or a week, or even a day. And it was clear in the way they moved in their Sentinel armour, in the way they wielded their Soulblades. Arden had been given two years before he'd been sent on task from the temple. Many of these men and women had been given little more than a day. They had been warriors in their past lives and so were well acquainted with death, but to be a Knight of Achyron was something different entirely. They no longer faced other men and woman but demons of Efialtír himself.

"Come, brothers," Ruon said. "Let us pray to Achyron this is the night we find it."

Kallinvar had said the convergence of the Taint in this Urak hold was the largest he had sensed since the Blood Moon had risen. They had spent hours carving their way through, trying to push towards the source. Six knights had fallen already, and many were injured.

As they drove further into the hold, the oily poison of the Taint grew thicker in the air, shifting in pulsing waves. It probed at Arden's mind, scratching over his skin and setting his hairs on end.

They came to a fork, the tunnel diverging. The core of the Taint lay ahead.

"Olyria, Ruon, Armites, Gandrid," Kallinvar called out, pointing his Soulblade towards the tunnel mouth on the left. "Take your chapters to the left. Reach through the Sigil if you find anything."

Ildris and Sylven pulled in beside Arden as the knighthood split, Sister Intara and Brother Endan alongside them. It was a strange thing to feel the pull of Daynin's and Mirken's Sigils but to know other souls held from Heraya's embrace were beneath the helmets.

Uraks flooded from side tunnels, howling and roaring, wielding their blackened steel, gemstones glowing red in the weapons' hilts. Arden carved through them with a fury, his Soulblade slicing flesh and bone alike. The further they pushed down the tunnel, the harder the Uraks fought and the greater their numbers. But Arden never stopped moving forwards, the others falling in behind him, Ruon, Ildris, and Varlin.

The tunnel opened into a small chamber with many levels rising upwards through the rock, connected by staircases of rough-hewn stone. Iron sconces and braziers stuffed with gemstones bathed the cold rock in crimson light, causing Arden to feel as though he had walked into the void itself.

Arden had never before seen the inside of an Urak hold. He had never even thought of where the beasts slept, where they ate or lived. In his mind, they had been akin to wild animals, sleeping in caves and surviving only for the sake of it. But this place had been carved over centuries, constructed with thought and care. This was their home. Rough-hewn benches of stone and iron were scattered about, along with chairs, baskets of half-rotted fruit, and buckets of salted meat. On the second level, deer carcasses hung from iron hooks alongside those of pigs and sheep – likely stolen from the farms nearby.

But any illusion that these beasts were anything other than monsters was shattered when he looked a little higher and saw the flayed bodies of men, women, and children hanging from more hooks.

A cacophony of roars echoed from the upper levels and the branching tunnels. Within a heartbeat, Uraks were leaping from above and swarming through the tunnels.

Before Arden even had the chance to move, a Bloodmarked crashed down onto the newly-inducted Brother Endan, its obsidian claws skewering him through the chest. The beast roared, and a pulse of Taint burst outwards, its runes igniting with crimson light.

Black fire swirled about the Bloodmarked's arm and through its claws, consuming Brother Endan. His screams lasted only seconds.

It was Brother Kevan who reached the creature first. His Soulblade carved through the Bloodmarked's arm, the runes blazing and smoke billowing. But the beast caught him with a backswing and sent him crashing into a group of Uraks.

Arden's feet moved even before his thoughts had fully formed. He charged forwards and leapt onto a rock before throwing himself into the crush of beasts that fell upon Brother Kevan. He summoned his Soulblade and drove it down through an Urak's back as he landed, releasing the weapon as the creature crashed to the ground. Arden rolled, freeing himself of the beast's lifeless body. Rising, he once more summoned the ancient weapon, green light bursting from his fist.

The Soulblade came into existence just in time to catch the downswing of a jet-black axe that had been destined to remove Kevan's head from his shoulders.

Arden swung his blade up the steel, then snapped it back down, severing the Urak's arms at the wrists. Without missing a beat, he twisted at the waist, threw his weight onto his back leg, and swung the light-wrought blade up through the creature's jaw in a burst of blood.

He reached back, felt a hand wrap around his forearm, and pulled. No words passed between Arden and Brother Kevan. The two knights stood back to back, Soulblades ignited in their fists. Together, they cut down anything that came close. Where Uraks moved, green light shone and bodies fell.

"Brothers!" Brother-Captain Armites strode through the thick of bodies, carving a path, six of his knights fighting beside him. They cut their way to Arden and Kevan, leaving a momentary stillness around them.

Arden released his Soulblade and grasped Brother-Captain Armites's pauldron. "Thank you, Brother-Captain."

"Don't thank me yet, brother. There is plenty more time to die. Though, the Bloodspawn look to be retreating." He glanced about at the emptying chamber. Any Bloodspawn that lingered were being cut down left and right.

"They're not retreating," Ruon called out as she approached, Ildris, Varlin, and Sylven with her. The new recruit, Sister Intara, knelt by Brother Endan's body.

Ruon pointed to a large tunnel mouth on the left side of the chamber, three levels up. "They're falling back. The Taint pulses from that direction. Whatever they are defending so ferociously lies there."

"I will summon the Grandmaster," Armites said, inclining his head to Ruon.

Ruon held up an open palm. "Not yet. This entire hold reeks of Efialtír's touch, and the Essence of stolen lives illuminates the very chamber we stand in. I would not call him until we are certain."

"Brother-Captain Gandrid," Ruon called, "Sister-Captain Olyria, take the rearguard. Armites and I will lead the way."

Olyria pulled her blade from the chest of a dead Bloodmarked and gave a sharp nod.

"Knights of The Seventh, form up!" Gandrid roared. "Nothing gets past us."

"Yes, Brother-Captain!" the knights answered.

Ruon lifted Intara to her feet, then knelt over Endan. "We will find you in his halls, brother," she whispered, her helmet receding as she looked down upon the man's blackened corpse. "Drink well."

She rose slowly and let out a soft sigh before pulling her gaze from the body of the man who had been called to serve The Warrior for little more than three days. "Whatever this place is," she said, her helmet reforming, eye slits glowing a vivid green, "none of these monsters are leaving it."

Ruon and Brother-Captain Armites led the knights of The Second and The Sixth to the third level and into the wide tunnel that sank deeper into the mountain.

"Knights of Achyron!" Ruon's voice echoed, and Arden looked ahead to see the tunnel opening and a tide of Uraks filling it, leathery skin glowing from the red light of the gemstones. "Pain is the path to strength!"

Even as Arden echoed the cry, he was charging. Ildris, Varlin, Sylven, Kevan, Ruon, and Intara matched his strides, the knights of The Sixth mingled between them.

Each step thundered through him, rattling his bones. But so too did each step bleed iron into his heart, solidifying his resolve.

"For Lyrin," Arden whispered as he slammed his shoulder into the wave of Uraks. Bone crunched. He leaned back, creating space, then thrust his blade into a beast's throat, blood sluicing as he ripped it free.

He fell into a rhythm, his Soulblade cleaving bones, rending flesh, and spilling blood. Knights died around him, his Sigil burning with each loss, his heart growing harder, his soul resolute. He would not allow Efialtír to destroy this world. Not while there was air in his lungs and blood in his veins.

"Ildris!" he roared. "Push!"

"Go! We're with you!" Ildris answered, taking an Urak's head from its shoulders as he did, blood splattering Intara's Sentinel armour.

Arden lunged forwards and swept his Soulblade in a wide arc, bone and flesh yielding to the might of a weapon wrought from the soul of a god. They needed to reach the chamber ahead. The Taint surged from it, like an overfull barrel of oil that leaked from a hundred cracks.

Forwards, he pushed, his Soulblade the guiding light and the vengeful hammer.

"For Achyron!" A wave of righteous fury overcame him, and for a moment he thought he could feel Achyron's will flowing through his body, The Warrior's voice resounding in his head. *"No mercy, my child. You are my sword in the mortal world. Give them no ground."*

As the knights pushed and the Uraks fell and the chamber grew ever closer, a brilliant red light shone from within.

A surge of pain swept through Arden's Sigil, and he felt two knights of The First fall in a single heartbeat – Brother Sangwen and Sister Helka. Beside him, Sister Intara fell to one knee, her Soulblade vanishing from her grasp. No cracks split her armour, no wound marred her flesh that he could see.

"Get up," Arden roared, grabbing her under the arms and hauling her upright. "Pain is the path to strength, sister."

"I can… I…" Her voice trembled. "I can feel them die… I felt Endan die?" She tapped the Sigil on her chest, her helmet turning to liquid metal and receding, her eyes raw and red, tears streaming.

"Recall your helm!" Arden snapped.

"I could… it… I… I can't do—" A black spear punched into Sister Intara's exposed face. The black steel ripped at her flesh and shattered her cheek, then burst from the back of her skull in a mist of blood and bone. Arden's Sigil once again burned with a fury.

He stood there for a moment, watching as the Sentinel armour that encased Intara's body turned to liquid and flowed back towards the Sigil in her chest.

His heart aflame, Arden turned and charged. "Knights of Achyron, with me!"

A chorus answered, and the knights surged forwards, forcing the Uraks back into the chamber beyond. The crimson glow of the gemstones was so bright it was as though, there, thousands of feet within the mountain, they fought beneath the light of the moon.

The chamber was massive, stretching off into the distance in all directions, the ceiling tall enough for ten men to stand on each other's shoulders.

Arden barely looked. He swung his Soulblade like a man possessed, cutting down everything that moved. An Urak axe skittered off his pauldron, and he swung his blade, leaving the beast's face dangling, jawless.

"Shaman!" a voice called out.

Arden snapped his head around to see a robed beast clutching a black staff, a gemstone pulsing at its top. A score of Bloodmarked stood alongside it.

Black fire surged from the Shaman's staff, and Arden's Sigil ignited once more as Brothers Inavor and Horun of The Third were ripped from the world.

Ruon cried out and charged, her Soulblade glistening. She slid on her knees and ducked the swing of the black-fire nithral that formed in the Shaman's hand. Rising, she cut a Bloodmarked's legs out from under it before spinning and carving through its thick neck.

All four chapters descended on the Bloodmarked and the Shaman. The Taint crashed through the chamber in waves, surging from the Shaman and from a pit at the chamber's centre. The oily tendrils scratched at Arden's mind as he fought, more Uraks pouring in from the connecting tunnels.

It was like nothing he'd ever felt, almost as though a voice whispered in the back of his mind. *"They're not brothers… They are your slavers. They keep you from your kin…"*

Arden pushed the thoughts back, shielding his mind.

"Do not listen!" Ildris shouted, his voice a distant echo. "Efialtír's whispers are poison!"

A burst of green light erupted in front of Arden and Kallinvar charged through the Rift, Soulblade ignited, the remainder of the knighthood at his back.

"For Achyron!" the Grandmaster bellowed.

Sister-Captain Emalia swept past him like a force of nature, The Tenth at her side, and the Uraks fell before them.

In what felt like heartbeats, the fighting was over, hundreds of bodies littering the ground.

Grandmaster Kallinvar held the Shaman by its throat, both of its arms severed, the bones of its right leg shattered a thousand ways.

"Where is it?" Kallinvar growled.

The Shaman spluttered and choked, the blood that dripped from its wounds as red as its eyes. "We have failed…" The Shaman's voice was akin to a stone dragged across rusted iron. "But… he will cross, and you will die."

"It's like Ilnaen," Olyria whispered. Arden followed her gaze to the pit at the centre of the chamber. Thousands of gemstones were piled at the centre, glowing with the light of a red sun.

"Strike them down and gain your freedom," a voice whispered in Arden's mind. *"I will protect you."*

"Get out of my head," Arden whispered, clenching his fingers into fists. He dragged his gaze from the pit. It was as though the entire chamber was submerged in the Taint itself.

"You hear it too?" Brother Kevan grabbed Arden's wrist. "Shut it out."

"What do you think I'm doing?" Arden snapped, yanking his hand away. He turned towards the far edges of the chamber. Water glistened in the red light, streaming from small passages in the rock into pools carved into the ground. He could still hear the Shaman choking, Kallinvar's voice harsh and cold.

"Don't be an idiot."

"What did you say?" Arden whipped his head around and stared at Brother Kevan.

"I didn't speak, Brother Arden."

"He thinks you a fool," the voice whispered.

Arden clenched his jaw and turned away from Kevan. He looked towards the rock pools. They lined the entire left wall, stretching onwards to the depths of the chamber's far end.

As he stepped closer, the Shaman's screams echoed, harsh and guttural.

"Tell me where it is!" Kallinvar's voice boomed.

Arden looked down into the nearest rock pool to see the water ran pink, tarnished by blood.

"What is it?" Sister-Captain Olyria asked, moving to Arden's side.

"I don't know…" Arden trailed off as his stare moved to a mound on the far side of the pool. The closer he got, the clearer it became. Bodies piled atop each other, tiny and fragile, the birth cords still attached to their navels. "That can't be…" He swallowed, his heart quickening. "That's not what I think it is."

"Don't go closer, *bastard*," Olyria said, resting a hand on Arden's chest.

"What did you call me?"

"I didn't." Olyria's helmet receded, her eyes narrowing in confusion. "I told you not to go closer."

"I…" Arden recalled his helmet and pressed a hand to his temple.

Olyria's expression softened. "Don't go closer. The sight is not one you want etched into your memories. Trust me."

Arden nodded vacantly, still staring at the mound of tiny bodies. They were so frail, their skin grey, eyes empty and white.

A shriek let Arden know that the Shaman had drawn his last breaths. He looked back just as Kallinvar roared and threw the broken corpse to the rock.

The Grandmaster stood over the dead Shaman, his Soulblade ignited, the crimson light of the gemstones glinting on his Sentinel armour.

"The Heart is not here," Kallinvar declared, staring down at the body. "They tried to create a crossing without it." He gestured towards the pit in the centre of the chamber.

"And sacrificed the lives of their young to do so…" Sister-Captain Airdaine of The Ninth whispered, just loud enough for Arden to hear. The realisation in Airdaine's voice sent a shiver through him, and he looked back towards the bodies.

He had known the Bloodspawn harvested Essence from those they slaughtered to give life to their young – a need birthed by a curse that befell them long ago. Though the Watchers and the priests said it was a curse set by Efialtír himself.

"Lies, lies, lies!" the voice screeched in Arden's mind.

Arden pushed it back, focusing on the bodies. He had known why they harvested, but… something felt wrong. Those bodies were not Uraks, not the beasts he knew. They were babies, innocent and gentle… betrayed.

A blinding crimson light filled the air as Kallinvar swept his Soulblade through the gemstones in the pit, shattering them with each swing. More knights joined and made short work of it until it was nothing but a hole filled with broken shards.

With the gemstones destroyed and the Essence released, the Taint all but evaporated from the air and the voice scratching at Arden's mind vanished.

"We return to the temple," Kallinvar called out, the Rift opening before him. "We will find new Sigil bearers, and we will strike again. Efialtír does not rest, and so neither will we."

"Pain is the path to strength," a voice answered, others joining.

A hand rested on Arden's shoulder – Ruon's. "Come, brother. There is no peace to be found here."

Arden nodded, then turned and walked with his captain back through the Rift.

CHAPTER SEVENTY-ONE

SLEEP WELL

20th Day of the Blood Moon

Temple of Achyron – Winter, Year 3081 After Doom

Kallinvar stood on the steps that led from Ardholm to the great temple, looking out over the city that had become his second home. The clouds covered everything beyond the cliff edge, seeming as immutable as the mountains they caressed. The moon's light bled into them, tarnishing any beauty they had once held.

He had heard Efialtír's voice in that chamber. Just as he knew every knight had. He could feel the fear radiating from their Sigils, the panic. Either Efialtír was growing stronger and closer to this world, or he was growing desperate. Neither option calmed Kallinvar's mind.

Kallinvar glanced up at the statues of the first knights that watched over the temple doors. Thousands of years those statues had stood, their watch unending, their will unbroken. Brother-Captain Arturius and Sister-Captain Cleotan.

Watch over us, brother and sister. I fear the night grows darker.

Red light spilled over Kallinvar's shoulder as he climbed the steps and passed through the wicket gate set into the temple doors. The halls echoed with the sound of footfalls and chatter, pots clanging, and young porters flitting about like bees. They were all welcome sounds to Kallinvar's ears. He'd never liked silence.

As Kallinvar walked, Ildris, Arden, and Kevan stepped from a doorway ahead that led to the Soul Vault.

"You acquitted yourselves well today, brothers. They would all be proud." Of the three, Arden's Sigil ached of pain the most. The man had taken Lyrin's loss as deep as a blade. The fault had lain with all three of them – Arden, Lyrin, and Kallinvar himself. Arden for separating from the rest of the chapter, Lyrin for following him, and Kallinvar for allowing it to happen. He was the Grandmaster. Their lives were his treasure to guard, his burden to hold.

"You were a Knight of Achyron today, more than any other day," Kallinvar said, grasping Brother Kevan's shoulder. Where Arden's Sigil held pain, Kevan's was wrapped in doubt and worry. "You were born for this, chosen by Achyron himself. Do not doubt that, brother."

When Kallinvar turned to continue on his way, Brother Arden touched his arm.

"A moment, Grandmaster?"

"Walk with me." Kallinvar gestured along the corridor that led to the Watchers' chambers. He knew what was coming. He didn't need to feel Arden's Sigil. "What plagues you?"

"My brother. While Ruon and the others eat, I would ask that I can see him. That I can ensure that he is all right, and my sister… I need to know how she is."

"He is well, brother. I watched the dragon vanish into the skies myself. And of your sister I can give you no reassurance other than your presence will do little for her recovery."

"I understand, Grandmaster, but if I can—"

"Listen to me carefully," Kallinvar said, stopping in front of Arden. He did not like the words he knew he must speak, but he had little choice. "Your duty is to this knighthood above all else. Do you understand?"

"Yes, Grandmaster." Conflict pulsed from the man.

"There is a reason we must shed our past lives, Arden. Being two people at once creates division in our minds, splits our loyalty – a loyalty that *must* be singular. You know why Lyrin died. I need not beat you round the head with it."

Arden's jaw slackened, his gaze shifting to the floor.

"I can accept mistakes. I have made thousands in my lifetime, tens of thousands. What I cannot accept is the repeating of a mistake. Wear your missteps like armour, brother. Wrap them around you so that you may always know them and not be doomed to suffer for them twice over. And so, I say again – your duty is to this knighthood."

"The duty of the strong is to protect the weak, Grandmaster." Arden pressed his fist to his chest. "I will be better."

"Each day, better than the last. That is all a man can strive for, all we are in control of." Kallinvar let out a soft sigh. "Your brother is a Draleid. His strength is vital to our cause. At this very moment, I go to Gildrick to see what they have uncovered in the remnants of what we found at Ilnaen. If there is something worthwhile, I will send you to your brother. But if not, I need you to know your place. If Efialtír crosses into this world, nothing else will matter. You do not water the plant while the whole village burns. We must focus on the task at hand. There is nothing else that matters. Go," Kallinvar said, placing his hand on Arden's back. "If you do not eat, you will not have the strength to fight. That makes you a liability to those around you."

Arden's eyes widened at that, his body growing tense.

"The others will be back from granting the new Sigils in little more than an hour. We will plan the next step then."

Arden acquiesced – though Kallinvar could see the reluctance in his features – and marched towards the kitchens. In the seven centuries Kallinvar had served Achyron, Arden was one of the greatest warriors he'd had the privilege of standing beside. The man still held the impetuosity of youth and the guilt-wracked soul of one who had not yet grown numb, but he was a ferocious warrior and his honour was without question. The conflict within him held him back, weighed him down. In the past, Kallinvar would have broken him, would have ground that conflict from his mind. But something had shifted in him of late. Perhaps it was losing Verathin, or perhaps it was finding Ruon. Whatever the cause, he found himself unable and unwilling to drive that love from Arden's heart.

When Kallinvar reached the Watchers' chambers, he paused a moment, allowing himself a deep breath of clean air and a moment of mental clarity. He twisted the doorknob and entered chaos incarnate.

The antechamber for the Watchers' chambers performed the dual function of entranceway and workshop. And at that moment, there wasn't a patch of stone left uncovered. Sheets of parchment were strewn about like autumn leaves on the forest floor, books stacked twenty-high. Chests were piled all about, some atop desks, others blocking doors or occupying chairs. Suits of old armour bearing The Order's sigil were in various stages of disassembly, propped on racks and hooks.

Bowls of Tarkin Stem sat on every table along with pots of tea, some steaming, some long-cold. Thirty or so Watchers moved about the room, stood over books, or sat cross-legged amidst the canopy of parchment on the floor. Watcher Kitra slept in an old wooden chair while Watcher Timkin had passed out on the floor with his legs to his chest.

"Grandmaster." Watcher Poldor bowed as he approached, a heavy leatherbound book in his grasp. The leather and the symbol of The Order embossed on the front were worn and tarnished, but the sewn binding still held and the pages looked fully intact.

"Poldor." Kallinvar inclined his head and looked about the chaotic room. "What can I get for you?"

"We will be fine, Grandmaster." Poldor kicked Watcher Kitra in the shin and she leapt from the chair, sending pages fluttering. "We will sleep when the knights sleep."

"But you are not knights, Poldor."

"No, Grandmaster, we are not. But we are Watchers. Our souls were not chosen by Achyron, but they belong to him. This is our place, and we will not shirk our duties."

"Have you found anything on Tarron? Anything that might help us find him?"

"Precious little, I'm afraid… but…" Poldor paused for a moment, scanning the room. He held up a finger. "There was something."

He gestured for Kallinvar to follow and stepped through the books and pages on the floor without even looking down. He led Kallinvar to the door on the left side of the chamber, stopping suddenly. "That's strange."

"What?"

"I left this door locked." He stared at the knob, the door slightly ajar. "At least, I thought I did. I always do because Watcher Yuni steals the biscuits that Marina in the kitchens makes for me." He shook his head and squeezed the bridge of his nose, then pushed into the door with his shoulder. "The lack of sleep, most likely."

Watcher Poldor's study was a perfect match for the disarray in the antechamber and the antithesis of everything that was Verathin's study. Kallinvar frowned at the half-eaten apple on the windowsill that had already gone brown as a column of ants scavenged its remnants.

Poldor laid the old leatherbound book on his desk atop a stack of parchment that was twice as high as the book itself.

"I found these in the quarters that had once belonged to the old Watchmasters. They are from long, long before my time – and yours. Though, they were not easy to find. In fact, it was complete chance that I came across them at all. They were locked in a chest set behind a wall." Poldor grunted like a mule as he hauled three stacks of books from the floor and placed them onto the desk. "I'd not visited those quarters. Not once in my lifetime. I don't believe anyone has. But I thought them worth a look in this case. I only found the books because the panel had come loose and stone dust had collected on the floor beneath it. The lock had rusted and broken. It must have fallen off."

Kallinvar studied the books. The leather and the bindings were in too good a condition to have been from the time of the old Watchmasters. That position had been abolished almost a thousand years ago. These books had been redrawn and rebound, though they were still old – older than Kallinvar.

"They are a collection of sorts…" Poldor tapped on the topmost book.

"Of what?"

"Everything we knew of Efialtír's workings in this world."

"Why would that be locked away?"

"Because, Grandmaster. There is more in these books than observations and musings. Watchmaster Arkustin felt that to defeat our enemy, we must know them. And so we recorded the composition of every blood rune, symbol, and writing the knights found in the field, asking them to sit and draw what they could and then combining the efforts into something cohesive. Rather ingenious."

"By Achyron…" Kallinvar reached out and touched the dark leather that covered the book closest to him.

"The Traitor's hand," Achyron whispered in his mind. *"It reaches even this place."*

"The Watchers keep meticulous records," Poldor said, folding his arms. "But I found no mention of these books." He scratched his chin. "I do not believe I would be far amiss if these records were the reason the Watchmasters were abolished. Though, that is just my speculation."

"Did you read them?" Kallinvar turned his full attention to Poldor.

Poldor looked at Kallinvar, a glint of uncertainty in his eyes. "Would it matter if I had?"

When Kallinvar said nothing, the man spoke again.

"I have looked through their pages in search of something that might lead us to Brother Tarron – under your command, Grandmaster. My loyalty and my soul belong to Achyron, to this temple, and to the knights over whom I watch. That is unwavering."

Kallinvar could feel Achyron watching from the depths of his mind, but the god remained silent. "Did you find anything?"

"There are records of old tears in the veil, of knights who closed them… but…"

"What is it?"

"The latter pages – those that I believe told of what truly happened – were torn from the books. As were a number of others. What's more, that seems to be a common trend. A trend we would not have noticed had you not set us to our task of searching for Brother Tarron."

"Does Watcher Gildrick know of this?"

"The rank of Watchmaster may have been abolished, Grandmaster, but in name only. There is nothing within these walls that Watcher Gildrick does not know."

"Where is he?"

"In his study. He spotted something in one of the books earlier today and has been studying it ever since."

"Something to do with Tarron?"

Poldor shook his head. "Something he believed might be of import in locating the Heart. Something about a fallen god. He said he wasn't sure."

Kallinvar nodded, staring down at the books on the desk. "There is wisdom in Watcher Arkustin's thoughts, Poldor. These books may yet guide us along the correct path. But so too are they a danger. Keep them safe. Seal them in chests and ensure this door is locked at all times. They are for your and Gildrick's eyes only. Understood?"

"Understood, Grandmaster."

Kallinvar stepped closer to Poldor. "Watcher, we are close to what could be the end of all we know. A feather alone could tip the balance."

"The duty of the strong is to protect the weak, Grandmaster Kallinvar. I remain faithful and resolute."

"Achyron guide us." Kallinvar inclined his head to the Watcher. "You have my trust, Poldor."

"And you have mine."

"Hmm. Let me know if you turn over anything that might be of import. I will see what Gildrick has found."

Kallinvar stepped from the room and walked carefully across the antechamber, avoiding the sleeping body of Watcher Timkin and trying not to tread on any of the loose sheets of parchment. He snatched some Tarkin Stem from a bowl on a nearby table and tossed the whole stem into his mouth. He bit down, and the stem cracked, the sour juice flooding his mouth. Kallinvar clenched his jaw and sucked in his cheeks. Chewing Tarkin Stem was like snorting fire and eating a raw lemon at the same time. But it kept him awake.

The main entrance door creaked, and Watcher Tallia slipped in, a satchel strapped around her shoulder. She smiled at Kallinvar, then knelt and shook Watcher Timkin by the shoulders until he jerked awake and slapped his head on a table leg.

Kallinvar carried on, rapping his knuckles on the door of Gildrick's study.

When no answer came, he knocked again. "Gildrick. It's Kallinvar."

No answer again. Kallinvar shook his head and turned the knob. As expected, Gildrick's study was pristine. The scrolls set in stone alcoves were well kept and orderly, the candle on the desk was fresh, any dripping wax scraped away. And the books and loose parchments were stacked neatly.

Gildrick was slumped, not behind his desk, but in a deep leather chair in the far corner, a blanket over his legs, a book open in his lap.

"Old age, my friend," Kallinvar said as he walked across the study and pulled over the book that sat at the top of the pile on Gildrick's desk. "An alphabetical list of all Watchers inducted? I would have fallen asleep too."

Kallinvar smiled. He shook his head and blew out the candle. Gildrick had earned his rest. Kallinvar could give him an hour or two, but there was no sense in burning the temple down.

He lifted the book from Gildrick's lap, the dim light drifting in through the half-open door to the antechamber.

"*A History of the People of Ardholm*," Kallinvar whispered, reading the title worked into the spine. He set the book on the desk, lifted the blanket up to Gildrick's shoulders, and turned for the door.

When Kallinvar's hand brushed the wood of the door's edge, he stopped, frigid fingers creeping up his spine. A tiny droplet of doubt in his mind.

Gildrick never sat in that chair. He hated it, said it was as uncomfortable as the void itself. He'd kept it only because his old mentor, Watcher Harthor, had loved it so.

"Gildrick?" Kallinvar called back into the room, far louder than before. No answer came.

Kallinvar looked back into the darkness, dread coiling around his heart like a viper. "Gildrick?"

Again, no answer.

His boots clapped against the stone as he walked, each step filling him with more darkness. The light from the antechamber shone over his shoulder, carving a thin strip through the dark and illuminating the grey hairs in Gildrick's beard.

"Gildrick?" Kallinvar's breaths trembled. He stood before Gildrick, eyes adjusting to the dark. His mind and his heart warred when he realised that Gildrick's chest did not rise or fall.

Please, Achyron, no. Please, no.

He reached out and touched his old friend's cold neck, tilting Gildrick's head and squinting to look more clearly upon his face.

There was no pulse, no beating heart.

Kallinvar dropped to his knees. He rested his hand on the side of his old friend's head, using his thumb to peel back Gildrick's eyelid. The eyes of a dead man.

He knelt there, his hand trembling against the cold skin of his dead friend's face, until the door creaked behind him.

"Watcher Gildrick?" Tallia's voice was soft. "Grandmaster, what are you doing here?"

Kallinvar held his gaze on Gildrick for a moment, then turned. "Where were you today, Tallia?"

He stood, the dread in his heart bubbling.

"What… what do you mean, Grandmaster? I was in the library in the temple. And… and out fetching tea."

"I don't believe her," Achyron's voice whispered.

"Where *were* you?" Kallinvar's voice rose, filling the room.

"I… I was in the library, I swear it."

His thoughts swirled as he approached the young Watcher. Gildrick never sat in that chair. The candle had been freshly changed. The book… Poldor had said Gildrick had been reading one of the old Watchmaster texts. "Where is the book?"

"What book?" She stared up at Kallinvar, fear in her eyes.

"We do not have time for this, my child."

Kallinvar grabbed Tallia by the shoulders and slammed her against the open door, roaring, "*Where* is the book?"

Shouts came from the antechamber and Watchers rushed in. Not one of them dared intervene. But Watcher Poldor called out, "Kallinvar, put her down. Whatever has happened, this is not the way."

Tallia's gaze flickered from Kallinvar to Poldor.

"Gildrick is dead," Kallinvar growled, staring into Tallia's eyes. There was something behind those eyes, something he hadn't quite figured out.

"She is hiding something," Achyron said in his mind.

"What did you do?" Kallinvar growled.

"I didn't do anything. I didn't, I promise. He's dead? He's really dead?" Tears streamed from Tallia's eyes.

"Grandmaster." Poldor's voice was steady. He didn't lay a hand on Kallinvar, but he stood less than a handspan away, his face between Kallinvar's and Tallia's. "She is a Watcher of Achyron."

"There are no wounds," a voice called from behind Kallinvar. "No blood. He died in his sleep."

"Did you hear Watcher Nandra?" Poldor's voice softened. "Let her go, Kallinvar. I understand your loss. Your rage. But Tallia hasn't been in the Watchers' chambers all day. Gildrick sent her to the library."

"That is true," Watcher Timkin called from behind the door.

Kallinvar loosened his grip, shame washing over him. "I… the candle… the book…" He swallowed hard, turning his head to look at Gildrick's lifeless body. "I… it can't be."

"Let her go, Grandmaster," Poldor said, finally resting a hand on Kallinvar's shoulder.

Kallinvar released his hold on Tallia, and the young Watcher squirmed away, dropping to the ground, tears streaming.

"You need rest." Poldor shifted so he looked into Kallinvar's eyes.

"He's dead, Poldor."

Poldor's jaw clenched at that, and he squeezed his eyes shut for a moment. "I'll have the rites prepared, and his name will be marked. Gildrick will watch over you always…" His fingers tightened on Kallinvar's shoulder. "Always."

"The book," Kallinvar said.

"What book?"

"The one he took in here to study…" Kallinvar tried to gather his thoughts. Gildrick was dead. The young boy he'd watched grow into a man. The man who had become his friend. The friend who had become a rock upon which Kallinvar leaned. "It wasn't what he was reading. Where is it?"

Poldor stared into Kallinvar's eyes, and Kallinvar wasn't sure whether it was because Poldor understood what he was saying or because the man just wanted to comfort him, but Poldor walked to Gildrick's desk. He pulled open the curtains, letting light wash over the room, then moved here and there, searching.

"It's not here," Poldor said finally. "It could be anywhere, Kallinvar."

"What is it you're looking for?" Tallia asked, still trembling, eyes red.

Poldor glanced at Kallinvar. "Just a book. One Watcher Gildrick had in his possession. Deep black leather, the edges frayed, some pages missing. It was thick and heavy."

She shook her head. "I don't know… That sounds like all the books."

Poldor sighed. "Go. Get some tea, some food, some rest."

The young Watcher was gone within a heartbeat of Poldor's words, scampering past Kallinvar like a terrified doe.

"I should speak to her," Kallinvar said, more to himself than to Poldor.

"Leave her be for now, Grandmaster. Hearts lash out when they are hurt. Go and rest until the others call. I will ensure Gildrick is taken care of. And I will find that book." Poldor paused for a moment. "At least he went in his sleep, quietly and peacefully. For those of us who do not carry blades and dreams of dying in the glory of battle, quietly and peacefully is the way all hope."

Kallinvar nodded absently, stepping past the three Watchers who surrounded Gildrick and kneeling beside his old friend. He pulled Gildrick's head closer and planted a kiss on the man's silvered hair. "Heraya will rejoice, for she has taken a shining star into her embrace this day. I'm sure she will be loath to let you go, but I would very much like a drink in Achyron's halls when I find my rest. Sleep well, my brother."

CHAPTER SEVENTY-TWO

THE CHOICES WE MAKE

21ˢᵗ Day of the Blood Moon

Mythníril, Aravell – Winter, Year 3081 After Doom

The drain sapped at Chora as she wove threads of Air through the wheels of her chair, pushing herself ever upwards along the staircases that led to the platform near the top of Mythníril. Two of the Dracurïn mages walked behind her, funnelling threads of Earth and Fire into the stone steps, forging them into a ramp as she moved, then back to steps as she passed over.

Before she'd lost Daiseer, she would not have needed their aid for such a usage of the Spark. But she was weaker now, and the towers of Mythníril were as tall as mountain peaks. Besides, before she'd lost Daiseer, she hadn't needed her chair either. She was a different person now, in a different world, and she'd come to terms with that… until she'd met Calen Bryer.

After what seemed like an eternity, she finally reached a landing that entered an enormous circular chamber. She paused for a moment, slowing her breaths as her lungs begged her for more air. She grunted and stretched, the pain in her lower back burning as though her bones were on fire. If Daiseer had taken her pain as well, she wouldn't have minded. How thoughtless of him. With a soft cotton cloth she pulled from a pouch at her waist, she wiped the sweat from her brow.

"Rakina." Hanvar, one of the Dracurïn who had helped her climb the tower, moved to stand beside her, his fist pressed to his breastplate. "We will wait for you here."

"Du haryn myia vrai, Hanvar."

You have my thanks, Hanvar.

"Din vrai é altinua atuya sin'vala, Rakina. Palín det er myia haydria ar myia thranuk."

Your thanks are always welcome here, One Who Survived. But it is my honour and my privilege.

Chora inclined her head and wheeled herself past the two elves.

Gaeleron Athis and five more Dracurïn stood guard at the wide arch that led out onto the platform. Each of them wore fine steel plate, white dragons emblazoned across the breasts and purple cloaks clasped at their shoulders by golden leaves. Finding that young smith, Valdrin, had been a stroke of luck, but the way Aeson had played the Triarchy against each other to contribute their own smiths had been masterful.

On the other side of the arch, Valerys stood tall, wings spread and head high, only Calen's lower half visible past the dragon's bulk.

"Rakina." Gaeleron bowed and gestured towards the arch.

From the platform, Chora could see for miles in all directions. The forest swept outwards in brushstrokes of deep green, dark clouds blotting the morning sky above. Here and there, rocky peaks burst through the dense canopy and fell away into sweeping valleys.

For centuries this woodland had remained untouched, a bastion against the carnage of the world beyond. A place that had been both her sanctuary and a prison. Now, streaks of black tore through the green, miles long and hundreds of feet wide. The dragonfire had scarred the land. What had once been vibrant and thriving was now ash and bones and char.

Her sanctuary was gone, her prison destroyed… and she wasn't sure which she missed more.

Only the subtlest of sounds alerted her to the presence of the two Fenryr Angan who stood on either side of the platform, watching with those golden eyes. Chora had spent hundreds of years around the Dvalin, but these Angan were different creatures, harsher, sharper, and more dangerous. She expected no less from creatures born of a wolf god.

Calen looked over his shoulder as Chora approached, and Valerys twisted his neck and lowered his head.

She paused and reached up a hand so that her fingers brushed the bottom of the dragon's jaw. Warm air rolled over her face from Valerys's nostrils, and she closed her eyes, feeling the rough, scarred scales beneath her fingers. It had been so long since she had seen a dragon whose fire still burned so bright. She would never grow tired of it.

Chora gasped as a wave of emotions flowed from Valerys - sorrow, loss, grief. She snapped her eyes open and stared up into those of the dragon. Without words, she knew Valerys's heart; she knew his sympathy for her pain, knew the ferocity with which he would protect her if he was ever called to.

She looked to Calen, and the young man stared back at her. In his eyes, she saw he had felt whatever had passed between Chora and the dragon. Something had shifted within him since Ilnaen. Something deep at his core. The simple fact that he had found his *níthral* was evidence of that. Most mages went their entire lives without being able to summon that weapon. Chora herself had never achieved the feat, and now, with only half a soul, she never would.

Calen frowned, realisation dawning in his eyes. "My head was elsewhere, Chora. I apologise for asking you to make the climb." His lips formed a regretful smile. "I should have come to you. Laël sanyin."

I am sorry.

"No apologies are needed. It was a simple thing," Chora lied. Her back still ached with a fury, and her lungs still burned. "Well, you asked me here alone, and now here I am. I'm assuming you've made a decision then?"

"I have."

Just over an hour earlier, as the sun broke the horizon, word had come from Coren Valmar in the North that a Lorian army some forty thousand strong had encircled them and that they called for Calen and Valerys.

When the Angan had relayed the message, Calen had asked for time to think. Time that Chora had granted him. She knew all too well how painful these decisions were. Duty to oneself against duty to a cause. In truth, Chora had expected the decision to take far longer.

"I don't mean to rush you," she said, twisting her hand so that her nail *clacked* off the chair.

Calen turned and stared back out at the vast expanse of the Aravell. "Dann and the others should be arriving in Salme any day now. I promised them I would be there, that I would fight by their side."

So that was his choice then. He would fly to protect his home, to protect the ones he held dear. Chora couldn't say she was surprised, but she had not yet given up. The young man had a sense of duty in him. It was simply buried beneath the fear of loss. "And what of Coren and Farwen and the five thousand souls who stand alone in Tarhelm? They have given everything to this rebellion. We cannot abandon them. If Daiseer still drew breath, I would fly myself, but he does not, and I cannot."

Without turning his head, Calen dropped his hand to a patch of silk knotted between his belt loops. It was deep red in colour, but plain. She'd noticed his brother – the knight, Arden – wearing something similar, but his was woven with vines of gold and cream leaves. The pattern mimicked that which Valdrin had marked into Calen's armour. It was a memory of something the two brothers shared – a loss, perhaps. That would seem the reasonable thing.

"I cannot be in two places at once," Calen said. Valerys craned his neck down and brushed the side of his jaw into Calen's shoulder. "No matter what we do," Calen said, looking to the dragon, "we abandon someone."

"Such is war." The words left a bitter taste on Chora's tongue. A time had once existed when she had not been so apathetic towards such things. That time was a distant memory, but she yearned for it so, just as she yearned for the touch of Daiseer's mind.

"Does it ever get easier?"

Chora shook her head. "Not in my experience. The choosing of who you save and who you do not should never be an easy thing. We must accept that we cannot save everyone and move forwards."

After a few moments passed, Chora nodded softly and clasped her hands together, resting them on her lap. In her many years roaming this land, Chora had learned that life was a fleeting thing. And there were things that were playing on her mind, things she would use this moment to say, lest she forever remain silent. "I know I have been harsh, and cold, and perhaps a little cruel in the way I have spoken to you since the battle for the city. But I want you to know it is only because I am afraid."

"Afraid?" Calen looked down at her, confusion on his face. "What is *Chora Sarn* afraid of?"

Chora ignored the mocking tone of his voice. He was young, and false arrogance was the shield of youth. She let her breath out in a long sigh. "I watched over hundreds of young souls who were tested for the Calling. It was my honour, my duty, and my privilege. I watched their soulkin hatch and stood by with pride in my heart as their bonds strengthened and they became everything I knew they could be. My heart was so full it was bursting."

Calen continued to stare back at her.

"There is something unique and special in watching a person grow – as you have." Chora pursed her lips as though this might hold back the tears that threatened her. When Daiseer had been taken from her, she had wept for almost three days and three nights without break. Her stomach had turned, her eyes had been dry as sand, and a hammer had pounded in her head. But after that, she had not shed a tear. This day might change that. "I watched every one of them die or have their soulkin be torn from them, their soul shattered. They were, each of them, like my own children. And there is nothing more savage, and brutal, and soul-rending to a parent than watching their children suffer. Aeson is the last, and he has lost more pieces of himself than any one man should be able to bear. Yet he perseveres. By some form of divine will, he puts one foot in front of the other, and he refuses to stop. Do not tell him, but he is the pride of my life. He should have been what you are. Do you see that?"

Calen raised a curious eyebrow.

"Aeson was the greatest prodigy we had ever seen. The bond he shared with Lyara was akin to the bond the moon shares with the stars. He was all pride and arrogance but equal parts honour and strength of will – much like someone else I know. He would have been a champion. His name would have danced in the greatest songs of the Age. He was destined to be Archon one day, to grace the skies with Lyara until time wore away at their hearts. That was taken from him. Everything was taken from him, and still he never faltered. Not once. His name will never be sung, his story seldom told, but if we win this war, it will be on Aeson's back we were carried."

Chora studied Calen, hoping her words were being heard. Understood. Calen needed to know who and what Aeson was. He needed to understand that no matter what strength flowed in his veins or how many marched at his back, he had been granted it all by the gift of Aeson's unwillingness to lie down and die. And he needed to understand that loss was a part of life.

"When I look at you, Calen, I see all of their faces. All of those young souls I failed to protect. I see the pride and hubris of youth, the hope and the fire. And it terrifies me, because I do not know if I can survive losing that hope again." Chora's gaze met Calen's, and a deep rumble resonated from Valerys's chest. "There are two shades of hope, Calen. One is the light that guides you forward, the other a noose around your neck. The more hope you let into your heart, the brighter the light, the longer the noose."

Calen gave a long sigh and nodded, more to himself than to Chora.

"Four hundred years ago, I would have stood here and I would have argued and roared and demanded you fly north to Tarhelm. Because without you, every soul in that mountain will die. Because it is your duty as a Draleid and your responsibility as a leader. But now I find myself in a place I have never before been, a place where I am afraid, and uncertain, and simply not myself. Because I have once more allowed hope into my heart. What if you fly to Tarhelm and Coren is wrong? What if Helios stands in your path, or Karakes, or Seleraine – or any of the elven dragons? Coren's message said the armies are alone, but what if she is wrong? If she is, then you will be dead and that hope will be gone, and I will see no more point in trudging through this world any longer. When hope dies, the light fades and the noose tightens."

She clicked her tongue off the roof of her mouth and shook her head.

"If I listened to myself, I would keep you sheltered in this place where you are safe, just as I have done to myself for these past four centuries while Aeson and Coren and Farwen refused to give in. So I will not listen to myself, and I will actively try not to tie you with those same chains I put on myself. I have been less than I am, and for that, I am sorry." Chora allowed a deep breath to swell in her chest, and she straightened her back in her chair, taking one last look at the woodland. "I will inform the others that you are to fly south to Salme. Perhaps there is something we can do for those in Tarhelm, perhaps not. As I said, this is war."

"We are going to fly north, Chora."

"North? You couldn't have led with that?"

"I didn't want to interrupt." Calen gave her a half-smile before reaching up and touching the scales of Valerys's neck. He stared into the dragon's eyes, going silent for a moment.

"Rise so that others rise with you." The words left Calen's lips in a whisper. Chora recognised them. Coren had repeated them over and over in those first years following The Fall, like a creed.

"Did you know a Draleid called Tarast?" Calen asked.

"Tarast?" Chora did little to keep the surprise from her tongue. "How do you know that name?"

"I watched him die." There was awe and admiration both in Calen's voice. "In the western hatchery tower, the night Ilnaen fell. He fought like a man possessed. He could have run. Could have taken Antala to wing and fled. But instead, he stood shoulder to shoulder with his brothers and sisters and faced his end. With fire and fury. He was a guardian until his dying breath."

Chora wanted to speak, but her voice twisted in her throat, refusing to come forth. She had not known how Tarast had died. She had simply never seen him again after that night.

"And Kollna, there was not a piece of her soul that considered doing anything other than save those eggs. She knew she would die, and yet she accepted it. That was why I did everything I could to bring them back, because it felt as though, in some way, it meant her death was for a reason."

"Calen, Calen, do not hold that weight." Chora knew she had been too harsh when he had returned with the eggs and left Alvira's possessions to the knights. She knew, and yet her own pride forbade her from saying so.

Calen shook his head, turning so he stared out at the morning sun that still hung low on the horizon, the Blood Moon beside it like a horrid mirror. "This Gift – if it is truly such a thing – shows me the darkest of memories. But there is something within them... I watched a Dracârdare refuse to allow fear to control him because his faith that the Draleid would protect him was so unshaking."

Those words sliced deep into Chora's shattered soul and carved into her pride and her guilt. The Draleid had not protected them. The Draleid had failed. *She* had failed. The city had fallen.

"When you told me I had a lot to learn about the world, you were right." Calen drew a long, slow breath. "I asked you here, Chora, not simply to tell you I will fly north, but because I need something from you first."

Calen's tone grew sombre, and his gaze fixed on hers. Above him, Valerys let out a low rumble that seemed to resonate in the stone around them. "I need you to allow Tivar and Avandeer to fly at my side."

Chora stared back at him. "We have already voted, Calen. You know this."

"I do. And if Farwen and Coren die at Tarhelm because I cannot save them alone, what then? I need Tivar and Avandeer at my side if I am to fly north and stand any chance of making a difference. And for that, I need you to change your vote. I need you to grant them life."

Chora gripped the rim of her right wheel reflexively, the muscles in her jaw tensing. "You ask this of me, when you know what they have done?"

"I do."

"Do you know how many of those young Draleid Tivar and Avandeer slew? How many of my friends? My family?"

Calen looked away for a moment, then turned back, his stare unflinching. "No, but no doubt countless. I don't ask this lightly, Chora. I understand the gravity of the decision. I understand what I am asking you to do."

"And what of Farda and the others?" Chora squeezed the rim of her wheel even harder, the knuckles in her hand and fingers growing stiff, her skin paling as she relived those moments from all those years ago. The night Ilnaen fell burned through her mind. Dragons shrieked as they were torn limb from limb, as their soulkin were ripped apart and slaughtered in their sleep. Screams echoed off white stone as the citizens she was meant to protect were savaged and butchered in the streets. "What of the man who murdered your mother, Calen? Are you as quick to forgive him as you ask me to be with Tivar?"

"I'm not asking you to forgive. I'm asking you to allow her to live so that she may die trying to save those who deserve saving." Calen drew a short breath, and as he did his eyes began to glow with a purple light, luminescent mist drifting outwards. "I've gone over this moment a thousand times in my head." His voice trembled with anger, and above him, Valerys pulled back his lips in a snarl. "I want Farda dead. I want to carve the black heart from his chest. And maybe one day I will…" Calen gripped that patch of silk hanging from his belt once more, twisting it in knots. "But not this day. You were right a thousand times over. My loss is not greater than yours. Tivar's hands are just as bloody as his. And if we do not bend, both of us, we risk everything we love breaking. Is punishing them more important than saving the others? If I can look past my hate and my pain and this rage that blazes in me, Chora, can you? Can we make that noose a little longer?"

"You would set Farda free as well?" The words were less a question and more a stunned realisation.

Calen nodded, clenching his jaw, the glow from his eyes redoubling. "If it means you would set Tivar and Avandeer free and allow them to fly with me… then yes, so long as they swear the same oath. Forty thousand strong lay siege to Tarhelm. I cannot even those odds alone. And if those men and women die because I could not look past my own hate, well, then I am not fit to be a Draleid."

"Do you truly trust Tivar to fight by your side?"

"If not for her, Valerys and I would already be dead. She came when she had no cause. I trust her shame, and her grief, and her guilt."

"And you have spoken to your sister?"

"She was the first person I spoke to. She does not like it, but she understands it."

"She doesn't strike me as the 'understanding' type."

"She's trying." Calen pulled at that patch of silk so hard Chora thought he might tear it in half. "I need an answer, Chora. If Tivar swears to fight at my side, to give her dying breath for this cause, and to not rest until the empire is nothing but ruin, will you change your vote?"

"And if she breaks her vow?"

"Then I will bear the weight of it, and I will kill her myself."

It was in that moment that Chora realised Aeson was wrong about Calen. He didn't have Alvira's heart. He had something stronger. She nodded. "I will do as you ask. I will change my vote."

Calen closed his eyes, a last rush of glowing purple mist slipping between his eyelids to drift upwards. He gave a short, bitter laugh and shook his head, then whispered, "Thank you."

"Is this not what you want?"

"What I want?" He pressed his fingers into his cheeks and ran a hand through his hair. "I have just arranged for the life of my mother's killer to be spared. A man I would strangle with my bare hands. It is the furthest thing in the world from what I want. But it is the choice I have to make."

"I will inform the others," Chora said. "There are many amongst the Rakina who will not be happy. I will keep them in line – for now. But if this decision goes sour, Calen, it will be you they turn on."

"I am aware."

Chora nodded to herself slowly. "Castor Kai, Aryana Torval, and the others. They will not be best pleased that you are leaving after all their time spent waiting, and I dare say I do not blame them."

"I go to speak with them now. After I fly to the North, I will go to Salme. I have asked the Illyanaran leaders to move south towards Drifaien. Alleron Helmund requires our aid. I will need someone to march with those armies. Someone I can trust. A Rakina, a warrior of legend to show them they do not fight alone."

"It is you they want, Calen, not me."

"They have seen me, they have seen Valerys, they have heard what I have to say. You are wiser than I and have far more experience in these things. It's time we start thinking about what we want the world to look like when this is all over, and I trust you to make those choices. Chora, if you truly want this world to change, it is time you leave this place and make that change happen. Let us not allow hope to die."

Chora gave Calen a soft smile, then nodded. Before she wheeled herself back towards the arch, she watched Calen for a moment. The young man turned back to look out at the woodland, his fingers still twisted in the silk scarf at his hip, his other hand resting on Valerys's side.

"Calen."

Calen turned back, his eyes still misting purple light.

"We are defined by the choices we make in our darkest hours. It is easy to be honourable and dutiful when it comes at no cost. In my darkest hours, I chose to hide, and it has shamed me for hundreds of years."

"There are plenty of dark hours left," Calen replied, finally releasing his iron grip on the patch of red silk. "You made the same choice I did today – the lives of others over your own pain. The same choice Tarast and Kollna made. The choice of a Draleid."

Chora gave Calen a nod, then turned and left. The two Dracurïn bowed and proceeded to funnel threads of Earth and Fire into the stairs, moulding them into a ramp. Chora thanked them and wove threads of Air around her wheels to slow her descent. At first, only her jaw trembled, but after a few moments, her eyes stung and tears fell, soft and soundless.

CHAPTER SEVENTY-THREE

WHAT WE MUST

21ˢᵗ Day of the Blood Moon

Salme – Winter, Year 3081 After Doom

ahlen's teeth chattered, and his breath plumed upwards. A frost coated the ground, crunching beneath his boots. This winter had not been as harsh as the others he'd known, but the past few days had changed that.

Smoke billowed from chimneys all about Salme, braziers burning in the streets. The chill had swept in overnight.

"We need to get you a coat," Nimara said, walking at his side, Conal on her left. "Should have done so a long time ago. You humans are fragile things. Always too warm or too cold."

"Mmm." Dahlen puffed out his lower lip. "And dwarves are as thick as rocks. We all have our shortcomings… some of us are just short."

"Watch your tongue," Nimara said with a wry smile.

Conal remained silent as they walked. The young lad was a quiet one, but he was always listening, always learning, much like Dahlen when he was younger. Erik had always said enough for the both of them. "You all right, Conal?"

The boy nodded, fingers gripped tightly around the Valtaran ordo shield Dahlen had given him, procured from Captain Kiron's last shipment.

"Getting heavy, is it?"

Conal shook his head, and Dahlen smiled.

"You're going to have to put it down eventually or you'll not have the strength to carry it when you need to." Dahlen inclined his head towards Ulrich, one of the Belduaran Kingsguard, who stood on the ramparts of the palisade wall.

"What's the report?" Dahlen asked when he'd crested the top of the stairs, looking out at the battered landscape beyond, stumps of felled trees providing a clear line of sight for hundreds of feet.

"Very little, Lord Captain. There was no attack last night."

"None? Not at all? I assumed I slept through the horns."

Ulrich shook his head. "First time in weeks." The man twisted his neck and narrowed his gaze at Dahlen. "What is it, Lord Captain? Is this not good news?"

Dahlen let out a long sigh.

"The Urak attacks have been light of late," Nimara said to Ulrich as Dahlen stared off at the horizon. "If they did not attack at all last night, that would suggest they have had other priorities."

"I'm not sure I follow."

"Camylin, Ulrich. It likely means they have focused their strength on Camylin."

"And that is a bad thing?"

"It is."

"Forgive me, Lord Captain, but I'm not understanding."

"Well," Dahlen said, folding his arms. "Firstly, there are tens of thousands of souls within Camylin. Souls that are facing their last days, and there is nothing we can do for them. Secondly, if Camylin falls, then the Uraks – along with their forces who took the city – will find a new priority. Us. And with their numbers at Camylin joining their ranks, they will flood over us. Our only chance will be if my brother arrives in time with this army he brings."

"Dahlen?" Conal stood with his hand resting on the tips of the palisade. "What's that?"

Dahlen followed Conal's gaze to a pair of horses that galloped over the low hill in the distance, breaths misting in deep snorts, hooves turning the soil. As the riders drew closer, Dahlen yelled, "Open the gates!"

He sprinted down the stairs to the yard, seeing the large wooden gates still shut.

"Open the fucking gates!" he called out again.

A short man with grey hair and a thick beard stood beside the drawbar, staring at Dahlen.

"Do you speak the Common Tongue?" Dahlen roared, rounding on him. "Open the damn gates."

"But what if it's a trap, my lord? What if—"

Dahlen pushed the man aside and removed the drawbar, Nimara, Conal, and three of the Belduarans helping him push the gate open just in time for the two horses to come galloping through.

"Please!" a young man shouted as he slid from the first horse. "My sister needs a healer." He gestured to the second horse, where a man held a young woman close to his chest, blood flowing freely from a wound in her side.

"Take her to the bloodhouse," Dahlen said to two of the guards. "And make sure she is brought to Anya. She doesn't have time." He turned back to the two men. One had not seen his twentieth summer, the other perhaps forty. "Speak."

"We're from a village east of Pirn, below the Cupped Mountains," the older man said. "We've been travelling for weeks. Uraks and brigands are everywhere. We'd heard from a ship captain of a safe place along the western coast, heard that Salme had become a fortress. Someone attacked us in the woods just east of here. They wrecked our wagons, left five of us dead. We rode here to get help."

"How far? And how many still live?"

"A few miles, no more. There are six families. Almost thirty of us… at least, there were. We're fur traders and farmers, not warriors. Please, there are many injured."

Others entered the yard: Erdhardt, Tharn Pimm, Lanan Halfhand, Yarik Tumber, and more.

"Tell me more," Dahlen said. "How were you attacked?"

"Archers at first, then they came in with spears. Broke the wagons, stole our furs, killed anyone who tried to stop them." The man held Dahlen's gaze as he spoke, ignoring the others. "My brother and his wife are there. That's their daughter you just took in. Please. What if the Uraks cross them?"

"So whoever attacked you brought your horses down, thinned your numbers, and then just left you there." Erdhardt's words were not a question.

Dahlen turned to Nimara. "Fetch Yoring and Almer." He looked at Ulrich. "Go. Find Thannon and Camwyn, along with five others. We leave now."

"This is clearly a trap," Erdhardt said. "I'll eat my shoe if there aren't fifty brigands waiting for us in the woods."

"So you're not coming then?"

"Oh, I'm coming," Erdhardt said with a smile. "I just thought I'd make sure we were all clear on what we were walking into."

"You can't go," Yarik Tumber said, stepping up beside Erdhardt.

"Can't?" Dahlen asked. "Are you going to stop me?"

Yarik flicked his tongue against the roof of his mouth in frustration. "Salme is our priority. You and your Belduarans are our best fighters. It would be idiocy to lose you by walking into a trap we already know is set."

"It's a good thing, Yarik, that it is not your courage that keeps these walls from falling." Dahlen looked to Conal, who still held his shield. "What do we do when people need us, Conal?"

"We do what we must, Lord Captain."

"And why do we do it?"

"We do it because we have to," Conal answered. "We do it because of what would happen if we didn't."

"Good lad. Good lad." Dahlen smiled at Yarik. "If I lived by your logic, Elder Tumber, I would not be in Salme. I would be with my brother and my father, and an Urak blade would likely have separated your head from your neck." Dahlen turned to the others. "Spread the word. I need fifty able bodies willing to ride. We leave at once."

Light filtered through the canopy above as Dahlen, Nimara, Thannon, Ulrich, and ten men and women of Salme rode along the dirt path that had been beaten into the ground through the forest.

The man who had asked for their aid, Owen Tah, rode on Dahlen's left.

"There," Owen whispered, pointing to a group in the distance huddled around wagons, pitchforks and scythes in their fists. At least six were propped against wagons, wounded, and more bodies lay about them.

Dahlen raised a hand, and the group stopped.

"Sixteen," Thannon whispered. "Four horses dead by the looks of it. Not Urak arrows, too small. We'd see those monstrous shafts even from here."

The group were all huddled about the central wagon, makeshift weapons pointed outwards.

Dahlen moved his horse closer to Owen's. "I didn't want to say this earlier and give that prick Yarik any sense of being right, but Owen, this is most certainly a trap. And if it is you who has laid it, you have made a grave error. I will kill you, make no mistake about it. In the defence of my people, I will not hesitate."

The man swallowed hard. "It's not of my making. I swear it by the gods."

Dahlen looked into his eyes. It had always been Aeson's belief that a man's soul lived in his eyes. Dahlen was inclined to agree. "Brigands?"

Owen nodded.

"What did they say to you?"

Owen looked at the ground, then back up. "They said to ride east. Said not to stop till we reached the city. Said we needed to bring you here or they'd kill my family."

Dahlen nodded slowly. He had suspected as much. The brigands in the region had grown increasingly restless. Food was scarce, safety and shelter even more so. Captured soldiers of Salme could be traded for quite a bit of meat and bread.

"I appreciate your honesty. But if you lie to me again, I will end your life. Do you understand?" When the man nodded, Dahlen carried on. "They will spring this trap as soon as they believe we are at our most vulnerable. When I shout your name, I want you to get as many of your people inside the wagons as you can, understand?"

"Yes. But... I can fight."

"Have you killed many men, Owen?" Dahlen ran his finger though his horse's mane as he spoke, savouring the soft touch.

"No... none."

"I have." And their blood stained his dreams. "You're a farmer, yes?"

"Fur trader, my lord."

"A good profession," Dahlen said with a half-smile. "This is mine. You get your people inside the wagons. I will keep them alive. And you can use those furs to help keep the people of Salme warm, agreed?"

Owen nodded.

Dahlen kept one hand held in the air as he patted his horse on the neck and whispered loud enough for the others to hear. "We are walking into an ambush.

These people are the bait. Stay tight. Use the wagons and the trees for cover, and do not get isolated. I do not intend to rescue these people, only to lose more of our own."

"What are we waiting for?" one of the men from Salme whispered.

Dahlen didn't answer, not until he heard a sharp 'hoot hoot' pierce the natural sounds of the forest.

"That," he whispered, gesturing for the others to follow him.

"Who goes there?" one of the men around the wagons called out, pointing a ragged-looking pitchfork at Dahlen.

"Dahlen Virandr of Salme. We were told you were in need of some assistance." As Dahlen spoke, he scanned the forest around them, seeing shadows shift behind bushes and trees. "Thirty or so," he whispered to Nimara, who pulled her horse beside his. "No more."

"Aye," she replied, her gaze never meeting his. "Swords, axes, and bows. I saw two wearing steel, the rest in leathers. Definitely brigands. Ill organised. Tired."

"What do you think they want?" Thannon whispered.

"Our gear and our coin, and trade us back to Salme for food and supplies, most likely. Let's make sure that doesn't happen." He inclined his head to Owen.

The man pushed his horse forwards. "Jackan, it's me. We made it!"

"Owen?" The man – Jackan – lowered his pitchfork, eyes widening. "Lana? Hakon?"

"Lana is with a healer. Hakon is all right."

As the two spoke, Dahlen slid from his horse, Nimara, Thannon, Camwyn, and Ulrich doing the same, the warriors of Salme not far behind. Dahlen had instructed them to do so. When springing a trap, it was important to make the bait as tempting as possible.

Owen looked to Dahlen, but Dahlen gave a gentle shake of his head, whispering the word 'wait'.

The man leaned into Jackan, whispering something in his ear.

This was the part Dahlen hated: the waiting. Fortunately, the brigands proved impatient. A branch snapped, followed by rustling leaves, over-eager feet and hands betraying their owners.

"Owen, now!" As Dahlen shouted, an arrow whistled past his head and buried itself in the side of a wagon, screams and shouts rising from the woods around them. Men and women in rough-worn leathers burst from hiding places, swords and axes in hand.

Owen and his group hid inside and under the wagons, some of them holding their ground, pitchforks and scythes in hand. The warriors of Salme gathered around Dahlen, Nimara, and the Belduarans.

Souls with steel in their hands were always dangerous, but these men were brigands, not soldiers, and they moved as such. Dahlen leapt forwards, sliding his blades from their scabbards and twirling them. His father had always hated when he'd done that. It was unnecessary and pointless, but it was habit.

The first brigand stabbed at him with their sword, but he twisted at the waist, turned the blade downwards with the sword in his right hand, then plunged his second into the man's chest. He ripped it free, then opened the man's throat with his other blade, blood splattering across a second brigand's face.

Before Dahlen could take another step, Erdhardt and Tharn Pimm charged from the trees behind the brigands, two score warriors with them. Erdhardt smashed a woman's face to pieces with the jagged face of his hammer, then swung the spike into another's chest.

Shouts rang out behind Dahlen as Jorvill Ehrnin, Kara Thain, and a handful of others attacked from the opposite flank. The best way to beat a trap was often by setting another.

Panic flared through the brigands. They were now outnumbered, outmanoeuvred, and utterly outmatched.

A scream rose to Dahlen's left, and he twisted to see four men in dark leathers, faces smeared with dirt and sweat, dragging two children and a man away from the wagons, knives and axes held to their throats.

"Make another fucking move and we'll slit their throats!" one of the men shouted, his hair shaved back with a blade, eyes wild.

Even as the man roared the threat, Erdhardt kicked another man in the chest and brought his hammer down on an exposed throat. Crunch. The body went limp. He lifted his hammer and pointed at the four men with the hostages. "You touch a hair on their heads, and I'll break every bone in your body. I'll start with your toes and work my way up."

Dahlen glanced sideways at Erdhardt. The man was a different beast in the heat of battle, as though a spirit took hold of him.

"You're outnumbered," Dahlen said, taking a step forwards, holding his blades out wide. Several of the brigands knelt around him, sharp steel at their necks. "You harm them, and we will run you down, and you will die. Let them go now, leave, and we'll settle your fate a different day."

The four brigands stared back at them, each unsure what to do.

The man who had spoken spat in the dirt, pulling the blade of his axe tight enough to draw blood from the throat of the young boy he held in his grip. "I don't fucking trust you as far as I could throw you. Lay your weapons down and get on your knees, or this boy will bleed."

"You think this is a negotiation?" Dahlen took another step, his gaze never leaving the man's. "You kill them, you have nothing. I've seen a lot of dead men in my life. You look like them."

He continued to move closer, the brigands shifting backwards.

"Your hand is shaking," Dahlen said, tilting his head to the side.

"Shut the fuck up!" the brigand roared, pulling his blade again and eliciting a scream from the child. The other brigands did the same, but instead of drawing tighter together, as trained soldiers might, they pushed further apart.

"I can tell the difference between true warriors and scum quite quickly in situations like these." Dahlen took another step, seeing the brush shift behind the brigands, everyone else standing and watching, Nimara drawing up only a few paces behind him, Erdhardt circling. "Would you like to know what it is?"

"Shut your fucking mouth, and drop your weapons!" one of the other brigands snarled, digging his fingers into the face of the man he held. "I swear to the gods!"

"True warriors shift inwards and stand tall. They look to those around them. Cowards, like you, assess their own chance of survival, of running, of leaving their companions to die." He pointed his blade at their feet. "It looks to me like you're each ready to run, but not one of you is thinking of the others. Not the kind of companion I'd want at my back."

As the brigands all looked at each other, Yoring and Almer leapt from the bushes behind them, axes hacking into flesh. Two of the men fell, captives jerking free with yelps.

Dahlen surged forwards and slammed his shoulder into the captive man, knocking the brigand off balance. He threw his weight into his left arm and slid his blade through the gap between the captive's arm and torso, finding flesh on the other side.

He pulled the blade free and turned to face the last man, only to watch in shock as the brigand drew the blade across the child's throat, blood spurting.

The child fell forwards, grasping at his neck. Dahlen froze for just a moment, his heart sinking. He saw the blood, knew the boy had no chance.

When the child hit the ground, he pushed everything down and leapt forwards, sliding his swords back in place and sprinting after the brigand. Dahlen caught the man in a matter of moments, slamming into his back. Both of them crashed to the ground, but Dahlen was quicker to react. He grabbed the brigand by the collar of his shirt and slammed a fist into his face. Again and again, bone crunched against bone and Dahlen felt his skin split. The boy's eyes flashed in his mind, blood pouring.

Something within him took over, something primal. He couldn't stop. By the time Dahlen found himself straddling the brigand's chest, hand throbbing, chest heaving, the man was a corpse with a face that looked as though it had been smashed by a horse's kick.

He dragged himself to his feet, turning to see Erdhardt standing behind him, the wails of a grieving father piercing the woodland.

"You all right?" Erdhardt asked, looking down at the battered corpse.

Dahlen shook his head. "Are you?"

Erdhardt did the same.

"But we carry on. We do what we must."

Erdhardt nodded, letting out a long sigh. "We do what we must."

"Eight captives," Thannon said, approaching Dahlen and Erdhardt. "The rest are dead. What do you want to do with them?"

Dahlen looked down at the kneeling brigands. They were savage-looking men, laced with cuts and rubbed with dirt and blood and grime. He drew a short breath, then called out to Camwyn while gesturing at Owen and his people. "Get these people back to Salme. See that they are fed and bathed, and find a roof for them."

"At once, Lord Captain."

Dahlen saw Conal mounting a horse and readying to leave, his eyes fixed on the bodies. Dahlen had commanded him to stay back during the fighting, but it was good for the young lad to see things like this. Aeson had done the same with Dahlen and Erik. The world was a place full of darkness and death. It would do no good to shy away from it. "Not you, Conal. You stay."

When the others had left, only Dahlen, Thannon, Erdhardt, Nimara, Conal, Yoring, Almer, and Kara Thain remained.

"We have no place for them in Salme," Kara said, looking down at the brigands, who were lined up on their knees. "We cannot have demons both inside the walls and out."

"Agreed." Dahlen clenched his jaw. A few moments' silence passed between them all, and Dahlen could point to the precise moment that Conal understood what would happen next, eyes widening.

"I will do it," Thannon said, placing his hand on the pommel of his sword.

Dahlen shook his head and stepped forwards. He looked down at the eight men. "Uraks savage these lands and Epheria is on fire. And yet you choose to prey on the weak. You choose to take the little others have instead of building something of your own. There are some men who would take your weapons and send you off into the wilds, who would stay their blades. I am not one of those men, and I cannot set you free only to see you torment and murder the souls who pass through these lands."

"Please," one of the brigands begged. "Please don't…"

Dahlen's throat tightened, and for a moment he heard the screams and saw the raging flames of Belduar and of the battles every night at Salme. He pushed it all down. "I take no pleasure in this, but I do what I must."

Hours later, Dahlen stood on the walls of Salme. As the sun set, it painted the Antigan Ocean in an array of sparkling yellows and oranges. The wind held a bitter chill, icy air tickling his skin.

His hand shook a little as he lifted the flask to his mouth and drank deeply, clenching his jaw as the spirit burned on the way down.

It seemed strange to him to have something as beautiful as that sparkling ocean in a world filled with so much horror. As the waves swashed against the docks, Dahlen heard the screams of the brigands in his mind, heard the chop of his blade biting into flesh and bone.

He'd made the right choice. Salme didn't have the capability to hold such men, and he could not set them free knowing they would only continue to kill and rob and slaughter anyone who passed through the woods. In another time, he would have let them walk away. But not this time. This was a time of war, a time when every choice mattered. The people of Salme were his charges, and he needed to do whatever was in their best interests. That didn't make it easier though.

After a while, Nimara joined him on the walls, arms folded as she watched the undulating waves coruscate like shattered glass.

"How many lives have you taken?" Dahlen asked, clasping his hands behind his back.

"Many," she answered.

"I can't even remember when I lost count. There are too many faces to remember. I'd killed fifty men by the time I had seen eighteen summers."

Nimara brushed her finger against several of the gold rings knotted into her hair. "You're a good man, Dahlen."

"I don't even know what that is anymore." Dahlen took another swig of the burning spirit Shola Holten had concocted at The Rusty Shell and offered it to Nimara.

The dwarf took it without hesitation. "Can you sleep at night? Soft and easy?" Dahlen shook his head.

"Then you are a good man. I would have made the same choice earlier. There was no path on which letting them live would have ended well."

"Mmm."

"Oh, also, I almost forgot. That fur trader – Owen – he asked me to give you this." Dahlen turned his head to see Nimara sliding a hefty canvas pack from her shoulders. She produced a thick grey and black wolfpineskin cloak. The thing was massive.

She handed the folded cloak to him and he let it unfurl, admiring the craftsmanship and the weight.

"He says there are thirty more where it came from, a gift to whoever you think deserves it. A thank you for saving his family."

Dahlen pulled the cloak around his shoulders, the warmth wrapping around his bones. He filled his lungs with frosted air.

"It suits you," Nimara said.

Dahlen gave her a half-smile. "Do you think we'll ever forget?"

"Forget what?"

"Everything we've done. Do you think when this is all over, we will be able to just... sit and... Sorry, I just..."

Nimara clasped his hand, fingers sliding between his. "I don't think I'll ever forget the faces or the screams... but I hope that one day I can forgive myself enough to die happy. War makes monsters of us all... but it also shows us who we are and the things worth fighting for."

"I've been at war all my life," he said, squeezing Nimara's hand.

"And yet, you are still kind, and hopeful, and true. Come, it's cold and I'm in need of warmth." Nimara tugged at Dahlen's hand, but he stayed firm.

"I just need a little longer."

She didn't argue or try to convince him otherwise. She simply stayed where she was, her fingers clasped in his.

"Do you know what scares me the most?" he asked, looking out at the waves. "I'm not sure who I am without this war. What am I without a sword in my hand? What if I need this? What if all I ever have to offer this world is death?"

CHAPTER SEVENTY-FOUR

RISE

21ˢᵗ Day of the Blood Moon

Aravell – Winter, Year 3081 After Doom

Calen sat astride Valerys as the dragon stood on a cliff edge that overlooked the sprawling valley ahead. The light of the sun and moon glistened in the spray of the waterfall that tumbled over the ledge on the opposite side of the vast chasm.

He replayed the conversation with Chora over and over in his mind. And each time he did, he remembered the flames consuming his home, remembered his mother's screams, remembered Farda's words.

"None of them had to die, but you had to play the hero, and fate made its choice."

There had not been even the slightest hint of guilt in the man's voice. He had killed her as though it cost him little more than the breath in his lungs. And Calen had agreed to spare Farda's life. He did not think a day would pass where he wouldn't question that decision. But he needed Tivar and Avandeer at his side if he was to have any hope of breaking the siege at Tarhelm.

Even as he thought of it, his mind shifted to Dann, and Vaeril, and Tarmon, and Erik, and all those who marched for Salme.

No matter what decision Calen made, he abandoned someone. But without him, Tarhelm would burn. With Queen Tessara and her army marching alongside them, Calen had to trust that Tarmon and the others could do what needed to be done. As this war spread and grew, he knew that he would not be able to protect everyone. He couldn't be everywhere. But that didn't make the choices any easier.

A warmth spread from Valerys, and the dragon's mind wrapped around his, settling his heart. They would fly to Tarhelm, and they would burn the Lorians to the ground. Then they would fly straight to Salme.

Calen closed his eyes and leaned forwards so that his head rested against the scales of Valerys's neck. "La'verkanet vidim dar la væi aver ata'du."

I don't know what I would do without you.

The heavy drum of footfalls drew Calen from his thoughts. He turned to see Gaeleron and the five Dracurïn the elf had selected as Calen's personal guard leading Castor Kai and his retinue up the winding path towards the cliff edge. Even then, two standard-bearers walked behind the High Lord, both holding banners bearing the six black stars of Illyanara on a yellow field.

Valerys let out a low rumble and lowered himself to the ground so that Calen could slide from his back. Dirt crunched beneath the weight of Calen's armoured boots as he landed. He looked down at the runes marked into his armour and whispered, "Dreskyr mit huartan. Dreskyr mit hnokle. Bante er vi, measter og osvarthe."

Protect my heart. Protect my bones. Bound are we, master and oath.

The runes ignited with a purple light, and the joints of the armour melded together as power flowed through him. He turned to where Aneera waited with Nuada and gave the Angan a sharp nod.

Aneera pressed her palm to her forehead, then folded her legs beneath her and closed her eyes.

"What is the meaning of this?" Castor Kai said, as the procession stopped before Calen and the others. The man was far taller than Calen had imagined he would be. "It had been arranged that we would meet at sunrise, and yet that is long past, and now I am 'summoned' to you without a word of explanation?"

"You will watch your tongue," Gaeleron snapped before Calen could say a word. The five other Dracurïn walked past the procession and formed up on either side of Calen.

Calen raised a hand and stepped forwards. Valerys stretched his neck out, allowing a deep growl to rumble in his chest. "My apologies, High Lord Kai. It appears that the war did not allow for our plans. How inconsiderate. We received word this morning that the Lorians lay siege to our allies in the North. I am called to give aid. Valerys and I fly within the hour."

Castor narrowed his gaze as though trying to discern whether Calen was joking or not. "You asked us here to discuss an alliance, then left us waiting for days while my army sits in the marshes, and now you are to traipse off across the continent once again and leave us waiting?"

Calen stared at the man for a moment, studying him, watching how he held himself, how his body shifted with the unfamiliar weight of the sword at his hip, and yet he stood with a wide base and the readiness of someone who knew battle. Castor could wield a sword, but it had been some time since he had worn one.

"I never said I would leave you waiting. I asked you to Aravell so that we could broker an alliance. Here we are."

"Where are the others?" A hint of trepidation crept into Castor's voice, and a murmur spread through his retinue of about fifty strong.

"I have already sent word to Aryana Torval and the other faction leaders. But I thought it best if we spoke face to face, given our history."

"Our history?"

Calen gave the man a soft smile but ignored the question. "I have little time, so I will be as direct as I can. What would it take for you to pledge your sword to me, High Lord Kai? What promise must I give?"

Castor's back straightened at that, and he lifted his chin a little higher. "You must support my claim to the crown of Illyanara."

"You wish to be a king?"

"I already am a king in all but name." He rested his hand on the pommel of his sword, though he had to look down to find it. "All across the province know it. If you support my claim, pledge your sword to me, then Illyanara will be united within a moon."

"Ah," Calen said with a half-smile. "You wish me to pledge my sword to *you*."

"You are from Illyanara, are you not? I have watched over you your entire life."

Again, Calen ignored him. "What would you have me do with Aryana and Tukul and all the others?"

Castor stepped closer, boldness in his voice. "They are traitors, Calen Bryer. I am the rightful High Lord of Illyanara. I am its natural king. And they have seized this moment, this strife, this darkness, to grab power for themselves. How do we trust people who do such things?"

"That does not answer my question, High Lord Kai."

"I would have their heads. That is the cost of treachery. Give me their heads, support my claim for the crown, and you will have a united Illyanara."

"I thought that might be your answer." Calen turned away for a moment and looked up at Valerys. The dragon was magnificent, the blended light of the moon and the sun glistening against his scales. A low rumble resonated in Valerys's chest as he lowered his head, eyes fixed on Castor Kai. Slowly, controlling its flow, Calen allowed the dragon's fury to seep into him.

Calen reached for his sword and pulled it free of its scabbard as he turned back to face the High Lord and his retinue.

A number of Castor's warriors stepped forwards and made to draw their swords, but Gaeleron and the Dracurïn moved like the wind, blades pressing into the leather that protected their chests.

"If the steel leaves your scabbard, your head leaves your shoulders," Gaeleron said, not so much as a tremble in his outstretched sword.

"What is this?" Castor demanded. The man pulled his hand away from his sword and looked about at the Dracurïn.

"Do you recognise this sword?" Calen held his sword in the air, his right hand on the hilt, his left balancing the flat of the blade. He couldn't help but admire it himself. The gleam of the steel, the swirls ornamenting the blade, the star crossguard, the coin pommel.

"Why would I recognise it?" Castor scoffed.

"It belonged to my father." Calen drew a long breath, allowing his memories to flow back to the day that Vars had handed him the sword wrapped in a bundle of cloth.

"It was given to me a long time ago," Vars had said as he'd gazed down at the sword. *"And now it's time that I pass it on to you."*

"He was a great man," Calen continued, passing his gaze along the length of the curved blade. "Greater than even I knew. More importantly, he was a good man. A man of principles."

"I'm afraid I did not know your father." The initial panic faded from the High Lord's voice. "You said he fought in the Varsund War? I'm sure he was a fine warrior, but I knew no man by the name Bryer."

Calen lifted his stare and smiled at Castor Kai. "He didn't go by that name."

Calen gestured towards the copse of trees that stood tall on the right of the cliff.

"You knew my father," Calen said, as the High Lord looked towards the copse, his gaze narrowing at the sound of shifting feet and murmurs coming from within.

"I did not know your father," the man reiterated. "I have had enough of these games. Whatever this is," he said, gesturing towards the trees, "be done with it. Pledge yourself to me, support my claim. We will make Illyanara whole."

"He slew Durin Longfang with this blade," Calen held his father's sword a little higher, savouring the look of shock on Castor Kai's face. "And Taran Shadesmire, and Rayce Garrin. He ended the Varsund War with this blade. My father's name, High Lord Kai, was Cassian Tal. He was the greatest swordsman Illyanara has ever seen. You knew him well. You betrayed him."

"I… That's not possible. How could you…"

Fenryr and a score of his Angan emerged from the trees, alongside Aryana Torval, Tukul Unger, and the other leaders of the Illyanaran factions. A clutch of Dracurïn walked among them.

"Your father murdered my son." Castor reached for his blade, fingers wrapping around the pommel.

"Please, do me the favour of drawing that sword." Calen's stare didn't falter as he looked into Castor's eyes. "I beg you."

Castor hesitated, his stare fixing on the sword in Calen's hand before shifting to Valerys, whose head now hovered just over Calen's.

"Let me introduce you to another name you know, High Lord Kai." Calen gestured towards Fenryr, who had stopped a few feet from the High Lord's retinue on the right. "This is Fenryr, Wolf God, blood of my blood, and the one you were willing to kill my father to chain."

Fenryr stepped forwards, armoured in that same black steel he had worn the other night, roaring wolf-head pauldrons adorning his shoulders. Castor Kai's retinue parted before the wolf god, shrinking at the sight of him.

A moment passed in which Fenryr stood over Castor Kai, seeming to grow before Calen's eyes. "You wanted to place a collar around my neck," the god said. "I can smell the fear in you, the greed. Such a small man."

Aryana Torval and the others approached Calen, each staring at the High Lord and his retinue.

"You heard his words?" Calen asked. "Heard the cost of his allegiance?"

"We are the traitors," Aryana said. "Our heads are to be taken from our shoulders, while a crown is to be placed upon his."

"That is not—"

"Speak when spoken to," Fenryr snapped, a dark claw pressing into Castor's neck, blood trickling.

"You have received my messages then?" Calen asked.

"We have," Tukul Unger responded.

"And what is your answer?"

One by one, in a semi-circle facing Calen, each of the leaders dropped to a knee and placed a closed fist across their chest. Aryana Torval was the last standing. She drew her sword slowly, then knelt, driving the blade into the ground as she did.

Calen gave a soft nod, then mimicked the gesture, his armour clinking against the hard earth. Behind him, Valerys dipped his head in a bow and extended his right forelimb. Calen looked to Gaeleron, who nodded.

"I hereby swear oath," Calen said, his voice loud and clear, "by witness of those here and the six who watch over us, to protect those before me with all my strength. To bleed for them, to fight by their side, and, if needs be, to die by it."

Aryana and the others repeated the words.

"It is with honour that your oath has been witnessed by those here and by the six who watch over us," Gaeleron said, pressing his fist to his chest and giving a slight bow.

Calen rose, leveraging his sword before pulling it from the earth and wiping it clean with his cloak. "I will lead you into the fires of war," he said, looking out at the leaders. "But I swear to always lead from the front and to never ask you to lay your life where I would not lay mine. This war encompasses more than just Illyanara, and so we must stray further from home to ensure that home is safe. And we will do so together."

Calen sheathed his sword but kept his left hand resting on the pommel. He turned his attention back to Castor Kai. The men and women in the High Lord's retinue shifted uneasily, watching as the other leaders stood.

"It appears, High Lord Kai, that we are at an impasse."

The man flicked his gaze to Calen, Fenryr's claw still pressed to his throat. "This was all some ploy."

Calen shook his head. "You give me too much credit. But you see, you yourself declared that the cost of treachery is death. You said you wanted their heads." Calen pointed at the other leaders. "What say you all?"

"I would have his head," a man called.

"Aye, stick it in the ashes of Argona!" another shouted.

Tukul Unger stepped forwards and spat on the ground. "A traitor pays the traitor's price."

"Agreed," Aryana Torval said.

"You cannot do this – you cannot!"

Calen gestured for Fenryr to lower his claw, then stepped closer. Gaeleron and those of the personal guard matched his step, swords still drawn.

The purple glow from Calen's eyes shone on the man's bronzed skin as they stood eye to eye. "And what would I do with a man I cannot trust? A man who betrayed my father and tried to put a god in chains? A man who would smile to my face and take my head from my shoulders when I turned?"

"You can trust me. I swear it."

"That army you have, High Lord Kai. Where was it you said?"

"In the marshes. Near sixteen thousand."

"That is strange," Calen said, turning down his bottom lip. "You see, I flew over the marshes. Twice. It is a large place, but from dragonback, an army of that size would have been quite a sight. So either you are lying about the numbers that follow you, or they have already abandoned you."

Castor took a step back as Calen reached forwards and pressed a gauntleted finger against one of the six black stars on his breastplate. "You wear the sigil of Illyanara, and yet, even now, as the empire crumbles, you still call yourself 'High Lord'. Your loyalty does not lie with the people of Illyanara but with whoever is most likely to grant you power."

Calen took a few steps away, then called back to the men and women of Castor's retinue. "If you wish to be judged by your High Lord's honour, stay where you are. If you would rather fight for your home, for Illyanara, and for Epheria, if you would rather join the songs our descendants will sing, step forwards."

To the last, each and every man and woman left Castor Kai's side and knelt in the patchy grass.

"You cowards!" Castor Kai roared. "The lot of you, rotten bastards!"

Calen turned back to Castor Kai, staring into the man's panicked eyes. "Our lives can be boiled down to a series of key choices, Castor. Choices that shape us, choices that mould our paths, choices that dictate how we will be remembered." Calen's mind flashed back to the night he'd followed Erik from The Two Barges, the night he'd taken his first life. He thought back to his decision to return to The Glade, a decision that had caused his parents' deaths. His decision to leave Rist in Camylin and then to cross the Burnt Lands in search of him. More memories washed through his mind until he finally settled on that moment when he'd looked down from dragonback at the army attacking Aravell. He could still hear the screams of the men and women he and Valerys had burned alive. "I've made many of my choices already, and I've had to live with them. I suggest you make your next choice carefully."

"You're just as arrogant as he was," Castor growled, wrapping his fingers around the hilt of his sword. "I will not die like some pig."

The man drew his sword and lunged at Calen.

This time it was not Gaeleron who drew steel quickest. Calen swept his blade across the lower part of Castor's abdomen, where the breastplate stopped and only leather protected. The leather yielded to the steel, and the steel bit into flesh.

"It's an elven blade," Vars's voice rang in his head. *"Better than anything I could make myself. The curve in the blade allows for smoother, cleaner strikes. Not as good at punching through armour, but if you're quick enough, that won't matter."*

One step had taken Calen past Castor Kai, and as the man stumbled, pressing a hand to his wound, Calen pivoted and, with a second swing, relieved the High Lord of his head.

He looked down at the corpse, blood pouring into the grass. That was not how he'd intended this to go, but neither would he mourn the man.

Gaeleron handed Calen a cloth.

"Take these warriors to the barracks." He gestured to Castor's former retinue and the faction leaders as he wiped the blood from his blade. "Give them as much food as they can eat and as much mead as they can drink."

"It will be done, Draleid."

As Gaeleron turned to leave, Calen grabbed his arm and met his gaze. "La uvahâr du val myia viël, Mahatirín Athis."

I trust you with my life, Warmarshal Athis.

Gaeleron straightened at the words, or more so at the new title Calen had just bestowed upon him. The title of Mahatirín was an ancient one amongst the elves, particularly those of Lunithír. It was given to one of unshaking faith and loyalty, to one whose honour was without question, to one who held no fear in the face of death.

Gaeleron stared into Calen's eyes and clenched his fingers into so tight a fist against his breastplate the blood drained, skin going pale. "Ar du val myialí… Calen."

And you with mine… Calen.

Calen turned to Aryana and Tukul, who both stared down at Castor Kai's headless body. "When you are fed and ready, I would have you gather your forces – along with Castor's retinue – and march to the Argonan Marshes and see to it that any remnants of the High Lord's support know that he is no longer with us."

"I thought you said you saw nothing in the marshes?" Aryana asked.

Calen smiled. "That's what I said. You will find them near the southeastern edge, near Fearsall. I will send Dracurïn with you. With Cardend and Stonehelm razed in Arkalen, Fearsall will be the first line against the Uraks and any who threaten Illyanara from the south. Ensure the city is held, then push south to Drifaien as agreed. Chora Sarn and two other Rakina will travel with you. When this war is over, Aryana, you will hold Fearsall and Tukul will hold Baylomon. All I ask is that you stop slaughtering each other."

"I will hold you to that promise," Aryana said.

"I expect you to."

Before mounting Valerys, Calen looked to Fenryr. "You are ready?"

The wolf god nodded. "We have remained in the shadows too long. It is time to teach this empire to fear the howl of the wolf. I am sure my brother waits for you."

"I'm sure he does too."

Calen mounted Valerys, casting one look over his shoulder as the Dracurïn collected Castor Kai's body, then let his mind drift into Valerys's as the dragon took flight.

CALEN FOUND KAYGAN – OR Rokka, or whatever name he chose to go by – precisely where he had said he would: in the courtyard by the empty barracks, the third on the right.

He slid from Valerys's back before the dragon alighted, softening his landing with the Spark.

The god stood alone, leaning on a long stick with grey robes over his shoulders. His lips twisted into a toothy grin as Calen approached. "What a surprise. How can I help you, Draleid?"

Calen didn't bother to answer. "When you said we would need you, this is what you meant, wasn't it?"

The god gave a shrug. "I knew there would be a choice and we would be needed either way."

Calen couldn't help but ask the question that had lingered in his mind. "If we go north, what happens to Salme?"

"That is not how the paths work, I'm afraid," Kaygan answered, moving the stick in circles, its butt pressed into the stone.

Anger flared in Valerys, and Calen did his best to keep it at bay as he took a step closer to the god. In the shadowed doorway of the barracks, he spotted Tamzin, her hand dropping to the head of the axe at her hip, that strange kat-like creature – Kerith – standing tall at her side.

That was good. It meant the god still didn't know whether he was safe or not.

"Does it weigh on you at all?" Calen asked, turning his gaze away from Tamzin. "All the lives lost because you choose to play games, choose to twist and turn everything so as to steer us along your path."

"All war is a game played with people's lives, Calen Bryer. I'm sure High Lord Castor Kai can tell you that." The god pulled back his upper lip and flicked his tongue against a sharp fang, giving Calen a knowing look. "As I said before, the path you are on will bring death beyond your wildest dreams. I simply wish to ensure that I and my kind are not amongst the bodies – that includes you, by the way."

"Well," Calen said, "seeing as you know everything before it happens. What is your answer to my question?"

The kat god's smile widened, his pupils sharpening to thin lines. It was still strange for Calen to look upon Kaygan's youthful features and broad shoulders and know this was the same old druid he'd met near the Burnt Lands. "Una will do as you ask," Kaygan said. "Or rather, will ask or were going to ask… She will carry a number of your warriors to Tarhelm. Consider it a show of faith. She cannot send any to Salme."

"Why not?"

"Because that path is not the correct path. You cannot have both things, Calen Bryer. You will not succeed at Tarhelm without us, and we cannot spare bodies for Salme. We can send twelve at most, perhaps fewer, or Una risks death. Passage through the aether comes with a price."

"Again with the games." Calen sighed. He had hoped for more. Fenryr had told him that some Aetherdruids, or Starchasers, could carry a much larger number through the aether, but some could move nothing more than themselves.

"I know you don't like when I talk of the paths, but I would suggest you bring the tall blue ones." He swirled his finger in the air. "The Jotnar, yes. There are four, if I remember correctly. And that sour-faced brother of mine, along with your sister and keeper, Tamzin and Kerith, of course myself, and Boud here."

Kaygan gestured to the doorway where Tamzin stood, and a dark-haired woman stepped forwards, red marks winding around her neck. She tilted her head ever so slightly. Calen didn't recognise her. She'd not been there the night before when Kaygan had come to the Eyrie.

"Who are you?" Calen asked, opening himself to the Spark just in case.

"I have heard much about you, Calen Bryer." The woman gave a half-smile and inclined her head but didn't answer his question.

"Boud is a Stormcaller. You will need her. Trust me. She has many Gifts."

"Trust is earned." It was difficult for Calen to argue with Kaygan's choices. He had already promised Ella. She had spent time in Tarhelm, fought alongside Coren and Farwen. And the Jotnar were powerful Spark users in their own right and mighty warriors. But Calen was wary of any advice the kat god gave. "I will leave behind Aelmar and take Therin Eiltris in his place." Calen looked at Tamzin. "You and your keeper will stay also. Two Fenryr Angan will go instead."

The frown on Kaygan's face let Calen know he had made the right choices. For better or worse, he trusted Fenryr more than he did Kaygan, and being outnumbered by the kat god's druids in the middle of Tarhelm didn't seem a wise move.

"It is decided then," Calen said, returning Kaygan's eternal grin. "With good wind, Valerys and I will reach the Firnin Mountains by daybreak tomorrow."

"We will be there."

Calen wanted to ask where he would see them. But he knew the question was pointless. Kaygan would answer in a riddle, as he always did. Calen would see them where he was meant to see them.

"Before I leave, I brought this for you." Calen reached into the pouch that hung from his shoulder and produced a bundle of cloths that he placed into Kaygan's hand.

The god stared down at the bundle, his thumb brushing over the outermost cloth. That usual sense of knowing was absent from his eyes.

"You do not see every path then."

Kaygan pulled open the bundle to reveal the two shattered segments of the metal disc the god had given Calen under the guise of Rokka in the hut near the Burnt Lands. "You play a dangerous game, Wolfchild."

"You began it," Calen answered. The god had given him that disc for a reason and, whatever that reason, Calen wanted nothing to do with it. "I am simply doing what I can."

As Calen walked towards Valerys, Kaygan called after him. "This disc was a gift. It was to save a life."

Calen staggered in his stride but continued walking as though he had not. He refused to give Kaygan the satisfaction of turning around. What was done was done. He had no choice but to believe the god was lying once more, trying to sow seeds of doubt into Calen's mind.

"That life is on your head now, Wolfchild. One more added to the scales."

Valerys leaned forwards and let out a roar, that familiar pressure building within him.

We have bigger battles to fight. Calen brushed his gauntlet-clad hand along a horn that framed Valerys's neck, the dragon bowing. Myia nithír til diar, Myia'ldryr.

My soul to yours, my fire.

"To the Eyrie."

THE SILENCE IN THE EYRIE was such that Calen could hear the beating of his own heart. The other Rakina had not said a word when he and Valerys had alighted on the stone, but Imala could have burned a hole through him with her stare. He had known the cost of asking Chora to change her vote and understood it, but he had seen no other way. He needed Tivar and Avandeer next to him in the battles to come.

And so he waited in the silence, counting the passing moments in heartbeats, Valerys standing over him, Varthear and Sardakes to his left. The enormous frames of the three dragons cast long shadows, strands of morning light streaming through in yellow and red. It was as though both of the Rakina dragons knew precisely what was about to happen.

Calen glanced over to Ella, who stood with Faenir and Therin. Her eyes were molten gold, and she refused to look at him. He didn't blame her. Farda had not only killed their mam, but he had been the cause of Rhett's death as well. Calen had hated asking her to allow him to live, but he'd not wanted to do it without her agreement.

In truth, Calen cared little for what Imala, or Danveer, or any of the other Rakina thought of him. His concern was for his sister.

The sound of deep wingbeats broke the silence, followed by a screeching roar. Avandeer surged upwards from the courtyard within the holding quarters. She swirled through the air before coming to land in the space between Calen and the arched passageway carved into the rock. Her eyes, yellow as the morning sun, looked to Valerys, a soft purr in her throat.

Valerys shook his head, frills raising on his neck, and mimicked the sound.

Moments later, four figures emerged from the passage, framed on both sides by a score of Dracurïn in gleaming plate.

Tivar walked at the front, garbed in the same white steel she had worn when Avandeer had fallen from the sky, but the black flame that had once adorned her breast was now gone, cut clean with the Spark.

Ella jerked forwards as Farda came into view, Faenir growling at her side. Therin rested a hand on her shoulder and whispered something Calen couldn't hear. She seemed to calm a little, but not much.

When Tivar and the others stopped in place, Chora looked to Calen and inclined her head.

Tivar lifted her gaze as Calen moved forwards. She glanced down at her armour, then tentatively at those around her, and whispered, "What is happening?"

"Tivar Savinír, I ask you again, will you fight by my side? Will you protect your brothers and sisters, protect the people of Epheria, until time takes you or a blade ends your watch? Will you forsake forgiveness and swear your dying breath to me and to everyone here?"

Calen turned and gestured towards Therin, who handed him an elven blade set into its scabbard.

"I offer you this last chance. Die by this blade, or wear it. Which do you choose?"

Tivar's lips moved, but no words came. Her eyes shifted from the sword in Calen's hands to the Rakina who watched her. "I…" She looked back to Calen, lowering her voice. "I do not understand. Have Coren and Farwen come?"

Calen shook his head. "Coren and Farwen sent word from the North. They are under siege and have called for aid. Chora Sarn has changed her mind and decided instead to grant you and Avandeer the chance to do something honourable with what is left of your life." Calen drew a deep breath and exhaled slowly. "If you accept, your life will not be your own. You and Avandeer will be sworn, by your honour, by your soul, by the blood in your veins, to spend every moment standing guard over this world. You will be Onuvrín. Unforgiven. From this day until your last day."

Slowly, Tivar's lips cracked into a soft smile, and she looked up at Avandeer, whose head was craned over her. The dragon twisted her neck so that her eyes met those of her soulkin, a deep rumble resonating in her chest.

Tivar dropped to her knees. "By The Father and The Mother, The Warrior and The Sailor, The Maiden and The Smith, we pledge the same vow to you that we did when I first knelt in this eyrie. We give you our dying breaths and every beat of our hearts until that moment. We will be both your sword and your shield. On the bond, we swear it."

"Then rise, Tivar Savinír, Onuvrín, Unforgiven. Take this sword, and with it be a guardian once more."

Calen held out the sword and scabbard. Tears welled in Tivar's eyes as she took it, her hand lingering on Calen's for just a moment. "You will never know what you have given me," she whispered, the tears rolling down her cheeks. "Vrail du nur haryníl asatrú en mír."

Thank you for having faith in me.

"Aver kanet nakil mír olkiran det," Calen replied. *Do not make me regret it.*

"Never." Tivar clipped the scabbard onto her belt and tugged on it firmly. Drawing a deep breath, she turned to face the other Rakina. "I know there is nothing I can do that will turn back the things I have already done. And it is you who have paid the price for my mistakes. I also know there are many who would rather take my head from my shoulders here and now. And I thank you for not bowing to the same darkness that took me."

A brief silence was followed by the sound of dirt crunching beneath wheels as Chora Sarn moved forwards. "I did not change my mind as Calen said. In my heart I would still rather have you dead. Protect him with your life, Onuvrín. Do not waste the chance we have given you."

Tivar pressed a fist to her chest and inclined her head.

With that, Chora looked to Calen and nodded once more.

Calen stepped past Tivar and stood before Farda, Hala, and Ilyain.

The elf and white-haired woman returned Calen's gaze, but Farda stared at the ground.

"Look at me." The words were barely louder than a whisper, but they were sharp and harsh.

Farda lifted his gaze. His eyes were as green as Ithrax's scales had been, the scars on his face now pale and pink.

This was the closest Calen had stood to the man since the day Farda had killed Freis. It took every drop of his strength to hold back the fury that swelled in Valerys.

The dragon ignored Calen's attempt at restraint and moved so that he loomed over his soulkin. Slowly, Valerys lowered his head, bringing his snout barely an arm's length from Farda's face. A puff of warm air swept back Farda's hair as Valerys bared his enormous teeth, a growl resonating in his throat.

Farda looked up at the dragon and did not flinch.

Calen reached down to the patch of red silk he'd tied to his belt loops, twisting it in his armoured fingers. It would never replace his mother's scarf; nothing could. But it gave him the slightest of reliefs. That was until her screams sounded in his mind.

"Farda Kyrana, Hala Nôri, and Ilyain Altair. You, too, are offered the same choice that has been offered to Tivar."

Therin and a Dracurïn moved to Calen's side, Therin handing him another sword and scabbard.

"Die by these blades," Calen said. "Or wear them. Forsake forgiveness and the lives you once led, and swear yourself to me, swear yourself to the brothers and sisters you betrayed, to the lives you destroyed. You will not be offered this chance again."

Calen's heart was a hammer in his chest, resounding thump after resounding thump, the sounds of his father's forge filling his mind, his mother's screams echoing. With those sounds, Valerys wrapped his soul around Calen, filling the cracks in his heart, warming the cold depths of his mind with a burning fury.

Farda stared at Calen for a moment, then turned his head to look at Ella.

Calen's sister had come a few steps closer, Faenir at her side. He wasn't sure which of the pair looked more savage. Ella's face twisted in an unnatural snarl, eyes glimmering gold, a pair of fangs jutting from her upper and lower jaws, and dark black claws extending from her fingers. There was none gathered there that day who would ever deny the wolf in her blood.

"I accept," Farda said, clear and loud. He dropped to one knee. "However long I have left in this world, I wish to spend it trying to reclaim the man I once was. I have no honour left to swear upon, only half a soul to give, cracked and broken as it is, and the blood in my veins is dark and worthless. I swear upon Shinyara's memory, upon the only piece of me that is good. If I betray that oath, she will never look upon me again, in this life or the next."

To Farda's right, Ilyain followed suit, his knees crunching in the dirt. "I am blind, and I am Broken. But I will give all that I am." He looked to where the

Rakina stood, his milky eyes seeming to see. "It means nothing to you, but I have waited a long time to say that I am truly sorry for what was done to this world and for my part in it. My life is yours for as long as you will allow me to walk the mortal plane."

"Have you ever taken a life with your blood cold?" Hala said once Ilyain grew quiet. "While they knelt before you? Hands empty, neck stretched?" When Calen didn't respond, she continued. "I am tempted to die by the blade you offer, if only to know if you have the steel in your heart to do it. It's not much of a choice, is it? Kneel and swear oath, or die."

"You would have us set you free after all you've done?"

"You don't know the half of what I've done. You've barely been alive for a breath."

Calen stared down at the fingers of Hala's left hand. They were bunched into a fist, as they had been every time he'd laid eyes on her. A result of being Rakina, most likely. He let his breath out slowly. "We offer you more choices than you offered the brothers and sisters you slaughtered the night Ilnaen fell. The night hatchlings were broken like twigs, eggs shattered like glass, and honourable Draleid died defending them." Calen set his stance and pulled the sword from its scabbard just enough to show glinting steel. "If you do not feel sorrow for those actions, then you have lived a long enough life already."

Hala returned his stare with an unsettling intensity, then nodded slowly, puffing out her bottom lip. She dropped to one knee. "I will swear oath."

Calen closed his eyes for just a moment, attempting to stop his hands from shaking as he slid the steel back into the scabbard. He gestured for Therin and the Dracurïn to step forwards. He would have asked two of the Rakina to stand in their place, but that had felt like an ask too far.

"Rise," Calen said, the word like poison on his tongue. "Farda Kyrana, Hala Nôri, and Ilyain Altair. Onuvrín. Unforgiven."

As Farda stood, Calen pressed the sword and scabbard into the man's arms and stared into his eyes.

"If you betray us," Calen whispered, leaning in closer, "if you so much as think of doing harm to anyone here, I will burn the Spark from your body myself. I will burn it, and I will cut out your tongue and I will drop you in a hole to rot."

"I cannot give back the things I've taken away," Farda said. "And—"

"No." Calen pushed the sword and scabbard harder so Farda leaned back on his heels. "No words. You do not deserve words, and I will not hear them." Calen started to pull away, then stopped. "You burned my mother alive. I hope I get the chance to do the same to you one day. But I will keep this oath as long as you do."

Calen pulled back from Farda and grasped Tivar's shoulder. "Are you ready to fly?"

"Whenever you call," she said, rolling her shoulders back and standing tall.

Calen nodded, looking at the other three. "You will remain here under the eyes of Chora Sarn and Warmarshal Gaeleron Athis. You will do as they say and nothing less."

Calen turned to Ella and could see by the tightness in her jaw that she did not find it easy to hold his gaze in that moment. "I will see you when the sun rises tomorrow. Be ready."

"I am."

Therin grasped Calen's forearm. "Fly well."

"I will see you there."

Chora wheeled herself to Calen's side, reaching up to grasp his forearm. "I'ldryr viel asatar. I sanvîr viel baralun. Iralíse alaith, akar."

In fire we are forged. In blood we are tempered. Fly well, brother.

"Du haryn myia vrai, vésani. Nur luienil."

You have my thanks, sister. For everything.

"I will continue to have the Dracârdare test the eggs you saved from Ilnaen for the Calling," Chora said. "Day and night. Every soul within the city will be tested."

Calen squeezed Chora's forearm a little tighter, inclining his head in thanks, then took his helmet from a nearby Dracurïn and mounted Valerys, the dragon bowing low. He waited as Tivar climbed to the nape of Avandeer's neck, then leaned closer to Valerys, the warmth of the dragon's scales flowing through him. "Nur il varsa vået, vir aver kanet iralíse untau."

For the first time, we do not fly alone.

A low rumble of recognition swept through the dragon, and he let out a roar, frills shaking on either side of Calen.

"Uora, Valerys."

Rise, Valerys.

Valerys's lungs and chest swelled, and the dragon shifted forwards, cracking his wings against the air. He moved towards the great ledge over which the river flowed and dove into the valley beyond.

The air ripped past Calen as Valerys plummeted, the tumbling river spraying over them. Calen pressed himself as tightly as he could to the dragon's neck, feeling Valerys's scales mould to his body. He felt Valerys's wings begin to unfurl, and he braced himself, pulling on threads of Air.

Valerys's wings caught the air, and the dragon's fall halted in an instant. He whipped forwards like a crack of lightning, the valley open before him.

A series of roars sounded behind them, and Calen twisted in place to see Avandeer launch herself over the edge. The dragon dropped like a gleaming gem, the mixture of the yellow morning sun and the crimson moon sparkling in the falling water around her.

In that moment, a truly unique warmth flowed from Valerys to Calen. A warmth that filled the dragon's heart and spread through their shared soul. Valerys was no longer alone. *They* were no longer alone.

As Avandeer unfurled her wings and entered the valley, another roar erupted from the ledge above.

Varthear stood in the waters of the river, her winged forelimbs spread wide, the hulking frame of Sardakes beside her. With a mighty roar, the dragon leapt. Calen's heart stopped for a moment as Varthear fell, only continuing to beat when the dragon spread her great vermillion wings and swept forwards.

Avandeer and Varthear swirled through the air around Valerys and Calen, moving like leaves in the wind. And with a surge of elation, Valerys joined them, and Calen smiled in a way he had not done in such a long time.

When Sardakes, who stood alone on the cliff's edge, unleashed a roar that shook the air, Valerys, Avandeer, and Varthear joined him. He could not fly – that had been taken from him when he had lost his soulkin – but his roar was not all sorrow and loss. Through Valerys, Calen could feel the triumph in it, the pride, as Varthear soared alongside the others.

While they flew to fight at Tarhelm, Sardakes would remain as Aravell's sole guardian. Something within him was awakened, and he would protect the place that had protected him.

CHAPTER SEVENTY-FIVE

THE COST OF FREEDOM

22nd Day of the Blood Moon

Achyron's Keep, western Valtara – Winter, Year 3081 After Doom

The wind at the top of the hill was sharp as a spear, cutting into the bare skin of Dayne's chest. Cold sweat dripped from his nose, the dirt-tacked cuts on his elbows and legs stinging. Loren had allowed him to ride the mare the entirety of the first day and again the next until they were a few hours' march from Achyron's Keep.

Once they'd drawn close, Dayne had been unceremoniously dismounted, the ground catching him in its embrace. Loren had proceeded to cut every shred of clothing from him, followed by his sandals.

The following ten miles they had all but dragged him behind the horses at a pace just faster than a walk, never allowing him to slow or catch his breath and pulling him across the dirt whenever he stumbled.

"Thirsty, Dayne?" Loren sat in the saddle to Dayne's right, a waterskin in his hand. The man didn't await Dayne's answer. He tipped the dregs into the dirt, then let the skin hang by his side. He gestured to the murky puddle. "Please, drink up. I wouldn't want you to pass out before the procession."

Dayne stared back at the man but didn't speak. Nor did he move to drink.

"Please, Dayne," Loren persisted. "The wind may be bitter, but the sun is high. I wouldn't have you go thirsty."

"You heard the High Lord." The Koraklon guard who held the rope tied to Dayne's shackles gave it a yank and hauled Dayne forwards, cutting at his wrists. "Drink up."

Dayne kept his gaze on Loren, stepped back, and pulled his shackles towards himself as hard as he could, ripping the guard from his saddle.

Before the others could respond, Dayne lunged forwards and planted his knee into the man's mouth as he tried to rise. Teeth chipped and shattered and sliced into the skin of Dayne's knee.

As the guard pulled his hands to his bleeding face, Dayne swung himself around and wrapped his arms around the man's neck in an iron grip, dropping to the ground. He twisted so the chains drew tight across the guard's throat and pulled with every fibre of his being while the guard flailed and thrashed.

Most men lasted ten heartbeats before passing out. This one lasted seven.

When the guard's legs finally stopped kicking and his hands stopped slapping at Dayne's arms, Dayne stared up at Loren, who sat unmoving in his saddle, his right hand raised to stop the other guards and the mages from intervening.

Dayne's muscles burned as the life drained from the guard's body, and still Loren made no motion to stop him.

Loren shrugged. "Any personal guard overpowered so easily is not one worth having."

Dayne squeezed tighter, clenching his jaw. After a few more moments, he let out a roar and tossed the man's limp body into the dirt beside him, face pressed into the sodden earth where Loren had spilled the water. The guard's back rose and fell slowly.

Dayne pressed his manacled hands into the dirt and pushed himself to his feet.

"Do you think me weak, Dayne?" Loren asked as he dropped from his saddle. He closed the distance between himself and Dayne in a breath, throwing a fist into Dayne's gut and then a second into the side of his head.

Dayne dropped to one knee, his vision blurring. He spat blood into the dirt, then rose.

Loren grabbed Dayne's face, fingernails clawing into his skin.

"Look at me, Dayne of House Ateres, dagger in my side." Loren pulled Dayne's head so they were looking eye to eye. "I am going to drag you behind my horse like the animal that you are, and every soul beneath my banners and those of the emperor will know that you are a man. You are not a ghost, or a demon, or some god-sent harbinger of death. You are a man."

"You sound like you're trying to convince yourself."

"Men bleed." Loren's right hand left Dayne's jaw, and moments later a knife blade was pressed to Dayne's throat, stinging as blood trickled. "And they will all see you bleed." He held the blade there. "I know you, Dayne. I know you because I knew your father and I knew your mother. I know the pain I inflict upon you will never be enough. And so if you try any more theatrics like you did here, I will chop your brother's hands into small pieces and feed them to you when you starve. Do you understand?" Loren lifted Dayne's chin. "Now be a good dog."

Loren turned, grabbed the rope connected to Dayne's shackles, and once more mounted his horse. He gestured to carry on, leaving the guard Dayne had choked unconscious in the dirt.

Before long, the fortress city of Achyron's Keep came into view, its walls massive, sharp, and grey. Thick cylindrical towers rose at every bend, banners of pale blue emblazoned with the Oranak squid beneath those of a deep crimson bearing the black lion of Loria. The Lorian Empire had forbidden the flying of House banners after the first Valtaran Rebellion, but it appeared they had made an exception for Loren.

Dayne had seen the city with its two enormous trenches and double walls many times in his youth. But at that moment, as he trudged behind Loren's horse, his hands bound, his attention was not on the city or the walls but on the thousands upon thousands gathered at the gates.

Each and every one was fully armoured as though marching to battle, the sun and moon glinting off polished helmets and shields. The coloured skirts of every Major House were present – even a few in the burnt orange of House Ateres. But the pale blue of House Koraklon and the yellow of House Thebal dominated the open plain next to the red and black of the Lorians. It was almost humorous to see that the two Houses had chosen this as their common ground upon which to stand. Centuries of infighting and war ceased only in opposition to a free Valtara.

"Make sure to smile," Loren called back, his horse picking up its pace and dragging Dayne along with it.

Dayne grunted, trying to keep his balance. His feet stung with every step, cuts opening along his soles, rocks and dirt finding every crevice.

As they drew closer, the sound of chatter and shifting feet that filled the air slowly died to a whisper. The clip of horse hooves accompanied the wind and low murmurs as Loren and his riders started down the long path towards the gates that split the massive crowd.

"All behold! Dayne of House Ateres, son of the traitors Arkin and Ilya Ateres. Here is your Ghost of Ankar, your Demon of the Pass! His blood runs red as yours! He bleeds like any man, and bleed he will!"

As Loren roared, his voice boomed, echoing all around in the most unnatural of ways. Dayne knew the Lorian mages carried the High Lord's words on threads of Air, but with the ward around him he could feel nothing.

Loren gave the rope a vicious yank, and Dayne stumbled forwards, his elbows crashing into the dirt as he brought his hands in front of him to protect his face.

The High Lord urged his mount on. Dayne tried to pull himself to his feet, but the rope grew taut and dragged him forwards through the dirt. He clenched his jaw even harder, the ground tearing at the exposed skin.

"This man has killed your brothers and sisters, your mothers and fathers, your children. His is the last face they saw. He has turned Valtara into a land of the dead and the dying. And if we allow him and his bitch sister to have their way, our home will be nothing but ash and bones."

Dayne pressed his elbows into the dirt, grunting as the ground peeled away the skin. He leveraged himself, pulling his legs up and planting his feet on the ground. He staggered forwards, trying to prevent the rope from dragging him back down. Just as he had gained his footing, something smashed into the side of his head and he hit the dirt once more, the horse dragging him forwards. Blood dripped into his eyes, and his head spun. Something else struck him in the side, then in the leg and the back: stones hurled by the watching crowd.

He lifted his gaze to see that, while some roared and howled, many of those in Valtaran garb stood straight, their chins high, their fists gripping valynas, their stares focused on him. Some took part, but mostly it was the Lorians who threw the stones.

A man in a red and black surcoat made to lunge forwards and was held back by another in the pale blue skirts of House Koraklon.

"An army of traitors marches on Achyron's Keep," Loren bellowed. "They will be here by the morning light. They believe they can scale the walls and put us to the sword. What say you?"

Spears clattered against shields amidst a thunderous cacophony of roars and shouts.

"This is their champion dragging in the dirt at my horse's back. This is the best of them. And he is ours!"

More shouts and clattering steel answered.

"When the pretender queen arrives at our walls, she will yield, or House Ateres will be put to the sword! Never again will they bring fire and ruin to our lands. By blade and by blood!"

"By blade and by blood!" came the chorus of replies. "By blade and by blood!"

Dayne dug his feet into the ground and pulled hard on the rope in Loren's hands. The force almost pulled the man from the saddle, but Loren managed to keep his balance.

A silence swept over the gathering. Loren stared down at Dayne, fury in his eyes. Dayne knew he would pay for what he was about to do.

"Valtara will be free!" he roared at the top of his lungs. "This is our home! Will you not fight for it? Do you call yourselves Valtarans?"

Loren yanked at the rope and hauled Dayne onto his knees. "I will not kill you yet. But I will happily watch you bleed. Yah!" Loren pulled at the reins and broke the horse into a fast walk, once more dragging Dayne onto his belly.

Dayne closed his eyes and tucked his head close to his manacled hands, gritting his teeth against every stone that found his sides, back, and legs.

Once through the giant gates of Achyron's Keep, two men in the pale blue of House Koraklon hauled Dayne upright. If they hadn't held him, he would have collapsed in a bloody heap. The tops of his feet, his shins, knees, chest, and elbows were scraped clean of skin, bruises already forming around gashes where thrown rocks had split him.

He slumped in their arms, eyelids drooping as they dragged him through the streets, past towers and temples, and up stairs, his bare feet trailing on the ground. As they moved, he caught glimpses of light and faces, his vision blurred. Sounds echoed in his ears: footfalls, hammers working steel, shouts, voices.

Eventually they reached the central keep, and the guards hauled him along countless corridors and up stairwells until they finally stopped in a large open chamber of grey stone. Candles in sconces added warm life to the cold grey.

The two guards held Dayne up against something hard, then unlocked his manacles and spread his arms, fastening each individually. Straps tightened around his ankles, and the two guards moved away.

Dayne's head lolled, his neck weak and aching, the strength sapped from his bones. His sweat-soaked hair fell over his eyes, and he allowed his lids to close, finding relief in the arms of sleep.

His eyes could only have been closed for a heartbeat when he was jolted awake by a bucket of frigid water that punched the breath from his lungs. He gasped for air, pulling against his restraints.

"Now, now, now. Is it really time to sleep?" A hand clutched Dayne's wet hair and lifted his head so he stared into the bright eyes of Loren Koraklon. "I thought you were eager for this family reunion?"

Dayne scanned the room, his heart stopping when he saw a bloody corpse strapped to an x-shaped wooden stand, wrists and ankles bound by thick leather straps and iron buckles.

"What did you do to him?" Dayne thrashed, his bonds tearing at his already frayed arms and legs. "Baren! Baren!"

"Just a few toes, a finger or two. Don't worry, he's only sleeping." Loren placed the bucket onto a low wooden table. "He's quite loyal. Did you know that? Surprised me as well. He never used to be. I always found him so agreeable. But this time around, no matter how much skin I took, or fingernails, or fingers, he refused to tell us anything."

Loren walked over to where Baren hung from the wooden stand. He grabbed Baren's hair and pulled back his head so Dayne could see the beaten, bruised, and bloody thing that was his brother's face. A raw patch of scabbed flesh marked Baren's chest where the emblem of House Ateres had once resided. Loren slapped Baren's cheek, eliciting a weak grunt.

"See? Alive. Just as I promised."

Loren let Baren's head loll once more, then gestured to someone Dayne couldn't see and pulled a stool before Dayne. As he took a seat, a porter shuffled in and unfolded a small table beside him. The young boy placed a bottle of wine and two cups on the table, then waited with his hands clasped before him. He tried his best not to look at Dayne, but his gaze kept sliding to the blood and the raw skin.

"Much obliged, Olim. Would you pour please? Thank you."

The porter poured the wine until it came just short of the rim of both cups, bowed, glanced once more towards Dayne, then left.

Dayne stared after the boy.

"He's not your nephew." Loren shook his head and folded one leg over the other. He leaned back in the chair and sipped at his wine. "No, that's my youngest. He's seen fifteen summers. Arkin has only seen six. Strange thing, to not even know what your nephew looks like. That happens when you abandon your family."

Arkin. Alina had named her boy after their father...

Loren shrugged, letting out a long sigh. "So, tell me Dayne, while we're chatting. How did you survive that night? I'd thought you surely dead when that Justicar sent you overboard. I suppose it doesn't truly matter. But I'm always intrigued." He pulled himself up from his slouched position. "Look at me, dithering. First thing's first. You can't see them, but there are Lorian mages standing guard at the doors – members of the Hand in fact. Your magic will be blocked every second of every day until your sister lays down her sword, so please don't exhaust yourself trying. Second." Loren rose, swirling the wine in his cup. "This is more a vanity thing than anything else, but I want you to know something. I want you to know that what I did all those years ago truly was for Valtara. And what I do now is *still* for Valtara."

Dayne hocked a mouthful of blood and saliva and spat at Loren's feet. "You are no Valtaran."

"You see, that's simply not true. And this is what irks me. I could torture you, break you down, and use you as a tool to force your sister's surrender. And don't get me wrong, I will do that. But I want more. Your father never understood. He never listened when I spoke to him. But I want *you* to understand, to listen. Can you do that for me?"

Dayne looked past Loren to where Baren hung limp. Half-healed scars and scabs covered his body. Two fingers were missing from his left hand, down to the first knuckle. A toe from each foot. Dayne gritted his teeth, then turned his gaze to Loren, who was staring at him while swirling the wine. "Tell me whatever you want. I'll listen. But I want *you* to understand that I *will* kill you. I will do things to you that will make your soul scream after I've torn it from your body. I will break you for what you have done to my family."

"Those are strong words for a man strapped to a post. I could kill you right now. In fact, a few more cups of wine and I just might. Though you're more use to me alive – lucky for you." Loren returned to his chair, leaning forwards with his elbows on his knees. "Your father was willing to start a civil war. He was willing to watch our people slaughter each other while the Lorian dragons burned the survivors to ash."

"He was willing to sacrifice anything for a free Valtara," Dayne snarled.

"Anything? What about his honour?" Loren pursed his lips and shook his head. "No," he said mockingly. "Arkin Ateres would never sacrifice his precious honour. Not even if it meant saving the lives of tens of thousands – hundreds of thousands. All he had to do was bend his knee, shut his fucking mouth, and eat from the silver spoon he had been gifted. Your family had *everything*. You didn't suffer like the others. You just used their plight to rally them."

"You let them burn Stormwatch." Every drop of hatred in Dayne's heart bled into those words.

"And you made it necessary!" Loren's rage came on in an instant, his face red, veins bulging. "Do you think I wanted that?" he asked, calming. "What kind of monster wants to watch thousands burned alive? I would have done *anything*, given *everything* to stop that. That was why I never wanted a rebellion. There comes a point where the cost in blood is not worth the freedom. We *are* free," he said, throwing out his arms. "Can you not wed who you want? Can you not live like a king in the comfort of Redstone?"

"They take two-fifths of everything. They take our firstborn. People starve all across Valtara. This is not freedom, Loren."

"They do that *because* of rebellion, Dayne. And what freedom does your sister offer? The freedom to die young beside the ones you love? More Valtarans have died in her rebellion than in all the years since the first rebellion. You see, Dayne, there is a distinct difference between your family and mine. You say that your father was willing to sacrifice anything for a free Valtara. And you are right. He was. That was the problem. He was willing to sacrifice any number of lives – lives he had no right to sacrifice – in order to claim Valtara's freedom. I was not. I will sacrifice anything that is my own. I will sacrifice my honour in the eyes of others, my name, my life – anything I have a right to give, I will give. That is why I do what I do. I don't care if you hate me. I just want my people to stop dying in your family's wars. You're already spilling enough blood to fill rivers, I may as well add a few drops to turn the tide."

Loren sat forwards and finished his cup, then stood, gaze narrowing as he studied Dayne. "You're just like him, you know. Not only in your face, but in that unshaking arrogance. In that unerring belief that you are always doing what's right."

Dayne leaned forwards, straining against the straps that held him. "Where is my nephew?"

"Ah, yes." Loren gestured to somebody Dayne couldn't see. A door creaked open, then clicked shut. "Your brother did well to track him down. I have to say, I was quite impressed. When the babe was taken from your sister, I pulled a few strings, greased a few palms. I had him switched with another. A young orphan of House Koruk. The Lorians never look too deeply. As long as they get their pound of flesh, they don't really care which animal it's carved from. And something gave me the feeling this particular young babe would be of much use one day. And look, I was right."

The door creaked open again and footsteps sounded. Dayne twisted his neck, trying to see. After a moment, a tall, broad man in the pale blue of House Koraklon walked into view holding the hand of a small child with a shock of dark brown hair.

"Come here, Arkin. Take my hand." Loren reached out and took the young child's hand in his.

"Arkin…" Dayne whispered his father's name as he studied the boy's face and eyes, hoping to find something that would show him this boy truly was Alina's son. But for the life of him, he had no idea.

"Ah, yes. Did you know she named him after your father? Fitting, I think." Loren knelt beside the boy. "Did you eat all your supper?"

Arkin nodded wordlessly, glancing up at Dayne.

"Good boy. You need your food so you can grow big and strong." Loren gripped the boy's bicep and squeezed. "Gods, maybe we should stop feeding you, or you'll grow big as a giant."

"No," the boy said, laughing and pulling his arm away. Dayne's heart melted a little as Arkin laughed.

"Run along now. I just wanted to check on you before you sleep. Your mother is waiting. And I have a bad man to deal with." Loren looked up at Dayne, who could only stare back in disbelief. "He's killed a lot of men. As many as there are stars in the sky. And that's a lot, isn't it?"

The boy nodded hesitantly, eyeing Dayne as though his life were now at risk. The fear in the young child's eyes cut deep into Dayne's heart.

As they started to leave, the Koraklon guard turned around. "Father, can…"

The man cut his sentence short at a glare from Loren, then escorted the young boy from the chamber. Loren stood back to his full height, letting out a sigh.

"Father?" Dayne asked, ignoring the pain as he pulled his lips into a smile. "What's his name? That's two sons of yours I've seen now. You touch a hair on that child's head and I will bleed your family's name from this world. The last face any Koraklon will see will be mine."

Loren's fist crunched into Dayne's face, blood coating Dayne's tongue as his teeth carved a gash into the inside of his cheek. "Speak of my sons again. I dare you."

"Olim and…" Dayne pondered a moment. "I'm guessing that was Gaimal? Your eldest?"

Loren punched Dayne again. More blood, more sounds of crunching bone.

Dayne laughed and spit his blood onto the floor. "I will mount their heads on spikes and set them atop the walls of this keep."

Loren punched him again, but Dayne just kept laughing.

"Little Arkin," Loren said, wrapping his fingers around Dayne's throat. "Speak of my sons again, and I will cut off his hands. Alina will still want him without hands, won't she? They're so pure at that age, so uncorrupted by those around them."

"You're a fucking monster."

"For ensuring a growing young boy eats enough before bed? Surely even you can see how that one is a little farfetched." Loren shook his head, then grabbed the bottle of wine and his cup. "I'll have someone come and clean you up and stitch the wounds closed." He leaned down and narrowed his eyes at Dayne's wounds. He gave an impressed downturn of his bottom lip. "You're a difficult man to kill, Dayne Ateres. It looks like the dirt has crusted around your wounds. Perfect for stopping the bleeding, but not ideal for infection. I hope you like the smell of brimlock sap. You're no use to me dead or festering."

As Loren made to leave, he turned back to Dayne one last time. "You know, Dayne. There is a piece of advice my father once passed on to me that I think would have benefitted you. When lords and kings and queens go to war, it is the common people who pay in blood. A king loses his temper, and thousands die in a field two hundred miles away. A queen makes a poor decision, and hundreds starve. When you think of what you've lost, I implore you to think on what you've taken from others. How many children have you left orphaned, waiting for a mother and a father who lie cold in the dirt? How many families have you broken? Ponder that while you dream of ways to kill me. And while you do, I'll dream of ways to stop the Lorian dragons from burning our home to the ground."

CHAPTER SEVENTY-SIX

THE BLOOD OF THE MOUNTAIN

22nd Day of the Blood Moon

*Dwarven outpost, Lodhar Mountains – Winter,
Year 3081 After Doom*

Kira gripped the haft of the axe, allowing her fingers to savour the familiar touch of the leather and the cold embrace of the steel. She was still less than half herself, but Hafaesir would grant her the strength to fight, as he always had.

She stood in the main chamber of the outpost headquarters. The silence was such that she would have almost thought she was alone were it not for the ten Queensguard standing about the room, the five stationed at the door, and the other ten at the headquarters' entrance. Vikmar, the new High Commander of her guard, was a statue by the main window, his hands clasped behind his back, his eyes watching everything that moved outside.

Footfalls sounded, boots slapping stone, and the door creaked open.

"Good," Erani said, her voice bouncing off the stone. "You're going to need that axe." Kira turned to see her sister setting a dwarf down in the chair on the opposite side of the central table, a thick black sack over his head and his hands bound. "Rikber Lars, scholar of Hafaesir."

Kira's uncle, Alrick, and her three cousins stood with Erani, as well as half a score of warriors from the various kingdoms.

"Are the sack and bindings necessary?" Kira asked, allowing the axe to hang by her side, ensuring her arm regained its familiarity with the weapon's weight.

"Well, he bit me, so yes." Erani pulled back her sleeve to show teeth marks in her forearm. "He wasn't gentle either."

"Remove the sack," Kira said, shaking her head.

Erani shrugged and pulled the black sack from the seated dwarf's head to reveal a knotted length of rope shoved into his mouth and tied tightly around the back of his head. Rikber Lars's eyes grew wide as soon as he saw Kira, and he tugged against his bonds. The dwarf's skin was time-touched, his beard thick and grey with no rings, his head bald as polished stone.

"Remove the rope, Erani."

"Let him bite you," she said as she pulled a knife from her belt and slid it between the rope and the back of Rikber's head. "See how you feel then."

She slit the rope, and the dwarf gasped for air, lurching in the chair.

Kira leaned forwards and pressed her left hand into the tabletop, the axe in her right clinking against the stone. "Rikber Lars, is it?"

The dwarf heaved in a breath. "Queen Kira..." He stared at her for a few moments, as though taking in a ghost. "I had heard tale that you were chained in Volkur's dungeons – or dead."

"As you can see, I am neither. Does that make you happy or sad?"

"Makes me curious." If Rikber held any fear at being captured, he did not show it.

"I've had you brought here because I've been told you are a scholar of Hafaesir."

"One of many, Your Majesty. If I may be so bold, why me in particular?"

Kira smiled. "What is your loyalty to King Hoffnar?"

"He is my king, Your Majesty."

Kira raised an eyebrow, and Rikber returned her smile.

"I do not know him, and from what I do know, I care little. Though I also do not know you. But I am a quick learner." He leaned his head back to look at the bonds that held his hands, then stared up at Erani and Alrick. "Did you attack me in my home and place a sack over my head because you thought I had some kind of blind loyalty to a king I've never met who suddenly proclaims himself ruler of all Lodhar?" In the brief silence that followed, Rikber shook his head and sighed. "Youth is wasted on the young."

"You bit me," Erani snapped.

"And I'll bite you again if you put your hands on me without warning. My only loyalty is to Hafaesir and to knowledge. Now, if you can please untie my hands, my fingers have been tingling for quite some time now." When Erani didn't move, Rikber looked to Kira. "I have seen over a hundred cycles. My right hip is as fragile as the skin on this one's hand," he said, nodding at Kira's sister. "And the only time I'm holding anything sharp is when I'm trying to open a letter. Even if I wanted your blood, I'd have trouble enough just climbing over this table."

Rikber leaned forwards and stretched his arms out.

Kira nodded to Erani, and her sister sighed before cutting the dwarf's bonds.

"Better?" Kira asked.

"Much." Rikber rubbed the red friction marks on his wrists. "Hoffnar wishes to lead us to the outer world, to have us claim lands beneath the sun's light." He let out a long, disgruntled sigh. "We are dwarves. Our ancestors were carved from the mountains, forged by Hafaesir. This is our home. Why would we leave it? To become like the other races? I think not. There is beauty and mystery enough beneath the rock of Lodhar. Hoffnar's preachings do not stir me. Now, what need have you for a scholar of Hafaesir?"

Kira glanced at Vikmar, who nodded and commanded two of the Queensguard to close and lock the main door while he drew the hastily erected curtains across the old, open window.

"Well," Rikber said, pressing his open palms against the table, "now I'm certainly intrigued."

"What would you say if I told you we had found the lost city of Vindakur?"

"I would say you were lying through your teeth."

"And what if we had excavated a mostly intact Portal Heart within the city limits?"

"I would say that Efialtír has touched your mind. And I would ask when we are leaving."

"That simple?"

Rikber let out a long sigh. He seemed to sigh a lot, though she supposed the older she got the more she sighed as well. "I already told you, I owe no loyalty to Hoffnar, nor anyone who sits on a throne and sends dwarves to carve each other apart. I have dedicated my entire life to the study and understanding of our people's history. If I can be the first dwarf to lay eyes on the lost city of Vindakur and a Portal Heart in over three hundred years, then I am yours, my queen."

"Hmm." Kira walked around the table until she stood beside the old scholar, leaning on the table's edge. "Tell me about the Portal Hearts."

"What do you want to know?"

"How many there are, where they go, can you use them?"

Rikber laughed. "Decades of my life, summarised in a few breaths."

"I don't want decades of your life. Simple answers. The stories say there are five portals, yes?"

Rikber nodded. "From my studies, there is one located in Vindakur and one in Drifaien at Mount Helmund – or Frostbone Hill as it was once called." He leaned forwards and tapped the map. "One buried deep in the Kolmir Mountains, lost with our brethren there. One in the dead city of Ulukar in Wolfpine Ridge and one in the Sea of Stone. Though the last time that was seen was millennia ago."

"And if we put you in front of one, do you think you could activate it? Take us where we need to go?"

Rikber gave a half-shrug. "Perhaps. Perhaps not. I've never actually seen one with my own eyes, only drawings and paintings that have seen more centuries than my mother has, and that dwarf simply won't die."

"Well then, what use are you?" Alrick's son, Lomak, asked, scratching at a cut on his face.

"More use than you, I'd wager." He frowned at the young dwarf, turning back to Kira. "I believe I can activate one, and that I have a reasonable chance of being able to utilise it with a degree of accuracy."

Kira stared down at the old dwarf for a moment, looking into his eyes. "I need you to be sure."

"I am what I am, my queen. I could not—"

"Thousands of lives depend on you telling me you are sure you can control a Portal Heart. This is no time for modesty. Are you the foremost living scholar of Hafaesir or not?"

Rikber's stare grew sombre. "If you take me to the lost city of Vindakur and put me before a true Portal Heart, I will not fail you."

"Good." Kira gestured to Ahktar, who stood watching by the door. "Have Rikber brought to where he can bathe and find a warm meal. And send for Turim Arlan. Tell him we will need every Wind Runner we have."

Ahktar nodded and gestured for Rikber to follow him.

Kira grasped Ahktar's arm and whispered in his ear. "Don't let him out of your sight. Understood?"

"My queen."

When Ahktar and Rikber left, Kira looked back to her sister and the others. "You did well finding him. We will need the others here as quickly as their legs can carry them. No matter how large the mountain, six thousand souls moving through the tunnels will not go unnoticed. We will need to arrange attacks to scatter Hoffnar's forces. How secure is the lost city?"

"We have no more than a hundred axes stationed there at this moment, but, sister…" Erani's voice took on a serious tone. "There is more."

"There is always more," Kira whispered to herself. "Speak."

"Our spies in Volkur bring news. We know why Hoffnar has been building the tunnels."

"Well," Kira said, impatient. "Out with it."

"He plans to assault Berona." Alrick stepped closer to the table, where the maps lay. "And Antiquar, and maybe more, by the sound of it. His tunnels are almost complete."

"And when is this assault to go ahead?"

"A matter of days," Alrick replied.

"Good."

"Good?" Erani narrowed her eyes at Kira. "I don't like the Lorians any more than I do the kerathlin, but Hoffnar is radicalising these dwarves. They don't want victory. They want blood, they want slaughter. There are thousands of innocents in those cities… hundreds of thousands."

"My concern is for my people and the Belduarans with whom we have broken bread for millennia, not the Lorians. Such is the weight of a crown." Kira folded her arms and looked at the maps. "This gives us time. While he is arranging his assaults, perhaps he will be less vigilant of what is closer to him."

"That is all well and good, sister. But it is the forces of Durakdur he will send first. Our people who will take the brunt of the Lorian mages. Why do we wait?

Why not attack now? There are many who stand beside you, ready to rally to your banner."

"Because first we must see the Belduarans safe from our halls. They have suffered too much already."

"And why is that *our* duty? We gave them sanctuary. *We* protected them. I was not here, but it was their boy-king who plotted with Pulroan, was it not?" Erani looked around the chamber at Alrick and the others. "Why do we continue to risk ourselves for their benefit?"

"Because that is who we are." Kira slammed her fist on the table. "The Belduarans have stood by us since long before you and I drew breath. I will not be the one to break that bond. Oleg has promised us half his fighting number to see Hoffnar dead and our home returned. All he has asked is that we ensure the Belduaran people escape this mountain and the torrent of horrors they have endured. They are our allies, and we *will* stand by them."

The door creaked open, and Turim Arlan, Guildmaster of the Wind Runners, strode in with those padded navigator glasses strapped to his head and two of Kira's Queensguard at his side.

"The Wind Runners Guild is ready when you are, my queen."

Kira nodded. "Then let us begin."

HOURS LATER, KIRA FOUND HERSELF standing in a place she never believed she would stand. A place part of her had only thought legend.

The lost city of Vindakur sprawled before her, golden domes and rooves glinting in the yellow light of the strange Heraya's Ward that covered the rock ceiling and spread down the sweeping pillars. If she didn't look too closely, it was as though the city stood still in time, just as awe-inspiring and wondrous as it had been in her mind when she'd heard the stories as a child. When she looked closer, however, she could see marks in the stone, the plants growing through the cracks, the bodies of the kerathlin littered about.

This place had once been the glittering gem of the Lodhar Freehold. And those creatures had slaughtered every soul within. It still made little sense to her. The kerathlin were vicious when provoked, an unrelenting wave of claw and mandible. And whenever mining parties strayed too close to the nests – which happened far too often for her liking – the results were savage. But they'd never attacked a city before. It had always been thought that the mass of sound and bodies kept them away. The kerathlin were ferociously defensive but not aggressive. And then, after everything, the creatures had simply abandoned their nest? Pieces of this puzzle were missing, of that she was sure.

Slowly, Kira pulled her attention from the golden rooves and sweeping walkways to the thousands of souls that filled the streets on the opposite side of the bridge upon which she stood. Blocks of red and purple marked her Queensguard and the Belduaran forces marching through the thick of bodies.

Just over half of the Belduaran refugees had made the journey so far, the Wind Runners in constant operation to bring them through. With care and patience, and more than a little luck, they could see the Belduarans through the portals before Hoffnar had any idea.

"Just a little longer," Kira whispered as she watched the sea of people. "Just a little longer."

Five shapes emerged from the crowd and crossed the bridge. Vikmar and four of her Queensguard stopped and bowed as they reached her. "The defensive lines are set, my queen, and we've blockaded the external Wind Tunnels. Twenty-nine watchposts have been placed between here and the other cities, virtuk riders at each. If Hoffnar's forces move, we will know about it."

"Good. Come."

Kira turned towards the ruined dome that had once enclosed the Portal Heart. The structure was enormous and dominated the island upon which they stood. Erani had told her they'd pulled several bodies from the rubble during the excavation, dwarven and Belduaran. This was how the Draleid had escaped the tunnels. Kira had made sure Rikber Lars would remain ignorant of the fact that he would not be the first person to activate a Portal Heart in centuries. That piece of information would help absolutely nobody.

The circular tunnel that led into the centre of the island was the only piece of the structure that had remained fully intact. Kira removed her gauntlet and brushed her fingers against the smooth rock as she stepped into the tunnel and walked its length. This place was more than just a structure. It was a holy thing, a gift from Hafaesir to her people – a gift she had thought lost.

When she reached the end of the tunnel, she just stopped and stared. Even with most of the roof gone and stacks of rock piled along the chamber's edges, the Portal Heart was still a sight to behold. Massive stone rings, some twenty feet across, etched with delicate carvings and marked with glyphs at the top. One had been crushed by the falling rocks, but three were still intact.

Rikber Lars and a score of other dwarves stood about a pedestal at the chamber's centre, as they had done for some time, books and sheets of parchment all about them.

"How goes the progress?" Kira asked Erani as her sister approached.

"As quickly as it can!" Rikber called out.

Erani just shrugged, and Kira gestured for her to follow.

"I understand it is a delicate process, Rikber," she said, moving to stand by Rikber's side. "But there are only four glyphs. Surely we could move a little faster."

Rikber shook his head, staring down at the markings on the topmost page of a thick sheaf of parchment in his hand. The dwarf stopped, gave a sharp '*tssk*', and turned to Kira. "There may only be four glyph markings, but each glyph is composed of several subsets with instructions contained within. These are glyphs in a language long lost, a language gifted to our ancestors by the gods themselves, one that is singular in its ability to record large quantities of information in a small space. I am the only living scholar who has even a semblance of an idea what they mean. If you want me to activate the rings, I can do so right now."

Rikber pressed his palm down onto one of the four glowing crystals. The ground beneath their feet shook, and the glyph marking atop the ring to Kira's left ignited with a golden light. A heartbeat passed and a *whoosh* swept through the chamber as molten gold poured from within the ring, forming into a floating pool.

"There," he said, gesturing towards the ring. "Step through. Go. I have no idea which Portal Heart I'm sending you to, but go. I'm sure it will only take hours or days to stumble your way through the tunnels on the other side and, with luck, you can determine where in the gods you actually are – as long as you don't starve or get murdered by something. And if you're in the wrong place, we can try again. Do we have days? Weeks? Not to mention Portal Hearts can *feel* intent and can alter their functions accordingly... at least, that's what the old writings say. But yes, go, step through, do what you want. What use am I anyway?"

"I get your point, Rikber."

"Do you? Good. Now can you stop looming over me and let me do my work?"

A part of Kira wanted to hack the old dwarf's head off and take her chances with a one-in-three guess. But she decided against it.

Kira gestured to her sister, and the pair marched back through the tunnel and out onto the island before crossing the last remaining bridge of what had once been four.

A block of Queensguard formed around her as she approached the boundary that separated the Belduarans from the island, marching in step, their crimson cloaks drifting behind them.

Oleg Marylin and Lumeera Arian stood in front of the line of wooden stakes that had been set across the main thoroughfare, a small gap left at the centre.

"Your Majesty," Oleg said with a bow, inclining his head to Erani as well. "Three thousand two hundred and fifty-one already evacuated to Vindakur and ready to step through the Portal Heart. Two thousand nine hundred and forty-three left at the outpost and on Wind Runners." The man gestured towards the Wind Tunnel docks about a hundred feet up the rock face behind her, where a line of refugees snaked down a long, narrow path towards the city. "Everything is running smoothly."

"Glad to hear it, Oleg. You will see the sun before long." She gave the man a soft smile.

"I believe I have grown rather fond of the Heraya's Ward."

Calls and shouts broke out in the crowd ahead, growing ever closer. The sea of people parted, and an armoured virtuk galloped through empty space, blood splattering its head and neck, a strip of flesh dangling from its beak. The creature ground to a halt before the line of wooden stakes, screeching as it did, its rider dropping to the ground like a stone.

Kira darted through the gap in the defensive line, Vikmar and her Queensguard following.

She dropped to the ground beside the dwarf. An arrow jutted from the gap in his armour below his breastplate, blood staining the mail and cloth.

"Get a Healer. Now!" Kira called to Vikmar, slipping an arm under the dwarf's head and tilting it up to look into his eyes. "What happened?"

"My queen." The dwarf grunted and coughed. "Hoffnar's forces. They came upon us so quickly... There was nothing we could do. They had mages and elves."

"Where were you stationed? How far?"

"There are thousands. They filled the tunnels. They knew we were here."

"It's all right, it's all right. Breathe. A Healer is coming. I need you to focus. What were their numbers? How many mages did you see?"

"Too many, my queen."

"You did well," Kira said as Vikmar returned with two Alamant Healers. "Hafaesir watches over you."

Kira stood as the two Healers took her place. "I thought we would have more time."

"He was stationed at the last watchpost," Vikmar said, staring down at the dwarf on the ground. "They will be upon us within the hour."

"How did they get past so many without a single warning?" Erani asked.

"Mages." Kira turned to Vikmar. "Send riders to scout the tunnels. We need to know what we're facing."

"At once, my queen."

She looked to Erani and Lumeera Arian. "What are our fighting numbers here?"

"Seven thousand," Lumeera answered. "Three thousand Belduarans, four thousand dwarves. Though many of our number are not warriors, just strong enough to hold steel in their hands."

"The rest of our forces are on the raids to draw Hoffnar's attention," Erani said.

"Gods dammit," Kira whispered. "Much good that did us." She closed her eyes for a moment, shaking her head. "We cannot let them have the Portal Heart. That is not an option."

"The Belduaran Highguard will take the main entrance," Lumeera said without room for argument. "Erani, if you can spare a few hundred, we can pile the rubble higher along the outside of the entrance and create a funnel. I'll set archers on the rooves. A hundred men there will be worth a thousand."

Kira held up a hand. "If they've brought elven Battlemages…" She sighed. "They'll cut through you like wheat."

"If you have a better plan, Your Majesty, I am all ears. But if you don't, my warriors and I will do what we must. There are three thousand Belduaran citizens here and more on the way – many injured, sick, old, or young. My sole purpose that remains in this life is protecting them. If time can be paid for in blood, we will do so. Just tell that scholar of yours the price we pay for every moment he takes. We don't have enough time to get them all safe from here. So we must stand."

Lumeera turned and set off for the main entrance, Belduaran warriors gathering around her. The crowd murmured and shifted, many still staring at the dwarf on the ground as the two Healers pulled the arrow from his gut.

Erani started to follow her, but Kira shook her head. "No. Ahktar, Kalik. The pair of you take four hundred and help Lord Captain Arian with that wall. Build it high and mighty." Kira turned to Oleg. "Move the refugees to the other side of the island. Keep them from the fighting and find a way to build a bridge on the other side."

The man nodded and set off with that strange waddling run he had.

When Kira looked at her sister, Erani knew what she intended immediately. "We don't need it."

"How long will we last against elven mages with just axes and steel, Erani? If it were Hoffnar alone, I'd say one of ours was worth ten of his. But the Spark... Hafaesir wove the soul of the bersekeer into our blood for a reason. He gave us the Rockblood *for a reason*."

"The cost is too high. Less than half survive. You said it yourself. The Wind Tunnels are still open. We can start evacuating now. Send as many as we can back to the outposts and take our chances with the Portal Heart. Live to fight another day."

"Look about you, sister." Kira gestured at the crowd of Belduarans and around at the city in which they stood. "We stand in Vindakur, the lost city of old. We seek to travel through a Portal Heart – a godgift. Our home is taken from us. We hide in caves and tunnels. Hoffnar leads our people to war and slaughter. I *will not* give him this place. I will not."

"It is rocks and ruin, sister. We can pick our battlefield more cleverly when we are not blindsided by elven mages. A good hunter takes their time. They make a plan with care. Let him have this place. We will find another way to see the Belduarans to safety. They will simply have to wait a little longer."

"Rocks and ruin?" Kira gave a laugh that was both sorrow and anger. "This is our history. It is *our people*. Hafaesir gave us two gifts – the Portal Hearts and the Rockblood. I will allow Hoffnar neither." She grasped Erani's pauldrons and looked into her eyes. "You are my blood, and I trust you with my soul. Tell me to grab my axe and stand right here. Tell me that you want us to fight and die side by side, here. Tell me this is the end and that you welcome it. Tell me all that, sister, and I will return to the stone with a bloody smile on my lips. My axe will be like Hafaesir's own, and we will burn ourselves a blazing glory in the fires of battle, side by side." Kira dropped her voice low. "Tell me that is what you want, and I will do it. But I will not run."

"Kira—"

"I will not run!" The rage that had been bubbling in Kira ever since Hoffnar had butchered Mirlak and her guards came screaming to the fore. "I watched his axe carve through Elenya's face. I stared into Mirlak's cold eyes when that piece of kerathlin shit threw my friend's severed head onto my table. He carved the hair and the rings from my head." Kira pulled at the short, ringless hair that grew from her head in clumps, breath shivering through her as her shoulders shook. She slammed her armour-clad fist to her breastplate. "I am a warrior of Hafaesir. I am the *queen* of Durakdur. And I will not give him any more! Today – here – we will make the first cut. Hoffnar thinks he has trapped us in this place. No doubt he has known of your discovery for some time and used it as bait. Draw us here, trap us, slaughter us. But it will be them trapped in here with us. We will show them Hafaesir's wrath. We will show that rotten coward the true strength of the dwarves of Durakdur."

Kira turned to Vikmar and the three score of Queensguard that stood about her. "What say you?"

Vikmar slipped his battleaxe from the loop on his back and slammed the butt into the stone, the other guards doing the same. "We are with you, my queen."

"And what of you, Uncle?" Kira looked to Alrick, his sons Lomak and Kandzal beside him.

"The bersekeer blood runs thick in our veins," Alrick said. "The dwarves of Durakdur are warriors from our skin to our bones. The only certainty is that blood will wet my axe. Let them come. We will be waiting. And if I can return to the stone with the blood of the rock in my veins, then even better."

Erani nodded slowly, letting out a sigh through her nostrils. "We all die eventually, I suppose. I would rather do it with an axe in my hand and a tale to tell when I return to the rock."

"Will you drink with me?" Kira asked, pulling her sister closer. "Will you drink the blood of the mountain? Will you set your soul free?"

Again, Erani drew a long breath. "I will." She swallowed. "At least if the Rockblood deems me unworthy, this place will be where I rest."

"That will not happen." Kira squeezed her sister's shoulder, holding her grip for a few moments. "Vikmar, spread the word. For the first time in almost a millennium, the children of Hafaesir will wield his hammer. All those who have the bersekeer blood in their veins and are willing to drink the blood of the mountain are to assemble here. Go now. We do not have time to linger."

CHAPTER SEVENTY-SEVEN

HAMMER OF HAFAESIR

22nd Day of the Blood Moon

Vindakur, Lodhar Mountains – Winter, Year 3081 After Doom

Lumeera Arian hefted her shield in her left hand, her sword hanging in its scabbard at her hip. Before her stood an enormous stone door set into the rock face of the cavern, framed on either side by walls of stone and rubble piled some twenty feet high.

The riders had returned with reports that Hoffnar's forces marching upon Vindakur numbered almost fifteen thousand, dwarves and elves between them. Over double their own number.

In all likelihood, Lumeera would die this day. She knew it, and she accepted it. Not in the wildest of her dreams would she ever have imagined that one day she would be Lord Captain of the Belduaran Kingsguard. Not ever. Tarmon Hoard had been a man cut from the cloth of the gods. She would have followed him wherever he led. And so too Baria Hawe before him. To be mentioned in the same breath as souls of that ilk was more than she had deserved in this life.

The Kingsguard may have been gone – they were the Highguard now – but their purpose, her purpose, remained the same. To stand shoulder to shoulder with the men and women around her, to lead them as their Lord Captain in the defence of the last bloodlines of Belduar… There was no greater honour, no more noble a thing for which a life could be given. That thought, those very words, brought a smile to her face as she remembered what Tarmon Hoard had said the night Belduar had fallen.

"We are the Kingsguard of Belduar!" he'd roared, his hand on the pommel of his sword as he'd looked out at the assembled Kingsguard. *"They sing of our deeds across Epheria! Those men and women marching on our home, they were raised on stories of our defiance. We are their legends! And tonight, we will be their nightmares! Some of us will not live to see the rising sun, and to those brave souls I say 'thank you for the honour of allowing me to stand by your side.' There is no greater purpose than to protect. And there is no more noble a thing than to give your life in the preservation of another. You are the Kingsguard of Belduar, and you will live in the stories told of this Age. You are immortal."*

Lumeera's blood had been pure fire that night, and every hair on her body had stood on end. She had given her entire life to defending the people of Belduar. She held no fear in giving them her death too.

"Lord Captain!"

Lumeera turned to see Oleg Marylin pushing through the rows of Highguard. He wore an ill-fitting set of dwarven plate, an axe hefted over his shoulder.

"What are you doing here, Oleg?" Lumeera looked down at the man, his scraggy beard poking through the bottom of the helmet, the chainmail beneath his breastplate bulging. "You are the Keeper. These people will need you on the other side."

Oleg simply smiled back at her. "The portal is open. The evacuation has begun."

"Thank Varyn." The beating of Lumeera's heart settled a little at that. Now she truly did have something to die for. Every swing of her blade would be another soul through, another moment bought for those still travelling the Wind Tunnels.

"Indeed." Oleg drew a long breath and shifted the axe on his shoulder. "I have no dreams of leaving this mountain," he said softly. "I was born atop it, and I'll be happy to die under it. My duty is to the people of Belduar. My duty is here."

"It's been an honour," Lumeera said. "You are a great man, Oleg Marylin."

"I'm a short man," he corrected. "A short man with an axe."

"You do yourself a disservice, my friend."

A silence of sorts held for a while, the sounds of chatter and armoured feet echoing in the vast cavern blending into the back of her mind. Every now and then a *whoosh* sounded, announcing the arrival of a Wind Runner in the docks, more Belduarans readying to find a new home.

A thunderous crack accompanied a tremor that swept through the stone beneath Lumeera's feet. Dust and loose rocks fell from around the giant stone door.

"They're here," Oleg whispered.

"They are." Lumeera tilted her neck side to side, receiving a few sharp cracks in reward. "I'm going to need you to step back, Oleg."

"I am more than willing, Lord Captain."

"I know you are. But you are not trained in the ranks of my guard. You will only break our lines. Step back, and keep that axe ready." She grasped the man's forearm. "I meant what I said. It has been an honour to serve you. You would have made a great king, and every man, woman, and child that steps through that portal will live a life granted to them by your wisdom, your strength, and your will."

"The honour has been mine, Lord Captain."

As Oleg stepped back, Lumeera slid her sword from its scabbard. "Kingsguard of Belduar!" she bellowed. King or no, they were still the Kingsguard. "If today is our last day, let us make it glorious!"

Steel clattered against steel all around her, men and women chanting.

"I grant you permission to die today, but only if you take ten with you. Do you hear me?"

The clamour rose, cheers and stomps echoing.

"For millennia, the Kingsguard have given their lives in service to the people of Belduar. If we are to be the last, let us ensure this song is the grandest ever written. It has been the pride and the privilege of my life to stand with you all. In the words of Tarmon Hoard – you are the Kingsguard of Belduar, and you are immortal!"

Cries and roars erupted, steel clattering.

"For Belduar!" Lumeera roared.

"For Belduar!" the cries answered.

The door shook again, a tremor sweeping through the stone, more rocks breaking free.

"Kingsguard, form up!"

Shields clicked together, feet shifting. Lumeera gripped her sword tight and pulled her shield close to her body. "Give no quarter, fight like demons, and die like heroes!"

The dwarves on either side of the Kingsguard lines slammed the butts of their axes against the ground and set themselves ready for the battle.

A tense silence hung in the air, and then the great stone door erupted inwards. Chunks of stone smashed into the ground and the walls of rock on either side of the doorway, clouds of dust spewing into the air.

A hunk of debris came to a stop only five or six feet in front of Lumeera. She clenched her jaw, steadying her racing heart.

Time stood still for all of a moment, the grey stone dust drifting outwards making it nearly impossible to see further than a few feet. Then shapes coalesced in the cloud of dust, and in a thunder of boots on stone, the dwarves of Volkur came charging.

A sharp whistle rang over Lumeera's head. Arrows fell, dwarves died.

"Hold the line!" Lumeera roared as the dwarves drew closer. "Hold the line!"

Kira had promised that if Lumeera and the others could buy them time, then she would even the odds with Hafaesir's hammer. And so that is what Lumeera would do.

Kira watched as the great doors of Vindakur turned to rubble. She stood at the centre of the main thoroughfare between the doors and the island upon which the Portal Heart resided. Just under three hundred dwarves stood around her – Erani, Vikmar, Ahktar, her uncle, and her cousins among them.

The vast majority of those who had come were of Kira's Queensguard, for the bersekeer blood ran in the veins of the greatest warriors. But so too did Kira see many faces she didn't recognise, some bearing the colours of the other kingdoms.

Each one of them had stripped themselves of their armour upon Kira's instruction, their weapons laid on the stone. And each one held a vial of shimmering Rockblood, veins of glowing gold rippling through the black.

She looked down at the markings drawn in Rockblood along her bare arms and chest, many more along her shoulders, legs, face, and back. Markings she had never drawn with her own hand until that day but had seen in the memories of those that had come before her.

The Rites of Leadership were as old as the mountain itself. The blood of the king or queen willingly cut fresh each day and crushed with Heraya's Ward, to be taken by the next in line, so that the histories of their people would never be lost. A chain unbroken.

Cries and shouts echoed through the enormous cavern, resounding off rock and stone. Flashes of lightning erupted at the doors, screams following, plumes of fire roaring. And still the Kingsguard of Belduar held their ground, as they always had. To a man they were some of the greatest warriors Kira had ever laid eyes on, and to a man they would be slaughtered were it not for Hafaesir's gift.

Kira walked through the two columns of waiting dwarves, the markings of the Rockblood on their skin glowing with a black and gold shimmer. "Each of you has the blood of the bersekeers in your veins. The ancient blood of our people emboldened with Hafaesir's fury. A fury you will need to wield his greatest weapon. It has been eight hundred years since the true form of the bersekeers has been witnessed. That changes today."

Kira nodded to a dwarf who stood on a nearby roof, and the call of horns filled the air: the signal for the Kingsguard and those at the doors to fall back and pull from the main street.

"Let us show these dwarves of Volkur the fury of our people," she roared. "Drink deep the blood of the mountain, and lay low those who threaten it. May Hafaesir guide you."

Kira lifted the vial of Rockblood into the air, the gold veins shimmering within. Around her, the others did the same.

A brief moment of panic touched her heart when she looked at Erani, but that panic died in an instant. This would not be the last time she looked upon her sister. Hafaesir would not allow it. They would serve his will together. She knew it in her bones. "I love you, my sister, even if I do not say it enough."

Erani inclined her head. "Where you lead, I follow."

Kira nodded to her sister, brought the vial to her lips, and drank deeply. As she did, so did those around her.

The first step had been taken. A line crossed that could not be uncrossed.

She reached over and grabbed her sister's hand as the burning started in her veins. "Listen to the rock."

"Silence is the sound of our home," Erani answered, pain twisting her words.

Kira's skin cracked and flaked, crimson blood seeping through, her bones feeling as though they would burst through her flesh. She squeezed Erani's hand. "Listen to the wind."

Erani's sudden scream cut off as she clamped her jaw shut. Her head jerked sideways, slivers of black rock slicing through the flesh of her neck. "For it breathes—Agh!" Her hand shook in Kira's, her shoulders snapping back. "For it breathes life into the soul of the mountain!"

To Kira's left, a blood-curdling scream erupted and a dwarf snapped backwards, his spine splitting so he stood like a crab, jagged rock bursting from his bones, steaming blood pouring onto the stone. More screams ripped through the cavern with the sound of bones splintering like dry kindling.

Kira gritted her teeth, her blood on fire. Her cracked skin blackened, shards of rock growing from her very flesh. She howled, her bones stretching.

More screams, and Kira watched as her cousins, Lomak and Kandzal, both twisted and broke, shoots of rock bursting from their skulls and spines.

She felt Erani let go of her hand, but her vision blurred and the burning in her blood rose to a new level of agony. Kira screamed until her throat went dry as dust, every piece of her shattering.

And then, from the depths of agony, her vision burst to life, illuminated with a golden light. A deep, seething rage blazed within her, and all she could do was dream of ripping the dwarves of Volkur limb from limb.

She took a lumbering step forwards, disoriented. Voices swirled in her head, voices she did not know, and yet she trusted them. They told her to lift Hafaesir's hammer and smite his enemies across the mountain.

Kira dropped to one knee, the golden light in her eyes burning and blurring. She pressed a hand against the ground, and something within her called to the mountain – a fury, a need, a desire. Her fingers sank into the stone as though it were water and wrapped around something solid. With a roar, she pulled back and ripped her hammer from the rock itself, veins of shimmering gold rippling through its surface.

She took another step forwards, the rage within her building as she watched the elves and the dwarves of Volkur flood into the lost city.

Another step, her limbs feeling less awkward, a constant buzz droning in her ears, the rage within her slowly rising and rising until two steps became three, became four, and she was charging. Kira roared. The voice that left her lips was not her own, and the words on her tongue were strange and ancient, and yet she knew them.

A chorus of thundering roars joined hers, and the bersekeers of Durakdur charged.

LUMEERA SHOVED HER SHIELD FORWARDS, throwing the dwarf back, then twisted and drove her sword down through the slit in the dwarf's helm, feeling the scrape of bone as the blade buried itself in his eye.

"To me!" she howled, ripping her sword free. A score of Kingsguard fell in beside her in an instant, shields levelled. Most of her warriors had cleared out to the side streets at the sound of the horn as Kira had instructed. But they couldn't all go, lest they be overrun. Some had to stay and hold back the tide. And she would never be the leader who stood in the back and shouted orders.

She threw her left shoulder forwards and rammed the rim of her shield into the mouth of a helmetless dwarf, teeth snapping and blood spraying. Within a heartbeat, another dwarf took its place, hacking and slashing with a long-hafted axe.

More Kingsguard fell in beside her as they recovered from the waves of lightning that had torn them apart. The elves had only sent a handful of mages, but they wielded the Spark with utter devastation.

"Do not let them pass!" Lumeera shouted. "Heave!"

Across the line, each of the Kingsguard pushed forwards with their shields, then stabbed down into the crush of dwarven bodies hemmed in by walls of rubble piled either side of the entranceway. The lines would not hold for long. The elven mages were toying with them. They could have ripped the formation in half with fire or lightning or whatever other manner of destruction the gods had granted them, but instead they seemed content to let the Volkuran dwarves throw themselves at the Belduaran shields.

Arrows rained down from the rooves of the nearby buildings. Many bounced and ricocheted off steel plate and shields, skittering across the stone. But some found their way through the thick dwarven armour, blood spraying.

"Heave!" she roared again, and in perfect unison the Kingsguard pushed forwards, stabbed, and fell back into the formation. As the dwarves gathered themselves, the second row struck through the gaps, steel slicing flesh and spilling blood.

A long, bearded axe blade flashed at the edge of Lumeera's vision, glinting in the golden light from the flowers on the chamber's ceiling. Lumeera swung her head back to avoid the full weight of the blow, but the blade cut a burning gash through the bridge of her nose and she let out a gasp.

The dwarf tried for a second swing, but Lumeera thrust her sword and buried the steel in the meat of his arm, piercing the rings of mail that had already been damaged. She pulled the blade free as the dwarf stumbled backwards.

Just as Lumeera fell back into formation, tightening her grip on her shield and readying herself, a sound like no other rumbled through the mountain city, as though the mountain itself raged and howled, and the ground beneath her shook.

"Behind us!" came a cry.

Lumeera glanced over her shoulder, bringing her shield high to protect the back of her head. "By the gods…"

Her heart stopped as she stared at the monstrous creatures that charged down Vindakur's main thoroughfare. Abominations plucked from the darkest stories of her childhood. They stood taller than even Uraks, bodies wrought from jagged rock, veins of glowing gold rippling through them. Horns of rock splintered out from their skulls, all twisted and harsh, and a golden light misted from their eyes.

"What manner of demon…" a voice whispered beside her, and it seemed even the dwarves of Volkur had stopped to stare at the dark manifestations.

The ground cracked beneath the creatures' steps, then reformed once they passed over. Each one of the beasts wielded an enormous spiked hammer as long as Lumeera was tall, wrought entirely of rock and shimmering light.

The fear rising within her stilled at the sound of cheers and the clapping of steel that rang out from the dwarves of Durakdur, who had pulled back at the horns. Could it be? Could these stone-forged demons be the great power Kira had spoken of?

The queen had been clear: do not stand in the way.

"Fall back!" Lumeera roared. She looked over her shield. The dwarves of Volkur stood with their mouths open, axes hanging loose at their sides. Lumeera shoved the soldiers next to her, shouting again, "Fall back!"

The Kingsguard broke off and sprinted towards the side streets, but some weren't fast enough. She watched in horror as a man tried desperately to escape the charging monsters' path, but one of the beasts caught him with a stone leg and sent him hurtling across the ground. Dread coiled in her stomach as a second creature brought its foot down and snapped the man in half without breaking stride, crushing his plate and bones in a single step.

The beasts crashed into the Volkuran lines with such devastating force that Lumeera thought she had stepped into the Godsrealm. Massive rock hammers crushed dwarven plate in single swings, golden light shimmering with each blow. They fought with a savage fury, roaring and howling words in a strange language as they ripped the Volkurans apart.

She watched in awe as one of the great monsters slammed an enormous fist down onto a dwarf in a horned helm and crushed him in an explosion of gore and bone, strips of flesh clinging to the jagged rock. The creature lifted its leg, then stomped on a fallen dwarf, shattering their legs, before swinging its hammer and tearing a body clean in half.

Lumeera had never seen carnage like it. These beasts were death incarnate.

Another horn blast sounded, but this one did not come from within the city.

A sharp *whoosh* was followed by a blur and an enormous bolt smashed into the arm of one of the stone beasts, tearing it free in a spray of dust and shards of rock. Another *whoosh*, a second bolt, and a leg was ripped from one of the creatures.

The bolts were followed by arcs of lightning that streaked from behind the destroyed doors, tearing strips of stone from the ground and ripping through dwarf and monster alike.

As one of the creatures fell to the ground, the horn sounded again, and the Volkuran dwarves let out a thunderous war cry and charged forwards. They swarmed around the creatures, hacking and slashing with renewed vigour, steel skittering off rock. Even more warriors swarmed past and towards the thoroughfare beyond. Towards the Portal Hearts. Towards the citizens of Belduar.

Lumeera surged forwards without hesitation, her fingers tight around the hilt of her sword.

Arrows continued to rain down from above, bouncing off dwarven armour. Deep, sonorous horns bellowed from further down the street, and Lumeera cast a glance to see the rest of the Durakdur forces breaking into a charge, crimson cloaks of the Queensguard fluttering, axes raised above their heads.

Lumeera pulled her shield tight and slammed it into the side of a charging Volkuran, sending him sprawling. She leaned backwards to avoid the swing of an axe, then opened the wielder's throat. More Kingsguard and Belduarans flooded around her. There were no lines drawn, no shield walls or slow advances. The battle descended into pure madness and slaughter. Lumeera stabbed down into a dwarf's open mouth and ripped the blade free in the same motion. "Do not let them pass! Do not let them reach the portal!"

A roar sounded near the entrance, and she watched one of the stone monsters sweep aside a score of Volkurans with one mighty swing of its hammer before taking a bolt to the chest and a second to the knee. It fell, reeling, and then an arc of lightning smashed into its head and shattered it to pieces.

RAGE WAS ALL KIRA KNEW. It was the blood in her veins, the beating of her heart, the song in her ears. She roared as she swung her axe and impaled two dwarves on the jagged spike that jutted from its end. Their blood soaked into the rock. It fed her, fuelled her, and drove her fury even deeper. She would have their blood. All of them. She would feed the mountain with it.

Something sharp whipped past her head, and a roar sounded behind her. She twisted around. One of her kin had fallen, a massive bolt piercing his chest. Volkurans climbed atop him, hacking with axes and smashing with hammers. She roared, her lungs burning and grating. Her existence was pain, and the pain drove the fury. She surged forwards, her legs devouring the ground beneath her.

Hafaesir's hammer ignited with golden light in her hand as she swung, killing three of the Volkurans in a heartbeat, their bodies crumpling. She swung the weapon high and brought it down atop a dwarf holding a wicked battleaxe, who burst apart like a bug squashed beneath a boot. With each kill, each drop of blood that seeped into her hammer, her fury burned brighter, and she welcomed it. She was a bersekeer. Her rage was her lifeblood.

Another bolt whipped past her head, slicing a groove through the rock that was her flesh. She snapped her head around and spotted three Bolt Throwers mounted on mobile platforms. She roared and launched her hammer through the air. It spun, golden light spilling from it, screams sounding as it smashed into the leftmost Bolt Thrower and shattered into a thousand shards. As the Bolt Thrower and the platform collapsed, the shards sliced through the flesh of anything nearby, ripping apart the dwarves that operated the other Throwers and tearing through the wooden supports of the weapons themselves.

Kira howled in triumph. She smashed her fists into the ground, crushing bodies everywhere she went.

Something crashed into her chest and sent her staggering backwards, followed by an arc of lightning that tore her right arm free from the elbow, shards of rock splintering. Pain and agony fed fury and rage. She found the mage standing amidst the chaos, golden armour swaddling its body like some pampered child, a crimson cloak swirling at its shoulders. With her vision flooded by Hafaesir's light, Kira could see the streams of power that swirled around the tiny creature, the threads of the Spark.

She bounded through the thick of battle, then slammed her severed arm into the ground. She called to the rock, to the mountain. She summoned it to her, and it answered. With a roar, Kira ripped her new arm free of the mountain, fresh rock forming joints and fingers.

The threads of power around the mage stiffened and pulsed, ready to strike. Kira lunged, and for a brief moment, she savoured the look of terror on the mage's face before she slammed her open hands together and crushed the horrid creature between them. Blood and organs spurted, bone and steel crunching.

Kira slammed her fist into the ground once more and ripped a new hammer free. She roared wildly, and her kin about her answered.

She could feel the terror in the hearts of those around her, as tangible as the ground beneath her feet. It was sweet as honey. Hafaesir was awakened, and she would teach these traitors to fear his wrath.

AN AXE SKITTERED off LUMEERA's pauldron as she twisted and turned amidst the swell of bodies. She swung her blade, only for it to bounce off heavy plate. She swung again, breaking chains on the mail that coated the dwarf's neck. Finally, Lumeera lifted her knee and planted her foot into the dwarf's shield, launching them backwards. The dwarf stumbled and fell, only for one of those stone monstrosities to slam its foot down and crush the dwarf inside their own armour.

Lumeera had to hold back the bile as shards of bone snapped through flesh and blood sprayed in a mist.

Those creatures may have fought on her side, but they killed anything that moved. More than once she had come within a hair's breadth of her own end by the stray swing of a jagged, rock-wrought hammer.

She looked back towards the central island where the Portal Heart was sheltered within the broken mound of stone. Rows of dwarves and Belduarans stood steadfast across the streets that gave access to the island and on the bridge at the far side. On the ledges above, citizens continued to stream down from the Wind Tunnels.

Lumeera stumbled backwards as a leg of jagged rock swept past her face and crushed two elves in their golden plate. One was broken from the waist up, and the other's skull became nothing but pulverized bone and brains.

The Volkurans and the elves had pushed them almost halfway down the main thoroughfare, and the fighting raged in the side streets and alleys. But the enemy's strength was waning. The might of Kira and her bersekeers was too much. Around her, she could see their numbers thinning, their resolve wavering. The sight brought a renewed vigour to her bones, and she let out a war cry, slamming the rim of her shield into the face of an elf who had turned to strike her down. The elf stumbled backwards, and Lumeera pressed her advantage. He turned her first two swings away, but she caught him with the third, steel hacking deep into the flesh of his neck. She shouldered her shield and pushed as she heaved the blade free, letting the body drop.

The triumphant cry had barely touched her lips when something hard punched into her lower abdomen. She stumbled backwards, the air catching in her lungs. An arrow jutted from just below her breastplate, the head buried in her flesh.

As she looked down at the wooden shaft, a horn rang out from the tunnels, followed by cries of "Fall back!"

The surviving Volkurans and the elves broke free from the melee and began their retreat, and cheers and war cries rose up from those who defended the city. The monstrous bersekeers paid no heed to horns or the fleeing. They carried on swinging their mighty hammers, crushing and killing everything within reach.

Amidst it all, Lumeera spotted an elf standing still, a bow in its hand, an arrow nocked and trained upon her, the string drawn. She drew a breath and prepared for the end, but before the elf loosed, Oleg Marylin – of all people – came swinging from the rush of bodies and slammed his axe clean into the elf's chest. The blow struck with such force the axe cleaved the steel and blood streamed around it.

The elf dropped the bow, the arrow skittering to the floor. It fell backwards, taking the axe with it.

Oleg reached down and ripped the axe free, a look of shock on his face. He stood there in that ill-fitting armour, a bloodied axe in his hands.

Lumeera dropped her shield and brought her fingers to the wooden shaft embedded in her stomach. Every breath she drew sent a surge of pain through her. She swallowed hard and looked to Oleg, giving him a nod of thanks.

A smile slowly spread across the man's face, and he pressed a hand to his breastplate. Oleg may not have been a warrior, but he had a warrior's heart.

Lumeera pressed her hand to her own plate in return, but coils of dread slithered through her veins as one of the giant monstrosities let out a roar and swung its hammer.

And then Oleg was gone.

The creature's hammer swept him aside as though he were nothing, and then it carried on, tearing through the Volkurans and the elves as they fled for the entrance.

Lumeera dropped her sword and broke into a sprint, her body screaming as the arrow scraped at her with every step. She threw herself to the ground to avoid the sweeping legs of another stone monster, then scrambled upright, only to drop to her knees beside Oleg's broken body.

His chestplate was caved in, his right arm hung on by threads of skin and muscle, and his neck was twisted and broken.

A pair of hands pulled at Lumeera's shoulders, but she ignored them, brushing her fingers across Oleg's bloodied, lifeless cheek.

"Lord Captain." The hands pulled at her again, a dwarf with a crimson cloak appearing at her side. "We need to go. The bersekeers will not stop. It's not safe here."

Lumeera clenched her jaw, the pain in her stomach burning. She grabbed the haft of Oleg's fallen axe and hacked down through the shaft jutting from her torso. The wood splintered and broke, leaving the head buried within her. She dropped the axe and slipped her hands beneath Oleg.

"I'm not leaving you here," she whispered as she lifted Oleg's lifeless body into her arms, his shattered arm dangling. "You will be returned to ash under the light of the sun."

Pankar, one of Lumeera's Kingsguard, rushed to her and tried to take Oleg's body, but she snapped at him and carried on, whispering to her dead friend as she hobbled through the street of corpses, the bersekeers still killing and butchering everything that moved behind her.

"I'll build you your own pyre," she whispered. "I'll take some of the ashes and spread them across Haftsfjord."

He'd spoken often about his love for the lake that glittered in the sunlight below Belduar. It seemed like a good place for him to rest, a gentle place.

Lumeera hobbled the length of the street, many of her Kingsguard and other Belduarans following as they saw whom she carried in her arms. By the time she'd crossed the bridge and entered the structure housing the Portal Heart, she was ready to collapse from the pain in her stomach, but she refused to stop.

The Belduaran refugees were still streaming down from the Wind Tunnels and through the Portal Heart, but they parted before her, whispering and pressing their hands to their hearts.

She walked past the pedestal at the centre of the shattered chamber and stopped before the ring filled with molten gold that rippled like water.

Sweat streaked her brow, and her vision had started to blur. She grunted at a dwarf who stood at the steps that fronted the portal. "I just walk through?"

"Yes," he said, his gaze never leaving Oleg.

Lumeera nodded in response, unable to muster any more words. She took the steps one at a time, then passed through. A wave of ice washed over her, and then she was on the other side.

People rushed to her, voices dull and distant in the back of her mind. She ignored them all and dropped to her knees, gently placing Oleg's body on the stone before collapsing, her vision going black.

KIRA SHIVERED AS SHE KNELT naked amidst the corpses. Her mind was dull and achey, her body screaming in pain with each movement. The rage that had consumed her still smouldered within. Crushed limbs and bone shards lay amidst pools of blood and innards. The sight was so visceral and raw, her stomach lurched.

Images flashed in her mind: her own hands ripping bodies in half, her hammer crushing and smashing bones and armour. She looked down at her arms and hands. Veins of gold marbled grey skin, bits of which were still cracked and split like rocks, blood coating every inch of her. She turned over her hands, tracing the gold that flowed across her palms and around her fingers.

What had she become?

"What I needed to be," she whispered to herself. She was not ignorant. She saw the bodies of Belduarans and her own kin, not slain by sword or axe or bow, but by the crushing blows of Hafaesir's hammer. Many others stood or knelt amidst the bodies, naked as the day they'd been born, grey skin shimmering with marbled veins of gold. Sixty or so, not many more.

"Sister?"

Kira's heart fluttered at the sound of Erani's voice. She had feared the worst. She turned to find her sister stumbling through the corpses, arms wrapped tight about herself. Tears streamed down Erani's cheeks, her eyes raw and red. She shivered, her lip trembling.

"Erani." Kira stumbled as she got to her feet. She pulled her sister in close, resting her chin on Erani's shoulder. "You're all right. Hafaesir bless us."

"Kira." Erani's voice trembled. She squeezed, her hands gripping Kira's back. "Kira, what have we done?"

CHAPTER SEVENTY-EIGHT

SACRIFICE

22nd Day of the Blood Moon

Elkenrim – Winter, Year 3081 After Doom

Eltoar stood with his arms folded behind his back, looking out the window at the city of Elkenrim, his armour stripped from him and laid out across a table on the far side of the room. In the distance, Helios soared through the skies over the Elkenwood, scales glinting in the light of a rare warm day, Karakes and Seleraine with him. Ever since he had been a child, there had been nothing that settled his mind more than watching dragons fly. There was a devastating beauty in it. These were creatures more powerful than anything else in existence, their fire so devastating the gods had taken it from them. And yet, even with the rage that burned inside them, the purest joy in their hearts came from being free with the air beneath their wings. They did not seek to destroy for the sake of doing so. When a dragon's wrath was unleashed, it was because something they loved was in danger.

His thoughts swirling in his mind, Eltoar reached out to the Spark and drew in threads of Air, Spirit, and Fire, weaving them through the air around himself, then pushing them outwards to create a ward of silence around the room. He turned to face Lyina and Voranur, who stood on either side of a sturdy wooden table, upon which sat a golden chest. The thing was about three feet across and the same in depth, the flaming egg insignia of the Dracárdare worked into each side. That chest had been used to carry dragon eggs once, a long time ago. It seemed fitting. "What would you give to see the eggs hatch again? What would you risk?"

"Anything and everything." Voranur's response was immediate.

Eltoar moved to the table's closest edge, meeting Lyina's gaze.

"What's in the chest, Eltoar?" He knew the sound of worry in her voice.

"Anything and everything," Eltoar said with a sigh.

He had kept his secret for centuries, not told a soul – not one. But the time for secrets had passed. Too much had been lost, and now the empire was crumbling, battered and broken, besieged on all sides. The eastern cities were ash, the elves held Catagan, the rebels had almost brought Berona to its knees, the South was aflame, and the Uraks tore everything apart. Even astride Helios, with the others at his wings, there was nothing he could do. Millions would die. Everything he had sacrificed, everything he had done, would be for nothing. The world he had given so much to create would be dust.

Eltoar slipped a key from his pocket and slid it into the lock set into the centre of the flaming egg. A *click* sounded. He grasped the lid with two hands and pulled it back.

A soft red glow emanated from the smooth gemstone that sat on a bed of purple silk. The stone was larger than a dragon egg, far larger than any gemstone in existence. The power of the Essence that radiated from it should not have been possible. The power to break open the world.

"How…" Lyina lifted her hand, the hairs on her arm all standing on end. She stared down at the gemstone, eyeing it as though it might spring forth and slit her throat. "I've never felt a power like that. What is it?"

"It's what Fane wants," Eltoar said, losing himself in the flickering glow of the enormous vessel. "The thing he hunts for – the Heart of Blood."

Lyina pulled her gaze from the gemstone, her mouth open wide. "And I'm sure there's a very good reason as to why you have it, Eltoar?"

Eltoar released a long sigh, and he felt Helios pull their minds together, their sorrow, loss, and grief blending. "The night it all happened. The night The Order fell… the night we tore it down. Fane held this gemstone atop the Sky Tower. The power he had was like nothing else. The skies opened. The world ignited."

Voranur looked at him, mouth agape. "The Burnt Lands…"

Eltoar nodded.

Lyina staggered backwards as though struck in the gut. She shook her head. "No, no… Eltoar, tell me this is not what I think it is…" She steadied herself, horror in her eyes as she looked down at the glowing gemstone. "Tell me this is not the Essence of every soul that perished at Ilnaen. Tell me that the strength of all our brothers and sisters that we betrayed does not reside within this thing. Please."

Eltoar stared at Lyina, wishing he could tell her what she wanted to hear. "I do not know…" He sucked in his cheeks, looking down at the pulsing light. "But I believe it is so. I cannot see how this much power could be harnessed any other way."

Voranur looked from Lyina to the gemstone, to Eltoar. "How does it now reside in your hands, brother?"

"I took it." In the depths of the gemstone, Eltoar saw the memories of that night. He watched as hundreds of arcs of lightning tore down from the warped sky, as the great wave of fire turned the city to ash and spread for hundreds of miles, wreaking death and destruction the likes of which he'd never known. That night, as he stood on the tower beside Fane, he'd feared he had made the greatest mistake that any soul had ever made. And now, as he stared down at the gemstone in that golden chest, this decision laid before him, he knew with every fibre of his being that he had.

"In the weeks following Ilnaen's fall, while Fane's mind was elsewhere, I made a choice. I took the vessel and hid it in the depths of the Sea of Stone. Fane had stood by me in everything. I trusted him. But no one soul could truly be trusted with that kind of power. I feared what he might do."

"What could have been darker than what we already did?" Lyina stared down at the stone as she spoke, her gaze lost in its light. "It's a strange thing when you look back at everything you've done and can't tell if you slayed the monster that threatened everything you loved or if you simply became it."

"We did what we needed to do," Voranur hissed, folding his arms across his chest. "Did we?"

"Yes. I know you think that I don't feel the shame and darkness of what we did, but I do. I simply don't allow it to consume me as you do. We can dwell on it, spend our lives pondering the choices we made, but we will never be the better for doing so. I regret many things, sister, but I do not regret choosing to fight for a better world… I just wish we had succeeded."

Lyina nodded softly but did not speak.

"Why show us this now?" Voranur asked. "You've held it for four centuries and said nothing. But now we are deemed worthy of your trust?"

"He is considering returning it to Fane." Lyina stared openly at Eltoar, and he heard Karakes roar in the distance. She held his gaze for a moment. "You are."

"I'm not sure," Eltoar said honestly. "That is why we are standing here. You are the last of my kin. You and Tivar, but she has made her choices. And Luka and Erdin haven't been seen in a long time."

Voranur spat on the ground at the mention of Tivar's name, and a fire burst to life within Eltoar.

"Do that again and I will rip your tongue from your head."

"She turned her back on us, Eltoar."

"She is still Tivar." Eltoar rounded on him. "She chose to stand by the first new Draleid in centuries. She chose to protect what could be the future of our entire race, a future you almost burned."

"Me?" Voranur snapped. "I did what I was ordered to do, and it cost me almost everything."

"Laël sanyin, myia'kar." *I am sorry, my brother.* Eltoar let out a long, mournful sigh. "My emotions overcome me. That hatchling is the first in so long… I cannot help but think if I could talk to the Draleid…"

"Then what?" Voranur asked, none of his anger fading. "Aeson Virandr has had his ear for a year at least. I would wager the man would sooner slit our throats than listen to a word from your lips."

"Shut up!" Lyina roared. "Both of you. This is not why we are here."

Voranur's lip curled, but he said nothing further.

"Eltoar, why now? After all these years, why now are you considering handing this power to Fane when by your own admission it is a power no soul should wield. What has changed?"

"Everything…" Eltoar closed his eyes as memories and emotions flooded into him from Helios. Memories of all those who had died across the years, of the first moment he had accepted that the eggs would no longer hatch, of Meranta falling from the sky… of watching Lyina hold Pellenor's lifeless body in her arms. "Everything has changed, Lyina," he repeated. "This world was not what we fought for, and now it lies on the brink of collapse. The empire is burning. The continent is in pieces. More than a million souls have been butchered in the past year alone. If this continues, there will be nothing left. Everything we did, everything we sacrificed will be for nothing if we allow that to happen. With this vessel, Fane could end the war. He could bring Efialtír across the veil between worlds."

"Is that something we want? Truly? What is to say the world we leave behind will be any better than this? Perhaps it is time to step aside, Eltoar."

"He claims that with the Heart he may be capable of breathing life back into the eggs." Eltoar looked into Lyina's eyes, then out the window behind him, where Helios, Karakes, and Seleraine still flew. "To bring the dragons back. If the gods truly did strip the life from the eggs as punishment for what we did, then a god who would give that life back is a god I would follow."

"Do you believe him?" Lyina asked.

"Does it matter? If there is even the slightest of chances—"

"Then we should take it." Voranur cut across Eltoar.

Eltoar turned his gaze to meet Voranur's, searching his eyes.

"I find little joy in this world anymore," Voranur said, "save for flying with Seleraine. Perhaps you are right. If it is true that the gods punished us for what we did, maybe it will take a god to lift that punishment." He stared down at the gemstone, then nodded softly. "If there is even a chance. Just the tiniest sliver, a grain of hope…" He stared into Eltoar's eyes. "Then you should take it. We owe them that much," he said, looking out at the dragons. "We owe them a chance."

Eltoar had never seen Voranur so open before. It stirred something within him.

Lyina sucked in her cheeks as she always did when she was thinking. "And what's to stop him from killing you when he learns of your theft?"

"It would be a good death if it meant life for the eggs. Though we would not simply lie down."

Lyina pressed her palms against the table and looked down at the glowing red light in the chest. "Is it worth it? Does one mistake fix another? I'm not—"

The door swung open, and a soldier all but fell into the room, panting and heaving. He stepped through the ward of silence without knowing, sweat dripping from the top of his nose and streaking down his face. "Commander Daethana," he said, dragging in deep lungfuls of air as he pulled himself upright. "The beacons near Merchant's Reach and Greenhills are lit."

Both Voranur and Lyina's eyes widened, and Eltoar slammed the lid of the chest shut, releasing the ward of silence around the room.

"How did they get as far as Greenhills without our knowing?" Lyina narrowed her gaze. "When were these beacons lit, Captain? And why haven't you come to us sooner?"

"I came as soon as the fire rose, Draleid. Only the beacons towards Greenhills lit first, those at Merchant's Reach after."

"That doesn't make any sense." Voranur strode towards the captain, looking down at the shorter man. "Are you sure that's what you saw?"

"Absolutely," the man answered, trying to avoid Voranur's gaze. He looked past Voranur to Eltoar. "The beacons towards Greenhills were set ablaze first, near an hour ago—"

"An *hour* ago?" Voranur rounded on the man. "They were lit an hour ago, and you are only here now?"

"We… we thought it an accident, Draleid." The man swallowed, his hands trembling. "We wanted to be sure before we sent word, and then the beacons at Merchant's Reach were lit and I came immediately."

Voranur pinched the bridge of his nose and turned away from the captain, looking at Eltoar. "So the elves will lay siege to two cities at once? They seek to split us."

Eltoar shook his head. "No… that still wouldn't explain how the beacons at Greenhills were lit first. Unless…"

"Unless what?"

"Unless it is not the elves."

"The new Draleid? You believe he is that brazen as to attack Merchant's Reach? With no army in support?"

"No. He has no interest in Merchant's Reach. He flies for the Firnin Mountains, for the army that marches on the rebel outpost." Eltoar placed a hand atop the chest. "Leave us, Captain."

The man looked as though he wanted to say more, but instead he bowed and left.

When the door had shut, Eltoar locked the chest, then carried it to the table where his armour lay on the far side of the room. He set the chest on the ground, then ran a finger across the black flame set into the white steel breastplate.

"If we go, we leave Elkenrim vulnerable," Voranur said.

"And if we don't, then we leave the forty thousand souls laying siege to the rebel outpost at the mercy of dragonfire. We make the choices we can live with." Eltoar turned to Voranur and Lyina. "Ready yourselves. We leave at once."

Lyina stood beside Eltoar as Voranur strode from the room. She looked into his eyes, her voice low. "Do we fly in aid of the armies or for another reason?"

"If I can talk to him, then I will. That is my hope. But if not, then I will do as I must."

She nodded slowly. "We need to know how the egg hatched, Eltoar. If something has changed…" She looked down at the chest. "We need to know."

"Agreed."

"What will you do with that? Surely you cannot leave it here."

"I will leave it somewhere safe." Eltoar laid a hand on the chest. "This gemstone may yet be the future of our race."

CHAPTER SEVENTY-NINE

THE LION AND THE DRAGON

22nd Day of the Blood Moon

Firnin Mountains – Winter, Year 3081 After Doom

ist and the others were about halfway up the mountain by the time the sun had joined the red moon in the sky. The mages of the First Army had set out in the middle of the night, divided into ten groups of ten. Each led a contingent of five hundred soldiers along narrow mountain paths discovered by Taya Tambrel's scouts the day before. Four of the Chosen had also joined Rist's contingent.

The mages of the other armies remained with the bulk of the force for the main assault that had begun at daybreak.

It was Garramon's plan. Taya Tambrel had discovered the main track on the first day, but the path was long and treacherous and the rebels were heavily dug in. With an army of forty thousand and near six hundred Battlemages, the rebel outpost would fall. But a full-frontal assault alone would take heavy casualties. However, if enough mages could find a way inside the mountain while the rebels were focused on the main assault, the rebels would be caught in a pincer and the battle would end swiftly.

It was a plan Rist agreed with. Pincer movements were among the most effective battle stratagems in history and often resulted in a dramatic reduction in the loss of life – at least from the attacking side. Sumara Tuzan's works spoke of them extensively. Besides, it was the defensive fortification of the mountain that made the assault so costly. If that factor was removed, more men and women would live to see another day – live to see their families again.

A gasp from behind him pulled Rist from his ponderings and he stuck out his hand by instinct. He grabbed hold of Samala's belt and had to dig his heels into the ground to stop the both of them from tumbling over the cliff edge. Dirt and rocks dropped over the edge, bouncing off the mountainside as they fell.

When he was sure his feet were stable, Rist leaned back to balance Samala's weight and tugged her away from the ledge.

"Thank you," she said, a tremble in her voice, her hands shaking before her. "I… my mind was elsewhere."

"Keep moving," Magnus called back.

"Don't look down," Rist said to Samala. "And if the path gets too narrow, turn your hips towards the mountain to keep your weight balanced. It's what goats do."

She looked at him as though he had two heads but thanked him again before he turned and continued on. He didn't know the woman well. She had seen five or six summers more than he had and had been drafted in from the Circle after the Battle of the Three Sisters. But he'd learned her name – as he had for every mage in the First Army. That was a promise he'd made to himself after Ilnaen, and he'd kept it. Of the nine that climbed with him, he only truly trusted Garramon, Magnus, and Neera, but at least he knew all their names.

"That hand was dangerously close to her arse," Neera whispered, dropping back to Rist, her eyes narrowing.

Rist knew it was a trap. It was always a trap. And yet, he had no idea how to avoid it. "Would you rather I let her fall?"

"Yes." Neera said nothing else. She simply turned to look back up the steep narrow path ahead to where Garramon, Magnus, and Yoric led the way, threads of Earth probing at the rock for any concealed entrances or hollow points.

Rist drew a long breath and let it out in a sigh. His father's words that women were 'equal parts confusing, irritating, and completely unavoidable' had made more and more sense the longer Rist had known Neera.

As they climbed, he looked out at the landscape beyond. The army was spread out in columns near the main path. The assault was already underway, but the bulk of the army stood in reserve as the path was only wide enough for five or six to walk abreast.

He had spent most of the night as they'd climbed thinking about the men and women who marched at the head of the army – those who walked the path first. No matter what he or anyone else did, those soldiers would be dead before the next sun. There was no path where that did not happen. They would face the full force of the rebel defences, and they would be cut down, only so that those behind them might push further and in turn be cut down, and so on and so forth.

"Magnus?" Rist whispered.

The man looked back at Rist with a raised eyebrow.

"The soldiers who led the assault."

"What of them?" Magnus asked.

"Did they know their only purpose was to die?"

"Fuck, lad. Do you ever ask a simple question?" Magnus frowned, then let out a long sigh. "Is this what bounces around in that head of yours when your lips aren't moving?"

Rist looked down at the ground, then back at the soldiers who walked behind him, careful to keep his voice low. "They're dead now. The assault would have begun a few hours ago. Surely, they had known their fate before they marched?"

Magnus puffed out his cheeks then ran his hand down his face, pinching the bridge of his nose. "Aye. They are, The Saviour's light upon them."

"But… why?" It was something Rist couldn't quite wrap his head around.

"A sense of honour," he suggested, though his eyes betrayed him. "Or more likely wilful ignorance. War is death. There is no escaping it."

"But why not wait? If we cut them off, eventually they will need food and supplies. We could take the outpost without any losses." Even as Rist spoke, his mind travelled back to what he had seen in the camps outside Berona, of the sick and the injured and the hungry, and of how cruel and hopeless it had all felt. And there he was, suggesting they do the same, or worse, to the souls within that mountain.

"Time," Magnus answered. "We have no idea what kind of stores they have in there, and we don't have weeks or months to wait. The emperor wants this place dealt with so we can focus on the Uraks and the elves. So, we do what must be done."

"But what—"

"Quiet," Garramon snapped in a hushed whisper.

"What is it?" As Magnus spoke, Rist heard something: the sound of dirt grinding beneath feet, of gently rustling leaves.

He barely had the time to take a breath before an arrow punched into Yoric's eye and the man went tumbling down the cliffside. Shouts erupted behind him, more bodies falling.

Neera threw herself across Rist and shrouded them both in threads of Air, creating a physical ward around them.

Rist glanced to the side, only to see an arrow ricochet off her ward and lodge itself into Samala's neck. The woman already had two in her leg and one in her chest, but her eyes rolled with the last one, and she collapsed, blood spilling from her open mouth. His heart raced as he stared into her dead, white eyes.

One of the other mages, Dremaine, was huddled behind a rock, an arrow jutting from just below his kneecap, soldiers both dead and alive all around him. And Rist thought he could see Yanda's body, along with a few others, tangled in the gnarled roots of a tree that grew from the mountainside over the cliff edge. The rest of the mages had raised their shields of Air in time to avoid injury. But they had lost scores of soldiers.

"Bastards," Magnus growled, threads of Air swirling around him. "Well, they know we're here now, and it looks like this path definitely leads somewhere. Find cover and engage!"

The man spun on his heels and launched streaks of lightning towards a cliff edge that twisted about the one upon which they stood. The rocks exploded in a cloud of dust, and three rebels fell from the ledge, the path they had stood on collapsing with them.

Rist pulled Neera down to the closest patch of boulders and opened himself to the Spark.

"Where are they?" Kalder, a mage who had been with the army since Rist had first met Magnus, shouted from some fifty feet down the path, back pressed to a tree.

"A score on the higher ledge to the right," Magnus answered. "More to the left, hiding in that bush. And a few more too, I'd guess. Rist, Neera, dragon's maw on the upper ledge. Keep them down. Hopefully cook them for dinner. Kalder, Lakrin. You do the same to those in the bush. Garramon and I will pick off whoever escapes. The rest of you, keep your heads down!"

"What about me?" Dremaine called out from behind his rock, his fingers pressing down around the arrow in his knee.

"Oh, Dremaine, you're alive? Great. Keep us from being killed, would you? On my mark. Three, two, one. Mark!"

Rist pulled threads of Fire and Air into his body, weaving them together as he rose from behind the rock. Neera followed him, her threads intertwining with his. He unleashed the threads, and a pillar of fire roared upwards to the ledge. Screams sounded, and blazing bodies plummeted into the open chasm below, bouncing off the cliffside as they fell. One body was impaled on a jagged peak, the rock bursting through his spine.

Rist stared down at the body, watching as the muscles and tendons snapped from the pressure and it ripped in half, both pieces tumbling out of sight. He did that. He killed that man, just as he had those people in Berona. And how many more would he kill before this day was over… in the name of what?

"Rist!" Neera grabbed his hand and squeezed. "I need you."

Rist snapped his focus back, realising his threads of Fire and Air had all but faded and the surviving rebel soldiers were nocking arrows and loosing.

He plucked another thread of Air from his mind just in time to redirect a hail of arrows meant for Neera and himself. This time he made certain to send them down the mountainside, unable to stop himself glancing at Samala's lifeless body, the arrow jutting from her neck.

Threads of Earth and Spirit whipped past Rist's face, and a chorus of screams filled the air as Garramon ripped the rock out from under the rebels' feet and sent them all into Heraya's embrace.

For a while, the only sound Rist could hear was the crashing of rocks as they cascaded down. A tense silence followed, broken only by the flames that crackled on nearby trees and bushes.

"Count?" Magnus called out.

A momentary silence was followed by Kalder's voice. "Six mages still breathing. Dremaine took an arrow to the neck. At least eighty soldiers dead."

"Fuck." Magnus tugged at the strap of his helmet. "These bastards are smarter than we gave them credit for." He drew a long breath, exhaling sharply. "All right. Rist, Neera, eyes open. Anything moves, kill it. After that racket, any element of surprise is well and truly gone. Don't fuck around. Bring the mountain down over them if you have to. The rest of you, prepare wards. Move out!"

They'd not been walking long when horns bellowed from the plains below, signalling the second phase of the assault.

"Pick up the pace, you sack of arse-licking donkeys," Magnus roared, raising a hand in the air. "I'll not have it said that we sucked each other's toes on the side of this fucking mountain while the rest of those bastards won all the glory."

"Sucked each other's toes?" Rist asked, sweat slicking his forehead, his helmet sliding as he tried to keep pace with Magnus.

"Don't question it, lad. It was the first thing that came to my mind." He twisted his head around and glared at Garramon, raising a finger. "Don't say a fucking word."

Rist fell into a rhythm, each step drumming up his legs, his muscles burning under the weight of his armour. Had he done this a year ago, he'd probably have keeled over long before the sun rose, his stomach emptied in the dirt. But he was stronger now, harder. All those steps Garramon had made him climb had been for a reason after all.

Out of the corner of his eye, Rist spotted something drifting between the clouds. He watched for a few moments, wondering if it had been a trick of the mind, but then he saw it again – like a shadow, barely visible. He stopped.

"What is it, lad?" Magnus called.

Rist tilted his head to the side, following the shape as it twisted in the sea of white above.

"Rist?" Garramon stepped into Rist's periphery.

"Dragon," Rist answered.

"What? Where?" The man followed his line of sight. "Are you sure?"

Rist pointed towards a gap in the clouds, judging the creature's trajectory. A moment later, something flashed across the sliver of blue sky before vanishing again.

"I think you might..." Garramon dropped his sentence short when a dragon covered in blue scales broke through the bottom of the cloud bank and roared before sweeping back upwards into the cover of the sky.

"I thought you said we wouldn't have the Dragonguard for this assault?" Magnus asked. Fear was not something Rist associated with Magnus. Fear, shame, nor the ability to say no to whiskey. But there was fear in his voice in that moment.

"We don't." Garramon stared up at the sky, his eyes narrowing. "Eltoar and the others are watching over Elkenrim and Merchant's Reach."

"Seleraine has blue scales," Magnus posed.

"She doesn't have red wings."

"Elves?"

Garramon shook his head. "I don't know. But it matters little."

As though responding to Garramon's words, the blue dragon burst through the clouds again, but this time it was followed by a second. A third creature followed, smaller than the others, its scales as pale as the clouds.

Murmurs spread through the soldiers and mages as the dragons wheeled around each other, soaring across the sky towards the columns of the Lorian armies below. Those murmurs soon became gasps when the creatures plummeted.

Gasps turned to utter silence as two of the dragons dropped low and unleashed rivers of dragonfire down over the men and women on the plains below. The third swooped and tore bloody paths through the columns before lifting into the air once more.

Not a word was spoken as they all stood and watched, helpless. Streaks of lightning tore upwards, shards of stone and spears of ice. In pockets, dragonfire washed over massive wards like water breaking over spheres of glass. Rist could feel the power of it all thrumming in the air. But the dragons were too fast, and the Draleid on their backs sliced through the Lorian threads with Spirit, fire pouring from their hands.

The smallest dragon soared from right to left and carved a path of fire through an entire column of soldiers.

There was something surreal about watching the devastation from so far away and yet seeing it so clearly. From above, with the wind whistling in his ears, everything seemed almost... calm. It was as though time moved more slowly. But even though he couldn't see the men and women thrashing about and burning, throwing themselves into the dirt, the skin peeling from their bones, he could still see it in his mind. His memories flashed back to the Battle of the Three Sisters. He could hear the screams of those around him as they were burned alive, see the incandescent light of the dragonfire as it raked through the army like the blade of a god.

"We need to move." Garramon's voice pulled Rist from his memories. "We need to get inside the mountain."

"What about them?" Rist hadn't intended for his voice to sound as sharp as it did, but neither did he apologise for it.

"There's nothing we can do for them up here."

"They're just dying down there, Garramon. We can't leave them."

Garramon grabbed Rist's shoulder. "The fighting would be long over by the time we got down. The Battlemages will hold the dragons off while the army gets inside the mountain. The rock is their best shield. Taya knows what she's doing."

"You need to have faith, lad," Magnus said. "Sometimes faith is the only armour we have." He motioned Rist on. "The Saviour will watch over them."

"I've never seen a god watch over anyone," Rist said, turning his gaze back to the battle below. He'd intended for the words to stay within the boundaries of his own mind, but his lips had stolen them.

Magnus's eyes sharpened for a moment, but he just nodded and turned. "Keep moving. We help them down there by killing everything inside. Go."

CoREN PRESSED HER BACK AGAINST the rock, arrows clattering off the mountainside above. Threads of each elemental strand swirled in the air around her as the Lorian mages laid siege to Tarhelm's main gates.

She drew a breath, then slipped an arrow from the bucket at her side and nocked it. She shifted to look over the ledge, found a black cloak, and loosed. The man dropped like a sack of stones. Coren repeated the motion, scanning the swell of bodies below, following the threads of the Spark to their sources.

For every arrow that found its mark, another ten were plucked from the air or set ablaze by threads of Fire. The main path from the gates to the plains below was inked with black Lorian leather, their number stretching outwards to the sea of tents beyond. The bodies had piled so high the Lorians had started to toss them back down the mountain just to find space to move.

At first she had wondered why they'd sent so many to simply die while beating themselves uselessly against the gates. Then she'd seen the shoddy, patched armour and the weary faces and understood they'd sent the auxiliaries first, those drawn from the refugees and citizens of Berona. The mages hadn't even arrived until a few thousand had been sent to Heraya's embrace.

A tremor swept through the rock, and Coren dropped back down behind the ledge, the vibrations sweeping through her. She could feel the power of the Spark pulsing in the air as the Lorian mages smashed threads of Air into the gates below and tried to crumble the rock with threads of Earth, all while the battering ram smashed at the wood unceasingly.

The only thing stopping the gates from caving in at the Spark's touch was Farwen and the ten mages who stood with her on the other side slicing through Lorian threads. And the only reason they stood a chance at all was because the Lorians were keeping most of their Battlemages in reserve – something Coren was well aware of. It had been clear for centuries how much higher the Lorians valued the life of a mage over that of the common people.

The power of the Spark pulsed below, and threads of Earth pushed into the ledge upon which Coren and the others stood. She opened herself to the Spark and fortified the ground with Earth while Tahro, one of the three other mages not holding the gates, sliced at the Lorian threads.

Another pulse of the Spark sent a tingle down Coren's spine, and arcs of lightning smashed through the ledge to her left.

A handful of rebels who had been hunkered behind the ledge were torn to pieces, shards of rock slicing through flesh and crushing limbs, while others were ripped apart by the lightning, the smell of burning flesh filling the air.

"We can't hold them here forever!" Varik shouted, scuttling over to Coren on all fours, pausing only briefly at the sight of a torso severed across the chest, the heart hanging from the open cavity, blood pumping.

Streams of blood flowed through the matted dirt on Varik's face. Almost three hundred souls were spread about the ledges that overlooked the main path, raining death from above. There had been over five hundred when they had begun.

"No," Coren answered. "But as long as Farwen can hold the gates together, we will do what we must. Understood?"

Varik gave a sharp nod and his lips moved, but the sound was drowned out by a monstrous roar.

Every hair on Coren's body stood on end, and she twisted, leveraging the rock behind her and staring up at the sky.

"He came." The tone in Varik's voice was equal parts relief and awe.

It can't be.

The awe within Coren however was not that Calen Bryer had answered her call, but that the dragon she saw above was not white. She knew Varthear instantly. The dragon's soulkin, Ilmirín, had been a close friend of Coren's master. And it had broken Coren's heart to watch Varthear sit about Alura's eyrie, the light gone from her eyes.

But this Varthear was all fury and power, her vermillion wings like streaks of blood against the clouds. This was the Varthear of old. Most astonishing of all though: she was here. She had left the Eyrie. Coren hadn't thought that possible.

The dragon lifted into the clouds once more before re-emerging only a few moments later. This time, Varthear was not alone.

And once more, Coren had more questions than answers. The clouds swirled around Avandeer's body as she dropped in the open sky above Varthear. Barely a few seconds later, a smaller dragon, white as the winter snow, streaked from the cloud cover, wings folded.

The white dragon unfurled a massive pair of black-veined wings and swooped forwards, its roar rippling across the sky.

"The white dragon!" a voice called out from somewhere on the ledge. "The Warden!"

More voices answered. "The Warden of Varyn! He's come!"

A cheer rose, steel clattering against rock. And as the cheers rose, the dragons dove. Avandeer and Valerys plummeted before unfurling their wings as a pair and raining fire down upon the Lorian army that waited in the plains below.

A rumble sounded in the back of her mind, a deep powerful thing that once more set her hairs on end. It was equal parts pride, joy, and rage.

Not yet. Coren drew a deep breath, settling herself. *Not yet.*

A roar of defiance echoed.

Horns bellowed from the Lorian forces below. It didn't take much for Coren to know what they meant: break through at all costs. The mountain would be the Lorians' only safe haven now.

She opened herself to the Spark and pulled in threads of Fire, Spirit, and Air. She roared, "Tahro, Makri, Ulyira – Eldingstír!"

Coren focused her threads forwards, feeling those of the other mages join hers. She was the conduit. With a breath, she let go, watching as the threads of Air crashed into the Lorian forces below, lifting soldiers from their feet, shattering legs, sending shards of broken stone slicing through the flesh as easily as steel.

The Lorian Battlemages were not used to facing others who could wield the Spark. In their eyes, there was nothing that could stand against them. The Circle taught them to kill, to destroy, and to crush everything in their path – and it taught them that such was their birthright.

But the Circle never taught them to face a Draleid, and a lion was not the predator when a dragon spread its wings.

Aldryn roared in the back of Coren's mind, defiant and furious. She pushed their power into the threads of Fire and Spirit, and arcs of chain lightning streaked from her hands and ripped the Lorian ranks to pieces.

As the other mages joined their threads to hers and the Spark wrought death and destruction below, a sharp, high-pitched horn shrieked from within the mountain, and her heart sank. Around her, faces paled.

The Lorians had found a way inside.

Coren looked out at the Lorian army that stretched down the mountain path and out to the plains, streaks of fire carving through the battlefield below. She turned back to the passage behind her, drew a short breath, then exhaled sharply. "Varik!"

The man loosed an arrow, then pressed himself to the rock beside Coren. He knew what she was going to say. There were no choices here. It didn't matter how long they held the gates if the Lorians got in behind them. They would be butchered. "Go," Varik said, his voice sombre. "We'll hold them here as long as we can."

"No. We go together. Farwen can hold the gates for a while longer. We need to secure whatever breach they have made and burn them from our home."

Varik smiled and rested a hand on Coren's shoulder. "It has been the greatest honour of my life standing beside you and Farwen in this war." He squeezed. "We will give you as much time as we can. Go. You'll owe me more than one bottle of rum after this."

Coren grasped Varik's forearm. "Give them fire and fury."

Varik nodded. "Wouldn't dream of anything else. Now go. If the gates fall, we'll collapse the rock and retreat to the sally port. Hopefully that Draleid clears the way."

Coren turned and sprinted towards the passage in the rock, calling out to Tahro as she did. He was young, and they'd found him before the empire could. His connection to the Spark was strong. He could hold them back for a time.

As she descended into the mountain and the rock swallowed her, she listened to the beating of her heart and pulled Aldryn's mind to hers.

It is time, my heart. Come.

She could feel the dirt sliding around Aldryn's talons, the rock scraping beneath. With a mighty roar, the great dragon lifted himself from the mountain eyrie that had been his fortress of solitude for so long. The time had finally come, and he would greet it with the fury of all he had lost.

CHAPTER EIGHTY

DAUGHTER OF THE SEA

22nd Day of the Blood Moon

Firnin Mountains – Winter, Year 3081 After Doom

Coren twisted to avoid the thrust of a Lorian blade, grabbed the man's wrist, then drove her own sword into his throat, blood sluicing as she ripped it free. She let the body drop, carving a path through six more of the leather-clad soldiers, opening their throats and bellies with clean strokes.

The bastards had found a way in through one of the scout tunnels. She had sealed each of the tunnels with the Spark herself two nights before – all but the sally port. She'd also set guards along the various mountain paths, but it clearly hadn't been enough.

Coren turned back and charged towards the tunnel mouth as more Lorians flooded through.

An arrow flashed past her and dropped the first man, a second hitting the floor just as fast. She lunged as more rushed through, turning the first swing of Lorian steel to her left, then bringing her blade across and opening the throat of a second soldier before driving it back and through the throat of the first.

She let go of the hilt and leapt backwards as a downstroke threatened to relieve her of her arms. Coren drove her back heel into the dirt, slid a knife from her belt, and rammed it up between the ribs of the woman who had swung the blade. She twisted the hilt, angling it upwards, before ripping it out, flipping into reverse grip, and driving it into the woman's neck.

The body dropped, and two more arrows flitted past in quick succession. Two more Lorians dead.

Coren pulled her sword from the corpse she'd left it in and carved a path to the tunnel mouth. These Lorians were green as newly ripened fruit. They were clumsy, hesitant, and fought as individuals. She felt guilt at the thought of slaughtering so many who were so young, men and women dying in a war that had started before their grandparents had been born. But that guilt did not extend to the blade in her hand.

She dropped low and sliced a furrow along the thigh of the nearest soldier. He screamed and fell, his lifesblood pouring into the rock as Coren moved past and opened another soldier's chest from clavicle to hip.

A soldier roared and charged at Coren, swinging a two-handed blade over his head. Coren stopped the sword mid-swing with a thread of Air, and as the shock spread across the man's face, she jabbed her blade into his neck, just enough to slice through the flesh and into the spine, then pulled it free.

The soldier choked on his own blood, dropping his blade and grasping at his throat. Coren stepped over him and stared into the tunnel mouth. The thing was black with shifting bodies, only the thinnest strands of light piercing through, voices and crunching dirt echoing.

She gave a soft sigh, then pulled threads of Earth into herself and spread them through the rock above the tunnel.

She felt mages within probing at her threads. That must have been how they'd gained entry, by searching for hollow points in the rock with the Spark. It was a clever tactic, but they were too late now. As they tried to sever her threads, Coren pulled on the elemental strand of Fire in her mind, its warmth filling her bones and sweeping over her skin.

Aldryn pushed his strength into hers as his mighty wings bore him across the sky. While the mages attempted to stop the tunnel from collapsing on top of them, Coren unleashed a plume of blazing fire from her hand, her heart bleeding just a little as the screams pierced her ears and the smell of burning flesh and leather filled her nostrils.

Those screams were soon swallowed by the crashing rocks as the tunnel's ceiling broke and the burning Lorians within were crushed.

She turned back and strode towards Suka, who stood on the other side of the chamber, pulling a knife from the last Lorian. As the guilt of snuffing out so many lives at once crept into her veins, she pushed it down and buried it deep. Her master had always told her to hold on to that guilt, lest it be lost, and that was what she had always tried to do. She let it in, then cut it down. These soldiers had come for the people she loved, and so they would die or she would die. There was no middle ground.

"We need to make sure Farwen and the others have a clear path back towards the sally port in case the gates fall. Take these warriors to the other tunnels and set defensive lines. We can't allow them to get in behind us. I will hunt down any still alive within and make my way back to the gates."

Suka wiped the blood from her knife and sprinted off down one of the interior tunnels, taking fifty or so with her.

Coren set off through the same tunnel but turned right where Suka had turned left. She gathered any and all souls she could as she passed. They moved from one tunnel to another, through the interconnecting chambers, following the shouts and sounds of crashing steel until they came to the common quarter, a massive cavern ringed with terraces that were split by Spark-carved steps. Buildings of brown stone littered the cavern, and a central plaza dominated the bottom level. Lorians had swarmed in from a different tunnel and were now slaughtering everything that moved. Man, woman, child, it didn't matter. For a moment, Coren was horrified at the butchery, but then she saw glowing red gemstones that hung from mages' necks, and her mind flickered back to the carnage the night Ilnaen fell.

Those gemstones twisted people, warped them into things they were not. And beneath the light of the Blood Moon, it seemed that gifted savagery was untethered. A strange sense of relief swept over her, for now there was nothing holding her back.

Coren sprinted forwards and leapt from the closest ledge. She drove her sword down into a Lorian mage's back as she fell, releasing the hilt as her feet hit the ground and she rolled. Coren sprang up and wrapped threads of air around a spear that lay in the dirt, then whipped the weapon through the air, past herself, and into the chest of a Lorian soldier, pinning them to the rock wall.

She turned and planted her foot into another soldier's chest, kicking him down into the plaza five terraces below. Arrows flitted past her head, slicing through the Lorian soldiers, but as Coren turned, two Battlemages appeared on the top terrace and unleashed pillars of fire down over a clutch of rebels.

"No!" Coren sprinted up the steps, snatching up a spear as she went.

The first Battlemage whirled threads of Fire and Spirit around himself, flames flickering in his palms. Coren hurled the spear, and as the man turned it to ash and cinders before it struck him, she pushed threads of Earth into his breastplate and crushed his ribs.

He dropped to his knees, coughing blood and choking.

Coren closed the distance between herself and the second mage in a heartbeat. A red glow emanated from beneath his breastplate.

She whipped a thread of Air into his right leg, bones snapping through flesh and blood spraying over the rock. As he dropped, howling, Coren reached out with threads of Earth and pulled shards of broken rock and stone into her fist, softening them with threads of Fire and forming them into a stone spear.

The Battlemage lifted his hand, the red gemstone glowing furiously beneath his breastplate. Before the man could take another breath, Coren drove the stone spear straight down into his open mouth, feeling the slightest resistance as it hit the back of his skull and burst out the other side. She released the spear and let the body fall.

Coren turned to find herself staring at a face she had once known, an Imperial Justicar by the name of Kalirist Mahkar. A red gemstone dangled from a chain around his neck, pulsing with a red glow, and something unseen wound around Coren, binding her tight.

Kalirist held out his sword so it pressed to the flesh of Coren's neck. "Coren Valmar. I knew you weren't dead. I'd heard tales."

The steel stung as it pressed deeper, drawing blood.

"Do you know how many people died when you attacked Berona?" He scoffed, deep blue eyes staring into Coren's. "You always thought yourself better, but you were only ever blind." Kalirist's lips curled at the edges, and the whites of his eyes took on a red hue. He drew back his sword. "Sleep well."

ELLA LEAPT THROUGH THE PORTAL that Una had opened, her hackles raised, the wolf howling in her blood. The chamber on the other side was all blood and steel and shouting. A tingling sensation ran up her spine, and she twisted at the waist, the wolf within demanding she do so. A sword sliced through the air where her abdomen had been, surprise painting the face of the Lorian soldier whose fingers were wrapped around the hilt.

The red mist fell over Ella's vision, the wolf within her coming to the fore. But no longer were they two parts of a whole; they were one. She let the creature's instincts take hold. She swept the Lorian aside with a ferocious backhand, her dark claws ripping through his leather helm as though it were mere paper.

Diango and Aneera rushed past her in their wolf forms, their eyes wild and claws rending whatever Lorian dared approach. Once more, a shiver ran down her spine, and she snapped her head around to find Fenryr holding a Lorian by the throat, the woman's sword arm still stretched towards Ella.

Fenryr, all clad in black plate with pauldrons wrought into roaring wolfheads, tilted his head to the side as Faenir often did, then rammed his fist through the woman's steel breastplate, obsidian claws breaking free of the flesh on her back. He tossed her to the ground, body still twitching, and proceeded to rip a Lorian Battlemage's throat out with a single swipe.

As Kaygan, Boud, and the three Jotnar stepped through the portal, Ella scanned the chamber, trying to find some semblance of order within the chaos. That was when she saw Coren floating in the air, a Battlemage's sword held to her neck, something almost imperceptible tangled around her. Only a faint shimmer let Ella know that some strange power held her friend, a distortion in the air where there should have been none. The wolf could smell it, *feel* it.

Ella did not need to utter so much as a whisper. Faenir bounded past her, his muscular legs launching him across the terraces with ease.

She broke into a run after him, the wolf growling within her, then skidded to a halt as a Lorian soldier leapt from the ledge to her right and came a heartbeat from cleaving her in two with a shimmering steel sword. She howled and thrust her left hand forwards, claws plunging into the man's wrist, slicing tendon and flesh and scraping bone.

Ella drove the claws of her right hand up beneath his chin, watching his eyes roll into the back of his head. She ripped her claws free of the man's skull, and the spray of blood that followed drove the wolf within her wild. Ella grabbed the back of the dying man's head, pulled him closer, wrapped her jaws around his neck, and ripped out his throat.

She spat the hunk of flesh into the dirt, twisting in the same motion to bound up the steps.

Another soldier leapt at her but fell from the air with an arrow bursting into his eye, blood and fluid spraying. At the edge of her vision, she saw Therin nocking another arrow, having stepped through the portal with the Aetherdruid, Una, at his side.

Ella focused ahead to where Faenir had wrapped his jaws around the Battlemage's head and Coren had dropped to her knees. Another Lorian blade came for Ella's shoulder as she reached the terrace, but the wolf in her blood pushed her knee to the ground and the blade slid over her head. She sprang upwards, raking her claws across the soldier's chest, then sweeping into a backhand that tore the man's face to ribbons of flesh.

Faenir gave a terrible wrench of the Battlemage's head, and Ella heard a bone snap and watched the man go limp.

Coren knelt before her, gasping for air as Faenir leapt past her and dragged another Lorian to the ground, tearing apart his breastplate as though it were made of clay.

Coren lifted her gaze, dark skin marred by dirt and blood. Ella gave a grim smile, opening her hand. "Try to keep up."

"What are you doing here?" Coren asked, taking Ella's arm and hauling herself upright. She glanced to where Faenir drained the last vestiges of life from the soldier behind her amidst a chorus of snapping and gurgling.

"You called. We answered," Ella said, picking a piece of flesh from between her teeth with her tongue and spitting it onto the ground.

"But how?" Coren looked down to the lower terraces where the three Jotnar cut down any Lorians that crossed their paths, then took a step backwards as Aneera and Diango drew closer, hackles raised and teeth bared.

"The how of it is best explained another time," Ella said, watching as Fenryr seized the last Lorian in the chamber. The god barely showed a semblance of effort as he grabbed the woman's skull and ripped it free from her body, her dangling spine still tethered to its base. Part of Ella wanted to vomit at the sight, but the wolf in her howled with abandon, revelling in the spilt blood. She turned back to Coren, whose eyes were wide. "We're here now. Tell us where you need us."

"The Lorians have found their way inside. I've sent warriors to hold the other tunnels in case of further breaches. Farwen holds the main gates, but she won't be able to do so for long," Coren said, gesturing towards a large tunnel on the other side of the chamber. "I'd hoped we could hold them longer. If we can somehow stem the tide, there's still a chance of holding Tarhelm while your brother breaks them outside."

Kaygan appeared at Ella's shoulder, Boud and Una beside him, both of their short swords wet with fresh-spilt blood. There wasn't a bone in Ella's body that trusted the kat god – or Una and Boud for that matter. She wasn't sure if it was the wolf within her or just her own nature, but all of them set her hackles on end. They smelled of deception. In truth, the only one her wolf didn't growl at was Tamzin.

"Ah," Kaygan said, stepping past Ella and staring at Coren. "You are… fabulous. Another living nexus. So many paths. So many possibilities… It's all coming together."

Ella's hackles rose once more, and Faenir turned, snapping and snarling as the god stared at Coren with an unsettling intensity. She stepped between the two, unflinching under Kaygan's gaze. "Dream of harming her," Ella said, the red mist descending over her vision, the wolf taking hold, "and I will know the taste of your heart."

Faenir moved to Ella's side, snarling, blood dripping from his jaws.

The god stared at her for a moment before his gaze softened and the tension evaporated from his muscles. "My, my, my. You truly are precisely what I had hoped you would be, Wolfchild."

"Speak again, brother, and I will have your tongue." Fenryr placed a hand on Kaygan's shoulder, stepping past without so much as glancing at him. He looked to Coren. "It is an honour to make your acquaintance, Coren Valmar, Daughter of the Sea."

Those words seemed to physically punch Coren in the gut. She stumbled backwards, staring at Fenryr as though she had seen a ghost in his eyes. "How did you…"

"She died with pride in her heart. You should know that. You were in her thoughts when her light faded."

Coren's jaw trembled, and she stared at Fenryr. "Kollna? How… She…" the woman stuttered, her words failing her. Ella had never seen Coren be anything but sure of herself. "What are you?"

"If we survive this, you will know more. But I thought you deserved to know this now. What is our next step?"

Coren stood in silence for a few moments, her eyes wide, blood dripping from the tip of her sword. "We…" She swallowed hard. "We need to get to Farwen and help her reinforce the gates. I've sent warriors to blockade any other potential entry points. The longer we can hold the gates, the more time we give Calen to break the army outside."

Therin gave a sharp nod. "Then let's go."

CoREN LED THE OTHERS THROUGH the maze-like tunnels of Tarhelm, gathering any scattered rebels as they went.

She couldn't get that man's words from her head. *"Coren Valmar, Daughter of the Sea…You were in her thoughts when her light faded… She died with pride in her heart."*

Only Kollna had ever called her 'Daughter of the Sea' and only on the night her old master had died… the night Ilnaen fell. How did this man know her words? Words that had dragged up wounds she'd thought long healed.

A swelling, pulsing sorrow flowed through Aldryn and into Coren. The dragon's heart ached, his wings feeling heavy, his soul bleeding at the memories of Kollna and Tinua – the only family they had ever known. So many nights had been spent wishing they had refused to leave their masters the night Ilnaen had fallen. That they should never have allowed it to be so, that they should have died that night, side by side with the ones they loved.

There are more we must protect now, my heart. That is what they would have wanted. You have waited long enough. It is time to rise so that others rise with us.

A fire burned in the dragon's heart, an unquenchable fury that seeped into Coren, and Coren found herself feeling just a touch of sympathy for the Lorians at the gates. For centuries, Aldryn had remained hidden, moving from eyrie to eyrie, from Dracaldryr to Stormwatch, to the Burnt Lands, and so on, and so on. He had done so at Coren's demand. She had refused to allow her soulkin to be ripped from the world like all the others.

"Our duty, above all else, is to our soulkin," Kollna had told her.

He had waited while she had fought with his strength in her veins. She could survive moving through the shadows, she could go unnoticed and still make a difference – he could not. And so they had waited, and waited, and waited, and now the time was here. The time when Aldryn's strength could make the difference, the time when the Dragonguard could not simply tear him from the skies.

She let her mind drift into his, feeling the powerful beats of his wings, the fire raging in his blood, the fury burning in his heart. All her doubts, all her fears and worries, melted away. Their purpose was singular: save as many lives as the gods would allow.

"There!" Ella called out as they exited a tunnel into the chamber that fronted the gates. Hundreds of rebels formed a shield wall, five rows deep, while more stood upon ledges higher up, arrows stacked in buckets, bows and javelins ready.

Farwen stood at the chamber's centre, seven mages around her, the power of the Spark pulsing furiously in the air, threads of each elemental strand winding and twisting in a storm of power. Three bodies lay on the ground around Farwen, their eye sockets black and scorched.

Coren could see the threads smashing into the gates on the other side, see them seeping into the rock and the wood and the metal, attempting to twist and snap and crumble.

She moved to stand before Farwen, lowering her voice to a whisper so as to not break the elf's concentration. "I'm here."

Farwen's eyes were closed, her jaw twitching with effort. "We won't hold it long," she said, voice trembling. "They're using Blood Magic. We can't see the threads."

As Coren looked closer, she could see two of the mages wove threads of Spirit and Earth through their bodies and those of the others, fortifying their bones and hardening their flesh to keep the Blood Magic from tearing them apart.

"Calen is here, and he's brought help. We—"

An enormous explosion sounded deeper in the mountain, screams and shouts echoing.

"We shall go." The one who spoke was the man Ella had threatened. The one who had stared into Coren's eyes with those irises of blue-grey. Two others went with him, women, both looking sharp and dangerous.

Coren turned to Asius, Thacia, Moras, and Therin. "Will you lend your strength to the gates?"

"It would be our honour, sister," Thacia said, her blood-red hair gleaming in the sunlight that shone down through the shafts carved into the mountain.

A sudden surge of the Spark erupted outside the gates, and the mountain itself seemed to shake, dust and debris breaking loose from the ceiling.

Therin leapt forwards and the power that flooded into him was like the light of the sun as he wove threads of Air and Spirit around himself, Ella, and Faenir.

A second explosion sounded, and the gates erupted inwards. Coren brought her hand to her face, opening herself to the Spark and erecting a ward around herself and anyone else she could reach – the Angan, Farwen, and a number of others. Stone dust filled the chamber, shards of wood and metal exploding inwards.

The mage nearest Coren ruptured in a cloud of blood and bone as a chunk of rock crashed down atop him. Another was skewered by a length of iron.

She stumbled forwards, thin strands of light spraying through the dust that filled the air. Screams and shouts rang out around her. She kicked something and looked down to see a woman's severed torso, spine shattered, innards spilling into the dirt.

The floor was littered with bodies.

Coren coughed as she dragged in a breath of dust. She called out, "Farwen?"

"Here." A hand pressed against the flat of Coren's back, and she looked up into Farwen's dark eyes, the panic in her heart settling.

More shapes appeared in the dust, gathering about her: Ella, Therin, Faenir, the man with the wolfhead pauldrons. Others appeared, men and women with shields and spears, blood clotting in the dirt that coated their skin.

Coren stood upright, placing a hand on Farwen's shoulder. "We need to fall back."

A chorus of chants and howls erupted, and a glowing red light carved through the dust-occluded air, joined by another, and another, until six shapes, illuminated by crimson runes, took form, each holding blood-red níthrals.

Arrows rained down from the ledges above, skittering harmlessly off silver armour.

The six warriors clad in rune-marked steel marched slowly into the chamber, crimson light swirling and flickering with the dust.

For a brief moment, there was silence, only dirt crunching beneath boots, and then the first of the warriors swung their crimson blade and carved a rising man in half with a single stroke, and the chamber descended into chaos. Lorian soldiers flooded in around the silver-clad warriors, hundreds of them.

Coren pulled on threads of each elemental strand and summoned her níthral in her fist, a spear that burned bright white. She grabbed Ella by the collar. "Take whoever you can and run. The sally port lies in a chamber behind the armoury, marked by a red stone. Go!"

Farwen stepped between them and pushed Coren towards the tunnel. "You go with her."

"I'm not—"

"You are whole, Coren. Aldryn needs you. Your fight is not over, but I am tired. Syndril calls to me." She looked to Moras and Thacia, the two Jotnar Rakina stepping from the dust. "We will hold them here, and we will leave them bloody."

Tears were already dripping from Coren's nose and chin. She knew the look in Farwen's eyes. Knew the acceptance and certainty for what it was. If they all stayed, they would all die. She grabbed the hair at the back of Farwen's head and pulled them both together. "I could never have survived without you."

"And I would never have wanted to without you." Farwen pulled away. "You are the greatest soul I have ever known. Being near you has been my privilege. You are not alone anymore. Escape this place and fly beside him."

"I was never alone," Coren whispered.

"Neither was I."

Coren wiped the tears from her cheeks and stood straight. She grasped Farwen's forearm. "Die well, sister."

The words brought a cracked smile to Farwen's lips. She nodded, tears welling in her eyes. "Live better."

With that, Farwen turned to face the monstrous steel-clad warriors, who were tearing a path through the surviving rebels, and the soldiers flowing through in their wake.

Both Thacia and Moras inclined their heads to Coren. But as Moras joined Farwen, Thacia paused and held Coren's gaze.

"Aldryn lives?" There was no judgement in her eyes, though Coren would have held nothing against her for it. She and Farwen had not told a soul.

"He does." Coren couldn't help but allow the shame and guilt to seep into her voice. She had lied to the others all these years, shared their pain when she knew nothing of it.

"Keep him safe," Thacia said. "I would give everything in this world to have Myrax by my side again. Now I will go to his instead. Tell Calen Bryer I am proud to have called him kin. And I am sorry for failing him."

Thacia gave a slight bow and opened herself to the Spark, threads swirling around her as she charged into the fray.

Coren allowed herself a heartbeat to watch as her friends, her kin, fought to give her and the others time.

Dragonbound by fire, Broken by death. Here we wait. Here we rest. Until we are called to make whole what is half.

She grabbed Ella by the arm and pushed her towards the tunnel mouth. "Go!"

"But we can help, we can—"

"Go, or they die for nothing! Tarhelm is lost. We must save as many as we can."

"We can make a difference," the man with wolfhead pauldrons said, his voice calm.

"Can you lay low ten thousand souls? Twenty? Thirty?"

He shook his head.

Ella stared at Coren, the gold in her eyes supplanted by a vivid blue for just a moment. She nodded and turned for the tunnel, shouting, "Fall back! With me!"

The Angan and the man with wolfhead pauldrons followed her, as did any warriors not embroiled in the fighting at the gates.

As Coren did the same, Asius came stumbling through suspended dust, a shard of wood the size of Coren's arm sticking from his right shoulder, blood smeared across his chest.

She pushed him towards the tunnel and ran, calling out for the others to fall back.

FARWEN SLICED HER BLADE ACROSS a Lorian throat, blood spilling, then dropped to one knee, spun, and cleaved a leg along the shin. The bone yielded to her elven steel, the soldier screaming as he hit the ground.

Dust still filled the air, constantly whipped about the chamber by threads of Air and Earth and stirred up by the unceasing slap of feet and dead bodies.

She got to her feet and carved a path towards the six warriors clad in silver steel. The glow of their níthrals and the runes in their armour shimmered in the dust, a beacon calling to her.

Farwen turned aside the swipe of a blade, then opened the wielder's throat with a backswing, shouting to Thacia and Moras. "None of us fall to a níthral, no matter what, understood?"

Thacia moved past her, shards of broken earth swirling about the Jotnar. "Do what needs to be done, sister."

Moras grabbed a Lorian mage's throat and slammed them down against the ground, splitting their skull, bone and blood smearing the stone. Every soldier that dared come close was sent to Achyron's halls as the three Rakina fought like demons.

The three of them fell upon the closest of the six rune-marked creatures. The monstrous warrior was almost as tall as Thacia and Moras and far broader with shoulders clad in silver plate.

Thacia blocked the first swing of the warrior's níthral with a thread of Air, holding it in place. As she did, Moras formed a spear of stone in his hand, threads of Earth, Air, and Fire pulling the rubble from the ground. He drove the spear through the warrior's chest, not letting up until it burst out the other side. And still the man did not fall.

This was no mortal creature.

The runes in its armour glowed with a furious light. It reached out a hand and pulled Moras through the air with threads unseen. The creature relinquished its níthral, only for Farwen to see the crimson light once again coming to life as it thrust its fist towards Moras's chest.

Farwen surged forwards. She knew her blade had no chance of piercing the creature's seamless armour, so instead she dropped it and grabbed hold of the creature's arm and dragged it down, the crimson blade scorching into the stone below.

Holding the blade arm down, Farwen reached within herself and pushed threads of Earth and Fire into the stone below the creature's feet. She moulded a spike as fine as a needle and pulled it upwards with all her strength, letting it widen as it moved.

The spike ripped through the creature's groin, into its stomach, then chest, before finally bursting out through that gleaming silver helmet, blood sluicing over the steel. Its arm went limp, and Farwen staggered backwards, the drain sapping the energy from her bones. She had already used so much holding the Lorians from the gates. The broken shards of her soul were aflame.

The rune-marked armour melted away, leaving the pale-skinned body of a young man, eyes black as a Fade's, flesh marked by deep-gouged runes into which the metal flowed. These *'things'* were human after all… and yet, they were not.

She turned her head to see Moras's feet hitting the ground, her lips curling in a fragile smile. A crimson light shimmered and Moras's head was cleaved from his shoulders, his soul shorn from the world. The Jotnar's knees hit the ground, his skull a moment later, then his body collapsed.

One of the rune-marked creatures stood over Moras's limp body, níthral blazing in its fist.

A roar sounded behind Farwen as Thacia threw herself at the creature. Threads of each element whirled around her, lightning crackling over her fists. The Jotnar slammed a fist into the creature's side, sparks flying, energy pulsing. The impact sent a web of cracks through the pristine plate, and the creature staggered backwards. Thacia roared again, this time smashing her fist into the creature's chest, sending more cracks shivering through the steel.

Farwen pushed down the pain that burned within her and joined Thacia. As the creature made to hack its níthral down into her collar, Farwen held its arm in place with threads of Air, fire igniting in her veins.

Thacia took advantage of the creature's immobilisation to grab hold of its helmet and unleash a surge of lightning so powerful the force of it rippled through Farwen. The Jotnar roared as sparks flickered around her hands, blue and white light sparkling in the shifting dust.

Farwen held the creature in place, her bones aching, soul screaming. Its silver helm began to glow a bright red. In a matter of moments, the helmet collapsed into globs of molten steel, smoke billowing into the air as the flesh beneath burned. And for the briefest of seconds, Farwen saw the soul beneath. It was a woman, her eyes deep and black, her face marked by runes. And then her flesh was slopping from her bones, lightning crackling, molten metal searing down to her bones.

She dropped to the ground, the armour already slithering back into the runes in her skin. A flash of motion signalled to Thacia's left, and Farwen leapt forwards. She grabbed the shaft of the spear before it pierced Thacia's back and drove the tip into the ground. Farwen threw her elbow back into the Lorian soldier's nose, rewarded with a *crunch* and a burst of blood. She whipped the spear around, the steel tip carving through the soldier's cheek and the bridge of his nose, his helmet lost somewhere in the chaos. As he flailed, Farwen stabbed the spear into his throat and turned back.

She pressed her back to Thacia's as more Lorian soldiers swarmed around them. Here and there, as the dust settled, she could see clutches of rebels holding their ground, shields and spears raised. But the Lorian numbers were too great, and the Battlemages simply carved paths before them, paths paved with blood and bone.

"Det er ata haydria na daui nai din siel, Farwen, davitir un Yanwë," Thacia said, the power of the Spark pulsing from her.

It is an honour to die by your side, Farwen, daughter of Yanwë.

"Ar det harys von myialí na solian nai diar," Farwen answered, gripping the spear shaft with both hands. "Draleid n'aldryr, myia yíar."

And it has been mine to live by yours. Dragonbound by fire, my friend.

"Rakina nai dauva."

The Lorian soldiers fell upon them like a flood. Farwen moved with every shred of strength in her body, twisting away from spear strikes and the swing of swords, pulling deeper and deeper on the Spark. Every second she lived was a second bought for Coren, for the one who had been her anchor, her pillar, her star. For the one who had pieced her soul back together when Syndril had been ripped from her. She owed Coren an eternity, but she could give her a few minutes. That would be enough. It had to be.

A burning sensation ignited in her side as a spear caught her, slicing through leather and flesh. She rammed the butt of her own spear into the wielder's jaw and sent them sprawling before opening the throats of two others and jabbing the tip into the fallen man's heart.

The drain pulled at her, and her legs begged her to stop, to lie down and die. She pulled the spear free of the man's chest, only for a sword to arc downwards and carve through her left forearm. She roared and reeled backwards, attempting to move fingers that were no longer attached.

Farwen found the sword's wielder and drove the spear through his cheek and up into his skull, yanking it free with her remaining hand and turning to call out for Thacia.

The Jotnar knelt in the dirt, two spears through her gut, one in her leg.

One of those silver-clad monsters stood over her, Soulblade igniting, arm poised to strike.

"I denír viël ar altinua," Farwen whispered. *In this life and always.* She pulled her arm back and launched the spear.

And for a brief moment, when the spearhead sliced into Thacia's back and then her heart, Farwen felt a shred of peace within her. The Jotnar collapsed on her side before the creature's níthral fell. Thacia would find warmth in Myrax's soul once more. That was the smallest of gifts Farwen could give her.

Farwen let out a grunt as pain flared through her, and she looked down to see the tip of a spear jutting from her belly. She dropped to her knees, drawing in rasping breaths. She closed her eyes and opened herself fully to the Spark, drawing more than she ever had in her existence. Her blood ignited, her bones screaming in agony as the power of the Spark flowed through her like lightning. And still she drew more. Her soul was broken and shattered. She was half of what she had ever been. But she was still a Draleid, and she would give everything she had left.

A dull pain throbbed in her back, more steel piercing her flesh.

As she pulled on each elemental strand, as the raw energy of the Spark burned through her and her eyes filled with a white light, Farwen heard a dragon's roar. It was a beautiful thing, as it always was.

She heard Syndril calling to her, felt his strength in her sundered soul. A dragon did not die quietly, and neither would she.

"Laël sanyin det panthar mír tiélahar," Farwen whispered. *I'm sorry it took me so long.*

Syndril roared in her mind, and Farwen gave one last push. The Spark burned through her, erupting in a blinding light. Every moment was pain and agony, and she cared little. The ground shook beneath her, and screams rang out in the periphery of her mind.

And finally, she rested.

CHAPTER EIGHTY-ONE

TRIAL OF WILL

22nd Day of the Blood Moon

Firnin Mountains – Winter, Year 3081 After Doom

alen looked through Valerys's eyes as the dragon carved a path of fire and fury through the Lorian ranks. The flames consumed everything they touched, the sheer force tearing chunks of earth from the ground, the power flooding Calen's veins.

To his right, Tivar sat astride Avandeer, the dragon soaring with her wings wide, mimicking Valerys's every movement, her fire blazing like the sun.

Arrows flitted past in waves, but none could touch Valerys's scales. The dragon streaked across the sky with the speed of a shooting star, twisting and turning. Calen had never felt him move so freely. Having Avandeer and Varthear by his side had untethered something within Valerys, a fear, an uncertainty. Streaks of lightning ripped upwards from mages below, but Tivar and Calen cut through the threads of any that came close. And wherever lightning rose, Varthear fell.

The dragon had lost her fire when Ilmirín died, but her fury remained. She crashed down atop the Lorian mages, tearing flesh and bone with her obsidian talons and slicing bodies in half with sweeps of her tail. Before the Lorians had a fraction of a moment to understand how and why they were dying, the dragon had already lifted herself into the air, readying for her next strike.

Valerys banked right hard, and Calen shifted in position, pressing himself low. Avandeer and Varthear fell in beside them, moving in perfect unity. They dropped low and angled towards the long mountain path that stretched towards the gates. The path would not even have been visible were it not for the river of Lorian soldiers that flowed upwards from the base of the mountain, all black leather and polished steel.

"Aldryr ar orimyn," Calen whispered, letting his mind drift into Valerys's. *Fire and fury.*

The dragon answered with a deep rumble and a crack of his wings. Valerys surged forwards, then dove, sweeping upwards only as he came to the foot of the mountain. Pressure built in their joined soul, burning through them, and Calen pulled on threads of Fire and Spirit. Lungs swelled with air, and dragonfire raged. Valerys swept left and right, flames pouring from his jaws. The path was long and winding, and Valerys flew at such speeds that the turns were impossible to match, and still hundreds burned. Sparkwards burst to life, spreading like spheres of glass over the soldiers below, flames washing over them. Those within were granted sanctuary from the fury of dragons, but those left exposed were turned to ash and dust as Avandeer wound along Valerys's path. They had not yet reached the gates when an enormous pulse of the Spark rippled outwards and an explosion shook the mountain. A blinding light burst from the cave mouth where the Lorian forces fought, chunks of rock soaring through the air and crashing down the mountainside.

Shouts and cries rose up from the Lorian forces as the cave collapsed and rocks crushed hundreds. Valerys swerved right to avoid a piece of debris as large as a horse. The dragon angled his wings and rose along the rock face, lifting towards the clouds.

He let out a roar, then swept back down the mountainside. He stayed close to the rock face, moving at such speed Calen had to bury his head in the dragon's scales, the air dragging at him.

Valerys angled his wings and swept outwards, a weightless feeling settling in Calen's stomach. The dragon soared across the plains towards the bulk of the Lorian forces and once more rained dragonfire down atop them before flying just low enough to slice three Varsundi Blackthorns in half with his tail and soaring up and away.

"What was that?" Calen roared at Tivar as Avandeer caught up to Valerys in the sky, his voice carried on threads of Air.

"A last stand," Tivar called back. "The Lorians must have found a way inside the mountain."

Through Valerys's eyes, Calen followed the long path of soldiers from the base of the mountain winding upwards towards the source of the explosion, where the Lorian forces were regrouping, everything around them burning, threads of Earth and Air clearing the debris. "We're too late."

"Not while souls within still breathe," Tivar called back. "There is only so much that can be done from dragonback. We need to get inside. I saw an oculus carved through the rock on the eastern—"

A fury rose within Valerys at Tivar's words, and he lurched and plummeted towards the ground. They would not be separated again. He would not allow it. Valerys spun as he unfurled his wings and raked dragonfire across the Lorian lines. Varthear followed, mimicking Valerys's movements. She crashed down into a column of Lorian soldiers, rending steel and bone with her talons and jaws, charging forwards before lifting into the air once more.

An arc of lightning streaked upwards, primed to tear into Varthear's wing before Calen erected a ward and redirected the lightning to the ground, tearing a contingent of Lorian soldiers to pieces.

Valerys roared in answer to the Lorian lightning, the pressure surging through him as he once more opened his jaws and rained death from above.

"Valerys," Calen whispered as they rose again, "it doesn't matter how many we kill out here if they all die in there."

A deep growl reverberated in Valerys's chest, and he unleashed a mighty roar.

"We didn't fly here to let them die, Valerys. If the Lorians have broken through, then Tivar and I need to get inside and do whatever we can."

Memories flooded from Valerys to Calen. Memories of Drifaien, the loneliness, the agony, the helplessness. Memories from the dungeons in Berona and from Ilnaen, and from every moment they'd spent apart. Every time they were separated, Valerys's soul bled. He could not keep Calen safe if they were apart, and every time they were apart, darkness swallowed them.

Calen leaned forwards and closed his eyes, resting his hands against Valerys's scales. "It is our purpose, Valerys. To fight, to save whomever we can. It is the reason we found each other. Ella and Therin are inside. Will you let them die? Or will you give the Lorians fire and fury while I fight within the mountain?" Calen drew a breath and pressed his helmet against Valerys's neck. It had often been the dragon who had given *him* warmth, Valerys who had filled the cracks in Calen. Now, it was Calen's turn to do the same. "Lumisín viel, viel ayar. I denír viël ar altinua. La'uva umirís tiastri du."

Wherever we are, we are one. In this life and always. I will never leave you.

Valerys unleashed another roar in answer, rage and fury surging through him. He swooped back across the battlefield, raking fire in his path as he went. The dragon angled his wings and swept upwards, tearing through the skies towards the mountain, Avandeer and Varthear in his wake.

Valerys soared around the eastern rock face of the Firnin Mountains, and Calen spotted the circular opening Tivar had spoken of, set into the top of a flat peak thousands of feet from the ground. It was barely five or six feet across.

The dragon swept forwards and alighted on the rock, Calen sliding from his back. Both Avandeer and Varthear landed to Valerys's left, Tivar dismounting and walking towards Calen.

"Their mages are learning to shield in groups," Tivar said as she approached. "But if the dragons can keep them occupied, wreak as much havoc as possible, then at the least we can find a way to get the others out. We need to move quickly. The longer we take, the more likely it is that Eltoar and the others will come. I saw beacons lit on one of the far hills. We get in. Save who we can. Get out. If the dragons can cause enough damage to the Lorian armies, they will be in no shape to pursue any rebels."

Calen inclined his head to Tivar before looking back to Valerys. "Myia nithír til diar, Valerys. Anataier aldryr ar orimyn."

My soul to yours, Valerys. Give them fire and fury.

The dragon let out a low rumble and pressed the side of his snout into Calen's chest. A wave of emotions flowed from Valerys's mind to Calen's, a rush of images and memories, all telling Calen one thing: protect the bond.

"Altinua," Calen whispered. *Always.*

The three dragons lifted towards the sky, wind swirling as they cracked their wings.

"Together," Tivar said, walking towards the edge of the circular opening in the rock.

"Together."

Calen drew a long breath, then dropped into the opening and wrapped himself in threads of Air. He exhaled slowly as he fell. Just before his feet touched the ground, he drove the threads downwards, cracks spreading out as his feet touched the rock. Tivar landed beside him less than a heartbeat later, light as a feather.

About them, rebels armed with swords and spears fought back a clutch of Lorians in red and black leather, the thrum of the Spark in the air.

Calen sprang forwards, reaching out with threads of Air as he did, wrapping them around the Lorian Battlemage who stood closest to him and pulling. As the man hurtled through the air towards him, Calen pulled on each elemental strand and summoned his níthral, a bright purple light bursting from his fist. With the blade forming in his fist, he swung and cleaved the man in half across the navel. The two pieces dropped to the ground, innards spilling into the dirt.

Valerys roared in Calen's mind as Calen kept moving, bounding over a corpse and cutting a second Lorian down before the woman had a chance to turn. A third charged him, but he caught the blow high while focusing a sphere of Air into his left hand and slamming it into the Lorian's chest. He could feel the soldier's ribs shatter with the force as the body soared backwards almost twenty feet.

Most of the Lorians had turned to face him and Tivar now. A pulse of the Spark sent a tingle down his spine, and Calen wove threads of Spirit, Fire, and Air together just in time to form a Sparkward. The lightning crashed against Calen's ward, breaking over its surface. Just as Calen had done when training with the others in Aravell, he pulsed Spirit through the ward and sent the Lorian hurtling back into the wall behind him.

Calen took the opportunity to close the distance between them. He drew his sword as the Battlemage recovered and surged forwards, steel in his fist. The first swing came at Calen's left thigh. He fell into the svidarya, his muscles acting on reflex. The second swing was a downstroke at Calen's skull. Calen blocked the strike and swept it left. As he twisted to make the killing blow, a fine thread of Air slammed into the Lorian's neck and snapped it clean, his eyes rolling to the back of his head as he collapsed.

Tivar pulled her sword from a Lorian chest, one hand outstretched towards Calen. The blood dripped from the steel as she approached, eyes scanning their surroundings.

They stood in a massive circular chamber, sparring pits set about the central area, chairs and benches lining the outer rim.

Men and woman of all ages stood staring, spears, swords, and axes clutched in their hands. It took one glance for Calen to see that these were hard people but not soldiers. They were garbed in mismatched patches of leather over tunics, covered in crusted-in dirt, blood and sweat marring their faces.

Two men and a woman approached, a tension in the way they moved, their eyes flitting from Calen to Tivar.

After a moment, the woman stepped forwards, pressed a fist to her chest, and bowed. "Warden of Varyn, thank the gods."

Across the chamber, others whispered the same thing. That damned name.

The woman was barely older than he was, her hair matted with blood.

"Are you all right?"

She nodded, swallowing hard. "They killed Tomas and Ferol, Mattea is injured. But the rest can keep fighting."

"What is your name?"

"Yandira, Warden."

"I am Calen Bryer, and this is Tivar Savinír," he said, gesturing towards Tivar, who stared at the ground, her sword returned to its scabbard. "Where are the others, Yandira? Farwen and Coren? What is the situation?"

"At the gates, I think. The Lorians broke through the scout tunnels. We were stationed here to watch over the children and the injured." Yandira motioned towards a low wall built from upturned boxes at the far side of the chamber.

Men and women lay on shoddy cots, wounds wrapped in bandages, limbs missing. Calen couldn't see any children, but he could hear their whimpers.

"If the soldiers get in behind the others… they won't stand a chance."

Calen nodded. "Is there a safe way out of the mountain?"

"There's a sally port near the armoury," one of the men said, stepping forwards. "That is where we're to go if Tarhelm is breached."

"Go. And gather anyone you see along the way. Tarhelm is lost but the people are not. We will cover your escape and ensure the Lorians have no desire to pursue. We will need one of you to guide us to the gates."

"I will go." Yandira stood tall and proud, her back straight, but Calen could see the fear in her eyes. "It would be my honour, Warden."

"The honour is mine." Calen gave the woman the slightest of bows, resting a hand on the pommel of his sword as he did. "Please, lead the way."

When they reached the tunnel mouth that led from the chamber, Calen stopped and turned back, searching for the man who had spoken of the sally port. He found him leading one of the injured rebels. "Keep them safe," Calen said, looking around at the others. "That is your task now. Get these people to the sally port. Don't look back."

"What do we do when we get there?"

"Get free of the mountain and find the nearest safe place. If nobody follows you through by the break of the next day, find shelter." Calen rested a hand on the man's shoulder. "We will not abandon you, I swear it."

Several men and women stepped forwards, hefting shields and spears, cold iron in their eyes.

"We will not fail you, Warden," a tall man said, shoulders broad, his left ear a bloody stump. He looked to be as old as Vars had been when he'd died.

"Nor I you."

Calen pressed a gauntleted hand to his breastplate, inclined his head, then turned and followed Yandira through the tunnel.

"You speak well," Tivar said as they entered the tunnel.

"I said what I needed to," Calen answered. His memories shifted to Kollna and Tarast, to their last moments, to the fire in their hearts, to their sense of purpose – his purpose. "We must be the light they look to. Nothing less." He turned to Yandira. "Lead the way."

RIST FOLLOWED GARRAMON THROUGH THE never-ending web of tunnels and chambers, Neera and Magnus at his side, Kalder and Lakrin trailing at the rear, the three hundred or so surviving soldiers in between them.

The four Chosen moved with them, never so much as uttering a word, the runes in their silver armour illuminating any shadow that dared stretch across the rock.

Garramon had found a sealed tunnel almost a mile further up the mountain, and they'd smashed through with the Spark. They lost quite a few of their number to the rebels on the other side.

They had not been long through the tunnel when a massive explosion shook the mountain, waves of the Spark rippling through the rock. Murmurs spread through the soldiers.

"What in the ever-loving fuck was that?" Magnus asked, looking about as dust and small chips of rocks fell from the ceiling.

"Nothing good," Garramon said. "But we need to keep moving."

As they went, the Chosen cut down any rebels that dared cross their path. The creatures had no hesitation within them, nor any mercy. Not that Rist expected mercy at a time like this, but their brutality unsettled him.

A few moments after they'd stepped into another chamber, cries rang out and arrows sliced through the air. One burst through Lakrin's hand, and Rist skidded to a stop, turning just in time to see another arrow punch into a soldier's neck, blood spraying in a plume.

"Rist!" Neera's voice was like a clap of distant thunder, echoing in Rist's mind as one of the Chosen threw itself in front of him, a pillar of fire spraying over its back. Those crimson eyes stared down at Rist, the flames causing the silver armour to burn with an incandescent glow.

The moment the flames faltered, the creature spun on its heels, the runes in its armour glowing, a pulse of Essence thrumming from it.

A man soared through the air, eyes wild, threads of Spirit and Fire whirling about him. The Chosen snatched him from the air, steel-clad fingers wrapping around his throat, and in that same instant snapped his neck with one flick of its wrist.

Rist stared at the body as it dropped, snapped bone protruding from the man's neck, his eyes vacant.

Dirt crunched to his left, followed by a shout. Rist's instincts took hold. He turned to meet a charging man clad in a tunic and breeches, sword raised above his head. Rist lunged forwards and wrapped the fingers of his left hand around the man's sword wrist, smashing his right elbow into the man's jaw. He slid his hand down and grabbed the hilt of the sword as the rebel's fingers slackened.

In a practiced motion from form five, movement nine, Rist ripped the sword free, shifted it into reverse grip, then drove it backwards past his left hip. He felt the blade bite on the leather, then felt the release as it slid through and into the flesh.

He pulled the sword free and let go of the hilt, the steel clanging. In less than a breath, he *felt* the man die, the gemstone beneath his breastplate pulsing. As it had before, a voice whispered in Rist's mind, not begging, but demanding he harness the Essence before it evaporated and was lost.

The voice was a tangible thing. *"You need it to keep them safe,"* it whispered. *"Take it."*

His throat tightened, his lungs seeming starved for air as he resisted the urge. It was like a hunger within him, and that terrified every part of Rist.

"No," he whispered back, setting his will in iron. The Essence faded, and the sounds of the world around him flooded his ears once more. He'd not even realised they'd gone. When Rist turned back to the others, the remaining rebels were dead, nothing but corpses in the dirt.

To him it had seemed the world had stopped, but nobody else looked to have even noticed. Nobody except Neera. She looked at him in only the way that she could, her eyes asking questions without words.

He nodded and looked back down at the dead man before turning to follow Garramon and the others into the next tunnel. A hand grabbed his shoulder and spun him.

One of the Chosen stood over Rist – the one who had saved him, he thought.

"Thank you," Rist said, looking up at the armoured giant.

"Does your faith falter?" There would never be a time when the eerie layered voices of the Chosen didn't set Rist's hair on end.

Rist didn't answer. The truth was pointless here. This was a creature of Efialtír, and he didn't think there would be much room for nuance.

The Chosen let out a long breath beneath its steel helmet, stared at him for a moment longer, then turned and walked towards the tunnel mouth.

Shouts erupted from the tunnel. "Forward!"

Rist looked to Neera, and the pair broke into a sprint, the straggling soldiers doing the same. They charged through the tunnel and emerged onto a platform that dropped down into an enormous cavern that stretched for hundreds of feet in all directions, buildings of brown stone rising all about. Rebels and Lorian soldiers alike were hacking each other to pieces in the narrow streets and atop the rooves, threads of each elemental strand whirling in the air.

Garramon and Magnus fought at the bottom of the stairs that led from the platform, rebels swarming around them, archers atop rooves loosing volley after volley. As the soldiers rushed past, Rist stopped for a moment, catching sight of something on a ledge above.

A man stood with his hands behind his back, watching over the fighting with the calm of a statue. Two women stood with him. The man tilted his head and stared directly at Rist, and Rist could have sworn a smile crept across his face.

The sound of clashing steel pulled Rist's attention back to the fighting. He opened himself to the Spark, pulled his sword from its scabbard, and charged down the stairs.

THE PURPLE LIGHT OF THE runes in Calen's armour shone against the smooth rock of the tunnels as Yandira guided him and Tivar through the maze within the mountain. There must have been hundreds of tunnels twisting in every direction, some climbing, others sloping down, shafts of light carved into their walls.

"How can you possibly find your way in here?" Calen said as they passed through a small chamber that branched off in six directions.

"I've been here for eleven years." Yandira didn't even break stride as she turned left and entered the third tunnel. She'd not looked much older than he. Had she truly been living in this place at only thirteen or fourteen summers? "Farwen and Coren built it this way on purpose. It meant that even if the imperials did get inside, we would still have an advantage."

The mountain shook, and Yandira stumbled, catching herself against the smooth wall. Tivar looked to him. He could feel the Spark pulsing through the rock. There was no doubt that Lorian mages were now within the mountain in large numbers.

Even with Kaygan and Fenryr at their side, there was little chance they could actually win this battle now. Gods they might be, but Calen had seen nothing of what they could do in battle. Either way, Aeson had taught him that sometimes winning meant surviving. He needed to find Ella and the others, needed to get as many people to safety as he could. That was victory.

He let his mind drift into Valerys's, let their hearts beat together. The dragon swept around the face of the mountain, twirled in the air as lightning streaked past, then dropped and poured fire over a force of Lorian cavalry that were moving around the foot of the mountain.

The horses split and scattered, only for Avandeer to drop low across them and set the ground alight, Varthear plunging through the flames to rip four of the mounted warriors to pieces with her talons. The three dragons soared back over the plains below, fires raging amidst the Lorian ranks. In the distance, through Valerys's eyes, he saw the army's tents and wagons. Valerys let out a roar and cracked his wings, surging forwards. No matter what happened within the mountain, these Lorians would pay for coming here. And without their supplies, they would not be hunting down any survivors.

Another quake shook the rock, and this time the pulse of the Spark was closer. Calen could feel it thrumming in the air. He pulled on threads of Air and Spirit, following the drift as Falmin had taught him. Sounds vibrated through the threads: clattering steel, screams, crackling fire.

"What's that way?" Calen asked, pointing to a tunnel on the opposite side of the chamber they'd just entered. He noticed a small green circle marked onto the rock.

"Many things," Yandira said, stopping. She licked her lips in thought. "The mushroom cellars, the grain stores, a section of living quarters…" She pointed towards a tunnel mouth on the right side of the cavern with a small orange square marked onto the rock beside it. "The gates are that way."

More screams vibrated along Calen's threads of Air, more pulses of the Spark thrumming. Something else called to him, something he could not explain… something familiar. It echoed in the Spark, like a shadow of a memory. He moved towards that echo, drawing his sword. "We go this way."

Neither Yandira nor Tivar argued, the latter sliding her sword from its scabbard.

Calen followed the shouts and screams, his feet pounding against the rock, his heart thumping, that familiar echo pulling at him. He stepped through into a new chamber, where rebels were gathering and readying themselves to enter the fray. Fifty or so, no more. "Fall back to the sally port!"

For a moment, they looked at him dumbstruck, then eyes widened and whispers spread.

He ignored them and looked to Yandira. "Get them to the sally port. Gather any you find along the way."

Calen didn't wait for her reply. He charged through the tunnel on the opposite side, releasing the threads of Air and Spirit, the clash of steel and shouts of battle carrying on their own now.

Tivar matched him stride for stride, her gaze forward.

The tunnel opened up to a ledge that overlooked an enormous cavern filled with rock-hewn buildings that rose two and three storeys. The fighting raged across the cavern, rebels loosing arrows from high ledges and rooves while others fought in the streets against Lorian soldiers. The rebels outnumbered the Lorians three to one at least, but the Battlemages were quickly evening out that discrepancy. In his periphery Calen caught the glimmer of red runes in silver steel, and he watched as one of the Chosen brought its crimson níthral down atop a man's head and split him from skull to groin, the two halves slopping to the ground.

"I'm with you," Tivar said, looking down at the pitched fighting below. She slid her sword into her scabbard and extended her arm. Calen felt her open to the Spark, threads of each elemental strand swirling around her. A moment passed, and then a sword of gleaming yellow light formed in her hand. Tivar let out a shivering sigh, staring down at the níthral in awe. "For almost four centuries, I was lost… and my níthral had ignored my call. Until you gave me purpose once more. I am yours."

"Uthikar, vésani," Calen said, turning back towards the fighting, his purple níthral igniting in his fist. *Together, sister.*

Pulling in threads of Air, Calen leapt from the ledge. He hit the ground hard, not softening his landing any more than he needed to.

The Lorian soldiers around him hesitated for just a moment. That was all he needed.

Calen swept forwards, dropping into Striking Dragon and allowing the svidarya to flow through him, the light of his níthral glowing across the rock. He cut down two men in red and black leather in quick succession. The third blocked his first swing in a burst of purple light, but the impact staggered him backwards and he tripped over a corpse. Calen was upon him in moments. He stared down into the Lorian's fear-filled eyes, steeled himself, then watched the man's light go out as he drove his níthral into his chest.

"To us!" Calen called out, moving through the forms of svidarya, carving the Lorians apart.

Tivar surged past, her níthral shimmering with yellow light as she sliced through a Lorian chest, then spun on her heels and extended a hand, threads of Air snapping outwards.

Calen turned to see a spear curve in the air and whip past his head, the blade grazing the side of his helmet with a rasping scrape. Within a heartbeat, Tivar had already wrapped the threads of Air around the soldier who had thrown the spear, his bones snapping in spurts of blood. As she moved to stand by Calen's side, the rebels rallied to them, snatching up dropped Lorian shields.

Lorian soldiers flooded from the side streets, and Calen could feel the Spark pulsing within their numbers.

Murmurs spread through the rebels about Calen, followed by shouts and pointed fingers as a Chosen leapt from a rooftop above, silver armour glinting in the light that poured through the thin shafts in the rock. The ground shook beneath Calen's feet as the Chosen crashed down, cracks spreading beneath its armoured boots.

The Chosen stood to its full height, towering over the Lorian soldiers, a burning red níthral forming in its hand. It charged, roaring in a voice that made Calen's skin crawl, "For The Saviour!"

The soldiers roared in response, clattering swords against shields, and charged after the monstrosity in silver plate.

"Stay together," Tivar called, the Spark crackling around her, níthral gleaming. "Today is not the day we die."

Calen's heart thumped against his ribs as the Chosen drew closer, its runes blazing.

"For those we've lost," Calen said, steadying himself. He reached out to Valerys, their minds blending. In the skies above the mountain, Valerys roared, and the dragon's strength flowed into Calen. Fire burned in his veins, and lightning crackled over his skin. This was his purpose. This was what it meant to be a Draleid, to be a guardian, to be a warrior. "With me!"

He broke into a charge, not needing to look to know that Tivar and the rebels charged alongside him.

The Chosen swung its crimson blade in a wide arc, trying to cleave Calen's head from his body. Calen fell into Howling Wolf, sliding beneath the glowing blade. As he twisted and struck down at the creature's knee, it threw its arm back and blocked the strike in a flash of purple and red.

Tivar lunged from the front, thrusting her níthral at the creature's gut. It twisted to avoid the blade.

Calen released his níthral and pushed threads of Fire and Spirit into his hand, lightning crackling over his gauntlet. He rammed his fist into the creature's side, sending cracks through the armour. It cried out in a twisted howl.

Again, Calen felt Tarast moving through him, the memories of a life once lived flashing across his mind.

The Chosen swung its blade where Calen's head had been only a heartbeat before, but Calen had dropped low and stepped right, Valerys roaring, their shared soul burning with a bright fury. His níthral burst to life in his fist, and he thrust it deep into the Chosen's chest as Tivar carved through its arm.

"Svidír i'il aldryrín un'il rastikar, Vitharnmír!" Calen roared as the níthral carved through steel and flesh, the runes in the Chosen's armour blazing with a blinding light. He had not intended to speak the words. They had simply flowed through him as though spoken by another. Burn in the fires of the void, Vitharnmír!

The rebels and Lorians crashed in around them, the clash of steel on steel echoing.

Calen pulled his níthral free, the Chosen's armour slithering back into the runes on its flesh as the body dropped to the floor.

"For Epheria," he roared, a fervour in his heart. "For freedom!"

Valerys's fury burned within him as he cut through the Lorians, his níthral shimmering, lightning crackling over his fist. He blocked a swing of Lorian steel overhead, ran his níthral up the blade, twisted his wrist at the top, then pushed the blade down before pivoting and carving open the Lorian's chest before him.

As the body dropped, Calen extended his hand and unleashed a maelstrom of death, lightning tearing holes through Lorian bodies and crashing into the rock beneath. The drain sapped at him, but as it did, Valerys roared from the sky outside and pushed his strength through the bond.

A pulse of the Spark surged outwards from within the Lorian numbers, and whips of Fire and Air streaked towards him.

The flames flickered and died before touching Calen's flesh as Tivar sliced through them with threads of Spirit.

"Mage," Tivar shouted, pointing her níthral towards a man rushing at them, black cloak billowing behind him, flames wreathing both hands.

A burst of crimson light ignited to the left, and a hulking man bounded forwards, a dense black beard covering his face, a shimmering níthral in his hand, his other arm cleaved just below the shoulder. A second mage joined him, the Spark pulsing.

"Uthikar," Calen shouted, moving to stand next to Tivar.

Together.

RIST BROUGHT HIS SWORD UP across his body, blocking the swing of the rebel blade. He sent a sphere of air into the man's chest, lifting him off his feet and slamming him into the brown stone wall at his back. He twisted at the waist, avoiding the stab of a spear while an arrow skittered off his helmet, then brought his blade back up the shaft, opening his attacker's face from the cheek through to the back of the skull. Essence pulsed all around him, and the gemstone hanging from his neck urged him to tap into its power, to give himself strength, to protect those he cared for, those he loved.

Neera and Garramon fought beside him, threads of Air, Fire, and Spirit whipping about them. The rebels had outnumbered them easily, but they were no match for the more heavily armoured soldiers. And the superior might of the Battlemages and Chosen had forced the rebels back, their numbers dwindling. He did not need the Essence.

Two parts of himself warred: the part that grew bold at watching those who had attacked Berona crumble and break, and the part that was horrified by the blood that poured onto the rock. But as the blood spilled, a sense of resolution set into him, and the former burned brighter than the latter. These rebels had murdered so many in Berona. Memories of the attack flashed across Rist's mind. Memories of the flames and the charred corpses, of that woman's blistered and burnt face, of her screams. These monsters had waited for the Healers to come, drawn them in, then set them all on fire again.

They had set their fate that day. This war needed to end, and it would end here in this mountain.

Rist pushed forwards, flowing through the movements he had spent countless hours memorising, his blade an extension of himself. He whipped threads of Air around his body, deflecting strikes as they came.

Shouts rang out, echoing in the enormous cavern. "It's the Warden of Varyn!"

Every hair on Rist's body pricked up. The Draleid was here, in this cavern. The one who all the soldiers talked of, the one who had set the entire city of Kingspass ablaze.

Ripples of the Spark surged in the air, and a sudden realisation came to Rist. "Where's Magnus?"

"What?" Garramon had been looking in the direction of the shouts.

"Magnus…" Rist scanned the street. The last of the rebels were falling, bodies littering the rock. He spotted Lakrin nearby. The mage was limping but alive. "Kalder and Magnus. They're not here."

More shouts echoed, sharper.

Both Rist and Garramon broke into a run, Neera following. Rist's heart had never beat so quickly, its thumps drowning out all other sounds in his ears. He rounded the corner of the nearest structure to see the fighting was far from over.

Soldiers and rebels tore pieces from each other, screams and clattering steel drumming in the back of Rist's mind.

His heart stopped in his chest when his gaze fell to the centre of it all. A purple nithral jutted from a man's back, the black cloak of a Battlemage knotted at their shoulders. The glowing light vanished as the blade was pulled back through, and the body dropped. Both relief and shame touched Rist's soul when he saw Kalder's face staring back at him with dead eyes. It wasn't Magnus.

The man who stood over Kalder's body was garbed entirely in blood-stained white steel plate marked with glowing purple runes. Golden leaves and vines were worked delicately into the breast in a pattern that struck Rist's mind… He knew it from somewhere. He could see it in his mind.

Rist understood why the Draleid had earned the name 'Warden of Varyn'. Even his eyes shimmered with a purple light, a luminescent mist drifting upwards. The man looked like the champion of a god.

Another warrior fought alongside him, but this one wore the same armour as Eltoar Daethana and the Dragonguard, except the sigil of the black flame had been carved from the breast.

Had one of them defected? Rist had watched what those elven Draleid had done at the Three Sisters, he'd seen Eltoar and the other Dragonguard's strength. There was no way they could stand against two of them.

In a blur of motion, the Draleid spun, his purple níthral crashing against another formed from a deep crimson light, sparks bursting.

Magnus.

Even with one arm, the man was a raging storm. He weaved between the two Draleid like a warrior half his size, turning away probing swords and spears from the surrounding rebels, the Spark pulsing from him.

Before Rist could think, his feet were moving, his fingers tightening around the hilt of his sword, his mind unconsciously reaching for the Spark. He would not let Magnus stand alone, no matter what. Both Garramon and Neera charged with him, the air thrumming with power.

CALEN SHIFTED FROM SVIDARYA TO valathír, then into fellensír and back again. The Burning Winds, the Frozen Soul, the Lonely Mountain, it mattered little. This Lorian Battlemage moved like a man possessed. Even with Tivar by his side, the beast of a man held his ground, the gemstone around his neck glittering with crimson light. Each swing of his blade fell like a hammer, and he moved with a speed no man should have. But Calen could see the lethargy creeping into his motions, the drain sapping at him, the light in the stone fading.

With each arc of lightning and whip of fire Calen smashed against the man's Sparkwards, with each thread he sliced, the mage grew weaker. No matter how strong this man was, he was no Draleid, and the well from which he drew was emptying.

Valerys's roar thundered in Calen's mind as the dragon once more swept over the battlefield below, raking fire across the Lorian remnants that had not fled into the mountain for cover or routed in all directions.

Calen drew a breath and pulled Valerys's strength into his. With the dragon's fury burning in his veins, he unleashed an unrelenting stream of lightning. The arcs of blue light smashed against an unseen shield, breaking like waves against a cliff. Calen roared as Valerys did, the dragon's power flowing through him.

The mage pushed out his left hand and sent a concussive wave slamming into Tivar. She careened backwards, crashing into a tangle of rebels and soldiers. Even still, Calen could feel the ward failing.

Something slammed into him hard, knocking the wind from his lungs and causing him to release his níthral. He barely had a chance to collect his thoughts when another mage charged at him, sword drawn.

Calen took a step back, his foot slamming into a mound of earth he'd sworn had not been there before. He twisted as he fell, forcing a thread of Air between himself and the ground. In that brief moment before he pushed himself back upright, he looked down at a spike jutting up from the rock barely a foot from his face. That had most definitely not been there.

Calen sent a pulse through the thread of Air and forced himself back to his feet, summoning his níthral in the same motion and blocking the swing of the mage's blade before it carved into his neck.

This man was different than the other, less fluid. Calen pushed onto the front foot, allowing the forms of the svidarya to flow through him. He struck high, meeting steel, then again, and again, pressing the man back.

He opened himself, waiting for the mage to strike, and when he did, Calen pounced, driving the tip of his níthral towards the man's gut.

Before the blade sliced into the mage's flesh, invisible coils wrapped around Calen, squeezing his body in a crunch.

Valerys's fury poured into him, liquid fire filling his veins, and he unleashed a pulse of Air that swept outwards in a wave of concussive force. The Blood Magic holding him in place evaporated, and he staggered forwards.

In a heartbeat, Tivar was at his side, and four mages pressed in around them. He could feel them probing with threads of Air and Spirit, see the gemstones around their necks glowing. Calen settled himself into fellensír, and just as he did, Valerys's mind crashed into his, urgent, panicking, the dragon's vision supplanting his own.

Through Valerys's eyes, a section of clouds whirled inwards, strands of red light piercing the dense canopy like the first light of dawn. And through the whirl of clouds came an enormous head covered in black and crimson scales, jaws large enough to swallow a wagon whole, eyes of smouldering red. Neck and shoulders followed, dense and broad, then deep crimson wings.

The enormous black dragon burst from the clouds like a god breaking through the veil, unleashing a roar that forced the world itself to tremble. Two more dragons broke through the clouds after him, scales deep blue and muted red.

"Helios," Tivar whispered beside him. "They have come."

The four mages surged forwards, and Calen pulled his mind back to his own body, the sword forms flowing through him as effortlessly as his lungs drew in breath. Tivar moved with him, her níthral ignited.

This ended now.

The first mage lunged, and Calen stepped into the space between them. He feigned a swing of his níthral, then released it as the man made to block. Tivar swept past him and sliced her blade along the man's side, causing him to cry out and stumble. Calen dropped his hand down onto the mage's shoulder and grabbed tight. With Valerys roaring in his mind, Calen unleashed a wreath of fire from his palm over the man's helmet-clad face.

The mage screamed and let out an eruption of Spirit and Air, knocking Calen back. Calen anchored threads of Air into the rock and stopped himself from careening through the air.

Again he moved forwards, turning aside each blade as it came, slicing through threads with his own, Tivar always beside him. An arc of lightning ignited to his left, and she threw herself in front of it. The lightning crashed into Tivar's pauldron and sent her to the ground, a crack in her plate, but she was on her feet in heartbeats.

The one-armed Battlemage rushed him with that crimson nithral in his fist, but the man was exhausted now. The drain had pulled the energy from his bones. And while the mage struggled to carry on, Valerys's fire still burned with a fury.

Calen sidestepped the man's half-hearted lunge, then swept his nithral across his back. The light-wrought blade sliced through the steel and bit into flesh, and the mage collapsed, howling. Calen spun, turning away the swing of another blade and knocking it free from its wielder's hands. Valerys's rage burning in him, he pushed threads of earth into the mage's breastplate, and she unleashed a horrendous shriek.

In that moment, Calen felt a surge of the Spark like nothing he'd ever felt. It swept outwards, rippling through the air and crackling over his skin. The entire cavern shook, and chunks of rock broke free from the ceiling, followed by clouds of dust and a deep, aching groan that reverberated through the mountain.

His threads of Earth were severed, and threads of each elemental strand bored into him, searing through his very core, Valerys roaring. Calen pushed back, the runes on his armour blazing. He charged the mage who was trying to burn him out, his nithral igniting as he did.

Their blades collided in a burst of purple light. Calen moved from form to form, feinting high, then striking low, slicing his nithral along the mage's side. The man staggered, but the energy that pulsed in waves did not falter. Calen could still feel it burning within him. Still, the man was no match for him with a blade.

Calen turned away a strike to his left, twisted his wrist, then dragged his nithral across the mage's breastplate, slicing through the steel and coming a hair's breadth from opening the man's chest.

Keeping his momentum, he set his back foot and lunged forwards for the killing blow, only for something to crash into him like a battering ram. He careened backwards, the sound of breaking rocks filling his ears as his head spun and every bone in his body felt as though it were melting from the inside. He pressed a fist into the ground, the purple light of his eyes glowing against the rock, and pushed himself upright.

One of the Chosen stood over him, its helm gone, deep black eyes staring at him. But before the creature could move, a mage strode past it, eyes gleaming beneath his helmet with the same red light that shone from the gemstone around his neck.

Tendrils of Blood Magic slithered around Calen's body, holding him in place while threads of the Spark pushed into him, ripping at his soul. Behind the Chosen, Tivar did everything she could to reach him, but two more Chosen fell upon her, crimson blades sweeping.

The mage wrapped his hand around Calen's throat and lifted him to his feet with the aid of the dark magic.

Valerys roared and thrashed in Calen's mind, sweeping around the western ridge of the mountain as Helios and the other dragons descended towards the battlefield. Fear. Fury. Sorrow. Panic. Calen could not leave him alone. He could not. Valerys wouldn't allow it. They were the same soul. They were together always.

The mage pushed harder and harder, the Spark burning in Calen. With Valerys's strength, Calen pushed back, the Spark rippling outwards. More rocks fell from the ceiling, the mountain crying out. And somewhere in the back of Calen's mind he heard men and women shouting.

"It's coming down!" someone called. Rebels and soldiers alike began to break and flee while Tivar fought ceaselessly against the two Chosen, rebels rallying around her.

As a white light began to burn in Calen's eyes, he pushed each strand into his fist, summoning his níthral. No matter how powerful this mage was, a níthral to the heart would surely see him dead.

And then, as the purple light formed in his fist and illuminated the man's face through his helmet, Calen saw it. The man roared and the bonds of dark magic crushed Calen's bones, but Calen looked past the red light that glowed in the mage's eyes. He knew that face. He knew those eyes. Calen released his níthral. Gasping for air, he choked out one word. "Rist?"

The bonds loosened, the Spark pulled back, and the crimson light vanished from Rist's eyes. A moment passed, a moment of strange silence as though Calen stood in a dream, one that could never be real.

"Calen?"

Even as the fighting raged about them, the utterance of Calen's name had blocked his ears to all other sounds except Rist's voice. He staggered forwards a step, searching the eyes he had known his entire life. Calen's hands trembled, his lip quivering, his mind racing. "You're alive? You… Is it really you?"

Rist reached up and pulled the helmet from his head, his jaw slack. He looked different than what Calen remembered – his cheeks fuller, neck thicker – but it was still Rist.

"Your eyes," Rist whispered. For a moment, he seemed to disappear into his own thoughts, just as he had always done.

"Rist, what are you doing here?" Calen shook his head as he spoke. He'd not wanted to believe what Ella had said. That Rist had joined the Lorian Empire… It couldn't be true. "How could you? How could you join them? What are you?"

"What am I? What are you? You are the one who burned Kingspass to the ground? You are the one who has spread this rebellion? Do you know how many lives you have destroyed, Calen?" Rist pressed a hand to his ribs where Calen had sliced into him. "This can't be real… it can't be."

"They killed my parents, Rist. They destroyed everything… How could you?"

"I didn't have a choice!" Rist snapped back.

"You *always* have a choice, Rist. Always."

Something in Rist's expression shifted, and he straightened. "It can't be…" he whispered. "This can't be real…"

"Rist, your mam and dad are alive. They're safe. They tortured them, Rist, but I broke them free. I—" Threads of Air pulled the breath from Calen's lungs and wrapped around his throat, lifting him from the ground.

Through watering eyes, he saw another mage step up beside Rist, a hand pressed to the burnt flesh on his face. The power of the Spark that rippled from the man was immense.

"Garramon, let him go!" Rist roared. "Let him go!"

"We need to end this now!" the other man shouted. "If he dies here, so does the rebellion."

"Let him go!" Rist roared again, and a surge of the Spark erupted outwards, knocking the man from his feet. Calen dropped like a sack of stones, his knees slamming against the ground. More shards broke free from the ceiling above, and a thunderous crack ripped through the rock.

Calen lifted his gaze to see Rist standing over him. He grunted and hauled himself to his feet, looking up at the ceiling as the cracks spread. Before he could say a word, a flash of motion blurred past and Rist was gone.

Calen looked down to see Ella standing over Rist, Faenir at her side. One of the Chosen broke away from Tivar, only for a black and gold wolf as large as a wagon to leap from a rooftop, wrap its jaws around the Chosen's helmet, and slam it to the ground. The runes in the Chosen's armour blazed as the monstrous wolf tore its head from its shoulders. Calen could feel the call of the wolf howling in his mind, could feel Fenryr's pull.

The giant wolf surged towards the second Chosen, shifting as it did, bones twisting and snapping, forming into the broad man in black plate Calen knew. A gleaming golden axe took shape in Fenryr's hand, and he buried its wicked blade into the Chosen's chest, tearing it free as the creature collapsed.

The other Lorian mages stood together, the Spark rippling around them, the gemstones gleaming at their necks. The man with one arm lay in a heap on the ground, his chest rising and falling slowly. But within a heartbeat, Aneera and Diango were there as well, and so too were Kaygan, his two druids, Asius, Therin, a Narvonan woman with her sword drawn, and a number of rebels.

More rocks broke free from the ceiling and crashed down, one smashing through a nearby building, the other crushing two Lorian soldiers beneath it.

"This place is crumbling," Kaygan said, gesturing towards Una.

Una's eyes turned a milky white, and a portal opened beside her. Through it, Calen saw blue skies tinged with the red light of the moon.

"*Now*," Kaygan said firmly as rocks continued to rain down, one impacting the ground beside Fenryr.

Boud was the first one through, followed by the rebels. Ella stared down at Rist for a moment, snarling, then whispered something in his ear and rose. She grabbed Calen's arm and pulled him towards the portal. He shrugged her off, and she growled like a wolf and stormed through the open portal, Faenir with her.

Calen looked down at Rist and extended a hand. "Come with me."

Rist stared back at him, then at the two mages who stood over the man on the ground.

"Rist, please."

Another voice called out – the man whose face Calen had burned. He'd lifted the one-armed mage up and slid a hand behind his back. "Rist, it's coming down. We need to go!"

Rist looked from the mage to Calen and back to the woman with dark hair, her breastplate partially crumpled. A rock smashed down between Calen and Rist, and a hand rested on Calen's pauldron.

"He's made his choice," Fenryr said, a growl in his voice.

"No." Calen stepped forwards, another rock crashing to the ground beside him. "Rist!"

Rist just stood there, his head shaking slightly from right to left, his jaw slack, eyes wide.

A monstrous crack sounded overhead, and threads of Air burst outwards from Rist to seize a large chunk of rock before it landed atop the other mages. He whipped the threads sideways and sent the rock crashing into a wall.

"I can't leave them…" Rist said, looking back towards the other mages.

"Rist, you have to come with me… you have to…"

"I'm sorry." Rist stared into Calen's eyes. "I can't leave them, Calen. They need me… I will find you, I swear it."

Rist turned and ran to the Lorian mages, threads of Air whipping at falling rocks.

"No! Rist!"

Fenryr grabbed Calen's shoulder and pulled him backwards, but Calen pushed his hand away. "Rist!"

Rist slipped his arm around the unconscious mage, looking back over his shoulder as the group fled for the nearest tunnel mouth.

"Rist…"

Valerys roared in Calen's mind. Where Calen's heart was sorrow and loss, Valerys's was fury and wrath. Everything Ella had said was true. *"I didn't leave him, Calen. He stayed."*

Valerys's fury burned Calen's agony away, devouring it, their minds pulling together. Helios and the other two dragons had alighted on an open plain on the western side of the mountain, and there they remained while Valerys, Avandeer, and Varthear perched on a mountain cliff.

As Rist vanished in the rockfall, Fenryr grabbed Calen once more and pushed him through the portal.

CHAPTER EIGHTY-TWO

OUR DUTY ABOVE ALL

22nd Day of the Blood Moon

Firnin Mountains – Winter, Year 3081 After Doom

The moment Calen emerged through the other side of the portal, Valerys was in the air, Avandeer and Varthear close behind.

Calen looked back as the portal collapsed, the white light along its rim vanishing. Voices called around him, but all he could hear was the beating of his heart and Rist's voice. *"I can't leave them. I'm sorry."*

Rist was alive. All this time, he had been alive… and Calen had given up looking. Guilt warred with anger in his heart. Rist had just walked away. He could have come, but instead he had chosen to stand by the people who had killed Vars and Freis, the people who had tortured Elia and Lasch to the point of breaking.

Valerys's mind crashed into his, swarming over his thoughts. In that same breath, their souls wrapped around each other, and Calen was looking through the dragon's eyes and hearing through his ears as a deep, booming voice thundered, "Calen Bryer. We wish only to talk."

Valerys and Avandeer dropped from the sky above, wings spreading wide.

Calen looked to Ella, her eyes shimmering gold, her face covered in blood. "Go. Find the others at the sally port. Move towards the Burnt Lands. Tivar and I will take Valerys and Avandeer and keep the Dragonguard occupied. We—"

A rush of air swept past Calen, causing him to stagger. A dense grey fog swept over him, and he could barely see his own hands in front of his face. Valerys's roar thundered in the grey, echoed by that of Avandeer and Varthear.

"Ella!"

"Calen?" As Ella's voice rang out, the grey fog pulled away in all directions, clearing an open space of almost fifty feet.

Fenryr, Kaygan, Ella, and all the others stood in the open, grass beneath them, soft, diffused light drifting through a wall of swirling grey that surrounded them.

At the centre of it all stood Boud, the woman who had appeared as if stepping from the shadows themselves only the day before. A 'Stormcaller' Kaygan had called her. Fenryr had spoken of Stormcallers that night in the Eyrie. *Our people were mighty. Our Stormcallers struck the dragons from the sky with lightning.*

The woman's eyes were bone white, and she stood with her hands thrust in the air, palms open.

"I told you that you would need her," Kaygan said, stepping between Boud and Calen. "The fog stretches for miles in all directions. Only around us is it clear."

A low rumble resonated in the air, and Valerys stepped through the fog behind Calen, eyes glowing with an incandescent purple light, Avandeer and Varthear emerging beside him.

Valerys moved so he stood over Calen, lowering his head, eyes fixed on Kaygan. The dragon trusted the god even less than Calen did, and he remembered the fear in Kaygan's eyes at the mention of dragonfire.

"The fog will obscure us for now," Kaygan said, narrowing his eyes at Valerys. "But the Lorians know we are few within here. If I sat astride Helios, I would burn everything."

"What good is it then?" The anger came upon Calen without warning, Rist still swirling in his mind, fire boiling in Valerys's veins.

"It will buy them and the others time," Tivar said, lowering her hand from the scales on Avandeer's jaw. She limped slightly as she walked towards Calen. "If Eltoar had meant us harm, he and the others would have fallen upon Valerys, Avandeer, and Varthear the moment they arrived. He wants to talk."

"And you trust him?" Calen spat, immediately regretting the venom in his voice. "And what if I choose to run? Will he tear me from the sky like he has all the others?"

"I make no excuses for Eltoar's deeds, just as I do not for mine. But beneath everything is a soul that aches. He does not want for more death. His heart is empty, and his soul wanders, him and Helios both. He does not want to see more of our kind slaughtered."

"Does he not?" The Narvonan woman that Calen had seen in the mountain had been silent until that moment, but now he could see a rage in her eyes to rival that of any dragon. She strode towards Tivar and slammed a fist into her face with enough force to send blood spraying and Tivar sprawling to the ground, her helmet coming free.

Avandeer roared as the woman leapt atop Tivar and wrapped her hands around the collar of Tivar's breastplate. But with a sudden shift, the dragon's roar turned to a whimper as the woman slammed her fist down into Tivar's face again and again. Tivar made no effort to defend herself. She just lay there, staring up at her attacker as knuckles crunched into bone.

Calen leapt forwards, grabbed the woman by the shoulders, and threw her to the ground. In a heartbeat, his níthral was in his hand, purple light glistening in the sweat that streaked the woman's face. "Lay a hand on her again," he said, a dragon's fury burning within him, "and it will be the last thing you do. I swear by the bond."

The woman stared at Calen, unflinching, the light gleaming in her eyes.

"Who are you?"

She leaned forwards, the flickering edge of Calen's níthral a finger's width from her throat. She spoke clear and true. "I am Coren Valmar, Daughter of the Sea, Soulkin to Aldryn, and I watched my whole world burn at her hands and the hands of those she stood beside. And now she speaks of empty hearts and wandering souls. She brings shame to everything that we are. And she owes me a debt of blood that can never be paid."

Calen released his níthral. He stared down at Coren Valmar and pushed away the rage that bubbled within. He knew that name. Chora had spoken of Coren Valmar. "Uvrín mír, Rakina. La'valkanet vidim."

Forgive me, Rakina. I didn't know.

"Uvríníl er kanet itharil," Coren said as she lifted herself to her feet, brushing the dirt from her elbows. *Forgiveness is not needed.* "You speak the Old Tongue well for one who was not born to it. Therin taught you well."

Calen must have given his thoughts away in his expression for Coren gave a soft laugh.

"You have his accent when you speak." The laughter vanished from her voice, the smile fading to a grim line, her eyes hard and cold as she stared at Tivar. "Last I heard, it was my word that would have taken your head from your shoulders." She rested her hand on the pommel of her sword. "If not my word, my steel will gladly perform the same task."

Calen stepped between the two. "Chora changed her vote. Tivar and Avandeer have sworn themselves to me, to Valerys, and to all the lives they have destroyed. They are Onuvrín."

"It is that simple, is it?" Coren asked, a mocking laugh on her tongue. "She swears an oath, and all her sins are forgotten? The lives she ended, the world she burned? She has made oaths before." Coren spat at Tivar's feet. "Oaths to stand by her brothers and sisters, oaths to protect those who looked to us. Those oaths did not stay her blade when Eltoar and Fane whispered in her ear. Her oath means *nothing*."

"It is never simple," Calen answered.

"Oh, it can be simple." Coren glared at Tivar. "She slaughtered her own kin. Turned her back on everything. She deserves death. That is simple."

Tivar stepped forwards, staring at Coren, blood streaming from her nose and across an open cut beneath her eye. "I do not ask for absolution."

"Good. You will not find any here," Coren answered.

"I wish I could change everything. Take it all back. But I can't. I—"

"Farwen is dead," Coren snapped, cutting Tivar short. "She sacrificed herself to give us time. She was tired, and her soul was broken, and she had fought long enough. Your precious Eltoar and his Dragonguard took her soulkin from her. He ripped her in half, and not once, not *ever*, despite everything she lost, did she think to turn her back on her brothers and sisters. She fought until her dying breath, and it should have been you in her place." Coren's jaw clenched as she shook her head. "How am I ever to trust a soul who has broken a vow so sacred? Tell me, Tivar, *how?*"

"You can't," Tivar said, her voice soft. Avandeer let out a low whine and tilted her head to brush her snout against Tivar. Tivar closed her eyes and ran her hand across Avandeer's scales. "You can never trust us, nor should you. But you *can* let us die for you. It is only in the sacrifice of that which we took from so many – our lives – that perhaps you can see the truth in my words."

Coren glared at Tivar for a few moments longer, nostrils flaring, then turned to Calen. She drew in a long breath, then let it out slowly. "You answered when I called."

"Always." He looked from Coren to Tivar. "I understand your fury. I do not ask you to forgive them, for I would be a hypocrite to do so. I have my own forgiveness to struggle with. But I do ask that you look past it for now, to focus on those who need us. Can you do that?"

Coren stared at Calen for a long moment. "I can."

"Laël sanyin, vésani, nur mandahír denír ove'du. Det vur il'uil dantuí."

I am sorry, sister, for forcing this upon you. It was the only way.

"La quinye," Coren said, the look in her eyes speaking of weariness. *I understand.* "You have clearly spent time around Aeson. It is an honour to meet you, brother." Her gaze turned up to Valerys, whose heart ached at hearing of Farwen's death. Neither Calen nor Valerys had ever met her, but she was kin and her loss was felt. Coren inclined her head. "And you, young one."

Valerys lowered his head so his jaw brushed the grass, his breath blowing over Coren.

"I thought I would never see a hatchling again… though he is far from that now." Coren rested a hand on the side of Valerys's scales. She looked to the group of rebels who stood a few feet back, then to Kaygan and Boud. "It appears we have little choice. Can you keep them covered while they lead you to the sally port and gather the others?"

Boud inclined her head. "I can do more than that."

"Then we will go and speak with Eltoar." She looked to Ella. "There is no place for the people of Tarhelm here in the North, not anymore, not while this war rages. If I don't return, I need you to promise me you will take them south. Aeson says the madness has left the Burnt Lands. That route would be my choice. It will be a hard road, but—"

"I swear it," Ella said, pressing a hand over her chest.

"We?" Calen asked. "You will come with us?" He turned to look at Varthear, who had slowly moved towards Coren, a low purr in her throat. The dragon had spread her vermillion wings and lowered her head. "Varthear may carry you, but Valerys and I would be honoured to do so as well."

Coren lowered her hand from Valerys's jaw, a smile spreading across her lips as she stared at Varthear. "Varthear, you are as beautiful as the first day I saw you, my sapphire queen." She took a few steps closer, staring up at the dragon in wonder. "I had thought I'd never again see the fire in your eyes. It would be the honour of my life to fly with you… but alas, I cannot, for the fire in my heart would not allow it."

At that moment, Valerys tilted his head, and the sound of heavy wingbeats drifted at the edge of the dragon's hearing.

Coren pressed a hand to her chest. "Calen Bryer, I do not know you, and yet I have already lied to you, and it is the greatest lie of my life."

Calen drew in a sharp breath, allowing the Spark to hover just out of reach, a pressure building within Valerys. He saw the same apprehension in Tivar and Avandeer. Even Fenryr took a step forwards.

"On the night I last saw my master, Kollna, daughter of Luan, she told me something that shaped everything from that day forward." Coren looked up at Varthear. "She said 'our duty, above all else, is to our soulkin.' Farwen and I, and Aldryn and Syndril, we fought for years. We watched hundreds of our kin perish… watched their souls shattered, their hearts torn to pieces. Have you ever seen the moments after a dragon loses their soulkin?" Tears rolled down Coren's cheeks. "It is a rage like no other. This whole world could burn, and it would not be enough. And that rage is followed by a darkness that swallows everything."

Coren stopped for a moment, steadying herself, the wingbeats growing louder. The fog above shifted and swirled, parting as a massive figure descended.

A dragon larger even than Sardakes emerged from the grey, thick tendrils of fog whipping around its silver-streaked orange scales. The membrane of its wings shimmered gold, and the horns that grew from its skull were three times as long as Calen was tall. The creature was immense, its muscles thick and powerful, eyes like swirling fire.

The dragon cracked its wings and alighted over Coren, a deep rumble in its throat followed by a high-pitched whine as it stretched its neck forwards and brushed its jaw against Varthear's.

The dragon lowered its head to Coren and nuzzled into her shoulder, like a horse nuzzling a mouse.

"For nearly three centuries, I kept Aldryn safe. A dead dragon cannot be killed. New eggs were not hatching, and dragons were dying in their scores. Aldryn was amongst the last." Coren shook her head, tears dripping from her chin. "I refused to let him die like all the others, pointlessly, needlessly… If we kept fighting as we were, Helios would have ripped him from the sky. The Dragonguard were too many, and we too few. I made a choice." She swallowed hard, running her tongue along her teeth. "When we found Aeson and the others, I told them Aldryn had died. I told them the Dragonguard had murdered my soulkin along with Farwen's. And for all these years, I pretended to know their pain, to know what it is to be Rakina."

"Why?"

"Because none of it made sense. When you watch dragons fall from the sky like rain, you understand that there is no rhyme nor reason, only death. Being stronger, more powerful, it meant nothing. So many dragons larger and stronger than Aldryn perished the night Ilnaen fell, without more than a whimper. Alvira's soulkin, Vyldrar, was a legend. His name was whispered in the halls where I apprenticed. And yet he died like all the rest. My master's soulkin, Tinua, she never saw another sky after Ilnaen."

"She died fighting," Calen said without a thought.

Coren stared at him for a moment as though she wanted to question what he'd said but continued. "It was Farwen who suggested it. After Karakes killed Syndril over the Aonan Wood and I found Farwen broken and alone, she made me promise to not throw Aldryn's life away, said there was no reason for him to die. That we could keep fighting while keeping him safe, in the hope that one day a time would come where every drop of blood we had spilled, every moment we had given, would amount to something. A time where Aldryn's strength could make the difference."

Aldryn lifted his head in the air, looking into Valerys's eyes.

"That time has come. The Dragonguard are only three now. Time has brought them low, and their numbers no longer swell the sky. No matter how little I trust her," she said, glancing at Tivar, "she is right in one thing. I know Eltoar, I know how he hunts and kills, I know the measure of his mercy. If he had wanted us dead, we would be dead. We could run, but there is no telling what course that might lead us on." She took a few steps towards Tivar, her soulkin, Aldryn, looming over her, a deep growl in his throat. "If you betray us, I will rip you apart piece by piece. I will break you. Believe me when I say there is no power in this world that could stand in my way."

"I will not," Tivar responded simply, returning Coren's stare.

Coren held Tivar's gaze for a few moments longer before offering her hand to Calen. "Det være myia haydria na iralíse nai din siel, akar."

It would be my honour to fly by your side, brother.

Calen moved forwards and offered his hand to Coren. "Ar myialí na iralíse nai diar, Coren Valmar, Davitir un il'Ilaríal."

And mine to fly by yours, Coren Valmar, Daughter of the Sea.

"Though perhaps Aldryn should stay hidden for just a little longer."

"What do you mean?"

Calen smiled.

CHAPTER EIGHTY-THREE

ALL PATHS CONVERGE

22nd Day of the Blood Moon

Firnin Mountains – Winter, Year 3081 After Doom

Eltoar stood on the open plain, his helmet in the crook of his arm, exhaling slowly through his nostrils as he stared at the vast expanse of grey fog that blanketed the foothills of the mountain. He had seen this magic before in the hands of the elves of Lynalion – which posed even more questions.

"Why do we wait?" Voranur growled, one hand resting on his sword pommel as he glared down at the fog. "Did you not see the destruction they have wrought? How many thousands burned alive? They are not our allies, Eltoar. Let us be done with them now, so that we need not look two ways. Tivar is no longer one of us. Stop letting her blind you. She is the reason Jormun and Ilkya are dead, and I will have my blood. She is a traitor, Eltoar."

"I caution you to take care with your words, Voranur." Eltoar stared into the elf's eyes. Without looking, he could feel Helios standing over him. "Tivar means more to me than you ever will. Understand that and you will be far closer to keeping your head."

"What will you do if I do not bow to you like a dog?" Voranur moved to stand in front of Eltoar, Seleraine shifting with him, a deep, resonant growl in her throat, her frills standing on end. "Will you strike me down? Do I not deserve to seek vengeance for the dead? What of you, Lyina? You slew Irulaian and Dravír over Antiquar, did you not? Is your bloodlust sated now? Would you shake hands with the elven Draleid if they stood before you?"

"I would carve open their throats and drink their blood." Lyina stared off into the distance at the wall of fog. She had not been the same since losing Pellenor. "What are we to do if Salara has gotten to him first?" She looked to Eltoar and then back at the fog. "That fog is their trick, is it not?"

"We will walk that path if it faces us. For now, we know too little."

"And how long do we stand here and wait?" Voranur asked. "A night? A year?"

"A breath," Eltoar said, watching as the surface of the fog shifted and three dragons rose.

Tendrils of grey swirled around them as they burst upwards, wings cracking against the air. Avandeer emerged first, and the sight of her lightened Eltoar's heart. The dragon was a beauty like no other. As she rose, a smaller white dragon with black-veined wings followed. Eltoar had seen the creature from atop Helios when he had first arrived, but he was closer now and through Helios's gaze he could see the dragon's pale lavender eyes and the thick horns that framed his skull. The dragon was much larger than he should have been, having hatched barely a summer or two ago.

A smile graced Eltoar's lips as he stared at the white dragon. He had seen many a hatchling in his time. Over a thousand. And he could tell by the structure of this one's shoulders, the depth of his chest, and width of his wings that he would one day be a force to be reckoned with. Eltoar only hoped that this was the first of many to come and not the last of what was.

A third dragon broke free of the fog's grasp, scales of deep blue with bright red wings and horns black as onyx.

"I know that dragon," Voranur said, taking a step forwards.

"Varthear." Eltoar followed Varthear's flight as she soared after Avandeer and the white dragon.

"Jormun and Hrothmundar killed her and Ilmirín centuries ago..." Voranur looked as though he was witnessing a ghost. "At least, I thought they did."

"There is no Draleid on her back," Lyina said. "She is Rakina."

"That's not possible."

Eltoar thought back to the many Rakina dragons he had known across the centuries. Far too many for his heart to ever feel true rest. Each of them had unleashed a fury like no other when their soulkin were torn from them. But in the time after, they were, each of them, lost, empty husks waiting for death. He had seen many Draleid carry on after such losses, find purpose and strength despite the shattered souls they were left with. But the dragons had never done so. It was as though when a soul shattered, the dragon always took less and suffered more. As it was in life, it was in death: the dragon took the pain to save their soulkin.

As the three dragons soared towards them, Eltoar felt something in his heart, something he hadn't realised until that moment he had not felt in a long time: hope. That feeling resonated within Helios and a warmth spread through the great dragon. It had been so many years since Helios had laid eyes on one so young.

Eltoar lifted his hand to his face, pressed the cold steel of his gauntlet against his cheek, then pulled it away to see a small drop of moisture. The sight of it surprised him. He had not shed many tears in his life. The last time he remembered was when he'd knelt in the hatchery tower over Dylain's body all those years ago. It was not his own sadness that brought the tears forth as he stood there staring into the sky at the white dragon, but that of Helios.

The sorrow and loss and agony crept into Helios slowly as he admired how the young dragon felt the currents of air and how he always moved to best protect his Draleid.

The white dragon never let his head drop lower than needed, always gave a subtle shift before changes of speed or sharp turns, and, crucially, always looked up. Most dragons never looked up. The greatest predators in the sky never needed to fear what came from above. A dragon that looked up cared more for its Draleid than for itself, always readying to turn and fight, leaving its own belly exposed.

Such a sight would have brought him joy in times past. But now, the only images that crossed Helios's mind were of the world they had ripped from this young dragon. A world they had sought to make better but instead had torn asunder.

"We can make it right," Eltoar whispered. "We can make it right."

Salara ran her hands along Vyrmír's golden scales, a fury burning within her as she looked through the dragon's eyes at Eltoar Daethana and the others stood upon the open plains at the base of the mountain.

"What is your command?" Taran called from the nape of Nymaxes's neck.

They stood upon a ledge hidden high in the mountain range, clouds circling. They had been there for some time, concealed by wards of sight and spirit. Warding a dragon was not a simple thing, near impossible. But high in the mountains, bolstered by the cloud cover, it was enough. They had flown by the cover of night, soaring silently through the dark clouds over the Lorian camp, careful to avoid the many beacons Eltoar had placed, setting their trap.

Salara turned her gaze to the thick grey fog and the three dragons that emerged from within. She flicked her tongue off the back of her teeth, squeezing her right hand into a fist.

"In two days, look to the Firnin Mountains. The path you wish to walk lies there." Those were the words that strange man had spoken the night he and his companions had taken Boud. Salara and Vandrien had agreed there was something deeper happening, that the man was weaving them into threads of his own making. Boud's fog confirmed this.

It was all far too coincidental for her liking and confirmed suspicions she had long held: Boud had allowed herself to be captured. Why and to what end, Salara could not work out. But a warrior with Boud's talents and strength did not simply find themselves wandering the depths of Lynalion, and they most certainly did not allow a collar to be placed around their neck so easily.

"Narvír?" Taran called again. "Dar er din narvan?"

Commander? What is your command?

Salara stared down at the three dragons that soared towards Eltoar and the others. Vandrien's plan had been for Salara and her kin to wreak havoc on the Lorian forces besieging the Firnin Mountains in hope of drawing Eltoar and the Dragonguard away from Elkenrim. But then they'd seen the Lorian beacons light, and they'd sat back and waited.

At that very moment, Vandrien and Warmarshal Luilin led a force of sixty thousand through the Elkenwood towards Anaduin – or Merchant's Reach as the human's had renamed it. All the while, the forces that had gathered in the east – over a hundred thousand strong – marched for Elkenrim.

By the time the sun left The Traitor's moon alone in the sky that night, two more cities would be reclaimed. And the human empire that had covered the continent in blood would be little more than ashes.

The astute course of action would have been to let the Dragonguard and these other dragons tear each other to pieces while Salara split forces and assisted with the reclamations of Anaduin and Elkenrim. She could hear Vandrien's voice in her mind. *"Patience, Salara, is an attribute all predators share."*

But Salara had been patient. She had waited centuries. She had let Eltoar and Voranur live at Darnírin's Hill. The time for patience was done. Salara wanted blood.

She reached down and collected her helm from where it sat between her legs and slid it into place. "What do you say, my light?"

A powerful rumble thrummed through Vyrmír, his rage flowing into Salara. Memories passed from the dragon's mind into Salara's, memories of the night Ilnaen fell, of how Eltoar had bound them on Driftstone while he slaughtered the ones they loved. More memories followed of the first time she'd met that same elf in the Üvrian un'Aldryr after Vyrmír had hatched. He had seemed a different soul then – lighter, full of compassion and joy. That Eltoar was dead, and the time had come for her to kill this one.

She drew a long breath, then raised a hand in the air. "Draleid un Numillíon. Hear me now. Hold courage in your hearts, and set it in steel. Hold fire in your veins, and let it burn through you. Today, we face the traitors who destroyed our world. We will not all leave this place. This will not be a day that is looked back upon with warm hearts. Our descendants will know this as a day of wrath and a day of reckoning. It has been my greatest pride to lead you forward into this new world and to fight alongside you. Leave the white dragon unharmed, but to the rest, show no mercy and give no quarter." Vyrmír shifted beneath Salara, his great golden wings spreading wide. "For Irulaian and Dravír, for all those we have lost, and for all those who deserve a future under free skies, fly with me now, my brothers and sisters. Forward unto victory!"

Vyrmír gave a mighty crack of his wings and leapt from the cliff, the wards of sight and sound shattering as he unleashed a roar that sent tremors through Salara's bones.

Behind them, Nymaxes answered with a roar of his own. And from further back, Andrax, Barathûr, Baerys, Rysírix, and Lauthín all roared like thunder as they lifted into the air.

Sorrow and fury burned in Salara's heart as the last of the dragons went to battle. There would be no victors, only survivors.

ELTOAR LOOKED TOWARDS THE MOUNTAINS at the sound of the rolling thunder that was the roar of dragons. His heart caught in his chest at the sight of Vyrmír's golden scales glinting in the light of the sun and the Blood Moon, the dragon's wings casting a gargantuan shadow across the mountainside. Six more flew in Vyrmír's wake.

"Please, Salara, no. Not now…" Eltoar gritted his teeth, clenching his fist at his side. They were so close. He needed to know how the egg had hatched. "Gods damn you."

"Is this enough then?" Voranur called as he mounted Seleraine. "Your old apprentice and this new Draleid have struck a deal. There is no denying it now, Eltoar. We are all that is left, and they would see us dead."

Eltoar shook his head, whispering. "No, no, no…"

"Voranur is right, Eltoar." As Lyina spoke, Avandeer, Varthear, and the young white dragon all turned in the sky, changing course to the west.

Eltoar watched them go, then pulled his helmet from the crook of his arm and slid it over his head. He drew one last long breath, then turned and mounted Helios, the great dragon's head resting on the grass beside him, a fire burning in Helios's veins. "Our focus is Salara and her Draleid. Leave Calen Bryer and the others. They can be dealt with another time."

"No!" Voranur roared from astride Seleraine, the blue dragon charging forwards and cracking her wings. "I will have my blood, Eltoar. I will have it!"

"Voranur! We're stronger together – Voranur!" Helios lurched forwards, but Seleraine had already lifted into the air. Seleraine had only ever been second to Eríthan when it came to speed, and now she tore across the sky like a streak of lightning, headed straight for Tivar and the others. Eltoar called to Lyina, who now sat at the nape of Karakes's neck. "Go after him!"

"I will not leave you alone in this," she called back. "Even Helios cannot stand against so many."

"Helios will do what he must, as will I. But if that dragon dies, so too may our hopes of ever gazing upon another hatchling. Go, Lyina! Protect our future. We will show them why Helios is known as The Shadow of Death." With that, Eltoar leaned forwards, and Helios unleashed a deep, primal roar, unfurling his wings.

The dragon surged forwards, wings cracking against the air, and then he was lifting, that familiar weightless feeling settling in Eltoar's stomach. A glance over his shoulder told him that Lyina had followed Voranur.

Good. Eltoar looked ahead to where the seven dragons bore down on him.

Vyrmír was the largest by a distance, larger even than Karakes. They would need to isolate him.

The red-scaled dragon who had fought at the Three Sisters and Andrax, with his yellow scales and pink wings, were the next largest threats. The three dragons with scales of purple, black, and blue were all far smaller.

The green-scaled dragon, the one streaked with silver on the left of the formation, as large as Meranta had been, this one would be Helios's first kill.

A part of Eltoar wanted to hold back, to find a way through to Salara. But over the course of his long life, Eltoar had learned that there were precious few things more unforgivable than making the same mistake twice. He had held back at the Three Sisters, and Pellenor had died for it. That thought ignited the fury within Helios, a pressure building within the great dragon, the beating of his wings rippling beneath Eltoar.

Tivar's voice echoed in his mind. *"I will not put another of our kind in the ground. I will not tear another soul in half."*

"I'm sorry," Eltoar whispered, the wind drowning his words. "I'm sorry I failed you. Keep them safe. I will do what I can."

Eltoar opened himself to the Spark and pulled his and Helios's minds together. They drew a breath, icy and sharp. Their heart beat, slow and steady. They settled their mind, resolute and steadfast. To survive this, they needed to be one.

Ayar elwyn, ayar uoré, ayar nithír.

One heart, one mind, one soul.

A series of roars filled the sky as the elven dragons angled their wings and streaked towards them. They fixed their gaze on the green dragon at the left of the formation. "Må Heraya tael du ia'sine ael."

May Heraya take you into her arms.

A brief moment of peace settled into them, and then Helios rose high, shifting, folding his wings and ripping through the sky. The other dragons were slow to react, all but Vyrmír, who twisted and cracked his wings, trying to intercept Helios's flight. But even he was not fast enough.

Helios crashed into the green dragon with the weight and power of a falling star. The creature let out a shriek as Helios's jaws wrapped around its throat and his talons tore at its belly. Streams of fire poured from the green dragon's jaw, weak and feeble, Helios's teeth cracking scales, warm blood flowing. Threads of Fire, Spirit, and Air whipped forwards from the Draleid on the creature's back, but Eltoar sliced through them and wrapped the elf in a ward as strong as steel. He could feel the Draleid pushing back, thrashing frantically with the Spark, all fear and panic.

"Du lirthín denír, akar."

You made this, brother.

Two of the smaller dragons tore at Helios's side, but as he and the green dragon fell, the wind flapping around them, they pulled away. Helios buried his talons into the dragon's belly, slicing through scale and flesh. He opened his jaws and poured fire down over the other dragon's head, unleashing a roar before sinking his teeth back into the creature's throat and deeper into its flesh. With a fury raging through him, Helios ripped the dragon's neck from its body, blood spraying into the wind.

He released his talons from the creature's belly and let the body fall before crunching down on the neck and throwing it to the wind. As the dragon's body spun and plummeted to the plains below, where the scattered remnants of the Lorian armies were falling back, a pang of guilt and pain twisted within Eltoar.

The Draleid clung to the severed neck of his Soulkin, face pressed against the scales. He made no effort to shield himself from the impact of the landing or to jump free.

"*I will not tear another soul in half,*" Tivar's voice echoed once more, carving Eltoar apart. He did not want to kill any more of his kind. He had hoped he'd seen the last of that years ago.

Eltoar forced himself to watch until the green dragon's body smashed into the ground below, a cloud of dust rising, chunks of dirt launching into the air.

A roar sounded behind him, and in that moment, Eltoar and Helios set that guilt alight and turned to face the others.

RIST'S LEGS MOVED WITH LITTLE thought, forwards and only forwards. He shifted Magnus with his shoulder, attempting to redistribute the man's weight, body aching. Magnus was awake, but barely. He had come close to burning himself out, and the drain had almost taken him. Shouting and chatter rang out across the fields around him, but it was all a blur.

"*Come with me… Rist, please…*"

Calen's voice plagued Rist's mind. His throat tightened at the thought, heart racing. Calen *was* the Draleid. What he had seen in the Well of Arnen had been true… or at least some of it. But how much? Had it been a vision of the future? His mind was a storm, nothing settled, everything raging and whirling.

Everything in his heart had wanted him to go with Calen. He had heard his own voice screaming at him in his mind to take Calen's hand… to go. But then he'd seen Magnus on the ground, Garramon calling out with his face burnt – burnt by Calen – and Neera struggling to breath with her armour twisted and bent. They had needed him. He couldn't have left them. He wouldn't. They had stood by him through everything, given him a purpose, cared for him, believed in him. Everything had just taken him off guard… The chamber had been collapsing… Magnus couldn't walk on his own. He'd had no choice.

Something grabbed at Rist's shoulders and pulled, a voice bellowing in his ears. Suddenly Magnus was gone. He turned to see Garramon, face burnt and scarred, throwing Magnus over his shoulder, lips moving, sounds echoing in Rist's ears.

Everyone around him was scattering, panic on their faces.

Something hard stung his face, then hands grabbed the sides of his head and he was staring down at Neera's bloodied and dirt-covered face. "Rist!"

She grabbed his hand with an iron grip and pulled him as she ran.

Rist looked over his shoulder to see Taya Tambrel and a score of her Blackwatch sitting astride their obsidian mounts, pointing and yelling. Taya glanced up towards the sky, then shouted, and the horses broke into a gallop.

Rist followed Taya's gaze to see a green-scaled dragon plummeting towards the earth. The enormous creature seemed to fall like a feather, its head and neck floating in the air beside its body, blood drifting around it. It was as though the falling dragon defied all sense of time and natural laws.

Taya shouted once more, her mighty horse churning the clay beneath its hooves. And then the dragon crashed into the earth, and Taya was gone. The dragon's limbs crushed scores of men and women as they slammed into the ground. The ground shook, and Rist stumbled, dust and dirt spewing into the air.

The dragon's head slammed into the earth before his eyes, snuffing soldiers' screams in an instant. Rist turned away as Neera wrapped her arms around him and opened herself to the Spark.

CALEN PUSHED HIS STRENGTH INTO Valerys as the dragon tore through the skies, Varthear and Avandeer with him. He glanced over his shoulder. Seleraine was gaining on them, blue scales gleaming in the light of the sun and the Blood Moon overhead.

Had the second dragon – likely Karakes and Lyina – not joined Voranur and Seleraine, Calen would have told Valerys to turn and tear them from the skies. With Avandeer and Varthear alongside him, the blue dragon wouldn't have stood a chance. But Karakes was even larger than Avandeer, and Varthear had no fire or Draleid on her back. There were too many risks.

"The hills!" Tivar roared, pointing towards a vast expanse of rolling hills that stretched southwards towards the Burnt Lands.

Calen was about to answer when a clap of thunder cracked above him. He looked up in awe to see dark storm clouds forming from thin air, rolling outwards like a sweeping wave and stretching across the sky. Within moments, he could no longer see the sun or moon, both shut out by a dark and ominous sky.

Boud. This was the power of a Stormcaller. Calen glanced over his shoulder once more to see Seleraine and Karakes were almost upon them. "Rise!" he shouted to Tivar. "We can lose them in the clouds!"

Valerys angled his wings and swept upwards. As he did, a roar sounded behind him and Seleraine slammed into them, sending them both reeling through the sky. The dragon was only atop them for a second, when Varthear crashed into Seleraine's side and ripped the dragon free.

Varthear roared, raking her talons along Seleraine's back and biting down into the dragon's forelimb.

Calen looked up at the dark storm clouds, then back towards Varthear and Seleraine rolling in the sky, Karakes hurtling towards them, Helios and the other dragons battling in the distance.

A small part of him whispered in the back of his mind. *"Go. Run!"* If they climbed and vanished into the storm clouds, they would be gone without a trace.

Calen took that part of himself and cut it to pieces, a fire rising within him, a fury flowing from Valerys. They would not leave Varthear to die. "Aldryr ar orimyn," Calen whispered, and Valerys lurched forwards, unleashing a primal roar, a pressure swelling within him.

Fire and fury.

Tivar and Avandeer swerved in the air and drew level with them.

"Laël val du, akar!" Tivar roared.

I'm with you, brother!

The two dragons descended on Seleraine together. Avandeer fell upon her from the top, talons slicing into the blue dragon's back. She snapped at Voranur, who sat at the nape of Seleraine's neck, but the man sent arcs of lightning streaking backwards.

Valerys took advantage of Voranur's distraction to fold his wings and crash into Seleraine's exposed belly, biting down into the dragon's throat, blood flowing into his open mouth. Varthear surged forwards to make the killing blow, only for the hulking form of Karakes to crash into her mid-flight.

The enormous red dragon tore strips through one of Varthear's wings, hooking her leg with a talon and swinging her through the air. Varthear snapped back and gave a vicious swing of her head, a black horn piercing Karakes's side. The dragon let out a shriek that sent a shiver through Calen's spine as he went hurtling through the air on Valerys's back.

Valerys, Seleraine, and Avandeer spun and flipped, talons slicing, jaws snapping, and blood flowing. In the madness, Calen lost sight of Varthear and Karakes, his head spinning. The Spark pulsed in the air, flashes of lightning igniting the sky.

The world spun, wings flapping. He saw smoke.

Valerys shrieked as Voranur pushed threads of Earth into his bones and scales. The dragon's pain turned to fury, and Valerys unleashed a torrent of fire over Voranur, causing Seleraine to thrash and roar. The Draleid had created a ward just in time to part the flames, but as he did, Calen pushed threads of Fire and Spirit into him, roaring. Images of Valerys's bones twisting and snapping flitted through Calen's mind, and rage like no other took him over.

He poured every ounce of his strength, his hatred, his fury, and his pain into the threads. Voranur pushed back, the air swirling about them, the world spinning as the dragons tore at each other across the sky, but Tivar joined her strength to Calen's, her threads winding around his.

Calen pulled from his memories, feeding on the searing images of the death and destruction Voranur had wrought at Aravell, of how his lightning had torn through Onymia's chest, sending the small grey dragon tumbling to the earth. Of how, one by one, he had witnessed each of the Rakina dragons fall, bellies torn open, scales cracked, bodies ravaged.

Valerys's rage swirled through him, the bond burning with white-hot fire. And as they spun and Voranur pushed back with every shred of power he had, Calen drew threads of Air through himself. A cracked blue scale drifted in the sky beside him, blood streaming in its wake. He wrapped the threads around the scale and launched it like an arrow.

The scale sliced through the flesh of Voranur's neck, and for a moment, the elf's eyes bulged and his mouth gaped open, blood pouring over his lips. Voranur's head separated from his body, and Seleraine let out a wail that froze even Calen's heart.

It was the cry of a soul being broken, the cry of a love shattered and a lifetime ended. But Valerys didn't share in Calen's sorrow. The dragon was all rage and fury. He rent Seleraine's chest, talons slicing through the scales of the blue dragon's underbelly. He kicked again and again, blood spraying into the wind, Seleraine's innards spilling. As she thrashed and roared, he crunched his jaws around her wing and ripped it free, that fury burning like the sun within him.

Memories flooded their shared mind from the Battle of Aravell: Seleraine's talons raking Valerys's side, her jaws coming inches from ripping Calen in half, her fire pouring over the city.

This dragon would have killed his soulkin in a heartbeat, would have torn him apart, broken the bond, just like she had done to so many others across the centuries. There was no mercy in Valerys's heart for Seleraine and Voranur. Not a shred, not a drop – none. He crunched the bones in her severed wing and released it into the air.

As the dragon fell, Voranur's headless body slowly spinning alongside it, a roar sounded above them.

Karakes had separated from Varthear and was hurtling towards Calen and Valerys. Still fuelled with rage, Valerys cracked his wings and rose to meet him.

At the same time, Avandeer turned in the air and unleashed a pillar of dragonfire.

But Karakes never reached either of them.

Aldryn didn't let out a roar. He barely gave a sound. The massive dragon burst from the dark clouds above, dropping with a speed the likes of which Calen had not thought possible for a creature so large. At the last moment, he unfurled his golden wings and hammered into Karakes's side, ripping him from the air.

Coren and Aldryn moved as one, their talons burying deep into Karakes's side, their fury an all-consuming thing. They bit down into Karakes's jaw, feeling scales snap and bones break, the sweet taste of blood on their tongue.

This was the dragon who had torn Syndril from the world, the dragon who had broken Farwen, the dragon who did not deserve to simply die but to feel the agony and pain Syndril felt. They had waited centuries for this moment.

When Aldryn and Karakes had first met in the sky over the old city of Mythavelion, Aldryn had been half the size of the older dragon. He had been but an adolescent, his fire little more than the flickering flame of a candle. But now he was larger by far, and the years had forged him into a warrior, into a dragon that had war in his veins. More than once, he had strayed from his isolation at the sight of a lone Dragonguard, and he had littered Epheria's coast with their bones. Even still, his hunger for vengeance had not been sated, nor would it be until every last one of the Dragonguard were broken and shattered.

As Karakes thrashed and kicked, Aldryn held him in place, biting down harder, gouging flesh and scales from his chest. From Karakes's back, Lyina lashed out with threads of each elemental strand. Fire plumed through the sky, arcs of lightning streaking. The woman drove threads of Earth into Aldryn's bones and tried to pull the breath from Coren's lungs with threads of Air. But her panic left her vulnerable, and Coren returned her onslaught tenfold.

Tears streamed down Coren's face, flowing freely and vanishing into the wind. Farwen was gone. The only family she had left. She and Aldryn were alone now. And these traitors had taken everything from her.

Memories from a time long ago drifted through her mind of Farwen's master, Dylain, in the northern hatchery tower, broken, his Soulkin, Soria, ripped from the sky.

"Keep her safe, Coren. Kollna has always spoken highly of you."

"I tried," Coren whispered. "We kept each other safe. For as long as we could."

Coren shook her head, allowing her sorrow to burn into rage. The roar she unleashed carried through Aldryn, and he bit down and ripped Karakes's jaw free, whipping his head left and right, then tearing at the dying dragon's throat, blood spraying into the wind.

As the ground rose to meet them, Aldryn watched the light fade in Karakes's eyes, then tossed the dragon aside, unfurling his wings as Karakes smashed into the ground.

Aldryn swept forwards, his talons trailing the grass. Coren leaned back and opened her arms, feeling the strength of the world pull against her. After a moment, Aldryn angled back around and alighted beside Karakes's broken body.

Coren slid from her soulkin's back, threads of Air allowing her feet to touch the grass as gently as the breeze. She passed Karakes's mutilated face, his lower jaw ripped free, shards of bone jutting outwards, blood pumping onto the ground.

The momentary pang of guilt and sadness was swallowed by the unyielding rage within her. Coren had spent many years weeping over the dragons she had been forced to kill. Over the bonds she had been forced to break. And she had spent many dark nights wondering what might have been if these traitors had not slaughtered her brothers and sisters.

She followed the wails to where she found Lyina lying broken beside Karakes's body. Both her legs were snapped, one twisted in a way that turned even Coren's stomach. The woman's cries carried on the wind, harsh and sharp. They were not cries of agony or pain, but of loss and emptiness. Coren had heard them enough times to know the difference.

She warded Lyina as she approached, then knelt beside her, staring down into those bloodshot, tear-filled eyes.

"Now you know how she felt," Coren said, wrapping her fingers in Lyina's hair and wrenching the woman's head up. Lyina shrieked in pain, but Coren slapped her. "Shhh... Look me in the eyes. That's it. I've waited for this moment for a very long time." Coren glared down at Lyina. "It should have been Farwen kneeling over you. But she finally rests now."

"I..." Lynia coughed, blood speckling her lip and catching in her throat. "I thought your soulkin had perished. I—"

Coren wrenched Lyina's head back again. "Shut your mouth. You shut your treacherous, fucking mouth."

"I am happy he lives," she choked out. "I am happy you are whole, Coren."

"Shut your damn mouth!" Coren roared, slamming her fist into Lyina's face. "Don't you dare. You did this. You caused all of this. Don't take this moment from me."

Lyina's head lolled, tears rolling from the corners of her eyes and mingling with the blood that coated her face. She hacked a cough again. "I'm sorry. For what it's worth, I'm—"

"It's worth nothing!" Coren roared, shaking Lyina's head. "You killed everything we loved! You will find no forgiveness now as you face Heraya."

A deep, visceral growl resonated in the air as Aldryn stepped across Karakes's corpse and loomed over Coren and Lyina. The dragon's rage was like the fires of the void. It poured into Coren, filling her bones, and she summoned her níthral.

She held the light-wrought spear to Lyina's throat, her hand shaking, her lip trembling.

"Do not keep me from him… please." Lyina choked on a bloody breath, convulsing. "Don't let yourself become that monster."

"You made me that monster," Coren growled. She drew in shallow breaths, blood trickling over her níthral as she pressed it into Lyina's flesh.

Lyina stared back at Coren, her eyes pleading. "You choose," she said, her voice weak. "You… choose… who you are. Nobody else."

Coren's entire body began to tremble, her and Aldryn's shared rage burning in her. The roar that left her, swept from her stomach up through her chest, and cut at her throat. She buried her níthral in the earth beside Lyina, holding it in place before releasing it.

She stared down into Lyina's eyes and slid a knife from her belt. "You are lucky that I am not you."

"I know." Lyina's eyes widened as Coren drove the knife into her heart.

Coren let the woman's head drop to the dirt and pressed a closed fist to her own face, all that rage and fury yielding to a wave of overwhelming loss and agony that wracked her body and ripped at her heart.

Farwen was gone.

She drew heavy breaths, letting them out slowly, then rose and mounted Aldryn, looking to the sky over the plains to the north, where Helios and the elven dragons tore each other apart.

To her left, Valerys, Avandeer, and Varthear – her wing badly torn and bleeding – descended towards her.

Aldryn let out a low rumble, staring down at Karakes one last time before lifting into the air and rising to meet the others.

She didn't speak as they came together. Aldryn simply angled his wings and soared towards the thick grey fog that had slowly begun shifting south towards the Burnt Lands.

This was not the end, but it was the beginning of it. Aldryn let out a low rumble beneath her, his powerful wings beating. No longer would Coren fight alone. No longer would she keep her soulkin in the shadows. They had waited and bided their time, and now the Lorian Empire would know their wrath.

CHAPTER EIGHTY-FOUR

MASTER AND APPRENTICE

22nd Day of the Blood Moon

Firnin Mountains – Winter, Year 3081 After Doom

Salara whipped threads of Spirit through the air around Vyrmír, slicing through Eltoar's threads of Air that aimed to pull Taran from Nymaxes's neck. Dark clouds swarmed about them where the sky had previously been clear and blue, claps of thunder booming. There wasn't a doubt in Salara's mind that this stormhead was Boud's work. The druid had failed to mention these abilities when they had found her, but the black clouds had emerged far too suddenly to be natural.

Salara looked through Vyrmír's eyes, tracing the warmth of each dragon that swirled through the storm, shadows bursting to life amidst the cracks of lightning.

Only five sources of heat darted back and forth through the dark clouds – the largest by a distance being Helios. Rysírix and Lauthín had already fallen, broken and shattered by the black dragon – their soulkin, Visenn and Falisín, with them. Her master's soulkin had only grown larger and more savage in the years she'd remained within Lynalion's bounds. And in the short time since their emergence, he had already slain four of her kin. She could not allow more to fall.

As Vyrmír circled around and prepared to take Helios head-on, Salara stilled her heart, the stormwinds battering against her. Vyrmír roared, defiant, and she roared with him. He spiralled as a stream of fire illuminated the dark clouds, so wide it would have swallowed them whole. He spread his wings and swept upwards as Barathûr, Andrax, Baerys, and Nymaxes all crashed into Helios together, talons and teeth tearing and slashing.

After rising, Vyrmír folded his wings and plummeted. Salara shifted so she stood at his neck, whirling threads of Air about herself to keep from being torn into the sky. With a roar, Vyrmír whipped to the left, and Salara launched herself from his back.

The wind howled in her ears, the clouds swallowing her as she dove, her vision nothing but black and grey. But she did not need her eyes. She saw Helios's warmth through Vyrmír, blazing like a burning city. And atop the monstrous dragon, she could see Eltoar's fire burning.

Salara adjusted her flight with threads of Air, holding her breath, feeling each beat of her heart hammering against her ribs.

A flash of lightning illuminated a black shadow so large she could not see its end.

Another push right, then left, adjusting. Something flitted past and skittered off her helmet; a scale torn free. Salara pulled Vyrmír's mind into hers, drawing on his courage, and his strength, and his will. She forged threads of Earth and Spirit into her bones and flesh, hardening them, whirling threads of Air to slow her pace.

A heartbeat passed and she crashed into Eltoar and ripped him from Helios's back, her shoulder slamming into his chest. Even with the Spark fortifying her body, the collision punched the air from her lungs and shook her to her core.

She gasped for air, the world whipping past as she spun over herself again and again, her arms wrapped around Eltoar's chest in an iron grip. He slammed his elbows down into her helmet, sending her head spinning. She twisted around him, coiling her legs about his waist and snaking an arm around his throat, squeezing with all her strength. As they fell, a glowing red pendant came loose from his breastplate, and Salara grabbed the crimson stone and ripped it free before tossing it into the sky.

"Your demon god cannot save you!" she roared, the wind devouring her words.

They came apart just as they broke free from the dark storm clouds that blanketed the sky. The world took shape around her in a moment of strange peace that was shattered when Eltoar crashed into her once more. She grabbed the back of his skull and rammed her helmet into his before lifting her knees to her chest, planting her feet into his stomach and kicking him free.

Above, Helios broke from the clouds, Vyrmír and the others swarming around him, tearing strips from his side, blood trailing. Salara watched in agony as Helios twisted his neck and closed his jaws around Baerys and his soulkin, Indivar.

Baerys was a brave dragon, and fierce, but he was a hatchling next to Helios, and the great black dragon bit him in half, crushing bone and scale both, blood and gore misting into the wind.

No...

Salara's heart broke as Baerys's severed body fell and Indivar was lost amidst the carnage. In that moment, the fury reignited within her, and Vyrmír dragged the shattered pieces of her heart together, binding them with fire as he crashed into Helios with a savage rage. Vyrmír was still smaller, but the difference was not as great as it had once been. Helios twisted to snap his jaws around Vyrmír's throat, but Vyrmír tore at the black dragon's side and opened a wicked gash through Helios's scales. He roared and redoubled his attack, tearing at the dragon he had once looked up to as a god.

As the battle above raged, Salara wound herself in threads of Air and bound threads of Earth and Spirit to her bones. Dropping from a height like this was no simple thing. She welled threads of Air into a sphere and slammed them down, wrapping others around herself and pulling upwards, slowing her descent as much as her body could stand.

A shockwave rippled through the ground below her, a cloud of dust pluming upwards as Eltoar made impact.

Salara settled her mind, stilled her heart, then slammed into the earth.

ELTOAR DREW IN A RAGGED, dust-filled breath, the air around him thick and clouded with dirt and broken rock. In the sky above, Helios's rage was only surpassed by his sorrow. This was not what either of them had wanted. The last thing this world needed was more dead dragons. Twice, Andrax had left his belly exposed and Helios had not the heart to make the final blow. They had flown together as hatchlings, fought side by side, hunted, and slept. Helios did not want to add Andrax to the list of friends he had laid low.

But it was the sight of Vyrmír's unabating fury that truly scored their shared soul. Vyrmír was a son to them, as Salara was a daughter.

Helios swept across the sky above, twisting and slamming his tail into the side of the crimson dragon that had fought at the Three Sisters, then unleashed a stream of dragonfire across the smaller black dragon that swept past him. Helios could have ripped it from the sky, but his heart was weak.

Eltoar pulled his mind back, staring through the dust to the western skies. He only hoped that Lyina had reached Voranur. Eltoar understood Voranur's pain, but the white dragon needed to be protected. The future of their entire race could depend on it.

He walked from the small crater that had formed in his landing, moving through still-drifting dust. He slid his sword from its scabbard at the sound of crunching dirt.

Salara stood before him, her burnished gold plate now coated in dirt and dust. She had shed her helmet, dark hair loose over shoulders.

"I offer you the right of Alvadrû," she said, sliding her sword from its scabbard, her voice cold and devoid of emotion.

"That right is offered *before* an attack." Eltoar circled, his eyes fixed on Salara. She held not a drop of fear in her heart.

"To those with honour," Salara corrected. "I offer you Alvadrû not because you deserve it, but so that the warriors who march from here, already bloody and broken, may live to see another sunrise. So that they may be spared. Otherwise, I will burn them myself."

"It doesn't have to be like this, Salara."

"It does." Salara wiped blood from her face, her stare fixing on Eltoar. "We are not in the skies, and you do not sit astride Helios's back as I had promised, but this will do. A blade in your hand, with nobody here to watch you die. Nobody here to sing any songs of your heroism."

"Salara, that young dragon – if we can understand *how*—"

"Quiet!" she roared, a sudden rage flaring in her voice. "I will not let you in again. I will not let you twist my mind with your false words. This ends here, *Master*. Will you accept Alvadrû, or will you fight without honour?"

Eltoar stared back at the elf he had once seen as the closest thing to a daughter he would ever have. He remembered teaching her how to hold a sword, how to fix her belt so it wouldn't slip, how to play Masari. He had carried her in his arms the first night she'd gotten too drunk. He had held her as she'd wept the first time her heart was broken. He had watched with pride as she'd carried her head high that next day. She had been his greatest joy… she still was.

"Did you see them fall?" Salara asked, not turning her gaze from Eltoar.

Eltoar narrowed his gaze before his pulse quickened.

"The young one ripped open Seleraine's belly and tore her wing from her body. It was beautiful." Her words were laced with venom. "To see the first of a new generation tear apart the last of those who betrayed the old. Poetic, don't you think?"

Eltoar's jaw clenched, and he tightened his grip on his sword's hilt. "Heraya take you," he whispered.

"Heraya? So you do still pray to the true gods. Was it all an act? All just a grab for power? Were you so jealous of Alvira and the love we had for her – so poisoned by Fane's words – that you saw no other path than to murder her?"

"Do not speak on what you do not know," Eltoar growled, Helios's fury burning in him as the dragon kept the others above at bay.

Salara shook her head, fresh blood streaming from her nose. "She loved you, you know? Not just as a companion. She told me one night when we'd drunk too much wine. You remember after the Battle of Alduin's Place? She didn't say it in words, not truly, but it was clear in her eyes, in the way she spoke of you, in the *trust* she had in you. She loved you, and you murdered her." Salara hocked a ball of spit and blood onto the cracked earth. "Karakes fell too."

Eltoar staggered backwards, the air fleeing his lungs, his throat tightening, and in the sky above Helios let out a heart-wrenching cry.

"I've never before found pleasure in someone else's pain…" She walked towards him, the tip of her blade hovering just above the grass. "How does it feel, Master? To be hunted? To be drawn into a snare and butchered one by one? At least we didn't do it while you slept. At least we didn't feign honour, only to set it on fire. Are you all that is left? How does it feel to be alone?"

Eltoar let out a long sigh, his heart cracked and bleeding at the thought of Lyina gone to rest in Achyron's halls. He hoped Salara was lying, trying to break him, trying to hurt him. But something in her voice told him it was true. "Salara… please…We cannot go on like this."

Salara only shook her head. "No. You do not know me. I owe you nothing. You made this," she said, shaking her head. "Eltoar Daethana is dead. You killed him. And I am here to seek vengeance for the death of the master I loved. Uvrín mír, Sainör, nur kanet cianilar hamín."

Forgive me, mentor, for not coming sooner.

Salara lifted her blade and fell into Howling Wolf. She had always favoured that form.

Eltoar set himself in Patient Wind.

Salara came at him with a rage, her steel blurring as it flashed left and right, pushing Eltoar backwards as she forced him into fellensír simply to keep her blade from opening his throat.

Good movement. Strong. You have grown. Eltoar twisted his back foot in the grass and flicked his blade into reverse grip, using Salara's momentum and aggression against her. She lunged, and he slipped past, her blade gliding along the strong of his with a rasp. He whipped his blade back and brought it down against the backplate of her cuirass.

She stumbled but regained her footing in a heartbeat, pivoting to meet his gaze, fury in her eyes. "Do not treat me like a child. Kill me as you would kill anyone else."

"Do not let your anger rule you," Eltoar said, shifting his stance into Striking Dragon. Above, Helios rose through the dark clouds, forcing the others to rise with him. He would not kill any more of his kind than he had to.

Salara drew in sharp breaths, the muscles in her jaw twitching. She charged once more, the fury of svidarya in her movements. The burning winds had always been a part of her, harnessing the rage in her heart. But her lack of control had held her back. That was no longer the case.

Eltoar parried her first strike at his neck by shifting into Rising Dawn, then swept his blade across and took the full force of her downward swing.

Salara leaned in, her face inches from his. "Stop holding back. You were Alvira's First Sword. The greatest swordsman in all Epheria. Tell me, ghost, was she surprised when you turned that same sword on her? Or did she see it coming?"

Eltoar threw his weight forwards and pushed Salara from him, holding down the rage that bubbled within and setting himself into Tenp i'il Uê. *Stone in the Water.*

Salara swung at his side, and as he turned the blade away, she smashed her elbow into his cheek with a *crunch.*

"I saw signs," she said, moving forwards as he staggered backwards. "I saw you change and darken, but I ignored it all." She brought her blade down twice in an overhead swing, smashing it against his in a fury before sweeping left then right and flicking the steel tip across his nose, slicing through flesh and grating bone. "I told myself I was seeing things. I told myself that if you were worried, you would talk to me. If you had fears, you would share them. Because we trusted each other." Salara feinted left, and Eltoar took the bait. She twisted her blade down and dropped her right shoulder, slamming into his chest and sending him backwards once more. "Because we were family."

When Eltoar caught his balance and looked at Salara's face, he found tears mingling with the blood on her cheeks.

"You were everything to me. You were a friend, a mentor, a father. I thought we were more. If you had come to me… we could have done something. We could have stopped all of this. You just had to come to me."

"You were too young, Salara. You didn't understand. Your heart was too full of dreams, your head too full of legends and stories."

"So you waited until the night you were to slaughter our kin? Was I suddenly old enough then? Or were you hoping to pull me into your shame and your darkness after my choices were already stripped from me?" Dried blood cracked at the corners of Salara's mouth. "Was I too naive to comprehend that you wanted people to look at you the way they looked at Alvira? She adored you, loved you, trusted you. And the entire time you craved what she was, what *she* had."

"That is not true." In the back of Eltoar's mind, Helios's rage overflowed at the thought of Alvira and Vyldrar. Darkness had never threatened to swallow Helios's heart more than the night he had killed Vyldrar.

"All great things require sacrifice," Fane had said, time and time again. Alvira and Vyldrar had been Eltoar and Helios's greatest sacrifice, the most necessary to ensure victory. The two dragons had been like brothers… and it had nearly broken him.

"It is true. But you always failed to understand one thing that I, in all my youth and lack of understanding, with my head of dreams and stories, saw clear as day. You could never have what she had because she was better than you. In her heart and in her soul."

"She was weak!" Eltoar roared, his blood burning, memories of Alvira flitting through his mind.

Salara closed her eyes and gave a soft sigh, a new tear carving its way through the blood and dirt on her cheek. "There it is," she whispered. "There's the anger I know consumes you. You always told me that I needed to control my fury and not let it control me. But you were wrong. It was *you* who was ruled by anger. You buried it deep down as you have always done, until it festered, until it clawed its way free and the world suffered. Your anger made you vulnerable, Master. It gave him cracks to pry open."

"She stood by and watched it all happen." Even as Eltoar tried to push his anger down, Helios refused. The black dragon roared in Eltoar's mind, then hurtled towards Vyrmír, the two of them crashing through the sky, lightning flashing about them. "I kept trying to tell her, Salara. I kept trying to show her that a gentle hand only walked us more slowly towards our graves. She allowed The Order to be torn down brick by brick, allowed it to rot, allowed it to—"

"At least she tried!" Salara surged forwards, swinging her blade at Eltoar's side, moving from Waiting Mantis into Still Night and then to Setting Sun. "You gave up on us!" Steel carved left and right as Salara moved into forms Eltoar had never seen, a movement he did not know. She flowed like water, the blade an extension of who and what she was, just as he had taught her. "You gave up on *me*!"

Salara stepped inside Eltoar's guard, throwing all form to the wind, and launched herself at him. Her shoulder connected with his breastplate, and they both went crashing to the ground.

She fell atop him, her sword lost in the tangle. She slammed a fist down into his face, his cheek *crunching*. "You took everything!" she roared again, punching him again, the steel of her gauntlet slicing open his flesh. "You're a monster! You will never be like her! You will never be loved because you are empty and cold, and—"

Eltoar swung his elbow and smashed it into Salara's face, feeling something *snap*, her cheek bursting open, blood spraying from her already-broken nose. He grabbed the arm loops in her chestplate and swung her to the ground, slamming her down. In an instant, the Spark filled him, and a glistening blue níthral took shape in his fist, the blade levelled at Salara's throat. "I loved you like a daughter! I loved her!"

A warning flashed in his mind from Helios. Vyrmír broke free from Helios's grasp and plummeted towards them, leaving Andrax and the other two dragons to slash at Helios.

Salara leaned forwards, blood dripping from her throat. "Kill me. Kill me, and add me to the list of Draleid you have slaughtered. But I want you to know now, you have lost…" A smile cracked her lips, and she laughed. "At this moment, Vandrien marches on Anaduin and Elkenrim. Berona will fall next, with or without me. It is already in motion. I tell you because you can do absolutely nothing to stop it. The empire you built on the bones of our kin is dead. For what is an empire without souls to name it so. You failed. And your name will forever be inked as he who bled the dragons from this world."

Eltoar's hand shook, his níthral scraping the skin from Salara's throat.

"Kill me!" she roared again, the veins popping in her head and neck. "You fucking coward! You are no Draleid. You are a demon."

Eltoar clenched his jaw, staring down at his old apprentice. In his mind, he saw back to that day in Ilnaen, in the northern hatchery tower, Dylain's broken body lying on the floor, Fane's voice in his ears. *"All great things require sacrifice."*

"No…" The words trembled as they left Eltoar's lips, his entire body shaking. He stared into Salara's fury-filled eyes. "I will not sacrifice you."

Eltoar released his Soulblade and stepped backwards. "I'm sorry… I caused all of this. I failed you and I am sorry and I know that it means nothing." He swallowed hard. "There is still something I can do. Whatever the cost. I can fill some of the cracks. I can give them a chance."

Eltoar savoured the sight of Salara's eyes, of her dark hair, of the proud warrior she had become. A warrior he would have given anything to have fought beside. "I didn't deserve you."

He turned and walked back towards where he had dropped his blade when Salara had tackled him.

"Don't walk away from me!" Salara roared, leaping to her feet, Vyrmír alighting behind her with a force that shook the ground.

The wind swirled around Eltoar, dirt and loose blades of grass whirling in the air as Helios landed, blood trickling from a thousand cuts, a score of deep gashes along his side and a tear in his right wing.

"Go," Eltoar called out as Helios lowered his head.

"We are not finished!" As Salara roared, the other three dragons landed on either side of Vyrmír. Andrax's pale yellow scales were crusted with deep wounds and clotted blood, his left eye savaged. The crimson dragon limped on one leg, and the smaller black dragon had a deep wound along his flank.

"I have two friends to mourn," Eltoar called back, resting a hand on Helios's neck. "You have three. Five dragons died today. We are done. Leave now. I do not want to add more to that number."

As Eltoar started to climb Helios's neck, Vyrmír leapt forwards, jaws opening, flames flickering in his throat. Helios was upon him in a heartbeat.

The great dragon clamped the talon of his winged forelimb down onto Vyrmír's throat and slammed Vyrmír's head into the ground. Helios loomed over Vyrmír and let out a monstrous roar. Nothing would harm his soulkin. Nothing.

Eltoar looked at Salara, who stood still as a statue, the power of the Spark pulsing from her as she gazed open-mouthed at Helios and Vyrmír.

"Take Vyrmír and go, Salara. I am done killing today."

"I am not!"

Slowly, Helios pulled away from Vyrmír, a low growl resonating in his chest as he backed away, the ground shaking beneath him.

As Vyrmír pulled himself back upright, Eltoar mounted Helios. He looked down at Salara for a moment longer before Helios cracked his wings and they lifted into the sky.

It hadn't taken Eltoar long to find Karakes's lifeless body splayed across a plain of grass, his lower jaw ripped free.

Helios whined, sorrow flowing from his heart to Eltoar's as he nuzzled his snout into the top of Karakes's head.

Eltoar had to close his eyes to stop the tears from flowing as Helios's grief overcame him. "Laël sanyinal, myia nithríen."

I am so sorry, my soulkin.

He rested a hand on one of Karakes's scales, waiting just a moment before walking slowly towards where Lyina lay, her legs snapped, blood coating her face and armour.

A physical ache set into Eltoar's chest, and his stomach felt as though it would turn. He knelt beside Lyina and dropped his gauntlet on the ground before brushing a strand of bloodied hair from her face. He cupped her cheek, leaned forwards, and pressed his lips to her forehead. "Du vyin alura anis, yíar'ydil. Duän il haydria i myia elwyn."

You can rest now, old friend. You were the honour in my heart.

As gently as he would a newborn babe, Eltoar slid his arms beneath Lyina's broken body and lifted her to his chest. He carried the woman he had flown beside for centuries to Karakes's chest and laid her against it, so that she might rest closer to his heart.

Eltoar brushed a thumb along Lyina's cheek. "Heraya væra alioner nåir aie vënai din nära."

Heraya will smile when she sees your light.

Eltoar needed to move, but he didn't want to. To move was to leave Lyina and Karakes, to accept they were gone, to face the truth of what was. His heart needed just a little longer.

He knelt there until his back ached and his legs lost feeling. The entire time, Helios curled around Karakes, a low whimper in his throat, his heart bleeding.

Eltoar nodded softly to himself, then brushed his hand along Lyina's cheek for the last time. "You were too good…"

He stood, collected his gauntlets, and walked to stand fifty or so feet away. Helios rose from where he was curled around Karakes, his red eyes speaking only of loss. The dragon moved behind Eltoar and stared down at their dead kin.

"I will make this right," he whispered.

Eltoar reached out to the Spark and pulled in threads of Earth, Spirit, Fire, and Water, pushing them into the ground. The earth beneath Eltoar's feet shook, cracks spreading. He wove the threads around Lyina and Karakes and deeper into the soil. He drew a breath, Helios's strength joining his as he dragged earth and rock and root from about him and forged a hill around the two soulkin. As the earth climbed, Helios leaned forwards, a pressure building within him, and he poured dragonfire down over Lyina and Karakes's bodies, so hot it melted the steel of Lyina's armour. The flames continued to rage until the hill swallowed them.

Eltoar slid his sword from its scabbard and climbed to the top of the formed hill. He wrapped both his hands around the hilt, then drove the blade into the earth. He leaned down and rested his forehead against the pommel for just a moment before turning, climbing back down, and mounting Helios.

He would find Voranur and Seleraine, and then he would do what needed to be done.

CHAPTER EIGHTY-FIVE

LOSS

22nd Day of the Blood Moon

Firnin Mountains – Winter, Year 3081 After Doom

ist walked through the ashes of the camp, bones and snapped wood crunching beneath his boots. Neera walked with him while many soldiers scoured the remnants around him.

The dragons had made sure to burn everything. *Calen* had made sure to burn everything.

In his mind he could still see that massive dragon crashing to the ground, crushing Taya Tambrel and so many others beneath it. Even in death the creatures were weapons of utter destruction.

He knew everything was gone. His books, his notes, everything except what he'd left in Berona. There was nothing that could have survived this. But still, he needed to see for himself. He knew where he'd pitched his tent. Precisely three hundred and forty-seven paces from the tree near the centre of the camp that was now nothing but a brittle husk.

"Rist," Neera said softly, taking his hand in hers. "You don't need to."

"I do." He squeezed her hand, running his thumb along hers. She'd removed her breastplate and wore only a loose linen tunic. He thanked Varyn no lasting damage had been done. Neera had been through enough.

When he found the remains of his tent, he drew a sharp breath, then swallowed hard.

"I can go." Neera cupped his cheek. "I'll go."

He shook his head, then gently pulled her hand away. He could see the spare breastplate Garramon had given him jutting from the pile of ash and charred bits.

He stepped past to the other side where he had placed the stake in the ground, where he had tethered Trusil. He stood there for a few moments, staring down at the horse's blackened bones and burnt flesh, the acrid smell still clinging to the air.

Rist moved to stand at the horse's head, the right side of which was barely recognisable. The left side, which had been pressed to the ground, still held some of his colouring. The blackened wooden handle of one of the long list of brushes Rist had acquired for keeping Trusil's coat clean and smooth stuck out from beneath the horse's neck. A dandy brush by the look of it.

He'd spent far too many hours reading about the proper care and tools needed to keep a horse healthy and happy. No, not far too many, he decided. Just enough.

"You were a good horse," Rist whispered, kneeling in the ashes.

"He was," Neera said from the other side of Trusil's remains. Tears rolled down her cheeks. "You took really good care of him, Rist."

"I did." Rist felt a tear of his own slowly run along the inside of his nose and drip onto Trusil's charred muzzle. He'd not lost many people in his life. He'd been lucky in that. Tommin, Anila... He'd barely known his grandparents. They'd died young. Seeing Trusil like that, helpless and alone, probably scared for his life... There was something different in that. "I wonder if he thought I left him," Rist whispered. He lifted his gaze to see Neera staring behind him, the sound of crunching ashes reaching his ears moments later.

A cold hand rested on the back of his neck.

"You had a bond with this creature?" The voice was harsh and layered, and Rist knew it immediately. He looked over his shoulder to see one of the Chosen standing there in a red shirt, black trousers tucked into muddied boots. He recognised the face of a young man, not much older than he, blue spiral tattoos snaking over his arms and winding up from his collar. This one called itself Azrim. It had barely left Rist's side during the battle.

"I did."

"Curious." Azrim dropped to his haunches beside Rist and stared down at Trusil's charred body for a moment before leaning forwards to touch the ashes.

Rist grabbed the Chosen's arm, his grip like iron. "Don't."

Azrim turned his head slowly, his deep black eyes staring into Rist's. "No?"

"No."

"Why?"

"Because that is not what you do to the dead."

"And what do you do to the dead, Rist Havel?"

"You respect them."

"How should I respect him?" Azrim looked down at the blackened bones of Trusil's ribs.

"Start with his name. He was called Trusil."

"Trusil..." Azrim spoke the name as though tasting it, staring at the ashes. "A name holds power."

"He liked carrots and apples," Rist said. "And he had a tendency to chew on fences if left next to them for too long. Only fences, never posts or trees."

"And he always licked my face," Neera added, wiping a tear from her eye.

Azrim just stared at Rist, tilting his head to the side, those black eyes betraying no emotion. "You will find *Trusil* again, Rist Havel. Efialtír treats life equally. This is only the mortal shell he was granted." Azrim raised a hand over Trusil's ashes, and threads of Air, Earth, Fire, and Spirit wove around his fingers. The threads of Air lifted some of Trusil's ashes into a vortex below Azrim's palm, swirling.

The threads of Fire, Earth, and Spirit wound about the thread of Air and all four pushed together. The vortex of ash collapsed in on itself, compressing into a tiny shape no bigger than the tip of Rist's pinky finger.

A low thrum sounded in Rist's head as the Spark pulsed from Azrim, and the small shape glowed white hot, the heat causing Rist to lean away.

After a moment, Azrim reached down and wrapped the floating ball of ash in his palm, the heat still bristling at Rist's skin. He squeezed his hand into a fist, and when he opened it, a small black diamond sat in the Chosen's palm.

Without a word, Azrim extended his hand and offered the diamond to Rist.

Rist took it into his hand and stared at the gleaming glass-like stone. He had seen a diamond once before, when a merchant's wife had passed through Milltown on the way to Skyfell. That one had been entirely transparent and reflected light in a multitude of colours. It had been fascinating.

The one Rist held in his palm was different. It was completely opaque and almost seemed to absorb the light instead of reflecting it.

Rist closed his fingers around the black diamond. "Thank you."

Azrim stood, continuing to stare down at the ashes.

"Rist." Rist turned at the sound of Garramon's voice. The Healers that had survived the dragonfire had seen to the burns on the man's face, but – despite many protestations – Garramon had insisted they leave the scars.

In general, Rist agreed with Garramon's belief that scars were reminders of the pain a person endured, that they should be left to never forget the darkness that had been overcome. But in this case, Rist most certainly would have let the Healers do their work. He still couldn't wrap his mind around the fact that it had been Calen who had caused that pain.

Despite calling his name, it wasn't Rist that Garramon was looking at. He stared directly at Azrim, his body tense, his hand resting on his sword pommel.

"The Saviour's light upon you, Brother Garramon." Azrim smiled from ear to ear in a way that sent a chill down Rist's spine, then strode away.

Garramon stared after him for a few moments. "Did you find him?"

Rist nodded, looking down at Trusil's remains. He held out the black diamond in his palm.

Garramon smiled, nodding softly. "Come," he said, gesturing to Neera as well. "We can't fall behind the main body. Without the wagons, the march will be faster, but food will be more scarce. They're not going to hold anything for us, not after a battle like that."

"How's Magnus?" Rist asked, slipping the black diamond into his pocket and keeping his hand there.

"Better, but still weak." A silence held for a few moments as they walked, the main body of the army – or at least, what was left of it – marching ahead. "Was that what you saw in your Trial of Will?"

Rist squeezed the diamond. "Is the trial a vision of the future?"

"I already told you, Rist. I don't know."

"No, you told me that some believe it is a warning from Efialtír of what will happen if we fail."

Garramon only grunted.

"Is that what you believe?"

"It is." Garramon stared off into the distance, his jaw clenching.

"What did you see in the well?"

Garramon drew a long breath and let it out in a sigh. "I saw my son. I saw Malyn. I killed him."

Before Rist could ask another question, Neera shuffled into the space on his left and gently squeezed his hand.

As they reached the tail of the army, Garramon dug his hand into his coat pocket and produced three carrots, each bearing scars and wounds of their own. "Most of the food got burned," he said with a weak smile, handing a carrot each to Rist and Neera. "These were the best I could get."

Rist opened his mouth to speak but couldn't find words.

"To Trusil," Garramon said, tapping the chopped end of his carrot against Rist's and then Neera's. He gave a soft mock neigh, which made Neera laugh, then he bit the end off and crunched.

Rist mimicked the gesture. "To Trusil."

Calen stood within the hollow section of the canopy of thick fog that spread for miles around, Boud's construct that obscured the land. The druid and her god had been true to their word and covered the others as they granted safe passage to the rebels who had escaped Tarhelm through the sally port – no more than a few hundred.

Kaygan, Fenryr, Ella, and the others all stood in a circle at the centre of the hollow, discussing the path forward, but their voices were nothing more than a dull throb in the back of his mind. The only sound that was clear was the thumping of his heart, and in his head all he saw was Rist walking away. None of it made any sense. No matter what way he looked at it.

He closed his eyes for a second and drew a long breath, steadying himself. When he opened them, Kaygan was looking directly at him.

"Una must rest," the god said, tilting his head sideways as he stared into Calen's eyes. He glanced at Una, who sat on the ground with her back against a tree, eyes closed. "The portals take their toll. We must return to Aravell now, lest she collapse here."

Fenryr eyed him askance, lip curling. "Your Starchaser's blood must be thin, brother. I have seen others carry half a thousand souls a dozen times."

"Well," Kaygan said with a mock bow, "the blood of the wolf is clearly much stronger than that of the kat, my dear brother. Perhaps your Starchaser should risk their life to carry more warriors to fight in a battle for a city that means nothing – oh apologies, none of yours yet live. Strange, that."

Calen snapped his head around and stared at the man who had once called himself Rokka. "That 'city that means nothing' is my home."

"But it is not *my* home." Kaygan took a step closer, fangs showing as he smiled. It still felt strange to Calen to think this was the same old man he had met in the hut near the Burnt Lands. "You must understand this, Calen Bryer. I walk the path that leads me to the future I need, and no other. If you did not need me – need Tamzin, and Boud, and Una – then you would not care if I lived or lay dead with my blood feeding the earth. You care little for the things that matter to me. Why should I care for the things that matter to you? I will not risk killing one of my own when it is completely avoidable. We will return to Aravell now. And we will take back those who travelled with us, and no more. Once we do, the fog will dissipate. If the rebels leave now, they will reach the Burnt Lands unscathed – more or less."

Kaygan leaned in a little closer, lowering his voice. "All actions have consequences, little Draleid. And it would be wise to think carefully before you believe yourself quick enough to play the great game of games. I've played a lot longer than you, and there are more players than you think."

Kaygan turned and left, Boud following him, the pair kneeling beside Una.

"My brother may call himself a kat, but he is a spider," Fenryr whispered to Calen. "It is always best to assume there is a deeper reason behind everything he does, lest you will be caught in his web."

"I'm beginning to see that," Calen said, watching Kaygan talk to the druids. He looked to Ella. "You haven't changed your mind?"

"About flying with you to Salme? I'm not sure Faenir would take too kindly to that," she said, scratching the massive wolfpine's cheek as he let out a low grumble.

"I'm sure Valerys could carry him in his talon."

Faenir snorted, glaring at Calen.

Calen only laughed, a laugh that died quickly. Rist consumed his thoughts.

"It's better I return to Aravell. Tanner and Yana will want to know what happened and that Farwen is gone. And Lasch and Elia need to be told that Rist is alive." Ella's eyes glossed over for a second, the molten gold fading to the blue she had been born with, then back again. She let out a soft sigh and nodded at Kaygan. "Besides, I don't trust that kat in the slightest. It's best someone watches over him."

Calen nodded but said nothing. Part of him wanted to be the one who told Lasch and Elia, but another part of him was thankful it would be Ella.

"I would have been honoured to fly with you," Coren said. "But my duty now is to see the survivors safe to Aravell." She inclined her head towards the few hundred rebels who had escaped Tarhelm through the sally port. He spotted the young woman, Yandira, near the edge of the group. "It is a long journey across the wasteland, even with the madness gone. I would see them safely across."

Coren moved so she stood just below Aldryn's jaw, brushing dirt from a long horn that scraped the ground. "You and Valerys fought like true warriors. I could not tell you how many of our kin were torn from this world by Seleraine and Voranur. There will not be a tear shed for them. And keeping Aldryn hidden was a wise stratagem. I can see why Aeson speaks so highly of you."

Something in Coren's stance shifted, and she looked down at the ground before returning her stare to Calen. "Earlier, there was something you said."

Calen nodded, knowing what was coming.

"You said that Tinua died fighting…"

"He did."

"How could you know that?" Coren looked at Fenryr. "You also. You told me that my master thought of me the night she died. I need to know."

Fenryr started to speak, but Calen cut across him. "I am a druid, like Ella, but we are different. I can see things, things that have already happened. I don't choose them, or when they happen, or what I see… but when I went to Ilnaen, we found dragon eggs buried in a hidden room in a vault below the western hatchery tower."

Coren's eyes widened. "How could you know of that? That place was—"

"I know that your master was Kollna, daughter of Luan, mother of Asius." Calen looked over to where Asius sat on a low rock, the wound in his shoulder cleaned and partially healed with Therin's aid. "I know that she called you Daughter of the Sea that night because that was where she found you – washed ashore after a shipwreck, no other survivors."

The woman who had seemed hard as steel faltered, her lip trembling. "H-how… how could you…"

"Alvira trusted Kollna. She asked her to hide dragon eggs in a room in that vault, surrounded by Jotnar runes. We found them."

"You found them?" Coren's eyes lit up.

Calen nodded. "They are being tested for the Calling as we speak. I can't see why they would be different to any other eggs in Epheria, but your master thought they were worth giving her life for." Calen sucked in his cheeks, tapping his foot against the ground. "She wanted you to know that you were ready. I could feel it in her heart that she believed you would be strong enough to survive."

Coren stared at Calen for a moment, but it wasn't what he saw in her eyes that betrayed the grief within her, it was Aldryn. The massive dragon craned his head down and pressed his snout into Coren's side. She snapped her eyes shut for just a second before opening them and grasping Calen's forearm. "Thank you."

"Thank *you* for saving our lives. Iralíse alaith, vésani. Aer varno."

Fly well, sister. Be safe.

"Ar du." *And you.* Coren grasped Calen's forearm. "We will see you in Aravell. And if you are not there, we will fly to Salme."

Calen made his way over to where Therin stood beneath Varthear's wing, threads of the Spark weaving into the dragon. Tivar stood beside him, both Avandeer and Valerys curled up at the dragon's head, watching, while Asius sat on a low rock to Tivar's right.

"Calen Bryer, son of Vars Bryer." Asius grunted as he tried to rise, his usually stony face grimacing.

"Rest," Calen said. Despite Asius sitting and Calen standing, Calen had to actually lift his hand to lay it on Asius's shoulder. "The portal will be open soon, and the Healers will look after you." Calen drew a short breath. "I am sorry for the loss of Thacia and Moras."

"They are part of the earth once more."

"As we were, so we will always be," Calen said, remembering the phrase Asius had used when they had first met.

Asius gave him a soft smile. "They can rest now. It is a rest they deserve. And many draw breath because of it. Gods willing, Larion will be in Aravell when I return. And for the first time in centuries, hundreds of my people will be together. It is only a shame that Senas, Thacia, and Moras will not be among them." Asius grimaced as he sat upright and stretched out his back. "When you return from Salme, I need you to promise me something, Calen Bryer, son of Vars Bryer, and Valerys, son of Valacia."

"Name it, Asius. If it is within our power, we will see it done."

"I need you to promise that my people will fight in the heart of the battles to come, that we will stand at the front of every line, and that we are beside you when we tear down Al'Nasla's walls."

Calen had never seen such fire in Asius's eyes, never heard such emotion in his voice. Calen wrapped his fingers around the Jotnar's pale blue forearm. "La'natal du myia vandíl."

I give you my oath.

"Ar du, myialí," Asius responded. *And you mine.*

Calen inclined his head to Asius, then looked over to where Therin and Tivar had been tending to Varthear. "How is she looking?"

"I'm not a strong enough Healer to see to these wounds on my own. Not properly," Therin answered, looking back at Calen with a sympathetic smile. Therin had seen Rist. "But this should get her to Salme. Tessara brought Healers with her." He looked over to Una, Kaygan, and Boud. "It would be simpler if we could bring a Healer here from Aravell."

"That it would," Calen responded. "For some reason, I don't think Kaygan wants this to be simple." Calen reached up and brushed his fingers along Varthear's scarred snout as she leaned down to greet him. "Thank you. Without you, we would be dead."

The dragon gave a low rumble, her nostrils flaring as she blew a warm breath over him. Flashes of memory passed through him, but they were not Varthear's… They were Ella's.

He saw himself through his sister's eyes as he lay unconscious in the snow, Rhett kneeling beside him. Panic flooded her heart, followed by warmth as Rhett picked Calen's body up from the snow.

The memory flashed forward to when they sat on the porch before The Proving, Calen sharpening his knife on the whetstone. He remembered that morning well.

"How sharp can a knife be?" Ella asked as she found Calen sitting on the porch.

Calen remembered his sister speaking those words in a mocking tone, but as he looked through her eyes, all he felt was worry and fear.

Calen pulled his mind away and stared into the dragon's red eyes. "How do you have those memories?"

"What's wrong?" Tivar asked, turning her head to look into Calen's eyes. She touched his cheek, cupped a hand to pull his eyes towards hers. Her touch was gentle and soft, her skin warm.

"I…" He looked into Tivar's eyes, finding genuine concern there. He pulled his cheek away, glancing over at Ella. "I'm all right," Calen answered, gathering his thoughts. "We need to be in the air."

"Avandeer is ready," Tivar responded, not looking away from his eyes.

Calen nodded slowly, reaching out to Valerys as both he and Avandeer rose from behind Varthear.

Therin turned and wiped the blood from his hands with a ragged old cloth. "Calen, if Valerys would have me, I would fly with you to Salme."

"What about Faelen?"

"Faelen is safe, but Salme is not. And it means I could take further care of Varthear along the way. There are people I care about there. I spoke to Faelen of this possibility before I left."

Calen looked up at Valerys, who shifted closer and lowered his head so the tip of his snout was barely half a foot from Therin's face, lavender eyes looking down at the elf. A brief moment of quiet passed between them, and Valerys pushed his snout into Therin's chest.

"We leave now," Calen said.

I'm coming, Dann.

CHAPTER EIGHTY-SIX

WALK THROUGH THE ASHES

23rd Day of the Blood Moon

Western villages of Illyanara – Winter, Year 3081 After Doom

The army had marched ceaselessly for three days, sleeping as little as they dared and moving as swiftly as their legs could carry them. The elves kept guard at night; they slept less than the others. Queen Tessara, Baralas, and Thurivîr had argued endlessly over who should have the 'honour' of holding the night's watch. An honour which Tarmon had happily ceded to them.

The Uraks' path had not been a difficult one to track. Every structure, every farm, inn, house, cottage – every single one – had been left burning, every soul within slaughtered, the land broken by the weight of the creatures' steps. Corpses had hung from trees, limbs hacked free. Rows upon rows of rotting severed heads were impaled on spikes running along on either side of the dirt road from Camylin to Erith. Dann's squire, Nala, had vomited at the sight. And then again a few moments later. Many of the other young squires and porters who travelled with the army did the same – along with a fair few of those who had seen many more summers. Dann didn't blame them. The fact that his own stomach didn't turn upset him in a way. It meant he had grown so accustomed to the horrors of war that even a sight as grotesque as severed heads on spikes had little effect other than setting an ache in his heart.

Smouldering cookfires and remnants of spiked trenches and makeshift fortifications of felled trees and iron signalled where the creatures had camped each night, the markings of their passage stretching for miles across.

All Dann had ever known of Uraks was that they were mindless beasts that killed and slaughtered. Everything he'd seen in his life had supported those thoughts. But seeing the fortifications they'd laid and the purposeful display of the mutilated bodies had shown him how wrong he'd been. These creatures moved with intent. They placed the bodies to brew terror. They laid their fortifications with care and thought. And for some reason, learning that he'd been wrong, learning that they were not the mindless animals he'd thought they were, had only served to strike even deeper fear into his heart.

The Uraks were terrifying enough when they were no better than beasts. But if they could plan, build fortifications, lay siege, set traps, it meant that these were not beasts who killed simply to eat and survive, monstrous from instinct alone. Nor did they do it for the reasons humans and elves did: land, glory, jealousy. It seemed to him the Uraks killed for nothing more than the sake of killing itself. They revelled in it, yearned for it.

His heart had sunk when they'd reached the long-broken and charred ruin of Erith. The village had been destroyed months ago, long before the Uraks who had razed Camylin had passed over it. The bodies were nothing but blackened husks, collapsing beneath the weight of the birds and animals that roamed the ruins. The rotting corpses of five children had been twisted about each other and pinned to a tree by a single black spear, forming some kind of gruesome rune shape. The skin had sloughed off their bones, ripped and torn where the birds had picked away at them. He'd only known they were children by the size of the corpses.

He didn't stop, nor did he dismount, but he whispered the blessings of the gods as he passed. A prayer to Heraya to take them into her embrace, to Varyn to watch over those who yet lived, to Neron to see their souls safely from the world, to Elyara in hope that she might gift him the wisdom to defeat what lay before them, to Achyron to grant him courage, and to Hafaesir to forge him into the man he needed to be.

The villages were his home. And in truth, he had not expected to ever see them again. But he had expected even less to find them in this state. The scouts had reported both Pirn and Ölm had shared the same fate. All he could think about is what if that had been young Lyna Styr, or Aren Ehrnin, or Tim Ferlok. That was something Dann had not prepared himself for; it was not something he thought he ever could prepare himself for. He knew the Uraks had attacked The Glade. He knew the place itself was gone – though he still couldn't spend too long thinking on it. But he had not asked Haem whose faces he'd seen amongst the dead. Dann wasn't ready for that.

They encountered small groups of Uraks as they travelled through Ölm forest. Scatterings of the creatures that had fallen behind the main body. After what the soldiers had seen in Erith and along the road… Dann had never witnessed such fervour in killing. The men and elves tore the Uraks limb from limb, hacking and slashing long after the beasts were dead.

As the sun sat high in the sky on the third day, they stopped by a stream nestled in the heart of Ölm Forest. At first glance, the woodland looked just as it had done during The Proving. The air was still thick and heavy. The trees still held sway, their vast, arthritic limbs creaking and groaning with the breeze. Gnarled roots stretched across the forest floor, mushrooms of vibrant yellows and blues sprouting in the damp soil around them. That same incessant, unrelenting buzz of insects filled the air.

And yet all was different. Bodies of men, women, and Uraks were scattered through the roots and foliage, all mashed and trampled, clawed footprints pressing into the soil everywhere Dann looked. The air may still have been heavy, but it no longer smelled the same; the ancient scent of time was gone, replaced with that of iron, and shit, and blood, and death. Birdsong no longer played chase with the breeze. No hares or squirrels scuttled about. He saw a wolfpine prowling through the thicket, but the animal had simply torn a chunk of flesh from a corpse and fled.

The air of magic and wonder with which he'd always viewed the forest was as dead as the bodies that now decorated its depths. And the fear he'd once felt was nothing but a lingering memory. What he feared now lay on the other side of the forest.

The sight of it all made Dann think back to that herd of stampeding deer he, Calen, and Rist had found when hunting. Those claw marks in the stag's ribs had been the first sign of what was to come. That seemed a lifetime ago now.

Dann dismounted, patting Drunir's neck. "Drink up."

Beside him, Nala dismounted from the bay mare Dann had gifted her – one of those he'd 'liberated' from the Lorian forces a while back. It was a fine animal with a good temperament. Probably would have cost an arm and a leg to buy in The Glade.

"How are you finding her?" Dann asked as he dropped to his haunches. He made to dip his waterskin into the stream but stopped at the sight of two bloated and rotting corpses pressed against the bank on the other side. All around him, men and elves were lined along both banks, thousands of them. Some filled their skins, others washed the accumulated dirt and sweat of constant travel from their face and hands, while others again stripped bare and dove into the water with alacrity. Either they hadn't seen the bodies or they had seen so many in the weeks of travel that they no longer cared.

At any other point in his life – were it not for the bodies – that likely would have been Dann. But he was tired, not just in his joints, muscles, and bones, but in his heart. He had seen what the Uraks had done to the other villages, knew what they'd do to Salme if Dann and the others didn't reach it in time.

"Can I be honest, my lord?"

Dann shook the dark thoughts from his head. "What did I say about the 'my lord'?"

When the porter in Durakdur – Conal, he thought his name was – had insisted on calling Calen m'lord every ten seconds, Dann had mocked Calen with every breath he could. He couldn't right well then turn around and allow Nala to call him the same. Dann had no problem if people called him an arsehole, but he wouldn't be named a hypocrite.

Besides, there was something 'wrong' about the word. He was the son of a tanner, not the son of a lord. There were no lords in the villages. The closest lords had resided in Camylin, and they were all dead now most likely. Not that he'd ever known their names in the first place. The only name he'd known was High Lord Castor Kai, and even then that had meant little. Nobody had ever really cared about the western villages, and that had suited everyone just fine.

"Sorry..." Nala dipped her head and pursed her lips. The girl was so timid. Though the sights of the past few days had knocked much of that out of her. Seeing grown men empty their stomachs at the sight of rotting corpses seemed to have made her feel a little better about doing it herself.

"It's fine." Dann waved her away, smiling. "You were saying?"

She nodded to herself. "I was saying... I was saying that I've never ridden a horse before, at least, not for long journeys, and I didn't know it hurt so much."

"Your arse sore? Insides of your legs burning? Stomach muscles cramping?"

Nala nodded again. "You too? It seemed like I was the only one."

"That's because you're the only squire with a horse," Dann pointed out. He'd started calling Nala his squire as opposed to his attendant after Tarmon had explained the difference. Many of the tasks were the same: look after the horses, clean and polish the armour, set up and take down the tents, wash his clothes and bedding, and all other manner of tasks Dann was more than happy to do himself. But the way Tarmon had put it was that a squire came with responsibility. Nala was Dann's to look after, to teach – not just in how to string a bow or hold a sword, but in how to live, and how to treat others, and how to carry herself. Which was a good thing, because Dann barely knew how to hold a sword himself. But something about it all appealed to him. He'd never had any siblings.

Nala had lost her parents to the Uraks, and her two brothers were a year and three years younger. The eldest of the two was squired elsewhere in the army, while the younger remained at Aravell.

"If you'd like," he said, opening his palms out, "I can see if someone else would like to take the horse off your hands?"

"No!" The sharpness of Nala's tone took Dann off guard. She stroked the mare's side. "Maria is a beautiful horse. I'm really thankful, I swear it. By Varyn and by Elyara. I've just got to get used to it is all – the riding that is."

Dann gave Nala a flat stare, looking from the young girl to the horse and then back again. "You named the horse Maria?"

The girl nodded. "Maria Brown."

"Because she's brown?"

Nala nodded again, a proud grin on her face.

"Maria the horse. Maria and Drunir... It doesn't exactly roll off the tongue. We can think of other names along the way."

"No, I like Maria." Nala frowned and stroked Maria's hair defensively.

"Well, not the hill I'd choose to die on, but Maria it is, I suppose."

Nala straightened, her eyes widening. "My lord." She pointed across the river.

Dann reflexively reached for the bow at his back, his fingers brushing the white wood, when his eyes fell on what Nala had seen. That stumpy little fucking bird. The creature had followed them all the way from the Darkwood, popping up out of nowhere like some kind of mole. How in the gods it kept up with the army on those little legs he'd never know. Another thing he'd never know is how in the gods he'd ended up in a battle of wits with a stumpy, kleptomaniacal, flightless bird. But he had, and he was losing.

Nala pulled her own bow from where it hung on Maria's saddle. She'd barely had it a week and never remembered to unstring it. She reached for an arrow, but Dann raised a hand.

"But my lo—Dann…" She paused after saying his name, as though she'd broken some kind of rule. "I thought we wanted to kill it."

He shook his head and lifted his chin. "I've chosen a path of peace, Nala."

"Very noble of you, my lord—I mean, Commander."

Dann stared across the bank at the bird. The little shit was staring right back at him, its beady eyes blending in with its brown and black feathers. He was reasonably sure the creature didn't blink. Or at least, if it did, he'd never seen it do so.

"Emm… Commander."

The tone in Nala's voice told Dann all he needed to know. He let out a long sigh. "What does it have?"

As though answering his question, the bird dipped its head and pulled up a section of white cloak trimmed with purple and gold.

He turned and glared at Nala. "Does that thing have my cloak?"

"Emm… It appears so, Commander Sureheart. It must have gotten into the wagon." She looked back at the wagon a few paces behind, which was being pulled by a stout horse while a man with a bowl-shaped hat held the reins.

"Nala." Dann pressed his tongue against his lip. "Did you lock the chest?"

"I… I… I thought I had. I did. I remember doing it."

"So you're telling me that bird – which has no hands, mind you – either picked the lock with its beak or stole your key?"

Nala patted at her pocket, relief spreading across her face. "It didn't steal my key."

"So you're sticking with the story that the bird picked the lock… with its beak."

"Yes, my lord—I mean, Commander."

"With its beak?" he repeated.

The girl stared back at him, her expression set in stone.

"Now I know how Aeson and Therin feel," he muttered.

"What did you say? I didn't hear you."

"I said go get my cloak."

The girl stared back at him for a minute, dumbfounded.

"Go!"

Nala set her bow back on Maria's saddle and leapt into the river where it was only knee deep. Upon spotting her, the bird attempted to snatch up the cloak and flee. But all it could do was shift the cloak an inch or so before stumbling over, giving up, and darting away through the shrubbery faster than it had any right to.

"This means war, bird," Dann whispered as Nala hauled herself onto the opposite bank and snatched up his cloak. "This means war."

Beside him Drunir snorted, stomping a hoof.

"Glad to have you with me. And you, Maria?" What a stupid name for a horse. Maria?

But even as Dann pressed his fingers into his cheeks, the horse stared back at him with what looked to be almost a smile, her top lip lifting.

Dann scratched at her neck. "You're not half bad."

After Nala made it back across the river, changed her trousers, and set Dann's sodden cloak back in the chest, she proceeded to triple-check it was locked. With a confident look on her face, she moved on to tend to the horses. As she combed Drunir's mane, Erik strode through the wood and stopped at Dann's side.

He looked out at those bathing in the stream, then turned to Dann, his gaze lingering. "How are you holding up? It can't have been easy seeing that village the way it was."

"I'm good." Dann tucked his thumbs in behind his belt, his mind picking back through the images of mutilated corpses and burnt houses. "It's just strange. I'd never even been to Erith before. Furthest I'd gone was Ölm. And that's gone too. We'll reach The Glade soon – what's left of it. That will be even stranger."

"We won't let them do the same to Salme."

"No," Dann said, shaking his head. "We won't." A few moments of silence passed, filled by chattering and the splashing of water. "I've not seen my mam and dad in almost two years." His throat constricted, the words growing heavy on his tongue. "I don't know if they're… What if…"

"We'll deal with each thing as it comes, Dann. That's all we can do. No more, no less."

Dann gave Erik a nod. He'd grown to appreciate the man over the past few months. "I found myself thinking last night, were it not for you and your brother and your father, Calen and I would likely be long dead. And at the same time, were it not for you, Calen would never have killed that soldier outside The Two Barges either and the past two years would have been very different."

"I never asked him to do that. He shouldn't have been there—"

"I'm glad he was there. Though, 'glad' isn't a strong enough word. Whether he had been or not, the Uraks still would have burned The Glade, but there likely wouldn't be an army marching to Salme's aid… and Calen and I and everyone we've ever known would be dead."

"It's funny how one moment, one single event, can change so much. If we'd arrived in Milltown a day earlier or a day later. Or stayed in a different inn—"

"Or you'd remembered your mantle."

Erik laughed. "Or you'd not gotten so drunk and made enough noise to wake the whole town throwing axes."

"What did me drinking have to do with anything?"

"You made it look like a good time. And I'd been in serious need of a good time that night. Something to take my mind off… everything. A lot of people died in Valacia."

Dann saw the pain in Erik's eyes, the darkness he knew so well. "So what you're saying is that me getting drunk is going to save Salme?"

"That's not even remotely…" Erik gave a resigned laugh, that pain momentarily fading. "Yes, Dann. You getting drunk is going to save Salme."

Shouts echoed through the forest. "Ready to march!"

Erik gave a long sigh, then rested a hand on Dann's shoulder. "We'll get there in time, Dann."

Dann nodded, giving Erik a half-smile, then turned to Nala. "Before we leave, take that cloak out of the chest and drape it over Drunir's back. How do you think it's going to dry stuffed in that chest?"

THE LAST TIME DANN HAD looked down at The Glade from the edge of Ölm Forest with the sun sinking into the horizon had been the night Therin had told the story of The Fall.

That night, columns of smoke had drifted languidly from chimneys and the sounds of the Moon Market had danced on the air. He'd always loved the view of the rooves under the light of the setting sun, the twilight glow spilling through the trees. That view – to him – was home.

That view was gone.

No smoke rose from chimneys, and the few rooves that remained to glow in the setting sun were coated in char and tainted by the light of that damned moon. He could see the remnants of his home amidst the ruin and death, three of the four walls collapsed, the roof caved in.

The army continued on a steady march down the hill and off along the dirt road towards Salme, keeping its distance from the ruins of The Glade.

"You go ahead," Dann said to Nala, gesturing for her to carry on with the others.

"This is your home?" the young squire asked.

"It is… or at least it was."

"Then I'm coming with you. You shouldn't be alone."

Dann didn't have the heart to argue with her. "Come on then."

He gave a *click* with the side of his mouth and tapped Drunir with his heels. The horse neighed and set off down the hill towards The Glade, his breath misting in the evening air.

Dann caught Tarmon's eye as he separated from the column, and the big man just nodded to him, holding his gaze for a few moments.

After a minute or so, Lyrei appeared at Drunir's side. She looked up at Dann and gave him a weak smile, not saying a word.

He dismounted at the village's edge and lead Drunir in by the reins. Nala and Maria stayed a few feet behind, the young girl's eyes drifting over Urak corpses that had been reduced to little more than bones and gnawed flesh. The wolfpines and kats must have scavenged the village after the fighting.

Strangely, Dann found no human corpses. Only Uraks and livestock, a few horses, bones peeking through rotted and torn flesh. The smell was horrid. The vomit-inducing stench of decaying flesh was so palpable it coated Dann's tongue and caused him to choke. That, blended with the 'wonderful' aroma of freshly laid shit, assaulted his senses.

Drunir walked alongside him without faltering, but he could hear Maria's complaints behind him, snorting and nickering. He didn't blame her. The Glade – the place that had always given him warm, fond memories – was a place of darkness and sorrow now, and animals had a way of feeling that more viscerally than most people did. They could sense things, feel the anguish in the air.

Partly-burnt wood cracked and split beneath Dann's feet as he walked the ruined street towards The Gilded Dragon. He stopped and pushed some of the blackened wood aside. His heart clenched when he unearthed what looked to be half a skull, cleaved clean from left temple to right jaw, the flesh burnt away. Whoever had cleared bodies had not found this. A hundred faces flashed across his mind's eye, from Verna Gritten to Marlo Egon to Iwan Swett – not that he cared much for Kurtis's father, but that didn't mean he'd wish death upon the man.

He dropped to his haunches and brushed the char from the severed skull, then picked it up and stood.

Lyrei reached out and took it from him gently, placing it into her satchel. She clasped his hand and squeezed. Only for a second, then let it go. Not a word passed between them, but it was like she could feel his soul.

"Why?" he heard Nala whisper to Lyrei as Dann brushed aside more of the rubble, finding no skeleton to go with the skull. He pretended he didn't hear and just kept moving.

"The dead should not be left alone in a place like this," Lyrei whispered back. "Someone took the other bodies. So maybe they're buried here, or maybe at Salme or somewhere along the way."

Ahead, at the end of the street scattered with broken spear shafts and Urak corpses, stood the remains of The Gilded Dragon. It would have broken Lasch's heart to see the ruin that it was. The entire building had collapsed in. What was left of the wood was brittle and black.

Amidst the death of his home, Dann allowed a smile to curl his lips. He dropped to one knee and pulled a large chunk of soot-covered wood from beneath the cover of a broken shield.

"What is it?" Lyrei asked, standing behind him.

Dann ran his fingers over the scales of the wooden dragon that had once stood atop one of the inn's balusters. Some slashes marred its surface, it was covered in soot and ash, and the tail was snapped where the baluster had been split, but he was pleasantly surprised at how intact it was – and how heavy it was. "A memory," he said, running his fingers along the wooden tail. "A dragon surviving the fire… almost poetic. It's something that will lift the weight in Lasch's heart a little bit."

Dann hauled the wooden dragon up and into his arms. He stopped and looked at Drunir. "What do you think? Can you take it?"

The horse stomped defiantly, as though saying 'What do you think I am, a donkey? Of course I can.'

Dann leaned in and touched the side of his head against Drunir's. "Good boy. That's what I thought."

Dann strapped the wooden dragon to the back of the saddle, propping a blanket at the back to make sure it didn't dig into Drunir.

They carried on through the village, passing the husk of the Fjorns' home, the Grittens', and many others.

A clear patch of earth sat where Calen's home had once been. The Lorians had set it aflame when they'd killed Vars and Freis. But someone had replanted Freis's lavender bushes, and they'd spread about the perimeter of the old home. The bushes looked dead, the deep green colouring turned a shade of silver. But that was how they always looked in winter. That silver would fade, and those purple flowers would bloom again.

Calen would find a lot of joy in knowing someone had replanted them, and Calen deserved a little joy.

The last place Dann stopped was the place he had been avoiding – his own home.

It was ash and broken things. The doorframe still stood, empty, a small section of wall allowing it to hold its place. But that was it.

He stared at that charred ruin in silence, the world fading around him. It wasn't until Lyrei's hand slipped into his that the gentle sound of the breeze touched his ears again. As she had an easy ability to do, she said a lot without speaking, her gaze fixed on the ashes, her shoulder pressed close to his.

Even Nala stayed quiet.

"I don't know if they're alive," Dann said after a long silence. He'd not said it out loud, not till then. The Angan hadn't said anything about who from The Glade had survived. And Dann had felt too selfish to ask. So many people had lost their loved ones in this war, and so many more people would continue to do so. Who was he to ask a question like that? He had no more right to solace than anyone else.

Though, as he stood there, the depth of his worry sinking in, he wished he had asked, right or no.

Lyrei squeezed his hand, but it was Nala who spoke.

"My father always used to say that there are things we can control and things we can't. And that it's best not to dwell on the things we can't because they'll drive us mad. I hope your parents are all right, my lord."

When Dann looked back at her, the young squire dropped her gaze. "I'm sorry, I shouldn't have spoken."

"My dad said something similar." He let go of Lyrei's hand and instead squeezed Nala's shoulder. "We're family now, Nala. You and your brothers aren't alone. I know it might feel like it sometimes, but you're not."

He let out a soft sigh, then turned and grabbed Drunir's reins. "Best not to linger. No telling if there are Uraks nearby."

When they neared the edge of the ruined village, Dann mounted Drunir, Nala doing the same with Maria. Not fifty feet past the last burnt husk of a home, Dann spotted something that turned his blood to ice and twisted his heart.

"What do you see?" Lyrei whispered from Drunir's right side.

Dann glanced at Nala on Maria to his left. She was staring away at the column of soldiers and banners marching up the dirt road. He gestured toward the rows and rows of graves just past the oak tree. Soil and rocks were scattered about the holes in the ground, upturned saplings half-buried, the ground turned to pieces.

"The graves have been dug up," he whispered. "The bodies have been taken."

THE ARMY MARCHED ALONG THE dirt road, passing more broken farms and burnt holds, heads skewered on spikes and limbs scattered about. Many of the corpses were Lorian, at least the ones whose breastplates were intact enough to make out the black lion.

Strangely, knowing the dead men and women were Lorian brought Dann no joy. Some of the soldiers kicked the corpses, or spat, or cursed, but he saw no point in it. Corpses were corpses, and it was a dark thing to look on any of them. Whatever they had been in life, they were dead now. And doubtless they'd left behind people who loved them. Dann would do what he needed to do, but he refused to take joy in seeing dead men.

When they reached the fork in the road that sprouted one direction towards Salme and the other towards Talin, he couldn't help but imagine Talin in the same state of ruin as The Glade had been. Dann had friends in Talin. Or more so his father had friends, and those friends had children. He hoped they'd made it to Salme.

Tarmon dropped back and spent some time riding beside Dann, Nala, and Lyrei. The man said little – as always – but the few words he did say were the right ones. As always.

They kept a steady clip as the sun sank into the horizon, yielding to the pale pink light of the moon. They would reach Salme in the next few hours but as of yet had seen little trace of the Urak horde besides the bodies and ruin it had left in its wake – though much of that had been done long before.

Dann was stroking the side of Drunir's neck when three riders came galloping along the outside of the column, bellowing for Tarmon.

"What news?" Tarmon asked after calling them over. "Uraks?"

"It's best if you see for yourself, Commander," one of the riders said.

"I'll have the meat of it now."

The man shook his head. "Bodies, my lord. It's... I would not speak of it. Please."

Elves in the black of Vaelen, crimson and gold of Luntihír, and green of Ardurän approached, all with curious faces.

Ilvalis, one of the Vaelen captains Dann recognised, raised a hand. "Need we prepare for battle, Narvír?"

Tarmon waved him away and focused on the scout. "Look at me, and breathe. Are we in danger?"

The man shook his head. "Not... not immediately, my lord. Please, it's best you come."

Tarmon gestured to Dann and Lyrei, then cracked his reins and galloped up the column with the scouts, calling out to halt the march.

Queen Tessara and the Ephorí joined them about halfway, on the backs of Dvalin Angan, along with Erik and Vaeril.

"What've they found?" Erik asked as he pulled his mount beside Dann.

Dann just shook his head and gave a slight shrug. But as they cleared the front of the marching column and Dann saw over the crest of the hill, he pulled on Drunir's reins and spun the horse around. "Nala, close your eyes."

"But I—"

"Close them, *now*. And don't let Maria take another step."

He understood that even children could not be spared from the horrors of war. Not in a world where they would have to face those horrors every day. But there were some things no child should ever have to witness, no matter what. Some things no soul at all should have to witness.

"What in all the gods…" Tarmon sat stunned on his mount, his jaw agape, his shoulders slumped.

Someone retched.

Once he was sure Nala's eyes were firmly closed and she wasn't going to move, Dann turned back and tapped Drunir's side. The horse continued to where Erik, Vaeril, Tarmon, and the others all waited, staring out.

Dread crept through Dann's veins and crawled over his skin.

Before him the hill levelled out into an open plain, split by the long dirt road to Salme. The Oak Road, it had always been called on account of the old oak trees that framed the path for miles, planted centuries ago. Some stood as high as seventy or eighty feet, their massive trunks almost six feet across, their branches gnarled and twisting. He'd walked the road before, a number of times, accompanying his dad as Tharn went to trade leather at Salme's port. He'd been in awe every time.

But that night, in the dark, the pale red light of the moon spilling through twisted branches, dismembered bodies were nailed to the ancient oaks, each in various stages of rot and decay. Arms and legs hacked free, massive bolts of iron holding them in place. The trees looked like voidspawn come alive.

Dann could only make out the first few trees on either side of the road, but something in the air told him those bodies went on for miles. He knew now why the bodies in The Glade had been dug up.

"Why?" one of the captains – Surin – asked.

"Fear." Tarmon held his reins slack in his lap, his stare unmoving from the corpse-covered trees.

"We can't march through that…" Ingvat said, sat astride a piebald gelding.

"Every moment we ponder here is a moment wasted." Thurivîr stood with his hand resting on his pommel. "These people are dead, and there is nothing we can do for them except enact vengeance."

Dann hated to even contemplate agreeing with the elf – especially considering Thurivîr was more motivated about returning to Aravell than he was saving Salme. And yet, he did agree. "The road is the quickest way." Dann looked back at Nala, who still sat in Maria's saddle with her eyes closed. "The land grows rough on both sides. The rocks are near impassable along the coast with a number this large, and if we try and take the hills near Talin, it will add a day at least. We don't have a day… Salme doesn't have a day."

Queen Tessara moved closer to the trees, staring up at the twisted bodies nailed to the gnarled limbs. She turned back to Tarmon. "You speak with the Draleid's voice, Narvír Hoard. This is his army. What say you?"

Tarmon shifted his gaze from the trees to Dann, then back down the hill to the massive column of souls that waited behind them. Shouts and murmurs echoed up the hill in the cold night. "I would rather not force this sight upon even a single pair of eyes. That is what the Uraks want. They want us to fear them, to fear what they will do to us. But no, we will march along this road. We will face the darkness they have set before us, and we will use it. We will show our people the kind of monsters we are fighting. We will show them the courage that is needed. And when we have slaughtered the dark beasts that did this, when we have ripped out their hearts and set their bones on fire, we will come back here and we will remove each and every body. And we will see them into Achyron's halls." Tarmon sat still astride his massive mount, nodding gently to himself, his breath rising in the cold air. "For now, there are others who need our blades, our courage, and our strength," he said, turning his horse. Tarmon roared, "Dracurïn, forward to Salme!"

CHAPTER EIGHTY-SEVEN

SALME

24th Day of the Blood Moon

Salme – Winter, Year 3081 After Doom

Dahlen filled his lungs with the frigid air, his hands clasped at his back. Salme was so silent he could have heard a feather touching the dirt at the base of the wall. It had been that way since the mass of torches had crested the hill a couple of miles north of the city. Thousands of Uraks, their roars and guttural cries carrying down the hill and through the night.

"Where did they all come from?" The young lad, Conal, stood to Dahlen's left with a spear in his fist, makeshift patches of leather armour on his chest, back, arms, and thighs. Dahlen had no intention of allowing Conal to fight on the walls, but when the Uraks did break through and the defences fell, it was better he had a spear in his hand.

"Camylin." Erdhardt folded his arms and stared up at the mass of torches. "The city has fallen."

Murmurs spread along packed walls and on the ground behind them. The horns had been blown, and every soul in Salme was awake, armoured, and ready. The city held just short of seven thousand souls, gathered from all the villages, farms, and holds across western Illyanara, along with many who had fled Camylin before the siege and travellers who had traversed the province in search of shelter – only to find themselves walled in against the coast. But of that number, many were injured, or too young, or too old, or too sick. The people of the villages were hard and strong, but spare few were true warriors.

A small part of him wished he had left for Aravell when he had intended to, and another part called him a fool for not taking passage on a merchant vessel to Valtara as others had. But the rest of him was proud of where he stood. If this place was to be where his bones rested, then so be it. He would die beside people he had grown to respect, people he trusted. He would die in the only place that had felt like home since he'd lost his mother. His only wish was that he could have shared one last night with Erik and his father.

Dahlen looked down at Nimara, who stood at his right. He could tell by her eyes that she knew the same as him: this would be their last night. There was no world in which the city could stand against a force this large.

The dwarf brushed her hand against his. She inclined her head, a resigned smile on her lips.

"Maybe the bards will tell stories of this night after we're long gone." Yoring could barely see over the parapet of the palisade, his hand resting on a thick spike.

"I'd rather prefer to be the one telling the story, dwarf," Tharn Pimm answered. "If that's all right with you."

As the others spoke, Erdhardt tapped Dahlen on the shoulder and gestured to the ground below where Lanan Halfhand stood with Kara Thain and the other elders, along with Exarch Dorman and the Lorian captains.

Dahlen, Erdhardt, Nimara, and Thannon descended to meet them, leaving Camwyn, Yoring, and Almer to watch over the walls. The open ground at the base of the walls was crammed with men and women grasping spears, axes, and shields. Most wore leather armour with rings of iron mail, while some were lucky enough to protect themselves with steel plate. It was a far cry from the equipment they'd all had before the Blood Moon had risen.

Captain Kiron, the merchant who sailed the waters between Valtara and Salme, had done right by them. The man had provided hoards of iron and leather, along with spears and axes and Valtaran ordo shields. Kiron had been fair about it too. He could have taken Salme for all it had, but he didn't.

"Be honest," Lanan said when Dahlen and the others approached, her arms folded, the brass rings in her nose glinting in the moonlight. "What are our chances?"

"Slim," Exarch Dorman replied before Dahlen had a chance. The mage looked at Dahlen and inclined his head. "I'd wager the reason the attacks have been light of late is that the Uraks had focused on Camylin. If they're here now in these numbers, Camylin is no more."

Dorman didn't need to continue. He'd said what he'd needed to without putting the rest into words: if Camylin had fallen, Salme stood no chance.

Silence descended, broken by Erdhardt. "Slim or no, we've not got much choice."

"There are ships in the port." Yarik Tumber looked over his shoulder in the direction of Salme's port, which was obscured by the houses and buildings. "We could—"

"We could what?" Dahlen snapped. "Those are boats, not ships, and there are enough to carry no more than a hundred, maybe two. What of the other seven thousand souls in this city?"

"I was only suggesting—"

"You were only suggesting we sneak away in the night and leave the others to die."

"And what else would you have us do? Stand and die like pigs when you yourself can clearly see there will be no dawn? Why should every soul here die when some can live?"

"Because that is what the villages do. We stand together." Erdhardt stepped forwards and loomed over Yarik, who – to his credit – didn't back down. The two men stood square to each other, moments away from coming to blows. "We do not leave others behind."

Dahlen moved between them and pushed them apart. He turned to two of the former Belduaran Kingsguard – Origal and Nayce – who had taken to following him on night watch as his personal guards. "Please escort Yarik Tumber to the great hall with the children and the elderly."

"At once, Lord Captain."

"What in the gods?" Yarik shuffled backwards at Origal and Nayce's approach. "You do not have that authority here!"

Dahlen rounded on the man. "You have just shown us that you are craven. I have no use for men who would run while others die, or worse, men who would push another onto a striking blade. You are nothing but a liability on those walls. And I will not have someone die for your cowardice. Do what you like, Elder Yarik, sip wine and eat cheese in the hall. But you will not hold a spear this night. Not while I breathe."

Yarik looked to Lanan, Ylinda, and the other elders, outraged. "Are you going to let this stand? He is not even *of* the villages. He does not belong here."

"I do not originally hail from the villages, Yarik." Kara Thain shrugged, her hand resting on the pommel of the sword at her hip. She was one of the few in the villages to wield one, outside of the Belduarans and the Lorians. "Would you say I have no voice here?"

"No. I… That's not what I meant."

Dahlen gestured to Origal and Nayce, who grabbed Yarik beneath the armpits and began to haul him away.

The man swiped at them and yanked his arms free. "I can walk myself."

"With all that said and done," Exarch Dorman said as Nayce and Origal escorted Yarik to the great hall. "What *is* our plan? I'm assuming you don't wish to lay down and die?"

"You're not taking the boats and fleeing then, no?" Dahlen folded his arms and held Dorman's gaze. There had been even less love lost between the Lorians and the people of the west since the brawl in The Rusty Shell – which had been followed by four more since. Dahlen would have had the ale cut off were it not the only thing providing any joy to most of those within Salme's walls.

"If we were going to take the ships and flee, Lord Captain, we would have done so. We stand with you."

Beside Dahlen, Thannon visibly tensed, his jaw twitching.

Dahlen nodded to himself, looking around at those gathered, taking everything in. "Dorman, we'll need half your infantry at the western wall, half at the east, ready for if the Uraks break through." Dahlen used the word 'if', but they all knew he meant 'when'. "We'll need soldiers who can hold a tight formation ready to face the tide. My Wolves will form the core at the main gate."

The 'Silver Wolves' was a nickname the people of Salme had granted Dahlen and the surviving Kingsguard ever since the fur trader, Owen, had gifted them the wolfpineskin cloaks. The burnished steel plate Thannon and the others wore had played no small part either. The name had been extended to include men and women of Salme who had distinguished themselves and joined Dahlen's guard in battle. They numbered just under a hundred in total, including the old Kingsguard. Each wore polished breastplates procured through Captain Kiron, while a few had scraps of steel covering their shoulders, arms, or legs. Dahlen like the name. It had been well earned.

"We can hold the cavalry in reserve in the plaza. We need them to have mobility," Dorman said. "A strong charge could be everything."

"What of your other mage, Jakson?" Dahlen asked.

Dorman shook his head. "The fever took him this morning. Nothing we could do. Just myself, Bahkter, and that Alamant... Polik." Dorman was loathe to say the name. "And he's too much of a coward to be of any use."

"Oaken will be busy trying to keep our walls from burning and collapsing. I'm going to need you and Bahkter to stay in motion, moving with the thickest fighting. Take horses. If those Bloodmarked break through and you're not there..."

"It'll be a bloodbath," Tharn Pimm finished.

They set about arranging the city's defences and planning out the route of tactical retreats through the streets should the need arise – or rather, 'when'.

When all was agreed, Dahlen turned to face the gates, looking about at those who manned the walls and the thousand or so crammed into the clearing before the gates.

Many heads had turned to face him, breaths misting into the night air beneath the glittering stars, the light of the Blood Moon painting everything in that strange ethereal hue.

His stomach twisted and turned. He drew one last long breath. "Warriors of Salme! Tonight we fight not just for our homes, for these logs and stones that we call Salme. We fight so that we may see the sun rise again. We fight so that our children will draw breath when that light comes, so that our lines do *not* end here. And if we do fail, if Salme falls, let the bards sing of our fury. Let them tell stories of what happened here for generations. Let them say that the men and women of the western villages did not go quietly into the night. For every soul they take, let us take ten. If this city is to burn, then let it burn brighter than any flame ever has." Dahlen pulled a sword from the scabbard across his back. "I was not born here. I was not raised here. I do not know these villages like you do. But I tell you now, I will go to Achyron's halls with pride in my heart if I am to die here!"

A chorus of roars and shouts ripped through the darkness, spears clattering against shields and feet stomping. Dahlen's skin goosefleshed at the sound, and his heart thumped. He raised his sword, catching the moonlight in the steel. "We will not run! We will not hide! We will not yield!"

The shouts and chanting redoubled, the crack of steel on steel like rippling thunder.

As Dahlen turned to ascend the steps to his position on the wall, the cheering unrelenting around him, Nimara grabbed his arm.

His jaw trembled as he looked down into her eyes, the blend of fear and fervour roaring in his veins.

"Do you love me, Dahlen Virandr?"

Those words were the last words he'd expected to leave her lips. He and Nimara had grown close over their time in Salme. Closer than he had grown to anyone outside of Erik and his father. She was steel and softness both. Fire and ice. Beauty, of the skin and the heart.

He nodded. "I do."

"You are brave, Dahlen. Strong. Noble." Nimara stared into his eyes. "My heart did not expect you. And yet now, on the night that will be our last, the only thing on my mind is not waking to you with the sun. The idea of never seeing your face again strikes a fear in me far worse than facing these beasts."

Nimara let go of Dahlen's hand. She pulled a short axe from her belt and cut a golden ring from her hair, letting strands of blonde and a chain of silver and copper rings fall to the ground. "When a dwarf finds the one who was carved from the same rock, it is custom that they offer a gift of their most treasured possession in exchange for a heart. This ring was given to me by my mother to mark my twenty-fifth kill. And it had been given to her by her own mother. This is a thing that holds value to me beyond anything else, and so I offer it to you."

"Nimara…" Dahlen looked down at the polished ring in the dwarf's open palm. "I cannot take this."

She smiled at Dahlen, strands of blonde hair falling across her face. "It is not something given for nothing. I ask for your heart. I ask for your loyalty, your courage, your devotion. I ask you to bind yourself to me, from this day until the day we return to the rock. And if you cannot, then do not take it."

"You have not known me even a year…"

"Must you know a flame a year to know it is warm?" Her smile softened, and she reached up and cupped Dahlen's cheek in her empty hand. "Unless Hafaesir smiles on us, we will not see the morning. I have found you, Dahlen, and I would not lose you. When we return to the rock, I would have it that our hearts do so together. My people do not have ceremonies like yours. We require nothing but truth in our hearts, the ground beneath our feet, and Hafaesir's blessing. If it is not what you want, I understand… but I refuse to die without asking."

Dahlen touched the gold ring in Nimara's palm. "And what if we live? What if we don't die?"

She laughed, brushing her fingers along his cheek. She didn't say a word, just stared into his eyes.

He did love her. Until that very moment he had not thought on it as love. He had not thought on it as anything. He had simply been content that she was at his side, that her body had warmed his on the cold nights and her voice had filled the silence. But his heart twisted at the idea of waking the next morning and not seeing her next to him, not feeling that warmth, not hearing that voice.

Dahlen cupped his hands around Nimara's and nodded. "I swear to fight for you with all my heart."

"And I you. Even though you snore like a drunk virtuk."

Dahlen brought his hands to Nimara's cheeks and pulled her close, kissing her deeply. "This was not how I saw this night beginning."

She shook her head. "I could not die without knowing... I could not let you die without knowing. Now, if we die here, we die together, two parts of a whole. And if we live, we will do that together also." She pulled back and placed the gold ring into Dahlen's hand. "Wear it, or don't. But keep it safe. It is my heart, and it belongs to you."

Dahlen took the ring and pressed it against his chest. "I don't have anything to give you in return... I don't own anything. Nothing except my clothes, my armour, and..."

His heart stopped at the thought of what he was about to do. His swords were everything. They were the last remnants of his mother, all he had to remember her by. No diamond, jewel, or precious metal was worth their price. Not even a wagonful. They were all he had. But then he thought back to his memories of Naia, of how fiercely she had loved both him and Erik and how bright that same love had burned for their father. He let out a long sigh and reached for the hilt of the blade over his right shoulder.

Nimara rested her hand on his elbow and stopped him, shaking her head. "Those blades are not possessions," she said, giving him a weak smile. "They are extensions of you. And I would rather they remain so. Use them to keep us both alive. There will be time to think on a gift, in this life or in the reforging. Right now, all I want is your heart. To be your equal and you mine."

"You have it."

Nimara lifted up onto her toes and pulled Dahlen into a passionate kiss, setting his heart to racing. He ran his fingers through the back of her hair and pulled her close, cheers and claps sounding around them. "I've seen your heart, Dahlen Virandr, and I would hold it fiercely for what little time we have."

The pair ascended to the battlements over the gates, where they found the Belduarans, Almer, Yoring, Erdhardt, and Tharn Pimm awaiting them.

Yoring stepped away from the parapet and looked down at the golden ring Dahlen had slid onto the middle finger of his right hand. "Did I just witness what I think I witnessed?"

Without waiting for a response, he looked to Almer with a broad grin on his face.

"Fuck." Almer shook his head.

"I knew it. I knew she would." Yoring shrugged and held out his hand, glaring at Almer when nothing dropped into it.

"Why would I have gold up here?"

"You wouldn't have paid anyway." Yoring moved forwards and grasped Dahlen's forearm. "From the walls of Belduar to the walls of Salme, Virandr. And now you've given your heart to a dwarf." He looked to Nimara. "It's only because you knew I'd say no, isn't it?"

"Even if Hafaesir himself blessed you, I wouldn't touch you with somebody else's hand, Yoring."

Almer stepped past the two, grasped Dahlen's forearm, and pulled him in close, clapping him on the back. "You are a lucky man. She would kill a god to keep you safe."

"I know I am."

"But she is lucky too. It's been an honour to fight at your side all this time, Dahlen Virandr. As it will be an honour to die by it." He looked out into the night and the mass of torches along the hilltop that had yet to move. "What more could a dwarf wish for than a glorious death? We all die somewhere. At least here they will sing songs of it."

"Am I the only one who would prefer not to die tonight?" Tharn Pimm was stringing his bow as he spoke, a frown carved into his face.

"I believe many here feel the same way." Thannon looked down to where a clutch of Lorian soldiers marched towards the western wall, heavy Valtaran shields strapped to their arms. "Though there are some who would not be missed."

Dahlen shot him a sharp look, and Thannon furrowed his brow in response. They'd had the conversation many times. Dahlen shared the man's sentiment, though in truth Dorman and many of his soldiers had proven themselves not only invaluable, but honourable. Still, they were Lorian, and he would not weep over the bodies. But sowing discontent would do no good.

"Thannon, Camwyn, ensure the rest of the Wolves are ready."

Thannon shook his head. "There is no—"

"At once, Lord Captain." Camwyn grabbed Thannon by the arm and pushed him along the battlements to where the other twelve surviving Kingsguard stood alongside the rest of the Silver Wolves.

"That was a rousing speech." Erdhardt Fellhammer stepped up beside Dahlen, his warhammer – Bonebreaker – in an iron grip around the neck. The weapon was a behemoth of a thing, larger and somehow sleeker than his previous, steel dark enough to be almost black, one side like a monstrous meat pounder, the other like a dragon's tooth. "You put a fire in the belly of every soul in this city. It's a pity nobody outside these walls will ever know what you said."

Dahlen followed Erdhardt's gaze to where the torches had started spilling down the hill like sparks from a flame, war drums thumping in the night.

This was it then. No matter how valiantly they fought, no matter how ferocious or brave, there was no overcoming a horde of Uraks that large. His thoughts shifted to his brother, Erik, who would arrive to find nothing but ash and broken things.

I love you, brother. And I'm sorry it's been so long. It should never have been this long. I just needed to find my feet.

As the flames of the torches drew closer, a thought came to Dahlen and he pushed through the wall's defenders until he found Lanan Halfhand standing with a wicked-looking sickle in each hand, the edges honed to a gleaming finish.

She narrowed her gaze at his approach and leaned in. "What?"

Dahlen whispered in her ear. "We should get as many of the children onto the boats as we can. Two at a time, without causing a stir."

She knew precisely what he meant. There were over a thousand children currently in the city and only space for a couple hundred on the boats. There was no sense in all of them dying. But if people heard the boats were leaving, some might allow their courage to falter and think they deserved a place aboard, just like Yarik.

"I'll have it done."

Dahlen grabbed her arm as she went to leave. "You should go with them. And Anya too. Maybe three or four you trust. The children will need people to guide them. The Valtarans will take you at Skyfall, I'm sure of it."

"This is my home, Dahlen. I will die here if I must, but I will not run." Lanan gestured towards a surly man with a polished head and thick beard. She whispered something to him, and he glared at her in return before eventually giving a gruff nod, glancing at Dahlen, then vanishing down the stairs. "It will be done."

He left Lanan to ready herself in peace and returned to Nimara and the others. The dwarf turned to him with that piercing stare of hers. A soft smile caressed her lips. And with the smile came the wish that death would not find him that night, because he truly desired to spend a lifetime learning Nimara's heart and soul.

"Keep looking at me like that," she said, grasping his hand. "May your fires never be extinguished."

"And your blade never dull."

Dahlen turned to the battlements and looked out at the charging mass of leathery skin and torches. Now, spread out from the top of the hill to the open plain at its feet, their number was uncountable.

"Give no ground!" Dahlen roared. "No mercy! Warriors of Salme, are you ready to die for your home?"

Spears and swords clattered against steel in answer, roars lifting into the night.

"When they tell stories of this night, let them say that we were the demons! That we were the monsters!"

A chorus of shouts answered, and Dahlen Virandr prepared himself to die.

CHAPTER EIGHTY-EIGHT

BROTHERS

24th Day of the Blood Moon

Salme – Winter, Year 3081 After Doom

"Take it down!" Dahlen roared, pointing towards the Bloodmarked that had hauled itself through the second trench, arrows jutting from its chest, a massive hole through its right arm where it had fallen on a spike.

Bowstrings snapped and arrows found their mark. Five in the chest, three in the left leg, four in the right, one through the neck. The beast kept moving, the runes etched into its skin glowing with a fury. Beneath the light of the red moon, the creatures were true monstrosities.

"Give it here!" Erdhardt bellowed beside him. He snatched a spear from another man's grasp, wrapped his gigantic hand around the wooden shaft, and launched it.

The spear punched into the Bloodmarked's face, sending the creature sprawling back into the trench behind it, stakes bursting through its chest. The Bloodmarked roared and thrashed, its runes billowing black smoke, until finally it went limp.

All along the walls, shouts and the twang of bowstrings filled the night. Young men and women darted up and down the stairs, carrying buckets of arrows and bundles of spears, sweat streaming down their faces. The bulk of the

Urak force were held behind the first trench, stretching back into the night, while the front lines pushed through the pit of wooden stakes.

Hundreds of the beasts already lay dead, studded with arrows, limbs snapped and broken, chests impaled. Those that made it across the first trench found the open bank between the two laced with crude bear traps hidden beneath piles of cracked winter leaves – the idea of a hunter from Talin. They were simple but horrifyingly effective. One wrong step and jagged bands of iron shattered legs in a single bite; but there were only so many.

"Lord Captain." A red-haired youth that Dahlen didn't recognise thrust a spear into his hand, then sprinted back down the stairs as fast as his legs could carry him.

Dahlen hefted the spear, turned, sighted his target, and hurled. The weapon slammed into an Urak's chest as it pulled itself from the first trench. He'd have a bow if there had been one to spare. Spears were simpler to craft and had multiple uses. There simply were not enough bows to go around and not enough arrows for all the Uraks.

A blinding flash erupted to the right, and arcs of purple lightning spiked into the Uraks swarming around towards the western wall. Everywhere Dahlen looked it seemed as though the Urak tide would be held at bay. Broken bodies lay in the first trench, piling higher and higher. Flames burned amidst their ranks where Dorman and Bahkter's lightning had torn them open, and arrows fell like rain from the walls. But slowly, the horde swallowed the first trench and swarmed into the second, trampling over the bodies of their fallen. For every one that fell, two took its place, unrelenting.

The creatures hurled their torches as they charged over the second trench. The first few fell harmlessly against the walls, but more and more rose up and over. A torch whirled past Dahlen's head and landed on a thatched roof behind him. Thankfully, rain had fallen for days, and the thatch was slow to ignite. But it would. More torches soared over the battlements, landing on rooves and dropping to the ground below.

As fires started to come to life, they were snuffed from existence, seemingly by nothing, smoke drifting upwards. That was when Dahlen noticed the Alamant, Oaken Polik, charging back and forth like a madman, waving his hands.

Dahlen took another spear from one of the runners, turned his attention back to the charging Uraks, and split a creature's skull with heavy iron and wood. They would reach the walls. And when they did, the Bloodmarked would smash everything to splinters and the fighting would truly begin. For now, he would settle for thinning their numbers.

⌒∽◎

ERIK STARED DOWN AT THE field of torches below, fires blooming all about the city walls. Tarmon, Lyrei, Vaeril, Dann, and the elves all stood around him, along with Syminil, chief of the Dvalin Angan sent with the army, and the two Rakina: Harken and Atara.

"They number at least ten thousand strong. Likely more." Thurivîr squinted. "The night obscures them. It would be prudent to wait until they have crushed themselves into the city walls. I see trenches below, a pair, both spiked. The bodies are piled high already. If we wait until half their number is across, we can crush the rear and leave the van exposed, caught between the walls and trenches, steel at their backs."

How the elf could see anything like that in the night, Erik couldn't fathom. Likely that moonsight Vaeril had taught Calen in Drifaien.

"It is a sound tactic," Baralas agreed.

"If we wait, we'll be saving a city of ash and bones," Atara said, her hand resting on the sword pommel at her hip. As they'd crossed Illyanara, the elf had thrown herself into the heart of every battle. She was the only soul Erik had ever seen who he believed could match Aeson blade to blade.

Erik clenched his jaw as he stared down at the city, flames slowly bursting to life across the walls.

"And if we don't, we may join them. Urak armies do not assemble in these numbers without Shamans amongst them," Thurivîr said. "We would do well to appreciate the situation we are in. This is by no means an assured victory. You've seen how these creatures fight beneath the Blood Moon."

"We must exercise caution, lest we throw lives away," Baralas agreed once again.

Dann moved forwards astride Drunir, his gaze fixed on the city below. "If my parents are alive, they are within those walls. Everything that is left of my home is there." He looked to Tarmon, who sat astride an enormous Blackthorn dense with muscle. "I will not wait. Not if it means leaving them to die. Even if I charge alone, I will not wait."

"You will not be alone." Erik pulled his mount up alongside Dann. The man had earned the name Baldon had given him a thousand times over. Sureheart. "Never alone. Not while I breathe."

Vaeril drew the star-pommelled sword from its scabbard, the pink moonlight blazing on the polished steel. "Vandasera, Sureheart."

That was all the elf needed to say. Oathsworn. Vaeril, Erik, Lyrei, Alea, Dann, Tarmon, Gaeleron, and Calen. Vandasera. Each of them bound by purpose, bound by an unbending loyalty to one another. Erik would die for them; they were his family. "Vandasera."

Queen Tessara bowed her head to Vaeril. She no longer wore her elaborate silken clothes and cut gems. The queen was clad in black steel ornamented with gleaming silver. A silver star adorned her breastplate, and she held a long glaive in her fist, the shaft stained black. She glanced at Thurivîr and Baralas before inclining her head to Vaeril. "The warriors of Vaelen march with their champion. You lead, Vaeril Ilyin, and we shall follow." She turned her head to Dann. "A home for a home, Sureheart."

"I will follow you," Atara said, turning to look at Dann atop Drunir.

Beside her, Harken Holdark grunted, nodding in agreement.

"I have my orders. We marched here to save the city of Salme," Tarmon said. "I will not stand by and watch it die. If you wish to do so, Thurivîr, I will not stop you. But let your honour be marked for it. Baralas?"

The Ephorí for Ardurän cast a glance at Thurivîr and drew his sword. "The elves of Ardurän hold fast to their vow. We will charge with you."

"I do not forsake my vows," Thurivîr spat. "I simply value prudence in the face of battle."

"Call it what you will, but allowing others to die while you stand and watch sounds more like cowardice than prudence to me." Tarmon pulled on his reins, the giant black beast of a horse shifting beneath him. The thing made even the other Blackthorns look small. He gestured to Ingvat, who rode towards him. "Spread the message. We march. No horns until my signal. I don't want them to hear us before they can see us. The cavalry will hit hard in the centre, along with the Angan. Those on foot will fall in around us with the archers thinning the flanks and raining voidfire down into the trenches. Go."

As Ingvat rode away, Tarmon looked to Vaeril. "You will lead the mages. Do as you see fit."

The elf nodded sharply.

Tarmon looked to Atara and Harken. "Where will you best be of use, Rakina?"

"Wherever it is bloodiest," Harken answered, giving a toothy grin.

"With me then," Erik said, inclining his head.

Once the word had been spread through the army, the march began down the hill. The cries of battle echoed in the empty night: crackling flames, clashing steel, dying wails. It killed Erik to not break his mount into a gallop and charge full speed into the Urak rear. But they needed to get closer and allow the archers and mages to get within range.

He leaned forwards in his saddle and ran his fingers along the black steel that barded his horse's neck. Erik had only seen Varsundi Blackthorns a handful of times in his short life. Never in a thousand years had he thought he'd find himself riding one. When they'd stolen the horses from the Lorians, Erik had given this one the name Shadow. It was a simple name, but he'd never been good at naming things. The beast seemed almost eager for battle, snorting as it walked, barded in black steel and leather. Behind him, some four hundred of the Dracurïn rode on horseback, almost half that number being Blackthorns. Atara rode astride an Angan, Harken on a bay gelding that looked like a pony beneath him. Fifty Triarchy mages, along with Vaeril and Queen Tessara herself, rode astride the white-furred stags that were the Dvalin Angan. It would be a cavalry charge to be feared.

A clap of thunder rolled through the sky overhead, dark stormclouds brewing.

Erik could feel the tension build in those around him as they drew closer, the screams and cries of battle rolling back up the hill. From there, sat astride his mount, it looked as though the Urak front lines had just reached the walls, swarming over the trenches like a wave of ants. His brother was in that city, and knowing Dahlen, he was standing at the heart of everything. They had never been apart this long.

"Just hold on," Erik whispered.

Just ahead, Tarmon lifted a horn to his lips and kicked his mount into a canter.

Erik tightened his grip on the reins and pushed Shadow forwards. The horse needed little encouragement.

Tarmon picked up the pace, Shadow and the other horses following suit.

The sound of the horn consumed all else, and Erik clenched his jaws and snapped at his reins. "Yah! Forward!"

The Blackthorn broke into a gallop, the earth churning beneath him. Erik drew slow breaths, his heart racing. He pulled himself low, grasping the reins with his left hand and sliding a sword from its scabbard with his right, the world shaking every time the horse's hooves smashed into the ground.

The air smelled of dirt and death. The only sounds were screams and thumping hooves. The light was that of the bleeding moon.

"For the world of men, we fight!" Tarmon roared, his voice carrying above even the thunder of hooves. "For the Draleid, we fight! Dracurïn, with me!"

A chorus of roars rose in response, and the hairs on Erik's neck and arms pricked, a shiver running through him, a fervour burning in his heart. He thrust his sword into the air and let his voice join the others. This was the war his father had prepared him for. This was the war he was born to fight.

The beasts at the Uraks' rear turned to face the charge, shock etched into their leathery faces.

Erik's heart hammered twice, and then the cavalry crashed into the Urak line. Even the Uraks couldn't stand in the face of Shadow's charge. The Blackthorn smashed through two of the creatures while Erik swung his steel and carved open another's jaw. Streams of lightning and fire plumed from the elven mages astride the Dvalin, ripping paths through the Urak horde.

He swung again, his blade splitting an Urak face from cheek to cheek, dark blood spraying.

Shadow reared and smashed his hoof into another of the beasts' throats, then slammed them down into the chest of an Urak that had fallen, bones shattering beneath the horse's weight. Erik turned to see a Bloodmarked cleave a horse in two with its claws, red eyes fixed on him.

"Yah!" He tugged at the reins and angled Shadow to face the beast. But as he did, an enormous white stag rammed into the Bloodmarked's side, gold-veined obsidian antlers splitting the creature's hide and lifting it from its feet.

The Dvalin Angan thrashed its head side to side, antlers shredding leathery flesh, runes burning with red light. Vaeril sat astride the Angan, that magnificent blade – Ünviril – glistening in his fist. He waved his empty hand, and the Bloodmarked was torn free of the Angan's antlers as though by the gods themselves.

"Imbahír, Dracurïn!" Vaeril roared. Forward, Dracurïn. "Aldryr ar Orimyn!" *Fire and fury.*

Cries sounded at Erik's back, and the infantry fell in around them, the white dragon tinted pink in the moon's hue, the Triarchy elves charging alongside them.

But as they did, arcs of purple lightning tore through a thick of bodies, ripping four riders apart along with their mounts, the acrid smell of burnt flesh filling the air.

Two Fades burst from the swell of Uraks, black-fire níthrals in their hands. Uraks flowed after them, and the creatures ripped into the infantry like demons unleashed.

Queen Tessara howled as she charged past Erik and sent a plume of fire from her palm, devouring three Uraks. She swung the glaive in her right fist and cleaved a Fade's arm at the elbow. But as she made to turn, an enormous black spear burst through the neck of the Dvalin Angan upon which she rode. The Angan stumbled sideways, blood pouring over its white fur, then collapsed into the dirt, Tessara leaping from its back. She swirled in the churned earth, swinging her glaive about her as though it were light as a feather. Uraks fell everywhere her steel moved, and warriors of Vaelen charged in around her, but the two Fades circled her like vipers.

"Imbahír!" Erik snapped at Shadow's reins. He doubted Shadow understood the Old Tongue, but the word had found its way to his lips without a thought and the horse understood his need nonetheless. Shadow broke into a savage charge, crushing an Urak beneath his hooves. "Inari!"

Tessara pivoted in reaction to Erik's shout, stepping aside as Shadow swept past and Erik's blade opened an Urak throat. The horse reared and kicked a beast in the face before bucking and thrusting its hind hoof into a Fade's jaw. The Fade crashed into the dirt, its jaw hanging lose, its nose and cheeks shattered and broken. And still the creature made to rise.

Before the Fade had climbed to its feet, Tessara surged past Shadow, her hands empty. A brilliant light burst from her right fist, taking the shape of a deep blue blade. The Queen brought the níthral above her head and drove it down into the Fade's chest, eliciting an otherworldly shriek from the creature as it thrashed and writhed.

"Yah!" Erik roared, and Shadow charged. He released the reins, pulled his feet from the stirrups, and launched himself from the horse's back. As he hit the ground, Erik rolled, rising to one knee between Tessara and the second Fade, its níthral poised to take her head. He drove his sword into the creature's thigh, released the handle, then ripped his second sword from its scabbard over his left shoulder and opened a gaping wound across the Fade's chest. Before the creature could react, Erik thrust the tip of his sword through the bottom of its jaw, the steel slicing through the cold flesh and up into the skull.

Even with the steel splitting its skull, the Fade's bottomless black eyes stared at him, its lips twisting.

The creature howled as steel carved through its neck from behind and left its head impaled on Erik's blade, body slumping. Erik snapped his sword down and flicked the Fade's severed head into the mud. He slid his first blade from the creature's thigh and looked up to see Atara already carving deeper into the Urak lines, moving like a herald of death, her blade tearing the Uraks to pieces.

"Du haryn myia vrai," Tessara said, approaching Erik, blood and dirt marring her previously pristine plate, her breaths heavy. *You have my thanks.*

"Det er myia haydria, Inari," Erik said with a dip of his head. *It is my honour, Queen.* He turned and found Shadow, leaping into the horse's saddle as the elves of Vaelen swarmed them, pushing the Uraks back.

Dann appeared beside him astride Drunir, Lyrei at his side. "You all right?"

Erik nodded, drawing a sharp breath. "To Salme."

Dahlen brought his left blade up, turned away the swing of an Urak sword, then slid his right blade deep into the creature's gut. He pulled the blade free, just until the tip left the flesh, then drove it back in anew and ripped it out. The Urak's intestines spilled onto the ramparts as it stumbled and fell to the ground below.

He spun on his heels and thrust his blade up through the jaw of another Urak attempting to crest the walls. The steel carved through its chin, lips, and nose, cleaving bone and flesh alike.

Before he could push the ladder from the palisade, a hand slapped against his chest and pushed him backwards. Nimara threw herself past Dahlen, swinging her wicked, double-bladed axe into an Urak's chest. She yanked the haft back towards herself, causing the creature to fall to a knee. In a flash, she released the axe's handle, then grabbed one of the short axes at her hip and slammed it down into the back of the Urak's head.

Nimara yanked the axe free and slid it back into its loop, pulled the Urak over onto its back, and heaved her weapon free of its chest. She planted her foot on the creature's side and pushed it over the ramparts.

"We can't hold the walls much longer." Erdhardt wiped blood from his eyes and looked out at the shifting sea of leathery skin that swept over the land. "As soon as one of those Bloodmarked makes it through, we're done."

At the rear of the Urak horde, the night ignited with flashes of lightning and pillars of fire. They'd all heard the horns, and even then Dahlen could see the purple banners bearing the white dragon jutting from blocks of archers who rained steel down upon the Urak flanks. Erik was here. He'd made it.

"Always at the last minute, little brother," Dahlen whispered.

Erdhardt swung his hammer into an Urak head rising above the parapet. It hit with a crunch. The beast fell in silence, and Erdhardt planted his foot on the ladder and kicked it free of the walls. "I say abandon the walls. Fall back into formation in the streets, funnel their numbers into smaller spaces. Spaces where the Lorian mages can rip them apart."

"No." Dahlen looked along the walls, where Salme's defenders were hurling spears and loosing arrows into the Urak onslaught below. "We need to make them bleed for every inch of this city. We need to hold these walls for as long as we can. Erik's arrival changes everything. Salme may yet live to see another sunrise, but only if we drag it through the night."

Erdhardt looked as though he disagreed, but he gave a sharp nod. "As you say, Lord Captain."

"Bloodmarked!" The cry rose somewhere to Dahlen's left. He looked over the ramparts to see the enormous creature hauling itself from the second trench. Its runes illuminated the mass of bodies that lay in the blood-soaked dirt. Two spears punched into its chest, causing it to stagger, while three more sank into the corpses at its feet.

The creature charged forwards, ripping one of the spears free as it did. It hurled the spear with inhuman strength, and a scream pierced the night as the steel slammed into a woman's chest and sent her soaring to the ground some twenty feet behind the walls.

Two arrows punched through the Bloodmarked's head in quick succession: one through the ear, the second barely a finger's width to the left of the first. The creature dropped, limp and lifeless. Dahlen looked to the roof of the wooden tower built into the walls on his left. Tharn Pimm knelt against the low parapet, already nocking another arrow. The man was a monster with a bow.

They fought tooth and nail for what felt like an eternity, until blood covered every inch of the walls and bodies had piled high on both sides. Dahlen's muscles burned from swinging his swords, and his bones ached. He'd seen Darda Vastion taken by a black spear to the head, and three of his Silver Wolves had fallen to Urak claws and steel. Yoring, Almer, Nimara, Erdhardt, and Jorvill Ehrnin all stayed tight to Dahlen, hacking and slashing at everything that dared come over the walls. And for every defender of Salme that fell, three Uraks did the same. Slowed by the trenches, the creatures were hammered with arrows and spears, dying in droves.

That was until cries erupted from the ground inside the walls.

Dahlen turned to see Uraks spilling into the city. The warriors he'd positioned on the ground slammed their shields together and levelled their spears, taking the charge head-on.

He'd barely reached for the horn around his neck when a column of the Lorian cavalry came blazing along the eastern section of the wall and smashed into the Urak flank like a hammer.

The spearmen surged forwards, drove steel through anything that still moved after the charge, and formed a new line across the now-shattered gates.

More screams broke out, and a section of the wall erupted to Dahlen's right, wood and bodies lifting into the air amidst a shockwave of fire. A second explosion sounded, and a third and fourth further in the distance at the western wall, plumes of fire burning in the night. The Bloodmarked had breached the walls.

Erdhardt whipped his head around and met Dahlen's gaze.

"Abandon the walls!" Dahlen roared, opening an Urak's throat as it reached the top of a ladder. He grabbed the horn and blew in four sharp bursts. "Fall back!"

Another explosion illuminated the night on the eastern wall, where Exarch Dorman was holding the ground.

"Abandon the walls!" Dahlen roared again, pushing two men towards the stairs. Below, the shield wall was holding across the gates and the cavalry were smashing through the Uraks that were beginning to trickle through the breaches.

Hands grabbed Dahlen's shoulder and spun him. He stared into Nimara's eyes as a black spear glanced off her thick pauldron – where his chest had been – and skittered upwards and off into the city.

Dahlen's heart froze in his chest, and the air caught in his lungs.

"Hafaesir forged you those eyes for a reason," Nimara said, grabbing the side of his head. "Use them. This city will fall if you do. I will fall."

Something cold touched Dahlen's cheek, then again, and again. And then the skies opened.

Erik sheathed his sword and yanked a spear free from an Urak corpse as Shadow charged. The rain sheeted down, falling as though the sky itself had been ripped open. It battered against him and hazed his vision, Shadow's hoofbeats slapping and sucking in the mud.

He drew a sharp breath, steadied himself, then threw his shoulder back and hurled the spear into a Bloodmarked's neck. The beast staggered but swung its obsidian claws and carved open two Dracurïn who fought on foot. The spear still jutting from its neck, the Bloodmarked rammed its claws through the gut of a Vaelen elf, slicing open the steel plate as though it were nothing. The creature pulled the elf close and ripped open her throat with a savage bite, then threw her into the legs of a charging horse. It clapped its hands together with a roar and sent a pillar of black fire swarming over a score of gold-armoured elves. It would have killed more if Atara hadn't sliced its legs out from under it, then twisted and took its head with a single clean swing as it fell.

Dann appeared astride Drunir, drawing an arrow from the quiver at his hip and loosing into an Urak's eye.

"We need to push through!" he roared, fear and panic in his voice. "The Uraks are inside!"

Erik glanced at the twenty-foot-high palisade wall that ringed the city of Salme. The western section had collapsed almost completely, flames billowing into the dark sky overhead while rain fell the other way. Several other breaches had been smashed into the wooden fortifications, one of the towers consumed in a blazing inferno.

Hold on, brother. Please, hold on. Erik drew his sword and pointed towards the city. "Tarmon!"

"Go!" The man swung his blade from the back of his black beast, carving through a loose arm. "Take the cavalry and the mages! We'll hold the line!"

"Vaeril, clear a path to the city!" Erik looked to the elf, who was carving apart Uraks from the back of his Angan mount, wielding that star-pommelled sword, elves in the black of Vaelen surging around him.

Vaeril nodded and shouted, "Imbahír, evalien un Aravell! Imbahír til haydria!"
Forward, elves of Aravell! Forward to honour!

Within seconds, Vaeril was charging towards the gates, white stags moving with him, mages bearing the silver star, the golden stag, and the green tree all answering his call. Even Thurivîr himself urged his Angan forwards and joined the charge.

Uraks were torn asunder by the air itself, consumed by fire that poured from elven hands, ripped apart by streaks of lightning, and crushed within their own armour. It was like a charge from the Age of War, that blade – Ünviril – coruscating in the crimson moonlight as Vaeril raised it above his head and roared another rallying cry.

"Vandasera," Erik whispered to himself. The word meant many things to him now. At that moment it was an acknowledgement of family found. It felt good to have so many souls he was willing to die for and so many who would do the same for him. Erik snapped his reins. "Cavalry! To the city! With me!"

Dann fell in beside Erik. Drunir was far smaller than Shadow, but the horse hadn't a drop of fear in its heart as it charged, trusting Dann to take down any beast that came close enough to touch it. Two arrows skittered off Dann's pauldron and breastplate in quick succession, but he didn't even notice, his white cloak flapping behind him. Ahead, Vaeril and the mages had sliced a bloody path through the swell of Urak bodies all the way to the second trench. Even those beasts couldn't stand in the way of the sheer destruction wrought by a contingent of elven mages. Erik had been around the Spark all his life. Known its power, seen it, feared it… but not in his wildest dreams had he ever truly comprehended the scale of wanton death and destruction that power would bring in war.

For a second, just a fleeting moment, Erik felt pity for the Uraks. That pity died as he watched a Bloodmarked rip open a horse from breast to rump with one swipe of its massive claws. The air seemed to shimmer, and then the horse burst into flames, the Bloodmarked igniting the creature with its Blood Magic.

"Yah!" he roared, snapping his reins again and again, urging Shadow onwards.

The first trench was so full of Urak corpses that Erik could barely see the tips of the wooden spikes poking through chests and limbs. It was as though there was no trench at all, just an overspilt grave.

The Dvalin Angan cleared the mound of corpses in a single leap, continuing their charge towards the gates, white fur striking against the blood-soaked corpses and blazing infernos. The Uraks were climbing the walls now, charging through the gates, swarming over the city like kerathlin.

Erik cast one last look over his shoulder to where Tarmon and the bulk of the army fought like beasts against the Urak horde. He drew a sharp breath, turned back to the city, and roared, "Forward!"

Shadow surged forwards and leapt over the twitching mound of bodies that filled the trench. The horse's front hooves slapped into the sodden ground, rain pouring down around him. His back hooves landed with a crunch, shattering the bones of a long-dead beast.

The world grew still in that moment before Shadow's next stride. The fires blazed from within the city now, and the walls were all but abandoned. Past the second trench, Uraks flooded through the gates.

The tiniest sliver of his heart felt the cold touch of fear. But that fear was not for himself. Erik was born to fight this war. He was born to wield a sword and stand where others would not. His father had built that kind of courage into him, forged it. The battlefield was his home. It was the only place he truly felt comfortable. No, the fear in his heart was for Dahlen. He could not lose his brother. He could lose anything in the world, but not Dahlen. He *would* not.

Beside him, Drunir charged forwards and cleared the trench, followed by Lyrei and Atara astride two massive Dvalin Angan.

"Forward!"

A Bloodmarked smashed through the shield wall that lined the gates, men and women hurtling through the air. One man landed beside Dahlen, his shield arm twisting and snapping against the ground, bone bursting through flesh. His scream sent a shiver through Dahlen. Another man landed on his head, the light vanishing in his eyes with the crack of his neck.

Dahlen leapt towards the break in the lines as Uraks flooded through. His Silver Wolves moved with him, Thannon and Camwyn tight at his side. Nimara, Yoring, Almer, and a clutch of Salme's defenders charged at his right. They'd separated from Erdhardt and the others somewhere in the thick of the fighting, but Dahlen could hear the behemoth of a man roaring over the sounds of death.

The Bloodmarked swung at Dahlen's head, and he dropped to the ground, sliding in the mud on his knees. He drove his left blade into the beast's thigh, then yanked it free and plunged his right into the opposite leg. The creature howled and swung down with its black claws. Dahlen threw himself back, losing his grip on the blade lodged in the beast's leg.

He slapped into the mud, and the Bloodmarked loomed over him, only for a double-bladed axe to whirl through the air and slice into the side of the creature's skull. The Bloodmarked stumbled, dazed and blinking wildly, steam rising as the rain hammered down and sizzled on its skin. The axe blade was lodged deep into the bone, the haft jutting upwards towards the rooves of the buildings that lined the street – and yet, the Bloodmarked didn't drop. The runes in its skin glowed furiously, red light spilling through the rainfall.

Nimara hurtled towards it. She rammed her foot down onto the pommel of Dahlen's sword lodged in its leg. The beast's knee twisted inwards, and it collapsed to the ground. As it fell, Nimara pulled a short, bearded axe from the loop on her belt and hacked it down into the Bloodmarked's neck.

The beast lashed out with its black claws, but Nimara was too quick. She ducked the strike, grabbed her second short axe from her left hip, and swung the blade upwards into the creature's chin. The steel cleaved the bone and burst through the Bloodmarked's mouth and up into its skull. It went limp and collapsed into the mud.

Nimara planted a foot on its head, then heaved her short axe free from its neck. She flipped the weapon in the air, shifting it into the correct orientation, then turned and launched it into a charging Urak's skull. The beast dropped dead instantly in a splash of mud.

As Yoring, Almer, and the others flowed around her and Dahlen, Nimara yanked Dahlen's blade free of the dead Bloodmarked's leg and tossed it to him.

Dahlen snatched the sword from the air as he rose, deflecting the swipe of a black steel blade and driving his second sword deep into the guts of the weapon's wielder.

"You've really got to look after those better." Nimara planted her foot on the dead Bloodmarked's skull and dragged her battle-axe free. As she did, another Bloodmarked charged through the swell of bodies at the gates and slammed its hands together. Men and Uraks alike were thrown into the air as a wave of concussive force erupted from the creature's hand, igniting the air in a wreath of flames. Dahlen swung his blades up and sheathed them with a practiced efficiency, then threw all his weight forwards and tackled Nimara to the ground.

The pair fell backwards over a mutilated corpse and hit the ground with a slap, the mud sucking at the dwarf's armour. He spread himself over Nimara as piercing screams sounded behind them and the ground shook.

Once the heat from the fire faded, he rolled off her and onto his back. The ground where they had stood was cracked, shattered, and burning, and upon it lay the corpses of both sides. He could tell by the armour that three of his Silver Wolves had been caught in the blast, alongside a score of others.

He threw himself to his feet and lunged forwards, pulling his swords from their scabbards and taking two Uraks' heads from their shoulders in quick succession. He twisted to avoid the thrust of a black spear, then drove his blade through the face of the wielder, splitting grey skin, blood pouring. He jammed an elbow into the creature's chest, turned, and pulled the blade free.

He looked about at the chaos that slowly consumed everything. The Uraks were no longer flooding through the gate alone. They surged through breaches in the broken palisade and leapt from the ramparts. All about, the men and women of Salme did everything they could to hold back the tide, but they would soon be overrun. Looking into the distance, he could see the same was true of the western and eastern walls.

They needed to pull back to the first boundaries. That had been his plan from the beginning. A staged retreat towards the central square. Before his brother had arrived with the army, there had been no chance of victory. Dahlen had known that. But he had planned to take as many Uraks with him from this world as he could.

"Fall back to the first boundary!" He grabbed the mud-smeared horn that hung around his neck and blew four sharp bursts. "We cannot hold them here! To the first boundary!"

Dahlen sheathed a blade and snatched up a round Valtaran shield from a man who wouldn't need it anymore. He turned to face the rush. "Silver Wolves. With me!"

Barely two heartbeats had passed by the time Thannon pressed hard against Dahlen's side, the other former Kingsguard doing the same.

Nimara fell in to Dahlen's left, a shield clutched in one hand, a bearded axe in the other, her massive battle-axe slung across her back. Others joined: Yoring, Almer, and the dwarves of Durakdur, along with Kara Thain, Lanan Halfhand, and – to Dahlen's surprise – the Alamant, Oaken Polik.

They fell back slow and steady, holding tight while the rest of the defenders about the gates retreated into the main thoroughfare that ran through the city. As they moved, Lanan called out, "The walls!"

Dahlen lifted his gaze to see Erdhardt Hammersmith charging across the blazing walls. The man swung his hammer at anything that moved, crushing Urak skulls as they climbed over ladders, smashing knees and jaws with monstrous backswings. The beasts were so caught off guard by the audacity that by the time any of them turned to face him head-on, he was leaping from the ramparts.

"He has a fucking death wish." Dahlen watched as Erdhardt was swallowed by the swell of Urak bodies.

"Don't do it." Nimara glared at him from behind her shield as an Urak axe smashed into the rim. "Don't fucking do it."

"He's going to do it." Almer swung his right hand over his shield and slapped his axe into an Urak's chest, pulling it free as the beast flopped to the ground.

Dahlen looked down into Nimara's eyes. "I have to." He drew a sharp breath, rolled his shoulders back, and heaved forwards. His shield crashed into a charging Urak, knocking it off balance. He drove his blade into the beast's groin, twisted, then yanked it free and opened the Urak's throat. "Fall back!" he roared as he charged forwards.

He couldn't leave Erdhardt to die, even though part of him believed the man couldn't be killed. Dahlen had never seen someone throw themselves into the heart of battle as wantonly as Erdhardt Fellhammer, with little thought of self-preservation. And yet, somehow, the gods refused to allow him to die.

Dahlen smashed his shield rim into an Urak jaw, then carved open the beast's belly with a single swing, innards steaming as they spilled onto the sodden earth. The massive creatures couldn't move as nimbly in the thick mud, and he took advantage of that. He swung and carved through an extended arm, then took a spear to the shield.

Nimara appeared at his side, blood trailing in the wake of her axe. She moved as though she always knew what would happen next, smooth and fluid, each step carefully chosen, each turn and twist of the body taken with meticulous care. From the very first moment he had seen her fight, he'd known that the gold and silver rings worked into her hair had been well earned. She was one of the most ferocious warriors he'd ever known.

She hacked and slashed through Urak limbs with a fury, and as her eyes met Dahlen's, he thought he could see a vibrant yellow tinge to her irises.

An Urak swung a wicked black hammer straight into the dwarf's shield, and Dahlen's heart skipped. But Nimara took the blow head-on, barely flinching when Dahlen himself would have been knocked to his arse. She twisted, dropped her lead shoulder, and opened the Urak's face with her axe. As she pulled it free, she turned to Dahlen. And in that moment, he saw that her irises *had* in fact taken on a hue of yellow, though her pupils had grown, leaving only the thinnest ring of colour. Her body shook, a fury in her voice. "Get him!"

To Dahlen's right, a circle had opened around Erdhardt, several bodies piled at his feet. The Uraks could have killed him then and there if they'd piled in, but instead they seemed to take some kind of sport in it, each stepping forwards one by one to see who could kill the giant with the black hammer. But Erdhardt moved like a demon, ducking below strikes, then crushing jaws and skulls in single blows.

In that moment, Erdhardt sidestepped the thrust of a spear from the edge of the circle, then brought the meat-grinder end of his hammer down onto the Urak's elbow before driving the spiked end into the creature's skull with a monstrous backswing. The heat of battle was one thing, but there was no man Dahlen knew who could go toe to toe with Uraks in that way without the Spark. His father, maybe, but Aeson lacked Erdhardt's raw strength.

Dahlen charged at the circle. He needed to give Erdhardt a way out. Yoring and Camwyn charged with him, along with three men of Salme. But before they'd reached the man, a thunderous roar erupted from the gates, and a column of cavalry crashed into the Urak mass. Streaks of lightning surged from a rider's hands, fire pluming. Elves rode on the backs of massive white stags, while others sat astride horses barded in the colours of Loria. The riders tore through the Urak ranks with abandon, the Spark wreaking utter havoc and devastation.

With the Uraks taken off guard, Dahlen charged forwards, carving a path to Erdhardt. When he grabbed the man's arm, Erdhardt spun on his heels, stopping with his hammer levelled in the air, his eyes wide with a murderous fury. The man's chest heaved, sweat and rain streaming down his face.

"We need to go!" Dahlen roared, tugging at Erdhardt's arm, but moving him was like trying to move a boulder. "Erdhardt. We need to go!"

"Lord Captain!" Camwyn surged past Dahlen and smashed her shoulder into the chest of a Bloodmarked that was only seconds away from ripping its claws through Erdhardt and Dahlen both.

The beast stumbled back half a step, its feet sliding in the mud, then drove its clawed hand into Camwyn's back. The obsidian claws burst out from the woman's steel breastplate, blood flowing in rivers.

"Camwyn!" Dahlen made to charge but hands grabbed him and pulled him back.

Nimara was at his side, her face and armour smeared with blood as though she'd bathed in it, those eyes still a vibrant yellow, her pupils wide as the moon. Nimara didn't speak, but she dragged Dahlen back, her grip like iron.

The Bloodmarked lifted Camwyn into the air by its claws, her body convulsing, and then it unleashed a guttural roar and flames burst outwards from its hand, consuming Camwyn entirely, her screams resounding in Dahlen's head.

In that brief moment, two others that had charged with him were hacked to pieces by Urak steel, chunks of flesh slapping into the forming puddles in the mud.

Nimara yanked Dahlen backwards, then moved past him and swung her axe upwards, cleaving through the skull of a lunging Urak.

With the battle raging around him, his mind lost itself in Camwyn's scream, in the blood and the death and the horror of it all. And for an instant, he was frozen, his heart galloping, his blood like ice in his veins.

No. Not now. No. Dahlen drew a sharp breath and steadied himself. And as he did, a group of riders atop massive black mounts crashed through the Uraks before him, the white stags at their side.

One of the riders in blood-splattered steel with a white dragon emblazoned on his breastplate opened an Urak's neck. Dahlen held his breath, spotting the triangular pommels of the man's swords. "Erik?"

Erik smiled beneath his helm. "It's good to see you, brother. I don't mean to rush you, but I'm going to need you to run."

As Erik spoke, the other riders fell in around him. The Uraks and Bloodmarked pushed forwards, but the elven mages ripped them apart, shards of earth and broken metal swirling in the air, slicing through anything that moved. Even then, mages fell from their mounts, black spears and arrows punching through their armour and flesh.

Nimara pulled on Dahlen once more, and they charged back towards the thoroughfare. Erdhardt appeared at their side, blood streaming from a wound in his side and a gash sliced along his left cheek. Bits of torn grey flesh clung to the face of his hammer.

They rushed down the street, buildings closing around them. Archers stood on the rooves, ready for what was to come. Ahead, a deep trench had been dug, a wooden bridge drawn across it, while many of the side streets had been lined with spiked blockades.

Dahlen glanced over his shoulder to see Erik and the cavalry moving towards the mouth of the street, hacking their way through any Uraks that dared come close. A black spear turned in the air, only inches from an elven mage's head, and lodged itself in the wall of the building behind. Three more spears flew, and each of them were turned away by something unseen, but the fourth found home and sank into the mage's chest, knocking him limp on his mount's back. Without wasting a moment, the white stag bucked its rider to the ground and charged down the thoroughfare. Erik and the others followed, arcs of purple lightning crashing into the sides of the buildings as they ran.

For a brief moment, Dahlen caught sight of a Fade standing amidst the Urak bodies, its light-drinking eyes fixed on him. The creature stood still as a statue, just staring. With an eerie rigidity, it lifted its hand and clenched its fingers into a fist. A scream rang out, and Dahlen watched as a score of the riders' breastplates dented and bent as though being struck by hammers, the white dragon collapsing inwards. Shrieks pierced the night as the metal split skin and cracked bone, the sounds cutting short as bodies fell from saddles, limp and lifeless, horses charging on without them.

Dahlen snapped his head back around and bounded across the makeshift bridge.

Lanan, Kara Thain, and the rest of the Silver Wolves waited on the other side, along with hundreds of men and women who had fallen back from the gates. They all stood ready with shields, spears, and swords, giving space for those who crossed.

Once over, Nimara dropped her shield, grabbed Dahlen by the sides of his head, and kissed him, her lips tasting of iron. The yellow had gone from her eyes, leaving them bloodshot, dark circles beneath. She drew in ragged breaths, rain carving paths in the blood on her cheeks. "Stop being a hero," she said through gritted teeth. "And start being a leader. Every soul here looks to you. You are their heart. That makes your life worth more, whether you like it or not. If they see you fall, they will break."

"What was that back there? Your eyes? That strength…"

"A gift of my people. Later." She hefted her shield back into place, then stared at him once more. "Stop being a hero."

As Erik and the riders approached the trench in the street, the archers above rained death on the Uraks giving chase. Many of the beasts took several arrows before falling, but they did fall. He spotted Tharn Pimm among the archers, nocking and loosing in rapid succession. Streaks of purple lightning smashed into the buildings, tearing chunks from stone and igniting those of wood, screams echoing.

The riderless horses were the first to reach the trench. The first of the animals skidded to a halt as it approached the spikes, stopping just long enough to take an Urak spear to the neck and stagger into the open pit. The horse squealed and kicked for barely a second before going limp, wooden stakes jutting through its body.

Erik and others followed, some bounding the gap, others charging over the bridge. Once the last of them was across, the defenders hauled the bridge back and formed a line of shields from building to building.

Erik swung his leg over the horse and dismounted. He pulled his helmet from his head, eyes searching for Dahlen.

Dahlen ran to his brother and wrapped his arms around him, pulling him into an iron grip.

"You didn't think I'd let you have all the fun, did you?" Erik returned Dahlen's embrace, his voice muffled through Dahlen's shoulder.

"You're a sight for sore eyes," Dahlen said, pulling away and looking over his brother. "The new armour could do with a bit of a polish."

"It was clean before I marched halfway across Illyanara to save your hide."

"Can you even move in that thing?"

"I'd still knock you on your arse."

Dahlen lifted his gaze and stared into Erik's eyes. He had almost forgotten how long it had been since he'd seen his brother's face. Over the course of their lives, they'd rarely spent even a night apart, and now a year had passed since last they'd laid eyes on each other. Even just the thought seemed incomprehensible. "I've missed you, brother."

He could hear his father's voice in his mind from when Erik had barely seen fourteen summers. *"If anything ever happens to me, boys, all you have is each other. Remember that. You are blood. No matter what happens, you protect each other. No matter what."*

Erik clasped Dahlen's cheek with his free hand. "I'm just happy we got here in time."

A figure approached from Dahlen's left, dropping from the back of a strangely coloured horse. "My parents, have you seen them? Are they all right?"

"Dann? Dann Pimm?" Dahlen pulled away from Erik to see the man who stood before them in blood-marred plate as fine as Erik's was the same man Dahlen had shared wine with in Belduar before it had fallen. The same smartmouthed, quick-witted man who had seemed barely more than a boy only a year ago.

"No kiss?" Dann gave a half-smile and grasped Dahlen's forearm. "Tharn and Ylinda Pimm, are they all right?"

"Your father—"

"Dann!" Tharn Pimm came charging out of one of the buildings that had been barred from the inside. He pushed through the throng of people and mounts who held back behind the front line and crashed into Dann with the weight of a bull. His hands trembled as he grabbed at Dann's head, voice shaking. "My boy. Ah gods, my boy."

Dann didn't say a word, which was probably the first time Dahlen had seen that happen. He just wrapped his arms around his father and held him close.

The sight made Dahlen think of his own father. Aeson had never been the type to show physical affection. At least not often. But Dahlen still loved him dearly. They argued and they fought and they bashed heads, but the time apart had shown him that mattered little. His father may not have been like Tharn Pimm, but he had given everything to Erik and Dahlen. And Dahlen was proud to say he was Aeson Virandr's son.

Dahlen looked to Erik, who talked to an elf clad all in black plate with a silver star enamelled on the breastplate. She sat on the back of one of the enormous white stags, two other riders close at her side, also in black and silver steel bearing the same star sigil.

A fourth elf, garbed in the same armour as Erik, sat astride another stag to Erik's right, his helmet in the crook of his arm, his golden hair tied with string. A star-pommeled sword rose up from his hip – a glorious-looking weapon. It took a moment, but Dahlen realised he knew the elf: Vaeril Ilyin.

Had Dahlen missed so much in the past year that even a ranger of Aravell now wore Calen's sigil on his breast?

"Lord Captain." The rain ran red down Thannon's helmet as it washed the blood from the steel. "We must continue—"

A crash followed by screams cut Thannon short.

Dahlen whipped his head around to see chunks of stone and burning wood tumbling down into the trench and over the ten-deep line of spears and shields who held the Uraks at bay.

Through the dust and thick of bodies, two Fades stood at the front of the great beasts, still and patient as Salme's defenders rushed to drag the injured from beneath the debris.

A moment later, Uraks charged and bounded over the trench, cutting down anything that moved.

"Hold!" Dahlen roared as he pushed his way through the ranks. "Hold!"

CHAPTER EIGHTY-NINE

THE TRUTH OF WAR

24th Day of the Blood Moon

Salme – Winter, Year 3081 After Doom

Anya crouched low as she moved through the streets, the rain hammering down over her so heavily it turned the ground to little more than sludge. Screams and clattering steel joined the crackling of fire that filled her ears. She turned down a side street, then pressed herself back against the building's wooden wall as three Uraks appeared at the other end and fell upon a group of defenders, black steel hacking them to pieces.

Isla and Kam stood across from her, their bodies still, their faces shrouded in shadow. There had been three others that night who had volunteered to venture out with her and drag the injured to safety. They were dead now. Tom had vanished without a trace, but she'd watched a Bloodmarked tear Jenna in half and another crush Samwell's skull beneath its feet while trying to drag one of the Lorians from an overturned wagon.

Those images flashed through her mind again and again, but she smothered them, focusing on her thumping heart and the feel of the coarse wood against her fingers as she pressed her hand into the wall. She drew a lungful of air through her nostrils, tasting the smell of burning wood at the back of her throat. Her tongue licked dirt and sweat from her lips. Anya had found, over the course of the months, that those senses grounded her, kept her fear from consuming everything.

"Let's move," she whispered to the others as the Uraks at the end of the street carried on. She crept through the mud as quickly as she dared, stopping where shadows met the light of the moon and the street opened up into a larger thoroughfare that ran perpendicular. She dropped to one knee and rested a hand on the neck of a man who lay in the mud, blood pooling about him. No pulse.

She lifted her gaze to look out across the street. A score of bodies were strewn about, unmoving. Not a single chest rose with breath, and many were so mutilated there was no possible way beneath the Enkara's light that they yet lived. The Uraks had a tendency to never leave anything living where they passed. Anya rarely found injured warriors anywhere other than where Salme's defenders had pushed the Uraks back. But that didn't stop her from searching.

She wasn't a fighter, and she never would be. But that didn't mean she couldn't do her part. She might not have the capacity to take lives, but she sure as damn well had the capacity to save them.

"Over there." Isla pointed towards another alley across the way, some twenty feet to the right. It took Anya a moment, but she saw something shifting in the shadow, something too small to be an Urak. She checked up and down the street, nodded to Isla and Kam, then darted down the street to the alley.

When she reached the alley's mouth, she found herself staring down at four youths who couldn't have seen more than fifteen summers. She recognised one immediately. "Conal!" she snapped in a whisper. "What are you doing here? You should be in the hall."

The young man knelt over a dead Lorian, a spear in his hand and a scrappy leather jerkin protecting his chest. Ever since Dahlen had taken Conal under his wing, the young man had only grown more and more eager to join the fighting.

"We wanted to help." He gestured back at the other three. One girl and two boys. Anya recognised their faces from walking through the city but didn't know their names. All three held spears in their fists, and one had a small wooden shield strapped to their arm.

"You're going to get yourselves killed. You need to come with us. We'll bring you back."

"But he's alive." Conal gestured at the body over which he knelt.

Anya squinted, trying to see through the dim light. The man coughed and spluttered, groaning. She dropped down beside him and checked him for wounds. Blood flowed through a slit in the leather just below the ribs, warm and thick. He was alive, but there was more chance of him succumbing to the wound in the next hour than there was of living to see the sun rise.

"You shouldn't be out here," Anya snapped at Conal, shaking her head. "It's not safe."

"Nowhere is safe."

Anya could hardly argue with that. She sighed. "We need to get this man back to the hall, and we need your help. Can you do that?"

Conal's face grew serious. "Of course we can, Lady Anya."

"Right. Help me lift him." Anya dropped a hand under the Lorian's armpit.

Like most others, the young required little more than a sense of purpose to give them strength.

The Lorian grunted, lurching upwards and clasping his hand to his gut. "Leave me."

"Not an option." She dropped one knee into the mud and hefted the man upright. "The hall isn't far. You'll be… safer there. Some stitches and some Brimlock sap and you'll be fine."

Anya hated lying. She could see now he'd lost too much blood. His face pale as ice, his skin almost as cold. But Conal and the other youths had risked their lives to drag this man from the street. She needed them to see that saving lives meant something.

"Conal." She gestured for the young lad to help.

He nodded and moved to wrap his left arm around the soldier when a scream erupted behind Anya, followed by a crash. Splinters spat at the back of her head, and Anya turned to see Isla swaying side to side, her jaw hanging loose, only clinging to her face by exposed muscle and strips of torn flesh on the right side. A massive black spear was embedded deep into the wooden wall beside her. She turned and stared at Anya, nothing but pure terror in her wide eyes.

A second spear burst through her chest, and she crashed forwards into the wall before collapsing into the mud with a splash.

Kam just stood there, awestruck. His lips moved as though he were attempting to speak, but no words left his mouth.

The youths all shrieked. All but Conal, who stared at Isla's mutilated face without a sound.

"Kam!" Anya scrambled to her feet and reached out to grab Kam by the shoulders, only to watch as a black axe hacked down into the man's clavicle, the *snap* of bone accompanying the blood that spurted around the steel.

"Go." The Lorian soldier was on his feet, one hand pressed to the wound in his gut, the other gripping the hilt of a sword. He grunted and coughed up blood, using the sword's pommel to hook Anya's shoulder and pull her back.

"You can barely stand."

"It's fine," he said, wiping mud from his eye, only to smear it with blood. "I won't have to stand for long." He glanced back at Conal and the others as the axe was wrenched free from Kam's body. "Take them and go."

"You can't—"

"Go!" The Lorian threw himself forwards as Kam's body dropped to the mud and two hulking Uraks took his place at the alley's mouth.

"Run!" Anya pushed Conal towards the other end of the alley, but the boy dug his heels in and looked set to charge after the Lorian.

"I'm not going to run!" he snapped when Anya grabbed his shoulder.

"Fight, Conal. By all means, fight. But don't be an idiot. Dahlen would never die for no reason. He uses his head. Live now, fight later. Go!"

The mention of Dahlen's name caught Conal's attention and the young lad looked from the Uraks to Anya, then turned and sprinted through the mud, following the other youths who had already set off like hounds unleashed.

Anya, too, ran. Her head told her it was the only option. She would be no help to the Lorian, nothing more than another corpse for the street. But her heart tugged at her. She threw a glance over her shoulder as she ran. The man had driven his sword into one of the Uraks' legs, but the beast grabbed him by the shoulders and tore a chunk of flesh from his neck with its teeth, tossing him to the ground.

Anya slipped in the mud, crashing down and scrambling back to her feet, terror wrapping itself around her pounding heart. She didn't dare look back. She had spent enough nights pulling the injured and maimed from the battles to know the Uraks would not give up the chase until either she died or they did.

Ahead, Conal and the youths sprinted out into the street, looking right, then left. A shriek like nothing Anya had ever heard left the young girl's mouth. Crimson light spilled through the deluge, followed by the monstrous shape of a Bloodmarked. One swipe of its claws and the girl fell in three pieces.

Conal and the other boys stood, staring in shock at the mutilated remains, all frozen in place.

"Run!" Anya screamed at the top of her lungs, but still they remained frozen. She buried her fear, darted from the alley, and barrelled into the three of them. The Bloodmarked slammed its fists into the ground and sent a shockwave of fire streaming past where the boys had just stood.

Anya slipped and slid in the mud, grabbing at each of them, ensuring they were still alive, before once more scrambling to her feet. The sounds of battle echoed down the street, followed by the slap of hooves.

Anya thought she was in a dream when she looked up to see a woman clad all in black armour riding a monstrous stag, white as snow. A host of other riders flanked her on either side, each grasping long spears with curved blades. The woman waved her hand, and the rain around the Bloodmarked froze in an instant.

The creature paused, staring at the shards of ice that hovered about it, but could do nothing when those same shards tore its thick hide to ribbons.

Anya watched in horror as the Bloodmarked was shredded alive, blood spraying in all directions, strips of flesh dropping to the mud. The runes in its flesh burned with bright crimson light, smoke pluming. Before she even had the time to understand what was happening, the two Uraks who had chased them down the alley burst out into the street.

The first was taken down by a launched spear to the chest, but the second careened into the side of a white stag, burying its claws into the animal's ribs again and again. The white fur turned pink from blood as the stag shrieked and thrashed, collapsing onto its side and taking its rider with it. More Uraks charged down the same street the riders had come from, the pommels of their black weapons glowing with red lights.

"Inari," one of the riders called to the woman, pointing his curved spear towards the Uraks. "Orin avûr!"

Anya didn't recognise the language they spoke, and the armour they wore was like nothing she knew.

The woman in black looked down at Anya and the youths. "Find shelter," she said, her voice soft and fair. "This battle is far from over." The great stag turned, and the woman charged towards the Uraks, roaring at the top of her lungs. "Imbahír til haydria!"

As the woman rode back towards the fighting, Anya grabbed Conal and the other boys. She cast a glance down at the three chunks of flesh that had once been a young girl. A young girl she should have kept safe. "*Stay* at my side."

None of them spoke, but they all nodded. More screams and the sound of fighting rose into the night. But these sounds came from deeper within the city, closer to the port and the great hall, where the children, elderly, and injured were being sheltered while the battle raged.

Anya looked over her shoulder where the riders and other warriors fought viciously with the Uraks, then back down the street before her. What was she to do? No matter which way she took the boys, death awaited them.

She made a choice and ushered them towards the port and the great hall. At least that way there was a chance. They passed clutches of Salme's defenders as they moved. Some charged the other way, back to where the riders had saved Anya and the boys; others sprinted through the alleys and side streets; and some simply sat and wept over the corpses of people they had once known, resigned to death.

This was not like the other nights. This felt like that night in The Glade. The night the Uraks had destroyed everything she had ever known and taken her mother from her. This felt like death come to life.

By the time they reached the main square that fronted the great hall, everything was chaos. The hall was ablaze, shrieks and screams rising from within, the flames climbing high as the tallest trees, bright and hot. Men and women scrambled about, tending to dead bodies and carrying buckets of water from the port.

"No, no, no…" Anya sprinted through the square, Conal and the boys following. She stopped the first man she came to, who knelt over the body of another, a hand resting on the dead man's breastplate. The copper rings in his nose marked him as a man of Salme from before the unification. "What happened here? The Uraks haven't broken through, have they?"

Panic flared in Anya's veins, and she scanned the square once more, seeing nothing but blood, bodies, and madness.

"Yarik Tumber." The man stood, swallowing as he looked down at his fallen companion. Ash and soot marred his face, hands, and hair. "He, Elder Benem, and a group of others decided to make for the boats. The guards stopped them, and a fight broke out. Somewhere in the middle of it, the hall caught fire. It went up like a tinder box." He shook his head, jaw slack as he watched the blazing building collapse inwards. "It all happened so fast. They must have set it ablaze to cover their escape… We got some of the children out, but… The flames grew too high too fast… There was nothing… nothing we could do."

The screams took on new meaning. The hall had not been the only place where those who couldn't fight had been sheltered, but it had been the largest. Almost a thousand souls had sheltered within, squashed shoulder to shoulder. The children, the elderly, the injured who were well enough to leave the Bloodhouse, and the guards set to keep them safe.

"How many got out?"

The man's lips moved, but what left his mouth was akin to a short choking sound.

"How many?" Anya roared, her own anger surprising her. She grabbed the collar of the man's leather cuirass. "*How many?*"

"Only those you see…"

Anya's throat tightened to the point that she could barely draw a breath. There were no more than a hundred in the yard. A group of children, some as young as two or three, were gathered on the far side of the square, being watched over by three guards who themselves looked distraught. A handful of injured men and women, all wrapped in bandages, were at the base of the old, gnarled oak only a few feet from the children. She didn't see any of the elderly. Most of those who'd made it out were guards and children.

A chill ran down Anya's spine as she realised the screaming had stopped.

"Heraya embrace you," she whispered, tears flowing freely down her cheeks. No soul was meant to die that way… The sorrow within her slowly boiled to rage. She turned back to the guard. "Yarik Tumber, where is he?"

"They made for the boats. They'd be long gone, Lady Gritten."

"You know my name?"

"You're the one who drags us from the field. There's not a man or woman who defends Salme that doesn't know your name."

She didn't know how to respond to that.

Shouts sounded over Anya's left shoulder. She looked to see a handful of guards drawing their swords and running towards the mouth of the main thoroughfare.

Riders streamed in. Warriors in bright steel bearing the marking of a white dragon on their chest rode atop a mixture of enormous black mounts and smaller bays and piebalds, all barded in the black and red of Loria. Beside them rode warriors in black steel atop stags like those she'd seen earlier.

This must have been the army Dahlen had been speaking of… Anya had never seen warriors garbed in such fine armour. They looked like something plucked from one of Therin's stories.

For a brief moment, a pang of hope rose within her, but that was quickly dashed when more screams came from the rooftops that overlooked the southern end of the square and lined the thoroughfare.

Two men soared from the rooves, falling for all of a second before smashing into the ground, bones twisted and broken. More men and women followed, arcing through the air as though launched from catapults.

Uraks soon appeared on the rooftops and wasted no time in vaulting into the square, dropping twenty feet or so as though it were nothing.

The creatures paused for a fraction of a second before charging at those lying about across the square.

A pair of them bounded towards her, Conal, and the two boys.

"Get back!" The guard darted forwards, drawing his sword, but as he blocked the strike of the first Urak's blade, the second creature hacked an axe into the side of his neck. The gemstone at the end of its weapon pulsed with a deep crimson light.

Anya had seen that light many times. And over the months, she had come to question what it was. She had not spoken those thoughts aloud to any others, but she could think of no explanation except that the Uraks claimed the souls of those they killed. And that thought terrified her.

"With me!" Conal roared and surged forwards.

"Conal, no!"

One of the two boys charged at Conal's side. The other dropped his spear and ran towards the port.

Conal stabbed out with his spear, but the Urak simply swatted it aside and planted its foot square into Conal's chest, sending him sprawling. The second creature split the other young boy's skull with its axe, the blade bedding deep into the bone. As it grabbed the boy's shoulder and ripped the axe free, the other Urak picked Conal up by his arms and held him in the air. It stared at him, then snapped both arms like twigs and tossed him to the ground.

Anya froze in place, staring at the two boys, then back to the Uraks. They moved towards her. The smaller of the two slammed its axe into the chest of a guard who ran to help her.

Run. Run. Run. Anya's legs didn't listen to a single word her mind spoke. She just kept staring down at Conal, who lay still on the ground. Her breaths quickened, and her heart felt as though it were going to explode out of her chest.

An arrow burst through the Urak's neck from left to right, followed by a second that crossed over the first. The beast staggered, then dropped to one knee. Before it had even hit the floor, a rider on a dappled grey mount charged past, a white bow in his hands. He nocked an arrow and loosed it straight into the eye of the axe-wielding Urak. The beast dropped like a sack of stones.

The rider drew his horse near. He wore armour as beautiful as the sky was blue, emblazoned with a white dragon on the breast. "Anya! Are you hurt?"

Anya stared up at him in complete shock. How in the gods did he know her name? She nodded.

The man gazed back at her for a moment, then over towards the mouth of the thoroughfare, where more and more soldiers were flooding into the square. Some trickled in through the other streets as well, but nowhere near as many. If they were all falling back to the square, then this was it. This was the end.

The man turned his horse around to where more of the Uraks were leaping from rooves, each getting cut down by the riders on the white stags. He gestured towards the children and the injured near the oak tree. "Can you get them to the port?"

"I think... I..."

"Anya, I'm going to need you to come back to me." He laid his bow across the saddle and removed his helmet to reveal a head of dark blond hair and eyes Anya had known since she was a child.

"Dann?" She took a subconscious step, still not sure she believed her eyes. "Dann, is that you?"

There were parts of him that were the same: his eyes, his hair, the way his lips always threatened to curl into a mischievous smile. But the passage of time had changed him. He looked harder, more fierce. His face was marked with pale cuts long healed. Even his voice had changed; he spoke like someone who expected others to listen.

"You can ask as many questions as you want once there's nothing trying to kill us. Please, Anya, take them from here."

"Erdhardt," Anya whispered as her eyes fell on the face of Erdhardt Hammersmith, who walked amongst the riders and warriors who spilled into the square. A sense of relief washed over her. The same way it did after every attack when she saw his face, saw him still walking amongst the living. They were a strange pair, the two of them, but they kept each other afloat.

Dahlen Virandr appeared beside Erdhardt. Less than half of the man's Silver Wolves walked with him, along with Nimara and her dwarves.

For every face that Anya recognised, two more were absent.

"Anya," Dann called down from his horse. "I'm going to need you to focus. I need you to get them to the port. Can you do that?"

She nodded sharply, finally regaining herself. "Dann?"

"Yes?"

"Calen?"

He shook his head. "He's always late, isn't he? Always." Dann must have seen the look on Anya's face, because he carried on, saying, "He's alive, and he's well, Anya. Now go so I can say the same about you."

With that, Dann rode to join the warriors forming together and cutting down any Uraks that launched themselves into the yard.

Anya watched for a moment, then grabbed three of the guards and did exactly what Dann Pimm had told her to do, and that wasn't a sentence she'd ever thought she'd say.

DAHLEN WEAVED THROUGH THE THICK of Urak bodies, his blades leaving arcs of blood in their wake. With Erik at his back, everything felt different – simpler. It was as though a piece of him had been missing since the Burning of Belduar, his balance shaken.

The square was chaos incarnate. There was no holding battle lines against an army of Uraks and Bloodmarked. Neither was there surrender. Whoever was left alive would be the victor. Everywhere he turned, axes, swords, and spears hacked, slashed, and stabbed. Everything was the colour of blood, and the rain continued to hammer down without respite, the ground sodden and squelching under foot.

All he cared about was keeping the Uraks away from the buildings along the port, where those who couldn't fight had been taken for safe keeping – those who hadn't been in the great hall. Despite the rain, the massive structure still blazed relentlessly. He pushed the thoughts to the back of his head as he turned an Urak spear to his left, then carved open the beast's leathery throat with a backswing.

He could do nothing for the dead, but he *could* save the living from joining them.

Dahlen spun his left blade into reverse grip and drove it into an Urak's chest while Erik swept past him, slid onto one knee, and raked his steel across thick, grey hamstrings.

To his right, Erdhardt fought alongside some of Dahlen's Wolves, that black hammer crushing Urak skulls and shattering limbs. The man was more a beast than any of the Uraks and dispensed even less mercy.

Nimara and the other dwarves stayed tight as well, never straying too far from Dahlen, while the elven mages wrought havoc with the Spark.

A realisation swept through him as another severed Urak head rolled to land at his feet: they would win this night. The horns that bellowed over the city told him as much. The remainder of Erik's army had crushed the Uraks at the walls and were now moving through the streets to catch the last of the beasts in the rear.

The moment should have brought joy beyond measure, but it was cold and empty. For it was a victory in name alone.

He stood still for a moment, the rain splattering his face, and watched a black spear punch through Jorvill Ehrnin's chest and another catch the Alamant – Oaken Polik – in the neck. With every second that passed, Heraya embraced another soul. 'Victory' might only be a short time away, but they would continue to die until that moment arrived, until the rest of the army flooded into the square and the Uraks were routed. The dead would number in their thousands come the morning, and the living would go on, broken and never quite the same.

And so Dahlen fought until his lungs burned and his limbs cried out for respite. He fought until he had spilled so much blood that he could have filled Haftsfjord twice over. And he fought until the sound of horns grew ever closer and a flood of warriors swept into the square, some bearing the white dragon, others a golden stag, or a silver star, or a green tree. They crashed down like a wave, and the Uraks broke beneath their weight.

The old Lord Captain of the Belduaran Kingsguard, Tarmon Hoard, charged astride a mountain of a horse, black and ferocious. The man was possibly the only match for Erdhardt in size and strength. But where Erdhardt was fury and raw power, Tarmon was precision and excellence, his years in the Kingsguard forging him into a warrior even Dahlen would have hesitated to face. He made every warrior around him appear like a hero of legend.

The Uraks fought like caged animals, taking three for every one they lost. Until Vaeril Ilyin charged on that white stag and drove his star-pommelled sword through the Shaman's heart after Erdhardt had smashed open its jaw.

And when the last of the Uraks fell, the remnants scattering at the sight of their dead Shaman, Dahlen dropped to his knees. He tilted back his head and let the rain wash the blood from his face, the flames of the great hall blazing in the night.

⌒⌒⊚

DANN RESTED HIS FOREHEAD AGAINST Drunir's muzzle, stroking the blood-matted hair on the horse's neck. "You did good."

The horse gave a soft snort, shaking his head. 'Of course I did,' Dann imagined the horse said.

He patted Drunir's neck and handed his reins to Nala, who had entered the city along with the other squires and porters after the Uraks had been thoroughly routed. "See that he's fed and watered, and scrub the blood from his coat. And Nala, give him as many carrots and apples as he wants. He's earned it."

The young girl smiled, scratching under Drunir's chin and leading him away, whispering in his ear.

Dann made his way through the square, where Urak bodies were being piled into carts to be burned outside the city limits. The place was still crowded, packed to the brim with the injured, who sat about having their wounds tended by the elven Healers. Without Healers capable of using the Spark, Salme's casualties would have doubled over the next few days. He couldn't help but think back at how many lives might have been saved in The Glade across the years if they'd had access to Healers. Freis Bryer was an incredible woman, and she'd pulled back more souls from the edge of death than Dann could count. But there was only so much a person could do with herbs, poultices, brimlock sap, and catgut.

The remains of the great hall still burned. The centre was a massive pile of smouldering embers, but flames licked the wooden frame and billowed smoke into the night. Had they not arrived with the army when they did, the entirety of Salme would have resembled the burning ruin that was the great hall. Even still, both Salme and the army had taken great losses.

A deep voice called out behind him. "Master Pimm."

Dann's skin prickled at the sound of Erdhardt Hammersmith's voice. He spun on his heels. The man was covered in blood and what looked to be small flecks of Urak flesh, and he carried a monstrous, spiked hammer, his massive fingers choking it around the neck. Somehow Erdhardt looked even larger than he once had. He was leaner, but his muscles were dense and strong. Dann would have paid good coin to see who would come out victorious in a brawl between Erdhardt, Tarmon, and Haem.

To Dann's surprise, Erdhardt stepped forwards and wrapped an enormous hand around Dann's forearm and stared into his eyes. The man had never greeted Dann that way. "You've grown up, Dann Pimm."

"So have you," Dann said, puffing out his cheeks. "What are they feeding you?"

Erdhardt cracked a broken smile. "It's good to see you, Dann." He looked at Dann as though he were appraising a new leather coat, his smile rising just a touch more at the edges. "It's good to see the man you've become. A man of The Glade."

Dann gave a soft nod. "I saw it... what's left of it."

"We are what's left of it." Erdhardt let go of Dann's forearm and slung his blood-coated hammer into the loop on his back. There was a pensive look on the man's face that Dann couldn't quite decipher. "How is Calen?"

"How long do you have?" Dann asked with a laugh.

"All the time in the world."

"He's alive. As is Ella."

"Ella?" Erdhardt's eyes widened. "After the soldiers killed Vars and Freis… and we didn't see her or Rhett, we just… We… we assumed the worst. Virandr told us that Rist was taken, but he said nothing of Ella."

"She's alive." Dann didn't feel the need to elaborate on the fact that Ella was alive but hadn't opened her eyes since the battle at Aravell. "With any luck, Calen will be here soon and you can talk to him yourself. Erdhardt, my mam and dad, have you seen them? I lost my dad in the fighting."

Erdhardt's expression grew grim, and fear raked its claws across Dann's heart.

"What's wrong? Erdhardt? Please…"

DANN FOUND HIS DAD STANDING at the edge of the docks, looking out over the water. Tharn's arms hung at his side, his shoulders drooped, the wind blowing at his loose clothes. Dann stopped a few paces behind him, his fragile heart trembling. He felt as though he was coming apart at the seams, his stomach churning and throat tight as a knot. "Dad?"

Tharn turned at the sound of his son's voice. His eyes were raw and red, tears glistening on his cheeks. He held out his arms. "Dann."

Without hesitation, Dann wrapped his arms around the man who had raised him, the man who had taught him what it was to be a man, what it was to be good and true. "I'm here, Dad."

At those three words, Tharn burst into tears. His dad squeezed him so tight Dann thought his eyes might pop out of his head.

"It's all right," Dann whispered. He tried his best to keep his voice from breaking. "She can rest now."

"I miss her already," Tharn sobbed, his wet nose burying into Dann's neck. "I miss her, Dann. She wasn't even fighting. She was meant to be safe in the hall…"

"I miss her too…" Dann pulled his dad in close and lifted his chin so it rested on the top of Tharn's head. He drew a long breath through his nose, tears rolling down his cheeks. All he wanted to do was break down and weep. But he couldn't. He needed to stay strong for his dad. Tharn had always been the strong one, always pushed Dann to be better. It was his turn to be the one taken care of.

They stood there on the docks for a long time. Dann didn't know how long, and he didn't care. He held his dad, and he saw his mam's face in his mind.

She was a sweet, kind, and – at times – fierce woman. And now she was gone, and he would never get to say goodbye. That's what hurt the most. He'd been away for so long. He'd seen so much of the world, so much death and horror and darkness. And he never got the chance to thank his mam for keeping him from all that, for allowing him the opportunity to live a life surrounded by love and light and laughter. And he'd never got to tell her about Camylin, or Midhaven, or Aravell, or Durakdur, or about all the beautiful things he'd seen. He'd never got to tell her about Lyrei.

Tharn may have taught Dann a lot of things, but Ylinda had taught him how to be kind and how to find the light in the dark. But he'd never told her that, never told her how thankful he was for everything she had given him.

By the time Lyrei found them standing on the docks, the warm golden light of the sun was starting to spill over the eastern horizon. Dann's heart had grown numb, a dark emptiness in his chest, and he shivered from the cold.

The pair of them walked Tharn back to the place he now called home: a wooden house near the dock with a small, covered porch and a slate roof.

"Jorvill lives right there." Tharn pointed to another house only a few paces away. Jorvill was dead now too. Dann had seen his body. He wasn't ready to find out who else they'd lost.

Dann helped his father remove his boots and leather armour. He took Tharn's shirt and trousers and planted a gentle kiss on his father's head.

Lyrei waited for him on the porch, her sword belt and bow set to the side, her knees pulled tight to her chest.

His muscles aching, Dann lowered himself to the step beside her. They sat there for a while, the rising sun slowly illuminating the corpse-filled streets of Salme. Lyrei rested her hand on Dann's leg and squeezed.

That was all it took to break him.

He leaned forwards, planted his elbows into his legs, put his face in his hands, and wept.

CHAPTER NINETY

THOSE WILLING TO DIE

24th Day of the Blood Moon

South of Achyron's Keep – Winter, Year 3081 After Doom

"Rise." Alina squeezed the handles of her saddle as Rynvar bolted upwards, the air attempting to rip her from his back. The buckles strapped to her hip pulled and jangled with the wyvern's flight.

Below, the army was setting up camp a day's march from Achyron's Keep. Shrieks rang out all around her as wyverns soared through the sky, their scales glinting in a myriad of colours as the sun hung high. The creatures were restless after leaving the camp they had settled in for so long.

She lifted her right hand and signalled for the patrols to head out, instructing the others to land and hunt. Feeding this many wyverns while moving across the land was no easy task. Staying a short flight from the coast was the only true solution. Fish were the only food source plentiful enough to not cause logistical issues, and as it happened wyverns were natural ocean hunters.

As the other Wyndarii dispersed, Alina stayed airborne with Mera, Lukira, and Amari, taking one last circuit around the perimeter. They'd already found some of Loren's scouts prowling about earlier that morning. The less knowledge Loren had on Alina's movements the better position they would be in. After sweeping the perimeter, Alina and her wing-sisters alighted near the command tent.

"Stay close," she said, running her hands along the scales of Rynvar's snout after dismounting.

The wyvern gave a soft purr and pressed the tip of his snout into Alina's chest. She laughed, scratching under his jaw. "Go," she said, pushing his snout away.

Rynvar, Audin, Syndel, and Urin all took flight as their riders made for the command tent.

"My queen." Both Olivian and Savrin inclined their heads from where they waited at the tent's entrance.

"The patrol was clear?" Savrin asked as they entered the command tent.

Alina nodded in response.

"I'll have fifty Wyndarii patrolling night and day." Mera unbuckled her helmet, holding it in the crook of her arm. "Nothing alive will get within ten miles of this camp without us knowing. Mistakes can be made once, never twice."

A long table was already set in the centre of the tent, cups and bottles of wine laid out, candles flickering. Six more of Alina's Royal Guard stood about the tent with backs rigid, hands resting on their sword pommels. The remaining two – Alcon and Vahir – guarded Alina's tent.

Everyone about the table rose as Alina entered.

Her High Commander, Joros, pressed a fist to his chest and bowed. "My queen, by blade and by blood."

"Sit, Joros." Alina gave the man a soft smile. He'd not been the same since the massacre at Myrefall. The man had lost five children and his wife in a single night, all while they'd slept. Anyone who experienced that and stayed the same was not human.

He gave Alina a sharp nod and returned to his chair, staring down into the wine cup before him.

"The rest of you as well." Alina gestured for the others to sit. They had all been marching double since Dayne had been taken – or since his departure. She still wasn't quite sure which was more accurate.

Anda Deringal and Tula Vakira, along with Tula's son Narek, were both seated across from Joros, with Rinek Larka to his left. The new head of House Herak – Vhin's eldest sister, Hakari – remained at Ironcreek to hold the blockade along the coast and to stop Lorian reinforcements by sea. But her two younger sisters, Savira and Vanda, were both seated at the table, along with her two eldest sons, Yerin and Vakar.

And Kirya of House Tallic – one of the large Minor Houses – now spoke for those who had once been vassals to House Thebal, since Aldon had defected.

A number of other heads of many Minor houses and some of the Wyndarii commanders took up the remaining seats, each of them staring at Alina intently as she walked to the head of the table and took her seat, her wing-sisters sitting alongside her. Alina would never not feel a warmth within her at seeing so many at her table, all bound together by the idea of a free Valtara. And yet, there was an emptiness too in the absence of Senya, Vhin, and Marlin.

After a few moments, porters brought out plates of roast rabbit and venison, pickled herring, fried potatoes, and roast vegetables on metal skewers. The cook fires had been the first things set up once the army had stopped; Alina had made sure of it. An army marched on its belly – a belly that, no matter what happened over the next few days, would soon go hungry.

Alina ripped a hunk of meat from a rabbit leg, chewed, and swallowed. She leaned in to Mera. "Dinekes and the others?"

Alina had asked Dinekes and the other Andurii captains to attend the meal. Not just to discuss plans for beginning the negotiations and the likely siege, but so they might rest with a warm meal and a cup of wine. The Andurii had turned solemn when they'd discovered Dayne was in Loren Koraklon's hands.

Mera shook her head. "They politely declined."

"I will see them after this."

"I'll go with you."

As the plates were cleared from the table, Rinek Larka sat forwards. "My queen. What are we to do if Loren does not wish to negotiate?"

Alina knew precisely what Rinek's words actually meant: what are we to do if Dayne is already dead and Loren is ready for battle?

"We do what we have always done, Rinek. We face what is in front of us with courage in our hearts."

"We lay siege," Narek Vakira declared, slapping his empty cup against the table. "We lay siege, and we tear Achyron's Keep to the ground. Then we mount the traitors' heads on spikes across the Hot Gates for any that might dare follow."

Alina raised an eyebrow at Tula Vakira, who simply gave a choked laugh at her son's words. Alina and the head of House Vakira argued more often than even she and Dayne, but the woman was direct, blunt, and fair. Those were qualities Alina needed at her side, regardless of whether they grated on her.

"Calm your fires, son." Tula sat back in her chair and took a long draught of her wine.

"Calm?" Anda Deringal shot upright, glaring at Tula, her fingers white around her cup. "Reinan Sarr and those traitors killed my aunt. They butchered Vhin and Sara. I will not be calm. I want their heads!"

Savrin, who had been standing in the back, glanced at Alina, but she shook her head. The night Senya and the others had been slaughtered, Anda had been but a timid girl, more used to dresses and dancing at sunset than spears and blood. And yet since that night, she had hardened. She had earned her third markings of spear and sword and been the first to volunteer for every assault. She had found the bottom of her cup this night, and Alina would not begrudge her that.

"To be calm does not mean to be timid." Alina sat forwards and rested on her arms. "But rushing head-on into a battle where we are vastly outnumbered will do nothing but see more of our kin entering Achyron's halls."

"Then what do you propose we do… Your Grace." Anda added the honorific with a touch of realisation in her voice, her eyes sobering.

"I too would like to hear what this plan is." Savira Herak had seen thirty summers and bore four rings of the blade. She was hard as iron and just as rigid. "We march on a keep legendary for its walls. We are vastly outnumbered, and the Lorians have brought Battlemages. I've seen the death when warriors try to storm the walls of a fortress. Each defender may as well be ten. Had the reinforcements Aeson Virandr promised arrived, I would say we stood a chance. But what now? What hope do we have?"

Murmurs spread about those gathered. Some agreeing with Savira, others arguing. One of the Wyndarii commanders was on her feet, hurling insults at the head of House Rudain.

"Our queen has not led us astray so far," Kirya of House Tallic called out, her voice swallowed by the arguing. "We have over seven hundred wyverns. All of Valtara is finally—"

"Oh, stop your rambling." The Head of the Minor House Joral rolled his eyes and emptied his cup. He shook his head. "It doesn't matter how many wyverns we have when Loren has a hundred Battlemages and outnumbers us two to one. All we—"

"Silence!" Joros threw his cup across the table, pushed his chair back, and stood. The man's hands trembled, and he stared at the ground, shaking his head. Joros had served in the Redstone guard for as many years as Alina had been alive. She trusted him completely. And her heart ached for everything he had lost.

Not a whisper left a single pair of lips as Joros's fist clenched and unclenched at his side, patches of sweat tacking his tunic to his muscular frame. He drew a long breath and lifted his gaze, glaring at all those sat about the table. "Alina Ateres is our queen. That I need remind you all of this simple fact is a sign of your ignorance and the arrogance that matches it."

Vhin Herak's son made to speak but silenced himself after a cold stare from Joros.

"Queen Alina Ateres," Joros repeated. "Let those words sink into your thick skulls. Queen. *Our* queen. A Valtaran queen for the first time in centuries. Freedom is within our grasp, and it is Alina who has brought us here. Alina who has united so many of the Houses and rides as First of the Wyndarii. If those at this table do not show her the respect she has rightfully earned in blood and sacrifice, then I will take it upon myself as High Commander of the queen's armies to teach you that respect."

Joros walked across the silent tent, collected his cup, and set it back down on the table. Slowly, he poured the wine.

"You are warriors of Valtara," he said, placing his palm over the mouth of the cup. "If your queen says that we lay siege to Achyron's Keep, then that is what we do. If she says that we scale the walls with nothing but our bare hands, then *that* is what we do. If Achyron himself stands guard over the keep, then we will cut him down and dance on his corpse. Dayne Ateres lies on the other side of those walls. Do you not think he would break the gates down himself if any of you were in his place? He is Andurios. He is the champion of Valtara. And I would rather die than leave him in Loren Koraklon's hands. I lost my dear wife, my sons, my daughters – I lost everything at Myrefall – and I would see those treacherous bastards bleed into the earth for what they have taken from me. If Aeson Virandr arrives in time, all the better. But if he does not, then we will fight like Valtarans, and if needs be, we will die like Valtarans. But I will not live another day with a Lorian blade to my neck."

Joros looked to Alina and pressed his hand to his chest. "I, Joros of House Myr, High Commander of the Valtaran armies, vow to follow my queen to the depths of the void. I vow to stand steadfast by her side, to fight in her name, to carry her banner, and to lay waste to her enemies. I vow to answer whenever she may call. The Warrior and The Sailor. By blade and by blood. I am yours, my queen. From this day until my last day."

Amari and Lukira followed Joros, the Wyndarii captains joining. And as they spoke the same words, so too did Anda Deringal and Kirya Tallic, and Rinek Larka and the heads of the other Minor Houses.

Tula Vakira stood, looking to Alina, her lips spreading into a thin but warm smile. "I'm too long in the tooth for vows. My time left is my own. But I truly believe that Queen Alina Ateres would do anything to bring the Houses of Valtara together, to unite us under one banner – strong and fierce. The Lorians have stood over us for so long because we have been divided, weak. But when we fight shield to shield, the wyvern of House Ateres next to the raven of House Vakira, the bull of House Deringal, the stallion of House Herak… we are more than the sum of our parts. I believe it is most certainly time for the rest of Epheria to once again fear the blademasters of Valtara." She grabbed her cup and raised it. "We are Valtarans! Long live the Wyvern Queen!"

"Long live the Wyvern Queen!"

As the chants settled, Alina pushed her chair back slowly, the wood creaking. When she stood, silence fell, the others still standing with her.

"My parents wanted nothing but the freedom of our home. They fought and died for that freedom. It was Loren Koraklon who sent them to their deaths, who hung them in the plaza for all to see. You have all faced your own losses, your own heartbreak. Our people have been fighting for generations. The other nations lay down and suckled on the Lorian teat, prayed at the altar of the lion. But not us. No. Valtaran blood runs hot. We are bronze, and steel, and scales, and we will *not* be bowed."

Alina drew a long, slow breath through her nostrils, exhaling as she cast her gaze around the tent.

"My brother lies within the walls of Achyron's Keep. I have not always given him the love he deserves. I was bitter, and weak, and stubborn. And it took me far too long to see the man he is. He is the firstborn child of Arkin and Ilya Ateres, the rightful heir to Redstone. When he returned, by right the head of House Ateres was his. He did not take it. He did not even ask for it. When Turik Baleer offered him the chance to take my place, he struck the man down, placed the crown on my head, and stood at my side. Dayne Ateres is not only Valtara's greatest champion, he is mine."

Mera stared into Alina's eyes, smiling softly.

"I ask you all gathered here. Will you let our champion die alone? In the hands of the man who betrays our very home with every breath he takes?"

"No." Joros hammered his hand against his chest, and in the corner of her eye, Alina saw Savrin Vander do the same, fire in his eyes.

"Will you lie down and let the Lorians place that collar around your neck once more?"

"No!" The chants grew louder now, cups slamming off the table, feet stamping, fists smashing into chests.

"By blade and by blood!"

WHEN CUPS HAD BEEN EMPTIED and bellies filled and the others had returned to their tents for a last night of good sleep, Alina strolled through the camp. Evrian, Glaukos, Olivian, and Baris marched in a square around her, orange cloaks drifting just above the dirt. Savrin and Mera walked alongside her.

"Has there been any further word from Aeson Virandr?" Mera asked.

Alina shook her head. "Not in some time. With the Lorian fleets patrolling the coast, there is no telling how long it might take him to reach Valtara." She looked up at the crimson moon that bled in the sky. "I had given him till the turning of the moon. But we cannot wait. Everything hangs on what happens tomorrow. If I feel Dayne's life is under threat, we will march on the keep, whether Belina has opened the gates or not. The Wyndarii will rain blood on the walls, and our warriors will mount ladders and smash the gates. We will take the keep, one way or another."

Savrin's face grew grim. "I will go wherever you send me, my queen. I will climb the walls alone if you will it. But to send our army crashing against Achyron's Keep, outnumbered against an entrenched foe… it is to welcome defeat."

"And what would you have me do, Savrin? Leave Dayne to die? Sue for peace, and live a life in chains?" Alina could do nothing to take the irritation from her voice, and yet she truly did wish to hear Savrin's counsel. He had kept his opinions close to his chest in the tent, and there were none in her court who knew war like Savrin Vander. He had been the champion of House Ateres in a time when all the Houses had been in constant quarrels. He had been the greatest of the Andurii – even greater than her father. He was not the same man now. His body not as quick or strong, and yet she would still favour him against any foe but her brother.

"I would have you wait, Your Grace. I would have you scrape every last moment you can in the hopes that Aeson Virandr reaches our shores in time."

"My parents waited on Aeson Virandr."

"That they did. May I speak plain?"

Alina inclined her head.

"You have never met the man. You base your opinions on the bleeding of your heart and little more. But I have met him. He is hard as steel, cold as ice, and in a world of souls that call themselves honourable, he stands above most else. I fought that night in Redstone. The night the Lorians attacked. The night Loren betrayed us and your parents – along with thousands of others – were slaughtered. We were caught off guard. We had no idea of Loren's betrayal. How could Aeson have known any better? We weren't expecting him for days. As much as I would love to lay the cause of that night at someone's feet, those feet are not Aeson's."

"Hmmm."

"If I may, Your Grace?"

Alina waved for Savrin to continue.

"Dayne gave me back my purpose. There are few in this camp that want him returned safely more than I."

Both Alina and Mera glanced at him with raised eyebrows.

"Present company being members of that few." The man raised his open palms, then continued. "When the Andurios left, he instructed patience, did he not? Belina Louna said to wait on her signal."

Savrin stopped in his tracks.

"What is it?" Alina asked, stopping with the man, Mera and the guards doing the same.

"If we march on that keep tomorrow with the numbers we have, if we throw ourselves against those grey walls and Lorian Battlemages, we will all die. You have fought enough battles to know this. And if you ask me to charge at those walls regardless, I will. I do not take the vows I swore to you lightly, so please do not take my words as disrespect."

Alina drew in a sharp breath and gave an even sharper nod. "I will take your words into consideration, Savrin."

The look on Savrin's face was one of relief. "Your Grace."

"Where are the Andurii camped?" Alina asked after a few paces.

"They are not at their tents, Your Grace," Savrin answered.

"Then where are they?"

"There is a spring nearby that trickles into a pool."

"And what in the gods are they doing there at nightfall?"

"Preparing, Your Grace."

"For?"

"Death, Your Grace."

Savrin led Alina, Mera, and the Royal Guard through the camp and up a slope to a dense wood nestled at the foot of a steep hill. Pale pink moonlight spilled through the canopy, illuminating the path. It wasn't long before the splashing and the rumble of a small waterfall reached Alina's ears.

Ahead the trees peeled away to reveal a clearing with a large pool at its centre, moss covered rocks arranged about its edges, and a small waterfall trickling.

"Oh…" Alina averted her gaze, more from surprise than embarrassment.

Each of the Andurii – men and women – were naked as the day they were brought into the world, the pink light cold on their skin. Some bathed in the pool's water, others sat about scrubbing their skin and combing their hair.

After a second or two, Alina lifted her gaze once more. "What in the gods are they doing?"

"I told you, Your Grace. Preparing to die. It is an old Andurii tradition from the Age of War. Some say from even before then, before our ancestors set foot on these lands."

"Your Grace." Dinekes Ilyon, one of Dayne's Andurii captains, rose from where he scrubbed his legs on a low rock by the pool. He wrapped a cloth around his waist and bowed. Alina had known him since she was a child in Redstone. He was a stern man, precise and level.

Alina inclined her head.

Dinekes gestured around at the other Andurii. "It is custom amongst the Andurii that when we have resigned ourselves to the arms of The Mother, we prepare our bodies for her embrace."

"You have resigned yourselves to dying? You think our odds so small?" Something in Alina's gut turned. The Andurii were the beating heart of her army. They were the symbol of Valtara reborn, of House Ateres arisen. There was not a soul who did not look on them almost as gods. If the Andurii had forsaken everything, what chance did they have?

"No, Your Grace. It is a commitment to ourselves and to each other that we are willing to give our lives in the battle to come. That we will die for each other. That we will die for the cause. That we will allow nothing to stop us. There will be no retreat, no surrender. Our Andurios lies on the other side of those walls. He would give his own life for us without a second's thought, without hesitation, or uncertainty, or question. And so we will do the same. We bathe our bodies and comb our hair so that when Heraya takes us, she knows that we gave ourselves willingly, that our deaths came with a conscious understanding. That we were not afraid."

When Alina once again studied the Andurii who sat about bare as babes, she no longer felt the compulsion to look away. Dinekes's words had changed the foundations of that moment.

"When I was told you had declined my offer for supper, I had feared… I had—"

"You had feared we'd abandoned you?"

"In a sense. I had feared you yourselves had felt abandoned by Dayne's choice to allow himself to be taken. I had feared your anger, feared you had thought it a betrayal."

Dinekes gave a half-laugh, clasping his hands behind his back. "It is not to us to question the heart of our Andurios's decisions. His wisdom, yes – I question that daily – but not his heart. If he made that choice, he made it for a reason. It is our charge now to see him safe from harm and to fight in his name."

"What is that?" Alina gestured towards a group of Andurii to the right of the pool. Some sat with their legs crossed and arms folded across their laps while others marked the chests of those seated with some kind of white and orange paint.

"The Andurii of old used to mark their bodies with ancient glyphs. Messages to the ones they loved should they die. Once the paint hardens and dries, it sticks to the skin for weeks. Sweat, rain, soap – nothing peels it away. It burns the skin, just a little. After a time, it becomes too brittle to hold its own form and peels free."

Dinekes turned so he stood with the pool on his right and Alina on his left. "Andurii," he bellowed. "Are you ready to die?"

"AH-OOH!"

Every man and woman roared their reply in unison, and a chill swept through Alina. Three hundred and forty-nine voices as one.

"Are you ready to fight in the name of House Ateres? In the name of Valtara?"

"AH-OOH!"

Even as they bathed and combed their hair, the Andurii shouts were as raw and deep as battle cries.

"Your Andurios is in need of your aid. Who or what will stand in your way?"

"Nothing!" Some of the Andurii beat their fists against their bare chests, others slapped stone or stomped their feet.

"What will you give to see him free? To see Valtara free?"

"Everything!"

"Andurii. By blade and by blood!"

"AH-OOH, AH-OOH, AH-OOH!"

"You see, Your Grace. We do not resign ourselves to dying. We resign ourselves to being *willing* to die. We resign our lives to the lives of the Andurii. We are your spears from now until we are taken from this world. We are the guardians of House Ateres, and we will never falter."

ALINA AND THE OTHERS WERE halfway between the wood and the camp when the screeches of wyverns tore through the night overhead.

A group of six flew low, marked in the sky by the moon's light.

Mera and Alina glanced at one another, and Savrin bellowed orders at the Royal Guard, each of them drawing their blades.

"Warn the Andurii!" Olivian shouted, ordering Glaukos back through the wood. She turned to Evrian. "Rouse the rest of the guard and sound the horns. The rest of you, nothing gets past your blades."

"Hold." Alina raised an open palm.

"My queen, if there is an attack, time is not our ally. We must act swiftly and decisively." Olivian's hand gripped the spherical pommel of her sword, which was still sheathed at her hip. She gestured for the remaining guards to spread out and take up a defensive position.

Alina pointed up at the sky. "Those Wyndarii each have horns to signal an attack. They've not yet used them."

"All the same, Your Grace, I would rather be prepared for a fight that does not come than face a fight we are not prepared for."

"As you will, but take us to the camp. If they're back from patrol, it's for a reason – reason enough to rouse me from the sleep they believe me to be enjoying."

By the time Alina and the others reached her tent, Ola Yarek, one of the Wyndarii commanders, was waiting alongside her night blue wyvern, Tuavast, and five other Wyndarii.

"My queen." Ola bowed and pressed her hand to her chest, the other Wyndarii following suit.

"What news, Commander?" Alina gestured for them all to rise.

"Ships, my queen. Hundreds."

Alina's skin goosefleshed, a twisted ball of dread forming in her stomach. "Whose?"

Ola shook her head. "I do not know the sigil, my queen. It's some kind of reptile, black and white, on a golden field lined with blue."

Alina looked to Savrin, who pursed his lips and shook his head.

"Sound the alarm. Better be prepared for a fight that does not come than face a fight we are not prepared for." She nodded at Olivian, then turned to Mera. "Ready yourself and summon Amari and Lukira. We ride for the coast."

Savrin started to object but stopped as soon as Alina raised a hand. "You're my guard, Savrin. Not my shadow."

"They're the same thing, Your Grace."

"Well unless you can fly, find a horse."

CHAPTER NINETY-ONE

OATHKEEPER

24ᵗʰ Day of the Blood Moon

South of Achyron's Keep – Winter, Year 3081 After Doom

Alina pulled in a breath of the salty, sea-tinged air, savouring the taste of it.

The ships numbered so many their golden sails spread across the entire horizon, the twilight of the Blood Moon marking them clearly. She had never before seen the sigil of the scaled beast emblazoned across them. It was like some wingless wyvern painted in strange colours.

Screeches and shrieks cut through the sound of the gently swashing waves. Alina had brought all but a hundred wyverns with her to the beach. She had wanted a show of force for whoever commanded those ships, but the camp needed enough Wyndarii to keep it safe. Six hundred would be enough to strike fear into anyone's heart.

Rynvar extended his head over Alina's right shoulder, and she reached back to scratch at the underside of his jaw. The wyvern purred, a series of clicks reverberating in his throat.

Alina shivered and rolled her shoulders. It took quite a bit for her to feel the cold in her bones. She was one of those people who lived with a warmth, her blood hotter than most. But when the cold did creep in, she despised it. Tonight was a particularly cold night.

"Are you sure we shouldn't send riders out? Glean what we can?" Amari folded her arms beside Alina, her breath forming in pale mist before her.

"What we would learn wouldn't be worth the risk. Those ships will be close enough soon. Friend or foe, it's better to make them face us on our terms, rather than theirs." She looked about at the hundreds of wyverns gathered on the cliff edges surrounding the short beach. "This beach is big enough for no more than three of those monstrous ships. If they want to land here, they'll be doing so three at a time, and if they mean us harm, the wyverns will tear them to pieces."

Alina stared out at the mass of ships on the dark waves. If she'd not received word from her fleet stationed around Stormwatch, then these ships had likely come from the south or west. It could be Aeson. It could be pirates. It could be sellswords from Ardan fighting in Loria's name. It could be an invading army from Karvos, or Narvona, or any of the other continents. The gods had always had a queer sense of humour. Regardless, caution was best.

Beside her Rynvar shook his head and spread his wings, screeching restlessly.

"Easy." She stroked his jaw.

Just as Alina had gauged, three of the foreign ships separated from the fleet as it drew in around the basin. Each of the three were built from wood black as coal, their hulls scraped free of lichen. All three were trimmed with gold that shone as though freshly polished, but one ship stood out. At least a hundred and fifty feet long and fifty feet wide along the central mast, she was monstrous yet beautiful, adorned with a golden figurehead that matched the banners. The form was nearly that of a dragon, but with a head far flatter and wider that tapered into a narrow, rounded snout. Its jaw swept out sharply at the back of its skull, and two enormous sapphires were set into the creature's golden eye sockets.

The massive ship carried on straight towards the sand as the other two drifted left and right, dropping anchor.

"My queen." Ursla Goan, a Wyndarii commander who had seen ten summers more than Alina, bowed her head. "That ship isn't dropping anchor."

"No," Alina responded. "It's not."

"We should move back, my queen."

"You are free to do so."

"My queen, I—"

Ursla's words were cut short by a low grumble from Rynvar. The wyvern tilted his head back to look at the woman, his teeth bared.

Ursla bowed and stepped back to her own wyvern – Ikuron – and led him away. She knew better than to press the point.

Amari, Lukira, and Mera all stood around Alina, Audin and the other wyverns with them.

The massive ship slowed as it approached the sand but continued on a forward course. It broke through the waves and hit the sand with a deep *thump*. The sound of grating wood filled the air as the vessel scraped across the beach, the hulking mass biting deep into the ground.

Alina filled her lungs as the ship continued towards her, its true size visible up close, the sapphire eyes of the figurehead glinting.

Amari and Lukira took a step back as the ship's bow drew ever closer, its enormity bearing down upon them. Alina held her ground along with Mera and the wyverns, her heart keeping its slow rhythm. The vessel finally came to a grinding halt about twenty feet from Alina, the wood creaking as it stopped.

Alina stared up at the golden head above her, into the sapphire eyes. After a few moments, she stepped back to get a better look at the ship.

The freeboard must have been forty feet, the hull a pristine black. Heads flitted about on the open deck above as deep groans and clangs came from within the belly.

Alina would never have beached a ship unless the hull had been compromised or it was an unavoidable obstacle. But the tide was at its lowest, and so when it came in, it would free the vessel from its lodging. Still, it was a needlessly reckless manoeuvre done clearly to make an impression. Whoever it was didn't plan on killing them, at least not right away.

Just as Alina turned to speak to Mera, a series of strange roars sounded from within the ship's belly. Deeper than a wyvern's, rougher – and yet not entirely dissimilar. That roar was answered by shrieks and chirps.

Mera placed her finger and thumb between her lips and gave a sharp whistle. The sound was answered by shrieks as fifty or so wyverns lifted from the overlooking cliffs and alighted across the beach, their Wyndarii drawing their javelins.

A wyvern with pale cream scales and blue wing membranes landed not two feet from Alina, Rynvar hissing as it did. The Wyndarii dismounted, bowing to Rynvar before doing the same to Alina. "My queen. It's Narvonans. The deck is thronged with them, all clad in gilded plate."

Alina nodded her thanks. She'd met many Narvonans in her lifetime, as was the case with most who lived along the southern and southwestern coasts of Epheria. The Valtarans were a people of the sea, but the Narvonans' love of the open water was even greater still. The Narvonans Alina had encountered had been smugglers, or traders, or pirates, or those come to make a home in Epheria. Many of the Wyndarii were descendants of Narvonan settlers. But whoever commanded these ships was no pirate or smuggler. These were some of the finest vessels Alina had ever laid eyes on. And there were hundreds of them.

Alina found herself praying to Achyron. If these Narvonans had aligned with the Lorians, then the rebellion was over. If they were here to invade, then the rebellion was over. She would not let that happen.

Alina turned to Amari. "Take ten Wyndarii and bring all of the Godfire we have left. If these Narvonans wish to do us harm, we will set their fleet alight from the sky."

"At once, my queen." Amari mounted Syndel and took to the sky, calling ten more Wyndarii to join her.

"If it comes to it," Alina said, talking to Mera. "We will hold them here at the beach as long as we can. It's better we take them slowly while their numbers are filtered through the narrow passage. We can pick them off from the boats as they try to land. If we retreat and allow them the freedom to come ashore, that will be our death."

"Agreed."

Mera relayed Alina's instructions to three of the Wyndarii commanders, who in turn took flight to arrange the defence in the event that things took a turn for the worst.

Alina cleared her throat and called out. "Who goes there? Who sails a fleet to the shores of Valtara?"

No answer came, but a horrible creaking sound groaned from the ship and a section of the starboard hull came away from the inside and slid to the left, leaving an enormous opening. After a moment, two beams of dark wood, each thicker than Alina's torso, slid from the opening on a set of hinged brackets, dropping down into the sand with a *thump*.

A pair of dark-skinned Narvonans appeared at the opening, both garbed in vibrant blue pantaloons and loose golden shirts marked with that same reptilian sigil. They were the finest dressed sailors she'd ever laid eyes on. The two sailors disappeared and reappeared as they loaded tethered slats into a groove in both beams of dark wood and slid them down one by one.

Upon seeing what had to be the largest gangway in existence, Alina had one thought and one thought only: what in all the gods required a gangway that large? It was at least twenty feet from edge to edge, thick and solid as a house.

It wasn't long before Alina's question was answered.

Those same deep roars echoed from within the ship, clearer this time, unmuffled by the wooden hull. Even stranger chirps followed, like that of a bird but more… otherworldly.

Commands in the Narvonan tongue sounded from within, and then the entire ship trembled where it stood, rattling in response to massive thumping steps.

"What in all that is sacred…"

A hulking scaled creature emerged from the hull of the ship. It walked on four thick-muscled legs, and its shoulders were easily twice as broad as that of a horse, its chest dense, its neck thick. The beast's skull was shaped precisely as that of the ship's figurehead: long and wide, its jaws curving out to the side, sharp and flat. Its curved snout tapered towards the end, fronted with two slits for nostrils.

Polished gold barding covered a large portion of the creature's body. An ornate helmet protected the top half of its head, leaving slits for the eyes, nostrils, and horns, which were also capped with gold. Articulated plates of golden armour stretched along the back of the creature's neck, the bottom covered in silver mail. More plates stretched across its back and legs, along with thick pauldron-like segments at the shoulders and rump. More silver mail, clipped to the plates, protected its belly.

A man in silver and gold armour was mounted on the creature's back, sitting in a gold and leather saddle that sat like that of a horse, adapted slightly to fit the curve of the reptile's spine. The man was heavily muscled and held a set of reins connected to the creature's helm. A massive, curved blade hung at his left hip, while a thick-shafted, eight-foot spear was clipped to the side of the saddle.

"That's a lot of gold," Mera whispered.

The gangway, thick as it was, groaned beneath the monstrous creature's weight as it disembarked. Something about the way the beast walked told Alina that although it seemed slow and cumbersome, it was anything but. The razor-sharp teeth that jutted down past the golden helm were those of a predator, and the short black claws on the ends of its feet were made for tearing prey to ribbons. Just as the beast stepped from the gangway onto the sand, a second followed it, equally as massive and imposing.

There wasn't a shield wall in the world that could stand against one of those creatures, never mind two.

Once both creatures had reached the sand, they walked side by side towards Alina and her Wyndarii, stopping a few feet short. They snorted and stomped, those strange chirping noises resonating in their chests.

One of the beasts reared onto its hind legs, nostrils flaring, but as it did, Rynvar stepped across Alina and roared, his frills rising. The wyvern puffed out his chest and hissed, shielding Alina protectively.

Beside her, Mera's wyvern, Audin, did the same, snaking his head low to the ground, his lips peeling back to show his razor teeth. Audin was far smaller than Rynvar but no less savage in the protection of his family. Urin and two other wyverns joined them, hissing and baring their teeth.

The man atop the reptilian beast made a clicking sound and slapped its side with a leather whip. The creature snorted but stepped back, its eyes darting between each of the wyverns.

All five of the wyverns' heads shot up as a fanfare of horns sounded and the two reptilian mounts separated, creating a space between them.

A stream of men and women marched down the gangway. The four at the front wore loose blue trousers and stiff golden shirts and blew long horns adorned with triangular flags. Brass rings hung from their ears and noses, each of their faces marked with a myriad of white-ink tattoos.

Two rows of ten warriors followed, clad in the most opulent armour Alina had ever laid eyes on, all polished black steel and gilding, embellishments of white enamel worked into the breastplates and pauldrons. Their helmets were formed from a single piece of metal lined with gold that broke up the black plate, almost like scales. A single slit two fingers thick ran from eye to eye.

The hornblowers and the warriors lined themselves in front of the mounts, twelve on either side. Once they were all in place, the horns sounded once again, and more souls poured from the opening.

These were not of Narvona. A man in black studded leather walked at their front, two swords slung across his back. A woman in a dark hooded cloak walked on his left, while a grey-haired beast of a man moved on his right, skin leathered, a well-kept grey beard covering his face. A column of others walked at their backs, several in mixed leathers and cloaks, followed by a number of warriors armoured in the black, gilded plate.

The man in the black leather stopped a foot or so before Alina, his chin tilted upwards as he stared at the five wyverns who stood over her protectively.

Rynvar leaned forwards, his black-scaled lips lifting in a snarl, his winged forelimbs pressing into the sand. The wyvern lowered his head, a growl resonating in his throat. Audin, Urin, and the other wyverns moved back, deferring to Rynvar.

The man didn't so much as flinch. He stared straight into the wyvern's eyes, then dropped to one knee, a fist across his chest, and looked to Alina. "Queen Alina Ateres, my name is Aeson Virandr, and I have come to keep an oath I made to your father and mother. I failed them, and that will haunt me for the rest of my days. But my oath is not dead. I will see Valtara free, or I will die in the trying, on this you have my solemn vow. I bring with me four thousand free Epherian swords pledged to rid this world of the Lorian Empire, five hundred of the finest Arkalen Stormguard sent by Aurelian Animar, and twenty thousand strong of the Latrakian Kingdom of Narvona. Allow us to fight by your side, and together we will drive your enemies from this land, and we will burn the Lorian Empire from Epheria."

The lines beneath his blue eyes creased as he stared at Alina, his hand firmly pressed to his chest, awaiting her response. Behind him, the others stood silent, and more soldiers marched down the gangway.

Alina allowed a few moments to pass, nodding slowly. Aeson had not mentioned that his swords would be those of a Narvonan kingdom. "Aeson Virandr. I have known your name since I was a child, yet I had never seen your face until this moment. You are not what I had imagined. Rise."

Aeson stood, bowing slightly at the waist. "What had you imagined, Your Grace?"

Something less. The man had an aura about him, a sense of strength and surety that radiated from every movement he made. For some reason, it irritated her.

"I'm not sure," Alina answered, feigning a smile.

Alina had been prepared for a battle of words the first time she would meet Aeson Virandr. For years she'd thought of what she'd say if she ever looked into his eyes. But in that moment, it all evaporated. She had not expected such deference from the man her parents had spoken of like a god. It had put her off balance.

"Where is Dayne?" Aeson looked past Alina at the other Wyndarii.

"Captured."

Aeson's expression shifted the moment the word left Alina's lips. "When? Where?"

"A few days past. Loren has him in Achyron's Keep. We march tomorrow."

"It is a good thing, then, that we arrived when we did. I had hoped to reach Valtara sooner, but the winds have not been kind, and Lorian ships patrol the waters all about the coasts of Varsund and Arkalen." He let out a short sigh. "Please, my manners."

Aeson turned to the side, the companions behind him parting.

A man and a woman stood at the head of a column of armoured Narvonan soldiers, flanked by four warriors in pearlescent plate astride two-legged reptilian mounts. These mounts were far smaller and leaner than the massive creatures that had first come down the gangplank, and they looked quick and ferocious. She had heard stories of the Narvonan darvakin, savage war mounts that could tear a man's arm free and outrun a horse.

The man was tall and wiry, though well-muscled. His head was shaved clean, and white-ink tattoos decorated his face. Armour gilded from top to bottom and bearing the face of one of those monstrous mounts fit his form perfectly, and the sapphire eyes in the breastplate sparkled fiercely in the sun. His pauldrons were shaped like snatching claws, the detail beyond anything Alina had ever seen wrought in metal. A long sword hung from the belt at his hip, a cut ruby set into the pommel.

The woman stood with her chin high, her right hand on the sapphire pommel of her sword. Thick braids adorned with sapphires and rings of gold hung nearly to her waist. A white dot was inked below each of her eyes, along with two white lines that moved from above her top lip and down over her chin. The armour she wore was wrought entirely from a smooth, pearlescent material that caught the light in many colours, gold worked into its edges. As she stared at the incomparable plate, Alina realised what it was: Atalus shell. The shell of the great Atalus turtles, hard as steel and capable of absorbing magic. Alina had only ever heard stories of it. It was granted to the greatest warriors of Narvona – the Isildans – and to royalty. It was said that Narvonans guarded it more closely than Godfire, more closely than their own souls. She looked back up at the warriors in the same plate mounted astride the darvakin. Were they truly Isildans?

The man stepped forwards. He nodded to Aeson before turning his attention to Alina. He bowed and pressed his two clenched fists together.

Alina knew the gesture: a Narvonan sign of respect. She mimicked it, drawing a smile from the man.

"Queen Alina Ateres of Valtara, First of the Wyndarii, it honours us to hunt by your side." His accent was thick, clinging to the vowels and rolling 'R's.

"The honour is ours. May our hunt be short and fruitful." Her father had taught her the words many summers ago, when he'd traded with Narvonan merchants to purchase the sapphire pendant she'd worn about her neck until the Lorians destroyed everything. She had been but a child then. And she would have paid a hundred times the price to have that pendant once more.

"My name is Akraf Latrak. Prince Consort, Commander of the armies of Princess Kayala Latrak, and Sworn Shield to the princess herself." The man smiled again before gesturing towards the woman. "May I introduce you to Princess Kayala Latrak, Blood of the Water, Scourge of the Antigan Ocean, and third in line to the royal house of Latrak."

Princess Kayala inclined her head and pressed her two fists together.

Alina stared back, unsure what to say. Aeson had not simply brought Narvonan warriors to her shores. Not sellswords or men and women looking for a new home. He had brought Narvonan royalty. There would be a price to that. "It is an honour to share the wind in your sails, Princess Kayala."

"And I yours, Queen Alina. On my journeys, I have received many reports of the Wyvern Queen of Valtara."

A tense silence passed between them, and Alina looked from Kayala to Aeson and back. "Forgive me," Alina said. "But our march has been long, my mind is weary, and my brother is in chains behind the walls of my enemy's keep. And so I apologise for my curtness when I ask why Aeson Virandr has brought a foreign army to my shores and what he has promised you in return for your aid."

Aeson made to speak but stopped at a glance from Kayala.

"Your people are foreign to these lands if I am not mistaken. We share the same ancestry. The first settlers of Valtara and Daris both come from the old lands, do they not?"

"That was three thousand years ago."

"So it was. And so in three thousand years, I will no longer be foreign, no?" The princess gave Alina a half-smile, looking towards Rynvar, who still loomed over Alina's shoulder, though the growl was long gone from his throat. "There is a price of blood I am owed. I wish to drain that blood from the heart of the black lion. To put it simply and in a way I believe you will understand, I want vengeance. For too long the Lorian Empire has burned our ships with impunity, killed my people, and hidden behind their dragons. If left unchecked, who is to say they would not turn their eyes on my homeland? I believe it is time to put them to the sword."

"And your queen or king? I know something of the histories of the Narvonan Kingdoms. Endless war. I cannot imagine they simply let you sail twenty thousand warriors across the Narvonan Sea? For what, vengeance? What do they seek?"

Kayala touched three fingers to her lips and laughed. "Perhaps we might discuss this over some wine and swordfish, but I feel that suggestion might not be one your ears wish for. No, they did not simply let me sail away. I am on what is called Aramuthíer. It is a word in my tongue that means 'in search of legacy'. I will never sit the throne of Latrak. I am third in line, and my Queen Mother will soon sail the River Trian – Akopa guide her. And as such, I must find my own way. To become Aramuthíer is an old tradition amongst the royal houses of Narvona, to allow the sons and daughters with no crown in their stars to find a glory of their own. And of course, were my mother to hear that the Lorian Empire was in ruins, she would no doubt find happiness in her heart."

Alina bit at her lip, tucking her thumb inside her right fist. There was more to this. She knew it. But without the warriors on those ships, Valtara would never smell the air of freedom and Dayne would die alone. She would be trading an enemy now and risking another later. But the choice had been taken from her.

She needed this Kayala Latrak and her army.

Alina exhaled slowly, counting her heartbeats and looking back at Mera. She nodded. "Swordfish, you said?"

"Indeed. Much swordfish, caught fresh by our fishermen as we journeyed. In fact, we have brought you hundreds of barrels of sausages, hard Narvonan cheese, salted beef and pork, smoked achkaret, pickled cabbage and beets, fresh apples and plums from the orchards of northern Unair – enough to fill every belly in your army. Consider it a sign of my intentions. Aeson Virandr said food was in short supply. Now it is not. Is your camp far?"

Alina shook her head.

"Trust is earned, Queen Alina. So tonight let us dine like gods. And come the morning, I will earn your trust in the blood of your enemies."

CHAPTER NINETY-TWO

CUTS THAT BLEED THE DEEPEST

25th Day of the Blood Moon

Salme – Winter, Year 3081 After Doom

The sun bled over the horizon at Calen's back as Valerys soared across the tall, harsh peaks of Wolfpine Ridge. He'd not seen those peaks in a long time, and something about them set a warmth within him. Far in the distance, through Valerys's eyes, he could see the green canopy of Ölm Forest stretching off towards the coast, The Glade somewhere along its edge.

The journey from the Firnin Mountains had taken longer than he'd hoped, but thanks to Therin, Varthear's deepest wounds were faring well. The elf sat behind Calen, arms wrapped around his waist, Varthear flying on their left, Avandeer and Tivar on their right.

They passed over the blackened remains of Talin as they flew, along with a few spread out homesteads, farms, and holds. Flocks of crows feasted on carrion and picked flesh from rotting severed heads left skewered along the roads.

Nothing had escaped the Urak destruction.

Just as the blend of sorrow and rage had begun to settle in Calen's stomach, Valerys caught sight of something in the distance: masses of black clouds swirling back and forth along a road that stretched for miles. Calen knew the hill that marked the fork in the road between Talin and Salme. The Oak Road.

Coils of dread slithered in his stomach and through his veins.

Before long, the squawking of crows had drowned out even the beating of the dragons' wings. The black birds filled the air, swirling around Calen and showing little fear of the three great dragons. It took Calen more than a few heartbeats to look through Valerys's eyes and see what lay below. Corpses. Hundreds of rotting, mutilated corpses bolted to every tree along the road, the birds picking the strips of decaying flesh.

Calen's stomach turned, and Valerys's rage burned so bright Calen could feel it searing his blood. The dragon unleashed a roar like rolling thunder, and Calen had to press himself to Valerys's scales and pull their minds together to stop him from setting every tree alight. The people of the villages burned their dead from time to time, but they preferred to bury them, to return them to earth, to allow life to grow anew.

Valerys let out another defiant roar, then ripped through the skies, scores of crows too slow to move crashing against his scales and whirling in his wake.

The dragon's fury was undercut by a fear that shifted between them. Fear of what they might find when they reached Salme.

Plumes of dark smoke came into view, scores of them billowing into the sky, black as onyx. The fear within him only faded when, through Valerys's eyes, Calen saw purple banners emblazoned with the image of the white dragon flapping in the wind. Some of the smoke came from within the city, but that smoke was grey and dwindling.

A pair of trenches – still half-filled with bodies – and spiked barricades ringed the broken palisade wall. Even further out, Urak bodies were piled high as houses, flames consuming them as more and more were added.

Horns bellowed in the distance. First one, then two, then many.

By the time Valerys, Avandeer, and Varthear alighted a few hundred feet from the closest pile of burning Uraks, a group of riders was already approaching.

Calen slid from Valerys's back, the dragon bowing low. He scanned the riders through Valerys's eyes. His heart skipped a beat as he counted Tarmon astride what could only be a Varsundi Blackthorn and again at the sight of Vaeril on the back of a Dvalin Angan. Erik rode with them, and Dahlen Virandr – it had been a long time since Calen had laid eyes on that man. A smile touched his lips at the sight of Atara and Harken jogging alongside the horses. Harken looked to have lost an ear and an eye, but Atara was fresh as a morning rose.

Another man moved alongside them, broad as a mountain, but his long, grey hair and beard covered most of his face.

"That couldn't be..." Calen whispered, taking a step forwards. "Erdhardt?"

Therin moved to stand beside Calen, worry etched into his eyes. Then Calen realised: he didn't see Dann or Lyrei. His heart plummeted, his arms and legs feeling as though they'd lost all strength.

The group of riders stopped before them, and even as Tarmon slid from his saddle with all the grace of a drunk donkey, Erdhardt pushed past him and moved straight for Calen.

Before a word was said, before even a whisper had dared leave a lip, Erdhardt crashed into Calen and wrapped his arms around him.

"Calen Bryer," the man said, pulling away and grabbing the sides of Calen's face. He held him at a distance, a broad smile on his face.

"You've got a few more scars since I last saw you." Calen hadn't truly realised how scared he was of discovering who had survived the attack on The Glade until that very moment. He'd also never expected to be quite so happy to see Erdhardt Hammersmith.

"And you've got a dragon," Erdhardt said, suddenly tentative as Valerys loomed over Calen. After a moment, the man looked back at Calen, staring into his eyes as though seeing a ghost. "You look exactly like him." He shook his head. "Your hair, your face, the way you hold yourself… not your eyes. When did that happen?" Erdhardt just smiled and pulled Calen back into the embrace. "It's so good to see you, my boy."

"Calen."

Calen pulled away from Erdhardt to see Tarmon, Vaeril, and Erik walking towards him.

"I'm sorry," Calen said, shaking his head. "I should have been here. I tried. The North was—"

"If you could have been here, you would have been." Tarmon grabbed the back of Calen's head and pressed their foreheads together. "You're alive, and Salme stands. That's what matters."

"And you brought friends." Erik looked up at Varthear and Avandeer, then over to Tivar, who stood at Avandeer's feet.

Erik pushed Tarmon aside and pulled Calen into an embrace. "You're always late, aren't you?"

"Ever since he was a child," Erdhardt said.

Calen laughed at them both, his eyes falling on Vaeril. The elf's lips held the subtlest of smiles, and he inclined his head. He grasped Calen's forearm. "Du sier ithnar, Draleid."

You look horrible, Draleid.

"Du sier mathon, evalír."

You look worse, elf.

That weak smile cracked into a laugh, and he pulled Calen close. "Det er aldin na vëna du, Calen."

It is good to see you, Calen.

"Ar du, akar."

And you, brother.

Calen pulled away from Vaeril. "Lumís é Dann ar Lyrei?"

The smile vanished from Vaeril's face, and panic flared within Calen.

"Lumís é'aiar, Vaeril?"

Where are they, Vaeril?

CALEN STEPPED ONTO THE COVERED porch of the small wooden house nestled into a row of similar structures near Salme's docks. Both Erdhardt and Therin waited for him at the bottom step. Neither had said a word as Erdhardt had led them through the city, heads turning as Calen walked the streets with his gaze down, white armour marred with dried blood and dirt. Some whispered 'Warden of Varyn' or 'Draleid', but he didn't lift his gaze. On a different day, perhaps, but not this day.

He'd thought he'd heard voices call his name – more than once – but when he did look up, he saw no faces he knew.

Calen wrapped his knuckles gently on the wooden door but got no response. After a few more knocks, he entered and found the house empty. When he stepped back out onto the porch, Erdhardt gestured towards the closest dock, where a lone man stood staring at the water.

"Give me a moment," Calen said to Therin and Erdhardt.

His skin itched, and his feet felt like they were filled with stones as he approached the man. "Tharn?"

Tharn Pimm turned slowly, as though afraid of what he might see. The man's eyes were bloodshot and ringed with dark circles. His hair was more grey than blond now, and a nasty scar wound from his chin up the right side of his face. "Calen?" He turned fully, looking as though he didn't truly believe what he saw. Tharn's lips moved to speak, but instead he just wrapped Calen in his arms and held him like that for a long moment. "You look even more like your father than you did before. I'm sorry for what happened to them, Calen."

"It wasn't your fault."

"I should have stepped in… I should have done something. I should have stopped it."

"Then you would have died with them… The past is the past, Tharn, and nothing any of us could have done would have changed anything." Calen pulled away from Tharn's embrace. He looked the man in the eye. For his entire life, Tharn Pimm had seemed solid as stone, strong as iron. He had been a man where Calen had been a boy. A lot had changed in the past couple of years. "Are you all right?" He grimaced. "The question seems kind of pointless now that I say it out loud."

"No, my boy. I am… shattered, like there are pieces of me everywhere wrapped in pieces of her." Tears welled in Tharn's eyes. He drew a sharp breath in through his nose and shook his head. "I *will* be all right. It'll just take a while to put all those pieces back together again, and I know some will always be missing. But you know all about that." He gave Calen a tender, sorrow-filled smile. "Dann is out by the woods with Lyrei. He's not good Calen. You know how he is, always acting like nothing phases him, always trying to be strong for everyone else."

"I know. The woods to the south?"

Tharn nodded.

THE COLD WINTER WIND BLEW in Calen's face as he walked from the city out towards the small wood that sat just past Salme's southern edge. He closed his eyes for a moment, letting the wind whistle in his ears, hearing the long grass shake. Salme may not have been The Glade, but this place sounded like home.

He spotted Dann and Lyrei sitting on the trunk of a fallen tree.

Lyrei noticed him immediately. She slid from her perch and walked towards him, pressing a hand to her chest and bowing at the waist. "Draleid. Alaith anar." *Well met.*

"Ar du," Calen responded. *And you.* He looked past her to where Dann still sat on the trunk. "How is he?"

Lyrei looked into Calen's eyes, then down at the grass. She stepped closer and rested a hand on Calen's shoulder, then left without a word.

Calen watched Lyrei as she walked back towards the city. Dann didn't speak as Calen approached. He didn't even lift his head. A green cloak was draped over his shoulders, the hood pulled up, casting his face in shadow. A small bird, plump and round with a sharp-looking beak and beady eyes, sat on the other side of the trunk, tilting its head to watch Calen.

Calen stood there in silence, staring out at the city and the thick columns of black smoke still pluming into the air.

"You're late," Dann said, his voice barely a whisper.

Calen looked back down at the grass. "I know."

Dann flicked a rock from his hand into the pile on the ground. "Where were you?"

"I had to fly north." Calen's heart felt as though it were cartwheeling, stopping and starting, skipping every second beat, his mouth going dry.

"You *had* to?" Dann lifted his head just enough for Calen to see his raw red eyes beneath the hood of his cloak.

Calen fought the urge to explain the choice. The explanation didn't matter. The reason didn't matter. Dann mattered. Calen had made a promise, and he had broken it. And it was Dann who had paid the cost for that choice, Dann and all the others who'd lost people they loved in the battle for Salme.

"You said you would be here Calen."

"I know, Dann."

"Then why weren't you?" Anger spilled into Dann's voice. Silence held between them for a few more minutes until Dann slid from the trunk, his feet landing softly. "She's dead... My mam's dead, Calen. She was breathing yesterday, and now she's dead." He shook his head, staring down at the ground. "You said you would be here... I trusted you... I needed you..."

"I'm sorry, Dann..."

"Sorry won't bring her back!" Dann rounded on Calen, his hood snapping back. His hair was still tacked with blood and dirt, his face filthy. "If you had been here..." He kept shaking his head and pressing his tongue against his teeth. "If you had been here like you said you would, she might still be alive. But you weren't, and she's not."

The tears flowed freely now, and Calen took a step forwards.

"Don't," Dann snapped, raising a finger.

Calen took another step, and Dann rammed his palms into Calen's breastplate and shoved him backwards.

"I said don't!" Dann roared. He lifted a shaking hand, extending his index finger. "I... I never..."

Calen took another step, and Dann shoved him again. Once more Calen stepped closer, but this time he brushed Dann's hand aside as Dann made to shove him for a third time.

"Don't fucking touch me," Dann snarled, tears rolling down his cheeks, his hands shaking. "You should have been here!"

Dann threw his fist and smashed it into Calen's cheek.

Calen staggered backwards, tasting blood on his tongue. In his mind, Valerys roared, but Calen silenced him.

"You're too good for me now, are you?" Dann's eyes glistened, tears flowing. Calen had never seen him like this. Dann had always been the one who others looked to. He was like his dad: stoic and resolute. Sure, he always made a joke of things, but when Calen needed him, Dann was always there, reliable as a mountain.

"No," Calen answered, shaking his head. "I'm sorry, Dann."

"Sorry? Sorry? You have no right to be sorry. All I needed you to be was *here!*" Dann threw another punch, but Calen slipped beneath it, moved closer, and threw his arms around Dann, squeezing him so tight his arms hurt.

Dann slammed his fists down onto Calen's shoulders and shoved at his chest. "Get off me! Get the fuck off me!"

The harder Dann struggled, the tighter Calen held him, until eventually Dann went still.

"I never got to say goodbye," he whispered through sobs, slowly squeezing Calen. "I never got to say goodbye."

"I know." Calen drew a slow breath through his nose as he held his friend close, staring blindly at the woods behind them.

"I never got to tell her that I saw Belduar…" He sniffled, snot and tears mashing into the crook of Calen's neck. "She'd never have believed me."

"Not for a second," Calen agreed, giving a short laugh. "But that's only because you're always talking shit."

"Does it ever stop?" Dann broke into sobs again. "Does it ever stop hurting?"

Calen shook his head, not able to find words, his own tears spilling down at the sight of his friend in such pain. "It never goes away – I wouldn't want it to – but it gets easier… Having you beside me made it easier." Calen drew a short breath. "Every time it hurts, I try to think of it like a hand on my shoulder. Like my mam or my dad are there, reminding me of all the good things, all the good memories."

"I miss Alea," Dann whispered, his tears finding new strength. "I didn't want to say it because I know Lyrei hurts more, but I miss her. And Baldon… Why… Why does everyone keep dying?"

"I don't know…" Calen's mind sifted through all the faces of those they'd lost. From Vars and Freis to Rhett, Falmin, Korik, Lopir… The list was endless, and it was only going to get longer as this war continued. He pulled a sharp breath into his lungs to centre himself. "Pain doesn't belong to anyone, Dann. Lyrei's grief is no less because of yours. And your dad's pain is no less. You loved your mam. You deserve to mourn her."

Dann clutched Calen tighter and sobbed. "I think she would have been proud of me… I'm not as much of a fuck up now."

"You were never a fuck up, Dann. And she was always proud of you." Calen grabbed Dann's head and pulled his friend in closer. "But you're right. She really would have been proud. She has a lot to be proud of."

Calen shifted away from Dann and climbed up to where Dann had been sitting on the fallen tree. He patted a spot beside him.

"Tell me something about her," Calen said when Dann had joined him.

"You knew her, Calen."

"Doesn't matter," Calen said, shaking his head. "Tell me something."

"She used to hit me with a wooden spoon."

"She's hit me with the same spoon."

"She did it with love," Dann said with a laugh, wiping tears from his eyes. "She always ran her finger down the bridge of my nose when I was sick. Really gently, back and forth. I never told her how much I loved that."

"She's listening." Calen wrapped an arm around Dann's shoulders and pulled him close. "They're always with us, Dann. Always."

Hours later, while the sun was setting across the Antigan Ocean, the Blood Moon clear and full in the sky, Calen stood by the water's edge, a mixture of dirt and wet stones by his feet.

He drew a long, slow breath in and let it out even slower, the gentle lapping of the waves swashing in his ears. He'd not spent much time by the water in his youth, but on the journey from Drifaien to Kingspass, aboard *The Enchantress,* Calen had learned to appreciate the beauty of the sunset across the open water. There was something serene about the way the warm orange glow sparkled silver across the ever-shifting waves.

Calen ran his thumb over the smooth stone in the palm of his hand, a brittle smile on his lips. Vars had made a point of always taking Calen to the water whenever they visited Milltown or Salme. They would skim stones for hours and talk about nothing in particular and everything at the same time. Whoever made their stone hop the most got to ride Drifter on the journey back to The Glade. Calen missed the horse. He hoped that someone in Milltown had found him and treated him well, maybe he was even somewhere in Salme at that very moment. He knew the odds were that Drifter lay dead in the ruins of Milltown, butchered by the Uraks, but ignorance hurt less.

He turned his wrist, angling the stone, then flicked it out over the water, watching as it skipped six times then sank.

"Not flat enough." Dahlen Virandr appeared at Calen's side, a heavy wolfpineskin cloak draped over his shoulders. He stared past Calen and out at the water, then dropped to his haunches and scanned the stones that littered the ground, eventually settling on one just under the size of his palm and smooth on all sides. Calen smiled as he heard his father's voice in his mind. *"Now that's a mighty fine stone."*

Dahlen drew a long breath, stepped forwards with his left leg, and launched the stone. It skipped nine times, catching the crest of a wave on the tenth and sinking.

He leaned down once more, selected another stone, and offered it to Calen.

Calen took it into his hand, brushing his thumb against edges so smooth they were almost polished. He gave Dahlen a half-smile and a nod of thanks before loosing the stone.

"Eleven," Dahlen said with a downturn of his lip. "I've never gotten more than ten, usually less than five or six. Erik's lucky if it doesn't just sink."

"My dad held the record. Twenty-seven times. He always rode the horse back."

"What?"

"Nothing, sorry…" Calen plucked another stone from the ground and launched it. Five skips. "Thank you. For everything you've done here. Erdhardt told me this place would be gone if you and the others hadn't arrived when you did."

Dahlen only gave him a nod, throwing another stone. Seven skips.

They continued like that without talking for a few minutes. Calen didn't think he'd ever spent as much time alone with Dahlen. "I was—"

"I didn't—"

They smiled awkwardly at each other.

"After you," Calen said, gesturing for Dahlen to speak.

Dahlen ran his thumb absently over the surface of the stone in his hand. "I was jealous of you… I had trained my entire life for the moment we would find an egg. Every morning, every night, I trained… to be everything my father wanted, everything he needed. And then you appeared, and the egg hatched. You didn't even want it." He shook his head, still rubbing his thumb over the stone. "You cared nothing about the rebellion I had spent my life bleeding for. That my brother, my father, and I had sacrificed everything to build. I was jealous, I blamed you, and I hated you…"

Dahlen looked up towards the sky, biting his top lip. He threw the stone. Twelve skips.

"A new record," Calen said in a half-whisper, staring out at the setting sun.

"That was until I realised what it was we took from you." Dahlen grabbed at the back of his neck. "The people of this place, the way they fight for each other… the way they pull together. I've never had anything like that outside of Erik and my father. The night we met you, that was taken away from you. And I see now why you wanted it back so badly. I see a lot of things I never did before."

"Like what?"

"That my father is a man and not some godlike hero of legend to be followed without question. He is a man with many flaws, who has made a thousand mistakes and will make a thousand more. And that still, to me, he is the greatest man who has ever lived. He has fought and lost and sacrificed for four hundred years, and he has never stopped. No matter what this world did to him or the people he loved, he always stood back up. I have seen twenty-four summers, and already I am tired and weary. I could not do what he has done, nor would I want to."

Dahlen grabbed another stone and squeezed it in his palm before looking into Calen's eyes. "All this is to say I was a man stuck in my father's shadow, trying desperately to be what he needed and blaming you because I wasn't. And I'm sorry for it. My father always taught me that a man holds himself accountable for his wrongs. It's about time I listened."

"I was wrong to blame you for Rist – since we're sharing." The laugh that touched Calen's lips never reached his heart. Rist's name alone saw to that. "I was more angry at myself than you. I left him. I should never have left him. Not because I didn't trust you, but because people of The Glade don't leave each other. If we'd stayed together that night, maybe everything would be different."

"Or maybe we'd all be dead." Dahlen scanned the ground and grabbed another smooth rock, passing it to Calen. "That's a good one."

Calen wound back his arm and let his anger at himself flow through him. Three skips and a squawk later and a terrified gull was flapping into the evening sky.

Dahlen watched the bird's flight. "The words 'if' and 'should have' can tear you apart quicker than any blade. You were a fucking arsehole that night. But I understand. If that had been Erik, I would've been the same."

"If what had been me?"

Calen turned to see Erik, Tarmon, and Vaeril approaching down the dirt track that led to the water.

Tarmon grasped Calen's forearm. "Queen Tessara invites us to eat with her this evening." He paused for a second. "The elves fought bravely and lost many in the battle for the city."

Calen nodded, letting out a short sigh. "Lead the way."

"Dann?" Erik asked.

"He's with Lyrei. He needs time."

Erik held Calen's gaze.

"He's not all right," Calen said, resting a hand on Erik's shoulder. "But he will be."

Dann sat on the first step below the porch of the place he supposed was now home. He could hear Lyrei and his dad laughing inside as they swapped stories and spent far too long cooking stew. Tharn had never been the cook; it had always been Ylinda. Lyrei wasn't much better, but she was trying, and she was making Tharn smile, which was all that mattered. In fact, Dann didn't think he'd heard Lyrei laugh so hard since the day he'd met her... which only made him worry about the stories his dad was telling.

He let out a long sigh and took a sip from the cup in his hand. Just the smell of the ale from The Rusty Shell made him appreciate the taste of Lasch's mead.

He'd wanted to find Calen, to apologise, but he simply didn't have it in him. Not that night. Better to say it with a sunrise at his back. Dann knew the weight of words, and he should never have put his mam's death on Calen. Calen dwelled on those kinds of things, let them chew him from the inside. He always had. "Why am I such a fucking idiot?"

"Don't be too harsh on yourself," Therin said, approaching the porch. "You're an idiot, but only from time to time."

"Where did you come from?"

"I'm always somewhere, watching," Therin said, taking a seat on the step beside Dann.

"That's creepy, Therin. You shouldn't be watching people like that." He sipped at his ale. "Besides, I'm pretty sure you've referred to me as 'the physical manifestation of a headache'."

"Did I say that out loud?"

"More than once."

Therin smiled, then narrowed his eyes. "Is that a weka?"

Dann lifted his head, then followed Therin's gaze to where the weka sat next to a low bush with a sock in its beak. "I call him Tom. He's a right little bastard."

"What is a weka doing all the way out here? Wait, Tom? Why Tom?"

Dann shrugged. "He looks like a Tom. Nala's horse is called Maria, so why not?"

For a moment Therin looked as though he were going to challenge Dann, then made a face that said he thought better of it. "I'll not stay long. I just wanted to tell you something."

"What?"

"Elves don't ride horses because we believe that to carry someone, to bear their weight, is one of the greatest burdens one soul can place on another. It requires a deep, trusting bond. As an ambassador to The Order, I spent much time outside of elven lands, outside of elven culture. I had to adapt. I ride horses, but infrequently and only those I have bonded with. I rode Vaen for almost thirty years. He died in the battle for Aravell – crushed by falling rocks."

"Therin…"

The elf shook his head. "The name Alea gave your horse – *Drunir* – it was a lesson. 'Companion'." Therin rested his hand on Dann's knee, squeezing. "We never truly lose the ones we love. They stay with us in everything we do. Those who affect us so deeply leave imprints that cannot be removed. We are who we are because of who we've loved and who we've lost – those things we do not decide. So never be afraid. Live boldly, love fiercely, and forgive quickly. Life is too short for anything else."

Therin squeezed Dann's knee one more time before standing while Dann sat with tears rolling down his cheeks.

As he turned to leave, Therin looked down at Dann. "And Dann."

Dann rubbed the heel of his hand into his eye. "What?"

"Elves can't grow beards, nor chest hair. But we do have hair beneath our arm pits and, some of us, on our feet – though most shave that off."

A laugh cracked through the pain in Dann's heart as Therin walked away and vanished over the lip in the land that led to the docks.

Wooden boards creaked as Lyrei sat down beside Dann. "Was that Therin?" She leaned closer. "Dann, what's wrong?"

Dann shook his head and wiped the tears from his eyes with his sleeve. "I just found out that elves can't grow beards," he said, laughing. "It's beautiful."

"Dann…" Lyrei let out a long sigh, setting her cup of mead in the dirt. "It's all right to hurt. You don't—"

"I know." He set his cup down beside Lyrei's, then turned to face her.

Lyrei narrowed her gaze, staring into his eyes. She pulled away at first as he cupped her hands in his, but then she held them in place, wrapping her fingers around the sides of his hands.

"I miss Alea, and I miss Baldon and Rist, and every time I think of my mam…" He paused for a moment, trying to stop the tears so he could speak. "Every time I think of her, I just feel empty."

Lyrei pulled a hand away and brushed the tears from his cheeks. "I miss them too."

Dann looked into Lyrei's golden eyes and remembered how awestruck he'd been the first time he'd seen them. He reached up, cautiously, and traced her cheekbone with his fingers, his pulse quickening when she didn't pull away. "Without you…"

"You'd still be alive," Lyrei said.

"But the world would be a lot darker."

Lyrei smiled. "So much darker. My people, they have a name for what you are, Dann."

"Arsehole?" Dann started to laugh at his joke but stopped when Lyrei didn't join him.

"Ayar Elwyn." A slight tremble ran through Lyrei's lips as she spoke the words.

"I don't speak elf," Dann whispered, wiping tears away, smiling.

"One Heart," she said, slapping his hand. "It is a word for when you realise you have found a soul whose heart is cracked in all the right ways that fit yours. They fill the gaps in you and you in them. They are the light that stops the world from going dark. Simply by being, they make you whole. It's not a thing that is earned, it's just something that *is*. Though it's not always easy to see. You have the purest heart of any soul I've ever known. You are gentle and kind and sweet, and still you are brave and strong, and you never let anyone suffer alone. You carry others, Dann."

"Are you calling me a horse? Because Therin explained that too."

"My Ayar Elwyn, whether I like it or not." Tears rolled slowly down Lyrei's cheeks, and she brushed her thumb through Dann's hair.

Dann stared into those golden eyes. "Ayar Elwyn."

Lyrei nodded and pressed her forehead to Dann's. In that moment, Dann understood completely. He took Lyrei's cheek in hand, lifted her head, and kissed her. His heartbeat slowed, and the world grew less empty as Lyrei's lips pressed against his and her fingers wrapped around the back of his neck.

"Commander Sureheart?"

Dann almost leapt from his skin, pulling away from Lyrei to see Nala standing in the house's doorway. "Sweet fucking Varyn, Nala. I forgot you were even here."

"I've been here all day," Nala said with a face of disbelief, looking a little deflated.

Dann let out a long, exasperated sigh that quickly turned to a laugh as he pressed his forehead to Lyrei's. "What is it, Nala?"

"Stew's ready." The squire all but pranced back inside to where her younger brother was helping Tharn with the stew.

Lyrei laughed, kissed Dann's forehead, then stood and followed Nala inside. As Dann lifted himself from the step, he looked down to see Tom the weka with his beak in Dann's cup of ale. "Get your filthy—you know what? Drink. With any luck, I'll find you passed out in a ditch tomorrow. Then you'll know what it feels like."

Dann paused in the doorway, letting himself linger over the sight of Lyrei helping his father dish the stew into bowls while Nala placed a spoon in each. He pulled a long, sad breath into his lungs and whispered, "You would have loved her, Mam. I'm sorry I wasn't here in time."

CHAPTER NINETY-THREE

WHAT WE BUILT

25th Day of the Blood Moon

Achyron's Keep – Winter, Year 3081 After Doom

The morning before a battle always had a distinct feeling to it, a stillness. Experience had taught Aeson this. Every soul, whether they were polishing steel, honing blades, checking straps, or readying horses, every one of them knew they might never see another sunrise. Achyron prepared his halls and set his tables, while Heraya reached into hearts and readied them.

As Aeson, Verma, and Akraf walked through the camp that morning, that familiar feeling clung to everything he saw. About him, the soldiers of Arkalen sat in clusters and prayed to Neron to guide them through the coming storm, while those of Narvona whispered blessings to Akopa, asking that he find them worthy of a place in the Eversea should they sail the River Trian that night.

"Do you not pray, Aeson Virandr?" Akraf asked when he saw Aeson staring at a large group of Narvonan warriors kneeling before a priest in gold and blue robes. The last time Aeson had seen the man had been in the port at Milltown after their return from Valacia – after Farda and the imperials had burned their ships. Akraf was a prince consort now, and he had swapped his leathers and trousers for a full suit of burnished black steel ornamented with gold.

Verma gave a knowing laugh.

"I prefer to keep my fate in my own hands."

"Blood of the water, this is the way." Akraf puffed out his bottom lip and nodded. "I am proud to hunt alongside you again, Aeson. It has been too long in the coming."

"And I you. May it be short and fruitful," Aeson said, giving the typical Narvonan response.

Akraf took a turn past two banners thrust into the ground bearing the roaring head of a tharnas marked in gold. They walked past a score of guards in black plate until they finally came upon Princess Kayala Latrak.

The woman awaited them with a wooden mug of steaming tea in her hands, a soft smile on her lips.

On either side of the princess, four Isildans clad in Atalus shell plate sat astride armoured darvakin, thick-shafted glaives in their fists. Where the tharnas - the great, powerful beasts that acted as the Latrakian Kingdom's emblem – were monstrous and indomitable, the darvakin were quick and ferocious. They stood on two powerful legs, the talons on their feet capable of rending steel with ease. The creatures' scaled bodies were lean and muscular, and Aeson had seen them reach speeds far past that of a horse. Each of them was barded in segmented plates of black steel. Darvakin were also known to be notoriously intelligent.

As he looked, one of the darvakin turned its head towards him, a sharp clicking in its throat. The creature pulled back its scaled lip to reveal rows of razor-sharp teeth.

Aeson snapped his gaze away. He had learned in the past that you didn't look a darvakin in the eye. He pressed his two fists together in the greeting of Narvona. As he had done for the entire duration of their journey along the southern coast, he fought his ingrained compulsion to kneel. Narvonans did not kneel. "Your Majesty. You asked for me?"

"Aeson Virandr," Kayala replied in her thick Narvonan accent. She inclined her head, pressing her two fists together. "I only wanted to wish you good fortune in the battle to come and to gift you this."

Kayala gestured to someone in a tent behind her, and a man came out holding a cuirass of black steel. It was plain and simple, but at its centre was the emblem of a roaring dragon worked into the plate in Atalus shell.

"Your Majesty, this is too much. I cannot accept it." The Narvonans guarded Atalus shell with even more ferocity than Godfire. It was bestowed upon only the greatest champions, the most valuable souls, harvested only once every generation from the holy animal. A shell with the power to absorb the Spark. Even a little was priceless. Aeson had once watched almost fifty Narvonans perish just to retrieve an Atalus-wrought pendant from a dead man's neck.

"You can accept it, Aeson. And you will." Kayala took the cuirass and offered it to Aeson. "This is not a gift from me. This is a gift from my mother, for Aeson Virandr, Blade of the Moon, the man that time cannot kill. She told me not to give it to you until we reached Epherian shores. She says to wear it and protect her daughter, as her mother protected you all those years ago."

Aeson reached out and took the cuirass, staring down at the Atalus dragon. "This is a gift like no other, Kayala."

"Blood of the water, this is the way." Kayala lifted her gaze at the sound of screeches overhead, shifting the topic in a heartbeat. She watched as some twenty wyverns soared across the sky, moving in tight formation. "This *Wyvern Queen,* she is fierce."

"She is."

"This will be a good hunt. We will find much glory here. I will let you go, Aeson Virandr. And when the night falls, may the shell of the Atalus keep you safe."

Aeson inclined his head, then turned and left, Verma at his side.

"Well, fuck me," she said, looking at the black steel cuirass in Aeson's arms.

"Not interested," Aeson replied, staring down at the gleaming dragon. As guarded as Atalus was, the craft of its working was even more so. Across the years, some pieces had been recovered during Narvonan invasions, and those that hadn't been lost to time were often shattered or destroyed by smiths arrogant enough to think themselves capable.

"Aeson Virandr, did you just tell a joke? I don't think I've ever heard you tell a joke."

"It wasn't a joke." Aeson held as straight as he could for a moment, then cracked a laugh. "Have you spoken to Ildur?"

"Mmm. His warriors are ready, as are the Stormguard. Calen Bryer made quite the impression on Animar. He made quite the impression on me. Five hundred Stormguard while Animar is fighting a war against Syrene Linas is nothing to sniff at."

"He grows with each day," Aeson said, once again looking down at the Atalus dragon on the cuirass and realising that white shell was a likeness for Valerys. He laughed. Coincidences had abandoned him long ago. "Come, it's a few miles to the lookout."

AESON HAD BEEN WITHIN THE walls of Achyron's Keep four times in his life. The fortress city's name had been hard earned. It was the choke point between Valtara and the rest of the continent, connected via the Hot Gates. Many an army had smashed itself against the walls trying to bring the fortress to its knees. Almost all had failed.

From where he stood upon the cliff ledge with the forest at his back, Aeson looked over a vast open plain of brown grass and cracked earth, the sun gleaming overhead. Plenty of space for arrows and spears to thin the numbers of any besieging army – plenty of space for Battlemages to wreak absolute destruction.

The city sat on the other side of the plain, embedded into the rock face of the rolling mountains, hundreds of wyvern Rests built about it. It was ringed by two sets of thick, grey stone walls, fortified by monstrous cylindrical towers, the keep rising above all else. The walls themselves were in turn ringed by a series of three trenches.

Screeches rang out in the sky above as formations of wyverns swept back and forth across the woodland, their wings smeared with white and orange paint. Alina's Wyndarii outnumbered those who stood by Loren Koraklon at least three to one. Even at that, and with the Stormguard and Kayala's army, the battle would be a bloody one.

"Have you heard word from Salme?" Verma had stood beside Aeson in silence, looking down over the city.

Aeson shook his head. He had hoped Dahlen would have sent word through the Angan, but Crokus – the Angan sent to Alina – had not been seen in days. The creatures were not pets to be kept on chains, but he did wish they were a little more reliable.

"They will be all right, Aeson. You and Naia raised two fine young men, fine warriors."

Aeson just nodded as he stared out at Achyron's Keep. Verma had been there through centuries, right from The Fall. She knew Aeson better than almost any soul that drew breath. Not just Aeson the Draleid, or Aeson the Rakina, but Aeson the man. She knew his truths and his lies, knew his fears. .

She laid a hand on his shoulder. "You cannot keep them strapped to your side forever, my friend."

"A little longer would have been nice."

Verma gave him a soft smile. "She is proud of you. I know she is. They both are."

He met Verma's gaze. "Should I have gone with Erik?"

"Perhaps," Verma said with a shrug. "We'll never know the outcomes of the decisions we do not make. Which I suppose is a good thing, because otherwise we'd all be driven mad. You have raised them to be each other's shields, to put one another above all else. You either trust them to do that, or you don't. You are one man, Aeson. You must do what you can and accept what you can't." She squeezed his shoulder. "I must check in with Fearn and Ildur to ensure we are ready for tonight."

Verma turned and walked back into the woods, and Aeson's thoughts fell to Naia and Lyara – his heart and his soul, shattered and broken, pieced together by his sons.

"To survive is not to live," he whispered, repeating Naia's words from the night before Heraya took his beloved into her arms. "I miss you more each day, my heart."

In his mind, he stared into her eyes, felt the touch of her skin, the warmth of her love.

And the question that had plagued Aeson in the years since Naia's death lurked behind those eyes. What if he had let go of his pain? What if he had burned the loss from his heart and instead focused on the things he had before him?

What then? If he had abandoned the rebellion and set free his burning need to see Eltoar and the others suffer for what they had done, perhaps Naia would still be alive. Perhaps the gods would not have chosen to take her from him. For the gods controlled all.

Aeson had stopped praying the day Naia died. At least with thought. By reflex he prayed to Varyn to watch over his children or to Neron for a safe journey, but they were empty prayers. He never expected the gods to answer. There were only three reasons men and women truly turned to the gods: hope, purpose, or absolution.

Hope that the ones they loved would not be taken from them and that if they were, there would be a place to find them in another life. Purpose so that a life might have meaning, something worth living for. And absolution for the dark deeds already committed and those yet to pass.

Aeson's hope had cracked with Lyara and died with Naia. And he would not leave the lives of his sons in the hands of absent gods. He would not leave something so important to the whims of creatures who clearly cared so little for what they claim to have created.

Aeson had no need for divine purpose. His purpose lay in Dahlen's and Erik's beating hearts and in the fires of vengeance.

And absolution? Not only did Aeson not seek it, but he did not deserve it either. He was happy to pay for the blood he'd spilled. All actions had consequences.

Aeson hoped that in the next life, or in some world beyond, or whatever awaited him, his soul would find Lyara and Naia once more, but he did not pray for it.

The only person Aeson prayed to was his wife. She would watch over them, as she always had.

Leaves and twigs crunched beneath boots at Aeson's back. He turned to find Alina Ateres, another woman, Dinekes Ilyon, Savrin Vander, and five of the queen's personal guard emerging from the trees.

It was strange to see Savrin after so long. Last Aeson had heard, the man was presumed dead. Apparently not. If nothing else, he would be happy to fight alongside Savrin in the battle for the Keep. He had never met a man or woman more gifted with a blade. Perhaps Atara.

Savrin inclined his head to Aeson.

"I was told I could find you here," Alina said, gesturing for Savrin and the guards to stay by the trees. "I realised you were not formally introduced last night. This is Mera. Mera Ateres."

"Mera…" Aeson whispered. The woman's eyes were blue as sapphires, her hair shaved at the side after the Valtaran fashion, and three pale scars ran from her forehead, across her left eye, and down to her jaw. She looked as fierce as Dayne. "It's good to finally put a face to the name. Wait, Ateres?"

Mera inclined her head. "Right before he decided to throw himself into Loren's arms so we could come and save him. Typical Dayne. Always living for the dramatic moments."

Aeson laughed at that.

A shriek sounded above, followed by screeching. Aeson looked to the sky to see four of Alina's wyverns chasing a fifth through the sky. He watched as a wyvern large enough to be a small dragon – Alina's wyvern, Rynvar – crashed into the fleeing creature and vanished from view. A heartbeat passed before something crashed down somewhere in the trees to the right.

Sounds of crunching leaves and snapping twigs erupted in the forest as soldiers moved like wolves through the brush.

"Loren knows we're here," Mera said, squinting through the trees. "But he need not know our number, nor that of the Arkalens and the Narvonans you have brought to our cause. The Andurii prowl the forest. The Wyndarii keep the skies empty."

"Why is it again you wish to wait until nightfall?" Aeson asked.

"Because they are scared of the dark," Alina answered, looking down at the keep. "Dayne made sure of it. Now all we need to do is wait for Belina Louna to give us the signal that the gates have been opened."

"She's going to set something on fire, isn't she?"

"Something big," Alina answered.

"That sounds like her," Aeson said, folding his arms.

"Now we just have to see if she's full of shit or not." Mera crouched low and ran her fingers in the dirt, her eyes fixed on the Keep. "I will not leave him in there another night."

"You will not have to. If those gates don't open, then Belina is dead. There is nothing in this world she wouldn't do for him. Either way, we will fight with you."

Aeson turned to Alina, who was already staring at him. She looked so much like her mother. Same eyes, same hair, same fury about her. That woman had been a force of nature. And by the looks of it, her daughter was no different. "Come the sunrise, Valtara will be free."

"I pray to Achyron you are right," Alina said.

"He is too busy to answer prayers," Aeson said, turning back to the fortress. "But we won't need him."

CHAPTER NINETY-FOUR

CHOICES

25th Day of the Blood Moon

Achyron's Keep – Winter, Year 3081 After Doom

lina sat astride Rynvar, her breath misting in the cold air before her. All across the ledge and in the forest behind her, seven hundred Wyndarii awaited her signal.

In the plains below, Olivian, Savrin, and her Royal Guard stood amongst her warriors and the Andurii, four Narvonan Ilsildans waiting within their numbers. She had never seen these mighty Narvonan champions before, never seen their Atalus armour. But if it worked as the stories told and as Aeson Virandr said it would, those champions would be what turned this battle. The bulk of the Narvonan forces, including their monstrous beasts – the tharnas – and the scaled darvakin mounts, waited just out of eyeline, behind the bend of the hill. It was best to keep their existence hidden from Loren until the last moment.

"How long do we wait?" Amari asked from astride Syndel.

"Until my patience wears thin." Alina sat forwards in her saddle, fingers tightening around the handles.

"Not long then," Lukira said.

"Give Belina time." Mera sat in Audin's saddle with her arms resting in her lap, eyes staring down at the lanterns that burned across the keep's walls. "This valley will run red this night, but the less of it that is ours the better."

"Mmm." Alina ran her fingers across Rynvar's scales. She could not say it aloud, but she held fear in her heart. Not fear of dying. She had accepted that a long time ago. But fear of losing Dayne, of losing the brother she had already lost. The brother who had come back to her. She had been so blinded by her own anger and her own loss that she had treated him as though he had drawn the blade across Kal's throat himself. She had pushed him away, and the thought of losing him before she could truly have him back tore her apart.

Baren could rot in the void for all she cared, but Dayne, Dayne she could not lose. She *would* not lose.

BELINA KEPT HER HEAD DOWN as she walked away from the gatehouse, the bridge of the Valtaran helmet scraping against her nose. She hated helmets. They made her feel claustrophobic. Though she didn't mind the Koraklon armoured skirts. Blue had always been her colour.

She hefted the circular shield on her left arm, her fingers gripped tightly around the clay jar of Godfire, the liquid spilling in a careful stream onto the ground. She would never let Dayne live this one down. She could have bought half a fleet with the amount of gold she'd spent on all the Godfire, nevermind the favours she'd called in. And now she only had three jars left.

Lorian and Valtaran soldiers buzzed about her, shifting in columns in the main square and lining the walls. She had to admit, this place was impressive. It would almost be a shame to burn it down. Almost.

A shout rose from behind her.

"Fuck," she muttered, not daring to glance over her shoulder. Someone knocked into her, sending her stumbling to the right.

"Watch where you're going," a man snapped, a heavy circular shield in one hand, a thick spear in the other.

"Suck my cock," Belina snapped back.

"What did you just say?"

Belina took the jar of Godfire into her free hand, swigged it, then sprayed it over the man's face.

He staggered backwards, rubbing at his eyes and shouting. Other soldiers turned and stared, moving towards them.

That had maybe not been her smartest move, but Belina never had been good at controlling her impulses. Well, she'd made her bed now. She might as well lie in it.

"Suck," she repeated, her mouth still half-full of the noxious liquid that appeared to be burning her tongue and cheeks. "My. Cock."

She reached over and snatched a flaming torch from a sconce. Her first instinct had been to spray the liquid through the flames over the man. She quickly realised that she wasn't quite sure whether that would set her own face on fire. She liked her face, so she decided instead to swing the torch into the man's hands as he rubbed his eyes while quickly spitting the rest of the Godfire on the ground behind her.

It didn't take even a second for the Koraklon soldier to burst into flames, screaming and shrieking. He fell backwards, slamming against the stone, thrashing as he did. The flames caught on the trail of Godfire she had marked from there to the gatehouse.

She watched the fire tear across the stone as the other soldiers levelled their spears, and more looked down from the ramparts and about the yard at the sound of the dying man's screams.

Belina decided she would leave this part out when she told Dayne about how she'd brought the gates down. He'd always said she made too much of a scene.

"Easy, easy," she said, pointing the torch towards the man who now lay still in the flames. "He was like that when I got here."

Three of the men raised their shields and strode forwards.

"Come now," Belina said, backing away slowly, her eyes never leaving the three men. "This is all a misunderstanding."

The three soldiers lunged in unison, pulling their spears back to skewer her like a fish. She glanced down to make sure her feet were clear, then dropped the torch.

The Godfire she'd spat on the ground erupted in flames, consuming all three of them. Half a second later, the entire keep shook and the Gatehouse exploded, flames pluming in all directions, chunks of stone crashing down all about the yard.

"Well," Belina whispered to herself, staring up at the bonfire that was the gates. "That worked a lot better than I expected."

In the ensuing chaos, Belina dropped her shield and vanished into a nearby doorway.

A FLASH OF LIGHT SHONE at the keep's gatehouse, followed less than a second later by an eruption of flame and stone that shook the earth. A clap of thunder swept through the valley, and Alina watched in awe as the gates of Achyron's Keep were torn asunder. Horns bellowed, and the defenders' shouts carried across the plains below.

More horns answered, and below, her warriors and the Andurii swept into motion, the light of the red moon reflecting on their shields.

"Well," Mera said, sitting up straight in Audin's saddle. "She said she'd set something on fire."

Beneath Alina, a rumble spread through Rynvar and turned to a roar as the wyvern reared and unfurled his wings, more wyverns answering through the forest at their back.

"Wyndarii of Valtara," Alina shouted, unclipping a javelin from the side of the saddle. "Tonight is the night we burn the Lorians from our home. Tonight, we set Valtara free!"

A chorus of cheers rang out behind her.

She raised her javelin into the air. "By blade and by blood!"

As Rynvar surged forwards and leapt from the ledge, spreading his wings, Alina heard Amari, Lukira, and Mera all answer her call, rising above the roars of the wyverns. "By blade and by blood!"

Alina pressed herself tight to Rynvar's neck as he plummeted down the cliffside, the buckles at her hip clinking, a weightless feeling in her stomach.

This was what she was born to do.

To her right, through watering eyes, she saw arcs of purple lightning tearing through the air towards her marching warriors. She watched with pain in her heart as some of the lightning tore holes into the ranks, shouts and screams rising. But most of the lightning swerved in the air, bending and twisting, funnelled towards four spots within the ranks before vanishing entirely.

In the purple glow, Alina just about made out the Narvonan Isildans, clad entirely in their gleaming Atalus-shell armour, riding astride their darvakin. The armour absorbed the lightning like a river did rain. If they'd had armour like that these past centuries, Valtara would already be free.

Alina squeezed her legs as Rynvar opened his wings and swept parallel to the ground some five or six hundred feet below them.

To her side, Mera's white-gloved hand flashed signals: split. Four. Above. Below. Attack. Question.

Yes, Alina signalled back. Both Amari and Lukira acknowledged the command.

They held superiority in numbers over the traitor Wyndarii, but the mages and archers on the ramparts could even that out in the blink of an eye if they weren't seen to.

"Take the walls!" Alina shouted to Rynvar, pressing herself to his neck so he could feel the vibrations above the wind. "Rip them from the ramparts."

The wyvern answered with a roar and streaked downwards towards the walls. More roars answered, and Alina looked about to see her Wyndarii breaking into the four squadrons they had decided upon before the battle.

Alina's blood burned with a fervour as the wyvern dropped lower, her fingers tightening around the wooden shaft of her javelin. Rynvar spun in the air, arrows skittering off his scales and whipping past Alina's head.

"Steady," she called, her face pressed to Rynvar's neck. She pulled herself upright, feeling Rynvar's movements beneath her. An arrow sliced past her head, the tip grazing her helmet. She could not hide now. A hunter needed to see their prey.

Alina drew a sharp breath and held it, feeling Rynvar do the same beneath her. Shrieks sounded overhead, letting her know that Mera and Amari had met the traitor Wyndarii in the air.

She tightened her grip on the left handle of the saddle until her knuckles went pale.

As Rynvar crashed down atop two Lorian soldiers on the ramparts, raking his talons through one and ripping the other's arm free with his jaws, he spun and angled upwards. The world shifted about Alina as she looked down sideways onto the ramparts, time standing still for just a heartbeat. She picked her target, drew back her arm, and launched her javelin. The steel tip punched into the face of a Lorian mage, sinking into her eye and ripping her from the walls.

Alina snapped her javelin hand down onto the free handle and gripped with all her strength as Rynvar tore upwards. The buckles and chains would have kept her from falling from the wyvern's back, but they didn't stop her bones from breaking or body from flailing. She cast a glance over her shoulder as the rest of the Wyndarii swept down over the walls. Alina had known she would lose sisters this night, but her heart still ached as she watched wyverns burned from the sky with plumes of fire and arcs of lightning. Every wyvern that fell was paid for with the blood of fifty defenders. But her Wyndarii were worth a hundred.

On the plains below, her forces were almost at the gates, the white crests of the Andurii visible from up high, and behind them marched the Narvonan host, glittering in gold.

Rynvar let out a shriek, and two wyverns crashed into him from the side, snapping and tearing at him with tooth and talon. He ripped out the throat of the first, but the second stretched its neck forwards and came but a blade's width from tearing Alina's head free.

Alina reached back and released a second javelin from its clip, and when the wyvern's head snaked forwards once more, she leaned back in the saddle and drove the javelin up through the soft flesh beneath its jaw. She pulled the tip free, then drove it back in again, blood sluicing from the wound and spraying over her face. The creature flapped and flailed before eventually going limp and dropping from the sky. The Wyndarii on its back screamed as they fell, and Alina watched her unbuckle herself from the saddle and drop like a stone to the courtyard below, her screams cutting short as she landed in the fire that blazed around the gatehouse.

"Rise!" Alina roared to Rynvar, and the wyvern swept upwards to where Mera's and Amari's Wyndarii battled in the sky.

DAYNE LIFTED HIS HEAD AND winced at the blazing light that shone through the window. He tugged gently against his bonds, feeling the straps burn at the raw skin beneath. He tried to reach out to the Spark, probing the ward that shrouded him. Dayne had done the same every day but found the same result: the ward remained in place.

"Well," Loren said, staring out at the city beyond. "It looks like your sister decided to forego negotiations." He gave a downturn of his lip. "Disappointing. It seems as though you were expendable after all. The mighty Dayne Ateres, a casualty of his sister's arrogance. That does seem to be a trait that runs in your family, doesn't it? Arrogance, followed by death."

"It's not me who'll be dying tonight," Dayne answered, cracking his neck. He looked over at Baren, who was still strapped to the x-shaped stand, head drooping, mumbling but barely conscious. In the three nights Dayne had been there, Baren had barely opened his eyes, let alone spoken. His wounds were red and pussing, infection setting in. Loren had cleaned Dayne's wounds but not Baren's. He didn't need Baren anymore. Baren had been bait for Dayne, and Dayne was bait for Alina.

"Is that so?" Loren walked from the window, stopping so he stood between Dayne and Baren. "That same Ateres arrogance. This is the night the bloodline of House Ateres dies. Your sister will lie broken against my walls, her wyvern food for the crows. You and your brother here will hang from these posts with your throats slit, and I will walk to young Arkin's chambers and drive a sword through his heart." He pursed his lips. "I'd rather not. He's a good boy. But you Ateres are like weeds. Even one left alive will smother the whole garden." He let out a long sigh. "Well, Dayne. I've enjoyed our time together, and I hope that, unlike your father, you have come to understand me a bit more."

"I'm going to cut your fucking heart from your chest while you're still breathing."

"Said the lamb to the wolf." Loren shook his head, smiling. He raised a finger, and a thin gash ripped open across Dayne's chest, blood trickling.

Dayne glanced over at the corner of the room towards the man who sat in a rickety wooden chair, eyes fixed on Dayne. One of the four Lorian mages he had seen over the nights. Two always inside, the others at the door. He would have to deal with them before he got to Loren.

Loren turned to face Baren, resting his hand on the pommel of a knife at his belt. "No matter how this night ends, neither of you are of use any longer." He glanced over his shoulder to Dayne. "What was it you said, Dayne? You would cut my heart from my chest while I was still breathing? That seems appropriate, seeing as you Ateres feel the need to mark where your heart is with that damn sigil."

"Don't touch him," Dayne roared. "Don't fucking touch him!"

"Stop me, Dayne." Loren slid the knife from its scabbard, turning to Baren.

At the sight of the steel, Dayne slowed his breathing. He could feel the Lorian gemstone pulsing in his stomach after he'd swallowed it at Fort Lukaris along with enough Urlin Leaf to twist his gut. A trick Belina had taught him many years ago. An uncomfortable but useful trick.

Loren placed the tip of the blade against Baren's chest.

Dayne had bided his time, waiting for Alina and the others to lay siege to the keep. Without them, there was no path by which Dayne could get both Baren and his nephew away from this place with their hearts still beating. Now that time had come, and Belina would be there shortly.

He honed in on that feeling of power that radiated from the gemstone and then opened himself to it.

Dayne let out a gasp as his veins filled with ice and his vision flashed black, nothing but the drum of his heart touching his ears. In an instant, the world came to life once more, light flooding into his eyes, sound crashing into his ears, and he felt stronger than he ever had.

Dayne wielded the Blood Magic as though it were the Spark, slicing threads of it through the leather bonds that held him.

A shout rang out behind him as Dayne fell forwards, his legs crumpling beneath him as they became reacquainted with his weight.

He could have snapped Loren's neck there and then, twisted a coil of this dark magic around the man's throat and pulled. But that would not be how he killed Loren Koraklon. He wanted to look the man in the eyes and do exactly as he had promised: cut out Loren's heart while there was still breath in his lungs.

He made to leap forwards, his legs still fumbling beneath him.

Loren turned, surprise and fear in his eyes. "How?" The man shifted so he stood square to Dayne, brandishing his knife.

The power of the gemstone flowing through Dayne, he dug his foot in and hurled himself at Loren, only for something to smash into his side and send him hurtling to the ground.

As Dayne's senses came back to him, his legs growing steadier, he hit the floor and rolled into a crouch. The two Lorian mages at the doors rushed into the room, while the two already within were charging towards him. Dayne sent a pulse of power rippling outwards from the gemstone. All he needed was a moment, just a fraction of a second – and he found it.

The pulse knocked the Lorian mages back a step, and their ward faltered. He tore through it with the savagery of a wyvern, the Spark flowing into him once more, the elemental strands pulsing in his mind.

"Do not hesitate." Dayne whispered Marlin's words as he wrapped threads of Air around one of the mage's throats and snapped her neck.

He surged forwards, dropping below the swing of Lorian steel, only to rise and wrap his hand around the man's throat. Dayne swung around the Lorian's back, interlocked the fingers of his left hand with those of his right, then dropped to the ground with all his strength, dragging the mage with him. With the Blood Magic flowing through his veins, Dayne brought the mage down with enough power to crack his skull.

"Do not contemplate mercy."

The gemstone called to him, urged him to breathe inwards, to capture the wisp of life that flowed from the dead Lorian. He pushed the voice down. *I am stronger than you.* He grabbed the Lorian's dropped sword, hurled himself to his feet, and charged at Loren and the two remaining mages.

All three hacked and slashed, but Dayne moved like a man possessed. One mage stabbed at Dayne's chest, the other at his leg. In the same motion, Dayne twisted at the hip and lifted his left leg. He brought his boot down, ripping the sword from one mage's hand while gliding his own sword down that of the other mage, slicing through her thumb and half her hand.

The first mage fell downwards, the momentum of Dayne's boot dragging him with it. Dayne twisted and drove his steel through the man's skull, wrenching it free in a spray of blood.

The last mage screamed and backed away, stumbling as she did. The woman sent threads of Fire whirling at Dayne, who split them in half with his own threads and stepped through the empty space.

When the flames died and Dayne stood over the screaming mage, Loren spoke.

"How fast are you, Dayne?"

Dayne turned his head slowly, his heart sinking at the sight of Loren having cut Baren free, holding him up with one arm, the other pressing a knife to his throat.

Loren dragged Baren across the room slowly, the steel never leaving Baren's flesh, blood trickling.

"Harm him, Loren, and I swear, I will kill every man, woman, and child that bears your name. I will burn every trace of your house from this world. I will cut out the tongues of bards who sing it and set fire to any books that dare record it. House Koraklon will not just die, it will never have existed."

Loren gave a crooked smile, his cheekbone shattered from Dayne's punch, blood dripping from two cuts. "And if I do nothing, you will what, let us live our lives in peace?"

"I'll only kill *you*," Dayne said, taking a tentative step towards Loren. "I'll make it quick."

"You'll make it quick," Loren said with a laugh. "How very kind of you. Do you like choices, Dayne?"

Dayne took a step closer, glancing at the Lorian mage who still lay on the ground, blood pumping from her severed hand.

"Ah ah," Loren hissed, lifting Baren's chin with the hilt of the knife. He kept shifting towards the door, then stopped when he stood between the mage and the door. "Here is your choice."

Loren dragged the knife across Baren's throat, blood pouring from the open wound, tossed Baren to the ground, then turned and ran through the open doors.

Dayne stared after Loren for just half a second, the rage deep within him telling him to chase the man, to kill him while he had a chance. Dayne gave in to that rage. He reached out to the Spark and launched a whip of Air, his heart racing. But before he could wrap that whip around Loren's legs, a thread of Spirit sliced through it. He looked down to see the Lorian mage staring at him.

Dayne tapped into the gemstone within him, his rage feeding it, and snapped the woman's neck as he dropped to the ground beside Baren.

Baren convulsed, blood pumping from his throat, his eyes rolling to the back of his head.

"Look at me." Dayne placed one hand behind his brother's head and the other over his throat, blood seeping through his fingers, panic trembling in his heart. "Baren, it's going to be all right. Hold on."

Baren choked, blood dripping from his open mouth and spilling over Dayne.

Dayne drew in sharp breaths, tears streaming. "I forgive you," he said, desperately trying to press his hand tighter around the wound. "I should have come back sooner. I should have... Ahhhh, Baren, no, please..."

Baren stared up at Dayne, his eyes glassy, his head lolling. He tried to speak but just coughed and spluttered, the colour draining from his face.

Dayne looked down at his little brother, the one he'd once held in his arms as a newborn babe.

"I'm sorry I wasn't better." Dayne let go of Baren's throat and pulled his brother close, warm blood spilling over his chest and arms. "I love you, and I will always love you. No matter what you did. You're my little brother, and I should have protected you."

Dayne squeezed Baren in his arms, holding him there for what felt like a lifetime before lowering him to the ground and looking into cold dead eyes.

"Dayne."

Belina stood in the doorway, staring down at Dayne, who knelt with his brother in his arms, both of them covered in blood.

She was too late.

The shrivelled pieces of her black heart cracked a little more as she looked down at Dayne sobbing and shaking. Her Exile. Her family.

Dayne leaned over his brother's lifeless body and planted a gentle kiss on Baren's forehead.

"He's gone…" Dayne whispered, looking up at Belina, his face smeared with blood, body covered in bruises and cuts.

Belina just stood there, staring down. She wasn't good with death. She was good at killing, but not death – not death that mattered. Death that cut pieces from the ones she loved, and there weren't many she loved. Just one. One flawed man whose entire life was built around others. One flawed man who had found a way through the armour she wore.

Dayne rose, stumbling forwards, his body weak. He looked past Belina to the doorway behind her. "I'm going to peel the skin from his bones," he said, voice trembling. Dayne leaned down and picked up a sword resting in the pool of blood. "He's taken everything, Belina… everything."

"No," Belina said, moving to force Dayne to look into her eyes. "He hasn't."

Dayne stared at her and through her, eyes raw and red.

"We will hunt him down, and we will make him understand the true meaning of pain. But not today, today—"

"Today!" Dayne rounded on her, a rage in his eyes untamed like she'd never seen. Dayne held a fury in his heart, but he had always been in control. That was not the case now.

Belina held her ground before turning back towards the door and holding out a hand. "Come here. Don't be shy, little one."

Dayne dropped the sword, steel clanging against stone, and he fell to his knees, cupping his hands around the cheeks of the small child who came at Belina's call.

"Arkin," Dayne whispered, pulling the boy in.

"I've been keeping track of him across the days."

"Where's my father?" the boy asked, trembling.

Dayne only squeezed him harder, and when Dayne stood, Belina could see the pain in his eyes.

"It will take time," Belina whispered. "For now, your sister needs you. I can get him somewhere safe."

"I can't just let Loren live."

"You choose now," she said, staring into his eyes. "Family or vengeance. You can't have both today. We *will* cross that last name off your list, I swear it. But your sister needs you. Choose what matters, Dayne."

Dayne clenched his jaw, then dropped to one knee in front of his nephew. "Belina will keep you safe, all right?" He kissed the boy's forehead. "Are you brave? You look brave."

The boy nodded, sniffling, tears staining his cheeks.

"Good, because I'm a little scared right now, and I need you to be brave for the both of us. Can you do that?"

The boy nodded again. "My father says you're a bad man… Are you?"

Dayne gave Arkin a sad smile. "I'm trying not to be."

"Come," Belina said, taking the boy's hand. She looked at Dayne. "I'll get him to safety, and then I'll come back. Don't die in the meantime."

"No promises."

ALINA STAYED TIGHT TO RYNVAR as the wyvern swooped and ripped two Lorians from the walls, dropping their bodies into the trenches on the other side. She had long used her last javelin, and the sword in her scabbard was bloody. She signalled her Wyndarii to rise – those that were left. Eighty or so in her squadron, almost half dead, slaughtered by the Lorian mages.

Amari's and Mera's squadrons still fought tooth and claw both in the air and on the ground. She'd seen Lukira and Urin fall, the wyvern pierced in the neck by a spear. The bulk of her army and the Narvonans fought on the walls in the yard, and they had already taken heavy losses. Even with the gates down, besieging a fortress of this scale took its toll. And so thick was the fighting that the Narvonan beasts were not yet through to the yard.

Rynvar let out a roar beneath her, his muscles twitching. She braced herself, and the wyvern rolled. A javelin whipped past her face, and a scream from behind let her know that one of her sisters had taken the steel meant for her.

"Down!" Alina shouted. Rynvar ignored her. Instead he cracked his wings and surged forwards towards the group of traitor Wyndarii that charged them in the sky. He twisted, raking his talons along a soft underbelly and spilling entrails onto the battle below.

"Down!" Alina roared again, but the wyvern had blood in his nostrils and a fury in his heart at seeing so many of his kin die. He tore three more from the sky, tearing out throats and snapping wings. As the wyvern spun, Alina pulled her sword free and sliced through the arm of a traitor Wyndarii, the world pulling at her as Rynvar dropped into a freefall.

Both Syndel and Audin swept in beside her, Amari and Mera on their backs.

"We need to break the lines!" Alina roared, the wind swallowing her voice. She looked down towards the main yard, where Loren's forces had consolidated and were protecting Lorian mages behind a shield wall. Belina had smashed open the gates, but the trenches were slowing her forces and the traitors were holding fast. The walls were chaos, and archers rained death from the towers and murder holes in the keep.

A sound like a thunderclap erupted to Alina's right, and she watched in horror as enormous boulders rolled down the side of the mountain at the Keep's eastern wall. A score of the giant chunks of stone swept down the mountainside and smashed into her forces traversing the trenches.

As she watched this new destruction, Rynvar let out a horrific shriek, and

Alina saw a spear jutting from his shoulder, buried deep. The wyvern flapped his wings and screamed, trying desperately to stay in the air, the world spinning.

They spiralled towards the ground, the wyvern thrashing to stay up, his wing failing him. Flames swept past Alina's vision, and before they crashed down into the yard, everything jerked upwards. Alina looked up to see Mera and Audin, Rynvar's harness in the other wyvern's talons.

Audin could only hold on for a second before Rynvar dragged them both down.

Rynvar let out another shriek and then spun, turning himself with his good wing so that Alina sat upright in the saddle when the wyvern slammed to the ground.

CHAPTER NINETY-FIVE

THE WYVERNS OF VALTARA

25th Day of the Blood Moon

Achyron's Keep – Winter, Year 3081 After Doom

Roars and shouts rang out, flames flickering in Alina's blurred vision. She shook her head, trying to loose the ringing. Beneath her, she felt Rynvar whine, and panic flared in her veins. She scrambled for the buckles and straps that held her in place on the wyvern's back, ripping them free. She slid to the ground, her ribs groaning as her feet touched stone.

Alina sprinted around to Rynvar's head, running her hands along his scales, his deep blue eyes searching hers.

"It's all right, it's all right," she whispered, staring into those eyes that had been her solace for so long. She looked down the length of his body to see one of his legs snapped and a broken spear shaft jutting from his shoulder. "You're going to be all right."

The wyvern hissed and whined, his chest wheezing.

"You fucking hold on, you understand me? You do not have permission to die. It's my turn to keep you safe. By blade and by blood." Alina slid her sword from its scabbard and pressed her head to the side of Rynvar's snout. "Do not hesitate," she whispered to herself, repeating the words she had heard Dayne speak every day. "Do not contemplate mercy."

She moved around Rynvar's flank to find eight warriors in bronzed cuirasses and white skirts standing with ordos and valynas in their hands, their backs to her. Aeson Virandr and three of his companions stood with them.

"Nothing gets past this line!" Savrin roared, beating his valyna against his ordo. Beyond him, over a hundred Koraklon warriors had broken away from the fighting and marched on them in a tight shield wall. "Protect your queen!"

Alina walked to join them, drawing in a long breath and letting it out slowly, her fingers tensing around the hilt of her sword. She slid her dardik shield from her back, small and light.

"How did you get to me so quickly?" Alina asked as she pushed between Savrin and Aeson, readying herself.

"He never let you out of his sight," Aeson said, tilting his head at Savrin without turning his gaze from the approaching warriors.

Savrin shrugged his ordo from his shoulder and handed it to Alina, taking her smaller dardik in return.

Alina tried to refuse, pushing the man's hand away, but he insisted.

"My purpose is to be your shield, my queen. Let me fulfil that purpose." The man cracked his neck and turned back to face the Koraklon warriors. Alina looked down the line to see which of her guard were missing: Saralis and Ravan.

"May Achyron welcome you into his halls," she whispered. She looked back at Rynvar, who had pulled himself upright, blood streaming from his shoulder, his weight on his right leg.

Streaks of purple lightning ripped down from a tower and were met by arcs of blue lightning that erupted from Verma Tallisair's fingers, the light blazing against the grey stone of the Keep.

"Can you handle this?" Verma asked Aeson, gesturing at the Koraklon warriors. He nodded.

"Pylvír, Andira, with me. Let's go take down a tower."

Alina looked up at the tower the mage ran towards. One of Achyron's three peaks. Three hundred feet tall and crafted from solid mountain stone.

As the Koraklon warriors drew closer, they broke into a slow charge, and Aeson stepped forwards. The air seemed to shift around the man's hands, hundreds of slivers of broken rock rising. A wave of air swept dust upwards and the slivers bolted forwards like loosed arrows, bouncing off shields and slicing through necks and legs. He charged and lifted his hand. A wave of concussive force tore a path through the Koraklon shield wall.

Alina snatched up a fallen spear and threw herself forwards. That shield wall could not be allowed to reform. Savrin, Glaukos, Olivian, and Alcon matched her stride for stride, two on the left, two on the right, while Vahir, Evrian, Baris, and Karilin took up the rear.

They smashed into the gap created by Aeson, scything down Koraklon soldiers as they tried to regain their footing. Alina dropped her shoulder, a spear slicing past her head, then rammed her spear up into the wielder's throat, ripping it free in a spray of blood. She twisted, ducking low to avoid the next thrust, then swung her arm back and smashed the rim of her shield into a Koraklon face, the nose guard of his helmet collapsing, nose breaking, jaw snapping.

Savrin swept past her. The man moved like some sort of spirit, his feet barely seeming to touch the ground, his spear painting death with every stroke. Alina had never seen him fight when she was a child, when he'd been at the peak of his powers, but she trembled to think of how this man could have been any greater a warrior. Achyron himself would be jealous of the sight.

As the Koraklon soldiers closed in around them and Lorians pushed in from the outside, shrieks rose above.

Scores of wyverns swooped down, crashing into the Koraklon ranks, ripping them apart, but even as they did, lightning tore down from the towers and more of the Keep's garrison poured into the main yard.

"Stay with me," Savrin shouted, pressing his back to Alina, Aeson and the others surrounding them as they protected Rynvar.

A shiver ran up Alina's spine as a voice thundered unnaturally across the sky. "Warriors of House Koraklon, your High Lord has turned tail and run! He leaves you to die while he flees like a coward. Ask yourselves, is this the leader you would follow? Or one who stands with you in the fires of battle?"

Alina lifted her head as a bright white light burst into existence atop the inner wall. Dayne stood on the crenelation, his chest bare and a glowing white spear in his hand.

Some of the Koraklon warriors looked from Dayne to Alina and the others. She could see the hesitation in their eyes. But it lasted only a moment before a streak of lightning tore upwards towards Dayne, collided against an invisible barrier, and smashed into an overlooking tower, and the fighting was ablaze once more.

The Koraklon soldiers pushed forwards, shields held high, spears stabbing.

"Warriors of Valtara!" Dayne roared again. "By blade and by blood, today is our day!"

A cry rose as, somewhere in the fighting, the Andurii answered. "AH-OOH, AH-OOH, AH-OOH!"

Dayne leapt from the wall, lightning streaking from his fingertips, that white spear glowing in his fist, and he vanished into the thick of the fighting.

A Koraklon spear stabbed at Alina's head. She slammed the shaft upwards with her shield, twisted, and drove her own spear forwards. The steel tip glanced off the man's cuirass and buried itself into the pit of his arm. Alina ripped the spear free and as she did, Rynvar craned his neck forwards and snapped his jaws shut around the man's torso, razor teeth slicing through steel. The wyvern lifted the man from the ground and shook him side to side until his body tore in half, blood and guts spraying over the Koraklon warriors.

Alina slammed her spear off her shield and roared, "For Valtara! For Freedom!"

BELINA SPRINTED THROUGH THE ARCHWAY and out onto the ramparts of the city's inner wall, a spear gripped in her fist. She'd left Dayne's nephew locked in a small granary store in the lower levels of the city's keep. She strongly doubted anyone would go rushing for a snack in the midst of all this, and if worse came to worst, the young boy would never go hungry.

Koraklon and Lorian soldiers lined the ramparts, staring down at the fighting in the main plaza. Archers were lined along the gaps in the parapet, nocking and loosing in a neverending cycle.

She stuck her hand into the pouch at her side, feeling three more clay jars of Godfire. She hadn't known there would be Narvonans here, and she didn't look forward to explaining how she'd come across enough Godfire to blow open a city gate. She just hoped nobody told them anything about the port of Ankar. She might be Narvonan by birth, but those people really didn't like finding Godfire anywhere but on their ships.

As Belina ran, the first soldier caught her out of the corner of his eye. He turned, and she slipped her left hand to her knife belt. A whir of steel and the man dropped backwards from the wall.

After leaving Arkin, Belina had run for the walls as quickly as her legs could carry her. And there she was. The only problem was that Belina hadn't quite thought through what she would do when she actually got there.

Something big, plenty of fire. That tended to work well. Things also had a way of simply working themselves out. She was lucky like that.

The second soldier noticed her. Another flash of steel. Another dead body falling from the walls. Unfortunately, that drew the attention of even more. And within seconds, arrows were slicing through the air past her head and shoulders. She thanked the gods these warriors had worse aim than a one-legged, blind goat with cockrot.

Belina reached into her pouch, grabbed a jar of Godfire, and launched it. The jar soared over heads, then smashed against the ground.

She twisted, an arrow *whooshing* past her head, then snatched a flaming torch from a sconce attached to the wall and hurled it after the jar of Godfire. She took a breath, and then the wall erupted in flames.

A Koraklon soldier charged at her, screaming, fire consuming him.

Belina hurled the spear, watching as it smashed into the man's face and sent him careening backwards.

The only problem now was that she was stuck on a wall covered in fire along with some very angry Valtarans. Shouts sounded behind her, and she turned to see Lorian soldiers charging through the arch, some kneeling and nocking arrows.

"Fuck."

Something swooped past the wall, and Belina got the worst idea of her life. At least, one of the worst. Fourth worst. That time in Karvos was definitely the worst.

She sprinted forwards and leapt onto the crenelations, having only half a second to pick her target before launching herself from the walls.

She slid two knives from her belt, the world seeming to grow still around her. At that point, as she hung in the air, nothing but a freefall of a few hundred feet separating her from hard stone, Belina elevated the situation to the third worst idea she'd ever had. Behind Karvos and that stunt with the chickens.

She glanced at the wyvern that swooped low, its wings unmarked by the orange and white that Alina's Wyndarii bore.

Belina slammed into the creature's side so hard the wind fled her lungs like an Ardanian at a whorehouse. She drove her knives down through the creature's hide, its wing slapping her in the face. The wyvern shrieked and howled, spinning in the air, Belina's stomach churning.

"Fuck, fuck, fuck."

Belina's legs swung, and it was all she could do to keep hold of her knives. She was seriously considering raising this idea above the chickens on her 'stupid list'.

When the wyvern levelled out, Belina pulled one knife free and slammed it back down, doing the same again as she hauled herself onto the creature's back. She ripped the knives free and crouched behind the Wyndarii in the saddle. Before the creature could twist or turn or spin, she leapt forwards. Belina wrapped her legs around the Wyndarii's waist, squeezing for dear life, and rammed her knives again and again into the woman's neck, blood spurting.

When the Wyndarii slumped forwards, Belina sliced through the straps that buckled the woman to the saddle and tossed her aside, quickly lunging forwards and grabbing the saddle's handles, leaving her knives to fall.

It took all of four heartbeats to realise why Wyndarii used straps and buckles. The wyvern dropped into a nosedive and Belina flopped upwards like a limp fish, legs flailing. Squeezing her stomach muscles as tight as she could, she pulled herself back into place and looked down at the battle below.

The Narvonans had fully joined the fray now, their monstrous tharnas crashing through the Lorian and Koraklon lines, their darvakin riders carving paths of blood. If these were the reinforcements Aeson had promised, he had delivered tenfold.

The wyvern jerked beneath Belina, twisting its neck back and trying to rip her from the saddle.

"Not food!" she roared, pulling another knife from her belt and slamming it down into the creature's shoulder. "Not. Food!"

The wyvern shrieked and swooped right. As Belina held on with every shred of strength she had, she looked down to see a column of blue and gold marching from the inner city. Thousands upon thousands. If they passed through the gates and smashed into Alina's flank, the battle would be a short one.

Belina reached back, relieved to still feel the two jars of Godfire firmly in her pouch.

"All right," she said to herself, looking from the unrelenting flames on the walls to the column of marching Koraklons. "How the fuck do you fly these things?"

She reached forwards and slammed a second knife into the wyvern's other shoulder. New handles. She yanked on the right, and the creature answered by swerving in the same direction. Delighted with herself, Belina steered the wyvern back towards the marching warriors.

The wind whipped past Belina's face, her eyes watering. As the wyvern dropped low and swept over the soldiers below, she reached into her satchel and grabbed a jar of Godfire and launched it backwards, doing so again in quick succession, the knuckles on her other hand pale and white around the hilt of the knife.

She glanced back to see the soldiers parting where the jars landed, then grabbed the second knife and steered the wyvern towards the closest roof. Unsurprisingly, the beast was uncooperative and swept straight past the roof.

It appeared she should have thought about getting off the wyvern before leaping on.

As the wyvern plummeted towards the ground, blood streaming around the knives driven into its hide, its wings flapping uselessly at its side, Belina drew slow breaths and readied herself.

One heartbeat passed, the wind battering her, her lungs swelling. Two heartbeats. Three. Four.

The wyverns swept over the soldiers, spear tips clinking against its underbelly.

Five heartbeats. Dayne better fucking thank her for this.

Just before the wyvern crashed down into the street, Belina leapt from the saddle, an unsuspecting soldier softening her landing. She slammed into the man, then hit the ground hard, something snapping in her left arm. She rolled, skin tearing, stone beating against her.

When she finally stopped rolling, her head spun and she could barely feel her arm – except for the excruciating pain. That, she could feel.

Belina hauled herself upright, looking down to see a sliver of broken bone jutting from her arm. "Fuuuck."

She grimaced, then looked up to see the entire column of Koraklon soldiers had stopped in their tracks, those at the rear now staring at her.

A torch sat in a sconce on the wall only a few feet away.

"Help!" she called out, glancing at the torch. "My arm's broken. My wyvern… she's gone."

Belina limped towards the soldiers, who were still hesitant, approaching her with caution. As they should. When those closest to her relaxed for just a moment, Belina broke into a sprint, snatched the torch with her good arm, and hurled it into the thick of the soldiers. As it whirled through the air, Belina prayed to every god she could think of. And when her mind landed on Elyara, screams pierced the night and a blazing inferno ignited.

The soldiers closest to her turned back to their companions who were being swallowed by the Godfire, and as they did, Belina fled down a side street into the night.

"Andurii! Break!" Dayne surged forwards, the Andurii breaking from their shield wall as the Narvonans atop their monstrous tharnas mounts smashed into the back of the Koraklon forces, ripping them from formation. Dayne had first encountered the tharnas and darvakin when he'd sailed with Belina to Daris. The creatures were akin to living battering rams, with teeth and claws that could rend steel.

Everywhere Dayne moved, Koraklons died, his níthral spraying blood in wide arcs. Iloen and Dinekes fell in beside him, as well as Tarine of House Valanis and Juna of House Toradin. They carved a path towards Alina and the others as Dayne roared Marlin's words. "Do not hesitate!"

"Do not contemplate mercy!" Dinekes answered, ripping his spear from a Koraklon throat.

"You are the Andurii of House Ateres!" he roared again, feeling the rush of battle overcome him, the thirst for blood. "You are death and deliverance! You are the darkness that all men fear!"

"AH-OOH!" came the reply.

Both pride and fervour swept through him. These men and women were Dayne's Andurii. The stories of legend would know their names, written in the blood of their enemies. They would be the spears that set Valtara free, or they would die in the trying.

Dayne leapt forwards, side-stepping a spear lunge, and slammed his shield into a Koraklon brow, feeling the skull split beneath the force.

He should have had no strength in his body, no power to lift his shield or swing his spear. But hate fuelled him, rage refusing to let him die. Loren Koraklon and all of his name would be burned from this earth.

In the thick of the fighting, Dayne saw a face that brought joy to his heart. The face of a man he'd seen only days before: Gaimal, Loren's eldest son.

Dayne charged forwards, deflecting a spear thrust with his shield, his eyes fixed on his target.

Gaimal turned just in time for Dayne's níthral to miss the man's chest and instead slice open the flesh on his upper arm. Gaimal twisted further and brought his shield down.

Dayne roared and planted a foot flat on the man's shield, kicking with all his strength.

Gaimal crashed backwards, slamming into the ground.

Dayne leapt atop him. He swung his shield arm down, the heavy rim snapping Gaimal's sword arm with a crunch, bone shredding skin, blood spurting. With a twist of his hip, Dayne drove his níthral into the man's shield arm and ripped it through the muscle and flesh.

He placed his foot on the breast of Gaimal's cuirass as the man screamed in agony. There was pity in Dayne's heart, but the memory of Baren bleeding out in his arms set that pity on fire.

"You will be the first," Dayne said, looking down at Gaimal. "The first to pay for your father's sins. But you will not be the last. You die today because your father set your path. A man should know why he died."

Dayne drove his níthral down into Gaimal's chest and stared into the man's eyes as his light vanished.

Around him, the battle was thinning. The Narvonans were in full force, sweeping through the yard in their gilded black plate, their monstrous steeds driving fear into Lorian and Koraklon hearts alike.

He watched as one of the Narvonan Isildans swung his massive glaive from the back of a darvakin, that glorious pearlescent plate of Atalus shell shimmering in the light of the blazing fires. Bolts of lightning and plumes of fire streaked towards him, only for the Atalus armour to drink them in. Dayne had seen the power of Atalus shell in Narvona, but only as a simple pendant. An entire suit of armour was something else entirely. It had been centuries since the last Narvonan invasion, and the Lorian mages had no answer to this kind of power.

"Andurii!" Dayne roared. "Tonight, the Wyvern of House Ateres will fly over Achyron's Keep. Valtara's freedom is here, will you take it?"

"AH-OOH."

Dayne's Andurii swept around him, carving through the Keep's defenders, the wyvern glistening on their shields.

He drove his níthral into a woman's throat, yanking it free, blood sluicing. As he did, he spotted Aeson weaving through the chaos, his blades ablur, bodies falling with every step he took. Verma charged with him, the pair moving as though intertwined.

Shouts rose to Dayne's right, and a wyvern smashed into the ground, crushing Lorian soldiers beneath it. Three more wyverns crashed, followed by a chorus of shrieks and roars in the sky.

Hundreds of wyverns alighted on the walls and patches of rock, their wings painted with streaks of orange and white. Alina's Wyndarii had secured the air.

The air hung thick with palpable tension, all eyes staring at the wyverns.

One by one, the defenders of Achyron's Keep dropped their weapons and fell to their knees, the sound of clinking ordo shields ringing out through the yard.

A Lorian mage opened himself to the Spark, but before he could release anything, Mera and Audin launched themselves from atop the ramparts of the outer wall and the wyvern clamped its jaws around the mage's head.

Audin tore the man's head and neck from his body, crunched on his skull, then spat the remnants onto the ground and roared.

Any Lorians or Koraklons who had remained standing dropped to their knees.

A chill swept through Dayne, setting his hairs on end, his legs giving way beneath him, his knees cracking off the stone.

Both Dinekes and Iloen grabbed at his shoulders.

"Andurios?" Dinekes looked him over. "Where are you hurt?"

Dayne's entire body ached and groaned, and scabs opened, blood trailing from a hundred cuts. Tears rolled from his eyes. Almost fourteen years since his parents had died. Years spent in exile, spent wandering and hoping.

He shook his head, wiping away the tears, fires blazing around him. "We're free. We're free."

ALINA STOOD BY RYNVAR'S SIDE after the battle had calmed and the Keep's defenders had laid down their weapons.

Verma Tallisair stood beneath the wyvern's wing, doing all she could to mend the damage. Though she had warned Alina that Rynvar might never take to the sky again.

"You will always be by my side," Alina whispered, resting a hand on Rynvar's scales.

After a few moments, she turned and looked out over the aftermath of the fighting. Flames still raged on the walls and all about the yard, illuminating bodies everywhere.

"How is he?" Savrin asked, blood covering every inch of the man's armour.

Alina didn't answer with words. She had no words. It was her task to protect Rynvar as much as it was his to protect her. She had failed in that task. "Saralis and Ravan," Alina said, changing the topic. "Any others?"

"Baris took a spear to the neck near the end."

"They fought like gods," Alina said, slowly walking past Savrin.

"That they did, Your Grace."

"As did you, Savrin." Alina paused and looked into the man's eyes. "You earned that armour, and you earned your place amongst the heroes of Valtara. You are everything my father always said you were."

"I am a shadow, Your Grace."

"We are not our mistakes, Savrin. Not entirely. I am honoured to have you at my side."

"The honour is mine and mine alone." Savrin looked at something behind her. "And it is a privilege to stand here to see that."

Alina followed Savrin's gaze up towards the gates to the inner city. Audin was perched upon a high tower, his red scales gleaming. And on that tower two banners flapped in the wind. One bore the wyvern of House Ateres marked in orange on a white field. The other held two black wyverns coiled around a white spear on an orange field. The emblem of a free Valtara.

"The wyverns of Valtara fly again," Savrin whispered, pressing a closed fist to his chest.

A shout rose behind Alina. "My queen!"

She turned to see a man pointing towards the inner gates.

Dayne walked towards her, battered and bloody. He stumbled, cradling someone in his arms. Belina was at his side, leading a young child with one hand, the other arm held tight to her abdomen.

Alina walked slowly towards her brother, slower with every step as she realised who he held.

Baren had used her like a tool, like a thing to be bargained. He had taken her son from her, taken her love. He had done so many things, and Alina hated him for them. She hated him. How could he have done those things to her? She was his sister, his little sister.

But even then, with all that hatred swirling in her, she felt her heart twist at the sight of Dayne holding their brother in his arms like a babe, blood smeared over Baren's broken body.

She had not even reached Dayne when he collapsed to his knees, holding Baren close.

The sight of it broke her.

Alina dropped to the ground before her brothers and brushed the hair from Baren's face. "We did it, big brother. We did it." The tears that flowed came upon her like a broken dam. "I wish everything had been different. I wish with all my heart that I didn't hate you and love you at the same time." She leaned over her dead brother's body and wrapped her arms around Dayne, pressing her cheek to his.

"We did it," Dayne whispered, repeating her words. "Valtara is free."

"Valtara is free," Alina answered.

Dayne pulled away for a moment, tears and blood marring his face. "There is something else."

Alina narrowed her eyes, but before Dayne could say a word, Belina came closer and she saw the child at the woman's side.

Alina shook, every piece of her body trembling, every shred of her soul and her heart bleeding. "Arkin?"

"Who are you?" the boy responded, his voice soft and full of uncertainty.

Alina knew her son. He had those same blue eyes, that dark brown hair that curled a little to the left. And he bore that same mark on his cheek that he'd been born with.

Alina shuffled forwards on her knees until she reached Arkin. She wiped her bloodied hands on her skirts, then wrapped her arms so tightly around him that it pained her battered bones. "I'm your mother," she said, drawing in a sniffling breath. "I'm your mother, Arkin. And I love you, and I'm never letting you go again." She drew another long breath, closing her eyes as she held the son she had thought long lost. "I'm your mother," she said again. The words were almost more for herself than for Arkin. "I'm yours."

CHAPTER NINETY-SIX

SHADES OF GREY

25th Day of the Blood Moon

Temple of Achyron – Winter, Year 3081 After Doom

Kallinvar rubbed his fingers into his temples, trying without success to ease the ache in his head. Even with the healing of Heraya's Well, his body groaned as he sat in the chair behind Verathin's desk.

Rain drummed against the window behind him, and the candle had run low, its flame the last source of light in the study. He pushed himself back in the chair and looked over the desk and the piles of books. Those he'd found in Gildrick's study, and others Poldor had brought to him – all with missing pages. The journals of the old Grandmasters were splayed about the desk, ribbons marking pages Kallinvar had thought important. There seemed to be about a thousand.

With Gildrick gone, Kallinvar had decided to spend his time in the temple, searching desperately for any hint of what the Watcher had found before he'd died. It seemed an impossible task, but so too was chasing every convergence that emerged across the continent while the Blood Moon tainted the sky.

If Poldor was right and Gildrick had indeed found something, Kallinvar needed to know what it was. Anything, any hint or clue, was better than sending the knights to die in battle after battle that meant nothing.

They had lost so many knights since the Blood Moon had risen that Kallinvar barely recognised his own brothers and sisters. And he finally understood why it had taken Verathin so long to replenish the knighthood. His old friend had been slow and careful in his selection, something Kallinvar could not afford to be. Many of these new knights held the hearts and minds of a knight but lacked the skills and battle constitution. Some had borne the Sigil less than a day before meeting their ends.

And many knew the ways of war but lacked the qualities of the heart and soul.

Kallinvar had tried to take the front foot, tried to stop sitting around and waiting, stop reacting and start *acting*. But now he knew he had been playing into Efialtír's hands. He had weakened his own position, and when the time came – *if* the time came – that Fane or the Bloodspawn tried to use the Heart to cross Efialtír, the knighthood would be too weak to fight them.

As he spoke, he could feel Sister-Captain Olyria and half the knighthood battling through a Lorian fort on the northern fringes of Lodhar.

The days were fast fading, and the Blood Moon would soon set. If they did not find the Heart before then, he would at least take solace in the fact that he would have four hundred more years to do so.

"I wasn't built for this, Verathin," Kallinvar whispered. "My place is in battle, beside my brothers and sisters, with a Soulblade in my fist and Bloodspawn beneath my boot. The pages of history were always your domain."

The lack of an answer cut into him.

"You always used silence to win our arguments." Kallinvar let out a long sigh. He couldn't remember the last time he'd slept for longer than an hour. His eyes stung, and his neck was stiff as a board.

"This is hopeless," he whispered to himself. He felt as though he had read through every book in the temple a thousand times, though he knew he'd barely scratched the surface.

They had yet to find the book Gildrick had been reading or any of the missing pages from all the others.

He and Poldor hadn't said it out loud, but they both knew the truth. There was a traitor inside the temple, or in Ardholm at least. Pages didn't simply tear themselves out. Had the missing pages been from Grandmaster Invictus's book of Andarsían recipes, Kallinvar would have thought little of it. But that was not the case. And if there was a traitor, then Kallinvar could not believe that Gildrick's death had not been a purposeful act.

Furthermore, if that traitor was not Watcher Tallia, then who was it? The thought that any in Ardholm could have betrayed them sent a chill down Kallinvar's spine.

He leaned forwards and pressed his forehead to the pages of the book in front of him. It was the same book he'd found on Gildrick's lap: *A History of the People of Ardholm.*

"Why was this the last book you were reading, old friend?"

Kallinvar knew he was missing something. Something that was right there in front of him.

The door creaked open, and Ruon pushed in with a steaming plate of roasted vegetables and sliced lamb. She was the only thing that brought him any semblance of peace.

"Fresh from the kitchens," Ruon said as she brushed aside the book before Kallinvar and laid the plate in its place.

"You should be sleeping." Kallinvar stared at the steam wafting from the food as he spoke, slowly moving his gaze to Ruon.

"I'll sleep when you sleep."

"You only got back an hour ago, Ruon."

"Don't lecture me, Kallinvar, you'll only turn yourself into more of a hypocrite than you already are." Ruon walked along the stone bookcase, tracing her fingers across the edges of scrolls. "I once asked Verathin whether he'd read all of these."

"What did he say?"

"He laughed." Ruon shook her head. She stopped, tapping her finger against the spine of a red leatherbound volume. "Eat that food while it's hot, and we will spar."

"I don't have time to be sparring, Ruon. None of us do."

"You've been sitting there with your head in those books for days on end. Sparring clears your mind. I told Ildris to meet us in the sparring pits. It's not a question."

Kallinvar began to argue but decided against it. He never won arguments with Ruon – nobody did.

Kallinvar devoured the food before him as Ruon stared at him with horror in her eyes.

"You could have at least taken a breath."

"No time for breathing." Kallinvar picked up the empty plate and made for the door before turning and cupping Ruon's cheek with his free hand. He stared into her eyes for a long moment, then kissed her. "Thank you for never doubting me."

She rested her hand atop his. "That cuts both ways."

The pair of them stepped from the study and walked through the great halls of the temple, their steps echoing.

"It is quiet tonight," Kallinvar said as they walked, looking about at the empty halls.

"Watcher Poldor is holding a vigil in Ardholm," Ruon said. "He came to me earlier to see if the other Watchers and temple hands could be given a few hours reprieve."

"He came to *you*?"

Ruon nodded. "The incident with Tallia has more than a few people on edge, Kallinvar."

Kallinvar gritted his teeth. "I was wrong to treat her as I did."

"You were. Have you apologised?"

Kallinvar shook his head, biting at his lip. "I wanted to... I should have." He bit at his lip. "I will."

Ruon led Kallinvar through the temple and down to the sparring pits, where they found Ildris. Ruon grabbed a sword from the racks and tossed it to him. "Best of five?"

Just as Ruon had said it would, the moving of bodies and the clash of steel settled Kallinvar's mind, focused him. The world around him grew quiet, the vibrations jarring his arms as he and Ruon whirled about one another.

Sweat slicked Kallinvar's entire body, his shirt clinging to his chest and arms, his hair tacked to his forehead. He blocked low as Ruon moved in, then brought his blade around to strike at her left shoulder.

Ruon turned the blow away and swept Kallinvar's blade down. And at that moment, Kallinvar finally understood. Hours upon hours of pouring over Gildrick's books and beating his head against the table and all he had found was a headache. But with his mind clear, he understood.

That brief moment of elation was cut short when Ruon's blunted blade smashed him in the stomach. The blow knocked the wind from his lungs, and he fell backwards into the sand, coughing and gasping for air.

As Ruon stood over him, the coughing turned to laughter.

"I didn't hit your head, did I?" Ruon asked as she offered her hand.

Kallinvar took her hand and hauled himself to his feet with Ruon's help. He shook his head. "*A History of the People of Ardholm*," he said, shaking his head.

"Are you sure she didn't hit your head?" Ildris asked.

"No…"

"No?"

"Yes, I'm sure. No, she didn't hit my head. The night Gildrick was killed—"

"Killed?" Ruon searched Kallinvar's eyes. "Go on."

"He had a number of books open in his study. *A History of the People of Ardholm* and a list of all people inducted into the Watchers."

Ruon gestured for Kallinvar to continue.

"If there is a traitor, one who…" He hesitated, not wishing to say the next words out loud but knowing they were true at the same time. "One who is tied to Efialtír, perhaps Gildrick believed they go back as far as the rebellion in five-twenty-one After Doom. Perhaps even that their ancestors were brought in after Grandmaster Invictus's decision to admit the refugees from Lurïnel." As Kallinvar spoke, he connected more threads in his mind. "Gildrick was trying to establish a connection, trying to make sense of it all." A heavy weight formed in his stomach. "Gildrick believed there was a traitor within the Watchers…"

"That cannot be…" Ruon stared back at him in disbelief. "Then what of the other book, the one that has gone missing, the one Poldor spoke of? And Gildrick's mention of a dead god?"

Kallinvar's heart sank. "I don't know."

Urgent footsteps slapped against the stone stairs that led down to the sparring chamber, and Watcher Poldor appeared at the entrance. "Grandmaster!"

"What is it, Poldor? What's wrong?"

"You need to see this now. You were right. It's Watcher Tallia," Poldor explained as he led Ruon, Kallinvar, and Ildris back through the temple to the Watcher's chambers. "I couldn't get it out of my head – Gildrick's death… the missing book… Tallia… everything."

"But you're the one who told me she hadn't been in the Watcher's chambers that day, Poldor. You defended her."

"I know, but I was always taught never to leave a question unasked. The pages were ripped from those books, Kallinvar, and I've searched everywhere for the book Gildrick had been reading. It's gone." Poldor turned left through a long corridor, then right through the next, the door to the Watcher's chambers up ahead. "I held the vigil tonight in Ardholm and told all the Watchers and all the temple hands that you had demanded they all attend. A vigil in remembrance of the lost knights, the brave souls who have given everything to preserve our world."

"And why are you not there?"

"Watcher Hatia leads it." Poldor stepped through the door into the Watcher's chambers. "I slipped out near the beginning." He stopped in the antechamber. "The books Gildrick was reading in his study, I believe—"

"That he thought the traitor was a Watcher."

Poldor smiled. "Precisely. Though I'm not sure he was *certain* there was a traitor, but he suspected one. Ever since he realised quite how many pages had been torn from certain books, knowledge obscured… There were threads."

"Why did he never come to me about this?"

"I'm afraid that was perhaps my doing, Grandmaster."

"Yours?"

"I convinced Gildrick that there was not enough evidence. That suggestions of a traitor inside the temple – of all places – were a thing to be handled with extreme care. That we shouldn't go to you until we had more."

And then Gildrick died. Kallinvar didn't say the words out loud. He did not want Poldor to bear the weight of them. The man was well intentioned.

"Please," Poldor said, gesturing for Ruon and Kallinvar to follow him. "While the others attended the vigil, I took the liberty of searching every room."

"You did what? Poldor, that is beyond your decision to make."

"And the weight you bear is beyond that any man should hold, Grandmaster. And yet, you do. Sometimes we must go beyond when times are dire."

Poldor led them through the various corridors of the Watcher's chambers, stopping outside an open door.

"Watcher Tallia's room," Poldor said, pushing open the door.

The room looked little different to any others, if a little scattered and in need of a clean. Though Kallinvar wouldn't fault Tallia for that in a time like this.

"I'm failing to see the need for your urgency, Poldor."

The man nodded. "I thought the same, at first. But when I made to leave. I kicked the bedpost, clumsy as I am… It's hollow."

Poldor knelt and tapped on the right leg at the foot of Tallia's bed. At first the man's knuckle produced a hard *thunk*, but as he moved down, a muffled echo sounded within.

"You claim her a traitor for having a hollow bed post?"

"No, I claim her a traitor for having these." Poldor manoeuvred the wooden panel at the inside of the bedpost until a segment slipped away with a click. When the man stood, Kallinvar's eyes widened.

Poldor held out tens of torn pages, all wrapped together with string. But the pages were nothing, not compared to the dull gemstone in his other hand.

Kallinvar couldn't believe what he was seeing. He could, but he didn't want to.

To consider the possibility that Tallia was a traitor and to know her as one were two different things, something Kallinvar had not realised until that moment.

Efialtír truly had found a way inside Achyron's temple. Kallinvar reached out and took the gemstone into his hand. It was empty. No red light glowed from its core, and he couldn't feel the Taint radiating from within. Perhaps it had never been used. But how had it found its way into Watcher Tallia's hands? How had it found its way to Ardholm at all?

Kallinvar turned and stormed from the room, holding the gemstone firmly in his hands. Ruon and Ildris sprinted after him, Poldor with them, and in that moment, Achyron awakened in his mind once more.

"This must end now, my child. Efialtír cannot set root in my sanctuary."

"Where is she?" Kallinvar demanded as he pushed through the doors from the Watcher's antechamber into the hall.

"She's in the village," Poldor answered, breathing heavy. "At the vigil."

"*Where?*"

"In the square before The Salted Sparrow."

Kallinvar pushed through the wicket gate set into the great temple doors and descended the stairs with a fury. The rain was cold against Kallinvar's skin, but the rage that pulsed within him cared little for it, part Achyron's, part his own. The people he had spent the last seven hundred years protecting had betrayed him, had killed one of the few people he had called 'friend'.

Lanterns blazed all about the city, the light of the Blood Moon drifting languidly over the rooftops. Villagers raised their fists to their foreheads as Kallinvar and the others passed, but Kallinvar didn't stop.

Hundreds were gathered at the square in front of The Salted Sparrow, candles lit all about them. They stood as a Watcher recounted a story, the words of which Kallinvar did not hear amid the pounding of his own heart.

"Watcher Tallia!" he roared, his Sentinel armour flowing from the Sigil in his chest.

Heads snapped around at the sound of Kallinvar's rage-filled shout. The crowd parted, leaving Tallia standing alone with a candle in her hands and a look of pure terror on her face. The young woman's hood was drawn, the rain splattering against it.

"What is this?" Kallinvar tossed the gemstone so it skittered across the ground and came to a stop at Tallia's feet.

This woman had betrayed them. She had betrayed Achyron, betrayed her people, but most of all she had betrayed Gildrick.

"I've never seen that before. I don't…. I don't…" She staggered backwards as Kallinvar approached, dropping her candle onto the stone, the wax splattering, the flame living on.

"Do *not* lie to me!" Kallinvar grabbed her by the throat and lifted her into the air, his Sentinel armour making it seem as though he were lifting a feather.

"I'm not," she choked, eyes wild with fear.

"How could you kill him?" Kallinvar did nothing to hide the seething rage in his voice. "He was good. He was kind. He treated you like an equal."

"Be done with this," Achyron said in his mind. "She is a slave of Efialtír. Destroy her!"

Kallinvar pushed the god's words away.

"Answer me!" he roared again.

"I didn't… I don't know what you're—"

"Do not dare lie!"

"I'm not, Grandmaster." Tallia pulled at the fingers of Kallinvar's gauntlet, her legs dangling, the rain beating harder against her. "Please."

"I know what you did. Your treachery is not in question here, child. Your reasons are."

Evidence could be planted. The pages might have been ripped by someone else, and the gemstone also. But that compartment in Tallia's bed, that told him of planning, of a need to hide.

Kallinvar released his hold on Tallia's throat and let her fall to the stone with a *thump.*

He turned and snatched the gemstone into his hand, looking into the dull red heart of it.

"Destroy it!" Achyron roared in his mind. The presence of Efialtír's touch in this place had set a fire in Achyron. *"Burn the Taint from my home!"*

Kallinvar squeezed his hand into a fist, and the gemstone shattered in his gauntlet. Memories of Gildrick flashed through his mind, of the man's kindness and generosity, of his thoughtfulness and selflessness. Kallinvar's mind slowed over the oldest memory, of a boy of fourteen summers, scraggy and small, but with a smile from ear to ear. That boy had grown into a man, and that man had grown into a friend, a friend that had trusted Kallinvar to keep him safe.

"Pain is the path to strength," Achyron said.

Kallinvar opened his hand and let the shattered remnants of the gemstone fall to the ground. A rage flowed through him like a river of molten fire that burned his veins and clouded his mind. He turned and unleashed a guttural roar, his Soulblade forming in his fist. He swung the mighty blade, green light gleaming in the falling rain.

Tallia screamed but went silent as Kallinvar stopped the arc of his Soulblade just short of taking her head. The blade hovered a hair's breadth from her neck as she knelt on the stone. Green mist drifted from its surface, a clap of thunder howling in the sky.

"Do it," Achyron demanded.

Kallinvar said nothing, holding his blade in place. Tallia stared up at him, eyes pleading.

All about him the citizens of Ardholm stood in a shattered circle, holding their breaths, staring. Even Ruon, who stood behind him, said nothing.

More memories of Gildrick drifted through Kallinvar's mind.

"She is a servant of Efialtír, and you will do as you are commanded." Achyron's voice was calm but absolute. *"She slaughtered Watcher Gildrick. She would have Efialtír cross the veil between worlds. It is your task to end her before she does."*

"No," Kallinvar whispered.

"You took an oath, Kallinvar. You will do what is required of you."

"I will not do this." Kallinvar's hand remained steady, the rain drumming against his Soulblade, green light misting. "The duty of the strong is to protect the weak."

"She is not the weak, my child."

"It is her weakness that has brought her here. She is a soul of Ardholm. It is our solemn duty to protect her from Efialtír. We have failed in that duty, but I will not fail her now."

"Do not defy me, Kallinvar. It is by my will that you still draw breath."

"A man should not simply wish to live. He should wish to live in a way that he deems to be right," Kallinvar whispered, the citizens of Ardholm still standing around him, staring at him as though he'd gone mad. It was Verathin who had spoken those words to him all those centuries ago, and they had bound to Kallinvar's soul. "This is not right."

"Then I will strip the life from your bones, burn the Sigil from your soul, and leave you to die as you should have before I saved your life. Efialtír is too close. I cannot allow defiance."

"Do it then!" Kallinvar roared, blood trickling from Tallia's neck as his Soulblade shook in his hand. "Do it and be done!"

Kallinvar's Sigil ignited in a pulse of burning energy, green light swallowing his vision.

In an instant he stood amidst an ocean of endless silver sand. Around him, towers of crystal jutted into the sky, hundreds of feet wide and twice again as tall.

Achyron stood before him, garbed in that gleaming green plate with blazing sun pauldrons, his features stern and harsh. "After all this time, you would turn your back on me?"

"Turn my back on you?" Kallinvar leaned into his anger. "I have given my life to you!"

"I gave you that life, Voran Thrace. I made you what you are."

"I made myself, forged my strength in the rivers of blood I spilled in your name. I have given you seven hundred years of service, of undying devotion. When Efialtír bore down on this world, I stood in his path and I did not yield. When my brothers and sisters were slaughtered at the last Blood Moon, I fought with every fibre of this life you gave. Where were you?"

Achyron stared back at Kallinvar, unyielding, his green eyes watching.

"Where were you?" Kallinvar roared. "When Verathin died in your name. Where were you? When Illarin died, when Tarron was pulled into that tear, when Gildrick was murdered, where were you, Achyron?"

"I was fighting the war you cannot see."

"When we die, do you even care?"

"Of course I care, my child. My love for your world is the only reason you exist."

"Do you? Truly? Or are we just tools to be worn and tossed away? Weapons to be wielded in a war between gods?"

"The duty of the strong is to protect the weak, Grandmaster Kallinvar."

"I know my gods damned oaths!" Kallinvar's rage burned through him. "Pain is the path to strength. I have held more pain than any soul has a right to. I have watched my brothers and sisters die again and again for centuries, and still I do not falter."

Kallinvar stepped closer to the god. "The duty of the strong is to protect the weak. I have embodied that oath since before I spoke the words."

"That woman is not 'the weak', my child. She is a slave to the god that betrayed us all."

"She is a child!"

"A child who killed Watcher Gildrick."

"No decision is straightforward," Kallinvar said, speaking Achyron's own words back to him, never straying from the god's gaze. "Black and white do not exist. We live in a world of ever-shifting grey."

Achyron stared back at him in silence.

"It is *my* soul that will bear the weight of every life I take. *My* soul. Not yours. I will fight for you, as I always have. I will stand against The Shadow, as I *always* have. I am a warrior, I am *your* warrior, but I am not your executioner. I will not slaughter a young woman of twenty summers in cold blood. I will not be that man. Because the day I become him is the day I do not deserve to bear this Sigil." Kallinvar pressed his hand to his chest. "The day I become that man is the day I lose sight of why I'm fighting in the first place. And since the Blood Moon rose, I have come too close to that. So you will have me as I am or kill me now. Strip the Sigil from my chest, and give it to someone you deem worthy."

Kallinvar clenched his hand into a fist and stared at the warrior god. "I am tired, and I would welcome rest."

Achyron drew a long breath, his expression still and unreadable, and silence hung between them until at last the god said, "It is not your time."

Kallinvar's Sigil pulsed again, the green light flashed across his eyes, and he once more stood in the square in Ardholm, the rain sheeting down over him. His Soulblade was still pressed slightly into the skin of Talia's neck, green mist drifting from its surface.

Kallinvar recalled his Soulblade and stared down at the young woman. "Sister-Captain Ruon, bring Watcher Tallia to the cells. The rest of you, sleep."

Kallinvar turned and walked back towards the great temple, ignoring the murmurs that rose about him. His heart galloped like a horse, and his hands shook.

Arden jolted awake in his bed as Kallinvar slammed open the door.

"Grandmaster, what is it?"

"You are to go to your brother. Tell him I need him here. There are five days left before the Blood Moon sets, and we must be ready. Nothing else matters."

CHAPTER NINETY-SEVEN

LIVES NEVER LIVED

26th Day of the Blood Moon

Salme – Winter, Year 3081 After Doom

Calen stood in the fields beyond Salme's walls, scratching at the scales that ran along the side of Valerys's jaw, watching as the piles of Urak bodies still burned in the morning sun, black smoke billowing relentlessly.

Tivar and Avandeer stood beside him, along with Varthear. The elven Healers had spent the better part of the morning since the sun had risen tending to Varthear's wounds. They had offered to do the same for Valerys and Avandeer, but Calen and Tivar had declined. The injured within the city were beyond count, and any wounds the two dragons had taken would heal with time.

In the distance, halfway between the city gates and where Calen stood, two riders moved towards them.

Valerys gave a low rumble and nudged Calen with his snout.

"Stay close," Calen said, looking away from the burning piles and up into Valerys's eyes. He patted the dragon's snout, and Valerys purred. Valerys lifted his head and nudged Avandeer's jaw before turning and lifting into the air. Both Avandeer and Varthear followed, shouts rising all about as the three dragons swept through the air towards the ocean.

"What are you thinking?" Tivar asked as they watched the three dragons.

"That if we'd not gone north, there would be a lot fewer graves here." Calen looked over past Salme's western walls, where the elves of Lunithír were burying bodies in their hundreds.

Closer, near a copse of trees, men and women lifted scores of bodies onto pyres. Even from a distance Calen knew those dead warriors were Belduarans, given to the flames as all Belduarans were.

From Tarmon's early report, of the fourteen thousand who had marched to Salme's aid, almost a third had perished in the battle. A more thorough count would come soon enough. *Wars are not won. They are ended.* Calen ran his hand through his hair, letting out a long sigh.

"And if we had not, every soul within Tarhelm would have perished. Coren and Aldryn would be dead. Choices cannot be viewed in hindsight. That path leads only to dark places." She clasped her hands behind her back. "That is the burden of being a Draleid. It is seldom that any choice we make will not come at a price."

Calen nodded but didn't speak. He knew what Tivar said was true, but that didn't help. The truth of things was seldom a comfort. These warriors had marched to war with his banner flying above them, and he had not been there. He stood by the decision he had made and knew it was a decision he would have to make again. But that didn't mean the guilt would ever leave his heart.

At that moment though, it was Dann and Rist that swirled in his mind. He knew he had to tell Dann what he had seen, but how and when? Their closest friend was alive. That was a thing he would cherish telling Dann. But the rest… that Rist had not only joined the Circle of Magii but actively killed in their name. Or that the man who was their brother by everything but blood had joined the army that murdered Calen's parents and tortured Rist's own. Or that it was Calen and Dann who had abandoned him to that fate… At that moment, the conversation would have been a selfish one, its only use to keep Calen from suffering with the knowledge alone. Dann needed to know and Calen would tell him, but these few days were for Ylinda. He could give Dann a few days.

"What you did in Aravell," Tivar said, stepping closer and looking out of the burning fields. "Thank you. We've not had a moment to speak on it, but I wanted to say that."

"I didn't do it for you." Calen looked from the Belduaran pyres to meet Tivar's gaze. "I am thankful for everything you've done. You saved our lives when you came to our aid that night. And I truly believe you when you say you want to make things right, but I did it for them," he said, pointing down at the city of Salme. "And for all the others who draw breath in these lands. I could never have faced the Dragonguard alone. Whatever rumours and stories spread, I am but one man and Valerys is but a single dragon. I still wish to rip Farda's heart from his chest, but I will swallow that hate. If it means having you and Avandeer fighting at our side, I will bury my darkest desires, because that is what is required of me."

Tivar's breath misted into the morning air. "I am thankful nonetheless. And I will show that thanks in blood and loyalty. Where do we go from here?"

"While the army recovers, we will fly south to Valtara, and I will send word to Alleron Helmund in Drifaien. First we clear the South. Then we look north. But for now, we will go and light the Belduaran pyres, and we will say prayers over the graves of the dead, and we will mourn with the others. And tonight, we will join the celebration."

"Celebration?"

"In the villages, we do not just mourn the loss of those who leave us, we celebrate their lives. Sometimes that is easier done than others. But tonight we not only celebrate those lives but the fact that the city still stands."

Before Tivar could say another word, the two riders drew closer and crested the slope upon which he and Tivar stood.

"Haem?"

Haem had slipped from his saddle before the horse had even come to a stop, while Erdhardt sat on his steed with a wide grin.

Calen wrapped his arms around his brother, squeezing tight.

"I thought you might be here." Haem pulled away and looked into Calen's eyes. "I'm sorry I've been gone so long, little brother. We have searched for the Heart night and day."

"Your Watchers found nothing amongst Alvira's possessions then?"

Haem shook his head. "Not yet. They don't sleep. They barely eat."

Calen nodded slowly.

Haem fixed his gaze on Calen once more. "I wanted to come to you... I tried... I just—"

"I understand," Calen said. "More than you know. It's not like it used to be, is it? When our choices were our own." Calen pushed the thoughts of Farda from his mind, realising he had something far more important to tell Haem. "Ella is awake."

Haem's eyes widened, his jaw dropping. "Is she all right? Is she—"

"She's all right... better than all right." A broad smile swept across Calen's face, and before he could say another word, Haem pulled him in tighter.

Calen closed his eyes for a moment and just savoured knowing his brother was so close.

"Come," Calen said, eventually pulling away from Haem. "First, we must pay our respects to the dead. But then we will talk, and tonight we can drink and eat with the others." He grabbed Haem's shoulder. "It's good to have you back... I needed you back."

"No, Calen. I came here to tell you that you must take Valerys now and fly with me. Grandmaster Kallinvar has asked that you come to the Temple of Achyron so that we may ready ourselves for the last day of the Blood Moon. It's not far, a day's flight at most."

Calen just stared back at his brother, dumbfounded. "Leave? Now?" He gestured towards Salme and the piles of burning Uraks and the pyres and the graves. "Do you not see this? Are you blind, or have I gone mad?"

"Calen, if Efialtír crosses into this world, there will be more dead than you can imagine. We need to go. None of this matters if The Traitor crosses."

"You sound like your Grandmaster now." Calen stared into Haem's eyes. "These are our people, Haem." He pointed at Erdhardt in the saddle. "*Our* people! The Glade is gone, but this is our home. Jorvill is dead – Dann's mam is dead."

"Ylinda…" The hardness that had set into Haem's eyes vanished in an instant. "Burned alive by cowards who fled on the boats."

"Calen, I didn't know. I'm—"

"I can't leave tonight. What am I if I do that?" Calen drew a slow breath in, trying to calm himself. It wasn't Haem he was mad at. "If I cannot honour the dead, what right have I to ask the living to keep fighting?"

In the back of Calen's mind Valerys's thoughts wrapped around his, the dragon's fire warming him, stilling the pain in his heart. Calen drew a breath to settle himself. "I asked fourteen thousand souls to march hundreds of miles to fight and die in a place far from their homes and the people they love. A third of them died here because I flew north when I could have flown south. I have accepted my choice. It was the choice I needed to make. But I *will not* fly away as though their deaths did not matter. Do you understand me? I will not be that man. They need me here, *Dann* needs me here, and this is where I will be."

Calen wrapped his fingers around Haem's forearm. "And if you are my brother, this is where you will be. I don't care what they told you at that temple. *This* is your home, your people. Erdhardt thought you were dead until I told him last night." Calen gestured up at Erdhardt. "Do as I ask today. Then tomorrow come with me to The Glade. Erdhardt buried Mam and Dad there. I want to plant saplings. Will you do that with me? Then I will fly. You have my word."

"Calen, we can't wait. We need to—"

"One fucking day!" Calen roared, trying desperately to quell the anger that burned within him. "Give me one day. Our parents' bones lie alone beneath the ashes of our home, and you will not come with me? Haem, or Arden… because that's who you are now, isn't it? You're not Haem anymore. You've not been Haem in a long time." Calen knew those words were harsh, but his fury burned too bright to take them back. "I'm going to watch as Valerys lights the Belduaran pyres. I'm going to say the Blessings of the Gods over the graves. And I'm going to drink and eat with those who were lucky enough to survive. Tomorrow I will go to The Glade, and I will bring saplings to plant where Mam and Dad rest. If you are still here, then Tivar and I will answer your master's call."

Calen didn't wait for an answer. He gestured to Tivar, whose face showed a recognition of his pain, and set off down the slope towards the city, nodding to Erdhardt as he went.

When night fell, Calen stood outside The Rusty Shell with a tankard of ale in his hand that he'd not touched and a weight in his heart that scratched at him. The streets were full, illuminated by wood-filled braziers and lanterns suspended between the buildings by lengths of chain. Even in the small space outside the inn, at least five different songs were being played by five different bards, and not one of them was as bad as the bard from The Two Barges in Milltown, who had sounded like a drunk man strumming a cat.

"The people of Belduar were honoured to see Valerys light the pyres," Tarmon said, his arms folded, a cup held firmly in his right hand. Much like Calen, the man hadn't touched his drink. "It was appreciated beyond measure."

"It was our honour." Calen stared across the wide street to where Dann stood with Tharn, Lyrei, Therin, Erik, and a young girl who'd seen fifteen or sixteen summers. All Calen wanted to do was take his friend and go drink by the water. They didn't have to talk. Sitting and staring out at the ocean would have been enough. But he needed to give Dann his space. He would be there whenever Dann needed him, as Dann had always been for him.

"Warden." Two men and three women approached and gave a slight bow before passing on and entering The Rusty Shell.

"It is strange," Vaeril said, sipping at his drink.

"What is?" Tarmon asked.

"To see so many souls from so many worlds all in one place."

Calen couldn't help but agree. Elves of Lunithír, Vaelen, and Ardurän laughed and drank and danced next to men and women of the villages and warriors of the Dracurïn who had come from all about the continent. Even a handful of dwarves walked among them.

"Stranger still to see Lorian soldiers." Calen narrowed his gaze at the men and women who all stood together on the far side of the street. Most wore loose shirts and trousers, but some were still clad in the black and red leather of Loria.

"I've heard tell there are two Battlemages amongst their number," Tarmon said.

"You have heard true." A dark-haired man of middling years stepped through the crowd and inclined his head to Calen and the others, a silver-trimmed black cloak about his shoulders. "I am Exarch Dorman of the Imperial Battlemages of the Forty-Third Army."

Every impulse in Calen's body told him to snap the man's neck, and in the distance Valerys roared, causing gasps to spread through the street as men and women lifted their heads to the sky.

As Calen stared at Dorman, who hadn't lifted his gaze, memories of Artim Valdock in that cell flickered in his mind. Nails being ripped from his fingers, ribs broken, blood dripping. A second roar from Valerys brought his mind back, and he steadied his breathing. "How did the Forty-Third Army find itself in Salme?"

"We were detached to aid in the relief of Camylin, but we were caught in an ambush and fell back through the villages." The man took a step closer, but the moment he did both Tarmon and Vaeril stepped between Dorman and Calen. Tarmon placed a hand on the mage's chest, and Vaeril's sword was half-free of its scabbard.

Dorman looked down at Tarmon's hand and gave a subdued laugh. "We have bled as much as anyone here."

He attempted to push Tarmon's hand down, but it stayed planted like a rock.

"And will you be staying here, Exarch Dorman? Or will you be leaving to rejoin the imperial armies?"

The question made Dorman visibly uncomfortable.

Calen gestured for Tarmon and Vaeril to stand down, moving close enough that he could smell the stew on Dorman's breath. He searched the man's eyes.

"Don't worry. You fought here and you defended my home, and so while you are within these walls, you are not my enemy." As Calen spoke, heavy wingbeats thumped in the air, and every head in the street turned to the sky. "If you choose to remain here and defend these people, live off this land, you will remain not my enemy. But as soon as your soldiers march from here, bearing that black lion on your chest, you are a threat to everything I hold dear and I will treat you accordingly."

Movement behind the Exarch drew Calen's attention, and he saw a face he never thought he would see again.

"Exarch, I do not have fond memories of Lorian mages. But I will say thank you for protecting my home and the people I love. If you'll excuse me."

Calen stepped past Exarch Dorman, Tarmon and Vaeril following close behind as he weaved through the crowd. He stopped when he found himself standing before Anya Gritten.

"You still smell like cherry blossoms." As soon as the words left his lips, Calen realised how much of an idiot he was. "I didn't mean… That was creepy, wasn't it? I'm sorry, I…"

He let his words fade as Anya threw her arms around him and squeezed him so tight he thought she might pop one of his ribs. For a moment, he stood there still as a tree, until a gentle push from Valerys in his mind told him to return the embrace.

When Anya finally released him, tears wet her cheeks. She brushed them aside, laughing. "Sorry… I just never thought…" She stopped herself and shook her head. "It's really good to see you, Calen." She gave him a broad smile. "You look taller."

"It's the boots."

Anya laughed, and Calen's heart suddenly felt lighter. Gods, he had missed her laugh. "This is Tarmon Hoard and Vaeril Ilyin, two of my closest friends."

Anya scrunched her brow and leaned a little to the left, pulling in her top lip as she laughed. "Are they now?"

"What?" Calen turned to see Vaeril and Tarmon had abandoned him and were looking back with shit-eating grins as they pushed through the crowd.

"Would you like to walk with me?"

"I'd love to."

TARMON FOLDED HIS ARMS AND just watched and listened with joy in his heart as Thannon, Origal, Nayce, Torka, and Leon told jokes and stories, ale flowing.

He and Vaeril had left Calen with the woman who clearly needed his time more than they did, and Tarmon brought Vaeril to meet the eight Belduaran Kingsguard who still drew breath within the city. Though it stung to know their number had been much larger only months before, it warmed his heart to see them again.

"You should have seen it, Lord Captain," Thannon said, puffing out his cheeks, ale sloshing in his cup. "Fellhammer just stood in the centre of them all, and the Uraks faced him one by one as though it were some kind of game. And one by one he crushed their skulls with that beast of a weapon. I've heard rumour he suckled on a bear's teat as a babe."

Tarmon had simply watched as Erdhardt Hammersmith had quietly walked up behind Thannon and stood there the entire time while Thannon wove his tale to the crowd around them – the Silver Wolves, he'd heard they were called, named after the cloaks they wore.

"You leave my mother out of this," Erdhardt said, slamming his hands down onto Thannon's shoulders and lowering his voice to a whisper. "And I'll leave this out of your mother."

Thannon's eyes bulged, and he leapt forwards. "You fucking son of a donkey-fucker."

Erdhardt and the others burst out laughing, and the mountain of a man clapped Thannon on the shoulders. Seeing this 'Fellhammer', Tarmon understood something of where Calen and Dann's strength of character came from.

"Have any of you seen Dahlen?" Erdhardt asked.

"He's at the bloodhouse," Nayce answered, his tone growing sombre. "An Urak snapped young Conal's arms. The elven Healers have done what they can but… there's no certainty he'll see the next sunrise."

Erdhardt nodded, then raised his cup. The others did the same and drank deeply.

As the drinks flowed, the jokes continued and the stories grew louder and more ridiculous. And as Thannon told tales of the great battle for the city, he said something Tarmon wished he hadn't.

"And now this Draleid prances around like he owns the place, after we've bled for months to keep the Uraks from slaughtering us all."

The other voices grew quiet, and Erdhardt flashed Tarmon a look.

"What?" Thannon asked, downing the remnants of his cup, looking at the faces around him. "He flies in on his big fucking dragon and expects us all to bow and nod and act as though he's actually done something. He wasn't here. He didn't stand by me, or you," he said, pointing his cup at Nayce. "I'm just sick of all these kings, and elders, and Draleid, and the fucking Lorians… They just do whatever they please, tell us to go die in some battle or leave us to starve like that little fuckwit Daymon."

Tarmon clenched his jaw, teeth grinding. "Thannon, that's enough."

"Arthur was a man I could follow. But that Daymon was a self-righteous prick. And what made him more than we were? Blood? A trinket on his head? This Draleid is no different. How is he anything better than the ones who burned this world in the first place? He doesn't give a shit about us."

Tarmon stepped forwards, but before he could do anything, Dann came striding from nowhere and slammed his fist into Thannon's face.

Thannon stumbled and fell, but Dann was on him in a heartbeat.

"Say that again," Dann roared, grabbing Thannon's collar. He punched the man in the face a second time, Thannon's cheek bursting. "Say another fucking word like that about Calen again and I will fucking gut you like a fish." Dann grabbed Thannon's shirt with both fists, dragging the man's face closer to his. "You're not fit to lick the shit from his boots. You know nothing."

Dann let Thannon drop back to the dirt, then stormed off into the crowd, swatting away Erdhardt's hand.

Thannon scrambled back to his feet, raging, fury in his eyes.

"Stand down," Tarmon said, grabbing Thannon by the shoulders.

"Stand down? Lord Captain, I'm going to fucking—"

"I am *not* your Lord Captain any longer. Stand down, Thannon, or I will put you down."

Thannon glared at Tarmon, then shoved him and started after Dann. Tarmon grabbed the man's shirt, spun him, and drove a fist into his face.

The former Kingsguard hit the ground like a sack of stones.

"Did you have to hit him so hard?" Erdhardt asked, standing next to Tarmon.

"I don't hit soft." Tarmon crouched down over Thannon, gently slapping the man's cheek until Thannon looked at him. "You've had too much ale. You said things a Kingsguard should be ashamed to say. Get up, go to bed, and tomorrow we'll forget it all."

"I'm not a Kingsguard anymore," Thannon said, spitting blood into the dirt, his words slurred.

"No, but you're better than this. Are we agreed?"

Thannon looked at the ground, then back to Tarmon, nodding.

Tarmon lifted his friend to his feet and passed him off to two of the others to take to bed.

"Forgive him, Lord Captain," Origal said. "King Daymon did a lot of harm."

"I am not your Lord Captain, and I know what Daymon did. He was only a boy. He should never have had to wear that crown alone."

Origal nodded, and Tarmon clapped him on the shoulder.

"I'm not your Lord Captain, Origal, but I am always your brother."

"Always," Origal agreed.

"I thought he was your friend," Erdhardt said, gesturing after Thannon.

"He is."

"If you do that to your friends, what do you do to your enemies?"

"My enemy wouldn't have gotten back up."

Erdhardt rested a hand on Tarmon's shoulder. "Come, I've always wanted to see if I could outdrink an elf and a Belduaran Kingsguard."

"You have?"

"No," Erdhardt answered. "But now I'm curious."

As CALEN AND ANYA WALKED through the streets of Salme, for the first time in a very, very long time, his mind fell quiet. He could still see Valerys as the dragon lay in the fields beyond with his head resting on Avandeer's side and his tail curled around Varthear's leg, but all he was focused on was Anya's voice.

She had become a healer, like his mother. Someone who saved lives instead of taking them. That might have been him had he never left The Glade. They walked and talked until they reached the docks, the sounds of music and dancing echoing from the city behind them.

They removed their shoes and sat with their feet dangling over the edge, staring out at the ocean.

Anya took his arm and looked down at the silver tattooed runes that ringed his forearms. "What are they?"

Calen looked into Anya's green eyes, then down at the markings. "Dreskyr mit huartan. Dreskyr mit hnokle. Bante er vi, measter og osvarthe."

Anya stared in wonder as the runes glowed with a purple light. Calen drew a sharp breath, feeling his armour pulse in his mind.

"They are Jotnar runes. They bind my armour to me. *Protect my heart. Protect my bones. Bound are we, master and oath.*"

Anya shook her head, smiling, then stared out at the water again.

"What?" Calen asked.

"I always imagined we'd fall in love, get married, and decide to have six children until we realised three was probably enough."

"You did?" Calen asked, laughing.

"Mm-hmm." Anya nodded, putting her hands on her knees. "We'd build a home on the edge of The Glade, with a big garden for all the flowers. You'd hunt with Faenir, because let's face it, you never really loved the forge. I'd start making soap with my mam, but eventually I'd learn to be a healer – Freis would teach me." A tear rolled down her cheek. "It was going to be a good life," she said. "Simple, but good."

"Simple sounds great."

"Is it all right to miss a life you never had?"

"I do every day." Calen rested a hand on Anya's knee, and she leaned over and laid her head on his shoulder. "Every day."

"Can we just sit here a while?"

Calen nodded. "I'd like that."

He drew a long breath tinged with the scent of cherry blossoms and closed his eyes. There would be no simple life, not anymore, but he could pretend for a few more hours.

CHAPTER NINETY-EIGHT

THE DEMON IN THE DETAILS

26th Day of the Blood Moon

The High Tower, Berona – Winter, Year 3081 After Doom

ain hammered down, echoing in the courtyard at the foot of the High Tower, drumming off Garramon's cloak.

They had returned to the city early that morning and provided a report to Fane. But the man had seemed more curious about Eltoar and Helios's whereabouts than the losses sustained in the fighting. Even the death of the two Dragonguard had seemed of little surprise to him. Garramon had gone to speak to his friend in private later, but he'd found the chambers empty.

Mages, apprentices, acolytes, and initiates of all affinities ran about the yard like headless chickens, trying desperately not to get saturated in the rain. Garramon walked slowly, the rain cold against his face and hands. When he had things to think on, Garramon enjoyed walking in the rain. The constant slap of rain on his hood was like the crackling of a fire in his mind. It calmed him, allowed his thoughts to drift.

At any other time, the battle at the Firnin Mountains would have been the thing that plagued him. He would have revisited it in his mind again and again, trying to understand, trying to learn, trying to see what might have been done differently. But it was not the battle that plagued his thoughts, it was Rist.

The young man had barely said a word since the battle. Seeing his friend, learning the truth, had broken him a little. And Trusil's death had affected him deeply. Rist might have been a quiet young man, may have seemed cold or distant to some, but Garramon knew different. Rist cared deeply for everyone and everything around him. He was a kind soul. The moment Garramon had handed over Trusil's reins to Rist, he had seen how much the young man would love that horse.

Drawing his hood back, Garramon stepped from the rain and through the doorway set into the wall that ringed the yard. He walked along the austere corridors until he found the staircase he was looking for and descended. The Craftsmages that ran the print houses – the Exucendi –preferred to keep their workshops below ground to avoid unnecessary distractions.

The stairs dropped some forty feet into the ground, the interwoven corridors carved with the Spark. Slow-burning oil lanterns sat in alcoves evenly spaced along the smooth stone walls, while iron-grated vents provided air flow. The network of tunnels and chambers beneath the Circle was far more intricate than the dungeons kept by the Inquisition, but Garramon could have walked them in his sleep. The elves had always been fond of subterranean systems and had worked them beneath nearly every major city under elven rule.

His steps echoed in the empty corridor as he walked, only a handful of young acolytes and porters crossing his path.

Garramon stepped through the corridor on his left and out into the antechamber that led to the Exucendi house of Berona. He pushed open the gilded door on the other side of the chamber and stepped into a cavernous hall ornamented with tapestries and banners woven from the finest Narvonan silk. Everything was gold. The doorhandles, the sconces, the banding on the tables – everything. And what precious little wasn't gold was rubies or sapphires or emeralds. The print houses of the Exucendi may as well have been royal houses themselves with the amount of coin that flowed through their coffers. Like-for-like perfect recreations of entire books, journals, manuscripts, and whatever else was needed were a rare and costly thing. And Fane kept the Beronan Exucendi well cared for. The preservation – and curation – of history was of great import.

He nodded at the porters who occupied the main hall and to the guards posted at every door. In six centuries, Garramon had not known of a single instance when anyone had been stupid enough to attempt a robbery of the Beronan Exucendi, but they retained a solid guard nonetheless.

"Exarch Kalinim." The guard posted outside Exucendi Adama's workshop inclined his head to Garramon, opening the door before him.

The workshop was as meticulous and organised as Rist's chambers, everything neatly placed where it would best suit its function. The entire right wall was an enormous bookcase that stretched some thirty feet long and fifteen feet high, blending into the vaulted ceiling above through arches of worked gold. The left side of the room was divided into two sections. One was dominated by open cabinets with large glass vessels of various inks and solutions and what seemed to be an endless supply of top-quality archival paper, the kind always used when important books were copied and bound. The other section contained a vast array of trinkets that Garramon was sure had absolutely nothing to do with books whatsoever. But Adama was known as a bit of a collector.

"They say that's the sword of Harken Holdark himself." Adama emerged from another door on the far side of the chamber, pushing his glasses back up onto the bridge of his nose. He stared up at an enormous greatsword with a bear head pommel. "I had to trade two kidneys for that."

Garramon raised an eyebrow. "Don't you need those?"

"They weren't mine." Adama stared at the sword for a moment longer, then raised a finger. "I have two pages left to transfer, and your books will be ready. Come, come. My apologies, I have been a bit distracted of late."

The Exucendi walked Garramon over to a bench that was just as meticulously arranged as the rest of the workshop. Inks, tools, books, and various binding materials were all organised in specific sections. The man stood beside a well-worn leather chair, two books laid out on the bench before him. He slid an enormous glass vessel of ink across the smooth stone bench and removed the lid.

"It will only be a moment," Adama said, once more pushing his glasses up the bridge of his nose. "As with most crafts, what you're paying for is the time it took to perfect the skill, not simply the time it takes to perform the task."

The Spark flowed from the man in a gentle ripple, threads of Air, Water, Fire, Earth, and Spirit whirling about his hand, each as thin as a strand of a spider's webbing. He wove the threads of Air, Water, and Earth into the vessel of ink and pulled a sheet of rippling dark liquid into the air, thinning it out so it looked like an almost solid pane of black glass. At the same time, the man wove threads of Spirit into the first book and onto the blank page of the second.

"What do threads of Spirit do?" Garramon whispered, looking over Adama's shoulder.

"They help my mind focus on what my eyes cannot see. The words, the inflections of the original penstrokes, the character and art in the craft. The near-imperceptible characteristics that make something unique. Now please, quiet."

The man created a triangle of Spirit between the two books and the ink. As he lowered the sheet of floating ink onto the second page, it thinned and pulled apart, creating hundreds of shapes: letters and punctuation marks. He pressed the ink onto the blank pages, weaving the threads of each element through them until they were set.

After a moment, the threads evaporated, and Adama closed both books. He set the newly inked book to the side, then pulled a second from a chest beneath the bench, laying them both in front of Garramon.

"A strange request," Adama said as he ran his fingers over the deep red leather atop the book closest to him. "*A History of Magii,* by Gandal Frendor, and *Druids, a Magic Lost,* by Duran Linold. There are not many who would pay my rates for books in such wide circulation."

"There are not many Exucendi who still hand bind and dye their own leather from Khergani goathide. Your work is worth the coin, Adama."

"I am pleased you think so, Exarch Kalinim. You put great care into these. Someone special?"

Garramon nodded. "My son."

The door creaked open on the other side of the room, and Garramon was surprised to see Brother Pirnil stepping into the workshop. The man looked like a ghost of himself, pale as bone, eyes sunken, clothes stained and torn. He bit at his lip as he walked, a persistent tremor in his hands.

Pirnil didn't even seem to notice Garramon. "Adama," he snapped. "Where is my commission?"

"I have it here, Lector Pirnil." Adama gave Garramon a look that let him know Brother Pirnil was not a particularly welcome client. The Exucendi bent down to another chest beneath the bench.

"If every detail is not perfect this time, I swear I will have you strung up by order of the emperor. Do you understand, Adama? *Perfect.* The illustrations could have been copied by a child. I was told you were the best the Exucendi had to offer, but I am yet to be impressed." Pirnil moved so he stood beside Garramon, still not seeming to notice Garramon even stood in the room.

"So you've told me, Lector." The man emerged with two thick black leather books, not dissimilar to the one Garramon had seen Fane with. "Here they are," he said, handing the books to Pirnil. "And my sincere apologies for the wait. It has been a busy period."

"Your apologies are not needed," Pirnil snapped, pulling the books close to his chest. "You will not be paid for tardiness and sloppy craftsmanship. You can consider this book a tribute to ensure the emperor allows you to keep your fingers. When I call again, Brother Adama, I will expect better."

Pirnil turned and strode from the room, muttering to himself as he did.

Garramon raised an eyebrow at Adama.

"He has a seal from the emperor himself. Waves the damn thing around like a sword." Adama handed the newly bound and inked books to Garramon. "He came to two of my colleagues first. They have subsequently vanished. I would like not to join them."

When Adama made to offer the original copies, Garramon waved a hand. "Would you keep them for me? Just for a few nights."

Adama agreed, and Garramon left the workshop as swiftly as he could without making a scene. He followed Brother Pirnil from the Exucendi antechamber and out into the tunnels beyond.

Pirnil was so absorbed in his own thoughts, Garramon didn't even have to pretend not to be following him. The man took turn after turn, ascending and descending staircase after staircase to a point that even Garramon wasn't quite sure where he was going. Eventually the man stopped at a thick iron door. Pirnil pulled a key from his pocket with his free hand, balancing the two thick books in the other. He unlocked the door and slipped through.

Garramon flitted across the stone and jammed his boot in the door before it closed.

The chamber within was enormous. The air clung to Garramon's throat, thick with the pungent smell of death and char and burning. He pinched his nostrils as he stepped into the windowless room. Stout candles sat all about, lodged into piles of melted wax, providing the barest touch of warmth.

Wooden benches lined the walls on either side of the room, each fitted with straps and buckles and occupied by bodies in various stages of mutilation, flies swarming about them. The sight on its own would have turned Garramon's stomach, but combined with the putrid stench, he had no choice but to swallow the vomit that flowed into his mouth.

"What in The Saviour's name is this place?" He stepped further into the dark, desolate chamber, his hand over his mouth.

Pirnil was perched over a desk at the far end of the room. He scribbled furiously into a journal while Garramon approached the body closest to the door. It was an older man. His hair was brittle and white, while his frame still held a notable amount of lean muscle. The flesh on his arms and legs had turned black, and his fingerbones had broken the skin, snapped and twisted at odd angles. Rough-carved runes marked a large portion of his body. The runes looked like those Pirnil had inscribed into the candidates who had volunteered to become hosts for the Chosen. But if that were true, why was Brother Pirnil still carrying out his work… and why did he have Fane's seal?

What have you done, old friend?

Garramon lifted his gaze to Brother Pirnil, who still hadn't even noticed Garramon had entered the room.

A noise drew Garramon's attention to the cot at Brother Pirnil's left. He approached to find a young man strapped to the table with a rag stuffed in his mouth. Judging by the loll of his head and his drooped eyelids, he had consumed enough Altweid Blood to dull a horse.

Garramon drew a sharp breath and rolled his shoulders back. "Brother Pirnil," he called, imbuing his voice with the same sense of authority he had wielded as the Arbiter all those years ago. "The emperor demands a report."

"What?" Pirnil twisted to look at Garramon, his eyes wide. "Garramon Kalinim? What are you doing here? You're not supposed—"

"Do you truly believe you have the power to question me, Drakus? The Arbiter is above questions from the likes of you." He moved closer to Pirnil, looking down at the notes the man was scribbling. "The emperor has sent me to procure an update from you, seeing as you are behind schedule. I would advise not wasting my time."

The man stared back at Garramon for a moment, clearly trying to decide what his wisest course of action was. But Garramon knew a thing or two about men like Pirnil. All cruel men were cowards at heart. A fear of their own pain led them to inflict it on others.

"I… I am… I am ready as he asked. The journals have been copied, and I am almost certain I have the runeset he has asked for, but I—"

"But what? Do you question the emperor?"

"No, no…" The man's hands trembled, but not from fear. Garramon knew the signs of excess Essence consumption. It was like a drug. The pale skin, the dark eyes, the short temper, and the constant state of panic and paranoia. He had seen it a thousand times over, particularly around the time of The Fall and the years after. Fane had made sure to curb such usages since. But clearly Pirnil was an exception.

"No," Pirnil muttered again. "I don't. I am simply trying to say the runeset he asked for is not optimal. There is a weakness in it. I cannot understand why—"

"You do not need to understand why, Drakus. Have you made your concerns clear in your notes?" Garramon nodded towards the man's scribblings.

"Yes, I have shown quite clearly that there is a stronger runeset and outlined my reasoning." He raised a finger in the air, seeming to entirely forget that Garramon shouldn't be there at all. "One more specimen." Pirnil glanced towards the semi-conscious young man strapped to the bench nearest him. "The same relative height and age as the candidate. I will inscribe the optimal runeset and make detailed notes. I believe that the emperor will see the error of his ways." He immediately looked to Garramon. "Not... not the error, but simply the miscalculation."

"Those are the same thing, Pirnil."

Pirnil moved across the room and opened a large chest sat atop an old wooden desk. The red glow of Essence shone over Pirnil's face as he opened the lid and removed a pulsing gemstone. "You can inform him that I will bring the report myself within the hour. We will be ready to move to the Sea of Stone as soon as the Heart is found. Please, step out of the way."

Pirnil pushed past Garramon and squeezed the young man's cheeks, moving his head left and right, inspecting him.

"Why has he taken so much Altweid Blood?"

"It makes them easier to handle. Now let me return to my work, and I will provide the report myself."

"I thought all hosts must volunteer for the—"

"Not in this case!" the man roared, a sudden rage blazing through him. The whites of his eyes had taken a reddish hue. "Now get out!"

Pirnil turned back to the young man, humming to himself as though Garramon had already left. The man had completely lost his mind.

Essence pulsed from Pirnil as he tapped into the gemstone in his hand.

Garramon looked down at the young man strapped to the chair and grabbed Pirnil's arm.

The man rounded on him, raging. "What do you—"

Garramon grabbed Pirnil by the throat and slammed him against the wall, the gemstone dropping from the man's grasp. He wrapped his fingers tighter around Pirnil's throat. Garramon already knew the answer to the question he was about to ask, but he needed to ask it. "Who is the candidate?"

"Your apprentice," Pirnil choked. "That little southern wretch." Even with Garramon's hand wrapped around his throat, Pirnil's lips twisted into a grin. "Fane thinks he is perfect. But I know he doesn't have the strength to accept The Saviour into his body. I will watch fondly as he is ripped apart from the inside out, and Fane will finally understand that he himself is the only true candidate. You will see, Garramon."

"You will see nothing. Not ever again." Garramon wove threads of Air and Fire about himself, then lashed them across Brother Pirnil, a hundred at a time. The man screamed and thrashed, but Garramon held him in place. "How does it feel, Drakus, to have your cruelty inflicted upon you?"

Garramon ripped and burned the flesh from Pirnil's body, searing through his tattered robes. "Scars over time can build a man, Drakus. But you don't have time. I will not let you come for my family again."

"I didn't," Pirnil screamed. "I never! Agh!"

"For every scar you gave Rist, I will give you a hundred. For every drop of pain you have inflicted on these poor souls, I will give you a thousand. This ends here."

"But the emperor… The Saviour! We are so close!"

"I can't believe you're the one I'm saying this to." The acrid smell of fresh-burnt flesh slithered into Garramon's nostrils as he held Pirnil against the wall, thousands of cuts lacing the man's body. "But it has taken me four hundred years to realise that I cannot place the will of a god above the lives of the flesh and blood, living people that I love. No… not that I cannot, but that I *will* not. Burn in the void, Drakus Pirnil. It is all you have ever deserved."

Garramon pulled threads of each elemental strand, weaving them into his fist until a shimmering blue nithral formed in his hand. He drove the blade into Pirnil's chest, watching as the light went out in the man's eyes.

He released his nithral and let Pirnil's body drop, then unbuckled the straps that held the young man in place and pulled the rag from his mouth. "Can you stand?"

Barely a grunt escaped his lips.

Garramon moved over to Pirnil's bench and grabbed the black leatherbound book he had been scribbling in, along with the one he had just had copied. With all four books stacked in one hand, Garramon hauled the young man upright and carried him from the chamber.

ALL BROKEN THINGS STARTED WITH tiny cracks. Some grew quickly, with little time to fix them. Others happened slowly and were never noticed until it was too late.

There were two broken things in the library that night: Rist and his understanding of the world.

Rist sat in a small nook on the top floor of the truly enormous Beronan Library, a curtain drawn. The Circle had its own library, but he'd wanted to be alone. Splayed out on the table before him was every letter he had ever received from his parents. He had spent hours going over them. Calen's words echoed in his mind.

"Rist, your mam and dad are alive. They're safe. They tortured them, Rist, but I broke them free."

Those words had sounded again and again and again. Even when Rist slept. They gnawed at him from the inside out. What had Calen meant?

Rist dropped his elbows to the table and clasped the back of his head.

Calen was the Draleid. Calen was the one who had burned Kingspass, the one who had incited the rebellion. How was that even possible? Nothing made sense. Nothing.

Pieces were missing. How could he solve a puzzle with the pieces missing? He needed to speak to Garramon. There were things the man hadn't told him, and he knew it. He'd always known it, but he simply hadn't realised quite how large those things were. He knew if he asked Garramon a straight question, the man would answer him. He would.

Where are my parents? Have you lied to me?

The curtain slid open, and Rist found himself staring up at Fane Mortem. Every fibre of his body told him to grab the letters and hide them, but it was too late.

"You and I are alike in so many ways, Rist." The emperor dropped himself into the armchair on the other side of the table as though he were Rist's oldest friend in the world. "The library was always where I went when I sought peace… or answers." He glanced down at the letters on the table. He smiled. "I wish I had parents as dedicated as yours to send so many letters. Mine sent me off to The Order when I was barely old enough to read. There was coin, you see, as reimbursement. I didn't see them again until I was… oh, perhaps in my twenty-sixth year? Cherish them, Rist. A mother and father like that are worth holding on to."

"Emperor Mortem…" Rist tried his hardest not to stare down at the letters. "I wasn't expecting to see you here."

"I'm not staying long. A little birdie told me you were here, and I just wanted to check in. I saw Garramon after his return from the battle, but not you. Azrim reported to me that you showed a great deal of strength in dealing with the Draleid. Perhaps it is time we see if you are fit to join the ranks of the Arcarians. What do you think?"

"Already? Now? Tonight?"

Fane stared at him a moment, tilting his head to the side, then smiled. "No, not tonight. But I believe we are very close." Fane leaned across the table. "You have the power within you, Rist. I felt it from the first day I met you. You have the power to change the world, just like I did, just like Garramon. I will guide you."

The curtain moved once again, and this time a Praetorian in ruby red plate stood in the nook's opening. He bowed to Fane. "Emperor, Helios has returned. Commander Daethana has sent a message."

"Good." Fane looked from the Praetorian to Rist. "It appears, Rist, that our stars are aligning. I will find you in the morning. There is much to talk about."

As Fane stood, Rist couldn't help but ask the question. "Do you find there is power in a name, Emperor Mortem?"

Fane looked at Rist with a raised eyebrow.

"I only ask because you used mine four times."

The man stared back at Rist for what felt like an eternity before giving a half-laugh and pulling the curtain closed behind him as he left.

Rist sat up straight, his heart thumping. Calen's words replayed in his mind once more. *"Your mam and dad are alive…"*

"Mam and Dad," Rist whispered. He flicked through the letters in his mind, falling all the way back to the first.

'We hope they are treating you all right up there. A mage? Your father had to read that part of your letter to me four times before I stopped calling him a liar.'

"Father…" Rist whispered. His mam rarely used the word 'father', only when she was mad at Lasch or Rist. The thought had come to him when Fane had said that 'a mother and father like that are worth holding on to'.

His mam had signed off the letter with *All our love, Mam and Dad*. But then she'd used the word 'father'… It was a small thing. Possibly nothing at all. But… it niggled at him.

He found the letter amongst those scattered across the table. Then something else struck him, and he lined up all the pages next to each other. In his mind he placed letters atop one another. 'A's and 'P's and 'F's from each letter.

His heart stopped and every hair on his body pricked.

"She never wrote these…"

Rist's throat suddenly felt dry as sand. How had he never seen it before? The writing was almost identical to his mam's, but as close as it was, each letter was just slightly different to the last. The inflections and subtle sweeps of the 'W's and 'R's… everything. The more letters he layered over the other in his mind, the deeper the chill set into his heart.

These letters had not been written by his mam, but by someone who had spent a long time learning to imitate Elia Havel's hand. Within a single letter, it was completely unnoticeable. But when set side by side and atop one another, the minute mistakes were obvious in their differences. Each attempt was near perfect but a failure in a different way.

Rist's hands began to tremble, and his breaths grew short. "No, no, no… I…"

He inhaled deeply, trying to calm himself, then exhaled slowly. He should have seen it, but he had been too distracted.

A part of him wanted to go to Garramon, to confront the man, to find one last shred of hope that he was just seeing something, that he was delusional.

But he didn't need to. Rist knew he was right. In his bones he knew. But one thing he didn't know was if Garramon knew.

Rist settled himself as best he could, folded each of the letters neatly, and placed them into his satchel before sprinting from the library.

CHAPTER NINETY-NINE

THE HANGED MAN

26th Day of the Blood Moon

Lake Berona – Winter, Year 3081 After Doom

Not a single cloud blemished the pure dark sky as Eltoar looked over Lake Berona. He stared into the depths of the black water, seeing Lyina's and Karakes's broken bodies in his mind. Behind him, Helios lay with his head resting by the lake's edge, a sorrow like no other drifting between them.

Everything they had ever loved in the world was dead or dying, the dragons themselves on the edge of extinction. And it was Eltoar's actions that had put them there. He could tell himself – as he had for centuries – that he was only doing what needed to be done, that he had made a choice, and that he had known it would never be easy.

But for a long time, in the depths of his heart, Eltoar had known he should have fought harder, should have convinced Fane there was another way, should have made Alvira see the truth. Fane had always had a way with words, a way of making his own path seem the only logical one. The truth was, the day Eltoar's blade took Alvira's head, it doomed the dragons as well, it doomed everything.

Everything had changed with the stroke of that blade. The entire world.

He could hear Salara in the back of his mind. *"She loved you, and you murdered her."*

Eltoar stared down into the dark lake, the light of the Blood Moon reflecting on its surface.

"I loved her too," he whispered to the wind. So many nights he had dreamt of what would have happened if he had stayed his blade… if he had lifted Alvira to her feet and taken a different path. But such things were the dreams of children. The past could not be changed. He had made his choice and now was reaping the consequences. But he could still make a difference. He could still save the dragons.

Helios lifted his head as the sound of crunching dirt broke the swashing of the lake's waves, followed by the nicker of a horse.

Eltoar drew a sharp breath and let it out slowly. This was another moment of clear and true choice that would affect the very fabric of the world. This time he would make the right one, no matter the cost.

Fane stopped his horse by the base of the rock upon which Eltoar stood and dismounted. The horse shook and snorted as Helios leaned closer.

"Shhh…" Fane whispered. "Be still."

Eltoar could feel the Spark rippling from his old friend as Fane calmed the horse with threads of Spirit.

"I received your message," Fane said as he stepped onto the rock beside Eltoar, black and red robes trailing. When Eltoar didn't answer, Fane spoke again. "I am truly sorry for your loss, old friend. I know there are no words that can bring you comfort, and so I will not try. This war has taken so many lives. With Elkenrim and Merchant's Reach lost, that is another half a million souls sent into The Saviour's light."

"And yet still you sit behind Berona's walls." Eltoar knew it was unwise to provoke Fane, but he was tired and he cared little for anything bar the choice that needed to be made.

"You know well why I do."

"Mmm. You search for this Heart of Blood. The vessel with the strength to cross Efialtír into this mortal world."

"I do. And I believe my search is finally at an end, is it not?"

Eltoar closed his eyes and gave a short sigh. "How long have you known?"

"I have suspected for some time now. But I was not absolutely certain until you asked me to meet you here." Fane looked up at Helios, who now loomed over the pair of them, the crimson light of the moon glinting off his scales. "Why?"

"I made a choice."

"You didn't trust me."

"I trusted you enough to follow you down this path. And I trusted you enough to call you here."

"You betrayed me." Fane clasped his hands behind his back, and Eltoar could feel a shift in Helios, a pressure building within him.

"I saw the power within that vessel. It was the kind of power no mortal should wield."

"You took it as insurance, Eltoar, as leverage for a day like today. Do not play coy or feign honour. I have not the patience for it. I am assuming you called me here because you have decided to return it?"

"And if I did… what is to stop you killing me the moment I give you what you want?"

"Do you think so little of me? That I would kill my oldest friend?"

"I think you would try."

Fane gave a laugh at that, a genuine laugh, the kind that had been so commonplace before the man had come back from Mar Dorul all those years ago. "Why now?"

Eltoar turned to face Fane, staring into the man's eyes. "I need you to be honest with me."

"Am I not always?"

"No. You are not even honest with yourself, old friend. I have followed you because I trust your heart. But your web of plans and your gilded words obscure the truth even from you. So I need you to be plain, and I need you to be honest. Can you do that?"

Fane nodded, staring back out at the lake. "There are few left living in this world who would speak to me with the honesty that you do. It is… refreshing." He ran his tongue across his lips. "Ask me what you will."

"If you had the Heart in your hands right now, could you breathe life back into the eggs? No maybes, or ifs, or convoluted stories. Yes or no."

The waves lapped against the rocks, mirroring a rumble resonating in Helios's chest.

"Yes."

Helios shifted in place, his heart quickening. Memories flooded from the dragon's mind into Eltoar's, memories of skies filled with dragons, of tiny hatchlings crawling from eggs, of fledglings finding their fire.

"And how am I to know you are not lying to me, simply because you believe I can give you the Heart?"

Fane grabbed Eltoar's arm and pulled him so they faced each other head-on. "You and I are brothers, Eltoar Daethana. I have bled for you and you for me. We sacrificed everything – *everything* – so that this world might see better days. When the eggs stopped hatching, my heart bled. That those gods, those monsters who pretend they care for this world would wreak such pain and horror… They are not fit to be called gods. They left this world to rot, to consume itself." He leaned closer. "I can bring the dragons back. Efialtír can *bring* the dragons back. On my life, on my heart, I swear it. But not without the Heart of Blood."

Eltoar stared back at Fane, his heart pounding. Helios stood at his full height now, talons raking the dirt, his emotions swirling through their shared soul. There was nothing else in this world worth anything except for the eggs. The eggs were their greatest shame, their greatest guilt… If those unborn souls could be given back the life that had been stolen from them, that was all that mattered.

The young Draleid and his soulkin were not enough. In a single day Eltoar had watched five dragons torn from the world, and he and Helios had been the cause of three. One dragon hatched in four hundred years was not enough to bring a species back from extinction. Fane had done as he had promised. He had reinstated the order of the Dracárdare. They had tested the eggs for the Calling.

Day after day, night after night. Tens of thousands had been brought through the vault in Venira. Nothing.

Eltoar could not sit around any longer. He did not share Fane's faith in Efialtír. But there were no other paths.

"This is it." A fire burned in Fane's eyes as he spoke. "This is what we have fought for every day. If you'd not taken the Heart all those years ago, Efialtír would already walk this world and the dragons would fill the skies. But that can still be. You have seen his power, Eltoar. Felt it in your veins. You cannot doubt him. You cannot doubt that which has been proven to you time and time again. The Chosen alone are proof of his strength. Even with the veil between worlds fighting against him, he reaches his hand into this world. Stand with me this last time."

Eltoar held his gaze on Fane, then stepped from the rock. Helios lowered his head as Eltoar approached, tilting to the side so Eltoar could unbuckle the chest from the straps that held it to the dragon's body.

As he held the chest in his hands, his mind warred on two sides. And then Helios pushed memories into Eltoar: Helios tearing Vyldrar from the side of the Tower of Faith, Alvira, Eltoar killing Dylain, Pellenor and Meranta, Lyina and Karakes. A thousand memories flitted through his vision, a thousand friends dead, a thousand dragons slaughtered. They had caused so much pain. They had made so many wrong choices. This was their chance to do something worthwhile, something good.

Both Helios and Eltoar knew that, despite Fane's words, the man might very well strike them down as soon as Eltoar handed him the chest. Eltoar had betrayed him, had stolen the Heart from beneath his nose. Fane had trusted him, and Eltoar had spurned that trust.

More than once, Eltoar had thought to use the Heart himself. With a well of Essence that deep, he and Helios could swat Fane aside as though the man were nothing. But could they breathe life back into the eggs? No. To take the Heart for himself would be a selfish choice, one amongst many. To preserve their lives at the cost of so many more.

Fane stepped down from the rock and stared at the chest without a word, his body still, his face expressionless, and yet Eltoar could feel the tension in him.

"I am sorry for not trusting you, old friend." Eltoar looked from Fane to the chest. "Perhaps if I had done sooner, so much death could have been avoided."

Fane's gaze never left the chest. "The past is both a poison and a gift, Eltoar. If we ignore it, we are destined to repeat it. But if we linger there, it will kill us."

"You've always known the right words to say, my friend. Always."

"It is my curse." Fane took a step closer, clasping his hands behind his back. "We can still make things right. I want you by my side. I *need* you by my side. As I always have. I don't care, Eltoar. I don't care that you took it. I don't care that you hid it. I understand your reasons. I would have made the same decision. The steps we've taken are behind us. All I care about is the next step. Will you take it with me? Will we finish this together?"

Eltoar placed the chest into Fane's arms, allowing his hands to linger for just a moment.

The thumping of his heart pounded in his ears as he pulled his hands away. It was done.

Fane wove threads of Air through the chest and cracked open the lid, a red glow washing over him. "Finally." He turned his gaze up at Eltoar, the light glinting in his eyes. "I will not fail you, my friend. The elves of Lynalion and this new Draleid will pay in blood for what they have taken from you. The dragons will once again fill the skies. And you will see that every sacrifice we have made was worth it. Epheria *will* find peace again. I swear it to you."

FANE STARED DOWN AT THE open chest that rested upon the desk in his study, the light of the Heart glowing with an unerring beauty.

Patience was always rewarded.

Eltoar had been a delicate piece of the puzzle. A soul so strong and filled with arrogance and yet burdened by a need to be loved, to be trusted, a need to protect. Such strong yearnings made for a malleable heart. That had always been Eltoar's weakness.

Alvira had those same needs, but she'd possessed a much stronger sense of self. She could never have been swayed. Fane had tried at first, but it was clear almost immediately that she did not have that same need for validation.

The inner workings of a mind, the strings that pulled at each heart and soul, those were the things Fane found the most fascinating. There was no puzzle more satisfying to complete.

Fane had not suspected Eltoar at first, and in the years following the fall of The Order, there had been other priorities. The veil between worlds wouldn't thin again for four hundred years. By the time he'd believed the thief to be Eltoar, the Blood Moon had been approaching once more.

Fane had known that all he needed to do was pluck away slowly at the things Eltoar cared for most. Create a sense of doubt within him. Apply an urgency, a need.

Even before The Fall, Vandrien had always walked around with her nose in the air. She was one of those elves who believed in the old days, in the superiority of elven blood. She had always thought herself smarter than every soul in the room. She was predictable, arrogant, and brutal. And all of those things had made her so easy to manipulate.

Fane had known the attack on Elkenrim was a ruse. He'd set scouts in the Elkenwood: Aldruids. Vethnir hunters. The elves had never come close to seeing them. Catagan had been a necessary sacrifice. Eltoar had needed to believe they were losing the war, needed to believe that *he* was failing.

The attack on the tower had been a masterstroke, if he dared say so himself. Which he did. He had allowed the Alamants to live freely for centuries, knowing how useful they could be if given the right push. And for centuries, he had filtered information into their network, tending them like a garden. They had truly believed their instructions had come from the rebels. The attack had served many purposes. It had made the empire look weaker so that Eltoar might be swayed. It had built a fervour within the armies for rebel blood. And it had also dampened Fane's boredom a little. But most of all, Fane had needed a way to draw the elven dragons from Catagan, a way to bring Eltoar and his old apprentice together. The raw power of dragons was such that when they met in the air, death would always follow. And the more dragons that died, the greater Eltoar's need would become. The arrival of Aeson Virandr's new protégé had been unexpected but surprisingly effective.

So many pieces all moving at once, so many threads interwoven. A thousand winding paths, one desired destination.

Allowing so many to die was not an easy thing to do. Fane truly did care for the souls that called the mortal plane home. They were his entire purpose. But to sacrifice a million to save everything… that was not even a question he contemplated. It was not a task in which he found joy, though. Joy was something that had long evaded him.

Everything was in place, and that was all that mattered.

Brother Pirnil was conducting the last of the tests, and now that the Heart was secure, the final step could be taken.

Fane shook his head as he looked down at the pulsing gemstone before him, power radiating from it like the heat of the sun. The irony was not lost on him that, in the hope of breathing life back into the dragon eggs, Eltoar had handed over that very thing.

Fane lifted his gaze from the Heart at the soft sound of footsteps.

Two of the Chosen stood at the chamber's centre, black eyes fixed on Fane. "We are at your command, Harbinger."

"Azrim, Tiamit. The time has come. Gather the others and bring Garramon and his apprentice here."

CHAPTER ONE HUNDRED

WHAT LURKS BENEATH

26th Day of the Blood Moon

Berona – Winter, Year 3081 After Doom

Rist darted about the room he and Neera had taken in the barracks, stuffing everything he could into his satchel and strapping his sword to his hip.

"Rist, slow down." Neera grabbed Rist's shoulders. "Talk to me. What is going on?"

"I need to leave," Rist answered. "And I'd like you to come with me. You don't have to, but I want you to."

"Stop, Rist. Breathe." Neera drew a slow breath in through her nostrils, exhaling at the same rate, gesturing for Rist to do the same. "The first thing we need to discuss is why you're only packing books and shoes."

"It's all I need."

"Food?"

"I can find some. Neera, we don't have time."

"Rist—"

"They took my parents, Neera."

"Who did?"

"Fane… or Garramon, or someone… Someone took them and tortured them and pretended that they were all right to keep me here. You… you saw what happened in that mountain. You saw the Draleid, saw Calen. I don't have all the pieces, but I can see it now… I've always seen it a little bit, but…"

"Rist, pieces of what? You need to slow down. I don't understand."

Rist remained quiet for a moment. His dad had always said that silence was the quickest way to get someone's attention. He laid the satchel on the ground and cupped Neera's cheeks in his hands. "Neera, I need you to trust me. Do you trust me?"

She nodded, pressing her cheek into Rist's hand. "Always."

"I can't stay here any longer. I need to go home. But I need to find Garramon first. There are things I must hear in his voice. Will you come with me?"

"I go where you go."

"I'm sorry," Rist said, kissing Neera on the forehead.

"For what?"

"For asking you to leave this place."

"This place is nothing to me. Not without you in it. I was brought here because I had nothing else, and I stayed for the same reason."

As Rist stared into Neera's eyes, an enormous explosion sounded and the room shook violently. The candle on the desk hit the floor, the flame catching on the cotton blanket Rist had left folded by the bedside.

He reached out with the Spark to snuff the flames when the room shook again, the walls cracking, dust falling from the ceiling.

"Rebels?" Neera stared up at the falling dust. "Again?"

Shouts and screams sounded from the yard, followed by a strange clicking sound, like thousands of steel spear tips bouncing off stone. *Click-clack. Click-clack.*

Rist grabbed Neera's hand. "We need to leave."

He allowed Neera to take a moment to pack whatever she needed before the pair of them headed for the door.

Rist had never quite seen anything like what awaited them when he stepped into the yard. Hundreds of stone-like spiders as large as hounds swarmed over the ground, leaping onto anything that moved, black-tipped claws slicing through leather and flesh. Threads of all elements whipped through the air as the mages of the First Army gathered themselves and tried desperately to save the soldiers, who were like sheep to wolves.

Where the stable had been, now an enormous hole gaped up to the sky, as though the world had caved inwards. More of the spiders flooded over the lip of the hole.

"What… what are they?" Neera stared in horror, the Spark pulsing from her.

"Kerathlin." Rist had read of them in *Devastating Creatures: Claw, Tooth, And Fang,* by Vace Entura. There had been no illustrations, but Vace had described them as spiders carved from stone, each leg tipped with claws sharp as steel and black as coal. They were native to the deep tunnels below the mountains in the dwarven realms. But what in all the gods were they doing here?

"Rist?" Neera tugged at Rist's shirt. "We need to move!"

Arcs of lightning left Neera's hand and smashed into three of the kerathlin who charged them. Both Neera and Rist broke into a run, pushing past soldiers as they made for the barracks gates.

"Dragon's Maw!" came a shout, and a column of fire ten feet across consumed scores of the stone spiders with hissing shrieks. A score of mages stood near the yard's centre, soldiers gathered behind them wearing nothing but smallclothes or linen shirts and trousers.

The kerathlin were swarming around them, threads of Air, Spirit, and Fire keeping them at bay. Rist could see clutches of the creatures scuttling up the buildings and across the rooves.

"Brother Havel!" Exarch Gurney called out, waving for Rist and Neera to run to them. "Sister Halar!"

For a fraction of a second, Rist's heart was torn. It was not these souls who had lied to him, not these men and women who had hurt his mam and dad. These were good people, people who had treated him with respect, who had fought beside him and broken bread with him. Even in that moment, they called to him to stand together.

Rist's choice was snatched from him when a creature unlike anything Rist had ever laid eyes on smashed through the barracks wall, sending chunks of stone hurtling through the air, crushing men, women, and kerathlin alike. This creature was not in Vace's book.

The monstrosity tore through the gathered mages and soldiers as though they were nothing. With one swipe of a spike-covered tail as long as four wagons, half the souls in the group were extinguished, blood, bone, and shattered limbs decorating the yard.

It stood on four legs with large interlinked, stone-like scales covering the entirety of its gargantuan body, as though it had been carved from a mountain. The crest of its back rose almost as tall as the buildings around it. Its head was flat and angular – like that of an arrow – with sharp slits for eyes that pulsated with a streaming yellow mist. Two ridges ran either side of its neck, sweeping across its back and then down into its long muscular tail covered in vicious-looking spikes.

"Rist?" Neera's voice was a mixture of panic and awe.

"I have absolutely no idea. Run!"

As the kerathlin and the enormous monster tore the surviving mages and soldiers apart, Rist and Neera sprinted through the open gates, only to be greeted by the same carnage in the streets.

Kerathlin were ripping apart everyone and everything. The stone spiders skittered from holes just like the one in the barracks yard that had appeared throughout the city, collapsing buildings and causing the earth to depress inwards.

"Garramon said he went to the tower!" Rist shouted over the screams of the dying and the clicking of the kerathlin claws. He looked through the gaps in the building to where the High Tower rose above everything.

"Rist, that's further into the city." Neera looked from the tower to the northern gates. "We'll never make it there and back."

"He wouldn't leave me, and I can't leave him."

A shriek sounded from above, and a swarm of kerathlin leapt from the windows of the buildings on the far side of the street. The creatures hit the ground with a crash, then bounded forwards with impossible speed, scuttling across the debris and bodies in the street.

Rist pulled on threads of Earth and Air and pushed them into the kerathlin. Shrieks pierced his ears, blue blood squirting as he crushed the creatures inside their own stone shells.

Neera raked lightning across more of the creatures that flooded from a side street, but they swarmed over their dead, unrelenting.

"Lightning Storm!" Four Battlemages charged from the building beside Rist and Neera, threads of Air, Spirit, and Fire whirling about them. Rist joined his threads to theirs, howling wind smashing the kerathlin against the walls and the ground, lightning tearing them to pieces.

"Justicar Irudan," one of the men said when the threads faded, grasping Rist's arm, then Neera's. "Where are you headed?"

"To the tower," Rist answered.

"Well, you're either fucking stupid or fucking crazy. Either way—"

The man's words were cut short by a roar that tore across the sky. Rist looked up to see a dark shape illuminated amidst the clouds by flashes of lightning. Slowly, the clouds began to glow with an incandescent light. They swirled apart as a pillar of dragonfire erupted from the dense canopy and poured down in the distance.

The dark clouds swirled again, the rain physically parting as the inconceivable shape of Helios descended, obscured by the buildings. Within a few heartbeats, the great dragon rose into Rist's field of vision once more. The dragon had one of those monstrous scaled creatures thrashing in its talons, luminous yellow eyes misting in the night.

With a crack of his wings, Helios rose higher and at the same time bit down into the creature's back, then unleashed dragonfire over it, rising higher and higher until Helios was once more swallowed by the stormclouds. A roar thundered, and the flaming body of the giant monster dropped like a meteor into the city.

"Depth Stalkers," Justicar Irudan muttered to himself. "What in the gods is happening?"

"You know those monsters?" Rist asked.

"We lost hundreds to one of those bastards in the scouring of Kolmir. They should not be here."

In the back of Rist's mind, he heard a high-pitched ringing noise, barely audible, as subtle as a whisper. "Can you hear that?"

"Hear what?"

"That noise… It's…" The ground shook beneath Rist's feet, gently at first, then stronger and stronger until cracks spread through the stone. "Go!"

Rist grabbed Neera and pushed her back towards the tower, shouting at the others. "Run!"

He glanced over his shoulder to see the ground falling away, cracks spreading, a hole forming. Two of the mages fell, the screams swallowed by that high pitched ring. Justicar Irudan and the other mage turned to look for their companions when kerathlin flooded from the newly formed hole in the ground, washing over them in a wave of stone carapace and black claw.

"They're making tunnels," Rist said to himself as he ran, lungs heaving.

Rist and Neera moved from street to street, making their way towards the High Tower near the city's centre.

"Please!" a voice called. "Help us! My wife is—"

Rist never even saw the man who had shouted. The only noise that followed was screams. Everywhere they went, citizens flooded the streets, screaming and shouting, trampling each other as they fled in the dark and the hammering rain, the clouds blocking out the moonlight from above. The streets ran red with blood, and bodies lay everywhere.

At first, Rist tried to help those he saw. He was a Battlemage, and they looked to him for protection. But no matter what he did, every soul he came across died. It was all he could do to keep himself and Neera safe as they moved.

They turned a corner into a wide street where Lorian soldiers stood in a tight circle around a group of screaming men and women. The soldiers hacked and slashed as the kerathlin scuttled around them and ripped at them with obsidian claws.

Rist was moving towards them before he even realised it, opening himself to the Spark, drawing in threads of Air, Earth, Fire, and Spirit.

Being a Battlemage had to mean something. Whether he'd been lied to or not, it meant something. He would never become an Arcarian. That would not be his mark on the world, his permanence. Nor did he want it to be.

He would not be remembered in the books and stories. He would be the only Rist Havel, and he would be remembered in the hearts and the minds of the people who knew him, the people he saved, and the people he loved.

That would be his permanence, and he would take pride in knowing he stood when he could have run.

Neera sprinted at his side. She didn't question him or tell him to turn back. All she said was, "Tell me what you need."

Rist lashed out with threads of Air, sending a wave of concussive force through the writhing swarm of kerathlin and carving a path to the soldiers and citizens. The creatures shrieked and hissed as they were launched into the air.

The soldiers stared open-mouthed at Rist and Neera as they charged through the channel created by the Spark.

"Pack in tight!" Rist roared, pointing to the soldiers and the men and women they shielded, a slew of bodies about them. The soldiers did as commanded, compacting in around the citizens, swords and shields held high.

Rist needed them closer, needed less ground to protect.

"Lightning Storm!" Rist shouted.

Rist pushed outwards with the Spark, Neera's threads weaving around his own. The wind howled about them, ripping back and forth, tearing the kerathlin from the ground as lightning burned through them. The creatures died in their scores, smoke pluming from where lightning cracked their shells.

But it wasn't enough. Even as the kerathlin fell, burning and shrieking, more swarmed over the dead. One of the creatures leapt through the wind and lightning, hurtling towards Neera.

The drain sapped at him, pulling the strength from his bones, and Rist did the only thing he could: he tapped into the vessel that hung around his neck. Ice flooded his veins, the world growing still and silent before exploding with light and raucous sound.

He pushed the Essence into his fist and punched through the leaping kerathlin's carapace. The creature thrashed and writhed, blue blood pouring around Rist's arm, warm innards tangled about his fingers. Rist flicked his arm down, the kerathlin sliding free, limbs curling inwards.

Rist pushed harder, funnelling the Essence through him, drawing deeper from the Spark, his veins burning, muscles screaming. He glanced over his shoulder to see Neera staggering, then collapsing, one of the soldiers catching her.

"Neera!"

He wanted to run to her, to make sure she was all right, but if he moved, if he stopped at all, the kerathlin would crash through the Lightning Storm and rip them all to shreds.

Rist pulled deeper from the Spark than he ever had before, feeling each elemental strand wind around him. The power poured into him like molten fire in his veins, and the Lightning Storm raged with a fury, the air itself seeming to shimmer and ripple as kerathlin careened off stone and were ripped apart by arcs of blue lightning.

He pulled deeper, the drain burning his soul, pain blending with euphoria. In their hundreds, the kerathlin died, shrieking and wailing, swirling about Rist and the others like leaves in a storm. And still they kept coming. Relentless. Savage.

Rist dropped to his knees and screamed, pushing the threads outwards with every drop of strength he could muster.

But there were simply too many.

Two kerathlin broke through his barrier of wind and lightning, one leaping from a window ledge above, the other scuttling along the ground.

The one above shrieked and crashed into his shoulder, a black claw plunging into the flesh of his left arm, mandibles carving through his shoulder and scraping bone.

Rist howled in pain, tapping deeper into the well of Essence in his gemstone. He reached over with his hand, grabbed the kerathlin, and ripped it free, smashing it against the ground. The creature's shell cracked and blue blood spilled, but still it twisted and lunged.

A flash of steel and a sword impaled the kerathlin, pinning it to the stone. The second creature launched itself upwards, and one of the Lorian soldiers leapt forwards, wrapped his arms around it, and hauled it to the ground. As the thing tore at him with black claws, Rist pushed the Essence into the ground beneath the kerathlin's abdomen, turned it to molten stone, then punched upwards. The creature went still, a solid spike piercing its carapace, barely a hair's breadth from the Lorian soldier's face.

"We've got you," a woman said to his left, pulling her sword from the first kerathlin's body.

The words had barely left her mouth when the ground shook once again and one of those monstrous Depth Stalkers burst through the building on the opposite side of the street.

The men and women who were huddled together screamed and wailed as they fled into the Lightning Storm. Above, chunks of stone fell, and the creature reared onto its hind legs.

Rist looked to Neera, who knelt in the street, two soldiers refusing to leave her. He let all other thoughts flood from his mind, releasing his hold on the Spark, the world dulling. But before he could take a step, a chunk of debris from above crashed down and plumed dust into the air, knocking Rist onto his back.

His entire body shook as he dragged himself to his feet, dust occluding the air and filling his lungs. "Neera!" He staggered forwards, hearing the *click-clack* of kerathlin around him, men and women screaming. "Neera!"

Through the dust a red light ignited, casting a man in shadow. Rist could feel the pulse of the Spark thrumming in the air. The red light flashed, and a kerathlin shrieked.

Rist staggered forwards, finally seeing the shape of Magnus down on one knee, a red níthral in his hand. The stump of his severed arm was pointed upwards, and in the haze, Rist thought he could see Magnus's arm, hand, and fingers wrought from the Spark, seeming to glow with threads of Spirit and Air. That Spark-wrought hand held up an enormous chunk of stone three times the size of a bear.

And there, pulling herself upright between Magnus and Rist, was Neera.

Rist's throat tightened, relief flooding him.

"Don't just fucking stand there, lad," Magnus shouted. With a pulse of Air, he sent the chunk of debris crashing to the ground behind him, then spun in the same motion and carved through a kerathlin with his níthral.

Rist sprinted forwards and wrapped his arms around Neera, who fell into him. "Rist…"

"It's all right. I've got you."

More Battlemages charged down the street behind Magnus, soldiers moving with them, whips of Air and Fire slicing through kerathlin.

Magnus clasped Rist's shoulder. "I've been fucking looking for you everywhere. We need to go. Now. The city is falling. The retreat's been sounded."

"Garramon," Rist said, coughing the last of the dust from his lungs. "He went to the tower. We need to—"

"No. We're not going to the tower. We're leaving. Do you understand me?"

"What?"

"We're leaving. We're taking the northern gates and following the river west. We'll catch a boat towards Antiquar."

"I… But Garramon… We need to get Garramon."

"Garramon's not coming, lad. He sent me."

"But…"

Magnus grabbed the sides of Rist's head, tight. "He's not coming. He's buying us time. Let's not waste it. We don't have time for those long chats you love. There are dwarves in the city as well. Ugly bastards with big axes."

Rist lifted his gaze and stared up at the High Tower, arcs of lightning streaking from its many windows and balconies, crashing down into the city. The shape of Helios soared in the clouds behind it, pouring fire down over whole sections of the city. He looked back down at Neera, who was slumped against his chest.

"Give her to me," Magnus said, wrapping an arm around Neera and slinging her over his shoulder. "She helped carry me from that mountain. I can return the favour." He looked Rist dead in the eye. "I need you to trust me, Rist. I'm all for dying a heroic death, but crushed by a fucking rock or eaten by some bastard of a spider is not how I want to go out. There are tunnels that can get us most of the way."

"No tunnels." Rist thought back to the holes in the yard, the kerathlin swarming upwards. "They're coming from underground."

"Right, fuck that. We can make it to the gates, but we need to go now."

Rist took one last look up at the High Tower, then nodded to Magnus, and they set off towards the northern gates.

GARRAMON PUSHED OPEN THE DOORS of the chamber to find Fane standing over his desk. Water dripped from Garramon's robes, trailing on the stone.

Fane turned to him, a look of relief in his eyes. "Garramon. You're here, good. I sent Chosen to find you before the attack. Kerathlin and Depth Stalkers? The elves are predictable but those dwarves, always full of surprises. I didn't think they had it in them." He gestured towards a chest that sat on the desk, cracking open the lid to release a warm red glow. "None of it matters. None of it. We have the Heart, Garramon. We have it. Everything we have worked towards, everything we have sacrificed for is here. Where is Rist? We leave for the Sea of Stone immediately."

Fane took a step towards Garramon, a broad smile forming on his face. That smile slowly faded as he looked at Garramon. "What is it? What's happened?"

"When were you going to tell me?" Garramon held Fane's gaze.

"Tell you what, brother?"

"I should have seen it," Garramon answered, shaking his head. "I did see it. But as you always have, you blinded me. Or I blinded myself to you. I do not know. I trusted you."

"Garramon. What did you do?" Fane took another step closer, eyes wide. "Where is Rist?"

"Dead," Garramon lied. Fane had always been able to tell when Garramon was lying, from the moment they had met. But Garramon had to try. "He was killed when the kerathlin broke through. He and Magnus both."

"I kept it from you because I know your heart," Fane said, ignoring Garramon's words. "You do not always see clearly when your heart is involved, and I know you care for the boy. But I also know that you understand the need for sacrifice. You always have. This is *our* path, Garramon, and we will walk it together as we always have. We are so close."

"Was there ever a word that left your lips that wasn't a lie?" Garramon stopped in the chamber's centre, cold water trickling down his face.

"A lie?" Fane answered. "You lie to yourself. You knew, Garramon. You always knew. Who trained him, knowing full well what he was? Who handed him those letters, knowing where they came from? You have known every step of the way. Why did you think I wanted him trained like an Arcarian? It wasn't for the title, and you know that. Deep down you had to know why I took such an interest in Rist."

"But this isn't about me, Fane. I'm asking you, has anything that wasn't a lie ever left your lips? Have we ever truly been friends, or am I just another tool for you to use and throw away? Am I just another necessity in this grand plan of yours?" Garramon looked to the window. "You preached the sacrifice of a few to save the many. You swore that you wanted to protect the people of Epheria, and now you are ready to leave while this city is torn apart? How many have died in this war, Fane? How many millions already? It will take thousands of years to recover. And all the while, you haven't fought in a single battle. Not in a hundred years. You stayed hidden, searching for this damn Heart, sending others to die in your name. You preach that all great things require sacrifice, but what have you sacrificed?"

For a moment Garramon thought he saw genuine sadness in Fane's eyes.

"I sacrificed Malyn… My son. My world. And you stood there with your hand on my back and your words in my ear, and you told me how noble I was, how honourable, how my sacrifice would be the difference. How it took the strongest of souls to make the hardest of choices. I lost Fulya… I gave everything to you, to this cause. And now you want Rist as well?" The rage that had been bubbling below the surface finally cracked through. "You cannot have him!"

Fane took a step closer, that glimpse of sadness vanishing from his eyes. "Where is he, Garramon?"

"Gone." Garramon didn't even try to stop the smile from spreading across his face. "He is gone, and you will never find him. Not in time. Not before the Blood Moon sets. I found Pirnil, found his notes." Garramon savoured the flash of fear on Fane's face. "You will never have Rist."

"What have you done, Garramon?" The rage came with terrible swiftness, the likes of which Garramon had not seen in centuries, the entire tower trembling as the Spark pulsed outwards from Fane. "What have you done, you damn fool?"

"What I should have done a long time ago." Garramon opened himself to the Spark, pulling as hard he could, drawing threads of each element into himself. "I could not go with him. Not after what I've done. Not after what I've taken from him, the pain I've caused, the darkness I spread while pretending to myself I was still a good man. I could not go with him, but neither will I let you have him. Not again, not like you took Malyn. You knew Solman Tuk was behind it all. I know you knew, I always did, deep down. From the day I met you, all I've ever done is lie to myself."

Garramon pulled so much of the Spark into himself that his veins felt as though they had caught fire and his soul burned. This was the only way. "I will *not* let you have him."

"You damn fool," Fane repeated, the anger in his voice fading to a low melancholy lament. The last thing Garramon had expected to see was tears in Fane's eyes.

A pulse of Essence burst outwards from Fane, wrapping around Garramon and completely severing him from the Spark.

"Why did you come here?" Fane asked, shaking his head. "You had to know as well as I do that you cannot leave this chamber alive."

"I had to look you in the eyes." Garramon didn't strain against the bonds of Essence that held him. He had known his fate before he had entered. "I am ready to die, Fane. No soul should see the number of summers we have seen. I am done. I want to go to my son now."

The bonds of Essence dragged Garramon to his knees, and he stared up at Fane.

"You were the only soul in this world I have ever truly called a brother. You were never just a tool to be used. Never. You were all I've ever had, all I've ever loved." Fane lowered himself to one knee before Garramon. "You ask me what I've sacrificed?" The smile that flitted over Fane's lips was broken and sorrowful. "Everything. I burned a good world to the ground. Every single soul weighs upon me. I have no peace in my heart, not a moment of solace in the waking world or the world of dreams. The screams of the dying are my lullaby, the cries of the damned my morning song. I see the flames of Ilnaen every time the sun sets. When I walked into that mountain all those years ago, do you want to know what I saw? A world on fire. A world that was nothing but pain and agony and endless suffering. Ten thousand futures, a hundred thousand, a thousand thousand. And in each of them, this world was ash. Only on this path could it be saved. What have I sacrificed, Garramon? Trust. Love. Solace. Hope. I will not know peace from now until the day I die, and I have not known it for four hundred years. I am haunted by the cost of my failure. I will sacrifice my soul and all the joy the living world brings… and now I must sacrifice the only man who truly knows me. The last tether to who I am. The last shred of what makes me human."

Fane shook his head, letting out a long sigh. "You will not see Malyn, my brother. You will not see anything. I sought Rist because he was the only other soul I had found that was capable of becoming Efialtír's vessel. I cannot take his place. If I do, this world burns. And so you take everything from me. And I make one more sacrifice."

"What do you mean?"

"You still can't see it, can you? I have searched for centuries to find another, to find a soul powerful enough to harbour Efialtír. By the time I understood what was needed, it was too late. The Arcarians were too few, and most had died in the fighting. The souls of the Draleid are not fit. Whatever magic Varyn has burned into them sees to that." Fane leaned forwards, placed his hands on Garramon's shoulders, then pressed their foreheads together. "The only one left, Garramon, the only one strong enough, has always been you. Rist was the last strand of hope I'd been clinging to. I am so sorry, old friend. I tried everything. You were a sacrifice I did not want to make. That is why I kept so much from you."

Garramon simply smiled. No joy or happiness lingered in that smile. It was not a smile born of any belief that he was a good man or that he deserved any form of absolution. It was a smile that existed only because he had been given a second chance to make the right choice, and he had done so. "You can have me, Fane. But you will not have him. I will not let you."

Fane stared into Garramon's eyes, searching for something, something Garramon thought the man found as he gave the softest of sighs. "You are the man I wish I had the chance to be."

A white light flickered in the air behind Fane, spreading until a window to another place appeared, and a woman stepped through.

"I wish you were standing at my side in what is to come," Fane whispered, resting his hand on Garramon's cheek. "It is time, my friend."

The bonds of Essence that held Garramon in place slithered over his body, pried open his mouth, and pushed into his eyes, ears, and nose until all he saw was black and all he heard was the sound of his own heart beating.

CHAPTER ONE HUNDRED AND ONE

EVERYTHING YOU SEEK

27th Day of the Blood Moon

Tahír un Ilyienë, Aravell – Winter, Year 3081 After Doom

A strange sense of peace seemed to hold the Tahír un Ilyienë in its grasp. It was more than a physical thing. Ella could *feel* the change in the air from the city beyond. That tree, with its glowing purple leaves, was an anchor between worlds, its heartbeat resounding within Ella's soul. She'd been sitting there, perched on the stone terraces with Faenir at her feet, since the sun had first risen.

Sennik and Balmyras sat a few rows back, while Luteir and Aneera lurked about somewhere.

Ella drew a sharp breath, staring down at the elves and Rakina who stood on the central platform at the tree's base. Hundreds came each day, thousands possibly. All to be closer to the ones they loved – the ones they'd lost.

A hand rested on Ella's shoulder, firm yet gentle.

"I thought I'd find you here," Tanner said, stepping down from the higher terrace to sit beside Ella. She had smelled him as soon as he'd entered the garden, the wolf within her pricking at his scent.

Ella gave him a half-smile, then turned back to staring at the Ilyienë tree.

"You've come here every day since returning. Sat in this same spot."

"Are you following me?"

"No," Tanner said with a weak shrug. "Yana is." He pointed a few terraces down to where Yana sat with her back to them, pretending she hadn't heard anything. "She thinks she's like some shapeshifting shadow or something."

"I've not seen her." Ella looked down at the woman, allowing a smile to touch her lips, the wolf within her grumbling gently, Faenir nuzzling against her leg. She had of course seen Yana follow her every morning without saying a word, but Tanner didn't need to know that.

"She's worried about you." Tanner leaned forwards, resting his elbows on his legs. "*We're* worried about you."

Ella laughed, shaking her head. "Nothing to be worried about." She leaned forwards, mimicking Tanner's stance, then looked down at Faenir, who gave her nose a lick with a wet tongue. She laughed, tilting her head to the side. The laughter died when her thoughts drifted. "Lasch and Elia's son…"

"What about him?"

"He's alive."

"He's what?"

"He's alive," Ella repeated with a sigh, sitting back up straight and staring down at the central yard, her gaze passing over the statues of the human and the Fenryr Angan.

"That's…" The man paused for a moment. "Not good news?"

"He fights for the empire. He almost killed Calen at Tarhelm. He's a mage."

Tanner puffed out his cheeks, nodding slowly. "That's a lot."

"It is. I need to tell them he's alive… but every time I try, I just… I can't. Elia is recovering so well, but she's so fragile. How do I tell her what Rist is? What he's become? It could break her."

"It could," Tanner agreed.

"That's not exactly what I'd hoped you'd say."

Tanner shrugged. "Few things in this life are simple or easy, Ella. That is just the way of it. Everything has a cost, and it all just depends on whether or not you're willing to pay it. What would you give for the truth, and is the truth worth it?"

"What are you saying?"

"I'm saying that right now, Elia is… she's in a good place, as good as can be. Perhaps it's worth waiting, allowing her to heal. How much do you know of Rist? Of the hows and the whys? Did you speak to him?"

"I… No. We didn't get a chance to speak while he was trying to murder my brother."

Tanner nodded. "What's the outcome if you tell her?"

"She'll know the truth."

"And what will that give her? Solace? Closure? Peace?"

"It will give her the truth. What more is there?"

"The truth for truth's sake is not always what a person needs."

"The truth is *always* what a person needs," Ella snapped, the wolf rising within her.

"It's your decision, Ella," Tanner said calmly. "Just make sure that you don't make it based on your own anger. Make it based on what Elia and Lasch need right now. The truth is important, but the timing of the truth can be just as much so."

Ella only grunted in response.

They sat there in silence for a while longer until Tanner spoke again. "Every time I come to this place, my mind drifts to Rhett…"

"Mine too." Just the mention of Rhett's name felt like a knife had been plunged into her heart. Faenir whimpered at her feet.

"I'm sorry." Tanner looked up at her from his hunched over position, his eyes already wet with tears. "I didn't mean to—"

"It's fine." Ella's throat clenched, that empty feeling she knew so well flooding her veins and filling her chest. "It's… I can go days, sometimes even a week, without thinking about him, as though he had never existed. And then, it just crashes down on me and breaks me all over again. And the guilt at forgetting him is like hot coals on my heart. It just… it rips at me. I could be sitting on a chair, staring into the fireplace, and thoughts of Rhett just consume me."

"That sounds about right." Tanner sat up straight. "I lost my mother almost twenty summers ago. Yesterday, I walked into the kitchen as Elia brought a fresh loaf of bread from the oven. She'd put rosemary in this one, like my mother used to. I had to walk straight out the door. Ended up drinking elven mead on my own in the middle of the city. Gods, I can't even remember the amount of people I've seen die, the number of friends and family I've lost. The last letter I got from my brother was over a year ago, telling me that an old friend, Forn Blackwell, was found dead in his own inn, throat slit. That was the same letter where he told me that Rhett had disappeared. I never responded. I was too busy… Rahlin could be dead, but it's Forn that hurts me. Explain that?"

"I remember him," Ella said, thinking back to the old innkeeper she and Rhett had met in The Twisted Oak. "We met him in Camylin at your suggestion. He was a lovely man."

"That would have been right before he died." Tanner shook his head, then let out a long regretful sigh. "I'll tell you one thing, Ella. The older you get, the more you appreciate what you have left." He squeezed Ella's knee and stood. "I'll leave you to it. The ones we lose, Ella, they're never really gone, just waiting."

Ella watched as Tanner climbed down the terraces and tapped Yana's left shoulder, promptly jumping to her right and receiving a light slap on the back of the head for his efforts. Yana looked up at Ella, smiling, as they made their way down and left.

The sight of it only made Ella miss Rhett more. Perhaps, if he'd lived, they might have grown apart, or argued, or screamed and roared at each other, and that would have been fine. Because that was human. They would have gotten through it; they would have gotten through anything. But he'd had to go and leave her alone, and so now all she had were memories of a man who loved her, who was kind and gentle, and selfless, and perfect. And that made her hate him a little bit, because no one else could ever live up to that.

Then, as she leaned back and stared at the Ilyienë, Ella could see Rhett's smiling face in her mind, those wrinkles forming at the corners of his eyes, that smile that was always so full.

"Fuck you, Rhett," she whispered, leaning her head back to stop herself from crying. "Fuck you."

When the threat of tears had diminished, Ella looked down at the Ilyienë tree and saw possibly the last person she'd expected to see: Farda. She'd completely avoided the man since returning to the city – since Calen had agreed to pardon him.

At her feet, Faenir sat upright, his hackles raised, lips pulling back in a snarl. She stood and walked down the stone stairs towards the central yard, crossing the bridge between the Jotnar and elf statues.

Farda stood with his eyes closed and one hand at his side, the other pressed to the trunk of the great tree, several elves around him.

Ella moved so she stood only a few feet to his left. She didn't know what she wanted to say, only that the wolf in her blood wanted to rip the man's throat out and that small pieces of her just wanted to know why. Why he had done all the things he'd done, why he'd stayed with her so long, why he'd brought her all the way to Aravell, knowing what would await him.

"Were you going to speak?" Farda said without opening his eyes. "Or just stand there staring at me? I can taste the smell of wet wolfpine."

Just the sound of his voice made her furious. "What are you doing here?"

"The same thing as all the others." Farda opened his eyes and stared up at the glowing canopy above. "Ella—"

"No," she snapped. "Don't even try."

Farda turned to face her, keeping his palm flat against the tree. "Why are *you* here? You approached me, and yet you won't let me speak. You want to kill me, but you won't let me die. Why are you here?"

"I don't know!"

Whispers sounded around Ella as she roared, elves staring at her and walking away to the other side of the tree.

"My nieces," Farda said, turning back to look up at the leaves overhead.

"What?"

"You wanted to know why I'm here – my nieces." Farda bit at his lip. "I'm going to talk. You can stay or you can go. But I would prefer if you stayed."

Ella wanted to leave, but her feet remained planted, the wolf within her growling.

"Hana and Valyianne." Farda paused for a moment, his throat tightening. "My brother's girls. My brother and his wife were killed by bandits on the road from Caelduin to Anthír. Apparently, the bandits had some kind of moral code, because they left the girls sitting at the side of the road. That's where I found them. I was late. I promised him I'd bring Shinyara and let the girls fly with me. But I was late. And… Torlan died because of it. The bandits took everything, stripped them of their clothes, coin, jewels, whatever was worth anything. But they left the girls."

Ella could smell the pain on Farda, hear the falter in his heartbeat. The moment of sympathy in her heart only served to light a rage at herself for allowing it to exist.

"I took them in, raised them. Taught them to hold swords, to hunt, taught them to sew and knit, how to cook. Hana couldn't tell a tomato from an apple, but Valyianne had a gift for it. You should have seen the smile on her face when she baked her first pie. It was godsawful, but I ate it. The second one was better. By the fifth, I was asking her to make pie every day. Hana might not have been a good cook, but by Elyara could she sing. They were the sweetest two girls in the world."

Farda ran his fingers down the bark of the tree. "They were everything. I'd always told myself I didn't want children. What if they were born without the Spark? There was something dark about that – about the chance that you might live to watch your children be born, to raise them, to bring them up in the world, and then watch them slowly grow old and wither, and then, eventually, lay them into the earth. But the girls, they made me see. To care for a child is a different kind of love… On the darkest days, just one smile from Hana or one laugh from Valyianne, and everything was better. They were joy, and love, and beauty. They were my girls."

Ella couldn't help but notice Farda's use of the word 'were'. She wanted to keep her rage flowing, to not let him in, but the smell of pain and loss filled her nostrils. "What happened to them?"

"They had only seen twelve summers when they died." Farda clenched his hand into a fist, the bark of the tree scraping away skin from his knuckles. "I'd left them with their grandparents – Sahira's mother and father – in the city of Orinhale. The city was burned to the ground the next night."

"Farda, I…"

"The Order knew about it before it happened. Orinhale and Aerilon were at war. The prince of Orinhale had taken the king of Aerilon's daughter and married her in secret. That daughter had a husband already. And The Order's spies had reported that the husband planned to set sail with an army and raze the city to the ground, his wife inside. We could have stopped it, but the council voted that Aerilon's support was too valuable." Farda drew a deep, trembling breath. "Alvira didn't tell me that we knew until a year after. She said that she 'didn't know Valyianne and Hana were in the city'… as though that made it better."

Farda leaned forwards and rested his forehead against the tree. "We let an entire city burn because the ones who burned it had a kingdom built atop a sapphire mine. I lost my girls that day, but hundreds of thousands of others died… and we just stood by."

Ella took a step closer, Faenir at her side. "Why are you telling me this?"

Farda drew a deep breath and pulled his hand away from the tree. He turned to look Ella in the eyes, the scars on his face catching the purple glow from above. "I know you hate me – rightly. But I needed to thank you."

"Thank me? For what?"

"For listening… and for giving me back my pain."

"I didn't give you anything."

"I've taken so much from you…" Farda's voice trembled. "I'd not thought of Hana and Valyianne since the day Shinyara died. It's like they were wiped from my heart. I'd forgotten the reason I was even fighting. I didn't care – I couldn't care. Shinyara took everything. But you gave me back my pain. You returned it to me."

"Farda, I didn't—"

"You did. I didn't understand it at first. But I see it now. You remind me of them. You remind me of Hana's fire, of Valyianne's heart. Watching over you gave me purpose again. I can't feel the cuts on my flesh, but I can feel the ones within." Farda's eyes glistened. "You let me remember the day my heart broke, and I'm so sorry that I'm the one who broke yours. But... I remember who I was now, and that is your doing whether you knew it or not. You gave me back my pain, Ella Fjorn, and that is a debt I can never repay."

Without another word, Farda stepped past Ella and walked across the bridge, and all Ella could do was stare after him.

Her legs felt weak, as though Farda's words had taken their strength. Faenir pressed his side against Ella's and held her upright, a low rumble in his chest. He tilted his head up and licked her chin.

Ella rested one hand on the wolfpine's head, scratching at his fur, then placed the other on the trunk of the Ilyienë tree.

Thump.

A heartbeat pulsed beneath the wood. The tree's heartbeat, rippling not through the mortal plane but through Níthianelle, through Ella's soul.

"Ella..."

A shiver ran across Ella's skin at the sound of her mother's voice.

"Mam?" Ella pressed her second hand to the tree. "Mam?"

Every bone in Ella's body told her to reach out, to step into Níthianelle, but fear cut into her heart. What if she fragmented again?

At the thought, the strangest of words came to her mind. Words from a long time ago. Erdhardt's words before The Proving.

"Everything you seek lies on the other side of fear," she whispered.

Beside Ella, Faenir growled, his hackles rising, and he stood to face away from her. Images and emotions flooded from the wolfpine to Ella, and she knew the meaning of his heart: he would protect her. He would keep her safe. He was her keeper.

The wolf within Ella howled, demanding she cross between the planes. Something inside it yearned to stand in the Sea of Spirits, and so Ella made her decision, whispering the words her mam had said to her before Tamzin had pulled her away. "Trust in the blood."

Ella called to the wolf in her blood, acquiescing. It howled in answer, and the world shifted.

CHAPTER ONE HUNDRED AND TWO

LOYALTY ABOVE ALL

27th Day of the Blood Moon

Tahír un Ilyienë, Aravell – Winter, Year 3081 After Doom

Farda had reached the entranceway to the Tahír un Ilyienë when a hand grabbed him by the shoulder and spun him, followed by a fist slamming into his face.

He staggered backwards from the force, nose crunching, the taste of blood in his mouth.

"Go near her again, and I swear it will be the last thing you do." Tanner Fjorn stood before Farda, a black tunic draped over his excessively large frame.

"I'd rather not hurt you, Tanner." Without a thought, Farda's hand fell to his pocket, his fingers clenching into a fist when he remembered the coin wasn't there. *I am the master of my own fate.*

Tanner glared at Farda, his hands clenched into fists, knuckles pale. "I don't have the same problem."

Farda stood straight, wiping the blood from his nose, then turned. Tanner grabbed his arm again, wrapped a hand around his throat, and heaved him against the wall of the tunnel, drawing a gasp from a cluster of passing elves.

Farda stared into Tanner's eyes as the man held him in place.

"Is the pain you've caused her not enough? What more do you want?"

"I want nothing from her."

"Then stay the fuck away from her, Kyrana. Am I clear?"

"I can't." Farda glanced down, allowing Tanner's gaze to follow his towards the knife he held against the man's side. Farda could have simply used the Spark, but he truly didn't want to hurt Tanner. There was no sense in it. He just wanted the man to fuck off.

Tanner looked down at the blade, then back up at Farda, his grip not loosening. The man turned his head at the sound of snarls coming from within the basin.

Faenir.

Tanner let go of Farda's throat, and both men sprinted back into the Tahír un Ilyienë and over the nearest bridge.

Elves were scattered around the central platform, all staring at Faenir, who stood beside Ella, hackles raised, snapping and snarling at anyone who came close.

The two Angan both stood a few feet from Ella, unmoving, eyes closed, while the druid that had been following her around like a sick puppy – Sennik – had his hand out, trying to calm Faenir, his black wolf standing between the two.

"What's happened?" Farda brushed past Sennik and then past Faenir, who barely gave him a passing glance. Ella's eyes were open and white as snow.

A voice sounded behind him, deep and unwavering. "She has entered Níthianelle after explicit instruction not to."

The man who stood behind Farda was tall and lean, his hair and beard a deep gold. Farda had seen him many times in the Eyrie and in Alura itself. "She is her mother's daughter."

ELLA DREW HER BREATHS IN slowly, the sound of waterfalls crashing in the back of her mind. Her hand rested on the enormous trunk of the Ilyienë tree before her, white mist drifting from its surface, the leaves glowing in a vast array of colours. "Mam? Please…"

"You listen as well as she does."

Ella had sensed Fenryr's presence before she'd heard his voice, her hackles rising, the wolf within her dipping its head. She turned to see him standing behind her, his body wreathed in black and gold smoke, eyes shimmering. Aneera and Luteir stood with him in their wolf forms, taller than any true wolf and wide as bears, smoke drifting from their bodies. Sennik was there too, watching her.

The entire terraced basin was empty save for small spheres of light flitting between the branches of the tree.

"I'm not going back," Ella said, pulling her hand from the tree and turning to face Fenryr. "Not without finding her."

"Your mother is dead, Ella. I felt her die."

"I don't care what you felt. I've heard her… I've *seen* her. She is here. I know it."

Fenryr took a step forwards, the smoke shifting around him as he moved. "To learn to navigate Níthianelle takes years, my child."

"I am *not* your child."

"Every moment you spend in this place," he said, ignoring her, "your scent drifts on the winds. Vethnir and Bjorna are not blind. They know the world is changing. They know I have left my den and that Kaygan weaves his webs. They hunt us. And these trees," Fenryr said, placing a palm on the bark of the Ilyienë, "are a magic older than time. They are a bridge of souls… they are a signal fire in the night."

"And what should we do? Cower? Run with our tails between our legs? Are we not wolves? Are we not the hunters?"

The words seemed to wound Fenryr, his lip rising in a snarl to reveal glistening fangs. Ella pushed harder.

"You are a *god*. You showed me our past, showed me the world as it once was. You keep saying how you are done hiding, yet all you want to do is hide. Let them come!" Ella roared. She looked about the ghostly basin of stone terraces, watching more Fenryr Angan appear, their bodies wisping grey and black smoke. She saw others too, Dvalin Angan with obsidian antlers and white fur phasing into existence, all watching.

"You speak with—"

"The arrogance born of youth, I know. But my mam is here. I have felt her, I have seen her, and, god or no, if you keep me from her, I will tear you apart."

"I can guide her." Ella turned to see Tamzin standing beside her, the woman's eyes gleaming a deep blue, her twin axes looped at her belt.

"She is a Blooddancer of Fenryr," Sennik snapped. "She is no kat. I will guide her."

"You couldn't guide a blind pig to slaughter if your balls were slathered in cheese." Tamzin looked back at Ella. "Understand this. When you reach out in Níthianelle, the entire realm can hear you. It is one thing to move through this place in silence. It is another to scream at the top of your lungs."

"I will take my chances."

"It is not just you who is at risk. Everyone here," she gestured around at the others. "And those in the mortal plane. I do not know what Gifts Bjorna's and Vethnir's Tuatha possess. This war between our clans has been cold as ice for centuries, because we have hidden and because we all fear what we do not know." Tamzin looked up at the Ilyienë. "This tree is something beyond what I understand. It is an anchor, an amplifier. If your mother is here, she will hear you. She just won't be the only one."

Fenryr looked at Ella, his eyes misting with golden light. Under the weight of the wolf god's stare, Ella's blood seemed to burn with fire, and the wolf within her snapped and snarled and thrashed, until eventually it whimpered, and Ella drew in a sharp breath. She could feel Fenryr's hands in her mind, in her soul. "What… what are you doing?"

Fenryr released his hold, and Ella dropped to her knees. "Searching. You truly believe your mother is still here."

It wasn't a question.

"She is alive."

"Loyalty above all," Fenryr whispered. He turned to Tamzin. "Where is your Bloodfather?"

She shook her head. "Wherever he needs to be. He does not tell me his every step."

"He does not tell himself… And he always seems to go missing precisely when he is needed." Fenryr drew a long breath, his gaze moving from Tamzin to Ella, then back. "I am trusting you, kat."

"And I am trusting you."

Fenryr helped Ella to her feet. "If we use this tree to reach out through Níthianelle, the others *will* come. It will cost lives." He looked into her eyes. "Your father freed me from my chains. He risked everything to do so. And so I will stand with you in this." The god nodded slowly, looking down at his feet. "And you speak true. I have been more words than actions. Let Bjorna and Vethnir come. Let them remember the power of the wolf." He drew a long breath. "Let it be done. I will not leave one of my pack behind. If your mother roams this place, we will find her. Loyalty above all."

Tamzin placed her hands on Ella's shoulders. "This will not be like before. Before, we were constantly in motion, moving quietly, not disturbing the aether. Now we will be lighting a fire on a mountainside in the dark of night. Vethnir hunters will come, Bjorna, wraiths. The hungry will find their food. I am not trying to dissuade you. That would be like trying to shift a mountain. I just want you to understand. We do not call out in the Sea of Spirits for a reason. When we do, it has a cost."

"I understand."

"In this plane *and* the waking world. If the Vethnir are close or they have a Starchaser amongst them… Is it worth it?"

"I will do this, with or without you."

Tamzin nodded and squeezed Ella's shoulders. "Close your eyes. And listen to my voice."

Ella did as she was told, feeling the beating of her heart alongside that of the Ilyienë, Faenir beside her in the waking world.

"There are… layers… to Níthianelle. Planes of existence wrapped around each other and buried within. Souls can drift between them, and Blooddancers can walk them. If your mother is here and Fenryr cannot sense her, she will be hidden within their depths. That night you thought you saw your mother, you were dreaming. What were you dreaming of?"

"A time when I was a child."

"Take me back to that memory. To that moment. To what you were feeling at that exact moment."

Ella nodded and closed her eyes. Her home took shape around her, the fire crackling, the smell of stew clinging to the air.

"Ella, could you fetch me a wooden spoon?" Freis's voice echoed.

"Can you tell us the story of Cassian Tal?" Calen's voice followed.

"Not again." Ella remembered being irritated. Calen had always asked for the same stories, the tales of Cassian Tal, of the man who slew Durin Longfang and Taran Shadesmire. Another lie from their parents. But Ella would have given the entire world just to hear her dad tell those stories again, more of those lies, just to hear his voice.

"Maybe a different one?" Freis's voice called out again and again. *"Maybe a different one? Maybe a different one?"*

"I can hear her," Ella whispered. As she did, white smoke swirled before her and took her mother's shape, and that of Calen's and Haem's and their dad's. "I can see them. They're right there."

Ella watched as her parents sat by the fire, Ella, Calen, and Haem beside them, and their father told story after story. As she watched, her mam's eyes flickered, and she stared at Ella.

Ella's skin goosefleshed. "Mam?" She tried to hug her mam, but Freis vanished in a wisp of smoke. "Mam!" Ella screamed, panic in her veins. "Mam!"

"Don't linger," Tamzin's voice echoed in Ella's mind, her hands squeezing tighter on Ella's shoulder. "Don't let yourself become lost. Hear my voice, feel the soul of the tree, let it anchor you. This memory will try and hold you. Don't let it."

A deep laugh sounded behind Ella. "Arrogant or stupid, Wolfchild?"

Ella knew the voice, the wolf in her blood snarling as she turned.

The man who had hunted her in Níthianelle before stood in her home, his grey hair falling over his shoulders, his eyes sharp and yellow. Six more stood with him, a mixture of men and women and three Angan in the forms of giant hawks, brown and white smoke misting from their figures.

Ella snapped her eyes open, seeing Tamzin before her. She once again stood in the Tahír un Ilyienë beneath the white light of Níthianelle. "They're here."

A scream sounded over her shoulder, and Ella turned to see Fenryr standing some twenty feet tall, his body covered in black and gold fur, his face a blend of wolf and man. The god ripped his claws through a giant hawk, tearing it into three pieces that hit the ground with wisps of smoke and vanished. A ripple swept through Ella, a shiver over her skin, a feeling of dread in her bones.

All about the platform, Angan and druids tore at each other. The other druids of Fenryr had arrived and stood beside the Fenryr Angan. There were far more Vethnir Angan and druids than those of the wolf god, but Fenryr himself carved through them as though they were nothing.

"Keep going," Fenryr snarled, his golden eyes fixing on Ella. "They know we are here now. They know *I* am here. Find her."

Tamzin squeezed Ella's shoulders. "Close your eyes."

FARDA RIPPED HIS SWORD FROM its scabbard at the sight of one of the Fenryr Angan dropping to the ground, blood spurting from a wound in its throat that seemed to form of its own volition. "What in the gods?"

Beside him, Tanner did the same, the rasp of steel ringing out. The elves who had occupied the platform with them had all run, screaming. Except for two Rakina, Willam and Ah-aela, who both opened themselves to the Spark at the sight of the dead Angan.

And yet nothing else moved. No attack came.

Farda dropped to one knee and ran his finger along the wound in the Angan's throat, blood coating his skin. "What is happening?"

A chilling scream pierced the air, and Farda snapped his head around to see a druid's body sliced in two across the navel, blood and innards spilling out, the two halves hitting the stone with a thump. He leapt to his feet, dropping into Howling Wolf.

"Kyrana, what in the fuck is going on?" Tanner stood to Farda's left, eyes scanning the enormous basin.

"Do I look like I have the slightest idea?"

"They're here," Sennik – the Aldruid – said, his eyes closed, that massive black wolf snarling at his side. "Ready yourselves."

"I'll get the others!" Willam called, sprinting towards the bridge.

As he ran, a white orb burst into life in his path and spread outwards into some sort of doorway. A vast mountainscape stood on the other side. A man stepped through, twice as tall as Tanner and broad as a bull. He roared and rammed his fist through Willam's gut, spreading his fingers as they burst through the man's back, blood dripping.

"Brother!" the man roared, a monstrous grin stretching his lips. "I've been looking for you!"

ELLA WAS BACK IN HER home, in The Glade, but the memory was not hers. Throngs of people were gathered around her home, faces she knew: Marlo Egon, Jorvill Ehrnin, Anya Gritten, Erdhardt Hammersmith, and so many others.

All of them stood around a circle of Lorian soldiers. Ella shoved through, white mist rising as she slipped to the front. "Mam… Dad…"

Ella's parents stood at the centre alongside Calen and two men… Farda.

The man beside Farda was touching his cheek, and her dad glared at him.

"Put a sword in my hand and show me who you are," Vars said.

Ella screamed as the man leapt forwards. She felt that same shift in the air she did when mages tried to wield their magic, and she saw her dad's hands start to move and then freeze as the man's sword pierced his chest.

"Dad!"

A shiver ran through Ella's spine as her mam's neck twisted and white eyes stared into hers. The world erupted in a cloud of smoke, then resettled as Freis leapt at Farda and the man sent her smashing through the wall of their home. Seconds later, the entire structure burst into flames.

Ella roared and charged, pushing through the crowd. To her left, Farda raised his sword over Calen and stopped when he saw her, his eyes staring into her soul. An arrow sliced through his arm, white blood spraying, and Ella darted into the flames of her home.

FARDA BROUGHT HIS BLADE DOWN with a crunch into the neck of a hawk large enough to pick up a horse. Blood spurted, and brittle bones gave way. The Angan screamed and thrashed, its talons slicing through Farda's shirt and gouging the flesh beneath.

Faenir crashed into the creature's chest, ripping and tearing, bloodied feathers and chunks of flesh coming away in his teeth. He brought the Angan to the ground and tore at its throat, thrashing his head left and right until the creature's shrieks died.

The wolfpine stood over the dead Angan and howled, blood dripping from his jaws.

A monstrosity of a man charged at Faenir, and the wolfpine turned and snarled, ready to leap, but Tanner swept across him and drove a sword through the man's skull, twisting the blade at the end. The druid went limp and dropped as Tanner pulled the sword free.

All three of them stood around Ella and Tamzin, who were frozen like statues, their eyes pure white.

Farda had seen many things across the centuries, but nothing like this.

Before him, wolves and bears and hawks – all far larger than they had a right to be – ripped each other to pieces, drenching the entire platform in blood and scattering body parts.

Here and there, druids and Angan dropped dead without a blade touching them, and at the centre of it all, two gods collided.

A wolf and a bear both as large as dragons smashed each other through the stone terraces of the basin, tearing strips of flesh from one another, the ground shaking beneath their weight.

Elven warriors rushed through the entrance, bows and swords in hand, gawking at the carnage within the basin.

Portals opened from thin air, showing a world of misty white on the other side, druids and Angan stepping through. Farda could see a battle raging beyond the portals, as though the fighting were happening in two worlds at one time.

In that moment, he heard something: Ella screaming, pain etched into her voice. The sound of it sent a shiver through him. He stared at the nearest portal, then back at Ella.

Farda grabbed Tanner's arm. "Protect her with your life."

"Always," Tanner answered.

Farda broke into a sprint, sliding across the stone as a bear large enough to bite a horse in half charged across his path. He slid beneath the creature, then wove threads of Air into a ball in his hand and slammed it down. Farda spun as he rose, the Air propelling him, his blade carving through the bear's leg.

The sword cut clean, blood streaming in its wake, and the bear collapsed on its side, howling and kicking.

Farda carried on into a sprint in the same motion and leapt through the portal before it collapsed behind him.

His entire body went cold as ice, his heartbeat thumping in his veins, every hair on his body standing on end. He stood in the same place, in the Tahír un Ilyienë, the Ilyienë tree looming over him. But here its leaves glowed with variegated light, shimmering and pulsing.

Tanner was gone, as were Faenir and the other wolves, and Ah-aela, but the Angan, the druids, and the two gods fought here with an even greater savagery. White mist trailed every movement, black, gold, and grey smoke shrouding the battling warriors.

The two gods were titans, two hundred feet tall, white blood spilling like rain. They stood on two legs, their faces looking part bear and wolf, part man.

Farda had never felt so insignificant, so powerless.

A shriek sounded above, and Farda lifted his head to see a hawk so large it covered the sky. The creature swooped down and latched its talons into the back of the wolf god, gold smoke pluming as white blood spilled.

Through it all, Farda saw Ella and Tamzin, two Fenryr Angan standing guard over them. He ran, his entire body feeling as though he'd dropped himself into a lake, his skin cold, veins cold, bones cold. This place did not want him. And yet, there was something *more* here. As though he were that little bit closer to being whole.

Ella stood with her eyes closed, hands grasping Tamzin's wrists while Tamzin's palms were flat on Ella's shoulders.

Tamzin's eyes narrowed as she saw Farda, her pupils sharpening to black slits. "You should not be here."

"Well, I am."

"You don't understand," Tamzin said, glancing back at Ella. "Souls like yours were not meant for Níthianelle. Mortal souls should not walk this place, let alone souls that are shattered."

Farda looked down at his hands and realised cracks spread through his body like a dropped vase, gleaming light slipping through the gaps.

"Listen to me."

"MAM!" Ella shrieked, her eyes still closed, her fingers visibly tightening around Tamzin's wrists.

"What is happening?"

"Let's have a chat about it when we're not all close to death. For now, listen. Think of something in the mortal plane, something that grounds you, that anchors you… something you can hold on to. If you don't, you will lose yourself here. Do that, turn around, and cut down anything that comes near us."

Farda nodded, then turned. He drew a slow breath, his fingers tightening around the hilt of his sword. In his mind, he pictured Ella standing with her hand on the tree. He would not let any harm come to her. He would be her shield.

A man with the shoulders of an ox charged at him, a Bjorna Angan at his side. Two Fenryr Angan leapt at the Bjorna, and Farda threw himself at the druid, his sword slicing through flesh and bone.

I will be the man I was. I will be worthy of her again.

⌒⌖

ELLA STOOD IN THE BLAZING white flames, the sound of crackling wood like thunder in her ears.

"Mam!"

She raised a hand over her eyes, the light blinding. She wanted to run, to pull herself from Níthianelle, to fight with the others, but the wolf within her howled in defiance. Its hackles rose, and the world shifted once more, and Ella stood on the front steps of her home. The flames were gone.

Her mam stood before her in the garden, staring wide-eyed. They both remained still for a brief moment, as though neither believed the other was real. And then they crashed together.

Ella squeezed her mam with every drop of strength she could find, clasping her hands together at Freis's back, fingers interlocking. She would not be ripped away again. She would not lose her mam again.

"My sweet girl," Freis whispered. "My sweet, sweet girl."

The sound of her mam's voice sent a tremble through Ella, her hands shaking, her mouth unable to form words. Real or not, she never wanted to leave that moment.

"I'm here, Ella." Freis ran a hand through Ella's hair, her fingers pressing into the back of Ella's head.

"You're alive?" Ella pulled away and looked over her mam's face. "This is real? You're real? You're here?"

Freis nodded. "I'm here. This is real. I'm real."

"How? I saw you die… Calen saw you die… You… You…" Ella's words kept catching in her throat, her breaths cut short by tears.

"I saw a thousand thousand futures, my girl. I looked through the stars and beyond, and on every path where your dad and I lived, you and your brothers died." Freis stroked Ella's cheek as though she might break. "We had no choice. There *was* no choice. Your dad and I agreed. Your lives above ours, always. But there are some things even Pathfinders can't see."

"How are you here? How are you alive?" Ella looked over her mam from head to toe as though expecting to find some crack or imperfection, some sign that this was all a dream, all some twisted piece of Níthianelle.

Freis smiled, continuing to stroke Ella's cheek. "You have become such a woman." Her mother puffed out her cheeks, tears glistening in her eyes. "Such a strong, fierce woman. There is so much to tell."

"Come with me, now, come with me… please."

The smile on Freis's lips curled downwards. "I have followed you from the moment you set foot in this place. Watched you as closely as I could."

"It was you," Ella whispered, thinking back to when something had scared that Vethnir hunter away and saved her life.

Freis nodded. "I've been here for a long time… But I've not always been me. With each day, we see more, we feel more. And we understand. We… there are rules, Ella. Laws, oaths that cannot be so easily broken… but can be bent, twisted."

"You're not making any sense. What rules? What do you mean 'we'?"

Freis brushed a strand of Ella's hair from her face. "Freis should have died…" Her mother stopped herself, her lips moving without sound, eyes staring into the distance for a moment. "*I should have died. On every path, I died. I needed to die for you to live. She saved me. She took me from death as I straddled the veil between worlds... She stretched the oaths to breaking.*"

"Who saved you? Mam, what's happening?"

"Elyara... I am her... We are..." As Freis looked at Ella, her eyes glowed with a brilliant white light and her voice shifted. The sound of Freis Bryer was gone. "There are oaths, young one. Oaths sworn millennia ago. To cross to the mortal world would have ripples... But to be here, in the folds of space and time, my kin never forbade that. To splinter myself between planes. To find a soul that could bear my own, one that could see how I see, to bind it to my own in this world... A soul that would charge towards its own doom, knowing the end and facing it anyway. I knew Efialtír was scheming, and I could not allow him free rein while the others sat and watched. I simply could not."

Ella stepped back, unable to look away from her mam. Elyara. The Maiden. "What are you?"

The voice shifted again, like two layered atop one another. "We are Freis, and we are Elyara. We are both." Freis's voice vanished once more. "Efialtír seeks to cross into your world. Many of my kin do not see the danger. They hold to the old oaths, oaths sworn with a purpose but ultimately flawed. If he crosses, we must be ready to fight. But to take form in the mortal plane would cost me half."

"Half of what?"

"Everything." Freis stared into Ella's eyes. "There may come a day soon where that sacrifice will be necessary, but we must bide our time. I can do more from here at this moment. I care for this world and I will not let him burn it."

A searing pain raked across Ella's back, and she lurched forwards, howling.

The light in Elyara's eyes vanished, and Freis's voice returned. "Ella!"

Freis wrapped her arms around Ella, her fingers coming away coated in glistening white blood.

Ella felt something tug at her, Tamzin's voice booming in her ears. "ELLA! Come back to us!"

The world around Ella began to collapse, and she reached out her hand, grasping for Freis.

"No!" Freis shouted. She grabbed hold of Ella, hands clasping Ella's shoulders. "I am here. I will never leave you. Your brother?"

"They're alive," Ella said, nodding frantically, Tamzin's voice clawing at the back of her mind.

"They?" Freis's mouth dropped open, her eyes widening, voice cracking. "Haem? He's alive? How?"

"He's alive, Mam. He came back to us."

"My boy..." Freis's eyes glistened, white light shimmering in her tears.

"Ella!" Tamzin's voice thundered again, and Ella's fingers slipped through Freis's.

"Mam, no!" Ella felt herself pulling away.

"I'm here, Ella. I won't leave you."

Everything collapsed in on itself in a plume of swirling smoke, and Ella once more stood in Níthianelle's mirror of Tahír un Ilyienë.

Screams and shouts and howls sounded all around her, Angan and druids battling.

A host of Aldithmar swarmed down the terraces, black smoke swirling around them. They tore through the Bjorna and Vethnir Angan, dark claws rending.

"Ella, can you fight?" Tamzin held Ella's face, staring into her eyes, white blood smeared across her.

Ella nodded, her mind swirling with a blend of loss, confusion, anger, and sorrow. The wolf within her snapped and snarled, furious to be torn from Freis.

Her eyes fell on something she could not understand. Farda knelt in front of her, his sword buried in the gut of an enormous bear, his shirt and trousers in tatters, white blood streaming from a hundred cuts. He ripped his blade free, then stood and cut down a woman who charged at him with gleaming green eyes, her shoulders as dense and muscled as Haem's.

Bodies lay all around him, the ground slick with white blood. Farda turned to her, grimacing and limping on one leg. "Are you hurt?"

Ella shook her head. She could feel the pain in her back where something had raked its claws across her, but she would live. Farda looked like he wouldn't.

"We need to leave this place," Tamzin said, looking about her. "The Bjorna and Vethnir have too many Angan, and they are too strong here."

A roar like booming thunder rang out, and Ella spun to see Fenryr standing like a mountain, his claws buried in an enormous hawk, the branches of the Ilyienë tree bowing around him. The god roared again, his eyes gleaming with golden light, and the hawk's body split, tearing from neck to feet, white blood streaming in rivers.

Shrieks rang all about, and Vethnir Angan dropped from the sky, smashing into the ground, lifeless.

Fenryr held the two pieces of Vethnir in the air and stared at a god that Ella knew could only be Bjorna. "You wanted me, brother. Here I am!"

He dropped the pieces of the dead god and lunged at Bjorna.

Ella stared in awe as the gods went to war. She pulled her gaze away, looking from Tamzin to Farda. "How do we get him out of here?"

"Leave me." Farda dropped to one knee, his sword skittering against the ground in a plume of white mist.

"How?" Ella repeated, staring at Tamzin.

"There!" She pointed towards a gateway that had just opened only a few feet away. "We need to get him back through to the waking world."

Ella grabbed at Farda, but the man swatted her away. "Leave me! I can hear them... I can hear them calling..."

The wolf in Ella's blood howled, and she felt it grab hold of her. She leaned down and thrust a shoulder into Farda's chest, hauling him up over her back, her legs burning beneath her. She broke into a run, the strength of the wolf surging through her, a rage burning in her veins.

The shape of a man emerged in the gateway, his eyes white as snow. Ella drew on the wolf's strength and launched herself at the man, hauling Farda on her shoulder. She crashed into the Starchaser, and all three of them hurtled back through the gateway.

In an instant, Ella was filled with a blinding pain, as though her soul was being ripped from her body.

About her, the fighting still raged. She was back in the waking world, but her body flickered, seeming to shift and change. She screamed, the agony burning through her. Then she saw herself standing with her hand on the trunk of the Ilyienë. Her true body.

Tamzin stood beside Ella's body, Faenir, Kerith, and Tanner with her. The woman turned and found Ella.

Ella couldn't hear a thing. All she saw was Tamzin screaming at her, face red, eyes wide.

The wolf within Ella howled and shrieked. Ella charged towards her physical body, feeling something pull at her with every step, trying to drag her away. A sword flashed before her face, then passed through as though she were not there. She kept moving until she crashed into herself, and the pain stopped, replaced by a shiver spreading from head to toe.

She gasped for air, stumbling backwards, Tamzin grabbing her.

"That was the most reckless thing I've ever seen in my life," Tamzin said, clasping Ella's face in her hands. "I can't believe you're alive."

The ground shook beneath Ella, and she turned her attention to where Bjorna and Fenryr smashed through the shattered remains of the terraces, chunks of stone tumbling into the streams that fed the central chamber.

A roar sounded over the ledge of the basin, resonating against the stone. A moment passed, and then the enormous frame of Sardakes appeared at the upper ledge and descended into the basin. The great black dragon spread his blue wings and hurled himself at Bjorna.

Sardakes smashed into the bear god, bit down into Bjorna's shoulder, and ripped a chunk free. He threw Bjorna backwards and roared again, Fenryr standing beside him.

Without a thought, Ella reached her mind outwards, half of her floating in Níthianelle, half in the waking world. Her sight flickered between the vivid colours before her and the pale whites of the Sea of Spirits. She could feel Sardakes's fury and his pain as clearly as she felt her own.

For a moment it looked as though Bjorna would charge into both Fenryr and the dragon, but the bear god stopped and stared up at something behind Ella.

There, at the top of the basin, standing on the ledge where a waterfall crashed down, was a stag larger than Valerys, its antlers black as coal, its fur white as sun-bleached bone.

"Dvalin…" Tamzin whispered. "All the Danuan have awoken."

Fenryr looked to Dvalin, then turned back to Bjorna. "What say you now, brother?"

Glistening white blood poured from wounds all about Bjorna's body, but even still, he looked as though he could tear through a mountain. The bear god stared at Fenryr for a few moments. A cloud of green and black smoke swirled around him, shifting and changing, until the largest man Ella had ever seen stood where the monstrous god had been.

"I've missed our battles, brother," Bjorna called out, his voice carrying in the broken basin of shattered terraces. "Let's not leave it so long."

A white light came to life behind Bjorna, spreading into a portal that showed a vast mountain on the other side. The god stepped through, and the portal collapsed behind him. Three more portals appeared across the central platform and the remaining Bjorna Angan and druids fled, leaving their dead behind. The surviving Vethnir druids did the same, their Angan already dead alongside their god.

Ella collapsed to the ground, her head resting against the trunk of the Ilyienë. From where she sat, she could see Farda's chest rising and falling in steady sweeps, and in her mind's eye, all she saw was her mother's face.

CHAPTER ONE HUNDRED AND THREE

THE NECESSARY PATH

27th Day of the Blood Moon

Western villages of Illyanara – Winter, Year 3081 After Doom

The light of the morning sun shone over the peaks of Wolfpine Ridge in the distance, glowing bright across the treeline of Ölm Forest. Calen and the others had set out on horseback at sunrise, Valerys soaring overhead. He had asked Tivar to remain at Salme to watch over the city with Avandeer and Varthear. Tivar and Avandeer agreed, Varthear however had other intentions.

The great blue dragon followed Valerys, vermillion wings pale and glowing in the morning light.

They had spent some hours helping to take the bodies down from the trees along the Oak Road. Calen could have used the Spark, but the thought of it made him feel empty. Those people deserved the care and attention of living hands. They deserved the respect that had been denied to them.

At that moment, Lanan Halfhand was coordinating the dig of the burial site. Calen and the others would return to pay their respects once they left The Glade.

Ahead, Calen could see the burnt remains of the place he had once called home, the place he had once believed he would spend the rest of his life. With every step the horse took, Calen's heart hammered heavier against his ribs.

"It's strange seeing it for the first time," Dann said, pulling his horse alongside Calen's.

"Do you remember the night Rist had his first mead?" Calen gestured towards the charred remains of a tree stump that had stood near the western edge of the village.

"Like it was yesterday," Dann answered. "Erdhardt stood in the puddle of puke the very next morning."

Erdhardt looked back from atop the mountain of a horse he rode, Erik and Tarmon riding beside him. "He handled it better than you did your first mead, Master Pimm."

"It's not a competition," Dann called back, a fleeting smile touching his lips.

The memory gave Calen a brief moment of joy, but it died as soon as his thoughts turned to the Firnin Mountains. To Rist. He still hadn't told Dann. How did you tell someone something like that? He knew he needed to… but he also needed to find the right moment.

Calen tilted his head back and looked to Valerys and Varthear in the sky, then brought his gaze back down to the burnt buildings that had begun to creep around them. He opened his mouth to speak, but the words caught in his throat when he noticed that Haem had dismounted ahead.

Haem stood before a line of thick, silvery lavender bushes, one hand gripping his horse's reins.

Calen threw one leg over and slid from his saddle, charred wood and ash crunching beneath him. He approached as slowly as he could without coming to a halt. As he walked, his mind drifted back to that day – the day everything had changed. The day Therin had saved his life. The day his mam and dad had died.

A hand rested on his back, and he turned and gave Anya a weak smile.

"Erdhardt planted the lavender," Anya said. "He took it from the bush Freis had planted by his own home. It was one of the only things that didn't burn when the Uraks attacked."

Calen looked over to try and find Erdhardt with his gaze. The man had drifted away and knelt amidst the charred remains of his home.

Haem had told Calen of Aela's death, of the night The Glade had been attacked, of how the man had fought like a god, only to lose the one thing he loved. Calen allowed Erdhardt to mourn in peace and went to join Haem by the silvered lavender bushes that now stood where their home had once been.

The silence stretched for what seemed like an eternity and yet could never truly have been long enough.

"I'm sorry you had to face that alone," Haem whispered, staring down at the patch of turned earth within the lavender bushes.

"I wasn't alone." Calen glanced at Dann, who stood only a few paces behind him, Lyrei at his side, Anya, Vaeril, and Tarmon close by. He looked back over at Haem, who stood in silence with his hands clasped behind his back, staring at the dirt.

Calen rested a hand on Haem's shoulder, then returned to the horse, where two saplings hung in a satchel from the saddle. They had been given to Erdhardt by a forester from Salme, and Erdhardt had given them to Calen. Seeds wouldn't grow this time of year without constant tending, but the saplings stood a chance.

Calen pulled out the clay pots from the satchels and handed one to Haem.

His brother took it as though being handed a newborn babe. He inclined his head and gave Calen a fragile smile.

"They'd stand a better chance in spring," Calen said, standing beside his brother.

"Calen, we had the same mam. I know what season is best to plant ash." Haem elbowed Calen in the shoulder gently, then looked down at the pot in his hand. "Thank you."

Calen nodded. "After this, we'll fly to your temple. I promise."

The air shook, wingbeats thumping overhead, and both Valerys and Varthear alighted on the other side of where Calen's home had once stood. Sorrow and loss radiated from Valerys as the dragon stared down at the patch of earth, a low rumble in his throat.

Valerys had never met Vars and Freis, never seen their love with his own eyes or heard it with his own ears or felt it with his own heart. But the dragon knew their love through Calen, and he mourned them the same.

Calen stepped forwards through the gaps in the lavender. He set the clay pot down and, with his hands, he dug a deep hole in the earth.

Beside him, Haem did the same.

Together they pulled their saplings free and set them gently in the ground, covering the roots with soil.

Anya handed Calen a waterskin, and he poured water onto the loose earth.

He knelt there with his hand pressed into the soil, his eyes fixed on the small sapling.

His mam and dad had been gone for so long now, but this was the first time Calen was truly saying goodbye. A hand came to rest on his back, and he didn't have to look to know it was Haem's.

After a few moments, Haem pulled his hand away, and when he returned it, he held a red silk scarf with vines of gold and cream leaves blowing in the wind.

Calen looked from the scarf to Haem, asking the question with his eyes.

"I thought it would be nice if you finally got a chance to give it to her."

Calen let out a soft laugh and took a piece of the scarf between his thumb and forefinger, feeling an immediate sense of relief at its soft touch. "You're sure?"

"It was never mine. I was just minding it," Haem answered. "You bought it for Mam. She should have it."

Calen nodded softly and took the scarf into his hands. He scooped a layer of earth away, placed the scarf down, and covered it.

"The sun will set," Haem whispered, pressing his hand to the ground beside where Calen had buried the scarf. "And it will rise again, and it will do so the next day and the next. The gods are in charge of such things, but it is by our own will that we pick ourselves up when we fall."

Haem's eyes glistened with tears, but none fell. He squeezed his hand into a fist, soil slipping through his fingers. "I've seen a lot since the day Kallinvar found me, but still our father is the greatest man I've ever known."

"Cassian Tal," Calen whispered. "Lies over lies."

"He was still Vars Bryer." Haem rubbed the dirt between his fingers, looking to Calen. "He still raised you, fed you, cared for you. He still held a damp cloth to your head for days on end when you got that fever, remember? You'd only seen five, maybe six, summers. He never left your side. Not for a minute. He slept on the floor beside you. Erdhardt was losing his mind because he needed horseshoes and Dad hadn't stepped foot in the forge for days. He will always be that man."

"I remember." Calen did remember. His mam had said he'd been lucky to keep his life with that fever. He only remembered flashes, but his dad was in all of them.

"He taught you to use that sword," Haem said, gesturing to the sword at Calen's hip. "And he did a damn good job."

Calen dropped his hand to the coin pommel of his father's sword, the cool touch of the steel calming him.

"Cassian Tal, Vars Bryer – the name doesn't matter. He was our dad, and he was a hero of legend to me long before I knew anything about Cassian Tal." Haem dropped the last of the dirt from his hand. "I wouldn't change a day."

Calen gripped the coin pommel tighter. "Neither would I." He drew a sharp breath. "I just miss him. I wish he was here."

"Me too."

Valerys lowered his neck, his snout brushing the ground beside the two saplings, a low rumble reverberating in his throat. The dragon blew a warm breath over the soil, a wave of loss cresting into Calen's mind. He let out a whine, Varthear watching from behind him.

That whine grew into a deep growl as Valerys lifted his head. The dragon spread his wings and roared at the sky, Varthear joining him.

The roar was sadness, and emptiness, and a deep sense of sorrow for a father he had never known. A father who had forged half of his soul.

Both Calen and Haem stood as the two dragons roared. And when their voices grew silent, Calen saw that Erdhardt, Dann, Tarmon, Anya, and Vaeril and all the others stood about them.

Tarmon still wore his steel plate, which he'd clearly polished the day before, white cloak clasped at his shoulders. The five Dracurïn who'd accompanied them all stood behind the High Commander, heads bowed.

"Nur temen vie'ryn valana," Vaeril said, loud and clear, a closed fist pressed to his chest. "Vir væra vëna aier andin i'il nära un ael Heraya. Du vyin alura anis."

Calen was about to translate when Vaeril took it upon himself.

"For those we have lost," Vaeril said. "We will see them again in the light of Heraya's arms. You can rest now."

"May The Mother embrace you," Calen said, tears falling slowly.

"And The Father protect you," Therin added.

Haem placed his hand on his chest. "May The Warrior guide your hand."

"And The Maiden guide your mind." Dann inclined his head to Calen.

"May The Smith keep your blade sharp." Anya's voice was barely louder than a whisper.

"And The Sailor see you to safe shores." It was Lyrei who added the last line, her hand wrapping around Dann's, their fingers interlocking.

One by one they all stepped away, leaving Calen and Haem standing over the ground beneath which their parents had been laid to rest.

After a while, Haem squeezed Calen's shoulder and left him alone by the saplings. Calen had no idea how long he stood there. The sun had moved across the sky but still burned bright when he heard Kaygan's voice.

"He really was something with a blade."

Calen snapped his head around to find the kat god standing beside him, staring down at the saplings. A portal closed behind him as Una stepped through.

"Why are you here?"

"The paths we walk are ever winding." Kaygan tilted his head to the side, his pupils narrowing to black slits. "The gods are waking, Calen Bryer. Efialtír stirs them from their slumber."

Calen said nothing, turning his gaze back to the saplings. He would not play Kaygan's games. He had done that enough already.

"Sometimes, Calen, you have to burn something down to build something better in its place. Sometimes you have to burn a whole world to create space for a new one. Our people have hidden for so long, and yet, even if we hadn't, we are so bent on killing one another we would have wiped ourselves out eventually."

Calen looked at Kaygan for a moment, then over at Valerys, who stared at the god with those lavender eyes.

"I have spent millennia carefully cultivating this path, meticulously pruning every weed that grew, filling every crack. Valerys was meant to be our first. A new dawn for our people, wielding the power that brought us to our knees. The souls of Cealtaí and the Evalien and all the mortal bloods are so easily steered. If you offer them what they want, what they *need*, they will ignore the cost, ignore any dangers that lie right before their eyes. But those born of Danuan blood are not the same. You are stubborn beyond measure. And sometimes what will not move must *be* moved. And let's not forget those damn Enkara. No path is clear when they meddle."

"This is not the time," Calen snapped, attempting to hold down the rage that burned within him, fed by Valerys. This moment was not his. It belonged to Vars and Freis.

Kaygan only smiled, a fang pinching his bottom lip. "Do you know the one truth I have learned in all these years, Calen Bryer?"

Calen pressed his tongue against the roof of his mouth, holding that anger down. He didn't answer.

The kat god let out a long, mournful sigh. "All great things require sacrifice. That is an immutable truth. You altered the path, Calen. Not I. You. For what little it matters, I did not want this. I wanted you to be the tip of our spear. I wanted you to be our future. But you chose to be the leaf that fought the wind. You forced my hand."

Calen turned to speak when a burning pain seared through his chest. His breath caught in his lungs, his body shaking.

He looked down to see Kaygan's claws buried in his chest, bloodstains forming in the tunic around them.

Pure fury and fear consumed everything within him as Valerys roared, and Calen felt pieces of himself begin to break.

"You strayed from the path, Wolfchild. That life you could have saved was your own… if only you had just listened."

"Valerys…" Calen's voice trembled, and he could feel Valerys screaming in his mind as the dragon leapt towards Kaygan. "Valerys…"

Something cracked, and the world went dark and cold.

HAEM'S ENTIRE WORLD STOPPED.

He heard Valerys roar, saw the man pull his hand from Calen's chest, saw Calen fall.

Valerys lunged at the man, Varthear with him, but he moved like a ghost, slipping past the dragons as talons raked earth. Dann and Therin ran to Calen, screaming. Tarmon and Vaeril charged the strange man, swords drawn.

The man raked his claws across Tarmon's chest, gouging the steel, then spun and slipped past Vaeril.

Valerys unleashed a pillar of fire, bright as the sun. The flames washed over the ruined homes but parted around the strange man.

A white portal opened like a tear in the world and the man slipped through, a woman with him. And then they were gone.

Screams sounded all around, and Haem could barely move. His heart felt as though it were going to split open his chest.

It was Valerys's roar that broke him free from his mind. The dragon was fury and loss, his roar shifting from clapping thunder to a hissing shriek. He swept his tail and smashed through the remnants of old houses, lifting char and dust into the air, shrieking and roaring.

The blue dragon, Varthear, shrieked back at him, but Valerys smashed his tail into her side and unleashed a torrent of fire over her.

The Dracur'in that had stood behind Tarmon drew their swords, and Valerys reduced them to ash. The roar that left his throat shook the earth itself, and Haem could feel the dragon's pain tearing his own heart.

Valerys whipped his head around to Calen's body, where Therin and Dann had dropped to their knees, screaming and shouting.

The dragon snapped his head forwards, jaws opening.

Haem leapt, his Sentinel armour pouring from his Sigil. He set himself between the dragon and Dann and Therin, slamming his gauntleted hands against Valerys's snout.

The dragon roared, and Haem roared back, memories flooding through him. Memories of an egg cracking, of eyes looking up at a young man who held him. Memories of riding at the nape of a horse's neck, of sleeping on Calen's shoulders, of feeling the pain in Calen's heart.

In that moment, Haem understood. Calen was everything to Valerys. He was his heart and his soul. He was his joy and his solace. And he was gone. He was dead, and Valerys was alone.

Haem gripped Valerys's snout, forced his helmet to recede into his collar, and stared deep into the dragon's lavender eyes. "We can save him. There's a chance. We can save him… We have to try."

Valerys stared back at him, talons carving into the earth, his breath like the heat of a forge. The dragon's eyes were two pools of agony and rage. Valerys let out a low whine and rested his head on the ground.

Haem turned immediately and pushed Dann and Therin out of the way, ignoring their shouts. He scooped his hands beneath Calen's lifeless body and carried him to Valerys.

Cradling Calen in one arm, Haem climbed atop the dragon's back, his Sentinel armour granting him the strength. He laid Calen before him and leaned forwards, pressing himself as close to the dragon as he could and wrapping his hands around small horns that grew about the dragon's scales.

Valerys roared and lifted into the air with such force Haem was almost ripped from his back.

CHAPTER ONE HUNDRED AND FOUR

THE WATERS OF LIFE

27th Day of the Blood Moon

Temple of Achyron – Winter, Year 3081 After Doom

allinvar stood in Brother Gildrick's study. He had not allowed the Watchers to move a thing after Gildrick had been given the rites and laid to rest. He had searched every inch of the room, every book, every shelf, chest, drawer – everything. And still he'd found nothing. Whatever book Gildrick had been reading before he died was lost to them. Tallia had likely burned it. But if it was a book worth burning, that meant it had something deeply important within its pages.

Gildrick's voice rang in Kallinvar's mind. *"Well, I've known you all my life. If I didn't have some idea what you were thinking, I wouldn't be a very good Watcher."*

Those were the words Gildrick had spoken when he had given Kallinvar the chronicles of the Grandmasters written by the Watchers. Perhaps if Kallinvar had paid half as much attention to Gildrick as Gildrick had to him, the man would still be alive. He tried not to dwell on the thought, but it was easier said than done. Outside, the rain had not ceased in days, thunder rumbling. He had asked Watcher Poldor and the others to speak to the people of Ardholm, to calm them and assuage their fears after the other night, but a tension still held in the air. The porters and servants in the temple stared at the ground as they passed him in the halls, and all conversations grew quiet whenever he approached.

Ruon and the other knights had reported similar. Kallinvar didn't blame the people. The knights were meant to be their protectors, paragons of honour and strength. And the other night, the people had watched Kallinvar draw a sacred weapon against one of their own, a weapon of the gods. Wounds from broken trust were a long time in healing.

A commotion sounded outside the door, and Ruon came bursting through, Ildris and a number of Watchers with her.

"Arden is back." Ruon didn't need to say more. Kallinvar reached out, and he could feel the hollowness in Arden's Sigil, the deep aching loss.

He pushed past the others and sprinted through the great halls of Achyron's temple, following the pulse of Arden's weeping Sigil.

HAEM HELD CALEN'S BODY IN the waters of Heraya's Well. Clusters of bright light swarmed around him, shimmering amidst the dark water, pulling the pain from his body… but not his heart.

Where the luminescent clusters shifted and reacted to Haem's movement, the water around Calen's body was still and dark.

The colour had drained from his little brother's face, and his lips were a pale blue. Haem brushed away a spot of dried blood from Calen's cheek. Claps of thunder answered Valerys's roars in the skies outside the temple. The dragon had shifted between pure rage and abject sorrow. As they had flown, he had set fire to entire forests, pouring flames from his jaws as they'd moved, roaring like the void itself had spilled open. And then he had been silent, drifting weakly on the air, dropping listlessly through the clouds.

And every movement of the dragon's heart had matched Haem's.

Haem wanted to scream and roar and cry, but his body did nothing. No tears came, no rage swept over him. Everything was just… still and empty.

He looked down at Calen, one arm wrapped around his brother's waist as Calen floated, the other resting behind his head.

The last time Haem had held Calen in his arms, Calen had only been a child – a baby, really. He had always loved having a brother. He loved Ella to the ends of the earth, but it was different. Ella had always been her own. She had always been twice as sharp as Haem, and she'd known it.

But Calen had followed Haem around from the very start and looked at him as though he were some kind of hero from the Age of Honour. Anything Haem did, Calen did too. As soon as Haem had been old enough to hold a sword, Calen had picked up a stick. When Vars had taken Haem hunting for the first time, Calen had snuck past Freis and tried to join them, only to trip on a rock less than a hundred feet into Ölm Forest and slice open his arm.

Haem gave a melancholy laugh as he held his brother's body in the Waters of Life. Freis had been furious with Calen that day, but Vars had just picked him up and placed him on the counter.

"*All real warriors fall, Calen,*" Vars had said, pretending to check the bandage Freis had applied.

"*No, they don't,*" Calen had said through sniffles. "*You didn't. Haem didn't. Just me. I wanted to help.*"

Vars had pulled his shirt off and counted off every scar that laced his chest, back, and arms. There had been so many.

"*You see this one?*" Vars had asked, pointing to a long thin scar across his ribs. "*I got this in the war. Not in a battle. Nothing heroic. I was told to dig a latrine pit. I ran to get a shovel, tripped, sliced myself open on a rock. Just like you.*"

"*You did?*" Calen had stopped sniffling at that.

"*I did. You're a warrior now, Calen. A true warrior. With a battle wound and all.*"

Haem clenched his eyes shut at the memory.

"I should have gotten to you sooner," he said, letting out a long sigh. "I'm sorry, little brother. It should have been me."

Footsteps sounded, and Haem didn't open his eyes.

A few moments passed before a splash sounded and he felt the waters shift around him.

"Brother." Kallinvar's voice was soft. "He's gone, brother. The well cannot bring back the dead."

"I know." Haem trembled, squeezing his hand a little tighter at the back of Calen's head. "I had to try. I had to do something…"

Haem felt Kallinvar place a hand at the back of his head and pull their heads together.

A second voice surprised him – Brother Ildris's. "You are not alone, brother."

Haem opened his eyes to see Ildris, Ruon, and Kallinvar standing in the well with him, the glowing lights of the pool swarming around them.

Ildris rested a hand on Haem's shoulder.

"I should have protected him." With those words, tears flowed from Haem's eyes and rolled over his cheeks, silent and cold.

"We cannot protect everyone," Ildris whispered. "That is something we must accept. It was something that took me a long time."

"He is my little brother," Haem whispered. "Protecting him was my only purpose. And I failed."

Holding Calen in his arms, Haem pushed past Kallinvar, Ruon, and Ildris, moving towards the pool's edge.

"Brother Arden. Where are you going?" Kallinvar asked.

"That's not my name." Haem laid Calen on the well's edge and climbed out of the water, his saturated clothes dragging him down. He lifted Calen back into his arms. "I'm taking him to Valerys."

Haem turned and walked away from the well.

Sylven, Varlin, and Kevan all stood in the garden, each of them bowing their head as Haem passed. The Watchers waited at the entranceway, whispering their blessings as Haem moved through them. Servants, porters, maids, cooks, and every other hand in the temple waited along the great halls. They had all seen him arrive on a dragon and walk through Ardholm with a body in his arms.

The rain poured down over him as he descended the stairs to Ardholm. The people were out in the streets, parting as he passed and walked towards the plateau where Valerys lay, listless.

As Haem walked, some of the children pulled closed fists to their foreheads in a sign of honour. The gesture was mimicked by every soul that Haem passed.

When he reached the plateau, Valerys lifted a wing and Haem sat on the cold stone, his back resting against the dragon's warm scales, the rain sheeting down over them, and his brother's body in his arms.

Valerys let out a low whine and shifted his neck so it curled around Calen and Haem, a lavender eye fixed on the pair of them.

"I'm sorry," Haem whispered to the dragon.

Valerys's only answer was to move his head closer, the scales of his jaw pressed against Calen's side.

Haem closed his eyes, pulled Calen close, and sat there in the rain with no intention of ever rising.

CHAPTER ONE HUNDRED AND FIVE

THE DARKNESS WITHIN

27th Day of the Blood Moon

Temple of Achyron – Winter, Year 3081 After Doom

Kallinvar stood at the top of the stairs that led from the temple, looking out at Arden and the dragon curled on the great plateau that overlooked the city.

He had not expected this. All men died. Death was a part of life. Even Kallinvar, with his immortality granted by Achyron's Sigil, would one day dine in The Warrior's halls. But seeing Calen Bryer fly astride that dragon, seeing him fight at the Battle of Kingspass and his strength in Ilnaen, Kallinvar had not even considered the young man's death.

The day truly was drawing near when Epheria would know the last dragon. He let out a long breath, then turned and re-entered the temple. He should have gone to sleep, should have given his body even a few hours of reprieve, but sleep eluded him. Only three days were left before the Blood Moon set. He would sleep then.

He passed Watcher Timkin in the halls. "Have you seen Watcher Poldor?"

"Not in some hours, Grandmaster. Last I checked, he was in the library."

Kallinvar nodded and carried on. Poldor could wait. He moved through the halls and descended several sets of stairs until the natural light vanished and the smaller corridors were lit by candles in sconces.

Two priests sat at the end of the long corridor that fronted the cell block. Thankfully, ever since Kallinvar had joined the knighthood, the cells had remained empty. There had never been a need for them. But back during the rebellion, thousands of years before Kallinvar's time, they had been a necessity.

The two priests greeted him, one – Toka – leading him through the cell block to where Tallia sat on a low cot in a cell barred by iron.

"Has she spoken?"

Toka shook his head. "Not a word, Grandmaster."

"Leave us."

The priest bowed and left.

Kallinvar stood there for a long while, looking down at Tallia, who had her knees pulled to her chest and her head down. "How are you?"

No answer came. Kallinvar had come to her both nights since she'd been placed in the cell, and the young woman had refused to say a word.

"Tallia, I need you to talk to me. I need you to tell me why."

Still no answer.

"Who turned you away from us? Was it your father?"

"My father is dead."

"I know." Kallinvar hadn't known who Tallia was when Rurik Andle had fallen and broken his neck three years before. His wife's heart had given out the year before that. "I'm sorry for your loss, Tallia. There is still a way back. I need you to give me answers."

Something in the air shifted, and a pulse of Essence swept through the temple, strong enough to set Kallinvar back a step. He drew in a sharp breath at the oily sickness of Taint that touched the air.

"Then ask the right questions." The voice that left Tallia's throat was harsher than before, deeper. "Gildrick asked the right questions. He came close. He did. Unfortunately for him."

When Tallia lifted her head, her eyes glowed with a deep red light. The sight of them twisted coils of dread around Kallinvar's heart.

The woman stepped from the bed, tilting her head to the side as she looked at Kallinvar. "You forced these people to live a life outside the natural world. You placed chains around them and called them safe. You robbed them of choice and of their futures. What did you expect?"

"How is this possible?" Kallinvar summoned his Soulblade, the green light illuminating the chamber. "This place is protected by Achyron himself."

"It *was*," Tallia said, staring at him with those gleaming red eyes. "But all things come to an end, little knight."

"What are you?"

"I am her saviour." Tallia smiled. "When you offered the people of Lurïnel sanctuary here, what did you expect, knight of Achyron? The illusion of choice is Achyron's finest deception, is it not? That has always been the way. He brandishes me as a traitor for wanting to protect the souls of a world I love. And yet he dangles sanctuary before the eyes of desperate men and women and pretends that it is true choice. You are his slave, not his warrior. He does not care about you. He simply hates me."

"Efialtír… How…"

"I have always been here. My blood is in the very crust of this world. I have known of this temple for a long time, but patience was needed. And now that the veil is thin enough to reach across…" Tallia stepped closer to the iron bars. "Your Watcher found my body. He understood."

"A fallen god…" Kallinvar whispered, remembering the old tales his mother used to tell him before she passed. Of how the Sea of Stone had been formed by the body of a dead god. "The Sea of Stone…"

"Well done, knight. But far too late. I tell you now only because you have already failed. I pity you. You are a slave, your choices bound by Achyron's desires. You are a bird in a cage that believes he can fly. I am not the coming shadow as you believe. I am not here to burn this world. I am here to preserve it, to bask in it. You have been lied to."

More pulses of Essence rippled through the temple above, and Kallinvar could feel his knights reaching out to him.

"What have you done?"

"I told you, *Grandmaster Kallinvar.* You are too late."

A convergence like nothing Kallinvar had ever felt erupted in his mind, bathing over the Sea of Stone, rippling outwards from its centre.

"No…"

"Yes."

"You found it…"

"Indeed."

Kallinvar staggered backwards as his Sigil ignited. He felt Brother Valdar of The Third be ripped from the world.

"I do not like to take chances. If you wish to save the people of this place – or at least to try – I would run now. Your brother-knight, Tarron, he told me of your heart. It took a while to pry open his soul… but he acquiesced eventually. Achyron did well in finding you, Kallinvar. I would have had you at my side. There is still time."

"I would rather burn in the void."

"Perhaps you will, but I hope not."

Kallinvar released his Soulblade, drew the sword at his hip, and drove it into Tallia's stomach. The woman screamed, and those red eyes shimmered with light before dulling.

"Grandmaster?" Tallia whispered, her hands around the blade in her chest, her voice once again what Kallinvar remembered.

"Yes, young one?"

"I'm sorry." Blood wet the young woman's tongue. "I didn't want to die here, in this place. I wanted to see the world, to see Valtara, and Loria, and all the places Watcher Gildrick used to tell me of. When he came to me and told me I had a choice… I…"

"When who came to you, Tallia? Who?" Kallinvar's heart stopped. "Watcher Gildrick?"

Tallia grunted, blood dripping from the blade in her gut. "Watcher Poldor. He came to me after my father died."

"Watcher Poldor? No, that can't be."

Tallia looked into Kallinvar's eyes. "I didn't kill Gildrick. I swear it." She drew a deep, hacking breath. "Do you think I'll see them? Will Heraya still take me?"

Kallinvar nodded gently. "The Mother understands mistakes, Tallia."

"It wasn't a mistake." Tallia gave one last breath and fell forwards against the bars.

Kallinvar looked down at her for a moment, pulled his sword free, and sprinted up the steps.

CANDLELIGHT FLICKERED ACROSS THE OPEN chamber, augmented by the crimson glow of Essence vessels and rune markings carved into the stone.

Fane's heart broke at the sight of Garramon floating at the chamber's centre, bare as the day he was born, runes carved into his flesh by Fane himself. Fane had wept as he'd done it.

In his mind, Garramon had always been there at the end. The two of them, standing side by side, looking out at the world they had saved. He had planned everything so meticulously. Sacrificed so much, so many lives, and every plan had fallen perfectly into place... except for this one piece.

"I will truly miss you, my friend. It was you who kept me anchored, reminded me who I was, where I came from. You were a better man than I will ever be. Perhaps I thought your soul would save mine." Fane drew a deep breath in through his nose and exhaled slowly. "But it is not good men this world needs right now. It needs someone who can make the choices others wouldn't dare dream of. I will do what you never could, but I will only be able to do it because of you."

He looked down at the five concentric circles of rune markings carved into both the ground below Garramon and the ceiling above. Fane had spent months carving those runes, taking all of Pirnil and Kiralla Holflower's research into account and blending it with his own learnings. This place was the beating heart of Essence in the world, shielded by the mountain around it. This was where Efialtír planted his seed into the crust of the world, where his mortal body fell, and the Sea of Stone was created.

And this was the night that all of Fane's plans, hundreds of years of waiting and weaving, would finally take their next step. He had seen the future that would come to pass without his actions, and he would not allow it. No matter the cost, for no cost could be greater.

Azrim entered the chamber from the passage on the far side, looking up at Garramon.

"It is done?" Fane asked.

"The knights will not be a problem," Azrim answered, his voice layered over that of his host.

"Good. The others?"

"On their way."

Fane would have rather sent every last one of the Vitharnmír to Achyron's temple and rid himself of these knights entirely. But he could not risk losing too many. Without their strength, he could not bring Efialtír through the veil, even with the Heart.

But Efialtír had long been twisting his way into that place. The temple may yet fall. For now, all Fane needed was to keep those knights from this place. No doubt many of the Urak clans had felt the pulse of the Essence as he'd awakened the Heart and were already on their way to set the whole mountainscape aflame. Eltoar and Helios would keep them at bay.

He turned back towards where the Heart of Blood sat atop a pedestal of brown stone, red light pulsing across its surface. Fane placed his hands on the smooth, glasslike exterior of the Heart, gasping as the power within swept through him like a bolt of lightning.

The power of every soul that died at Ilnaen. The power of every dragon that fell. The power of the life Essence of every dragon that would never draw breath.

It had softened the blow, in a way, commanding the Uraks to destroy the eggs in Ilnaen while knowing that none would ever hatch anyway. He'd needed the eggs to be destroyed, for he'd needed that blend of rage and guilt burning in the hearts of Eltoar and the Dragonguard, needed the power that Essence would bring. The Essence of Varyn's greatest creations, the only creatures that could have stood in his way.

"All great things require sacrifice," Fane whispered to himself, as he had done a thousand times.

Only with the Blood Moon in the sky could the life Essence be captured in such a way, and only with Efialtír's guidance.

Eltoar had given Fane the Heart of Blood in the hopes that Fane could bring life back to the dragons of Epheria. And so it was ironic that, with that very act, he had assured the exact opposite.

Fane usually appreciated irony. He saw it as the world's way of laughing at the living. But he found no amusement in this. Once the Essence within the Heart was used to bring Efialtír across the veil, it would be gone, spent, extinguished. And with it, so too the dragons. He held no love for the creatures, the living weapons of indomitable fury. But neither did he hate them. Their extinction was simply a necessity.

Helios and the few others that were left would be the last of their dying race now. There was no doubt their sacrifice would be the greatest of all.

As Fane stared down into the shifting light of the Heart, power surging through him, the remaining Vitharnmír entered the chamber, armoured boots clinking against the stone.

With a short exhale, Fane lifted the Heart from its pedestal and turned back to face his old friend, seeing the Vitharnmír take their places around Garramon. Forty in total, precisely what he needed.

They all stood there in their silver armour, red runes blazing with light. Efialtír's champions, his most trusted warriors. Fane smiled as he looked at them, taking in their hubris. They believed themselves above all mortal things, untouchable. They would learn better soon enough.

"It is time," Fane called out, stepping closer to Garramon. He held the Heart before himself, tapping into its core. Every hair on Fane's body stood on end, his robes lifting as though suspended in water. The power of hundreds of thousands of souls poured through him, the roar of dragons sounding in his mind, the screams of the dying, the crackling of flames.

Fane's eyes wet with tears at the millions of lives lost to reach this moment, his soul held together by the billions that would be saved.

He channelled the power of the Essence through him and pushed it into Garramon. Fane drew a sharp breath into his lungs as Garramon's eyes snapped open and the runes carved into his bare skin shone like the sun, red light blazing.

All forty Vitharnmír stood about him, the power of Essence crackling like lightning in the air.

"I call to you, Efialtír, bringer of life. Take this vessel as your own, see this light, and let it guide you through the darkness."

As Fane spoke, the Vitharnmír added their strength to his, and the runes carved into the stone around them burst to life, crimson light gleaming.

Screams ripped Haem from his thoughts as he sat on the plateau with Calen's body cradled in his arms, the rain hammering down. At first, it was just one, but one turned to many in a heartbeat.

He lowered Calen to the stone, and before he had taken more than three steps, Valerys had curled around Calen's body and covered him with a massive white wing. The dragon cared little for anything outside of Calen. Not even the shrieks and howls pulled him from his misery.

Haem summoned his Sentinel armour and Soulblade, the green light-wrought sword taking shape in his fist as the liquid metal flowed over his fingers. He bounded down the steps and through the gate at the eastern wall into the city.

Men and women sprinted in all directions, fleeing for their homes as three warriors clad in shimmering steel plate carved through everything that moved with glowing red Soulblades.

Even as Haem watched in horror, a red orb burst into life behind them, spreading into a disc of rippling black liquid. The Rift.

More of the Chosen charged through. Ten by Haem's count.

A second Rift opened above them, its edges a shimmering green light, and Grandmaster Kallinvar dropped from the sky, Ruon and the rest of The Second with him.

"Go!" Haem roared at three men who came charging from their homes with spears in their fists.

"We can help!" one of them called back.

"Protect your families," Haem said, recalling his helm so they might see his face. "Let Achyron protect you."

Haem replaced his helm and charged into the fray.

KALLINVAR RAMMED HIS SHOULDER INTO a Chosen's breastplate, stepped back, and sliced his Soulblade through the creature's knee. The Chosen howled and collapsed backwards, only for Ruon and Varlin to fall atop it and drive their blades into its chest and head, the runes in its armour igniting with a burning fury.

He should have known they had access to the Rift. Or at least some form of it. But they should never have been able to open it in Ardholm or the temple. The entire city was warded against such things, and that ward had not been violated in the thousands of years the temple had stood.

A crimson Soulblade swept past Kallinvar's face. He leaned back, then brought his own blade up to block a strike from a second Chosen in a burst of green and red light.

He drew his fist back and rammed it into the Chosen's ribs, feeling the plate crack beneath the weight of the blow.

Kallinvar pushed forwards, Arden sweeping in beside him like a man possessed. The young knight moved with the grace of a bird and struck with the strength of an ox, his Sigil radiating pure fury and loss. Arden swept past the Chosen's guard, released his Soulblade, and swung around the creature's waist. He pressed his fist against the Chosen's hip, and his Soulblade burst to life once more, ripping through the creature's body from side to side. Arden twisted and hauled the blade free of flesh and steel through the Chosen's gut, blood spilling onto stone, runes blazing.

With each passing moment, Kallinvar screamed in his mind to Achyron but heard nothing in return. Surely now, of all moments, he had not abandoned them?

A roar sounded behind Kallinvar, and he twisted to see a Chosen slicing through four citizens with a single swipe of his Soulblade, tearing their souls in half. Scores more men, women, and children scattered through the streets, running for their lives as more knights flooded from the temple.

Gandrid and Emalia, along with their chapters, charged down the great steps, crashing into four Chosen that raced towards the temple.

Kallinvar's Sigil ignited, and he opened the Rift beside himself, letting Olyria and The Third through.

"Airdaine and Arlena are still within the temple. Fades and Chosen both roam the halls." Olyria stared into Kallinvar's eyes. "Is it true? I felt it Kallinvar. We all did."

"They have the Heart." Kallinvar grasped Olyria's arm and pulled her close. "The duty of the strong is to protect the weak. That duty does not die, Olyria. Do you understand me? It does not die. No matter what we face, our duty never ends."

"I am always with you, Kallinvar. Always. My Grandmaster, my friend."

"And I you. Clear them from the city. Keep the people safe. That is all that matters."

Olyria nodded, then turned and joined the battle, Soulblade blazing to life in her hands.

"Ruon! Knights of The Second, with me!" Kallinvar opened the Rift and leapt through, the icy embrace washing over him, the darkness shrouding his vision, until he emerged on the other side into the chaos of the Heart Chamber.

His Sigil pulsed as knights fell: Sisters Jurea and Larwain of The First, Brother Yurin of The Ninth, Brother Kandir of The Eight. All in quick succession. The knights of The Second flowed into the chamber at Kallinvar's back, crashing into the Fades and Chosen.

Kallinvar surged forwards, dipping below the swing of a crimson blade before carving a Fade in half with his Soulblade, a shriek ringing out. He turned and swept aside another strike meant to take his head from his shoulders before a second blade carved a deep furrow across the breast of his plate. As the two Chosen fell upon him, Kevan, Sylven, and Varlin charged in, smashing into the creatures' flanks.

A pulse of the Taint erupted deeper in the temple, and Kallinvar broke into a run. He smashed through the doors of the Heart Chamber and out into the great halls beyond. Bodies lay scattered about the floor, blood smearing the stone.

He followed the oily tendrils of Taint through the halls until he reached the Tranquil Garden. Before he stepped onto the soft grass, some part of him already knew what he would find within, but his heart still cracked when he saw Brother Tarron standing over a score of headless bodies, Watcher Poldor to his right. The blood from the bodies pooled into the many streams that fed Heraya's Well, tainting it.

The rest of the Watchers and priests of the temple were all lined around the well, shaking and whimpering with their heads bowed.

Two more Chosen stood between Kallinvar and Tarron, the runes in their silver armour burning stark against the vibrant purple flowers of the Hallow trees.

"Brother!" Kallinvar roared, stepping further into the temple, his Soulblade blazing in his hand.

Tarron turned to face him slowly. He wore his Sentinel armour, though the plate was cracked and worn, crimson light shining through. When he lifted his gaze to Kallinvar, his eyes glowed with a deep red and his skin was pale as stretched parchment.

"No… No, brother, no." Kallinvar lifted his Soulblade and pointed it at Tarron. "Let him go!"

"Let me go?" Tarron said, raising an eyebrow. "I chose this, Kallinvar. I see clearly now. The wool is lifted from my eyes."

"The Great Deceiver, Devourer of Souls." The ground sank against Kallinvar's weight as he moved. "I will not let you into my heart. I will not swallow your lies."

"You are too late." Tarron shrugged. "It is done."

As the last of Tarron's words left his lips, a surge of Essence swept through the air, so great that it brought Kallinvar to his knees, and for a moment his vision went black and all sounds drowned in his ears.

"He is here."

THE VERY AIR IN THE chamber crackled with power, the runes on Garramon's body burning with such a fury that smoke rose from the man's flesh. Black tears ripped through the fabric of the world, taking tangible form in the air around Garramon, spreading like cracks through a broken bowl.

About him, all the Vitharnmír stood with their armour receded, bare flesh and runes open to the air, eyes glowing with red light.

Tendrils of black and red burst from the tears in the world and clung to the runes in Garramon's flesh. The black gashes spread, cracking through the air until Garramon vanished entirely, enveloped by a black sphere.

For a brief moment, just a fraction of a second, Fane felt a tinge of hesitation, a touch of uncertainty. This was a god he was summoning. A creature so powerful it had ascended from the mortal plane – and he was calling it back. What if he had been wrong? What if the future he saw would never come to pass? What Efialtír had been pulling the strings all along, twisting Fane's mind, carving out Fane's path with the illusion of choice and hope?

Those doubts flickered and died. If that were the case, then the path was already too long trodden. He would face whatever stood before him. Nothing would stand in his way. Not even a god. He would be what this world needed and kill the pieces of himself that it did not.

A pulse of Essence swept outwards from the black sphere that surrounded Garramon. The force of it knocked Fane back a step and shook the entire chamber. The Heart ignited in Fane's hands, and a beam of crimson light burst from within and crashed into the black sphere, swirling around it like sweeping fire.

The flames consumed the black, revealing Garramon within. As the sphere burned away, Garramon slowly lowered to the ground, his arms outstretched, the Chosen beginning to chant in a tongue foreign to Fane's ear.

Garramon's bare feet touched the stone, the runes carved into the ground reacting to his touch, billowing black smoke around glistening red light.

Fane stared in awe at the power that radiated from his old friend, at the way it rippled in the air as heat did across stone on a hot day.

Garramon's gaze fell on Fane, and Fane dropped to one knee, holding the Heart of Blood out in his hands.

"Rise." The words were spoken in a deep, powerful voice. The same voice Fane had heard speak in his mind a thousand times.

He did as commanded, slowly lifting to his feet and pulling the Heart to his chest. "My lord, Efialtír. Today is a day that will be spoken of throughout time. You have returned to us."

"You have done everything I've ever asked of you." Efialtír stood before Fane in his bare skin. "And you shall have everything you were promised."

"I live to serve, my lord."

"No, you do not."

Those words sent a spark of fear through Fane.

"But I do not wish for a servant," Efialtír said. "I wish for a general. I have crossed the veil between worlds for the first time in millennia. I am weak. My body is still frail and new. The others will not simply lay down now that I have crossed. There is much still to come, my child. And we will see how quickly they abandon their sacred oaths now that I have returned. Their hypocrisy unsheathed."

Efialtír reached out a hand and grasped Fane's shoulder. "I have searched an endless sea of souls to find you. You are singular. And together, we will rid this world of those who call themselves gods. Let them come. Let us finish this war they started so long ago."

KALLINVAR LET OUT HIS BREATHS slowly, his knees pressing into the soft earth, his hands hanging at his sides.

"It is over, Kallinvar," Tarron said, walking past the trembling Watchers and priests. "You have lost. Your god has abandoned you."

Kallinvar stared back at his old friend. He knew the voice that spoke was not Tarron's. This was the voice of a demon, a Vitharnmír, a Chosen. How? He did not know, but it didn't matter.

"Pain is the path to strength," Kallinvar said as he lifted one foot up.

"The duty of the strong is to protect the weak." Kallinvar placed his hands on his knee and hauled himself upright.

"Pretty words," Tarron spat, staring at Kallinvar. "But you have still lost. The Saviour has crossed the veil. This world is his domain once more. It is over, slave of Achyron."

Kallinvar stared past Tarron at the Watchers and priests, who looked back at him with pure terror in their eyes.

"It is never over." Kallinvar ignited his Soulblade, green light blazing. "And I will never yield. Not while there is air in my lungs and blood in my veins. Heraya embrace you, brother. I will save your soul."

"Heraya will burn!" Tarron roared.

"You first." Kallinvar charged forwards. The two Vitharnmír who stood between him and Tarron bounded forwards. He slid between them both, Soulblades crashing together in flashes of green and red light.

One blade sliced across his breastplate, the other scoring his helmet. He twisted, releasing his Soulblade as he had seen Arden do so many times, then reignited it with his hand pressed to one of the Vitharnmír's chests. The creature howled and shrieked, its runes blazing as it fell to the ground.

Kallinvar ripped his Soulblade free and pushed the second Vitharnmír backwards. Tarron smashed into his side, causing Kallinvar to stagger. When he caught his footing, Tarron and the Vitharnmír stood facing him, each walking in a circle about him, one on the left, one on the right.

The Soulblade in Tarron's fist flickered from red to green, its light weak and crackling.

A heartbeat passed, and both of them fell upon Kallinvar, blades slicing through the air.

He turned away blow after blow until a crimson blade plunged into his thigh, then ripped free. He staggered backwards, Tarron and the Vitharnmír stalking him like wolves.

Bursts of light erupted as their blades collided, again and again, each time pushing Kallinvar back further, each time getting closer to a killing blow.

I will find you in the void, Verathin. At least if we are to drift, we will drift together, old friend.

Kallinvar turned away a swing of Tarron's blade, only to have the Vitharnmír's carve clean through the plate on his chest and into the flesh beneath.

I had always thought that when we were to die, we would do so side by side, as brothers, in the fire of battle. But I will find you in death, as you found me.

He turned away three more blows before a fourth scored his ribs, slicing through his plate.

Kallinvar opened his Sigil to Ruon's, feeling the fear in her heart, the rage in her soul, as she fought.

I love you. I have always loved you. And I will love you until the breaking of time. You are the beating of my heart. You are my goodness and my light. You are my eternity, my constant. I'm sorry I waited so long.

Two more strikes came down over Kallinvar's head. He raised his Soulblade and took the full weight of both but collapsed backwards onto his knee from the force.

As Tarron struck down with his Soulblade, a blazing fire ignited in Kallinvar's Sigil and Achyron's voice boomed in his mind.

"Rise, Kallinvar, Champion of Achyron. You will never stand alone! Be my herald in this world, my avatar. Be my strength. I will not stand by any longer."

The chamber illuminated with a brilliant green light that shone from Kallinvar's left hand, and a glistening green shield burst into existence, catching the killing blow of Tarron's flickering Soulblade.

All pain fled Kallinvar's body as he felt Achyron surging through him. He hauled himself to his feet, sword and shield in hand.

"The duty of the strong is to protect the weak," Achyron's voice boomed. *"You are a paragon of those words."*

Kallinvar caught Tarron's blade on his Soulshield, then drove his blade through Tarron's arm.

"Pain is the path to strength," Achyron bellowed. *"And you have suffered for near a millennium."*

Kallinvar ripped his sword free and twisted, slicing through the Vitharnmír's neck and relieving it of its head.

"The mark of the righteous is to rise when you would rather fall, to stand when your legs beg you to kneel." Achyron's voice dropped to a whisper. *"I am sorry, my child. Efialtír held me at bay in the Godsrealm."*

"You are here now," Kallinvar answered, power thrumming from his Sigil.

"You are what I once was, Kallinvar. Give me one last war, my child. Give me Efialtír's head."

Footsteps sounded, and Ruon charged into the chamber, the knights of The Second at her back.

"It cannot be..." Ruon whispered, staring at Tarron.

"Stay back," Kallinvar called. He moved towards Tarron, who staggered backwards, his Soulblade forming in his other hand.

Kallinvar surged forwards, catching Tarron on his back foot. The man turned away two swings before Kallinvar sliced through the flesh of Tarron's remaining arm.

Tarron roared and howled, but Kallinvar lifted his foot and planted it into Tarron's chest, sending the man crashing to the ground.

Releasing his Soulblade and shield, Kallinvar dropped onto Tarron's chest and placed a hand over the cracked Sigil of Achyron marked onto his Sentinel armour.

"You will burn!" Tarron roared. "Your god will die, and this world will be as it should!"

Kallinvar wrapped the fingers of his free hand around Tarron's throat and stared into the man's black eyes. "Listen to me, demon. Tell your god I am coming for his soul. He is in my world now. He is not free. He is trapped in this mortal plane with me, and I will have my vengeance for every soul he has torn apart."

"To kill me, you must kill him." Tarron's lips pulled into a wicked smile. His expression shifted, eyes flickering from pure red to the blue irises of Tarron, and the demon's voice was gone. "Kallinvar? Brother? I'm sorry. Kill me, please. Kill me."

As quickly as Tarron had returned, he was gone, and his eyes filled with a brimming red light once more. "We are one," the demon within Tarron said, laughing. A helm of liquid metal poured from Tarron's collar and formed around his head. "Tear my soul free, and do the same to his."

"No." Kallinvar reached out to Tarron's Sigil, pushing through the layers of oily Taint that wrapped around the man's soul, and commanded it to recall his Sentinel armour. Something deep within snapped back, but Kallinvar pushed harder and the armour slithered over Tarron's skin, revealing scores of deep runes carved into the flesh.

Holding the man's throat, Kallinvar removed his hand from above Tarron's Sigil, drew his sword from his hip, and drove the blade deep into Tarron's gut.

Tarron thrashed and screamed, pushing against Kallinvar's weight, until eventually the red in his eyes faded to blue and white.

"Kallinvar?" Tarron convulsed, struggling to draw breath.

"You can rest now, brother. Dine in Achyron's halls. You have earned it. I will see you soon." Kallinvar slipped his hand behind the back of Tarron's head as his friend's body stopped moving, his chest growing still, eyes rolling.

A pulse of Taint rippled from Tarron, and Kallinvar could see the black, oily shape that peeled away from his friend's body. Kallinvar snatched it with his left hand, feeling it writhe and thrash in his grip, green light spreading from his fingers.

"Show them the strength of The Warrior," Achyron's voice sounded in his mind.

Kallinvar dropped his sword, and his Soulblade burst to life in his fist. He drove the shimmering green blade into the heart of the writhing black manifestation of the demon, feeling it shriek as it died and its soul was torn from the world.

He relinquished his Soulblade and leaned forwards, pressing his forehead to Tarron's before laying the man on the stone. "What did they do to you? Oh, brother. I am sorry for your pain. I am sorry I failed you."

When Kallinvar finally rose, his brothers and sisters stood around him, staring down at their lost companion.

Ildris knelt beside Tarron, pulling the man into his arms, helmet receding.

Kallinvar looked up and found Watcher Poldor standing like a stunned deer, his mouth ajar.

The man tried to run as Kallinvar approached, but Watcher Timkin and one of the priests clambered to their feet and grabbed him.

"I didn't…" Poldor stammered. "Kallinvar, you need to understand—"

"No," Kallinvar said, wrapping his gauntleted hand around Poldor's throat. "I don't need to understand. I don't need to know why. You're a coward. You should have come to me. You didn't. You listened to the whispers of the god we have been fighting since the birth of this knighthood. You took the lives of the people who meant the most to me. You stripped me of them. And there are no words that can bring them back. You killed Gildrick."

"There are others, Kallinvar," Poldor said, gasping for breath. "I can tell you—"

"I'm sure there are, and I'm sure you can. I'm also sure you'd say anything to save your own skin. I trusted you, Poldor. *He* trusted you." Kallinvar ignited his Soulblade and drove it through Poldor's stomach. He stared into Poldor's eyes, then ripped the blade free down through the man's groin and tossed his ravaged body to the ground.

Kallinvar turned and stared down at Tarron, Ildris and Ruon kneeling beside him. Kallinvar dropped to his knees and let his Sentinel armour flow back into his Sigil. As he did, he closed his eyes and ran his hands through his sweat-soaked hair, clasping his fingers behind the back of his head.

"The Godwar is here, my child. Efialtír has crossed the veil and taken a body of flesh and blood in the mortal world."

"Good," Kallinvar whispered. "Now I can kill him."

CHAPTER ONE HUNDRED AND SIX

TWO SHADES OF HONOUR

27th Day of the Blood Moon

Berona – Winter, Year 3081 After Doom

Salara walked through the ruins of Berona as dwarves cleared corpses and debris from the street. Ervian, Vandrien, and Cala all walked ahead of her, alongside the dwarven king, Hoffnar, and his guard. Vyrmír, Andrax, Nymaxes, and Barathûr soared above the city – the only survivors of their encounter with Eltoar and Helios at the Firnin Mountains. Four centuries they had waited in Lynalion, only to watch so many of their kin die in a matter of months.

Salara had not slept since, not truly. Every time she did, she watched Indivar be ripped to shreds. She saw Helios tear Baerys in half, blood spraying into the wind. Nothing could have prepared her for that day. There was no stopping Eltoar and Helios. They were a force created by the gods.

While the dragons had fought, Vandrien and the eastern forces had captured Elkenrim and Anaduin, and all lands east of the Kolmir Mountains now belonged to the elves of Numillíon, the banner of the golden stag standing proud. The armies cheered and celebrated, but Salara had no heart for it. Nothing within her felt a shred of victory.

Something brushed against Salara's hand, and she looked down to see Ervian's fingers sliding between hers. No words passed between them. Ervian knew the workings of Salara's mind, the bleeding of her heart.

"It appears your plan worked perfectly," Vandrien said to Hoffnar as she surveyed the sheer devastation around her. "Casualties on your side?"

"Minimal," Hoffnar responded, pressing the tip of his boot into the breastplate of a dead Lorian. "The kerathlin and Depth Stalkers tenderised the meat, and we finished the scraps. Your aid in fine-tuning the frequency of the crystals was invaluable. And your mages helped to keep the Durakduran traitors at bay. I believe our peoples have a bright future together, Queen Vandrien."

"As do I."

Salara could tell by the tone in the queen's voice that she was wary of King Hoffnar – a sentiment Salara shared. Any soul willing to force a nest of kerathlin into a city of innocents was one with deep-rooted darkness. Salara had not known the explicit details of the plan. If she had, she would have objected fiercely.

The act was dishonourable to the highest degree.

The queen had justified it all by claiming that it was Hoffnar's hand that had done the deed and not hers. Vandrien had simply helped create the crystal amplifier that controlled the swarms.

But to Salara, distance from the act itself did not create distance from the dishonour. Their souls had been tarnished.

Vandrien and her Sunguard stopped before the ruins of the High Tower, her sister, Cala, beside her. "Now I will require you to complete your side of the bargain, King Hoffnar."

"First," Hoffnar said, brushing dust from his tabard, "we must rid ourselves of the menace beneath the mountains. Then we will move forwards to the next step."

Vandrien's eyes narrowed. "That is not what we agreed."

"As circumstances change, so too must our priorities. Surely you understand that, honourable queen? If Kira and her rabble are left unchecked at our back door, everything we have achieved may come undone. Once my flanks are secure, I will be in a position to push forwards. My soldiers report that she has discovered a unique power... one thought long dead."

"My scouts have told me of the monstrosities forged from rock."

"Enlightened bersekeers," the king said. "Not only will killing Kira secure our flanks, but if we can pry this power from her corpse... well, Queen Vandrien, this alliance of elves and dwarves will find no equal."

When Hoffnar and Vandrien had parted ways and the elves had set back on the road for Anaduin, Salara took to the sky with Vyrmír. Andrax and Nymaxes flew on her left, while the crimson dragon, Barathûr, soared on her right.

And when the procession stopped to set up camp near the Firnin Mountains, the four dragons alighted on a high cliff thousands of feet above the level of the ground.

Salara slid from Vyrmír's back and stood at the cliff edge, staring through the dragon's eyes at the red and gold tents pitched below.

"Did you know? About the kerathlin?" Lomari, Andrax's soulkin, asked, clasping his hands at his back. The elf had seen almost seven centuries, and still his dark skin was untouched by the markings of time, his hair black as coal. Lomari's left eye was a mess of knotted flesh. He had carved it out himself after Andrax had lost his eye in the battle.

Salara shook her head.

Barathûr's soulkin, Havírl, let out a sigh on Salara's other side. She rested her hand on her sword pommel. "What are we? All these years we have waited… for vengeance, for honour… and still he tears us apart. And now, we commit the same atrocities as those we hate?"

As Havírl spoke, the words the man who rescued Boud had spoken in Salara's chamber occupied every corner of her mind. *"But your fate is not yet decided. It is in your own hands. What do you want to be? A hero or a monster?"*

"What would you do?" Salara asked, looking to both Lomari and Havírl, then to Taran, who remained silent.

"I would stop following blindly." Lomari's expression didn't change as he stared out at the horizon. He knew the meaning of those words, knew the risk of speaking them.

"Be careful of your next words, Lomari."

"Or what, Salara? You will strike me down? I've lived far too long to care about death. Death is an old friend. I will smile when I see them." After a moment, he looked at Salara. "Alvira followed the council blindly when she allowed The Order to slowly rot – we all did. And Eltoar and the traitors followed Fane blindly when they butchered their own kin. I am tired of being blind. Blinded by honour, by fate, by vengeance. I wish to see. Do you not?"

Salara hesitated, then gave a slow nod. "I believe it is time we sit down with this new Draleid and see if a future can be found for our kind in which we don't tear each other apart."

CHAPTER ONE HUNDRED AND SEVEN

OF GODS AND ASHES

28th Day of the Blood Moon

Temple of Achyron – Winter, Year 3081 After Doom

Haem found Kallinvar in the Soul Vault, staring at all the Sigils that had returned to their alcoves – staring at Brother Tarron's.

"What is it, brother?" Kallinvar asked without turning his head, his voice steeped in loss.

"I want to speak to him."

"To who?"

"Achyron. I want to speak to him."

Kallinvar turned his gaze from the Sigils and looked into Haem's eyes. "Why?"

"This cannot be it, Kallinvar." Haem clenched his hand into a fist behind his back. "It can't. You said you can hear his voice, that you talk to him."

"Your brother is dead, Arden. You must accept that."

"Why? Why must I accept it?"

"Because there are things in this life that just are. Calen is not the only one we lost this day. What has brought this on?"

"What has brought it on?" Haem's throat tightened, and he clenched his jaw. "I woke with my little brother's dead body in my arms." That was the moment the tears flowed, rolling gently down his cheeks. There was nothing he could do to stop them. They were a symptom of a broken heart. "I watched him grow, Kallinvar. I watched him take his first step and speak his first word. I held him in my arms. He was mine to protect – *mine*. I promised our dad that I would watch over them both, that I would keep them safe. And this morning, as the sun rose, I held Calen's cold body and I looked into his dead eyes… and I just cannot accept it. I will not."

"Achyron cannot bring back the dead, Arden."

"Look at us." Haem said, opening his arms. "What are *we*?"

"That is not the same."

"How do you know?" Haem roared. "How do we know anything at all? I need to try!"

Kallinvar stared back at Haem, tilting his head slightly. He closed his eyes. A few moments passed, and he nodded. "Say what you must."

Haem's Sigil burned in his chest, ice flowing through his veins. The world flashed with a green light, and when the light faded, he stood atop a cliff, the wind blowing against him, the waves of a sparkling silver ocean stretching out before him.

He stood there in silence, watching in awe as the light from a sunless sky sparkled across the ocean. When he looked to one side, he found himself staring at a man with a head of thick black hair and dark beard. He wore a long purple cloak over a marble-white cuirass, his hands clasped behind his back.

Haem knew without speaking a word that this was not Achyron, but Varyn. The Father.

He wanted to speak, but his words clung to his throat. He stood before a god. The protector of all things, the giver of light, the Father of all.

The pair of them stood in silence for what felt like an eternity until Varyn finally spoke. "What is it you seek, Haem Bryer? I know it in your heart, but I must hear it on your lips."

"I want my brother back."

"The giving and taking of life is fundamental to the existence of the mortal world. What is born must die to make way for what comes after. Life cannot simply be given back. If it could, it would lose all value. And even if that were not the case, why, of all the souls that have been taken from the world, does this single one deserve it above all others?"

"Because it was you who set him on this path. I saw your light in his eyes – the world did. He is your champion."

"And now he is dead."

Haem stared at the god, who looked out at the sea of silver. His heart burned as though set aflame. "Why am I here if there is no chance? Why bother listening to me?"

"I never said that."

⚬

CALEN'S EYES OPENED TO A glistening silver ocean. His last memory had been of falling, of pain burning in his chest, of Valerys screaming in his mind. Calen pressed a hand to his chest, an emptiness within him, a hollow that could never be filled.

"You are dead."

Calen turned at the voice. The speaker stood a head taller than him and was garbed in white plate and purple robes, his hair and beard thick and black. He knew the man without thought or words. "You are Varyn."

"I am. And this is the Aethersea. Where souls pass through the realms between the living and the dead. Normally it would be Heraya meeting you here."

"What will happen to Valerys?" With every second that passed, Calen fought his body's need to weep. He had never felt a thing like this. His soul was shattered. "He's alone. He shouldn't be alone. Please don't leave him alone."

Varyn gave Calen a soft, brittle smile. "There are many things that should not be. Are you happy with what you did in the time you had, Calen Bryer?"

"I'm not done." Calen shook his head. "What of Haem? And of Vaeril and Dann and Tarmon and Erik? Do they live?"

"They do." Varyn looked out over the silver ocean. "I chose you for the same reason Valerys did. Not for the man you are, but for the man you have the potential to be. And I created the dragons of Valacia for the same reason. When I tempered the fires of my creations in Epheria, I did so to limit their potential for destruction, to balance their lesser qualities with those of other souls. But what I did not see was that limiting a soul's light limits everything that they are. Ignoring our lesser qualities, burying our rage and our fury, it does not make us stronger. We must learn to control the darker pieces of ourselves, not destroy them. And so you and Valerys are unique amongst my creations, the tethers of your potential unbound. Together you could have been something greater than anything that has come before."

VARYN LOOKED OUT AT THE ocean of silver as he spoke to Haem. "After we almost tore the mortal world apart, my kin and I swore oaths, oaths that forbid us from weaving our wills into your world. We did so for your sake. We were no longer mortal, and your world did not deserve to burn at our whims."

"Then what am I except a manifestation of Achyron's will? Has he not broken those oaths? Has not Efialtír?"

Varyn let out a long sigh. "We allowed Achyron some semblance of excess as a counter to Efialtír. A weight to keep the scales balanced. To give back life to the dead, Haem Bryer, that is not a feather on the scales, it is a rock. What meaning has death and life if it can be changed on a whim?"

"Not every death. Just one."

"IF YOU HAD ANOTHER CHANCE at life, Calen Bryer, what would you do with it?"

"What is it you want from me?" Calen asked. "Chances like that do not come without strings."

"And you do not like strings."

"No, not particularly."

"Efialtír has crossed from our realm through the veil into the mortal plane. He has taken corporeal form."

"How is that possible?"

"Much can change in a short time. Efialtír has broken every oath my kind have made. He claims to love the mortal world. But it is not the world he loves, rather control over it. The last time gods warred in your world, we almost tore it asunder. I would not have that happen a second time. If you had another chance, would you be the blade that strikes back? Would you stand against Efialtír, fight with all your strength? Would you do whatever was needed to keep your world from burning?"

"I would."

"ALL LIFE COMES AT A COST, Haem Bryer." Varyn let out a long sigh.

"I will pay it."

"You do not even know what it is."

"I will pay it."

"A god cannot simply grant life to the dead, no matter how powerful they are. It requires more. Shards of who we are."

"I will pay it," Haem repeated again.

"Shards of me… shards of you. To mend a shattered soul so it will stay as one… When things break, they do not go back together in the same way. New pieces are required to fill the cracks. I will be weakened. You will be…"

"Lost," Haem finished.

Varyn nodded. "I need you to understand. My powers have limits. To do this is no simple thing. Not for either of us. I must break the oaths I swore, become the thing I stood against. But if I do not, Efialtír will tear that world into oblivion. And so I am faced with a choice."

"I will pay the cost," Haem said for a fourth time, his resolve strengthening. "Will you?"

CALEN STARED OUT AT THE silver ocean as Varyn stood in silence.

"I will," the god said.

"You will what?"

Varyn rested a hand on Calen's shoulder. "This is our last chance, Calen Bryer. If we fail now, Efialtír will hold eternal dominion over your world. He will burn the veil between worlds. To give a sliver of what I am, a piece of my soul, that is a sacrifice I never thought I would make. But if I cross the veil myself, I know the world will break beneath me." He sighed once more, something that might have been a smile cracking across his lips. "What is a god, if they are not willing to give pieces of themselves for the world they created?" A resignation set into Varyn's voice. "I will not be what we once were. I will pay the cost."

"Calen?"

Calen's heart stopped at the sound of his brother's voice. He looked to the other side of Varyn, and Haem stepped forwards to seize Calen in the deepest of embraces.

"I'm sorry," Calen whispered. "For everything. I… I'm sorry for arguing. I'm sorry for—"

"Shhh…" Haem squeezed Calen tighter. "I love you, little brother. Please don't be mad. This was always my purpose. I only ever took the Sigil so I could keep you safe. I love you so much, and I could never be prouder of the man you've become."

"Haem? Haem, what's wrong? Why would I be mad?"

"You were always stronger," Haem said, pulling his arm inwards and pressing a fist to Calen's heart. "In here. You never gave up. Not once. We would train for hours, and no matter how many times you went down, you stood right the fuck back up. Covered in mud, blood on your face. You always stood back up. And I was so gods damn proud of you every time. I need you to stand back up again, little brother."

"Haem, why are you crying? You're scaring me."

"This is what I was made for, Calen. I would always give my life for you and Ella, always. This is my purpose. To protect you, to keep you safe. Tell her I'm sorry, I'm sorry we got so little time. Ask her to forgive me. She's yours to keep safe now, and you're hers." Haem clasped his hands to the sides of Calen's face. "You better protect her. I'll come find you if you don't."

A sudden realisation dawned on Calen. "Haem, no…" Calen clutched at Haem and glared at Varyn. "I don't want it. I won't take it. I won't pay this cost. I won't!"

"It's already been paid," the god replied.

"No, no… Haem."

"The sun will set, Calen," Haem said, pulling Calen in close. "And it will rise again, and it will do so the next day and the next. The gods are in charge of such things, but it is by our own will that we pick ourselves up when we fall. I will always be there. A piece of me will always be there."

"Haem, don't do this, please… please don't do this."

Even as he said the words, a brilliant white light consumed everything, and a storm raged in Calen's mind.

For a heartbeat everything was quiet, and then he woke with a gasp, dragging air into his lungs, his body stiff and aching, his chest burning.

He placed a hand over his chest, feeling four scars over his heart. A wave of fear, of agony and joy and hope and every emotion he could have imagined crashed into him with a weight that bore down on his soul, and he found himself staring up into pale lavender eyes.

Valerys's heart beat so fast Calen thought the dragon would collapse. Valerys twisted and turned, hauling himself upright, his winged forelimbs pressing into the stone, his frills standing on end. The weight of the dragon's heart consumed him, drowning him.

"I'm here. I'm here." Calen wrapped his arms around the dragon's snout as Valerys pushed against him, high-pitched shrieks in his throat. Calen held on and squeezed, closing his eyes, pulling their minds together and bathing in the warmth that flowed through them.

Something within them was different, harsher, more primal. But the bond was there, and that was all he cared about. Valerys wouldn't be alone.

"Myia nithír til diar, Valerys. I denír vïel ar altinua. Uvrín mír, myia'nära."

My soul to yours, Valerys. In this life and always. Forgive me, my light.

In that moment, as their minds drifted together, as their heart beat and their soul savoured its bond, one thought flowed through them: Haem.

Calen broke into a run and vaulted down the steps of the plateau. He had no idea where he was. He'd never seen this place before. He grabbed a man in the short street. "Haem Bryer? Where is he?"

The man shoved Calen away and walked off, glaring back at him. Up high, Calen saw two statues garbed in the same armour Haem wore atop an enormous stone staircase. He sprinted through the city and up the stairs, his legs screaming at him, his lungs threatening to burst. When he reached the top and stepped through the small wicket gate set into the giant doors, he found himself staring at a familiar face.

"Ruon, where is Haem? Arden, where is he?"

"Calen…" Ruon stared at him wide-eyed, mouth ajar. Her skin went pale as snow. "You… you're…"

"Ruon," Calen snapped, cutting her off. "Where is Haem?"

The woman continued to stare at him as though she didn't believe he was real. "He's in the Soul Vault with Kallinvar. How are you alive?"

"Take me to him, please."

Ruon led Calen through a series of enormous halls and down a wide staircase before leading him into a chamber with alcoves spread across the entire far wall.

Calen dropped to his knees the moment the door was opened, his legs collapsing beneath the weight of his shattered heart. He tried to stand, but his body ignored his commands, tears rolling down his cheeks. "No…" he whispered as he looked at Haem's body lying on the floor at Kallinvar's feet. "No, please, not again."

"You're alive," Kallinvar whispered.

Calen planted one foot and dragged himself upright. He shook his head as he stumbled towards Haem.

He dropped to the ground once more, trembling as he slipped one arm behind Haem's head and pulled his brother in close. "I said no…" Calen rocked back and forth, Valerys roaring in his mind. "I said no… I can't do this again."

He drew a long, settling breath, then lifted his brother into his arms and turned for the door. Calen's leg gave way, but he gritted his teeth and pulled himself back to his feet, taking another step.

"Let me," Kallinvar said, moving to stand next to Calen. To Calen's surprise, tears rolled down the man's cheeks and his eyes were raw and red.

Calen shook his head. "He's my brother. He carried me all my life. I can carry him a little further."

"Where are you taking him?"

"Home."

CHAPTER ONE HUNDRED AND EIGHT

THICKER THAN WATER

29th Day of the Blood Moon

West of Berona – Winter, Year 3081 After Doom

Rist stared into the crackling flames of the fire nestled within a deep cave near the foot of the Kolmir Mountains. Magnus had insisted they not take the western road and wouldn't allow a fire unless they could find a cave deep enough to keep them from unwanted eyes.

They'd barely stopped at all for three days, moving every hour they could stay awake. They had no way of knowing if they'd been followed or not. Magnus had said few words except that Garramon had been insistent they leave and that Fane had planned to use Rist as Efialtír's host, which in hindsight Rist should have anticipated. For now, there was a plan to reach Antiquar and sail south. What happened after that was up to the wind.

Neera sat at Rist's side, staring into the flames as he did, hands clasped together.

"Stop staring at me," Neera whispered.

"I'm not."

"You are." She reached over and squeezed his hand.

Magnus grunted as he walked from the cave mouth and dropped himself to the ground beside Rist. He stared into the flames for a moment before reaching over and grabbing one of the two large packs he'd brought with him.

"Garramon told me to give you these when we were far enough away," Magnus said, handing the pack to Rist. "I'm not sure if we're far enough away yet, but I'm sick of fucking carrying them."

Rist took the pack from Magnus, his injured shoulder groaning at the weight. He laid it down beside him and undid the brass buckle, producing four heavy books – two bound in red leather and two bound in black – along with a folded letter sealed with black wax.

The first book bound in black leather was plain and simple, filled with hundreds of pages of detailed sketches of runes and musing and experiments. It was research into Blood Magic and runecraft, far more detailed than anything Rist had seen in the libraries in Berona. It appeared to have been written by a Scholar named Kiralla Holflower.

Rist opened the second black book.

The complete findings and conclusions of the study of Essence-Empowered Runecraft, collated and written by Drakus Pirnil, Lector of the Affinity of Scholars of the Imperial Circle of Magii.

Rist stared at the name, his jaw clenching. He closed his eyes for a moment, calming himself, then set the two black books down atop the pack. The two books bound in red leather were far more elaborately constructed. The leather was smooth to the touch, embellished with gold, titles embossed on the spines.

A History of Magii, by Gandal Frendor, and *Druids, a Magic Lost*, by Duran Linold.

Rist had lost his copies in the fires that had burned the forward camps near the Firnin Mountains. The sight of these new ones warmed his heart.

He opened the first page of *Druids, A Magic Lost* to find a note written inside, along with a bookmark forged from red steel.

To the most curious mind I have ever known. To have met you was a pleasure. To have watched you grow was a privilege.

Those words carved deep into Rist's chest, and his throat grew tight. He closed the book and set both down atop the others before opening the letter.

Rist,

I had hoped all of this would have unfolded differently. By now, you should be two hundred miles from Berona, but knowing Magnus, you are barely half that.

The day you came to me, you were scared and alone and lost. It was my pride to watch that change. In a short time, you have grown to become a man with a powerful sense of self, an indomitable will, and a light that draws others in.

Rist, I am sorry that I am less than you thought I was. I could say that I didn't come with you because I went to stop Fane. That would be a lie. I didn't go with you because I was ashamed. You are someone who cherishes honesty and rewards it with unyielding loyalty. And I have lied to you. From the moment I met you, I have lied.

I always knew who you were. I never sent your letters, not to your friends, not to your family. My task was to teach you the value of the Circle, to gain your trust, to shape you into what we needed you to be… to manipulate you and bend your will.

I tell you this now because the likelihood is that by the time you read it, I will be dead. And even in death I am still a coward, too ashamed to look into your eyes as I give you the truth you deserve.

It was I who was to shape and mould you, but in the end, it was you who shaped me. You showed me the man I had once been, the man I wanted to be again. And so I tell you that I may have lied about my intentions, but that is where the lies ended.

I am proud of you. I am proud of everything you have accomplished and everything you have overcome. You are a special soul.

I had hoped to give you the books in person. May they bring endless hours of escape. And please, for the love of all things sacred, use the bookmark.

The black books are every record kept of Fane's research into blood runes. I was wrong. All those years ago, I was wrong. Study the books. Brother Pirnil mentioned there was a weakness in Fane's plan. With luck, you will find the answers you need.

I do not expect you to forgive me. Please do not think on it. Live a long life, Rist. Surround yourself with the people you love, and never let them go. That was my first mistake. This world, this life, is nothing but the sum of our experiences and those we share them with. What happens in the end means little. What matters are the things we do along the way. The only joy is the joy we create. The only hope is the hope we refuse to let go.

I would keep writing this letter until time broke, because I know that when I put the pen down, I will never speak to you again. And so, I keep writing, because our talks were the greatest happiness I've had in a long time. I will miss your musings, my brother. I will miss the simple way you see the world. I will miss your conviction. But most of all, I will miss watching you grow into the man I know you will become. Do not let this world change you.

And so now I put the pen down, and I walk towards the only honourable thing I've done in a very long time. Magnus will always be there for you. Remember that.

Never stop questioning.

Garramon

Rist brushed his thumb back and forth across the paper, his mind blank. He didn't know what to feel, what to think. For perhaps the first time in his life, a thousand questions didn't swirl around his head. He was just sad.

Neera grasped his arm.

"He cared about you, lad," Magnus said.

"I know."

"All he wanted was to get you out of that city. There was nothing else."

"Why did you come with me, Magnus? Why not stay?"

"For what? To keep fighting wars I lost interest in centuries ago? Anila is gone. Garramon is gone. People – they are what's important, lad. And when you live long enough, you learn to choose your people carefully. Fane was always a prick anyway." Magnus grasped a stick and poked a log in the fire, sending a shower of sparks into the air. "When we finally reach the South, where do you want to go?"

"Me?"

"No, the fucking shrub behind you. Of course you. Where are we going, Rist?"

Rist stared into the flames for a few more moments, reading over Garramon's letter again in his mind. "Home," he said. "I'd like to go home."

CHAPTER ONE HUNDRED AND NINE

THE MOON AND THE STARS

29th Day of the Blood Moon

Salme – Winter, Year 3081 After Doom

Distant cracks of thunder rumbled in the dark skies above Salme as Dann sat on the trunk of the fallen tree upon the hill that overlooked the city. The fire crackled, and the branches of nearby trees creaked and groaned.

Tarmon sat on the far side of the fire, knees pulled to his chest, his stare lost in the flames. Vaeril and Erik were opposite him, while Lyrei sat with her back to the trunk.

Therin was perched atop a flat rock, staring up at the star-studded sky, charcoal and parchment in his lap, the young smith – Valdrin – beside him. Therin hadn't lifted the charcoal even once. He'd just sat in silence; they all had. Not a single word had passed since before night had fallen.

Dann had gone to that spot first.

"If you had been here like you said you would, she might still be alive. But you weren't, and she's not."

This was the spot he had spoken those words. Those words that would forever be burned into his mind. Calen had not deserved them, but he had taken them and said nothing. And now he was gone. Both Calen and Rist… gone.

Dann didn't have words to describe the pain that sundered his heart. His brothers were gone. Without them he was not whole. He was nothing, and he was numb. Lyrei had tried to drag him from the pit of his own depression, but he had snapped at her, and now all they had was silence.

Even then he looked down from the tree trunk and watched her as she stared into the night. His heart told him to drop himself beside her and apologise, but his body did not answer the command.

The sound of crunching dirt drifted from behind him, and he tilted his head to see Vaeril climbing atop the trunk. The elf sat to Dann's left and stared down at the fire.

After a few minutes' silence, he made to speak, but all that left his lips was a breath. Vaeril closed his eyes for a moment, dragging air in through his nostrils. "He trusted me…"

Dann pressed his fingers into his temple as he looked over at Vaeril, the firelight glistening in tears that rolled slow and steady down the elf's cheek.

"It wasn't your fault," Dann said, his aching heart redoubling in pain. There was a time when he'd thought Vaeril incapable of emotion. To see the elf cry was like watching a mountain crumble.

"He was… he was my friend, and he trusted me. We were Vandasera…"

"Vaeril…"

"I should have died with him."

Dann grasped Vaeril's shoulder and squeezed hard enough for his fingers to go stiff. "Never say that. Do you hear me? Never."

"It's true, I—"

"It's not," Dann snapped. He swallowed hard. "Calen would never have wanted that."

"There is a saying amongst my people," Vaeril said as he stared down at the flames that burned in the firepit. "Det er il uvían uru anatli il varahín olinivíl til vírna."

Dann didn't have to ask for the translation.

"It is the moon that gives the stars permission to shine," Vaeril whispered. "Calen showed me who I was. Without him… what am I?"

Dann wanted to say something. He wanted to offer Vaeril words of comfort, but nothing came. For the first time in his life, words had abandoned him.

It is the moon that gives the stars permission to shine. Normally, Dann would have to ask Rist what in the gods that meant. But somehow he knew. It was the moon that dimmed the sun's light, the moon that dared shine in the face of the greatest fire. The moon inspired the stars to become what they needed to be, to light the way.

A silence fell between them. After Haem had left with Valerys, all of them had fallen apart. They'd slept in the ruins of The Glade that night, none of them having the will to stand and walk away. They'd only returned to Salme that morning as the sun rose, and Tarmon had gone to the city to tell the others what had happened. Dann hadn't seen the reaction, but Tarmon had said that warriors had dropped to their knees in the muddied ground of Salme. That grown men and women who had never even laid eyes on Calen had wept in the streets.

Half of his heart understood their grief, but the other half was repulsed by it. Who were they to weep over a man they did not truly know? Calen was a symbol them, a symbol of hope and change, a symbol of strength, but he was not their brother. They did not care for him. They cared only for what he could do for them. The thought scratched at him until his eyes were once again raw and wet.

A roar sounded from the city, and Dann jolted upwards. He watched as two enormous shapes rose in the night, the pink moonlight washing lazily over Varthear's and Avandeer's scaled bodies.

Vaeril stiffened, looking out towards the dragons. "What stirs them? If they—"

The elf's words were drowned out by another roar, one that came from the skies behind Dann. A shiver swept through Dann, his spine tingling at the sight of Valerys dropping through the dark canopy above, clouds swirling about him.

The dragon soared overhead, sweeping around to the left before alighting not a hundred feet from the fallen tree upon which Dann sat.

Dann slid from the trunk, Lyrei rising as he hit the ground. He set off into a run before anyone spoke a word. Shouts rang out from Salme, torches gathering on the broken walls.

Valerys's white scales glistened pink beneath the red moon. Dust and ashes swirled into the air beneath the dragon's wings.

Dann stopped some twenty feet from Valerys, the others gathering around him. Both Varthear and Avandeer alighted nearby, Tivar sliding from Avandeer's back.

Valerys lowered his neck, and in the dark of night, a shape dropped to the ground, dust whipping up around it.

Dann moved closer, lifting his hand to keep the dust from his eyes. As he moved, he saw a man kneeling, the moonlight drifting down from above, casting his face in shadow.

Another crack spread through Dann's heart at the sight of the man cradling a body in his arms. The pain was a tangible thing that spread through him, stiffening his limbs and slowing his heart.

He didn't want to do it. He didn't want to look at Calen's body, to see the lights gone from those eyes he'd known for so long. He didn't think he could.

Valerys lifted his head, and those lavender eyes stared into Dann's, a soft whine in his throat.

Dann took a few steps, heard sobs drifting on the gentle night breeze.

"We're here, Haem," Dann whispered, moving closer again, his heart the only thing causing him to slow.

"I said no…"

The blood in Dann's veins turned to ice, the hairs on his arms and neck standing on end.

"I said no, Dann… He just… He's gone…" Calen lifted his head, meeting Dann's gaze, voice trembling.

Now that Dann stood closer, he could see the body being cradled was not Calen, but Haem, head lolling.

Footsteps sounded about him, Lyrei, Tarmon, and the others gathering in a circle.

Dann began to shake, his body doing so of its own volition. He wanted to speak, but instead he dropped to his knees before Calen and clasped either side of the man's head, desperately trying to understand if what was happening was real or a dream.

Calen's skin was warm, his eyes bright and wet with tears.

"How…" was the only word that escaped Dann's lips.

Calen didn't answer. He only lifted his gaze so that they stared into each other's eyes. The loss in his friend's eyes was like a bottomless well that dragged him in.

"Calen, how are you here? How is Haem… What happened?"

"I need to take him home, Dann," Calen whispered, tears quietly rolling down his cheeks. "I need to… I need to lay him next to them."

"By Varyn…" Tarmon whispered over Dann's shoulder.

Dann looked over Calen's body, still unable to see how any of this could truly be real. "I watched you die, Calen. I saw it."

Calen leaned down and pressed his forehead to Haem's, his shoulders convulsing. He lifted his gaze and once more stared into Dann's eyes, and in that moment, Dann threw his arms around the brother he had lost and pulled Calen closer, Haem's body between them.

"Can you help me?" Calen asked, cold tears rubbing against Dann's cheek. "Can you help me bury him?" Calen shook his head. "I can't do it alone."

Dann nodded. A thousand questions floated in his mind, and for the first time in his life, he knew not to ask them. There would be a time, but that was not this time. "We'll do it together."

More sounds shuffled around them, and Tarmon dropped to a knee beside Calen without uttering a word, his hand resting on Calen's shoulder. Lyrei, Erik, and Vaeril followed.

Dann glanced over his shoulder, noticing Therin's absence. He found the elf just standing there, staring down at Calen and Haem, cheeks wet, eyes wide.

Above, thunder cracked again, rolling across the skies, and for a short while, even the dragons were silent.

CHAPTER ONE HUNDRED AND TEN

THE EVERSNOW

29th Day of the Blood Moon

The Hearth, Drifaien – Winter, Year 3081 After Doom

Alleron Helmund lifted his shield, sending an arrow bouncing off the iron boss and skittering into the snow. He dropped his left shoulder, twisted, then hacked his axe into the torso of the man before him, the blade burying between two ribs.

Baird swooped past him, wielding twin bearded axes, a patch over one eye, Audun and Destin with him.

Through the dense snowfall, Alleron could just about see Gudrun and Sigrid leading their warriors through the second gate.

The fortress of The Hearth protected the mouth of Drifaien. It was the province's most important chokepoint. If they could take it, they would cut off Alleron's father's supplies from the rest of the continent – at least by land. They would control all who entered and left Drifaien, and Calen's reinforcements could enter freely. They had failed in taking Arisfall, but there was more than one way to skin a kat.

The battle was already a bloody one, but his father had long hoarded the vast majority of his might in Arisfall and the surrounding regions, leaving sparse few warriors garrisoning the ancient fortress. Were it not for the Lorian forces that had ventured south following a fierce battle on the Arythn Plain, The Hearth would already belong to the rebellion.

"These Northern bastards have never fought in the snow," Baird shouted as he ripped his axe from a Lorian face, blood spurting from the trench carved from eyebrow to mouth. "I bet they've never even seen their piss freeze." He looked down at the dead Lorian. "Should have stayed at home, little lion."

Alleron looked down at the maimed corpse, then about the blood-stained yard. Bodies lay everywhere. Most bore the black lion of Loria on their breasts, though many were his own warriors, his friends, his followers.

A brief pang of guilt probed at his heart, finding an icy wall formed by the memory of Leif's head rolling in the snow. Rebellions had a cost that could only be paid in blood. But that did not mean a man should shy away from what must be done. If a man didn't stand for what he believed in, didn't stand for what was right, then what was the point in standing at all?

Frozen blood would glitter across Drifaien, and Alleron would be the hand that spilled it. His soul would bear the weight because someone's had to. His father could not be allowed to keep bleeding their people dry. The Lorian parasite needed to be killed. The people of Drifaien deserved a chance at life, and for that Alleron was willing to carry the burden of death.

"We must take the keep swiftly," Destin said, drawing up beside Alleron, his face splattered with fresh blood. "It will be easy for us to lose far too many lives. I suggest..." Destin trailed off as he spoke, tilting his head sideways. "What in the gods is that?"

A sphere of light floated near the far wall of The Hearth's main yard, spreading outwards with each passing heartbeat until it looked as though Alleron were staring out through a window framed in white light. But there was no snow on the other side, only rocks and green trees. Four men and two women stepped through, boots crunching in the bloodied snow.

"Tssk, tssk, tssk." One man stepped forwards, lean and tall. He looked about the yard, ignoring Alleron and the five hundred strong who stood alongside him. "This is not the path at all."

"Who are you?" Alleron called out.

"I have been called many names," the man responded, glancing up briefly towards Alleron. "I suggest you order the retreat, little Lord Helmund. Otherwise you will not like what happens next." He turned to one of the women with a ring of worn red skin around her neck. "Boud, the night is a bit clear, don't you think? Surely the 'Eversnow' should be ever snowing?"

"Indeed," Boud responded. She raised her arms, and her eyes turned a milky white. In the span of a breath, the snowfall grew heavier as though a blizzard had formed from thin air.

The man turned to another, who stood almost a head and a half taller than Alleron, with wiry muscles and a deep scowl on his face. "Vhorkel, if you please."

"At once, my lord." Just as the woman's had, Vhorkel's eyes shifted to a pure white.

Baird leaned closer. "I don't like this."

The snowfall grew heavier again, to the point that Alleron could barely see these new strangers through the wall of white.

"We all have choices to make, Alleron Helmund. Yours is simple – live or die." The leader stepped closer. "I'm very sorry. This war is not yours to win."

Screams sounded outside the walls, horrible shrieks. And then cries came from the ramparts: "Wyrms!"

Even as the shout rang out, a white-tipped hawk swept down through the barrage of snow and plunged its claws into a warrior's face, shrieking a loud 'kee-aah' as it tore strips of flesh free.

The ground shook, and Alleron turned back towards the gates to see blue-scaled bodies wriggling through the snow. Two wyrms burst outwards and ripped towards a clutch of soldiers on the far side of the yard, more following.

"This is above us, Alleron." Baird gripped Alleron's shoulder. "There is strange magic here. Old magic. We must fall back and live to fight another day." By the time Baird had spoken, ten more wyrms had burst from the snow to tear men and women apart.

"Listen to Baird," the man called out through the snowfall. "Your path does not end here, but it can."

Alleron stared back at the figures that were now little more than dark silhouettes through the blizzard. "Fuck…" About him, more and more wyrms emerged as though drawn by something. "We were so damn close." He gripped the hilt of his axe. "Fall back!"

He looked to Baird and gave a sharp nod, the man echoing his cry.

"Fall back!"

KAYGAN STOOD WITH HIS HANDS behind his back, staring out at the city of Arisfall before him. It had always amused him how much knowledge had been lost across the centuries. In Terroncia, the Cealtaí had built structures of polished stone so grand and beautiful it had quite often taken his breath away.

These people – these Drifaienin – had come from that place, his old homeland, their ancestry stretching back for thousands of mortal years. And yet now they built structures with stuck-together grey blocks, with rooves of thatch and battered shingles. There was no eloquence to it, no art. And everything was smaller, much smaller.

That was the way of things with mortals. When they warred, they killed so many of each other that ideas, moments of genius, knowledge passed down from generation to generation, were often lost.

As he stared out at the light snow dusting the rooves, he found himself mildly sorrowful at having to take Calen Bryer's life. The Cealtaí and the Tuatha alike needed souls like him, souls with wills strong enough to break the bonds of the paths. But unfortunately, young Bryer's will had proven too strong and the path he had been straying from was one that could not be altered. Regardless of the respect Kaygan had for the mortal, no one life could be placed above the path.

The options were now limited, the margin for error thin as a hair. There were few paths without Calen Bryer that ended in anything but destruction.

He let out a long sigh and flicked his tongue against a sharp fang.

Footsteps sounded behind him, and Lothal Helmund stepped out onto the parapet beside Kaygan.

"Your son's attempt on The Hearth has been dealt with," Kaygan said without looking at Lothal. The man was a necessary evil. His heart was dark but extremely pliable, and Kaygan needed pliable hearts. "Can I assume you will clean up your own mess from here?"

"Whom do you think you're speaking to? I'm not some child you can—"

"Oh, but you *are* a child," Kaygan said, cutting Lothal off and allowing his pupils to shift to black slits. "And I *can* order you about, and yes, Alleron is still alive, and no, I will not kill him for you. He is your son, clean his blood off your hands if you want it shed."

Kaygan didn't need to look to know Lothal glared at him – he'd already seen it.

"We have a deal, Lothal. I keep you in power. You do as I say. Has that changed? Please let me know if it has, and I can act accordingly."

"No," the man growled, the smell of whiskey on his breath.

"Well, our business is concluded then. I just wanted you to come out here and understand your position so that you would not do the stupid things I know you are planning."

"I wouldn't... I..."

"Calm yourself," Kaygan whispered, shaking his head. "You have my trust. For now. Leave me. I wanted you to understand your situation. You do."

Lothal Helmund may have been a drunk, but he was no fool. There were only a few paths on which he would ever cross Kaygan, and Kaygan had steered wide of each of those. So long as all remained untouched, the path would survive.

The man grunted and left, allowing both Boud and Una to step from the shadows.

They remained quiet for a moment until Boud finally plucked up the courage to ask the question Kaygan already knew she would ask.

"What of Tamzin?"

"She made her choice."

"Did she? Did you ask her?"

Kaygan raised an eyebrow at that.

"Surely you must hear the words from her mouth. Are the paths always so set?"

"You question my steering of the paths, Boud?"

"You know I don't. But she has earned the respect of making her own choice."

"She did, Boud. The further we walked, the fewer the paths became where she would walk with us... until there were none."

"But she knows of this place. What if she tells of it?"

"We will do what we must, Boud. This is my word."

Boud inclined her head reluctantly, giving a short grunt and ending the conversation.

Kaygan preferred to always allow his Tuatha to walk their paths unimpeded. He could have steered Tamzin where he wanted her, told her of the future she needed to know, as he had done to others so many times. But futures and prophecy were powerful things. A prophecy could fulfil itself simply by existing. Telling a man he had five days to live more often than not put a recklessness in his heart that would lead to a death that might otherwise not have existed.

A desired future could be manifested simply by the speaking of it. His Tuatha deserved free will. Kaygan had known from the moment that Tamzin had found Ella what the woman's choice would be. And he was happy for her to make it. Had he told her of Calen Bryer's impending demise, he would have taken her agency from her. That was not the soul he was.

"We are almost there," Kaygan said, staring out at the city. "For over a thousand years, I have steered these paths towards this point. The way forward is a haze. There are too many hands, too many forces meddling. I can feel them even now. But we will find our path. If all has gone well, both Fenryr and Vethnir have drawn their last breaths, the dragons are all but extinct, and the Cealtaí and elves march towards a mutual destruction. We will stand from the ashes, my children, and a new dawn will rise for our people."

CHAPTER ONE HUNDRED AND ELEVEN

FROM ASHES WE STAND

30th Day of the Blood Moon

The Glade – Winter, Year 3081 After Doom

Calen knelt in the rain, his hand pressed to the wet soil before him. Above, grey clouds wept as the skies themselves joined him in mourning.

He drew slow breaths, staring at the third sapling he had planted behind the lavender.

Haem was gone. Calen had barely had him back, and now he was gone. Truly gone.

A dark shadow loomed over him, the rain stopping as Valerys extended his wings like an awning to shield him. The dragon leaned over Calen, a low rumble in his throat as he pressed his snout to the ground, ash and brittle leaves shifting beneath his breath.

Calen gasped at the river of emotions that flowed across the bond. Everything from love to loss to despair and myriad others in between. But most of all, a deep appreciation ripped at Valerys's core. Haem had given him back his soulkin. Haem had been strong enough to reach through Valerys's grief and centre his mind when his world was spiralling. Were it not for the brother he had barely known, he would be completely and entirely alone. Haem was gone, but his sacrifice had meant the preservation of Valerys's entire world.

Valerys owed Haem everything, and he would protect that gift with a fury the likes of which Epheria had never known. Kaygan would burn beneath an ocean of dragonfire. His soul would scream for eternity.

The dragon leaned his neck up into the rain and roared with such force that Calen's bones shook. And with the roar, Valerys pushed memories of Haem's words through their shared soul. *"You always stood back up. And I was so gods damn proud of you every time. I need you to stand back up again, little brother."*

Calen buried his hands in the sodden earth before him, tears mingling with the rain that dripped from his hair. "I will never stop," he whispered. "I promise. Never." His voice trembled. "We will kill them all. We will end this war no matter the cost. You will not die for nothing."

Calen's jaw trembled, images of Kaygan flashing through his mind. He curled his fingers into a fist, grabbing a handful of wet dirt. He stood and looked down over the small sapling where he had laid Haem's body. "I didn't say it to you enough, but all I ever wanted was to be like you. Strong, kind, brave – calm. I won't fail you, I swear it. If I can be half of what you were, I'll be lucky. I love you, brother. With all my heart. And I'm sorry for any moment I made you feel otherwise. Wait for me. This war needs to end."

Calen drew one last, long breath, dropped the dirt slowly back to the ground, then turned and walked through the ruins of his old home amid the blackened husks of long-burnt houses.

The column of purple and white banners had ground to a halt just ahead, waiting. It stretched off into the distance, thousands strong.

Tarmon, Dann, Vaeril, Lyrei, Therin, and the others waited at its head. Queen Tessara sat astride her Dvalin Angan mount, rain splattering against the black hooded cloak drawn over her head.

Dann slid from Drunir's back and looked into Calen's eyes. He didn't speak. Tharn sat on a horse a few feet back, having decided to stay by his son's side.

All of them still stared at Calen as though he were some kind of apparition. And the soldiers looked at him with awe in their eyes.

"We march for Valtara," Calen called out. "We crush the Lorians gathering at the Hot Gates, then we burn every trace of them from Epheria."

Valerys alighted behind Calen, the rain swirling in the draft of his wings. Calen grasped Dann's forearm. "You have always been a brother to me. I love you like my own blood, and I'm sorry I wasn't there when you needed me. I will be from now on."

Calen would not die again without saying those words.

Dann nodded slowly, his grip tightening around Calen's forearm. "I thought I lost you."

"I know..." Calen let out a heavy sigh. He pulled Dann into an embrace, then mounted Valerys. The white dragon let out a low whine as he gazed back at the saplings, then roared and lifted into the air.

Calen looked down at the column of soldiers as they started into a march, banners bearing the white dragon flapping in the breeze. This path was never what he had dreamt of, but it was his now, and he would not shy away from it.

Gods and demons warred over the world he loved, and he would burn them all to save it.

As Valerys twisted in the air, Avandeer and Varthear rose from amidst the column, swirling about the white dragon, matching his roars. Valerys angled his wings and swooped down so that he soared over the marching soldiers. A pressure built within him, burning in their shared soul, bound anew by Varyn himself. A raw power surged within them and Valerys unleashed a river of bright purple dragonfire into the sky, luminescent mist drifting from his eyes, cheers and clanging steel sounding below.

"Aldryr ar orimyn, Valerys," Calen whispered, allowing Valerys's power to surge through him. "Denuvír latuá væra vidim rakaril."

Fire and fury, Valerys. These gods will know fear.

The End

of the fourth book of
The Bound and The Broken

ACKNOWLEDGEMENTS

I believe that if each book isn't more difficult than the last, then I'm not pushing my limits hard enough. And I suppose that extends to most things in life. Our comfort zone is warm and cosy; it has cookies. Everyone loves cookies. It's a tempting place to stay. But if we don't reach outside that zone and test ourselves, how can we grow? How can we become better versions of ourselves?

With that said, this book was, without a shadow of a doubt, the most difficult endeavour of my life. I am truly and genuinely both exhausted and proud in equal measure. I believe this is the best work of fiction I have ever produced, and I also need to sleep for about seventeen days. And I'd really like one of those cookies I mentioned earlier. These past two years have been crammed with life experiences: I got married, went on a honeymoon, had two six-week-long tours where I met hundreds of readers across five separate countries, wrote a novella and a short story, got a puppy, and became the father to a beautiful baby girl. All of this while trying to write, edit, and publish this monstrosity of a book. I almost broke multiple times. But I didn't. And that is in no small part due to my:

Amazing wife, Amy. You are my anchor, and you always will be.

Parents who flew ten thousand miles across the world to support Amy and me when our beautiful baby, Ella, was born (Note: Amy chose Ella's name. I was just happy to agree).

Editor and Proofreader, Taya and Izzy, who worked around the clock to make sure these deadlines were met.

Beta Readers: Colin, Graham, Brian, Elli, Carrie, Viv, Brandon, Kristin, Sannie, Claudia, Corey, Kate, Brent, Jonica, Ariana, Adam, Alicia, Rory, and Will.

Advance Readers: Anthony, Nikki, Spencer, Jonica, Rory, Ariana, Amina, Harry, Cooper, Debbie, Beki, Silver, Michael, Chuck, Mike, Kira, Cooper, Andrés, Tabor, Linda, Nashelton, Mitchell, Vivian, Lesley, Pauline, Wes, Justin, Alexander, Haney, Jessica, Casey, Eric, Callum, Karin, Cynthia, Isabelle, Antonio, Joe, Panex, Tina, Andrew, Timothy, Ognjana, Graham, Eric J, Scott F, Nathan, Ola, Danielle, Scott M, Eric L, Zak, Nicole, Sam, Kaitlin, Daniel, Tracey, Jacqueline, Adriana, Alina, Yaniv, Danny, Francesca, Sandra, Eddie, Marie, Ty, Luke, Brandon, Jeremy, Jonathon, James, Denise, James C, Terry, Pati, Trevor, Todd D, Nick, Dale, Josh, Anthony, Ghastly Magician, Joey, Aaron, Blaine, Todd, Vignesh, Ciprian, Mel, Charlie, Tianna, Petra, ChillyOne, Beren, Cole, Kendyll, Sunwish, Joe G, Brandon, Lianne, Chris, Alexander, Jeff, Roli, Alicia, Courtney S, Michael S, Austin, Taylor, David, April, Tony, Brendan, Sean, Rohit, Dave C.

Holy shit that was a lot of names. The passion with which you share this series with others is the reason for its success. You are the beating heart of everything.

One more step, many more left.